1

Beyond the Zero

Nature does not know extinction; all it knows is transformation. Everything science has taught me, and continues to teach me, strengthens my belief in the continuity of our spiritual existence after death.

—WERNHER VON BRAUN

□

A screaming comes across the sky. It has happened before, but there is nothing to compare it to now.

It is too late. The Evacuation still proceeds, but it's all theatre. There are no lights inside the cars. No light anywhere. Above him lift girders old as an iron queen, and glass somewhere far above that would let the light of day through. But it's night. He's afraid of the way the glass will fall—soon—it will be a spectacle: the fall of a crystal palace. But coming down in total blackout, without one glint of light, only great invisible crashing.

Inside the carriage, which is built on several levels, he sits in velveteen darkness, with nothing to smoke, feeling metal nearer and farther rub and connect, steam escaping in puffs, a vibration in the carriage's frame, a poising, an uneasiness, all the others pressed in around, feeble ones, second sheep, all out of luck and time: drunks, old veterans still in shock from ordnance 20 years obsolete, hustlers in city clothes, derelicts, exhausted women with more children than it seems could belong to anyone, stacked about among the rest of the things to be carried out to salvation. Only the nearer faces are visible to all, and at that only as half-silvered images in a view finder, green-stained VIP faces remembered behind bulletproof windows speeding through the city....

They have begun to move. They pass in line, out of the main station, out of downtown, and begin pushing into older and more desolate parts of the city. Is this the way out? Faces turn to the windows, but no one dares ask, not out loud. Rain comes down. No, this is not a disentanglement from, but a progressive *knotting into*—they go in under archways, secret entrances of rotted concrete that only looked like loops of an underpass ... certain trestles of blackened wood have moved slowly by overhead, and the smells begun of coal from days far to the past, smells of naphtha winters, of Sundays when no traffic came through, of the coral-like and mysteriously vital growth, around the blind curves and out the lonely spurs, a sour smell of rolling-stock absence, of maturing rust, developing

3

through those emptying days brilliant and deep, especially at dawn, with blue shadows to seal its passage, to try to bring events to Absolute Zero . . . and it is poorer the deeper they go . . . ruinous secret cities of poor, places whose *names he has never heard* . . . the walls break down, the roofs get fewer and so do the chances for light. The road, which ought to be opening out into a broader highway, instead has been getting narrower, more broken, cornering tighter and tighter until all at once, much too soon, they are under the final arch: brakes grab and spring terribly. It is a judgment from which there is no appeal.

The caravan has halted. It is the end of the line. All the evacuees are ordered out. They move slowly, but without resistance. Those marshaling them wear cockades the color of lead, and do not speak. It is some vast, very old and dark hotel, an iron extension of the track and switchery by which they have come here. . . . Globular lights, painted a dark green, hang from under the fancy iron eaves, unlit for centuries . . . the crowd moves without murmurs or coughing down corridors straight and functional as warehouse aisles . . . velvet black surfaces contain the movement: the smell is of old wood, of remote wings empty all this time just reopened to accommodate the rush of souls, of cold plaster where all the rats have died, only their ghosts, still as cave-painting, fixed stubborn and luminous in the walls . . . the evacuees are taken in lots, by elevator—a moving wood scaffold open on all sides, hoisted by old tarry ropes and cast-iron pulleys whose spokes are shaped like Ss. At each brown floor, passengers move on and off . . . thousands of these hushed rooms without light. . . .

Some wait alone, some share their invisible rooms with others. Invisible, yes, what do the furnishings matter, at this stage of things? Underfoot crunches the oldest of city dirt, last crystallizations of all the city had denied, threatened, lied to its children. Each has been hearing a voice, one he thought was talking only to him, say, "You didn't really believe you'd be saved. Come, we all know who we are by now. No one was ever going to take the trouble to save *you*, old fellow. . . ."

There is no way out. Lie and wait, lie still and be quiet. Screaming holds across the sky. When it comes, will it come in darkness, or will it bring its own light? Will the light come before or after?

But it is already light. How long has it been light? All
this while, light has come percolating in, along with the
cold morning air flowing now across his nipples: it has begun to reveal an assortment of drunken wastrels, some in
uniform and some not, clutching empty or near-empty
bottles, here draped over a chair, there huddled into a cold
fireplace, or sprawled on various divans, un-Hoovered
rugs and chaise longues down the different levels of the
enormous room, snoring and wheezing at many rhythms,
in self-renewing chorus, as London light, winter and elastic
light, grows between the faces of the mullioned windows,
grows among the strata of last night's smoke still hung,
fading, from the waxed beams of the ceiling. All these
horizontal here, these comrades in arms, look just as rosy
as a bunch of Dutch peasants dreaming of their certain
resurrection in the next few minutes.

His name is Capt. Geoffrey ("Pirate") Prentice. He is
wrapped in a thick blanket, a tartan of orange, rust, and
scarlet. His skull feels made of metal.

Just above him, twelve feet overhead, Teddy Bloat is
about to fall out of the minstrels' gallery, having chosen to
collapse just at the spot where somebody in a grandiose
fit, weeks before, had kicked out two of the ebony balusters. Now, in his stupor, Bloat has been inching through
the opening, head, arms, and torso, until all that's keeping
him up there is an empty champagne split in his hip
pocket, that's got hooked somehow—

By now Pirate has managed to sit up on his narrow
bachelor bed, and blink about. How awful. How bloody
awful . . . above him, he hears cloth rip. The Special
Operations Executive has trained him to fast responses. He
leaps off of the cot and kicks it rolling on its casters in
Bloat's direction. Bloat, plummeting, hits square amidships
with a great strum of bedsprings. One of the legs collapses.
"Good morning," notes Pirate. Bloat smiles briefly and
goes back to sleep, snuggling well into Pirate's blanket.

Bloat is one of the co-tenants of the place, a maisonette
erected last century, not far from the Chelsea Embankment,
by Corydon Throsp, an acquaintance of the Rossettis' who
wore hair smocks and liked to cultivate pharmaceutical
plants up on the roof (a tradition young Osbie Feel has
lately revived), a few of them hardy enough to survive
fogs and frosts, but most returning, as fragments of

peculiar alkaloids, to rooftop earth, along with manure from a trio of prize Wessex Saddleback sows quartered there by Throsp's successor, and dead leaves off many decorative trees transplanted to the roof by later tenants, and the odd unstomachable meal thrown or vomited there by this or that sensitive epicurean—all got scumbled together, eventually, by the knives of the seasons, to an impasto, feet thick, of unbelievable black topsoil in which anything could grow, not the least being bananas. Pirate, driven to despair by the wartime banana shortage, decided to build a glass hothouse on the roof, and persuade a friend who flew the Rio–to–Ascension–to–Fort-Lamy run to pinch him a sapling banana tree or two, in exchange for a German camera, should Pirate happen across one on his next mission by parachute.

Pirate has become famous for his Banana Breakfasts. Messmates throng here from all over England, even some who are allergic or outright hostile to bananas, just to watch—for the politics of bacteria, the soil's stringing of rings and chains in nets only God can tell the meshes of, have seen the fruit thrive often to lengths of a foot and a half, yes amazing but true.

Pirate in the lavatory stands pissing, without a thought in his head. Then he threads himself into a wool robe he wears inside out so as to keep his cigarette pocket hidden, not that this works to well, and circling the warm bodies of friends makes his way to French windows, slides outside into the cold, groans as it hits the fillings in his teeth, climbs a spiral ladder ringing to the roof garden and stands for a bit, watching the river. The sun is still below the horizon. The day feels like rain, but for now the air is uncommonly clear. The great power station, and the gasworks beyond, stand precisely: crystals grown in morning's beaker, stacks, vents, towers, plumbing, gnarled emissions of steam and smoke. . . .

"Hhahh," Pirate in a voiceless roar watching his breath slip away over the parapets, "hhaahhh!" Rooftops dance in the morning. His giant bananas cluster, radiant yellow, humid green. His companions below dream drooling of a Banana Breakfast. This well-scrubbed day ought to be no worse than any—

Will it? Far to the east, down in the pink sky, something

has just sparked, very brightly. A new star, nothing less noticeable. He leans on the parapet to watch. The brilliant point has already become a short vertical white line. It must be somewhere out over the North Sea ... at least that far ... icefields below and a cold smear of sun. ...

What is it? Nothing like this ever happens. But Pirate knows it, after all. He has seen it in a film, just in the last fortnight ... it's a vapor trail. Already a finger's width higher now. But not from an airplane. Airplanes are not launched vertically. This is the new, and still Most Secret, German rocket bomb.

"Incoming mail." Did he whisper that, or only think it? He tightens the ragged belt of his robe. Well, the range of these things is supposed to be over 200 miles. You can't see a vapor trail 200 miles, now, can you.

Oh. Oh, yes: around the curve of the Earth, farther east, the sun over there, just risen over in Holland, is striking the rocket's exhaust, drops and crystals, making them blaze clear across the sea. ...

The white line, abruptly, has stopped its climb. That would be fuel cutoff, end of burning, what's their word ... Brennschluss. We don't have one. Or else it's classified. The bottom of the line, the original star, has already begun to vanish in red daybreak. But the racket will be here before Pirate sees the sun rise.

The trail, smudged, slightly torn in two or three directions, hangs in the sky. Already the rocket, gone pure ballistic, has risen higher. But invisible now.

Oughtn't he to be doing something ... get on to the operations room at Stanmore, they must have it on the Channel radars—no: no time, really. Less than five minutes Hague to here (the time it takes to walk down to the teashop on the corner ... for light from the sun to reach the planet of love ... no time at all). Run out in the street? Warn the others?

Pick bananas. He trudges through black compost in to the hothouse. He feels he's about to shit. The missile, sixty miles high, must be coming up on the peak of its trajectory by now ... beginning its fall ... *now*. ...

Trusswork is pierced by dáylight, milky panes beam beneficently down. How could there be a winter—even this one—gray enough to age this iron that can sing in the wind, or cloud these windows that open into another season, however falsely preserved?

Pirate looks at his watch. Nothing registers. The pores of his face are prickling. Emptying his mind—a Commando trick—he steps into the wet heat of his bananery, sets about picking the ripest and the best, holding up the skirt of his robe to drop them in. Allowing himself to count only bananas, moving barelegged among the pendulous bunches, among these yellow chandeliers, this tropical twilight. . . .

Out into the winter again. The contrail is gone entirely from the sky. Pirate's sweat lies on his skin almost as cold as ice.

He takes some time lighting a cigarette. He won't hear the thing come in. It travels faster than the speed of sound. The first news you get of it is the blast. Then, if you're still around, you hear the sound of it coming in.

What if it should hit *exactly*—ahh, no—for a split second you'd have to feel the very point, with the terrible mass above, strike the top of the skull. . . .

Pirate hunches his shoulders, bearing his bananas down the corkscrew ladder.

□

Across a blue tile patio, in through a door to the kitchen. Routine: plug in American blending machine won from Yank last summer, some poker game, table stakes, B.O.Q. somewhere in the north, never remember now. . . . Chop several bananas into pieces. Make coffee in urn. Get can of milk from cooler. Puree 'nanas in milk. Lovely. *I would coat all the booze-corroded stomachs of England.* . . . Bit of marge, still smells all right, melt in skillet. Peel more bananas, slice lengthwise. Marge sizzling, in go long slices. Light oven *whoomp* blow us all up someday oh, ha, ha, yes. Peeled whole bananas to go on broiler grill soon as it heats. Find marshmallows. . . .

In staggers Teddy Bloat with Pirate's blanket over his head, slips on a banana peel and falls on his ass. "Kill myself," he mumbles.

"The Germans will do it for you. Guess what I saw from the roof."

"That V-2 on the way?"

"A4, yes."

"I watched it out the window. About ten minutes ago.
Looked queer, didn't it. Haven't heard a thing since, have
you. It must have fallen short. Out to sea or something."

"Ten minutes?" Trying to read the time on his watch.

"At least." Bloat is sitting on the floor, working the
banana peel into a pajama lapel for a boutonniere.

Pirate goes to the phone and rings up Stanmore after
all. Has to go through the usual long, long routine, but
knows he's already stopped believing in the rocket he saw.
God has plucked it for him, out of its airless sky, like a
steel banana. "Prentice here, did you have anything like a
pip from Holland a moment ago. Aha. Aha. Yes, we *saw*
it." This could ruin a man's taste for sunrises. He rings off.
"They lost it over the coast. They're calling it premature
Brennschluss."

"Cheer up," Teddy crawling back toward the busted
cot. "There'll be more."

Good old Bloat, always the positive word. Pirate for a
few seconds there, waiting to talk to Stanmore, was thinking, Danger's over, Banana Breakfast is saved. But it's
only a reprieve. Isn't it. There will indeed be others, each
just as likely to land on top of him. No one either side of
the front knows exactly how many more. Will we have to
stop watching the sky?

Osbie Feel stands in the minstrels' gallery, holding one
of the biggest of Pirate's bananas so that it protrudes out
the fly of his striped pajama bottoms—stroking with his
other hand the great jaundiced curve in triplets against
4/4 toward the ceiling, he acknowledges dawn with the
following:

> Time to gather your arse up off the floor,
>   (have a bana-na)
> Brush your teeth and go toddling off to war.
> Wave your hand to sleepy land,
> Kiss those dreams away,
> Tell Miss Grable you're not able,
> Not till V-E Day, oh,
> Ev'rything'll be grand in Civvie Street
>   (have a bana-na)
> Bubbly wine and girls wiv lips so sweet—
> But there's still the German or two to fight,

So show us a smile that's shiny bright,
And then, as we may have suggested once before—
Gather yer blooming arse up off the floor!

There's a second verse, but before he can get quite into
it, prancing Osbie is leaped upon and thoroughly pum-
meled, in part with his own stout banana, by Bartley
Gobbitch, DeCoverley Pox, and Maurice ("Saxophone")
Reed, among others. In the kitchen, black-market marshmallows slide languid into syrup atop Pirate's double
boiler, and soon begin thickly to bubble. Coffee brews.
On a wooden pub sign daringly taken, one daylight raid,
by a drunken Bartley Gobbitch, across which still survives
in intaglio the legend SNIPE AND SHAFT, Teddy Bloat is
mincing bananas with a great isosceles knife, from beneath
whose nervous blade Pirate with one hand shovels the
blonde mash into waffle batter resilient with fresh hens'
eggs, for which Osbie Feel has exchanged an equal number of golf balls, these being even rarer this winter than
real eggs, other hand blending the fruit in, not overvig-
orously, with a wire whisk, whilst surly Osbie himself,
sucking frequently at a half-pint milk bottle filled with
Vat 69 and water, tends to the bananas in the skillet and
broiler. Near the exit to the blue patio, DeCoverley Pox
and Joaquin Stick stand by a concrete scale model of the
Jungfrau, which some enthusiast back during the twenties
spent a painstaking year modeling and casting before finding out it was too large to get out of any door, socking the
slopes of the famous mountain with red rubber hot-water
bags full of ice cubes, the idea being to pulverize the ice
for Pirate's banana frappés. With their nights' growths of
beard, matted hair, bloodshot eyes, miasmata of foul
breath, DeCoverley and Joaquin are wasted gods urging
on a tardy glacier.
    Elsewhere in the maisonette, other drinking companions
disentangle from blankets (one spilling wind from his,
dreaming of a parachute), piss into bathroom sinks, look at
themselves with dismay in concave shaving mirrors, slap
water with no clear plan in mind onto heads of thinning
hair, struggle into Sam Brownes, dub shoes against rain
later in the day with hand muscles already weary of it,
sing snatches of popular songs whose tunes they don't

always know, lie, believing themselves warmed, in what patches of the new sunlight come between the mullions, begin tentatively to talk shop as a way of easing into whatever it is they'll have to be doing in less than an hour, lather necks and faces, yawn, pick their noses, search cabinets or bookcases for the hair of the dog that not without provocation and much prior conditioning bit them last night.

Now there grows among all the rooms, replacing the night's old smoke, alcohol and sweat, the fragile, musaceous odor of Breakfast: flowery, permeating, surprising, more than the color of winter sunlight, taking over not so much through any brute pungency or volume as by the high intricacy to the weaving of its molecules, sharing the conjuror's secret by which—though it is not often Death is told so clearly to fuck off—the living genetic chains prove even labyrinthine enough to preserve some human face down ten or twenty generations . . . so the same assertion-through-structure allows this war morning's banana fragrance to meander, repossess, prevail. Is there any reason not to open every window, and let the kind scent blanket all Chelsea? As a spell, against falling objects. . . .

With a clattering of chairs, upended shell cases, benches, and ottomans, Pirate's mob gather at the shores of the great refectory table, a southern island well across a tropic or two from chill Corydon Throsp's mediaeval fantasies, crowded now over the swirling dark grain of its walnut uplands with banana omelets, banana sandwiches, banana casseroles, mashed bananas molded in the shape of a British lion rampant, blended with eggs into batter for French toast, squeezed out a pastry nozzle across the quivering creamy reaches of a banana blancmange to spell out the words *C'est magnifique, mais ce n'est pas la guerre* (attributed to a French observer during the Charge of the Light Brigade) which Pirate has appropriated as his motto . . . tall cruets of pale banana syrup to pour oozing over banana waffles, a giant glazed crock where diced bananas have been fermenting since the summer with wild honey and muscat raisins, up out of which, this winter morning, one now dips foam mugsfull of banana mead . . . banana croissants and banana kreplach, and banana oatmeal and banana jam and banana bread, and bananas

flamed in ancient brandy Pirate brought back last year
from a cellar in the Pyrenees also containing a clandestine
radio transmitter . . .

The phone call, when it comes, rips easily across the
room, the hangovers, the grabassing, the clatter of dishes,
the shoptalk, the bitter chuckles, like a rude metal double-
fart, and Pirate knows it's got to be for him. Bloat, who's
nearest, takes it, forkful of *bananes glacées* poised fashionably in the air. Pirate takes up a last dipper of mead, feels
it go valving down his throat as if it's time, time in its
summer tranquility, he swallows.

"Your employer."

"It's not fair," Pirate moans, "I haven't even done me
morning pushups yet."

The voice, which he's heard only once before—last year
at a briefing, hands and face blackened, anonymous
among a dozen other listeners—tells Pirate now there's a
message addressed to him, waiting at Greenwich.

"It came over in a rather delightful way," the voice
high-pitched and sullen, "none of *my* friends are that
clever. All *my* mail arrives by post. Do come collect it,
won't you, Prentice." Receiver hits cradle a violent whack,
connection breaks, and now Pirate knows where this morning's rocket landed, and why there was no explosion. Incoming mail, indeed. He gazes through sunlight's but-
tresses, back down the refectory at the others, wallowing
in their plenitude of bananas, thick palatals of their
hunger lost somewhere in the stretch of morning between
them and himself. A hundred miles of it, so suddenly.
Solitude, even among the meshes of this war, can when it
wishes so take him by the blind gut and touch, as now,
possessively. Pirate's again some other side of a window,
watching strangers eat breakfast.

He's driven out, away, east over Vauxhall Bridge in a
dented green Lagonda by his batman, a Corporal Wayne.
The morning seems to grow colder the higher the sun
rises. Clouds begin to gather after all. A crew of American
sappers spills into the road, on route to clear some ruin
nearby, singing:

> It's . . .
> Colder than the nipple on a witch's tit!

> Colder than a bucket of penguin shit!
> Colder than the hairs of a polar bear's ass!
> Colder than the frost on a champagne glass!

No, they are making believe to be narodnik, but *I* know, they are of Iasi, of Codreanu, *his* men, men of the League, they . . . they kill for him—they have *oath!* They try to kill me . . . Transylvanian Magyars, they know *spells* . . . at night they whisper. . . . Well, hrrump, heh, heh, here comes Pirate's Condition creeping over him again, when he's least expecting it as usual—might as well mention here that much of what the dossiers call Pirate Prentice is a strange talent for—well, for getting inside the fantasies of others: being able, actually, to take over the burden of *managing* them, in this case those of an exiled Rumanian royalist who may prove needed in the very near future. It is a gift the Firm has found uncommonly useful: at this time mentally healthy leaders and other historical figures are indispensable. What better way to cup and bleed them of excess anxiety than to get someone to take over the running of their exhausting little daydreams for them . . . to live in the tame green lights of their tropical refuges, in the breezes through their cabañas, to drink their tall drinks, changing your seat to face the entrances of their public places, not letting their innocence suffer any more than it already has . . . to get their erections for them, at the oncome of thoughts the doctors feel are inappropriate . . . fear all, all that they cannot afford to fear . . . remembering the word of P. M. S. Blackett, "You can't run a war on gusts of emotion." Just hum the nitwit little tune they taught you, and try not to fuck up:

> Yes—I'm—the—
> Fellow that's hav-ing other peop-le's fan-tasies,
> Suffering what they ought to be themselves—
> No matter if Girly's on my knee—
> If Kruppingham-Jones is late to tea,
> I don't even get to ask for whom the bell's . . .
> [Now over a lotta tubas and close-harmony trombones]
> It never does seem to mat-ter if there's daaaanger,
> For Danger's a roof I fell from long ago—

I'll be out-one-day and never come back,
Forget the bitter you owe me, Jack,
Just piss on m' grave and car-ry on the show!

He will then actually *skip* to and fro, with his knees
high and twirling a walking stick with W. C. Fields'
head, nose, top hat, and all, for its knob, and surely
capable of magic, while the band plays a second chorus.
Accompanying will be a phantasmagoria, a real one, rushing
toward the screen, in over the heads of the audiences, on
little tracks of an elegant Victorian cross section
resembling the profile of a chess knight conceived fancifully
but not vulgarly so—then rushing back out again, in and
out, the images often changing scale so quickly, so
unpredictably that you're apt now and then to get a bit of
lime-green in with your rose, as they say. The scenes are
highlights from Pirate's career as a fantasist-surrogate, and go
back to when he was carrying, everywhere he went, the mark
of Youthful Folly growing in an unmistakable Mongoloid
point, right out of the middle of his head. He had known
for a while that certain episodes he dreamed could not be
his own. This wasn't through any rigorous daytime analysis
of content, but just because he *knew*. But then came the
day when he met, for the first time, the real owner of a
dream he, Pirate, had had: it was by a drinking fountain
in a park, a very long, neat row of benches, a feeling of
sea just over a landscaped rim of small cypresses, gray
crushed stone on the walks looking soft to sleep on as the
brim of a fedora, and here comes this buttonless and
drooling derelict, the one you are afraid of ever meeting,
to pause and watch two Girl Guides trying to adjust the
water pressure of the fountain. They bent over, unaware,
the saucy darlings, of the fatal strips of white cotton
knickers thus displayed, the undercurves of baby-fat little
buttocks a blow to the Genital Brain, however pixilated.
The tramp laughed and pointed, he looked back at Pirate
then and said something extraordinary: "Eh? Girl Guides
start pumping water ... *your sound will be the sizzling
night* ... eh?" staring directly at no one but Pirate now, no
more pretense. . . . Well, Pirate had dreamed these very
words, morning before last, just before waking, they'd
been part of the usual list of prizes in a Competition grown

crowded and perilous, out of some indoor intervention of charcoal streets . . . he couldn't remember that well . . . scared out of his wits by now, he replied, "Go away, or I will call a policeman."

It took care of the immediate problem for him. But sooner or later the time would come when someone else would find out his gift, someone to whom it mattered—he had a long-running fantasy of his own, rather a Eugène Sue melodrama, in which he would be abducted by an organization of dacoits or Sicilians, and used for unspeakable purposes.

In 1935 he had his first episode *outside* any condition of known sleep—it was during his Kipling Period, beastly Fuzzy-Wuzzies far as eye could see, dracunculiasis and Oriental sore rampant among the troops, no beer for a month, wireless being jammed by other Powers who would be masters of these horrid blacks, God knows why, and all folklore broken down, no Cary Grant larking in and out slipping elephant medicine in the punchbowls out here . . . not even an Arab With A Big Greasy Nose to perform on, as in that wistful classic every tommy's heard . . . small wonder that one fly-blown four in the afternoon, open-eyed, in the smell of rotting melon rinds, to the seventy-seven-millionth repetition of the outpost's only Gramophone record, Sandy MacPherson playing on his organ "The Changing of the Guard," what should develop for Pirate here but a sumptuous Oriental episode: vaulting lazily and well over the fence and sneaking in to town, to the Forbidden Quarter. There to stumble into an orgy held by a Messiah no one has quite recognized yet, and to know, as your eyes meet, that you are his John the Baptist, his Nathan of Gaza, that it is you who must convince him of his Godhead, proclaim him to others, love him both profanely and in the Name of what he is . . . it could be no one's fantasy but H. A. Loaf's. There is at least one Loaf in every outfit, it is Loaf who keeps forgetting that those of the Moslem faith are not keen on having snaps taken of them in the street . . . it is Loaf who borrows one's shirt runs out of cigarettes finds the illicit one in your pocket and lights up in the canteen at high noon, where presently he is reeling about with a loose smile, addressing the sergeant commanding the red-cap section by his

Christian name. So of course when Pirate makes the mistake of verifying the fantasy with Loaf, it's not very long at all before higher echelons know about it too. Into the dossier it goes, and eventually the Firm, in Their tireless search for negotiable skills, will summon him under Whitehall, to observe him in his trances across the blue baize fields and the terrible paper gaming, his eyes rolled back into his head reading old, glyptic old graffiti on his own sockets. . . .

The first few times nothing clicked. The fantasies were O.K. but belonged to nobody important. But the Firm is patient, committed to the Long Run as They are. At last, one proper Sherlock Holmes London evening, the unmistakable smell of gas came to Pirate from a dark street lamp, and out of the fog ahead materialized a giant, organlike form. Carefully, black-shod step by step, Pirate approached the thing. It began to slide forward to meet him, over the cobblestones slow as a snail, leaving behind some slime brightness of street-wake that could not have been from fog. In the space between them was a crossover point, which Pirate, being a bit faster, reached first. He reeled back, in horror, back past the point—but such recognitions are not reversible. *It was a giant Adenoid.* At least as big as St. Paul's, and growing hour by hour. London, perhaps all England, was in mortal peril!

This lymphatic monster had once blocked the distinguished pharynx of Lord Blatherard Osmo, who at the time occupied the Novi Pazar desk at the Foreign Office, an obscure penance for the previous century of British policy on the Eastern Question, for on this obscure sanjak had once hinged the entire fate of Europe:

Nobody knows-where, it is-on-the-map,
Who'd ever think-it, could start-such-a-flap?
Each Montenegran, and Serbian too,
Waitin' for some-thing, right outa the blue—oh honey
Pack up my Glad-stone, 'n' brush off my suit,
And then light me up my bigfat, cigar—
If ya want my address, it's
That O-ri-ent Express,
To the san-jak of No-vi Pa-zar!

Chorus line of quite nubile young women naughtily attired in Busbies and jackboots dance around for a bit here while in another quarter Lord Blatherard Osmo proceeds to get *assimilated* by his own growing Adenoid, some horrible transformation of cell plasma it is quite beyond Edwardian medicine to explain ... before long, tophats are littering the squares of Mayfair, cheap perfume hanging ownerless in the pub lights of the East End as the Adenoid continues on its rampage, not swallowing up its victims at random, no, the fiendish Adenoid has a *master plan*, it's choosing only certain personalities useful to it—there is a new election, a new preterition abroad in England here that throws the Home Office into hysterical and painful episodes of indecision ... no one knows *what* to do ... a halfhearted attempt is made to evacuate London, black phaetons clatter in massive ant-cortege over the trusswork bridges, observer balloons are stationed in the sky, "Got it in Hampstead Heath, just sitting *breathing*, like ... going in, and out ..." "Any sort of *sound* down there?" "Yes, it's horrible ... like a stupendous *nose* sucking in snot ... wait, now it's ... beginning to ... oh, *no* ... oh, God, I can't describe it, it's so beast—" the wire is snapped, the transmission ends, the balloon rises into the teal-blue daybreak. Teams come down from the Cavendish Laboratory, to string the Heath with huge magnets, electric-arc terminals, black iron control panels full of gauges and cranks, the Army shows up in full battle gear with bombs full of the latest deadly gas—the Adenoid is blasted, electric-shocked, poisoned, changes color and shape here and there, yellow fat-nodes appear high over the trees ... before the flash-powder cameras of the Press, a hideous green pseudopod crawls toward the cordon of troops and suddenly *sshhlop!* wipes out an entire observation post with a deluge of some disgusting orange mucus in which the unfortunate men are *digested*—not screaming but actually laughing, *enjoying* themselves. ...

Pirate/Osmo's mission is to establish liaison with the Adenoid. The situation is now stable, the Adenoid occupies all of St. James's, the historic buildings are no more, Government offices have been relocated, but so dispersed that communication among them is highly uncertain—postmen are being snatched off of their rounds by stiff-pimpled Adenoid tentacles of fluorescent beige, telegraph wires are apt to go down at any whim of the Adenoid. Each morning Lord Blatherard Osmo must put on his bowler, and take his briefcase out to the Adenoid to make his daily *démarche*. It is taking up so much of his time he's begun to neglect Novi Pazar, and F.O. is worried. In the thirties balance-of-power thinking was still quite strong, the diplomats were all down with Balkanosis, spies with foreign hybrid names lurked in all the stations of the Ottoman rump, code messages in a dozen Slavic tongues were being tattooed on bare upper lips over which the operatives then grew mustaches, to be shaved off only by authorized crypto officers and skin then grafted over the messages by the Firms' plastic surgeons . . . their lips were palimpsests of secret flesh, scarred and unnaturally white, by which they all knew each other.

Novi Pazar, anyhow, was still a *croix mystique* on the palm of Europe, and F.O. finally decided to go to the Firm for help. The Firm knew just the man.

Every day for 2½ years, Pirate went out to visit the St. James Adenoid. It nearly drove him crazy. Though he was able to develop a pidgin by which he and the Adenoid could communicate, unfortunately he wasn't nasally equipped to make the sounds too well, and it got to be an awful chore. As the two of them snuffled back and forth, alienists in black seven-button suits, admirers of Dr. Freud the Adenoid clearly had no use for, stood on stepladders up against its loathsome grayish flank shoveling the new wonderdrug cocaine—bringing *hods* full of the white substance, in relays, up the ladders to smear on the throbbing glandcreature, and into the germ toxins bubbling nastily inside its crypts, with no visible effects at all (though who knows how that *Adenoid* felt, eh?).

But Lord Blatherard Osmo was able at last to devote all of his time to Novi Pazar. Early in 1939, he was discovered mysteriously suffocated in a bathtub full of tapioca pudding, at the home of a Certain Viscountess. Some have seen in this the hand of the Firm. Months passed, World War II started, years passed, nothing was heard from Novi Pazar. Pirate Prentice had saved Europe from the Balkan Armageddon the old men dreamed of, giddy in their beds with its grandeur—though not from World War II, of course. But by then, the Firm was allowing Pirate only tiny homeopathic doses of peace, just enough to keep his defenses up, but not enough for it to poison him.

□

Teddy Bloat's on his lunch hour, but lunch today'll be, ack, a soggy banana sandwich in wax paper, which he's packing inside his stylish kangaroohide musette bag and threaded around the odd necessities—midget spy-camera, jar of mustache wax, tin of licorice, menthol and capsicum Meloids for a Mellow Voice, gold-rim prescription sunglasses General MacArthur style, twin silver hairbrushes each in the shape of the flaming SHAEF sword, which Mother had Garrard's make up for him and which he considers exquisite.

His objective this dripping winter noon is a gray stone town house, neither large nor historic enough to figure in any guidebook, set back just out of sight of Grosvenor Square, somewhat off the official war-routes and corridors about the capital. When the typewriters happen to pause (8:20 and other mythical hours), and there are no flights of American bombers in the sky, and the motor traffic's not too heavy in Oxford Street, you can hear winter birds cheeping outside, busy at the feeders the girls have put up.

Flagstones are slippery with mist. It is the dark, hard, tobacco-starved, headachy, sour-stomach middle of the day, a million bureaucrats are diligently plotting death and some of them even know it, many about now are already into the second or third pint of highball glass, which produces a certain desperate aura here. But Bloat, going in the sandbagged entrance (provisional pyramids erected to gratify curious gods' offspring indeed), can't feel a bit of it: he's too busy running through plausible excuses should he happen to get caught, not that he will, you know. . . .

Girl at the main desk, gumpopping, good-natured bespectacled ATS, waves him on upstairs. Damp woolen aides on the way to staff meetings, W.C.s, an hour or two of earnest drinking, nod, not really seeing him, he's a well-known face, what's'isname's mate, Oxford chums aren't they, that lieutenant works down the hall at ACHTUNG. . . .

The old house has been subdivided by the slummakers of war. ACHTUNG is Allied Clearing House, Technical

Units, Northern Germany. It's a stale-smoke paper warren, at the moment nearly deserted, its black typewriters tall as grave markers. The floor is filthy lino, there are no windows: the electric light is yellow, cheap, merciless. Bloat looks into the office assigned to his old Jesus College friend, Lt. Oliver ("Tantivy") Mucker-Maffick. No one's about. Tantivy and the Yank are both at lunch. Good. Out wiv the old camera then, on with the gooseneck lamp, now aim the reflector just so . . .

There must be cubicles like this all over the ETO: only the three dingy scuffed-cream fiberboard walls and no ceiling of its own. Tantivy shares it with an American colleague, Lt. Tyrone Slothrop. Their desks are at right angles, so there's no eye contact but by squeaking around some 90°. Tantivy's desk is neat, Slothrop's is a godawful mess. It hasn't been cleaned down to the original wood surface since 1942. Things have fallen roughly into layers, over a base of bureaucratic smegma that sifts steadily to the bottom, made up of millions of tiny red and brown curls of rubber eraser, pencil shavings, dried tea or coffee stains, traces of sugar and Household Milk, much cigarette ash, very fine black debris picked and flung from type-writer ribbons, decomposing library paste, broken aspirins ground to powder. Then comes a scatter of paperclips, Zippo flints, rubber bands, staples, cigarette butts and crumpled packs, stray matches, pins, nubs of pens, stubs of pencils of all colors including the hard-to-get heliotrope and raw umber, wooden coffee spoons, Thayer's Slippery Elm Throat Lozenges sent by Slothrop's mother, Nalline, all the way from Massachusetts, bits of tape, string, chalk . . . above that a layer of forgotten memoranda, empty buff ration books, phone numbers, unanswered letters, tattered sheets of carbon paper, the scribbled ukulele chords to a dozen songs including "Johnny Doughboy Found a Rose in Ireland" ("He does have some rather snappy arrangements," Tantivy reports, "he's a sort of American George Formby, if you can imagine such a thing," but Bloat's decided he'd rather not), an empty Kreml hair tonic bottle, lost pieces to different jigsaw puzzles showing parts of the amber left eye of a Weimaraner, the green velvet folds of a gown, slate-blue veining in a distant cloud, the orange nimbus of an explosion (perhaps a sunset), rivets in the skin of a Flying Fortress, the pink inner thigh of a pouting pin-up girl ... a few old Weekly Intelligence Summaries from G-2, a busted corkscrewing ukulele string, boxes of gummed paper stars in many colors, pieces of a flashlight, top to a Nugget shoe polish can in which Slothrop now and then studies his blurry brass reflection, any number of reference books out of the ACHTUNG library back down the hall—a dictionary of technical German, an F.O. *Special Handbook* or *Town Plan*—and usually, unless it's been pinched or thrown away, a *News of the World* somewhere too—Slothrop's a faithful reader.

Tacked to the wall next to Slothrop's desk is a map of London, which Bloat is now busy photographing with his tiny camera. The musette bag is open, and the cubicle begins to fill with the smell of ripe bananas. Should he light a fag to cover this? air doesn't exactly stir in here, they'll know someone's been in. It takes him four exposures, click zippety click, my how very efficient at this he's become—anyone nips in one simply drops camera into bag where banana-sandwich cushions fall, telltale sound and harmful G-loads alike.

Too bad whoever's funding this little caper won't spring for color film. Bloat wonders if it mightn't make a difference, though he knows of no one he can ask. The stars pasted up on Slothrop's map cover the available spectrum, beginning with silver (labeled "Darlene") sharing a constellation with Gladys, green, and Katharine, gold, and as the eye strays Alice, Delores, Shirley, a couple of Sallys—mostly red and blue through here—a cluster near Tower Hill, a violet density about Covent Garden, a nebular streaming on into Mayfair, Soho, and out to Wembley and up to Hampstead Heath—in every direction goes this glossy, multicolored, here and there peeling firmament, Carolines, Marias, Annes, Susans, Elizabeths.

But perhaps the colors are only random, uncoded. Perhaps the girls are not even real. From Tantivy, over weeks of casual questions (*we know he's your schoolmate but it's too risky bringing him in*), Bloat's only able to report that Slothrop began work on this map last autumn, about the time he started going out to look at rocket-bomb disasters for ACHTUNG—having evidently the time, in his travels among places of death, to devote to girl-chasing. If there's a reason for putting up the paper stars every few days the man hasn't explained it—it doesn't seem to be for publicity, Tantivy's the only one who even glances at the map and that's more in the spirit of an amiable anthropologist— "Some sort of harmless Yank hobby," he tells his friend Bloat. "Perhaps it's to keep track of them all. He does lead rather a complicated social life," thereupon going into the story of Lorraine and Judy, Charles the homosexual constable and the piano in the pantechnicon, or the bizarre masquerade involving Gloria and her nubile mother, a quid wager on the Blackpool–Preston North End game, a naughty version of "Silent Night," and a providential fog. But none of these yarns, for the purposes of those Bloat reports to, are really very illuminating. . . .

   Well. He's done now. Bag zipped, lamp off and moved back in place. Perhaps there's time to catch Tantivy over at the Snipe and Shaft, time for a comradely pint. He moves back down the beaverboard maze, in the weak yellow light, against a tide of incoming girls in galoshes, aloof Bloat unsmiling, no time for slap-and-tickle here you see, he still has his day's delivery to make. . . .

□

Wind has shifted around to the southwest, and the barometer's falling. The early afternoon is already dark as evening, under the massing rainclouds. Tyrone Slothrop is gonna be caught out in it, too. Today it's been a long, idiot chase out to zero longitude, with the usual nothing to show. This one was supposed to be another premature airburst, the lumps of burning rocket showering down for miles around, most of it into the river, only one piece in any kind of shape and that well surrounded, by the time Slothrop arrived, with the tightest security he's seen yet, and the least friendly. Soft, faded berets against the slate clouds, Mark III Stens set on automatic, mustaches mouth-wide covering enormous upper lips, humorless—no chance for any American lieutenant to get a look, not today.

   ACHTUNG, anyhow, is the poor relative of Allied intelligence. At least this time Slothrop's not alone, he's had the cold comfort of seeing his opposite number from T.I., and shortly after that even the man's section chief, come fussing onto the scene in a '37 Wolseley Wasp, both turned back too. Ha! Neither of them returning Slothrop's amiable nod. Tough shit, fellas. But shrewd Tyrone hangs around, distributing Lucky Strikes, long enough to find at least what's up with this Unlucky Strike, here.

What it is is a graphite cylinder, about six inches long and two in diameter, all but a few flakes of its Army-green paint charred away. Only piece that survived the burst. Evidently it was meant to. There seem to be papers stashed inside. Sergeant-major burned his hand picking it up and was heard to holler *Oh fuck,* causing laughter among the lower paygrades. Everybody was waiting around for a Captain Prentice from S.O.E. (*those* prickly bastards take their time about everything), who does presently show up. Slothrop gets a glimpse—windburned face, big mean mother. Prentice takes the cylinder, drives away, and that's that.

In which case, Slothrop reckons, ACHTUNG can, a bit wearily, submit its fifty-millionth interbranch request to that S.O.E., asking for some report on the cylinder's contents, and, as usual, be ignored. It's O.K., he's not bitter. S.O.E. ignores everybody, and everybody ignores ACHTUNG. A-and what does it matter, anyhow? It's his last rocket for a while. Hopefully for good.

This morning in his IN basket were orders sending him TDY some hospital out in the East End. No explanation beyond an attached carbon copy of a note to ACHTUNG requesting his reassignment "as part of the P.W.E. Testing Programme." Testing? P.W.E. is Political Warfare Executive, he looked that up. Some more of that Minnesota Multiphasic shit, no doubt. But it will be a change from this rocket-hunting routine, which is beginning to get a little old.

Once upon a time Slothrop cared. No kidding. He thinks he did, anyway. A lot of stuff prior to 1944 is getting blurry now. He can remember the first Blitz only as a long spell of good luck. Nothing that Luftwaffe dropped came near him. But this last summer they started in with those buzzbombs. You'd be walking on the street, in bed just dozing off suddenly here comes this farting sound over the rooftops—if it just keeps on, rising to a peak and passing over why that's fine, then it's somebody else's worry . . . but if the engine cuts off, look out Jackson—it's begun its dive, sloshing the fuel aft, away, from the engine burner, and you've got 10 seconds to get under something. Well, it wasn't really too bad. After a while you adjusted—found yourself making small bets, a shilling or two, with Tantivy Mucker-Maffick at the next desk, about where the next doodle would hit. . . .

But then last September the rockets came. Them fucking rockets. You couldn't adjust to the bastards. No way. For the first time, he was surprised to find that he was really scared. Began drinking heavier, sleeping less, chain-smoking, feeling in some way he'd been taken for a sucker. Christ, it wasn't supposed to keep on like *this*. . . .

"I say Slothrop, you've already got one in your mouth—"

"Nervous," Slothrop lighting up anyway.

"Well not *mine*," Tantivy pleads.

"Two at a time, see?" making them point down like comicbook fangs. The lieutenants stare at each other through the beery shadows, with the day deepening outside the high cold windows of the Snipe and Shaft, and Tantivy about to laugh or snort oh God across the wood Atlantic of their table.

Atlantics aplenty there've been these three years, often rougher than the one William, the first transatlantic Slothrop, crossed many ancestors ago. Barbarities of dress and speech, lapses in behavior—one horrible evening drunken Slothrop, Tantivy's guest at the Junior Athenaeum, got them both 86'd feinting with the beak of a stuffed owl after the jugular of DeCoverley Pox whilst Pox, at bay on a billiard table, attempted to ram a cue ball down Slothrop's throat. This sort of thing goes on dismayingly often: yet kindness is a sturdy enough ship for these oceans, Tantivy always there blushing or smiling and Slothrop surprised at how, when it's really counted, Tantivy hasn't ever let him down.

He knows he can spill what's on his mind. It hasn't much to do with today's amorous report on Norma (dimply Cedar Rapids subdeb legs), Marjorie (tall, elegant, a build out of the chorus line at the Windmill) and the strange events Saturday night at the Frick Frack Club in Soho, a haunt of low reputation with moving spotlights of many pastel hues, OFF LIMITS and NO JITTERBUG DANCING signs laid on to satisfy the many sorts of police, military and civilian, whatever "civilian" means nowadays, who look in from time to time, and where against all chance, through some horrible secret plot, Slothrop, who was to meet one, walks in sees who but *both*, lined up in a row, the angle deliberately just for him, over the blue wool shoulder of an engineman 3rd class, under the bare lovely armpit of a lindy-hopping girl swung and posed, skin stained lavender by the shifting light just there, and then, paranoia flooding up, the two faces beginning to turn his way. . . .

Both young ladies happen to be silver stars on Slothrop's map. He must've been feeling silvery both times—shiny, jingling. The stars he pastes up are colored only to go with how he feels that day, blue on up to golden. Never to rank a single one—how can he? Nobody sees the map but Tantivy, and Christ they're *all* beautiful . . . in leaf or flower around his wintering city, in teashops, in the queues babushkaed and coatwrapped, sighing, sneezing, all lisle legs on the curbstones, hitchhiking, typing or filing with pompadours sprouting yellow pencils, he finds them— dames, tomatoes, sweater girls—yes it is a little obsessive maybe but . . . "I know there is wilde love and joy enough in the world," preached Thomas Hooker, "as there are wilde Thyme, and other herbes; but we would have garden love, and garden joy, of Gods owne planting." How Slothrop's garden grows. Teems with virgin's-bower, with forget-me-nots, with rue—and all over the place, purple and yellow as hickeys, a prevalence of love-in-idleness.

He likes to tell them about fireflies. English girls don't know about fireflies, which is about all Slothrop knows for sure about English girls.

The map does puzzle Tantivy. It cannot be put down to the usual loud-mouthed American ass-banditry, except as a fraternity-boy reflex in a vacuum, a reflex Slothrop can't help, barking on into an empty lab, into a worm-holing of echoing hallways, long after the need has vanished and the brothers gone to WW II and their chances for death. Slothrop really doesn't like to talk about his girls: Tantivy has to steer him diplomatically, even now. At first Slothrop, quaintly gentlemanly, didn't talk at all, till he found out how shy Tantivy was. It dawned on him then that Tantivy was looking to be fixed up. At about the same time, Tantivy began to see the extent of Slothrop's isolation. He seemed to have no one else in London, beyond a multitude of girls he seldom saw again, to talk to about *anything*.

Still Slothrop keeps his map up daily, boobishly conscientious. At its best, it does celebrate a flow, a passing from which—among the sudden demolitions from the sky, mysterious orders arriving out of the dark laborings of nights that for himself are only idle—he can save a moment here or there, the days again growing colder, frost in the morning, the feeling of Jennifer's breasts inside cold sweater's wool held to warm a bit in a coal-smoke hallway he'll never know the daytime despondency of . . . cup of Bovril a fraction down from boiling searing his bare knee as Irene, naked as he is in a block of glass sunlight, holds up precious nylons one by one to find a pair that hasn't laddered, each struck flashing by the light through the winter trellis outside . . . nasal hep American-girl voices singing out of the grooves of some disc up through the thorn needle of Allison's mother's radiogram . . . snuggling for warmth, blackout curtains over all the windows, no light but the coal of their last cigarette, an English firefly, bobbing at her whim in cursive writing that trails a bit behind, words he can't read. . . .

"What happened?" Silence from Slothrop. "Your two Wrens . . . when they saw you . . ." then he notices that Slothrop, instead of going on with his story, has given himself up to shivering. Has been shivering, in fact, for some time. It's cold in here, but not that cold. "Slothrop—"

"I don't know. Jesus." It's interesting, though. It's the weirdest feeling. He can't stop. He turns his Ike jacket collar up, tucks hands inside sleeves, and sits that way for a while.

Presently, after a pause, cigarette in motion, "You can't hear them when they come in."

Tantivy knows which "they." His eyes shift away. There is silence for a bit.

"Of course you can't, they go faster than sound."

"Yes but—that's not it," words are bursting out between the pulses of shivering—"the other kind, those V-1s, you can hear them. Right? Maybe you have a chance to get out of the way. But these things explode first, a-and *then* you hear them coming in. Except that, if you're dead, you *don't* hear them."

"Same in the infantry. You know that. You never hear the one that gets you."

"Uh, but—"

"Think of it as a very large bullet, Slothrop. With fins."

"Jesus," teeth chattering, "you're such a comfort."

Tantivy, leaning anxiously through the smell of hops and the brown gloom, more worried now about Slothrop's shaking than any specter of his own, has nothing but established channels he happens to know of to try and conjure it away. "Why not see if we can get you out to where some of them have hit. . . ."

"What for? Come on, Tantivy, they're completely destroyed. Aren't they?"

"I don't know. I doubt even the Germans know. But it's the best chance we'll have to one-up that lot over in T.I. Isn't it."

Which is how Slothrop got into investigating V-bomb "incidents." Aftermaths. Each morning—at first—someone in Civil Defence routed ACHTUNG a list of yesterday's hits. It would come round to Slothrop last, he'd detach its pencil-smeared buck slip, go draw the same aging Humber from the motor pool, and make his rounds, a Saint George after the fact, going out to poke about for droppings of the Beast, fragments of German hardware that wouldn't exist, writing empty summaries into his notebooks—work-ther-apy. As inputs to ACHTUNG got faster, often he'd show up in time to help the search crews—following restless-muscled RAF dogs into the plaster smell, the gas leaking, the leaning long splinters and sagging mesh, the prone and noseless caryatids, rust already at nails and naked thread-surfaces, the powdery wipe of Nothing's hand across wall-paper awhisper with peacocks spreading their fans down deep lawns to Georgian houses long ago, to safe groves of holm oak . . . among the calls for silence following to where some exposed hand or brightness of skin waited them, survivor or casualty. When he couldn't help he stayed clear, praying, at first, conventionally to God, first time since the other Blitz, for life to win out. But too many were dying, and presently, seeing no point, he stopped.

Yesterday happened to be a good day. They found a

child, alive, a little girl, half-suffocated under a Morrison shelter. Waiting for the stretcher, Slothrop held her small hand, gone purple with the cold. Dogs barked in the street. When she opened her eyes and saw him her first words were, "Any gum, chum?" Trapped there for two days, gumless—all he had for her was a Thayer's Slippery Elm. He felt like an idiot. Before they took her off she brought his hand over to kiss anyway, her mouth and cheek in the flare lamps cold as frost, the city around them at once a big desolate icebox, stale-smelling and no surprises inside ever again. At which point she smiled, very faintly, and he knew that's what he'd been waiting for, wow, a Shirley Temple smile, as if this exactly canceled all they'd found her down in the middle of. What a damn fool thing. He hangs at the bottom of his blood's avalanche, 300 years of western swamp-Yankees, and can't manage but some nervous truce with their Providence. A *détente.* Ruins he goes daily to look in are each a sermon on vanity. That he finds, as weeks wear on, no least fragment of any rocket, preaches how indivisible is the act of death . . . Slothrop's Progress: London the secular city instructs him: turn any corner and he can find himself inside a parable.

He has become obsessed with the idea of a rocket with his name written on it—if they're really set on getting him ("They" embracing possibilities far far beyond Nazi Germany) that's the surest way, doesn't cost them a thing to paint his name *on every one, right?*

"Yes, well, that can be useful," Tantivy watching him funny, "can't it, especially in combat to, you know, *pretend* something like that. Jolly useful. Call it 'operational paranoia' or something. But—"

"Who's pretending?" lighting a cigarette, shaking his forelock through the smoke, "jeepers, Tantivy, listen, I don't want to upset you but . . . I mean I'm four years overdue's what it is, it could happen *any time,* the next second, right, just suddenly . . . shit . . . just zero, just nothing . . . and . . ."

It's nothing he can see or lay hands on—sudden gases, a violence upon the air and no trace afterward . . . a Word, spoken with no warning into your ear, and then silence forever. Beyond its invisibility, beyond hammerfall and

doomcrack, here is its real horror, mocking, promising him
death with German and precise confidence, laughing down
all of Tantivy's quiet decencies . . . no, no bullet with fins,
Ace . . . not the Word, the one Word that rips apart the
day. . . .

It was Friday evening, last September, just off work,
heading for the Bond Street Underground station, his
mind on the weekend ahead and his two Wrens, that
Norma and that Marjorie, whom he must each keep from
learning about the other, just as he was reaching to pick
his nose, suddenly in the sky, miles behind his back and
up the river *memento-mori* a sharp crack and a heavy
explosion, rolling right behind, almost like a clap of
thunder. But not quite. Seconds later, this time from in
front of him, it happened again: loud and clear, all over
the city. Bracketed. Not a buzzbomb, not that Luftwaffe.
"Not thunder either," he puzzled, out loud.

"Some bloody gas main," a lady with a lunchbox, puffy-
eyed from the day, elbowing him in the back as she
passed.

"No it's the *Germans*," her friend with rolled blonde
fringes under a checked kerchief doing some monster
routine here, raising her hands at Slothrop, "coming to get
him, they especially *love* fat, plump Americans—" in a
minute she'll be reaching out to pinch his cheek and
wobble it back and forth.

"Hi, glamorpuss," Slothrop said. Her name was Cynthia.
He managed to get a telephone number before she was
waving ta-ta, borne again into the rush-hour crowds.

It was one of those great iron afternoons in London: the
yellow sun being teased apart by a thousand chimneys
breathing, fawning upward without shame. This smoke is
more than the day's breath, more than dark strength—it is
an imperial presence that lives and moves. People were
crossing the streets and squares, going everywhere. Busses
were grinding off, hundreds of them, down the long concrete viaducts smeared with years' pitiless use and no
pleasure, into haze-gray, grease-black, red lead and pale
aluminum, between scrap heaps that towered high as
blocks of flats, down side-shoving curves into roads
clogged with Army convoys, other tall busses and canvas
lorries, bicycles and cars, everyone here with different

destinations and beginnings, all flowing, hitching now and
then, over it all the enormous gas ruin of the sun among
the smokestacks, the barrage balloons, power lines and
chimneys brown as aging indoor wood, brown growing
deeper, approaching black through an instant—perhaps
the true turn of the sunset—that is wine to you, wine and
comfort.

The Moment was 6:43:16 British Double Summer Time:
the sky, beaten like Death's drum, still humming, and
Slothrop's cock—say what? yes lookit inside his GI undershorts here's a sneaky *hardon* stirring, ready to jump—
well great God where'd *that* come from?

There is in his history, and likely, God help him, in his
dossier, a peculiar sensitivity to what is revealed in the
sky. (But a *hardon*?)

On the old schist of a tombstone in the Congregational
churchyard back home in Mingeborough, Massachusetts,
the hand of God emerges from a cloud, the edges of the
figure here and there eroded by 200 years of seasons' fire
and ice chisels at work, and the inscription reading:

> *In Memory of Conſtant*
> *Slothrop, who died March*
>
> *y̆ 4ᵗʰ 1766, in y̆ 29ᵗʰ*
> *year of his age.*
>
> *Death is a debt to nature due,*
> *Which I have paid, and ſo muſt you.*

Constant saw, and not only with his heart, that stone
hand pointing out of the secular clouds, pointing directly
at him, its edges traced in unbearable light, above the
whispering of his river and slopes of his long blue Berkshires, as would his son Variable Slothrop, indeed all of
the Slothrop blood one way or another, the nine or ten
generations tumbling back, branching inward: every one,
except for William the very first, lying under fallen leaves,
mint and purple loosestrife, chilly elm and willow shadows
over the swamp-edge graveyard in a long gradient of rot,
leaching, assimilation with the earth, the stones showing
round-faced angels with the long noses of dogs, toothy and
deep-socketed death's heads, Masonic emblems, flowery
urns, feathery willows upright and broken, exhausted hour-

glasses, sunfaces about to rise or set with eyes peeking
Kilroy-style over their horizon, and memorial verse running
from straight-on and foursquare, as for Constant Slothrop,
through bouncy Star Spangled Banner meter for Mrs.
Elizabeth, wife of Lt. Isaiah Slothrop (d. 1812):

> Adieu my dear friends, I have come to this grave
> Where Insatiate Death in his reaping hath brought me.
> Till Christ rise again all His children to save,
> I must lie, as His Word in the Scriptures hath taught me.
> Mark, Reader, my cry! Bend thy thoughts on the Sky,
> And in midst of prosperity, know thou may'st die.
> While the great Loom of God works in darkness above,
> And our trials here below are but threads of His Love.

To the current Slothrop's grandfather Frederick (d. 1933),
who in typical sarcasm and guile bagged his epitaph from
Emily Dickinson, without a credit line:

> Because I could not stop for Death
> He kindly stopped for me

Each one in turn paying his debt to nature due and leaving the excess to the next link in the name's chain. They
began as fur traders, cordwainers, salters and smokers of
bacon, went on into glassmaking, became selectmen, builders of tanneries, quarriers of marble. Country for miles
around gone to necropolis, gray with marble dust, dust
that was the breaths, the ghosts, of all those fake-Athenian
monuments going up elsewhere across the Republic. Always elsewhere. The money seeping its way out through
stock portfolios more intricate than any genealogy: what
stayed at home in Berkshire went into timberland whose
diminishing green reaches were converted acres at a clip
into paper—toilet paper, banknote stock, newsprint—a
medium or ground for shit, money, and the Word. They
were not aristocrats, no Slothrop ever made it into the
Social Register or the Somerset Club—they carried on
their enterprise in silence, assimilated in life to the dynamic that surrounded them thoroughly as in death they
would be to churchyard earth. Shit, money, and the Word,
the three American truths, powering the American mobility, claimed the Slothrops, clasped them for good to the
country's fate.

But they did not prosper ... about all they did was
persist—though it all began to go sour for them around
the time Emily Dickinson, never far way, was writing

> Ruin is formal, devil's work,
> Consecutive and slow—
> Fail in an instant no man did,
> Slipping is crash's law,

still they would keep on. The tradition, for others, was
clear, everyone knew—mine it out, work it, take all you
can till it's gone then move on west, there's plenty more.
But out of some reasoned inertia the Slothrops stayed east
in Berkshire, perverse—close to the flooded quarries and
logged-off hillsides they'd left like signed confessions across
all that thatchy-brown, moldering witch-country. The
profits slackening, the family ever multiplying. Interest
from various numbered trusts was still turned, by family
banks down in Boston every second or third generation,
back into yet another trust, in long rallentando, in infinite
series just perceptibly, term by term, dying ... but never
quite to the zero. ...

The Depression, by the time it came, ratified what'd
been under way. Slothrop grew up in a hilltop desolation
of businesses going under, hedges around the estates of
the vastly rich, half-mythical cottagers from New York
lapsing back now to green wilderness or straw death, all
the crystal windows every single one smashed, Harrimans
and Whitneys gone, lawns growing to hay, and the
autumns no longer a time for foxtrots in the distances,
limousines and lamps, but only the accustomed crickets
again, apples again, early frosts to send the hummingbirds
away, east wind, October rain: only winter certainties.

In 1931, the year of the Great Aspinwall Hotel Fire,
young Tyrone was visiting his aunt and uncle in Lenox.
It was in April, but for a second or two as he was coming
awake in the strange room and the racket of big and little
cousins' feet down the stairs, he thought of winter, because so often he'd been wakened like this, at this hour of
sleep, by Pop, or Hogan, bundled outside still blinking
through an overlay of dream into the cold to watch the
Northern Lights.

They scared the shit out of him. Were the radiant curtains just about to swing open? What would the ghosts of the North, in their finery, have to show him?

But this was a spring night, and the sky was gusting red, warm-orange, the sirens howling in the valleys from Pittsfield, Lenox, and Lee—neighbors stood out on their porches to stare up at the shower of sparks falling down on the mountainside . . . "Like a meteor shower," they said, "Like cinders from the Fourth of July . . ." it was 1931, and those were the comparisons. The embers fell on and on for five hours while kids dozed and grownups got to drink coffee and tell fire stories from other years.

But what Lights were these? What ghosts in command? And suppose, in the next moment, all of it, the complete night, *were* to go out of control and curtains part to show us a winter no one has guessed at. . . .

6:43:16 BDST—*in the sky right now* here is the same unfolding, just about to break through, his face deepening with its light, everything about to rush away and he to lose himself, just as his countryside has ever proclaimed . . . slender church steeples poised up and down all these autumn hillsides, white rockets about to fire, only seconds of countdown away, rose windows taking in Sunday light, elevating and washing the faces above the pulpits defining grace, swearing *this is how it does happen—yes the great bright hand reaching out of the cloud.* . . .

☐

On the wall, in an ornate fixture of darkening bronze, a gas jet burns, laminar and gently singing—adjusted to what scientists of the last century called a "sensitive flame": invisible at the base, as it issues from its orifice, fading upward into smooth blue light that hovers several inches above, a glimmering small cone that can respond to the most delicate changes in the room's air pressure. It registers visitors as they enter and leave, each curious and civil as if the round table held some game of chance. The circle of sitters is not at all distracted or hindered. None of your white hands or luminous trumpets here.

Camerons officers in parade trews, blue puttees, dress

kilts drift in conversing with enlisted Americans ... there
are clergymen, Home Guard or Fire Service just off duty,
folds of wool clothing heavy with smoke smell, everyone
grudging an hour's sleep and looking it ... ancient Edwardian ladies in crepe de Chine, West Indians softly
plaiting vowels round less flexible chains of Russian-Jewish
consonants. ... Most skate tangent to the holy circle, some
stay, some are off again to other rooms, all without breaking in on the slender medium who sits nearest the sensitive
flame with his back to the wall, reddish-brown curls tightening close as a skullcap, high forehead unwrinkled, dark
lips moving now effortless, now in pain:

"Once transected into the realm of Dominus Blicero,
Roland found that all the signs had turned against him. ...
Lights he had studied so well as one of you, position and
movement, now gathered there at the opposite end, all in
dance ... irrelevant dance. None of Blicero's traditional
progress, no something new ... alien. ... Roland too became conscious of the wind, as his mortality had never
allowed him. Discovered it so ... so joyful, that the arrow
must veer into it. The wind had been blowing all year
long, year after year, but Roland had felt only the secular
wind ... he means, only his personal wind. Yet ... Selena,
the wind, the wind's everywhere. ..."

Here the medium breaks off, is silent awhile ... one
groan ... a quiet, desperate moment. "Selena. Selena.
Have you gone, then?"

"No, my dear," her cheeks mottled with previous tears,
"I'm listening."

"It's control. All these things arise from one difficulty:
control. For the first time it was *inside*, do you see. The
control is put inside. No more need to suffer passively
under 'outside forces'—to veer into any wind. As if ...

"A market needed no longer be run by the Invisible
Hand, but now could *create itself*—its own logic, momentum, style, from *inside*. Putting the control inside was
ratifying what de facto had happened—that you had dis-
pensed with God. But you had taken on a greater, and
more harmful, illusion. The illusion of control. That A
could do B. But that was false. Completely. No one can
do. Things only happen, A and B are unreal, are names
for parts that ought to be inseparable. ..."

"More Ouspenskian nonsense," whispers a lady brushing by on the arm of a dock worker. Odors of Diesel fuel and Sous le Vent mingle as they pass. Jessica Swanlake, a young rosy girl in the uniform of an ATS private, noticing the prewar perfume, looks up, hmm, the frock she imagines is about 15 guineas and who knows how many coupons, probably from Harrods *and would do more for me,* she's also sure. The lady, suddenly looking back over her shoulder, smiles oh, yes? My gosh, did she hear? Around *this* place almost certainly.

Jessica's been standing near the séance table with a handful of darts idly plucked from the board on the wall, her head bent, pale nape and top vertebra visible above the brown wool collar and through some of her lighter brown hair, fallen either side along her cheeks. Brass throats and breasts warm to her blood, quake in the hollow of her hand. She seems herself, gentling their feathered crosses, brushing with fingertips, to have slid into a shallow trance. . . .

Outside, rolling from the east, comes the muffled rip of another rocket bomb. The windows rattle, the floor shakes. The sensitive flame dives for shelter, shadows across the table sent adance, darkening toward the other room—then it leaps high, the shadows drawing inward again, fully two feet, and disappears completely. Gas hisses on in the dim room. Milton Gloaming, who achieved perfect tripos at Cambridge ten years ago, abandons his shorthand to rise and go shut the gas off.

It seems the right moment now for Jessica to throw a dart: one dart. Hair swinging, breasts bobbing marvelously beneath each heavy wool lapel. A hiss of air, whack: into the sticky fibers, into the dead center. Milton Gloaming cocks an eyebrow. His mind, always gathering correspondences, thinks it has found a new one.

The medium, irritable now, has begun to drift back out of his trance. Anybody's guess what's happening over on the other side. This sitting, like any, needs not only its congenial circle here and secular, but also a basic, four-way entente which oughtn't, any link of it, be broken: Roland Feldspath (the spirit), Peter Sachsa (the control), Carroll Eventyr (the medium), Selena (the wife and survivor). Somewhere, through exhaustion, redirection,

gusts of white noise out in the aether, this arrangement has
begun now to dissolve. Relaxation, chairs squeaking, sighs
and throatclearings ... Milton Gloaming fusses with his
notebook, shuts it abruptly.

Presently Jessica comes wandering over. No sign of
Roger and she's not sure he wants her to come looking for
him, and Gloaming, though shy, isn't as horrid as some of
Roger's other friends. ...

"Roger says that now you'll count up all those words
you copied and graph them or something," brightly to head
off any comment on the dart incident, which she'd rather
avoid. "Do you do it only for séances?"

"Automatic texts," girl-nervous Gloaming frowns, nods,
"one or two Ouija-board episodes, yes yes ... we-we're
trying to develop a vocabulary of curves—certain pa-
thologies, certain characteristic shapes you see—"

"I'm not sure that I—"

"Well. Recall Zipf's Principle of Least Effort: if we plot
the frequency of a word P sub n against its rank-order n
on logarithmic axes," babbling into her silence, even her
bewilderment graceful, "we should of course get something like a straight line ... however we've data that suggest the curves for certain—conditions, well they're
actually quite different—schizophrenics for example tend
to run a bit flatter in the upper part then progressively
steeper—a sort of bow shape ... I think with this chap,
this Roland, that we're on to a classical paranoiac—"

"Ha." *That's* a word she knows. "Thought I saw you
brighten up there when he said 'turned against.'"

"'Against,' 'opposite,' yes you'd be amazed at the frequency with this one."

"What's the *most* frequent word?" asks Jessica. "Your
number one."

"The same as it's always been at these affairs," replies
the statistician, as if everyone knew: "death."

An elderly air-raid warden, starchy and frail as organdy,
stands on tiptoe to relight the sensitive flame.

"Incidentally, ah, where's your mad young gentleman
gone off to?"

"Roger's with Captain Prentice." Waving vaguely. "The
usual Mysterious Microfilm Drill." Being transacted in
some distant room, across a crown-and-anchor game with

which chance has very little to do, billows of smoke and chatter, Falkman and His Apache Band subdued over the BBC, chunky pints and slender sherry glasses, winter rain at the windows. Time for closeting, gas logs, shawls against the cold night, snug with your young lady or old dutch or, as here at Snoxall's, in good company. Here's a shelter— perhaps a real node of tranquillity among several scattered throughout this long wartime, where they're gathering for purposes not entirely in the martial interest.

Pirate Prentice feels something of this, obliquely, by way of class nervousness really: he bears his grin among these people here like a phalanx. He learned it at the films—it is the exact mischievous Irish grin your Dennis Morgan chap goes about cocking down at the black smoke vomiting from each and every little bucktooth yellow rat he shoots down.

It's as useful to him as he is to the Firm—who, it is well known, will use anyone, traitors, murderers, perverts, Negroes, even women, to get what They want. They may not've been that sure of Pirate's usefulness at first, but later, as it developed, They were to grow very sure, indeed.

"Major-General, you can't actually give your support to this."

"We're watching him around the clock. He certainly isn't leaving the premises physically."

"Then he has a confederate. Somehow—hypnosis, drugs, I don't know—they're getting to his man and tranquilizing him. For God's sake, next you'll be consulting horoscopes."

"Hitler does."

"Hitler is an inspired man. But you and I are employees, remember. . . ."

After that first surge of interest, the number of clients assigned to Pirate tapered off some. At the moment he carries what he feels is a comfortable case load. But it's not what he really wants. They will not understand, the gently bred maniacs of S.O.E. *ah very good, Captain* rattling sitreps, shuffling boots, echoes off of Government eyeglasses *jolly good and why not do it actually for us sometime at the Club.* . . .

Pirate wants Their trust, the good-whisky-and-cured-Latakia scent of Their rough love. He wants understand-

ing from his *own* lot, not these bookish sods and rationalized freaks here at Snoxall's, so dedicated to Science, so
awfully tolerant that this (he regrets it with all his heart)
may be the only place in the reach of war's empire that he
does feel less than a stranger. . . .

"It's not at all clear," Roger Mexico's been saying,
"what they have in mind, not at all, the Witchcraft Act's
more than 200 years old, it's a relic of an entirely different
age, another way of thinking. Suddenly here we are 1944
being hit with convictions right and left. Our Mr. Eventyr," motioning at the medium who's across the room
chatting with young Gavin Trefoil, "could be fallen upon
at any moment—pouring in the windows, hauling dangerous tough Eventyr away to the Scrubs on pretending - to -
exercise - or - use - a - kind - of - conjuration - to - cause - the -
spirits - of - deceased - persons - to - be - present - in - fact -
at- the - place - where - he - then - was - and - that - those -
spirits - were - communicating - with - living - persons - then -
and - there - present my God what imbecile Fascist *rot* . . ."

"Careful, Mexico, you're losing the old objectivity
again—a man of science shouldn't want to do that, should
he. Hardly scientific, is it."

"Ass. You're on *their* side. Couldn't you feel it tonight,
coming in the door? It's a great swamp of paranoia."

"That's my talent, all right," Pirate as he speaks knowing it's too abrupt, tries to file off the flash with: "I don't
know that I'm really up to the *multiple* sort of thing. . . ."

"Ah. Prentice." Not an eyebrow or lip out of place.
Tolerance. Ah.

"You ought to come down this time and have our Dr.
Groast check it out on his EEG."

"Oh, if I'm in town," vaguely. There's a security problem here. Loose talk sinks ships and he can't be sure, even
about Mexico. There are too many circles to the current
operation, inner and outer. Distribution lists growing narrower as we move ring by ring toward the bull's eye, Instructions To Destroy gradually encompassing every scrap,
idle memo, typewriter ribbon.

His best guess is that Mexico only now and then sup-
ports the Firm's latest mania, known as Operation Black
Wing, in a statistical way—analyzing what foreign-morale

data may come in, for instance—but someplace out at the
fringes of the enterprise, as indeed Pirate finds himself
here tonight, acting as go-between for Mexico and his
own roommate Teddy Bloat.

He knows that Bloat goes somewhere and microfilms
something, then transfers it, via Pirate, to young Mexico.
And thence, he gathers, down to "The White Visitation,"
which houses a catchall agency known as PISCES—
Psychological Intelligence Schemes for Expediting Surrender. Whose surrender is not made clear.

Pirate wonders if Mexico isn't into yet another of the
thousand dodgy intra-Allied surveillance schemes that
have sprung up about London since the Americans, and a
dozen governments in exile, moved in. In which the German curiously fades into irrelevance. Everyone watching
over his shoulder, Free French plotting revenge on Vichy
traitors, Lublin Communists drawing beads on Varsovian
shadow-ministers, ELAS Greeks stalking royalists, un-
repatriable dreamers of all languages hoping through will,
fists, prayer to bring back kings, republics, pretenders,
summer anarchisms that perished before the first crops
were in ... some dying wretchedly, nameless, under ice-
and-snow surfaces of bomb craters out in the East End not
to be found till spring, some chronically drunk or opiated
for getting through the day's reverses, most somehow
losing, losing what souls they had, less and less able to
trust, seized in the game's unending chatter, its daily self-
criticism, its demands for total attention ... and what
foreigner is it, exactly, that Pirate has in mind if it isn't
that stateless lascar across his own mirror-glass, that poorest of exiles. ...

Well: he guesses They have euchred Mexico into some
such Byzantine exercise, probably to do with the Americans. Perhaps the Russians. "The White Visitation," being
devoted to psychological warfare, harbors a few of each, a
Behaviorist here, a Pavlovian there. It's none of Pirate's
business. But he notes that with each film delivery, Roger's
enthusiasm grows. Unhealthy, unhealthy: he has the sense
of witnessing an addiction. He feels that his friend, his
provisional wartime friend, is being used for something not
quite decent.

What can he do? If Mexico wanted to talk about it he

could find a way, security or not. His reluctance is not Pirate's own over the machinery of Operation Black Wing. It looks more like shame. Wasn't Mexico's face tonight, as he took the envelope, averted? eyes boxing the corners of the room at top speed, a pornography customer's reflex . . . hmm. Knowing Bloat, perhaps that's what it is, young lady gamming well-set-up young man, several poses—more wholesome than anything this war's ever photographed . . . life, at least. . . .

There's Mexico's girl, just entering the room. He spots her immediately, the clarity around her, the absence of smoke and noise . . . is he seeing auras now? She catches sight of Roger and smiles, her eyes enormous . . . dark-lashed, no make-up or none Pirate can see, her hair worn in a roll down to the shoulders—what the hell's she doing in a mixed AA battery? She ought to be in a NAAFI canteen, filling coffee cups. He is suddenly, dodderer and ass, taken by an ache in his skin, a simple love for them both that asks nothing but their safety, and that he'll always manage to describe as something else—"concern," you know, "fondness. . . ."

In 1936, Pirate ("a T. S. Eliot April" she called it, though it was a colder time of year) was in love with an executive's wife. She was a thin, speedy stalk of a girl named Scorpia Mossmoon. Her husband Clive was an expert in plastics, working out of Cambridge for Imperial Chemicals. Pirate, the career soldier, was having a year or two's relapse or fling outside in civilian life.

He'd got the feeling, stationed east of Suez, places like Bahrein, drinking beer watered with his own falling sweat in the perpetual stink of crude oil across from Muharraq, restricted to quarters after sundown—98% venereal rate anyway—one sunburned, scroungy unit of force preserving the Sheik and the oil money against any threat from east of the English Channel, horny, mad with the itching of lice and heat rash (masturbating under these conditions is exquisite torture), bitter-drunk all the time—even so there had leaked through to Pirate a dim suspicion that life was passing him by.

Incredible black-and-white Scorpia confirmed not a few Piratical fantasies about the glamorous silken-calved English realworld he'd felt so shut away from. They got together while Clive was away on a troubleshooting mission for ICI in, of all places, Bahrein. The symmetry of this helped Pirate relax about it some. They would attend parties as strangers, though she never learned to arm herself against unexpected sight of him across a room (trying to belong, as if he were not someone's employee). She found him touching in his ignorance of everything—partying, love, money—felt worldly and desperately caring for this moment of boyhood among his ways imperialized and set (he was 33), his pre-Austerity, in which Scorpia figured as his Last Fling—though herself too young to know *that*, to know, like Pirate, what the lyrics to "Dancing in the Dark" are *really* about....

He will be scrupulous about never telling her. But there are times when it's agony not to go to her feet, knowing she won't leave Clive, crying *you're my last chance ... if it can't be you then there's no more time....* Doesn't he wish, against all hope, that he *could* let the poor, Westernman's timetable go ... but how does a man ... where does he even begin, at age 33.... "But that's just *it*," she'd have laughed, not so much annoyed (she *would have* laughed) as tickled by the unreality of the problem—herself too lost at the manic edge of him, always at *engage*, so taking, cleaving her (for more than when jerking off into an Army flannel in the Persian Gulf was some collar of love's nettles now *at* him, at his cock), too unappeasable for her not to give in to the insanity of, but too insane really even not to think of as any betrayal of Clive....

Convenient as hell for her, anyway. Roger Mexico is now going through much the same thing with Jessica, the Other Chap in this case being known as Beaver. Pirate has looked on but never talked about it to Mexico. Yes he is waiting, to see if it will end for Roger the same way, part of him, never so cheery as at the spectacle of another's misfortune, rooting for Beaver and all that he, like Clive, stands for, to win out. But another part—an alternate self?—one that he mustn't be quick to call "decent"—does *seem* to want for Roger what Pirate himself lost....

"You *are* a pirate," she'd whispered the last day—neither of them knew it was the last day—"you've come and taken me off on your pirate ship. A girl of good family and the usual repressions. You've raped me. And I'm the

Red Bitch of the High Seas. . . ." A lovely game. Pirate
wished she'd thought it up sooner. Fucking the last (already the last) day's light away down afternoon to dusk,
hours of fucking, too in love with it to uncouple, they
noticed how the borrowed room rocked gently, the ceiling
obligingly came down a foot, lamps swayed from their
fittings, some fraction of the Thameside traffic provided
salty cries over the water, and nautical bells. . . .

But back over their lowering sky-sea behind, Government hounds were on the track—drawing closer, the cutters are coming, the cutters and the sleek hermaphrodites
of the law, agents who, being old hands, will settle for her
safe return, won't insist on his execution or capture. Their
logic is sound: give him a bad enough wound and he'll
come round, round to the ways of this hard-boiled old egg
of world and timetables, cycling night to compromise
night. . . .

He left her at Waterloo Station. A gala crowd was
there, to see Fred Roper's Company of Wonder Midgets
off to an imperial fair in Johannesburg, South Africa. Midgets in their dark winter clothes, exquisite little frocks and
nip-waisted overcoats, were running all over the station,
gobbling their bonvoyage chocolates and lining up for
news photos. Scorpia's talc-white face, through the last
window, across the last gate, was a blow to his heart. A
flurry of giggles and best wishes arose from the Wonder
Midgets and their admirers. Well, thought Pirate, guess
I'll go back in the Army. . . .

□

They're bound eastward now, Roger peering over the
wheel, hunched Dracula-style inside his Burberry, Jessica
with bright millions of droplets still clinging in soft net to
her shoulders and sleeves of drab wool. They want to be
together, in bed, at rest, in love, and instead it's eastward
tonight and south of the Thames to rendezvous with a
certain high-class vivisectionist before the clock of St.
Felix chimes one. And when the mice run down, who
knows tonight but what they've run for good?

Her face against the breath-fogged window has become
another dimness, another light-trick of the winter. Beyond

her, the white fracture of the rain passes. "Why does he go out and pinch all his dogs in person? He's an administrator, isn't he? Wouldn't he hire a boy or something?"

"We call them 'staff,'" Roger replies, "and I don't know why Pointsman does anything he does, he's a Pavlovian, love. He's a Royal Fellow. What am I supposed to know about any of those people? They're as difficult as the lot back in Snoxall's."

They're both of them peevish tonight, whippy as sheets of glass improperly annealed, ready to go smash at any indefinite touch in a whining matrix of stresses—

"Poor Roger, poor lamb, he's having an awful war."

"All right," his head shaking, a fuming b or p that refuses to explode, "ahh, you're so clever aren't you," raving Roger, hands off the wheel to help the words out, windscreen wipers clicking right along, "you've been able to shoot back now and then at the odd flying buzz bomb, you and the boy friend dear old Nutria—"

"*Beaver.*"

"Quite right, and all that magnificent esprit you lot are so justly famous for, but you haven't brought down many *rockets* lately have you, haha!" gurning his most spiteful pursed smile up against wrinkled nose and eyes, "any more than I, any more than Pointsman, well who's that make purer than whom *these* days, eh mylove?" bouncing up and down in the leather seat.

By now her hand's reaching out, about to touch his shoulder. She rests her cheek on her own arm, hair spilling, drowsy, watching him. Can't get a decent argument going with her. How he's tried. She uses her silences like stroking hands to divert him and hush their corners of rooms, bedcovers, tabletops—accidental spaces. . . . Even at the cinema watching that awful *Going My Way*, the day they met, he saw every white straying of her ungauntleted hands, could feel in his skin each saccade of her olive, her amber, her coffee-colored eyes. He's wasted gallons of paint thinner striking his faithful Zippo, its charred wick, virility giving way to thrift, rationed down to a little stub, the blue flame sparking about the edges in the dark, the many kinds of dark, just to see what's happening with her face. Each new flame, a new face.

And there've been the moments, more of them lately too—times when face-to-face there has been no way to

tell which of them is which. Both at the same time feeling
the same eerie confusion ... something like looking in a
mirror by surprise but ... more than that, the feeling of
actually being joined ... when after—who knows? two
minutes, a week? they realize, separate again, what's been
going on, that Roger and Jessica were merged into a joint
creature unaware of itself.... In a life he has cursed,
again and again, for its need to believe so much in the
trans-observable, here is the first, the very first real magic:
data he can't argue away.

It was what Hollywood likes to call a "cute meet," out in
the neat 18th-century heart of downtown Tunbridge Wells,
Roger motoring in the vintage Jaguar up to London,
Jessica at the roadside struggling prettily with a busted
bicycle, murky wool ATS skirt hiked up on a handle bar,
most nonregulation black slip and clear pearl thighs above
the khaki stockings, well—

"Here love," brakes on in a high squeak, "it's not backstage at the old Windmill or something, you know."

She knew. "Hmm," a curl dropping down to tickle her
nose and put a bit more than the usual acid in her reply,
"are they letting little boys into places like that, I didn't
know."

"Well nobody's," having learned by now to live with
remarks about his appearance, "called up the Girl Guides
yet either, have they."

"I'm twenty."

"Hurrah, that qualifies you for a ride, in this Jaguar
here you see, all the way to London."

"But I'm going the other way. Nearly to Battle."

"Oh, round trip of course."

Shaking hair back out of her face, "Does your mother
know *you're* out like this."

"My mother is the war," declares Roger Mexico, leaning
over to open the door.

"That's a queer thing to say," one muddy little shoe
pondering on the running board.

"Come along, love, you're holding up the mission, leave
the machine where it is, mind your skirt getting in, I
wouldn't want to commit an unspeakable act out here in
the streets of Tunbridge Wells—"

At which moment the rocket falls. Cute, cute. A thud, a
hollow drumroll. Far enough toward the city to be safe,

but close and loud enough to send her the hundred miles between herself and the stranger: long-swooping, balletic, her marvelous round bottom turning to settle in the other seat, hair in a moment's fan, hand sweeping Army-colored skirt under graceful as a wing, all with the blast still reverberating.

He thinks he can see a solemn gnarled something, deeper or changing faster than clouds, rising to the north. Will she snuggle now cutely against him, ask him to protect her? He didn't even believe she'd get in the car, rocket or no rocket, accordingly now puts Pointsman's Jaguar somehow into reverse instead of low, yes, backs over the bicycle, rendering it in a great crunch useless for anything but scrap.

"I'm in your power," she cries. "*Utterly.*"

"Hmm," Roger at length finding his gear, dancing among the pedals rrrn, snarl, off to London. But Jessica's not in his power.

And the war, well, she *is* Roger's mother, she's leached at all the soft, the vulnerable inclusions of hope and praise scattered, beneath the mica-dazzle, through Roger's mineral, grave-marker self, washed it all moaning away on her gray tide. Six years now, always just in sight, just where he can see her. He's forgotten his first corpse, or when he first saw someone living die. That's how long it's been going on. Most of his life, it seems. The city he visits nowadays is Death's antechamber: where all the paperwork's done, the contracts signed, the days numbered. Nothing of the grand, garden, adventurous capital his childhood knew. He's become the Dour Young Man of "The White Visitation," the spider hitching together his web of numbers. It's an open secret that he doesn't get on with the rest of his section. How can he? They're all wild talents—clairvoyants and mad magicians, telekinetics, astral travelers, gatherers of light. Roger's only a satistician. Never had a prophetic dream, never sent or got a telepathic message, never touched the Other World directly. If anything's there it will show in the experimental data won't it, in the numbers . . . but that's as close or clear as he'll ever get. Any wonder he's a bit short with Psi Section, all the definitely 3-sigma lot up and down his basement corridor? Jesus Christ, wouldn't you be?

That one clear need of theirs, so patent, exasperates

him. . . . *His* need too, all right. But how are you ever going to put anything "psychical" on a scientific basis with your mortality always goading, just outside the chi-square calculations, in between the flips of the Zener cards and the silences among the medium's thick, straining utterances? In his mellower moments he thinks that continuing to try makes him brave. But most of the time he's cursing himself for not working in fire control, or graphing Standardized Kill Rates Per Ton for the bomber groups . . . *anything* but this thankless meddling into the affairs of invulnerable Death. . . .

They have drawn near a glow over the rooftops. Fire Service vehicles come roaring by them, heading the same direction. It is an oppressive region of brick streets and silent walls.

Roger brakes for a crowd of sappers, firefighters, neighbors in dark coats over white nightclothes, old ladies who have a special place in their night-thoughts for the Fire Service *no please you're not going to use that great Hose on me . . . oh no . . . aren't you even going to take off those horrid rubber boots . . . yesyes that's—*

Soldiers stand every few yards, a loose cordon, unmoving, a bit supernatural. The Battle of Britain was hardly so formal. But these new robot bombs bring with them chances for public terror no one has sounded. Jessica notes a coal-black Packard up a side street, filled with dark-suited civilians. Their white collars rigid in the shadows.

"Who're they?"

He shrugs: "they" is good enough. "Not a friendly lot."

"Look who's talking." But their smile is old, habitual. There was a time when his job had her a bit mental: lovely little scrapbooks on the flying bombs, how sweet. . . . And his irritated sigh: Jess don't make me out some cold fanatical man of science. . . .

Heat beats at their faces, eye-searing yellow when the streams shoot into the fire. A ladder hooked to the edge of the roof sways in the violent drafts. Up top, against the sky, figures in slickers brace, wave arms, move together to pass orders. Half a block down, flare lamps illuminate the rescue work in the charry wet wreckage. From trailer pumps and heavy units, canvas hoses run fat with pressure, hastily threaded unions sending out stars of cold spray, bitter cold, that flash yellow when the fire leaps. Somewhere over a radio comes a woman's voice, a quiet Yorkshire girl, dispatching other units to other parts of the city.

Once Roger and Jessica might have stopped. But they're both alumni of the Battle of Britain, both have been drafted into the early black mornings and the crying for mercy, the dumb inertia of cobbles and beams, the profound shortage of mercy in those days.... By the time one has pulled one's nth victim or part of a victim free of one's nth pile of rubble, he told her once, angry, weary, it has ceased to be that personal ... the value of n may be different for each of us, but I'm sorry: sooner or later ...

And past the exhaustion with it there is also this. If they have not quite seceded from war's state, at least they've found the beginnings of gentle withdrawal ... there's never been the space or time to talk about it, and perhaps no need—but both know, clearly, it's better together, snuggled in, than back out in the paper, fires, khaki, steel of the Home Front. That, indeed, the Home Front is something of a fiction and lie, designed, not too subtly, to draw them apart, to subvert love in favor of work, abstraction, required pain, bitter death.

They have found a house in the stay-away zone, under the barrage balloons south of London. The town, evacuated in '40, is still "regulated"—still on the Ministry's list. Roger and Jessica occupy the place illegally, in a defiance they can never measure unless they're caught. Jessica has brought an old doll, seashells, her aunt's grip filled with lace knickers and silk stockings. Roger's managed to scare up a few chickens to nest in the empty garage. Whenever they meet here, one always remembers to bring a fresh flower or two. The nights are filled with explosion and motor transport, and wind that brings them up over the downs a last smack of the sea. Day begins with a hot cup and a cigarette over a little table with a weak leg that Roger has repaired, provisionally, with brown twine. There's never much talk but touches and looks, smiles together, curses for parting. It is marginal, hungry, chilly—most times they're too paranoid to risk a fire—but it's something they want to keep, so much that to keep it they will take on more than propaganda has ever asked them for. They are in love. Fuck the war.

□

Tonight's quarry, whose name will be Vladimir (or Ilya,
Sergei, Nikolai, depending on the doctor's whim), slinks
carefully toward the cellar entrance. This jagged opening
ought to lead to something deep and safe. He has the
memory, or reflex, of escaping into similar darkness from
an Irish setter who smells of coal smoke and will attack
on sight . . . once from a pack of children, recently from a
sudden blast of noiselight, a fall of masonry that caught
him on the left hindquarter (still raw, still needs licking).
But tonight's threat is something new: not so violent, instead a systematic stealth he isn't used to. Life out here is
more direct.

It's raining. The wind hardly flickers. It brings a scent
he finds strange, never having been near a laboratory in
his life.

The smell is ether, it emanates from Mr. Edward W. A.
Pointsman, F.R.C.S. As the dog vanishes around the
broken remnant of a wall, just as the tip of his tail flicks
away, the doctor steps into the white waiting throat of a
toilet bowl he has not, so intent on his prey, seen. He
bends over, awkwardly, tugging loose the bowl from its
surrounding debris, muttering oaths against all the care-
less, meaning not himself, particularly, but the owners of
this ruined flat (if they weren't killed in the blast) or
whoever failed to salvage this bowl, which seems, actually,
to be wedged on rather tight. . . .

Mr. Pointsman drags his leg over to a shattered staircase, swings it quietly, so as not to alarm the dog, against
the lower half of a fumed-oak newel post. The bowl only
clanks back, the wood shudders. Mocking him—all right.
He sits on stairsteps ascending to open sky and attempts to
pull the damned thing loose of his foot. It will not come.
He hears the invisible dog, toenails softly clicking, gain
the sanctuary of the cellar. He can't reach inside the
toilet bowl even to untie his fucking *boot.* . . .

Settling the window of his Balaclava helmet snug and
tickling just under his nose, resolved not to give way to
panic, Mr. Pointsman stands up, has to wait for blood to

drain, resurge, bounce up and down its million branches
in the drizzly night, percolate to balance—then limping,
clanking, he heads back toward the car to get a hand from
young Mexico, who did remember, he hopes, to bring the
electric lantern. . . .

Roger and Jessica found him a bit earlier, lurking at the
end of a street of row houses. The V-bomb whose mutila-
tion he was prowling took down four dwellings the other
day, four exactly, neat as surgery. There is the soft smell
of house-wood down before its time, of ashes matted
down by the rain. Ropes are strung, a sentry lounges
silent against the doorway of an intact house next to where
the rubble begins. If he and the doctor have chatted at
all, neither gives a sign now. Jessica sees two eyes of no
particular color glaring out the window of a Balaclava
helmet, and is reminded of a mediaeval knight wearing a
casque. What creature is he possibly here tonight to fight
for his king? The rubble waits him, sloping up to broken
rear walls in a clogging, an open-work of laths pointlessly
chevroning—flooring, furniture, glass, chunks of plaster,
long tatters of wallpaper, split and shattered joists: some
woman's long-gathered nest, taken back to separate straws,
flung again to this wind and this darkness. Back in the
wreckage a brass bedpost winks; and twined there someone's brassiere, a white, prewar confection of lace and
satin, simply left tangled. . . . For an instant, in a vertigo
she can't control, all the pity laid up in her heart flies to
it, as it would to a small animal stranded and forgotten.
Roger has the boot of the car open. The two men are
rummaging, coming up with large canvas sack, flask of
ether, net, dog whistle. She knows she must not cry: that
the vague eyes in the knitted window won't seek their
Beast any more earnestly for her tears. But the poor lost
flimsy thing . . . waiting in the night and rain for its
owner, for its room to reassemble round it . . .

The night, full of fine rain, smells like a wet dog. Pointsman seems to've been away for a bit. "I've lost my mind.
I ought to be cuddling someplace with Beaver this very
minute, watching him light up his Pipe, and here instead
I'm with this *gillie* or something, this spiritualist, statistician, what *are* you anyway—"

"Cuddling?" Roger has a tendency to scream. "*Cuddling?*"

"Mexico." It's the doctor, sighing, toilet bowl on his foot and knitted helmet askew.

"Hello, doesn't that make it difficult for you to walk? should think it would . . . up here, first get it in the door, this way, and, ah, good," then closing the door again around Pointsman's ankle, the bowl now occupying Roger's seat, Roger half-resting on Jessica's lap, "tug now, hard as ever you can."

Thinking *young prig* and *mocking ass* the doctor rocks back on his free leg, grunting, the bowl wallowing to and fro. Roger holds the door and peers attentively into where the foot vanished. "If we had a bit of Vaseline, we could— something slippery. Wait! Stay there, Pointsman, don't move, we'll have this resolved. . . ." Under the car, impulsive lad, in search of the crankcase plug by the time Pointsman can say, "There isn't *time* Mexico, he'll escape, he'll escape."

"Quite right." Up again fumbling a flashlight from his jacket pocket. "I'll flush him out, you wait with the net. Sure you can get about all right? Nasty if you fell or something just as he made his break for the open."

"For pity's sake," Pointsman thumping after him back into the wreckage. "Don't frighten him Mexico, this isn't Kenya or something, we need him as close to normative, you know, as possible."

Normative? *Normative?*

"Roger," calls Roger, giving him short-long-short with the flash.

"Jessica," murmurs Jessica, tiptoeing behind them.

"Here, fellow," coaxes Roger. "Nice bottle of *ether* here for you," opening the flask, waving it in the cellar entrance, then switching on his beam. Dog looks up out of an old rusted pram, bobbing black shadows, tongue hanging, utter skepticism on his face. "Why it's Mrs. Nussbaum!" Roger cries, the same way he's heard Fred Allen do, Wednesday nights over the BBC.

"You vere ekshpecting maybe *Lessie?*" replies the dog.

Roger can smell ether fumes quite strongly as he starts his cautious descent. "*Come* on mate, it'll be over before you know it. Pointsman just wants to count the old drops of saliva, that's all. Wants to make a wee incision in your cheek, nice glass tube, nothing to bother about, right? Ring a bell now and then. Exciting world of the laboratory, you'll love it." Ether seems to be getting to him. He tries to stopper the flask: takes a step, foot plunges into a hole. Lurching sideways, he gropes for something to steady himself. The stopper falls back out of the flask and in forever among the debris at the bottom of the smashed house. Overhead Pointsman cries, "The sponge, Mexico, you forgot the *sponge!*" down comes a round pale collection of holes, bouncing in and out of the light of the flash. "Frisky chap," Roger making a two-handed grab for it, splashing ether liberally about. He locates the sponge at last in his flashlight beam, the dog looking on from the pram in some confusion. "Hah!" pouring ether to drench the sponge and go wisping cold off his hand till the flask's empty. Taking the wet sponge between two fingers he staggers toward the dog, shining the light up from under his chin to highlight the vampire face he thinks he's making. "Moment—of truth!" He lunges. The dog leaps off at an angle, streaking past Roger toward the entrance while Roger keeps going with his sponge, headfirst into the pram, which collapses under his weight. Dimly he hears the doctor above whimper, "He's getting away. Mexico, do hurry."

"Hurry." Roger, clutching the sponge, extricates himself from the infant's vehicle, taking it off as if it were a shirt, with what seems to him not unathletic skill.

"Mexico-o-o," plaintive.

"Right," Roger blundering up the cellar's rubble to the outside again, where he beholds the doctor closing in on the dog, net held aloft and outspread. Rain falls persistently over this tableau. Roger circles so as to make with Pointsman a pincer upon the animal, who now stands with paws planted and teeth showing near one of the pieces of rear wall still standing. Jessica waits halfway into it, hands in her pockets, smoking, watching.

"Here," hollers the sentry, "you. You idiots. Keep away from that bit of wall, there's nothing to hold it up."

"Do you have any cigarettes?" asks Jessica.

"He's going to bolt," Roger screams.

"For God's sake, Mexico, slowly now." Testing each

footstep, they move upslope over the ruin's delicate balance. It's a system of lever arms that can plunge them into deadly collapse at any moment. They draw near their quarry, who scrutinizes now the doctor, now Roger, with quick shifts of his head. He growls tentatively, tail keeping up a steady slap against the two sides of the corner they've backed him into.

As Roger, who carries the light, moves rearward, the dog, some circuit of him, recalls the other light that came from behind in recent days—the light that followed the great blast so seethed through afterward by pain and cold. Light from the rear signals death / men with nets about to leap can be avoided—

"Sponge," screams the doctor. Roger flings himself at the dog, who has taken off in Pointsman's direction and away toward the street whilst Pointsman, groaning, swings his toiletbowl foot desperately, misses, momentum carrying him around a full turn, net up like a radar antenna. Roger, snoot full of ether, can't check his lunge—as the doctor comes spinning round again Roger careens on into him, toilet bowl hitting Roger a painful thump in the leg. The two men fall over, tangled in the net now covering them. Broken beams creak, chungs of rain-wet plaster tumble. Above them the unsupported wall begins to sway.

"Get out of there," hollers the sentry. But the efforts of the pair under the net to move away only rock the wall more violently.

"We're for it," the doctor shivers. Roger seeks his eyes to see if he means it, but the window of the Balaclava helmet now contains only a white ear and fringe of hair.

"Roll," Roger suggests. They contrive to roll a few yards down toward the street, by which time part of the wall has collapsed, in the other direction. They manage to get back to Jessica without causing any more damage.

"He's run down the street," she mentions, helping them out of the net.

"It's all right," the doctor sighs. "It doesn't make any difference."

"Ah but the evening's *young*," from Roger.

"No, no. Forget it."

"What will you do for a dog, then."

They are under way again, Roger at the wheel, Jessica

between them, toilet bowl out a half-open door, before the answer. "Perhaps it's a sign. Perhaps I should be branching out."

Roger gives him a quick look. Silence, Mexico. Try not to think about what *that* means. He's not one's superior after all, both report to the old Brigadier at "The White Visitation" on, so far as he knows, equal footing. But sometimes—Roger glances again across Jessica's dark wool bosom at the knitted head, the naked nose and eyes—he thinks the doctor wants more than his good will, his collaboration. But wants *him*. As one wants a fine specimen of dog. . . .

Why's he here, then, assisting at yet another dognapping? What stranger does he shelter in him so mad—

"Will you be going back down tonight, doctor? The young lady needs a ride."

"I shan't, I'll be staying in. But you might take the car back. I must talk with Dr. Spectro."

They are approaching now a lengthy brick improvisation, a Victorian paraphrase of what once, long ago, resulted in Gothic cathedrals—but which, in its own time, arose not from any need to climb through the fashioning of suitable confusions toward any apical God, but more in a derangement of aim, a doubt as to the God's actual locus (or, in some, as to its very existence), out of a cruel network of sensuous moments that could not be transcended and so bent the intentions of the builders not on any zenith, but back to fright, to simple escape, in whatever direction, from what the industrial smoke, street excrement, windowless warrens, shrugging leather forests of drive belts, flowing and patient shadow states of the rats and flies, were saying about the chances for mercy that year. The grimed brick sprawl is known as the Hospital of St. Veronica of the True Image for Colonic and Respiratory Diseases, and one of its residents is a Dr. Kevin Spectro, neurologist and casual Pavlovian.

Spectro is one of the original seven owners of The Book, and if you ask Mr. Pointsman what Book, you'll only get smirked at. It rotates, the mysterious Book, among its co-owners on a weekly basis, and this, Roger gathers, is Spectro's week to get dropped in on at all hours. Others, in Pointsman's weeks, have come the same way to "The

White Visitation" in the night, Roger has heard their earnest, conspirators' whispering in the corridors, the smart rattle of all their shoes, like dancing pumps on marble, destroying one's repose, refusing ever to die with distance, Pointsman's voice and stride always distinct from the rest. How's it going to sound now with a toilet bowl?

Roger and Jessica leave the doctor at a side entrance, into which he melts, leaving nothing but rain dripping from slopes and serifs of an unreadable legend on the lintel.

They turn southward. Lights on the dash glow warmly. Searchlights rake the raining sky. The slender machine shivers over the roads. Jessica drifts toward sleep, the leather seat creaking as she curls about. Windscreen wipers brush the rain in a rhythmic bright warp. It is past two, and time for home.

□

Inside St. Veronica's hospital they sit together, just off the war-neurosis ward, these habitual evenings. The autoclave simmers its fine clutter of steel bones. Steam drifts into the glare of the gooseneck lamp, now and then becoming very bright, and the shadows of the men's gestures may pass through it, knife-edged, swooping very fast. But both faces are usually reserved, kept well back, in the annulus of night.

Out of the blackness of the ward, a half-open file drawer of pain each bed a folder, come cries, struck cries, as from cold metal. Kevin Spectro will take his syringe and spike away a dozen times tonight, into the dark, to sedate Fox (his generic term for any patient—run three times around the building without thinking of a fox and you can cure anything). Pointsman will sit each time waiting for their talking to resume, glad to rest these moments in the half-darkness, the worn gold-leaf letters shining from the spines of books, the fragrant coffee mess besieged by roaches, the winter rain in the downspout just outside the window. . . .

"*You're* not looking any better."

"Ah, it's the old bastard again, he's got me down. This

fighting, Spectro, every *day*, I don't . . ." pouting downward at his eyeglasses that he's wiping on his shirt, "there's
more to damned Pudding than I can *see*, he's always
springing his . . . senile little surprises. . . ."

"It's his age. Really."

"Oh, *that* I can deal with. But he's so damned—such a
bastard, he *never* sleeps, he *plots*—"

"Not senility, no, I meant the position he's working
from. Pointsman? You don't have the priorities he does
quite yet, do you? You can't take the chances he can.
You've treated them that age, surely you know that
strange . . . *smugness*. . . ."

Pointsman's own Fox waits, out in the city, a prize of
war. In here the tiny office space is the cave of an oracle:
steam drifting, sybilline cries arriving out of the darkness
. . . Abreactions of the Lord of the Night. . . .

"I don't like it, Pointsman. Since you did ask."

"Why not." Silence. "Unethical?"

"For pity's sake, is *this* ethical?" raising an arm then
toward the exit into the ward, almost a Fascist salute.
"No, I'm only trying to think of ways to justify it, experimentally. I can't. It's only one man."

"It's Slothrop. You know what he is. Even Mexico
thinks . . . oh, the usual. Precognition. Psychokinesis. They
have their own problems, *that* lot. . . . But suppose *you*
had the chance to study a truly classical case of . . . some
pathology, a perfect mechanism. . . ."

One night Spectro asked: "If he hadn't been one of
Laszlo Jamf's subjects, would you be all this keen on
him?"

"Of course I would."

"Hmm."

Imagine a missile one hears approaching only *after* it
explodes. The reversal! A piece of time neatly snipped
out . . . a few feet of film run backwards . . . the blast of
the rocket, fallen faster than sound—then growing *out of
it* the roar of its own fall, catching up to what's already
death and burning . . . a ghost in the sky. . . .

Pavlov was fascinated with "ideas of the opposite." Call
it a cluster of cells, somewhere on the cortex of the brain.
Helping to distinguish pleasure from pain, light from dark,
dominance from submission. . . . But when, somehow—

starve them, traumatize, shock, castrate them, send them over into one of the transmarginal phases, past borders of their waking selves, past "equivalent" and "paradoxical" phases—you weaken this idea of the opposite, and here all at once is the paranoid patient who would be master, yet now feels himself a slave . . . who would be loved, but suffers his world's indifference, and, "I think," Pavlov writing to Janet, "it is precisely the *ultraparadoxical phase* which is the base of the weakening of the idea of the opposite in our patients." Our madmen, our paranoid, maniac, schizoid, morally imbecile—

Spectro shakes his head. "You're putting response before stimulus."

"Not at all. Think of it. He's out there, and he can *feel them coming*, days in advance. But it's a reflex. A reflex to something that's in the air *right now*. Something we're too coarsely put together to sense—but *Slothrop can*."

"But that makes it extrasensory."

"Why not say 'a sensory cue we just aren't paying attention to.' Something that's been there all along, something we could be looking at but no one is. Often, in our experiments . . . I believe M. K. Petrova was first to observe it . . . one of the women, quite early in the game really . . . the act merely of bringing the dog *into the laboratory*—especially in our experimental neurosis work . . . the first sight of the test stand, of the technician, a stray shadow, the touch of a draft of air, some cue we might never pin down would be enough to send him over, send him transmarginal.

"So, Slothrop. Conceivably. Out in the city, the ambience alone—suppose we considered the war itself as a *laboratory*? when the V-2 hits, you see, first the blast, then the sound of its falling . . . the normal order of the stimuli reversed that way . . . so he might turn a particular corner, enter a certain street, and for no clear reason feel suddenly . . ."

Silence comes in, sculptured by spoken dreams, by pain-voices of the rocketbombed next door, Lord of the Night's children, voices hung upon the ward's stagnant medicinal air. Praying to their Master: sooner or later an abreaction, each one, all over this frost and harrowed city . . .

. . . as once again the floor is a giant lift propelling you with no warning toward your ceiling—replaying now as the walls are blown outward, bricks and mortar showering down, your sudden paralysis as death comes to wrap and stun *I don't know guv I must've blacked out when I come to she was gone it was burning all around me head was full of smoke* . . . and the sight of your blood spurting from the flaccid stub of artery, the snowy roofslates fallen across half your bed, the cinema kiss never completed, you were pinned and stared at a crumpled cigarette pack for two hours in pain, you could hear them crying from the rows either side but couldn't move . . . the sudden light filling up the room, the awful silence, brighter than any morning through blankets turned to gauze no shadows at all, only unutterable two-o'clock dawn . . . and . . .

. . . this transmarginal leap, this surrender. Where ideas of the opposite have come together, and lost their oppositeness. (And is it really the rocket explosion that Slothrop's keying on, or is it exactly *this depolarizing,* this neurotic "confusion" that fills the wards tonight?) How many times before it's washed away, these iterations that pour out, reliving the blast, afraid to let go because the letting go is so final *how do I know Doctor that I'll ever come back?* and the answer *trust us,* after the rocket, is so hollow, only mummery—trust you?—and both know it. . . . Spectro feels so like a fraud but carries on . . . only because the pain continues to be real. . . .

And those who do let go at last: out of each catharsis rise new children, painless, egoless for one pulse of the Between . . . tablet erased, new writing about to begin, hand and chalk poised in winter gloom over these poor human palimpsests shivering under their government blankets, drugged, drowning in tears and snot of grief so real, torn from so deep that it surprises, seems more than their own. . . .

How Pointsman lusts after them, pretty children. Those drab undershorts of his are full to bursting with need humorlessly, worldly to use their innocence, to write on them new words of himself, his own brown Realpolitik dreams, some psychic prostate ever in aching love promised, ah hinted but till now . . . how seductively they lie ranked in their iron bedsteads, their virginal sheets, the darlings so artlessly erotic. . . .

St. Veronica's Downtown Bus Station, their crossroads

(newly arrived on this fake parquetry, chewing-gum scuffed charcoal black, slicks of nighttime vomit, pale yellow, clear as the fluids of gods, waste newspapers or propaganda leaflets no one has read in torn scythe-shaped pieces, old nose-pickings, black grime that blows weakly in when the doors open . . .).

You have waited in these places into the early mornings, synced in to the on-whitening of the interior, you know the Arrivals schedule by heart, by hollow heart. And where these children have run away from, and that, in this city, there is no one to meet them. You impress them with your gentleness. You've never quite decided if they can see through to your vacuum. They won't yet look in your eyes, their slender legs are never still, knitted stockings droop (all elastic has gone to war), but charmingly: little heels kick restless against the canvas bags, the fraying valises under the wood bench. Speakers in the ceiling report departures and arrivals in English, then in the other, exile languages. Tonight's child has had a long trip here, hasn't slept. Her eyes are red, her frock wrinkled. Her coat has been a pillow. You feel her exhaustion, feel the impossible vastness of all the sleeping countryside at her back, and for the moment you really are selfless, sexless . . . considering only how to shelter her, you are the Traveler's Aid.

Behind you, long, night-long queues of men in uniform move away slowly, kicking AWOL bags along, mostly silent, toward exit doors painted beige, but with edges smudged browner in bell-curves of farewell by the generation of hands. Doors that only now and then open let in the cold air, take out a certain draft of men, and close again. A driver, or a clerk, stands by the door checking tickets, passes, furlough chits. One by one men step out into this perfectly black rectangle of night and disappear. Gone, the war taking them, the man behind already presenting his ticket. Outside motors are roaring: but less like transport than like some kind of stationary machine, very low earthquake frequencies coming in mixed with the cold—somehow intimating that out there your blindness, after this bright indoors, will be like a sudden blow. . . . Soldiers, sailors, marines, airmen. One by one, gone. Those who happen to be smoking might last an instant longer, weak little coal swinging in orange arc once, twice—no more. You sit, half-turned to watch them, your soiled sleepy darling beginning to complain, and it's no use— how can your lusts fit inside this same white frame with so much, such endless, departure? A thousand children are shuffling out these doors tonight, but only rare nights will even one come in, home to your sprung, spermy bed, the wind over the gasworks, closer smells of mold on wet coffee grounds, cat shit, pale sweaters with the pits heaped in a corner, in some accidental gesture, slink or embrace. This wordless ratcheting queue . . . thousands going away . . . only the stray freak particle, by accident, drifting against the major flow. . . .

Yet for all his agonizing all Pointsman will score, presently, is an octopus—yes a gigantic, horror-movie devilfish name of Grigori: gray, slimy, never still, shivering slow-motion in his makeshift pen down by the Ick Regis jetty . . . a terrible wind that day off the Channel, Pointsman in his Balaclava helmet, eyes freezing, Dr. Porkyevitch with greatcoat collar up and fur hat down around his ears, their breaths foul with hours-old fish, and what the hell can Pointsman do with this animal?

Already, by itself, the answer is growing, one moment a featureless blastulablob, the next folding, beginning to differentiate. . . .

One of the things Spectro said that night—surely it was that night—was, "I only wonder if you'd feel the same way without all those dogs about. If your subjects all along had been human."

"You ought to be offering me one or two, then, instead of—are you serious?—giant octopi." The doctors are watching each other closely.

"I wonder what you'll do."

"So do I."

"Take the octopus." Does he mean "forget Slothrop"? A charged moment.

But then Pointsman laughs the well-known laugh that's done him yeoman service in a profession where too often it's hedge or hang. "I'm *always* being told to take animals." He means that years ago a colleague—gone now—told him he'd be more human, warmer, if he kept a dog of his own, outside the lab. Pointsman tried—God knows he

did—it was a springer spaniel named Gloucester, pleasant
enough animal, he supposed, but the try lasted less than
a month. What finally irritated him out of all tolerance
was that the dog didn't know how to reverse its behavior.
It could open doors to the rain and the spring insects, but
not close them . . . knock over garbage, vomit on the floor,
but not clean it up—how could *anyone* live with such a
creature?

"Octopi," Spectro wheedles, "are docile under surgery.
They can survive massive removals of brain tissue. Their
unconditioned response to prey is *very* reliable—show
them a crab, WHAM! out wiv the old tentacle, home to
poisoning and supper. And, Pointsman, they don't *bark*."

"Oh, but. No . . . tanks, pumps, filtering, special food . . .
that may be fine up in Cambridge, that lot, but everyone here's so damned tightfisted, it's the damned Rundstedt offensive, has to be. . . . P.W.E. won't fund anything
now unless it pays off tactically, immediately—last week
you know, if not sooner. No an octopus is much too
elaborate, not even Pudding would buy it, no not even
old delusions-of-grandeur himself."

"No limit to the things you can teach them."

"Spectro, you're not the devil." Looking closer, "Are
you? You know we're set for sound stimuli, the whole
thrust of this Slothrop scheme *has* to be auditory, the
reversal is auditory. . . . I've seen an octopus brain or two
in my time, mate, and don't think I haven't noticed those
great blooming optic lobes. Eh? You're trying to palm off a
visual creature on me. What's there to *see* when the
damned things come down?"

"The glow."

"Eh?"

"A fiery red ball. Falling like a meteor."

"Rot."

"Gwenhidwy saw one the other night, over Deptford."

"What I want," Pointsman leaning now into the central
radiance of the lamp, his white face more vulnerable than
his voice, whispering across the burning spire of a hypodermic set upright on the desk, "what I really need, is not
a dog, not an octopus, but one of your fine Foxes. *Damn
it*. One, little, *Fox!*"

□

Something's stalking through the city of Smoke—gathering up slender girls, fair and smooth as dolls, by the handful. *Their piteous cries ... their dollful and piteous cries ...* the face of one is suddenly very close, and *down!* over the staring eyes come cream lids with stiff lashes, slamming loudly shut, the long reverberating of lead counterweights tumble inside her head as Jessica's own lids now come flying open. She surfaces in time to hear the last echoes blowing away on the heels of the blast, austere and keen, a winter sound. . . . Roger wakes up briefly too, mutters something like "Fucking madness," and nods back to sleep.

She reaches out, blind little hand grazing the ticking clock, the worn-plush stomach of her panda Michael, an empty milk bottle holding scarlet blossoms from a spurge in a garden a mile down the road: reaches to where her cigarettes ought to be but aren't. Halfway out now from under the covers, she hangs, between the two worlds, a white, athletic tension in this cold room. Oh, well ... she leaves him in their warm burrow, moves shivering vuhvuh-vuh in grainy darkness over winter-tight floorboards, slick as ice to her bare soles.

Her cigarettes are on the parlor floor, left among pillows in front of the fire. Roger's clothing is scattered all about. Puffing on a cigarette, squinting with one eye for the smoke, she tidies up, folding his trousers, hanging up his shirt. Then wanders to the window, lifts the blackout curtain, tries to see out through frost gathering on the panes, out into the snow tracked over by foxes, rabbits, long-lost dogs, and winter birds but no humans. Empty canals of snow thread away into trees and town whose name they still don't know. She cups the cigarettes in her palm, leery of showing a light though blackout was lifted weeks and weeks ago, already part of another time and world. Late lorry motors rush north and south in the night, and airplanes fill the sky then drain away east to some kind of quiet.

Could they have settled for hotels, AR-E forms, being frisked for cameras and binoculars? This house, town,

crossed arcs of Roger and Jessica are so vulnerable, to
German weapons and to British bylaws . . . it doesn't *feel*
like danger here, but she does wish there were others
about, and that it could really be a village, her village.
The searchlights could stay, to light the night, and barrage balloons to populate fat and friendly the daybreak—
everything, even the explosions in the distances might
stay as long as they were to no purpose . . . as long as no
one had to die . . . couldn't it be that way? only excitement, sound and light, a storm approaching in the summer (to live in a world where *that* would be the day's
excitement . . .), only kind thunder?

Jessica has floated out of herself, up to watch herself
watching the night, to hover in widelegged, shoulderpadded white, satin-polished on her nightward surfaces.
Until something falls here, close enough to matter, they do
have their safety: their thickets of silverblue stalks reaching after dark to touch or sweep clouds, the green-brown
masses in uniform, at the ends of afternoons, stone, eyes
on the distances, bound in convoy for fronts, for high
destinies that have, strangely, so little to do with the two
of them here . . . don't you know there's a war on, moron?
yes but—here's Jessica in her sister's hand-me-down
pajamas, and Roger asleep in nothing at all, but where *is*
the war?

Until it touch them. Until something falls. A doodle
will give time to get to safety, a rocket will hit before
they can hear it coming. Biblical, maybe, spooky as an
old northern fairy tale, but not The War, not the great
struggle of good and evil the wireless reports everyday.
And no reason not just to, well, to keep on. . . .

Roger has tried to explain to her the V-bomb statistics:
the difference between distribution, in angel's-eye view,
over the map of England, and their own chances, as seen
from down here. She's almost got it: nearly understands
his Poisson equation, yet can't quite put the two together—
put her own enforced calm day-to-day alongside the pure
numbers, and keep them both in sight. Pieces keep slipping in and out.

"Why is your equation only for angels, Roger? Why
can't *we* do something, down here? Couldn't there be an
equation for us too, something to help us find a safer
place?"

"Why am I surrounded," his usual understanding self today, "by statistical illiterates? There's no way, love, not as long as the mean density of strikes is constant. Pointsman doesn't even understand that."

The rockets *are* distributing about London just as Poisson's equation in the textbooks predicts. As the data keep coming in, Roger looks more and more like a prophet. Psi Section people stare after him in the hallways. It's not precognition, he wants to make an announcement in the cafeteria or something . . . have I ever pretended to be anything I'm not? all I'm doing is plugging numbers into a well-known equation, you can look it up in the book and do it yourself. . . .

His little bureau is dominated now by a glimmering map, a window into another landscape than winter Sussex, written names and spidering streets, an ink ghost of London, ruled off into 576 squares, a quarter square kilometer each. Rocket strikes are represented by red circles. The Poisson equation will tell, for a number of total hits arbitrarily chosen, how many squares will get none, how many one, two, three, and so on.

An Erlenmeyer flask bubbles on the ring. Blue light goes rattling, reknotting through the seedflow inside the glass. Ancient tatty textbooks and mathematical papers lie scattered about on desk and floor. Somewhere a snapshot of Jessica peeks from beneath Roger's old Whittaker and Watson. The graying Pavlovian, on route with his tautened gait, thin as a needle, in the mornings to his lab, where dogs wait with cheeks laid open, winter-silver drops welling from each neat raw fistula to fill the wax cup or graduated tube, pauses by Mexico's open door. The air beyond is blue from cigarettes smoked and as fag-ends later in the freezing black morning shifts resmoked, a stale and loathsome atmosphere. But he must go in, must face the habitual morning cup.

Both know how strange their liaison must look. If ever the Antipointsman existed, Roger Mexico is the man. Not so much, the doctor admits, for the psychical research. The young statistician is devoted to number and to method, not table-rapping or wishful thinking. But in the domain of zero to one, not-something to something, Pointsman can only possess the zero and the one. He cannot, like Mexico, survive anyplace in between. Like his master I. P. Pavlov before him, he imagines the cortex of the brain as a mosaic of tiny on/off elements. Some are always in bright excitation, others inhibited. The contours, bright and dark, keep changing. But each point is allowed only the two states: waking or sleep. One or zero. "Summation," "transition," "irradiation," "concentration," "reciprocal induction"—all Pavlovian brain-mechanics—assumes the presence of these bi-stable points. But to Mexico belongs the domain *between* zero and one—the middle Pointsman has excluded from his persuasion—the probabilities. A chance of 0.37 that, by the time he stops his count, a given square on his map will have suffered only one hit, 0.17 that it will suffer two. . . .

"Cant you . . . *tell*," Pointsman offering Mexico one of his Kyprinos Orients, which he guards in secret fag fobs sewn inside all his lab coats, "from your map here, which places would be safest to go into, safest from attack?"

"No."

"But surely—"

"Every square is just as likely to get hit again. The hits aren't clustering. Mean density is constant."

Nothing on the map to the contrary. Only a classical Poisson distribution, quietly neatly sifting among the squares exactly as it should . . . growing to its predicted shape. . . .

"But squares that have already *had* several hits, I mean—"

"I'm sorry. That's the Monte Carlo Fallacy. No matter how many have fallen inside a particular square, the odds remain the same as they always were. Each hit is independent of all the others. Bombs are not dogs. No link. No memory. No conditioning."

Nice thing to tell a Pavlovian. Is it Mexico's usual priggish insensitivity, or does he know what he's saying? If there *is* nothing to link the rocket strikes—no reflex arc, no Law of Negative Induction . . . then . . . He goes in to Mexico each morning as to painful surgery. Spooked more and more by the choirboy look, the college pleasantries. But it's a visit he must make. How can Mexico play, so at his ease, with these symbols of randomness and fright? Innocent as a child, perhaps unaware—perhaps—that in this play he wrecks the elegant rooms of history, threatens the idea of cause and effect itself. What if Mexico's whole *generation* have turned out like this? Will Postwar be nothing but "events," newly created one moment to the next? No links? Is it the end of history?

"The Romans," Roger and the Reverend Dr. Paul de la Nuit were drunk together one night, or the vicar was, "the ancient Roman priests laid a sieve in the road, and then waited to see which stalks of grass would come up through the holes."

Roger saw the connection immediately. "I wonder," reaching for pocket after pocket, why are there never any damned—ah here, "if it would follow a Poisson . . . let's see . . ."

"Mexico." Leaning forward, definitely hostile. "They used the stalks that grew through the holes to cure the sick. The sieve was a very sacred item to them. What will you do with the sieve you've laid over London? How will you use the things that grow in your network of death?"

"I don't follow you." It's just an equation. . . .

Roger really wants other people to know what he's talking about. Jessica understands that. When they don't, his face often grows chalky and clouded, as behind the smudged glass of a railway carriage window as vaguely silvered barriers come down, spaces slide in to separate him that much more, thinning further his loneliness. She knew their very first day, he leaning across to open the Jaguar door and so sure she'd never get in. She saw his loneliness: in his face, between his red nail-bitten hands. . . .

"Well, it isn't fair."

"It's eminently fair," Roger now cynical, looking very young, she thinks. "Everyone's equal. Same chances of getting hit. Equal in the eyes of the rocket."

To which she gives him her Fay Wray look, eyes round as can be, red mouth about to open in a scream, till he has to laugh. "Oh, stop."

"Sometimes . . ." but what does she want to say? That he must always be lovable, in need of her and never, as now, the hovering satistical cherub who's never quite been to hell but speaks as if he's one of the most fallen. . . .

"Cheap nihilism" is Captain Prentice's name for that. It was one day by the frozen pond near "The White Visitation," Roger off sucking icicles, lying flat and waving his arms to make angels in the snow, larking.

"Do you mean that he hasn't paid . . . ," looking up, up, Pirate's wind-burned face seeming to end in the sky, her own hair finally in the way of his gray, reserved eyes. He was Roger's friend, he wasn't playing or undermining, didn't know the first thing, she guessed, about such dancing-shoe wars—and anyway didn't have to, because she was already, terrible flirt . . . well, nothing serious, but those eyes she could never quite see into were so swoony, so utterly terrif, really. . . .

"The more V-2s over there waiting to be fired over here," Captain Prentice said, "obviously, the better his chances of catching one. Of course you can't say he's not paying a minimum dues. But aren't we all."

"Well," Roger nodding when she told him later, eyes out of focus, considering this, "it's the damned Calvinist insanity again. Payment. Why must they always put it in terms of exchange? What's Prentice want, another kind of Beveridge Proposal or something? Assign everyone a Bitterness Quotient! lovely—up before the Evaluation Board, so many points earned for being Jewish, in a concentration camp, missing limbs or vital organs, losing a wife, a lover, a close friend—"

"I knew you'd be angry," she murmured.

"I'm not angry. No. He's right. It is cheap. All right, but what does he want then—" stalking now this stuffed, dim little parlor, hung about with rigid portraits of favorite gun dogs at point in fields that never existed save in certain fantasies about death, leas more golden as their linseed oil ages, even more autumnal, necropolitical, than pre-war hopes—for an end to all change, for a long static afternoon and the grouse forever in blurred takeoff, the sights taking their lead aslant purple hills to pallid sky, the good dog alerted by the eternal scent, the explosion over his head always just about to come—these hopes so patently, defenselessly there that Roger even at his most cheaply nihilistic couldn't quite bring himself to take the pictures down, turn them to the wallpaper—"what do you all expect from me, working day in day out among raving lunatics," Jessica sighing *oh gosh*, curling her pretty legs up into the chair, "they believe in survival after death, communication mind-to-mind, prophesying, clairvoyance, teleportation—they *believe,* Jess! and—and—" something is blocking his speech. She forgets her annoyance, comes up out of the fat paisley chair to hold him, and *how does she know,* warm-skirted thighs and mons pushing close to heat and rouse his cock, losing the last of her lipstick across his shirt, muscles, touches, skins confused, high, blooded—know so exactly what Roger meant to say?

Mind-to-mind, tonight up late at the window while he sleeps, lighting another precious cigarette from the coal of the last, filling with a need to cry because she can see so plainly her limits, knows she can never protect him as much as she must—from what may come out of the sky, from what he couldn't confess that day (creaking snow lanes, arcades of the ice-bearded and bowing trees . . . the wind shook down crystals of snow: purple and orange creatures blooming on her long lashes), and from Mr. Pointsman, and from Pointsman's . . . his . . . a bleakness whenever she meets him. Scientist-neutrality. Hands that— she shivers. There are chances now for enemy shapes out of the snow and stillness. She drops the blackout curtain. Hands that could as well torture people as dogs and never feel their pain . . .

A skulk of foxes, a cowardice of curs are tonight's traffic whispering in the yards and lanes. A motorcycle out on the trunk road, snarling cocky as a fighter plane, bypasses the village, heading up to London. The great balloons drift in the sky, pearl-grown, and the air is so still that this morning's brief snow still clings to the steel cables, white goes twisting peppermint-stick down thousands of feet of night. And the people who might have been asleep in the empty houses here, people blown away, some already forever . . . are they dreaming of cities that shine all over with lamps at night, of Christmases seen again from the vantage of children and not of sheep huddled so vulnerable on their bare hillside, so bleached by the Star's awful radiance? or of songs so funny, so lovely or true, that they can't be remembered on waking . . . dreams of peacetime. . . .

"What was it like? Before the war?" She knows she was alive then, a child, but it's not what she means. Wireless, staticky Frank Bridge Variations a hairbrush for the tangled brain over the BBC Home Service, bottle of Montrachet, a gift from Pirate, cooling at the kitchen window.

"Well, now," in his cracked old curmudgeon's voice, palsied hand reaching out to squeeze her breast in the nastiest way he knows, "girly, it depends *which* war you *mean*," and here it comes, ugh, ugh, drool welling at the corner of his lower lip and over and down in a silver string, he's so clever, he's practiced all these disgusting little—

"Don't be ridic, I'm serious, Roger. I don't remember." Watches dimples come up either side of his mouth as he considers this, smiling at her in an odd way. *It'll be like this when I'm thirty* . . . flash of several children, a garden, a window, voices *Mummy, what's* . . . cucumbers and brown onions on a chopping board, wild carrot blossoms sprinkling with brilliant yellow a reach of deep, very green lawn and his voice—

"All *I* remember is that it was silly. Just overwhelmingly silly. Nothing happened. Oh, Edward VIII abdicated. He fell in love with—"

"I know that, I can read magazines. But what was it *like?*"

"Just . . . just damned silly, that's all. Worrying about things that don't—Jess, can't you really remember?"

Games, pinafores, girl friends, a black alley kitten with white little feet, holidays all the family by the sea, brine, frying fish, donkey rides, peach taffeta, a boy named Robin . . .

"Nothing that's really gone, that I can't ever find again."

"Oh. Whereas *my* memories—"

"Yes?" They both smile.

"One took lots of aspirin. One was drinking or drunk much of the time. One was concerned about getting one's lounge suits to fit properly. One despised the upper classes but tried desperately to behave like them. . . ."

"And one cried wee, wee, wee, all the way—" Jessica breaking down in a giggle as he reaches for the spot along her sweatered flank he knows she can't bear to be tickled in. She hunches, squirming, out of the way as he rolls past, bouncing off the back of the sofa but making a nice recovery, and by now she's ticklish all over, he can grab an ankle, elbow—

But a rocket has suddenly struck. A terrific blast quite close beyond the village: the entire fabric of the air, the time, is changed—the casement window blown inward, rebounding with a wood squeak to slam again as all the house still shudders.

Their hearts pound. Eardrums brushed taut by the overpressure ring in pain. The invisible train rushes away close over the rooftop. . . .

They sit still as the painted dogs now, silent, oddly unable to touch. Death has come in the pantry door: stands watching them, iron and patient, with a look that says *try to tickle me.*

□

(1)

> TDY Abreaction Ward
> St. Veronica's Hospital
> Bonechapel Gate, E1
> London, England
> Winter, 1944

The Kenosha Kid
General Delivery
Kenosha, Wisconsin, U.S.A.

Dear Sir:
Did I ever bother you, *ever*, for anything, in your life?

> Yours truly,
> Lt. Tyrone Slothrop

————

> General Delivery
> Kenosha, Wisc., U.S.A.

few days later

Tyrone Slothrop, Esq.
TDY Abreaction Ward
St. Veronica's Hospital
Bonechapel Gate, E1
London, England

Dear Mr. Slothrop:
You never did.

> The Kenosha Kid

(2)   Smartass youth: Aw, I did all them old-fashioned
dances, I did the "Charleston," a-and the "Big Apple,"
too!
   Old veteran hoofer: Bet you never did the "Kenosha,"
kid!

(2.1)   S.Y.: Shucks, I did all them dances, I did the
"Castle Walk," and I did the "Lindy," too!
   O.V.H.: Bet you never did the "Kenosha Kid."

(3)   Minor employee: Well, he has been avoiding me,
and I thought it might be because of the Slothrop Affair.
If he somehow held me responsible—
   Superior (haughtily): You! never did the Kenosha Kid
think for one instant that *you* . . .

(3.1)   Superior (incredulously): You? Never! Did the
Kenosha Kid think for one instant that *you* . . . ?

(4)   And at the end of the mighty day in which he gave
us in fiery letters across the sky all the words we'd ever
need, words we today enjoy, and fill our dictionaries with,
the meek voice of little Tyrone Slothrop, celebrated ever
after in tradition and song, ventured to filter upward to
the Kid's attention: "You never did '*the*,' Kenosha Kid!"
   These changes on the text "You never did the Kenosha
Kid!" are occupying Slothrop's awareness as the doctor
leans in out of the white overhead to wake him and begin
the session. The needle slips without pain into the vein
just outboard of the hollow in the crook of his elbow: 10%
Sodium Amytal, one cc at a time, as needed.

(5)   Maybe you did fool the Philadelphia, rag the
Rochester, josh the Joliet. But you never did the Kenosha
kid.

(6)   (The day of the Ascent and sacrifice. A nation-wide
observance. Fats searing, blood dripping and burning to a
salty brown . . .) You did the Charlottesville shoat, check,
the Forest Hills foal, check. (Fading now . . .) The
Laredo lamb. Check. Oh-oh. Wait. What's this, Slothrop?
You never did the Kenosha kid. Snap to, Slothrop.

Got a hardon in my fist,
Don't be pissed,
Re-enlist—
Snap—to, Slothrop!

Jackson, I don't give a fuck,
Just give me my "ruptured duck!"
Snap—to, Slothrop!

No one here can love or comprehend me,
They just look for someplace else to send . . . me . . .

Tap my head and mike my brain,
Stick that needle in my vein,
Slothrop, snap to!

PISCES: We want to talk some more about Boston today, Slothrop. You recall that we were talking last time about the Negroes, in Roxbury. Now we know it's not all that comfortable for you, but do try, won't you. Now— where are you, Slothrop? Can you see anything?

Slothrop: Well no, not *see* exactly . . .

Roaring in by elevated subway, only in Boston, steel and a carbon shroud over the ancient bricks—

Rhy-thm's got me,
Oh baby dat swing, swing, swing!
Yeah de rhythm got me
Just a-thinkin' that whole-wide-world-can-sing,
Well I never ever heard-it, sound-so-sweet,
Even down around the corner-on, Ba-sin Street,
As now dat de rhythm's got me, chillun let's
Swing, swing, swing,
Come on . . . chillun, let's . . . swing!

Black faces, white tablecloth, gleaming *very sharp knives* lined up by the saucers . . . tobacco and "gage" smoke richly blended, eye-reddening and tart as wine, yowzah gwine smoke a little ob dis hyah sheeit gib de wrinkles in mah *brain* a process! straighten 'em all raht out, sho nuf!

PISCES: That was "sho nuf," Slothrop?

Slothrop: Come on you guys . . . don't make it too . . .

White college boys, hollering requests to the "combo" up

on the stand. Eastern prep-school voices, pronouncing
asshole with a certain sphinctering of the lips so it comes
out *ehisshehwle* ... they reel, they roister. Aspidistras,
giant philodendrons, green broad leaves and jungle palms
go hanging into the dimness ... two bartenders, a very
fair West Indian, slight, with a mustache, and his running-
mate black as a hand in an evening glove, are moving
endlessly in front of the deep, the oceanic mirror that
swallows most of the room into metal shadows ... the
hundred bottles hold their light only briefly before it
flows away into the mirror ... even when someone bends
to light a cigarette, the flame reflects back in there only
as dark, sunset orange. Slothrop can't even see his own
white face. A woman turns to look at him from a table.
Her eyes tell him, in the instant, what he is. The mouth
harp in his pocket reverts to brass inertia. A weight. A
jive accessory. But he packs it everywhere he goes.

Upstairs in the men's room at the Roseland Ballroom he
swoons kneeling over a toilet bowl, vomiting beer, ham-
burgers, homefries, chef's salad with French dressing, half
a bottle of Moxie, after-dinner mints, a Clark bar, a pound
of salted peanuts, and the cherry from some Radcliffe
girl's old-fashioned. With no warning, as tears stream out
his eyes, PLOP goes the harp into the, *aagghh*, the loathsome *toilet!* Immediate little bubbles slide up its bright
flanks, up brown wood surfaces, some varnished some lip-
worn, these fine silver seeds tripping loose along the harp's
descent toward stone-white cervix and into lower night. . . .
Someday the U.S. Army will provide him with shirts whose
pockets he can button. But in these prewar days he can
rely only on the starch in his snow-white Arrow to hold
the pocket stuck together enough to keep objects from ...
But no, no, fool, the harp *has* fallen, remember? the low
reeds singing an instant on striking porcelain (it's raining
against a window somewhere, and outside on top of a
sheet-metal vent on the roof: cold Boston rain) then
quenched in the water streaked with the last bile-brown
coils of his vomit. There's no calling it back. Either he
lets the harp go, his silver chances of song, or he has to
follow.

Follow? Red, the Negro shoeshine boy, waits by his
dusty leather seat. The Negroes all over wasted Roxbury

wait. Follow? "Cherokee" comes wailing up from the
dance floor below, over the hi-hat, the string bass, the
thousand sets of feet where moving rose lights suggest not
pale Harvard boys and their dates, but a lotta dolled-up
redskins. The song playing is one more lie about white
crimes. But more musicians have floundered in the channel to "Cherokee" than have got through from end to end.
All those long, long notes . . . what're they up to, all that
time to do something inside of? is it an Indian spirit plot?
Down in New York, drive fast maybe get there for the
last set—on 7th Ave., between 139th and 140th, tonight,
"Yardbird" Parker is finding out how he can use the notes
at the higher ends of these very chords to break up the
melody into *have* mercy what is it a fucking machine gun
or something man he must be out of his *mind* 32nd notes
demisemiquavers say it very (demisemiquaver) fast in a
Munchkin voice if you can dig *that* coming out of Dan
Wall's Chili House and down the street—shit, out in all
kinds of streets (his trip, by '39, well begun: down inside
his most affirmative solos honks already the idle, amused
dum-de-dumming of old Mister fucking Death he self)
out over the airwaves, into the society gigs, someday as
far as what seeps out hidden speakers in the city elevators and in all the markets, his bird's singing, to gainsay
the Man's lullabies, to subvert the groggy wash of the endlessly, gutlessly over-dubbed strings. . . . So that prophecy,
even up here on rainy Massachusetts Avenue, is beginning
these days to work itself out in "Cherokee," the saxes
downstairs getting now into some, oh really weird shit. . . .

If Slothrop follows that harp down the toilet it'll have
to be headfirst, which is not so good, cause it leaves his
ass up in the air helpless, and with Negroes around that's
just what a fella doesn't want, his face down in some fetid
unknown darkness and brown fingers, strong and sure, all
at once undoing his belt, unbuttoning his fly, strong hands
holding his legs apart—and he feels the cold Lysol air on
his thighs as down come the boxer shorts too, now, with
the colorful bass lures and trout flies on them. He struggles
to work himself farther into the toilet hole as dimly, up
through the smelly water, comes the sound of a whole
dark gang of awful Negroes come yelling happily into the
white men's room, converging on poor wriggling Slothrop,

jiving around the way they do singing, "Slip the talcum to me, Malcolm!" And the voice that replies is who but that Red, shoeshine boy who's slicked up Slothrop's black patents a dozen times down on his knees jes poppin' dat rag to beat the band . . . now Red the very tall, skinny, extravagantly conked redhead Negro shoeshine boy who's just been "Red" to all the Harvard fellas—"Say Red, any of those Sheiks in the drawer?" "How 'bout another luck-changin' phone number there, Red?"—this Negro whose true name now halfway down the toilet comes at last to Slothrop's hearing—as a thick finger with a gob of very slippery jelly or cream comes sliding down the crack now toward his asshole, chevroning the hairs along like topo lines up a river valley—*the true name is Malcolm,* and all the black cocks know him, Malcolm, have known him all along—Red Malcolm the Unthinkable Nihilist sez, "Good golly he sure is *all* asshole ain't he?" Jeepers Slothrop, what a position for you to be in! Even though he has succeeded in getting far enough down now so that only his legs protrude and his buttocks heave and wallow just under the level of the water like pallid domes of ice. Water splashes, cold as the rain outside, up the walls of the white bowl. "Grab him 'fo' he gits away!" "Yowzah!" Distant hands clutch after his calves and ankles, snap his garters and tug at the argyle sox Mom knitted for him to go to Harvard in, but these insulate so well, or he has progressed so far down the toilet by now, that he can hardly feel the hands at all. . . .

Then he has shaken them off, left the last Negro touch back up there and is free, slick as a fish, with his virgin asshole preserved. Now some folks might say whew, thank God for *that,* and others moaning a little, aw shucks, but Slothrop doesn't say much of anything cause he didn't *feel* much of anything. A-and there's *still* no sign of his lost harp. The light down here is dark gray and rather faint. For some time has been aware of shit, elaborately crusted along the sides of this ceramic (or by now, iron) tunnel he's in: shit nothing can flush away, mixed with hardwater minerals into a deliberate brown barnacling of his route, patterns thick with meaning, Burma-Shave signs of the toilet world, icky and sticky, cryptic and glyptic, these shapes loom and pass smoothly as he continues on down

the long cloudy waste line, the sounds of "Cherokee" still
pulsing very dimly above, playing him to the sea. He finds
he can identify certain traces of shit as belonging definitely
to this or that Harvard fellow of his acquaintances. Some
of it too of course must be Negro shit, but that all looks
alike. Hey, here's that "Gobbler" Biddle, must've been the
night we all ate chop suey at Fu's Folly in Cambridge
cause there's bean sprouts around here someplace and even
a hint of that wild plum sauce . . . say, certain senses then
do seem to grow sharper . . . wow . . . Fu's Folly, weepers,
that was months ago. A-and here's Dumpster Villard, he
was constipated that night, wasn't he—it's black shit mean
as resin that will someday clarify forever to dark amber.
In its blunt, reluctant touches along the wall (which speak
the reverse of its own cohesion) he can, uncannily shit-
sensitized now, read old agonies inside poor Dumpster,
who'd tried suicide last semester: the differential equations
that would not weave for him into any elegance, the
mother with the low-slung hat and silk knees leaning
across Slothrop's table in Sidney's Great Yellow Grille to
finish for him his bottle of Canadian ale, the Radcliffe
girls who evaded him, the black professionals Malcolm
touted him on to who dealt him erotic cruelty by the
dollar, up to as much as he could take. Or if Mother's
check was late, only afford. Gone away upstream, bas-
relief Dumpster lost in the gray light as now Slothrop is
going past the sign of Will Stonybloke, of J. Peter Pitt, of
Jack Kennedy, the ambassador's son—say, where the heck
is that *Jack* tonight, anyway? If anybody could've saved
that harp, betcha Jack could. Slothrop admires him from
a distance—he's athletic, and kind, and one of the most
well-liked fellows in Slothrop's class. Sure is daffy about
that history, though. Jack . . . might Jack have kept it from
falling, violated gravity somehow? Here, in this passage
to the Atlantic, odors of salt, weed, decay washing to him
faintly like the sound of breakers, yes it seems Jack might
have. For the sake of tunes to be played, millions of possible blues lines, notes to be bent from the official frequencies, bends Slothrop hasn't really the breath to do . . . not
yet but someday . . . well at least if (when . . .) he finds
the instrument it'll be well soaked in, a lot easier to play.
A hopeful thought to carry with you down the toilet.

Down the toilet, lookit me,
What a silly thing ta do!
Hope nobody takes a pee,
Yippy dippy dippy doo . . .

At which precise point there comes this godawful surge
from up the line, noise growing like a tidal wave, a jam-
packed wavefront of shit, vomit, toilet paper and dingle-
berries in mind-boggling mosaic, rushing down on panicky
Slothrop like an MTA subway train on its own hapless
victim. Nowhere to run. Paralyzed, he stares back over
his shoulder. A looming wall stringing long tendrils of
shitpaper behind, the shockwave is on him—*GAAHHH!*
he tries a feeble frog kick at the very last moment but
already the cylinder of waste has wiped him out, dark as
cold beef gelatin along his upper backbone, the paper
snapping up, wrapping across his lips, his nostrils, everything gone and shit-stinking now as he has to keep batting
micro-turds out of his eyelashes, it's worse than being
torpedoed by Japs! the brown liquid tearing along, carrying him helpless . . . seems he's been tumbling ass over tea-
kettle—though there's no way to tell in this murky shit-
storm, no visual references . . . from time to time he will
brush against shrubbery, or perhaps small feathery trees.
It occurs to him he hasn't felt the touch of a hard wall
since he started to tumble, if that indeed is what he's
doing.

At some point the brown dusk around him has begun
to lighten. Like the dawn. Bit by bit his vertigo leaves
him. The last wisps of shitpaper, halfway back to slurry,
go . . . sad, dissolving, away. An eerie light grows on him,
a watery and marbled light he hopes won't last for long
because of what it seems to promise to show. But "contacts" are living in these waste regions. People he knows.
Inside shells of old, what seem to be fine-packed masonry
ruins—weathered cell after cell, many of them roofless.
Wood fires burn in black fireplaces, water simmers in rusty
institutional-size lima-bean cans, and the steam goes up
the leaky chimneys. And they sit about the worn flagstones, transacting some . . . he can't place it exactly . . .
something vaguely religious. . . . Bedrooms are fully furnished, with lights that turn and glow, velvet hung from
walls and ceiling. Down to the last ignored blue bead

clogged with dust under the Capehart, the last dried spider
and complex ruffling of the carpet's nap, the intricacy of
these dwellings amazes him. It is a place of sheltering
from disaster. Not necessarily the flushings of the Toilet—
these occur here only as a sort of inferred disturbance,
behind this ancient sky, in its corroded evenness of tone—
but something else has been terribly *at* this country, something poor soggy Slothrop cannot see or hear . . . as if
there is a Pearl Harbor every morning, smashing invisibly
from the sky. . . . He has toilet paper in his hair and a
fuzzy thick dingleberry lodged up inside his right nostril.
Ugh, ugh. Decline and fall works silently on this landscape. No sun, no moon, only a long smooth sinewaving
of the light. It is a Negro dingleberry, he can tell—stubborn as a wintertime booger as he probes for it. His fingernails draw blood. He stands outside all the communal
rooms and spaces, outside in his own high-desert morning,
a reddish-brown hawk, two, hanging up on an air current
to watch the horizon. It's cold. The wind blows. He can
feel only his isolation. They want him inside there but he
can't join them. Something prevents him: once inside, it
would be like taking some kind of blood oath. They would
never release him. There are no guarantees he might not
be asked to do something . . . something so . . .

Now every loose stone, every piece of tinfoil, billet of
wood, scrap of kindling or cloth is moving up and down:
rising ten feet then dropping again to hit the pavement
with a sharp clap. The light is thick and water-green. All
down the streets, debris rises and falls in unison, as if at
the mercy of some deep, regular wave. It's difficult to see
any distance through the vertical dance. The drumming
on the pavement goes for eleven beats, skips a twelfth,
begins the cycle over . . . it is the rhythm of some traditional American tune. . . . The streets are all empty of
people. It's either dawn or twilight. Parts of the debris that
are metal shine with a hard, nearly blue persistence.

> Now don't you remember Red Malcolm up there,
> That kid with the Red Devil Lye in his hair . . .

Here now is Crutchfield or Crouchfield, the westwardman. Not "archetypical" westwardman, but *the only*.
Understand, there was only one. There was only one

Indian who ever fought him. Only one fight, one victory, one loss. And only one president, and one assassin, and one election. True. One of each of everything. You had thought of solipsism, and imagined the structure to be populated—on your level—by only, terribly, one. No count on any other levels. But it proves to be not quite that lonely. Sparse, yes, but a good deal better than solitary. One of each of everything's not so bad. Half an Ark's better than none. This Crutchfield here is browned by sun, wind and dirt—against the deep brown slats of the barn or stable wall he is wood of a different grain and finish. He is good-humored, solid-set against the purple mountainslope, and looking half into the sun. His shadow is carried strained coarsely back through the network of wood inside the stable—beams, lodgepoles, stall uprights, trough-trestlework, rafters, wood ceiling-slats the sun comes through: blinding empyrean even at this failing hour of the day. There is somebody playing a mouth harp behind an outbuilding—some musical glutton, mouth-sucking giant five-note chords behind the tune of

RED RIVER VALLEY

Down this toilet they say you are flushin'—
Won'tchew light up and set fer a spell?
Cause the toilet it ain't going nowhar,
And the shit hereabouts shore is swell.

Oh, it's the Red River all right, if you don't believe it just ask that "Red," wherever he may be (tell you what Red means, FDR's little asshole buddies, they want to take it all away, women all have hair on their legs, give it all to them or they'll blow it up round black iron in the middle of the night bleeding over Polacks in gray caps okies niggers yeh niggers especially . . .)

Well, back here, Crutchfield's little pard has just come out of the barn. His little pard of the moment, anyway. Crutchfield has left a string of broken-hearted little pards across this vast alkali plain. One little feeb in South Dakota,

One little hustler in San Berdoo,
One little chink run away from the railroad

With his ass just as yellow as Fu Manchu!
One with the clap and one with a goiter,
One with the terminal lepro-see,
Cripple on the right foot, cripple on the left foot,
Crippled up both feet 'n' that makes three!
Well one little fairy, even one bull dyke,
One little nigger, one little kike,
One Red Indian with one buffalo,
And a buffalo hunter from New Mexico . . .

And on, and on, one of each of everything, he's the White
Cocksman of the *terre mauvais*, this Crouchfield, doing it
with both sexes and all animals except for rattlesnakes
(properly speaking, "rattlesnake," since there's only one),
but lately he's been havin' these fantasies about that
rattlesnake, too! Fangs just tickling the foreskin . . . the
pale mouth open wide, and the horrible joy in the crescent
eyes. . . . His little pard of the moment is Whappo, a
Norwegian mulatto lad, who has a fetish for horsy paraphernalia, likes to be quirt-whipped inside the sweat-and-
leather tackrooms of their wandering, which is three
weeks old today, pretty long time for a little pard to've
lasted. Whappo is wearing chaps of imported gazelle hide
that Crutchfield bought for him in Eagle Pass from a faro
dealer with a laudanum habit who was crossing the great
Rio forever, in the blank furnace of the wild Mexico.
Whappo also sports a bandanna of the regulation magenta
and green (Crutchfield is supposed to have a closetful of
these silken scarves back home at "Rancho Peligroso" and
never rides out into the rock-country and riverbed trails
without a dozen or two stashed in his saddlebags. This
must mean that the one-of-each rule applies only to forms
of life, such as little pards, and not to objects, such as
bandannas). And Whappo tops off with a high shiny
opera hat of Japanese silk. Whappo is quite the dandy
this afternoon in fact, as he comes sauntering out from
the barn.

"Ah, Crutchfield," flipping a hand, "how nice of you to
show up."

"You knew I'd show up, you little rascal," shit that
Whappo is such a caution. Always baiting his master in
hopes of getting a leather-keen stripe or two across those
dusky Afro-Scandinavian buttocks, which combine the

callipygian rondure observed among the races of the Dark
Continent with the taut and noble musculature of sturdy
Olaf, our blond Northern cousin. But this time Crutchfield
only turns back to watching the distant mountains.
Whappo sulks. His top hat reflects the coming holocaust.
What the white man does not have to utter, however
casually, is anything like "Toro Rojo's gonna be riding in
tonight." Both pardners know about *that*. The wind, bringing them down that raw Injun smell, ought to be enough
for anybody. Oh God it's gonna be a shootout and bloody
as hell. The wind will be blowing so hard blood will glaze
on the north sides of the trees. The redskin'll have a dog
with him, the only Indian dog in these whole ashen
plains—the cur will mix it up with little Whappo and end
hung on the meathook of an open meat stall in the dirt
plaza back in Los Madres, eyes wide open, mangy coat
still intact, black fleas hopping against the sunlit mortar
and stone of the church wall across the square, blood
darkened and crusting at the lesion in his neck where
Whappo's teeth severed his jugular (and maybe some
tendons, for the head dangles to one side). The hook
enters in the back, between two vertebrae. Mexican ladies
poke at the dead dog, and it sways reluctantly in the forenoon market-smell of platanos for frying, sweet baby
carrots from the Red River Valley, trampled raw greens of
many kinds, cilantro smelling like animal musk, strong
white onions, pineapples fermenting in the sun, about to
blow up, great mottled shelves of mountain mushroom.
Slothrop moves among the bins and hung cloths, invisible,
among horses and dogs, pigs, brown-uniformed militia,
Indian women with babies slung in shawls, servants from
the pastel houses farther up the hillside—the plaza is
seething with life, and Slothrop is puzzled. Isn't there
supposed to be only one of each?

A. Yes.

Q. Then one Indian girl . . .

A. One *pure* Indian. One *mestiza*. One *criolla*. Then:
one Yaqui. One Navaho. One Apache—

Q. Wait a minute, there was only one Indian to begin
with. The one that Crutchfield killed.

A. Yes.

Look on it as an optimization problem. The country
can best support only one of each.

Q. Then what about all the others? Boston. London. The ones who live in cities. Are those people real, or what?

A. Some are real, and some aren't.

Q. Well are the real ones necessary? or unnecessary?

A. It depends what you have in mind.

Q. Shit, I don't have anything in mind.

A. *We* do.

For a moment, ten thousand stiffs humped under the snow in the Ardennes take on the sunny Disneyfied look of numbered babies under white wool blankets, waiting to be sent to blessed parents in places like Newton Upper Falls. It only lasts a moment. Then for another moment it seems that all the Christmas bells in the creation are about to join in chorus—that all their random pealing will be, this one time, coordinated, in harmony, present with tidings of explicit comfort, feasible joy.

But segway into the Roxbury hillside. Snow packs into the arches, the crosshatchings of his black rubber soles. His Ar'tics clink when he moves his feet. The snow in this slum darkness has the appearance of soot in a negative . . . it flows in and out of the night. . . . The brick surfaces by daylight (he only sees them in very early dawn, aching inside his overshoes, looking for cabs up and down the Hill) are flaming corrosion, dense, deep, fallen upon by frosts again and again: historied in a way he hasn't noticed in Beacon Street. . . .

In the shadows, black and white holding in a panda-pattern across his face, each of the regions a growth or mass of scar tissue, waits the connection he's traveled all this way to see. The face is as weak as a housedog's, and its owner shrugs a lot.

Slothrop: Where is he? Why didn't he show? Who are you?

Voice: The Kid got busted. And you know me, Slothrop. Remember? I'm Never.

Slothrop (peering): *You,* Never? (A pause.) *Did* the Kenosha Kid?

□

"Kryptosam" is a proprietary form of stabilized tyrosine, developed by IG Farben as part of a research contract with OKW.

An activating agent is included which, in the presence of some component of the seminal fluid to date [1934] unidentified, promotes conversion of the tyrosine into melanin, or skin pigment. In the absence of seminal fluid, the "Kryptosam" remains invisible. No other known reagent, among those available to operatives in the field, will alter "Kryptosam" to visible melanin. It is suggested, in cryptographic applications, that a proper stimulus be included with the message which will reliably produce tumescence and ejaculation. A thorough knowledge of the addressee's psychosexual profile would seem of invaluable aid.

—PROF. DR. LASZLO JAMF,
"Kryptosam" (advertising brochure), Agfa, Berlin, 1934

The drawing, on heavy cream paper under the black-letter inscription GEHEIME KOMMANDOSACHE, is in pen and ink, very finely textured, somewhat after the style of von Bayros or Beardsley. The woman is a dead ringer for Scorpia Mossmoon. The room is one they talked about but never saw, a room they would have liked to live in one day, with a sunken pool, a silken tent draped from the ceiling—a De Mille set really, slender and oiled girls in attendance, a suggestion of midday light coming through from overhead, Scorpia sprawled among fat pillows wearing exactly the corselette of Belgian lace, the dark stockings and shoes he daydreamed about often enough but never—

No, of course he never told her. He never told anyone. Like every young man growing up in England, he was conditioned to get a hardon in the presence of certain fetishes, and then conditioned to feel shame about his new reflexes. Could there be, somewhere, a dossier, could They (They)? somehow have managed to monitor everything he saw and read since puberty ... how *else* would They know?

"Hush," she whispers. Her fingers stroke lightly her long olive thighs, bare breasts swell from the top of her garment. Her face is toward the ceiling, but her eyes are looking into Pirate's own, long, narrow with lust, two points of light glittering through the thick lashes ... "I'll leave him. We'll come here and live. We'll never stop making love. I belong to you, I've known that for a long time. . . ." Her tongue licks out over her little sharpened teeth. Her furry quim is at the center of all the light, and there is a taste in his mouth he would feel again. . . .

Well, Pirate nearly doesn't make it, barely gets his cock out of his trousers before he's spurting all over the place. Enough sperm saved, though, to rub over the blank scrap enclosed with the picture. Slowly then, a revelation through the nacreous film of his seed, in Negro-brown, comes his message: put in a simple Nihilist transposition whose keywords he can almost guess. Most of it he does in his head. There is a time given, a place, a request for help. He burns the message, fallen on him from higher than Earth's atmosphere, salvaged from Earth's prime meridian, keeps the picture, hmm, and washes his hands. His prostate is aching. There is more to this than he can see. He has no recourse, no appeal: he has to go over there and bring the operative out again. The message is tantamount to an order from the highest levels.

Far way, through the rain, comes the crack-blast of another German rocket. The third today. They hunt the sky like Wuotan and his mad army.

Pirate's own robot hands being to search drawers and folders for necessary vouchers and forms. No sleep tonight. Probably no chance even to catch a cup or cigarette on route. Why?

□

In Germany, as the end draws upon us, the incessant walls read WAS TUST DU FÜR DIE FRONT, FÜR DEN SIEG? WAS HAST DU HEUTE FÜR DEUTSCHLAND GETAN? At "The White Visitation" the walls read ice. Graffiti of ice the sunless day, glazing the darkening blood brick and terra cotta as if the house is to be preserved weatherless in some skin of clear museum plastic, an architectural document, an old-fashioned apparatus whose use is forgotten. Ice of varying thickness, wavy, blurred, a legend to be deciphered by lords of the winter, Glacists of the region, and argued over in their journals. Uphill, toward the sea, snow gathers like light at all windward edges of the ancient Abbey, its roof long ago taken at the manic whim of Henry VIII, its walls left to stand and mitigate with saintless window-hollows the salt wind, blowing as the seasons replay the grass floor in great cowlicks, green to blonde, to snow. From the Palladian house down in its resentful and twilit hollow this is the only view: the Abbey or else gentle, broadly mottled swoops of upland. View of the sea denied, though certain days and tides you can smell it, all your vile ancestry. In 1925 Reg Le Froyd, an inmate at "The White Visitation," escaped—rushed through the upper town to stand teetering at the edge of the cliff, hair and hospital garment flickering in the wind, the swaying miles of south coast, pallid chalk, jetties and promenades fading right and left into brine haze. After him came a Constable Stuggles, at the head of a curious crowd. "Don't jump!" cries the constable.

"I never thought of that," Le Froyd continuing to stare out to sea.

"Then what are you doing here. Eh?"

"Wanted to look at the sea," Le Froyd explains. "I've never seen it. I am, you know, related, by blood, to the sea."

"Oh aye," sly Stuggles edging up on him all the while, "visiting your relatives are you, how nice."

"I can hear the Lord of the Sea," cries Le Froyd, in wonder.

"Dear me, and what's his name?" Both of them wet-faced, shouting for the wind.

"Oh, I don't know," yells Le Froyd, "what would be a good name?"

"Bert," suggests the constable, trying to remember if it's right hand graps left arm above elbow or left hand grasps . . .

Le Froyd turns, and for the first time sees the man, and the crowd. His eyes grow round and mild. "Bert is fine," he says, and steps back into the void.

That's all the townsfolk of Ick Regis had from "The White Visitation" in the way of relief—from summers of staring at the pink or sun-freckled overflow from Brighton, Flotsam and Jetsam casting each day of wireless history into song, sunsets on the promenade, lens openings forever changing for the sea light, blown now brisk, now sedate about the sky, aspirins for sleep—only Le Froyd's leap, that single entertainment, up till the outbreak of this war.

At the defeat of Poland, ministerial motorcades were suddenly observed at all hours of the night, putting in at

"The White Visitation," silent as sloops, exhausts well muffled—chromeless black machinery that shone if there were starlight, and otherwise enjoyed the camouflage of a face about to be remembered, but through the act of memory fading too far. . . . Then at the fall of Paris, a radio transmitting station was set up on the cliff, antennas aimed at the Continent, themselves heavily guarded and their landlines back mysteriously over the downs to the house patrolled night and day by dogs specially betrayed, belted, starved into reflex leaps to kill, at any human approach. Had one of the Very High gone higher—that is, dotty? Was Our Side seeking to demoralize the German Beast by broadcasting to him random thoughts of the mad, naming for him, also in the tradition of Constable Stuggles that famous day, the deep, the scarcely seen? The answer is yes, all of the above, and more.

Ask them at "The White Visitation" about the master plan of the BBC's eloquent Myron Grunton, whose melted toffee voice has been finding its way for years out the fraying rust bouclé of the wireless speakers and into English dreams, foggy old heads, children at the edges of attention. . . . He's had to keep putting his plan off, at first only a voice alone, lacking the data he really needed, no support, trying to get at the German soul from whatever came to hand, P/W interrogations, Foreign Office Handbooks, the brothers Grimm, tourist memories of his own (young sleepless Dawes-era flashes, vineyards sunlit very green bearding the south valley-slopes of the Rhine, at night in the smoke and worsted cabarets of the capital long frilled suspenders like rows of carnations, silk stockings highlighted each in one long fine crosshatching of light . . .). But at last the Americans came in, and the arrangement known as SHAEF, and an amazing amount of money.

The scheme is called Operation Black Wing. My what a careful construction, five years in the making. No one could claim it all as his own, not even Grunton. It was General Eisenhower who laid down the controlling guideline, the "strategy of truth" idea. Something "real," Ike insisted on: a hook on the war's pocked execution-wall to hang the story from. Pirate Prentice of the S.O.E. came back with the first hard intelligence that there were indeed in Germany real Africans, Hereros, ex-colonials from South-West Africa, somehow active in the secret-weapons program. Myron Grunton, inspired, produced on the air one night completely ad lib the passage that found its way into the first Black Wing directive: "Germany once treated its Africans like a stern but loving stepfather, chastising them when necessary, often with death. Remember? But that was far away in Südwest, and since then a generation has gone by. Now the Herero lives in his stepfather's house. Perhaps you, listening, have seen him. Now he stays up past the curfews, and watches his stepfather while he sleeps, invisible, protected by the night which is his own colour. What are they all thinking? Where are the Hereros tonight? What are they *doing*, this instant, your dark, secret children?" And Black Wing has even found an American, a Lieutenant Slothrop, willing to go under light narcosis to help illuminate racial problems in his own country. An invaluable extra dimension. Toward the end, as more foreign morale data began to come back—Yank pollsters with clipboards and squeaky new shoe-pacs or galoshes visiting snow-softened liberated ruins to root out the truffles of truth created, as ancients surmised, during storm, in the instant of lightning blast—a contact in American PWD was able to bootleg copies and make them available to "The White Visitation." No one is sure who suggested the name "Schwarzkommando." Myron Grunton had favored "Wütende Heer," that company of spirits who ride the heaths of the sky in furious hunt, with great Wuotan at their head—but Myron agreed that was more a northern myth. Effectiveness in Bavaria might be less than optimum.

They all talk effectiveness, an American heresy, perhaps overmuch at "The White Visitation." Loudest of all, usually, is Mr. Pointsman, often using for ammo statistics provided him by Roger Mexico. By the time of the Normandy landing, Pointsman's season of despair was well upon him. He came to understand that the great continental pincers was to be, after all, a success. That this war, this State he'd come to feel himself a citizen of, was to be adjourned and reconstituted as a peace—and that, professionally speaking, he'd hardly got a thing out of it. With funding available for all manner of radars, magic torpedoes, aircraft and missiles, where was Pointsman in the scheme of

things? He'd had a moment's stewardship, that was all:
his Abreaction Research Facility (ARF), early on snaring
himself a dozen underlings, dog trainer from the variety
stage, veterinary student or two, even a major prize, the
refugee Dr. Porkyevitch, who worked with Pavlov himself at the Koltushy institute, back before the purge trials.
Together the ARF team receive, number, weigh, classify
by Hippocratic temperament, cage, and presently experiment on as many as a dozen fresh dogs a week. And there
are one's colleagues, co-owners of The Book, all now—
all those left of the original seven—working in hospitals
handling the battle-fatigued and shell-shocked back from
across the Channel, and the bomb- or rocket-happy this
side. They got to watch more abreactions, during these
days of heavy V-bombardment, than doctors of an earlier
day were apt to see in several lifetimes, and they are able
to suggest ever new lines of inquiry. P.W.E. allows a
stingy dribble of money, desperate paper whispering down
the corporate lattice, enough to get by on, enough that
ARF remains a colony to the metropolitan war, but not
enough for nationhood.... Mexico's statisticians chart for
it drops of saliva, body weights, voltages, sound levels,
metronome frequencies, bromide dosages, number of
afferent nerves cut, percentages of brain tissue removed,
dates and hours of numbing, deafening, blinding, castra-
tion. Support even comes from Psi Section, a colony
dégagé and docile, with no secular aspirations at all.

Old Brigadier Pudding can live with this spiritualist
gang well enough, he's tendencies himself in that direction. But Ned Pointsman, with his constant scheming after
more money—Pudding can only stare back at the man, try
to be civil. Not as tall as his father, certainly not as wholesome looking. Father was M.O. in Thunder Prodd's regiment, caught a bit of shrapnel in the thigh at Polygon
Wood, lay silent for seven hours before they, without a
word before, in that mud, that terrible smell, in, yes
Polygon Wood ... or was that—who *was* the ginger-
haired chap who slept with his hat on? ahhh, come back.
Now Polygon Wood ... but it's fluttering away. Fallen
trees, dead, smooth gray, swirlinggrainoftreelikefrozen-
smoke ... ginger ... thunder ... no use, no bleeding use,
it's gone, another gone, another, oh dear ...

The old Brigadier's age is uncertain, though he must be

pushing 80—reactivated in 1940, set down in a new space
not only of battlefield—where the front each day or hour
changes like a noose, like the gold-lit borders of consciousness (perhaps, though it oughtn't to get too sinister
here, *exactly like them* . . . better, then, "like a noose")—
but also of the War-state itself, its very structure. Pudding finds himself wondering, at times aloud and in the
presence of subordinates, what enemy disliked him enough
to assign him to Political Warfare. One is supposed to be
operating in concert—yet too often in amazing dissonance—with other named areas of the War, colonies of that
Mother City mapped wherever the enterprise is systematic
death: P.W.E. laps over onto the Ministry of Information,
the BBC European Service, the Special Operations Executive, the Ministry of Economic Warfare, and the F.O.
Political Intelligence Department at Fitzmaurice House.
Among others. When the Americans came in, their OSS,
OWI, and Army Psychological Warfare Department had
also to be coordinated with. Presently there arose the joint,
SHAEF Psychological Warfare Division (PWD), reporting direct to Eisenhower, and to hold it all together a
London Propaganda Coordinating Council, which has no
real power at all.

Who can find his way about this lush maze of initials,
arrows solid and dotted, boxes big and small, names
printed and memorized? Not Ernest Pudding—that's for
the New Chaps with their little green antennas out for the
usable emanations of power, versed in American politics
(knowing the difference between the New Dealers of
OWI and the eastern and moneyed Republicans behind
OSS), keeping brain-dossiers on latencies, weaknesses, tea-
taking habits, erogenous zones of all, all who might someday be useful.

Ernest Pudding was brought up to believe in a literal
Chain of Command, as clergymen of earlier centuries believed in the Chain of Being. The newer geometries confuse him. His greatest triumph on the battlefield came in
1917, in the gassy, Armageddonite filth of the Ypres
salient, where he conquered a bight of no man's land
some 40 yards at its deepest, with a wastage of only
70% of his unit. He was pensioned off around the beginning of the Great Depression—went to sit in the study of

an empty house in Devon, surrounded by photos of old comrades, none of whose gazes quite met one's own, there to go at a spot of combinatorial analysis, that favorite pastime of retired Army officers, with a rattling intense devotion.

It occurred to him to focus his hobby on the European balance of power, because of whose long pathology he had labored, deeply, all hope of waking lost, in the nightmare of Flanders. He started in on a mammoth work entitled *Things That Can Happen in European Politics*. Begin, of course, with England. "First," he wrote, "Bereshith, as it were: Ramsay MacDonald can die." By the time he went through resulting party alignments and possible permutations of cabinet posts, Ramsay MacDonald had died. "Never make it," he found himself muttering at the beginning of each day's work—"it's changing out from under me. Oh, dodgy—very dodgy."

When it had changed as far as German bombs falling on England, Brigadier Pudding gave up his obsession and again volunteered his services to his country. Had he known at the time it would mean "The White Visitation" . . . not that he'd expected a combat assignment you know, but wasn't there something mentioned about intelligence work? Instead he found a disused hospital for the mad, a few token lunatics, an enormous pack of stolen dogs, cliques of spiritualists, Ouspenskians, Skinnerites, lobotomy enthusiasts, Dale Carnegie zealots, all exiled by the outbreak of war from pet schemes and manias damned, had the peace prolonged itself, to differing degrees of failure—but their hopes *now* focusing on Brigadier Pudding and possibilities for funding: more hope than Prewar, that underdeveloped province, ever offered. Pudding could only respond by adopting rather an Old Testament style with everyone, including the dogs, and remaining secretly baffled and hurt by what he imagined as treachery high inside Staff.

Snowlight comes in through tall, many-paned windows, a dark day, a light burning only here and there among the brown offices. Subalterns encrypt, blindfolded subjects call Zener-deck guesses to hidden microphones: "Waves . . . Waves . . . Cross . . . Star . . ." While someone from Psi

Section records them from a speaker down in the cold basement. Secretaries in woolen shawls and rubber galoshes shiver with the winter cold being inhaled through the madhouse's many crevices, their typewriter keys chattery as their pearlies. Maud Chilkes, who looks from the rear rather like Cecil Beaton's photograph of Margot Asquith, sits dreaming of a bun and a cup of tea.

In the ARF wing, the stolen dogs sleep, scratch, recall shadowy smells of humans who may have loved them, listen undrooling to Ned Pointsman's oscillators and metronomes. The drawn shades allow only mild passages of light from outdoors. Technicians are moving behind the thick observation window, but their robes, greenish and submarine through the glass, flutter more slowly, less brightly. . . . A numbness has taken over, or a felt darkening. The metronome at 80 per second breaks out in wooden echoes, and Dog Vanya, bound atop the test stand, begins to salivate. All other sounds are damped severely: the beams underpinning the lab smothered in sand-filled rooms, sandbags, straw, uniforms of dead men occupying the spaces between the windowless walls . . . where the country bedlamites sat around, scowling, sniffing nitrous oxide, giggling, weeping at an E-major chord modulating to a G-sharp minor, now are cubical deserts, stand-rooms, keeping the metronome sovereign here in the lab, behind the iron doors, closed hermetically.

The duct of Dog Vanya's submaxillary gland was long ago carried out the bottom of his chin through an incision and sutured in place, leading saliva outside to the collecting funnel, fixed there with the traditional orange Pavlovian Cement of rosin, iron oxide and beeswax. Vacuum brings the secretion along through shining tubework to displace a column of light red oil, moving to the right along a scale marked off in "drops"—an arbitrary unit, probably not the same as the actually fallen drops of 1905, of St. Petersburg. But the number of drops, for this lab and Dog Vanya and the metronome at 80, is each time predictable.

Now that he has moved into "equivalent" phase, the first of the transmarginal phases, a membrane, hardly noticeable, stretches between Dog Vanya and the outside. Inside and outside remain just as they were, but the *inter-*

face—the cortex of Dog Vanya's brain—is changing, in
any number of ways, and that is the really peculiar thing
about these transmarginal events. It no longer matters now
how loudly the metronome ticks. A stronger stimulus no
longer gets a stronger response. The same number of
drops flow or fall. The man comes and removes the metronome to the farthest corner of his muffled room. It is
placed inside a box, beneath a pillow with the machine-
sewn legend *Memories of Brighton*, but the drops do not
fall off . . . then played into a microphone and amplifier so
that each tick fills the room up like a shout, but the drops
do not increase. Every time, the clear saliva pushes the
red line over only to the same mark, the same number of
drops. . . .

Webley Silvernail and Rollo Groast go sneaky-Peteing
away down the corridors, nipping into people's offices to
see if there are any smokable fag-ends to be looted. Most
offices right now are empty: all personnel with the patience
or masochism for it are going through a bit of ritual with
the doddering Brigadier.

"That old-man *has, no-shame*," Géza Rózsavölgyi,
another refugee (and violently anti-Soviet, which creates
a certain strain with ARF) flicking his hands up Brigadier
Puddingward in gay despair, the lilting Hungarian gypsy-
whisper bashing like tambourines all around the room,
provoking, in one way or another, everyone here except
for the aged Brigadier himself, who just goes rambling
on from the pulpit of what was a private chapel once,
back there on the maniac side of the 18th century, and is
now a launching platform for "The Weekly Briefings," a
most amazing volley of senile observations, office paranoia,
gossip about the War which might or might not include
violations of security, reminiscences of Flanders . . . the
coal boxes in the sky coming straight down on you with a
roar . . . the drumfire so milky and luminous on his birthday night . . . the wet surfaces in the shell craters for miles
giving back one bleak autumn sky . . . what Haig, in the
richness of his wit, once said at mess about Lieutenant
Sassoon's refusal to fight . . . the gunners in springtime, in
their flowing green robes . . . roadsides of poor rotting
horses just before apricot sunrise . . . the twelve spokes of
a stranded artillery piece—a mud clock, a mud zodiac,

clogged and crusted as it stood in the sun its many shades
of brown. The mud of Flanders gathered into the curd-
clumped, mildly jellied textures of human shit, piled, duck-
boarded, trenched and shell-pocked leagues of shit in all
directions, not even the poor blackened stump of a tree—
and the old blithering gab-artist tries to shake the cherry-
wood pulpit here, as if that had been the worst part of
the whole Passchendaele horror, that absence of vertical
interest. . . . On he goes, gabbing, gabbing, recipes for
preparing beets in a hundred tasty ways, or such cucurbi-
taceous improbabilities as Ernest Pudding's Gourd Surprise—yes, there *is* something sadistic about recipes with
"Surprise" in the title, chap who's hungry wants to just
eat you know, not be Surprised really, just wants to bite
into the (sigh) the old potato, and be reasonably sure
there's nothing inside *but* potato you see, certainly not
some clever nutmeg "Surprise!", some mashed pulp all
magenta with *pomegranates* or something . . . well but
this is just the doubtful sort of joke that Brigadier Pudding loves to play: how he's *chuckled,* as unsuspecting
dinner-guests go knifing into his notorious Toad-in-the-
Hole, through the honest Yorkshire batter into—*ugh!* what
is it? a beet *rissolé*? a *stuffed* beet *rissolé*? or perhaps today some lovely pureed samphire, reeking of the sea
(which he obtains once a week from the same fat fish-
monger's son wheeling his bicycle, puffing, up the chalk-
white cliff)—none of these odd, odd vegetable rissoles do
resemble any ordinary "Toad," but rather the depraved,
half-sentient creatures that Young Chaps from Kings Road
have Affairs With in limericks—Pudding has *thousands* of
these recipes and no shame about sharing any of them
with the lot at PISCES, along with, later in the weekly
soliloquy, a line or two, eight bars, from "Would You
Rather Be a Colonel with an Eagle on Your Shoulder, or
a Private with a Chicken on Your Knee?" then perhaps a
lengthy recitation of all his funding difficulties, all, dating
back to long before the emergence of even the Electra
House group . . . letter-feuds he has carried on in the
Times with critics of Haig. . . .

    And they all *sit* there, in front of the very high, blacked,
lead-crossed windows, allowing him his folly, the dog
people skulking over in one corner, passing notes and
leaning to whisper (they plot, they plot, sleeping or afoot

they never let up), the Psi Section lot clear over the other side of the room—as if we have a parliament of some kind here . . . everyone for years has occupied his own unique pew-seat and angle in to the ravings of reddish and liver-spotted Brigadier Pudding—with the other persuasions-in-exile spread between these two wings: the balance of power, if any power existed at "The White Visitation."

Dr. Rózsavölgyi feels that there well might, if the fellows "play their cards right." The only issue now is survival—on through the awful interface of V-E Day, on into the bright new Postwar with senses and memories intact. PISCES must not be allowed to go down under the hammer with the rest of the bawling herd. There must arise, and damned soon, able to draw them into a phalanx, a concentrated point of light, some leader or program powerful enough to last them across who knows how many years of Postwar. Dr. Rózsavölgyi tends to favor a powerful program over a powerful leader. Maybe because this is 1945. It was widely believed in those days that behind the War—all the death, savagery, and destruction—lay the Führer-principle. But if personalities could be replaced by abstractions of power, if techniques developed by the corporations could be brought to bear, might not nations live rationally? One of the dearest Postwar hopes: that there should be no room for a terrible disease like charisma . . . that its rationalization should proceed while we had the time and resources. . . .

Isn't that what's really at stake for Dr. Rózsavölgyi here in this latest scheme, centered on the figure of Lieutenant Slothrop? All the psychological tests in the subject's dossier, clear back to his college days, indicate a diseased personality. "Rosie" slaps the file with his hand for emphasis. The staff table shudders. "For ex*am*-ple: his Minne*so*-ta, Mul-ti*pha*-sic Person*ali*ty *In*ventory is tre*men*-dously lop*si*-ded, always in *fa*-vor of, the psycho-pathic, and, the un-*whole*-some."

But the Reverend Dr. Paul de la Nuit is not fond of the MMPI. "Rosie, are there scales for measuring inter-personal traits?" Hawk's nose probing, probing, eyes lowered in politic meekness, "*Human* values? Trust, honesty, love? Is there—forgive me the special pleading—a religious scale, by any chance?"

No way, padre: the MMPI was developed about 1943.

In the very heart of the War. Allport and Vernon's Study
of Values, the Bernreuter Inventory as revised by Flana-
gan in '35—tests from before the War—seem to Paul de
la Nuit more humane. All the MMPI appears to test for
is whether a man will be a good or bad soldier.

"Soldiers are much in demand these days, Reverend
Doctor," murmurs Mr. Pointsman.

"I only hope that we don't put too much emphasis on
his MMPI scores. It seems to me very narrow. It omits
large areas of the human personality."

"Pre*cise*-ly *why*," leaps Rózsavölgyi, "we are now pro-
*pos*ing, to give, Sloth-rop a com*plete*-ly *dif*-ferent sort, of
test. We are now de*sign*-ing for him, a so-*called*, 'projec-
tive' test. The most fam*il*-iar ex*am*-ple of the *type*, is the
Rorschach *ink*-blot. The *ba*-sic theory, is, that when given
an un*struc*-tured stimulus, some shape-less *blob* of experience, the subject, will seek to impose, *struc*-ture *on* it.
How, he goes a-*bout struc*-turing this blob, will reflect his
needs, his hopes—will pro*vide*, us with *clues*, to his
dreams, *fan*-tasies, the deepest *re*-gions of his mind." Eyebrows going a mile a minute, extraordinarily fluid and
graceful hand gestures, resembling—most likely it is deliberate, and who can blame Rosie for trying to cash in—
those of his most famous compatriot, though there're the
inevitable bad side-effects: staff who swear they've seen him
crawling headfirst down the north façade of "The White
Visitation," for example. "So we are *re*-ally, quite, in a*gree*-
ment, Reverend Doctor. A test, like the MMPI, is, in this
respect, not adequate. It is, a *struc*-tured stimulus. The
sub-ject can *fal*-sify, consciously, or repress, *un*-consciously.
But with the projec-tive tech*nique*, nothing he can do, conscious or otherwise, can pre-*vent* us, from fin-ding what we
wish, to know. We, are in control. He, cannot *help*, himself."

"Must say it doesn't sound like your cup of tea, Pointsman," smiles Dr. Aaron Throwster. "Your stimuli are more
the structured sort, aren't they?"

"Let's say I find a certain shameful fascination."

"Let's not. Don't tell me you're going to keep your fine
Pavlovian hand completely out of this."

"Well, not completely, Throwster, no. Since you've
brought it up. We *also* happen to have in mind a very

structured stimulus. Same one, in fact, that got us interested to begin with. We want to expose Slothrop to the German rocket. . . ."

Overhead, on the molded plaster ceiling, Methodist versions of Christ's kingdom swarm: lions cuddle with lambs, fruit spills lushly and without pause into the arms and about the feet of gentlemen and ladies, swains and milkmaids. No one's expression is quite right. The wee creatures leer, the fiercer beasts have a drugged or sedated look, and none of the humans have any eye-contact at all. The ceilings of "The White Visitation" aren't the only erratic thing about the place, either. It is a classic "folly," all right. The buttery was designed as an Arabian harem in miniature, for reasons we can only guess at today, full of silks, fretwork and peepholes. One of the libraries served, for a time, as a wallow, the floor dropped three feet and replaced with mud up to the thresholds for giant Gloucestershire Old Spots to frolic, oink, and cool their summers in, to stare at the shelves of buckram books and wonder if they'd be good eating. Whig eccentricity is carried in this house to most unhealthy extremes. The rooms are triangular, spherical, walled up into mazes. Portraits, studies in genetic curiosity, gape and smirk at you from every vantage. The W.C.s contain frescoes of Clive and his elephants stomping the French at Plassy, fountains that depict Salome with the head of John (water gushing out ears, nose, and mouth), floor mosaics in which are tessellated together different versions of Homo Monstrosus, an interesting preoccupation of the time—cyclops, humanoid giraffe, centaur repeated in all directions. Everywhere are archways, grottoes, plaster floral arrangements, walls hung in threadbare velvet or brocade. Balconies give out at unlikely places, overhung with gargoyles whose fangs have fetched not a few newcomers nasty cuts on the head. Even in the worst rains, the monsters only just manage to drool—the rainpipes feeding them are centuries out of repair, running crazed over slates and beneath eaves, past cracked pilasters, dangling Cupids, terra-cotta facing on every floor, along with belvederes, rusticated joints, pseudo-Italian columns, looming minarets, leaning crooked chimneys—from a distance no two observers, not matter how close they stand, see quite the same building in that orgy

of self-expression, added to by each succeeding owner,
until the present War's requisitioning. Topiary trees line
the drive for a distance before giving way to larch and
elm: ducks, bottles, snails, angels, and steeplechase riders
they dwindle down the metaled road into their fallow
silence, into the shadows under the tunnel of sighing trees.
The sentry, a dark figure in white webbing, stands port-
arms in your masked headlamps, and you must halt for
him. The dogs, engineered and lethal, are watching you
from the woods. Presently, as evening comes on, a few
bitter flakes of snow begin to fall.

□

Better behave yourself or we'll send you back to Dr. Jamf!

When Jamf conditioned *him*, he threw away the stimulus.

Looks like Dr. Jamf's been to see *your* little thing
    today, hasn't he?

> —Neil Nosepicker's Book of 50,000 Insults,
> §6.72, "Awful Offspring,"
> The Nayland Smith Press,
> Cambridge (Mass.), 1933

PUDDING: But isn't this—

POINTSMAN: Sir?

PUDDING: Isn't it all rather shabby, Pointsman? Meddling with another man's mind this way?

POINTSMAN: Brigadier, we're only following in a long
line of experiment and questioning. Harvard University,
the U.S. Army? Hardly shabby institutions.

PUDDING: We can't, Pointsman, it's beastly.

POINTSMAN: But the Americans have already been *at*
him! don't you see? It's not as if we're corrupting a virgin
or something—

PUDDING: Do we have to do it because the Americans
do it? Must we allow them to corrupt *us*?

Back around 1920, Dr. Laszlo Jamf opined that if Watson and Rayner could successfully condition their "Infant
Albert" into a reflex horror of everything furry, even of his
own Mother in a fur boa, then Jamf could certainly do the

same thing for his Infant Tyrone, and the baby's sexual reflex. Jamf was at Harvard that year, visiting from Darmstadt. It was in the early part of his career, before he phased into organic chemistry (to be as fateful a change of field as Kekulé's own famous switch into chemistry from architecture, a century before). For the experiment he had a slender grant from the National Research Council (under a continuing NRC program of psychological study which had begun during the World War, when methods were needed for selecting officers and classifying draftees). Shoestring funding may have been why Jamf, for his target reflex, chose an infant hardon. Measuring secretions, as Pavlov did, would have meant surgery. Measuring "fear," the reflex Watson chose, would have brought in too much subjectivity (what's fear? How much is "a lot"? Who decides, when it's on-the-spot-in-the-field, and there isn't time to go through the long slow process of referring it up to the Fear Board?). Instrumentation just wasn't available in those days. The best he might've done was the Larson-Keeler three-variable "lie detector," but at the time it was still only experimental.

But a hardon, that's either there, or it isn't. Binary, elegant. The job of observing it can even be done by a *student*.

Unconditioned stimulus = stroking penis with antiseptic cotton swab.

Unconditioned response = hardon.

Conditioned stimulus = x.

Conditioned response = hardon whenever x is present, stroking is no longer necessary, all you need is that x.

Uh, x? well, what's x? Why, it's the famous "Mystery Stimulus" that's fascinated generations of behaviorial-psychology students, is what it is. The average campus humor magazine carries 1.05 column inches per year on the subject, which ironically is the exact mean length Jamf reported for Infant T.'s erection.

Now ordinarily, according to tradition in these matters, the little sucker would have been de-conditioned. Jamf would have, in Pavlovian terms, "extinguished" the hardon reflex he'd built up, before he let the baby go. Most likely he did. But as Ivan Petrovich himself said, "Not only must we speak of partial or of complete extinction of a condi-

tioned reflex, but we must realize that extinction can proceed *beyond* the point of reducing a reflex to zero. We
cannot therefore judge the degree of extinction *only* by
the magnitude of the reflex or its absence, since there can
still be a *silent extinction beyond the zero*." Italics are Mr.
Pointsman's.

Can a conditioned reflex survive in a man, dormant,
over 20 or 30 years? Did Dr. Jamf extinguish only to
zero—wait till the infant showed zero hardons in the presence of stimulus *x*, and then stop? Did he forget—or ignore—the "silent extinction beyond the zero"? If he ignored it, why? Did the National Research Council have
anything to say about that?

When Slothrop was discovered, late in 1944, by "The
White Visitation"—though many there have always known
him as the famous Infant Tyrone—like the New World,
different people thought they'd discovered different things.

Roger Mexico thinks it's a statistical oddity. But he feels
the foundations of that discipline trembling a bit now,
deeper than oddity ought to drive. Odd, odd, odd—think
of the word: such white finality in its closing clap of
tongue. It implies moving past the tongue-stop—beyond
the zero—and into the other realm. Of course you don't
move past. But you do realize, intellectually, that's how
you *ought* to be moving.

Rollo Groast thinks it's precognition. "Slothrop is able
to predict when a rocket will fall at a particular place. His
survival to date is evidence he's acted on advance information, and avoided the area at the time the rocket was
supposed to fall." Dr. Groast is not sure how, or even if,
sex comes into it.

But Edwin Treacle, that most Freudian of psychical
researchers, thinks Slothrop's gift is psychokinesis. Slothrop is, with the force of his mind, *causing* the rockets to
drop where they do. He may not be physically highballing
them about the sky: but maybe he is fooling with the
electrical signals inside the rocket's guidance system.
However he's doing it, ṡex *does* come into Dr. Treacle's
theory. "He subconsciously needs to abolish all trace of
the sexual Other, whom he symbolizes on his map, most
significantly, as a *star*, that anal-sadistic emblem of class-
room success which so permeates elementary education in
America. . . ."

It's the map that spooks them all, the map Slothrop's been keeping on his girls. The stars fall in a Poisson distribution, just like the rocket strikes on Roger Mexico's map of the Robot Blitz.

But, well, it's a bit more than the distribution. The two patterns also happen to be identical. They match up square for square. The slides that Teddy Bloat's been taking of Slothrop's map have been projected onto Roger's, and the two images, girl-stars and rocket-strike circles, demonstrated to coincide.

Helpfully, Slothrop has dated most of his stars. A star always comes *before* its corresponding rocket strike. The strike can come as quickly as two days, or as slowly as ten. The mean lag is about 4½ days.

Suppose, Pointsman argues, that Strobe's stimulus x was some loud noise, as it was in the Watson-Rayner experiment. Suppose that, in Slothrop's case, the hardon reflex wasn't completely extinguished. In that case he ought to be getting one on at any loud noise that's preceded by the same kind of ominous buildup he would've found in Jamf's lab—as dogs to this day find in Pointsman's own lab. The points to the V-1: any doodle close enough to make him jump ought to be giving him an erection: the sound of the motor razzing louder and louder, then the cutoff and silence, suspense building up—then the explosion. Boing, a hardon. But oh, no. Slothrop instead only gets erections when this sequence happens *in reverse*. Explosion first, then the sound of approach: the V-2.

But the stimulus, somehow, *must* be the rocket, some precursor wraith, some rocket's double present for Slothrop in the percentage of smiles on a bus, menstrual cycles being operated upon in some mysterious way—what *does* make the little doxies do it for free? Are there fluctuations in the sexual market, in pornography or prostitutes, perhaps tying into prices on the Stock Exchange itself, that we clean-living lot know nothing about? Does news from the front affect the itch between their pretty thighs, does desire grow directly or inversely as the real chance of sudden death—damn it, what cue, right in front of our eyes, that we haven't the subtlety of heart to see? . . .

But if it's in the air, right here, right now, then the rockets follow from it, 100% of the time. No exceptions. When we find it, we'll have shown again the stone

determinacy of everything, of every soul. There will be
precious little room for any hope at all. You can see how
important a discovery like that would be.

They walk down past the snow-drifted kennel runs,
Pointsman in Glastonburys and fawn-colored British warm,
Mexico wearing a scarf Jessica's lately knitted him whipping landward a scarlet dragon's tongue—this day the
coldest so far of the winter, 39 degrees of frost. Down to
the cliffs, faces freezing, down to the deserted beach.
Waves run up, slide away to leave great crescents of ice
fine as skin and dazzling in the weak sunlight. The boots
of the two men crunch through to sand or shingle. The
very bottom of the year. They can hear the guns in Flanders today, all the way across the Channel on the wind. The
Abbey's ruin stands gray and crystal up on the cliff.

Last night, in the house at the edge of the stay-away
town, Jessica, snuggling, afloat, just before sleep was to
take them, whispered, "Roger . . . what about the girls?"
That was all she said. But it brought Roger wide awake.
And bone-tired as he was, he lay staring for another hour,
wondering about the girls.

Now, knowing he ought to let it go, "Pointsman, what if
Edwin Treacle is right? That it's PK. What if Slothrop's—
not even consciously—*making* them fall where they do?"

"Well. You lot'd have something then, wouldn't you."

"But . . . *why* should he. If they are falling wherever
he's been—"

"Perhaps he hates women."

"I'm serious."

"Mexico. Are you actually worried?"

"I don't know. Perhaps I wondered if it might tie in, in
any way, with your ultraparadoxical phase. Perhaps . . . I
want to know what you're really looking for."

Above them now throb a flight of B-17s, bound somewhere uncommon today, well out of the usual corridors of
flight. Behind these Fortresses the undersides of the cold
clouds are blue, and their smooth billows, are veined in
blue—elsewhere touched with grayed-out pink or purple. . . . Wings and stabilizers are shadowed underneath
in dark gray. The shadows softly feather lighter up around
curves of fuselage or nacelle. Spinners emerge from hooded
dark inside the cowlings, spinning props invisible, the

light of the sky catching all vulnerable surfaces a uniform
bleak gray. The planes drone along, stately, up in the zero
sky, shedding frost as it builds, sowing the sky behind in
white ice-furrows, their own color matching certain degrees of cloud, all the tiny windows and openings in soft
blackness, the perspex nose shining back forever warped
and streaming cloud and sun. Inside it is black obsidian.

Pointsman has been talking about paranoia and the "idea
of the opposite." He has scribbled in The Book exclama-
tion points and *how trues* all about the margins of Pavlov's open letter to Janet concerning the *sentiments d'emprise,* and of Chapter LV, "An Attempt at a Physiological
Interpretation of Obsessions and of Paranoia"—he can't
help this bit of rudeness, although the agreement among
the seven owners was not to mark up The Book—it was
too valuable for that sort of thing, they'd had to put in a
guinea apiece. It was sold him on the sly, in the dark,
during a Luftwaffe raid (most existing copies had been
destroyed in their warehouse early in the Battle of Britain).
Pointsman never even saw the seller's face, the man vanishing into the hoarse auditory dawn of the all-clear, leaving the doctor and The Book, the dumb sheaf already heating up, moistening in his tight hand . . . yes it might have
been a rare work of erotica, certainly that coarse hand-set
look to the type . . . the crudities in phrasing, as if Dr.
Horsley Gantt's odd translation were in cipher, the plain-
text listing shameful delights, criminal transports. . . . And
how much of the pretty victim straining against her bonds
does Ned Pointsman see in each dog that visits his test
stands . . . and aren't scalpel and probe as decorative, as
fine extensions as whip and cane?

Surely the volume preceding The Book—the first
Forty-one Lectures—came to him at age 28 like a man-
date from the submontane Venus he could not resist: to
abandon Harley Street for a journey more and more
deviant, deliciously on, into a labyrinth of conditioned-
reflex work in which only now, thirteen years along the
clew, he's beginning to circle back, trip across old evidence
of having come that path before, here and there to confront consequences of his younger, total embrace. . . . But
she did warn him—did she not? was he ever listening?—
of the deferred payment, in its full amount. Venus and

Ariadne! She seemed worth any price, the labyrinth looking, in those days, too intricate for *them*—the twilit pimps
who made the arrangement between a version of himself,
a crypto-Pointsman, and his fate . . . too varied, he thought
then, ever to find him in. But he knows now. Too far in,
preferring not to face it just yet, he knows that they only
wait, stone and sure—these agents of the Syndicate she
must also pay—wait in the central chamber, as he draws
closer. . . . They own everything: Ariadne, the Minotaur,
even, Pointsman fears, himself. He gets flashes of them
these days, naked, athletes poised and breathing about the
chamber, terrible penises up mineral as their eyes, which
glisten with frost or flakes of mica, but not with lust, or
for him. It's only a job they have. . . .

"Pierre Janet—sometimes the man talked like an Oriental mystic. He had no real grasp of the opposites. 'The act
of injuring and the act of being injured are joined in the
behavior of the whole injury.' Speaker and spoken-of,
master and slave, virgin and seducer, each pair most conveniently coupled and inseparable— The last refuge of the
incorrigible lazy, Mexico, is just sort of yang-yin rubbish.
One avoids all manner of unpleasant lab work that way,
but what has one *said?*"

"I don't want to get into a religious argument with you,"
absence of sleep has Mexico more cranky than usual, "but
I wonder if you people aren't a bit too—well, strong, on
the virtues of analysis. I mean, once you've taken it all
apart, fine, I'll be first to applaud your industry. But
other than a lot of bits and pieces lying about, what have
you said?"

It isn't the sort of argument Pointsman relishes either.
But he glances sharply at this young anarchist in his red
scarf. "Pavlov believed that the ideal, the end we all
struggle toward in science, is the true mechanical explanation. He was realistic enough not to expect it in his lifetime. Or in several lifetimes more. But his hope was for a
long chain of better and better approximations. His faith
ultimately lay in a pure physiological basis for the life of
the psyche. No effect without cause, and a clear train of
linkages."

"It's not my forte, of course," Mexico honestly wishing
not to offend the man, but really, "but there's a feeling

about that cause-and-effect may have been taken as far as it will go. That for science to carry on at all, it must look for a less narrow, a less . . . sterile set of assumptions. The next great breakthrough may come when we have the courage to junk cause-and-effect entirely, and strike off at some other angle."

"No—not 'strike off.' Regress. You're 30 years old, man. There are no 'other angles.' There is only forward—*into it*—or backward."

Mexico watches the wind tugging at the skirts of Points-man's coat. A gull goes screaming away sidewise along the frozen berm. The chalk cliffs rear up above, cold and serene as death. Early barbarians of Europe who ventured close enough to this coast saw these white barriers through the mist, and knew then where their deed had been taken to.

Pointsman has turned now, and . . . oh, God. He is smiling. There is something so ancient in its assumption of brotherhood that—not now, but a few months from now, with spring prevailing and the War in Europe ended—Roger will remember the smile—it will haunt him—as the most evil look he has ever had from a human face.

They've paused in their walking. Roger stares back at the man. The Antimexico. "Ideas of the opposite" themselves, but on what cortex, what winter hemisphere? What ruinous mosaic, facing outward into the Waste . . . outward from the sheltering city . . . readable only to those who journey outside . . . eyes in the distance . . . barbarians . . . riders. . . .

"We both have Slothrop," is what Pointsman has just said.

"Pointsman—what are you expecting out of this? Besides glory, I mean."

"No more than Pavlov. A physiological basis for what seems very odd behavior. I don't care which of your P.R.S. categories it may fit into—oddly enough none of you's even suggested telepathy: perhaps he's tuned in to someone over there, someone who knows the German firing schedule ahead of time. Eh? And I don't care if it's some terrible Freudian revenge against his mother for trying to castrate him or something. I am not grandiose, Mexico. I am modest, methodical—"

"Humble."

"I have set myself limitations in this. I have only the reversal of rocket sounds to go on ... his clinical history of sexual conditioning, *perhaps* to auditory stimuli, and what *appears* to be a reversal of cause-and-effect. I'm not as ready as you to junk cause-and-effect, but if it does need modifying—so be it."

"But what are you *after?*"

"You've seen his MMPI. His F Scale? Falsifications, distorted thought processes. ... The scores show it clearly: he's psychopathically deviant, obsessive, a latent paranoiac—well, Pavlov believed that obsessions and paranoid delusions were a result of certain—call them cells, neurons, on the mosaic of the brain, being excited to the level where, through reciprocal induction, all the area around becomes inhibited. One bright, burning point, surrounded by darkness. Darkness it has, in a way, called up. Cut off, this bright point, perhaps to the end of the patient's life, from all other ideas, sensations, self-criticisms that might temper its flame, restore it to normalcy. He called it a 'point of pathological inertia.' We're working right now with a dog ... he's been through the 'equivalent' phase, where any stimulus, strong or weak, calls up exactly the same number of saliva drops ... and on through the 'paradoxical' phase—strong stimuli getting weak responses and vice versa. Yesterday we got him to go ultraparadoxical. Beyond. When we turn on the metronome that used to stand for food—that once made Dog Vanya drool like a fountain—now he turns away. When we shut off the metronome, oh *then* he'll turn to it, sniff, try to lick it, bite it—seek, in the silence, for the stimulus that is not there. Pavlov thought that all the diseases of the mind could be explained, eventually, by the ultraparadoxical phase, the pathologically inert points on the cortex, the confusion of ideas of the opposite. He died at the very threshold of putting these things on an experimental basis. But I live. I have the funding, and the time, and the will. Slothrop is a strong imperturbable. It won't be easy to send him into any of the three phases. We may finally have to starve, terrorize, I don't know ... it needn't come to that. But I will find his spots of inertia, I will find what they are if I have to open up his damned skull, and how they are isolated, and perhaps solve the mystery of why the rockets are falling as they do—though I admit that was more of a sop to get your support."

"Why?" A bit uneasy, there, Mexico? "Why do you need. me?"

"I don't know. But I do."

"*You're* obsessed."

"Mexico." Standing very still, seaward half of his face seeming to have aged fifty years in the instant, watching the tide of three full times leave behind its sterile film of ice. "Help me."

I can't help any one, Roger thinks. Why is he so tempted? It's dangerous and perverse. He does want to help, he feels the same unnatural fear of Slothrop that Jessica does. *What about the girls?* It may be his loneliness in Psi Section, in a persuasion he can't in his heart share, nor quite abandon... their faith, even smileless Gloaming's, that there must be more, beyond the senses, beyond death, beyond the Probabilities that are all Roger has to believe in.... *Oh Jessie,* his face against her bare, sleeping, intricately boned and tendoned back, *I'm out of my depth in this....*

Halfway between the water and the coarse sea-grass, a long stretch of pipe and barbed wire rings in the wind. The black latticework is propped up by longer slanting braces, lances pointing out to sea. An abandoned and mathematical look: stripped to the force-vectors holding it where it is, doubled up in places one row behind another, moving as Pointsman and Mexico begin to move again, backward in thick moiré, repeated uprights in parallax against repeated diagonals, and the snarls of wire below interfering more at random. Far away, where it curves into the haze, the openwork wall goes gray. After last night's snowfall, each line of the black scrawl was etched in white. But today wind and sand have blown the dark iron bare again, salted, revealing, in places, brief steaks of rust... in others, ice and sunlight turn the construction to electric-white lines of energy.

Farther up, past buried land mines and antitank posts of corroding concrete, up in a pillbox covered with netting and sod, halfway up the cliff, young Dr. Bleagh and his nurse Ivy are relaxing after a difficult lobotomy. His

scrubbed and routinized fingers dart in beneath her suspender straps, pull outward, release in a sudden great
smack and ho-ho-ho from Bleagh as she jumps and laughs
too, trying not too hard to squirm away. They lie on a bed
of faded old nautical charts, maintenance manuals, burst
sandbags and spilled sand, burned matchsticks and un-
raveled cork-tips from cigarettes long decomposed that
comforted through the nights of '41 and the sudden rush
of heart at any glimpse of a light at sea. "You're mad," she
whispers. "I'm randy," he smiles, and snaps her garter
again, boy-and-slingshot.

In the uplands a line of cylindrical blocks to cripple
the silent King Tigers that now will never roll the land
chains away like so many white muffins across the dun
pasture, among the low patches of snow and the pale lime
outcrops. Out on a little pond the black man is down from
London, ice-skating, improbable as a Zouave, riding his
blades tall, dignified, as if born to them and ice not desert.
Small townschildren scatter before him, close enough to
have their cheeks stung by curved wakes of powdered ice
whenever he turns. Until he smile they dare not speak,
only follow, tag, flirt, wanting the smile, fearing it, wanting it. . . . He has a magic face, a face they know. From
the shore, Myron Grunton and Edwin Treacle, both chain-
smoking, brooding over Operation Black Wing and the
credibility of the Schwarzkommando, watch their magic
Negro, their prototype, neither caring to risk the ice, loping Fen or any style, in front of these children.

The winter's in suspense—all the sky a bleak, luminous
gel. Down on the beach, Pointsman fishes a roll of toilet
paper, each sheet stenciled PROPERTY OF H.M. GOVERN-
MENT, from a pocket to blow his nose. Roger now and
then pushes hair back under his cap. Neither speaks. So,
the two of them: trudging, hands in and out of pockets,
their figures dwindling, fawn and gray and a lick of
scarlet, very sharp-edged, their footprints behind them a
long freezing progress of exhausted stars, the overcast reflecting from the glazed beach nearly white. . . . We have
lost them. No one listened to those early conversations—
not even an idle snapshot survives. They walked till that
winter hid them and it seemed the cruel Channel itself
would freeze over, and no one, none of us, could ever com-

pletely find them again. Their footprints filled with ice, and a little later were taken out to sea.

□

In silence, hidden from her, the camera follows as she moves deliberately nowhere longlegged about the rooms, an adolescent wideness and hunching to the shoulders, her hair not bluntly Dutch at all, but secured in a modish up-sweep with an old, tarnished silver crown, yesterday's new perm leaving her very blonde hair frozen on top in a hundred vortices, shining through the dark filigree. Widest lens-opening this afternoon, extra tungsten light laid on, this rainiest day in recent memory, rocket explosions far away to south and east now and then visiting the maison-ette, rattling not the streaming windows but only the doors, in slow three- and fourfold shudderings, like poor spirits, desperate for company, asking to be let in, only a moment, a touch . . .

She's alone in the house, except for the secret camera-man and Osbie Feel, who's out in the kitchen, doing some-thing mysterious with a harvest of mushrooms from up on the roof. They have shiny red-orange cups with raised patches of whitish-gray veil. Now and then the geometry of her restlessness brings her to glace in a doorway at his boyish fussing with the *Amanita muscaria* (for it is this peculiar relative of the poisonous Destroying Angel that claims Osbie's attention, or what passes with him for at-tention)—flash him a smile she means to be friendly but which to Osbie seems terribly worldly, sophisticated, wicked. She being the first Dutch girl he's ever spoken to, he's surprised at finding high heels instead of wooden shoes, struck in fact a bit witless by her so groomed and (he imagines) Continental style, the intellect behind the fair-lashed eyes or dark glasses she affects out on the street, behind the traces of baby fat, the dimples counter-sunk each side of her mouth. (In closeup her skin, though nearly perfect, is seen to be lightly powdered and rouged, the eyelashes a touch darkened, brows reshaped a matter of two or three empty follicles. . . .)

What *can* young Osbie possibly have in mind? He is

carefully scraping out the inside of each persimmon-colored mushroom cup and shredding the rest. Dispossessed elves run around up on the roof, gibbering. He now has a growing heap of orange-gray fungus, which he proceeds to add in fistfuls to a pot of steaming water. A previous batch also simmers atop the stove, reduced to a thick gruel covered with yellow scum, which Osbie now removes and purees further in Pirate's blending machine. Then he spreads the fungoid mush over a tin cookie sheet. He opens the oven, removes with asbestos potholders another sheet covered with dark caked dust, and replaces it with the one he has just prepared. With a mortar and pestle he pulverizes the substance and dumps it into an old Huntley & Palmers biscuit tin, reserving only enough to roll deftly up in a Rizla liquorice cigarette paper, light, and inhale the smoke of.

But she happens to've glanced in just at the instant Osbie opened the echoing oven. The camera records no change in her face, but why does she stand now so immobile at the door? as if the frame were to be stopped and prolonged into just such a lengthwise moment of gold fresh and tarnished, innocence microscopically masked, her elbow slightly bent, hand resting against the wall, fingers fanned on the pale orange paper as if she touches her own skin, a pensive touch. . . . Outside, the long rain in silicon and freezing descent smacks, desolate, slowly corrosive against the mediaeval windows, curtaining like smoke the river's far shore. This city, in all its bomb-pierced miles: this inexhaustibly knotted victim . . . skin of glistening roofslates, sotted brick flooded high about each window dark or lit, each of a million openings vulnerable to the gloom of this winter day. The rain washes, drenches, fills the gutters singing, the city receives it, lifting, in a perpetual shrug. . . . With a squeak and metal slam the oven is closed again, but for Katje it will never close. She has posed before the mirrors too often today, knows her hair and make-up are perfect, admires the frock they have brought her from Harvey Nicholls, a sheer crepe that flows in from padded shoulders down to a deep point between her breasts, a rich cocoa shade known as "nigger" in this country, yards and yards of this delicious silk spun and thrown, tied loosely at the waist, soft pleats falling to her knees. The cameraman is pleased at the unexpected effect of so much flowing crepe, particularly when Katje passes before a window and the rainlight coming through changes it for a few brief unshutterings to murky glass, charcoal-saturated, antique and weather-worn, frock, face, hair, hands, slender calves all gone to glass and glazing, for the celluloid instant poised—the translucent guardian of a rainfall shaken through all day by rocket blasts near and far, downward, dark and ruinous behind her the ground which, for the frames' passage, defines her.

At the images she sees in the mirror Katje also feels a cameraman's pleasure, but knows what he cannot: that inside herself, enclosed in the *soignée* surface of dear fabric and dead cells, she is corruption and ashes, she belongs in a way none of them can guess cruelly to the Oven ... to *Der Kinderofen* ... remembering now his teeth, long, terrible, veined with bright brown rot as he speaks these words, the yellow teeth of Captain Blicero, the network of stained cracks, and back in his nightbreath, in the dark oven of himself, always the coiled whispers of decay. . . . She recalls his teeth before any other feature, teeth were to benefit most directly from the Oven: from what is planned for her, and for Gottfried. He never uttered it clearly as threat, nor ever addressed to either of them directly, but rather across her trained satin thighs to the evening's guests, or down the length of Gottfried's docile spine ("the Rome-Berlin Axis" he called it the night the Italian came and they were all on the round bed, Captain Blicero plugged into Gottfried's upended asshole and the Italian at the same time into his pretty mouth) Katje only passive, bound and gagged and false-eyelashed, serving tonight as human pillow for the Italian's whitening perfumed curls (roses and fat just at the edge of turning rancid) ... each utterance a closed flower, capable of exfoliation and infinite revealing (she thinks of a mathematical function that will expand for her bloom-like into a power series *with no general term*, endlessly, darkly, though never completely by surprise) ... his phrase *Padre Ignacio* unfolding into Spanish inquisitor, black robes, brown arching nose, the suffocating smell of incense + confessor/executioner + Katje and Gottfried both kneeling, side by side in dark confessional + children out of old Märchen kneeling, knees

cold and aching, before the Oven, whispering to it secrets
they can tell no one else + Captain Blicero's witch-
paranoia, suspecting them both, Katje despite her NSB
credentials + the Oven as listener/avenger + Katje
kneeling before Blicero in highest drag, black velvet and
Cuban heels, his penis squashed invisible under a flesh-
colored leather jockstrap, over which he wears a false
cunt and merkin of sable both handcrafted in Berlin by
the notorious Mme. Ophir, the mock labia and bright purple clitoris molded of—Madame had been abject, pleading
shortages—synthetic rubber and Mipolam, the new polyvinyl chloride . . . tiny blades of stainless steel bristle from
lifelike pink humidity, hundreds of them, against which
Katje, kneeling, is obliged to cut her lips and tongue, and
then kiss blood-abstracts across the golden ungessoed back
of her "brother" Gottfried. Brother in play, in slavery . . .
she had never seen him before coming to the requisitioned house near the firing sites, hidden in the woods and
parkland of this settled tongue of small farms and estates
that reaches eastward from the royal city, between two
expanses of polder, toward Wassenaar—yet his face, for
that first time, seen in autumn sunlight through the great
west window of the drawing-room, kneeling naked except
for a studded dog collar, masturbating metronomic, at
shouted commands from Captain Blicero, all his fair skin
stained by afternoon a luminous synthetic orange she has
never before associated with skin, his penis a blood monolith, its thickly gasping mouth audible in the carpeted
silence, his face raised to none of them, but as if to something on the ceiling, or in the sky which ceilings may in
his vision stand for, eyes-down as he seems most of the
time to be—his face, ascending, tightening, coming, is so
close to what she's been seeing all her life in mirrors, her
own studied mannequin's stare, that she catches her breath,
feels for a moment the speeded percussion of her heart,
before just such a stare toward Blicero. He is delighted.
"Perhaps," he tells her, "I will cut your hair." He smiles at
Gottfried. "Perhaps I'll have him grow his." The humiliation would be good for the boy each morning at quarters,
ranked with his battery near Schußstelle 3, where horses
thundered once before the frantic, the losing railbirds of
the old peace—failing inspections time after time yet pro-

tected by his Captain from Army discipline. Instead, between firings, day or night, short of sleep, odd hours,
suffering the Captain's own "Hexeszüchtigung." But did
Blicero also cut her hair? She can't remember now. She
knows she wore Gottfried's uniforms once or twice (pushing her hair, yes, up under his forage cap), looking easily
his double, spending these nights "in the cage," as Blicero
has set the rules, while Gottfried must wear her silk stockings, her lace apron and cap, all her satin and her ribboned organdy. But afterward he must always go back
again to the cage. That's how it is. Their Captain allows
no doubt as to which, brother or sister, really is maid-
servant, and which fattening goose.

How seriously is she playing? In a conquered country,
one's own occupied country, it's better, she believes, to
enter into some formal, rationalized version of what, outside, proceeds without form or decent limit day and night,
the summary executions, the roustings, beatings, subterfuge, paranoia, shame . . . though it is never discussed
among them openly, it would seem Katje, Gottfried, and
Captain Blicero have agreed that this Northern and ancient form, one they all know and are comfortable with—
the strayed children, the wood-life in the edible house,
the captivity, the fattening, the Oven—shall be their preserving routine, their shelter, against what outside none of
them can bear—the War, the absolute rule of chance,
their own pitiable contingency here, in its midst. . . .

It isn't safe, even inside, in the house . . . nearly every
day a rocket misfires. Late in October, not far from this
estate, one fell back and exploded, killing 12 of the
ground crew, breaking windows for hundreds of meters all
around, including the west window of the drawing-room
where Katje first saw her golden game-brother. The official
rumor stated that only fuel and oxidizer had gone off. But
Captain Blicero, with a trembling—she must say nihilistic—pleasure, said that the Amatol charge in the warhead
had also exploded, making them as much target as launch
site. . . . That they were all condemned. The house lies
west of the Duindigt racecourse, quite the other direction
from London, but no bearing is exempt—often the rockets,
crazed, turn at random, whinnying terribly in the sky, turn
about and fall according each to its madness so unreach-

able and, it is feared, incurable. When there's time to, their owners destroy them, by radio, in mid-convulsion. Between rocket launches there are the English raids. Spitfires come roaring in low over the dark sea at suppertime, the searchlights in the city staggering on, the after-hum of sirens hangs in the sky high above the wet iron seats in the parks, the AA guns chug, searching, and the bombs fall in woodland, in polder, among flats thought to be billeting rocket troops.

It adds an overtone to the game, which changes the timbre slightly. It is she who, at some indefinite future moment, must push the Witch into the Oven intended for Gottfried. So the Captain must allow for the real chance she's a British spy, or member of the Dutch underground. Despite all German efforts, intelligence inputs still flow from Holland back to RAF Bomber Command in a steady torrent, telling of deployments, supply routes, of which dark-green crumble of trees may hide an A4 emplacement—data changing hour-to-hour, so mobile are the rockets and their support equipment. But the Spitfires will settle for a power station, a liquid-oxygen supply, a battery commander's billet . . . that's the intriguing question. Will Katje feel her obligation canceled by someday calling down English fighter-bombers on this very house, her game's prison, though it mean death? Captain Blicero can't be sure. Up to a point he finds the agony delightful. Certainly her record with Mussert's people is faultless, she's credited with smelling out at least three crypto-Jewish families, she attends meetings faithfully, she works at a Luftwaffe resort near Scheveningen, where her superiors find her efficient and cheerful, no shirker. Nor, like so many of them, using party fanaticism to cover a lack of ability. Perhaps there's the only shadow of warning: her commitment is not emotional. She appears to have reasons for being in the Party. A woman with some background in mathematics, and with *reasons*. . . . "Want the Change," Rilke said, "O be inspired by the Flame!" To laurel, to nightingale, to wind . . . *wanting* it, to be taken, to embrace, to fall toward the flame growing to fill all the senses and . . . not to love because it was no longer possible to act . . . but to be helplessly in a condition of love. . . .

But not Katje: no mothlike plunge. He must conclude that secretly she fears the Change, choosing instead only trivially to revise what matters least, ornament and clothing, going no further than politic transvestism, not only in Gottfried's clothing, but even in traditional masochist uniform, the French-maid outfit so inappropriate to her tall, longlegged stride, her blondeness, her questing shoulders like wings—she plays at this only . . . plays at playing.

He can do nothing. Among dying Reich, orders lapsing to paper impotence he needs her so, needs Gottfried, the straps and whips leathern, real in his hands which still feel, her cries, the red welts across the boy's buttocks, their mouths, his penis, fingers and toes—in all the winter these are sure, can be depended on—he can give you no reason but in his heart he trusts, perhaps only, by now, in the form, this out of all Märchen und Sagen, trusts that this charmed house in the forest will be preserved, that no bombs could ever fall here by accident, only betrayal, only if Katje really were a spotter for the English and bade them—and he knows she cannot: that through some magic, below the bone resonance of any words, a British raid is the one prohibited shape of all possible pushes from behind, into the Oven's iron and final summer. It will come, it will, his Destiny . . . not that way—but it will come. . . . *Und nicht einmal sein Schritt klingt aus dem tonlosen Los.* . . . Of all Rilke's poetry it's this Tenth Elegy he most loves, can feel the bitter lager of Yearning begin to prickle behind eyes and sinuses at remembering any passage of . . . the newly-dead youth, embracing his Lament, his last link, leaving now even her marginally human touch forever, climbing all alone, terminally alone, up and up into the mountains of primal Pain, with the wildly alien constellations overhead. . . . *And not once does his step ring from the soundless Destiny.* . . . It's he, Blicero, who climbs the mountain, has been so climbing for nearly 20 years, since long before he embraced the Reich's flame, since Südwest . . . alone. No matter what flesh was there to appease the Witch, cannibal, and sorcerer, flourishing implements of pain—alone, alone. He doesn't even know the Witch, can't understand the hunger that defines him/her, is only, in times of weakness, bewildered that it should coexist in the same body as himself. An athlete and his

skill, separate awarenesses. . . . Young Rauhandel at least
had said so . . . how many years back into the peace . . .
Blicero had watched his young friend (even then already
so blatantly, so pathetically doomed to some form of Eastern Front) inside a bar, out in the street, wearing whatever tight or awkward suit, whatever fragile shoes, react
in all grace to the football which jokers would recognizing
him toss out of nowhere—the deathless performances! that
one impromptu boot so impossibly high, so perfectly parabolic, the ball soaring miles to pass exactly between the
two tall, phallic electric columns of the Ufa-theatre on the
Friedrichstrasse . . . the head-control he could keep up for
city blocks, for hours, the feet articulate as poetry. . . . Yet
he could only shake his head, wanting to be a good fellow
when they asked, but unable really to say—"It's . . . it
happens . . . the muscles do it—" then recalling an old
trainer's words—"it's muscular," smiling beautifully and
already, by the act, conscripted, already cannon fodder,
the pale bar-light across the grating of his close-shaved
skull—"it's reflexes, you see. . . . Not me. . . . Just the reflexes." When did it begin to change for Blicero, among
those days, from lust to simple sorrow, dumb as Rauhandel's amazement with his own talent? He has seen so many
of these Rauhandels, especially since '39, harboring the
same mysterious guests, strangers, often no more bizarre
than a gift for being always where shells were not . . . do
any of *them*, this raw material, "want the Change"? Do
they even know? He doubts it. . . . Their reflexes are only
being used, hundreds of thousands at a time, by others—
by royal moths the Flame has inspired. Blicero has lost,
years ago, all his innocence on this question. So his Destiny is the Oven: while the strayed children, who never
knew, who change nothing but uniforms and cards of
identity, will survive and prosper long beyond his gases
and cinders, his chimney departure. So, so. A Wandervogel
in the mountains of Pain. It's been going on for much too
long, he has chosen the game for nothing if not the kind
of end it will bring him, nicht wahr? too old these days,
grippes taking longer to pass, stomach too often in day-
long agony, eyes measurably blinder with each examina-
tion, too "realistic" to prefer a hero's death or even a
soldier's. He only wants now to be out of the winter, in-

side the Oven's warmth, darkness, steel shelter, the door
behind him in a narrowing rectangle of kitchen-light gonging shut, forever. The rest is foreplay.

Yet he cares, more than he should and puzzled that he
does, about the children—about their motives. He gathers
it is their freedom they look for, yearningly as he for the
Oven, and such perversity haunts and depresses him ...
he returns again and again to the waste and senseless
image of what was a house in the forest, reduced now to
crumbs and sugar-smears, the black indomitable Oven all
that remains, and the two children, the peak of sweet
energy behind them, hunger beginning again, wandering
away into a green blankness of trees. . . . Where will they
go, where shelter the nights? The improvidence of children ... and the civil paradox of this their Little State,
whose base is the same Oven which must destroy it. . . .

But every true god must be both organizer and destroyer. Brought up into a Christian ambience, this was
difficult for him to see until his journey to Südwest: until
his own African conquest. Among the abrading fires of the
Kalahari, under the broadly-sheeted coastal sky, fire and
water, he learned. The Herero boy, long tormented by
missionaries into a fear of Christian sins, jackal-ghosts,
potent European strand-wolves, pursuing him, seeking to
feed on his soul, the precious worm that lived along his
backbone, now tried to cage his old gods, snare them in
words, give them away, savage, paralyzed, to this scholarly
white who seemed so in love with language. Carrying in
his kit a copy of the *Duino Elegies,* just off the presses
when he embarked for Südwest, a gift from Mother at the
boat, the odor of new ink dizzying his nights as the old
freighter plunged tropic after tropic ... until the constellations, like the new stars of Pain-land, had become all unfamiliar and the earth's seasons reversed ... and he came
ashore in a high-powered wooden boat that had 20 years
earlier brought blue-trousered troops in from the iron
roadstead to crush the great Herero Rising. To find, back
in the hinterland, up in an outstretch of broken mountains
between the Namib and the Kalahari, his own faithful
native, his night-flower.

An impassable waste of rock blasted at by the sun ...
miles of canyons twisting nowhere, drifted at the bottoms

with white sand turning a cold, queenly blue as the afternoons lengthened. . . . *We make Ndjambi Karunga now,
omuhona* . . . a whisper, across the burning thorn branches
where the German conjures away energies present outside
the firefight with his slender book. He looks up in alarm.
The boy wants to fuck, but he is using the Herero name
of God. An extraordinary chill comes over the white man.
He believes, like the Rhenish Missionary Society who corrupted this boy, in blasphemy. Especially out here in the
desert, where dangers he can't bring himself to name even
in cities, even in daylight, gather about, wings folded,
buttocks touching the cold sand, waiting. . . . Tonight he
feels the potency of every word: words are only an eye-
twitch away from the things they stand for. The peril of
buggering the boy under the resonance of the sacred
Name fills him insanely with lust, lust in the face—the
mask—of instant talion from outside the fire . . . but to the
boy Ndjambi Karunga is what happens when they couple,
that's all: God is creator and destroyer, sun and darkness,
all sets of opposites brought together, including black and
white, male and female . . . and he becomes, in his innocence, Ndjambi Karunga's child (as are all his preterite
clan, relentlessly, beyond their own history) here underneath the European's sweat, ribs, gut-muscles, cock (the
boy's own muscles staying fiercely tight for what seems
hours, as if he intends to kill, but not a word, only the
long, clonic, thick slices of night that pass over their
bodies).

What did I make of him? Captain Blicero knows that
the African at this moment is halfway across Germany,
deep in the Harz, and that, should the Oven this winter
close behind him, why they have already said auf Wiedersehen for the last time. He sits, stomach crawling, glands
stuffed with malaise, bowed over the console, inside the
swarm-painted launch-control car. The sergeants at motor
and steering panels are out taking a cigarette break—he's
alone at the controls. Outside, through the dirty periscope, gnarled fog unloosens from the bright zone of frost
that belly-bands the reared and shadowy rocket, where the
liquid-oxygen tank's being topped off. Trees press close:
overhead you see barely enough sky for the rocket's ascent.
The Bodenplatte—concrete plate laid over strips of steel—

is set inside a space defined by three trees, blazed so as to triangulate the exact bearing, 260°, to London. The symbol used is a rude mandala, a red circle with a thick black cross inside, recognizable as the ancient sun-wheel from which tradition says the swastika was broken by the early Christians, to disguise their outlaw symbol. Two nails are driven into the tree at the center of the cross. Next to one of the painted blaze-marks, the most westerly, someone has scratched in the bark with the point of a bayonet the words IN HOC SIGNO VINCES. No one in the battery will admit to this act. Perhaps it is the work of the Underground. But it has not been ordered removed. Pale yellow stump-tops wink around the Bodenplatte, fresh chips and sawdust mix with older fallen leaves. The smell, childlike, deep, is confused by petrol and alcohol. Rain threatens, perhaps, today, snow. The crews move nervously gray-green. Shiny black India-rubber cables snake away into the forest to connect the ground equipment with the Dutch grid's 380 volts. *Erwartung.* . . .

For some reason he finds it harder these days to remember. What is framed, dirt-blurry, in the prisms, the ritual, the daily iteration inside these newly cleared triangles in the forests, has taken over what used to be memory's random walk, its innocent image-gathering. His time away, with Katje and Gottfried, has become shorter and more precious as the tempo of firings quickens. Though the boy is in Blicero's unit, the captain hardly sees him when they're on duty—a flash of gold helping the surveyors chain the kilometers out to the transmitting station, the guttering brightness of his hair in the wind, vanishing among trees. . . . How strangely opposite to the African— a color-negative, yellow and blue. The Captain, in some sentimental overflow, some precognition, gave his African boy the name "Enzian," after Rilke's mountainside gentian of Nordic colors, brought down like a pure word to the valleys:

Bringt doch der Wanderer auch vom Hange des Bergrands nicht eine Hand voll Erde ins Tal, die alle unsägliche, sondern ein erworbenes Wort, reines, den gelben und blaun Enzian.

"Omuhona. . . . Look at me. I'm red, and brown . . . *black*, omuhona. . . ."

"Liebchen, this is the other half of the earth. In Germany you would be yellow and blue." Mirror-metaphysics. Self-enchanted by what he imagined elegance, his bookish symmetries. . . . And yet why speak so purposeless to the arid mountain, the heat of the day, the savage flower from whom he drank, so endlessly . . . why lose *those* words into the mirage, the yellow sun and freezing blue shadows in the ravines, unless it was prophesying, beyond all predisaster syndrome, beyond the terror of contemplating his middle age however glancingly, however impossible the chance of any "providing"—*beyond* was something heaving, stirring, forever below, forever before his words, something then that could see a time coming terrible, *at least* as terrible as this winter and the shape to which the War has now grown, a shape making unavoidable the shape of one last jigsaw piece: this Oven-game with the yellowhaired and blueeyed youth and silent doubleganger Katje (who was *her* opposite number in Südwest? what black girl he never saw, hidden always in the blinding sun, the hoarse and cindered passage of the trains at night, a constellation of dark stars no one, no anti-Rilke, had named . . .)—but 1944 was much too late for any of it to matter. Those symmetries were all prewar luxury. Nothing's left him to prophesy.

Least of all her sudden withdrawal from the game. The one variation he didn't provide for, perhaps indeed because he never saw the black girl either. Perhaps the black girl is a genius of meta-solutions—knocking over the chessboard, shooting the referee. But after the act of wounding, breaking, what's to become of the little Oven-state? Can't it be fixed? Perhaps a new form, one more appropriate . . . the archer and his son, and the shooting of the apple . . . yes and the War itself as tyrant king . . . it can still be salvaged can't it, patched up, roles reassigned, no need to rush outside where . . .

Gottfried, in the cage, watches her slip her bonds and go. Fair and slender, the hair on his legs only visible in sunlight and then as a fine, imponderable net of gold, his eyelids already wrinkling in oddly young/old signatures, flourishes, the eyes a seldom-encountered blue that on certain days, in sync with the weather, is too much for these almond fringes and brims over, seeps, bleeds out to illuminate the boy's entire face, virgin-blue, drowned-man blue, blue drawn so insatiably into the chalky walls of Mediterranean streets we quietly cycled through in noontimes of the old peace. . . . He can't stop her. If the Captain asks, he'll tell what he saw. Gottfried has seen her sneak out before, and there are rumors—she's with the Underground, she's in love with a Stuka pilot she met in Scheveningen. . . . But she must love Captain Blicero too. Gottfried styles himself a passive observer. He has waited for his present age, and the conscription notice, to catch him, with an impudent terror like watching the inrush of a curve you mean to take for the first time in a controlled skid, *take me*, gathering speed till the last possible moment, *take me* his good-nights' one prayer. The danger he thinks he needs is still fictional for him: in what he flirts and teases with, death is not a real outcome, the hero always walks out of the heart of the explosion, sooty-faced but grinning—the blast is noise and change, and diving for cover. Gottfried hasn't yet seen a stiff, not up close. He hears now and then from home that friends have died, he's watched long, flabby canvas sacks being handled in the distances into the poisoned gray of the trucks, and the headlamps cutting the mist . . . but when the rockets fail, and try to topple back on you who fired them, and a dozen of you press down, bodies jammed together in the slit trenches waiting all sweat-stunk wool and tense with laughter held in, you only think—What a story to tell at mess, to write to Mutti. . . . These rockets are his pet animals, barely domesticated, often troublesome, even apt to revert. He loves them in the way he would have loved horses, or Tiger tanks, had he pulled duty somewhere else.

Here he feels *taken*, at true ease. Without the War what could he have hoped for? But to be part of *this* adventure . . . *If you cannot sing Siegfried at least you can carry a spear*. On what mountainslope, from what tanning and adored face did he hear that? All he remembers is the white sweep upward, the quilted meadows mobbed with cloud. . . . Now he's learning a trade, tending the rockets, and when the War ends he'll study to be an engineer. He

understands that Blicero will die or go away, and that he
will leave the cage. But he connects this with the end of
the War, not with the Oven. He knows, like everyone,
that captive children are always freed in the moment of
maximum danger. The fucking, the salt length of the
Captain's weary, often impotent penis pushing into his
meek mouth, the stinging chastisements, his face reflected
in the act of kissing the Captain's boots, their shine mottled, corroded by bearing grease, oil, alcohol spilled in
fueling, darkening his face to the one he can't recognize—
these are necessary, they make specific his captivity, which
otherwise would hardly be different from Army stifling,
Army repression. He's ashamed that he enjoys them so
much—the word *bitch*, spoken now in a certain tone of
voice, will give him an erection he cannot will down—
afraid that, if not actually judged and damned, he's gone
insane. The whole battery knows of the arrangement:
though they still obey the Captain it's there, in their faces,
felt trembling out along the steel tape-measures, splashing
onto his tray at mess, elbowed into his right sleeve with
each dressing of his squad. He dreams often these days of
a very pale woman who wants him, who never speaks—
but the absolute confidence in her eyes . . . his awful certainty that she, a celebrity everyone recognizes on sight,
knows him and has no reason to speak to him beyond the
beckoning that's in her face, sends him vibrating awake in
the nights, the Captain's exhausted face inches away across
the silk of wrinkled silver, weak eyes staring as his own,
whiskers he suddenly must scrape his cheek against, sobbing, trying to tell how she was, how she *looked at
him*. . . .

The Captain's seen her, of course. Who hasn't? His idea
of comfort is to tell the child, "She's real. You have no say
in this. You must understand that she means to have you.
No use screaming awake, bothering me this way."

"But if she comes *back*—"

"Submit, Gottfried. *Give it all up.* See where she takes
you. Think of the first time I fucked you. How tight you
were. Until you knew I meant to come inside. Your little
rosebud bloomed. You had nothing, not even by then your
mouth's innocence, to lose. . . ."

But the boy continues to cry. Katje won't help him. Perhaps she's asleep. He never knows. He wants to be her friend, but they hardly ever speak. She's cold, mysterious, he's jealous of her sometimes and at others—usually when he wants to fuck her and through some ingenuity of the Captain's cannot—at such times he thinks he loves her desperately. Unlike the Captain, he has never seen her as the loyal sister who'll free him from the cage. He dreams *that* release, but as a dark exterior Process that will happen, no matter what any of them may want. Whether she goes or stays. So, when Katje quits the game for good, he is silent.

Blicero curses her. He flings a boot-tree at a precious TerBorch. Bombs fall to the west in the Haagsche Bosch. The wind blows, ruffling the ornamental ponds outside. Staff cars snarl away, down the long drive lined with beeches. The half-moon shines among hazy clouds, its dark half the color of aged meat. Blicero orders everyone down into the shelter, a cellarful of gin in brown crocks, open-slat crates of anemone bulbs. The slut has put his battery in the British crosshairs, the raid can come at any moment! Everybody sits around drinking oude genever and peeling cheeses. Telling stories, mostly funny ones, from before the War. By dawn, they're all drunk and sleeping. Scraps of wax litter the floor like leaves. No Spitfires come. But later that morning Schußstelle 3 is moved, and the requisitioned house is abandoned. And she is gone. Crossed over the English lines, at the salient where the great airborne adventure lies bogged for the winter, wearing Gottfried's boots and an old dress, black moiré, calf-length, a size too large, dowdy. Her last disguise. From here on she will be Katje. The only debt outstanding is to Captain Prentice. The others—Piet, Wim, the Drummer, the Indian—have all dropped her. Left her for dead. Or else this is her warning that—

"Sorry, no, we need the bullet," Wim's face in shadows her eye can't compensate for bitterly whispering underneath the Scheveningen pier, ragged crowd-footfalls on the wood overhead, "every fucking bullet we can get. We need the silence. We couldn't spare a man to get rid of the body. I've wasted five minutes with you already . . ." so he will take up their last meeting with technical matters she can no longer share. When she looks around, he's

gone, guerrilla-silent, and she has no way to bring this
together with how he felt last year for a while under the
cool chenille, in the days before he got so many muscles,
and the scars on shoulder and thigh—a late bloomer, a
neutral man goaded finally past his threshold, but she'd
loved him before that . . . she must have. . . .

She's worth nothing to them now. They were after
Schußstelle 3. She gave them everything else, but kept
finding reasons not to pinpoint the Captain's rocket site,
and there is too much doubt by now as to how good the
reasons were. True, the site was often moved about. But
she could've been placed no closer to the decision-making:
it was her own expressionless servant's face that leaned in
over their schnapps and cigars, the charts coffee-ringed
across the low tables, the cream papers stamped purple as
bruised flesh. Wim and the others have invested time and
lives—three Jewish families sent east—though wait now,
she's more than balanced it, hasn't she, in the months out
at Scheveningen? They were kids, neurotic, lonely, pilots
and crews they all loved to talk, and she's fed back who
knows how many reams' worth of Most Secret flimsies
across the North Sea, hasn't she, squadron numbers, fueling stops, spin-recovery techniques and turning radii,
power settings, radio channels, sectors, traffic patterns—
hasn't she? What more do they want? She asks this
seriously, as if there's a real conversion factor between
information and lives. Well, strange to say, there is. Written down in the Manual, on file at the War Department.
Don't forget the real business of the War is buying and
selling. The murdering and the violence are self-policing,
and can be entrusted to non-professionals. The mass nature
of wartime death is useful in many ways. It serves as
spectacle, as diversion from the real movements of the
War. It provides raw material to be recorded into History,
so that children may be taught History as sequences of
violence, battle after battle, and be more prepared for the
adult world. Best of all, mass death's a stimulus to just
ordinary folks, little fellows, to try 'n' grab a piece of that
Pie while they're still here to gobble it up. The true war is
a celebration of markets. Organic markets, carefully styled
"black" by the professionals, spring up everywhere. Scrip,
Sterling, Reichsmarks continue to move, severe as classical

ballet, inside their antiseptic marble chambers. But out here, down here among the people, the truer currencies come into being. So, Jews are negotiable. Every bit as negotiable as cigarettes, cunt, or Hershey bars. Jews also carry an element of guilt, of future blackmail, which operates, natch, in favor of the professionals. So Katje here is hollering into a silence, a North Sea of hopes, and Pirate Prentice, who knows her from hurried meetings—in city squares that manage to be barracksfaced and claustrophobic, under dark, soft-wood smells of staircases steep as ladders, on a gaffrigger by an oily quai and a cat's amber eyes staring down, in a block of old flats with rain in the courtyard and a bulky, ancient Schwarzlose stripped to toggle links and oil pump littered about the dusty room—who has each time seen her as a face belonging with others he knows better, at the margin of each enterprise, now, confronted with this face out of context, an enormous sky all sea-clouds in full march, tall and plum, behind her, detects danger in her loneliness, realizes he's never heard her name, not till the meeting by the windmill known as "The Angel." . . .

She tells him why she's alone—more or less—why she can't ever go back, and her face is somewhere else, painted on canvas, hung with other survivals back in the house near Duindigt, only witnessing the Oven-game—centuries passing like the empurpled clouds, darkening an infinitesimal layer of varnish between herself and Pirate, granting her the shield of serenity she needs, of classic irrelevance. . . .

"But where will you go?" Both of them hands in pockets, scarves tightly wrapped, stones the water has left behind shining black wait like writing in a dream, about to make sense printed here along the beach, each fragment so amazingly clear yet . . .

"I don't know. Where would be a good place?"

" 'The White Visitation,' " Pirate suggested.

" 'The White Visitation' is fine," she said, and stepped into the void. . . .

"Osbie, have I gone mad?" a snowy night, five rocket bombs since noon, shivering in the kitchen, late and candlelit, Osbie Feel the house idiot-savant so far into an encounter with nutmeg this evening that the inquiry seems

quite proper, the pale cement Jungfrau asquat, phlegmatic
and one gathers nettled in a dim corner.

"Of course, of course," sez Osbie, with a fluid passage
of fingers and wrist based on the way Bela Lugosi handed
a certain glass of doped wine to some fool of a juvenile
lead in *White Zombie,* the first movie Osbie ever saw and in
a sense the last, ranking on his All-Time List along with *Son
of Frankenstein, Freaks, Flying Down to Rio* and perhaps
Dumbo, which he went to see in Oxford Street last night
but midway through noticed, instead of a magic feather,
the humorless green and magenta face of Mr. Ernest
Bevin wrapped in the chubby trunk of the longlashed baby
elephant, and decided it would be prudent to excuse himself. "No," since Pirate meantime has misunderstood whatever it was Osbie said, "not 'of course you've gone mad,
Prentice,' that wasn't it at all. . . ."

"What then," Pirate asks, after Osbie's lapse has passed
the minute mark.

"Ah?" sez Osbie.

Pirate is having second thoughts, is what it is. He keeps
recalling that Katje now avoids all mention of the house in
the forest. She has glanced into it, and out, but the truth's
crystal sheets have diffracted all her audible words—often
to tears—and he can't quite make sense of what's spoken,
much less infer to the radiant crystal itself. Indeed, why
did she leave Schußstelle 3? We are never told why. But
now and then, players in a game will, lull or crisis, be
reminded how it is, after all, really play—and be unable
then to continue in the same spirit. . . . Nor need it be
anything sudden, spectacular—it may come in gentle—and
regardless of the score, the number of watchers, their
collective wish, penalties they or the Leagues may impose,
the player will, waking deliberately, perhaps with Katje's
own tough, young isolate's shrug and stride, say *fuck it*
and quit the game, quit it cold. . . .

"All right," he continues alone, Osbie lost in a moon-
ing doper's smile, tracking the mature female snow-skin
of the Alp in the corner, he and the frozen peak above
and the blue night . . . "it's a lapse of character then, a
crotchet. Like carrying the bloody Mendoza." Everyone
else in the Firm packs a Sten you know. The Mendoza
weighs three times as much, no one's even *seen* any 7 mm

Mexican Mauser bullets lately, even in Portobello Road: it hasn't the grand Garage Simplicity or the rate of fire and still he loves it (yes, most likely it's love these days) "you see, it's a matter of trade-off, i'n't i'," the nostalgia of its Lewis-style straight pull, and being able to lift the barrel off in a second (ever tried to take the barrel off of a Sten?), and having a double-ended striker in case one breaks. . . . "Am I going to let the extra weight make a difference? It's my *crotchet*, I'm indifferent to weight, or I wouldn't have brought the girl back out, would I."

"I am not your responsibility." A statue in wine-colored *façonné* velvet from neck to wrists and insteps, and how long, gentlemen, has she been watching from the shadows?

"Oh," Pirate turning sheepish, "you are, you know."

"The happy couple!" Osbie roars suddenly, taking another pinch of nutmeg like snuff, eyeballs rolling white as the miniature mountain. Sneezing now loudly about the kitchen, it strikes him as incredible that he has both these people inside the same field of vision. Pirate's face darkening with embarrassment, Katje's unchanging, half struck by light from the next room, half in slate windows.

"Should I have left you, then?" and when she only compresses her mouth, impatient, "or do you think someone over here owed it to you to bring you out?"

"*No.*" That reached her. Pirate only asked because he's begun to suspect, darkly, any number of Someones Over Here. But to Katje a debt is for wiping out. Her old, intractable vice—she wants to cross seas, to connect countries between whom there is no possible rate of exchange. Her ancestors sang, in Middle Dutch,

> ic heb u liever dan ên everswîn,
> al waert van finen goude ghewracht,

love incommensurate with gold, golden calf, even in this case golden swine. But by the middle of the 17th century there were no more pigs of gold, only of flesh mortal as that of Frans Van der Groov, another ancestor, who went off to Mauritius with a boatlead of these live hogs and lost thirteen years toting his haakbus through the ebony forests, wandering the swamps and lava flows, systematically killing off the native dodoes for reasons he could not explain. The Dutch pigs took care of eggs and younger birds. Evans carefully drew beads on the parents at 10 or 20 meters, the piece propped on its hook, slowly squeezing the trigger, eye focused on the molting ugliness while closer in the slowmatch, soaked in wine, held in the jaws of the serpentine, came blooming redly downward, its heat on his cheek *like my own small luminary*, he wrote home to Hendrik the older brother, *the ruler of my Sign* . . . uncovering the priming-powder he'd been keeping shielded with his other hand—sudden flash in the pan, through the touchhole, and the loud report echoing off the steep rocks, recoil smashing the butt up along his shoulder (the skin there at first raw, blistered, then callused over, after the first summer). And the stupid, awkward bird, never intended to fly or run at any speed—what *were* they good for?—unable now even to locate his murderer, ruptured, splashing blood, raucously dying. . . .

At home, the brother skimmed the letters, some crisp, some seastained or faded, spanning years, delivered all at once—understanding very little of it, only anxious to spend the day, as usual, in the gardens and greenhouse with his tulips (a reigning madness of the time), especially one new variety named for his current mistress: blood-red, finely tattooed in purple. . . . "Recent arrivals all carrying the new snaphaan . . . but I stick to my clumsy old matchlock . . . don't I deserve a clumsy weapon for such a clumsy prey?" But Frans got no closer to telling what kept him out among the winter cyclones, stuffing pieces of old uniform down after the lead balls, sunburned, bearded and filthy—unless it rained or he was in the uplands where the craters of old volcanoes cupped rainfall blue as the sky in upward offering.

He left the dodoes to rot, he couldn't endure to eat their flesh. Usually, he hunted alone. But often, after months of it, the isolation would begin to change him, change his very perceptions—the jagged mountains in full daylight flaring as he watched into freak saffrons, streaming indigos, the sky his glass house, all the island his tulipomania. The voices—he insomniac, southern stars too thick for constellations teeming in faces and creatures of fable less likely than the dodo—spoke the words of sleepers, singly, coupled, in chorus. The rhythms and timbres were Dutch, but made no waking sense. Except that he thought they were warning him . . . scolding, angry that he couldn't understand. Once he sat all day staring at a single white dodo's egg in a grass hummock. The place was too remote for any foraging pig to've found. He waited for scratching, a first crack reaching to net the chalk surface: an emergence. Hemp gripped in the teeth of the steel snake, ready to be lit, ready to descend, sun to black-powder sea, and destroy the infant, egg of light into egg of darkness, within its first minute of amazed vision, of wet down stirred cool by these southeast trades. . . . Each hour he sighted down the barrel. It was then, if ever, he might have seen how the weapon made an axis potent as Earth's own between himself and this victim, still one, inside the egg, with the ancestral chain, not to be broken out for more than its blink of world's light. There they were, the silent egg and the crazy Dutchman, and the hookgun that linked them forever, framed, brilliantly motionless as any Vermeer. Only the sun moved: from zenith down at last behind the snaggleteeth of mountains to Indian ocean, to tarry night. The egg, without a quiver, still unhatched. He should have blasted it then where it lay: he understood that the bird would hatch before dawn. But a cycle was finished. He got to his feet, knee and hip joints in agony, head gonging with instructions from his sleeptalkers droning by, overlapping, urgent, and only limped away, piece at right shoulder arms.

When loneliness began to drive him into situations like this, he often returned to a settlement and joined a hunting party. A drunken, university hysteria would take hold of them all, out on night-rampages where they'd be presently firing at anything, treetops, clouds, leather demon bats screaming up beyond hearing. Tradewinds moving upslope to chill their nights' sweating, sky lit half crimson by a volcano, rumblings under their feet as deep as the bats' voices were high, all these men were caught in the spectrum between, trapped among frequencies of their own voices and words.

This furious host were losers, impersonating a race chosen by God. The colony, the venture, was dying—like the ebony trees they were stripping from the island, like the poor species they were removing totally from the earth. By 1681, *Didus ineptus* would be gone, by 1710 so would every last settler from Mauritius. The enterprise here would have lasted about a human lifetime.

To some, it made sense. They saw the stumbling birds ill-made to the point of Satanic intervention, so ugly as to embody argument against a Godly creation. Was Mauritius some first poison trickle through the sheltering dikes of Earth? Christians must stem it here, or perish in a second Flood, loosed this time not by God but by the Enemy. The act of ramming home the charges into their musketry became for these men a devotional act, one whose symbolism they understood.

But if they were chosen to come to Mauritius, why had they also been chosen to fail, and leave? Is that a choosing, or is it a passing-over? Are they Elect, or are they Preterite, and doomed as dodoes?

Frans could not know that except for a few others on the island of Reunion, these were the only dodoes in the Creation, and that he was helping exterminate a race. But at times the scale and frenzy of the hunting did come through to trouble his heart. "If the species were not such a perversion," he wrote, "it might be profitably husbanded to feed our generations. I cannot hate them quite so violently as do some here. But what now can mitigate this slaughter? It is too late.... Perhaps a more comely beak, fuller feathering, a capacity for flight, however brief ...details of Design. Or, had we but found savages on this island, the bird's appearance might have then seemed to us no stranger than that of the wild turkey of North America. Alas, their tragedy is to be the dominant form of Life on Mauritius, but incapable of speech."

That was it, right there. No language meant no chance of co-opting them in to what their round and flaxen invaders were calling Salvation. But Frans, in the course of morning lights lonelier than most, could not keep from finally witnessing a miracle: a Gift of Speech...a Conversion of the Dodoes. Ranked in thousands on the shore, with a luminous profile of reef on the water behind them, its roar the only sound on the morning, volcanoes at rest, the wind suspended, an autumn sunrise dispensing light glassy and deep over them all...they have come from their nests and rookeries, from beside the streams bursting out the mouths of lava tunnels, from the minor islands awash like debris off the north coast, from sudden waterfalls and the wasted rain-forests where the axeblades are rusting and the rough flumes rot and topple in the wind, from their wet mornings under the shadows of mountain-stubs they have waddled in awkward pilgrimage to this assembly: to be sanctified, taken in.... *For as much as they are the creatures of God, and have the gift of rational discourse, acknowledging that only in His Word is eternal life to be found* ... And there are tears of happiness in the eyes of the dodoes. They are all brothers now, they and the humans who used to hunt them, brothers in Christ, the little baby they dream now of sitting near, roosting in his stable, feathers at peace, watching over him and his dear face all night long....

It is the purest form of European adventuring. What's it all been for, the murdering seas, the gangrene winters and starving springs, our bone pursuit of the unfaithful, midnights of wrestling with the Beast, our sweat become ice and our tears pale flakes of snow, if not for such moments as this: the little converts flowing out of eye's field, so meek, so trusting—how shall any craw clench in fear, any recreant cry be offered in the presence of our blade, our necessary blade? Sanctified now they will feed us, sanctified their remains and droppings fertilize our crops. Did we tell them "Salvation"? Did we mean a dwelling forever in the City? Everlasting life? An earthly paradise restored, their island as it used to be given them back? Probably. Thinking all the time of the little brothers numbered among our own blessings. Indeed, if they save us from hunger in this world, then beyond, in Christ's kingdom, our salvations must be, in like measure, inextricable. Otherwise the dodoes would be only what they appear as in the world's illusory light—only our prey. God could not be that cruel.

Frans can look at both versions, the miracle and the hunt of more years than he can remember now, as real, equal possibilities. In both, eventually, the dodoes die. But as for faith ... he can believe only in the one steel reality of the firearm he carries. "He knew that a snaphaan would weigh less, its cock, flint, and steel give him

surer ignition—but he felt a nostalgia about the haakbus... he didn't mind the extra weight, it was *his*
crotchet...."

Pirate and Osbie Feel are leaning on their roof-ledge, a
magnificent sunset across and up the winding river, the
imperial serpent, crowds of factories, flats, parks, smoky
spires and gables, incandescent sky casting downward
across the miles of deep streets and roofs cluttering and
sinuous river Thames a drastic stain of burnt orange to
remind a visitor of his mortal transience here, to seal or
empty all the doors and windows in sight to his eyes
that look only for a bit of company, a word or two in the
street before he goes up to the soap-heavy smell of the
rented room and the squares of coral sunset on the floorboards—an antique light, self-absorbed, fuel consumed in
the metered winter holocaust, the more distant shapes
among the threads or sheets of smoke now perfect ash
ruins of themselves, nearer windows, struck a moment by
the sun, not reflecting at all but containing the same destroying light, this intense fading in which there is no
promise of return, light that rusts the government cars at
the curbsides, varnishes the last faces hurrying past the
shops in the cold as if a vast siren had finally sounded,
light that makes chilled untraveled canals of many streets,
and that fills with the starlings of London, converging by
millions to hazy stone pedestals, to emptying squares and
a great collective sleep. They flow in rings, concentric
rings on the radar screens. The operators call them
"angels."

"He's haunting you," Osbie puffing on an Amanita
cigarette.

"Yes," Pirate ranging the edges of the roof-garden,
irritable in the sunset, "but it's the last thing I want to
believe. The other's been bad enough...."

"What d'you think of her, then."

"Someone can use her, I think," having decided this
yesterday at Charing Cross Station when she left for "The
White Visitation." "An unforeseen dividend, for somebody."

"Do you know what they have in mind, down there?"

Only that they're brewing up something that involves
a giant octopus. But no one up here in London knows

with any precision. Even at "The White Visitation" there's this sudden great coming and going, and a swampy ambiguity as to why. Myron Grunton is noted casting less than comradely looks at Roger Mexico. The Zouave has gone back to his unit in North Africa, back under the Cross of Lorraine, all that the German might find sinister in his blackness recorded on film, sweet-talked or coerced out of him by none less than Gerhardt von Göll, once an intimate and still the equal of Lang, Pabst, Lubitsch, more lately meshed in with the affairs of any number of exile governments, fluctuations in currencies, the establishment and disestablishment of an astonishing network of market operations winking on, winking off across the embattled continent, even as the firefights whistle steel up and down the streets and the firestorms sweep oxygen up in the sky and the customers fall smothered like bugs in the presence of Flit . . . but commerce has not taken away von Göll's Touch: these days it has grown more sensitive than ever. In these first rushes the black man moves about in SS uniform, among the lath and canvas mockups of rocket and Meillerwagen (always shot through pines, through snow, from distant angles that don't give away the English location), the others in plausible blackface, recruited for the day, the whole crew on a lark, Mr. Pointsman, Mexico, Edwin Treacle, and Rollo Groast, ARF's resident neurosurgeon Aaron Throwster, all playing the black rocketeers of the fictional Schwarzkommando—even Myron Grunton in a nonspeaking role, a blurry extra like the rest of them. Running time of the film is three minutes, 25 seconds and there are twelve shots. It will be antiqued, given a bit of fungus and ferrotyping, and transported to Holland, to become part of the "remains" of a counterfeit rocket-firing site in the Rijkswijksche Bosch. The Dutch resistance will then "raid" this site, making a lot of commotion, faking in tire-tracks and detailing the litter of hasty departure. The inside of an Army lorry will be gutted by Molotov cocktails: among ashes, charred clothing, blackened and slightly melted gin bottles, will be found fragments of carefully forged Schwarzkommando documents, and of a reel of film, only three minutes and 25 seconds of which will be viewable. Von Göll, with a straight face, proclaims it to be his greatest work.

"Indeed, as things were to develop," writes noted film critic Mitchell Prettyplace, "one cannot argue much with his estimate, though for vastly different reasons than von Göll might have given or even from his peculiar vantage foreseen."

At "The White Visitation," because of erratic funding, there is only one film projector. Each day, about noon, after the Operation Black Wing people have watched their fraudulent African rocket troops, Webley Silvernail comes to carry the projector back down the chilly scuffed-wood corridors again to the ARF wing, in to the inner room where octopus Grigori oozes sullenly in his tank. In other rooms the dogs whine, bark shrilly in pain, whimper for a stimulus that does not, will never come, and the snow goes whirling, invisible tattooing needles against the nerveless window glass behind the green shades. The reel is threaded, the lights are switched off, Grigori's attention is directed to the screen, where an image already walks. The camera follows as she moves deliberately nowhere long-legged about the rooms, an adolescent wideness and hunching to the shoulders, her hair not bluntly Dutch at all, but secured in a modish upsweep with an old, tarnished silver crown. . . .

☐

It was very early morning. He stumbled out alone into a wet brick street. Southward the barrage balloons, surf-riders on the combers of morning, were glowing, pink and pearl, in the sunrise.

They've cut Slothrop loose again, he's back on the street, shit, last chance for a Section 8 'n' he blew it. . . .

Why didn't they keep him on at that nut ward for as long as they said they would—wasn't it supposed to be a few weeks? No explanation—just "Cheerio!" and the onion-skin sending him back to that ACHTUNG. The Kenosha Kid, and that Crouchfield the Westwardman and his side-kick Whappo have been all his world for these recent days . . . there were still problems to be worked out, adventures not yet completed, coercions and vast deals to be made on the order of the old woman's arrangement for getting her pig home over the stile. But now, rudely, here's that London again.

But something's different . . . something's . . . been *changed* . . . don't mean to bitch, folks, but—well for instance he could almost swear he's being followed, or watched anyway. Some of the tails are pretty slick, but others he can spot, all right. Xmas shopping yesterday at that Woolworth's, he caught a certain pair of beady eyes in the toy section, past a heap of balso-wood fighter planes and little-kid-size Enfields. A hint of constancy to what shows up in the rearview mirror of his Humber, no color or model he can pin down but *something* always present inside the tiny frame, has led him to start checking out other cars when he goes off on a morning's work. Things on his desk at ACHTUNG seem not to be where they were. Girls have found excuses not to keep appointments. He feels he's being gently separated from the life he lived before going into St. Veronica's. Even in movies there's always someone behind him being careful not to talk, rattle paper, laugh too loud: Slothrop's been to enough movies that he can pick up an anomaly like that right away.

The cubicle near Grosvenor Square begins to feel more and more like a trap. He spends his time, often whole days, ranging the East End, breathing the rank air of Thameside, seeking places the followers might not follow.

One day, just as he's entering a narrow street all ancient brick walls and lined with costermongers, he hears his name called—and hubba hubba what's this then, here she comes all right, blonde hair flying in telltales, white wedgies clattering on cobblestones, an adorable tomato in a nurse uniform, and her name's, uh, well, oh—Darlene. Golly, it's Darlene. She works at St. Veronica's hospital, lives nearby at the home of a Mrs. Quoad, a lady widowed long ago and since suffering a series of antiquated diseases—greensickness, tetter, kibes, purples, imposthumes and almonds in the ears, most recently a touch of scurvy. So, out in search of limes for her landlady, the fruit beginning to jog and spill from her straw basket and roll yellowgreen back down the street, young Darlene comes running her nurse's cap, her breasts soft fenders for this meeting on the gray city sea.

"You come back! Ah Tyrone, you're *back*," a tear or two, both of them down picking up citrus, the starch khaki dress rattling, even the odd sniffle from Slothrop's not unsentimental nose.

"It's me love . . ."

Tire tracks in the slush have turned to pearl, mellow pearl. Gulls cruise slowly against the high windowless brick walls of the district.

Mrs. Quoad's is up three dark flights, with the dome of faraway St. Paul's out its kitchen window visible in the smoke of certain afternoons, and the lady herself tiny in a rose plush chair in the sitting-room by the wireless, listening to Primo Scala's Accordion Band. She looks healthy enough. On the table, though, is her crumpled chiffon handkerchief: feathered blots of blood in and out the convolutions like a floral pattern.

"You were here when I had that horrid quotidian ague," she recalls Slothrop, "the day we brewed the wormwood tea," sure enough, the very taste now, rising through his shoe-soles, taking him along. They're reassembling . . . it must be outside his memory . . . cool clean interior, girl and woman, independent of his shorthand of stars . . . so many fading-faced girls, windy canalsides, bed-sitters, bus-stop good-bys, how can he be expected to remember? but this room has gone on clarifying: part of whoever he was inside it has kindly remained, stored quiescent these months outside of his head, distributed through the grainy shadows, the grease-hazy jars of herbs, candies, spices, all the Compton Mackenzie novels on the shelf, glassy ambro-types of her late husband Austin night-dusted inside gilded frames up on the mantel where last time Michaelmas daisies greeted and razzled from a little Sèvres vase she and Austin found together one Saturday long ago in a Wardour Street shop. . . .

"He was my good health," she often says. "Since he passed away I've had to become all but an outright witch, in pure self-defense." From the kitchen comes the smell of limes freshly cut and squeezed. Darlene's in and out of the room, looking for different botanicals, asking where the cheesecloth's got to, "Tyrone help me just reach down that—no next to it, the tall jar, thank you love"—back into the kitchen in a creak of starch, a flash of pink. "I'm the only one with a memory around here," Mrs. Quoad sighs. "We help each other, you see." She brings out from behind its cretonne camouflage a great bowl of candles. "*Now*," beaming at Slothrop. "Here: wine jellies. They're prewar."

"Now I remember you—the one with the graft at the Ministry of Supply!" but he knows, from last time, that no gallantry can help him now. After that visit he wrote home to Nalline: "The English are kind of weird when it comes to the way things taste, Mom. They aren't like us. It might be the climate. They go for things we would never dream of. Sometimes it is enough to turn your stomach, boy. The other day I had one of these things they call 'wine jellies.' That's their idea of *candy*, Mom! Figure out a way to feed some to that Hitler 'n' I betcha the war'd be over *tomorrow!*" Now once again he finds himself checking out these ruddy gelatin objects, nodding, he hopes amiably, at Mrs. Quoad. They have the names of different wines within on them in bas-relief.

"Just a touch of menthol too," Mrs. Quoad popping one into her mouth. "Delicious."

Slothrop finally chooses one that says Lafitte Rothschild and stuffs it on into his kisser. "Oh yeah. Yeah. Mmm. It's great."

"If you *really* want something peculiar try the Bernkastler Doktor. Oh! Aren't you the one who brought me those lovely American slimy elm things, maple-tasting with a touch of sassafras—"

"Slippery elm. Jeepers I'm sorry, I ran out yesterday."

Darlene comes in with a steaming pot and three cups on a tray. "What's that?" Slothrop a little quickly, here.

"You don't really want to know, Tyrone."

"Quite right," after the first sip, wishing she'd used more lime juice or something to kill the basic taste, which is ghastly-bitter. These people are really insane. No sugar, natch. He reaches in the candy bowl, comes up with a black, ribbed licorice drop. It looks safe. But just as he's biting in, Darlene gives him, and it, a peculiar look, great timing this girl, sez, "Oh, I thought we got rid of all *those*—" a blithe, Gilbert & Sullivan ingenue's *thewse*— "*years* ago," at which point Slothrop is encountering this dribbling liquid center, which tastes like mayonnaise and orange peels.

"You've taken the last of my Marmalade Surprises!"

cries Mrs. Quoad, having now with conjuror's speed produced an egg-shaped confection of pastel green, studded all
over with lavender nonpareils. "Just for that I shan't let you
have any of these marvelous rhubarb creams." Into her
mouth it goes, the whole thing.

"Serves me right," Slothrop, wondering just what he
means by this, sipping herb tea to remove the taste of the
mayonnaise candy—oops but that's a mistake, right, here's
his mouth filling once again with horrible alkaloid desolation, all the way back to the soft palate where it digs in.
Darlene, pure Nightingale compassion, is handing him a
hard red candy, molded like a stylized raspberry . . . mm,
which oddly enough even tastes like a raspberry, though
it can't begin to take away that bitterness. Impatiently, he
bites into it, and in the act knows, fucking idiot, he's been
had once more, there comes pouring out onto his tongue
the most godawful crystalline concentration of Jeez it
must be pure nitric acid, "Oh mercy that's really *sour*,"
hardly able to get the words out he's so puckered up,
exactly the sort of thing Hop Harrigan used to pull to get
Tank Tinker to quit playing his ocarina, a shabby trick
then and twice as reprehensible coming from an old lady
who's supposed to be one of our Allies, shit he can't even
see it's up his nose and whatever it is won't dissolve, just
goes on torturing his shriveling tongue and crunches like
ground glass among his molars. Mrs. Quoad is meantime
busy savoring, bite by dainty bite, a cherry-quinine *petit
four*. She beams at the young people across the candy
bowl. Slothrop, forgetting, reaches again for his tea. There
is no graceful way out of this now. Darlene has brought a
couple-three more candy jars down off the shelf, and now
he goes plunging, like a journey to the center of some
small, hostile planet, into an enormous bonbon *chomp*
through the mantle of chocolate to a strongly eucalyptus-
flavored fondant, finally into a core of some very tough
grape gum arabic. He fingernails a piece of this out from
between his teeth and stares at it for a while. It is purple
in color.

"Now you're getting the idea!" Mrs. Quoad waving at
him a marbled conglomerate of ginger root, butterscotch,
and aniseed, "you see, you also have to enjoy the way it
looks. Why are Americans so impulsive?"

"Well," mumbling, "usually we don't get any more complicated than Hershey bars, see. . . ."

"Oh, try *this*," hollers Darlene, clutching her throat and swaying against him.

"Gosh, it must really be something," doubtfully taking this nasty-looking brownish novelty, an exact quarter-scale replica of a Mills-type hand grenade, lever, pin and everything, one of a series of patriotic candies put out before sugar was quite so scarce, also including, he notices, peering into the jar, a .455 Webley cartridge of green and pink striped taffy, a six-ton earthquake bomb of some silver-flecked blue gelatin, and a licorice bazooka.

"Go on then," Darlene actually taking his hand with the candy in it and trying to shove it into his mouth.

"Was just, you know, looking at it, the way Mrs. Quoad suggested."

"And no fair squeezing it, Tyrone."

Under its tamarind glaze, the Mills bomb out to be luscious pepsin-flavored nougat, chock-full of tangy candied cubeb berries, and a chewy camphor-gum center. It is unspeakably awful. Slothrop's head begins to reel with camphor fumes, his eyes are running, his tongue's a hopeless holocaust. Cubeb? He used to *smoke* that stuff. "Poisoned . . ." he is able to croak.

"Show a little backbone," advises Mrs. Quoad.

"Yes," Darlene through tongue-softened sheets of caramel, "don't you know there's a war on? Here now love, open your mouth."

Through the tears he can't see it too well, but he can hear Mrs. Quoad across the table going "Yum, yum, yum," and Darlene giggling. It is enormous and soft, like a marshmallow, but somehow—unless something is now going seriously wrong with his brain—it tastes like gin. "Wha's 'is," he inquires thickly.

"A gin marshmallow," sez Mrs. Quoad.

"Awww . . ."

"Oh that's nothing, have one of *these*—" his teeth, in some perverse reflex, crunching now through a hard sour gooseberry shell into a wet spurting unpleasantness of, he hopes it's tapioca, little glutinous chunks of something all saturated with powdered cloves.

"More tea?" Darlene suggests. Slothrop is coughing violently, having inhaled some of that clove filling.

"Nasty cough," Mrs. Quoad offering a tin of that least believable of English coughdrops, the Meggezone. "Darlene, the tea is lovely, I can feel my scurvy going away, really I can."

The Meggezone is like being belted in the head with a Swiss Alp. Menthol icicles immediately begin to grow from the roof of Slothrop's mouth. Polar bears seek toenail-holds up the freezing frosty-grape alveolar clusters in his lungs. It hurts his teeth too much to breathe, even through his nose, even, necktie loosened, with his nose down inside the neck of his olive-drab T-shirt. Benzoin vapors seep into his brain. His head floats in a halo of ice.

Even an hour later, the Meggezone still lingers, a mint ghost in the air. Slothrop lies with Darlene, the Disgusting English Candy Drill a thing of the past, his groin now against her warm bottom. The one candy he did not get to taste—one Mrs. Quoad withheld—was the Fire of Paradise, that famous confection of high price and protean taste—"salted plum" to one, "artificial cherry" to another . . . "sugared violets" . . . "Worcestershire sauce" . . . "spiced treacle" . . . any number of like descriptions, positive, terse—never exceeding two words in length—resembling the descriptions of poison and debilitating gases found in training manuals, "sweet-and-sour eggplant" being perhaps the lengthiest to date. The Fire of Paradise today is operationally extinct, and in 1945 can hardly be found: certainly nowhere among the sunlit shops and polished windows of Bond Street or waste Belgravia. But every now and then one will surface, in places which deal usually other merchandise than sweets: at rest, back inside big glass jars clouded by the days, along with objects like itself, sometimes only one candy to a whole jar, nearly hidden in the ambient tourmalines in German gold, carved ebony finger-stalls from the last century, pegs, valve-pieces, threaded hardware from obscure musical instruments, electronic components of resin and copper that the War, in its glutton, ever-nibbling intake, has not yet found and licked back into its darkness. . . . Places where the motors never come close enough to be loud, and there are trees outside along the street. Inner rooms and older faces developing under light falling through a skylight, yellower, later in the year. . . .

Hunting across the zero between waking and sleep, his halfway limp cock still inside her, their strengthless legs bent the same angle . . . The bedroom deepens into water and coolness. Somewhere the sun is going down. Just enough light to see the darker freckles on her back. In the parlor Mrs. Quoad is dreaming she's back in the gardens at Bournemouth, among the rhododendrons, and a sudden rain, Austin crying *Touch her throat, Majesty. Touch!* and Yrjö—a pretender but the true king, for a very doubtful branch of the family usurped the throne in 1878 during the intrigues over Bessarabia—Yrjö in an old-fashioned frock coat with golden galloons shining at the sleeves, bending toward her in the rain to cure her forever of King's Evil, looking exactly as he does in the rotogravure, his lovely Hrisoula a step or two behind kindly, seriously waiting, around them the rain thundering down, the King's white ungloved hand bending like a butterfly to touch the hollow of Mrs. Quoad's throat, the miracle touch, gently . . . touch . . .

The lightning—

And Slothrop is yawning "What time is it?" and Darlene is swimming up from sleep. When, with no warning, the room is full of noon, blinding white, every hair flowing up from her nape clear as day, as the concussion drives in on them, rattling the building to its poor bones, beating in the windowshade, gone all to white and black lattice of mourning-cards. Overhead, catching up, the rocket's rush comes swelling, elevated express down, away into ringing silence. Outside glass has been breaking, long, dissonant cymbals up the street. The floor has twitched like a shaken carpet, and the bed with it. Slothrop's penis has sprung erect, aching. To Darlene, suddenly awake, heart pounding fast, palms and fingers in fear's pain, this hardon has seemed reasonably part of the white light, the loud blast. By the time the explosion has died to red strong flickering on the shade, she's begun to wonder . . . about the two together . . . but they're fucking now, and what does it matter, but God's sake why shouldn't this stupid Blitz be good for something?

And who's that, through the crack in the orange shade,

breathing carefully? Watching? And where, keepers of
maps, specialists at surveillance, would you say the next
one will fall?

□

The very first touch: he'd been saying something mean, a
bit of the usual Mexico self-reproach—ah you don't know
me I'm really a bastard sort of thing—"No," she went to
put her fingers to his lips, "don't say that...." As she
reached, without thinking he grabbed her waist, moved
her hand away, pure defense—but kept holding her, by
the wrist. They were eyes-to-eyes, and neither would look
away. Roger brought her hand to his lips and kissed it
then, still watching her eyes. A pause, his heart in sharp
knocks against the front of his chest..."Ohh..." the
sound rushing out of her, and she came in to hug him,
completely let-go, open, shivering as they held each other.
She told him later that as soon as he took her wrist that
night, she came. And the first time he touched her cunt,
squeezed Jessica's soft cunt through her knickers, the
trembling began again high in her thighs, growing, taking
her over. She came twice before cock was ever officially
put inside cunt, and this is important to both of them
though neither has figured out why, exactly.

Whenever it happens, though, the light always gets very
red for them.

Once they met at a teashop: she was wearing a red
sweater with short sleeves, and her bare arms glowed red
by her sides. She hadn't any make-up on, the first time
he'd seen her so. Walking to the car, she takes his hand
and puts it, for a moment, lightly between her moving
legs. Roger's heart grows erect, and comes. That's really
how it feels. Up sharply to skin level in a V around his
centerline, washing over his nipples... it is love, it is
amazing. Even when she isn't there, after a dream, at a
face in the street that might against chance be Jessica's,
Roger can never control it, he's in its grasp.

About Beaver, or Jeremy, as he is known to his mother,
Roger tries not to think any more than he has to. Of course
he agonizes over technical matters. She cannot possibly—

can she?—be Doing The Same Things with Jeremy. Does Jeremy ever kiss her cunt, for example? Could that *prig* actually—does she reach around as they're fucking a-and slide a mischievous finger, his English rose, into *Jeremy's* asshole? Stop, stop this (but does she suck his cock? Has he ever had his habitually insolent face between her lovely buttocks?) no use, it's youthful folly time here and you're better off up at the Tivoli watching Maria Montez and Jon Hall, or looking for leopards or peccaries in Regents Park Zoo, and wondering if it'll rain before 4:30.

The time Roger and Jessica have spent together, totaled up, still only comes to hours. And all their spoken words to less than one average SHAEF memorandum. And there is no way, first time in his career, that the statistician can make these figures mean anything.

Together they are a long skin interface, flowing sweat, close as muscles and bones can press, hardly a word beyond her name, or his.

Apart is for all their flip flim-dialogue, scenarios they make up to play alone for themselves in the nights with the Bofors door-knocking against her sky, with his wind humming among the loops of barbed wire down along the beach. The Mayfair Hotel. "We *are* quite the jet-propelled one aren't we, only half an hour late."

"Well," Wrens and NAAFI girls, jeweled young widows side-glancing on by, "I'm sure *you've* put the time to good use."

"Time enough for several assignations," he replies, looking elaborately at his watch, worn WW II style on the inside of his wrist, "and by *now,* I should say, a confirmed pregnancy or two, if not indeed—"

"Ah," she blithely jumps (but upward, not on), "that *reminds* me . . ."

"Yaaahhh!" Roger reeling back to a potted plant, among the lilting saxophones of Roland Peachey and his Orchestra playing "There, I Said It Again," and cowering.

"So, *that's* on your mind. If mind is the word I want."

They confuse everyone. They look so innocent. People immediately want to protect them: censoring themselves away from talk of death, business, duplicity when Roger and Jessica are there. It's all shortages, songs and boy friends, films and blouses . . .

With her hair pulled back of her ears, her soft chin in profile, she looks only 9 or 10, alone by windows, blinking into the sun, turning her head on the light counterpane, coming in tears, child's reddening wrinkling face about to cry, going *oh, oh* . . .

One night in the dark quilt-and-cold refuge of their bed, drowsing to and fro himself, he licked Jessica to sleep. When she felt his first warm breaths touch her labia, she shivered and cried like a cat. Two or three notes, it seemed, that sounded together, hoarse, haunted, blowing with snowflakes remembered from around nightfall. Trees outside sifting the wind, out of her sight the lorries forever rushing down the streets and roads, behind houses, across canals or river, beyond the simple park. Oh and the dogs and cats who went padding in the fine snow. . . .

". . . pictures, well scenes, keep flashing *in,* Roger. By themselves, I mean I'm not *making* them. . . ." A bright swarm of them is passing by, against the low isotonic glimmer of the ceiling. He and she lie and breathe mouth-up. His soft cock drools down around his thigh, the downhill one, closest to Jessica. The night room heaves a sigh, yes Heaves, a Sigh—old-fashioned comical room, oh me I'm hopeless, born a joker never change, flirting away through the mirrorframe in something green-striped, pantalooned, and ruffled—meantime though, it *is* quaint, most rooms today hum you know, have been known also to "breathe," yes even *wait in hushed expectancy* and that ought to be the rather sinister tradition here, long slender creatures, heavy perfume and capes in rooms assailed by midnight, pierced with spiral stairways, blue-petaled pergolas, an ambience in which no one, however provoked or out of touch, my dear young lady, ever, Heaves, a Sigh. It is not done.

But here. Oh, *this* young lady. Checked gingham. Ragged eyebrows, grown wild. Red velvet. On a dare once, she took off her blouse, motoring up on the trunk road near Lower Beeding.

"My God she's gone insane, what *is* this, why do they all come to *me?*"

"Well, ha, ha," Jessica twirling the necktie of her Army blouse like a stripper, "you uh, said I was afraid to. Di'n't you. Called me 'cowardly, cowardly custard' or something, 's I recall—" No brassiere of course, she never wears one.

"Look here," glaring sideways, "do you know you can get arrested? Never mind *you*," just occurring to him, here, "*I'll* get arrested!"

"They'll blame it all on you, la, la." Lower teeth edging out in a mean-girl's smile. "I'm just an innocent lamb and this—" flinging a little arm out, striking light from the fair hairs on her forearm, her small breasts bouncing free, "this Roger-the-rake! here, this awful beast! makes me perform, these degrading . . ."

Meantime, the most gigantic lorry Roger has ever seen in his *life* has manoeuvred steel-shuddering nearby, and now not only the driver, but also several—well, what appear to be horrid . . . *midgets*, in strange operetta uniforms actually, some sort of Central European government-in-exile, all of them crammed somehow into the high-set cab, all are staring down, scuffling like piglets on a sow for position, eyes popping, swarthy, mouths leaking spit, to take in the spectacle of his Jesicca Swanlake scandalously bare-breasted and himself desperately looking to slow down and drop behind the lorry—except that now, behind Roger, pressing him on, in fact, at a speed identical with the lorry's, has appeared, oh shit it *is*, a military police car. He can't slow down, and if he speeds up, they'll *really* get suspicious. . . .

"Uh, Jessie, please get dressed, um, would you love?" Making a show of looking for his comb which is, as usual, lost, suspect is known as a notorious ctenophile . . .

The driver of the huge, loud lorry now tries to get Roger's attention, the other midgets crowding at the windows calling, "Hey! Hey!" and emitting oily, guttural laughs. Their leader speaks English with some liquid, unspeakably nasty European accent. Lot of winking and nudging up there now, too: "Meester! Ay, zhu! Wet a meeneh', eh?" More laughter. Roger in the rearview mirror sees English cop-faces pink with rectitude, red insignia leaning, bobbing, consulting, turning sharply now and then to stare ahead at the couple in the Jaguar who're acting so—"What *are* they *doing*, Prigsbury, can you make it out?"

"Appears to be a man and a woman, sir."
"Ass." And it's out with the black binoculars.

Through rain ... then through dreaming glass, green
with the evening. And herself in a chair, old-fashioned
bonneted, looking west over the deck of Earth, inferno
red at its edges, and further in the brown and gold
clouds. . . .

Then, suddenly, night: The empty rocking chair lit
sharing chalk blue by—is it the moon, or some other light
from the sky? just the hard chair, empty now, in the very
clear night, and this cold light coming down. . . .

The images go, flowering, in and out, some lovely, some
just awful ... but she's snuggled in here with her lamb,
her Roger, and how she loves the line of his neck all at
once so—why there it is right *there*, the back of his
bumpy head like a boy of ten's. She kisses him up and
down the sour salt reach of skin that's taken her so, taken
her nightlit along this high tendoning, kisses him as if
kisses were flowing breath itself, and never ending.

One morning—he had not seen her for about a fortnight—he woke in his hermit's cell at "The White Visitation" with a hardon, scratchy eyelids and a long pale
brown hair tangled in his mouth. It wasn't one of his own
hairs. It wasn't anybody's he could think of but Jessica's.
But it couldn't be—he hadn't seen her. He sniffed a couple
of times, then sneezed. Morning developed out the window. His right canine ached. He unreeled the long hair,
beaded with saliva, tooth-tartar, mouth-breather's morning
fur, and stared at it. How'd it get here? Eerie, dearie. A
bit of the je ne sais quoi de sinistre, all right. He had to
piss. Shuffling to the lavatory, his graying government flannel tucked limply inside the cord of his pajamas, it came to
him: what if it's some mauve turn-of-the-century tale of
ghostly revenge and this hair here's some First Step . . .
Oh, paranoia? You should've seen him going through all
the combinations as he moved around doing lavatory
things among the stumbling, farting, razor-scraping, hack-
ing, sneezing and snot-crusted inmates of Psi Section. Only
later in this did he even begin to think of Jessica—of her
safety. Thoughtful Roger. What if, if she'd died in the

night, an accident at the magazines . . . with this hair the only good-by her ghostly love had been able to push back through to this side, to the only one who'd ever mattered. . . . Some spider-statistician: his eyes had actually filled with tears before the Next Idea—*oh. Oboy.* Turn off that faucet, Dorset, and get hep to *this.* He stood, half-stooped, over the washbasin, paralyzed, putting his worry for Jessica on Hold for a bit, wanting very much to look back over his shoulder, even into the, the old mirror, you know, see what they're up to, but too frozen to risk even that . . . *now* . . . oh yes a most superb possibility has found seedbed in his brain, and here it is. What if they are all, all these Psi Section freaks here, ganged up on him in secret? O.K.? Yes: suppose they *can* see into your mind! a-and how about—what if it's *hypnotism?* Eh? Jesus: then a whole number of *other* occult things such as: astral projection, brain control (nothing occult about *that*), secret curses for impotence, boils, madness, yaaahhh—*potions!* (as he straightens at last and back in his mind's eyes to his office now glances, *very* gingerly, at the coffee mess, oh *God* . . .), psychic-unity-with-the-Controlling-Agency such that Roger would be he and he Roger, yes yes a number of these notions rambling through his mind here, none of them really pleasant, either—especially inside this staff latrine, with Gavin Trefoil's face this morning colored bright magenta, a clover blossom flashing in the wind, Ronald Cherrycoke hawking fine-marbled amber phlegm into the basin—what's all this, who *are all these people.* . . . Freaks! *Freeeeaks!* He's surrounded! they've been out there night and day all the war long tapping his brain, telepaths, witches, Satanic operators of all descriptions tuning in on *everything*—even when he and Jessica are in bed *fucking*—

Try to hold it down old man, panic if you must but later, not here. . . . Faint washroom light bulbs deepen the thousands of old clustered water and soap spots on the mirrors to an interfeathering of clouds, of skin and smoke as he swings his head past, lemon and beige, oilsmoke black and twilight brown in here, very loosely crumbled, that's the texture. . . .

Lovely morning, World War Two. All he can keep in front of his mind are the words *I want a transfer,* kind of

humming tunelessly at the mirror, yes sir got to put in a
chit right away. I'll volunteer for duty in Germany's what
I'll do. Dum de dum, de dum. Right, there was an ad only
Wednesday in the classified section of *Nazis in the News*,
sandwiched between a Merseyside Labour branch that was
looking for a publicist, and a London advertising agency
with positions open immediately on demob, they said. This
ad in the middle was placed by some arm of the G-5-to-be,
trying to round up a few "re-education" experts. Vital, vital
stuff. Teach the German Beast about the Magna Carta,
sportsmanship, that sort of thing, eh? Out inside the works
of some neurotic Bavarian cuckoo clock of a village, were-
elves streaking in out of the forests at night to leave subversive handbills at door and window—"Anything!" Roger
groping back to his narrow quarters, "anything at all's
better than this. . . ."

That's how bad it was. He knew he'd feel more at home
in mad Germany with the Enemy than here in Psi Section.
The time of year makes it even worse. Christmas.
Bwweeeaaaagghh, clutching to his stomach. Jessica was all
that made it human or tolerable. Jessica . . .

He was taken over then, for half a minute, shivering and
yawning in his long underwear, soft, nearly invisible in the
December-dawn enclosure, among so many sharp edges of
books, sheafs and flimsies, charts and maps (and the chief
one, red pockmarks on the pure white skin of lady London, watching over all . . . *wait* . . . disease on skin . . . *does*
she carry the fatal infection inside herself? are the sites
predestined, and does the flight of the rocket actually follow from the fated eruption *latent in the city* . . . but he
can't hold it, no more than he understands Pointsman's
obsession with the reversal of sound stimuli and please,
please can't we just drop it for a bit . . .), visited, not
knowing till it passed how clearly he was seeing the honest
half of his life that Jessica was now, how fanatically his
mother the War must disapprove of her beauty, her cheeky
indifference to death-institutions he'd not so long ago believed in—her unflappable hope (though she hated to
make plans), her exile from childhood (though she refused ever to hold on to memories). . . .

His life had been tied to the past. He'd seen himself a
point on a moving wavefront, propagating through sterile

history—a known past, a projectable future. But Jessica was the breaking of the wave. Suddenly there was a beach, the unpredictable . . . new life. Past and future stopped at the beach: that was how he'd set it out. But he wanted to believe it too, the same way he loved her, past all words— believe that no matter how bad the time, nothing was fixed, everything could be changed and she could always deny the dark sea at his back, love it away. And (selfishly) that from a somber youth, squarely founded on Death— along for Death's ride—he might, with her, find his way to life and to joy. He'd never told her, he avoided telling himself, but that was the measure of his faith, as this seventh Christmas of the War came wheeling in another charge at his skinny, shivering flank. . . .

She trips fussing about the dormitory, bothering other girls for puffs off of stale Woodbines, nylon-repair kits, sparrow-bright war-wisecracks passing for sympathy. To-night she'll be with Jeremy, her lieutenant, but she wants to be with Roger. Except that, really, she doesn't. Does she? She can't remember ever being so confused. When she's with Roger it's all love, but at any distance—any at *all,* Jack—she finds that he depresses and even frightens her. Why? On top of him in the wild nights riding up and down his cock her axis, trying herself to stay rigid enough not to turn to cream taper-wax and fall away melting to the coverlet coming there's only room for *Roger, Roger, oh love* to the end of breath. But out of bed, walking talking, his bitterness, his darkness, run deeper than the War, the winter: he hates England so, hates "the System," gripes endlessly, says he'll migrate when the War's over, stays inside his paper cynic's cave hating himself . . . and does she *want* to bring him out, really? Isn't it safer with Jeremy? She tries not to allow this question in too often, but it's there. Three years with Jeremy. They might as well be married. Three years ought to count for something. Daily, small stitches and easings. She's worn old Beaver's bathrobes, brewed his tea and coffee, sought his eye across lorry-parks, day rooms and rainy mud fields when all the day's mean, dismal losses could be rescued in the one look—familiar, full of trust, in a season when the word is invoked for quaintness or a minor laugh. And to rip it all

out? three years? for this erratic, self-centered—*boy*, really.
Weepers, he's supposed to be past thirty, he's years older
than she. He ought to've learned *something*, surely? A
man of experience?

The worst of it's that she has no one to talk to. The
politics of this mixed battery, the professional incest, the
unwholesome obsessions with who said what to whom in
the spring of 1942 for God's sake, outside of Grafty Green,
Kent, or someplace, and who ought to have answered what
but didn't but told someone else instead thus provoking
hatreds that have thrived wonderfully down to the present
day—six years of slander, ambition and hysteria make
confiding anything to anyone around here an act of pure
masochism.

"Girl in distress, Jess?" Maggie Dunkirk on the way by,
smoothing her gauntlets. On the Tannoy a BBC swing
band is blaring hotly syncopated Christmas music.

"Got a fag, Mag?" pretty automatic by now, you guess,
Jess?

Well— "Thought it looked somewhat like a bloody
Garbo film around here, not at all the usual nicotine
starvation, sorry wrong again, ta-ta. . . ."

Oh be on your way. "Thinking about me Xmas shopping."

"What're you getting the Beaver then."

Concentrating on gartering her nylons, the older pair,
up-in-front-down-in-back mnemonically stirring in wafts
among her fingers, laundry-white puckered elastic being
stretched fine and tangent now to the gentle front curve
of her thigh, suspender-clips glittering silver under or behind her lacquered red fingernails, passing like distant
fountains behind red topiary trees, Jessica replies, "Oh.
Mm. A Pipe, I suppose. . . ."

Near her battery one night, driving Somewhere in Kent,
Roger and Jessica came upon a church, a hummock in the
dark upland, lamplit, growing out of the earth. It was
Sunday evening, and shortly before vespers. Men in great-
coats, in oilskins, in dark berets they slipped off at the
entrance, American fliers in leather lined with sheep's
wool, a few women in clinking boots and wide-shouldered
swagger coats, but no children, not a child in sight, just

grownups, trudging in from their bomber fields, balloon-
bivouacs, pillboxes over the beach, through the Norman
doorway shaggy with wintering vines. Jessica said, "Oh, I
remember..." but didn't go on. She was remembering
other Advents, and hedges snowy as sheep from her window, and the Star ready to be pasted up on the sky again.

Roger pulled over, and they watched the scuffed and
dun military going in to evensong. The wind smelled of
fresh snow.

"We ought to be home," she said, after a bit, "it's late."

"We could just pop in here for a moment."

Well, *that* surprised her, but def, after weeks of his snide
comments? His unbeliever's annoyance with the others in
Psi Section he thought were out to drive him dotty as they
were, and his Scroogery growing as shopping days till
Xmas dwindled—"You're not supposed to be the sort,"
she told him. But she did want to go in, nostalgia was
heavy in tonight's snow-sky, her own voice ready to betray
her and run to join the waits whose carols we're so apt to
hear now in the distances, these days of Advent dropping
one by one, voices piping across frozen downs where the
sown mines crowd thick as plums in a pudding... often
above sounds of melting snow, winds that must blow not
through Christmas air but through the substance of time
would bring her those child-voices, singing for sixpences,
and if her heart wasn't ready to take on quite all the
stresses of her mortality and theirs, at least there was the
fear that she was beginning to lose them—that one winter
she would go running to look, out to the gate to find them,
run as far as the trees but in vain, their voices fading....

They walked through the tracks of all the others in the
snow, she gravely on his arm, wind blowing her hair to
snarls, heels slipping once on ice. "To hear the music," he
explained.

Tonight's scratch choir was all male, epauletted shoulders visible under the wide necks of the white robes, and
many faces nearly as white with the exhaustion of soaked
and muddy fields, midwatches, cables strummed by the
nervous balloons sunfishing in the clouds, tents whose lights
inside shone nuclear at twilight, soullike, through the
cross-hatched walls, turning canvas to fine gauze, while
the wind drummed there. Yet there was one black face, the

counter-tenor, a Jamaican corporal, taken from his warm
island to this—from singing his childhood along the rum-
smoky saloons of High Holborn Street where the sailors
throw mammoth red firecrackers, quarter of a stick of
dynamite man, over the swinging doors and run across the
street giggling, or come walking out with high-skirted girls,
girls of the island, Chinese and French girls . . . lemon
peels crushed in the gutters of the streets scented the early
mornings where he used to sing, O have you seen my
darlin' Lola, with a shape like a bottle of Coca-Cola,
sailors running up and down in the brown shadows of
alleys, flapping at neckerchief and pants-leg, and the girls
whispering together and laughing . . . each morning he
counted out half a pocket full of coins of all nations. From
palmy Kingston, the intricate needs of the Anglo-American
Empire (1939–1945) had brought him to this cold field-
mouse church, nearly in earshot of a northern sea he'd
hardly glimpsed in crossing, to a compline service, a program tonight of plainsong in English, forays now and then
into polyphony: Thomas Tallis, Henry Purcell, even a
German macaronic from the fifteenth century, attributed to
Heinrich Suso:

> *In dulci jubilo*
> Nun singet und seid froh!
> Unsers Herzens Wonne
> Leit in *praesipio,*
> Leuchtet vor die Sonne
> *Matris in gremio.*
> *Alpha es et O.*

With the high voice of the black man riding above the
others, no head falsetto here but complete, out of the
honest breast, a baritone voice brought over years of wood-
shedding up to this range . . . he was bringing brown girls
to sashay among these nervous Protestants, down the ancient paths the music had set, Big and Little Anita, Stiletto
May, Plongette who loves it between her tits and will do
it that way for free—not to mention the Latin, the *German?* in an English church? These are not heresies so
much as imperial outcomes, necessary as the black man's
presence, from acts of minor surrealism—which, taken in
the mass, are an act of suicide, but which in its pathology,

in its dreamless version of the real, the Empire commits by the thousands every day, completely unaware of what it's doing. . . . So the pure counter-tenor voice was soaring, finding its way in to buoy Jessica's heart and even Roger's she guessed, risking glances at his face sideways and up through brown ghosts of her hair, during recitatives or releases. He wasn't looking nihilistic, not even cheaply so. He was . . .

No, Jessica's never seen his face exactly like this, in the light of a few hanging oil lamps, the flames ungutterng and very yellow, on the nearest the verger's two long fingerprints in fine, pollen V-for-victory up around the belly of the glass, Roger's skin more child-pink, his eyes more glowing than the lamplight alone can account for—isn't it? or is that how she wants it to be? The church is as cold as the night outside. There's the smell of damp wool, of bitter on the breaths of these professionals, of candle smoke and melting wax, of smothered farting, of hair tonic, of the burning oil itself, folding the other odors in a maternal way, more closely belonging to Earth, to deep strata, other times, and listen . . . listen: this is the War's evensong, the War's canonical hour, and the night is real. Black great-coats crowd together, empty hoods full of dense, church-interior shadows. Over on the coast the Wrens work late, down inside cold and gutted shells, their blue torches are newborn stars in the tidal evening. Hullplates swing in the sky, like great iron leaves, on cables that creak in splinters of sound. At ease, on standby, the flames of the torches, softened, fill the round glass faces of the gauges with apricot light. In the pipefitters' sheds, icicled, rattling when the gales are in the Straits, here's thousands of old used toothpaste tubes, heaped often to the ceilings, thousands of somber man-mornings made tolerable, transformed to mint fumes and bleak song that left white spots across the quicksilver mirrors from Harrow to Gravesend, thousands of children who pestled foam up out of soft mortars of mouths, who lost easily a thousand times as many words among the chalky bubbles—bed-going complaints, timid announcements of love, news of fat or translucent, fuzzy or gentle beings from the country under the counterpane—uncounted soapy-liquorice moments spat and flushed down to sewers and the slow-scumming gray estuary, the morning mouths growing with the day tobacco and fish-furred, dry with fear, foul with idleness, flooded at thoughts of impossible meals, settling instead for the week's offal in gland pies, Household Milk, broken biscuits at half the usual points, and isn't menthol a marvelous invention to take just enough of it away each morning, down to become dusty oversize bubbles tessellating tough and stagnant among the tar shorelines, the intricate draftsmanship of outlets feeding, multiplying out to sea, as one by one these old toothpaste tubes are emptied and returned to the War, heaps of dimly fragrant metal, phantoms of peppermint in the winter shacks, each tube wrinkled or embossed by the unconscious hands of London, written over in interference-patterns, hand against hand, waiting now—it is true return—to be melted for solder, for plate, alloyed for castings, bearings, gasketry, hidden smokeshriek linings the children of that other domestic incarnation will never see. Yet the continuity, flesh to kindred metals, home to hedgeless sea, has persisted. It is not death that separates these incarnations, but paper: paper specialties, paper routines. The War, the Empire, will expedite such barriers between our lives. The War needs to divide this way, and to subdivide, though its propaganda will always stress unity, alliance, pulling together. The War does not appear to want a folk-consciousness, not even of the sort the Germans have engineered, ein Volk ein Führer—it wants a machine of many separate parts, not oneness, but a complexity. . . . Yet who can presume to say *what* the War wants, so vast and aloof is it . . . so *absentee*. Perhaps the War isn't even an awareness—not a life at all, really. There may only be some cruel, accidental resemblance to life. At "The White Visitation" there's a long-time schiz, you know, who believes that *he* is World War II. He gets no newspapers, refuses to listen to the wireless, but still, the day of the Normandy invasion somehow his temperature shot up to 104°. Now, as the pincers east and west continue their slow reflex contraction, he speaks of darkness invading his mind, of an attrition of self. . . . The Rundstedt offensive perked him up though, gave him a new lease on life—"A beautiful Christmas gift," he confessed to the resident on his ward, "it's the season of birth, of fresh beginnings." Whenever the rockets fall—those which are audible—he smiles, turns out to pace the ward, tears about to splash from the corners of his merry eyes, caught up in a ruddy high tonicity that can't help cheering his fellow patients. His days are numbered. He's to die on V-E Day. If he's not in fact the War then he's its child-surrogate, living high for a certain term but come the ceremonial day, look out. The true king only dies a mock death. Remember. Any number of young men may be selected to die in his place while the real king, foxy old bastard, goes on. Will he show up under the Star, slyly genuflecting with the other kings as this winter solstice draws on us? Bring to the serai gifts of tungsten, cordite, high-octane? Will the child gaze up from his ground of golden straw then, gaze into the eyes of the old king who bends long and unfurling overhead, leans to proffer his gift, will the eyes meet, and what message, what possible greeting or entente will flow between the king and the infant prince? Is the baby smiling, or is it just gas? Which do you want it to be?

Advent blows from the sea, which at sunset tonight shone green and smooth as iron-rich glass: blows daily upon us, all the sky above pregnant with saints and slender heralds' trumpets. Another year of wedding dresses abandoned in the heart of winter, never called for, hanging in quiet satin ranks now, their white-crumpled veils begun to yellow, rippling slightly only at your passing, spectator . . . visitor to the city at all the dead ends. . . . Glimpsing in the gowns your own reflection once or twice, halfway from shadow, only blurred flesh-colors across the peau de soie, urging you in to where you can smell the mildew's first horrible touch, which was really the idea—covering all trace of her own smell, middleclass bride-to-be perspiring, genteel soap and powder. But virgin in her heart, in her hopes. None of your bright-Swiss or crystalline season here, but darkly billowed in the day with cloud and the snow falling like gowns in the country, gowns of the winter, gentle at night, a nearly windless breathing around you. In the stations of the city the prisoners are back from Indo-China, wandering their poor visible bones, light as dreamers or men on the moon, among chrome-sprung prams of black hide resonant as drumheads, blonde wood high-chairs pink and blue with scraped and mush-spattered floral decals, folding-cots and bears with red felt tongues, baby-blankets making bright pastel clouds in the coal and stream smells, the metal spaces, among the queued, the drifting, the warily asleep, come by their hundreds in for the holidays, despite the warnings, the gravity of Mr. Morrison, the tube under the river a German rocket may pierce now, even now as the words are set down, the absences that may be waiting them, the city addresses that surely can no longer exist. The eyes from Burma, from Tonkin, watch these women at their hundred perseverances—stare out of blued orbits, through headaches no Alasils can ease. Italian P/Ws curse underneath the mail sacks that are puffing, echo-making in now each hour, in seasonal swell, clogging the snowy trainloads like mushrooms, as if the trains have been all night underground, passing through the country of the dead. If these Eyeties sing now and then you can bet it's not "Giovinezza" but something probably from *Rigoletto* or *La Bohème*—indeed the Post Office is considering issuing a list of Nonacceptable Songs, with ukulele chords as an aid to ready identification. Their cheer and songfulness, this lot, is genuine up to a point—but as the days pile up, as this orgy of Christmas greeting grows daily beyond healthy limits, with no containment in sight before Boxing Day, they settle, themselves, for being more professionally Italian, rolling the odd eye at the lady evacuees, finding techniques of balancing the sack with one hand whilst the other goes playing "dead"—*cioé*, conditionally alive—where the crowds thicken most feminine, directionless . . . well, most promising. Life has to go on. Both kinds of prisoner recognize that, but there's no *mano morto* for the Englishmen back from CBI, no leap from dead to living at mere permission from a likely haunch or thigh—no *play*, for God's sake, about life-and-death! They want no more adventures: only the old dutch fussing over the old stove or warming the old bed, cricketers in the wintertime, they want the semi-detached Sunday dead-leaf sommolence of a dried garden. If the brave new world should also come about, a kind of windfall, why there'll be time to adjust certainly to that. . . . But they want the nearly postwar luxury this week of buying an electric train set for the kid, trying that way each to light his own set of sleek little faces here,

calibrating his strangeness, well-known photographs all,
brought to life now, oohs and aahs but not yet, not here
in the station, any of the moves most necessary: the War
has shunted them, earthed them, those heedless destroying
signalings of love. The children have unfolded last year's
toys and found reincarnated Spam tins, they're hep this
may be the other and, who knows, unavoidable side to the
Christmas game. In the months between—country springs
and summers—they played with real Spam tins—tanks,
tank-destroyers, pillboxes, dreadnoughts deploying meat-
pink, yellow and blue about the dusty floors of lumber-
rooms or butteries, under the cots or couches of their exile.
Now it's time again. The plaster baby, the oxen frosted
with gold leaf and the human-eyed sheep are turning real
again, paint quickens to flesh. To believe is not a price
they pay—it happens all by itself. He is the New Baby.
On the magic night before, the animals will talk, and the
sky will be milk. The grandparents, who've waited each
week for the Radio Doctor asking, What Are Piles? What
Is Emphysema? What Is A Heart Attack? will wait up
beyond insomnia, watching again for the yearly impossible
not to occur, but with some mean residue—this *is* the hillside, the sky *can* show us a light—like a thrill, a good time
you wanted too much, not a complete loss but still too far
short of a miracle . . . keeping their sweatered and shawled
vigils, theatrically bitter, but with the residue inside going
through a new winter fermentation every year, each time a
bit less, but always good for a revival at this season.
. . . All but naked now, the shiny suits and gowns of their
pubcrawling primes long torn to strips for lagging the hot-
water pipes and heaters of landlords, strangers, for holding the houses' identities against the winter. The War
needs coal. They have taken the next-to-last steps, attended the Radio Doctor's certifications of what they
knew in their bodies, and at Christmas they are naked as
geese under this woolen, murky, cheap old-people's swad-
dling. Their electric clocks run fast, even Big Ben will be
fast now until the new spring's run in, all fast, and no one
else seems to understand or to care. The War needs electricity. It's a lively game, Electric Monopoly, among the
power companies, the Central Electricity Board, and other
War agencies, to keep Grid Time synchronized with

Greenwich Mean Time. In the night, the deepest concrete wells of night, dynamos whose locations are classified
spin faster, and so, responding, the clock-hands next to all
the old, sleepless eyes—gathering in their minutes whining,
pitching higher toward the vertigo of a siren. It is the
Night's Mad Carnival. There is merriment under the shadows of the minute-hands. Hysteria in the pale faces between the numerals. The power companies speak of loads,
war-drains so vast the clocks will slow again unless this
nighttime march is stolen, but the loads expected daily do
not occur, and the Grid runs inching ever faster, and the
old faces turn to the clock faces, thinking *plot*, and the
numbers go whirling toward the Nativity, a violence, a
nova of heart that will turn us all, change us forever to
the very forgotten roots of who we are. But over the sea
the fog tonight still is quietly scalloped pearl. Up in the
city the arc-lamps crackle, furious, in smothered blaze up
the centerlines of the streets, too ice-colored for candles,
to chill-dropleted for holocaust . . . the tall read busses sway,
all the headlamps by regulation newly unmasked now
parry, cross, traverse and blind, torn great fistfuls of wetness blow by, desolate as the beaches beneath the nacre
fog, whose barbed wire that never knew the inward sting
of current, that only lay passive, oxidizing in the night,
now weaves like underwater grass, looped, bitter cold,
sharp as the scorpion, all the printless sand miles past
cruisers abandoned in the last summers of peacetime that
once holidayed the old world away, wine and olive-grove
and pipe-smoke evenings away the other side of the War,
stripped now to rust axles and brackets and smelling inside of the same brine as this beach you cannot really
walk, because of the War. Up across the downs, past the
spotlights where the migrant birds in autumn choked the
beams night after night, fatally held till they dropped exhausted out of the sky, a shower of dead birds, the compline worshipers sit in the unheated church, shivering,
voiceless as the choir asks: where are the joys? Where else
but there where the Angels sing new songs and the bells
ring out in the court of the King. *Eia*—strange thousand-
year sigh—*eia, wärn wir da!* were we but there. . . . The
tired men and their black bellwether reaching as far as
they can, as far from their sheeps' clothing as the year will

let them stray. Come then. Leave your war awhile, paper or iron war, petrol or flesh, come in with your love, your fear of losing, your exhaustion with it. All day it's been at you, coercing, jiving, claiming your belief in so much that isn't true. Is that who you are, that vaguely criminal face on your ID card, its soul snatched by the government camera as the guillotine shutter fell—or maybe just left behind with your heart, at the Stage Door Canteen, where they're counting the night's take, the NAAFI girls, the girls named Eileen, carefully sorting into refrigerated compartments the rubbery maroon organs with their yellow garnishes of fat—oh Linda come here feel this one, put your finger down in the ventricle here, isn't it swoony, it's still *going. . . .* Everybody you don't suspect is in on this, everybody but you: the chaplain, the doctor, your mother hoping to hang that Gold Star, the vapid soprano last night on the Home Service programme, let's not forget Mr. Noel Coward so stylish and cute about death and the afterlife, packing them into the Duchess for the fourth year running, the lads in Hollywood telling us how grand it all is over here, how much fun, Walt Disney causing Dumbo the elephant to clutch to that feather like how many carcasses under the snow tonight among the white-painted tanks, how many hands each frozen around a Miraculous Medal, lucky piece of worn bone, half-dollar with the grinning sun peering up under Liberty's wispy gown, clutching, dumb, when the 88 fell—what do you think, it's a children's story? There aren't any. The children are away dreaming, but the Empire has no place for dreams and it's Adults Only in here tonight, here in this refuge with the lamps burning deep, in pre-Cambrian exhalation, savory as food cooking, heavy as soot. And 60 miles up the rockets hanging the measureless instant over the black North Sea before the fall, ever faster, to orange heat, Christmas star, in helpless plunge to Earth. Lower in the sky the flying bombs are out too, roaring like the Adversary, seeking whom they may devour. It's a long walk home tonight. Listen to this mock-angel singing, let your communion be at least in listening, even if they are not spokesmen for your exact hopes, your exact, darkest terror, listen. There must have been evensong here long before the news of Christ. Surely for as long as there have

been nights bad as this one—something to raise the possibility of another night that could actually, with love and
cockcrows, light the path home, banish the Adversary,
destroy the boundaries between our lands, our bodies, our
stories, all false, about who we are: for the one night,
leaving only the clear way home and the memory of the
infant you saw, almost too frail, there's too much shit in
these streets, camels and other beasts stir heavily outside,
each hoof a chance to wipe him out, make him only another Messiah, and sure somebody's around already taking
bets on that one, while here in this town the Jewish
collaborators are selling useful gossip to Imperial Intelligence, and the local hookers are keeping the foreskinned
invaders happy, charging whatever the traffic will bear,
just like the innkeepers who're naturally delighted with
this registration thing, and up in the capital they're wondering should they, maybe, give everybody a *number*,
yeah, something to help SPQR Record-keeping . . . and
Herod or Hitler, fellas (the chaplains out in the Bulge are
manly, haggard, hard drinkers), what kind of a world is
it ("You forgot Roosevelt, padre," come the voices from
the back, the good father can never see them, they harass
him, these tempters, even into his dreams: "Wendell
Willkie!" "How about Churchill?" "'Arry Pollitt!") for a
baby to come in tippin' those Toledos at 7 pounds 8 ounces
thinkin' he's gonna redeem it, why, he oughta have his
head examined. . . .

But on the way home tonight, you wish you'd picked
him up, held him a bit. Just held him, very close to your
heart, his cheek by the hollow of your shoulder, full of
sleep. As if it were you who could, somehow, save him.
For the moment not caring who you're supposed to be
registered as. For the moment anyway, no longer who the
Caesars say you are.

> *O Jesu parvule,*
> Nach dir ist mir so weh . . .

So this pickup group, these exiles and horny kids, sullen
civilians called up in their middle age, men fattening
despite their hunger, flatulent because of it, pre-ulcerous,
hoarse, runny-nosed, red-eyed, sore-throated, piss-swollen

men suffering from acute lower backs and all-day hangovers, wishing death on officers they truly hate, men you
have seen on foot and smileless in the cities but forgot,
men who don't remember you either, knowing they ought
to be grabbing a little sleep, not out here performing for
strangers, give you this evensong, climaxing now with its
rising fragment of some ancient scale, voices overlapping
three- and fourfold, up, echoing, filling the entire hollow
of the church—no counterfeit baby, no announcement of
the Kingdom, not even a try at warming or lighting this
terrible night, only, damn us, our scruffy obligatory little
cry, our maximum reach outward—*praise be to God!*—for
you to take back to your war-address, your war-identity,
across the snow's footprints and tire tracks finally to the
path you must create by yourself, alone in the dark.
Whether you want it or not, whatever seas you have
crossed, the way home. . . .

□

Paradoxical phase, when weak stimuli get strong responses. . . . When did it happen? A certain early stage of
sleep: you had not heard the Mosquitoes and Lancasters
tonight on route to Germany, their engines battering apart
the sky, shaking and ripping it, for a full hour, a few puffs
of winter cloud drifting below the steel-riveted underside
of the night, vibrating with the constancy, the terror, of so
many bombers outward bound. Your own form immobile,
mouth-breathing, alone face-up on the narrow cot next to
the wall so pictureless, chartless, mapless: so *habitually
blank*. . . . Your feet pointed toward a high slit window at
the far end of the room. Starlight, the steady sound of the
bombers' departure, icy air seeping in. The table littered
with broken-spined books, scribbled columns headed
Time / Stimulus / Secretion (30 sec) / Remarks, teacups,
saucers, pencils, pens. You slept, you dreamed: thousands
of feet above your face the steel bombers passed, wave
after wave. It was indoors, some great place of assembly.
Many people were gathered. In recent days, at certain
hours, a round white light, quite intense, has gone sliding
along and down in a straight line through the air. Here,

suddenly, it appears again, its course linear as always, right to left. But this time it isn't constant—instead it lights up brilliantly in short bursts or jangles. The apparition, this time, is taken by those present as a warning—something wrong, drastically wrong, with the day. . . . No one knew what the round light signified. A commission had been appointed, an investigation under way, the answer tantalizingly close—but now the light's behavior has changed. . . . The assembly adjourns. On seeing the light jangling this way, you begin to wait for something terrible—not exactly an air raid but something close to that. You look quickly over at a clock. It's six on the dot, hands perfectly straight up and down, and you understand that six is the hour of the appearance of the light. You walk out into the evening. It's the street before your childhood home: stony, rutted and cracked, water shining in puddles. You set out to the left. (Usually in these dreams of home you prefer the landscape to the right—broad night-lawns, towered over by ancient walnut trees, a hill, a wooden fence, hollow-eyed horses in a field, a cemetery. . . . Your task, in these dreams, is often to cross—under the trees, through the shadows—before something happens. Often you go into the fallow field just below the graveyard, full of autumn brambles and rabbits, where the gypsies live. Sometimes you fly. But you can never rise above a certain height. You may feel yourself being slowed, coming inexorably to a halt: not the keen terror of falling, only an interdiction, from which there is no appeal . . . and as the landscape begins to dim out . . . you *know . . . that . . .*) But this evening, this six o'clock of the round light, you have set out leftward instead. With you is a girl identified as your wife, though you were never married, have never seen her before yet have known her for years. She doesn't speak. It's just after a rain. Everything glimmers, edges are extremely clear, illumination is low and very pure. Small clusters of white flowers peep out wherever you look. Everything blooms. You catch another glimpse of the round light, following its downward slant, a brief blink on and off. Despite the apparent freshness, recent rain, flower-life, the scene disturbs you. You try to pick up some fresh odor to correspond to what you see, but cannot. Everything is silent, odorless. Because of the light's behavior something is going to happen, and you can only wait. The landscape shines. Wetness on the pavement. Settling a warm kind of hood around the back of your neck and shoulders, you are about to remark to your wife, "This is the most sinister time of evening." But there's a better word than "sinister." You search for it. It is someone's name. It waits behind the twilight, the clarity, the white flowers. There comes a light tapping at the door.

You sat bolt upright in bed, your heart pounding in fright. You waited for it to repeat, and became aware of the many bombers in the sky. Another knock. It was Thomas Gwenhidwy, come down all the way from London, with the news about poor Spectro. You slept through the loud squadrons roaring without letup, but Gwenhidwy's small, reluctant tap woke you. Something like what happens on the cortex of Dog during the "paradoxical" phase.

Now ghosts crowd beneath the eaves. Stretched among snowy soot chimneys, booming over air-shafts, too tenuous themselves for sound, dry now forever in this wet gusting, stretched and never breaking, whipped in glassy French-curved chase across the rooftops, along the silver downs, skimming where the sea combs freezing in to shore. They gather, thicker as the days pass, English ghosts, so many jostling in the nights, memories unloosening into the winter, seeds that will never take hold, so lost, now only an every-so-often word, a clue for the living—"Foxes," calls Spectro$_E$ across astral spaces, the word intended for Mr. Pointsman who is not present, who won't be told because the few Psi Section who're there to hear it get cryptic debris of this sort every sitting—if recorded at all it finds its way into Milton Gloaming's word-counting project—"Foxes," a buzzing echo on the afternoon, Carroll Eventyr, "The White Visitation"'s resident medium, curls thickly tightened across his head, speaking the word "Foxes," out of very red, thin lips . . . half of St. Veronica's hospital in the morning smashed roofless as the old Ick Regis Abbey, powdered as the snow, and poor Spectro picked off, lighted cubbyhole and dark ward subsumed in the blast and he never hearing the approach, the sound too late, after the blast, the rocket's ghost calling to ghosts it newly made. Then silence. Another "event" for Roger Mexico, a round-

headed pin to be stuck in his map, a square graduating
from two up to three hits, helping fill out the threes pre-
diction, which lately's being lagged behind. . . .

A pin? not even that, a pinhole in paper that someday
will be taken down, when the rockets have stopped their
falling, or when the young statistician chooses to end his
count, paper to be hauled away by the charwomen, torn
up, burned. . . . Pointsman alone, sneezing helplessly in
his dimming bureau, the barking from the kennels flat now
and diminished by the cold, shaking his head *no* . . . inside me, in my memory . . . more than an "event" . . . our
common mortality . . . these tragic days. . . . But by now he
is shivering, allowing himself to stare across his office space
at the Book, to remind himself that of an original seven
there are now only two left, himself and Thomas Gwenhidwy tending his poor out past Stepney. The five ghosts
are strung in clear escalation: Pumm in a jeep accident,
Easterling taken early in a raid by the Luftwaffe, Dromond
by German artillery on Shellfire Corner, Lamplighter by a
flying bomb, and now Kevin Spectro . . . auto, bomb, gun,
V-1, and now V-2, and Pointsman has no sense but terror's,
all his skin aching, for the mounting sophistication of this,
for the dialectic it seems to imply. . . .

"Ah, yes indeed. The mummy's curse, you idiot. Christ,
Christ, I'm ready for D Wing."

Now D Wing is "The White Visitation"'s cover, still
housing a few genuine patients. Few of the PISCES people go near it. The skeleton of regular hospital staff have
their own canteen, W.C.s, sleeping quarters, offices, carrying on as under the old place, suffering the Other Lot in
their midst. Just as, for their part, PISCES staff suffer the
garden or peacetime madness of D Wing, only rarely
finding opportunity to swap information on therapies or
symptoms. Yes, one would expect more of a link. Hysteria
is, after all, is it not, hysteria. Well, no, come to find out,
it's not. How does one feel legitimist and easy for very
long about the transition? From conspiracies so mild, so
domestic, from the serpent coiled in the teacup, the hand's
paralysis or eye's withdrawal at words, *words* that could
frighten that much, to the sort of thing Spectro found
every day in his ward, extinguished now . . . to what
Pointsman finds in Dogs Piotr, Natasha, Nikolai, Sergei,

Katinka—or Pavel Sergevich, Varvara Nikolaevna, and
then ther children, and— When it can be read so clearly
in the faces of the physicians... Gwenhidwy inside his
fluffy beard never as impassive as he might have wished,
Spectro hurrying away with a syringe for his Fox, when
nothing can really stop the Abreaction of the Lord of the
Night unless the Blitz stops, rockets dismantle, the entire
film runs backward: faired skin back to sheet steel back to
pigs to white incandesence to ore, to Earth. But the reality
is not reversible. Each firebloom, followed by blast then
by sound of arrival, is a mockery (how can it not be
deliberate?) of the reversible process: with each one the
Lord further legitimizes his State, and we who cannot find
him, even to see, come to think of death no more often,
really, than before... and, with no warning when they
will come, and no way to bring them down, pretend to
carry on as in Blitzless times. When it does happen, we
are content to call it "chance." Or we have been per-
suaded. There do exist levels where chance is hardly recognized at all. But to the likes of employees such as Roger
Mexico it is music, not without its majesty, this power
series Ne$^{-m}\left(1 + m + \dfrac{m^2}{2!} + \dfrac{m^3}{3!} + \cdots + \dfrac{m^{n-1}}{(n-1)!}\right)$,
terms numbered according to rocketfalls per square, the
Poisson dispensation ruling not only these annihilations no
man can run from, but also cavalry accidents, blood
counts, radioactive decay, number of wars per year....

Pointsman stands by a window, his own vaguely reflected face blown through with the driven snow outside
in the darkening day. Far across the downs cries a train
whistle, grainy as late fog: a cockcrow — • — • ——, a
long whistle, another crow, fire at trackside, a rocket,
another rocket, in the woods or valley...

Well... Why *not* renounce the Book then Ned, give it
up that's all, the obsolescent data, the Master's isolated
moments of poetry, it's paper that's all, you don't need it,
the Book and its terrible curse... before it's too late....
Yes, recant, grovel, oh fabulous—but before whom? Who's
listening? But he has crossed back to the desk and actually
laid hands on it....

"Ass. Superstitious *ass*." Wandering, empty-headed...

these episodes are coming more often now. His decline, creeping on him like the cold. Pumm, Easterling, Dromond, Lamplighter, Spectro . . . what should he've done then, gone down to Psi Section, asked Eventyr to get up a séance, try to get on to one of them at least . . . perhaps . . . yes . . . What holds him back? "Have I," he whispers against the glass, the aspirate, the later plosives clouding the cold pane in fans of breath, warm and disconsolate breath, "so much pride?" One cannot, *he* cannot walk down that particular corridor, cannot even suggest, no not even to Mexico, how he misses them . . . though he hardly knew Dromond, or Easterling . . . but . . . misses Allen Lamplighter, who would bet on anything, you know, on dogs, thunderstorms, tram numbers, on street-corner wind and a likely skirt, on how far a given doodle would get, perhaps . . . oh God . . . even the one that fell on him. . . . Pumm's arranger-style piano and drunken baritone, his adventuring among the nurses. . . . Spectro . . . Why *can't* he ask? When there are a hundred ways to put it. . . .

I should . . . should have. . . . There are, in his history, so many of these unmade moves, so many "should haves"—should have married her, let her father steer him, should have stayed in Harley Street, been kinder, smiled more at strangers, even smiled back this afternoon at Maudie Chilkes . . . why couldn't he? A silly bleeding smile, why not, what inhibits, what snarl of the mosaic? Pretty, amber eyes behind those government spectacles . . . Women avoid him. He knows in a general way what it is: he's creepy. He's even aware, usually, of the times when he's *being* creepy—it's a certain set to his face-muscles, a tendency to sweat . . . but he can't seem to *do* anything about it, can't ever concentrate for long enough, they distract him so—and next thing he knows he's back to radiating the old creepiness again . . . and their response to it is predictable, they run uttering screams only they, and he, can hear. Oh but how he'd like someday to give them something *really to scream about.* . . .

Here's an erection stirring, he'll masturbate himself to sleep again tonight. A joyless constant, an institution in his life. But goading him, just before the bright peak, what images will come whirling in? Why, the turrets and blue waters, the sails and churchtops of Stockholm—the yellow telegram, the face of a tall, cognizant, and beautiful woman turned to watch him as he passes in the ceremonial limousine, a woman who will later, hardly by chance, visit him in his suite at the Grand Hotel ... it's not *all* ruby nipples and black lace cami-knickers, you know. There are hushed entrances into rooms that smell of paper, satellite votes on this Committee or that, the Chairs, the Prizes ... what could compare! *Later, when you're older, you'll know,* they said. Yes and it grows upon him, each war year equal to a dozen of peacetime, oh my, how right they were.

As his luck has always known, his subcortical, brute luck, this gift of survival while other and better men are snatched away into Death, here's the door, one he's imagined so often in lonely Thesean brushings down his polished corridors of years: an exit out of the orthodox-Pavlovian, showing him vistas of Norrmalm, Södermalm, Deer Park and Old City....

One by one they are being picked off around him: in his small circle of colleagues the ratio slowly grows top-heavy, more ghosts, more each winter, and fewer living ... and with each one, he thinks he feels patterns on his cortex going dark, settling to sleep forever, parts of whoever he's been now losing all definition, reverting to dumb chemistry....

Kevin Spectro did not differentiate as much as he between Outside and Inside. He saw the cortex as an interface organ, mediating between the two, but *part of them both.* "When you've looked at how it really is," he asked once, "how can we, any of us, be separate?" He is my Pierre Janet, Pointsman thought....

Soon, by the dialectic of the Book, Pointsman will be alone, in a black field lapsing to isotropy, to the zero, waiting to be last to go.... Will there be time? He *has* to survive ... to try for the Prize, not for his own glory, no— but to keep a promise, to the human field of seven he once was, the ones who didn't make it.... Here's a medium shot, himself backlit, alone at the high window in the Grand Hotel, whisky glass tipped at the bright subarctic sky and *here's to you then, chaps, it'll be all of us up there onstage tomorrow, Ned Pointsman only happened to survive that's all* ... TO STOCKHOLM his banner and cry, and after Stockholm a blur, a long golden twilight....

Oh yes once you know, he did believe in a Minotaur
waiting for him: used to dream himself rushing into the
last room, burnished sword at the ready, screaming like
a Commando, letting it all out at last—some true marvelous peaking of life inside him for the first and last time,
as the face turned his way, ancient, weary, seeing none of
Pointsman's humanity, ready only to assume him in another
long-routinized nudge of horn, flip of hoof (but this time
there would be struggle, Minotaur blood the fucking beast,
cries from far inside himself whose manliness and violence
surprise him). . . . This was the dream. The settings, the
face changed, little of it past the structure survived the
first cup of coffee and flat beige Benzedrine pill. It might
be a vast lorry-park just at dawn, the pavement newly
hosed, mottled in grease-browns, the hooded olive trucks
standing each with a secret, each waiting . . . but he knows
that inside one of these . . . and at last, sifting among
them, finds it, the identifying code beyond voicing, climbs
up into the back, under the canvas, waits in the dust and
brown light, until through the cloudy oblong of the cab
window a face, a face *he knows* begins to turn . . . but the
underlying structure is the turning face, the meeting of
eyes . . . stalking Reichssieger von Thanatz Alpdrücken,
that most elusive of Nazi hounds, champion Weimaraner
for 1941, bearing studbook number 416832 tattooed inside
his ear along through a Londonized Germany, his liver-
gray shape receding, loping at twilit canalsides strewn
with debris of war, rocket blasts each time missing them,
their chase preserved, a plate etched in firebursts, the map
of a sacrificial city, of a cortex human and canine, the
dog's ear-leather mildly aswing, top of his skull brightly
reflecting the winter clouds, into a shelter lying steel-clad
miles below the city, an opera of Balkan intrigue, in whose
hermetic safety, among whose clusters of blue dissonance
unperiodically stressed he's unable to escape completely
because of how always the Reichssieger persists, leading,
serene, uncancelable, and to the literal pursuit of whom he
thus returns, must return time and again in a fever-rondo,
until at last they are on some hillside at the end of a long
afternoon of dispatches from Armageddon, among scarlet
bangs of bougainvillea, golden pathways where dust is
rising, pillars of smoke far away over the spidery city

they've crossed, voices in the air telling of South America burned to cinders, the sky over New York glowing purple with the new all-sovereign death-ray, and here at last is where the gray dog can turn and the amber eyes gaze into Ned Pointsman's own. . . .

Each time, each turning, his own blood and heart are stroked, beaten, brought jubilantly high, and triggered to the icy noctiluca, to flare and fusing Thermite as he begins to expand, an uncontainable light, as the walls of the chamber turn a blood glow, orange, then white and begin to slip, to flow like wax, what there is of labyrinth collapsing in rings outward, hero and horror, engineer and Ariadne consumed, molten inside the light of himself, the mad exploding of himself. . . .

Years ago. Dreams he hardly remembers. The intermediaries come long since between himself and his final beast. They would deny him even the little perversity of being in love with his death. . . .

But now with Slothrop in it—sudden angel, thermodynamic surprise, whatever he is . . . will it change now? Might Pointsman get to have a go at the Minotaur after all?

Slothrop ought to be on the Riviera by now, warm, fed, well-fucked. But out in this late English winter the dogs, thrown over, are still ranging the back-streets and mews, sniffing the dustbins, skidding on carpets of snow, fighting, fleeing, shivering in their wet pools of Prussian blue . . . seeking to avoid what cannot be smelled or seen, what announces itself with the roar of a predator so absolute they sink to the snow whining and roll over to give it their soft and open bellies. . . .

Has Pointsman renounced them in favor of one untried human subject? Don't think he hasn't doubts as to the validity of this scheme, at least. Let Vicar de la Nuit worry about its "rightness," he's the staff chaplain. But . . . what about the dogs? Pointsman knows them. He's deftly picked the locks of their awareness. They have no secrets. He can drive them mad, and with bromides in adequate doses he can bring them back. But Slothrop . . .

So the Pavlovian dithers about his office, feeling restless and old. He should sleep but he can't. It has to be more than the simple conditioning of a child, once upon a time.

How can he've been a doctor this long and not developed reflexes for certain conditions? He knows better: he knows it is more. Spectro is dead, and Slothrop (*sentiments d'emprise*, old man, softly now) was with his Darlene, only a few blocks from St. Veronica's, two days before.

When one event happens after another with this awful regularity, of course you don't automatically assume that it's cause-and-effect. But you do look for some mechanism to make sense of it. You probe, you design a modest experiment. . . . He owes Spectro that much. Even if the American's not legally a murderer, he is sick. The etiology ought to be traced, the treatment found.

There is to this enterprise, Pointsman knows, a danger of seduction. Because of the symmetry. . . . He's been led before, you know, down the garden path by symmetry: in certain test results . . . in assuming that a mechanism must imply its mirror image—"irradiation," for example and "reciprocal induction" . . . and who'd ever said that either had to exist? Perhaps it will be so this time, too. But how it haunts him, the symmetry of these two secret weapons, Outside, out in the Blitz, the sounds of V-1 and V-2, one the reverse of the other. . . . Pavlov showed how mirror-images Inside could be confused. Ideas of the opposite. But what new pathology lies Outside now? What sickness to events—to History itself—can create symmetrical opposites like these robot weapons?

Sign and symptoms. Was Spectro right? Could Outside and Inside be part of the same field? If only in fairness . . . in fairness . . . Pointsman ought to be seeking the answer at the interface . . . oughtn't he . . . on the cortex of Lieutenant Slothrop. The man will suffer—perhaps, in some clinical way, be destroyed—but how many others tonight are suffering in his name? For pity's sake, every *day* in Whitehall they're weighing and taking risks that make his, in this, seem almost trivial. Almost. There's something here, too transparent and swift to get a hold on—Psi Section might speak of ectoplasms—but he knows that the time has never been better, and that the exact experimental subject *is* in his hands. He must seize now, or be doomed to the same stone hallways, whose termination he knows. But he must remain open—even to the possibility that the Psi people are right. "We may all be right," he puts in his journal tonight, "so may be all we have speculated, and more. Whatever we may find, there can be no doubt that he is, physiologically, historically, a monster. *We must never lose control.* The thought of him lost in the world of men, after the war, fills me with a deep dread I cannot extinguish. . . ."

□

More and more, these days of angelic visit and communiqué, Carroll Eventyr feels a victim of his freak talent. As Nora Dodson-Truck once called it, his "splendid weakness." It showed late in life: he was 35 when out of the other world, one morning on the Embankment, between strokes of a pavement artist's two pastels, salmon darkening to fawn, and a score of lank human figures, ragsorrowful in the distances interlacing with ironwork and river smoke, all at once someone was speaking through Eventyr, so quietly that Nora caught hardly any of it, not even the identity of the soul that took and used him. Not then. Some of it was in German, some of the words she remembered. She would ask her husband, whom she was to meet that afternoon out in Surrey—arriving late though, all the shadows, men and women, dogs, chimneys, very long and black across the enormous lawn, and she with a dusting of ocher, barely noticeable in the late sun, making a fan shape near the edge of her veil—it was that color she'd snatched from the screever's wood box and swiftly, turning smoothly, touching only at shoe tip and the creamy block of yellow crumbling onto the surface, never leaving it, drew a great five-pointed star on the pavement, just upriver from an unfriendly likeness of Lloyd George in heliotrope and sea-green: pulling Eventyr by the hand to stand inside the central pentagon, seagulls in a wailing diadem overhead, then stepping in herself, an instinctive, a motherly way, her way with anyone she loved. She'd drawn her pentagram not even half in play. One couldn't be too safe, there was always evil. . . .

Had he felt her, even then, beginning to recede . . . called up the control from across the Wall as a way of holding on? She was deepening from his waking, his social

eye like light at the edge of the evening when, for perhaps a perilous ten minutes, nothing helps: put on your
glasses and light lamps, sit by the west window and still it
keeps going away, you keep losing the light and perhaps
it is forever this time . . . a good time of day for learning
surrender, learning to diminish like the light, or like certain music. This surrender is his only gift. Afterward he
can recall nothing. Sometimes, rarely, there may be tantalizing—not words, but halos of meaning around words
his mouth evidently spoke, that only stay behind—if they
do—for a moment, like dreams, can't be held or developed,
and, presently, go away. He's been under Rollo Groast's
EEG countless times since first he came to "The White
Visitation," and all's normal-adult except for, oh once or
twice perhaps a stray 50-millivolt spike off a temporal
lobe, now left now right, really no pattern to it—indeed a
kind of canals-of-Mars controversy has been in progress for
these years among the different observers—Aaron Throwster swears he's seen slow delta-wave shapes out of the left
frontal and suspects a tumor, last summer Edwin Treacle
noted a "subdued petitmal spike-and-wave alternation,
curiously much slower than the usual three per second"—
though admittedly Treacle was up in London all the night
before debauching with Allen Lamplighter and his gambling crowd. Less than a week later the buzzbomb gave
Lamplighter his chance: to find Eventyr from the other
side and prove to him to be what others had said: an
interface between the worlds, a sensitive. Lamplighter had
suffered 5-to-2 odds. But so far he's been silent: nothing
in the soft acetate/metal discs or typed transcripts that
mightn't be any of a dozen other souls. . . .

They've come, in their time, from as far way as the
institute at Bristol to gape at, to measure and systematically doubt the freaks of Psi Section. Here's Ronald Cherrycoke, the noted psychometrist, eyes lightly fluttering, hands
a steady inch away framing the brown-wrapped box in
which are securely hidden certain early-War mementos, a
dark-maroon cravat, a broken Schaeffer fountain pen, a
tarnished pince-nez of white gold, all belonging to a Group
Captain "Basher" St. Blaise, stationed far away north of
London . . . as this Cherrycoke, a normal-looking lad, perhaps a bit overweight, begins now to recite in his lathe-

humming Midland accents an intimate résumé of the Group Captain, his anxieties about his falling hair, his enthusiasm over the Donald Duck cinema cartoons, an incident during the Lübeck raid which only he and his wingman, now passed on, shared and agreed not to report—nothing that violated security: confirmed later, in fact, by St. Blaise himself smiling a bit openmouthed well the joke's certainly on me and now tell me how'd you do it? Indeed, how does Cherrycoke do it? How do any of them? How does Margaret Quartertone produce voices on discs and wire recorders miles distant without speaking or physically touching the equipment? And what speakers are now beginning to assemble? Where are the five-digit groups coming from which the Reverend Dr. Paul de la Nuit, chaplain and staff automatist, has been writing for weeks now, and which, it is felt ominously, no one up in London quite knows how to decrypt? What do Edwin Treacle's recent dreams of flight mean, especially as time-correlated with Nora Dodson-Truck's dreams of falling? What gathers among them all, that each in his own freak way can testify to but not in language, not even the lingua franca of the offices? Turbulences in the aether, uncertainties out in the winds of karma. Those souls across the interface, those we call the dead, are increasingly anxious and evasive. Even Carroll Eventyr's own control, the habitually cool and sarcastic Peter Sachsa, the one who found him that day long ago on the Embankment and thereafter—whenever there are messages to be passed across—even Sachsa's become nervous. . . .

Lately, as if all tuned in to the same aethereal Xth Programme, new varieties of freak have been showing up at "The White Visitation," all hours of the day and night, silent, staring, expecting to be taken care of, carrying machines of black metal and glass gingerbread, off on waxy trances, hyperkinetically waiting only the right trigger-question to start blithering 200 word a minute about their special, terrible endowments. An assault. What are we to make of Gavin Trefoil, for whose gift there's not even a name yet? (Rollo Groast wants to call it *autochromatism*.) Gavin, the youngest here, only 17, can somehow metabolize at will one of his amino acids, tyrosine. This will produce melanin, which is the brown-black pig-

ment responsible for human skin color. Gavin can also
inhibit this metabolizing by—it appears—varying the level
of his blood phenylalanine. So he can change his color
from most ghastly albino up through a smooth spectrum
to very deep, purplish, black. If he concentrates he can
keep this up, at any level, for weeks. Usually he is distracted, or forgets, and gradually drifts back to his rest
state, a pale freckled redhead's complexion. But you can
imagine how useful he was to Gerhardt von Göll during
the shooting of the Schwarzkommando footage: he helped
save literally hours of make-up and lighting work, acting
as a variable reflector. The best theory of *how* is Rollo's,
but it's hopelessly vague—we do know that the dermal
cells which produce melanin—the melanocytes—were
once, in each of us, at an early stage of embryonic growth,
part of the central nervous system. But as the embryo
grows, as tissue goes on differentiating, some of these nerve
cells move away from what will be the CNS, and migrate
out to the skin, to become melanocytes. They keep their
original tree-branch shapes, the axon and dendrites of the
typical nerve cell. But the dendrites are used now to
carry not electric signals but skin pigment. Rollo Groast
believes in some link, so far undiscovered—some surviving
cell-memory that will, retrocolonial, still respond to messages from the metropolitan brain. Messages that young
Trefoil may not consciously know of. "It is part," Rollo
writes home to the elder Dr. Groast in Lancashire, in
elaborate revenge for childhood tales of Jenny Greenteeth
waiting out in the fens to drown him, "part of an old and
clandestine drama for which the human body serves only
as a set of very allusive, often cryptic programme-notes—
it's as if the body we can measure is a scrap of this programme found outside in the street, near a magnificent
stone theatre we cannot enter. The convolutions of language denied us! the great Stage, even darker than Mr.
Tyrone Guthrie's accustomed murk.... Gilt and mirror-
ing, red velvet, tier on tier of box seats all in shadows too,
as somewhere down in that deep proscenium, deeper than
geometries we know of, the voices utter secrets we are
never told...."
    —Everything that comes out from CNS we have to file
here, you see. It gets to be a damned nuisance after a

while. Most of it's utterly useless. But you never know when they'll want something. Middle of the night, or during the worst part of an ultraviolet bombardment you know, it makes no difference to them back there.

—Do you ever get out much to . . . well, up to the Outer Level?

(A long pause in which the older operative stares quite openly, as several changes flow across her features—amusement, pity, concern—until the younger one speaks again.) I-I'm sorry, I didn't mean to be—

—(Abruptly) I'm supposed to tell you, eventually, as part of the briefing.

—Tell me what?

—Just as I was told once. We hand it on, one generation to the next. (There is no piece of business plausible enough for her to find refuge in. We sense that this has not yet become routine for her. Out of decency now, she tries to speak quietly, if not gently.) We *all* go up to the Outer Level, young man. Some immediately, others not for a while. But sooner or later everyone out here has to go Epidermal. No exceptions.

—Has to—

—I'm sorry.

—But isn't it . . . I thought it was only a—well, a *level*. A place you'd visit. Isn't it . . . ?

—Outlandish scenery, oh yes so did I—unusual formations, a peep into the Outer Radiance. But it's all of *us*, you see. Millions of *us*, changed to interface, to horn, and no feeling, and silence.

—Oh, God. (A pause in which he tries to take it in—then, in panic, pushes it back.) No—how can you say that—you can't feel the *memory?* the tug . . . we're in exile, we do have a home! (Silence from the other.) Back there! Not up at the interface. Back in the CNS!

—(Quietly) It's been a prevalent notion. Fallen sparks. Fragments of vessels broken at the Creation. And someday, somehow, before the end, a gathering back to home. A messenger from the Kingdom, arriving at the last moment. But I tell you there is no such message, no such home—only the millions of last moments . . . no more. Our history is an aggregate of last moments.

She crosses the complex room dense with its supple

hides, lemon-rubbed teak, rising snarls of incense, bright
optical hardware, faded Central Asian rugs in gold and
scarlet, hanging open-ribbed wrought-ironwork, a long,
long downstage cross, eating an orange, section by acid
section, as she goes, the faille gown flowing beautifully, its
elaborate sleeves falling from very broadened shoulders till
tightly gathered into long button-strung cuffs all in some
nameless earth tone—a hedge-green, a clay-brown, a touch
of oxidation, a breath of the autumnal—the light from the
street lamps comes in through philodendron stalks and
fingered leaves arrested in a grasp at the last straining
away of sunset, falls a tranquil yellow across the cut-steel
buckles at her insteps and streaks on along the flanks and
down the tall heels of her patent shoes, so polished as to
seem of no color at all past such mild citrus light where
it touches them, and they refuse it, as if it were a masochist's kiss. Behind her steps the carpet relaxes ceiling-
ward, sole and heel-shapes disappearing visibly slow out
of the wool pile. A single rocket explosion comes thudding
across the city, from far east of here, east by southeast.
The light along her shoes flows and checks like afternoon
traffic. She pauses, reminded of something: the military
frock trembling, silk filling-yarns shivering by crowded
thousands as the chilly light slides over and off and touching again their unprotected backs. The smells of burning
musk and sandalwood, of leather and spilled whisky,
thicken in the room.

And he—passive as trance, allowing her beauty: to
enter him or avoid him, whatever's to be her pleasure.
How shall he be other than mild receiver, filler of silences?
All the radii of the room are hers, watery cellophane,
crackling tangential as she turns on her heel-axis, lancing
as she begins to retrace her path. Can he have loved her
for nearly a decade? It's incredible. This connoisseuse of
"splendid weaknesses," run not by any lust or even velleity
but by vacuum: by the absence of human hope. She is
frightening. Someone called her an erotic nihilist . . . each
of them, Cherrycoke, Paul de la Nuit, even, he would
imagine, young Trefoil, even—so he's heard—Margaret
Quartertone, each of them *used* for the ideology of the
Zero . . . to make Nora's great rejection that much more
awesome. For . . . if she does love him: if all her words,

this decade of rooms and conversations meant anything . . .
if she loves him and still will deny him, on the short end
of 5-to-2 deny his gift, deny what's distributed in his every
cell . . . then . . .

If she loves him. He's too passive, he hasn't the nerve
to reach in, as Cherrycoke has tried to. . . . Of course
Cherrycoke is odd. He laughs too often. Not aimlessly
either, but *directed at* something he thinks everyone else
can see too. All of us watching some wry newsreel, the
beam from the projector falling milky-white, thickening
with smoke from briers and cheroots. Abdullas and Woodbines . . . the lit profiles of military personnel and young
ladies are the edges of clouds: the manly crepe of an overseas cap knifing forward into the darkened cinema, the
shiny rounding of a silk leg tossed lazily toe-in between
two seats in the row ahead, the keen-shadowed turbans of
velvet and feathering eyelashes beneath. Among these
nights' faint and lusting couples, Ronald Cherrycoke's
laughing and bearing his loneliness, brittle, easily crazed,
oozing gum from the cracks, a strange mac of most unstable plastic. . . . Of all her splendid weaklings, it is he
who undertakes the most perilous trips into her void, looking for a heart whose rhythms *he* will call. It must astonish
her, Nora-so-heartless, Cherrycoke kneeling, stirring her
silks, between his hands old history flowing in eddy-cur-
rents—scarves of lime, aqua, lavender passing, pins,
brooches, opalescent scorpions (her birth sign) inside gold
mountings in triskelion, shoe-buckles, broken nacre fans
and theatre programs, suspender-tabs, dark, lank, pre-
austerity stockings . . . on his unaccustomed knees, hands
swimming, turning, seeking out her past in molecular
traces so precarious among the flow of objects, the progress through his hands, she delighted to issue her denials,
covering up his hits (close, often dead on) skillfully as if
it were drawing-room comedy. . . .

It's a dangerous game Cherrycoke's playing here. Often
he thinks the sheer volume of information pouring in
through his fingers will saturate, burn him out . . . she
seems determined to overwhelm him with her history and
its pain, and the edge of it, always fresh from the stone,
cutting at his hopes, at all their hopes. He does respect
her: he knows that very little of this is female theatricals,

really. She *has* turned her face, more than once, to the
Outer Radiance and simply seen nothing there. And so each
time has taken a little more of the Zero into herself. It
comes down to courage, at worst an amount of self-deluding that's vanishingly small: he has to admire it, even if
he can't accept her glassy wastes, her appeals to a day
not of wrath but of final indifference. . . . Any more than
she can accept the truth he knows about himself. He does
receive emanations, impressions . . . the cry inside the
stone . . . excremental kisses stitched unseen across the
yoke of an old shirt . . . a betrayal, an informer whose
guilt will sicken one day to throat cancer, chiming like
daylight through the fourchettes and quirks of a tattered
Italian glove . . . Basher St. Blaise's angel, miles beyond
designating, rising over Lübeck that Palm Sunday with the
poison-green domes underneath its feet, an obsessive cross-flow of red tiles rushing up and down a thousand peaked
roofs as the bombers banked and dived, the Baltic already
lost in a poll of incendiary smoke behind, here was the
Angel: ice crystals swept hissing away from the back edges
of wings perilously deep, opening as they were moved into
new white abyss. . . . For half a minute radio silence broke
apart. The traffic being:

St. Blaise: Freakshow Two, *did you see that*, over.

Wingman: This is Freakshow Two—affirmative.

St. Blaise: Good.

No one else on the mission seemed to've had radio communication. After the raid, St. Blaise checked over the
equipment of those who got back to base and found nothing wrong: all the crystals on frequency, the power supplies rippleless as could be expected—but others remembered how, for the few moments the visitation lasted, even
static vanished from the earphones. Some may have heard
a high singing, like wind among masts, shrouds, bedspring
or dish antennas of winter fleets down in the dockyards . . .
but only Basher and his wingman saw it, droning across
in front of the fiery leagues of face, the eyes, which went
towering for miles, shifting to follow their flight, the irises
red as embers fairing through yellow to white, as they
jettisoned all their bombs in no particular pattern, the
fussy Norden device, sweat drops in the air all around its
rolling eyepiece, bewildered at their unannounced need to
climb, to give up a strike at earth for a strike at heaven. . . .

Group Captain St. Blaise did not include an account of this angel in his official debriefing, the W.A.A.F. officer who interrogated him being known around the base as the worst sort of literal-minded dragon (she had reported Blowitt to psychiatric for his rainbowed Valkyrie over Peenemünde, and Creepham for the bright blue gremlins scattering like spiders off of his Typhoon's wings and falling gently to the woods of The Hague in little parachutes of the same color). But damn it, this was not a cloud. Unofficially, in the fortnight between the fire-raising at Lübeck and Hitler's order for "terror attacks of a retaliatory nature"—meaning the V-weapons—word of the Angel got around. Although the Group Captain seemed reluctant, Ronald Cherrycoke was allowed to probe certain objects along on the flight. Thus the Angel was revealed.

Carroll Eventyr attempted then to reach across to Terence Overbaby, St. Blaise's wingman. Jumped by a skyful of MEs and no way out. The inputs were confusing. Peter Sachsa intimated that there were in fact many versions of the Angel which might apply. Overbaby's was not as available as certain others. There are problems with levels, and with Judgment, in the Tarot sense. . . . This is part of the storm that sweeps now among them all, both sides of Death. It is unpleasant. On his side, Eventyr tends to feel wholly victimized, even a bit resentful. Peter Sachsa, on his, falls amazingly out of character and into nostalgia for life, the old peace, the Weimar decadence that kept him fed and moving. Taken forcibly over in 1930 by a blow from a police truncheon during a street action in Neukölln, he recalls now, sentimentally, evenings of rubbed darkwood, cigar smoke, ladies in chiseled jade, panne, attar of damask roses, the latest angular pastel paintings on the walls, the latest drugs inside the many little table drawers. More than any mere "Kreis," on most nights full mandalas came to bloom: all degrees of society, all quarters of the capital, palms down on that famous blood veneer, touching only at little fingers. Sachsa's table was like a deep pool in the forest. Beneath the surface things were rolling, slipping, beginning to rise. . . . Walter Asch ("Taurus") was visited one night by something so unusual it took three "Hieropons" (250 mg.) to bring him back, and even so he seemed reluctant to sleep. They all stood watching him, in ragged rows resembling athletic

formations, Wimpe the IG-man who happened to be holding the Hieropon keying on Sargner, a civilian attached
to General Staff, flanked by Lieutenant Weissmann, recently back from South-West Africa, and the Herero aide
he'd brought with him, staring, staring at them all, at
everything . . . while behind them ladies moved in a sibilant
weave, sequins and high-albedo stockings aflash, black-
and-white make-up in daintily nasal alarm, eyes wide
going *oh.* . . . Each face that watched Walter Asch was a
puppet stage: each a separate routine.

. . . shows good hands yes droop and wrists as far up as
muscle relaxant respiratory depression . . .

. . . same . . . same . . . my own face white in mirror three
threethirty four march of the Hours clock ticking room no
can't go in no not enough light not enough no *aaahhh—*

. . . theatre nothing but Walter really look at head phony
angle wants to catch light good fill-light throw a yellow
gel . . .

(A pneumatic toy frog jumps up onto a lily pad
trembling: beneath the surface lies a terror . . . a late captivity . . . but he floats now over the head of what would
take him back . . . his eyes cannot be read. . . .)

. . . mba rara m'eroto ondyoze . . . mbe mu munine
m'oruroto ayo u n'omuinyo . . . (further back than this is a
twisting of yarns or cordage, a giant web, a wrenching of
hide, of muscles in the hard grip of something that comes
to wrestle when the night is deep . . . and a sense, too, of
visitation by the dead, afterward a sick feeling that they
are not as friendly as they seemed to be . . . he has wakened, cried, sought explanation, but no one ever told him
anything he could believe. The dead have talked with him,
come and sat, shared his milk, told stories of ancestors, or
of spirits from other parts of the veld—for time and space
on their side have no meaning, all is together).

"There are sociologies," Edwin Treacle, his hair going
all directions, attempts to light a pipeful of wretched left-
overs—autumn leaves, bits of string, fag-ends, "that we
haven't even begun to look into. The sociology of our own
lot, for example. Psi Section, the S.P.R., the old ladies in
Altrincham trying to summon up the Devil, all of us on
this side, you see, are still only half the story."

"Careful with that 'we,'" Roger Mexico distracted today

by a hundred things, chi-square fittings that refuse to jibe, textbooks lost, Jessica's absence. . . .

"It makes no sense unless we also consider those who've passed over to the other side. We do transact with them, don't we? Through specialists like Eventyr and their controls over there. But all together we form a single subculture, a psychical community, if you will."

"I won't," Mexico says dryly, "but yes I suppose someone ought to be looking into it."

"There are peoples—these Hereros for example—who carry on business every day with their ancestors. The dead are as real as the living. How can you understand them without treating both sides of the wall of death with the same scientific approach?"

And yet for Eventyr it's not the social transaction Treacle hopes it is. There's no memory on his side: no personal record. He has to read about it in the notes of others, listen to discs. Which means he has to trust the others. *That's* a complicated social setup. He must base the major part of his life on the probity of men charged with acting as interface between what he is supposed to be and himself. Eventyr knows how close he is to Sachsa on the other side, but he doesn't *remember*, and he's been brought up a Christian, a Western European, believing in the primacy of the "conscious" self and its memories, regarding all the rest as abnormal or trivial, and so he is troubled, deeply. . . .

The transcripts are a document on Peter Sachsa as much as on the souls he puts in touch. They tell, in some detail, of his obsessive love for Leni Pökler, who was married to a young chemical engineer and also active with the K.P.D., shuttling between the 12th District and Sachsa's sittings. Each night she came he wanted to cry at the sight of her captivity. In her smudged eyes was clear hatred of a life she would not leave: a husband she didn't love, a child she had not learned to escape feeling guilty for not loving enough.

The husband Franz had a connection, too vague for Sachsa to pass across, with Army Ordnance, and so there were also ideological barriers that neither one found energy enough to climb. She attended street actions, Franz reported to the rocket facility at Reinickendorf after swal-

lowing his tea in an early-morning room full of women
he thought were sullen and waiting for him to leave:
bringing their bundles of leaflets, their knapsacks stuffed
with books or political newspapers, filtering through the
slum courtyards of Berlin at sunrise. . . .

□

They are shivering and hungry. In the Studentenheim
there's no heat, not much light, millions of roaches. A
smell of cabbage, old second Reich, grandmothers' cabbage, of lard smoke that has found, over the years, some
détente with the air that seeks to break it down, smells of
long illness and terminal occupation stir the crumbling walls.
One of the walls is stained yellow with waste from the broken
lines upstairs. Leni sits on the floor with four or five others,
passing a dark chunk of bread. In a damp nest of *Die
Faust Hoch,* back issues no one will read, her daughter
Ilse sleeps, breathing so shallow it can hardly be seen. Her
eyelashes make enormous shadows on the upper curves of
her cheeks.

They have left for good this time. This room will be all
right for another day, even two . . . after that Leni doesn't
know. She took one valise for both of them. Does he know
what it means for a woman born under the Crab, a mother,
to have all her home in a valise? She has a few marks with
her, Franz has his toy rockets to the moon. It is really
over.

As she used to dream it, she'd go directly to Peter
Sachsa. If he didn't take her in, he'd at least help her to
find a job. But now that she's really broken away from
Franz . . . there's something, some nasty earth-sign belliger-
ence that will rise up in Peter now and then. . . . Lately
she isn't sure about his moods. He's under pressure from
levels she guesses to be higher than usual, and he isn't
handling it well. . . .

But Peter's worst infantile rages are still better than
the most tranquil evenings of her Piscean husband, swimming his seas of fantasy, deathwish, rocket-mysticism—
Franz is just the type they want. They know how to use
that. They know how to use nearly everybody. What will
happen to the ones they can't use?

Rudi, Vanya, Rebecca, here we are a slice of Berlin life, another Ufa masterpiece, token La Bohème Student, token Slav, token Jewess, look at us: the Revolution. Of course there is no Revolution, not even in the Kinos, no German *October,* not under this "Republic." The Revolution died—though Leni was only a young girl and not political—with Rosa Luxemburg. The best there is to believe in right now is a Revolution-in-exile-in-residence, a continuity, surviving at the bleak edge over these Weimar years, waiting its moment and its reincarnated Luxemburg. . . .

AN ARMY OF LOVERS CAN BE BEATEN. These things appear on the walls of the Red districts in the course of the night. Nobody can track down author or painter for any of them, leading you to suspect they're one and the same. Enough to make you believe in a folk-consciousness. They are not slogans so much as texts, revealed in order to be thought about, expanded on, translated into action by the people. . . .

"It's true," Vanya now, "look at the forms of capitalist expression. Pornographies: pornographies of love, erotic love, Christian love, boy-and-his-dog, pornographies of sunsets, pornographies of killing, and pornographies of deduction—*ahh,* that sigh when we guess the murderer— all these novels, these films and songs they lull us with, they're approaches, more comfortable and less so, to that Absolute Comfort." A pause to allow Rudi a quick and sour grin. "The self-induced orgasm."

" 'Absolute'?" Rebecca coming forward on her bare knees to hand him the bread, damp, melting from the touch of her wet mouth, "Two people are—"

"Two people is what you are told," Rudi does not quite smirk. Through her attention, sadly and not for the first time around here, there passes the phrase *male supremacy* . . . why do they cherish their masturbating so? "but in nature it is almost unknown. Most of it's solitary. You know that."

"I know there's coming together," is all she says. Though they have never made love she means it as a reproach. But he turns away as we do from those who have just made some embarrassing appeal to faith there's no way to go into any further.

Leni, from inside her wasted time with Franz, knows
enough about coming alone. At first his passivity kept her
from coming at all. Then she understood that she could
make up anything at all to fill the freedom he allowed her.
It got more comfortable: she could dream such tender-
nesses between them (presently she was dreaming also of
other men)—but it became more solitary. Yet her lines
will not deepen fast enough, her mouth not learn hardening past a face she keeps surprising herself with, a daydreaming child's face, betraying her to anyone who'll look,
exactly the sort of fat-softened, unfocused weakness that
causes men to read her as Dependent Little Girl—even in
Peter Sachsa she's seen the look—and the dream is the
same one she went to find while Franz groaned inside his
own dark pain-wishes, a dream of gentleness, light, her
criminal heart redeemed, no more need to run, to struggle,
a man arriving tranquil as she and strong, the street becoming a distant memory: exactly the one dream that out
here she can least allow herself. She knows what she has
to impersonate. Especially with Ilse watching her more.
Ilse is not going to be used.

Rebecca's been carrying on an argument with Vanya,
half flirting, Vanya trying to keep it all in intellectual code,
but the Jewess reverting, time and again, to the bodily . . .
so sensual: the insides of her thighs, just above the knee,
smooth as oil, the tenseness of all her muscles, the alert
face, the Judenschnautze feinting, pushing, the flashes of
tongue against thick lips . . . what would it be like, to be
taken to bed by her? To do it not just with another women,
but *with a Jewess.* . . . Their animal darkness . . . sweating
hindquarters, pushing aggressively toward her face, black
hairs darkening in fine crescent around each buttock from
the crevice . . . the face turned over a shoulder smiling in
coarse delight . . . all by surprise, really, during a moment's
refuge in a pale yellow room, while the men wandered the
halls outside with drugged smiles . . . "No, not that hard.
Be gentle. I'll tell you when to do it harder. . . ." Leni's
fair skin, her look of innocence, and the Jewess's darker
coloring, her rawness, contrasting with Leni's delicacy of
structure and skin, pelvic bones stretching cobwebs
smoothly down groins and around belly, the two women
sliding, snarling, gasping . . . *I know there's coming to-*

gether . . . and Leni waking alone—the Jewess out already
in some other room of the place—never having known the
instant at which she fell into her true infant sleep, a soft
change of state that just didn't happen with Franz. . . . So
she brushed and batted with fingertips her hair to show
something of how she felt about the night's clientele and
strolled down to the baths, stripped without caring what
eyes were on her and slid into the body-warmth, the conventional perfume of it. . . . All at once, through a shouting
and humidity that might have made it hard to concentrate,
she saw, there, up on one of the ledges, looking down at
her . . . Yes he was Richard Hirsch, from the Mausigstrasse,
so many years ago . . . she knew immediately that her face
had never looked more vulnerable—she could see it in his
eyes. . . .

All round them the others splashed, made love, carried
on comic monologues, perhaps they were friends of his—
yes wasn't that Siggi frog-kicking by, we called him "the
Troll," he hasn't grown a centimeter since then . . . since
we ran home along the canal, tripped and fell on the
hardest cobblestones in the world, and woke in the mornings to see snow on the spokes of the wagon wheels, steam
out the old horse's nose. . . . "Leni. Leni." Richard's hair
pushed all the way back, his body golden, leaning to lift
her from the cloudy bath, to sit beside him.

"You're supposed to be . . ." she's flustered, doesn't know
how to put this. "Someone told me you hadn't come back
from France. . . ." She stares at her knees.

"Not even the French girls could have kept me in
France." He's still there: she feels him trying to look in her
eyes: and he speaks so simply, he's so alive, sure that
French girls must be more coercive than English machine
guns . . . she knows, filled with crying for his innocence,
that he can't have been with anyone there, that French
girls still are to him beautiful and remote agents of
Love. . . .

In Leni, now, nothing of her long employment shows,
nothing. She is the child he looked at across park pathways, or met trudging home down the gassen in the
crust-brown light, her face, rather broad then, angled
down, fair eyebrows troubled, bookpack on her back,
hands in apron pockets . . . some of the stones in the walls

were white as paste . . . she may have seen him coming
the other way, but he was older, always with friends. . . .

Now they all grow less raucous around them, more
deferent, even shy, happy for Richard and Leni. "Better
late than never!" pipes Siggi in his speeded-up midget's
voice, reaching on tiptoe to pour May wine in all their
glasses. Leni goes to get her hair restyled and lightened a
shade, and Rebecca comes with her. They talk, for the
first time, of plans and futures. Without touching, Richard
and she have fallen in love, as they should have then.
It's understood he'll take her away with him. . . .

Old Gymnasium friends have been showing up in recent
days, bringing exotic food and wine, new drugs, much
ease and honesty in sexual matters. No one bothers to
dress. They show one another their naked bodies. No one
feels anxious, or threatened about the size of her breasts or
his penis. . . . It is all beautifully relaxing for everyone.
Leni practices her new name, "Leni Hirsch," even sometimes when she's sitting with Richard at a café table in the
morning: "Leni Hirsch," and he actually smiles, embarrassed, tries to look away but can't escape her eyes and
finally he turns full into her own look, laughs out loud, a
laugh of pure joy, and reaches his hand, the palm of his
dear hand, to hold her face. . . .

On a multi-leveled early evening of balconies, terraces,
audiences grouped at the different levels, all looking downward, in toward a common center, galleries of young
women with green leaves at their waists, tall evergreen
trees, lawns, flowing water and national solemnity, the
President, in the middle of asking the Bundestag, with his
familiar clogged and nasal voice, for a giant war appropriation, breaks down suddenly: "Oh, fuck it . . ." *Fickt es*, the
soon-to-be-immortal phrase, rings in the sky, rings over
the land, *Ja, fickt es!* "I'm sending all the soldiers home.
We'll close down the weapon factories, we'll dump all the
weapons in the sea. I'm sick of war. I'm sick of waking
up every morning afraid I'm going to die." It is suddenly
impossible to hate him any more: he's as human, as mortal
now, as any of the people. There will be new elections.
The Left will run a woman whose name is never given,
but everyone understands it is Rosa Luxemburg. The other
candidates will be chosen so inept or colorless that no one

will vote for them. There will be a chance for the Revolution. The President has promised.

Incredible joy at the baths, among the friends. True joy: events in a dialectical process cannot bring this explosion of the heart. Everyone is in love. . . .

AN ARMY OF LOVERS CAN BE BEATEN.

Rudi and Vanya have fallen to arguing street tactics. Somewhere water is dripping. The street reaches in, makes itself felt everywhere. Leni knows it, hates it. The impossibility of any rest . . . needing to trust strangers who may be working for the police, if not right now then a little later, when the street has grown for them more desolate than they can bear . . . She wishes she knew of ways to keep it from her child, but already that may be too late. Franz—Franz was never much in the street. Always some excuse. Worried about security, being caught on a stray frame by one of the leather-coated photographers, who will be always at the fringes of the action. Or it was, "What'll we do with Ilse? What if there's violence?" If there's violence, what'll we do with Franz?

She tried to explain to him about the level you reach, with both feet in, when you lose your fear, you lose it all, you've penetrated the moment, slipping perfectly into its grooves, metal-gray but soft as latex, and now the figures are dancing, each pre-choreographed exactly where it is, the flash of knees under pearl-colored frock as the girl in the babushka stoops to pick up a cobble, the man the black suitcoat and brown sleeveless sweater grabbed by policemen one on either arm, trying to keep his head up, showing his teeth, the older liberal in the dirty beige overcoat, stepping back to avoid a careening demonstrator, looking back across his lapel how-dare-you or look-out-not-*me*, his eyeglasses filled with the glare of the winter sky. There is the moment, and its possibilities.

She even tried, from what little calculus she'd picked up, to explain it to Franz as Δt approaching zero, eternally approaching, the slices of time growing thinner and thinner, a succession of rooms each with walls more silver, transparent, as the pure light of the zero comes nearer. . . .

But he shook his head. "Not the same, Leni. The important thing is taking a function to its limit. Δt is just a convenience, so that it can happen."

He has, had, this way of removing all the excitement
from things with a few words. Not even well-chosen words:
he's that way by instinct. When they went to movies he
would fall asleep. He fell asleep during *Nibelungen*. He
missed Attila the Hun roaring in from the East to wipe
out the Burgundians. Franz loved films but this was how
he watched them, nodding in and out of sleep. "You're
the cause-and-effect man," she cried. How did he connect
together the fragments he saw while his eyes were open?

He was the cause-and-effect man: he kept at her
astrology without mercy, telling her what she was supposed to believe, then denying it. "Tides, radio interference, damned little else. There is no way for changes
out there to produce changes here."

"Not produce," she tried, "not cause. It all goes along
together. Parallel, not series. Metaphor. Signs and symptoms. Mapping on to different coordinate systems, I don't
know . . ." She didn't know, all she was trying to do was
reach.

But he said: "Try to design anything that way and
have it work."

They saw *Die Frau im Mond*. Franz was amused, condescending. He picked at technical points. He knew some
of the people who'd worked on the special effects. Leni
saw a dream of flight. One of many possible. Real flight
and dreams of flight go together. Both are part of the
same movement. Not A before B, but all together. . . .

Could anything with him ever have lasted? If the
Jewish wolf Pflaumbaum had not set the torch to his own
paint factory by the canal, Franz might have labored out
their days dedicated to the Jew's impossible scheme of
developing patterned paint, dissolving crystal after patient
crystal, controlling the temperatures with obsessive care
so that on cooling the amorphous swirl might, this time
might, suddenly shift, lock into stripes, polka-dots, plaid,
stars of David—instead of finding one early morning a
blackened waste, paint cans exploded in great bursts of
crimson and bottle-green, smells of charred wood and
naphtha, Pflaumbaum wringing his hands oy, oy, oy, the
sneaking hypocrite. All for the insurance.

So Franz and Leni were very hungry for a time, with
Ilse growing in her belly each day. What jobs came along

were menial and paid hardly enough to matter. It was breaking him. Then he met his old friend from the T.H. Munich one night out in the swampy suburbs.

He'd been out all day, the proletarian husband, out pasting up bills to advertise some happy Max Schlepzig film fantasy, while Leni lay pregnant, forced to turn when the pain in her back got too bad, inside their furnished dustbin in the last of the tenement's Hinterhöfe. It was well after dark and bitter cold by the time his paste bucket was empty and the ads all put up to be pissed on, torn down, swastikaed over. (It may have been a quota film. There may have been a misprint. But when he arrived at the theatre on the date printed on the bill, he found the place dark, chips of plaster littering the floor of the lobby, and a terrible smashing far back inside the theatre, the sound of a demolition crew except that there were no voices, nor even any light that he could see back there . . . he called, but the wrecking only went on, a loud creaking in the bowels behind the electric marquee, which he noticed now was blank. . . .) He had wandered, bone-tired, miles northward into Reinickendorf, a quarter of small factories, rusted sheeting on the roofs, brothels, sheds, expansions of brick into night and disuse, repair shops where the water in the vats for cooling the work lay stagnant and scummed over. Only a sprinkling of lights. Vacancy, weeds in the lots, no one in the streets: a neighborhood where glass breaks every night. It must have been the wind that was carrying him down a dirt road, past the old army garrison the local police had taken over, among the shacks and tool cribs to a wire fence with a gate. He found the gate open, and pushed through. He'd become aware of a sound, somewhere ahead. One summer before the World War, he'd gone to Schaffhausen on holiday with his parents, and they'd taken the electric tram to the Rhine Falls. They went down a stairway and out on to a little wood pavilion with a pointed roof—all around them were clouds, rainbows, drops of fire. And the roar of the waterfall. He held on to both their hands, suspended in the cold spray-cloud with Mutti and Papi, barely able to see above to the trees that clung to the fall's brim in a green wet smudge, or the little tour boats below that came up nearly to where the cataract crashed into the Rhine.

But now, in the winter heart of Reinickendorf, he was
alone, hands empty, stumbling over frozen mud through
an old ammunition dump grown over with birch and willow, swelling in the darkness to hills, sinking to swamp.
Concrete barracks and earthworks 40 feet high towered in
the middle distance as the sound beyond them, the sound
of a waterfall, grew louder, calling from his memory.
These were the kinds of revenants that found Franz, not
persons but forms of energy, abstractions. . . .

Through a gap in the breastwork he saw then a tiny
silver egg, with a flame, pure and steady, issuing from
beneath, lighting the forms of men in suits, sweaters, overcoats, watching from bunkers or trenches. It was a rocket,
in its stand: a static test.

The sound began to change, to break now and then.
It didn't sound ominous to Franz in his wonder, only
different. But the light grew brighter, and the watching
figures suddenly started dropping for cover as the rocket
now gave a sputtering roar, a long burst, voices screaming
get down and he hit the dirt just as the silver thing blew
apart, a terrific blast, metal whining through the air where
he'd stood, Franz hugging the ground, ears ringing, no
feeling even for the cold, no way for the moment of
knowing if he was still inside his body. . . .

Feet approached running. He looked up and saw Kurt
Mondaugen. The wind all night, perhaps all year, had
brought them together. This is what he came to believe,
that it was the wind. Most of the schoolboy fat was replaced now by muscle, his hair was thinning, his complexion darker than anything Franz had seen in the street
that winter, dark even in the concrete folds of shadow
and the flames from the scattered rocket fuel, but it was
Mondaugen sure enough, seven or eight years gone but
they knew each other in the instant. They'd lived in the
same drafty mansarde in the Liebigstrasse in Munich.
(Franz had seen the address then as a lucky omen, for
Justus von Liebig had been one of his heroes, a hero of
chemistry. Later, as confirmation, his course in polymer
theory was taught by Professor-Doctor Laszlo Jamf, who
was latest in the true succession, Liebig to August Wilhelm von Hofmann, to Herbert Ganister to Laszlo Jamf, a
direct chain, cause-and-effect.) They'd ridden the same

rattling Schnellbahnwagen with its three contact arms frail as insect legs squeaking along the wires overhead to the T.H.: Mondaugen had been in electrical engineering. On graduating he'd gone off to South-West Africa, on some kind of radio research project. They had written for a while, then stopped.

Their reunion went on till very late, in a Reinickendorf beer hall, undergraduate hollering among the working-class drinkers, a jubilant and grandiose past-mortem on the rocket test—scrawling on soggy paper napkins, all talking at once around the glass-cluttered table, arguing through the smoke and noise heat flux, specific impulse, propellant flow. . . .

"It was a failure," Franz weaving under their electric bulb at three or four in the morning, a loose grin on his face, "it failed, Leni, but they talk only of success! Twenty kilograms of thrust and only for a few seconds, but *no one's ever done it before.* I couldn't believe it Leni I saw something that, that no one ever did before. . . ."

He meant to accuse her, she imagined, of conditioning him to despair. But she only wanted him to grow up. What kind of Wandervögel idiocy is it to run around all night in a marsh calling yourselves the Society for Space Navigation?

Leni grew up in Lübeck, in a row of kleinbürger houses beside the Trave. Smooth trees, spaced evenly all along the riverward edge of her cobbled street, arched their long boughs over the water. From her bedroom window she could see the twin spires of the Dom rising above the housetops. Her fetid back-court existence in Berlin was only a decompression lock—*must* be. Her way out of that fussy Biedermeier strangulation, her dues payable against better times, after the Revolution.

Franz, in play, often called her "Lenin." There was never any doubt about who was active, who possive—still she had hoped he'd grow beyond it. She has talked to psychiatrists, she knows about the German male at puberty. On their backs in the meadows and mountains, watching the sky, masturbating, yearning. Destiny waits, a darkness latent in the texture of the summer wind. Destiny will betray you, crush your ideals, deliver you into the same detestable Bürgerlichkeit as your father, sucking at his

pipe on Sunday strolls after church past the row houses by
the river—dress you in the gray uniform of another family
man, and without a whimper you will serve out your time,
fly from pain to duty, from joy to work, from commitment
to neutrality. Destiny does all this to you.

Franz loved her neurotically, masochistically, he belonged to her and believed that she would carry him on
her back, away to a place where Destiny couldn't reach.
As if it were gravity. He had half-awakened one night
burrowing his face into her armpit mumbling, "Your
wings . . . oh, Leni, your wings . . ."

But her wings can only carry her own weight, and she
hopes Ilse's, for a while. Franz is a dead weight. Let him
look for flight out at the Raketenflugplatz, where he goes
to be used by the military and the cartels. Let him fly to
the dead moon if he wants to. . . .

Ilse is awake, and crying. No food all day. They ought
to try Peter's after all. He'll have milk. Rebecca holds out
what's left of the end crust she's been eating. "Would she
like this?"

Not much of the Jew in her. Why are half the Leftists
she knows Jewish? She immediately reminds herself that
Marx was one. A racial affinity for the books, the theory, a
rabbinical love of loud argument . . . She gives the crust
to her child, picks her up.

"If he comes here, tell him you haven't seen me."

They arrive at Peter Sachsa's well after dark. She finds a
séance just about to begin. She is immediately aware of
her drab coat and cotton dress (hemline too high), her
scuffed and city-dusted shoes, her lack of jewelry. More
middle-class reflexes . . . vestiges, she hopes. But most of
the women are old. The others are *too* dazzling. Hmm.
The men look more affluent than usual. Leni spots a silver
lapel-swastika here and there. Wines on the tables are the
great '20s and '21s. Schloss Vollrads, Zeltinger, Pies-
porter—it is an Occasion.

The objective tonight is to get in touch with the late
foreign minister Walter Rathenau. At the Gymnasium,
Leni sang with the other children the charming anti-
Semitic street refrain of the time:

> Knallt ab den Juden Rathenau,
> Die gottverdammte Judensau . . .

After he was assassinated she sang nothing for weeks, certain that, if the singing hadn't brought it about, at least it had brought it about, at least it had been a prophecy, a spell. . . .

There are specific messages tonight. Questions for the former minister. A gentle sorting-out process is under way. Reasons of security. Only certain guests are allowed to go on into Peter's sitting room. The preterite stay outside, gossiping, showing their gums out of tension, moving their hands. . . . The big scandal around IG Farben this week is the unlucky subsidiary Spottbilligfilm AG, whose entire management are about to be purged for sending to OKW weapons procurement a design proposal for a new airborne ray which could turn whole populations, inside a ten-kilometer radius, stone blind. An IG review board caught the scheme in time. Poor Spottbilligfilm. It had slipped their collective mind what such a weapon would do to the dye market after the next war. The Götterdämmerung mentality again. The weapon had been known as L-5227, L standing for light, another comical German euphemism, like the A in rocket designations which stands for aggregate, or IG itself, Interessengemeinschaft, a fellowship of interests . . . and what about the case of catalyst poisoning in Prague—was it true that the VI b Group Staffs at the Chemical Instrumentality for the Abnormal have been flown east on emergency status, and that it's a complex poisoning, both selenium and tellurium . . . the names of the poisons sober the conversation, like a mention of cancer. . . .

The elite who will sit tonight are from the corporate Nazi crowd, among them Leni recognizes who but Generaldirektor Smaragd, of an IG branch that was interested, for a time, in her husband. But then abruptly there'd been no more contact. It would have been mysterious, a little sinister, except that everything in those days could reasonably be blamed on the economy. . . .

In the crowd her eyes meet Peter's. "I've left him," she whispers, nodding, as he shakes hands.

"You can put Ilse to sleep in one of the bedrooms. Can we talk later?" There is to his eyes tonight a definite faunish slant. Will he accept that she is not *his*, any more than she belonged to Franz?

"Yes, of course. What's going on?"

He snorts, meaning *they haven't told me*. They are

using him—have been, various theys, for ten years. But he never knows how, except by rare accident, an allusion, an interception of smiles. A distorting and forever clouded mirror, the smiles of clients. . . .

Why do they want Rathenau tonight? What did Caesar really whisper to his protégé as he fell? Et tu, Brute, the official lie, is about what you'd expect to get from them—it says exactly nothing. The moment of assassination is the moment when power and the ignorance of power come together, with Death as validator. When one speaks to the other then it is not to pass the time of day with et-tu-Brutes. What passes is a truth so terrible that history—at best a conspiracy, not always among gentlemen, to defraud—will never admit it. The truth will be repressed or in ages of particular elegance be disguised as something else. What will Rathenau, past the moment, years into a new otherside existence, have to say about the old dispensation? Probably nothing as incredible as what he might have said just as the shock flashed his mortal nerves, as the Angel swooped in. . . .

But they will see. Rathenau—according to the histories—was prophet and architect of the cartelized state. From what began as a tiny bureau at the War Office in Berlin, he had coordinated Germany's economy during the World War, controlling supplies, quotas and prices, cutting across and demolishing the barriers of secrecy and property that separated firm from firm—a corporate Bismarck, before whose power no account book was too privileged, no agreement too clandestine. His father Emil Rathenau had founded AEG, the German General Electric Company, but young Walter was more than another industrial heir—he was a philosopher with a vision of the postwar State. He saw the war in progress as a world revolution, out of which would rise neither Red communism nor an unhindered Right, but a rational structure in which business would be the true, the rightful authority—a structure based, not surprisingly, on the one he'd engineered in Germany for fighting the World War.

Thus the official version. Grandiose enough. But Generaldirektor Smaragd and colleagues are not here to be told what even the masses believe. It might almost—if one were paranoid enough—seem to be a collaboration here, between both sides of the Wall, matter and spirit. What

is it they know that the powerless do not? What terrible
structure behind the appearances of diversity and enterprise?

Gallows humor. A damned parlor game. Smaragd cannot really believe in any of this, Smaragd the technician
and manager. He may only want signs, omens, confirma-
tions of what's already in being, something to giggle over
among the Herrenklub—"We even have the Jew's blessing!" Whatever comes through the medium tonight they
will warp, they will edit, into a blessing. It is contempt
of a rare order.

Leni finds a couch in a quiet corner of a room full of
Chinese ivory and silk hangings, lies on it, one calf dangling, and tries to relax. Franz now will be home from the
rocket-field, blinking under the bulb as Frau Silberschlag
next door delivers Leni's last message. Messages tonight,
borne on the lights of Berlin . . . neon, incandescent, stel-
lar . . . messages weave into a net of information that no
one can escape. . . .

"The path is clear," a voice moving Sachsa's lips and
rigid white throat. "You are constrained, over there, to
follow it in time, one step after another. But here it's possible to see the whole shape at once—not for me, I'm not
that far along—but many know it as a clear presence . . .
'shape' isn't really the right word. . . . Let me be honest
with you. I'm finding it harder to put myself in your
shoes. Problems you may be having, even those of global
implication, seem to many of us here only trivial side-
trips. You are off on a winding and difficult road, which
you conceive to be wide and straight, an Autobahn you
can travel at your ease. Is it any use for me to tell you
that all you believe real is illusion? I don't know whether
you'll listen, or ignore it. You only want to know about
your path, your Autobahn.

"All right. Mauve: that's in the pattern. The invention
of mauve, the coming to your level of the color mauve.
Are you listening, Generaldirektor?"

"I am listening, Herr Rathenau," replies Smaragd of
IG Farben.

"Tyrian purple, alizarin and indigo, other coal-tar dyes
are here, but the important one is mauve. William Perkin
discovered it in England, but he was trained by Hofmann,
who was trained by Liebig. There is a succession involved.

If it is karmic it's only in a very limited sense . . . another Englishman, Herbert Ganister, and the generation of chemists he trained. . . . Then the discovery of Oneirine. Ask your man Wimpe. He is the expert on cyclized benzyl-isoquinilines. Look into the clinical effects of the drug. I don't know. It seems that you might look in that direction. It converges with the mauve-Perkin-Ganister line. But all I have is the molecule, the sketch . . . Methoneirine, as the sulfate. Not in Germany, but in the United States. There is a link to the United States. A link to Russia. Why do you think von Maltzan and I saw the Rapallo treaty through? It was necessary to move to the east. Wimpe can tell you. Wimpe, the V-Mann, was always there. Why do you think we wanted Krupp to sell them agricultural machinery so badly? It was also part of the process. At the time I didn't understand it as clearly as I do now. But I knew what I had to do.

"Consider coal and steel. There is a place where they meet. The interface between coal and steel is coal-tar. Imagine coal, down in the earth, dead black, no light, the very substance of death. Death ancient, prehistoric, species *we will never see again*. Growing older, blacker, deeper, in layers of perpetual night. Above ground, the steel rolls out fiery, bright. But to make steel, the coal tars, darker and heavier, must be taken from the original coal. Earth's excrement, purged out for the ennoblement of shining steel. Passed over.

"We thought of this as an industrial process. It was more. We passed over the coal-tars. A thousand different molecules waited in the preterite dung. This is the sign of revealing. Of unfolding. This is one meaning of mauve, the first new color on Earth, leaping to Earth's light from its grave miles and aeons below. There is the other meaning . . . the succession . . . I can't see that far yet. . . .

"But this is all the impersonation of life. The real movement is not from death to any rebirth. It is from death to death-transfigured. The best you can do is to polymerize a few dead molecules. But polymerizing is not resurrection. I mean your IG, Generaldirektor."

"*Our* IG, I should have thought," replies Smaragd with more than the usual ice and stiffness.

"That's for you to work out. If you prefer to call this a liaison, do. I am here for as long as you need me. You don't have to listen. You think you'd rather hear about what you call 'life': the growing, organic Kartell. But it's only another illusion. A very clever robot. The more dynamic it seems to you, the more deep and dead, in reality, it grows. Look at the smokestacks, how they proliferate, fanning the wastes of original waste over greater and greater masses of city. Structurally, they are strongest in compression. A smokestack can survive any explosion— even the shock wave from one of the new cosmic bombs"— a bit of a murmur around the table at this—"as you all must know. The persistence, then, of structures favoring death. Death converted into more death. Perfecting its reign, just as the buried coal grows denser, and overlaid with more strata—epoch on top of epoch, city on top of ruined city. This is the sign of Death the impersonator.

"These signs are real. They are also symptoms of a process. The process follows the same form, the same structure. To apprehend it you will follow the signs. All talk of cause and effect is secular history, and secular history is a diversionary tactic. Useful to you, gentlemen, but no longer so to us here. If you want the truth—I know I presume—you must look into the technology of these matters. Even into the hearts of certain molecules— it is they after all which dictate temperatures, pressures, rates of flow, costs, profits, the shapes of towers. . . .

"You must ask two questions. First, what is the real nature of synthesis? And then: what is the real nature of control?

"You think you know, you cling to your beliefs. But sooner or later you will have to let them go. . . ."

A silence, which prolongs itself. There is some shifting in the seats around the table, but the sets of little fingers stay in touch.

"Herr Rathenau? Could you tell me one thing?" It is Heinz Rippenstoss, the irrepressible Nazi wag and gadabout. The sitters begin to giggle, and Peter Sachsa to return to his room. "Is God really Jewish?"

□

Pumm, Easterling, Dromond, Lamplighter, Spectro are stars on the doctor's holiday tree. Shining down on this holiest of nights. Each is a cold announcement of dead ends, suns that will refuse to stand, but flee south, ever south, leaving us to north-without-end. But Kevin Spectro is brightest, most distant of all. And the crowds they swarm in Knightsbridge, and the wireless carols drone, and the Underground's a mob-scene, but Pointsman's all alone. But he's got his Xmas present, fa la la, he won't have to settle for any Spam-tin dog this year mates, he's got his own miracle and human child, grown to manhood but carrying, someplace on the Slothropian cortex now a bit of Psychology's own childhood, yes pure history, inert, encysted, unmoved by jazz, depression, war—a survival, if you will, of a piece of the late Dr. Jamf himself, past death, past the reckoning of the, the old central chamber you know. . . .

He has no one to ask, no one to tell. My heart, he feels, my heart floods now with such virility and hope. . . . News from the Riviera is splendid. Experiments *here* begin to run smoothly for a change. From some dark overlap, a general appropriation or sinking fund someplace, Brigadier Pudding has even improved the funding for ARF. Does he feel Pointsman's power too? Is he buying some insurance?

At odd moments of the day Pointsman, fascinated, discovers himself with an erect penis. He begins making jokes, English Pavlovian jokes, nearly all of which depend on one unhappy accident: the Latin *cortex* translates into English as "bark," not to mention the well-known and humorous relation between dogs and trees (these are bad enough, and most PISCES folk have the good sense to avoid them, but they are dazzling witticisms compared with jokes *out* of the mainstream, such as the extraordinary "What did the Cockney exclaim to the cowboy from San Antonio?"). Sometime during the annual PISCES Christmas Party, Pointsman is led by Maudie Chilkes to a closet full of belladonna, gauze, thistle tubes, and the scent of surgical rubber, where in a flash she's down on her red knees, unbuttoning his trousers, as he, confused, good God, strokes her hair, clumsily shaking much of it loose from its wine-colored ribbon—here what's this, an actual, slick and crimson, hot, squeak-stockinged slavegirl "gam" yes right among these winter-pale clinical halls, with the distant gramophone playing rumba music, basses, wood-blocks, wearied blown sheets of tropic string cadences audible as everyone dances back there on the uncarpeted floors, and the old Palladian shell, conch of a thousand rooms, gives, resonates, shifting stresses along walls and joists . . . bold Maud, this is incredible, taking the pink Pavlovian cock in as far as it will go, chin to collarbone vertical as a sword-swallower, releasing him each time with some small ladylike choking sound, fumes of expensive Scotch rising flowerlike, and her hands up grabbing the loose wool seat of his pants, pleating, unpleating—it's happening so fast that Pointsman only sways, blinks a bit drunkenly you know, wondering if he's dreaming or has found the perfect mixture, try to remember, amphetamine sulphate, 5 mg q 6 h, last night amobarbital sodium 0.2 Gm. at bedtime, this morning assorted breakfast vitamin capsules, alcohol an ounce, say, per hour, over the past . . . how many cc.s is that and oh, Jesus I'm coming. Am I? yes . . . well . . . and Maud, dear Maudie, swallowing, wastes not a drop . . . smiling quietly, unplugged at last, she returns the unstiffening hawk to its cold bachelor nest but kneels still a bit longer in the closet of this moment, the drafty, white-lit moment, some piece by Ernesto Lecuona, "Siboney" perhaps, now reaching them down corridors long as the sealanes back to the green shoals, slime stone battlements, and palm evenings of Cuba . . . a Victorian pose, her cheek against his leg, his high-veined hand against her face. But no one saw them, then or ever, and in the winter ahead, here and there, her look will cross his and she'll begin to blush red as her knees, she'll come to his room off the lab once or twice perhaps, but somehow they're never to have this again, this sudden tropics in the held breath of war and English December, this moment of perfect peace. . . .

No one to tell. Maud knows something's up all right, the finances of PISCES pass through her hands, nothing escapes her. But he *can't* tell her . . . or not everything, not the *exact terms of his hope*, he's never, even to himself . . . it lies ahead in the dark, defined inversely, by horror, by ways all hopes might yet be defeated and he find only his death, that dumb, empty joke, at the end of this Pavlovian's Progress.

Now Thomas Gwenhidwy too senses change fibrillating
in the face and step of his colleague. Fat, prematurely
white Santa Claus beard, a listing, rumpled showman, performing every instant, trying to speak a double language,
both Welsh comic-provincial and hard diamond gone-a-
begging truth, hear what you will. His singing voice is
incredible, in his spare time he strolls out past the wire-
mesh fighter runways looking for bigger planes—for he
loves to practice the bass part to "Diadem" as the Flying
Fortresses take off at full power, and even so you can
hear him, bone-vibrating and pure above the bombers, all
the way to Stoke Poges, you see. Once a lady even wrote
in to the *Times* from Luton Hoo, Bedfordshire, asking who
was the man with the lovely deep voice singing "Diadem." A Mrs. Snade. Gwenhidwy likes to drink a lot,
grain alcohol mostly, mixed in great strange mad-scientist
concoctions with beef tea, grenadine, cough syrup, bitter
belch-gathering infusions of blue scullcap, valerian root,
motherwort and lady's-slipper, whatever's to hand really.
His is the hale alcoholic style celebrated in national legend and song. He is descended directly from the Welshman in *Henry V* who ran around forcing people to eat his
Leek. None of your sedentary drinkers though. Pointsman
has never seen Gwenhidwy off of his feet or standing
still—he fusses endlessly pitch-and-roll avast you scum
down the long rows of sick or dying faces, and even Pointsman has noted rough love in the minor gestures, changes
of breathing and voice. They are blacks, Indians, Ashke-
nazic Jews speaking dialects you never heard in Harley
Street: they have been bombed out, frozen, starved,
meanly sheltered, and their faces, even the children's, all
possess some ancient intimacy with pain and reverse that
amazes Pointsman, who is more polarized upon West End
catalogues of genteel signs and symptoms, headborn ano-
rexias and constipations the Welshman could have little
patience with. On Gwenhidwy's wards some BMRs run
low as —35, —40. The white lines go thickening across the
X-ray ghosts of bones, gray scrapings from underneath
tongues bloom beneath his old wrinkle-black microscope
into clouds of Vincentesque invaders, nasty little fangs
achop and looking to ulcerate the vitamin-poor tissue they
came from. A quite different domain altogether, you see.

"I don't know, man—no, I don't," flinging a fat slow-motion arm out of his hedgehog-colored cape, back at the hospital, as they walk in the falling snow—to Pointsman a clear separation, monks here and cathedral there, soldiers and garrison—but not so to Gwenhidwy, part of whom remains behind, hostage. The streets are empty, it's Christmas day, they are tramping uphill to Gwenhidwy's rooms as the quiet snow curtains fall on and on between themselves and the pierced wall of the institution marching in stone parallax away into a white gloom. "How they *persist*. The poor, the black. And the Jews! The Welsh, the Welsh once upon a time were *Jewish* too? one of the Lost Tribes of Israel, a black tribe, who wandered overland, centuries? oh an incredible journey. Until at last they reached Wales, you see."

"Wales . . ."

"Stayed on, and became the Cymri. What if we're all Jews, you see? all scattered like seeds? still flying outward from the primal fist so long ago. Man, I believe that."

"Of course you do, Gwenhidwy."

"Aren't we then? What about you?"

"I don't know. I don't feel Jewish today."

"I meant flying outward?" He means alone and forever separate: Pointsman knows what he means. So, by surprise, something in him is touched. He feels the Christmas snow now at crevices of this boots, the bitter cold trying to get in. The brown wool flank of Gwenhidwy moves at the edge of his sight, a pocket of color, a holdout against this whitening day. Flying outward. Flying . . . Gwenhidwy, a million ice-points falling at a slant across his caped immensity, looking so improbable of extinction that now, from where it's been lying, the same yawing-drunk chattering fear returns, the Curse of the Book, and here is someone he wants, truly, with all his mean heart, to see preserved . . . though he's been too shy, or proud, ever to've smiled at Gwenhidwy without some kind of speech to explain and cancel out the smile. . . .

Dogs run barking at their approach. They get the Professional Eye from Pointsman. Gwenhidwy is humming "Aberystwyth." Out comes the doorkeeper's daughter Estelle with a shivering kid or two underfoot and a Christ-

mas bottle of something acrid but very warming inside
the breast after about the first minute it's down. Smells of
coal smoke, piss, garbage, last night's bubble-and-squeak,
fill the hallways. Gwenhidwy is drinking from the bottle,
carrying on a running slap-and-tickle with Estelle and
getting in a fast game of where'd-he-go-there-he-is with
Arch her youngest around the broad mouton hipline of his
mother who keeps trying to smack him but he's too fast.

Gwenhidwy breathes upon a gas meter which is frozen
all through, too tight to accept coins. Terrible weather. He
surrounds it, curses it, bending like a screen lover, wings
of his cape reaching to enfold—Gwenhidwy, radiating like
a sun. . . .

Out the windows of the sitting-room are a row of bare
Army-colored poplars, a canal, a snowy trainyard, and
beyond it a long sawtooth pile of scrap coal, still smoldering from a V-bomb yesterday. Ragged smoke is carried
askew, curling, broken and back to earth by the falling
snow.

"It's the closest yet," Gwenhidwy at the kettle, the sour
smell of a sulfur match in the air. After a moment, still on
watch over the gas ring, "Pointsman, do you want to hear
something really paranoid?"

"You too?"

"Have you consulted a map of London lately? All this
great me-teoric plague of V-weapons, is being dumped
out *here*, you see. Not back on Whitehall, where it's supposed to be, but on me, and I think it is beast-ly?"

"What a damned unpatriotic thing to say."

"Oh," hawking and spitting into the washbowl, "you
don't want to believe it. Why should you? Harley Street
lot, my good Jesus Christ."

It's an old game with Gwenhidwy, Royal Fellow—baiting. Some unaccustomed wind or thermocline along the
sky is bringing them down the deep choral hum of American bombers: Death's white Gymanfa Ganu. A switching-
locomotive creeps silently across the web of tracks below.

"They're falling in a Poisson distribution," says Pointsman in a small voice, as if it was open to challenge.

"No doubt man, no doubt—an excellent point. But all
over the fucking *East End*, you see." Arch, or someone,
has drawn a brown, orange, and blue Gwenhidwy carrying

a doctor's bag along a flat horizon-line past a green gas-works. The bag's full of gin bottles, Gwenhidwy is smiling, a robin is peeking out from its nest in his beard, and the sky is blue and the sun yellow. "But have you ever thought of why? Here is the City Paranoiac. All these long centuries, growing over the country-side? like an intelligent creature. An actor, a fantastic *mimic*, Pointsman! Counterfeiting all the correct forces? the eco-nomic, the demo-graphic? oh yes even the ran-dom, you see."

"What do you mean 'I see'? I *don't* see." Against the window, backlit by the white afternoon, Pointsman's face is invisible except for a tiny bright crescent glowing off each eyeball. Should he fumble behind him for the window catch? Is the woolly Welshman gone raving mad, then?

"You don't see *them*," steam in tight brocade starting to issue from the steel-blotched swan's mouth, "the blacks and Jews, in their darkness. You can't. You don't hear their silence. You became so used to talking, and to light."

"To barking, anyway."

"Nothing comes through my hos-pital but fail-ure, you see." Staring with a fixed, fool-alcoholic smile. "What can I cure? I can only send them back, outside again? Back to *that*? It might as well be Europe here, com-bat, splint-ing and drug-ging them all into some mini-mum condition to get on with the kill-ing?"

"Here, don't you know there's a war on?" Thus Points-man receives, with his cup, a terrible scowl. In truth, he is hoping with nitwit irrelevancies to discourage Gwen-hidwy from going on about his City Paranoiac. Pointsman would rather talk about the rocket victims admitted today to the hospital down there. But this is exorcism man, it is the poet singing back the silence, adjuring the white riders, and Gwenhidwy knows, as Pointsman cannot, that it's part of the plan of the day to sit inside this mean room and cry into just such a deafness: that Mr. Pointsman is to play exactly himself—stylized, irritable, uncomprehending. . . .

"In some cities the rich live upon the heights, and the poor are found below. In others the rich occupy the shore-line, while the poor must live inland. Now in London, here is a gra-dient of wretchedness? increasing as the river widens to the sea. I am only ask-ing, why? Is it because of

the ship-ping? Is it in the pat-terns of land use, especially
those relating to the Industrial Age? Is it a case of an-cient
tribal tabu, surviving down all the Eng-lish generations?
No. The true reason is the Threat From The East, you
see. And the South: from the mass of Eu-rope, certainly.
The people out there were *meant to go down first.* We're
expendable: those in the West End, and north of the river
are not. Oh, I don't mean the Threat has this or that
specific shape. Political, no. If the City Paranoiac dreams,
it's not accessible to *us.* Perhaps the Ci-ty dreamed of
another, en-emy city, float-ing across the sea to invade the
es-tuary . . . or of waves of darkness . . . waves of fire. . . .
Perhaps of being swallowed again, by the immense, the
si-lent Mother Con-tinent? It's none of *my* business, city
dreams. . . . But what if the Ci-ty were a growing neo-
plasm, across the centuries, always chang-ing, to meet
exactly the chang-ing shape of its very worst, se-cret fears?
The raggedy pawns, the disgraced bish-op and cowardly
knight, all we condemned, we irreversibly lost, are left
out here, exposed and wait-ing. It was known, don't deny
it—*known,* Pointsman! that the front in Eu-rope someday
must develop like this? move away east, make the rock-ets
necessary, and *known* how, and where, the rockets would
fall short. Ask your friend Mexico? look at the densities
on his map? east, east, and south of the river too, where
all the bugs live, that's who's getting it *thick*-est, my
friend."

"You're right, Gwenhidwy," judicious, sipping his tea,
"that is very paranoid."

"It's true." He is out with the festive bottle of Vat 69
now, and about to pour them a toast.

"To the babies." Grinning, completely mad.

"Babies, Gwenhidwy?"

"Ah. I've been keep-ing my *own* map? Plot-ting da-ta
from the maternity wards. The ba-bies born during this
Blitz are al-so fol-lowing a Poisson distribution, you see."

"Well—to the oddness of it, then. Poor little bastards."

Later, toward dusk, several enormous water bugs, a very
dark reddish brown, emerge like elves from the wainscot-
ing, and go lumbering toward the larder—pregnant
mother bugs too, with baby translucent outrider bugs
flowing along like a convoy escort. At night, in the very

late silences between bombers, ack-ack fire and falling
rockets, they can be heard, loud as mice, munching
through Gwenhidwy's paper sacks, leaving streaks and
footprints of shit the color of themselves behind. They
don't seem to go in much for soft things, fruits, vegetables,
and such, it's more the solid lentils and beans they're into,
stuff they can gnaw at, paper and plaster barriers, hard
interfaces to be pierced, for they are agents of unification,
you see. Christmas bugs. They were deep in the straw of
the manger at Bethelehem, they stumbled, climbed, fell
glistening red among a golden lattice of straw that must
have seemed to extend miles up and downward—an edible
tenement-world, now and then gnawed through to disrupt
some mysterious sheaf of vectors that would send neighbor
bugs tumbling ass-over-antennas down past you as you
held on with all legs in that constant tremble of golden
stalks. A tranquil world: the temperature and humidity
staying nearly steady, the day's cycle damped to only a
soft easy sway of light, gold to antique-gold to shadows,
and back again. The crying of the infant reached you,
perhaps, as bursts of energy from the invisible distance,
nearly unsensed, often ignored. Your savior, you see. . . .

□

Inside the bowl, the two goldfish are making a Pisces sign,
head-to-tail and very still. Penelope sit and peers into their
world. There is a little sunken galleon, a china diver in a
diving suit, pretty stones and shells she and her sisters
have brought back from the sea.

Aunt Jessica and Uncle Roger are out in the kitchen,
hugging and kissing. Elizabeth is teasing Clare in the hallway. Their mother is in the W.C. Sooty the cat sleeps in a
chair, a black thundercloud on the way to something else,
who happens right now to look like a cat. It's Boxing Day.
The evening's very still. The last rocket bomb was an
hour ago, somewhere south. Claire got a golliwog, Penelope a sweater, Elizabeth a frock that Penelope will grow
into.

The pantomine Roger took them all to see this afternoon was *Hansel and Gretel*. Claire immediately took off

under the seats where others were moving about by secret
paths, a flash of braid or white collar now and then among
the tall attentive uncles in uniform, the coat-draped backs
of seats. On stage Hansel, who was supposed to be a boy
but was really a tall girl in tights and smock, cowered inside the cage. The funny old Witch foamed at the mouth
and climbed the scenery. And pretty Gretel waited by the
Oven for her chance. . . .

Then the Germans dropped a rocket just down the street
from the theatre. A few of the little babies started crying.
They were scared. Gretel, who was just winding up with
her broom to hit the Witch right in the bum, stopped:
put the broom down, in the gathering silence stepped to
the footlights, and sang:

> Oh, don't let it get you,
> It will if they let you, but there's
> Something I'll bet you can't see—
> It's big and it's nasty and it's right over there,
> It's waiting to get its sticky claws in your hair!
> Oh, the greengrocer's wishing on a rainbow today,
> And the dustman is tying his tie . . .
> And it all goes along to the same jolly song,
> With a peppermint face in the sky!

"Now sing along," she smiled, and actually got the audience, even Roger, to sing:

> With a peppermint face in the sky-y,
> And a withered old dream in your heart,
> You'll get hit with a piece of the pie-ie,
> With the pantomime ready to start!
> Oh, the Tommy is sleeping in a snowbank tonight,
> And the Jerries are learning to fly—
> We can fly to the moon, we'll be higher than noon,
> In our polythene home in the sky. . . .
>
> Pretty polythene home in the sky,
> Pretty platinum pins in your hand—
> Oh your mother's a big fat machine gun,
> And your father's a dreary young man. . . .
> (Whispered and staccato):
> Oh, the, man-a-ger's suck-ing on a corn-cob, pipe,
> And the bank-ers are, eat-ing their, wives,
> All the world's in a daze, while the orchestra plays,
> So turn your pockets and get your surprise—

Turn your pockets and get-your surpri-ise,
There was nobody there af-ter all!
And the lamps up the stairway are dying,
It's the season just after the ball . . .
Oh the palm-trees whisper on the beach somewhere,
And the lifesaver's heaving a sigh,
And those voices you hear, Boy and Girl of the Year,
Are of children who are learning to die. . . .

Penelope's father's chair, in the corner, next to the table
with the lamp, is empty. It faces her now. She can see the
crocheted shawl over the back, many knots of gray, tan,
black, and brown, with amazing clarity. In the pattern, or
in front of it, something is stirring: at first no more than
refraction, as if there were a source of heat directly in
front of the empty chair.

"No," she whispers out loud. "I don't want to. You're
not him. I don't know who you are but you're not my
father. Go away."

Its arms and legs are silent and rigid. She stares into it.
I only want to visit you.

"You want to possess me."

Demonic possessions in this house are not unknown. Is
this really Keith, her father? taken when she was half her
present age, and returned now as not the man she knew,
but only the shell—with the soft meaty slug of soul that
smiles and loves, that feels its mortality, either rotted
away or been picked at by the needle mouths of death-by-
government—a process by which living souls unwillingly
become the demons known to the main sequence of Western magic as the Qlippoth, Shells of the Dead. . . . It is
also what the present dispensation often does to decent
men and women entirely on this side of the grave. In
neither process is there any dignity, or any mercy. Mothers and fathers are conditioned into deliberately dying in
certain preferred ways: giving themselves cancer and
heart attacks, getting into motor accidents, going off to
fight in the war—leaving their children alone in the forest.
They'll always tell you fathers are "taken," but fathers
only leave—that's what it really is. The fathers are all
covering for each other, that's all. Perhaps it's even better
to have this presence, rubbing the room dry as glass,
slipping in and out of an old chair, than a father who still

hasn't died yet, a man you love and have to watch it happening to. . . .

In the kitchen, the water in the kettle shakes, creaks toward boiling, and outside the wind blows. Somewhere, in another street, a roofslate slides and falls. Roger has taken Jessica's cold hands in to warm against his breast, feeling them, icy, through his sweater and shirt, folded in against him. Yet she stands apart, trembling. He wants to warm all of her, not just comic extremities, wants beyond reasonable hope. His heart shakes like the boiling kettle.

It has begun to reveal itself: how easily she might go. For the first time he understands why this is the same as mortality, and why he will cry when she leaves. He is learning to recognize the times when nothing really holds her but his skinny, 20-pushup arms. . . . If she leaves, then it ceases to matter how the rockets fall. But the coincidence of maps, girls, and rocketfalls has entered him silently, silent as ice, and Quisling molecules have shifted in latticelike ways to freeze him. If he could be with her more . . . if it happened when they were together—in another time that might have sounded romantic, but in a culture of death, certain situations are just more hep to the jive than others—but they're apart so much. . . .

If the rockets don't get her there's still her lieutenant. Damned Beaver/Jeremy *is* the War, he is every assertion the fucking War has ever made—that we are meant for work and government, for austerity: and these shall take priority over love, dreams, the spirit, the senses and the other second-class trivia that are found among the idle and mindless hours of the day. . . . Damn them, they are wrong. They are insane. Jeremy will take her like the Angel itself, in his joyless weasel-worded come-along, and Roger will be forgotten, an amusing maniac, but with no place in the rationalized power-ritual that will be the coming peace. She will take her husband's orders, she will become a domestic bureaucrat, a junior partner, and remember Roger, if at all, as a mistake thank God she didn't make. . . . Oh, he feels a raving fit coming on—how the bloody hell can he survive without her? She is the British warm that protects his stooping shoulders, and the wintering sparrow he holds inside his hands. She is his deepest innocence in spaces of bough and hay before wishes were given a separate name to warn that they might not come true, and his lithe Parisian daughter of joy, beneath the eternal mirror, forswearing perfumes, capeskin to the armpits, all that is too easy, for his impoverishment and more worthy love.

You go from dream to dream inside me. You have passage to my last shabby corner, and there, among the debris, you've found life. I'm no longer sure which of all the words, images, dreams or ghosts are "yours" and which are "mine." It's past sorting out. We're both being someone new now, someone incredible. . . .

His act of faith. In the street the children are singing:

> Hark, the herald angels sing:
> Mrs. Simpson's pinched our King . . .

Up on the mantelpiece Sooty's son Kim, an alarmingly fat crosseyed Siamese, lurks waiting to do the only thing he enjoys these days. Beyond eating, sleeping or fucking his chief obsession is to jump, or topple, on his mother, and lie there laughing while she runs screaming around the room. Jessica's sister Nancy comes out of the loo to break up what's becoming a full-scale row between Elizabeth and Claire. Jessica steps away from Roger to blow her nose. The sound is as familiar to him as a bird's song, ip-ip-ip-ip NGUNNGG as the handkerchief comes away . . . "Oh sooper dooper," she says, "think I'm catching a cold."

You're catching the War. It's infecting you and I don't know how to keep it away. Oh. Jess. Jessica. Don't leave me. . . .

2

Un Perm' au Casino
Hermann Goering

You will have the tallest, darkest leading man in Hollywood.
—MERIAN C. COOPER to Fay Wray

□

This morning's streets are already clattering, near and far, with woodsoled civilian feet. Up in the wind is a scavenging of gulls, sliding, easy, side to side, wings hung out still, now and then a small shrug, only to gather lift for this weaving, unweaving, white and slow faro shuffle off invisible thumbs. . . . Yesterday's first glance, coming along the esplanade in the afternoon, was somber: the sea in shades of gray under under gray clouds, the Casino Hermann Goering flat white and the palms in black sawtooth, hardly moving. . . . But this morning the trees in the sun now are back to green. Leftward, far away, the ancient aqueduct loops crumbling, dry yellow, out along the *Cap*, the houses and villas there baked to warm rusts, gentle corrosions all through Earth's colors, pale raw to deeply burnished.

The sun, not very high yet, will catch a bird by the ends of his wings, turning the feathers brightly there to curls of shaved ice. Slothrop rattles his teeth at the crowd of birds aloft, shivering down on his own miniature balcony, electric fire deep in the room barely touching the backs of his legs. They have filed him high on the white sea-façade, in a room to himself. Tantivy Mucker-Maffick and his friend Teddy Bloat are sharing one down the hall. He takes back his hands into ribbed cuffs of a sweatshirt, crosses his arms, watches the amazing foreign morning, the ghosts of his breathing into it, feeling first sunwarmth, wanting a first cigarette—and perversely he waits for a sudden noise to begin his day, a first rocket. Aware of all the time he's in the wake of a great war gone north, and that the only explosions around here will have to be champagne corks, motors of sleek Hispano-Suizas, the odd amorous slap, hopefully. . . . No London? No Blitz? Can he get used to it? Sure, and by then it'll be just time to head back.

"Well, he's awake." Bloat in uniform, sidling into the room gnawing on a smoldering pipe, Tantivy behind in a pin-striped lounge suit. "Up at the crack, reconnoitering the beach for the unattached mamzelle or two, no doubt . . ."

"Couldn't sleep," Slothrop yawning back down into the room, birds in the sunlight kiting behind him.

"Nor we," from Tantivy. "It must take years to adjust."

"God," Bloat really pushing the forced enthusiasm this morning, pointing theatrically at the enormous bed, collapsing onto it, bouncing vigorously. "They must have had advance word about you, Slothrop! Luxury! They gave us some disused closet, you know."

"Hey, what are you telling him?" Slothrop forages around for cigarettes. "I'm some kind of a Van Johnson or something?"

"Only that, in the matter of," Tantivy from the balcony tossing his green pack of Cravens, "girls, you know—"

"Englishmen being rather reserved," Bloat explains, bouncing for emphasis.

"Oh, raving maniacs," Slothrop mumbles, heading for his private lavatory, "been invaded by a gang of those section 8s, all right. . . ." Stands pleased, pissing no-hands, lighting up, but wondering a little about that Bloat. Supposed to be oldtime pals with Tantivy. He snaps the match into the toilet, a quick hiss: yet something about the way he talks to Slothrop, patronizing? maybe nervous . . .

"You're expecting me to fix you guys up?" he yells over the crash of the toilet flushing, "I thought the minute you guys get across that Channel, set foot on that France, you all turn into Valentinos."

"I hear there was some prewar tradition," Tantivy hanging plaintive now in the doorway, "but Bloat and I are members of the New Generation, we have to depend on Yank expertise. . . ."

Whereupon Bloat leaps from the bed and seeks to enlighten Slothrop with a song:

THE ENLISHMAN'S VERY SHY (FOX-TROT)

(Bloat):   The Englishman's very shy,
             He's none of your Ca-sa-no-va,
             At bowling the ladies o-ver,
             A-mericans lead the pack—

(Tantivy):   —You see, your Englishman tends to lack
             That recklessness transatlantic,
             That women find so romantic
             Though frankly I can't see why . . .

(Bloat):   The polygamous Yank with his girls galore
                       Gives your Brit-ish rake or carouser fits,

(Tantivy):   Though he's secretly held in re-ve-rent awe
                       As a sort of e-rot-ic Clausewitz. . . .

(Together):   If only one could al-ly
                       A-merican bedroom know-how
                       With British good looks, then *oh* how
                       Those lovelies would swoon and sigh,
                       Though you and I know the Englishman's
                             very shy.

"Well you've sure come to the right place," nods Slothrop, convinced. "Only don't expect me to put it in for you."

"Just the initial approach," Bloat says.

"Moi," Tantivy has meanwhile been screaming down from the balcony, "Moi Tantivy, you know. Tantivy."

"Tantivy," replies a dim girl-chorus from outside and below.

"J'ai deux amis, aussi, by an odd coincidence. Par un bizarre coincidence, or something, oui?"

Slothrop, at this point shaving, wanders out with the foamy badger brush in his first to see what's happening, and collides with Bloat, who's dashing to peer down over his compatriot's left epaulet at three pretty girls' faces, upturned, straw-haloed each by a giant sun-hat, smiles all dazzling, eyes mysterious as the sea behind them.

"I say où," inquires Bloat, "où, you know, déjeuner?"

"Glad I could help you out," Slothrop mutters, lathering Tantivy between the shoulderblades.

"But come with us," the girls are calling above the waves, two of them holding up an enormous wicker basket out of which lean sleek green wine bottles and rough-crusted loaves still from under their white cloth steaming in little wisps feathering off of chestnut glazes and paler split-streaks, "come—sur la plage . . ."

"I'll just," Bloat half out the door, "keep them company, until you . . ."

"Sur la plage," Tantivy a bit dreamy, blinking in the sun, smiling down at their good-morning's wishes come true, "oh, it sounds like a painting. Something by an Impressionist. A Fauve. Full of light. . . ."

Slothrop goes flicking witch hazel off his hands. The smell in the room brings back a moment of Berkshire Saturdays—bottles of plum and amber tonics, fly-studded paper twists swayed by the overhead fan, twinges of pain from blunt scissors. . . . Struggling out of his sweatshirt, lit cigarette in his mouth, smoke coming out the neck like a volcano, "Hey could I bum one of your—"

"You've already got the pack," cries Tantivy—"God almighty, what is *that* supposed to be?"

"What's what?" Slothrop's face nothing but innocent as he slips into and begins to button the object in question.

"You're joking, of course. The young ladies are waiting, Slothrop, do put on something civilized, there's a good chap—"

"All set," Slothrop on the way past the mirror combing his hair into the usual sporty Bing Crosby pompadour.

"You can't expect us to be *seen* with—"

"My brother Hogan sent it to me," Slothrop lets him know, "for my birthday, all the way from the Pacific. See on the back? under the fellows in that outrigger canoe there, to the left of those hibiscus blossoms, it sez SOUVENIR OF HONOLULU? This is the authentic item, Mucker-Maffick, not some cheap imitation."

"Dear God," moans Tantivy, trailing him forlornly out of the room, shading his eyes from the shirt, which glows slightly in the dimness of the corridor. "At least tuck it in and cover it with something. Here, I'll even lend you this Norfolk jacket. . . ." Sacrifice indeed: the coat is from a Savile Row establishment whose fitting rooms are actually decorated with portraits of all the venerable sheep—some nobly posed up on crags, others in pensive, soft close-ups—from whom the original fog-silvered wool was sheared.

"Must be woven out of that barbed wire," is Slothrop's opinion, "what girl'd want to get near anything like that?"

"Ah, but, but would any woman in her right mind want to be within ten miles of that-that ghastly shirt, eh?"

"Wait!" From someplace Slothrop now produces a gaudy yellow, green and orange display handkerchief, and over Tantivy's groans of horror arranges it in his friend's jacket pocket so as to stick out in three points. "There!" beaming, "that's what you call *real sharp!*"

They emerge into sunlight. Gulls begin to wail, the garment on Slothrop blazes into a refulgent life of its own. Tantivy squeezes his eyes shut. When he opens them, the girls are all attached to Slothrop, stroking the shirt, nibbling at its collar-points, cooing in French.

"Of course." Tantivy picks up the basket. "Right."

The girls are dancers. The manager of the Casino Hermann Goering, one César Flebótomo, brought in a whole chorus-line soon as the liberators arrived, though he hasn't yet found time to change the place's occupation name. Nobody seems to mind it up there, a pleasant mosaic of tiny and perfect seashells, thousands of them set in plaster, purple, pink and brown, replacing a huge section of roof (the old tiles still lie in a heap beside the Casino), put up two years ago as recreational therapy by a Messerschmitt squadron on furlough, in German typeface expansive enough to be seen from the air, which is what they had in mind. The sun now is still too low to touch the words into any more than some bare separation from their ground, so that they hang suppressed, no relation any more to the men, the pain in their hands, the blisters that grew black under the sun with infection and blood—only receding as the party now walk down past sheets and pillowcases of the hotel, spread to dry on the slope of the beach, fine wrinkles edged in blue that will flow away as the sun climbs, six pairs of feet stirring debris never combed for, an old gambling chip half bleached by the sun, translucent bones of gulls, a drab singlet, Wehrmacht issue, torn and blotted with bearing grease. . . .

They move along the beach, Slothrop's amazing shirt, Tantivy's handkerchief, girls' frocks, green bottles all dancing, everyone talking at once, boy-and-girl lingua franca, the girls confiding quite a lot to each other with side glances for their escorts. This ought to be good for a bit of the, heh, heh, early paranoia here, a sort of pick-me-up to help face what's sure to come later in the day. But it isn't. Much too good a morning for that. Little waves are rolling in, breaking piecrustwise along a curve of dark shingle, farther off foaming among the black rocks that poke up along the *Cap.* Out at sea wink twin slivers of a boat's sails being sucked along in the sun and distance, over toward Antibes, the craft tacking gradual, cockle-frail among low swells whose touch and rowdy hiss along the chines Slothrop can feel this morning, reminded of prewar Comets and Hamptons sighted from the beach at Cape Cod, among land odors, drying seaweed, summer-old cooking oil, the feel of sand on sunburn, the sharp-pointed dune grass under bare feet. . . . Closer to shore a *pédalo* full of soldiers and girls moves along— they dangle, splash, sprawl in green and white striped lounge chairs back aft. At the edge of the water small kids are chasing, screaming, laughing in that hoarse, helplessly tickled little-kid way. Up on the esplanade an old couple sit on a bench, blue and white and a cream-colored parasol, a morning habit, an anchor for the day. . . .

They go as far as the first rocks, finding there an inlet partly secluded from the rest of the beach, and from the looming Casino. Breakfast is wine, bread, smiling, sun diffracting through the fine gratings of long dancers' hair, swung, flipped, never still, a dazzle of violet, sorrel, saffron, emerald. . . . For a moment you can let the world go, solid forms gone a-fracturing, warm inside of bread waiting at your fingertips, flowery wine in long, easy passage streaming downward around the root of your tongue. . . .

Bloat cuts in. "I say Slothrop, is she a friend of yours too?"

Hmm? what's happening . . . she, what? Here sits Bloat, smug, gesturing over at the rocks and a tide pool nearby. . . .

"You're getting 'the eye,' old man."

Well . . . she must have come out of the sea. At this distance, some 20 meters, she is only a dim figure in a black bombazine frock that reaches to her knees, her bare legs long and straight, a short hood of bright blonde hair keeping her face in shadow, coming up in guiches to touch her cheeks. She's looking at Slothrop, all right. He smiles, sort of waves. She only continues to stand, the breeze pushing at her sleeves. He turns back to draw the cork from a wine bottle, and its pop arrives as a grace note for a scream from one of the dancers. Tantivy's already halfway to his feet, Bloat gaping out in the girl's direction, the danseuses snapshot in defense reflexes, hair flying, frocks twisted, thighs flashing—

Holy shit it's *moving*—an octopus? Yes it is the biggest fucking octopus Slothrop has ever seen outside of the movies, Jackson, and it has just risen up out of the water and squirmed halfway onto one of the black rocks. Now, cocking a malignant eye at the girl, it reaches out, wraps one long sucker-studded tentacle around her neck as everyone watches, another around her waist and begins to drag her, struggling, back under the sea.

Slothrop's up, bottle in hand, running down past Tantivy who's doing a hesitant dance step, hands patting lounge-suit pockets for weapons that aren't there, more and more of the octopus revealed the closer he comes and wow it's a *big* one, holycow—skids to a halt alongside, one foot in the tide pool, and commences belting the octopus in the head with the wine bottle. Hermit crabs slide in death-struggle around his foot. The girl, already half in the water, is trying to cry out, but the tentacle, flowing and chilly, barely allows her windway enough to breathe. She reaches out a hand, a soft-knuckled child's hand with a man's steel ID bracelet on the wrist, and clutches at Slothrop's Hawaiian shirt, begins tightening her own grip there, and who was to know that among her last things would be vulgar-faced hula girls, ukuleles, and surfriders all in comic-book colors . . . *oh God God please*, the bottle thudding again and again wetly into octopus flesh, no fucking use, the octopus gazes at Slothrop, triumphant, while he, in the presence of certain death, can't quit staring at her hand, cloth furrowing in tangents to her terror, a shirt button straining at a single last thread—he sees the name on the bracelet, scratched silver letters each one clear but making no sense to him before the slimy gray stranglehold that goes tightening, liquid, stronger than he and she together, framing the poor hand its cruel tetanus is separating from Earth—

"Slothrop!" Here's Bloat ten feet away offering him a large crab.

"What th' fuck . . ." Maybe if he broke the bottle on the rock, stabbed the bastard between the eyes—

"It's hungry, it'll go for the crab. *Don't kill it, Slothrop.* Here, for God's sake—" and here it comes spinning through the air, legs cocked centrifugally outward: dithering Slothrop drops the bottle just before the crab smacks

against his other palm. Neat catch. Immediately, through
her fingers and his shirt, he can feel the reflex to food.

"O.K." Shaking Slothrop waves the crab at the octopus.
"Chow time, fella." Another tentacle moves in. Its corrugated ooze touches his wrist. Slothrop tosses the crab a
few feet along the beach, and what do you know, that
octopus goes for it all right: dragging along the girl and
Slothrop staggering for a bit, then letting her go. Slothrop
quickly snatches up the crab again, dangling it so the
octopus can see, and begins to dance the creature away,
down the beach, drool streaming from its beak, eyes held
by the crab.

In their brief time together Slothrop forms the impression that this octopus is not in good mental health, though
where's his basis for comparing? But there is a mad ex-
uberance, as with inanimate objects which fall off of tables
when we are sensitive to noise and our own clumsiness
and don't *want* them to fall, a sort of wham! ha-ha you
hear that? here it is *again*, WHAM! in the cephalopod's
every movement, which Slothrop is glad to get away from
as he finally scales the crab like a discus, with all his
strength, out to sea, and the octopus, with an eager splash
and gurgle, strikes out in pursuit, and is presently gone.

The frail girl lies on the beach, taking in great breaths
of air, surrounded now by the others. One of the dancers
is holding her in her arms and speaking, r's and nasals
still French, in a language Slothrop, moseying back into
earshot, can't quite place.

Tantivy smiles and flips a small salute. "Good show!"
cheers Teddy Bloat. "I wouldn't have wanted to try that
myself!"

"Why not? You had that crab. Saaay—where'd you *get*
that crab?"

"Found it," replies Bloat with a straight face. Slothrop
stares at this bird but can't get eye contact. What th'
fuck's going on?

"I better have some of that wine," Slothrop reckons.
He drinks out of the bottle. Air goes splashing upward in
lopsided spheres inside the green glass. The girl watches
him. He stops for breath and smiles.

"Thank you, lieutenant." Not a tremor in the voice, and
the accent is Teutonic. He can see her face now, soft nose

of a doe, eyes behind blonde lashes full of acid green. One of those thin-lipped European mouths. "I had almost stopped breathing."

"Uh—you're not German."

Shaking her head no emphatically, "Dutch."

"And have you been here—"

Her eyes go elsewhere, she reaches, takes the bottle from his hand. She is looking out to sea, after the octopus. "They are very optical, aren't they. I hadn't known. It *saw* me. Me. I don't look like a crab."

"I guess not. You're a swell-looking lady." In the background, delighted Bloat nudges Tantivy. That recklessness transatlantic. Slothrop takes her wrist, finds no problem now reading that ID bracelet. Sez KATJE BORGESIUS. He can feel her pulse booming. Does she know him from someplace? strange. A mixture of recognition and sudden shrewdness in her face . . .

So it is here, grouped on the beach with strangers, that voices begin to take on a touch of metal, each word a hard-edged clap, and the light, though as bright as before, is less able to illuminate . . . it's a Puritan reflex of seeking other orders behind the visible, also known as paranoia, filtering in. Pale lines of force whir in the sea air . . . pacts sworn to in rooms since shelled back to their plan views, not quite by accident of war, suggest themselves. Oh, that was no "found" crab, Ace—no random octopus or girl, uh-uh. Structure and detail come later, but the conniving around him now he feels instantly, in his heart.

They all stay a bit longer on the beach, finishing breakfast. But the simple day, birds and sunlight, girls and wine, has sneaked away from Slothrop. Tantivy is getting drunk, more relaxed and funnier as the bottles empty. He's staked out not only the girl he first had his eye on, but also the one Slothrop would be no doubt sweet-talking right now if that octopus hadn't shown up. He is a messenger from Slothrop's innocent, pre-octopus past. Bloat, on the other hand, sits perfectly sober, mustache unruffled, regulation uniform, watching Slothrop closely. His companion Ghislaine, tiny and slender, pin-up girl legs, long hair brushed behind her ears falling all the way down her back, shifts her round bottom in the sand, writing marginal commentaries around the text of Bloat. Slothrop, who believes that women, like Martians, have antennas men do not, keeps an eye on her. She looks over only once, and her eyes grow wide and cryptic. He'd swear she knows something. On the way back to the Casino, toting their empties, and the basket full of the debris of the morning, he manages a word with her.

"Some picnic, nessay-pah?"

Dimples appear next to her mouth. "Did you know all the time about the octopus? I thought so because it was so like a dance—all of you."

"No. Honestly, I didn't. You mean you thought it was just a practical joke or something?"

"Little Tyrone," she whispers suddenly, taking his arm with a big phony smile for the others. Little? He's twice her size. "Please—be very careful. . . ." That's all. He has Katje by the other hand, two imps, contrary, either side. The beach is empty now except for fifty gray gulls sitting watching the water. White heaps of cumulus pose out at sea, hard-surfaced, cherub-blown—palm leaves stir, all down the esplanade. Ghislaine drops away, back down the beach, to pick up prim Bloat. Katje squeezes Slothrop's arm and tells him just what he wants to hear about now: "Perhaps, after all, *we were meant to meet. . . .*"

☐

From out at sea, the Casino at this hour is a blazing bijou at the horizon: its foil of palms already shadows in the dwindling light. Deepening go the yellowbrown of these small serrated mountains, sea colored the soft inside of a black olive, white villas, perched châteaux whole and ruined, autumn greens of copses and solitary pines, all deepening to the nightscape latent across them all day. Fires are lit on the beach. A faint babble of English voices, and even occasional songs, reaches across the water to where Dr. Porkyevitch stands on deck. Below, Octopus Grigori, having stuffed himself with crab meat, frisks happily in his special enclosure. The reaching radius of the lighthouse on the headland sweeps by, as tiny fishing craft head out to sea. Grischa, little friend, you have performed your last trick for a while. . . . Is there any hope for further support from Pointsman, now that Porkyevitch and His Fabulous Octopus have done their part?

He gave up questioning orders long ago—even questioning his exile. The evidence linking him to the Bukharin conspiracy, whose particulars he has never heard, might somehow be true—the Trotskyite Bloc might have known of him, by reputation, used him in ways forever secret . . . *forever secret:* there are forms of innocence, he knows, that cannot conceive of what that means, much less accept it as he has. For it might, after all, be only another episode in some huge pathological dream of Stalin's. At least he had physiology, something outside the party . . . those who had nothing but the party, who had built their whole lives upon it, only to be purged, must go through something very like death . . . and never to know anything for certain, never to have the precision of the laboratory . . . it's been his own sanity, God knows, for twenty years. At least they can never—

No, no they wouldn't, there's never been a case . . . unless it's been hushed up, you'd never read it in the journals of course—

Would Pointsman—

He might. Yes.

Grischa, Grischa! It's come true. On us so quickly: foreign cities, comedians in broken hats, cancan girls, fountains of fire, a noisy pit band . . . Grischa, with the flags of all the nations curled in your arms . . . fresh shellfish, a warm pirozhok, hot glasses of tea in the evenings, between performances . . . learn to forget Russia, to take comfort from what mean, falsified bits of her we wander across. . . .

Now, the sky stretches to admit a single first star. But Porkyevitch makes no wish. Policy. Signs of arrival do not interest him, nor even signs of departure. . . . As the boat's engine goes full ahead, their own wake goes lifting, pink with sunset, to obscure the white Casino on shore.

Electricity is on tonight, the Casino back in France's power grid. Chandeliers shaggy with crystal needles flare overhead, and softer lamps shine among the gardens outside. Going in to dinner with Tantivy and the dancers, Slothrop is brought to a round-eyed halt by the sight of

Katje Borgesius, hair in one of those emerald tiaras, the rest of her rigged out in a long Medici gown of sea-green velvet. Her escort's a two-star general and a brigadier.

"RHIP," sings Tantivy, shuffling off sarcastic buffaloes along the carpet, "*oh*, RHIP indeed."

"You're trying to get my goat," Slothrop smiles, "but it's not working."

"I can tell." His own smile freezes. "Oh, no, Slothrop, please, no, we're going in to dinner—"

"Well, I know we're going in to dinner—"

"No, this is very embarrassing, you've got to take it off."

"You like that? She's genuine hand-painted! Look! Nice tits, huh?"

"It's the Wormwood Scrubs School Tie."

In the main dining room they merge into a great coming and going of waiters, officers and ladies. Slothrop, young dancer by the hand, caught up in the eddying, manages at last to slide with her into a pair of seats just vacated: to find who but Katje his left-hand partner. He puffs out his cheeks, crosses his eyes, brushes his hair industriously with his hands by which time the soup has showed up, which he goes at as if disarming a bomb. Katje is ignoring him, talking earnestly instead across her general with some bird colonel about his prewar profession, managing a golf course in Cornwall. Holes and hazards. Gave one a feel for terrain. But he did like most to be there at night, when the badgers came out of their sets to play. . . .

By the time the fish has come and gone, something funny is happening. Katje's knee seems to be rubbing Slothrop's, velvet-warm, under the table.

Weeell, opines Slothrop, watch this: I will employ some of that *subterfuge*, I mean I'm in that Europe, aren't I? He raises his wineglass and announces, " 'The Ballad of Tantivy Mucker-Maffick.' " Cheers go up, bashful Tantivy tries not to smile. It's a song everyone knows: one of the Scotsmen goes dashing down the room to the grand piano, César Flebótomo, twirling his slick mustache in a saber-point, nips behind a palm in a tub to turn the lights up a notch, sticks his head back out winking, and hisses for his maître d'hôtel. Wine is gargled, throats are cleared and a good number of the company commence singing

THE BALLAD OF TANTIVY MUCKER-MAFFICK

Oh Italian gin is a mother's curse,
And the beer of France is septic,
Drinking Bourbon in Spain is the lonely domain
Of the saint and the epileptic.
White lightning has fueled up many a hearse
In the mountains where ridge-runners dwell—
It's a brew begot in a poison pot,
And mulled with the hammers of Hell!

(Refrain): Oh—Tantivy's been drunk in many a place,
From here to the Uttermost Isle,
And if he should refuse any chance at the booze,
May I die with an hoary-eyed smile!

There are what sound like a hundred—but most likely
only two—Welshmen singing, tenor from the south and
bass from the north of the country, you see, so that all
conversation sub rosa or not is effectively drowned out.
Exactly what Slothrop wants. He leans in Katje's direction.

"Meet me in my room," she whispers, "306, after midnight."

"Gotcha." And Slothrop is upright in time to join in
again right on bar one:

He's been ossified in oceans of grog,
In the haunts of the wobbly whale—
He's been half-seas over from Durban to Dover,
Wiv four shaky sheets to the gale.
For in London fog or Sahara's sun,
Or the icebound steeps of Zermatt,
Loaded up for a lark to 'is Plimsoll mark
He's been game to go off on a bat!

Yes, Tantivy's been drunk in many a place . . . &c.

After dinner Slothrop gives Tantivy the high-sign.
Their dancers go off arm in arm to the marble lounges
where the toilet stalls are equipped with a network of
brass voice-tubes, all acoustic, to make stall-to-stall conversation easier. Slothrop and Tantivy head for the nearest
bar.

"Listen," Slothrop talking into his highball glass, bouncing words off of ice cubes so they'll have a proper chill, "either I'm coming down with a little psychosis here, or something funny is going on, right?"

Tantivy, who is feigning a relaxed air, breaks off humming "You Can Do a Lot of Things at the Sea-side That You Can't Do in Town" to inquire, "Ah, yes, do you really think so?"

"Come on, that octopus."

"The devilfish is found quite commonly on Mediterranean shores. Though usually not so large—is it the *size* that bothers you? Don't Americans *like*—"

"Tantivy, it was no accident. Did you hear that Bloat? 'Don't kill it!' He had a crab *with* him, m-maybe inside that musette bag, all set to lure that critter away with. And where'd he go tonight, anyhow?"

"I think he's out on the beach. There's a lot of drinking."

"He drinks a lot?"

"No."

"Look, you're his friend—"

Tantivy moans. "God, Slothrop, *I* don't know. I'm your friend too, but there's always, you know, an element of Slothropian paranoia to contend with. . . ."

"Paranoia's ass. Something's up, a-and you know it!"

Tantivy chews ice, sights along a glass stirring rod, rips up a small napkin into a snowstorm, all sorts of bar business, he's an old hand. But at last, in a soft voice, "Well, he's receiving messages in code."

"Ha!"

"I saw one in his kit this afternoon. Just a glimpse. I didn't try to look closer. He is with Supreme Headquarters, after all—I suppose that could be it."

"No, that's not it. Now what about *this*—" and Slothrop tells about his midnight date with Katje. For a moment they might almost be back in the bureau at ACHTUNG, and the rockets falling, and tea in paper cups, and everything right again. . . .

"Are you going?"

"Shouldn't I? You think she's dangerous?"

"I think she's delightful. If I hadn't Françoise, not to mention Yvonne to worry about, I'd be racing you to her door."

"But?"

But the clock over the bar only clicks once, then presently again, ratcheting time minutewise into their past.

"Either what you've got is contagious," Tantivy begins, "or else they've an eye on me too."

They look at each other. Slothrop remembers that except for Tantivy he's all alone here. "Tell me."

"I wish I could. He's changed—but I couldn't give you a single bit of evidence. It's been since . . . I don't know. Autumn. He doesn't talk politics any more. God, we used to get into these— He won't discuss his plans after he's demobbed either, it's something he used to do all the time. I thought the Blitz might have got him rattled . . . but after yesterday, I think it must be more. Damn it, it makes me sad."

"What happened?"

"Oh. A sort of—not a threat. Or not a serious one. I mentioned, only joking, that I was keen on your Katje. And Bloat became very cold, and said, 'I'd stay clear of that one if I were you.' Tried to cover it with a laugh, as if he had his eye on her too. But that wasn't it. I-I don't have his confidence any more. I'm— I feel I'm only useful to him in a way I can't see. Being tolerated for as long as he can use me. The old University connection. I don't know if you ever felt it at Harvard . . . from time to time back in Oxford, I came to sense a peculiar *structure* that no one admitted to—that extended far beyond Turl Street, past Cornmarket into covenants, procuring, accounts due . . . one never knew who it would be, or when, or how they'd try to collect it . . . but I thought it only idle, only at the fringes of what I was *really* up there for, you know. . . ."

"Sure. In that America, it's the first thing they tell you. Harvard's there for other reasons. The 'educating' part of it is just sort of a front."

"We're so very innocent here, you see."

"Some of you, maybe. I'm sorry about Bloat."

"I still hope it's something else."

"I guess so. But what do we do right now?"

"Oh, I'd say—keep your date, be careful. Keep me posted. Perhaps tomorrow I'll have an adventure or two to tell you about, for a change. And if you need help," teeth flashing, face reddening a bit, "well, I'll help you."

"Thanks, Tantivy." Jesus, a British ally. Yvonne and

Françoise peek in, beckoning them outside. On to the
Himmler-Spielsaal and chemin-de-fer till midnight. Slothrop breaks even, Tantivy loses, and the girls win. No sign
of Bloat, though dozens of officers go drifting in and out,
brown and distant as rotogravure, through the evening.
Nor any sight of his girl Ghislaine. Slothrop asks. Yvonne
shrugs: "Out with your friend? Who knows?" Ghislaine's
long hair and tanned arms, her six-year-old face in a
smile. . . . If it turns out she does know something, is she
safe?

At 11:59 Slothrop turns to Tantivy, nods at the two
girls, tries to chuckle lewdly, and gives his friend a quick,
affectionate punch in the shoulder. Once, back in prep
school, just before sending him into a game, young Slothrop's football coach socked him the same way, giving
him confidence for at least fifty seconds, till being
trampled flat on his ass by a number of red-dogging
Choate boys, each with the instincts and mass of a killer
rhino.

"Good luck," says Tantivy, meaning it, hand already
reaching for Yvonne's sweet chiffon bottom. Minutes of
doubt, yes yes . . . Slothrop ascending flights of red-
carpeted stairway (Welcome Mister Slothrop Welcome
To Our Structure We Hope You Will Enjoy Your Visit
Here), malachite nymphs and satyrs paralyzed in chase,
evergreen, at the silent landings, upward toward a single
staring bulb at the top. . . .

At her door he pauses long enough to comb his hair.
Now she wears a white pelisse, with sequins all over,
padded shoulders, jagged white ostrich plumes at the
neckline and wrists. The tiara is gone: in the electricity
her hair is new snowfall. But inside a single scented candle burns, and the suite is washed in moonlight. She pours
brandy in old flint snifters, and as he reaches, their fingers
touch. "Didn't know you were so daffy about that golf!"
Suave, romantic Slothrop.

"He was pleasant. I was being pleasant to him," one eye
kind of squinched up, forehead wrinkled. Slothrop wonders if his fly's open.

"And ignore me. Why?" Clever pounce there, Slothrop—but she only evaporates before the question, re-
forms in another part of the room. . . .

"Am I ignoring you?" She's at her window, the sea below and behind her, the midnight sea, its individual waveflows impossible at this distance to follow, all integrated into the hung stillness of an old painting seen across the deserted gallery where you wait in the shadow, forgetting why you are here, frightened by the level of illumination, which is from the same blanched scar of moon that wipes the sea tonight. . . .

"I don't know. But you're fooling around a lot."

"Perhaps I'm supposed to be."

"As 'Perhaps we were meant to meet'?"

"Oh, you think I'm more than I am," gliding to a couch, tucking one leg under.

"I know. You're only a Dutch milkmaid or something. Closet full o' those starched aprons a-and wooden shoes, right?"

"Go and look." Spice odors from the candle reach like nerves through the room.

"O.K., I will!" He opens her closet, and in moonlight reflected from the mirror finds a crowded maze of satins, taffetas, lawn, and pongee, dark fur collars and trimming, buttons, sashes, passementerie, soft, confusing, womanly tunnel-systems that must stretch back for miles—he could be lost inside of half a minute . . . lace glimmers, eyelets wink, a crepe scarf brushes his face . . . Aha! wait a minute, the operational scent in here is carbon tet, Jackson, and this wardrobe here's mostly props. "Well. Pretty snazzy."

"If that's a compliment, thank you."

Let Them thank me, babe. "An Americanism."

"You're the first American I've met."

"Hmm. You must've got out by way of that Arnhem, then, right?"

"My, you're quick," her tone warning him not to go after it. He sighs, ringing the snifter with his fingernail. In the dark room, with the paralyzed and silent sea at his back, he tries singing:

Too Soon to Know (Fox-trot)

It's still too soon,
It's not as if we'd kissed and kindled,
Or chased the moon

Through midnight's hush, as dancing dwindled
Into quiet dawns,
Over secret lawns . . .

Too soon to know
If all that breathless conversation
A sigh ago
Was more than casual flirtation
Doomed to drift away
Into misty gray . . .

How can we tell,
What can we see?
Love works its spells in hiding,
Quite past our own deciding . . .

So who's to say
If joyful love is just beginning,
Or if its day
Just turned to night, as Earth went spinning?
Darling, maybe so—
It's TOO SOON TO KNOW.

Knowing what is expected of her, she waits with a
vapid look till he's done, mellow close-harmony reeds
humming a moment in the air, then reaches out a hand,
melting toward him as he topples in slow-motion toward
her mouth, feathers sliding, sleeves furling, ascending bare
arms finely moongrained slipping around and up his back,
her tacky tongue nervous as a moth, his hands rasping
over sequins . . . then her breasts flatten against him as
her forearms and hands go away folding up behind her
to find a zipper, bring it snarling down her spineline. . . .
Katje's skin is whiter than the white garment she rises
from. *Born again* . . . out the window he can almost see
the spot where the devilfish crawled in from the rocks.
She walks like a ballerina on her toes, thighs long and
curving, Slothrop undoing belt, buttons, shoelaces hopping
one foot at a time, oboy oboy, but the moonlight only
whitens her back, and there is still a dark side, her ventral
side, her face, that he can no longer see, a terrible beast-
like change coming over muzzle and lower jaw, black
pupils growing to cover the entire eye space till whites
are gone and there's only the red animal reflection when
the light comes to strike *no telling when the light—*

She has sunk to the deep bed, pulling him along, into down, satin, seraphic and floral embroidery, turning immediately to take his erection into her stretched fork, into a single vibration on which the night is tuning . . . as they fuck she quakes, body strobing miles beneath him in cream and night-blue, all sound suppressed, eyes in crescents behind the gold lashes, jet earrings, long, octahedral, flying without a sound, beating against her cheeks, black sleet, his face above her unmoved, full of careful technique—is it for her? or wired into the Slothropian Runtogether they briefed her on—she will move him, she will not be mounted by a plastic shell . . . her breathing has grown more hoarse, over a threshold into sound . . . thinking she might be close to coming he reaches a hand into her hair, tries to still her head, needing to see her face: this is suddenly a struggle, vicious and real—she will not surrender her face—and out of nowhere she does begin to come, and so does Slothrop.

For some reason now, she who never laughs has become the top surface of a deep, rising balloon of laughter. Later as she's about to go to sleep, she will also whisper, "Laughing," laughing again.

He will want to say, "Oh, They let you," but then again maybe They don't. But the Katje he's talking to is already gone, and presently his own eyes have closed.

Like a rocket whose valves, under remote control, open and close at prearranged moments, Slothrop, at a certain level of his re-entry into sleep, stops breathing through his nose and commences breathing through his mouth. This soon grows to snores that have been known to rattle storm windows, set shutters to swinging and chandeliers into violent tintinnabulation, yes indee-eed. . . . At the first of these tonight, Katje wakes up belts him in the head with a pillow.

"None of that."

"Hmm."

"I'm a light sleeper. Every time you snore, you get hit with this," waving the pillow.

No kidding, either. The routine of snore, get belted with pillow, wake up, say hmm, fall back to sleep, goes on well into the morning. "Come on," finally, "cut it out."

"Mouth-breather!" she yells. He grabs his own pillow and swings it at her. She ducks, rolls, hits the deck feint-

ing with her pillow, backing toward the sideboard where
the booze is. He doesn't see what she has in mind till she
throws her pillow and picks up the Seltzer bottle.

The what, *The Seltzer Bottle?* What shit is this, now?
What other interesting props have They thought to plant,
and what other American reflexes are They after? Where's
those *banana cream pies*, eh?

He dangles two pillows and watches her. "One more
step," she giggles. Slothrop dives in goes to hit her across
the ass whereupon she lets him have it with the Seltzer
bottle, natch. The pillow bursts against one marble hip,
moonlight in the room is choked with feathers and down
and soon with hanging spray from jets of Seltzer. Slothrop
keeps trying to grab the bottle. Slippery girl squirms
away, gets behind a chair. Slothrop takes the brandy de-
canter off of the sideboard, unstoppers it, and flings a
clear, amber, pseudopodded glob across the room twice
in and out of moonlight to splash around her neck, between her black-tipped breasts, down her flanks. "Bastard," hitting him with the Seltzer again. Settling feathers
cling to their skins as they chase around the bedroom,
her dappled body always retreating, often in this light,
even at close range, impossible to see. Slothrop keeps
falling over the furniture. "Boy, when I get my hands on
you!" At which point she opens the door to the sitting
room, skips through, slams it again so Slothrop runs right
into it, bounces off, sez shit, opens the door to find her
waving a big red damask tablecloth at him.

"What's this," inquires Slothrop.

"Magic!" she cries, and tosses the tablecloth over him,
precisely wrinkling folds propagating swift as crystal
faults, redly through the air. "Watch closely, while I make
one American lieutenant disappear."

"Quit fooling," Slothrop flailing around trying to reach
the outside again. "How can I watch closely when I'm in
here." He can't find an edge anyplace and feels a little
panicky.

"That's the idea," suddenly inside, next to him, lips at
his nipples, hands fluttering among the hairs at the back
of his neck, pulling him slowly to deep carpeting, "My
little chickadee."

"Where'd you see that one, hey? Remember when he
gets in bed w-with that *goat?*"

"Oh, don't ask . . ." This time it is a good-natured coordinated quickie, both kind of drowsy, covered with sticky feathers . . . after coming they lie close together, too liquefied to move, mm, damask and pile, it's so cozy and just as red as a womb in here. . . . Curled holding her feet in his, cock nestled in the warm cusp between her buttocks, Slothrop trying earnestly to breathe through his nose, they drop off to sleep.

Slothrop wakes to morning sunlight off of that Mediterranean, filtered through a palm outside the window, then red through the tablecloth, birds, water running upstairs. For a minute he lies coming awake, no hangover, still belonging Slothropless to some teeming cycle of departure and return. Katje lies, quick and warm, S'd against the S of himself, beginning to stir.

From the next room he hears the unmistakable sound of an Army belt buckle. "Somebody," he observes, catching on quickly, "must be robbing my pants." Feet patter by on the carpet, close to his head. Slothrop can hear his own small change jingling in his pockets. "Thief!" he yells, which wakes up Katje, turning to put her arms around him. Slothrop, managing now to locate the hem he couldn't find last night, scoots from under the tablecloth just in time to see a large foot in a two-tone shoe, coffee and indigo, vanish out the door. He runs into the bedroom, finds everything else he had on is gone too, down to shoes and skivvies.

"My clothes!" running back out past Katje now emerging from the damask and making a grab for his feet. Slothrop flings open the door, runs out in the hall, recollects that he is *naked* here, spots a laundry cart and grabs a purple satin bedsheet off of it, drapes it around him in a sort of toga. From the stairway comes a snicker and the pad-pad of crepe soles. "Aha!" cries Slothrop charging down the hall. The slippery sheet will not stay on. It flaps, slides off, gets underfoot. Up the stairs two at a time, only to find at the top another corridor, just as empty. Where is everybody?

From way down the hall, a tiny head appears around a corner, a tiny hand comes out and gives Slothrop the tiny finger. Unpleasant laughter reaches him a split second later, by which time he's sprinting toward it. At the stairs, he hears footsteps heading down. The Great Purple

Kite races cursing down three flights, out a door and onto a little terrace, just in time to see somebody hop over a stone balustrade and vanish into the upper half of a thick tree, growing up from somewhere below. "Treed at last!" cries Slothrop.

First you have to get into the tree, then you can climb it easy as a ladder. Once inside, surrounded by pungent leaflight, Slothrop can't see farther than a couple of limbs. The tree is shaking though, so he reckons that that thief is in here someplace. Industriously he climbs on, sheet catching and tearing, skin stuck by needles, scraped by bark. His feet hurt. He's soon out of breath. Gradually the cone of green light narrows, grows brighter. Close to the top, Slothrop notes a saw-cut or something partway through the trunk, but doesn't stop to ponder what it might mean till he's reached the very top of the tree and clings swaying, enjoying the fine view of the harbor and headland, paint-blue sea, whitecaps, storm gathering off at the horizon, the tops of people's heads moving around far below. Gee. Down the trunk he hears the sound of wood beginning to crack, and feels vibration here in his slender perch.

"Aw, hey . . ." That *sneak*. He climbed *down* the tree, not up! He's down there now, watching! They knew Slothrop would choose up, not down—they were counting on *that* damned American reflex all right, bad guy in a chase always heads up—why up? and they sawed the trunk nearly through, a-and now—

They? *They*?

"Well," opines Slothrop, "I had better, uh . . ." About then the point of the tree cracks through, and with a great rustle and whoosh, a whirl of dark branches and needles breaking him up into a few thousand sharp falling pieces, down topples Slothrop, bouncing from limb to limb, trying to hold the purple sheet over his head for a parachute. Oof. Nnhh. About halfway to the ground, terrace-level or so, he happens to look down, and there observes many senior officers in uniform and plump ladies in white batiste frocks and flowered hats. They are playing croquet. It appears Slothrop will land somewhere in their midst. He closes his eyes and tries to imagine a tropical island, a secure room, where this cannot be happening. He opens them about the time he hits the ground. In the silence, before he can even register pain, comes the loud *thock* of wood hitting wood. A bright-yellow striped ball comes rolling past an inch from Slothrop's nose and on out of sight, followed a second later by a burst of congratulations, ladies enthusiastic, footfalls heading his way. Seems he's, unnhh, wrenched his back a little, but doesn't much feel like moving anyhow. Presently the sky is obscured by faces of some General and Teddy Bloat, gazing curiously down.

"It's Slothrop," sez Bloat, "and he's wearing a purple sheet."

"What's this my lad," inquires the General, "costume theatricals, eh?" He is joined by a pair of ladies beaming at, or perhaps through, Slothrop.

"Whom are you talking to, General?"

"That blighter in the toga," replies the General, "who is lying between me and my next wicket."

"Why how extraordinary, Rowena," turning to her companion, "do *you* see a 'blighter in a toga'?"

"Goodness no, Jewel," replies blithe Rowena. "*I* believe the General has been *drink*ing." The ladies begin to giggle.

"If the General made *all* his decisions in this state," Jewel grasping for breath, "why there'd, there'd be *sauerkraut in the Strand!*" The two of them shriek, very loudly, for an unpleasant length of time.

"And your name would be Brun*hild*e," the two faces now a strangled rose, "instead of—of Jewel!" They are clutching each other for dear life. Slothrop glares up at this spectacle, augmented now by a cast of dozens.

"We-e-e-ell, you see, somebody swiped all my clothes, and I was just on my way to complain to the management—"

"But decided to put on a purple bedsheet and climb a tree instead," nods the General. "Well—I dare say we can fix you up with something. Bloat, you're nearly this man's size, aren't you?"

"Oh," croquet mallet over his shoulder, posed like an advertising display for Kilgour or Curtis, smirking down at Slothrop, "I've a spare uniform somewhere. Come along, Slothrop, you're all right, aren't you. Didn't break anything."

"Yaagghh." Wrapped in his tattered sheet, helped to

his feet by solicitous croqueteers, Slothrop goes limping after Bloat, off the turf and into the Casino. They stop first at Slothrop's room. He finds it newly cleaned, perfectly empty, ready for new guests. "Hey . . ." Yanking out drawers empty as drums: every stitch of clothing he owns is gone, including his Hawaiian shirt. What the fuck. Groaning, he rummages in the desk. Empty. Closets empty. Leave papers, ID, everything, taken. His back muscles throb with pain. "What is this, Ace?" going to check out the number on the door again, everything now for form's sake. He knows. Hogan's shirt bothers him most of all.

"First put on something respectable," Bloat's tone full of headmasterish revulsion. Two subalterns come crashing in carrying their valises. They halt goggling at Slothrop. "Here mate, you're in the wrong theatre of operations," cries one. "Show a bit of respect," the other haw-haws, "it's Lawrence of Arabia!"

"Shit," sez Slothrop. Can't even lift his arm, much less swing it. They proceed to Bloat's room, where they put together a uniform.

"Say," it occurs to Slothrop, "where's that Mucker-Maffick this morning?"

"I've no idea, really. Off with his girl. Or girls. Where've *you* been?"

But Slothrop's looking around, tightening rectal fear belatedly taking hold now, neck and face beading in a surge of sweat, trying to find in this room Tantivy shares with Bloat some trace of his friend. Bristly Norfolk jacket, pinstripe suit, anything. . . . Nothing. "Did that Tantivy move out, or what?"

"He may have moved in, with Françoise or What's-her-name. Even gone back to London early, I don't keep a file on him, I'm not the missing-persons bureau."

"You're his friend. . . ." Bloat, with an insolent shrug, for the very first time since they met, now looks Slothrop in the eyes. "Aren't you? What are you?"

The answer's in Bloat's stare, the dim room become rationalized, nothing to it of holiday, only Savile Row uniforms, silver hairbrushes and razor arranged at right angles, a shiny spike on an octagonal base impaling half an inch of pastel flimsies, all edges neatly squared . . . a piece of Whitehall on the Riviera.

Slothrop drops his eyes away. "See if I can find him," he mumbles, retreating out the door, uniform ballooning at the ass and too tight at the waist. Live wi' the way it feels mate, you'll be in it for a while. . . .

He begins at the bar they talked in last night. It is empty except for a colonel with a great twisted mustache, with his hat on, sitting stiffly in front of something large, fizzing, opaque, and garnished with a white chrysanthemum. "Didn't they teach you at Sandhurst to salute?" this officer screams. Slothrop, hesitating only a moment, salutes. "Damned O.C.T.U. must be full of Nazis." No bartender in sight. Can't remember what— "Well?"

"Actually, what I am is, uh, is an American, I only borrowed the uniform, and well I was looking for a Lieutenant, or actually Leftenant, Mucker-Maffick. . . ."

"You're a what?" roars the colonel, pulling leaves from the chrysanthemum with his teeth. "What kind of Nazi foolishness is that, eh?"

"Well, thank you," Slothrop backing out of the room, saluting again.

"This is incredible!" the echo following him down the corridors to the Himmler-Spielsaal. "It's Nazi!"

Deserted in noon's lull, here are resonant reaches of mahogany, green baize, hanging loops of maroon velvet. Long-handled wood money rakes lie fanned out on the tables. Little silver bells with ebony handles are turned mouth-down on the russet veneer. Around the tables, Empire chairs are lined up precise and playerless. But some are taller than the rest. These are no longer quite outward and visible signs of a game of chance. There is another enterprise here, more real than that, less merciful, and sytematically hidden from the likes of Slothrop. Who sits in the taller chairs? Do They have names? What lies on Their smooth baize surfaces?

Brass-colored light seeps in from overhead. Murals line the great room: pneumatic gods and goddesses, pastel swains and shepherdesses, misty foliage, fluttering scarves. . . . Everywhere curlicued gilt festoonery drips—from moldings, chandeliers, pillars, window frame . . . scarred parquetry gleams under the skylight . . . From the ceiling, to within a few feet of the tabletops, hang long chains, with hooks at the ends. What hangs from these hooks?

For a minute here, Slothrop, in his English uniform, is

alone with the paraphernalia of an order whose presence
among the ordinary debris of waking he has only lately
begun to suspect.

There may, for a moment, have been some golden,
vaguely rootlike or manlike figure beginning to form
among the brown and bright cream shadows and light
here. But Slothrop isn't to be let off so easy. Shortly, unpleasantly so, it will come to him that everything in this
room is really being used for something different. Meaning
things to Them it has never meant to us. Never. Two
orders of being, looking identical . . . but, but . . .

> Oh, THE WORLD OVER THERE, it's
> So hard to explain!
> Just-like, a dream's-got, lost in yer brain!
> Dancin' like a fool through that Forbid-den Wing,
> Waitin' fer th' light to start shiver-ing—well,
> Who ev-ver said ya couldn't move that way,
> Who ev-ver said ya couldn't try?
> If-ya find-there's-a-lit-tle-pain,
> Ya can al-ways-go-back-a-gain, cause
> Ya don't-ev-er-real-ly-say, good-by!

Why here? Why should the rainbow edges of what is
almost on him be rippling most intense here in this amply
coded room? say why should walking in here be almost the
same as entering the Forbidden itself—here are the same
long rooms, rooms of old paralysis and evil distillery, of
condensations and residues you are afraid to smell from
forgotten corruptions, rooms full of upright gray-feathered
status with wings spread, indistinct faces in dust—rooms
full of dust that will cloud the shapes of inhabitants
around the corners or deeper inside, that will settle on
their black formal lapels, that will soften to sugar the
white faces, white shirt fronts, gems and gowns, white
hands that move too quickly to be seen . . . what game do
They deal? What passes are these, so blurred, so old and
perfect?

"Fuck you," whispers Slothrop. It's the only spell he
knows, and a pretty good all-purpose one at that. His
whisper is baffled by the thousands of tiny rococo surfaces. Maybe he'll sneak in tonight—no not at night—
but sometime, with a bucket and brush, paint FUCK YOU in

a balloon coming out the mouth of one of those little pink shepherdesses there. . . .

He steps back out, backward out the door, as if half, his ventral half, were being struck in kingly radiance: retreating from yet facing the Presence feared and wanted.

Outside, he heads down toward the quay, among funseekers, swooping white birds, an incessant splat of seagull shit. As I walk along the Bwa-deboolong with an independent air . . . Saluting everybody in uniform, getting it to a reflex, don't ask for extra trouble, try for invisible . . . bringing his arm each time a bit more stupidly to his side. Clouds now are coming up fast, out of the sea. No sign of Tantivy out here, either.

Ghosts of fishermen, glassworkers, fur traders, renegade preachers, hilltop patriarchs and valley politicians go avalanching back from Slothrop here, back to 1630 when Governor Winthrop came over to America on the *Arbella,* flagship of a great Puritan flotilla that year, on which the first American Slothrop had been a mess cook or something—there go that *Arbella* and its whole fleet, sailing backward in formation, the wind sucking them east again, the creatures leaning from the margins of the unknown *sucking in* their cheeks, growing crosseyed with the effort, in to black deep hollows at the mercy of teeth no longer the milky molars of cherubs, as the old ships zoom out of Boston Harbor, back across an Atlantic whose currents and swells go flowing and heaving in reverse . . . a redemption of every mess cook who ever slipped and fell when the deck made an unexpected move, the night's stew collecting itself up out of the planks and off the indignant shoes of the more elect, slithering in a fountain back into the pewter kettle as the servant himself staggers upright again and the vomit he slipped on goes bushing back into the mouth that spilled it . . . Presto change-o! Tyrone Slothrop's English again! But it doesn't seem to be redemption exactly that *this* They have in mind. . . .

He's on a broad cobbled esplanade, lined with palms shifting now to coarse-grained black as clouds begin to come over the sun. Tantivy isn't out on the beach, either—nor are any of the girls. Slothrop sits on a low wall, feet swinging, watching the front, slate, muddy purple, advancing from the sea in sheets, in drifts. Around him the air is cooling. He shivers. What are They doing?

He gets back to the Casino just as big globular raindrops, thick as honey, begin to splat into giant asterisks
on the pavement, inviting him to look down at the bottom
of the text of the day, where footnotes will explain all. He
isn't about to look. Nobody ever said a day has to be
juggled into any kind of sense at day's end. He just runs.
Rain grows in wet crescendo. His footfalls send up fine
flowers of water, each hanging a second behind his flight.
It is flight. He comes in speckled, pied with rain, begins a
frantic search through the great inert Casino, starting again
with the same smoky, hooch-fumed bar, proceeding through
the little theatre, where tonight will play an abbreviated
version of *L'Inutil Precauzione* (that imaginary opera with
which Rosina seeks to delude her guardian in *The Barber of
Seville*), into its green room where girls, a silkenness of
girls, but not the three Slothrop wants most to see, tease
hair, arrange garters, glue on eyelashes, smile at Slothrop.
No one has seen Ghislaine, Françoise, Yvonne. From
another room the orchestra rehearses a lively Rossini tarantella. The reeds are all something like a half tone flat.
At once Slothrop understands that he is surrounded by
women who have lived a good fraction of their lives at war
and under occupation, and for whom people have been
dropping out of sight every day . . . yes, in one or two
pairs of eyes he finds an old and European pity, a look he
will get to know, well before he loses his innocence and
becomes one of them. . . .

So he drifts, through the bright and milling gaming
rooms, the dining hall and its smaller private satellites,
busting up tête-à-têtes, colliding with waiters, finding only
strangers wherever he looks. *And if you need help, well,
I'll help you.* . . . Voices, music, and shuffling of cards all
grow louder, more oppressive, till he stands looking into
the Himmler-Spielsaal again, crowded now, jewels flashing, leather gleaming, roulette spokes whirling blurring—
it's here that saturation hits him, it's all this playing games,
too much of it, too many games: the nasal, obsessive voice
of a croupier he can't see—messieurs, mesdames, les jeux
sont faits—is suddenly speaking out of the Forbidden
Wing directly to him, and about what Slothrop has been
playing against the invisible House, perhaps after all for
his soul, all day—terrified he turns, turns out into the rain

again where the electric lights of the Casino, in full holocaust, are glaring off the glazed cobbles. Collar up, Bloat's
hat down over his ears, saying *shit* every few minutes,
shivering, his back aching from that fall out of that tree,
he goes stumbling along in the rain. He thinks he might
begin to cry. How did this all turn against him so fast?
His friends old and new, every last bit of paper and clothing connecting him to what he's been, have just, fucking,
vanished. How can he meet this with any kind of grace?
Only much later, worn out, snuffling, cold and wretched in
his prison of soggy Army wool, does he think of Katje.

He gets back to the Casino near midnight, her hour,
tramping upstairs leaving wet footprints behind, loud as a
washing machine—stops at her door, rain pattering onto
the carpet, afraid even to knock. Has she been taken too?
Who's waiting behind the door and what machinery have
They brought with Them? But she's heard him, and opens
with a dimpled, chiding smile for being so wet. "Tyrone,
I missed you."

He shrugs, convulsive, helpless, showering both of
them. "It's the only place I knew to come." Her smile
slowly unpurses. Gingerly he steps across the sill then, not
sure if it's door or high window, into her deep room.

□

Good mornings of good old lust, early shutters open to the
sea, winds coming in with the heavy brushing of palm
leaves, the wheezing break to surface and sun of porpoises
out in the harbor.

"Oh," Katje groans, somewhere under a pile of their
batistes and brocade, "Slothrop, you *pig*."

"Oink, oink, oink," sez Slothrop cheerfully. Seaglare
dances up on the ceiling, smoke curls from black-market
cigarettes. Given the precisions of light these mornings,
there are forms of grace to be found in the rising of the
smoke, meander, furl, delicate fade to clarity. . . .

At certain hours the harbor blue will be reflected up on
the whitewashed sea-façade, and the tall windows will be
shuttered again. Wave images will flicker there in a
luminous net. By then Slothrop will be up, in British uni-

form, gobbling down croissants and coffee, already busy at a refresher course in technical German, or trying to dope out the theory of arrow-stable trajectories, or tracing nearly with the end of his nose some German circuit schematic whose resistors look like coils, and the coils like resistors—"What bizarre shit," once he got hep to it, "why would they go and switch it around like that? Trying to camouflage it, or what?"

"Recall your ancient German runes," suggests Sir Stephen Dodson-Truck, who is from the Foreign Office P.I.D. and speaks 33 languages including English with a strong Oxonian blither to it.

"My what?"

"Oh," lips compressing, some kind of brain nausea here, "that coil symbol there happens to be very like the Old Norse rune for 'S,' *sól*, which means 'sun.' The Old High German name for it is *sigil*."

"Funny way to draw that *sun*," it seems to Slothrop.

"Indeed. The Goths, much earlier, had used a circle with a dot in the center. This broken line evidently dates from a time of discontinuities, tribal fragmenting perhaps, alienation—whatever's analogous, in a social sense, to the development of an independent ego by the very young child, you see. . . ."

Well, no, Slothrop doesn't see, not exactly. He hears this sort of thing from Dodson-Truck nearly every time they get together. The man just materialized one day, out on the beach in a black suit, shoulders starred with dandruff from thinning carrot hair, coming into view against the white face of the Casino, which trembled over him as he approached. Slothrop was reading a Plasticman comic. Katje was dozing in the sun, face-up. But when his footpads reached her hearing, she turned on one elbow to wave hello. The peer flung himself to full length, Attitude 8.11, Torpor, Undergraduate. "So this is Lieutenant Slothrop."

Four-color Plasticman goes oozing out of a keyhole, around a corner and up through piping that leads to a sink in the mad Nazi scientist's lab, out of whose faucet Plas's head now, blank carapaced eyes and unplastic jaw, is just emerging. "Yeah. Who're you, Ace?"

Sir Stephen introduces himself, freckles roused by the

sun, eyeing the comic book curiously. "I gather this isn't a study period."

"Is he cleared?"

"He's cleared," Katje smiling/shrugging at Dodson-Truck.

"Taking a break from that Telefunken radio control. That 'Hawaii I.' You know anything about that?"

"Only enough to wonder where they got the name from."

"The *name?*"

"There's a poetry to it, engineer's poetry . . . it suggests *Haverie*—average, you know—certainly you have the two lobes, don't you, symmetrical about the rocket's intended azimuth . . . *hauen*, too—smashing someone with a hoe or a club . . ." off on a voyage of his own here, smiling at no one in particular, bringing in the popular wartime expression *ab-hauen*, quarterstaff technique, peasant humor, phallic comedy dating back to the ancient Greeks. . . . Slothrop's first impulse is to get back to what that Plas is into, but something about the man, despite obvious membership in the plot, keeps him listening . . . an innocence, maybe a try at being friendly in the only way he has available, sharing what engages and runs him, a love for the Word.

"Well, it might be just Axis propaganda. Something to do with that Pearl Harbor."

Sir Stephen considers this, seeming pleased. Did They choose him because of all those word-smitten Puritans dangling off of Slothrop's family tree? Were They trying to seduce his brain now, his reading eye too? There are times when Slothrop actually can find a clutch mechanism between him and Their iron-cased engine far away up a power train whose shape and design he has to guess at, a clutch he can disengage, feeling then all his inertia of motion, his real helplessness . . . it is not exactly unpleasant, either. Odd thing. He is almost sure that whatever They want, it won't mean risking his life, or even too much of his comfort. But he can't fit any of it into a pattern, there's no way to connect somebody like Dodson-Truck with somebody like Katje. . . .

Seductress-and-patsy, all right, that's not so bad a game. There's very little pretending. He doesn't blame her:

the real enemy's somewhere back in that London, and this
is her job. She can be versatile, gay, and kind, and he'd
rather be warm here with her than freezing back under
the Blitz. But now and then . . . too insubstantial to get a
fix on, there'll be in her face a look, something not in her
control, that depresses him, that he's even dreamed about
and so found amplified there to honest fright: the terrible
chance that she might have been conned too. As much a
victim as he is—an unlucky, an unaccountably *futureless*
look. . . .

One gray afternoon in where but the Himmler-Spielsaal,
where else, he surprises her alone by a roulette wheel.
She's standing, head bent, gracefully hipshot, playing
croupier. An employee of the House. She wears a white
peasant blouse and a rainbow-striped dirndl skirt of satin,
which shimmers underneath the skylight. The ball's tattoo,
against the moving spokes, gathers a long, scratchy resonance here in the muraled space. She doesn't turn till Slothrop is beside her. To her breathing there is a grave
slow-beating tremor: she nudges at the shutters of his
heart, opening to him brief flashes of an autumn country
he has only suspected, only feared, outside him, inside
her. . . .

"Hey Katje . . ." Making a long arm, hooking a finger
on a spoke to stop the wheel. The ball drops in a compartment whose number they never see. Seeing the number is supposed to be the point. But in the game behind
the game, it is not the point.

She shakes her head. He understands that it's something
back in Holland, before Arnhem—an impedance permanently wired into the circuit of themselves. How many
ears smelling of Palmolive and Camay has he crooned
songs into, outside-the-bowling-alley songs, behind-the-
Moxie-billboard songs, Saturday-night open-me-another-
quart songs, all saying, honey, it don't matter where you've
been, let's not live in the past, right now's all there is. . . .

Fine for back there. But not in here, tapping on her
bare shoulder, peering in at her European darkness, bewildered with it, himself with his straight hair barely combable and shaven face without a wrinkle such a chaste in-
trusion in the Himmler-Spielsaal all crowded with Ger-
man-Baroque perplexities of shape (a sacrament of hands

in every last turn each hand must produce, because of
what the hand was, had to become, to make it all come out
exactly this way . . . all the cold, the trauma, the departing
flesh that has ever touched it. . . .) In the twisted gilt play-
ing-room his secret motions clarify for him, some. The
odds They played here belonged to the past, the past only.
Their odds were never probabilities, but frequencies *already observed*. It's the past that makes demands here.
It whispers, and reaches after, and, sneering disagreeably,
gooses its victims.

When They chose numbers, red, black, odd, even, what
did They mean by it? What Wheel did They set in motion?

Back in a room, early in Slothrop's life, a room forbidden
to him now, is something very bad. Something was done
to him, and it may be that Katje knows what. Hasn't he, in
her "futureless look," found some link to his own past,
something that connects them closely as lovers? He sees
her standing at the end of a passage in her life, without
any next step to take—all her bets are in, she has only the
tedium now of being knocked from one room to the next,
a sequence of numbered rooms whose numbers do not
matter, till inertia brings her to the last. That's all.

Naïve Slothrop never thought anybody's life could end
like that. Nothing so bleak. But by now it's grown much
less strange to him—he's been snuggling up, masturbatorily
scared-elated, to the disagreeable chance that exactly such
Control might already have been put over him.

The Forbidden Wing. Oh, the hand of a terrible croupier is that touch on the sleeves of his dreams: all in his
life of what has looked free or random, is discovered to've
been under some Control, all the time, the same as a fixed
roulette wheel—where only destinations are important,
attention is to long-term statistics, not individuals: and
where the House always does, of course, keep turning a
profit. . . .

"You were in London," she will presently whisper, turning back to her wheel and spinning it again, face averted,
womanly twisting the night-streaked yarn of her past,
"while they were coming down. I was in 's Graven-
hage"—fricatives sighing, the name spoken with exile's
lingering—"while they were going up. Between you and
me is not only a rocket trajectory, but also a life. You will

come to understand that between the two points, in the five minutes, *it* lives an entire life. You haven't even learned the data on our side of the flight profile, the visible or trackable. Beyond them there's so much more, so much none of us know. . . ."

But it is a curve each of them feels, unmistakably. It is the parabola. They must have guessed, once or twice—guessed and refused to believe—that everything, always, collectively, had been moving toward that purified shape latent in the sky, that shape of no surprise, no second chances, no return. Yet they do move forever under it, reserved for its own black-and-white bad news certainly as if it were the Rainbow, and they its children. . . .

As the War's front moves away from them, and the Casino becomes more and more a rear area, as the water grows more polluted and the prices rise, so the personnel coming down on leave get noisier and more dedicated to pure assholery—none of Tantivy's style about them, his habit of soft-shoe dancing when drunk, his make-believe foppishness and shy, decent impulses to conspire, however marginally, whenever possible, against power and indifference. . . . There hasn't been a word about him. Slothrop misses him, not just as an ally, but as a presence, a kindness. He continues to believe, here on his French leave, and at his ease, that the interference is temporary and paper, a matter of messages routed and orders cut, an annoyance that will end when the War ends, so well have They busted the sod prairies of his brain, tilled and sown there, and subsidized him not to grow anything of his own. . . .

No letters from London, not even news of ACHTUNG. All gone. Teddy Bloat one day just vanished: other conspirators, like a chorus line, will show up off and on behind Katje and Sir Stephen, dancing in, all with identical Corporate Smiles, the multiplication of whose glittering choppers is to dazzle him, they think, distract him from what they're taking away, his ID, his service dossier, his past. Well, fuck . . . you know. He lets it happen. He's more interested, and sometimes a little anxious, about what they seem to be adding on. At some point, apparently on a whim, though how can a fellow be sure, Slothrop decides to raise a mustache. Last mustache he had was at age 13, he sent away to that Johnson Smith for a whole Mustache Kit, 20 different shapes from Fu Manchu to Groucho Marx. They were made of black cardboard, with hooks that fit into your nose. After a while snot would soak into these hooks, and they'd grow limp, and the mustache would fall off.

"What kind?" Katje wants to know, soon as this one is visible.

"Bad-guy," sez Slothrop. Meaning, he explains, trimmed, narrow, and villainous.

"No, that'll give you a negative attitude. Why not raise a good-guy mustache instead?"

"But good guys don't *have*—"

"Oh no? What about Wyatt Earp?"

To which one might've advanced the objection that Wyatt wasn't all that good. But this is still back in the Stuart Lake era here, before the revisionists moved in, and Slothrop believes in that Wyatt, all right. One day a General Wivern, of SHAEF Technical Staff, comes in and sees it. "The ends droop down," he observes.

"So did that Wyatt's," explains Slothrop.

"So did John Wilkes Booth's," replies the general. "Eh?"

Slothrop ponders. "He was a bad guy."

"Precisely. Why don't you twist the ends *up?*"

"You mean English style. Well, I tried that. It must be the weather or something, the old duster just keeps droopin' down again, a-and I need to bite those *ends* off. It's really annoying."

"It's disgusting," sez Wivern. "Next time I come round I shall bring you some wax for it. They make it with a bitter taste to discourage, ah, end-chewers, you know."

So as the mustache waxes, Slothrop waxes the mustache. Every day there's something new like this. Katje's always there, slipped by Them into his bed like nickels under the pillow for his deciduous Americanism, innocent incisors 'n' Momworshiping molars just left in a clattering trail back down these days at the Casino. For some odd reason he finds himself with hardons right after study sessions. Hm, that's peculiar. There is nothing specially erotic about reading manuals hastily translated from the German— brokenly mimeographed, even a few salvaged by the Polish underground from the latrines at the training site at Blizna, stained with genuine SS shit and piss . . . or memorizing conversion factors, inches to centimeters, horsepower to Pferdestärke, drawing from memory schematics and isometrics of the snarled maze of fuel, oxidizer, steam, peroxide and permanganate lines, valves, vents, chambers—what's sexy about that? still he emerges from each lesson with great hardon, tremendous pressure inside . . . some of that temporary insanity, he reckons, and goes looking for Katje, hands to crabwalk his back and silk stockings squealing against his hipbones. . . .

During the lessons he will often look over and catch Sir Stephen Dodson-Truck consulting a stopwatch and taking notes. Jeepers. He wonders what that's all about. Never occurs to him it might have to do with these mysterious erections. The man's personality was chosen—or designed—to sidetrack suspicions before they have a chance to gather speed. Winter sunlight hitting half his face like a migraine, trouser cuffs out of press, wet and sandy because he's up every morning at six to walk along the strand, Sir Stephen makes perfectly accessible his disguise, if not his function in the conspiracy. For all Slothrop knows he's an agronomist, a brain surgeon, a concert oboist—in that London you saw all levels of command seething with these multidimensional geniuses. But as with Katje, there hangs about Dodson-Truck's well-informed zeal an unmistakable aura of the employee and loser. . . .

One day Slothrop gets a chance to check this out. Seems Dodson-Truck is a chess fanatic. Down in the bar one afternoon he gets around to asking Slothrop if he plays.

"Nope," lying, "not even checkers."

"Damn. I've hardly had time till now for a good game."

"I do know a game," has something of Tantivy been sheltering inside all this time? "a drinking game, it's called Prince, maybe the English even invented it, cause you have those princes, right? and we don't, not that that's wrong understand, but everybody takes a number, a-and you start off the Prince of Wales has lost his tails, no offense now, the numbers going clockwise around the table, and number two has found them, clockwise from that Prince, or whatever number he wants to call out actually, he, that's the Prince, six or anything, see, you pick a Prince first, he starts it off, then that number two, or whoever

that Prince called, sez, but first he goes, the Prince does,
Wales, tails, two sir, after saying that about how that
Prince of Wales has lost his tails, and number two answers,
not I, sir—"

"Yes yes but—" giving Slothrop a most odd look, "I
mean I'm not quite sure I really see, you know, the point
to it all. How does one *win?*"

Ha! How does one win, indeed. "One doesn't win,"
easing into it, thinking of Tantivy, one small impromptu
counter-conspiracy here, "one loses. One by one. Whoever's *left* is the winner."

"It sounds rather negative."

"Garçon." Drinks here are always on the house for
Slothrop—They are springing for it, he imagines. "Some
of that champagne! Wantcha to just keep it coming, and
any time we run out, go get more, comprendez?" Any
number of slack-jawed subalterns, hearing the magic word,
drift over and take seats while Slothrop explains the
rules.

"I'm not sure—" Dodson-Truck begins.

"Baloney. Come on, do you good to get outa that chess
rut."

"Right, right," agree the others.

Dodson-Truck stays in his seat, a bit tense.

"Bigger glasses," Slothrop hollers at the waiter. "How
about those *beer mugs* over there! Yeah! They'd be just
fine." The waiter unblasts a jeroboam of Veuve Clicquot
Brut, and fills everybody up.

"Well, the Prince o' Wales," Slothrop commences, "has
lost his tails, and number three has found them. Wales,
tails, three sir!"

"Not I, sir," replies Dodson-Truck, kind of defensive
about it.

"Who, sir?"

"Five, sir."

"Say what?" inquires Five, a Highlander in parade
trews, with a sly look.

"You fucked up," commands princely Slothrop, "so you
got to drink up. All the way now, 'n' no stopping to breathe
or anything."

On it goes. Slothrop loses Prince position to Four, and
all the numbers change. The Scot is first to drop, making

mistakes at first deliberate but soon inevitable. Jeroboams come and go, fat, green, tattered gray foil at the necks giving back the bar's electric radiance. Corks grow straighter, less mushroomy, dates of *degorgement* move further into the war years as the company gets drunker. The Scot has rolled chuckling from his chair, remaining ambulatory for some ten feet, where he goes to sleep against a potted palm. At once another junior officer slides beaming into his place. The word has osmosed out into the Casino, and there is presently a throng of kibitzers gathered around the table, waiting for casualties. Ice is being hauled in by the giant block, fern-faulted inside, breathing white off of its faces, to be sledged and chipped into a great wet tub for the procession of bottles being run up from the cellar now in relays. It soon becomes necessary for the harassed waiters to stack empty tankards in pyramids and pour fountain-style from the top, the bubble-shot cascades provoking cheers from the crowd. Some joker is sure to reach in and grab one of the mugs on the bottom, sending the whole arrangement swaying, everybody else jumping to salvage what they can before it all comes down, crashing, soaking uniforms and shoes—so that it can be set up all over again. The game has switched to Rotating Prince, where each number called out immediately becomes Prince, and all the numbers shift accordingly. By this time it is impossible to tell who's making mistakes and who isn't. Arguments arise. Half the room are singing a vulgar song:

VULGAR SONG

Last night I poked the Queen of Transylvan-ia,
Tonight I'll poke the Queen of Burgundee—
I'm bordering on the State of Schizophren-ia,
But Queenie is so very nice to me. . . .
It's pink champagne and caviar for break-fast,
A spot of Chateaubriand wiv me tea—
Ten-shilling panatelas now are all that I can smoke,
I laugh so much you'd think the world was just a silly joke,
So call me what you will, m' lads, but make way for the
    bloke
That's poked the love-ly lit-tle Queen of Transyl-vaayn-yaa!

Slothrop's head is a balloon, which rises not vertically but horizontally, constantly across the room, whilst staying in one place. Each brain cell has become a bubble: he's been transmuted to black Epernay grapes, cool shadows, noble cuvées. He looks across at Sir Stephen Dodson-Truck, who is still miraculously upright though with a glaze about the eyes. Aha, right, s'posed to be counter-conspiring here, yes yes uh, now . . . he gets involved watching another pyramidal fountain, this time of sweet Taittinger with no date on the label. Waiters and off-duty dealers sit like birds along the bar, staring. Noise in the place is incredible. A Welshman with an accordion stands on a table playing "Lady of Spain," in C, just zooming up and down that wheezebox like a maniac. Smoke hangs thick and swirling. Pipes glow in the murk. At least three fist-fights are in progress. The Prince game is difficult to locate any more. Girls crowd at the door, giggling and pointing. The light in the room has gone bear-brown with swarming uniforms. Slothrop, clutching his tankard, struggles to his feet, spins around once, falls with a crash into a floating crown-and-anchor game. Grace, he warns himself: grace. . . . Roisterers pick him up by the armpits and back pockets, and fling him in the direction of Sir Stephen Dodson-Truck. He makes his way on under a table, a lieutenant or two falling over him on route, through the odd pond of spilled bubbly, the odd slough of vomit, till he finds what he imagines to be Dodson-Truck's sand-filled cuffs.

"Hey," getting himself threaded among the legs of a chair, angling his head up to locate Dodson-Truck's face, haloed by a hanging fringe-shaded lamp. "Can you walk?"

Carefully swinging his eyes down on Slothrop, "Not sure, actually, that I can stand. . . ." They spend some time at the business of untangling Slothrop from the chair, then standing up, which is not without its complications—locating the door, aiming for it. . . . Staggering, propping each other up, they push through a bottle-wielding, walleyed, unbuttoned, roaring, white-faced and stomach-clutching mob, in among the lithe and perfumed audience of girls at the exit, all sweetly high, a decompression lock for the outside.

"Holy shit." This is the kind of sunset you hardly see any more, a 19th-century wilderness sunset, a few of which got set down, approximated, on canvas, landscapes of the American West by artists nobody ever heard of, when the land was still free and the eye innocent, and the presence of the Creator much more direct. Here it thunders now over the Mediterranean, high and lonely, this anachronism in primal red, in yellow purer than can be found anywhere today, a purity begging to be polluted . . . of course Empire took its way westward, what other way was there but into those virgin sunsets to penetrate and to foul?

But out at the horizon, out near the burnished edge of the world, who are these visitors standing . . . these robed figures—perhaps, at this distance, hundreds of miles tall—their faces, serene, unattached, like the Buddha's, bending over the sea, impassive, indeed, as the Angel that stood over Lübeck during the Palm Sunday raid, come that day neither to destroy nor to protect, but to bear witness to a game of seduction. It was the next-to-last London took before her submission, before that liaison that would bring her at length to the eruption and scarring of the wasting pox noted on Roger Mexico's map, latent in this love she shares with the night-going rake Lord Death . . . because sending the RAF to make a terror raid against civilian Lübeck was the unmistakable long look that said *hurry up and fuck me,* that brought the rockets hard and screaming, the A4s, which were to've been fired anyway, a bit sooner instead. . . .

What have the watchmen of world's edge come tonight to look for? deepening on now, monumental beings, stoical, on toward slag, toward ash the color the night will stabilize at, tonight . . . what is there grandiose enough to witness? only Slothrop here, and Sir Stephen, blithering along, crossing shadow after long prison-bar shadow cast by the tall trunks of palms lining the esplanade. The spaces between the shadows are washed a very warm sunset-red now, across grainy chocolate beach. There seems to be nothing happening of any moment. No traffic whispering in the circular driveways, no milliards of francs being wagered because of a woman or an entente of nations at any of the tables inside. Only the somewhat formal weeping of Sir Stephen, down now on one knee in the sand still warm from the day: soft and strangled cries of despair held in, so testifying to all the repression he ever underwent that even Slothrop can feel, in his own throat, sympathetic flashes of pain for the effort it is clearly costing the man. . . .

"Oh yes, yes you know, I, I can't. No. I assumed that you knew—but then why should they tell you? *They* all know. I'm an office joke. The people even know. Nora's been the sweetheart of the psychic crowd for years and years. That's always good for some bit of copy in the *News of the World*—"

"Oh! Yeah! Nora!—that's that dame that was caught that time with the kid who-who can *change his color*, right? Wow! Sure, that Nora Dodson-Truck! I knew your name was familiar—"

But Sir Stephen has gone on: ". . . had a son, yes we came complete with sensitive son, boy about your age. Frank . . . I think they sent him to Indo-China. They're very polite when I ask, very polite but, they won't let me find out where he is. . . . They're good chaps at Fitzmaurice House, Slothrop. They mean well. It's been, most of it's been my fault. . . . I did love Nora. I did. But there were other things. . . . Important things, I believed they were. I still do. I must. As she got along, you know . . . they do get that way. You know how they are, demanding, always trying to-to drag you into bed. I couldn't," shaking his head, his hair now incandescent orange in this twilight, "I couldn't. I'd climbed too far. Another branch. Couldn't climb back down to her. She-she might even have been happy with a, even a *touch* now and then. . . . Listen Slothrop, your girl, your Katje, sh-she's very *lovely*, you know."

"I know."

"Th-they think I don't *care*, any more. 'You can observe without passion.' Bastards . . . No I didn't mean that. . . . Slothrop, we're all such mechanical men. Doing our jobs. That's all we are. Listen—how do you think I *feel*? When you're off with her after every lesson. I'm an impotent *man*—all I have to look forward to is a book, Slothrop. A report to write . . ."

"Hey, Ace—"

"Don't get angry. I'm harmless. Go ahead hit me, I'll only fall over and bounce right up again. Watch." He demonstrates. "I care about you, both of you. I do care, believe me, Slothrop."

"O.K. Tell me what's going on."

"I *care!*"

"Fine, fine . . ."

"My 'function' is to observe you. That's my function. You like my function? You like it? *Your* 'function' . . . is, learn the rocket, inch by inch. *I* have . . . to send in a daily log of your progress. And that's all I know."

But that's not all. He's holding something back, something deep, and fool Slothrop is too drunk to get at it with any kind of style. "Me and Katje too? You looking through the keyhole?"

Sniffling, "What difference's it make? I'm the perfect man for it. Perfect. I can't even masturbate half the time . . . no nasty jissom getting all over their reports, you know. Wouldn't want that. Just a neuter, just a recording eye. . . . They're so cruel. I don't think they even know, really. . . . They aren't even sadists. . . . There's just *no passion at all.* . . ."

Slothrop puts a hand on his shoulder. The suit padding shifts and bunches over the warm bone beneath it. He doesn't know what to say, what to do: himself, he feels empty, and wants to sleep. . . . But Sir Stephen is on his knees, just about, quaking at the edge of it, to tell Slothrop a terrible secret, a fatal confidence concerning:

THE PENIS HE THOUGHT WAS HIS OWN

(lead tenor):	'Twas the penis, he thought-was, his own—
	Just a big playful boy of a bone . . .
	With a stout purple head,
	Sticking up from the bed,
	Where the girlies all played Telephone—
(bass):	Te-le-phone. . . .
(inner voices):	But They came through the hole in the night,
(bass):	And They sweet-talked it clear out of sight—
(inner voices):	Out of sight . . .
(tenor):	Now he sighs all alone,
	With a heartbroken moan,
	For the pe-nis, he thought-was, his, owwwwn!
(inner voices):	Was, his, own!

The figures out to sea have been attending, growing now even more windy and remote as the light goes cold and out. . . . They are so difficult to reach across to—difficult to grasp. Carroll Eventyr, trying to confirm the Lübeck angel, learned how difficult—he and his control Peter Sachsa both, floundering in the swamp between the worlds. Later on, in London, came the visit from that most ubiquitous of double agents, Sammy Hilbert-Spaess, whom everyone had thought in Stockholm, or was at Paraguay?

"Here then," the kindly scombroid face scanning Eventyr, quick as a fire-control dish antenna and even less mercy, "I thought I'd—"

"You thought you'd just check in."

"Telepathic too, God he's amazing i'n't he." But the fishy eyes will not let up. It is a rather bare room, the address behind Gallaho Mews ordinarily reserved for cash transactions. They have summoned Eventyr up from "The White Visitation." They know in London how to draw pentacles too, and cry conjurations, how to bring in exactly the ones they want. . . . The tabletop is crowded with glasses, smudged, whitish, emptied or with residues of deep brown and red drinks, with ashtrays and with debris from artificial flowers which old Sammy here has been plucking, unpeeling, twisting into mysterious curves and knots. Train-smoke blows in a partly opened window. One wall of the room, though blank, has been eroded at, over years, by shadows of operatives, as certain mirrors in public easing-places have been by the images of customers: a surface gathering character, like an old face. . . .

"But then you don't actually *talk* to him," ah, Sammy's so good at this, softly-softly, "I mean it's none of your telegraphers in the middle of the night having a bit of a chat sort of thing. . . ."

"No. No." Eventyr understanding now that they've been seeing transcripts of everything that comes through from Peter Sachsa—that what Eventyr himself gets to read is already censored. And that it may have been this way for a while now. . . . So relax, grow passive, watch for a shape to develop out of Sammy's talking, a shape that really Eventyr knows already, as we do working out acrostics— he's called up to London, but they aren't asking to be put in touch with anyone, so it's Sachsa himself they're interested in, and the purpose of this meeting is not to commission Eventyr, but to warn him. To put a part of his own hidden life under interdiction. Bits, tones of voice, choices of phrasing now come flying together: ". . . must've been quite a shock to find himself over there . . . had a Zaxa or two of me own to worry about . . . keep *you* out of the street at least . . . see how you're holding up, old Zaxa too of course, need to filter out *personalities* you see from the data, easier for us that way. . . ."

Out of the street? Everyone knows how Sachas died. But no one knows why he was out there that day, what led up to it. And what Sammy is telling Eventyr here is: *Don't ask.*

Then will they try to get to Nora too? If there are analogies here, if Eventyr does, somehow, map on to Peter Sachsa, then does Nora Dodson-Truck become the woman Sachsa loved, Leni Pökler? Will the interdiction extend to Nora's smoky voice and steady hands, and is Eventyr to be kept, for the duration, perhaps for his life, under some very sophisticated form of house arrest, for crimes that will never be told him?

Nora still carries on her Adventure, her "Ideology of the Zero," firm among the stoneswept hair of the last white guardians at the last stepoff into the black, into the radiant. . . . But where will Leni be now? Where will she have wandered off to, carrying her child, and her dreams that will not grow up? Either we didn't mean to lose her—either it was an ellipsis in our care, in what some of us will even swear is our love, or someone has taken her, deliberately, for reasons being kept secret, and Sachsa's death is part of it too. She has swept with her wings another life—not husband Franz, who dreamed of, prayed for exactly such a taking but instead is being kept for something quite different—Peter Sachsa, who was passive in a different way . . . is there some mistake? Do They never make mistakes, or . . . why is he here rushing with her toward her own end (as indeed Eventyr has been sucked along in Nora's furious wake) her body blocking from his sight everything that lies ahead, the slender girl strangely grown oaken, broad, maternal . . . all he has to go by is the debris of their time sweeping in behind from either side, looping away in long helices, into the dusty

invisible where a last bit of sunlight lies on the stones of
the road.... Yes: however ridiculously, he is acting out
Franz Pökler's fantasy for him, here crouched on her back,
very small, being *taken:* taken forward into an aether-wind
whose smell ... no *not that smell* last encountered just before his birth ... the void long before he ought to be
remembering ... which means, if it's here again ... then
... *then* ...

They are being pushed backward by a line of police.
Peter Sachsa is jammed inside it, trying to keep his footing, no escape possible ... Leni's face moving, restless,
against the window of the Hamburg Flyer, concrete roads,
pedestals, industrial towers of the Mark flying away at
over a hundred miles an hour the perfect background,
brown, blurred, any least mistake, in the points, in the
roadbed at this speed and they're done for ... her skirt is
pulled up in back, the bare bottoms of her thighs, marked
red from the train seat, turn toward him ... yes ... in
the imminence of disaster, yes, whoever's watching yes....
"Leni, where are you?" She was at his elbow not ten
seconds ago. They'd agreed beforehand to try and keep
together. But there are two sorts of movement out here—
as often as the chance displacements of strangers, across a
clear skirmish-line from the Force, will bring together
people who'll remain that way for a time, in love that can
even make the oppression seem a failure, so too love, here
in the street, can be taken centrifugally apart again: faces
seen for the last time here, words spoken idly, over your
shoulder, taking for granted she's there, already last
words—"Will Walter be bringing wine tonight? I forgot
to—" it's a private joke, his forgetting, going around in
some adolescent confusion, hopelessly in love too by now
with the little girl. She is his refuge from society, parties,
clients ... often she is his sanity. He's taken to sitting for
a little while each night beside her bed, late at night,
watching her sleep, with her bottom up in the air and
face in the pillow ... the purity, the *rightness* of it ...
But her mother, in her own sleep, grinds her teeth often
these nights, frowns, talks in a tongue he cannot admit he
might, some time or place, know and speak fluently. Just
in this past week ... what does he know of politics? but
he can see that she has crossed a threshold, found a

branching of the time, where he might not be able to follow—

"You're her mother . . . what if they arrest you, what happens to her?"

"That's what they—Peter can't you see, they *want* a great swollen tit with some atrophied excuse for a human, bleating around somewhere in its shadows. How can I be *human* for her? Not her *mother*. 'Mother,' that's a civil-service category, Mothers work for *Them!* They're the policemen of the soul . . ." her face darkened, Judaized by the words she speaks, not because it's out loud but because she means it, and she's right. Against her faith, Sachsa can see the shallows of his own life, the bathtub stagnancy of those soirees where for years not even the faces changed . . . too many tepid years. . . .

"But I love you . . ." she brushes hair back from his sweating forehead, they lie beneath a window through which street- and advertising-light blow constantly, lapping at their skins, at their roundings and shadows, with spectra colder than those of the astrologers' Moon. . . . "You don't have to be anything you aren't, Peter. I wouldn't be here if I didn't love who you are. . . ."

Did she goad him into the street, was she the death of him? In his view from the other side, no. In love, words can be taken too many ways, that's all. But he does feel he was sent across, for some particular reason. . . .

And Ilse, vamping him with her dark eyes. She can say his name, but often, to flirt with him, she won't, or she'll call him *Mama*.

"No-no, that's Mama. I'm Peter. Remember? Peter."

"Mama."

Leni only gazes, a smile held between her lips almost, he must say, smug, allowing the mix-up in names to fall, to set up male reverberations she can't be ignorant of. If she doesn't want him out in the street, why does she only keep her silence at such moments?

"I was only glad she wasn't calling *me* Mama," Leni thought she'd explain. But that's too close to ideology, it's nothing he can be comfortable with yet. He doesn't know how to listen to talk like that as more than slogans strung together: hasn't learned to hear with the revolutionary heart, won't ever, in fact, be given enough time to gather

a revolutionary heart from the bleak comradely love of
the others, no, no time for it now, or for anything but one
more breath, the rough breath of a man growing afraid
in the street, not even enough time to lose his fear in the
time-honored way, no, because here comes Schutzmann
Jöche, truncheon already in backswing, the section of
Communist head moving into view for him stupidly, so
unaware of him and his power . . . the Schutzmann's first
clear shot all day . . . oh, his timing is perfect, he feels it
in arm and out the club no longer flabby at his side but
tensed back now around in a muscular curve, at the top
of his swing, peak of potential energy . . . far below that
gray vein in the man's temple, frail as parchment, standing
out so clear, twitching already with its next to last pulse-
beat . . . and, SHIT! Oh—*how*—

How beautiful!

During the night, Sir Stephen vanishes from the Casino.
But not before telling Slothrop that his erections are of
high interest to Fitzmaurice House.

Then in the morning Katje comes storming in madder
than a wet hen, to tell Slothrop that Sir Stephen's gone.
Suddenly everybody is telling Slothrop things, and he's
barely awake. Rain rattles at the shutters and windows.
Monday mornings, upset stomachs, good-bys . . . he blinks
out at the misted sea, the horizon mantled in gray, palms
gleaming in the rain, heavy and wet and very green. It
may be that the champagne is still with him—for ten
extraordinary seconds there's nothing in his field but simple
love for what he's seeing.

Then, perversely aware of it, he turns away, back into
the room. Time to play with Katje, now. . . .

Her face is as pale as her hair. A rain-witch. Her hat
brim makes a chic creamy green halo around her face.

"Well, he's gone then." Keenness of this order might
work to provoke her. "It's too bad. Then again—maybe
it's good."

"Never mind him. How much do you know, Slothrop?"

"What's that mean, never mind him? What do you do,
just throw people away?"

"Do you want to find out?"

He stands twisting his mustache. "Tell me about it."

"You bastard. You've sabotaged the whole thing, with your clever little collegiate drinking game."

"What whole thing, Katje?"

"What did he tell you?" She moves a step closer. Slothrop watches her hands, thinking of army judo instructors he's seen. It occurs to him he's naked and also, hmm, seems to be getting a hardon here, look out, Slothrop. And nobody here to note it, or speculate why. . . .

"Sure didn't tell me you knew any of that *judo*. Must of taught you it in that *Holland*, huh? Sure—little things," singing in descending childish thirds, "give you away, you know. . . ."

"Aahh—" exasperated she rushes in, aims a chop at his head which he's able to dodge—goes diving in under her arm, lifts her in a fireman's carry, throws her against the bed and comes after her. She kicks a sharp heel at his cock, which is what she should've done in the first place. Her timing, in fact, is drastically off all through this, else she would likely be handing Slothrop's ass to him . . . it may be that she wants her foot to miss, only scraping Slothrop along the leg as he swerves now, grabs her by the hair and twists an arm behind her, pushing her, face-down, on the bed. Her skirt is up over her ass, her thighs squirming underneath him, his penis in terrific erection.

"Listen, cunt, don't make me lose my temper with you, got no problems at all hitting women, I'm the Cagney of the French Riviera, so look out."

"I'll kill you—"

"What—and sabotage the whole thing?"

Katje turns her head and sinks her teeth in his forearm, up near the elbow where the Pentothal needles used to go in. "Ow, *shit*—" he lets go the arm he's been twisting, pulls down underwear, takes her by one hip and pentrates her from behind, reaching under to pinch nipples, paw at her clitoris, rake his nails along inside her thighs, Mister Technique here, not that it matters, they're both ready to come—Katje first, screaming into the pillow, Slothrop a second or two later. He lies on top of her, sweating, taking great breaths, watching her face turned ¾ away, not even a profile, but the terrible Face That Is No Face, gone too abstract, unreachable: the notch of eye socket, but never the labile eye, only the anonymous curve of cheek, convexity of mouth, a noseless mask of the Other Order of Being, of Katje's being—the lifeless nonface that is the only face of hers he really knows, or will ever remember.

"Hey, Katje," 's all he sez.

"Mm." But here's only her old residual bitterness again, and they are not, after all, to be lovers in parachutes of sunlit voile, lapsing gently, hand in hand, down to anything meadowed or calm. Surprised?

She has moved away, releasing his cock into the cold room. "What's it like in London, Slothrop? When the rockets come down?"

"What?" After fucking he usually likes to lie around, just smoke a cigarette, think about food, "Uh, you don't know it's there till it's there. Gee, till *after* it's there. If it doesn't hit you, then you're O.K. till the next one. If you hear the explosion, you know you must be alive."

"That's how you know you're alive."

"Right." She sits up, pulling underpants back up and skirt back down, goes to the mirror, starts rearranging her hair. "Let's hear the boundary-layer temperatures. While you're getting dressed."

"Boundary-layer temperature T sub e, what *is* this? rises exponentially till Brennschluss, around 70 miles range, a-and then there's a sharp cusp, 1200 degrees, then it drops a little, minimum of 1050, till you get out of the atmosphere, then there's another cusp at 1080 degrees. Stays pretty steady till re-entry," blablabla. The bridge music here, bright with xylophones, is based on some old favorite that will comment, ironically but gently, on what is transpiring—a tune such as "School Days, School Days," or "Come, Josephine, in My Flying Machine," or even "There'll Be a HOT TIME in the Old Town Tonite!" take your pick—slowing and fading to a glassed-in porch downstairs, Slothrop and Katje tête-à-tête, alone except for a number of musicians in the corner groaning and shaking their heads, plotting how to get César Flebótomo to pay them for a change. Bad gig, bad gig. . . . Rain bats against the glass, lemon and myrtle trees outside shake in the wind. Over croissants, strawberry jam, real butter, real coffee, she has him running through the flight profile in terms of wall temperature and Nusselt heart-transfer coefficients, computing in his head from Reynolds numbers she flashes him . . . equations of motion, damping, restoring moments . . . methods of computing Brennschluss by IG and radio methods . . . equations, transformations . . .

"Now jet expansion angles. I'll give you altitude, you tell me the angle."

"Katje, why don't you tell *me* the angle?"

She was pleased, once, to think of a peacock, courting, fanning his tail . . . she saw it in the colors that moved in the flame as it rose off the platform, scarlet, orange, iridescent green . . . there were Germans, even SS troops, who called the rocket *Der Pfau*. 'Pfau Zwei.' Ascending, programmed in a ritual of love . . . at Brennschluss it is done—the Rocket's purely feminine counterpart, the zero point at the center of its target, has submitted. All the rest will happen according to laws of ballistics. The Rocket is helpless in it. Something else has taken over. Something beyond what was designed in.

Katje has understood the great airless arc as a clear allusion to certain secret lusts that drive the planet and herself, and Those who use her—over its peak and down, plunging, burning, toward a terminal orgasm . . . which is certainly nothing she can tell Slothrop.

They sit listening to gusts of rain that's nearly sleet. Winter gathers, breathes, deepens. A roulette ball goes rattling, somewhere back in another room. She's running. Why? Has he come too close again? He tries to remember if she always needed to talk this way, in draw-shots, rebounding first before she could touch him. Fine time to start asking. He's counter-conspiring in the dark, jimmying doors at random, no telling what'll come out. . . .

Dark basalt pushes up out of the sea. A vaporous scrim hangs across the headland and its châteaux, turning it all to a grainy antique postcard. He touches her hand, moves his fingers up her bare arm, reaching. . . .

"Hm?"

"Come on upstairs," sez Slothrop.

She may have hesitated, but so briefly that he didn't notice: "What have we been talking about all this time?"

"That A4 rocket."

She looks at him for a long time. At first he thinks she's about to laugh at him. Then it looks like she'll cry. He doesn't understand. "Oh, Slothrop. No. You don't want

me. What they're after may, but *you* don't. No more than
A4 wants London. But I don't think they know . . . about
other selves . . . yours or the Rocket's . . . no. No more than
you do. If you can't understand it now, at least remember.
That's all I can do for you."

They go back up to her room again: cock, cunt, the
Monday rain at the windows. . . . Slothrop spends the rest
of the morning and early afternoon studying Professors
Schiller on regenerative cooling, Wagner on combustion
equations, Pauer and Beck on exhaust gases and burning
efficiency. And a pornography of blueprints. At noon the
rain stops. Katje is off on chores of her own. Slothrop
passes a few hours downstairs in the bar, waiters who
catch his eye smiling, holding up bottles of champagne,
wiggling them invitingly—"No, merci, non. . . ." He's
trying to memorize the organization charts at that Peenemünde.

As light begins to spill from the overcast sky, he and
Katje are out taking a walk, an end-of-the-day stroll along
the esplanade. Her hand is gloveless and icy in his, her
narrow black coat making her taller, her long silences helping to thin her for him nearly to fog. . . . They stop, lean
against a railing, he watching the midwinter sea, she the
blind and chilly Casino poised behind them. Colorless
clouds slide by, endlessly, in the sky.

"I was thinking of the time I came in on you. That afternoon." He can't quite bring himself to get specific out
loud, but she knows he means the Himmler-Spielsaal.

She has looked around sharply. "So was I."

Their breaths are torn into phantoms out to sea. She
has her hair combed high today in a pompadour, her fair
eyebrows, plucked to wings, darkened, eyes rimmed in
black, only the outboard few lashes missed and left
blonde. Cloudlight comes slanting down across her face,
taking away color, leaving little more than a formal snapshot, the kind that might appear on a passport. . . .

"A-and you were so far away then . . . I couldn't reach
you. . . ."

Then. Something like pity comes into her face and goes
again. But her whisper is lethal and bright as sudden wire:
"Maybe you'll find out. Maybe in one of their bombed-out
cities beside one of their rivers or forests, even one day in

the rain, it will come to you. You'll remember the Himmler-Spielsaal, and the skirt I was wearing ... memory will dance for you, and you can even make it my voice saying what I couldn't say then. Or now." Oh what is it she smiles here to him, only for that second? already gone. Back to the mask of no luck, no future—her face's rest state, preferred, easiest. . . .

They are standing among black curly skeletons of iron benches, on the empty curve of this esplanade, banked much more steeply than the waking will ever need: vertiginous, trying to spill them into the sea and be rid of this. The day has grown colder. Neither of them can stay balanced for long, every few seconds one or the other must find a new footing. He reaches and turns up the collar of her coat, holds her cheeks then in his palms ... is he trying to bring back the color of flesh? He looks down trying to see into her eyes, and is puzzled to find tears coming up to fill each one, soaking in among her lashes, mascara bleeding out in fine black swirls ... translucent stones, trembling in their sockets. . . .

Waves crash and drag at the stones of the beach. The harbor has broken out in whitecaps, so brilliant they can't be gathering their light from this drab sky. Here it is again, that identical-looking Other World—is he gonna have *this* to worry about, now? What th'—lookit these *trees*—each long frond hanging, stung, dizzying, in laborious drypoint against the sky, each *so perfectly placed*. . . .

She has moved her thighs and the points of her hips up to touch him, through her coat—it might still, after all, be to help bring him back—her breath a white scarf, her tear-trails, winter-lit, ice. She feels warm. But it's not enough. Never was—nope, he understands all right, she's been meaning to go for a long time. Braced for the wind the whitecaps imply, or for the tilt of the pavement, they hold each other. He kisses her eyes, feels his cock again begin to swell with good old, bad old—old, anyhow—lust.

Out at sea a single clarinet begins to play, a droll melody joined in on after a few bars by guitars and mandolins. Birds huddle bright-eyed on the beach. Katje's heart lightens, a little, at the sound. Slothrop doesn't yet have the European reflexes to clarinets, he still thinks of Benny Goodman and not of clowns or circuses—but wait . . .

aren't these *kazoos* coming? Yeah, a *lotta* kazoos! A Kazoo *Band!*

Late that night, back in her room, she wears a red gown of heavy silk. Two tall candles burn an indefinite distance behind her. He feels the change. After making love she lies propped on an elbow watching him, breathing deep, dark nipples riding with the swell, as buoys ride on the white sea. But a patina has formed on her eyes: he can't even see her accustomed retreat, this last time, dimmed, graceful, to the corner of some inner room. . . .

"Katje."

"Sshh," raking dreamy fingernails down the morning, over the Côte d'Azur toward Italy. Slothrop wants to sing, decides to, but then can't think of anything that'd work. He reaches an arm, without wetting his fingers snuffs the candles. She kisses the pain. It hurts even more. He falls asleep in her arms. When he wakes she is gone, completely, most of her never-worn clothes still in the closet, blisters and a little wax on his fingers, and one cigarette, stubbed out before its time in an exasperated fishhook. . . . She never wasted cigarettes. She must have sat, smoking, watching him while he slept . . . until something, he'll never be asking her what, triggered her, made it impossible to stay till cigarette's end. He straightens it out, finishes it, no point wasting smokes is there, with a war on. . . .

□

"Ordinarily in our behavior, we react not singly, but complexly, to fit the ever present contents of our environment. In old people," Pavlov was lecturing at the age of 83, "that matter is altogether different. Concentrating on one stimulus we exclude by negative induction other collateral and simultaneous stimuli because they often do not suit the circumstances, are not complementary reactions in the given setting."

> Thus [Pointsman never shows these excursions of his to
>   anyone], reaching for some flower on my table,
> I know the cool mosaic of my room
> Begin its slow, inhibitory dissolve

Around the bloom, the stimulus, the need
That brighter burns, as brightness, quickly sucked
From objects all around, now concentrates
(Yet less than blinding), focuses to flame.
Whilst there yet, in the room's hypnotic evening,
The others lurk—the books, the instruments,
The old man's clothes, an old *gorodki* stick,
Glazed now but with their presences. Their spirits,
Or memories I kept of where they were,
Are canceled, for this moment, by the flame:
The reach toward the frail and waiting flower . . .
And so, one of them—pen, or empty glass—
Is knocked from where it was, perhaps to roll
Beyond the blank frontiers of memory . . .
Yet this, be clear, is no "senile distraction,"
But concentrating, such as younger men
Can easily and laughing dodge, their world
Presenting too much more than one mean loss—
And out here, eighty-three, the cortex slack,
Excitatory processes eased to cinders
By Inhibition's tweaking, callused fingers,
Each time my room begins its blur I feel
I've looked in on some city's practice blackout
(Such as must come, should Germany keep on
That road of madness). Each light, winking out . . .
Except at last for one bright, stubborn bloom
The Wardens cannot quench. Or not this time.

The weekly briefings at "The White Visitation" are all but abandoned. Hardly anyone sees the old Brigadier about these days. There is evidence of a budgetary insecurity begun to filter in among the cherub-crusted halls and nooks of the PISCES facility.

"The old man's funking," cries Myron Grunton, none too stable himself these days. The Slothrop group are gathered for their regular meeting in the ARF wing. "He'll shoot down the whole scheme, all it'll take is one bad night. . . ."

A degree of well-bred panic can be observed among those present. In the background, laboratory assistants move about cleaning up dog shit and calibrating instruments. Rats and mice, white and black and a few shades of gray, run clattering on their wheels in a hundred cages.

Pointsman is the only one here maintaining his calm. He appears unruffled and strong. His lab coats have even begun lately to take on a Savile Row serenity, suppressed waist, flaring vents, finer material, rather rakishly notched lapels. In this parched and fallow time, he gushes affluence. After the baying has quieted down at last, he speaks, soothing: "There's no danger."

"No danger?" screams Aaron Throwster, and the lot of them are off again muttering and growling.

"Slothrop's knocked out Dodson-Truck and the girl in one day!"

"The whole thing's falling apart, Pointsman!"

"Since Sir Stephen came back, Fitzmaurice House has dropped out of the scheme, and there's been embarrassing inquiries down from Duncan Sandys—"

"That's the P.M.'s son-in-law, Pointsman, not good, not good!"

"We've already begun to run into a deficit—"

"Funding," IF you can keep your head, "is available, and will be coming in before long . . . certainly before we run into any serious trouble. Sir Stephen, far from being 'knocked out,' is quite happily at work in Fitzmaurice House, and is At Home there should any of you wish to confirm. Miss Borgesius is still active on the program, and Mr. Duncan Sandys is having all his questions answered. But best of all, we *are* budgeted well into fiscal '46 before anything like a deficit begins to rear its head."

"Your Interested Parties again?" sez Rollo Groast.

"Ah, I noticed Clive Mossmoon from Imperial Chemicals closeted with you day before yesterday," Edwin Treacle mentions now. "Clive and I took an organic chemistry course or two together back at Manchester. Is ICI one of our, ah, sponsors, Pointsman?"

"No," smoothly, "Mossmoon, actually, is working out of Malet Street these days. I'm afraid we were up to nothing more sinister than a bit of routine coordination over this Schwarzkommando business."

"The hell you were. I happen to know Clive's at ICI, managing some sort of polymer research."

They stare at each other. One is lying, or bluffing, or both are, or all of the above. But whatever it is Pointsman has a slight advantage. By facing squarely the extinction of his program, he has gained a great bit of Wisdom: that if there is a life force operating in Nature, still there is

nothing so analogous in a bureaucracy. Nothing so mystical. It all comes down, as it must, to the desires of individual men. Oh, and women too of course, bless their
empty little heads. But survival depends on having strong
enough desires—on knowing the System better than the
other chap, and how to use it. It's work, that's all it is, and
there's no room for any extrahuman anxieties—they only
weaken, effeminize the will: a man either indulges them,
or fights to win, und so weiter. "I do wish ICI *would*
finance part of this," Pointsman smiles.

"Lame, lame," mutters the younger Dr. Groast.

"What's it matter?" cries Aaron Throwster. "If the old
man gets moody at the wrong time this whole show can
prang."

"Brigadier Pudding will not go back on any of his
commitments," Pointsman very steady, calm, "we have
made arrangements with him. The details aren't important."

They never are, in these meetings of his. Treacle has
been comfortably sidetracked onto the Mossmoon Issue,
Rollo Groast's carping asides never get as far as serious
opposition, and are useful in presenting the appearance of
open discussion, as are Throwster's episodes of hysteria
for distracting the others.... So the gathering breaks up,
the conspirators head off for coffee, wives, whisky, sleep,
indifference. Webley Silvernail stays behind to secure his
audiovisual gear and loot the ashtrays. Dog Vanya, back
for the moment in an ordinary state of mind if not of kidneys (which are vulnerable after a while to bromide
therapy), has been allowed a short break from the test
stand, and he goes sniffing now over to the cage of Rat
Ilya. Ilya puts his muzzle against the galvanized wire, and
the two pause this way, nose to nose, life and life....
Silvernail, puffing on a hook-shaped stub, lugging a 16 mm
projector, leaves ARF by way of a long row of cages,
exercise wheels strobing under the fluorescent lights. Careful youse guys, here comes da screw. Aw he's O.K. Looie,
he's a regular guy. The others laugh. Den what's he doin'
in here, huh? The long white lights buzz overhead. Gray-
smocked assistants chat, smoke, linger at various routines.
Look out, Lefty, dey're comin' fer you dis time. Watch dis,
chuckles Mouse Alexei, when he picks me up I'm gonna

shit, right'n his hand! Better not hey, ya know what happened ta Slug, don'tcha? Dey *fried* him when he did dat,
man, da foist time he fucked up runnin' dat maze. A
hundrit volts. Dey said it wuz a "accident." Yeah . . . *sure*
it wuz!

From overhead, from a German camera-angle, it occurs
to Webley Silvernail, this lab here is also a maze, i'n't it
now . . . behaviorists run these aisles of tables and consoles
just like rats 'n' mice. Reinforcement for them is not a
pellet of food, but a successful experiment. But who
watches from above, who notes *their* responses? Who hears
the small animals in the cages as they mate, or nurse, or
communicate through the gray quadrilles, or, as now, begin
to sing . . . come out of their enclosures, in fact, grown to
Webley Silvernail–size (though none of the lab people
seem to be noticing) to dance him down the long aisles
and metal apparatus, with conga drums and a peppy tropical orchestra taking up the very popular beat and melody
of:

PAVLOVIA (BEGUINE)

> It was spring in Pavlovia-a-a,
> I was lost, in a maze . . .
> Lysol breezes perfumed the air,
> I'd been searching for days.
> I found you, in a cul-de-sac,
> As bewildered as I—
> We touched noses, and suddenly
> My heart learned how to fly!
>
> So, together, we found our way,
> Shared a pellet, or two . . .
> Like an evening in some café,
> Wanting nothing, but you . . .
>
> Autumn's come, to Pavlovia-a-a,
> Once again, I'm alone—
> Finding sorrow by millivolts,
> Back to neurons and bone.
> And I think of our moments then,
> Never knowing your name—
> Nothing's left in Pavlovia,
> But the maze, and the game. . . .

They dance in flowing skeins. The rats and mice form circles, curl their tails in and out to make chrysanthemum and sunburst patterns, eventually all form into the shape of a single giant mouse, at whose eye Silvernail poses with a smile, arms up in a V, sustaining the last note of the song, along with the giant rodent-chorus and orchestra. One of PWD's classic propaganda leaflets these days urges the Volksgrenadier: SETZT V-2 EIN!, with a footnote, explaining that "V-2" means to raise both arms in "honorable surrender"—more gallows-humor—and telling how to say, phonetically, "ei ssörrender." Is Webley's V here for victory, or ssörrender?

They have had their moment of freedom. Webley has only been a guest star. Now it's back to the cages and the rationalized forms of death—death in the service of the one species cursed with the knowledge that it will die. . . . "I would set you free, if I knew how. But it isn't free out here. All the animals, the plants, the minerals, even other kinds of men, are being broken and reassembled every day, to preserve an elite few, who are the loudest to theorize on freedom, but the least free of all. I can't even give you hope that it will be different someday—that They'll come out, and forget death, and lose Their technology's elaborate terror, and stop using every other form of life without mercy to keep what haunts men down to a tolerable level—and be like you instead, simply here, simply alive. . . ." The guest star retires down the corridors.

Lights, all but a sprinkling, are out at "The White Visitation." The sky tonight is deep blue, blue as a Navy greatcoat, and the clouds in it are amazingly white. The wind is keen and cold. Old Brigadier Pudding, trembling, slips from his quarters down the back stairs, by a route only he knows, through the vacant orangery in the starlight, along a gallery hung to lace dandies, horses, ladies with hard-boiled eggs for eyes, out a small entresol (point of *maximum danger* . . .) and into a lumber-room, whose stacks of junk and random blacknesses, even this far from his childhood, are good for a chill, out again and down a set of metal steps, singing, he hopes quietly, for courage:

Wash me in the water
That you wash your dirty daughter,
And I shall be whiter than the whitewash on the wall. . . .

at last to D Wing, where the madmen of the '30s persist. The night attendant is asleep under the *Daily Herald*. He is a coarse-looking fellow, and has been reading the leader. It is an indication of things to come, next election? Oh, dear . . .

But orders are to let the Brigadier pass. The old man tiptoes by, breathing fast. Mucus rattles back in his throat. He's at the age where mucus is a daily companion, a culture of mucus among the old, mucus in a thousand manifestations, appearing in clots by total surprise on a friend's tablecloth, rimming his breath-passages at night in hard venturi, enough to darken the outlines of dreams and send him awake, pleading. . . .

A voice from some cell too distant for us to locate intones: "I am blessed Metatron. I am keeper of the Secret. I am guardian of the Throne. . . ." In here, the more disturbing Whig excesses have been chiseled away or painted over. No point disturbing the inmates. All is neutral tones, soft draperies, Impressionist prints on the walls. Only the marble floor has been left, and under the bulbs it gleams like water. Old Pudding must negotiate half a dozen offices or anterooms before reaching his destination. It hasn't yet been a fortnight, but there is already something of ritual to this, of iteration. Each room will hold a single unpleasantness for him: a test he must pass. He wonders if Pointsman hasn't set these up too. Of course, of course he must . . . how did the young bastard ever find out? Have I been talking in m' sleep? Have they been slipping in at night with their truth serums to—and just at the clear emergence of the thought, here is his first test tonight. In the first room: a hypodermic outfit has been left lying on a table. Very clear and shining, with the rest of the room slightly out of focus. Yes mornings I felt terribly groggy, couldn't wake, after dreaming—were they dreams? I was talking. . . . But it's all he remembers, talking while someone else was there listening. . . . He is shivering with fear, and his face is whiter than whitewash.

In the second antechamber is an empty red tin that held coffee. The brand name is Savarin. He understands that it means to say "Severin." Oh, the filthy, the mocking scoundrel. . . . But these are not malignant puns against an intended sufferer so much as a sympathetic magic, a repetition high and low of some prevailing form (as, for instance,

no sane demolition man at his evening dishwater will wash
a spoon between two cups, or even between a glass and a
plate, for fear of the Trembler it implies . . . because it's a
trembler-tongue he really holds, poised between its two
fatal contacts, in fingers aching with having been so suddenly reminded). . . . In the third, a file drawer is left ajar,
a stack of case histories partly visible, and an open copy of
Krafft-Ebing. In the fourth, a human skull. His excitement
grows. In the fifth, a Malacca cane. I've been in more wars
for England than I can remember . . . haven't I paid
enough? Risked it all for them, time after time. . . . Why
must they torment an old man? In the sixth chamber,
hanging from the overhead, is a tattered tommy up on
White Sheet Ridge, field uniform burned in Maxim holes
black-rimmed as the eyes of Cléo de Mérode, his own left
eye shot away, the corpse beginning to stink . . . no . . . no!
an overcoat, someone's old coat that's all, left on a hook
in the wall . . . but couldn't he *smell* it? Now mustard
gas comes washing in, into his brain with a fatal buzz
as dreams will when we don't want them, or when we
are suffocating. A machine-gun on the German side
sings *dum diddy da da,* an English weapon answers
dum dum, and the night tightens coiling round his body,
just before H-Hour. . . .

At the seventh cell, his knuckles feeble against the dark
oak, he knocks. The lock, remotely, electrically commanded, slams open with an edge of echo trailing. He
enters, and closes the door behind him. The cell is in semi-
darkness, with only a scented candle burning back in a
corner that seems miles away. She waits for him in a tall
Adam chair, white body and black uniform-of-the-night.
He drops to his knees.

"Domina Nocturna . . . shining mother and last love . . .
your servant Ernest Pudding, reporting as ordered."

In these war years, the focus of a woman's face is her
mouth. Lipstick, among these tough and too often shallow
girls, prevails like blood. Eyes have been left to weather
and to tears: these days, with so much death hidden in the
sky, out under the sea, among the blobs and smears of
recco photographs, most women's eyes are only functional.
But Pudding comes out of a different time, and Pointsman
has considered this detail too. The Brigadier's lady has

Un Perm' au Casino Hermann Goering 271

spent an hour at her vanity mirror with mascara, liner, shadow, and pencil, lotions and rouges, brushes and tweezers, consulting from time to time a looseleaf album filled with photographs of the reigning beauties of thirty and forty years ago, so that her reign these nights may be authentic if not—it is for her state of mind as well as his— legitimate. Her blonde hair is tucked and pinned beneath a thick wig. When she sits with her head down, forgetting the regal posture, the hair comes forward, over her shoulders, below her breasts. She is naked now, except for a long sable cape and black boots with court heels. Her only jewelry is a silver ring with an artificial ruby not cut to facets but still in the original boule, an arrogant gout of blood, extended now, waiting his kiss.

His clipped mustache bristles, trembling, across her fingers. She has filed her nails to long points and polished them the same red as her ruby. Their ruby. In this light the nails are almost black. "That's enough. Get ready."

She watches him undress, medals faintly jingling, starch shirt rattling. She wants a cigarette desperately, but her instructions are not to smoke. She tries to keep her hands still. "What are you thinking, Pudding?"

"Of the night we first met." The mud stank. The Archies were chugging in the darkness. His men, his poor sheep, had taken gas that morning. He was alone. Through the periscope, underneath a star shell that hung in the sky, he saw her . . . and though he was hidden, she saw Pudding. Her face was pale, she was dressed all in black, she stood in No-man's Land, the machine guns raked their patterns all around her, but she needed no protection. "They knew you, Mistress. They were your own."

"And so were you."

"You called to me, you said, 'I shall never leave you. You belong to me. We shall be together, again and again, though it may be years between. And you will always be at my service.'"

He is on his knees again, bare as a baby. His old man's flesh creeps coarse-grained in the light from the candle. Old scars and new welts group here and there over his skin. His penis stands at present arms. She smiles. At her command, he crawls forward to kiss her boots. He smells wax and leather, and can feel her toes flexing beneath his

tongue, through the black skin. From the corner of his
eye, on a little table, he can see the remains of her early
evening meal, the edge of a plate, the tops of two bottles,
mineral water, French wine. . . .

"Time for pain now, Brigadier. You shall have twelve of
the best, if your offering tonight pleases me."

Here is his worst moment. She has refused him before.
His memories of the Salient do not interest her. She doesn't
seem to care for mass slaughter as much as for myth, and
personal terror . . . but please . . . please let her accept. . . .

"At Badajoz," whispering humbly, "during the war in
Spain . . . a bandera of Franco's Legion advanced on the
city, singing their regimental hymn. They sang of the bride
they had taken. It was you, Mistress: they-they were proclaiming you as their bride. . . ."

She's silent for a bit, making him wait. At last, eyes
holding his, she smiles, the component of evil in it she has
found he needs taking care of itself as usual: "Yes. . . .
Many of them did become my bridegrooms that day," she
whispers, flexing the bright cane. There seems to be a
winter wind in the room. Her image threatens to shake
apart into separate flakes of snow. He loves to listen to her
speak, hers is the voice that found him from the broken
rooms of the Flemish villages, he knows, he can tell from
the accent, the girls who grew old in the Low Countries,
whose voices went corrupted from young to old, gay to
indifferent, as that war drew out, season into ever more
bitter season. . . . "I took their brown Spanish bodies to
mine. They were the color of the dust, and the twilight,
and of meats roasted to a perfect texture . . . most of them
were so very young. A summer day, a day of love: one of
the most poignant I ever knew. Thank you. You shall have
your pain tonight."

It's a part of her routine she can enjoy, at least. Though
she has never read any classic British pornography, she
does feel herself, sure as a fish, well in the local mainstream. Six on the buttocks, six more across the nipples.
Whack where's that Gourd Surprise now? Eh? She likes
the way the blood leaps to cross last night's welts. Often
it's all she can do to keep from moaning herself at each of
his grunts of pain, two voices in a dissonance which would
be much less accidental than it sounded. . . . Some nights

she's gagged him with a ceremonial sash, bound him with a gold-tasseled fourragère or his own Sam Browne. But tonight he lies humped in the floor at her feet, his withered ass elevated for the cane, bound by nothing but his need for pain, for something real, something pure. They have taken him so far from his simple nerves. They have stuffed paper illusions and military euphemisms between him and this truth, this rare decency, this moment at her scrupulous feet . . . no it's not guilt here, not so much as amazement—that he could have listened to so many years of ministers, scientists, doctors each with his specialized lies to tell, when she was here all the time, sure in her ownership of his failing body, his true body: undisguised by uniform, un-cluttered by drugs to keep from him her communiqués of vertigo, nausea and pain. . . . Above all, pain. The clearest poetry, the endearment of greatest worth. . . .

He struggles to his knees to kiss the instrument. She stands over him now, legs astride, pelvis cocked forward, fur cape held apart on her hips. He dares to gaze up at her cunt, that fearful vortex. Her pubic hair has been dyed black for the occasion. He sighs, and lets escape a small shameful groan.

"Ah . . . yes, I know." She laughs. "Poor mortal Brigadier, I know. It is my last mystery," stroking with fingernails her labia, "you cannot ask a woman to reveal her last mystery, now, can you?"

"Please . . ."

"No. Not tonight. Kneel here and take what I give you."

Despite himself—already a reflex—he glances quickly over at the bottles on the table, the plates, soiled with juices of meat, Hollandaise, bits of gristle and bone. . . . Her shadow covers his face and upper torso, her leather boots creak softly as thigh and abdominal muscles move, and then in a rush she begins to piss. He opens his mouth to catch the stream, choking, trying to keep swallowing, feeling warm urine dribble out the corners of his mouth and down his neck and shoulders, submerged in the hissing storm. When she's done he licks the last few drops from his lips. More cling, golden clear, to the glossy hairs of her quim. Her face, looming between her bare breasts, is smooth as steel.

She turns. "Hold up my fur." He obeys. "Be careful.

Don't touch my skin." Earlier in this game she was nervous, constipated, wondering if this was anything like male impotence. But thoughtful Pointsman, anticipating this, has been sending laxative pills with her meals. Now her intestines whine softly, and she feels shit begin to slide down and out. He kneels with his arms up holding the rich cape. A dark turd appears out the crevice, out of the absolute darkness between her white buttocks. He spreads his knees, awkwardly, until he can feel the leather of her boots. He leans forward to surround the hot turd with his lips, sucking on it tenderly, licking along its lower side . . . he is thinking, he's sorry, he can't help it, thinking of a Negro's penis, yes he knows it abrogates part of the conditions set, but it will not be denied, the image of a brute African who will make him behave. . . . The stink of shit floods his nose, gathering him, surrounding. It is the smell of Passchendaele, of the Salient. Mixed with the mud, and the putrefaction of corpses, it was the sovereign smell of their first meeting, and her emblem. The turd slides into his mouth, down to his gullet. He gags, but bravely clamps his teeth shut. Bread that would only have floated in porcelain waters somewhere, unseen, untasted—risen now and baked in the bitter intestinal Oven to bread we know, bread that's light as domestic comfort, secret as death in bed . . . Spasms in his throat continue. The pain is terrible. With his tongue he mashes shit against the roof of his mouth and begins to chew, thickly now, the only sound in the room. . . .

There are two more turds, smaller ones, and when he has eaten these, residual shit to lick out of her anus. He prays that she'll let him drop the cape over himself, to be allowed, in the silk-lined darkness, to stay a while longer with his submissive tongue straining upward into her asshole. But she moves away. The fur evaporates from his hands. She orders him to masturbate for her. She has watched Captain Blicero with Gottfried, and has learned the proper style.

The Brigadier comes quickly. The rich smell of semen fills the room like smoke.

"Now go." He wants to cry. But he has pleaded before, offered her—absurdly—his life. Tears well and slide from his eyes. He can't look into hers. "You have shit all over your mouth now. Perhaps I'll take a photograph of you like that. In case you ever get tired of me."

"No. No, I'm only tired of *that*," jerking his head back out of D Wing to encompass the rest of "The White Visitation." "So bloody tired. . . ."

"Get dressed. Remember to wipe your mouth off. I'll send for you when I want you again."

Dismissed. Back in uniform, he closes the cell door and retraces his way in. The night attendant is still asleep. Cold air hits Pudding like a blow. He sobs, bent, alone, cheek resting a moment against the rough stone walls of the Palladian house. His regular quarters have become a place of exile, and his real home is with the Mistress of the Night, with her soft boots and hard foreign voice. He has nothing to look forward to but a late-night cup of broth, routine papers to sign, a dose of penicillin that Pointsman has ordered him to take, to combat the effects of *E. coli*. Perhaps, though, tomorrow night . . . perhaps then. He can't see how he can hold out much longer. But perhaps, in the hours just before dawn . . .

□

The great cusp—green equinox and turning, dreaming fishes to young ram, watersleep to firewaking, bears down on us. Across the Western Front, up in the Harz in Blei-cheröde, Wernher van Braun, lately wrecked arm in a plaster cast, prepares to celebrate his 33rd birthday. Artillery thunders through the afternoon. Russian tanks raise dust phantoms far away over the German leas. The stroks are home, and the first violets have appeared.

At "The White Visitation," days along the chalk piece of seacoast now are fine and clear. The office girls are bundling into fewer sweaters, and breasts peaking through into visibility again. March has come in like a lamb. Lloyd George is dying. Stray visitors are observed now along the still-forbidden beach, sitting among obso-lescent networks of steel rod and cable, trousers rolled to the knee or hair unsnooded, chilly gray toes stirring the shingle. Just offshore, underwater, run miles of secret piping, oil ready at a valve-twist to be released and roast

German invaders who belong back in dreams already
old . . . fuel waiting hypergolic ignition that will not come
unless now as some junior-bureaucratic rag or May uprising of the spirit, to Bavarian tunesmith Carl Orff's lively

O, O, O,
To-tus flore-ol
Iam amore virginali
Totus ardeo . . .

all this fortress coast alight, Portsmouth to Dungeness,
blazing for the love of spring. Plots to this effect hatch
daily among the livelier heads at "The White Visitation"—
the winter of dogs, of black snowfalls of issueless words, is
ending. Soon it will be behind us. But once there, behind
us—will it still go on emanating its hooded cold, however
the fires burn at sea?

At the Casino Hermann Goering, a new regime has been
taking over. General Wivern's is now the only familiar
face, though he seems to've been downgraded. Slothrop's
own image of the plot against him has grown. Earlier the
conspiracy was monolithic, all-potent, nothing he could
ever touch. Until that drinking game, and that scene with
that Katje, and both the sudden good-bys. But now—

Proverbs for Paranoids, 1: You may never get to touch
the Master, but you can tickle his creatures.

And then, well, he is lately beginning to find his way
into one particular state of consciousness, not a dream certainly, perhaps what used to be called a "reverie," though
one where the colors are more primaries than pastels . . .
and at such times it seems he has touched, and stayed
touching, for a while, a soul we know, a voice that has
more than once spoken through research-facility medium
Carroll Eventyr: the late Roland Feldspath again, long-
co-opted expert on control systems, guidance equations,
feedback situations for this Aeronautical Establishment
and that. Seems that, for personal reasons, Roland has remained hovering over this Slothropian space, through sunlight whose energy he barely feels and through storms
that tickled his back with static electricity has Roland been
whispering from eight kilometers, the savage height, stationed as he has been along one of the Last Parabolas—

flight paths that must never be taken—working as one of the invisible Interdictors of the stratosphere now, bureaucratized hopelessly on that side as ever on this, he keeps his astral meathooks in as well as can be expected, curled in the "sky" so tense with all the frustrations of trying to reach across, with the impotence of certain dreamers who try to wake or talk and cannot, who struggle against weights and probes of cranial pain that it seems could not be borne waking, he waits, not necessarily for the aimless entrances of boobs like Slothrop here—

Roland shivers. Is *this* the one? This? to be figurehead for the latest passage? Oh, dear. God have mercy: what storms, what monsters of the Aether could this Slothrop ever charm away for anyone?

Well, Roland must make the best of it, that's all. If they get this far, he has to show them what he knows about Control. That's one of his death's secret missions. His cryptic utterances that night at Snoxall's about economic systems are merely the folksy everyday background chatter over here, a given condition of being. Ask the Germans especially. Oh, it is a real sad story, how shoddily their Schwärmerei for Control was used by the folks in power. Paranoid Systems of History (PSH), a short-lived periodical of the 1920s whose plates have all mysteriously vanished, natch, has even suggested, in more than one editorial, that the whole German Inflation was created deliberately, simply to drive young enthusiasts of the Cybernetic Tradition into Control work: after all, an economy inflating, upward bound as a balloon, its own definition of Earth's surface drifting upward in value, uncontrolled, drifting with the days, the feedback system expected to maintain the value of the mark constant having, humiliatingly, failed. . . . Unity gain around the loop, unity gain, zero change, and hush, that way, forever, these were the secret rhymes of the childhood of the Discipline of Control—secret and terrible, as the scarlet histories say. Diverging oscillations of any kind were nearly the Worst Threat. You could not pump the swings of these playgrounds higher than a certain angle from the vertical. Fights broke up quickly, with a smoothness that had not been long in coming. Rainy days never had much lightning or thunder to them, only a haughty glass grayness collect-

ing in the lower parts, a monochrome overlook of valleys
crammed with mossy deadfalls jabbing roots at heaven
not entirely in malign playfulness (as some white surprise
for the elitists up there paying no mind, no . . .), valleys
thick with autumn, and in the rain a withering, spinsterish
brown behind the gold of it . . . very selectively blighted
rainfall teasing you across the lots and into the back
streets, which grow ever more mysterious and badly paved
and more deeply platted, lot giving way to crooked lot
seven times and often more, around angles of hedge, across
freaks of the optical daytime until we have passed, fevered,
silent, out of the region of streets itself and into the
countryside, into the quilted dark fields and the wood, the
beginning of the true forest, where a bit of the ordeal
ahead starts to show, and our hearts to feel afraid . . . but
just as no swing could ever be thrust above a certain
height, so, beyond a certain radius, the forest could be
penetrated no further. A limit was always there to be
brought to. It was so easy to grow up under that dispensation. All was just as wholesome as could be. Edges
were hardly ever glimpsed, much less flirted at or with.
Destruction, oh, and demons—yes, including Maxwell's—
were there, deep in the woods, with other beasts vaulting
among the earthworks of your safety. . . .

So was the Rocket's terrible passage reduced, literally,
to bourgeois terms, terms of an equation such as that elegant blend of philosophy and hardware, abstract change
and hinged pivots of real metals which describes motion
under the aspect of yaw control:

$$\theta \, \frac{d^2\phi}{dt^2} + \delta^\circ \, \frac{d\phi}{dt} + \frac{\partial L}{\partial \alpha} \, (s_1 - s_2)\, \alpha = - \, \frac{\partial R}{\partial \beta} \, s_3 \beta,$$

preserving, possessing, steering between Scylla and Cha-
rybdis the whole way to Brennschluss. If any of the young
engineers saw correspondence between the deep conserva-
tism of Feedback and the kinds of lives they were coming
to lead *in the very process* of embracing it, it got lost, or
disguised—none of them made the connection, at least not
while alive: it took death to show it to Roland Feldspath,
death with its very good chances for being Too Late, and
a host of other souls feeling themselves, even now, Rocket-

like, driving out toward the stone-blue lights of the Vacuum under a Control they cannot quite name . . . the illumination out here is surprisingly mild, mild as heavenly robes, a feeling of population and invisible force, fragments of "voices," glimpses into *another order of being.* . . .

Afterward, Slothrop would be left not so much with any clear symbol or scheme to it as with some alkaline aftertaste of lament, an irreducible *strangeness,* a self-sufficiency nothing could get inside. . . .

Yes, sort of *German,* these episodes here. Well, these days Slothrop is even dreaming in the language. Folks have been teaching him dialects, Plattdeutsch for the zone the British plan to occupy, Thuringian if the Russians happen not to drive as far as Nordhausen, where the central rocket works is located. Along with the language teachers come experts in ordnance, electronics, and aerodynamics, and a fellow from Shell International Petroleum named Hilary Bounce, who is going to teach him about propulsion.

It seems that early in 1941, the British Ministry of Supply let a £10,000 research contract to Shell—wanted Shell to develop a rocket engine that would run on something besides cordite, which was being used in those days to blow up various sorts of people at the rate of oodles 'n' oodles of tons an hour, and couldn't be spared for rockets. A team ramrodded by one Isaac Lubbock set up a static-test facility at Langhurst near Horsham, and began to experiment with liquid oxygen and aviation fuel, running their first successful test in August of '42. Engineer Lubbock was a double first at Cambridge and the Father of British Liquid Oxygen Research, and what he didn't know about the sour stuff wasn't worth knowing. His chief assistant these days is Mr. Geoffrey Gollin, and it is to Gollin that Hilary Bounce reports.

"Well, I'm an Esso man myself," Slothrop thinks he ought to mention. "My old short was a gasgobbler all right, but a gourmet. Any time it used that Shell I had to drop a whole bottle of that Bromo in the tank just to settle that poor fucking Terraplane's plumbing down."

"Actually," the eyebrows of Captain Bounce, a 110% company man, going up and down earnestly to help him out, "we handled only the transport and storage end of things then. In those days, before the Japs and the Nazis you know, production and refining were up to the Dutch office, at The Hague."

Slothrop, poor sap, is remembering Katje, lost Katje, saying the name of her city, whispering Dutch love-words as they moved down seamornings now another age, another dispensation.... *Wait a minute.* "That's Bataafsche Petroleum Maatschappij, N.V.?"

"Right."

It's also the negative of a recco photograph of the city, darkbrown, festooned with water-spots, never enough time to let these dry out completely—

"Are you blokes *aware,*" they're trying to teach him English English too, heaven knows why, and it keeps coming out like Cary Grant, "that Jerry—old Jerry, you know—has been *in* that The Hague there, shooting his bloody rockets at that London, a-and *using,* the ... Royal Dutch Shell headquarters *building,* at the Josef Israelplein if I remember correctly, for a radio *guidance* transmitter? What bizarre shit is *that,* old man?"

Bounce stares at him, jingling his gastric jewelry, not knowing what to make of Slothrop, exactly.

"I mean," Slothrop now working himself into a fuss over something that only disturbs him, dimly, nothing to kick up a row over, is it? "doesn't it strike you as just a bit odd, you Shell chaps working on *your* liquid engine *your* side of the Channel you know, and *their* chaps firing *their* bloody things at you with your own ... blasted ... Shell trans*mitter* tower, you see."

"No, I can't see that it makes—what are you getting at? Surely they'd simply have picked the tallest building they could find that's in a direct line from their firing sites to London."

"Yes, and at the right *distance* too, don't forget that— exactly twelve kilometers *from* the firing site. Hey? That's exactly what I mean." Wait, oh wait. Is *that* what he means?

"Well, I'd never thought of it that way."

Neither have I, Jackson. Oh, me neither folks. ...

Hilary Bounce and his Puzzled Smile. Another innocent, a low-key enthusiast like Sir Stephen Dodson-Truck. But: Proverbs for Paranoids, 2: The innocence of the crea-

tures is in inverse proportion to the immortality of the
Master.

"I hope I haven't said anything wrong."

"Whyzat?"

"You look—" Bounce aspirating what he means to be a
warm little laugh, "worried."

Worried, all right. By the jaws and teeth of some Creature, some Presence so large that nobody else can see it—
there! that's that monster I was telling you about. —That's
no monster, stupid, that's *clouds!* —No, can't you *see?* It's
his *feet*— Well, Slothrop can feel this beast in the sky: its
visible claws and scales are being mistaken for clouds and
other plausibilities . . . or else everyone has agreed to *call
them other names* when Slothrop is listening. . . .

"It's only a 'wild coincidence,' Slothrop."

He will learn to hear quote marks in the speech of
others. It is a bookish kind of reflex, maybe he's genetically
predisposed—all those earlier Slothrops packing Bibles
around the blue hilltops as part of their gear, memorizing
chapter and verse the structures of Arks, Temples, Vision-
ary Thrones—all the materials and dimensions. Data behind which always, nearer or farther, was the numinous
certainty of God.

Well, what more appropriate way for Tyrone to Get It
one cold morning than this:

It's a blueprint of a German parts list, reproduced so
crummy he can hardly read the words—"Vorrichtung für
die Isolierung, 0011-5565/43," now what's this? He knows
the number by heart, it's the original contract number for
the A4 rocket as a whole. What's an "insulation device"
doing with the Aggregat's contract number? And a DE
rating too, the highest Nazi priority there is? Not good.
Either a clerk at OKW fucked up, which is not unheard-of,
or else he just didn't know the number, and put the
rocket's in as the next best thing. Claim, part and work
numbers all have the same flagnote, which directs Slothrop
to a Document SG-1. Flagnote on the flagnote sez "Geheime Kommandosache! This is a state secret, in the meaning of § 35 R5138."

"Say," he greets General Wivern nipping in through the
door, "like to get ahold of a copy of that Document SG-1."

"Haw, haw," replies the General. "So would our chaps,
I imagine."

"Quit fooling." Every piece of Allied intelligence on the A4, however classified, gets stuffed into a secret funnel back in London and all comes out in Slothrop's fancy cell at the Casino. So far they've held back nothing.

"Slothrop, there are no 'SG' documents."

First impulse is to rattle the parts list in the man's face, but today he is the shrewd Yankee foxing the redcoats. "Oh. Well, maybe I read it wrong," making believe look around the paper-littered room, "maybe it was a '56' or something, jeepers it was just *here*. . . ."

The General goes away again. Leaving Slothrop with a puzzle, kind of a, well not an obsession really . . . not yet . . . Opposite the parts listing, over in the Materials column now, here's "Imipolex G." Oh really. Insulation device made of Imipolex G eh? He kicks around the room looking for his handbook of German trade names. Nothing even close to it there . . . he locates next a master materials list for the A4 and all its support equipment, and there's sure no Imipolex G in that either. Scales and claws, and footfalls no one else seems to hear. . . .

"Something wrong?" Hilary Bounce again, with his nose in the doorway.

"It's about this liquid oxygen, need some more of that specific impulse data, there."

"Specific . . . do you mean specific thrust?"

"Oops, thrust, thrust," English English to the rescue, Bounce diverted:

"For LOX and alcohol it's about 200. What more do you need to know?"

"But didn't you chaps use petrol at Langhurst?"

"Among other things, yes."

"Well it's about those other things. Don't you know there's a war on? You can't be proprietary about stuff like that."

"But all our company reports are back in London. Perhaps my next time out—"

"Shit, this red tape. I need it *now*, Cap'n!" He goes around assuming they've assigned him a limitless Need To Know, and Bounce confirms it:

"I could send back by teletype, I suppose. . . ."

"*Now* yer talkin'!" Teletype? Yes, Hilary Bounce has his own, private, Shell International Network Teletype Rig or

Terminal, just what Slothrop was hoping for, right in his hotel room, back in the closet behind a rack of Alkit uniforms and stiff shirts. Slothrop finesses his way in with the help of his friend Michele, whom he's noticed Bounce has an eye on. "Howdy babe," up in a brown stocking-hung garret where the dancing girls sleep, "how'd you like to get fixed up with a big oilman tonight?" Some language problem here, she's thinking of getting connected through metal fittings to a gross man dripping somehow with crude oil, a sex angle she's not sure she'd enjoy, but they get that one straightened out, and presently Michele is raring to go sweet-talk the man away from his teletype long enough for Slothrop to get on to London and ask about Imipolex G. Indeed, she has noted Captain Bounce now and then among her nightly admirers, noted in particular an item of belly-brass that Slothrop's seen too: a gold benzene ring with a formée cross in the center—the IG Farben Award for Meritorious Contributions to Synthetics Research. Bounce got that one back in '32. The industrial liaison it suggests was indeed dozing at the bottom of Slothrop's mind when the Rocket Guidance Transmitter Question arose. It has even, in a way, inspired the present teletype plot. Who'd know better than an outfit like Shell, with no real country, no side in any war, no specific face or heritage: tapping instead out of that global stratum, most deeply laid, from which all the appearances of corporate ownership really spring?

Okay. Now there is a party tonight over on the *Cap,* chez Raoul de la Perlimpinpin, young madcap heir of the Limoges fireworks magnate Georges ("Poudre") de la Perlimpinpin—if "party" is the word for something that's been going on nonstop ever since this piece of France was liberated. Slothrop is allowed—under the usual surveillance—to drop in to Raoul's whenever the mood strikes him. It's a giddy, shiftless crowd out there—they drift in from all corners of Allied Europe, linked by some network of family, venery and a history of other such parties whose complexity his head's never quite been able to fit around. Here and there faces will go by, old American faces from Harvard or from SHAEF, names he's lost—they are revenants, maybe accidental, maybe . . .

It is to this party that Michele has seduced Hilary

Bounce, and for which Slothrop, soon as his reply from
London has come nattering through, in clear, on Bounce's
machine, now proceeds to dude himself up for. He'll read
the information through later. Singing,

> With my face shined up-like a microphone
> And uh Sta-Comb on my hair,
> I'm just as suave-as, an ice-cream cone, say,
> I'm Mis-ter Debo-nair. . . .

and turned out in a green French suit of wicked cut with
a subtle purple check in it, broad flowered tie won at the
trente-et-quarante table, brown and white wingtip shoes
with golf cleats, and white socks, Slothrop tops off now
with a midnight-blue snap-brim fedora and is away, click-
ety clack out the foyer of the Casino Hermann Goering,
looking sharp. As he exits, a wiry civilian, disguised as the
Secret Service's notion of an Apache, eases away from a
niche in the porte-cochere, and follows Slothrop's cab out
the winding dark road to Raoul's party.

□

Turns out that some merrymaker has earlier put a hundred grams of hashish in the Hallandaise. Word of this has
got around. There has been a big run on broccoli. Roasts
lie growing cold on the room-long buffet tables. A third of
the company are already asleep, mostly on the floor. It is
necessary to thread one's way among bodies to get to
where anything's happening.

What's happening is not clear. There are the usual tight
little groups out in the gardens, dealing. Not much spectacle tonight. A homosexual triangle has fizzed over into
pinches and recriminations, so as to block the door to the
bathroom. Young officers are outside vomiting among the
zinnias. Couples are wandering. Girls abound, velvet-
bowed, voile-sleeved, underfed, broad-shouldered and
permed, talking in half a dozen languages, sometimes
brown from the sun here; others pale as Death's Vicar
from more eastern parts of the War. Eager young chaps
with patent-leather hair rush about trying to vamp the

ladies, while older heads with no hair at all prefer to wait,
putting out only minimal effort, eyes and mouths across
the rooms, talking business in the meantime. One end of
the salon is occupied by a dance band and an emaciated
crooner with wavy hair and very red eyes, who is singing:

JULIA (FOX-TROT)

Ju-lia,
Would you think me pe-cul-iar,
If I should fool ya,
In-to givin' me—just-a-little-kiss?

Jool-yaaahh,
No one else could love you tru-lier,
How I'd worship and bejewel ya,
If you'd on-ly give-me just-a-little-kiss!

Ahh *Jool*-yaaahhhh—
My poor heart grows un-ru-lier,
No one oolier or droolier,
Could I be longing for—
What's more—

Ju-lia,
I would shout hallelujah,
To have my Jool-yaaahh,
In-my-arms forevermore.

Saxophony and Park Lane kind of tune, perfect for certain states of mind. Slothrop sees Hilary Bounce, clearly a
victim of the hallucinogenic Hollandaise, nodded out on a
great pouf with Michele, who's been fondling his IG
Farben trinket for the past two or three hours. Slothrop
waves, but neither one notices him.

Dopers and drinkers struggle together without shame at
the buffet and in the kitchens, ransacking the closets, licking out the bottoms of casseroles. A nude bathing party
passes through on the way down the sea-steps to the beach.
Our host, that Raoul, is roaming around in a ten-gallon
hat. Tom Mix shirt and brace of sixguns with a Percheron
horse by the bridle. The horse is leaving turds on the
Bokhara rug, also on the odd supine guest. It is all out of
shape, no focus to it until a sarcastic flourish from the

band, and here comes the meanest customer Slothrop has seen outside of a Frankenstein movie—wearing a white zoot suit with reet pleats and a long gold keychain that swings in flashing loops as he crosses the room with a scowl for everybody, in something of a hurry but taking the time to scan faces and bodies, head going side to side, methodical, a little ominous. He stops at last in front of Slothrop, who's putting together a Shirley Temple for himself.

"You." A finger the size of a corncob, an inch from Slothrop's nose.

"You bet," Slothrop dropping a maraschino cherry on the rug then squashing it as he takes a step backward, "I'm the man all right. Sure. What is it? Anything."

"Come on." They proceed outside to a eucalyptus grove, where Jean-Claude Gongue, notorious white slaver of Marseilles, is busy white-slaving. "Hey you," hollering into the trees, "you wanna be a white slave, huh?" "Shit no," answers some invisible girl, "I wanna be a *green* slave!" "Magenta!" yells somebody from up in an olive tree. "Vermilion!" "Think I'll take up dealing dope," sez Jean-Claude.

"Look," Slothrop's friend producing a kraft-paper envelope that even in the gloom Slothrop can tell is fat with American Army yellow-seal scrip, "I want you to hold this for me, till I ask for it back. It looks like Italo is going to get here before Tamara, and I'm not sure which one—"

"At this rate, Tamara's gonna get here before tonight," Slothrop interjects in a Groucho Marx voice.

"Don't try to undermine my confidence in you," advises the Large One. "You're the man."

"Right," Slothrop tucking envelope inside pocket. "Say, where'd you get that zoot you're wearing, there?"

"What's your size?"

"42, medium."

"You shall have one," and so saying he rumbles off back inside.

"A-and a *sharp keychain!*" Slothrop calls after. What th' heck's going on? He wanders around asking a question or two. The fella turns out to be Blodgett Waxwing, well-known escapee from the Caserne Martier in Paris, the worst stockade in the ETO. Waxwing's specialty is phonying documents of various sorts—PX ration cards, passports,

Soldbücher—whilst dealing in Army hardware also as a sideline. He has been AWOL off and on since the Battle of the Bulge, and with a death rap for that over his head he still goes into U.S. Army bases at night to the canteens to watch the movies—provided they're westerns, he loves those shit-kickers, the sound of hoofbeats through a metal speaker across a hundred yards of oildrums and deuce 'n' a half ruts in the foreign earth makes his heart stir as if a breeze blew there, he's got some of his many contacts to run him off a master schedule of every movie playing in every occupation town in the Theatre, and he's been known to hot-wire a general's jeep just to travel up to that Poitiers for the evening to see a good old Bob Steele or Johnny Mack Brown. His picture may hang prominently in all the guardrooms and be engraved in thousands of snow-drops' brains, but he has seen *The Return of Jack Slade* twenty-seven times.

The story here tonight is a typical WW II romantic in-trigue, just another evening at Raoul's place, involving a future opium shipment's being used by Tamara as security against a loan from Italo, who in turn owes Waxwing for a Sherman tank his friend Theophile is trying to smuggle into Palestine but must raise a few thousand pounds for pur-poses of bribing across the border, and so has put the tank up as collateral to borrow from Tamara, who is using part of her loan from Italo to pay him. But meantime the opium deal doesn't look like it's going to come through, because the middleman hasn't been heard from in several weeks, along with the money Tamara fronted him, which she got from Raoul de la Perlimpinpin through Waxwing, who is now being pressured by Raoul for the money be-cause Italo, deciding the tank belongs to Tamara now, showed up last night and took it away to an Undisclosed Location as payment on his loan, thus causing Raoul to panic. Something like that.

Slothrop's tail is being made indecent propositions by two of the homosexuals who've been fighting in the bath-room. Bounce and Michele are nowhere in sight, and neither's that Waxwing. Raoul is talking earnestly to his horse. Slothrop is just settling down next to a girl in a prewar Worth frock and with a face like Tenniel's Alice, same forehead, nose, hair, when from outside comes this

most godawful clanking, snarling, crunching of wood, girls
come running terrified out of the eucalyptus trees and into
the house and right behind them what comes crashing
now into the pallid lights of the garden but—why the
Sherman Tank itself! headlights burning like the eyes of
King Kong, treads spewing grass and pieces of flagstone as
it manoeuvres around and comes to a halt. Its 75 mm cannon swivels until it's pointing through the French windows
right down into the room. "Antoine!" a young lady focusing in on the gigantic muzzle, "for heaven's sake, not
now...." A hatch flies open and Tamara—Slothrop
guesses: wasn't Italo supposed to have the tank?—uh—
emerges shrieking to denounce Raoul, Waxwing, Italo,
Theophile, and the middleman on the opium deal. "But
now," she screams, "I have you all! One coup de foudre!"
The hatch drops—oh, Jesus—there's the sound of a 3-inch
shell being loaded into its breech. Girls start to scream
and make for the exits. Dopers are looking around, blinking, smiling, saying yes in a number of ways. Raoul tries
to mount his horse and make his escape, but misses the
saddle and slides all the way over, falling into a tub
of black-market Jell-o, raspberry flavor, with whipped
cream on top. "Aw, no . . ." Slothrop having about decided to make a flanking run for the tank when
YYYBLAAANNNGGG! the cannon lets loose an enormous
roar, flame shooting three feet into the room, shock wave
driving eardrums in to middle of brain, blowing everybody
against the far walls.

A drape has caught fire. Slothrop, tripping over partygoers, can't hear anything, knows his head hurts, keeps
running through the smoke at the tank—leaps on, goes to
undog the hatch and is nearly knocked off by Tamara
popping up to holler at everybody again. After a struggle
which shouldn't be without its erotic moments, for Tamara
is a swell enough looking twist with some fine moves,
Slothrop manages to get her in a come-along and drag her
down off of the tank. But loud noise and all, look—he
doesn't seem to have an erection. Hmm. This is a datum
London never got, because nobody was looking.

Turns out the projectile, a dud, has only torn holes in
several walls, and demolished a large allegorical painting
of Virtue and Vice in an unnatural act. Virtue had one of

those dim faraway smiles. Vice was scratching his shaggy head, a little bewildered. The burning drape's been put out with champagne. Raoul is in tears, thankful for his life, wringing Slothrop's hands and kissing his cheeks, leaving trails of Jell-o wherever he touches. Tamar is escorted away by Raoul's bodyguards. Slothrop has just disengaged himself and is wiping the Jell-o off of his suit when there is a heavy touch on his shoulder.

"You were right. You are the man."

"That's nothing." Errol Flynn frisks his mustache. "I saved a dame from an octopus not so long ago, how about that?"

"With one difference," sez Blodgett Waxwing. "This really happened tonight. But that octopus didn't."

"How do you know?"

"I know a lot. Not everything, but a few things you don't. Listen Slothrop—you'll be needing a friend, and sooner than you think. Don't come here to the villa—it may be too hot by then—but if you can make it as far as Nice—" he hands over a business card, embossed with a chess knight and an address on Rue Rossini. "I'll take the envelope back. Here's your suit. Thanks, brother." He's gone. His talent is just to fade when he wants to. The zoot suit is in a box tied with a purple ribbon. Keychain's there too. They both belonged to a kid who used to live in East Los Angeles, named Ricky Gutiérrez. During the Zoot Suit Riots in 1943, young Gutiérrez was set upon by a carload of Anglo vigilantes from Whittier, beaten up while the L.A. police watched and called out advice, then arrested for disturbing the peace. The judge was allowing zoot-suiters to choose between jail and the Army. Gutiérrez joined up, was wounded on Saipan, developed gangrene, had to have his arm amputated, is home now, married to a girl who works in the kitchen at a taco place in San Gabriel, can't find any work himself, drinks a lot during the day. . . . But his old zoot, and those of thousands of others busted that summer, hanging empty on the backs of all the Mexican L.A. doors, got bought up and have found their way over here, into the market, no harm turning a little profit, is there, they'd only have hung there in the fat smoke and the baby smell, in the rooms with shades pulled down

against the white sun beating, day after day, on the dried
palm trees and muddy culverts, inside these fly-ridden and
empty rooms. . . .

□

Imipolex G has proved to be nothing more—or less—sinister than a new plastic, an aromatic heterocyclic polymer,
developed in 1939, years before its time, by one L. Jamf
for IG Farben. It is stable at high temperatures, like up to
900°C., it combines good strength with a low power-loss
factor. Structurally, it's a stiffened chain of aromatic rings,
hexagons like the gold one that slides and taps above
Hilary Bounce's navel, alternating here and there with
what are known as heterocyclic rings.

The origins of Imipolex G are traceable back to early
research done at du Pont. Plasticity has its grand tradition
and main stream, which happens to flow by way of du
Pont and their famous employee Carothers, known as The
Great Synthesist. His classic study of large molecules
spanned the decade of the twenties and brought us directly
to nylon, which not only is a delight to the fetishist and a
convenience to the armed insurgent, but was also, at the
time and well within the System, an announcement of
Plasticity's central canon: that chemists were no longer to
be at the mercy of Nature. They could decide now what
properties they wanted a molecule to have, and then go
ahead and build it. At du Pont, the next step after nylon
was to introduce aromatic rings into the polyamide chain.
Pretty soon a whole family of "aromatic polymers" had
arisen: aromatic polyamides, polycarbonates, polyethers,
polysulfanes. The target property most often seemed to be
strength—first among Plasticity's virtuous triad of Strength,
Stability and Whiteness (*Kraft, Standfestigkeit, Weiße:*
how often these were taken for Nazi graffiti, and indeed
how indistinguishable they commonly were on the rain-
brightened walls, as the busses clashed gears in the next
street over, and the trams creaked of metal, and the people were mostly silent in the rain, with the early evening
darkened to the texture of smoke from a pipe, and the
arms of young passersby not in the sleeves of their coats

but inside somewhere, as if sheltering midgets, or ecstatically drifted away from the timetable into a tactile affair with linings more seductive even than the new nylon . . .).
L. Jamf, among others, then proposed, logically, dialectically, taking the parental polyamide sections of the new chain, and looping *them* around into rings too, giant "heterocyclic" rings, to alternate with the aromatic rings. This principle was easily extended to other precursor molecules. A desired monomer of high molecular weight could be synthesized to order, bent into its heterocyclic ring, clasped, and strung in a chain along with the more "natural" benzene or aromatic rings. Such chains would be known as "aromatic heterocyclic polymers." One hypothetical chain that Jamf came up with, just before the war, was later modified into Imipolex G.

Jamf at the time was working for a Swiss outfit called Psychochemie AG, originally known as the Grössli Chemical Corporation, a spinoff from Sandoz (where, as every schoolchild knows, the legendary Dr. Hofmann made his important discovery). In the early '20s, Sandoz, Ciba, and Geigy had got together in a Swiss chemical cartel. Shortly after, Jamf's firm was also absorbed. Apparently, most of Grössli's contracts had been with Sandoz, anyway. As early as 1926 there were oral agreements between the Swiss cartel and IG Farben. When the Germans set up their cover company in Switzerland, IG Chemie, two years later, a majority of the Grössli stock was sold to them, and the company reconstituted as Psychochemie AG. The patent for Imipolex G was thus cross-filed for both the IG and for Psychochemie. Shell Oil got into it through an agreement with Imperial Chemicals dated 1939. For some curious reason, Slothrop will discover, no agreements between ICI and the IG seem to be dated any later than '39. In this Imipolex agreement, Icy Eye could market the new plastic inside the Commonwealth in exchange for one pound and other good and valuable consideration. That's nice. Psychochemie AG is still around, still doing business at the same old address in the Schokoladestrasse, in that Zurich, Switzerland.

Slothrop swings the long keychain of his zoot, in some agitation. A few things are immediately obvious. There is even more being zeroed in on him from out there than

he'd thought, even in his most paranoid spells. Imipolex G
shows up on a mysterious "insulation device" on a rocket
being fired with the help of a transmitter on the roof of
the headquarters of Dutch Shell, who is co-licensee for
marketing the Imipolex—a rocket whose propulsion system
bears an uncanny resemblance to one developed by British
Shell at around the same time . . . and oh, oh boy, it just
occurs to Slothrop now where all the rocket intelligence is
being *gathered*—into the office of who but Mr. Duncan
Sandys, Churchill's own son-in-law, who works out of the
Ministry of Supply located where but at Shell Mex *House,
for Christ's sake*. . . .

Here Slothrop stages a brilliant Commando raid, along
with faithful companion Blodgett Waxwing, on Shell Mex
House itself—right into the heart of the Rocket's own
branch office in London. Mowing down platoons of heavy
security with his little Sten, kicking aside nubile and
screaming WRAC secretaries (how else is there to react,
even in play?), savagely looting files, throwing Molotov
cocktails, the Zootsuit Zanies at last crashing into the final
sanctum with their trousers up around their armpits, smelling singed hair, spilled blood, to find not Mr. Duncan
Sandys cowering before their righteousness, nor open window, gypsy flight, scattered fortune cards, nor even a test
of wills with the great Consortium itself—but only a rather
dull room, business machines arrayed around the walls
calmly blinking, files of cards pierced frail as sugar faces,
frail as the last German walls standing without support
after the bombs have been and now twisting high above,
threatening to fold down out of the sky from the force of
the wind that has blown the smoke away. . . . The smell of
firearms is in the air, and there's not an office dame in
sight. The machines chatter and ring to each other. It's
time to snap down your brims, share a postviolence cigarette and think about escape . . . do you remember the way
in, all the twists and turns? No. You weren't looking. Any
of these doors might open you to safety, but there may
not be time. . . .

But Duncan Sandys is only a name, a function in this,
"How high does it go?" is not even the right kind of
question to be asking, because the organization charts have
all been set up by Them, the titles and names filled in by
Them, because

Proverbs for Paranoids, 3: If they can get you asking
the wrong questions, they don't have to worry about
answers.

Slothrop finds he has paused in front of the blue parts
list that started all this. *How high does it go . . . ahhhh.*
The treacherous question is not meant to apply to *people*
after all, but to the *hardware!* Squinting, moving a finger
carefully down the columns, Slothrop finds that Vorrichtung für die Isolierung's Next Higher Assembly.

"S-Gerät, 11/00000."

If this number is the serial number of a rocket, as its
form indicates, it must be a special model—Slothrop hasn't
even heard of any with four zeroes, let alone five . . . nor
an S-Gerät either, there's an I- and a J-Gerät, they're in
the guidance . . . well, Document SG-1, which isn't supposed to exist, must cover that. . . .

Out of the room: going noplace special, moving to a
slow drumbeat in his stomach muscles *see what happens,
be ready. . . .* In the Casino restaurant, not the slightest
impedance at all to getting in, no drop in temperature
perceptible to his skin, Slothrop sits down at a table
where somebody has left last Tuesday's London *Times.*
Hmmm. Hasn't seen one of *them* in a while. . . . Leafing
through, dum, dum, de-doo, yeah, the War's still on, Allies
closing in east and west on Berlin, powdered eggs still
going one and three a dozen, "Fallen Officers," MacGregor,
Mucker-Maffick, Whitestreet, Personal Tributes . . . *Meet
Me in St. Louis* showing at the Empire Cinema (recalls
doing the penis-in-the-popcorn-box routine there with one
Madelyn, who was less than—)—

Tantivy . . . Oh shit no, no wait—

"True charm . . . humble-mindedness . . . strength of
character . . . fundamental Christian cleanness and goodness . . . we all loved Oliver . . . his courage, kindness of
heart and unfailing good humour were an inspiration to all
of us . . . died bravely in battle leading a gallant attempt
to rescue members of his unit who were pinned down by
German artillery . . ." And signed by his most devoted
comrade in arms, Theodore Bloat. *Major* Theodore Bloat
now—

Staring out the window, staring at nothing, gripping a
table knife so hard maybe some bones of his hand will
break. It happens sometimes to lepers. Failure of feed-

back to the brain—no way to know how fiercely they may be making a fist. You know these lepers. Well—

Ten minutes later, back up in his room, he's lying face-down on the bed, feeling empty. Can't cry. Can't do *anything*.

They did it. Took his friend out to some deathtrap, probably let him fake an "honourable" death . . . and then just *closed up his file.* . . .

It will occur to him later that maybe the whole story was a lie. They could've planted it easy enough in that London *Times*, couldn't they? Left the paper for Slothrop to find? But by the time he figures that one out, there'll be no turning around.

At noon Hilary Bounce comes in rubbing his eyes wearing a shit-eating grin. "How was your evening? Mine was remarkable."

"Glad to hear it." Slothrop is smiling. *You're on my list too, pal.* This smile asks from him more grace than anything in his languid American life ever has, up till now. Grace he always imagined himself short on. But it's working. He's surprised, and so grateful that he almost starts crying then. The best part of all is not that Bounce appears fooled by the smile, but that Slothrop knows now that it will work for him again. . . .

So he does make it to Nice, after a fast escape down the Corniche through the mountains fishtailing and rubber softly screeching at the sun-warmed abysses, tails all shaken back on the beach where he was thoughtful enough to lend his buddy Claude the assistant chef, about the same height and build, his own brand-new pseudo-Tahitian bathing trunks, and while they're all watching that Claude, find a black Citroën with the keys left in, nothing to it, folks— rolling into town in his white zoot, dark glasses, and a flopping Sydney Greenstreet Panama hat. He's not exactly inconspicuous among the crowds of military and the mam-zelles already shifted into summer dresses, but he ditches the car off Place Garibaldi, heads for a bistro on the old-Nice side of La Porte Fausse and takes time to nab a roll and coffee before setting out to find the address Waxwing gave him. It turns out to be an ancient four-story hotel with early drunks lying in the hallways, eyelids like tiny loaves brushed with a last glaze of setting sun, and summertime dust in stately evolutions through the taupe light, summertime ease to the streets outside, April summertime as the great vortex of redeployment from Europe to Asia hoots past leaving many souls each night to cling a bit longer to the tranquillities here, this close to the drain-hole of Marseilles, this next-to-last stop on the paper cyclone that sweeps them back from Germany, down the river-valleys, beginning to drag some from Antwerp and the northern ports too now as the vortex grows more sure, as preferential paths are set up. . . . Just for the knife-edge, here in the Rue Rossini, there comes to Slothrop the best feeling dusk in a foreign city can bring: just where the sky's light balances the electric lamplight in the street, just before the first star, some promise of events without cause, surprises, a direction at right angles to every direction his life has been able to find up till now.

Too impatient to wait for the first star, Slothrop enters the hotel. The carpets are dusty, the place smells of alcohol and bleach. Sailors and girls come ambling through, together and separate, as Slothrop paranoids from door to door looking for one that might have something to tell him. Radios play in the heavy wood rooms. The stairwell doesn't appear to be plumb, but *tilted* at some peculiar angle, and the light running down the walls is of only two colors: earth and leaf. Up on the top floor Slothrop finally spots an old motherly femme de chambre on the way into a room carrying a change of linen, very white in the gloom.

"Why did you leave," the sad whisper ringing as if through a telephone receiver from someplace far away, "they wanted to help you. They wouldn't have done anything bad. . . ." Her hair is rolled up, George Washington style, all the way around. She gazes at 45° to Slothrop, a patient, parkbench chessplayer's gaze, very large, arching kindly nose and bright eyes: she is starch, sure-boned, the toes of her leather shoes turn up slightly, she's wearing red-and-white striped socks on enormous feet that give her the look of a helpful critter from one of the other worlds, the sort of elf who'd not only make shoes while you slept but also sweep up a little, have the pot on when you awoke, and maybe a fresh flower by the window—

"I beg your pardon?"

"There's still time."

"You don't understand. They've killed a friend of mine."
But seeing it in the *Times* that way, so public . . . how
could any of that be real, real enough to convince him
Tantivy won't just come popping in the door some day,
howdyfoax and a bashful smile . . . hey, Tantivy. Where
were you?

"Where *was* I, Slothrop? That's a good one." His smile
lighting the time again, and the world all free. . . .

He flashes Waxwing's card. The old woman breaks into
an amazing smile, the two teeth left in her head under the
night's new bulbs. She thumbs him upstairs and then gives
him either the V-for-victory sign or some spell from distant
countryside against the evil eye that sours the milk. Whichever it is, she is chuckling sarcastically.

Upstairs is a roof, a kind of penthouse in the middle.
Three young men with Apache sideburns and a young
woman packing a braided leather sap are sitting in front of
the entrance smoking a thin cigarette of ambiguous odor.
"You are lost, mon ami."

"Uh, well," out with Waxwing's card again.

"Ah, bien. . . ." They roll aside, and he passes into a
bickering of canary-yellow Borsalini, corksoled comicbook
shoes with enormous round toes, lotta that saddle-stitching
in contrasting colors (such as orange on blue, and the
perennial favorite, green on magenta), workaday groans of
comforted annoyance commonly heard in public toilets,
telephone traffic inside clouds of cigar smoke. Waxwing
isn't in, but a colleague interrupts some loud dealing soon
as he sees the card.

"What do you need?"

"Carte d'identité, passage to Zürich, Switzerland."

"Tomorrow."

"Place to sleep."

The man hands over a key to one of the rooms downstairs. "Do you have any money?"

"Not much. I don't know when I could—"

Count, squint, riffle, "Here."

"Uh . . ."

"It's all right, it's not a loan. It comes out of overhead.
Now, don't go outside, don't get drunk, stay away from
the girls who work here."

"Aw . . ."

"See you tomorrow." Back to business.

Slothrop's night passes uncomfortably. There is no position he can manage to sleep in for more than ten minutes. The bugs sally out onto his body in skirmish parties not uncoordinated with his level of wakefulness. Drunks come to the door, drunks and revenants.

" 'Rone, you've gotta let me in, it's Dumpster, Dumpster Villard."

"What's 'at—"

"It's really bad tonight. I'm sorry. I shouldn't impose this way, I'm more trouble than I'm worth . . . listen . . . I'm cold . . . I've been a long way. . . ."

A sharp knock. "Dumpster—"

"No, no, it's Murray Smile, I was next to you in basic, company 84, remember? Our serial numbers are only two digits apart."

"I had to let . . . let Dumpster in . . . where'd he go? Was I asleep?"

"Don't tell them I was here. I just came to tell you you don't have to go back."

"Really? Did they say it was all right?"

"It's all right."

"Yeah, but did *they say* it was?" Silence. "Hey? Murray?" Silence.

The wind is blowing in the ironwork very strong, and down in the street a vegetable crate bounces end over end, wooden, empty, dark. It must be four in the morning. "Got to get back, shit I'm late. . . ."

"No." Only a whisper. . . . But it was her "no" that stayed with him.

"Whozat. Jenny? That you, Jenny?"

"Yes it's me. Oh love I'm so glad I found you."

"But I have to . . ." Would They ever let her live with him at the Casino . . . ?

"No. I can't." But *what's wrong with her voice?*

"Jenny, I heard your block was hit, somebody told me, the day after New Year's . . . a rocket . . . and I meant to go back and see if you were all right, but . . . I just *didn't* . . . and then They took me to that Casino. . . ."

"It's all right."

"But not if I didn't—"

"Just don't go back to them."

And somewhere, dark fish hiding past angles of refraction in the flow tonight, are Katje and Tantivy, the two visitors he wants most to see. He tries to bend the voices that come to the door, bend them like notes on a harmonica, but it won't work. What he wants lies too deep. . . .

Just before dawn knocking comes very loud, hard as steel. Slothrop has the sense this time to keep quiet.

"Come on, open up."

"MPs, open up."

American voices, country voices, high-pitched and without mercy. He lies freezing, wondering if the bedsprings will give him away. For possibly the first time he is hearing America as it must sound to a non-American. Later he will recall that what surprised him most was the fanaticism, the reliance not just on flat force but on the *rightness* of what they planned to do . . . he'd been told long ago to expect this sort of thing from Nazis, and especially from Japs—*we* were the ones who always played fair—but this pair outside the door now are as demoralizing as a close-up of John Wayne (the angle emphasizing how slanted his eyes are, funny you never noticed before) screaming "BANZAI!"

"Wait a minute Ray, there he goes—"

"Hopper! You asshole, come back here—"

"You'll never get me in a strait jacket agaaaaain. . . ." Hopper's voice goes fading around the corner as the MPs take off in pursuit.

It dawns on Slothrop, literally, through the yellowbrown window shade, that this is his first day Outside. His first free morning. He *doesn't* have to go back. Free? What's free? He falls asleep at last. A little before noon a young woman let herself in with a passkey and leaves him the papers. He is now an English war correspondent named Ian Scuffling.

"This is the address of one of our people in Zürich. Waxwing wishes you good luck and asks what kept you so long."

"You mean he wants an answer?"

"He said you'd have to think about it."

"Sa-a-aay." It's just occurred to him. "Why are all you folks helping me like this? For free and all?"

"Who knows? We have to play the patterns. There must be a pattern you're in, right now."

"Uh ..."

But she's already left. Slothrop looks around the place: in the daylight it's mean and anonymous. Even the roaches must be uncomfortable here. ... Is he off so quickly, like Katje on her wheel, off on a ratchet of rooms like this, to be in each one only long enough to gather wind or despair enough to move on to the next, but no way backward now, ever again? No time even to get to know the Rue Rossini, which faces holler from the windows, where's a good place to eat, what's the name of the song everybody's whistling these premature summer days. ...

A week later he's in Zürich, after a long passage by train. While the metal creatures in their solitude, days of snug and stable fog, pass the hours at mime, at playing molecules, imitating industrial synthesis as they are broken up, put together, coupled and recoupled, he dozes in and out of a hallucination of Alps, fogs, abysses, tunnels, bone-deep laborings up impossible grades, cowbells in the darkness, in the morning green banks, smells of wet pasture, always out the windows an unshaven work crew on the way to repair some stretch of track, long waits in marshaling-yards whose rails run like layers of an onion cut end to end, gray and desolate places, nights of whistles, coupling, crashes, sidings, staring cows on the evening hillsides, army convoys waiting at the crossings as the train puffs by, never a clear sense of nationality anywhere, nor even of belligerent sides, only the War, a single damaged landscape, in which "neutral Switzerland" is a rather stuffy convention, observed but with as much sarcasm as "liberated France" or "totalitarian Germany," "Fascist Spain," and others. ...

The War has been reconfiguring time and space into its own image. The track runs in different networks now. What appears to be destruction is really the shaping of railroad spaces to other purposes, intentions he can only, riding through it for the first time, begin to feel the leading edges of. ...

He checks in to the Hotel Nimbus, in an obscure street in the Niederdorf or cabaret section of Zürich. The room's in an attic, and is reached by ladder. There's also a ladder outside the window, so he reckons it'll be O.K. When

night comes down he goes out looking for the local Waxwing rep, finds him farther up the Limmatquai, under a
bridge, in rooms full of Swiss watches, clocks and altim-
eters. He's a Russian named Semyavin. Outside boats hoot
on the river and the lake. Somebody upstairs is practicing
on a piano: stumbling, sweet lieder. Semyavin pours gentian brandy into cups of tea he's just brewed. "First thing
you have to understand is the way everything here is
specialized. If it's watches, you go to one café. If it's
women, you go to another. Furs are subdivided into Sable,
Ermine, Mink, and Others. Same with dope: Stimulants,
Depressants, Psychomimetics. . . . What is it you're after?"

"Uh, information?" Gee, this stuff tastes like Moxie. . . .

"Oh. Another one." Giving Slothrop a sour look. "Life
was simple before the first war. You wouldn't remember.
Drugs, sex, luxury items. Currency in those days was no
more than a sideline, and the term 'industrial espionage'
was unknown. But I've seen it change—oh, how it's
changed. The German inflation, that should've been my
clue right there, zeros strung end to end from here to
Berlin. I would have stern talks with myself. 'Semyavin,
it's only a temporary lapse away from reality. A small
aberration, nothing to worry about. Act as you always
have—strength of character, good mental health. *Courage*,
Semyavin! Soon all will be back to normal.' But do you
know what?"

"Let me guess."

A tragic sigh. "Information. What's wrong with dope
and women? Is it any wonder the world's gone insane,
with information come to be the only real medium of exchange?"

"I thought it was cigarettes."

"You dream." He brings out a list of Zürich cafés and
gathering spots. Under Espionage, Industrial, Slothrop
finds three. Ultra, Lichtspiel, and Sträggeli. They are on
both banks of the Limmat, and widely spaced.

"Footwork," folding the list in an oversize zoot-suit
pocket.

"It'll get easier. Someday it'll all be done by machine.
Information machines. You are the wave of the future."

Begins a period of shuttling among the three cafés,
sitting a few hours over coffee at each one, eating once a

day, Zürich baloney and rösti at the People's Kitchens . . .
watching crowds of businessmen in blue suits, sun-black
skiers who've spent the duration schussing miles of glacier
and snow hearing nothing of campaigns or politics, reading nothing but thermometers and weathervanes, finding
their atrocities in avalanches or toppling séracs, their victories in layers of good powder . . . ragged foreigners in
oil-stained leather jackets and tattered fatigues, South
Americans bundled in fur coats and shivering in the clear
sunlight, elderly hypochondriacs who were caught out
lounging at some spa when the War began and have been
here since, women in long black dresses who don't smile,
men in soiled overcoats who do . . . and the mad, down
from their fancy asylums on weekend furlough—oh, the
mental cases of Switzerland: Slothrop is known to them,
all right, among all the somber street faces and colors only
he is wearing white, shoes zoot 'n' hat, white as the
cemetery mountains here. . . . He's also the New Mark In
Town. It's difficult for him to sort out the first wave of
corporate spies from the

LOONIES ON LEAVE!

(The Chorus line is divided not into the conventional Boys and
Girls but into Keepers and Nuts, without regard to sex, though all
four possibilities are represented on stage. Many are wearing sunglasses with black lenses and white rims, not so much to be fashionable as to suggest snow-blindness, the antiseptic white of the
Clinic, perhaps even the darkness of the mind. But all seems
happy, relaxed, informal . . . no sign of repression, not even a
distinction in costume so that at first there is some problem telling
Nuts from Keepers as they all burst in from the wings dancing
and singing):

> Here we come foax—ready or not!
> Put your mask on, and plot your plot,
> We're just laughin' and droolin', all—*over*
>   the sleigh,
> Like a buncha happy midgets on a holiday!
>
> Oh we're the LOONIES ON LEAVE, and
> We haven't a care—
> Our brains at the cleaners, our souls at the Fair,
> Just freaks on a fur-lough, away from the blues,
> As daffy and sharp as—the taps on our shoes!
> Hey, we're passin' the hat for—your frowns and
>   your tears,

And the fears you thought'd never go 'way—
Oh take it from a loony, life's so dear and swoony,
So just hug it and kiss it to-day!
La-da-da, ya-ta ya-ta ta-ta &c . . . (They go on
    humming the tune behind what follows):

First Nut (or maybe Keeper): Got an amazing deal for you here,
American? I thought so, always tell a face from home, saaay, like
your suit there, go far enough up the glacier 'n' nobody'd be able
to see ya! Well yes now, I know how you feel about these street-
vendors keep coming by, it's the old three-card monte on the sidewalk [trucks across the stage for a while, back and forth, waving
his finger in the air, singing "Three-card monte on-the *side, walk*,"
over and over in the same obsessive monotone, for as many repetitions as he can get away with] and you can spot right away what's
wrong, every one promises ya somethin' fer nothin', right? yes
now oddly enough, that's the main objection engineers and scientists have always had to the idea of [lowering his voice] perpetual
motion or as we like to call it Entropy Management—here, here's
our card—well, sure, they've got a point. At least they *had* a
point. Up till now. . . .

Second Nut or Keeper: Now you've heard about the two-hundred-
mile-per-gallon carburetor, the razor edge that never gets dull,
the eternal bootsole, the mange pill that's good to your glands,
engine that'll run on sand, ornithopters and robobopsters—you
heard me, got a little goatee made out of steel wool—jivey, that's
fine, but *here's* one for yo' *mind!* Are you ready? It's Lightning-
Latch, The Door That Opens *You!*

Slothrop: Think I'll go take my nap now. . . .

Third N. or K.: Transmogrify common air into diamonds through
Cataclysmic Carbon Dioxide Reducti-o-o-o-o-n-n-n. . . .

If he were sensitive about such things, it'd all be pretty
insulting, this first wave. It passes, gesturing, accusative,
pleading. Slothrop manages to stay calm. There is a
pause—then on come the real ones, slowly at first but
gathering, gathering. Synthetic rubber or gasoline, electronic calculators, aniline dyes, acrylics, perfumes (stolen
essences in vials in sample cases), sexual habits of a hundred selected board members, layouts of plants, code-
books, connections and payoffs, ask for it, they can get it.
    At last, one day at the Sträggeli, Slothrop eating on a
bratwurst and hunk of bread he's been toting around all
morning in a paper bag, suddenly from noplace appears
one Mario Schweitar in a green frogged waistcoat, just
popped out of the echoing cuckoo clock of Dubya Dubya
Two here, the endless dark corridors at his back, with a

change of luck for Slothrop. "Psst, Joe," he begins, "hey, mister."

"Not me," replies Slothrop with his mouth full.

"You interested in some L.S.D.?"

"That stands for pounds, shillings, and pence. You got the wrong café, Ace."

"I think I've got the wrong country," Schweitar a little mournful. "I'm from Sandoz."

"Aha, Sandoz!" cries Slothrop, and pulls out a chair for the fella.

Turns out Schweitar is very tight indeed with Psychochemie AG, being one of those free-floating trouble-shooters around the Cartel, working for them on a per diem basis and spying on the side.

"Well," Slothrop sez, "I'd sure like anything they got on L. Jamf, a-and on that Imipolex G."

"Gaaah—"

"Pardon me?"

"That stuff. Forget it. It's not even our line. You ever try to develop a polymer when there's nothing but indole people around? With our giant parent to the north sending in ultimatums every day? Imipolex G is the company albatross, Yank. They have vice-presidents whose only job is to observe the ritual of going out every Sunday to spit on old Jamf's grave. You haven't spent much time with the indole crowd. They're very elitist. They see themselves at the end of a long European dialectic, generations of blighted grain, ergotism, witches on broomsticks, community orgies, cantons lost up there in folds of mountain that haven't known an unhallucinated day in the last 500 years—keepers of a tradition, aristocrats—"

"*Wait* a minute. . . ." Jamf dead? "You say Jamf's *grave*, now?" It ought to be making more of a difference to him, except that the man was never really alive so how can he be really—

"Up in the mountains, toward the Uetliberg."

"You ever—"

"What?"

"Did you ever meet him?"

"Before my time. But I know that there's a lot of data on him in the classified files at Sandoz. It would be some job getting you what you want. . . ."

"Uh . . ."

"Five hundred."

"Five hundred what?"

Swiss francs. Slothrop hasn't got 500 anything, unless it's worries. The money from Nice is almost gone. He heads toward Semyavin's, across the Gemüse-Brücke, deciding he'll walk everywhere from now on, chewing his white sausage and wondering when he'll see another.

"First thing you want to do," Semyavin advises him, "is go to a pawnshop and raise a few francs on that, ah," pointing to the suit. Aw no, not the suit. Semyavin goes rummaging in a back room, comes out with a bundle of workmen's clothes. "You should start thinking more about your visibility. Come back tomorrow, I'll see what else I can find."

White zoot in a bundle under his arm, a less visible Ian Scuffling goes back outside, down into the mediaeval afternoon of the Niederdorf, stone walls now developing like baking bread in the failing sun, oboy oboy he can see it now: gonna turn into another of them Tamara/Italo drills here, 'n' then he'll be in so deep he'll just never get out. . . .

At the entrance to his street, in the wells of shadow, he notes a black Rolls parked, motor idling, its glass tinted and afternoon so dark he can't see inside. Nice car. First one he's seen in a while, should be no more than a curiosity, except for

Proverbs for Paranoids, 4: *You* hide, they seek.

Zunnggg! diddilung, diddila-ta-ta-ta, ya-ta-ta-ta William Tell Overture here, back in the shadows, hope nobody was looking through that one-way glass—zoom, zoom, dodging around corners, scooting down alleys, no sound of pursuit but then it's the quietest engine on the road except for the King Tiger tank. . . .

Forget that Hotel Nimbus, he reckons. His feet are already starting to bother him. He gets to the Luisentrasse and the hockshop just before closing time, and manages to raise a little, baloney for a day or two maybe, on the zoot. So long zoot.

This town sure closes up early. What does Slothrop do tonight for a bed? He has a moment's relapse into optimism: ducks in a restaurant and rings up the desk at the Hotel Nimbus. "Ah, yes," English English, "can you possibly tell me if the British chap who's been waiting in the foyer is still *there*, you know . . ."

In a minute on comes a pleasant, awkward voice with an are-you-there. Oh, so seraphic. Slothrop funks, hangs up, stands looking at all the people at dinner staring at him—blew it, blew it, now They know he's on to Them. There is the usual chance his paranoia's just out of hand again, but the coincidences are running too close. Besides, he knows the sound of Their calculated innocence by now, it's part of Their style. . . .

Out again in the city: precision banks, churches, Gothic doorways drilling by . . . he must avoid the hotel and the three cafés now, right, right. . . . The permanent Zürchers in early-evening blue stroll by. Blue as the city twilight, deepening blue. . . . The spies and dealers have all gone indoors. Semyavin's place is out, the Waxwing circle have been kind, no point bringing any heat down on them. How much weight do the Visitors have in this town? Can Slothrop risk checking in to another hotel? Probably not. It's getting cold. A wind is coming in now off the lake.

He finds that he has drifted as far as the Odeon, one of the great world cafés, whose specialty is not listed any-where—indeed has never been pinned down. Lenin, Trotsky, James Joyce, Dr. Einstein all sat out at these tables. Whatever it was *they* all had in common: whatever they'd come to this vantage to score . . . perhaps it had to do with the people somehow, with pedestrian mortality, restless crisscrossing of needs or desperations in one fateful piece of street . . . dialectics, matrices, archetypes all need to connect, once in a while, back to some of that prole-tarian blood, to body odors and senseless screaming across a table, to cheating and last hopes, or else all is dusty Dracularity, the West's ancient curse. . . .

Slothrop finds he has enough spare change for coffee. He goes sits inside, choosing a seat that'll face the en-trance. Fifteen minutes and he's getting the spy-sign from a swarthy, curly-headed alien in a green suit a couple tables away. Another front-facer. On his table is an old newspaper that appears to be in Spanish. It is open to a peculiar political cartoon of a line of middle-aged men wearing dresses and wigs, inside the police station where a cop is holding a loaf of white . . . no it's a baby, with a label on its diaper sez LA REVOLUCIÓN . . . oh, they're all claiming the infant revolution as their own, all these poli-ticians bickering like a bunch of putative mothers, and

somehow this cartoon here is supposed to be some kind of
a touchstone, this fella in the green suit, who turns out to
be an Argentine named Francisco Squalidozzi, is looking
for a reaction . . . the key passage is at the very end of the
line where the great Argentine poet Leopoldo Lugones is
saying, "Now I'm going to tell you, in verse, how I conceived her free from the stain of Original Sin. . . ." It is
the Uriburu revolution of 1930. The paper is fifteen years
old. There is no telling what Squalidozzi is expecting from
Slothrop, but what he gets is pure ignorance. This seems
to be acceptable, and presently the Argentine has loosened
up enough to confide that he and a dozen colleagues,
among them the international eccentric Graciela Imago
Portales, hijacked an early-vintage German U-boat in Mar
del Plata a few weeks ago, and have sailed it back across
the Atlantic now, to seek political asylum in Germany, as
soon as the War's over there. . . .

"You say *Germany?* You gone goofy? It's a mess there,
Jackson!"

"Not nearly the mess we left back home," the sad
Argentine replies. Long lines have appeared next to his
mouth, lines learned from living next to thousands of horses,
watching too many doomed colts and sunsets south of
Rivadavia, where the true South begins. . . . "It's been a
mess since the colonels took over. Now, with Perón on his
way . . . our last hope was Acción Argentina," *what's he
talking about, Jesus I'm hungry,* ". . . suppressed it a
month after the coup . . . now everybody waits. Attending
the street actions out of habit. No real hope. We decided
to move before Perón got another portfolio. War, most
likely. He already has the *descamisados,* this will give him
the Army too you see . . . it's only a matter of time . . . we
could have gone to Uruguay, waited him out—it's a tradition. But perhaps he will be in for a long time. Montevideo
is swarming with failed exiles, and failed hopes. . . ."

"Yeah, but Germany—that's the last place you want to
go."

"*Pero ché, no sós argentino.* . . ." A long look away,
down the engineered scars of Swiss avenues, looking for
the South he left. Not the same Argentine, Slothrop, that
that Bob Eberle's seen toasts to Tangerine raised in ev'ry
bar across, now. . . . Squalidozzi wants to say: *We of all*

*magical precipitates out of Europe's groaning, clouded
alembic, we are the thinnest, the most dangerous, the
handiest to secular uses. . . . We tried to exterminate our
Indians, like you: we wanted the closed white version of
reality we got—but even into the smokiest labyrinths, the
furthest stacked density of midday balcony or courtyard
and gate, the land has never let us forget. . . .* But what he
asks aloud is: "Here—you look hungry. Have you eaten?
I was about to go to supper. Would you do me the honor?"

In the Kronenhalle they find a table upstairs. The evening rush is tapering off. Sausages and fondue: Slothrop's
starving.

"In the days of the gauchos, my country was a blank
piece of paper. The pampas stretched as far as men could
imagine, inexhaustible, fenceless. Wherever the gaucho
could ride, that place belonged to him. But Buenos Aires
sought hegemony over the provinces. All the neuroses
about property gathered strength, and began to infect the
countryside. Fences went up, and the gaucho became less
free. It is our national tragedy. We are obsessed with
building labyrinths, where before there was open plain and
sky. To draw ever more complex patterns on the blank
sheet. We cannot abide that *openness:* it is terror to us.
Look at Borges. Look at the suburbs of Buenos Aires. The
tyrant Rosas has been dead a century, but his cult flourishes. Beneath the city streets, the warrens of rooms and
corridors, the fences and the networks of steel track, the
Argentine heart, in its perversity and guilt, longs for a
return to that first unscribbled serenity . . . that anarchic
oneness of pampas and sky. . . ."

"But-but bobwire," Slothrop with his mouth full of that
fondue, just gobblin' away, "that's *progress*—you, you
can't have open range forever, you can't just stand in the
way of progress—" yes, he is actually going to go on for
half an hour, quoting Saturday-afternoon western movies
dedicated to Property if anything is, at this foreigner who's
springing for his meal.

Squalidozzi, taking it for mild insanity instead of rudeness, only blinks once or twice. "In ordinary times," he
wants to explain, "the center always wins. Its power grows
with time, and that can't be reversed, not by ordinary
means. Decentralizing, back toward anarchism, needs ex-

traordinary times . . . this War—this incredible War—just
for the moment has wiped out the proliferation of little
states that's prevailed in Germany for a thousand years.
Wiped it clean. *Opened it.*"

"Sure. For how long?"

"It won't last. Of course not. But for a few months . . .
perhaps there'll be peace by the autumn—*discúlpeme*, the
spring, I still haven't got used to your hemisphere—for a
moment of spring, perhaps. . . ."

"Yeah but—what're you gonna do, take over land and
try to hold it? They'll run you right off, podner."

"No. Taking land is building more fences. We want to
leave it open. We want it to grow, to change. In the
openness of the German Zone, our hope is limitless." Then,
as if struck on the forehead, a sudden fast glance, not at
the door, but *up at the ceiling*— "So is our danger."

The U-boat right now is cruising around somewhere off
of Spain, staying submerged for much of the day, spending nights on the surface to charge batteries, sneaking in
now and then to refuel. Squalidozzi won't go into the fueling arrangements in much detail, but there are apparently
connections of many years' standing with the Republican
underground—a community of grace, a gift of persistence.
. . . Squalidozzi is in Zürich now contacting governments
that might be willing, for any number of reasons, to assist
his anarchism-in-exile. He must get a message to Geneva
by tomorrow: from there word is relayed to Spain and the
submarine. But there are Peronist agents here in Zürich.
He is being watched. He can't risk betraying the contact
in Geneva.

"I can help you out," Slothrop licking off his fingers,
"but I'm short of cash and—"

Squalidozzi names a sum that will pay off Mario Schweitar and keep Slothrop fed for months to come.

"Half in front and I'm on the way."

The Argentine hands over message, addresses, money,
and springs for the check. They arrange to meet at the
Kronenhalle in three days. "Good luck."

"You too."

A last sad look from Squalidozzi alone at his table. A
toss of forelock, a fading of light.

The plane is a battered DC-3, chosen for its affinity for

moonlight, the kind expression on its windowed face,
its darkness inside and outside. He wakes up curled among
the cargo, metal darkness, engine vibration through his
bones . . . red light filtering very faint back through a bulkhead from up forward. He crawls to a tiny window and
looks out. Alps in the moonlight. Kind of small ones,
though, not as spectacular as he figured on. Oh, well. . . .
He settles back down on a soft excelsior bed, lighting up
one of Squalidozzi's corktips thinking, Jeepers, not bad,
guys just jump in the airplane, go where they want . . .
why stop at Geneva? Sure, what about—well, that Spain?
no wait, they're Fascists. South Sea Islands! hmm. Full of
Japs and GIs. Well Africa's the Dark Continent, nothing
there but natives, elephants, 'n' that Spencer Tracy. . . .

"There's nowhere to go, Slothrop, nowhere." The figure
is huddled against a crate, and shivering. Slothrop squints
through the weak red light. It is the well-known frontis-
piece face of insouciant adventurer Richard Halliburton:
but strangely altered. Down both the man's cheeks runs a
terrible rash, palimpsested over older pockmarks, in whose
symmetry Slothrop, had he a medical eye, could have read
drug reaction. Richard Halliburton's jodhpurs are torn and
soiled, his bright hair greasy now and hanging. He appears
to be weeping silently, bending, a failed angel, over all
these second-rate Alps, over all the night skiers far below,
out on the slopes, crisscrossing industriously, purifying and
perfecting their Fascist ideal of Action, Action, Action,
once his own shining reason for being. No more. No more.

Slothrop reaches, puts the cigarette out on the deck.
How easy these angel-white wood shavings can go up. Lie
here in this rattling and wrenched airplane, lie still as you
can, damn fool, yup they've conned you—conned you
again. Richard Halliburton, Lowell Thomas, Rover and
Motor Boys, jaundiced stacks of *National Geographics* up
in Hogan's room must've all lied to him, and there was no
one then, not even a colonial ghost in the attic, to tell him
different. . . .

Bump, skid, slew, pancake landing, fucking washouts
from kite-flying school, gray Swiss dawn light through little
windows and every joint, muscle, and bone in Slothrop is
sore. It's time to punch back in.

He gets off of the plane without incident, mingling into

a yawning, sour flock of early passengers, delivery agents, airfield workers. Cointrin in the early morning. Shocking green hills one side, brown city on the other. Pavements are slick and wet. Clouds blow slowly in the sky. Mont Blanc sez hi, lake sez howdy too, Slothrop buys 20 cigarettes and a local paper, asks directions, gets in a tram that comes and with cold air through doors and windows to wake him up goes rolling into the City of Peace.

He's to meet his Argentine contact at the Café l'Éclipse, well off the trolley lines, down a cobblestone street and into a tiny square surrounded by vegetable and fruit stalls under beige awnings, shops, other cafés, window-boxes, clean hosed sidewalks. Dogs go running in and out of the alleys. Slothrop sits with coffee, croissants, and newspaper. Presently the overcast burns off. The sun throws shadows across the square nearly to where he's sitting with all antennas out. Nobody seems to be watching. He waits. Shadows retreat, sun climbs then begins to fall, at last his man shows up, exactly as described: suit of Buenos Aires daytime black, mustache, goldrim glasses, and whistling an old tango by Juan d'Arienzo. Slothrop makes a show of searching all his pockets, comes up with the foreign bill Squalidozzi told him to use: frowns at it, gets up, goes over.

Como no, señor, no problem changing a 50-peso note— offering a seat, coming out with currency, notebooks, cards, pretty soon the tabletop's littered with pieces of paper that eventually get sorted back into pockets so that the man has Squalidozzi's message and Slothrop has one to bring back to Squalidozzi. And that's that.

Back to Zürich on an afternoon train, sleeping most of the way. He gets off at Schlieren, some ungodly dark hour, just in case They're watching the Bahnhof in town, hitches a ride in as far as the St. Peterhofstatt. Its great clock hangs over him and empty acres of streets in what he now reads as dumb malignity. It connects to Ivy League quadrangles in his distant youth, clock-towers lit so dim the hour could never be read, and a temptation, never so strong though as now, to surrender to the darkening year, to embrace what he can of real terror to the hour without a name (unless it's . . . no . . . NO . . .): it was vanity, vanity as his Puritan forerunners had known it, bones and heart alert to Nothing, Nothing underneath the college saxophones melding sweetly, white blazers lipsticked about the lapels, smoke from nervous Fatimas, Castile soap vaporizing off of shining hair, and mint kisses, and dewed carnations. It was being come for just before dawn by pranksters younger than he, dragged from bed, blind-folded, Hey Reinhardt, led out into the autumnal cold, shadows and leaves underfoot, and the moment then of doubt, the real possibility that they are something else—that none of it was real before this moment: only elaborate theatre to fool you. But now the screen has gone dark, and there is absolutely no more time left. The agents are here for you at last. . . .

What better place than Zürich to find vanity again? It's Reformation country, Zwingli's town, the man at the end of the encyclopedia, and stone reminders are everywhere. Spies and big business, in their element, move tirelessly among the grave markers. Be assured there are ex-young men, here in this very city, faces Slothrop used to pass in the quads, who got initiated at Harvard into the Puritan Mysteries: who took oaths in dead earnest to respect and to act always in the name of *Vanitas,* Emptiness, their ruler . . . who now according to life-plan such-and-such have come to Switzerland to work for Allen Dulles and his "intelligence" network, which operates these days under the title "Office of Strategic Services." But to initiates OSS is also a secret acronym: as a mantra for times of immediate crisis they have been taught to speak inwardly *oss . . . oss,* the late, corrupt, Dark-age Latin word for bone. . . .

Next day, when Slothrop meets Mario Schweitar at the Sträggeli to front him half his fee, he asks also for the location of Jamf's grave. And that's where they arrange to close the deal, up in the mountains.

Squalidozzi doesn't show up at the Kronenhalle, or the Odeon, or anyplace Slothrop will think to look in the days that follow. Disappearances, in Zürich, are not unheard of. But Slothrop will keep going back, just in case. The message is in Spanish, he can't make out more than a word or two, but he'll hold on to it, there might be a chance to pass it on. And, well, the anarchist persuasion appeals to him a little. Back when Shays fought the federal troops across Massachusetts, there were Slothrop Regulators patrolling Berkshire for the rebels, wearing sprigs of hemlock in their hats so you could tell them from the Government soldiers. Federals stuck a tatter of white paper in theirs. Slothrops in those days were not yet so much involved with paper, and the wholesale slaughtering of trees. They were still for the living green, against the dead white. Later they lost, or traded away, knowledge of which side they'd been on. Tyrone here has inherited most of their bland ignorance on the subject.

Back behind him now, wind blows through Jamf's crypt. Slothrop's been camped here these past few nights, nearly out of money, waiting for word from Schweitar. Out of the wind, huddled inside a couple of Swiss army blankets he managed to promote, he's even been able to sleep. Right on top of Mister Imipolex. The first night he was afraid to fall asleep, afraid of a visit from Jamf, whose German-scientist mind would be battered by Death to only the most brute reflexes, no way to appeal to the dumb and grinning evil of the shell that was left . . . voices twittering with moonlight around his image, as step by step he, It, the Repressed, approaches. . . . *waitaminute* up out of sleep, face naked, turning to the foreign gravestones, *the what? what was it* . . . back again, almost to it, up again . . . up, and back, that way, most of the early night.

There's no visit. It seems Jamf is only dead. Slothrop woke next morning feeling, in spite of an empty stomach and a runny nose, better than he had in months. Seemed like he'd passed a test, not somebody else's test, but one of his own, for a change.

The city below him, bathed now in a partial light, is a necropolis of church spires and weathercocks, white castle-keep towers, broad buildings with mansard roofs and windows glimmering by thousands. This forenoon the mountains are as translucent as ice. Later in the day they will be blue heaps of wrinkled satin. The lake is mirror-smooth but mountains and houses reflected down there remain strangely blurred, with edges fine and combed as rain: a dream of Atlantis, of the Suggenthal. Toy villages, desolate city of painted alabaster. . . . Slothrop hunkers down here in the cold curve of a mountain trail, packing and lobbing idle snowballs, not much to do around here but smoke the last butt of what for all he knows is the last Lucky Strike in all Switzerland. . . .

Footfalls down the trail. Clinking galoshes. It is Mario Schweitar's delivery boy, with a big fat envelope. Slothrop pays him, chisels a cigarette and some matches, and they part. Back to the crypt Slothrop relights a small pile of kindling and pine boughs, warms up his hands, and begins to thumb through the data. The absence of Jamf surrounds him like an odor, one he knows but can't quite name, an aura that threatens to go epileptic any second. The information is here—not as much as he wanted (aw, how much was that?) but more than he hoped, being one of those practical Yankees. In the weeks ahead, in those very few moments he'll be allowed to wallow in his past, he may even have time to wish he hadn't read any of it. . . .

□

Mr. Pointsman has decided to spend Whitsun by the sea. Feeling a bit megalo these days, nothing to worry about really, never gets worse than, oh perhaps the impression, whilst zooming along through the corridors of "The White Visitation," that all the others seem to be frozen in attitudes of unmistakable parkinsonism, with himself the only alert, unpalsied one remaining. It is peacetime again now, no room for the pigeons in Trafalgar Square on V-E Night, everyone at the facility that day mad drunk and hugging and kissing, except for the Blavatskian wing of Psi Section, who were off on a White Lotos Day pilgrimage to 19 Avenue Road, St. John's Wood.

Now there's time again for holidays. Though Pointsman does feel a certain obligation to go relax, there is also, of course, The Crisis. A leader must show self-possession, up to and including a holiday mood, in the midst of Crisis.

There's now been no word of Slothrop for nearly a month, since the fumbling asses in military intelligence lost him in Zürich. Pointsman is a bit browned-off with the Firm. His clever strategy appears to've failed. In first discussions with Clive Mossmoon and the others, it seemed foolproof: to let Slothrop escape from the Casino Hermann Goering, and then rely on Secret Service to keep him under surveillance instead of PISCES. An economy move. The surveillance bill is the most excruciating thorn in the crown of funding problems he seems condemned to wear for the duration of this project. Damned funding is going to be his downfall, if Slothrop doesn't drive him insane first.

Pointsman has blundered. Hasn't even the Tennysonian comfort of saying "someone" has blundered. No, it was he and he alone who authorized the Anglo-American team of Harvey Speed and Floyd Perdoo to investigate a random sample of Slothropian sex adventures. Budget was available, and what harm could it do? They went off practically *skipping*, obsessive as Munchkins, out into the erotic Poisson. Don Giovanni's map of Europe—640 in Italy, 231 in Germany, 100 in France, 91 in Turkey *but*, but, but—in Spain! in Spain, 1003!—is Slothrop's map of London, and the two gumshoes become so infected with the prevailing fondness out here for mindless pleasures that they presently are passing whole afternoons sitting out in restaurant gardens dawdling over chrysanthemum salads and mutton casseroles, or larking at the fruit monger's—"Hey Speed, look, *canteloupes!* I haven't seen one of them since the Third Term—wow, smell this one, it's beautiful! Say, how about a canteloupe, Speed? Huh? Come on."

"Excellent idea, Perdoo, excellent."

"Uh . . . Oh, well you pick out the one *you* want, okay?"

"The *one?*"

"Yeah. This is the one," turning it to show him as the faces of threatened girls are roughly turned by villains, "that *I* picked out, see?"

"But but I thought we were both going to—" gesturing feebly toward what he still cannot quite accept as Perdoo's melon, in whose intaglio net now, as among craters of the pale moon, a face is indeed emerging, the face of a captive woman with eyes cast downward, lids above as smooth as Persian ceilings. . . .

"Well, no, I usually, uh—" this is *embarrassing* for Perdoo, it's like being called on to, to justify eating an apple, or even popping a *grape* into your mouth—"just, well, sort of, eat them . . . whole, you know," chuckling in

what he hopes is a friendly way, to indicate politely the
social *oddness* of this discussion—

—but the chuckle is taken the wrong way by Speed:
taken as evidence of mental instability in this slightly buck-
toothed and angular American, who is dancing now from
stoop to English stoop, lank as a street-puppet in the wind.
Shaking his head, he nevertheless selects his own whole
canteloupe, realizes he's been left to pay the bill, which is
exorbitant, and goes skipping off after Perdoo, hippety hop
both of them, tra-la-la-la *slam* right into another dead end:

"Jenny? No—no Jenny here. . . ."

"A Jennifer, perhaps? Genevieve?"

"Ginny" (it could've been misspelled), "Virginia?"

"If you gentlemen are looking for a good time—" Her
grin, her red, maniacally good-morning-and-I-mean-*good!*
grin, is wide enough to hold them both right, shivering,
smiling, here, and she's *old* enough to be their Mother—
their joint Mother, combining the worst traits of Mrs.
Perdoo and Mrs. Speed—in fact she is turning now into
just that, even as they watch. These wrecked seas are full
of temptresses—it's watery and wanton out here all right.
As the two gawking soft-boiled shamuses are drawn along
into her aura, winking right here in the street, brassy with
henna-glare, with passion-flowers on rayon—just before
the last stumbling surrender into the lunacy of her purple
eyes, they allow themselves, for the sinful tickle of it, a
last thought of the project they're supposed to be here
on—Slothropian Episodic Zone, Weekly Historical Observations (SEZ WHO)—a thought that comes running out in
the guise of a clown, a vulgar, loose-ends clown be-
spangled with wordless jokes about body juices, bald-
headed, an amazing fall of nose-hair out both nostrils
which he has put into braids and tied with acid-green
bows—a scrabbling dash now out past sandbags and falling
curtain, trying to get back his breath, to garble to them
in a high unpleasant screech: "No Jenny. No Sally W. No
Cybele. No Angela. No Catherine. No Lucy. No Gretchen.
When are you going to see it? When are you going to
see it?"

No "Darlene" either. That came in yesterday. They
traced the name as far as the residence of a Mrs. Quoad.
But the flashy young divorcée never, she declared, even

knew that English children were named "Darlene." She
was dreadfully sorry. Mrs. Quoad spent her days lounging
about a rather pedicured Mayfair address, and both investigators felt relieved to be out of the neighborhood. . . .

When are you going to see it? Pointsman sees it immediately. But he "sees" it in the way you would walking
into your bedroom to be jumped on, out of a bit of penum-
bra on your ceiling, by a gigantic moray eel, its teeth in
full imbecile death-smile, breathing, in its fall onto your
open face, a long human sound that you know, horribly, to
be a *sexual sigh.* . . .

That is to say, Pointsman avoids the matter—as re-
flexively as he would any nightmare. Should this one turn
out not to be a fantasy but *real*, well . . .

"The data, so far, are incomplete." This ought to be
prominently stressed in all statements. "We admit that the
early data seem to show," remember, *act sincere*, "a number of cases where the names on Slothrop's map do not
appear to have counterparts in the body of fact we've
been able to establish along his time-line here in London.
Establish *so far*, that is. These are mostly all first names,
you see, the, the Xs without the Ys so to speak, ranks
without files. Difficult to know how far into one 'far
enough' really is.

"And what if many—even if most—of the Slothropian
stars *are* proved, some distant day, to refer to sexual fantasies instead of real events? This would hardly invalidate
our approach, any more than it did young Sigmund
Freud's, back there in old Vienna, facing a similar violation of probability—all those Papi-has-raped-me stories,
which might have been lies evidentially, but were certainly
the truth *clinically*. You must realize: we are concerned,
at PISCES, with a rather strictly defined, clinical version
of truth. We seek no wider agency in this."

So far, it is Pointsman's burden alone. The solitude of a
Führer: he feels himself growing strong in the rays of this
dark companion to his public star now on the rise . . . but
he doesn't want to share it, no not just yet. . . .

Meetings of the staff, his staff, grow worse and worse
than useless. They bog down into endless arguments about
trivia—whether or not to rename PISCES now that the
Surrender has been Expedited, what sort of letterhead, if

any, to adopt. The representative from Shell Mex House, Mr. Dennis Joint, wants to put the program under Special Projectiles Operations Group (SPOG), as an adjunct of the British rocket-scavenging effort, Operation Backfire, which is based out of Cuxhaven on the North Sea. Every other day brings a fresh attempt, from some quarter, to reconstitute or even dissolve PISCES. Pointsman is finding it much easier of late to slip into a l'état c'est moi frame of mind—who *else* is doing anything? *isn't* he holding it all together, often with nothing beyond his own raw will . . . ?

Shell Mex House, naturally, is frantic about Slothrop's disappearance. Here's a man running loose who knows everything it's possible to know—not only about the A4, but about what *Great Britain* knows about the A4. Zürich teems with Soviet agents. What if they've already got Slothrop? They took Peenemünde in the spring, it appears now they will be given the central rocket works at Nordhausen, another of the dealings at Yalta. . . . At least three agencies, VIAM, TsAGI, and NISO, plus engineers working out of other commissariats, are even now in Soviet-occupied Germany with lists of personnel and equipment to be taken east. Inside the SHAEF sphere of influence, American Army Ordnance, and a host of competing research teams, are all busy collecting everything in sight. They've already rounded up von Braun and 500 others, and interned them at Garmisch. What if *they* get hold of Slothrop?

There have also been, aggravating the Crisis, defections: Rollo Groast assumed back into the Society for Psychical Research, Treacle setting up a practice, Myron Grunton again a full-time wireless personality. Mexico has begun to grow distant. The Borgesius woman still performs her nocturnal duties, but with the Brigadier ill now (has the old fool been forgetting his antibiotics? Must Pointsman do everything?) she's beginning to fret. Of course Géza Rózsavölgyi is still with the project. A fanatic. Rózsavölgyi will *never* leave.

So. A holiday by the sea. For political reasons, the party is made up of Pointsman, Mexico, Mexico's girl, Dennis Joint, and Katje Borgesius. Pointsman wears rope-soled shoes, his prewar bowler, and a rare smile. The weather is not ideal. An overcast, a wind that will be chilly by midafternoon. A smell of ozone blows up from the Dodgem cars out of the gray steel girderwork along the promenade, along with smells of shellfish on the barrows, and of salt sea. The pebbled beach is crowded with families: shoeless fathers in lounge suits and high white collars, mothers in blouses and skirts startled out of war-long camphor sleep, kids running all over in sunsuits, nappies, rompers, short pants, knee socks, Eton hats. There are ice cream, sweets, Cokes, cockles, oysters and shrimps with salt and sauce. The pinball machines writhe under the handling of fanatical servicemen and their girls, throwing body-english, cursing, groaning as the bright balls drum down the wood obstacle courses through ka-chungs, flashing lights, thudding flippers. The donkeys hee-haw and shit, the children walk in it and their parents scream. Men sag in striped canvas chairs talking business, sports, sex, but most usually politics. An organ grinder plays Rossini's overture to *La Gazza Ladra* (which, as we shall see later, in Berlin, marks a high point in music which everybody ignored, preferring Beethoven, who never got further than statements of intention), and here without snaredrums or the sonority of brasses the piece is mellow, full of hope, promising lavender twilights, stainless steel pavilions and everyone elevated at last to aristocracy, and love without payment of any kind. . . .

It was Pointsman's plan today not to talk shop, but to let the conversation flow more or less organically. Wait for others to betray themselves. But there is shyness, or constraint, among them all. Talk is minimal. Dennis Joint is watching Katje with a horny smile, with now and then a suspicious stare for Roger Mexico. Mexico meantime has his troubles with Jessica—more and more often these days—and at the moment the two aren't even looking at each other. Katje Borgesius has her eyes far out to sea, and there is no telling *what* is going on with this one. In some dim way, Pointsman, though he can't see that she has any leverage at all, is still afraid of her. There is still a lot he doesn't know. Perhaps what's bothering him most right now is her connection, if any, with Pirate Prentice. Prentice has been down to "The White Visitation" several times asking rather pointed questions about her. When PISCES recently opened its new branch office in London

(which some wag, probably that young imbecile Webley
Silvernail, has already dubbed "Twelfth House") Prentice
began hanging heavily around up there, romancing secretaries, trying for a peep into this file or that. . . . What's
up? What afterlife have the Firm found, this side of V-E
Day? What does Prentice want . . . what's his price? Is he
in love with La Borgesius here? Is it possible for this
woman to be in love? *Love?* Oh, it's enough to make you
scream. What would her idea of love be. . . .

"Mexico," grabbing the young statistician's arm.

"Eh?" Roger interrupted eying a lovely looks a bit like
Rita Hayworth in a one-piece floral number with straps
that X across her lean back. . . .

"Mexico, I think I am hallucinating."

"Oh, really? You think you are? What are you seeing?"

"Mexico, I see . . . I see . . . What do you mean, what
am I *seeing*, you nit? It's what I'm *hearing*."

"Well, what are you hearing, then." A touch of peevish-
ness to Roger now.

"Right now I'm hearing *you*, saying, 'What are you
hearing, then.' And I *don't like it!*"

"Why not."

"Because, unpleasant as this hallucination is, I find I still
much prefer it to the sound of your voice."

Now this is odd behavior from anybody, but from
usually correct Mr. Pointsman, it is enough to stop this
mutually-paranoid party in their tracks. Nearby is a Wheel
of Fortune, with Lucky Strike packs, kewpie dolls and
candy bars stuffed among the spokes.

"I say, what d'you think?" blond, hale-fellow Dennis
Joint nudges Katje with an elbow as broad as a knee. In
his profession he has learned to make instant evaluations
of those with whom he deals. He judges old Katje here to
be a jolly girl, out for a spot of fun. Yes, leadership material here, definitely. "Hasn't he gone a bit mental suddenly?" Trying to keep his voice down, grinning in athletic
paranoia vaguely over in the peculiar Pavlovian's direction—not *right* at him you understand, eye contact might
be suicidal folly given his state of mind. . . .

Meantime, Jessica has gone into her Fay Wray number.
This is a kind of protective paralysis, akin to your own
response when the moray eel jumps you from the ceiling.

But this is for the Fist of the Ape, for the lights of electric
New York white-waying into the room you thought was
safe, could never be penetrated . . . for the coarse black
hair, the tendons of need, of tragic love. . . .

"Yeah well," as film critic Mitchell Prettyplace puts it
in his definitive 18-volume study of *King Kong*, "you know,
he *did* love her, folks." Proceeding from this thesis, it appears that Prettyplace has left nothing out, every shot including out-takes raked through for every last bit of symbolism, exhaustive biographies of everyone connected with
the film, extras, grips, lab people . . . even interviews with
King Kong Kultists, who to be eligible for membership
must have seen the movie at least 100 times and be prepared to pass an 8-hour entrance exam. . . . And yet, and
yet: there is Murphy's Law to consider, that brash Irish
proletarian restatement of Gödel's Theorem—*when everything has been taken care of, when nothing can go wrong,
or even surprise us . . . something will.* So the permutations 'n' combinations of Pudding's *Things That Can Happen in European Politics* for 1931, the year of Gödel's
Theorem, don't give Hitler an outside chance. So, when
laws of heredity are laid down, mutants will be born.
Even as determinist a piece of hardware as the A4 rocket
will begin spontaneously generating items like the "S-Gerät" Slothrop thinks he's chasing like a grail. And so, too,
the legend of the black scapeape we cast down like Lucifer from the tallest erection in the world has come, in the
fullness of time, to generate its own children, running
around inside Germany even now—the Schwarzkommando,
whom Mitchell Prettyplace, even, could not anticipate.

At PISCES it is widely believed that the Schwarzkommando have been summoned, in the way demons may
be gathered in, called up to the light of day and earth by
the now defunct Operation Black Wing. You can bet Psi
Section was giggling about this for a while. Who could
have guessed there'd be *real* black rocket troops? That a
story made up to scare last year's enemy should prove to
be literally true—and no way now to stuff them back in
the bottle or even say the spell backward: no one ever
knew the complete spell—different people knew different
parts of it, that's what teamwork *is*. . . . By the time it occurs to them to look back through the Most Secret docu-

mentation surrounding Operation Black Wing, to try and
get some idea of how this all might've happened, they
will find, curiously, that certain critical documents are
either missing or have been updated past the end of the
Operation, and that it is impossible at this late date to re-
construct the spell at all, though there will be the usual
elegant and bad-poetic speculation. Even earlier speculation will be lopped and tranquilized. Nothing will remain,
for example, of the tentative findings of Freudian Edwin
Treacle and his lot, who toward the end even found themselves at odds with their own minority, the psychoanalytic
wing of Psi Section. It began as a search for some measur-
able basis for the common experience of being haunted by
the dead. After a while colleagues began to put in chits
requesting they be transferred out. Unpleasantries such as
"It's beginning to sound like the Tavistock Institute around
here" began muttering up and down the basement halls.
Palace revolts, many of them conceived in ornamentally
splendid flashes of paranoia, brought locksmiths and weld-
ers in by droves, led to mysterious shortages of office supplies, even of water and heat . . . none of which kept Treacle and lot from carrying on in a Freudian, not to mention
Jungian frame of mind. Word of the Schwarzkommando's
real existence reached them a week before V-E Day. Individual events, who really said what to whom, have been
lost in the frenzy of accusation, crying, nervous break-
downs, and areas of bad taste that followed. Someone
remembers Gavin Trefoil, face as blue as Krishna, running
through the topiary trees stark naked, and Treacle chasing
him with an ax, screaming "Giant *ape?* I'll show *you* a
giant ape all right!"

Indeed he would show the critter to many of us, though
we would not look. In his innocence he saw no reason why
co-workers on an office project should not practice self-
criticism with the same rigor as revolutionary cells do. He
had not meant to offend sensibilities, only to show the
others, decent fellows all, that their feelings about blackness were tied to feelings about shit, and feelings about
shit to feelings about putrefaction and death. It seemed to
him so clear . . . why wouldn't they listen? Why wouldn't
they admit that their repressions *had,* in a sense that Europe in the last weary stages of its perversion of magic has

lost, *had* incarnated real and living men, likely (according
to the best intelligence) in possession of real and living
weapons, as the dead father who never slept with you,
Penelope, returns night after night to your bed, trying to
snuggle in behind you . . . or as your unborn child wakes
you, crying in the night and you feel its ghost-lips at your
breast . . . they are real, they are living, as you pretend to
scream inside the Fist of the Ape . . . but looking over now
at the much more likely candidate, cream-skinned Katje
under the Wheel of Fortune, who is herself getting ready
now to bolt down the beach and into the relative calm of
the switch-back railway. Pointsman is hallucinating. He
has lost control. Pointsman is supposed to have absolute
control over Katje. Where does this leave her? In a control
that is out of control. Not even back in the leather and
pain of gemütlich Captain Blicero's world has she felt as
terrified as now.

Roger Mexico is taking it personally, oh-I-say, only trying to help. . . .

What the somewhat disconnected Mr. Pointsman has
been hearing all this time is a voice, strangely familiar, a
voice he once imagined a face in a well-known news
photograph from the War to have:

"Here is what you have to do. You need Mexico now,
more than ever. Your winter anxieties about the End of
History seem now all well comforted to rest, part of your
biography now like any old bad dream. But like Lord
Acton always sez, History is not woven by innocent hands.
Mexico's girl friend there is a threat to your whole enterprise. He will do anything to hold on. Scowling and even
cursing him she will nevertheless seduce him away, into
a civilian fogbank in which you will lose him and never
find him—not unless you act now, Pointsman. Operation
Backfire is sending ATS girls out to the Zone now. Rocket
girls: secretarial and even minor technical duties at the
Cuxhaven test range. You have only to drop a word to
SPOG, through Dennis Joint here, and Jessica Swanlake
is out of your way. Mexico may complain for a while, but
all the more reason for him, given the proper direction, to
Lose Himself In His Work, eh? Remember the eloquent
words of Sir Denis Nayland Smith to young Alan Sterling,
whose fiancée is in the clutches of the insidious yellow

Adversary: 'I have been through the sort of fires which are burning you now, Sterling, and I have always found that work was the best ointment for the burns.' And we both know what Nayland Smith represents, mm? don't we."

"*I* do," sez Pointsman, aloud, "but I can't really say that *you* do, can I, if I don't even know who you *are*, you see."

This strange outburst does not reassure Pointsman's companions. They begin to edge away, in definite alarm. "We should find a doctor," murmurs Dennis Joint, winking at Katje like a blond crewcut Groucho Marx. Jessica, forgetting her sulk, takes Roger's arm.

"You see, you see," the voice starts up again, "she feels that she's protecting him, *against you*. How many chances does one get to *be* a synthesis, Pointsman? East and West, together in the same bloke? You can not only be Nayland Smith, giving a young lad in a funk wholesome advice about the virtues of work, but you also, at the same time, get to be *Fu Manchu*! eh? the one who has the young lady in his power! How's *that*? Protagonist and antagonist in one. I'd jump at it, if I were you."

Pointsman is about to retort something like, "But you're *not* me," only he sees how the others all seem to be goggling at him. "Oh, ha, ha," he sez instead. "Talking to myself, here. Little—sort of—eccentricity, heh, heh."

"Yang and Yin," whispers the Voice, "Yang and Yin. . . ."

3

In the Zone

*Toto, I have a feeling we're not in Kansas
any more....*
— Dorothy, arriving in Oz

□

We are safely past the days of the Eis-Heiligen—St. Pan-
cratius, St. Servatius, St. Bonifacius, die kalte Sophie . . .
they hover in clouds above the vineyards, holy beings of
ice, ready with a breath, an intention, to ruin the year
with frost and cold. In certain years, especially War years,
they are short on charity, peevish, smug in their power:
not quite saintly or even Christian. The prayers of growers,
pickers and wine enthusiasts must reach them, but there's
no telling how the ice-saints feel—coarse laughter, pagan
annoyance, who understands this rear-guard who preserve
winter against the revolutionaries of May?

They found the countryside, this year, at peace by a
scant few days. Already vines are beginning to grow back
over dragon's teeth, fallen Stukas, burned tanks. The sun
warms the hillsides, the rivers fall bright as wine. The
saints have refrained. Nights have been mild. The frost
didn't come. It is the spring of peace. The vintage, God
granting at least a hundred days of sun, will be fine.

Nordhausen puts less credence in the ice-saints than do
wine regions farther south, but even here the season looks
promising. Rain blows scattering out over the town as
Slothrop comes in in the early morning, bare feet, blister-
ing and reblistering, cooled here in the wet grass. There's
sunlight up on the mountains. His shoes got lifted by some
DP with fingers lighter than dreams, on one of the many
trains since the Swiss border, someplace rolling across
Bavaria fast asleep. Whoever it was left a red tulip between Slothrop's toes. He has taken it for a sign. A reminder of Katje.

Signs will find him here in the Zone, and ancestors will
reassert themselves. It's like going to that Darkest Africa to
study the natives there, and finding their quaint superstitions taking you over. In fact, funny thing, Slothrop just
the other night ran into an African, the first one he ever
met in his life. Their discussion on top of the freight car
in the moonlight lasted only a minute or two. Small talk
for the sudden background departure of Major Duane
Marvy over the side bounce-clatter down the cobbled fill

into the valley—well, certainly nothing was said then of any Herero beliefs about ancestors. Yet he feels his own, stronger now as borders fall away and the Zone envelops him, his own WASPs in buckled black, who heard God clamoring to them in every turn of a leaf or cow loose among apple orchards in autumn. . . .

Signs of Katje, and doubles too. One night he sat in a children's play house on an abandoned estate, feeding a fire from the hair of a blonde doll with lapis lazuli eyes. He kept those eyes. A few days later he traded them for a ride and half a boiled potato. Dogs barked far away, summerwind blew in the birches. He was on one of the main arterials of the spring's last dissolution and retreat. Somewhere nearby, one of Major-General Kammler's rocket units had together found corporate death, leaving in their crippled military rage pieces, modules, airframe sections, batteries rotting, paper secrets rained back into slurry. Slothrop follows. Any clue's good enough to hop a train for. . . .

The doll's hair was human. The smell of it burning is horrible. Slothrop hears movement from the other side of the fire. A ratcheting noise—he grabs his blanket, ready to vault away out the empty window frame, expecting a grenade. Instead one of these little brightly painted German toys, an orangutan on wheels, comes ki-ki-ki-ing into the firelight, spastic, head lolling, face in an idiot's grin, steel knuckles scraping the floor. It rolls nearly into the fire before the clockwork runs down, the wagging head coming to dead center to stare at Slothrop.

He feeds the fire another tuft of golden hair. "Evening."

Laughter, somewhere. A child. But old laughter.

"Come on out, I'm harmless."

The ape is followed by a tiny black crow with a red beak, also on wheels, hopping, cawing, flapping metal wings.

"Why are you burning my doll's hair?"

"Well, it's not her own hair, you know."

"Father said it belonged to a Russian Jewess."

"Why don't you come in to the fire?"

"Hurts my eyes." Winding again. Nothing moves. But a music box begins to play. The tune is minor and precise. "Dance with me."

"I can't see you."

"Here." Out of the fire's pale, a tiny frost-flower. He reaches and just manages to find her hand, to grasp her little waist. They begin their stately dance. He can't even tell if he's leading.

He never saw her face. She felt like voile and organdy. "Nice dress."

"I wore it for my first communion." The fire died presently, leaving starlight and a faint glow over some town to the east, through windows whose panes were all gone. The music box still played, beyond the running time, it seemed, of an ordinary spring. Their feet moved over clouded, crumbled old glass, torn silks, bones of dead rabbits and kittens. The geometrical path took them among ballooning, ripped arrases, smelling of dust and an older bestiary than the one by the fire ... unicorns, chimaeras ... and what had he seen festooning the child-sized entranceway? Garlic bulbs? Wait—weren't they to keep away *vampires?* A faint smell reached him exactly then, an inbreaking of Balkan blood on the air of his north, as he turned back to her to ask if she really was Katje, the lovely little Queen of Transylvania. But the music had run down. She had vaporized from his arms.

Well here he is skidded out onto the Zone like a planchette on a Ouija board, and what shows up inside the empty circle in his brain might string together into a message, might not, he'll just have to see. But he can feel a sensitive's fingers, resting lightly but sure on his days, and he thinks of them as Katje's.

He's still Ian Scuffling, war (peace?) correspondent, though back in British uniform these days, with plenty of time on these trains to hash over in his mind the information Mario Schweitar bootlegged for him back there in Zürich. There is a fat file on Imipolex G, and it seems to point to Nordhausen. The engineer on the customer end of the Imipolex contract was one Franz Pökler. He came to Nordhausen in early '44, as the rocket was going into mass production. He was billeted in the Mittelwerke, an underground factory complex run largely by the SS. No word on where he went when the plant was evacuated in February and March. But Ian Scuffling, ace reporter, will be sure to find a clue down in the Mittelwerke.

Slothrop sat in the swaying car with thirty other cold
and tattered souls, eyes all pupil, lips cratered with sores,
They were singing, some of them. A lot of them kids. It is
a Displaced Person's song, and Slothrop will hear it often
around the Zone, in the encampments, out on the road, in
a dozen variations:

> If you see a train this evening,
> Far away against the sky,
> Lie down in your wooden blanket,
> Sleep, and let the train go by.
>
> Trains have called us, every midnight,
> From a thousand miles away,
> Trains that pass through empty cities,
> Trains that have no place to stay.
>
> No one drives the locomotive,
> No one tends the staring light,
> Trains have never needed riders,
> Trains belong to bitter night.
>
> Railway stations stand deserted,
> Rights-of-way lie clear and cold:
> What we left them, trains inherit,
> Trains go on, and we grow old.
>
> Let them cry like cheated lovers,
> Let their cries find only wind.
> Trains are meant for night and ruin.
> We are meant for song, and sin.

Pipes are passing around. Smoke hangs from the damp
wood slats, is whipped out cracks into the night slipstream.
Children wheeze in their sleep, the rachitic babies cry . . .
now and then the mothers exchange a word. Slothrop huddles inside his paper misfortune.

The Swiss firm's dossier on L. (for Laszlo) Jamf listed
all his assets at the time he came to work in Zürich. Apparently he had sat—as token scientist—on the board of
directors of the Grössli Chemical Corporation as late as
1924. Among stock options and pieces of this firm and
that back in Germany—pieces to be gathered in over the
next year or two by the octopus IG—was the record of a

transaction between Jamf and Mr. Lyle Bland, of Boston, Massachusetts.

On the beam, Jackson. Lyle Bland is a name he knows, all right. And a name that also shows up often in the private records Jamf kept of his own business deals. Seems that Bland, during the early twenties, was heavily involved with the Hugo Stinnes operation in Germany. Stinnes, while he lasted, was the Wunderkind of European finance. Based out of the Ruhr, where his family had been coal barons for generations, young Stinnes built up a good-sized empire of steel, gas, electric and water power, street-cars and barge lines before he was 30. During the World War he worked closely with Walter Rathenau, who was ramrodding the whole economy then. After the war Stinnes managed to put the horizontal electrical trust of Siemens-Schuchert together with the coal and iron supplies of the Rheinelbe Union into a super-cartel that was both horizontal and vertical, and to buy into just about everything else—shipyards, steamship lines, hotels, restaurants, forests, pulp mills, newspapers—meantime also speculating in currency, buying foreign money with marks borrowed from the Reichsbank, driving the mark down and then paying off the loans at a fraction of the original figure. More than any one financier he was blamed for the Inflation. Those were the days when you carried marks around in wheelbarrows to your daily shopping and used them for toilet paper, assuming you had anything to shit. Stinnes's foreign connections went all over the world—Brazil, the East Indies, the United States—businessmen like Lyle Bland found his growth rate irresistible. The theory going around at the time was that Stinnes was conspiring with Krupp, Thyssen, and others to ruin the mark and so get Germany out of paying her war debts.

Bland's connection was vague. Jamf's records mention that he had negotiated contracts for supplying tons of private currency known as Notgeld to Stinnes and colleagues, as well as "Mefo bills" to the Weimar Republic—another of Hjalmar Schacht's many bookkeeping dodges to keep official records clear of any hint of weapons procurement banned under the terms of Versailles. Some of these banknote contracts were let to a certain Massachusetts paper mill, on whose board Lyle Bland happened to sit.

The name of this contractor was the Slothrop Paper Company.

He reads his name without that much surprise. It belongs here, as do the most minor details during déjà vu. Instead of any sudden incidence of light (even in the shape of a human being: golden and monitory light), as he stares at these eight ink marks, there passes a disagreeable stomach episode, a dread tangible as vomit beginning to assert itself—the same vertigo that overtook him one day long ago in the Himmler-Spielsaal. A gasbag surrounds his head, rubbery, vast, pushing in from all sides, that feeling we know, yes, but . . . He is also getting a hardon, for no immediate reason. And there's that *smell* again, a smell from before his conscious memory begins, a soft and chemical smell, threatening, haunting, not a smell to be found out in the world—*it is the breath of the Forbidden Wing* . . . essence of all the still figures waiting for him inside, daring him to enter and find a secret he cannot survive.

Once something was done to him, in a room, while he lay helpless. . . .

His erection hums from a certain distance, like an instrument installed, wired by Them into his body as a colonial outpost here in our raw and clamorous world, another office representing Their white Metropolis far away. . . .

A sad story, all right. Slothrop, very nervous by now, reads on. Lyle Bland, eh? Well, sure, that fits. He can recall dimly once or twice having seen Uncle Lyle. The man used to come to visit his father, affable, fair-haired, a hustler in the regional Jim Fisk style. Bland was always picking young Tyrone up and swinging him around by his feet. That was O.K.—Slothrop had no special commitment at the time to right side up.

From what it sez here, Bland either saw the Stinnes crash coming before most of its other victims, or was just naturally nervous. Early in '23 he began to sell off his interests in the Stinnes operations. One of these sales was made through Laszlo Jamf to the Grössli Chemical Corporation (later Psychochemie AG). One of the assets transferred in this sale was "all interest in Schwarzknabe enterprise. Seller agrees to continue surveillance duties until such time as Schwindel operative can be relieved by purchaser equivalent, acceptability to be determined by seller."

Jamf's codebook happens to be in the dossier. Part of the man's personality structure, after all. "Schwindel" was his code name for Hugo Stinnes. Clever sense of humor, the old fart. Across from "Schwarzknabe," now, are the initials "T.S."

Well, holy cow, Slothrop reckons, that must be me, huh. Barring the outside possibility of Tough Shit.

Listed as a "Schwarzknabe" liability is the unpaid remainder of a bill to Harvard University, about $5000 worth including the interest, "as per agreement (oral) with Schwarzvater."

"Schwarzvater" is the code for "B.S." Which, barring the outside possibility of Bull Shit, seems to be Slothrop's own father, Broderick. Blackfather Slothrop.

Nice way to find out your father made a deal 20 years ago with somebody to spring for your education. Come to think of it, Slothrop never could quite put the announcements, all through the Depression, of imminent family ruin, together with the comfort he enjoyed at Harvard. Well, now, what *was* the deal between his father and Bland? I've been sold, Jesus Christ I've been sold to IG Farben like a side of beef. Surveillance? Stinnes, like every industrial emperor, had his own company spy system. So did the IG. Does this mean Slothrop has been under their observation—m-maybe since he was *born?* Yaahhh . . .

The fear balloons again inside his brain. It will not be kept down with a simple Fuck You. . . . A smell, a forbidden room, at the bottom edge of his memory. He can't see it, can't make it out. Doesn't want to. It is allied with the Worst Thing.

He knows what the smell has to be: though according to these papers it would have been too early for it, though he has never come across any of the stuff among the daytime coordinates of his life, still, down here, back here in the warm dark, among early shapes where the clocks and calendars don't mean too much, he knows that what's haunting him now will prove to be the smell of Imipolex G.

Then there's this recent dream he is afraid of having again. He was in his old room, back home. A summer afternoon of lilacs and bees, and warm air through an open window. Slothrop had found a very old dictionary of technical German. It fell open to a certain page prickling with black-face type. Reading down the page, he would come to JAMF. The definition would read: I. He woke begging It *no*—but even after waking, he was sure, he would remain sure, that It could visit him again, any time It wanted. Perhaps you know that dream too. Perhaps It has warned you never to speak Its name. If so, you know about how Slothrop'll be feeling now.

What he does is lurch to his feet, over to the door of the freight car, which is going up a grade. He drags open the door, slips out—action, action—and mounts a ladder to the roof. A foot from his face, this double row of shiny bright teeth hangs in the air. Just what he needs. It is Major Marvy of U.S. Army Ordnance, leader of Marvy's Mothers, the meanest-ass technical intelligence team in this whole fuckin' Zone, mister. Slothrop can call him Duane, if he wants. "Boogie, boogie, boogie! Catch all 'em *jungle* bunnies back 'ere in 'at *next car!* Sheee-*oo!*"

"Wait a minute," sez Slothrop, "I think I've been asleep or something." His feet are cold. This Marvy is really fat. Pants bloused into shiny combat boots, roll of fat hanging over a web belt where he keeps his sunglasses and .45, hornrims, hair slicked back, eyes like safety valves that pop out at you whenever—as now—the pressure in his head gets too high.

Marvy hitched a lift on a P-47 from Paris far as Kassel, got coupled onto this train here west of Heiligenstadt. He's headed for the Mittelwerke, like Ian Scuffling. Needs to coordinate with some Project Hermes people from General Electric. Sure makes him nervous, those niggers next door. "Hey, ought to be a good story for you people. Warn the folks back home."

"Are they GIs?"

"Shit no. Kraut. South-West African. Something. You mean you don't know about that? Come on. Aw. Limey intelligence sure ain't too intelligent, hahah, no offense understand. I thought the whole world knew." Follows a lurid tale—which sounds like something SHAEF made up,

Goebbels's less than giddy imagination reaching no further than Alpine Redoubts and such—of Hitler's scheme for setting up a Nazi empire in black Africa, which fell through after Old Blood 'n' Guts handed Rommel's ass to him in the desert. " 'Here's yer ass, General.' 'Ach du lieber! Mein Arsch! YAH—hahaha . . .' " clutching comically at the seat of his own large trousers. Well, the black cadres had no more future in Africa, stayed on in Germany as governments-in-exile without even official recognition, drifted somehow into the ordnance branch of the German Army, and pretty soon learned how to be rocket technicians. Now they were just running loose. Wild. Haven't been interned as P/Ws, far as Marvy knows they haven't even been disarmed. "Not enough we have to worry about Russkys, frogs, limeys—hey, beg pardon, buddy. Now we got not just niggers you see, but *kraut* niggers. Well, Jesus. V-E Day just about everyplace you had a rocket, you had you a nigger. Never any all-boogie batteries, understand. Even the krauts couldn't be *that* daffy! One battery, that's 81 men, *plus* all your support, your launch-control, power, propellants, your surveying— champ, that'd sure be one heap o' niggers all in one place. But are they still all scattered out, like they were? You find out, you got you a *scoop*, friend. Cause if they're gettin' together now, oh dat's *bi-i-i-g* trouble! There's at least two dozen in that car—right down there, look. A-and they're *headin' for Nordhausen*, pal!" a fat finger-poke in the chest with each word, "hah? Whatcha think they have in mind? You know what I think? They have a *plan*. Yeah. I think it's rockets. Don't ask me how, it's just something I feel here, in m'heart. A-and you know, that's *awful* dangerous. You can't trust *them*— With *rockets*? They're a childlike race. Brains are smaller."

"But our patience," suggests a calm voice now out of the darkness, "our patience is enormous, though perhaps not unlimited." So saying, a tall African with a full imperial beard steps up grabs the fat American, who has time to utter one short yell before being flung bodily over the side. Slothrop and the African watch the Major bounce down the embankment behind them, arms and legs flying, out of sight. Firs crowd the hills. A crescent moon has risen over one ragged crest.

The man introduces himself in English, as Oberst Enzian, of the Schwarzkommando. He apologizes for his show of temper, notes Slothrop's armband, declines an interview before Slothrop can get in a word. "There's no story. We're DPs, like everybody else."

"The Major seemed worried that you're headed for Nordhausen."

"Marvy is going to be an annoyance, I can tell. Still, he doesn't pose as much of a problem as—" He peers at Slothrop. "Hmm. Are you really a war correspondent?"

"No."

"A free agent, I'd guess."

"Don't know about that 'free,' Oberst."

"But you are free. We all are. You'll see. Before long." He steps away down the spine of the freighttop, waving a beckoning German good-by: "Before long. . . ."

Slothrop sits on the rooftop, rubbing his bare feet. A friend? A good omen? *Black rocket troops?* What bizarre shit?

> Well good mornin' gang, let's start it
> Off with a bang, so long to
> Double-u Double-u Two-o-o-o!
> Now the fightin's over and we're all in clover
> And I'm here ta bring sunshine to you—
> Hey there Herman the German, stop yer fussin'
>   and squirmin',
> Don'tcha know you're goin' home ta stay—
> No, there's never a frown, here in Rocket,
>   Sock-it Town,
> Where ev'ry day's a beautiful day—
> (Quit kvetchin', Gretchen!)
> Go on and have a beautiful daa-aay!

Nordhausen in the morning: the lea is a green salad, crisp with raindrops. Everything is fresh, washed. The Harz hump up all around, dark slopes bearded to the tops with spruce, fir and larch. High-gabled houses, sheets of water reflecting the sky, muddy streets, American and Russian GIs pouring in and out of the doors of the taverns and makeshift PXs, everybody packing a sidearm. Meadows and logged-off wedges up on the mountainsides flow with mottled light as rainclouds blow away over Thuringia.

Castles perch high over the town, sailing in and out of
torn clouds. Old horses with smudged knobby knees, short-
legged and big-chested, pull wagonloads of barrels, necks
straining at twin collars chained together, heavy horse-
shoes sending mudflowers at each wet clop, down from
the vineyards to the taverns.

Slothrop wanders into a roofless part of town. Old people in black are bat-flittering among the walls. Shops and
dwellings here are all long-looted by the slave laborers
liberated from the Dora camp. Lotta those *fags* still
around, with baskets and 175 badges out on display, staring moistly from doorways. From the glassless bay window of a dress shop, in the dimness behind a plaster
dummy lying bald and sprawled, arms raised to sky, hands
curved for bouquets or cocktail glasses they'll never hold
again, Slothrop hears a girl singing. Accompanying herself
on a balalaika. One of those sad little Parisian-sounding
tunes in 3/4:

> Love never goes away,
> Never completely dies,
> Always some souvenir
> Takes us by sad surprise.
>
> You went away from me,
> One rose was left behind—
> Pressed in my Book of Hours,
> That is the rose I find. . . .
>
> Though it's another year,
> Though it's another me,
> Under the rose is a drying tear,
> Under my linden tree. . . .
>
> Love never goes away,
> Not if it's really true,
> It can return, by night, by day,
> Tender and green and new
> As the leaves from a linden tree, love,
>   that I left with you.

Her name turns out to be Geli Tripping, and the balalaika belongs to a Soviet intelligence officer named Tchitcherine. In a way, Geli does too—part-time, anyhow.

Seems this Tchitcherine maintains a harem, a girl in every rocket-town in the Zone. Yup, another rocket maniac. Slothrop feels like a tourist.

Geli talks about her young man. They sit in her roofless room drinking a pale wine known hereabouts as Nordhäuser Schattensaft. Overhead, black birds with yellow beaks lace the sky, looping in the sunlight from their nests up in the mountain castles and down in the city ruins. Far away, perhaps in the marketplace, a truck convoy is idling all its engines, the smell of exhaust washing over the maze of walls, where moss creeps, water oozes, roaches seek purchase, walls that baffle the motor sound so that it seems to come in from all directions.

She's thin, a bit awkward, very young. Nowhere in her eyes is there any sign of corrosion—she might have spent all her War roofed and secure, tranquil, playing with small forest animals in a rear area someplace. Her song, she admits, sighing, is mostly wishful thinking. "When he's away, he's away. When you came in I almost thought you were Tchitcherine."

"Nope. Just a hard-working newshound, is all. No rockets, no harems."

"It's an arrangement," she tells him. "It's so unorganized out here. There have to be arrangements. You'll find out." Indeed he will—he'll find thousands of arrangements, for warmth, love, food, simple movement along roads, tracks and canals. Even G-5, living its fantasy of being the only government in Germany now, is just the arrangement for being victorious, is all. No more or less real than all these others so private, silent, and lost to History. Slothrop, though he doesn't know it yet, is as properly constituted a state as any other in the Zone these days. Not paranoia. Just how it is. Temporary alliances, knit and undone. He and Geli reach their arrangement hidden from the occupied streets by remnants of walls, in an old fourposter bed facing a dark pier glass. Out the roof that isn't there he can see a long tree-covered mountain ascending. Wine or her breath, nests of down in the hollows of her arms, thighs with the spring of saplings in wind. He's barely inside her before she comes, a fantasy about Tchitcherine in progress, clear and touchingly, across her face. This irritates Slothrop, but doesn't keep him from coming himself.

The foolishness begins immediately on detumescence, amusing questions like, what kind of word has gone out to keep everybody away from Geli but me? Or, is it that something about me reminds her of Tchitcherine, and if so, *what*? And, say, where's that Tchitcherine right now? He dozes off, is roused by her lips, fingers, dewy legs sliding along his. The sun jumps across their section of sky, gets eclipsed by a breast, is reflected out of her child's eyes . . . then clouds, rain for which she puts up a green tarp with tassels she's sewn on, canopy style . . . rain sluices down off the tassels, cold and loud. Night. She feeds him boiled cabbage with an old heirloom of a spoon with a crest on it. They drink more of that wine. Shadows are soft verdigris. The rain has stopped. Somewhere kids go booting an empty gas can over the cobblestones.

Something comes flapping in out of the sky: talons scrabble along the top of the canopy. "What's that?" half awake and she's got the covers again, c'mon Geli. . . .

"My owl," sez Geli. "Wernher. There's a candy bar in the top drawer of the chiffonier, Liebchen, would you mind feeding him?"

Liebchen indeed. Staggering off the bed, vertical for the first time all day, Slothrop removes a Baby Ruth from its wrapper, clears his throat, decides not to ask her how she came by it because he knows, and lobs the thing up on the canopy for that Wernher. Soon, lying together again, they hear peanuts crunching, and a clacking beak.

"Candy bars," Slothrop grouches. "What's the matter with him? Don't you know he's supposed to be out foraging, for live mice or some shit? You've turned him into a house owl."

"You're pretty lazy yourself." Baby fingers creeping down along his ribs.

"Well—I bet—cut it out—I bet that *Tchitcherine* doesn't have to get up and feed that owl."

She cools, the hand stopping where it is. "He loves Tchitcherine. He never comes to be fed, unless Tchitcherine's here."

Slothrop's turn to cool. More correctly, freeze. "Uh, but, you don't mean that Tchitcherine is actually, uh . . ."

"He was supposed to be," sighing.

"Oh. When?"

"This morning. He's late. It happens."

Slothrop's off the bed halfway across the room with a softoff, one sock on and the other in his teeth, head through one armhole of his undershirt, fly zipper jammed, yelling *shit*.

"My brave Englishman," she drawls.

"Why didn't you bring this up earlier, Geli, huh?"

"Oh, come back. It's nighttime, he's with a woman someplace. He can't sleep alone."

"I hope you can."

"Hush. Come here. You can't go out with nothing on your feet. I'll give you a pair of his old boots and tell you all his secrets."

"Secrets?" Look out, Slothrop. "Why should I want to know—"

"You're not a war correspondent."

"Why does everybody keep saying that? Nobody believes me. Of course I'm a war correspondent." Shaking the brassard at her. "Can't you read? Sez 'War Correspondent.' I even have a mustache, here, don't I? Just like that Ernest Hemingway."

"Oh. Then I imagine you wouldn't be looking for Rocket Number 00000 after all. It was just a silly idea I had, I'm sorry."

Oh boy, am I gonna get out of *here*, sez Slothrop to himself, this is a badger game if I ever saw one, man. Who else would be interested in the one rocket out of 6000 that carried the Imipolex G device?

"And you couldn't care less about the Schwarzgerät, either," she keeps on. She keeps on.

"The what?"

"They also called it S-Gerät."

Next higher assembly, Slothrop, remember? Wernher, up on the canopy, is hooting. A signal to that Tchitcherine, no doubt.

Paranoids are not paranoids (Proverb 5) because they're paranoid, but because they keep putting themselves, fucking idiots, deliberately into paranoid situations.

"Now how on earth," elaborately uncorking a fresh bottle of Nordhäuser Schattensaft, *thoppp*, best Cary Grant imitation he can summon up with bowels so echoing tight, suavely refilling glasses, handing one to her, "would a sweet, young, thing, like you, know anything, about rocket, *hahd*-weah?"

"I read Vaslav's mail," as if it's a dumb question, which it is.

"You shouldn't be blabbing to random strangers like this. If he finds out, he'll murder you."

"I like you. I like intrigue. I like playing."

"Maybe you like to get people in trouble."

"All right." Out with the lower lip.

"O.K., O.K., tell me about it. But I don't know if the *Guardian* will even be interested. My editors are a rather stuffy lot, you know."

Goose bumps crowd her bare little breasts. "I posed once for a rocket insignia. Perhaps you've seen it. A pretty young witch straddling an A4. Carrying her obsolete broom over her shoulder. I was voted the Sweetheart of 3/Art. Abt. (mot) 485."

"Are you a real witch?"

"I think I have tendencies. Have you been up to the Brocken yet?"

"Just hit town, actually."

"I've been up there every Walpurgisnacht since I had my first period. I'll take you, if you like."

"Tell me about this, this 'Schwarzgerät.' "

"I thought you weren't interested."

"How can I know if I'm interested or not if I don't even know what I'm supposed or not supposed to be interested *in*?"

"You must be a correspondent. You have a way with words."

Tchitcherine comes roaring through the window, a Nagant blazing in his fist. Tchitcherine lands in a parachute and fells Slothrop with one judo chop. Tchitcherine drives a Stalin tank right into the room, and blasts Slothrop with a 76 mm shell. Thanks for stalling him, Liebchen, he was a spy, well, cheerio, I'm off to Peenemünde and a nubile Polish wench with tits like vanilla ice cream, check you out later.

"I have to go, I think," Slothrop sez, "typewriter needs a new ribbon, gotta sharpen pencils, you know how it is—"

"I told you, he won't be here tonight."

"Why? Is he out after that *Schwarzgerät*, eh?"

"No. He hasn't heard the latest. The message came in from Stettin yesterday."

"In clear, of course."

"Why not?"

"Couldn't be very important."

"It's for sale."

"The message?"

"The S-Gerät, you pill. A man in Swinemünde can get it. Half a million Swiss francs, if you're in the market. He waits on the Strand-Promenade, every day till noon. He'll be wearing a white suit."

Oh yeah? "Blodgett Waxwing."

"It didn't give the name. But I don't think it's Waxwing. He sticks close to the Mediterranean."

"You get around."

"Waxwing is already a legend around the Zone. So is Tchitcherine. For all I know, so are you. What was your name?"

"Cary Grant. Ge-li, Ge-li, Ge-li. . . . Listen, Swinemünde, that's in that Soviet zone, ain't it."

"You sound like a German. Forget frontiers now. Forget subdivisions. There aren't any."

"There are soldiers."

"That's right." Staring at him. "But that's different."

"Oh."

"You'll learn. It's all been suspended. Vaslav calls it an 'interregnum.' You only have to flow along with it."

"Gonna flow outa here now, kid. Thanx for the info, and a tip of the Scuffling hat to ya—"

"Please stay." Curled on the bed, her eyes about to spill over with tears. Aw, shit, Slothrop you sucker . . . but she's just a little kid. . . . "Come here. . . ."

The minute he puts it in, though, she goes wicked and a little crazy, slashing at his legs, shoulders, and ass with chewed-down fingernails sharp as a saw. Considerate Slothrop is trying to hold off coming till she's ready when all of a sudden something heavy, feathered, and many-pointed comes crashing down onto the small of his back, bounces off triggering him and as it turns out Geli too ZONNGGG! eeeeee . . . oh, gee whiz. Wings flap and Wernher—for it is he—ascends into the darkness.

"Fucking bird," Slothrop screams, "he tries that again I'll give him a Baby Ruth right up his ass, boy—" it's a plot it's a plot it's *Pavlovian conditioning!* or something, "Tchitcherine trained him to do that, right?"

"Wrong! *I* trained him to do that." She's smiling at him so four-year-old happy and not holding a thing back, that Slothrop decides to believe everything she's been telling him.

"You are a witch." Paranoid that he is, he snuggles down under the counterpane with the long-legged sorceress, lights a cigarette, and despite endless Tchitcherines vaulting in over the roofless walls with arsenals of disaster all for him, even falls asleep, presently, in her bare and open arms.

□

It's a Sunday-funnies dawn, very blue sky with gaudy pink clouds in it. Mud across the cobblestones is so slick it reflects light, so that you walk not streets but these long streaky cuts of raw meat, hock of werewolf, gammon of Beast. Tchitcherine has big feet. Geli had to stuff pieces of an old chemise in the toes of his boots so they'd fit Slothrop. Dodging constantly for jeeps, ten-ton lorries, Russians on horseback, he finally hitches a ride from an 18-year-old American first lieutenant in a gray Mercedes staff car with dents all over it. Slothrop frisks mustaches, flashes his armband, feeling defensive. The sun's already warm. There's a smell of evergreens on the mountains. This rail driving, who's attached to the tank company guarding the Mittelwerke, doesn't think Slothrop should have any trouble getting inside. English SPOG have come and gone. Right now American Army Ordnance people are busy crating and shipping out parts and tools for a hundred A4s. A big hassle. "Trying to get it all out before the Russians come to take over." Interregnum. Civilians and bureaucrats show up every day, high-level tourists, to stare and go wow. "Guess nobody's seen 'em this big before. I don't know what it is. Like a burlesque crowd. Not gonna do anything, just here to look. Most of them bring cameras. Notice you didn't. We have them for rent at the main gate, if you're interested."

One of many hustles. Yellow James the cook has got him a swell little sandwich wagon, you can hear him in the tunnels calling, "Come an' get 'em! Hot 'n' cold and drippin' with greens!" And there'll be grease on the glasses of half these gobbling fools in another five minutes. Nick De Profundis, the company lounge lizard, has surprised everybody by changing, inside the phone booth of factory spaces here, to an energetic businessman, selling A4 souvenirs: small items that can be worked into keychains, money clips or a scatter-pin for that special gal back home, burner cups of brass off the combustion chambers, ball bearings from the servos, and this week the hep item seems to be SA 100 acorn diodes, cute little mixing valves looted out of the Telefunken units, and the even rarer SA 102s, which of course fetch a higher price. And there's "Micro" Graham, who's let his sideburns grow and lurks in the Stollen where the gullible visitors stray: "Pssst."

"Pssst?"

"Forget it."

"Well now you've got me curious."

"Thought you looked like a sport. You taking the tour?"

"I-I only stepped away for a second. Really, I'm going right back. . . ."

"Finding it a little dull?" Oily Micro moves in on his mark. "Ever wonder to yourself: 'What *really* went on in here?'?"

The visitor who is willing to spend extravagant sums is rarely disappointed. Micro knows the secret doors to rock passages that lead through to Dora, the prison camp next to the Mittelwerke. Each member of the party is given his own electric lantern. There is hurried, basic instruction on what to do in case of any encounter with the dead. "Remember they were always on the defensive here. When the Americans liberated Dora, the prisoners who were still alive went on a rampage after the material— they looted, they ate and drank themselves sick. For others, Death came like the American Army, and liberated them spiritually. So they're apt to be on a spiritual rampage now. Guard your thoughts. Use the natural balance of your mind against them. They'll be coming at you off-balance, remember."

A popular attraction is the elegant Raumwaffe spacesuit wardrobe, designed by famous military couturier Heini of Berlin. Not only are there turnouts dazzling enough to thrill even the juvenile leads of a space-operetta, down to the oddly-colored television images flickering across their toenails, but Heini has even thought of silks for the amusing little Space-Jockeys (Raum-Jockeier) with their electric whips, who will someday zoom about just outside the barrier-glow of the Raketen-Stadt, astride "horses" of polished meteorite all with the same stylized face (a high-contrast imago of the horse that follows you, emphasis on its demented eyes, its teeth, the darkness under its hindquarters . . .), with the propulsive gases blowing like farts out their tail ends—the juvenile leads giggle together at this naughty bathroom moment, and slowly, in what's hardly more than a sigh of gravity here, go bobbing, each radiant in a display of fluorescent plastics, back in to the Waltz, the strangely communal Waltz of the Future, a slightly, disquietingly grainy-dissonant chorale implied here in the whirling silence of faces, the bare shoulderblades slung so space-Viennese, so jaded with Tomorrow. . . .

Then come—the Space Helmets! At first you may be alarmed, on noticing that they appear to be fashioned from skulls. At least the upper dome of this unpleasant headgear is certainly the skull of some manlike creature built to a larger scale. . . . Perhaps Titans lived under this mountain, and their skulls got harvested like giant mush-rooms. . . . The eye-sockets are fitted with quartz lenses. Filters may be slipped in. Nasal bone and upper teeth have been replaced by a metal breathing apparatus, full of slots and grating. Corresponding to the jaw is a built-up section, almost a facial codpiece, of iron and ebonite, perhaps housing a radio unit, thrusting forward in black fatality. For an extra few marks you are allowed to slip one of these helmets on. Once inside *these* yellow caverns, looking out now through neutral-density orbits, the sound of your breath hissing up and around the bone spaces, what you thought was a balanced mind is little help. The compartment the Schwarzkommando were quartered in is no longer an amusing travelogue of native savages taking on ways of the 21st century. The milk calabashes appear only to be made from some plastic. On the spot where tradition sez Enzian had his Illumination, in the course of a wet dream where he coupled with a slender white rocket, there is the dark stain, miraculously still

wet, and a smell you understand is meant to be that of
semen—but it is really closer to soap, or bleach. The wall-
paintings lose their intended primitive crudeness and take
on primitive spatiality, depth and brilliance—transform,
indeed, to dioramas on the theme "The Promise of Space
Travel." Lit sharply by carbide light which hisses and
smells like the bad breath of someone quite familiar to
you, the view commands your stare. After a few minutes
it becomes possible to make out actual movement down
there, even at the immense distances implied by the scale:
yes, we're hanging now down the last limb of our trajectory in to the Raketen-Stadt, a difficult night of magnetic storm behind us, eddy currents still shimmering
through all our steel like raindrops that cling to vehicle
windows . . . yes, it is a City: vegetable "Ho-*ly!*"s and
"Isn't that something!"s go away echoing as we crowd
about the bloom of window in this salt underground. . . .
Strangely, these are not the symmetries we were programmed to expect, not the fins, the streamlined corners,
pylons, or simple solid geometries of the official vision at
all—*that's* for the ribbon clerks back on the Tour, in the
numbered Stollen. No, this Rocket-City, so whitely lit
against the calm dimness of space, is set up deliberately
To Avoid Symmetry, Allow Complexity, Introduce Terror
(from the Preamble to the Articles of Immachination)—
but tourists have to connect the look of it back to things
they remember from their times and planet—back to the
wine bottle smashed in the basin, the bristlecone pines
outracing Death for millennia, concrete roads abandoned
year ago, hairdos of the late 1930s, indole molecules,
especially *polymerized* indoles, as in Imipolex G—

Wait—which one of them was thinking that? Monitors,
get a fix on it, *hurry up*—

But the target slips away. "They handle their own
security down inside," the young rail is telling Slothrop,
"we're here for Surface Guard only. Our responsibility
ends at Stollen Number Zero, Power and Light. It's really
a pretty soft racket for us." Life is good, and nobody's
looking forward much to redeployment. There are fräuleins for screwing, cooking, and doing your laundry. He
can put Slothrop on to champagne, furs, cameras, cigarettes. . . . Can't just be interested in rockets, can he,
that's crazy. He's right.

One of the sweetest fruits of victory, after sleep and
looting, must be the chance to ignore no-parking signs.
There are struck Ps in circles up all over the place, nailed
on trees, wired on girderwork, but the main tunnel entrances are pretty well blocked with vehicles by the time
the dimpled Mercedes arrives. "Shit," hollers the young
tanker, turns off his engine and leaves the German short
at no particular angle on the broad muddy apron. Leaving
keys in the car too, Slothrop's learning to notice items
like this. . . .

The entrance to the tunnel is shaped like a parabola.
The Albert Speer Touch. Somebody during the thirties
was big on parabolas anyhow, and Albert Speer was in
charge of the New German Architecture then, and later
he went on to become Minister of Munitions, and nominal
chief customer for the A4. This parabola here happens
to be the inspiration of a Speer disciple named Etzel
Ölsch. He had noted this parabola shape around on Autobahn overpasses, sports stadiums u.s.w., and thought it
was the most contemporary thing he'd ever seen. Imagine
his astonishment on finding that the parabola was also
the shape of the path intended for the rocket through
space. (What he actually said was, "Oh, that's nice.")
It was his mother who'd named him after Attila the Hun,
and nobody ever found out why. His parabola has a high
loft to it, and the railroad tracks run in underneath, steel
into shadows. Battened cloth camouflage furls back at the
edges. The mountain goes sloping away above, rock crop-
ping out here and there among the bushes and the trees.

Slothrop presents his sooper dooper SHAEF pass,
signed off by Ike and even more authentic, by the colonel
heading up the American "Special Mission V-2" out of
Paris. A Waxwing specialty of the house. B Company,
47th Armored Infantry, 5th Armored Division appears to
be up to something besides security for this place. Slothrop is shrugged on through. There is a lot of moseying,
drawling, and country humor around here. Somebody
must've been picking his nose. A couple days later Slothrop will find a dried piece of snot on the card, a crystal
brown visa for Nordhausen.

In past the white-topped guard towers. Transformers
buzz through the spring morning. Someplace chains rattle
and a tailgate drops. Between ruts, high places, ridges

of mud are beginning to dry out in the sun, to lighten and crumble. Nearby the loud wake-up yawn and stretch of a train whistle cuts loose. In past a heap of bright metal spheres in daylight, with a comical sign PLEEZ NO SQUEEZ-A DA OXYGEN-A UNIT, EH? how long, how long you sfacim-a dis country. . . . In under parabola and parable, straight into the mountain, sunlight gone, into the cold, the dark, the long echoes of the Mittelwerke.

There is that not-so-rare personality disorder known as Tannhäuserism. Some of us love to be taken under mountains, and not always with horny expectations—Venus, Frau Holda, her sexual delights—no, many come, actually, for the gnomes, the critters smaller than you, for the sepulchral way time stretches along your hooded strolls down here, quietly through courtyards that go for miles, with no anxiety about getting lost . . . no one stares, no one is waiting to judge you . . . out of the public eye . . . even a Minnesinger needs to be alone . . . long cloudy-day indoor walks . . . the comfort of a closed place, where everyone is in complete agreement about Death.

Slothrop knows this place. Not so much from maps he had to study at the Casino as knowing it in the way you know *someone is there.* . . .

Plant generators are still supplying power. Rarely a bare bulb will hollow out a region of light. As darkness is mined and transported from place to place like marble, so the light bulb is the chisel that delivers it from its inertia, and has become one of the great secret ikons of the Humility, the multitudes who are passed over by God and History. When the Dora prisoners went on their rampage, the light bulbs in the rocket works were the first to go: before food, before the delights to be looted out of the medical lockers and the hospital pharmacy in Stollen Number 1, these breakable, socketless (in Germany the word for electric socket is also the word for Mother—so, motherless too) images were what the "liberated" had to take. . . .

The basic layout of the plant was another inspiration of Etzel Ölsch, a Nazi inspiration like the parabola, but again also a symbol belonging to the Rocket. Picture the letters SS each stretched lengthwise a bit. These are the two main tunnels, driven well over a mile into the mountain. Or picture a ladder with a slight S-shaped ripple in it, lying flat: 44 runglike Stollen or cross-tunnels, linking the two main ones. A couple hundred feet of rock mountain, at the deepest, press down overhead.

But the shape is more than an elongated SS. Apprentice Hupla comes running in one day to tell the architect. "Master!" he's yelling, "Master!" Ölsch has taken up quarters in the Mittelwerke, insulated from the factory down a few private drifts that don't appear on any map of the place. He's getting into a grandiose idea of what an architect's life should be down here, insisting now on the title "Master" from all his helpers. That isn't his only eccentricity, either. Last three designs he proposed to the Führer all were visually in the groove, beautifully New German, except that none of the buildings will stay up. They look normal enough, but they are designed to fall down, like fat men at the opera falling asleep into someone's lap, shortly after the last rivet is driven, the last forms removed from the newly set allegorical statue. This is Ölsch's "deathwish" problem here, as the little helpers call it: it rates a lot of gossip in the commissary at meals, and beside the coffee urns out on the gloomy stone loading docks. . . . It's well after sunset now, each desk in this vaulted, almost outdoor bay has its own incandescent light on. The gnomes sit out here, at night, with only their bulbs shining conditionally, precariously . . . it all might go dark so easily, in the next second. . . . Each gnome works in front of his drawing board. They're working late. There's a deadline—it's not clear if they're working overtime to meet it, or if they have already failed and are here as punishment. Back in his office, Etzel Ölsch can be heard singing. Tasteless, low beer-hall songs. Now he is lighting a cigar. Both he and the gnome Apprentice Hupla who's just run in know that this is an exploding cigar, put in his humidor as a revolutionary gesture by persons unknown but so without power that it doesn't matter—"Wait, Master, don't light it—Master, put it out, please, it's an *exploding cigar!*"

"Proceed, Hupla, with the intelligence that prompted your rather rude entrance."

"But—"

"Hupla . . ." Puffing masterful clouds of cigar smoke.

"It-it's about the shape of the tunnels here, Master."

"Don't flinch like that, I based that design on the double lightning-stroke, Hupla—the SS emblem."

"But it's also a double integral sign! Did you know that?"

"Ah. Yes: Summe, Summe, as Leibniz said. Well, isn't that—"

BLAM.

All right. But Etzel Ölsch's genius was to be fatally receptive to imagery associated with the Rocket. In the static space of the architect, he might've used a double integral now and then, early in his career, to find volumes under surfaces whose equations were known—masses, moments, centers of gravity. But it's been years since he's had to do with anything that basic. Most of his calculating these days as with marks and pfennigs, not functions of idealistic r and θ, naïve x and y. . . . But in the dynamic space of the living Rocket, the double integral has a different meaning. To integrate here is to operate on a rate of change so that time falls away: change is stilled. . . . "Meters per second" will integrate to "meters." The moving vehicle is frozen, in space, to become architecture, and timeless. It was never launched. It will never fall.

In the guidance, this is what happened: a little pendulum was kept centered by a magnetic field. During launch, pulling gs, the pendulum would swing aft, off center. It had a coil attached to it. When the coil moved through the magnetic field, electric current flowed in the coil. As the pendulum was pushed off center by the acceleration of launch, current would flow—the more acceleration, the more flow. So the Rocket, on its own side of the flight, sensed acceleration first. Men, tracking it, sensed position or distance first. To get to distance from acceleration, the Rocket had to integrate twice—needed a moving coil, transformers, electrolytic cell, bridge of diodes, one tetrode (an extra grid to screen away capacitive coupling inside the tube), an elaborate dance of design precautions to get to what human eyes saw first of all—the distance along the flight path.

There was that backward symmetry again, one that Pointsman missed, but Katje didn't. "A life of its own," she said. Slothrop remembers her reluctant smile, the

Mediterranean afternoon, the peeling twist of a eucalyptus
trunk, the same pink, in that weakening light, as the
American officer's trousers Slothrop wore once upon a
time, and the acid, the pungent smell of the leaves. . . .
The current, flowing in the coil, passed a Wheatstone
bridge and charged up a capacitor. The charge was the
time integral of the current flowing in the coil and bridge.
Advanced versions of this so-called "IG" guidance integrated twice, so that the charge gathering on one side
of the capacitor grew directly as the distance the Rocket
had traveled. Before launch, the other side of the cell
had been charged up to a level representing the distance
to a particular point out in space. Brennschluss exactly
here would make the Rocket go on to hit 1000 yards east
of Waterloo Station. At the instant the charge (B_{IL})
accumulating in flight equaled the preset charge (A_{IL}) on
the other side, the capacitor discharged. A switch closed,
fuel cut off, burning ended. The Rocket was on its own.

That is one meaning of the shape of the tunnels down
here in the Mittelwerke. Another may be the ancient rune
that stands for the yew tree, or Death. The double integral
stood in Etzel Ölsch's subconscious for the method of
finding hidden centers, inertias unknown, as if monoliths
had been left for him in the twilight, left behind by some
corrupted idea of "Civilization," in which eagles cast in
concrete stand ten meters high at the corners of the stadiums where the people, a corrupted idea of "the People"
are gathering, in which birds do not fly, in which imaginary centers far down inside the solid fatality of stone
are thought of not as "heart," "plexus," "consciousness,"
(the voice speaking here grows more ironic, closer to
tears which are not all theatre, as the list goes on . . .)
"Sanctuary," "dream of motion," "cyst of the eternal present," or "Gravity's gray eminence among the councils of
the living stone." No, as none of these, but instead a
point in space, a point hung precise as the point where
burning must end, never launched, never to fall. And
what is the specific shape whose center of gravity is the
Brennschluss Point? Don't jump at an infinite number of
possible shapes. There's only one. It is most likely an
interface between one order of things and another. There's
a Brennschluss point for every firing site. They still hang

up there, all of them, a constellation waiting to have a 13th sign of the Zodiac named for it . . . but they lie so close to Earth that from many places they can't be seen at all, and from different places inside the zone where they can be seen, they fall into completely different patterns. . . .

Double integral is also the shape of lovers curled asleep, which is where Slothrop wishes he were now—all the way back with Katje, even lost as he might feel again, even more vulnerable than now—even (because he still honestly misses her), preserved by accident, in ways he can't help seeing, accident whose own much colder honesty each lover has only the other to protect him from. . . . *Could* he live like that? Would They ever agree to let him and Katje live like that? He's had nothing to say to anyone about her. It's not the gentlemanly reflex that made him edit, switch names, insert fantasies into the yarns he spun for Tantivy back in the ACHTUNG office, so much as the primitive fear of having a soul captured by a likeness of image or by a name. . . . He wants to preserve what he can of her from Their several entropies, from Their softsoaping and Their money: maybe he thinks that if he can do it for her he can also do it for himself . . . although that's awful close to nobility for Slothrop and The Penis He Thought Was His Own.

In the sheet-metal ducting that snakes like a spine along the overhead, plant ventilation moans. Now and then it sounds like voices. Traffic from somewhere remote. It's not as if they were discussing Slothrop *directly*, understand. But he wishes he could hear it better. . . .

Lakes of light, portages of darkness. The concrete facing of the tunnel has given way to whitewash over chunky fault-surfaces, phony-looking as the inside of an amusement-park cave. Entrances to cross-tunnels slip by like tuned pipes with an airflow at their mouths . . . once upon a time lathes did screech, playful machinists had shootouts with little brass squirt cans of cutting oil . . . knuckles were bloodied against grinding wheels, pores, creases and quicks were stabbed by the fine splinters of steel . . . tubeworks of alloy and glass contracted tinkling in air that felt like the dead of winter, and amber light raced in phalanx among the small neon bulbs. Once, all this did happen. It is hard down here in Mittelwerke to live in the present for very long. The nostalgia you feel is not your own, but it's potent. All the objects have grown still, drowned, enfeebled with evening, terminal evening. Tough skins of oxides, some only a molecule thick, shroud the metal surfaces, fade out human reflection. Straw-colored drive belts of polyvinyl alcohol sag and release their last traces of industrial odor. Though found adrift and haunted, full of signs of recent human tenancy, this is not the legendary ship *Marie-Celeste*—it isn't bounded so neatly, these tracks underfoot run away fore and aft into all stilled Europe, and our flesh doesn't sweat and pimple here for the domestic mysteries, the attic horror of What Might Have Happened so much as for our knowledge of what likely *did happen* . . . it was always easy, in open and lonely places, to be visited by Panic wilderness fear, but these are the urban fantods here, that come to get you when you are lost or isolate inside the way time is passing, when there is no more History, no time-traveling capsule to find your way back to, only the lateness and the absence that fill a great railway shed after the capital has been evacuated, and the goat-god's city cousins wait for you at the edges of the light, playing the tunes they always played, but more audible now, because everything else has gone away or fallen silent . . . barn-swallow souls, fashioned of brown twilight, rise toward the white ceilings . . . they are unique to the Zone, they answer to the new Uncertainty. Ghosts used to be either likenesses of the dead or wraiths of the living. But here in the Zone categories have been blurred badly. The status of the name you miss, love, and search for now has grown ambiguous and remote, but this is even more than the bureaucracy of mass absence—some still live, some have died, but many, many have forgotten which they are. Their likenesses will not serve. Down here are only wrappings left in the light, in the dark: images of the Uncertainty. . . .

Post-A4 humanity is moving, hammering, and shouting among the tunnels. Slothrop will catch sight of badged civilians in khaki, helmet liners with GE stenciled on, sometimes getting a nod, eyeglasses flashing under a distant light bulb, most often ignored. Military working parties go at route-step bitching in and out, carrying crates. Slothrop is hungry and Yellow James is nowhere in sight.

But there is nobody down here even going to say howdy to, much less feed, the free lance Ian Scuffling. No, wait, by golly here comes a delegation of girls in tight pink lab coats reaching just to the tops of bare thighs, tripping up the tunnel on stylish gold wedgies "Ah, so reizend ist!" too many to hug at once, "Hübsch, was?" now now ladies one at a time, they are giggling and reaching to drape around his neck lush garlands of silvery B nuts and flange fittings, scarlet resistors and bright-yellow capacitors strung like little sausages, scraps of gasketry, miles of aluminum shavings as curly-bouncy 'n' bright as Shirley Temple's head—hey Hogan ya can keep yer hula girls— and where are they taking him here? into an empty Stollen, where they all commence a fabulous orgy, which goes on for days and days, full of poppies, play, singing, and carrying on.

Moving into Stollen 20 and up, traffic grows heavier. This was the A4 part of the factory, which the Rocket shared with V-1 and turboprop assemblies. Out of these Stollen, the 20s, 30s, and 40s, Rocket components were fed out crosswise into the two main assembly lines. As you walk deeper, you retrace the Rocket's becoming: superchargers, center sections, nose assemblies, power units, controls, tail sections . . . lotta these tail sections still around here, stacked alternately fins up/fins down, row on row identical, dimpled ripply metal surfaces. Slo- throp moseys along looking at his face in them, watching it warp and slide by, just a big underground fun house here folks. . . . Empty dollies with small metal wheels chain away back down the tunnel: they carry four-bladed arrowhead shapes that point at the ceiling—oh. Right— the pointed holders must've fit inside the expansion noz- zles of the thrust chambers, sure enough here comes a bunch of them, *big* fucking things tall as Slothrop, capital As painted in white near the burner cups. . . . Overhead the fat and sinuous white-lagged pipes are lurking, and the steel lamps give no light out of their scorched skullcap reflectors . . . down the tunnel's centerline run Lally columns, slender, gray, the exposed threads locked in rust of long standing . . . blue shadows wash through the spare-parts cages, set on planking and I beams hung from damp and chimney-sized columns of brick . . . glasswool insulation lies beside the tracks, heaped like snow. . . .

Final assembly went on in Stollen 41. The cross-tunnel is 50 feet deep, to accommodate the finished Rocket. Sounds of carousing, of voices distinctly unbalanced, come welling up, reverberating off of the concrete. Personnel are weaving back up the main tunnel with a glassy and rubicund look to their faces. Slothrop squints down into this long pit, and makes out a crowd of Americans and Russians gathered around a huge oak beer barrel. A gnome-size German civilian with a red von Hindenburg mustache is dispensing steins of what looks to be mostly head. Ordnance smoke-puffs flicker on nearly every sleeve. The Americans are singing

ROCKET LIMERICKS

There once was a thing called a V-2,
To pilot which you did not need to—
You just pushed a button,
And it would leave nuttin'
But stiffs and big holes and debris, too.

The tune is known universally among American fraternity boys. But for some reason it is being sung here in German Storm Trooper style: notes clipping off sharp at the end of each line, then a pulse of silence before the attack on the next line.

[Refrain:] Ja, ja, ja, ja!
In Prussia they never eat pussy!
There ain't hardly cats enough,
There's garbage and that's enough,
So waltz me around again, Russky!

Drunks are hanging from steel ladders and draped over catwalks. Beer fumes crawl in the long cavern, among pieces of olive-drab rocket, some upright, some lying on their sides.

There was a young fellow named Crockett,
Who had an affair with a rocket.
If you saw them out there
You'd be tempted to stare,
But if you ain't tried it, don't knock it!

Slothrop is hungry and thirsty. Despite the clear and present miasma of evil in Stollen 41, he starts looking for some way to go down there and maybe score some of that lunch. Turns out the only way down is by a cable, hooked to an overhead hoist. A fat cracker Pfc. lounges at the controls, sucking on a bottle of wine. "Go ahead, Jackson, I'll give you a good ride. They taught me how to run these in the WPA." Bracing his mustache in what he figures to be a stiff upper lip, Ian Scuffling climbs on, one foot through an eye-splice, the other hanging free. An electric motor whines, Slothrop lets go the last steel railing and clutches on to the cable as 50 feet of twilit space appears underneath him. Uh . . .

Rolling out over Stollen 41, heads milling far below, beer foam bobbing like torches in the shadows—suddenly the motor cuts off and he's falling like a rock. Oh fuck, "Too young!" he screams, voice pitched way too high so it comes out like a teenager on the radio, which ordinarily would be embarrassing, but here's the concrete floor rushing up at him, he can see every shuttering mark, every dark crystal of Thuringian sand he's going to be splashed over—not even a body nearby to get him off with only multiple fractures. . . . With about ten feet to go the Pfc. puts on the brakes. Maniacal laughter from above and behind. The cable, brought up taut, sings under Slothrop's hand till he loses his grip on it, falls, and is carried gently upside down and hanging by the foot, in among fun-seekers around the beer keg who, used to this form of arrival by now, only continue their singing:

> There was a young fellow named Hector,
> Who was fond of a launcher-erector.
> But the squishes and pops
> Of acute pressure drops
> Wrecked Hector's hydraulic connector.

Each young American in turn getting to his feet (optional), raising his tankard, and singing about different ways of Doing It with the A4 or its related hardware. Slothrop does not know that they are singing to him, and neither do they. He eyes the inverted scene with a certain unease: with his brain approaching the frontiers of red-out, there comes to him the peculiar notion that

it's Lyle Bland who has hold of his ankle here. So he
is borne stately into the fringes of the party. "Hey!"
observes a crewcut youth, "i-it's *Tarzan* or something! Ha!
Ha!" Half a dozen Ordnance people, juiced and roaring
happily, grab for Slothrop. After a lot of twisting and
shoving, the foot is freed from its wire loop. The hoist
whines back the way it came, to its prankish operator
and the next fool he can talk into riding it.

> There once was a fellow named Moorehead,
> Who had an affair with a warhead.
> His wife moved away
> The very next day—
> She *was* always kind of a sorehead.

The Russians are drinking relentlessly and in silence,
shuffling boots, frowning, maybe trying to translate these
limericks. It isn't clear whether the Americans are here
on Russian sufferance or vice versa. Somebody presses on
Slothrop a shell-case, ice cold, foaming down the sides.
"Gee, we weren't expecting the English too. Some party,
huh? Stick around—he'll be along in a minute."

"Who's that." Thousands of these luminous worms are
wriggling all over Slothrop's field of vision, and his foot
is beginning to prickle awake again. Oh, this beer here
is *cold*, cold and hop-bitter, no point coming up for air,
gulp, till it's all—hahhhh. His nose comes up drowned
in foam, his mustache white and bubbly too. All at once
comes shouting from the edges of the company. "Here
he is, here he is!" "Give him a beer!" "Hi there, Major,
babes, sir!"

> There was a technician named Urban,
> Who had an affair with a turbine.
> "It's much nicer," he said,
> "Than a woman in bed,
> And it's sure as hell cheaper than bourbon!"

"What's happening," inquires Slothrop through the
head of another beer just materialized in his hand.
"It's Major Marvy. This is his going-away party."
Marvy's Mothers are all singing "For He's a Jolly Good
Fellow," now. Which nobody can deny if they know

what's good for them, is the impression one cannot help
receiving. . . .

"Uh, where's he going?"

"Away."

"Thought he was here to see that GE."

"Sure, who do ya think's pickin' up the tab f'r this?"

Marvy here by subterranean light is even less engaging
than he was in the moonlight on top of that boxcar. The
rolls of fat, bulging eyes and glistening teeth are grayer
here, screened more coarsely. A strip of adhesive tape
plastered athletically over the bridge of his nose, and a
purple, yellow, and green decoration around one eye
testify to his rapid journey down the railroad embankment the other night. He is shaking hands with his well-
wishers, booming male endearments, paying special attention to the Russians—"Well, bet *you've* spiked *that* with
a little vodka! Hah?" moving on "Vlad, fella, how's yer
ass!" The Russians do not appear to understand, which
leaves them only the fanged smile, the Easter-egg eyes,
to make sense of. Slothrop is just snorting foam out of
his nose when Marvy spots him, and those eyes bug out
in earnest.

"*There* he is," in a great roar, indicating Slothrop with
a trembling finger, "by God the limey sonofabitch go *git*
him, boys!" Go *git him,* boys? Slothrop continuing to gaze
a moment here at this finger, illuminated in cute flourishes
and curlicues of cherubic fat.

"There, there, my man," begins Ian Scuffling, by which
point hostile faces have begun to close in. Hmm. . . . Oh,
that's right, escape—he sloshes beer at the head nearest,
heaves the empty shell case at another, finds a gap in
the crowd, slithers through and flees, across florid faces
of drunks asleep, vaulting khaki paunches festooned with
splashes of vomit, away down the deep cross-tunnel,
among the pieces of Rocket.

"Reveille you hammerheads," Marvy's screaming, "don't
let that 'sucker git away!" A sergeant with a boy's face
and gray hair, dozing with a grease gun cradled against
him, wakes up crying, "Krauts!" lets loose a deafening
burst from his weapon straight into the beer barrel, which
destroys the bottom half and sends a great gush of wet
amber and foam surging among the pursuing Americans,

half of whom promptly slip and go down on their ass. Slothrop reaches the other end of the Stollen with a good lead, and goes sprinting up a ladder there, taking rungs two at a time. *Shots*— Terrific blasts in this soundbox. Either Marvy's Mothers are too drunk, or the darkness is saving him. He hits the top out of breath.

In the other main tunnel now, Slothrop falls into a jog down the long mile to the outside, trying not to wonder if he has the wind to make it. He hasn't gone 200 feet when the vanguard comes clambering up off of that ladder behind him. He dodges into what must be a paint shop, skids on a patch of wet Wehrmacht green, and goes down, proceeding through big splashes of black, white, and red before coming to rest against the combat boots of an elderly man in a tweed suit, with white, water-buffalo mustaches. "Gruss Gott."

"Say, I think they're trying to kill me back there. Is there someplace—"

The old man winks, motions Slothrop through the Stollen and on into the other main tunnel. Slothrop notices a pair of coveralls streaked with paint, and thinks to grab them. Past four more Stollen, then a sharp right. It's a metal storage area. "Watch this." The old man goes chuckling down the long shop among blue racks of cold-rolled sheets, heaps of aluminum ingots, sheafs of 3712 bar stock, 1624, 723. . . . "This is going to be *good*."

"Not *that* way, man, that's the one they're coming *down*." But this oversize elf already has set about hitching cable from a hoist overhead to a tall bundle of Monel bars. Slothrop climbs into those coveralls, combs his pompadour down over his forehead, takes out a pocket-knife and saws off pieces of mustache on both sides.

"You look like Hitler now. Now they will *really* want to kill you!" German humor. He introduces himself as Glimpf, Professor of Mathematics of the Technische Hochschule, Darmstadt, Scientific Advisor to the Allied Military Government, which takes a while. "Now—we bring them this way."

I am in the hands of a raving maniac—"Why not just hide out in here, till they forget it?" But here comes dim shouts up-tunnel now: "All clear in 37 and 38, Chuckie babes!" "O.K., old hoss, you guys take odds we'll take evens." They are not going to forget it, they are making a tunnel-by-tunnel search instead. It's peacetime, they can't shoot you in peacetime . . . but they're drunk . . . oh boy. Slothrop is scared shitless.

"What do we do?"

"You will be the expert in idiomatic English. Say something provocative."

Slothrop sticks his head out in the long tunnel and hollers, in his most English accent, "Major Marvy sucks!"

"Up this way!" Sounds of galloping GI boots, nailheads smacking the concrete and a lot of other ominous metal too going snick . . . snick . . .

"Now," beams mischievous Glimpf, setting the hoist in motion.

A fresh thought occurs to Slothrop. He puts his head back out and hollers "Major Marvy sucks NIGGERS!"

"I think we should hurry," sez Glimpf.

"Aw, I just thought of a good one about his mother." Slack has been disappearing inch by inch from the bight of cable between the hoist and the bar stock, which Glimpf has rigged to topple across the doorway, hopefully about the time the Americans show up.

Slothrop and Glimpf light out through the opposite exit. About the time they reach the first curve in the tunnel, all the lights go out. The ventilation whines on. The phantom voices inside it gain confidence from the dark.

The bundle of Monel falls with a great crash. Slothrop touches rock wall, and uses the wall then for guidance through this absolute blackness. Glimpf is still someplace in the middle of the tunnel, on the tracks. He is not breathing hard, but he *is* chuckling to himself. Behind are the hollow staggerings of the pursuit, but no light yet. There is a soft clang and sharp "Himmel" from the old professor. Sounds of yelling have grown louder and now here are the first flashlights, and it's time to get out of the bathtub—

"What's happening? For Christ's sake . . ."

"Come here." Glimpf has collided with some kind of miniature train, just visible now in outline—it was used once to show visitors from Berlin around the factory. They climb aboard the tractor in front, and Glimpf fiddles with switches.

Well here we go, all aboard, lights must've been all that Marvy cut, sparks are crackling out behind and there's even a little wind now. Good to be rolling.

> Ev'ry little Nazi's shootin' pool or playin' potsy
> On the Mittel-werk Ex-press!
> All the funny Fascists just a-twirlin' their mustaches
> Where we goin'? Can't you guess?
> Headin' for the country just down the tracks,
> Never heard o' shortages or in-come-tax,
> Gonna be good-times, for Minnie and-Max,
> On the Mittel-werk Ex-press!

Glimpf has switched on a headlamp. From side-tunnels booming by, figures in khaki stare. Whites of eyes give back the light for an instant before flicking past. A few people wave. Shouts go dopplering *Hey-eyyy-y-y-y* like car horns at the crossings going home at night on the Boston and Maine. . . . The Express is rolling at a fair clip. Damp wind rushes by in a whistle. In the lamp's backscatter, silhouettes of warhead sections can be made out, stacked on the two little flatcars the engine's towing. Local midgetry scuttle and cringe alongside the tracks, nearly out of the light. They think of the little train as their own, and feel hurt whenever the big people come to commandeer it. Some sit on stacks of crates, dangling their legs. Some practice handstands in the dark. Their eyes glow green and red. Some even swing from ropes secured to the overhead, in mock Kamikaze attacks on Glimpf and Slothrop, screaming, "Banzai, banzai," before vanishing with a giggle. It's all in play. They're really quite an amiable—

Right behind, loud as megaphones, in massed chorale:

> There once was a fellow named Slattery

"Oh, shit," sez Slothrop.

> Who was fond of the course-gyro battery.
> With that 50-volt shock,
> What was left of his cock
> Was all slimy and sloppy and spattery.
>
> Ja, ja, ja, ja,
> In Prussia they never eat pussy, u.s.w.

"Can you get back and uncouple those cars?" Glimpf
wants to know.

"Reckon so. . . ." But he seems to fumble at it for
hours. Meantime:

> There was a young fellow named Pope,
> Who plugged into an *oscilloscope*.
> The cyclical trace
> Of their carnal embrace
> Had a damn nearly infinite slope.

"Engineers," Glimpf mutters. Slothrop gets the cars uncoupled and the engine speeds up. Wind is tearing at all
Irish pennants, collarpoints, cuffs, buckles, and belts.
Back behind them there's a tremendous crash and clank,
and a few shouts in the dark.

"Think that stopped 'em?"

Right up their ass, in four-part harmony:

> There was a young fellow named Yuri,
> Fucked the nozzle right up its venturi.
> He had woes without cease
> From his local police,
> And a hell of a time with the jury.

"O.—K., Jocko babes! Got that old phosphorus flare?"
"Stand by, good buddy!"

With only that warning, in blinding concussion the Icy
Noctiluca breaks, floods through the white tunnel. For a
minute or two nobody in here can see. There is only the
hurtling on, through amazing perfect whiteness. Whiteness without heat, and blind inertia: Slothrop feels a
terrible *familiarity* here, a center he has been skirting,
avoiding as long as he can remember—never has he been
as close as now to the true momentum of his time: faces
and facts that have crowded his indenture to the Rocket,
camouflage and distraction fall away from the white
moment, the vain and blind tugging at his sleeves *it's
important . . . please . . . look at us . . .* but it's already
too late, it's only wind, only g-loads, and the blood of his
eyes has begun to touch the whiteness back to ivory, to
brushings of gold and a network of edges to the broken
rock . . . and the hand that lifted him away sets him
back in the Mittelwerke—

"Whoo-wee! *There's* 'at 'sucker now!"

Out of the flare, inside easy pistol range, emerges a lumbering diesel engine, pushing ahead of it the two cars Slothrop uncoupled, itself stuffed with bloodshot, disheveled, bloated Americans, and at an apex, perched lopsided on their shoulders, Major Marvy himself, wearing a giant white Stetson, and clutching two .45 automatics.

Slothrop ducks down behind a cylindrical object at the rear of the tractor. Marvy starts shooting, wildly, inspired by hideous laughter from the others. Slothrop happens to notice now that what he's chosen to hide behind, actually, seems to be another warhead. If the Amatol charges are still in—say, Professor, could the shock wave from a .45 bullet at this range succeed in detonating this warhead here if it struck the casing? e-even if there was no fuze installed? Well, Tyrone, now that would depend on many things: muzzle velocity, wall thickness and composition—

Counting at least on a pulled arm muscle and hernia, Slothrop manages to tip and heave the warhead off onto the track while Marvy's bullets go whanging and crashing all over the tunnel. It bounces and comes to rest tilted against one of the rails. Good.

The flare has begun to die. Shadows are reoccupying the mouths of the Stollen. The cars ahead of Marvy hit the obstacle a solid WHONK! doubling up in an inverted V—diesel brakes screech in panic *yi-i-i-ke* as the big engine derails, slews, begins to tip, Americans grabbing frantically for handholds, each other, empty air. Then Slothrop and Glimpf are around the last curve of the integral sign, and there is another huge crash behind them, screaming that prolongs, echoing, as they see now the entrance ahead, growing parabola of green mountain-slopes, and sunlight. . . .

"Did you have a car when you came?" inquires the twinkling Glimpf.

"What?" Slothrop recalls the keys still in that Mercedes. "*Oh. . . .*"

Glimpf eases on the brakes as they coast out under the parabola into daylight, and roll to a smooth and respectable stop. They flip salutes at the B Company sentries and proceed to hijack the Mercedes, which is right where that rail left it.

Out on the road, Glimpf gestures them north, watching
Slothrop's driving with a leery eye. They wind snarling
up into the Harz, in and out of mountain shadows, pine
and fir odors enveloping them, screeching around curves
and sometimes nearly off of the road. Slothrop has the
inborn gift of selecting the wrong gear for all occasions,
and anyhow he's jittery, eye in the mirror and out the
back of his head aswarm with souped-up personnel carriers and squadrons of howling Thunderbolts. Coming
around a blind corner, using the whole width of the pavement to make it—a sharp road-racing trick he happens
to know—they nearly buy it from a descending American
Army deuce-and-a-half, the words *fucking idiot* clearly
visible on the mouth of the driver as they barely scoot
past, heartbeats slamming low in their throats, mud from
the truck's rear tires slapping over them in a great wing
that shakes the rig and blots out half the windshield.

The sun is well past its zenith when they pull up,
finally, below a forested dome with a small dilapidated
castle on top, hundreds of doves, white teardrops, dripping from its battlements. The green breath of the woods
has sharpened, grown colder.

They climb a switchbacking path strewn with rocks,
among dark firs toward the castle in the sunlight, jagged
and brown above as a chunk of bread left out for all its
generations of birds.

"This is where you're staying?"

"I used to work here. I think Zwitter might still be
around." There wasn't enough room in the Mittelwerke
for many of the smaller assembly jobs. Control systems
mainly. So they were put together in beerhalls, shops,
schools, castles, farmhouses all around Nordhausen here,
any indoor lab space the guidance people could find.
Glimpf's colleague Zwitter is from the T.H. in Munich.
"The usual Bavarian approach to electronics." Glimpf begins to frown. "He's bearable, I suppose." Whatever
mysterious injustices spring from a Bavarian approach to
electronics now remove Glimpf's twinkle, and keep him
occupied in surly introspection the rest of the way up.

Mass liquid cooing, damped in white fluff, greets them
as they slip in a side entrance to the castle. Floors are
dirty and littered with bottles and scraps of papers. Some
of the papers are stamped with the magenta GEHEIME

KOMMANDOSACHE. Birds fly in and out of broken windows. Thin beams of light come in from chinks and erosions. Dust motes, fanned by the doves' wings, never stop billowing here. Walls are hung with dim portraits of nobles in big white Frederick the Great hairdos, ladies with smooth faces and oval eyes in low-necked dresses whose yards of silk spill out into the dust and wingbeats of the dark rooms. There is dove shit all over the place.

By contrast, Zwitter's laboratory uptsairs is brightly lit, well-ordered, crammed with blown glass, work tables, lights of many colors, speckled boxes, green folders—a mad Nazi scientist lab! Plasticman, where are you?

There's only Zwitter: stocky, dark hair parted down the middle, eyeglass lenses thick as the windows of a bathysphere, the fluorescent hydras, eels, and rays of control equations swimming seas behind them. . . .

But when they see Slothrop, there is immediate clearing there, and glazed barriers come down. Hmm, T.S., what's this? Who are these people? What's happened to the apples in old Glimpf's cheeks? What's a Nazi guidance expert doing this side of the fence at Garmisch, with his lab intact?

> OH . . . thur's . . .
> Nazis in the woodwork,
> Fascists in the walls,
> Little Japs with bucktooth grins
> A-gonna grab yew bah th' balls.
> Whin this war is over,
> How happy Ah will be,
> Gearin' up fer thim Rooskies
> And Go-round Number Three. . . .

□

In the days when the white engineers were disputing the attributes of the feeder system that was to be, one of them came to Enzian of Bleicheröde and said, "We cannot agree on the chamber pressure. Our calculations show that a working pressure of 40 atü would be the most desirable. But all the data we know of are grouped around a value of only some 10 atü."

"Then clearly," replied the Nguarorerue, "you must listen to the data."

"But that would not be the most perfect or efficient value," protested the German.

"Proud man," said the Nguarorerue. "What are these data, if
not direct revelation? Where have they come from, if not from
the Rocket which is to be? How do you presume to compare a
number you have only derived on paper with a number that is
the Rocket's own? Avoid pride, and design to some compromise
value."

—from *Tales of the Schwarzkommando*,
collected by Steve Edelman

In the mountains around Nordhausen and Bleicheröde,
down in abandoned mine shafts, live the Schwarzkommando. These days it's no longer a military title: they
are a people now, Zone-Hereros, in exile for two generations from South-West Africa. Early Rhenish missionaries
began to bring them back to the Metropolis, that great
dull zoo, as specimens of a possibly doomed race. They
were gently experimented with: exposed to cathedrals,
Wagnerian soirées, Jaeger underwear, trying to get them
interested in their souls. Others were taken back to Germany as servants, by soldiers who went to put down the
great Herero rising of 1904–1906. But only after 1933
did most of the present-day leadership arrive, as part
of a scheme—never openly admitted by the Nazi party—
for setting up black juntas, shadow-states for the eventual
takeover of British and French colonies in black Africa,
on the model of Germany's plan for the Maghreb. Südwest by then was a protectorate administered by the
Union of South Africa, but the real power was still with
the old German colonial families, and they cooperated.

There are several underground communities now near
Nordhausen/Bleicheröde. Around here they are known
collectively as the Erdschweinhöhle. This is a Herero joke,
a bitter one. Among the Ovatjimba, the poorest of the
Hereros, with no cattle or villages of their own, the totem
animal was the Erdschwein or aardvark. They took their
name from him, never ate his flesh, dug their food from
the earth, just as he does. Considered outcasts, they lived
on the veld, in the open. You were likely to come across
them at night, their fires flaring bravely against the wind,
out of rifle range from the iron tracks: there seemed no
other force than that to give them locus out in that
emptiness. You knew what they feared—not what they
wanted, or what moved them. And you had business up-

country, at the mines: so, presently, as the sputtering lights slipped behind, so did all further need to think of them. . . .

But as you swung away, who was the woman alone in the earth, planted up to her shoulders in the aardvark hole, a gazing head rooted to the desert plane, with an upsweep of mountains far behind her, darkly folded, far away in the evening? She can feel the incredible pressure, miles of horizontal sand and clay, against her belly. Down the trail wait the luminous ghosts of her four stillborn children, fat worms lying with no chances of comfort among the wild onions, one by one, crying for milk more sacred than what is tasted and blessed in the village calabashes. In preterite line they have pointed her here, to be in touch with Earth's gift for genesis. The woman feels power flood in through every gate: a river between her thighs, light leaping at the ends of fingers and toes. It is sure and nourishing as sleep. It is a warmth. The more the daylight fades, the further she submits—to the dark, to the descent of water from the air. She is a seed in the Earth. The holy aardvark has dug her bed.

Back in Südwest, the Erdschweinhöhle was a powerful symbol of fertility and life. But here in the Zone, its real status is not so clear.

Inside the Schwarzkommando there are forces, at present, who have opted for sterility and death. The struggle is mostly in silence, in the night, in the nauseas and crampings of pregnancies or miscarriages. But it is political struggle. No one is more troubled with it than Enzian. He is Nguarorerue here. The word doesn't mean "leader" exactly, but "one who has been proven."

Enzian is also known, though not to his face, as Otyikondo, the Half-breed. His father was a European. Not that it makes him unique among the Erdschweinhöhlers here: there's German, Slavic and Gypsy blood mixed in by now too. Over the couple of generations, moved by accelerations unknown in the days before the Empire, they have been growing an identity that few can see as ever taking final shape. The Rocket will have a final shape, but not its people. Eanda and oruzo have lost their force out here—the bloodlines of mother and father were left behind, in Südwest. Many of the early emigrants had even gone over to the faith of the Rhenish Missionary Society long before they left. In each village, as noon flared the shadows in tightly to their owners, in that moment of terror and refuge, the omuhona took from his sacred bag, soul after converted soul, the leather cord kept there since the individual's birth, and untied the birth-knot. Untied, it was another soul dead to the tribe. So today, in the Erdschweinhöhle, the Empty Ones each carry one knotless strip of leather: it is a bit of the old symbolism they have found useful.

They call themselves Otukungurua. Yes, old Africa hands, it *ought* to be "Omakungurua," but they are always careful—perhaps it's less healthy than care—to point out that *oma-* applies only to the living and human. *Otu-* is for the inanimate and the rising, and this is how they imagine themselves. Revolutionaries of the Zero, they mean to carry on what began among the old Hereros after the 1904 rebellion failed. They want a negative birth rate. The program is racial suicide. They would finish the extermination the Germans began in 1904.

A generation earlier, the declining number of live Herero births was a topic of medical interest throughout southern Africa. The whites looked on as anxiously as they would have at an outbreak of rinderpest among the cattle. How provoking, to watch one's subject population dwindling like this, year after year. What's a colony without its dusky natives? Where's the fun if they're all going to die off? Just a big hunk of desert, no more maids, no field-hands, no laborers for the construction or the mining—wait, wait a minute there, yes it's Karl Marx, that sly old racist skipping away with his teeth together and his eyebrows up trying to make believe it's nothing but Cheap Labor and Overseas Markets. . . . Oh, no. Colonies are much, much more. Colonies are the outhouses of the European soul, where a fellow can let his pants down and relax, enjoy the smell of his own shit. Where he can fall on his slender prey roaring as loud as he feels like, and guzzle her blood with open joy. Eh? Where he can just wallow and rut and let himself go in a softness, a receptive darkness of limbs, of hair as woolly as the hair on his own forbidden genitals. Where the poppy, and cannabis and coca grow full and green, and not to the

colors and style of death, as do ergot and agaric, the
blight and fungus native to Europe. Christian Europe was
always death, Karl, death and repression. Out and down
in the colonies, life can be indulged, life and sensuality
in all its forms, with no harm done to the Metropolis,
nothing to soil those cathedrals, white marble statues,
noble thoughts. . . . No word ever gets back. The silences
down here are vast enough to absorb all behavior, no
matter how dirty, how animal it gets. . . .

Some of the more rational men of medicine attributed
the Herero birth decline to a deficiency of Vitamin E in
the diet—others to poor chances of fertilization given the
peculiarly long and narrow uterus of the Herero female.
But underneath all this reasonable talk, this scientific
speculating, no white Afrikaner could quite put down
the way it *felt*. . . . Something sinister was moving out
in the veld: he was beginning to look at their faces,
especially those of the women, lined beyond the thorn
fences, and he knew beyond logical proof: there *was* a
tribal mind at work out here, and it had chosen to commit
suicide. . . . Puzzling. Perhaps we weren't as fair as we
might have been, perhaps we did take their cattle and
their lands away . . . and then the work-camps of course,
the barbed wire and the stockades. . . . Perhaps they feel
it is a world they no longer want to live in. Typical of
them, though, giving up, crawling away to die . . . why
won't they even negotiate? We could work out a solution,
some solution. . . .

It was a simple choice for the Hereros, between two
kinds of death: tribal death, or Christian death. Tribal
death made sense. Christian death made none at all. It
seemed an exercise they did not need. But to the Europeans, conned by their own Baby Jesus Con Game, what
they were witnessing among these Hereros was a mystery
potent as that of the elephant graveyard, or the lemmings
rushing into the sea.

Though they don't admit it, the Empty Ones now
exiled in the Zone, Europeanized in language and thought,
split off from the old tribal unity, have found the why
of it just as mysterious. But they've seized it, as a sick
woman will seize a charm. They calculate no cycles, no
returns, they are in love with the glamour of a whole

people's suicide—the pose, the stoicism, and the bravery. These Otukungurua are prophets of masturbating, specialists in abortion and sterilization, pitchmen for acts oral and anal, pedal and digital, sodomistical and zoophiliac— their approach and their game is pleasure: they are spieling earnestly and well, and Erdschweinhöhlers are listening.

The Empty Ones can guarantee a day when the last Zone-Herero will die, a final zero to a collective history fully lived. It has appeal.

There is no outright struggle for power. It is all seduction and counterseduction, advertising and pornography, and the history of the Zone-Hereros is being decided in bed.

Vectors in the night underground, all trying to flee a center, a force, which appears to be the Rocket: some immachination, whether of journey or of destiny, which is able to gather violent political opposites together in the Erdschweinhöhle as it gathers fuel and oxidizer in its thrust chamber: metered, helmsmanlike, for the sake of its scheduled parabola.

Enzian sits this evening under his mountain, behind him another day of schemes, expediting, newly invented paperwork—forms he manages to destroy or fold, Japanese style, before the day's end, into gazelles, orchids, hunter-hawks. As the Rocket grows toward its working shape and fullness, so does he evolve, himself, into a new configuration. He feels it. It's something else to worry about. Late last night, among the blueprints, Christian and Mieczislav looked up, abruptly smiled, and fell silent. A transparent reverence. They study the drawings as if they were his own, and revelations. This is not flattering to him.

What Enzian wants to create will have no history. It will never need a design change. Time, as time is known to the other nations, will wither away inside this new one. The Erdschweinhöhle will not be bound, like the Rocket, to time. The people will find the Center again, the Center without time, the journey without hysteresis, where every departure is a return to the same place, the only place. . . .

He has thus himself found a strange rapprochement

with the Empty Ones: in particular with Josef Ombindi
of Hannover. The Eternal Center can easily be seen as
the Final Zero. Names and methods vary, but the movement toward stillness is the same. It has led to strange
passages between the two men. "You know," Ombindi's
eyes rolled the other way, looking up at a mirror-image
of Enzian that only he can see, "there's . . . well, something you ordinarily wouldn't think of as erotic—but it's
really the most erotic thing there is."

"Really," grins Enzian, flirting. "I can't think of what
that would be. Give me a clue."

"It's a non-repeatable act."

"Firing a rocket?"

"No, because there's always another rocket. But there's
nothing—well, never mind."

"Ha! Nothing to follow it with, that's what you were
going to say."

"Suppose I give you another clue."

"All right." But Enzian has already guessed: it's there
in the way he holds his jaw and is just about to laugh. . . .

"It embraces all the Deviations in one single act."
Enzian sighs, irritated, but does not call him on this use
of "Deviations." Bringing up the past is part of Ombindi's
game. "Homosexuality, for example." No rise. "Sadism *and*
masochism. Onanism? Necrophilia. . . ."

"All those in the same act?"

All those, and more. Both know by now that what's
under discussion is the act of suicide, which also includes
bestiality ("Think how sweet," runs the pitch, "to show
mercy, sexual mercy to *that* hurt and crying animal"),
pedophilia ("It is widely reported that just at the edge
you grow glaringly younger"), lesbianism ("Yes, for as the
wind blows through all the emptying compartments the
two shadow-women at last can creep out of their chambers in the dying shell, at the last ashen shoreline, to
meet and embrace . . ."), coprophilia and urolagnia ("The
final convulsions . . ."), fetishism ("A wide choice of
death-fetishes, naturally . . ."). Naturally. The two of
them sit there, passing a cigarette back and forth, till
it's smoked down to a very small stub. Is it idle talk, or
is Ombindi really trying to hustle Enzian here? Enzian's
got to be sure before he moves. If he comes out sez,

"This is a hustle, right?" and turns out it isn't, well— But the alternative is so *strange*, that Enzian is, in some way, being

SOLD ON SUICIDE

> Well I don't care-for, th' things I eat,
> Can't stand that boogie-woogie beat—
> But I'm sold, on, *suicide!*
>
> You can keep Der Bingle too, a-
> And that darn "bu-bu-bu-boo,"
> Cause I'm sold on suicide!
>
> *Oh!* I'm not too keen on ration stamps,
> Or Mothers who used to be baby vamps,
> But I'm sold, on, *suicide!*
>
> Don't like either, the Cards or Browns,
> Piss on the country and piss on the town,

But I'm S.O.S., yes well actually this goes on, verse after verse, for quite some time. In its complete version it represents a pretty fair renunciation of the things of the world. The trouble with it is that by Gödel's Theorem there is bound to be some item around that one has omitted from the list, and such an item is not easy to think of off the top of one's head, so that what one does most likely is go back over the whole thing, meantime correcting mistakes and inevitable repetitions, and putting in new items that will surely have occurred to one, and—well, it's easy to see that the "suicide" of the title might have to be postponed indefinitely!

Conversations between Ombindi and Enzian these days are thus a series of commercial messages, with Enzian not so much mark as unwilling shill, standing in for the rest of the tip, who may be listening and maybe not.

"Ahh, do I see your cock growing, Nguarorerue? . . . no, no, perhaps you are only thinking of someone you loved, somewhere, long ago . . . back in Südwest, eh?" To allow the tribal past to disperse, all memories ought to be public record, there's no point in preserving history with that Final Zero to look forward to. . . . Cynically, though, Ombindi has preached this in the name of the old Tribal Unity, and it's a weakness in his pitch all right—it looks bad, looks like Ombindi's trying to make believe the Christian sickness never touched us, when everyone knows it has infected us all, some to death. Yes it is a little bit jive of Ombindi here to look back toward an innocence he's really only heard about, can't himself believe in—the gathered purity of opposites, the village built like a mandala. . . . Still he will profess and proclaim it, as an image of a grail slipping through the room, radiant, though the jokers around the table be sneaking Whoopee Cushions into the Siege Perilous, under the very descending arse of the grailseeker, and though the grails themselves come in plastic these years, a dime a dozen, penny a gross, still Ombindi, at times self-conned as any Christian, praises and prophesies that era of innocence he just missed living in, one of the last pockets of Pre-Christian Oneness left on the planet: "Tibet is a special case. Tibet was deliberately set aside by the Empire *as* free and neutral territory, a Switzerland for the spirit where there is no extradition, and Alp-Himalayas to draw the soul upward, and danger rare enough to tolerate. . . . Switzerland and Tibet are linked along one of the *true* meridians of Earth, true as the Chinese have drawn meridians of the body. . . . We will have to learn such new maps of Earth: and as travel in the Interior becomes more common, as the maps grow another dimension, so must we. . . ." And he tells too of Gondwanaland, before the continents drifted apart, when Argentine lay snuggled up to Südwest . . . the people listen, and filter back to cave and bed and family calabash from which the milk, unconsecrated, is swallowed in cold whiteness, cold as the north. . . .

So, between these two, even routine greeting does not pass without some payload of meaningfulness and the hope of Blitzing the other's mind. Enzian knows that he is being used for his name. The name has some magic. But he has been so unable to touch, so neutral for so long . . . everything has flowed away but the name, Enzian, a sound for chanting. He hopes it will be magic enough for one thing, one good thing when the time comes, however short of the Center. . . . What are these persistences among a people, these traditions and offices, but traps? the sexual fetishes Christianity knows how to flash, to lure us in, meant to remind us of earliest infant love. . . . Can his name, can "Enzian" break *their* power? Can his *name* prevail?

The Erdschweinhöhle is in one of the worst traps of all, a dialectic of word made flesh, flesh moving toward something else. . . . Enzian sees the trap clearly, but not the way out. . . . Sitting now between a pair of candles just lit, his gray field-jacket open at the neck, beard feathering down his dark throat to shorter, sparser glossy black hairs that go running in a whirl, iron filings about the south pole of his Adam's apple . . . pole . . . axis . . . axle-tree. . . . Tree . . . Omumborombanga . . . Mukuru . . . first ancestor . . . Adam . . . still sweating, hands from the working day gone graceless and numb, he has a minute to drift and remember this time of day back in Südwest, above ground, participating in the sunset, out watching the mist gather, part fog, part dust from the cattle returning to the kraals to milking and sleep . . . his tribe believed long ago that each sunset is a battle. In the north, where the sun sets, live the one-armed warriors, the one-legged and one-eyed, who fight the sun each evening, who spear it to death until its blood runs out over the horizon and sky. But under the earth, in the night, the sun is born again, to come back each dawn, new and the same. But we, Zone-Hereros, under the earth, how long will we wait in this north, this locus of death? Is it to be reborn? or have we really been buried for the last time, buried facing north like all the rest of our dead, and like all the holy cattle ever sacrificed to the ancestors? North is death's region. There may be no gods, but there is a pattern: names by themselves may have no magic, but the *act* of naming, the physical utterance, obeys the pattern. Nordhausen means dwellings in the north. The Rocket had to be produced out of a place called Nordhausen. The town adjoining was named Bleicheröde as a validation, a bit of redundancy so that the message would not be lost. The history of the old Hereros is one of lost messages. It began in mythical times, when the sly hare who nests in the Moon brought death among men, instead of the Moon's true message. The true message has never come. Perhaps the Rocket is meant to take us there some-day, and then Moon will tell us its truth at last. There are those down in the Erdschweinhöhle, younger ones who've only known white autumn-prone Europe, who believe Moon is their destiny. But older ones can remember that Moon, like Ndjambi Karunga, is both the bringer of evil and its avenger. . . .

And Enzian's found the name Bleicheröde close enough to "Blicker," the nickname the early Germans gave to Death. They saw him white: bleaching and blankness. The name was later Latinized to "Dominus Blicero." Weissmann, enchanted, took it as his SS code name. En-zian was in Germany by then. Weissmann brought the new name home to his pet, not showing it off so much as indicating to Enzian yet another step to be taken toward the Rocket, toward a destiny he still cannot see past this sinister cryptography of naming, a sparse pattern but one that harshly will not be denied, that cries and nags him on stumbling as badly as 20 years ago. . . .

Once he could not imagine a life without return. Be-fore his conscious memories began, something took him, in and out of his mother's circular village far out in the Kakau Veld, at the borders of the land of death, a de-parture and a return. . . . He was told about it years later. Shortly after he was born, his mother brought him back to her village, back from Swakopmund. In ordinary times she would have been banished. She'd had the child out of wedlock, by a Russian sailor whose name she couldn't pronounce. But under the German invasion, protocol was less important than helping one another. Though the murderers in blue came down again and again, each time, somehow, Enzian was passed over. It is a Herod myth his admirers still like to bring up, to his annoyance. He had been walking only for a few months when his mother took him with her to join Samuel Maherero's great trek across the Kalahari.

Of the stories told about these years, this is the most tragic. The refugees had been on the desert for days. Khama, king of the Bechuanas, sent guides, oxen, wagons and water to help them. Those who arrived first were warned to take water only little by little. But by the time the stragglers arrived, everyone else was asleep. No one

to warn them. Another lost message. They drank till they
died, hundreds of souls. Enzian's mother was among them.
He had fallen asleep under a cowhide, exhausted from
hunger and thirst. He woke among the dead. It is said
that he was found there by a band of Ovatjimba, taken
and cared for. They left him back at the edge of his
mother's village, to walk in alone. They were nomads,
they could have taken any other direction in that waste
country, but they brought him back to the place he'd left.
He found hardly anyone remaining there. Many had gone
on the trek, some had been taken away to the coast and
herded into kraals, or to work on the railroad the Germans
were building through the desert. Many others had died
eating cattle dead of rinderpest.

No return. Sixty per cent of the Herero people had been
exterminated. The rest were being used like animals. Enzian grew up into a white-occupied world. Captivity, sudden death, one-way departures were the ordinary things
of every day. By the time the question occurred to him, he
could find no way to account for his own survival. He
could not believe in any process of selection. Ndjambi
Karunga and the Christian God were too far away. There
was no difference between the behavior of a god and the
operations of pure chance. Weissmann, the European
whose protégé he became, always believed he'd seduced
Enzian away from religion. But the gods had gone away
themselves: the gods had left the people.... He let
Weissmann think what he wanted to. The man's thirst for
guilt was insatiable as the desert's for water.

It's been a long time now since the two men have seen
each other. Last time they spoke was during the move from
Peenemünde down here to the Mittelwerke. Weissmann is
probably dead by now. Even in Südwest, 20 years ago,
before Enzian could even speak his language, he'd seen
that: a love for the last explosion—the lifting and the
scream that peaks past fear.... Why should Weissmann
want to survive the war? Surely he'd have found something splendid enough to match his thirst. It could not
have ended for him rationalized and meek as his hundred
glass bureaus about the SS circuit—located in time and
space always just to miss grandeur, only to be in its
vacuum, to be tugged slightly along by its slipstream but

finally left to lie still again in a few tarnished sequins of
wake. Bürgerlichkeit played to Wagner, the brasses faint
and mocking, the voices of the strings drifting in and out
of phase. . . .

At night down here, very often lately, Enzian will wake
for no reason. Was it really Him, pierced Jesus, who came
to lean over you? The white faggot's-dream body, the
slender legs and soft gold European eyes . . . did you
catch a glimpse of olive cock under the ragged loincloth,
did you want to reach to lick at the sweat of his rough,
his wooden bondage? Where is he, what part of our Zone
tonight, damn him to the knob of that nervous imperial
staff. . . .

There are few such islands of down and velvet for him
to lie and dream on, not in these marble passages of power.
Enzian has grown cold: not so much a fire dying away as
a positive coming on of cold, a bitter taste growing across
the palate of love's first hopes. . . . It began when Weissmann brought him to Europe: a discovery that love, among
these men, once past the simple feel and orgasming of it,
had to do with masculine technologies, with contracts, with
winning and losing. Demanded, in his own case, that he
enter the service of the Rocket. . . . Beyond simple steel
erection, the Rocket was an entire system *won*, away from
the feminine darkness, held against the entropies of lovable
but scatterbrained Mother Nature: that was the first thing
he was obliged by Weissmann to learn, his first step toward citizenship in the Zone. He was led to believe that
by understanding the Rocket, he would come to understand truly his manhood. . . .

"I used to imagine, in some naïve way I have lost now,
that all the excitement of those days was being put on for
me, somehow, as a gift from Weissmann. He had carried
me over his threshold and into his house, and this was the
life he meant to bring me to, these manly pursuits, devotion to the Leader, political intrigue, secret re-arming in
naughty defiance of the aging plutocracies all around us
. . . they were growing impotent, but we were young and
strong . . . to be *that* young and strong, at such a time in
the life of a nation! I could not believe so many fair young
men, the way the sweat and dust lay on their bodies as
they lengthened the Autobahns day into ringing day: we

drove among trumpeters, silk banners impeccably tailored
as suits of clothes ... the woman seemed to move all docile, without color ... I thought of them in ranks, down on
all fours, having their beasts milked into pails of shining
steel. ..."

"Was he ever jealous of the other young men—the way
you felt about them?"

"Oh. It was still very physical for me then. But he had
already moved past that part of it. No. No, I don't think
he minded. ... I loved him then. I could not see into him,
or the things he believed in, but I wanted to. If the
Rocket was his life, then I would belong to the Rocket."

"And you never doubted him? He certainly hadn't the
most ordered personality—"

"Listen—I don't know how to say this ... have you ever
been a Christian?"

"Well ... at one time."

"Did you ever, in the street, see a man that you knew,
in the instant, *must* be Jesus Christ—not hoped he was, or
caught some resemblance—but *knew*. The Deliverer, returned and walking among the people, just the way the
old stories promised ... as you approached you grew more
and more certain—you could see nothing at all to con-
tradict that first amazement ... you drew near and passed,
terrified that he would speak to you ... your eyes grap-
pled ... it was confirmed. And most terrible to all, *he
knew*. He saw into your soul: all your make-believe ceased
to matter. ..."

"Then ... what's happened, since your first days in
Europe, could be described, in Max Weber's phrase, almost as a 'routinization of charisma.'"

"Outase," sez Enzian, which is one of many Herero
words for shit, in this case a large, newly laid cow turd.

Andreas Orukambe sits in front of any army-green,
wrinkle-finished transmitter/receiver rig, off in a rock al-
cove of the room. A pair of rubber headphones covers his
ears. The Schwarzkommando use the 50 cm band—the
one the Rocket's Hawaii II guidance operated on. Who
but rocket-maniacs would listen in at 53 cm? Schwarzkommando can be sure, at least, that they're being monitored by every competitor in the Zone. Transmissions from
the Erdschweinhöhle begin around 0300 and run till dawn.

Other Schwarzkommando stations broadcast on their own schedules. Traffic is in Herero, with a German loan-word now and then (which is too bad, since these are usually technical words, and valuable clues for whoever's listening).

Andreas is on the second dog watch, now, copying mostly, answering when he has to. Keying any transmitter is an invitation to instant paranoia. There springs into being an antenna pattern, thousands of square kilometers full of enemies out in their own night encampments in the Zone, faceless, monitoring. Though they are in contact with one another—the Schwarzkommando try to listen in to as much as they can—though there can be no illusion about their plans for the Schwarzkommando, still they are holding off, waiting for the optimum time to move in and destroy without a trace. . . . Enzian believes they will wait for the first African rocket to be fully assembled and ready for firing: it will look better if they move against a real threat, real hardware. Meantime Enzian tries to keep security tight. Here at the home base it's no problem: penetration by less than a regiment would be impossible. But farther out in the Zone, rocket-towns like Celle, Enschede, Hachenburg—they can pick us off out there one by one, first a campaign of attrition, then a coordinated raid . . . leaving then only this metropolis, under siege, to strangle. . . .

Perhaps it's theater, but they *seem* no longer to be Allies . . . though the history they have invented for themselves conditions us to *expect* "postwar rivalries," when in fact it may all be a giant cartel including winners and losers both, in an amiable agreement to share what is there to be shared. . . . Still, Enzian has played them off, the quarreling scavengers, one against the other . . . it *looks* genuine enough. . . . Marvy must be together with the Russians by now, and with General Electric too—throwing him off the train the other night bought us—what? a day or two, and how well have we used the time?

It comes down to this day-to-day knitting and unraveling, minor successes, minor defeats. Thousands of details, any one of which carries the chance of a fatal mistake. Enzian would like to be more out of the process than he is—to be able to see where it's going, to know, in real

time, at each splitting of the pathway of decision, which
would have been right and which wrong. But it is *their*
time, *their* space, and he still expects, naïvely, outcomes
the white continuum grew past hoping for centuries ago.
The details—valves, special tools that may or may not exist,
Erdschweinhöhle jealousies and plots, lost operating manuals, technicians on the run from both East and West,
food shortages, sick children—swirl like fog, each particle
with its own array of forces and directions . . . he can't
handle them all at the same time, if he stays too much
with any he's in danger of losing others. . . . But it's not
only the details. He has the odd feeling, in moments of
reverie or honest despair, that he is speaking lines prepared somewhere far away (not far away in space, but
in levels of power), and that his decisions are not his own
at all, but the flummeries of an actor impersonating a
leader. He has dreamed of being held in the pitiless
emprise of something from which he cannot wake . . .
he is often aboard a ship on a broad river, leading a
rebellion which must fail. For reasons of policy, the rebellion is being allowed to go on for a bit. He is being
hunted, his days are full of narrow escapes which he finds
exciting, physically graceful . . . and the Plot itself! it
has a stern, an intense beauty, it is music, a symphony
of the North, of an Arctic voyage, past headlands of very
green ice, to the feet of icebergs, kneeling in the grip of
this incredible music, washed in seas blue as blue dye,
an endless North, vast country settled by people whose
old culture and history are walled off by a great silence
from the rest of the world . . . the names of their penin-
sulas and seas, their long and powerful rivers are unknown
down in the temperate world . . . it is a return, this
voyage: he has grown old inside his name, the sweeping
music of the voyage is music he wrote himself, so long
ago that he has forgotten it completely . . . but now it is
finding him again. . . .

"Trouble in Hamburg—" Andreas is scribbling away,
lifting one earpiece back *smock* damp with sweat so that
he can be on both ends of the link at once. "Sounds like
it might be the DPs again. Got a bad signal. Keeps
fading—"

Since the surrender there have been these constant
skirmishes between the German civilians and foreign

prisoners freed from the camps. Towns in the north have
been taken over by displaced Poles, Czechs, Russians
who've looted the arsenals and granaries and mean to hold
what they've taken. But nobody knows how to feel about
the local Schwarzkommando. Some see only the ragged
pieces of SS uniform, and respond to that one way or
another—others take them for Moroccans or Indians
drifted somehow over the mountains from Italy. Germans
still remember the occupation of the Rhineland 20 years
ago by French colonial units, and the posters screaming
SCHWARZE BESATZUNG AM RHEIN! Another stress in the
pattern. Last week in Hamburg, two Schwarzkommando
were shot. Others were badly beaten. The British military
government sent in some troops, but only after the killing
was over. Their main interest seemed to be in enforcing
a curfew.

"It's Onguruve." Andreas hands over the earphones and
swivels to roll out of Enzian's way.

". . . can't tell if it's us they want, or the oil refinery
. . ." the voice goes crackling in and out, ". . . hundred,
maybe two hundred . . . so many . . . —fles, clubs, hand-
guns—"

Bl-bleep and a burst of hissing, then in laps a familiar
voice. "I can bring a dozen men."

"Hannover's answering," Enzian murmurs, trying to
sound amused.

"You mean Josef Ombindi." Andreas is not amused.

Now Onguruve, calling for help, is neutral on the
Empty Ones Question, or tries to be. But if Ombindi can
bring a relief force to Hamburg, he may decide to stay.
Hannover, even with the Volkswagen plant there, is only
a stepping-stone for him. Hamburg would give the Empty
Ones a stronger power base, and this could be the opportunity. The north ought to be their native element, anyway . . .

"I'll have to go," handing the phones back to Andreas.
"What's wrong?"

"Could be the Russians, trying to draw you out."

"It's all right. Stop worrying about Tchitcherine. I don't
think he's up there."

"But your European said—"

"Him? I don't know how far to trust him. Remember,
I did hear him talking with Marvy on the train. Now

he's with Tchitcherine's girl in Nordhausen. I mean, would you trust him?"

"But if Marvy's chasing him now, it might mean he's worth something."

"If he is, we're sure to see him again."

Enzian grabs his kit, swallows two Pervitins for the road, reminds Andreas of a business detail or two for tomorrow, and climbs the long salt and stone ramps to the surface.

Outside, he breathes the evergreen air of the Harz. In the old villages, it would be the time of evening for the milking. The first star is out, okanumaihi, the little drinker of sweet milk. . . .

But this must be a different star, a northern star. There is no comfort. What has happened to us? If choices have never been our own, if the Zone-Hereros are meant to live in the bosom of the Angel who tried to destroy us in Südwest . . . then: have we been passed over, or have we been chosen for something even more terrible?

Enzian has to be in Hamburg before another spearing of the sun. Security on the trains is troublesome, but the sentries know him. The long freights are rolling out from the Mittelwerke day and night, carrying A4 hardware west to the Americans, north to the English . . . and soon, when the new map of the occupation goes into effect, east to the Russians too. . . . Nordhausen will be under Russian administration and we should have some action then . . . will it give him a chance at Tchitcherine? Enzian has never seen the man, but they are meant to come together. Enzian is his half-brother. They are the same flesh.

His sciatic nerve is throbbing now. Too much sitting. He goes limping, alone, head still down for the low clearances back down in the Erdschweinhöhle—who knows what waits out here for the head held too high? Down the road to the railway overpass, tall and gray in the growing starlight, Enzian is heading into the North. . . .

☐

Just before dawn. A hundred feet below flows a pallid sheet of cloud, stretching west as far as they can see.

Here are Slothrop and the apprentice witch Geli Tripping, standing up on top of the Brocken, the very plexus of German evil, twenty miles north by northwest of the Mittelwerke, waiting for the sun to rise. Though May Day Eve's come and gone and this frolicking twosome are nearly a month late, relics of the latest Black Sabbath still remain: Kriegsbier empties, lace undergarments, spent rifle cartridges, Swastika-banners of ripped red satin, tattooing-needles and splashes of blue ink— "What the heck was *that* for?" Slothrop wondered.

"For the devil's kiss, of course," Geli snuggling oh-you-old-silly up to his armpit there, and Slothrop feeling a little icky and square for not knowing. But then he knows next to nothing about witches, even though there was, in his ancestry, one genuine Salem Witch, one of the last to join the sus. per coll. crowd dangling, several of them back through the centuries' couplings, off of the Slothrop family tree. Her name was Amy Sprue, a family renegade turned Antinomian at age 23 and running mad over the Berkshire countryside, ahead of Crazy Sue Dunham by 200 years, stealing babies, riding cows in the twilight, sacrificing chickens up on Snodd's Mountain. Lot of ill will about those chickens, as you can imagine. The cows and babies always, somehow, came back all right. Amy Sprue was not, like young skipping Dorothy's antagonist, a mean witch.

> She headed for Rhode Island, seeking some of that
>   asylum,
> And she thought she'd stop by Salem on her way,
> But they didn't like her style, and they didn't like
>   her smile,
> So she never saw that Narragansett Bay. . . .

They busted her for witchery and she got death. Another of Slothrop's crazy kinfolks. When she was mentioned aloud at all it was with a shrug, too far away really to be a Family Disgrace—more of a curiosity. Slothrop grew up not quite knowing what to think about her. Witches were certainly not getting a fair shake in the thirties. They were depicted as hags who called you dearie, not exactly a wholesome lot. The movies had not prepared him for this Teutonic version here. Your kraut witch, for example, has six toes on each foot and no hair at all on her cunt. That is how the witches look, anyhow, in the stairway murals inside the one-time Nazi transmitter tower up on the Brocken here, and government murals are hardly places to go looking for irresponsible fantasy, right? But Geli thinks the hairless cunt derives from the women von Bayros drew. "Aw, you just don't wanna shave *yours*," crows Slothrop. "Ha! Ha! Some witch!"

"I'll show *you* something," she sez, which is why they are now awake at this ungodly hour, side by side, holding hands, very still as the sun begins to clear the horizon. "Now watch," Geli whispers: "out there."

As the sunlight strikes their backs, coming in nearly flat on, it begins developing on the pearl cloudbank: two gigantic shadows, thrown miles overland, past Clausthal-Zelterfeld, past Seesen and Goslar, across where the river Leine would be, and reaching toward Weser. . . . "By golly," Slothrop a little bit nervous, "it's the Specter." You got it up around Greylock in the Berkshires too. Around these parts it is known as the Brockengespenst.

God-shadows. Slothrop raises an arm. His fingers are cities, his biceps is a province—of course he raises an arm. Isn't it expected of him? The arm-shadow trails rainbows behind as it moves reaching eastward for a grab at Göttingen. Not ordinary shadows, either—*three-dimensional* ones, cast out on the German dawn, yes and Titans *had* to live in these mountains, or under them. . . . Impossibly out of scale. Never to be carried by a river. Never to look to a horizon and think that it might go on forever. No trees to climb, no long journeys to take . . . only their deep images are left, haloed shells lying prone above the fogs men move in. . . .

Geli kicks a leg out straight as a dancer, and tilts her head to the side. Slothrop raises his middle finger to the west, the headlong finger darkening three miles of cloud per second. Geli grabs for Slothrop's cock. Slothrop leans to bite Geli's tit. They are enormous, dancing the floor of the whole visible sky. He reaches underneath her dress. She twines a leg around one of his. The spectra wash red to indigo, tidal, immense, at all their edges. Under the clouds out there it's as still, and lost, as Atlantis.

But the Brockengespenstphänomen is confined to dawn's slender interface, and soon the shadows have come shrinking back to their owners.

"Say, did that Tchitcherine ever—"

"Tchitcherine's too busy for this."

"Oh, and I'm some kind of a drone or something."

"You're different."

"We-e-e-ll . . . he *ought* to see it."

She looks at him curiously, but doesn't ask why—her teeth halt on her lower lip, and the *warum* (varoom, a Plasticman sound) hovers trapped in her mouth. Just as well. Slothrop doesn't *know* why. He's no help to anybody who's fixing to interrogate. Last night he and Geli blundered onto a Schwarzkommando picket outside one of the old mine entrances. The Hereros threw questions at him for an hour. Oh, just wandering about you know, looking for a bit of the odd, what we call "human interest," fascinating of course, we're always interested in what you chaps are up to. . . . Geli snickering in the darkness. They must have known her. They didn't ask *her* anything.

When he brought it up later, she wasn't sure just what this is between Tchitcherine and the Africans, but whatever it is it's being carried on with high passion.

"It's hate, all right," she said. "Stupid, stupid. The war's over. It isn't politics or fuck-your-buddy, it's old-time, pure, personal hate."

"Enzian?"

"I think so."

They found the Brocken occupied both by American and by Russian troops. The mountain lay on what was to be the border of the Soviet zone of occupation. The brick and stucco ruins of the radio transmitter and a tourist hotel loomed up just outside the firelight. Only a couple of platoons here. Nobody higher than noncoms. The officers were all down in Bad Harzburg, Halberstadt, someplace comfortable, getting drunk or laid. There is a certain air of resentment up on the Brocken all right, but the boys like Geli and tolerate Slothrop, and luckiest of all, nobody seems to be connected with that Ordnance.

It's only a moment's safety, though. Major Marvy is gnashing about the Harz, sending thousands of canaries into cardiac episodes, dropping in yellow droves belly-up

out of the trees as he marauds on by hollering *Git* that
limey 'sucker I don't care how many men it takes I want
a fucking *division* you hear me boy? Only a matter of time
before he picks up the trail again. He's out of his mind.
Slothrop's a little daffy, but not like this—this is really
unhealthy, this Marvy persecution. Is it possible . . .
yup, the thought has certainly occurred to him—that
Marvy's in tight with those Rolls Roycers who were after
him in Zürich? There may be no limit to their connections.
Marvy is buddies with GE, that's Morgan money, there's
Morgan money in Harvard, and surely an interlock someplace with Lyle Bland . . . who *are* they, hey? why do
they want Slothrop? He knows now for sure that Zwitter
the mad Nazi scientist is one of them. And that kindly
old Professor Glimpf was only waiting down in the Mittelwerke to pick up Slothrop if he showed. Jesus. If Slothrop
hadn't snuck out after dark back down into Nordhausen
to Geli's place, they'd have him locked up by now for
sure, maybe beaten up, maybe dead.

Before they head back down the mountain, they manage to chisel six cigarettes and some K-rations off of the
sentries. Geli knows a friend of a friend who stays out on
a farm in the Goldene Aue, a ballooning enthusiast named
Schnorp, who is heading toward Berlin.

"But I don't want to go to Berlin."

"You want to go where Marvy isn't, Liebchen."

Schnorp is beaming, eager enough for company, just
back from a local PX with an armload of flat white boxes:
merchandise he plans to move in Berlin. "No trouble," he
tells Slothrop, "don't worry. I've done this trip hundreds
of times. Nobody bothers a balloon."

He takes Slothrop out in back of the house, and here
in the middle of a sloping green field is a wicker gondola
beside a great heap of bright yellow and scarlet silk.

"Real unobtrusive getaway," Slothrop mutters. A gang
of kids have appeared running out of an apple orchard
to help them carry tin jerricans of grain alcohol out to
the gondola. All shadows are being thrown uphill by the
afternoon sun. Wind blows from the west. Slothrop gives
Schnorp a light from his Zippo to get the burner going
while kids straighten out the folds in the gasbag. Schnorp
turns up the flame till it's shooting sideways and with a

steady roar into the opening of the great silk bag. Children visible through the gap break up into wiggly heat waves. Slowly the balloon begins to expand. "Remember me," Geli calls above the rumbling of the burner. "Till I see you again . . ." Slothrop climbs in the gondola with Schnorp. The balloon rises a little off the ground and is caught by the wind. They start to move. Geli and the kids have taken hold of the gondola all around its gunwales, the bag still not all the way up but gathering speed, dragging them all as fast as their feet can move, giggling and cheering, uphill. Slothrop keeps as much out of the way as he can, letting Schnorp see that the flame's pointed into the bag and that lines to the basket are clear. At last the bag swings vertical, across the sun, the inside of it going a riotous wreathing of yellow and scarlet heat. One by one the ground crew fall away, waving good-by. The last to go is Geli in her white dress, hair brushed back over her ears into pigtails, her soft chin and mouth and big serious eyes looking into Slothrop's for as long as she can before she has to let go. She kneels in the grass, blows a kiss. Slothrop feels his heart, out of control, inflate with love and rise quick as a balloon. It is taking him longer, the longer he's in the Zone, to remember to say *aw quit being a sap*. What is this place doing to his brain?

They soar up over a stand of firs. Geli and the children go dwindling to shadow-strokes on the green lawn. The hills fall away, flatten out. Soon, looking back, Slothrop can see Nordhausen: Cathedral, Rathaus, Church of St. Blasius . . . the roofless quarter where he found Geli. . . .

Schnorp nudges and points. After a while Slothrop makes out a convoy of four olive-drab vehicles dusting along toward the farm in a hurry. Marvy's Mothers, by the looks of things. And Slothrop hanging from this gaudy beach ball. Well, all right—

"I'm bad luck," Slothrop hollers over a little later. They've found a steady course now northeastward, and are huddling close to the alcohol flame, collars turned up, with a gradient of must be 50° between the wind at their backs and the warmth in front. "I should've mentioned that. You don't even know me, and here we're flying into that Russian zone."

Schnorp, his hair blown like holidays of hay, does a wistful German thing with his upper lip: "There are no zones," he sez, which is also a line of Geli's. "No zones but the Zone."

Before too long Slothrop has begun checking out these boxes here that Schnorp brought along. There are a dozen of them, and each contains a deep, golden custard pie, which will fetch a fantastic price in Berlin. "Wow," cries Slothrop, "holy shit. Surely I hallucinate," and other such eager junior sidekick talk.

"You ought to have a PX card." A sales pitch.

"Right now I can't afford a ration stamp for an ant's jockstrap," replies Slothrop, forthrightly.

"Well, I'll split this one pie here with you," Schnorp reckons after a time, "because I'm getting kind of hungry."

"Oboy, oboy."

Well, Slothrop is just chowing on that pie! enjoying himself, licking custard off his hands, when he happens to notice off in the sky, back toward Nordhausen, this funny dark object, the size of a dot. "Uh—"

Schnorp looks around, "Kot!" comes up with a brass telescope and braces it blazing on the gunwale. "Kot, Kot—no markings."

"I wonder . . ."

Out of air so blue you can take it between your fingers, rub, and bring them back blue, they watch the dot slowly grow into a rusty old reconnaissance plane. Presently they can hear its engine, snarling and sputtering. Then, as they watch, it banks and starts a pass.

Along the wind between them, faintly, comes the singing of Furies:

> There was a young man named McGuire,
> Who was fond of the pitch amplifier.
> But a number of shorts
> Left him covered with warts,
> And set half the bedroom on fire.
>
> Ja, ja, ja, ja!
> In Prussia they never eat pussy—

The plane buzzes by a yard or two away, showing its underbelly. It is a monster, about to give birth. Out of a little access opening peers a red face in leather helmet and goggles. "You limey 'sucker," going past, "we fixin' to hand your *ass* to *you*."

Without planning to, Slothrop has picked up a pie. "Fuck you." He flings it, perfect shot, the plane peeling slowly past and *blop* gets Marvy right in the face. Yeah. Gloved hands paw at the mess. The Major's pink tongue appears. Custard drips into the wind, yellow droplets fall in long arcs toward earth. The hatch closes as the recon plane slides away, slow-rolls, circles and heads back. Schnorp and Slothrop heft pies and wait.

"There's no cowling around that engine," Schnorp has noticed, "so we'll aim for that." Now they can see the dorsal side of the plane, its cockpit jammed to capacity with beer-sodden Americans, singing:

> There once was a fellow named Ritter,
> Who slept with a guidance transmitter.
> It shriveled his cock,
> Which fell off in his sock,
> And made him exceedingly bitter.

A hundred yards and closing fast. Schnorp grabs Slothrop's arm and points off to starboard. Providence has contrived to put in their way a big white slope of cloud, and the wind is bringing them swiftly into it: the seething critter puts out white tentacles, beckoning hurry . . . hurry . . . and they are inside then, inside its wet and icy reprieve. . . .

"Now they'll wait."

"No," Schnorp cupping an ear, "they've cut the motor. They're in here with us." The swaddled silence goes on for a minute or two, but sure enough:

> There once was a fellow named Schroeder,
> Who buggered the vane servomotor.
> He soon grew a prong
> On the end of his schlong,
> And hired himself a promoter.

Schnorp is fiddling with the flame, a rose-gray nimbus, trying for less visibility, but not too much loss of altitude. They float in their own wan sphere of light, without co-

ordinates. Outcrops of granite smash blindly upward like
fists into the cloud, trying to find the balloon. The plane
is somewhere, with its own course and speed. There is no
action the balloon can take. Binary decisions have lost
meaning in here. The cloud presses in, suffocating. It con-
denses in fat drops on top of the pies. Suddenly, raucous
and hungover:

> There was a young man from Decatur,
> Who slept with a LOX generator.
> His balls and his prick
> Froze solid real quick,
> And his asshole a little bit later.

Curtains of vapor drift back to reveal the Americans,
volplaning along well inside ten meters and only a little
faster than the balloon.

"Now!" Schnorp yells, heaving a pie at the exposed
engine. Slothrop's misses and splatters all over the windscreen in front of the pilot. By which time Schnorp has
commenced flinging ballast bags at the engine, leaving
one stuck between two of the cylinders. The Americans,
taken by surprise, reach in confusion for sidearms, grenades, machine guns, whatever it is your Ordnance types
carry around in the way of light armament. But they have
glided on past, and now the fog closes in again. There
are a few shots.

"Shit, man, if they hit that bag—"

"Shh. I think we got the wire from the booster mag-
neto." Off in the middle of the cloud can be heard the
nagging whicker of an engine refusing to start. Linkage
squeaks desperately.

"Oh, fuck!" A muffled scream, far away. The inter-
mittent whining grows fainter until there is silence.
Schnorp is lying on his back, slurping pie, laughing bitterly. Half of his inventory's been thrown away, and Slothrop feels a little guilty.

"No, no. Stop worrying. This is like the very earliest
days of the mercantile system. We're back to that again.
A second chance. Passages are long and hazardous. Loss
in transit is a part of life. You have had a glimpse of the
Ur-Markt."

When the clouds fall away a few minutes later, they

find themselves floating quietly under the sun, shrouds dripping, gasbag still shiny with the moist cloud. No sign at all of Marvy's plane. Schnorp adjusts the flame. They begin to rise.

Toward sundown, Schnorp gets thoughtful. "Look. You can see the edge of it. At this latitude the earth's shadow races across Germany at 650 miles an hour, the speed of a jet aircraft." The cloud-sheet has broken up into little fog-blankets the color of boiled shrimp. The balloon goes drifting, over countryside whose green patchwork the twilight is now urging toward black: the thread of a little river flaming in the late sun, the intricate-angled pattern of another roofless town.

The sunset is red and yellow, like the balloon. On the horizon the mild sphere goes warping down, a peach on a china plate. "The farther south you go," Schnorp continues, "the faster the shadow sweeps, till you reach the equator: a thousand miles an hour. Fantastic. It breaks through the speed of sound somewhere over southern France—around the latitude of Carcassonne."

The wind is bundling them on, north by east. "Southern France," Slothrop remembers then. "Yeah. That's where *I* broke through the speed of sound. . . ."

□

The Zone is in full summer: souls are found quiescent behind the pieces of wall, fast asleep down curled in shell-craters, out screwing under the culverts with gray shirt-tails hoisted, adrift dreaming in the middles of fields. Dreaming of food, oblivion, alternate histories. . . .

The silences here are retreats of sound, like the retreat of the surf before a tidal wave: sound draining away, down slopes of acoustic passage, to gather, someplace else, to a great surge of noise. Cows—big lummoxes splotched black and white, harnessed now for the plowing because German horses in the Zone are all but extinct—will drudge with straight faces right on into minefields, sown back in the winter. The godawful blasts go drumming over the farmland, horns, hide and hamburger come showering down all over the place, the dented bells lie

quiet in the clover. Horses might have known to
keep clear—but the Germans wasted their horses, squan-
dered the race, hearding them into the worst of it,
the swarms of steel, the rheumatic marshes, the un-
blanketed winter chills of our late Fronts. A few might
have found safety with the Russians, who still care for
horses. You hear them often in the evenings. Their camp-
fires send up rays for miles from behind the stands of
beech, through northern-summer haze that's almost dry,
only enough of it to give a knife's edge to the firelight,
a dozen accordions and concertinas all going at once in
shaggy chords with a reed-ringing to it, and the songs
full of plaintive *stvyehs* and *znyis* with voices of the girl
auxiliaries clearest of all. The horses whicker and move
in the rustling grass. The men and women are kind, resourceful, fanatical—they are the most joyous of the
Zone's survivors.

In and out of all the vibrant flesh moves the mad
scavenger Tchitcherine, who is more metal than anything
else. Steel teeth wink as he talks. Under his pompadour
is a silver plate. Gold wirework threads in three-dimensional tattoo among the fine wreckage of cartilage and
bone inside his right knee joint, the shape of it always
felt, pain's hand-fashioned seal, and his proudest battle
decoration, because it is invisible, and only he can feel
it. A four-hour operation, and in the dark. It was the
Eastern Front: there were no sulfa drugs, no anaesthesia.
Of course he's proud.

He has marched here, with his limp as permanent as
gold, out of coldness, meadows, mystery. Officially he reports to TsAGI, which is the Central Aero and Hydrodynamics Institute in Moscow. His orders mention technical intelligence. But his real mission in the Zone is private,
obsessive, and not—so his superiors have let him know,
in a number of delicate ways—in the people's interest.
Tchitcherine guesses that this, taken literally, may be true
enough. But he is not sure about the interests of those
who warned him. They could have their own reasons for
wanting Enzian liquidated in spite of what they say. Their
differences with Tchitcherine may be over the timing, or
the motives. Tchitcherine's motives are not political. The
little State he is building in the German vacuum is

founded on a compulsive need he has given up trying to understand, a need to annihilate the Schwarzkommando and his mythical half-brother, Enzian. He comes from Nihilist stock: there are in his ancestry any number of bomb throwers and jubilant assassins. He is no relation at all to the Tchitcherine who dealt the Rapallo Treaty with Walter Rathenau. There was a long-term operator, a Menshevik turned Bolshevik, in his exile and his return believing in a State that would outlive them all, where someone would come to sit in his seat at the table just as he had slipped into Trotsky's—sitters would come and go but the seats would remain . . . well, fine. There is *that* kind of State. But then again, there is this other Tchitcherine's kind, a mortal State that will persist no longer than the individuals in it. He is bound, in love and in bodily fear, to students who have died under the wheels of carriages, to eyes betrayed by nights without sleep and arms that have opened maniacally to death by absolute power. He envies their loneliness, their willingness to go it alone, outside even a military structure, often without support or love from anyone. His own faithful network of fräuleins around the Zone is a compromise: he knows there's too much comfort in it, even when the intelligence inputs are good. But the perceptible hazards of love, of attachment, are still light enough for him to accept, when balanced against what he has to do.

During the early Stalin days, Tchitcherine was stationed in a remote "bear's corner" *(medvezhy ugolok),* out in Seven Rivers country. In the summer, irrigation canals sweated a blurry fretwork across the green oasis. In the winter, sticky teaglasses ranked the windowsills, soldiers played *preference* and stepped outside only to piss, or to shoot down the street at surprised wolves with a lately retooled version of the Moisin. It was a land of drunken nostalgia for the cities, silent Kirghiz riding, endless tremors in the earth . . . because of the earthquakes, nobody built higher than one story and so the town looked like a Wild West movie: a brown dirt street, lined with grandiose two- and three-story false fronts.

He had come to give the tribesmen out here, this far out, an alphabet: it was purely speech, gesture, touch among them, not even an Arabic script to replace. Tchitcherine coordinated with the local Likbez center, one of a string known back in Moscow as the "red džurts." Young and old Kirghiz came in from the plain, smelling of horses, sour milk and weed-smoke, inside to stare at slates filled with chalk marks. The stiff Latin symbols were almost as strange to the Russian cadre—tall Galina in her cast-off Army trousers and gray Cossack shirts . . . marcelled and soft-faced Luba, her dear friend . . . Vaslav Tchitcherine, the political eye . . . all agents—though none thought of it this way—representing the NTA (New Turkic Alphabet) in uncommonly alien country.

In the mornings after mess, Tchitcherine will usually mosey down to the red džurt there, fixing to look in on that Galina the schoolmarm—who appeals to what must be a feminine linkage or two in his personality . . . well . . . often he'll come outside to find his morning skies full of sheet-lighting: gusting, glaring. Awful. The ground shudders just below his hearing. It might be the end of the world, except that it is a fairly average day, for Central Asia. Pulse after heavenwide pulse. Clouds, some in very clear profile, black and jagged, sail in armadas toward the Asian arctic, above the sweeping dessiatinas of grasses, of mullein stalks, rippling out of sight, green and gray in the wind. An amazing wind. But he stands in the street, out in it, hitching his pants, lapelpoints whipped rattling against his chest, cursing Army, Party, History— whatever has put him here. He will not come to love this sky or plain, these people, their animals. Nor look back, no not even in the worst marsh-bivouacs of his soul, in naked Leningrad encounters with the certainty of his death, of the deaths of comrades, never keep any memory of Seven Rivers to shelter with. No music heard, no summer journey taken . . . no horse seen against the steppe in the last daylight. . . .

Certainly not Galina. Galina won't even be a proper "memory." Already she is more like the shape of an alphabet, the procedure for field-stripping a Moisin—yes, like remembering to hold back trigger with forefinger of left hand as you remove bolt with right, a set of interlocking precautions, part of a process among the three exiles Galina/Luba/Tchitcherine which is working out its changes, its little dialectic, until it ends, with nothing past the structure to remember. . . .

Her eyes hide in iron shadows, the orbits darkened as if by very precise blows. Her jaw is small, square, levered forward, the lower teeth more apt to show when she speaks. . . . Hardly ever a smile. Bones in her face strongly curved and welded. Her aura is chalkdust, laundry soap, sweat. With desperate Luba about the edges, always, of her room, at her window, a pretty hawk. Galina has trained her—but it's only Luba who flies, who knows the verst-long dive, the talon-shock and the blood, while her lean owner must stay below in the schoolroom, shut in by words, drifts and frost-patterns of white words.

Light pulses behind the clouds. Tchitcherine tracks mud off the street into the Center, gets a blush from Luba, a kind of kowtow and mopflourish from the comical Chinese swamper Chu Piang, unreadable stares from an early pupil or two. The traveling "native" schoolteacher Džaqyp Qulan looks up from a clutter of pastel survey maps, black theodolites, bootlaces, tractor gaskets, plugs, greasy tierod ends, steel map-cases, 7.62 mm rounds, crumbs and chunks of lepeshka, about to ask for a cigarette which is already out of Tchitcherine's pocket and on route.

He smiles thank you. He'd better. He's not sure of Tchitcherine's intentions, much less the Russian's friendship. Džaqyp Qulan's father was killed during the 1916 rising, trying to get away from Kuropatkin's troops and over the border into China—one of about 100 fleeing Kirghiz massacred one evening beside a drying trickle of river that might be traceable somehow north to the zero at the top of the world. Russian settlers, in full vigilante panic, surrounded and killed the darker refugees with shovels, pitchforks, old rifles, any weapon to hand. A common occurrence in Semirechie then, even that far from the railroad. They hunted Sarts, Kazakhs, Kirghiz, and Dungans that terrible summer like wild game. Daily scores were kept. It was a competition, good-natured but more than play. Thousands of restless natives bit the dust. Their names, even their numbers, lost forever. Colors of skin, ways of dressing became reasonable cause to jail, or beat and kill. Even speaking-voices—because rumors of German and Turkish agents swept along these plains, not without help from Petrograd. This native uprising was supposed to be the doing of foreigners, an international conspiracy to open a new front in the war. More Western paranoia, based solidly on the European balance of power. How could there be Kazakh, Kirghiz—Eastern—reasons? Hadn't the nationalities been happy? Hadn't fifty years of Russian rule brought progress? enrichment?

Well, for now, under the current dispensation in Moscow, Džaqyp Qulan is the son of a national martyr. The Georgian has come to power, power in Russia, ancient and absolute, proclaiming Be Kind To The Nationalities. But though the lovable old tyrant does what he can, Džaqyp Qulan remains somehow as much a "native" as before, gauged day-to-day by these Russians as to his degree of restlessness. His sorrel face, his long narrow eyes and dusty boots, where he goes on his travels and what really transpires inside the lonely hide tents Out There, among the auls, out in that wind, these are mysteries they don't care to enter or touch. They throw amiable cigarettes, construct him paper existences, use him as an Educated Native Speaker. He's allowed his function and that's as far as it goes . . . except, now and then, a look from Luba suggesting falconhood—jesses, sky and earth, voyages. . . . Or from Galina a silence where there might have been words. . . .

Here she has become a connoisseuse of silences. The great silences of Seven Rivers have not yet been alphabetized, and perhaps never will be. They are apt at any time to come into a room, into a heart, returning to chalk and paper the sensible Soviet alternatives brought out here by the Likbez agents. They are silences NTA cannot fill, cannot liquidate, immense and frightening as the elements in this bear's corner—scaled to a larger Earth, a planet wilder and more distant from the sun. . . . The winds, the city snows and heat waves of Galina's childhood were never so vast, so pitiless. She had to come out here to learn what an earthquake felt like, and how to wait out a sandstorm. What would it be like to go back now, back to a city? Often she will dream some dainty pasteboard model, a city-planner's city, perfectly detailed so tiny her bootsoles could wipe out neighborhoods at a step—at the same time, she is also a dweller, down inside the little city, coming awake in the very late night, blinking up into painful daylight, waiting for the annihilation, the blows from the sky, drawn terribly tense with the waiting, unable to name whatever it is approaching, knowing—too awful to say—it is herself, her Central Asian giantness self, that is the Nameless Thing she fears. . . .

These tall, these star-blotting Moslem angels . . . *O, wie spurlos zerträte ein Engel den Trostmarkt.* . . . He is constant back there, westward, the African half-brother and his poetry books furrowed and sown with Teutonic lettering burntwood-black—he waits, smudging the pages one by one, out across the unnumbered versts of lowland and of zonal light that slants as their autumns come around again each year, that leans along the planet's withers like an old circus rider, tries to catch their attention with nothing more than its public face, and continues to fail at each slick, perfect pass around the ring.

But didn't Džaqyp Qulan, now and then—not often—across the paper schoolroom, or by surprise in front of windows into the green deep open, give Tchitcherine a certain look? Didn't the look say, "Nothing you do, nothing he does, will help you in your mortality"? And, "You are brothers. Together, apart, why let it matter this much? Live. Die someday, honorably, meanly—but not by the other's hand. . . ." The light of each common autumn keeps bringing the same free advice, each time a little less hopefully. But neither brother can listen. The black must have found, somewhere in Germany, his own version of Džaqyp Qulan, some childish native to stare him out of German dreams of the Tenth-Elegy angel coming, wingbeats already at the edges of waking, coming to trample spoorless the white marketplace of his own exile. . . . Facing east, the black face keeping watch from some winter embankment or earth-colored wall of a fine-grained stone into low wastes of Prussia, of Poland, the leagues of meadow waiting, just as Tchitcherine grows each month now more taut and windsmooth at his westward flank, seeing History and Geopolitics move them surely into confrontation as the radios go screaming higher, new penstocks in the night shudder to the touch with hydroelectric rage, mounting, across the empty canyons and passes, skies in the day go thick with miles of falling canopies, white as visions of rich men's heavenly džurts, gaming now and still awkward, but growing, each strewn pattern, less and less at play. . . .

Out into the bones of the backlands ride Tchitcherine and his faithful Kirghiz companion Džaqyp Qulan. Tchitcherine's horse is a version of himself—an Appaloosa from the United States named Snake. Snake used to be some kind of remittance horse. Year before last he was in Saudi Arabia, being sent a check each month by a zany (or, if you enjoy paranoid systems, a horribly rational) Midland, Texas oil man to stay off of the U.S. rodeo circuits, where in those days the famous bucking bronco Midnight was flinging young men right and left into the sun-beat fences. But Snake here is not so much Midnight-wild as methodically homicidal. Worse, he's unpredictable. When you go to ride him he may be indifferent, or docile as a maiden. But then again, with no warning, seized out of the last ruffling of a great sigh, he could manage to kill you simply as the gesture of a hoof, the serpent tuck of a head toward the exact moment and spot on the ground that you'll cease to live. No way to tell: for months he can be no trouble at all. So far he's ignored Tchitcherine. But he's tried for Džaqyp Qulan three times. Twice dumb luck preserved the Kirghiz, and the third time he actually hung on and rode the colt a long time down to a fair kind of obedience. But each time Tchitcherine goes up to Snake's jingling picket on the hillside, he carries, with his leather gear and his bit of scarred tapestry for the horse's back, the doubt, the inconsolable chance that the Kirghiz didn't really break him last time. That Snake is only waiting his moment. . . .

They're riding away from the railroad: farther away from the kinder zones of Earth. Black and white stars explode down the Appaloosa's croup and haunch. At the center of each of these novae is a stark circle of vacuum, of no color, into which midday Kirghiz at the roadsides have taken looks, and grinned away with a turn of the head to the horizon behind.

Strange, strange are the dynamics of oil and the ways of oilmen. Snake has seen a lot of changes since Arabia,

on route to Tchitcherine, who may be his other half—lot
of horse thieves, hard riding, confiscation by this government and that, escapes into ever more remote country.
This time, the Kirghiz pheasants scattering now at the
sound of hooves, birds big as turkeys, black and white
with splashes of blood-red all around the eyes, lumbering
for the uplands, Snake is going out into what could be
the last adventure of all, hardly remembering now the
water-pipes at the oases crawling with smoke, the bearded
men, the carved, nacred and lacquered saddles, the neck-
reins of twisted goat-hide, the women pillioned and wailing with delight up into Caucasian foothills in the dark,
carried by lust, by storm along streaks of faintest trail . . .
only traces spread back in a wake now over these terminal
grasslands: shadows damping and passing to rest among
the rout of pheasants. Momentum builds as the two riders
plunge ahead. The smell of forests on the night slowly
disappears. Waiting, out in sunlight which is not theirs
yet, is the . . . The . . . Waiting for them, the unimagined
creature of height, and burning . . .

. . . even now in her grown up dreams, to anxious
Galina comes the winged rider, red Sagittarius off the
childhood placards of the Revolution. Far from rag, snow,
lacerated streets she huddles here in the Asian dust with
her buttocks arched skyward, awaiting the first touch of
him—of *it*. . . . Steel hooves, teeth, some whistling sweep
of quills across her spine . . . the ringing bronze of an
equestrian statue in a square, and her face, pressed into
the seismic earth. . . .

"He's a soldier," Luba simply meaning Tchitcherine,
"and far away from home." Posted out to the wild East,
and carrying on quiet, expressionless, and clearly under
some official curse. The rumors are as extravagant as this
country is listless. In the dayroom the corporals talk about
a woman: an amazing Soviet courtesan who wore cami-
soles of white kid and shaved her perfect legs every morning all the way to the groin. Horse-fucking Catherine,
ermined and brilliant, brought up to date. Her lovers ran
from ministers down to the likes of Captain Tchitcherine,
naturally her truest. While neo-Potemkins ranged the deep
Arctic for her, skilled and technocratic wolves erecting

settlements out of tundra, entire urban abstractions out of ice and snow, bold Tchitcherine was back at the capital, snuggled away in her dacha, where they played at fisherman and fish, terrorist and State, explorer and edge of the wavegreen world. When official attention was finally directed their way, it did not mean death for Tchitcherine, not even exile—but a thinning out of career possibilities: that happened to be how the vectors ran, in those days. Central Asia for a good part of his prime years, or attaché someplace like Costa Rica (well—he wishes it *could* be Costa Rica, someday—a release from this purgatory, into shuffling surf, green nights—how he misses the sea, how he dreams of eyes dark and liquid as his own, colonial eyes, gazing down from balconies of rotting stone . . .).

Meanwhile, another rumor tells of his connection with the legendary Wimpe, the head salesman for Ostarznei-kunde GmbH, a subsidiary of the IG. Because it is common knowledge that IG representatives abroad are actually German spies, reporting back to an office in Berlin known as "NW7," this story about Tchitcherine is not so easy to believe. If it were literally true, Tchitcherine wouldn't be here—there's no possible way his life could have been spared in favor of this somnambulism among the eastern garrison towns.

Certainly he *could* have known Wimpe. Their lives, for a while, ran close enough in space and time. Wimpe was a Verbindungsman in the classic style, with a streak of unhealthy enthusiasm: charming, handsome in a way that came at you in shelves or terraces of strength: amiable gray eyes, vertical granite nose, mouth that never quivered, chin incapable of fantasies . . . dark suits, immaculate leather belts and silver studs, horsehide shoes that gleamed under the skylights in the Czarist entrance-halls and across the Soviet concrete, always dapper, usually correct, informed and passionate about organic chemistry, his specialty and, it's been suggested, his faith.

"Think of chess," in his early days around the capital looking for a comparison that Russians might take to, "an extravagant game of chess." Going on to show, if his audience was receptive (he had salesman reflexes, knew to steer automatically along lines of least indifference) how each molecule had so many possibilities open to it, possibilities for bonding, bonds of different strengths, from carbon the most versatile, the queen, "the Great Catherine of the periodic table," down to the little hydrogens numerous and single-moving as pawns . . . and the brute opposition of the chessboard yielding, in this chemical game, to dance-figures in three dimensions, "four, if you like," and a radically different idea of what winning and losing meant. . . . Schwärmerei, his colleagues back home had muttered, finding excuses to drift away into other conversations. But Tchitcherine would have stayed. Foolish and romantic, he would have kept listening, even egged the German on.

How could they have failed to be observed? By and by, as the affair in its repressed and bloodless way proceeded, the Soviet chain of command, solicitous as any 19th-century family, would begin to take simple steps to keep the two apart. Conservative therapy. Central Asia. But in the weeks of vague and soft intelligence, before the watchers quite caught the drift of things . . . what heads and tails went jingling inside the dark pockets of *that* indeterminacy? Since his earliest days as a detail man, Wimpe's expertise had been focused in cyclized benzylisoquinolines. Those of major interest being the opium alkaloids and their many variations. Right. The inner rooms of Wimpe's office—a suite at an older hotel— were full of samples, German dope in amazing profusion, Wimpe the jinni of the West holding them up, vial after vial, for little Tchitcherine's face to wonder at: "Eumecon, a 2% solution of morphine . . . Dionine (we add on an ethyl group, here, to the morphine, as you see) . . . Holopon and Nealpon, Pantopon and Omnopon, all mixtures of opium alkaloids as the soluble hydrochlorides . . . and Glycopon, as glycero-phosphates. . . . Here is Eucodal—a codeine with two hydrogens, a hydroxyl, a hydrochloride"—gesturing in the air around his basic fist— "hanging off different parts of the molecule." Among these patent medicines, trappings and detailing were half the game—"As the French do with their dresses, nicht wahr? a ribbon here, a pretty buckle there, to help sell a sparer design. . . . Ah, this? Trivalin!" One of the jewels of his line. "Morphine, and caffeine, and cocaine, all in solution,

as the valerates. Valerian, ja—root and rhizome: you may
have older relatives who took it years ago as a nerve
tonic . . . a bit of passementerie, you might say—some
trimming over these bare molecules."

What did Tchitcherine have to say? Was Tchitcherine
there at all? sitting back in the dingy room while the lift
cables slapped and creaked through the walls, and down
in the street, rarely enough to matter, a droshky rattled
whip-snapping over these black old cobbles? Or while
snow beat at the grimy windows? How far, in the eyes
of those who would send him to Central Asia, was too
far: would his simple presence in these rooms have gotten
him death automatically . . . or was there still, even at
this stage of things, enough slack to let him reply?

"But once the pain has been taken care of . . . the simple pain . . . beyond . . . below that zero level of feeling . . . I have heard . . ." He has heard. Not the subtlest
way to get into it, and Wimpe must have known every
standard opener there is. Some military men are only
blunt, while others are of such reckless blood there is
never a question of "holding back"—it's a positive insanity, they not only will commit horse against cannon,
they will lead the charge themselves. It's magnificent, but
it's not war. Wait until the Eastern Front. By his first
action, Tchitcherine will have gained his reputation as a
suicidal maniac. German field commanders from Finland
to the Black Sea will develop for him a gentlemanly distaste. It will be seriously wondered if the man has any
sense of military decency at all. They will capture him
and lose him, wound him, take him for killed in action,
and he will go on, headlong, a raving snowman over the
winter marshes—there'll be no wind adjustment, no field-
change to the bottleneck fairing or deadly ogive of their
Parabellum rounds that can ever bring him down. He is
fond, as was Lenin, of Napoleon's *on s'engage, et puis,
on voit,* and as for plunging ahead, well, that IG man's
hotel room may have been one of his earlier rehearsals.
Tchitcherine has a way of getting together with unde-
sirables, sub rosa enemies of order, counterrevolutionary
odds and ends of humanity: he doesn't plan it, it just
happens, he is a giant supermolecule with so many open
bonds available at any given time, and in the drift of

things . . . in the dance of things . . . howsoever . . . others latch on, and the pharmacology of the Tchitcherine thus modified, its onwardly revealed side-effects, can't necessarily be calculated ahead of time. Chu Piang, the Chinese factotum in the red džurt, knows something of this. The first day Tchitcherine came to report in to the place, Chu Piang knew—and tripped over his mop, not so much to divert attention as to celebrate the meeting. Chu Piang has a bond or two available himself. He is a living monument to the success of British trade policy back during the last century. This classic hustle is still famous, even today, for the cold purity of its execution: bring opium from India, introduce it into China—howdy Fong, this here's opium, opium, this is Fong—ah, so, me eatee!—no-ho-ho, Fong, you smokee, *smokee*, see? pretty soon Fong's coming back for more and more, so you create an inelastic demand for the shit, get China to make it illegal, then sucker China into a couple-three disastrous wars over the right of your merchants to sell opium, which by now you are describing as sacred. You win, China loses. Fantastic. Chu Piang being a monument to all this, nowadays whole tourist caravans come through to look at him, usually while he's Under The Influence . . . "Here ladies and gentlemen, as you may have observed, the characteristic sooty-gray complexion. . . ." They all stand peering into his dreamstruck facies, attentive men with mutton-chop sideburns, holding pearl-gray morning hats in their hands, the women lifting their skirts away from where horrid Asian critters are seething microscopically across the old floorboards, while their tour leader indicates items of interest with his metal pointer, an instrument remarkably thin, thinner than a rapier in fact, often flashing along much faster than eyes can really follow—"His Need, you will notice, retains its shape under all manner of stresses. No bodily illness, no scarcity of supply seems to affect it a whit . . ." all their mild, their shallow eyes following gently as piano chords from a suburban parlor . . . the inelastic Need turns luminous this stagnant air: it is an ingot beyond price, from which sovereigns yet may be struck, and faces of great administrators engraved and run off to signify. It was worth the trip, just to see this shining, worth the long passage by sleigh, over the frozen steppe in an enormous closed sleigh, big as a ferryboat, bedizened all over with Victorian gingerbread—inside are decks and levels for each class of passenger, velvet saloons, well-stocked galleys, a young Dr. Maledetto whom the ladies love, an elegant menu including every-thing from Mille-Feuilles à la Fondue de la Cervelle to La Surprise du Vésuve, lounges amply fitted out with stereo-opticons and a library of slides, oak toilets rubbed to a deep red and hand-carved into mermaid faces, acanthus leaves, afternoon and garden shapes to remind the sitter of home when he needs it most, hot insides poised here so terribly above the breakneck passage of crystalline ice and snow, which may be seen also from the observation deck, the passing vistas of horizontal pallor, the wheeling snowfields of Asia, beneath skies of metal baser by far than this we have come to watch. . . .

Chu Piang is also watching them, as they come, and stare, and go. They are figures in dreams. They amuse him. They belong to the opium: they never come if it's anything else. He tries not to smoke the hashish out here, actually, any more than courtesy demands. That chunky, resinous Turkestan phantasmagoric is fine for Russian, Kirghiz, and other barbaric tastes, but give Chu the tears of the poppy any time. The dreams are better, not so geo-metrical, so apt to turn everything—the air, the sky—to Persian rugs. Chu prefers situations, journeys, comedy. Finding the same appetite in Tchitcherine, this stocky, Latin-eyed emissary from Moscow, this Soviet remittance man, is enough to make anybody trip over his mop, suds hissing along the floor and the bucket gong-crashing in astonishment. In delight!

Before long these two wretched delinquents are skulk-ing out to the edges of town to meet. It is a local scandal. Chu, from some recess within the filthy rags and shreds that hang from his unwholesome yellow body, produces a repulsive black gob of the foul-smelling substance, wrapped in a scrap torn from an old *Enbekši Qazaq* for 17 August of last year. Tchitcherine brings the pipe—being from the West he's in charge of the technology of the thing a—charred, nasty little implement in red and yellow repetitions over Britannia metal, bought used for a handful of kopecks in the Lepers' Quarter of Bukhara, and yes, nicely broken in too by that time. Reckless Captain Tchitcherine. The two opiomaniacs crouch behind a bit of wall wrecked and tilted from the last earthquake. Occasional riders pass by, some noting them and some not, but all in silence. Stars overhead crowd the sky. Far into the country, grasses blow, and the waves move on through, slow as sheep. It's a mild wind, carrying the last smoke of the day, the odors of herds and jasmine, of standing water, settling dust . . . a wind Tchitcherine will never remember. Any more than he can now connect this raw jumble of forty alkaloids with the cut, faceted, polished, and foiled molecules that salesman Wimpe showed him once upon a time, one by one, and told the histories of. . . .

"Oneirine, and Methoneirine. Variations reported by Laszlo Jamf in the ACS Journal, year before last. Jamf was on loan again, this time as a chemist, to the Americans, whose National Research Council had begun a massive program to explore the morphine molecule and its possibilities—a Ten-Year Plan, coinciding, most oddly, with the classic study of large molecules being carried on by Carothers of du Pont, the Great Synthesist. Connection? Of course there's one. But we don't talk about it. NRC is synthesizing new molecules every day, most of them from pieces of the morphine molecule. Du Pont is stringing together groups such as amides into long chains. The two programs seem to be complementary, don't they? The American vice of modular repetition, combined with what is perhaps our basic search: to find something that can kill intense pain without causing addiction.

"Results have not been encouraging. We seem up against a dilemma built into Nature, much like the Heisenberg situation. There is nearly complete parallelism between analgesia and addiction. The more pain it takes away, the more we desire it. It appears we can't have one property without the other, any more than a particle physicist can specify position without suffering an uncertainty as to the particle's velocity—"

"I could have told you that. But why—"

"*Why*. My dear captain. *Why?*"

"The money, Wimpe. To pour funds down the latrine on such a hopeless search—"

A man-to-man touch then on his buttoned epaulet. A middle-aged smile full of Weltschmerz. "Trade-off, Tchitcherine," whispers the salesman. "A question of balancing priorities. Research people come cheap enough, and even an IG may be allowed to dream, to hope against hope. . . . Think of what it would mean to find such a drug—to abolish pain rationally, without the extra cost of addiction. A *surplus* cost—surely there is something in Marx and Engels," soothe the customer, "to cover this. A demand like 'addiction,' having nothing to do with real pain, real economic needs, unrelated to production or labor . . . we need fewer of these unknowns, not more. We know how to produce real pain. Wars, obviously . . . machines in the factories, industrial accidents, automobiles built to be unsafe, poisons in food, water, and even air— these are quantities tied directly to the economy. We know them, and we can control them. But 'addiction'? What do we know of that? Fog and phantoms. No two experts will even agree on how to define the word. 'Compulsion'? Who is not compelled? 'Tolerance'? 'Dependence'? What do they mean? All we have are the thousand dim, academic theories. A rational economy cannot depend on psychological quirks. We could not *plan*. . . ."

What premonition has begun to throb in Tchitcherine's right knee? What direct conversion between pain and gold?

"Are you really this evil, or is it just an act? Are you really trafficking in pain?"

"Doctors traffick in pain and no one would dream of critizing their noble calling. Yet let the Verbindungsman but reach for the latch on his case, and you all start to scream and run. Well—you won't find many addicts among us. The medical profession is full of them, but we salesmen believe in real pain, real deliverance—we are knights in the service of that Ideal. It must all be real, for the purposes of our market. Otherwise my employer—and our little chemical cartel is the model for the very structure of nations—becomes lost in illusion and dream, and one day vanishes into chaos. Your own employer as well."

"My 'employer' is the Soviet State."

"Yes?" Wimpe did say "*is* the model," not "will be." Surprising they could have got this far, if indeed they did—being of such different persuasions and all. Wimpe, however, being far more cynical, would have been able to admit more of the truth before starting to feel uncomfortable. His patience with Tchitcherine's Red Army version of economics may have been wide enough. They did part amiably. Wimpe was reassigned to the United States (Chemnyco of New York) shortly after Hitler became Chancellor. Tchitcherine's connection, according to the garrison gossip, ceased then, forever.

But these are rumors. Their chronology can't be trusted. Contradictions creep in. Perfect for passing a winter in Central Asia, if you happen not to be Tchitcherine. If you *are* Tchitcherine, though, well, that puts you in more of a peculiar position. Doesn't it. You have to get through the winter on nothing but paranoid suspicions about why you're here. . . .

It's because of Enzian, it's got to be damned Enzian. Tchitcherine has been to the Krasnyy Arkhiv, has seen the records, the diaries and logs from the epical, doomed voyage of Admiral Rozhdestvenski, some still classified even after 20 years. And now he knows. And if it's all in the archives, then They know, too. Nubile young ladies and German dope salesmen are reason enough to send a man east in any period of history. But They would not be who or where They are without a touch of Dante to Their notions of reprisal. Simple talion may be fine for wartime, but politics between wars demands symmetry and a more elegant idea of justice, even to the point of masquerading, a bit decadently, as mercy. It is more complicated than mass execution, more difficult and less satisfying, but there are arrangements Tchitcherine can't see, wide as Europe, perhaps as the world, that can't be disturbed very much, between wars. . . .

It seems that in December, 1904, Admiral Rozhdestvenski, commanding a fleet of 42 Russian men-o'-war, steamed into the South-West African port of Lüderitzbucht. This was at the height of the Russo-Japanese War. Rozhdestvenski was on route to the Pacific, to relieve the other Russian fleet, which had been bottled up for months in Port Arthur by the Japanese. Out of the Baltic, around Europe and Africa, bound across the whole Indian Ocean and then north along the final coast of Asia, it was to be

among the most spectacular sea voyages of history: seven
months and 18,000 mlies to an early summer day in the
waters between Japan and Korea, where one Admiral
Togo, who'd been lying in wait, would come sailing out
from behind the island of Tsushima and before nightfall
hand Rozhdestvenski's ass to him. Only four Russian ships
would make it in to Vladivostok—nearly all the rest would
be sunk by the wily Jap.

Tchitcherine's father was a gunner on the Admiral's
flagship, the *Suvorov*. The fleet paused in Lüderitzbucht
for a week, trying to take on coal. Storms lashed through
the crowded little harbor. The *Suvorov* kept smashing up
against her colliers, tearing holes in the sides, wrecking
many of her own 12-pound guns. Squalls blew in, clammy
coal dust swirled and struck to everything, human and
steel. Sailors worked around the clock, with searchlights
set up on deck at night, hauling coal sacks, half blind in
the glare, shoveling, sweating, coughing, bitching. Some
went crazy, a few tried suicide. Old Tchitcherine, after
two days of it, went AWOL, and stayed away till it was
over. He found a Herero girl who'd lost her husband in
the uprising against the Germans. It was nothing he had
planned or even dreamed about before going ashore. What
did he know of Africa? He had a wife back in Saint Petersburg, and a child hardly able to roll over. Up till then
Kronstadt was the farthest he'd been from home. He only
wanted a rest from the working parties, and from the way
it looked . . . from what the black and white of coal and
arc-light were about to say . . . no color, and the unreality
to go with it—but a *familiar* unreality, that warns This Is
All Being Staged To See What I'll Do So I Mustn't Make
One Wrong Move . . . on the last day of his life, with
Japanese iron whistling down on him from ships that are
too far off in the haze for him even to see, he will think
of the slowly carbonizing faces of men he thought he
knew, men turning to coal, ancient coal that glistened,
each crystal, in the hoarse sputter of the Jablochkov
candles, each flake struck perfect . . . a conspiracy of carbon, though he never phrased it as "carbon," it was
power he walked away from, the feeling of too much
meaningless power, flowing wrong . . . he could smell
Death in it. So he waited till the master-at-arms turned to

light a cigarette, and then just walked away—they were all too black, artificially black, for it to be easily noticed—and found ashore the honest blackness of the solemn Herero girl, which seemed to him a breath of life after long confinement, and stayed with her at the edge of the flat sorrowful little town, near the railroad, in a one-room house built of saplings, packing-cases, reeds, mud. The rain blew. The trains cried and puffed. The man and woman stayed in bed and drank kari, which is brewed from potatoes, peas, and sugar, and in Herero means "the drink of death." It was nearly Christmas, and he gave her a medal he had won in some gunnery exercise long ago in the Baltic. By the time he left, they had learned each other's names and a few words in the respective languages—afraid, happy, sleep, love . . . the beginnings of a new tongue, a pidgin which they were perhaps the only two speakers of in the world.

But he went back. His future was with the Baltic fleet, it was something neither he nor the girl questioned. The storm blew out, fog covered the sea. Tchitcherine steamed away, shut back down in a dark and stinking compartment below the *Suvorov*'s waterline, drinking his Christmas vodka and yarning about his good times in a space that didn't rock, back at the edge of the dry veld with something warm and kind around his penis besides his lonely fist. He was already describing her as a sultry native wench. It is the oldest sea story. As he told it he was no longer Tchitcherine, but a single-faced crowd before and after, all lost but not all unlucky. The girl may have stood on some promontory watching the gray ironclads dissolve one by one in the South Atlantic mist, but even if you'd like a few bars of *Madame Butterfly* about here, she was more probably out hustling, or asleep. She was not going to have an easy time. Tchitcherine had left her with a child, born a few months after the gunner went down in sight of the steep cliffs and green forests of Tsushima, early in the evening of 27 May.

The Germans recorded the birth and the father's name (he had written it down for her, as sailors do—he had given her his name) in their central files at Windhoek. A travel pass was issued for mother and child to return to her tribal village, shortly after. A census by the colonial government to see how many natives they'd killed, taken just after Enzian was returned by Bushmen to the same village, lists the mother as deceased, but her name is in the records. A visa dated December 1926 for Enzian to enter Germany, and later an application for German citizenship, are both on file in Berlin.

It took no small amount of legwork to assemble all these pieces of paper. Tchitcherine had nothing to start with but a brief word or two in the Admiralty papers. But this was in the era of Feodora Alexandrevna, she of the kidskin underwear, and the access situation was a little better for Tchitcherine than it is now. The Rapallo Treaty was also in force, so there were any number of lines open to Berlin. That weird piece of paper . . . in his moments of sickest personal grandeur it is quite clear to him how his own namesake and the murdered Jew put together an elaborate piece of theatre at Rapallo, and that the real and only purpose was to reveal to Vaslav Tchitcherine the existence of Enzian . . . the garrison life out east, like certain drugs, makes these things amazingly clear. . . .

But alas, seems like the obsessive is his own undoing. The dossier that Tchitcherine put together on Enzian (he'd even got to see what Soviet intelligence had on then Lieutenant Weissmann and his political adventures in Südwest) was reproduced by some eager apparatchik and stashed in Tchitcherine's *own* dossier. And so it transpired, no more than a month or two later, that somebody equally anonymous had cut Tchitcherine's orders for Baku, and he was grimly off to attend the first plenary session of the VTsK NTA (Vesoynznyy Tsentral'nyy Komitet Novogo Tyurkskogo Alfavita), where he was promptly assigned to the Γ Committee.

Γ seems to be a kind of G, a voiced uvular plosive. The distinction between it and your ordinary G is one Tchitcherine will never learn to appreciate. Come to find out, all the Weird Letter Assignments have been reserved for ne'er-do-wells like himself. Shatsk, the notorious Leningrad nose-fetishist, who carries a black satin handkerchief to Party congresses and yes, more than once has been unable to refrain from reaching out and actually *stroking* the noses of powerful officials, is here—banished to the θ Committee, where he keeps forgetting that θ in the NTA, *is*

Œ, not Russian F, thus retarding progress and sowing confusion at every working session. Most of his time is taken up with trying to hustle himself a transfer to the N Committee, "Or actually," sidling closer, breathing heavily, "just a plain, N, or even an M, will, do. ..." The impetuous and unstable practical joker Radnichny has pulled the ə Committee, ə being a schwa or neutral *uh*, where he has set out on a megalomaniac project to replace every spoken word vowel in Central Asia—and why stop there, why not even a consonant or two? with these schwas here ... not unusual considering his record of impersonations and dummy resolutions, and a brilliant but doomed conspiracy to hit Stalin in the face with a grape chiffon pie, in which he was implicated only enough to get him Baku instead of worse.

Naturally Tchitcherine gravitates into this crew of irredeemables. Before long, if it isn't some scheme of Radnichny's to infiltrate an oil-field and disguise a derrick as a giant penis, it's lurking down in Arab quarters of the city, waiting with the infamous Ukrainian doper Bugnogorkov of the glottal K Committee (ordinary K being represented by Q, whereas C is pronounced with a sort of *tch* sound) for a hashish connection, or fending off the nasal advances of Shatsk. It occurs to him that he is, in reality, locked up in some military nut ward back in Moscow, and only hallucinating this plenary session. No one here seems quite right in the head.

Most distressing of all is the power struggle he has somehow been suckered into with one Igor Blobadjian, a party representative on the prestigious G Committee. Blobadjian is fanatically attempting to steal ⲓs from Tchitcherine's Committee, and change them to Gs, using loan-words as an entering wedge. In the sunlit, sweltering commissary the two men sneer at each other across trays of zapekanka and Georgian fruit soup.

There is a crisis over which kind of g to use in the word "stenography." There is a lot of emotional attachment to the word around here. Tchitcherine one morning finds all the pencils in his conference room have mysteriously vanished. In revenge, he and Radnichny sneak in Blobadjian's conference room next night with hacksaws, files and torches, and reform the alphabet on his typewriter. It is some fun

in the morning. Blobadjian runs around in a prolonged
screaming fit. Tchitcherine's in conference, meeting's
called to order, CRASH! two dozen linguists and bureaucrats go toppling over on their ass. Noise echoes for a full
two minutes. Tchitcherine, on his ass, notes that pieces of
chair leg all around the table have been sawed off, re-
attached with wax and varnished over again. A professional
job, all right. Could Radnichny be a double agent? The
time for lighthearted practical jokes is past. Tchitcherine
must go it alone. Painstakingly, by midwatch lantern light,
when the manipulations of letters are most apt to produce
other kinds of illumination, Tchitcherine transliterates the
opening sura of the holy Koran into the proposed NTA,
and causes it to be circulated among the Arabists at the
session, over the name of Igor Blobadjian.

This is asking for trouble, all right. These Arabists are
truly a frenzied bunch. They have been lobbying passion-
ately for a New Turkic Alphabet made up of Arabic letters.
There are fistfights in the hallways with unreconstructed
Cyrillicists, and whispers of a campaign to boycott,
throughout the Islamic world, any Latin alphabet. (Actually nobody is really too keen on a Cyrillic NTA. Old
Czarist albatrosses still hang around the Soviet neck.
There is strong native resistance in Central Asia these days
to anything suggesting Russification, and that goes even
for the look of a printed language. The objections to an
Arabic alphabet have to do with the absence of vowel
symbols, and no strict one-to-one relation between sounds
and characters. So this has left Latin, by default. But the
Arabists aren't giving up. They keep proposing reformed
Arabic scripts—mostly on the model of one ratified at
Bukhara in 1923 and used successfully among the Uzbeks.
Palatal and velar vocalics of spoken Kazakh can be got
round by using diacritical marks.) And there is a strong
religious angle in all this. Using a non-Arabic alphabet is
felt to be a sin against God—most of the Turkic peoples
are, after all, Islamic, and Arabic script is the script of
Islam, it is the script in which the word of Allah came
down on the Night of Power, the script of the Koran—
Of the *what*? Does Tchitcherine know what he's doing
with this forgery of his? It is more than blasphemy, it is
an invitation to holy war. Blobadjian, accordingly, is pur-

sued through the black end of Baku by a passel of screaming Arabists waving scimitars and grinning horribly. The
oil towers stand sentinel, bone-empty, in the dark. Hunchbacks, lepers, hebephrenics and amputees of all descriptions have come popping out of their secret spaces to
watch the fun. They loll back against the rusting metal
flanks of refinery hardware, their whole common sky in a
tessellation of primary colors. They occupy the chambers
and bins and pockets of administrative emptiness left after
the Revolution, when the emissaries from Dutch Shell were
asked to leave, and the English and Swedish engineers all
went home. It is a period now in Baku of lull, of retrenchment. All the oil money taken out of these fields by the
Nobels has gone into Nobel Prizes. New wells are going
down elsewhere, between the Volga and the Urals. Time
for retrospection here, for refining the recent history that's
being pumped up fetid and black from other strata of
Earth's mind. . . .

"In here, Blobadjian—quickly." Close behind, Arabists
are ululating, shrill, merciless, among the red-orange stars
over the crowds of derricks.

Slam. The last hatch is dogged. "Wait—what is this?"

"Come. Time for your journey now."

"But I don't want—"

"You don't want to be another slaughtered infidel. Too
late, Blobadjian. Here we go. . . ."

The first thing he learns is how to vary his index of
refraction. He can choose anything between transparent
and opaque. After the thrill of experimenting has worn off,
he settles on a pale, banded onyx effect.

"It suits you," murmur his guides. "Now hurry."

"No. I want to pay Tchitcherine what he's got coming."

"Too late. You're no part of what he's got coming. Not
any more."

"But he—"

"He's a blasphemer. Islam has its own machineries for
that. Angels and sanctions, and careful interrogating.
Leave him. He has a different way to go."

How alphabetic is the nature of molecules. One grows
aware of it down here: one finds Committees on molecular
structure which are very similar to those back at the NTA
plenary session. "See: how they are taken out from the

coarse flow—shaped, cleaned, rectified, just as you once redeemed your letters from the lawless, the mortal streaming of human speech. . . . These are our letters, our words: they too can be modulated, broken, recoupled, redefined, co-polymerized one to the other in worldwide chains that will surface now and then over long molecular sliences, like the seen parts of a tapestry."

Blobadjian comes to see that the New Turkic Alphabet is only one version of a process really much older—and less unaware of itself—than he has ever had cause to dream. By and by, the frantic competition between ¶ and G has faded away to trivial childhood memories. Dim anecdotes. He has gone beyond—once a sour bureaucrat with an upper lip as clearly demarcated as a chimpanzee's, now he is an adventurer, well off on a passage of his own, by underground current, without any anxiety over where it may be taking him. He has even lost, an indefinite distance upstream, his pride in feeling once a little sorry for Vaslav Tchitcherine, destined never to see the things Blobadjian is seeing. . . .

And print just goes marching on without him. Copy boys go running down the rows of desks trailing smeared galleys in the air. Native printers get crash courses from experts airlifted in from Tiflis on how to set up that NTA. Printed posters go up in the cities, in Samarkand and Pishpek, Verney and Tashkent. On sidewalks and walls the very first printed slogans start to show up, the first Central Asian fuck you signs, the first kill-the-police-commissioner signs (and somebody does! this alphabet is really something!) and so the magic that the shamans, out in the wind, have always known, begins to operate now in a political way, and Džaqyp Qulan hears the ghost in his own lynched father with a scratchy pen in the night, practicing As and Bs. . . .

But right about now, here come Tchitcherine and Džaqyp Qulan riding up over some low hills and down into the village they've been looking for. The people are gathered in a circle: there's been a feast all day. Fires are smoldering. In the middle of the crowd a small space has been cleared, and two young voices can be heard even at this distance.

It is an ajtys—a singing-duel. The boy and girl stand in the eye of the village carrying on a mocking well - I - sort - of - like - you - even - if - there's - one - or - two - weird - things - about - you - for - instance—kind of game while the tune darts in and out of qobyz and dombra strummed and plucked. The people laugh at the good lines. You have to be on your toes for this: you trade four-line stanzas, first, second, and last lines all have to rhyme though the lines don't have to be any special length, just breathable. Still, it's tricky. It gets insulting too. There are villages where some partners haven't spoken to each other for years after an ajtys. As Tchitcherine and Džaqyp Qulan ride in, the girl is making fun of her opponent's horse, who is just a little—nothing serious, but kind of heavy-set . . . well, fat, really. *Really* fat. And it's getting to the kid. He's annoyed. He zips back a fast one about bringing all his friends around and demolishing her and her family too. Everybody sort of goes hmm. No laughs. She smiles, tightly, and sings:

> You've been drinking a lot of qumys,
> I must be hearing the words of qumys—
> For where were you the night my brother
> Came looking for his stolen qumys?

Oh-oh. The brother she mentioned is laughing fit to bust. The kid singing is not so happy.

"This could go on for a while." Džaqyp Qulan dismounts, and sets about straightening his knee joints. "That's him, over there."

A very old aqyn—a wandering Kazakh singer—sits with a cup of qumys, dozing near the fire.

"Are you sure he'll—"

"He'll sing about it. He's ridden right through that country. He'd betray his profession if he didn't."

They sit down and are passed cups of the fermented mare's milk, with a bit of lamb, lepeshka, a few strawberries. . . . The boy and girl go on battling with their voices—and Tchitcherine understands, abruptly, that soon someone will come out and begin to write some of these down in the New Turkic Alphabet he helped frame . . . and this is how they will be lost.

Now and then he glances over at the old aqyn, who only appears to be sleeping. In fact he radiates for the singers a sort of guidance. It is kindness. It can be felt as unmistakably as the heat from the embers.

Slowly, turn by turn, the couple's insults get gentler, funnier. What might have been a village apocalypse has gone on now into comic cooperation, as between a pair of vaudeville comedians. They are out of themselves, playing it all for the listeners to enjoy. The girl has the last word.

> Did I hear you mention a marriage?
> Here there has been a marriage—
> This warm circle of song,
> Boisterous, loud as any marriage. . . .

And I like you, even if there are one or two things— For a little while the feast gathers momentum. Drunks holler and women talk, and the little kids totter in and out of the huts, and the wind has picked up some speed. Then the wandering singer begins to tune his dombra, and the Asian silence comes back.

"Are you going to get it all?" asks Džaqyp Qulan.

"In stenography," replies Tchitcherine, his g a little glottal.

THE AQYN'S SONG

> I have come from the edge of the world.
> I have come from the lungs of the wind,
> With a thing I have seen so awesome
> Even Džambul could not sing it.
> With a fear in my heart so sharp
> It will cut the strongest of metals.
>
> In the ancient tales it is told
> In a time that is older than Qorqyt,
> Who took from the wood of Šyrghaj
> The first qobyz, and the first song—
> It is told that a land far distant
> Is the place of the Kirghiz Light.
>
> In a place where words are unknown,
> And eyes shine like candles at night,

And the face of God is a presence
Behind the mask of the sky—
At the tall black rock in the desert,
In the time of the final days.

If the place were not so distant,
If words were known, and spoken,
Then the God might be a gold ikon,
Or a page in a paper book.
But It comes as the Kirghiz Light—
There is no other way to know It.

The roar of Its voice is deafness,
The flash of Its light is blindness.
The floor of the desert rumbles,
And Its face cannot be borne.
And a man cannot be the same,
After seeing the Kirghiz Light.

For I tell you that I have seen It
In a place which is older than darkness,
Where even Allah cannot reach.
As you see, my beard is an ice-field,
I walk with a stick to support me,
But this light must change us to children.

And now I cannot walk far,
For a baby must learn to walk.
And my words are reaching your ears
As the meaningless sounds of a baby.
For the Kirghiz Light took my eyes,
Now I sense all Earth like a baby.

It is north, for a six-day ride,
Through the steep and death-gray canyons,
Then across the stony desert
To the mountain whose peak is a white džurt.
And if you have passed without danger,
The place of the black rock will find you.

But if you would not be born,
Then stay with your warm red fire,
And stay with your wife, in your tent,
And the Light will never find you,
And your heart will grow heavy with age,
And your eyes will shut only to sleep.

"Got it," sez Tchitcherine. "Let's ride, comrade." Off again, the fires dying at their backs, the sounds of string music, of village carousing, presently swallowed behind the wind.

And on into the canyons. Far away to the north, a white mountaintop winks in the last sunlight. Down here, it is already shadowed evening.

Tchitcherine will reach the Kirghiz Light, but not his birth. He is no aqyn, and his heart was never ready. He will see It just before dawn. He will spend 12 hours then, face-up on the desert, a prehistoric city greater than Babylon lying in stifled mineral sleep a kilometer below his back, as the shadow of the tall rock, rising to a point, dances west to east and Džaqyp Qulan tends him, anxious as child and doll, and drying foam laces the necks of the two horses. But someday, like the mountains, like the young exiled women in their certain love, in their innocence of him, like the morning earthquakes and the cloud-driving wind, a purge, a war, and millions after millions of souls gone behind him, he will hardly be able to remember It.

But in the Zone, hidden inside the summer Zone, the Rocket is waiting. He will be drawn the same way again. . . .

☐

Last week, in the British sector someplace, Slothrop, having been asshole enough to drink out of an ornamental pond in the Tiergarten, took sick. Any Berliner these days knows enough to boil water before drinking, though some then proceed to brew it with various things for tea, such as tulip bulbs, which is not good. Word is out that the center of the bulb is deadly poison. But they keep doing it. Once Slothrop—or Rocketman, as he is soon to be known—thought he might warn them about things like tulip bulbs. Bring in a little American enlightenment. But he gets so desperate with them, moving behind their scrims of European pain: he keeps pushing aside gauze after wavy gauze but there's always still the one, the impenetrable. . . .

So there he is, under the trees in summer leaf, in flower, many of them blasted horizontal or into chips and splinters—fine dust from the bridle paths rising in the sunrays by itself, ghosts of horses still taking their early-morning turns through the peacetime park. Up all night and thirsty, Slothrop lies on his stomach and slurps up water, just an old saddle tramp at the water hole here. . . . Fool. Vomiting, cramps, diarrhea, and who's he to lecture about tulip bulbs? He manages to crawl as far as an empty cellar, across the street from a wrecked church, curls up and spends the next days feverish, shivering, oozing shit that burns like acid—lost, alone with that sovereign Nazi movie-villain fist clamping in his bowels ja—you vill *shit* now, ja? Wondering if he'll ever see Berkshire again. Mommy, Mommy! The War's over, why can't I go home now? Nalline, the reflection from her Gold Star brightening her chins like a buttercup, smirks by the window and won't answer. . . .

A terrible time. Hallucinating Rolls Royces and bootheels in the night, coming to get him. Out in the street women in babushkas are lackadaisically digging trenches for the black iron water pipe that's stacked along the curbside. All day long they talk, shift after shift, into evening. Slothrop lies in the space where sunlight visits his cellar for half an hour before going on to others with mean puddles of warmth—sorry, got to go now, schedule to keep, see you tomorrow if it doesn't rain, heh heh. . . .

Once Slothrop wakes to the sound of an American work detail marching down the street, cadence being counted by a Negro voice—yo lep, yo lep, yo lep O right O lep . . . kind of little German folk tune with some sliding upscale on the word "right"—Slothrop can imagine his mannered jog of arm and head to the left as he comes down hard on that heel, the way they teach it in Basic . . . can see the man's smile. For a minute he has the truly unbalanced idea of running out in the street and asking them to take him back, requesting political asylum in America. But he's too weak. In his stomach, in his heart. He lies, listening to the tramping and the voice out of earshot, the sound of his country fading away. . . . Fading like the WASP ghosts, the old-time DPs trailing rootless now down the roads out of his memory, crowding the

rooftops of the freights of forgetfulness, knapsacks and
poor refugee pockets stuffed with tracts nobody'd read,
looking for another host: given up for good on Rocketman
here. Somewhere between the burning in his head and
the burning in his asshole, if the two can be conveniently
separated, and paced to that dying cadence, he elaborates
a fantasy in which Enzian, the African, finds him again—
comes to offer him a way out.

Because it seems a while back that they did meet again,
by the reedy edge of a marsh south of the capital. Unshaven, sweating, stinking Rocketman restlessly tripping
out to the suburbs, among his people: there is haze over
the sun, and a rotting swamp odor worse than Slothrop's
own. Only two or three hours' sleep in the last couple of
days. He stumbles on the Schwarzkommando, busy dredg-
ing for pieces of rocket. Formations of dark birds are
cruising in the sky. The Africans have a partisan look:
pieces here and there of old Wehrmacht and SS uniform,
tattered civilian clothes, only one insigne in common, worn
wherever it will show, a painted steel device in red, white
and blue, thus:

Adapted from insignia the German troopers wore in
South-West Africa when they came in 1904 to crush the
Herero Rebellion—it was used to pin up half the brim of
a wide-awake hat. For the Zone-Hereros it has become
something deep, Slothrop gathers, maybe a little mystical.
Though he recognizes the letters—Klar, Entlüftung, Zündung, Vorstufe, Haupstufe, the five positions of the launching switch in the A4 control car—he doesn't let on to
Enzian.

They sit on a hillside eating bread and sausages. Children from the town move by in every direction. Someone
has set up an army tent, someone has brought beer in
kegs. A scratch band, a dozen brasses in tasseled, frayed
gold and red uniforms play selections from *Die Meister-
singer*. Fat-smoke drifts in the air. Choruses of drinkers in
the distance break from time to time into laughter or a
song. It's a Rocket-raising: a festival new to this country.
Soon it will come to the folk-attention how close Wernher

von Braun's birthday is to the Spring Equinox, and the same German impulse that once rolled flower-boats through the towns and staged mock battles between young Spring and deathwhite old Winter will be erecting strange floral towers out in the clearings and meadows, and the young scientist-surrogate will be going round and round with old Gravity or some such buffoon, and the children will be tickled, and laugh. . . .

Schwarzkommando struggle knee-deep in mud, engaged entirely with the salvage, with the moment. The A4 they're about to uncover was used in the last desperate battle for Berlin—an abortive firing, a warhead that didn't explode. Around its grave they're driving in planks for shoring, sending back mud in buckets and wood casks along a human chain to be dumped on shore, near where their rifles and kits are stacked.

"So Marvy was right. They didn't disarm you guys."

"They didn't know where to find us. We were a surprise. There are even now powerful factions in Paris who don't believe we exist. And most of the time I'm not so sure myself."

"How's that?"

"Well, I think we're here, but only in a statistical way. Something like that rock over there is just about 100% certain—it knows it's there, so does everybody else. But our own chances of being right here right now are only a little better than even—the slightest shift in the probabilities and we're gone—schnapp! like that."

"Peculiar talk, Oberst."

"Not if you've been where we have. Forty years ago, in Südwest, we were nearly exterminated. There was no reason. Can you understand that? *No reason.* We couldn't even find comfort in the Will of God Theory. These were Germans with names and service records, men in blue uniforms who killed clumsily and not without guilt. Search-and-destroy missions, every day. It went on for two years. The orders came down from a human being, a scrupulous butcher named von Trotha. The thumb of mercy never touched his scales.

"We have a word that we whisper, a mantra for times that threaten to be bad. Mba-kayere. You may find that it will work for you. Mba-kayere. It means 'I am passed over.' To those of us who survived von Trotha, it also

means that we have learned to stand outside our history
and watch it, without feeling too much. A little schizoid.
A sense for the statistics of our being. One reason we
grew so close to the Rocket, I think, was this sharp awareness of how contingent, like ourselves, the Aggregat 4
could be—how at the mercy of small things ... dust that
gets in a timer and breaks electrical contact ... a film of
grease you can't even see, oil from a touch of human
fingers, left inside a liquid-oxygen valve, flaring up soon
as the stuff hits and setting the whole thing off—I've seen
that happen ... rain that swells the bushings in the servos
or leaks into a switch: corrosion, a short, a signal grounded
out, Brennschluss too soon, and what was alive is only an
Aggregat again, an Aggregat of pieces of dead matter, no
longer anything that can move, or that has a Destiny with
a shape—stop doing that with your eyebrows, Scuffling. I
may have gone a bit native out here, that's all. Stay in the
Zone long enough and you'll start getting ideas about
Destiny yourself."

A cry from down in the marsh. Birds swirl upward,
round and black, grains of coarse-cut pepper on this bouilla-
baisse sky. Little kids come skidding to a halt, and the
brass band fall silent in mid-bar. Enzian is on his feet and
loping down to where the others are gathering.

"Was ist los, meinen Sumpfmenschen?" The others,
laughing, scoop up fistfuls of mud and start throwing them
at their Nguarorerue, who ducks, dodges, grabs him some
of that mud and starts flinging it back. The Germans on
shore stand blinking, politely aghast at this lack of discipline.

Down in the plank enclosure, a couple of muddy trim-
tabs poke up now out of the marsh, with twelve feet of
mud between them. Enzian, spattered and dripping, his
white grin preceding him by several meters, vaults over
the shoring and into the hole, and grabs a shovel. The
moment has become roughly ceremonial: Andreas and
Christian have moved up to either side to help him scrape
and dig till about a foot of one fin-surface is exposed. The
Determination of the Number. The Nguarorerue crouches
and brushes away mud, revealing part of a slashmark, a
white 2, and a 7.

"Outase." And glum faces on the others.

Slothrop's got a hunch. "You expected der Fünffachnullpunkt," he proposes to Enzian a little later, "the quintuple zero, right? Haa-*aaah!*" Gotcha, gotcha—

Throwing up his hands, "It's insane. I don't believe there is one."

"Zero probability?"

"I think it will depend on the number of searchers. Are your people after it?"

"I don't know. I only heard by accident. I don't have any people."

"Schwarzgerät, Schwarzkommando. Scuffling: suppose somewhere there were an alphabetical list, someone's list, an input to some intelligence arm, say. Some country, doesn't matter. But suppose that on this list, the two names, Blackinstrument, Blackcommand, just happened to be there, juxtaposed. That's all, an alphabetical coincidence. We wouldn't have to be real, and neither would it, correct?"

The marshes streak away, patched with light under the milk overcast. Negative shadows flicker white behind the edges of everything. "Well, this is all creepy enough here, Oberst," sez Slothrop. "You're not helping."

Enzian is staring into Slothrop's face, with something like a smile under his beard.

"O.K. Who *is* after it, then?" Being enigmatic, won't answer—is this bird *looking* to be needled? "That Major Marvy," opines Slothrop, "a-and that Tchitcherine, too!"

Ha! That did it. Like a salute, a boot-click, Enzian's face snaps into perfect neutrality. "You would oblige me," he begins, then settles for changing the subject. "You were down in the Mittelwerke. How did Marvy's people seem to be getting along with the Russians?"

"Ace buddies, seemed like."

"I have the feeling that the occupying Powers have just about reached agreement on a popular front against the Schwarzkommando. I don't know who you are, or how your lines are drawn. But they're trying to shut us down. I'm just back from Hamburg. We had trouble. It was made to look like a DP raid, but the British military government was behind it, and they had Russian cooperation."

"I'm sorry. Can I help?"

"Don't be reckless. Let's all wait and see. All anyone knows about you is that you keep showing up."

Toward dusk, the black birds descend, millions of them,

to sit in the branches of trees nearby. The trees grow heavy with black birds, branches like dendrites of the Nervous System fattening, deep in twittering nerve-dusk, in preparation for some important message. . . .

Later in Berlin, down in the cellar among fever-dreams with shit leaking out of him at gallons per hour, too weak to aim more than token kicks at the rats running by with eyes fixed earnestly noplace, trying to make believe they don't have a newer and dearer status among the Berliners, at minimum points on his mental health chart, when the sun is gone so totally it might as well be for good, Slothrop's dumb idling heart sez: The Schwarzgerät is no Grail, Ace, that's not what the G in Imipolex G stands for. And you are no knightly hero. The best you can compare with is Tannhäuser, the Singing Nincompoop—you've been under one mountain at Nordhausen, been known to sing a song or two with uke accompaniment, and don'tcha feel you're in a sucking marshland of sin out here, Slothrop? maybe not the same thing William Slothrop, vomiting a good part of 1630 away over the side of that *Arbella*, meant when he said "sin." . . . But what you've done is put yourself on somebody's else's voyage—some Frau Holda, some Venus in some mountain—playing her, its, game . . . you know that in some irreducible way it's an evil game. You play because you have nothing better to do, but that doesn't make it right. And where is the Pope whose staff's gonna bloom for you?

As a matterof fact, he is also just about to run into his Lisaura: someone he will be with for a while and then leave again. The Minnesinger abandoned his poor woman to suicide. What Slothrop will be leaving Greta Erdmann to is not so clear. Along the Havel in Neubabelsberg she waits, less than the images of herself that survive in an indeterminate number of release prints here and there about the Zone, and even across the sea. . . . Every kind technician who ever threw a magenta gel across her key light for her has gone to war or death, and she is left nothing but God's indifferent sunlight in all its bleaching and terror. . . . Eyebrows plucked to pen-strokes, long hair streaked with gray, hands heavy with rings of all colors, opacities and uglinesses, wearing her dark prewar Chanel suits, no hat, scarves, always a flower, she is haunted by Central European night-whispers that blow, like the skin curtains of Berlin, more ghostly around her fattening, wrecked beauty the closer she and Slothrop draw. . . .

This is how they meet. One night Slothrop is out raiding a vegetable garden in the park. Thousands of people living in the open. He skirts their fires, stealthy— All he wants is a handful of greens here, a carrot or mangel-wurzel there, just to keep him going. When they see him they throw rocks, lumber, once not long ago an old hand-grenade that didn't go off but made him shit where he stood.

This evening he is orbiting someplace near the Grosser Stern. It is long after curfew. Odors of woodsmoke and decay hang over the city. Among pulverized heads of stone margraves and electors, reconnoitering a likely-looking cabbage patch, all of a sudden Slothrop picks up the scent of an unmistakable no it can't be yes it is it's a REEFER! A-and it's burning someplace close by. Gold-shot green of the Rif's slant fields here, vapor-blossoms resinous and summery, charm his snoot on through bushes and matted grass, under the blasted trees and whatever sits in their branches.

Sure enough, in the hollow of an upended trunk, long roots fringing the scene like a leprechaun outpost, Slothrop finds one Emil ("Säure") Bummer, once the Weimar Republic's most notorious cat burglar and doper, flanked by two beautiful girls, handing around a cheerful little orange star. The depraved old man. Slothrop's on top of them before they notice. Bummer smiles, reaches up an arm, offering the remainder of what they've been smoking to Slothrop, who receives it in long dirty finger-nails. Oboy. He hunkers down.

"Was ist los?" sez Säure. "We've had a windfall of kif. Allah has smiled on us, well actually he was smiling at everybody, we just happened to be in his direct line of sight. . . ." His nickname, which means "acid" in German, developed back in the twenties, when he was carrying around a little bottle of schnapps which, if he got in a tight spot, he would bluff people into thinking was fuming nitric acid. He comes out now with another fat Moroccan reefer. They light up off of Slothrop's faithful Zippo.

Trudi, the blonde, and Magda, the sultry Bavarian, have spent the day looting a stash of Wagnerian opera costumes. There is a pointed helmet with horns, a full cape of green velvet, a pair of buckskin trousers.

"Saaaay," sez Slothrop, *"that* rig looks pretty *sharp!"*

"They're for you," Magda smiles.

"Aw . . . no. You'd get a better deal at the Tausch-zentrale. . . ."

But Säure insists. "Haven't you ever noticed, when you're this Blitzed and you want somebody to show up, they always do?"

The girls are moving the coal of the reefer about, watching its reflection in the shiny helmet changing shapes, depths, grades of color . . . hmm. It occurs to Slothrop here that without those horns on it, why this helmet would look just like the nose assembly of the Rocket. And if he could find a few triangular scraps of leather, figure a way to sew them on to Tchitcherine's boots . . . yeah, a-and on the back of the cape put a big, scarlet, capital R— It is as pregnant a moment as when Tonto, after the legendary ambush, attempts to—

"Raketemensch!" screams Säure, grabbing the helmet and unscrewing the horns off of it. Names by themselves may be empty, but the *act of naming*. . . .

"You had the same idea?" Oh, strange. Säure carefully reaches up and places the helmet on Slothrop's head. Ceremonially the girls drape the cape around his shoulders. Troll scouting parties have already sent runners back to inform their people.

"Good. Now listen, Rocketman, I'm in a bit of trouble."

"Hah?" Slothrop has been imagining a full-scale Rocketman Hype, in which the people bring him food, wine and maidens in a four-color dispensation in which there is a lot of skipping and singing "La, la, la, la," and beefsteaks blossoming from these strafed lindens, and roast turkeys thudding down like soft hail on Berlin, sweet potatoes a-and melted marshmallows, bubbling up out of the ground. . . .

"Do you have any armies?" Trudi wants to know. Slothrop, or Rocketman, hands over half a withered pack.

The reefer keeps coming around: darts and stabs through this root shelter. Everybody forgets what it is

they've been talking about. There's the smell of earth.
Bugs rush through, aerating. Magda has lit one of Slothrop's cigarettes for him and he tastes raspberry lipstick.
Lipstick? Who's got lipstick these days? What are all these
people here *into*, anyway?

Berlin is dark enough for stars, the accustomed stars
but never so clearly arranged. It is possible also to make
up your own constellations. "Oh," Säure recalls. "I had
this problem . . ."

"I'm really hungry," it occurs to Slothrop.

Trudi is telling Magda about her boy friend Gustav,
who wants to live inside the piano. "All you could see
was his feet sticking out, he kept saying, 'You all hate
me, you hate this piano!'" They're giggling now.

"Plucking on the strings," sez Magda, "right? He's so
paranoid."

Trudi has these big, blonde Prussian legs. Tiny blonde
hairs dance up and down in the starlight, up under her
skirt and back, all through the shadows of her knees,
around under the hollows behind them, this starry jittering. . . . The stump towers above and cups them all, a
giant nerve cell, dendrites extended into the city, the
night. Signals coming in from all directions, and from back
in time too, probably, if not indeed forward. . . .

Säure, who is never able entirely to lay off business,
rolls, flows to his feet, clutching on to a root till his head
decides where it is going to come to rest. Magda, her ear
at its entrance, is banging on Rocketman's helmet with a
stick. It gongs in chords. The separate notes aren't right
on pitch, either: they sound *very odd* together. . . .

"I don't know what time it is," Säure Bummer gazing
around. "Weren't we supposed to be at the Chicago Bar?
Or was that last night?"

"I forget," Trudi giggles.

"Listen, Kerl, I really have to talk to that American."

"Dear Emil," Trudi whispers, "don't worry. He'll be at
the Chicago."

They decide on an intricate system of disguise. Säure
gives Slothrop his jacket. Trudi wears the green cape.
Magda puts on Slothrop's boots, and he goes in his socks,
carrying her own tiny shoes in his pockets. They spend
some time gathering plausible items, kindling and greens,

to fill the helmet with, and Säure carries that. Magda and
Trudi help stuff Slothrop into the buckskin pants, both
girls down on pretty knees, hands caressing his legs and
ass. Like the ballroom in St. Patrick's Cathedral, there is
none in these trousers here, and Slothrop's hardon, en-
larging, aches like thunder.

"Fine for you folks." The girls are laughing. Grandiose
Slothrop limps along after everybody, a network of clear
interweaving ripples now like rain all through his vision,
hands turning to stone, out of the Tiergarten, past shell-
struck lime and chestnut trees, into the streets, or what is
serving for them. Patrols of all nations keep coming by,
and this mindless quartet have to hit the dirt often, trying
not to laugh too much. Slothrop's sox are sodden with dew.
Tanks manoeuvre in the street, chewing parallel ridges of
asphalt and stonedust. Trolls and dryads play in the open
spaces. They were blasted back in May out of bridges,
out of trees into liberation, and are now long citified. "Oh,
that drip," say the subdeb trolls about those who are not
as hep, "he just isn't out-of-the-tree about *anything.*"
Mutilated statues lie under mineral sedation: frock-coated
marble torsos of bureaucrats fallen pale in the gutters. Yes,
hmm, here we are in the heart of downtown Berlin, really,
uh, a little, Jesus Christ what's *that*—

"Better watch it," advises Säure, "it's kind of rubbery
through here."

"What *is* that?"

Well, what it is—is? what's "is"?—is that King Kong, or
some creature closely allied, squatting down, evidently
just, taking a shit, right in the street! and everything!
a-and being ignored, by truckload after truckload of
Russian enlisted men in pisscutter caps and dazed
smiles, grinding right on by—"Hey!" Slothrop wants
to shout, "hey lookit that giant *ape!* or whatever it
is. You guys? Hey . . ." But he doesn't, luckily. On closer
inspection, the crouching monster turns out to be the
Reichstag building, shelled out, airbrushed, fire-brushed
powdery black on all blastward curves and projections,
chalked over its hard-echoing carbon insides with Cyrillic
initials, and many names of comrades killed in May.

Berlin proves to be full of these tricks. There's a big

chromo of Stalin that Slothrop could swear is a girl he
used to date at Harvard, the mustache and hair only in-
cidental as makeup, *damn* if that isn't what's her name . . .
but before he can quite hear the gibbering score of little
voices—hurry, hurry, get it in place, he's almost around
the corner—here, laid side by side on the pavement, are
these enormous loaves of bread dough left to rise under
clean white cloths—boy, is everybody hungry: the same
thought hits them all at once, wow! *Raw dough!* loaves of
bread for that *monster* back there . . . oh, no that's right,
that was a building, the Reichstag, so these aren't bread
. . . by now it's clear that they're human bodies, dug from
beneath today's rubble, each inside its carefully tagged
GI fartsack. But it was more than an optical mistake. They
are rising, they are transubstantiated, and who knows, with
summer over and hungry winter coming down, what we'll
be feeding on by Xmas?

What the notorious Femina is to cigarette-jobbing circles
in Berlin, the Chicago is to dopers. But while dealing at
the Femina usually gets under way around noon, the
Chicago here only starts jiving after the 10:00 curfew.
Slothrop, Säure, Trudi and Magda come in a back entrance, out of a great massif of ruins and darkness lit only
here and there, like the open country. Inside, M.O.s and
corpsmen run hither and thither clutching bottles of fluffy
white crystalline substances, small pink pills, clear ampoules the size of pureys. Occupation and Reichsmarks
ruffle and flap across the room. Some dealers are all
chemical enthusiasm, others all business. Oversize photos
of John Dillinger, alone or posed with his mother, his pals,
his tommygun, decorate the walls. Lights and arguing are
kept low, should the military police happen by.

On a wire-backed chair, blunt hair hands picking quietly
at a guitar, sits an American sailor with an orangutan look
to him. In 3/4 time and shit-kicking style, he is singing:

THE DOPER'S DREAM

Last night I dreamed I was plugged right in
To a bubblin' hookah so high,
When all of a sudden some Arab jinni
Jump up just a-winkin' his eye.
"I'm here to obey all your wishes," he told me,

As for words I was trying to grope.
"Good buddy," I cried, "you could surely oblige me
By turnin' me on to some *dopel*"
With a bigfat smile he took ahold of my hand,
And we flew down the sky in a flash,
And the first thing I saw in the land where he took me
Was a whole solid mountain of hash!
All the trees was a-bloomin' with pink 'n' purple pills,
Whur the Romilar River flowed by,
To the magic mushrooms as wild as a rainbow,
So pretty that I wanted to cry.
All the girls come to greet us, so sweet in slow motion,
Morning glories woven into their hair,
Bringin' great big handfuls of snowy cocaine,
All their dope they were eager to share.
Well we dallied for days, just a-ballin' and smokin',
In the flowering Panama Red,
Just piggin' on peyote and nutmeg tea,
And those brownies so kind to your head.
Now I could've passed that good time forever,
And I really was fixing to stay,
But you know that
                    jinni turned out, t'be a narco man,
And he busted me right whur I lay.
And he took me back, to this cold, cold world,
'N' now m' prison's whurever I be . . .
And I dream of the days back in Doperland
And I wonder, will I ever go free?

The singer is Seaman Bodine, of the U.S. destroyer
John E. Badass, and he's the contact Säure is here to see.
The *Badass* is docked in Cuxhaven and Bodine is semi-
AWOL, having hit Berlin night before last for the first
time since the early weeks of American occupation. "Things
are so tight, man," he's groaning, "Potsdam, I couldn't
believe it over there. Remember how the Wilhelmplatz
used to be? Watches, wine, jewels, cameras, heroin, fur
coats, everything in the world. Nobody *gave* a shit, right?
You ought to see it now. Russian security all over the
place. Big mean customers. You couldn't get near it."

"Isn't there supposed to be something going on over
there?" sez Slothrop. He's heard scuttlebutt. "A conference
or some shit?"

"They're deciding how to cut up Germany," sez Säure.
"All the Powers. They should call in the Germans, Kerl,
we've been doing *that* for centuries."

"You couldn't get a gnat in there now, man," Seaman Bodine shaking his head, dexterously rolling a reefer one-handed on a cigarette paper he has first torn, with straight-faced bravura, in half.

"Ah," smiles Säure, flinging an arm over Slothrop, "but what if *Rocketman* can?"

Bodine looks over, skeptical. "That's Rocketman?"

"More or less," sez Slothrop, "but I'm not sure I want to go into that Potsdam, right now. . . ."

"If you only knew!" cries Bodine. "Listen, Ace, right this minute, hardly 15 miles away, there is six *kilos!* of pure, top-grade Nepalese hashish! Scored it from my buddy in the CBI, government seals 'n' everything, buried it myself back in May, so safe nobody'll ever find it without a map. All you got to do is fly over there or whatever it is you do, just go in and get it."

"That's all."

"A kilo for you," offers Säure.

"They can cremate it with me. All those Russians can stand around the furnace and get loaded."

"Perhaps," the most decadent young woman Slothrop has ever seen in his life, wearing fluorescent indigo eye-shadow and a black leather snood, comes slithering past, "the pretty American is not a devotee of the Green Hershey Bar, mm? ha-ha-ha. . . ."

"A million marks," Säure sighs.

"Where are you going to get—"

Holding up an elfin finger, leaning close, "I print it."

Sure enough, he does. They all troop out of the Chicago, half a mile down through rubble piles, over pathways twisting invisible in the dark to all but Säure, down at last in a houseless cellar with filing cabinets, a bed, an oil-lamp, a printing-press. Magda cuddles close to Slothrop, her hands dancing over his erection. Trudi has formed an inexplicable attachment to Bodine. Säure begins to crank his clattering wheel, and sheets of Reichsmarks do indeed come fluttering off into the holder, thousands on thousands. "All authentic plates and paper, too. The only detail missing is a slight ripple along the margins. There was a special stamp-press nobody managed to loot."

"Uh," Slothrop sez.

"Aw, come on," sez Bodine. "Rocketman, jeepers. You don't want to do nothing no more."

They help jog and square the sheets while Säure chops them up with a long glittering cutter blade. Holding out a fat roll of 100s, "You could be back tomorrow. No job is too tough for the Rocketman."

A day or two later, it will occur to Slothrop that what he should have said at that point was, "But I wasn't Rocketman, until just a couple hours ago." But right now he is beguiled at the prospect of 2.2 pounds of hashish and a million nearly-real marks. Nothing to walk away from, or fly or whatever it is, right? So he takes a couple thousand in front and spends the rest of the night with round and moaning Magda on Säure's bed, while Trudi and Bodine lark in the bathtub, and Säure slips back on some other mission, out into the three-o'clock waste that presses, oceanic, against their buoyed inner space. . . .

□

Säure to and fro, bloodshot and nagging, with a wreathing pot of tea. Slothrop's alone in bed. The Rocketman costume waits on a table, along with Seaman Bodine's treasure map—oh. Oh, boy. Is Slothrop really going to have to go through with this?

Outside, birds whistle arpeggios up the steps, along the morning. Trucks and jeeps sputter in the distances. Slothrop sits drinking tea and trying to scrape dried sperm off of his trousers while Säure explains the layout. The package is stashed under an ornamental bush outside a villa at 2 Kaiserstrasse, in Neubabelsberg, the old movie capital of Germany. That's across the Havel from Potsdam. It seems prudent to stay off the Avus Autobahn. "Try to get past the checkpoint just after Zehlendorf instead. Come up on Neubabelsberg by canal."

"How come?"

"No civilians allowed on VIP Road—here, this one, that runs on across the river to Potsdam."

"Come on. I'll need a boat, then."

"Ha! You expect improvisation from a German? No, no, that's—that's Rocketman's problem! ha-ha!"

"Unnhh." Seems the villa fronts on the Griebnitz See. "Why don't I hit it from that side?"

"You'll have to go under a couple of bridges first, if you do. Heavily guarded. Plunging fire. Maybe—maybe even mortars. It gets very narrow opposite Potsdam. You won't have a chance." Oh, German humor's a *fine* way to start the morning. Säure hands Slothrop an AGO card, a trip ticket, and a pass printed in English and Russian. "The man who forged these has been in and out of Potsdam on them a dozen times since the Conference began. That's how much faith he has in them. The bilingual pass is special, just for the Conference. But you mustn't spend time gawking like a tourist, asking celebrities for autographs—"

"Well say look Emil, if you've got one of these and they're so good, why don't *you* go?"

"It's not my *specialty*. I stick to dealing. Just an old bottle of acid—and even that's make-believe. Buccaneering is for *Rocketmen*."

"Bodine, then."

"He's already on his way back to Cuxhaven. Won't he be upset, when he comes back next week, only to find that Rocketman, of all people, has shown the white feather."

"Oh." Shit. Slothrop stares awhile at that map, then tries to memorize it. He puts on his boots, groaning. He bundles his helmet in that cape, and the two, conner and connee, set out through the American sector.

Mare's-tails are out seething across the blue sky, but down here the Berliner Luft hangs still, with the odor of death inescapable. Thousands of corpses fallen back in the spring still lie underneath these mountains of debris, yellow mountains, red and yellow and pale.

Where's the city Slothrop used to see back in those newsreels and that National Geographic? Parabolas weren't all that New German Architecture went in for—there were the spaces—the necropolism of blank alabaster in the staring sun, meant to be filled with human harvests rippling out of sight, making no sense without them. If there is such a thing as the City Sacramental, the city as outward and visible sign of inward and spiritual illness or health, then there may have been, even here, some continuity of sacrament, through the terrible surface of May. The emptiness of Berlin this morning is an inverse mapping of the white and geometric capital before the destruction—the fallow and long-strewn fields of rubble, the same weight of too much featureless concrete . . . except that here everything's been turned inside out. The straight-ruled boulevards built to be marched along are now winding pathways through the waste-piles, their shapes organic now, responding, like goat trails, to laws of least discomfort. The civilians are outside now, the uniforms inside. Smooth facets of buildings have given way to cobbly insides of concrete blasted apart, all the endless-pebbled rococo just behind the shuttering. Inside is outside. Ceilingless rooms open to the sky, wall-less rooms pitched out over the sea of ruins in prows, in crow's-nests. . . . Old men with their tins searching the ground for cigarette butts wear their lungs on their breasts. Advertisements for shelter, clothing, the lost, the taken, once classified, folded bürgerlich inside newspapers to be read at one's ease in the lacquered and graceful parlors are now stuck with Hitler-head stamps of blue, orange, and yellow, out in the wind, when the wind comes, stuck to trees, door-frames, planking, pieces of wall—white and fading scraps, writing spidery, trembling, smudged, thousands unseen, thousands unread or blown away. At the Winterhilfe one-course Sundays you sat outside at long tables under the swastika-draped winter trees, but outside has been brought inside and that kind of Sunday lasts all week long. Winter is coming again. All Berlin spends the daylight trying to make believe it isn't. Scarred trees are back in leaf, baby birds hatched and learning to fly, but winter's here behind the look of summer—Earth has turned over in its sleep, and the tropics are reversed. . . .

Like the walls of the Chicago Bar brought outside, giant photographs are posted out in the Friedrichstrasse—faces higher than a man. Slothrop recognizes Churchill and Stalin all right, but isn't sure about the other one. "Emil, who's that guy in the glasses?"

"The American president. Mister Truman."

"Quit fooling. Truman is vice-president. Roosevelt is president."

Säure raises an eyebrow. "Roosevelt died back in the spring. Just before the surrender."

They get tangled in a bread queue. Women in worn plush coats, little kids holding on to frayed hems, men in caps and dark double-breasted suits, unshaven old faces,

foreheads white as a nurse's leg. . . . Somebody tries to
grab Slothrop's cape, and there's a brief tugging match.

"I'm sorry," Säure offers, when they're clear again.

"Why didn't anybody tell me?" Slothrop was going into
high school when FDR was starting out in the White
House. Broderick Slothrop professed to hate the man, but
young Tyrone thought he was brave, with that polio and
all. Liked his voice on the radio. Almost saw him once
too, in Pittsfield, but Lloyd Nipple, the fattest kid in
Mingeborough, was standing in the way, and all Slothrop
got to see was a couple wheels and the feet of some guys
in suits on a running-board. Hoover he'd heard of, dimly—
something to do with shack towns or vacuum cleaners—
but Roosevelt was *his* president, the only one he'd known.
It seemed he'd just keep getting elected, term after term,
forever. But somebody had decided to change that. So he
was put to sleep, Slothrop's president, quiet and neat,
while the kid who once imaged his face on Lloyd's
T-shirted shoulderblades was jiving on the Riviera, or in
Switzerland someplace, only half aware of being extinguished himself. . . .

"They said it was a stroke," Säure sez. His voice is arriving from some quite peculiar direction, let us say from
directly underneath, as the wide necropolis begins now to
draw inward, to neck down and stretchout into a Corridor,
one known to Slothrop though not by name, a deforma-
tion of space that lurks inside his life, latent as a heredi-
tary disease. A band of doctors in white masks that cover
everything but eyes, bleak and grown-up eyes, move in
step down the passage toward where Roosevelt is lying.
They carry shiny black kits. Metal rings inside the black
leather, rings as if to speak, as if a ventriloquist were
playing a trick, help-let-me-out-of-here. . . . Whoever it
was, posing in the black cape at Yalta with the other leaders, conveyed beautifully the sense of Death's wings, rich,
soft and black as the winter cape, prepared a nation of
starers for the passing of Roosevelt, a being They assembled, a being They would dismantle. . . .

Someone here is cleverly allowing for parallax, scaling,
shadows all going the right way and lengthening with the
day—but no, Säure can't be real, no more than these dark-
clothed extras waiting in queues for some hypothetical

tram, some two slices of sausage (sure, sure), the dozen half-naked kids racing in and out of this burned tenement so amazingly detailed—They sure must have the budget, all right. Look at this desolation, all built then hammered back into pieces, ranging body-size down to powder (please order by Gauge Number), as that well-remembered fragrance Noon in Berlin, essence of human decay, is puffed on the set by a hand, lying big as a flabby horse up some alley, pumping its giant atomizer. . . .

(By Säure's black-market watch, it's nearly noon. From 11 to 12 in the morning is the Evil Hour, when the white woman with the ring of keys comes out of her mountain and may appear to you. Be careful, then. If you can't free her from a spell she never specifies, you'll be punished. She is the beautiful maiden offering the Wonderflower, and the ugly old woman with long teeth who found you in that dream and said nothing. The Hour is hers.)

Black P-38s fly racketing in formation, in moving openwork against the pale sky. Slothrop and Säure find a café on the sidewalk, drink watered pink wine, eat bread and some cheese. That crafty old doper breaks out a "stick" of "tea" and they sit in the sun handing it back and forth, offering the waiter a hit, who can tell? that's how you have to smoke armies too, these days. Jeeps, personnel carriers, and bicycles go streaming by. Girls in fresh summer frocks, orange and green as fruit ices, drift in to sit at tables, smiling, smiling, checking the area continuously for early business.

Somehow Säure has got Slothrop to talking about the Rocket. Not at all Säure's specialty, of course, though he's been keeping an ear tuned. If it's wanted, then it has a price. "I could never see the fascination. We kept hearing so much about it on the radio. It was our Captain Midnight Show. But we grew disillusioned. Wanting to believe, but nothing we saw giving us that much faith. Less and less toward the end. All I know is it brought disaster down on the cocaine market, Kerl."

"How's that?"

"Something in that rocket needed potassium permanganate, right?"

"Turbopump."

"Well, without that Purpurstoff you can't deal cocaine honestly. Forget honesty, there just wasn't any *reality*. Last winter you couldn't find a cc of permanganate in the whole fucking Reich, Kerl. *Oh* you should've seen the burning that was going on. Friends, understand. But what friend hasn't wanted to—in terms you can recognize—*push a pie in your face?* eh?"

"Thank you." Wait a minute. Is he talking about *us?* Is he getting ready to—

"So," having continued, "there crept over Berlin a gigantic Laurel and Hardy film, silent, silent . . . because of the permanganate shortage. I don't know what other economies may have been affected by the A4. This was not just pie-throwing, not just anarchy on a market, this was chemical irresponsibility; Clay, talcum, cement, even, it got this perverse, flour! Powdered milk, diverted from the stomachs of little sucklings! Look-alikes that were worth even more than cocaine—but the idea was that someone should get a sudden noseful of milk, hahahahah!" breaking up here for a minute, "and that was *worth the loss!* Without the permanganate there was no way to tell anything for sure. A little novocain to numb the tongue, something bitter for the taste, and you could be making enormous profits off of sodium bicarbonate. Permanganate is the touchstone. Under a microscope, you drop some on the substance in question, which dissolves—then you watch how it comes out of solution, how it recrystallizes: the cocaine will appear first, at the edges, then the vegetable cut, the procaine, the lactose at other well-known positions—a purple target, with the outer ring worth the most, and the bull's-eye worth nothing. An anti-target. Certainly not the A4's idea of one, *eh, Rocketman.* That machinery of yours was not exactly the doper's friend. What do you want it for? Will your country use it against Russia?"

"I don't want it. What do you mean, 'my country'?"

"I'm sorry. I only meant that it looks like the Russians want it badly enough. I've had connections all over the city taken away. Interrogated. None of them know any more about rockets than I do. But Tchitcherine thinks we do."

"Oboy. Him again?"

"Yes he's in Potsdam right now. Supposed to be. Set up a headquarters in one of the old film studios."

"Swell news, Emil. With my luck . . ."

"You don't look too good, Rocketman."

"Think that's horrible? Try this!" and Slothrop proceeds
to ask if Säure has heard anything about the Schwarzgerät.

Säure does not exactly scream *Aiyee!* and run off down
the street or anything, but squeeeak goes a certain valve all
right, and something is routed another way. "I'll tell you
what," nodding and shifting in his seat, "you talk to der
Springer. Ja, you two would get on fine. I am only a retired cat burglar, looking to spend my last several decades
as the sublime Rossini did his: comfortable. Just don't
mention me at all, O.K., Joe?"

"Well, who is that der Springer, and where do I find
him, Emil?"

"He is the knight who leaps perpetually—"

"Wow."

"—across the chessboard of the Zone, is who he is. Just
as Rocketman flies over obstacles today." He laughs nastily.
"A fine pair. How do I know where he is? He could be
anyplace. He is everywhere."

"Zorro? The Green Hornet?"

"Last I heard, a week or two ago, he was up north on
the Hanseatic run. You will meet. Don't worry." Abruptly
Säure stands up to go, shaking hands, slipping Rocketman
another reefer for later, or for luck. "I have medical officers
to see. The happiness of a thousand customers is on your
shoulders, young man. Meet me at my place. Glück."

So the Evil Hour has worked its sorcery. The wrong
word was Schwarzgerät. Now the mountain has closed
again thundering behind Slothrop, damn near like to crush
his heel, and it might just be centuries before that White
Woman appears again. Shit.

The name on the special pass is "Max Schlepzig." Slothrop, feeling full of pep, decides to pose as a vaudeville
entertainer. An illusionist. He has had a good apprentice-
ship with Katje, her damask tablecloth and magical body,
a bed for her salon, a hundred soirées fantastiques. . . .

He's through Zehlendorf by midafternoon, inside his
Rocketman rig and ready to cross. The Russian sentries
wait under a wood archway painted red, toting Suomis or
Degtyarovs, oversize submachine guns with drum magazines. Here comes also a Stalin tank now, lumbering in
low, soldier in earflapped helmet standing up in the 76

mm mount yelling into walkie-talkie . . . uh, well. . . . On
the other side of the arch is a Russian jeep with a couple
officers, one talking earnestly into the mike of *his* radio
set, and the air between quickens with spoken Russian at
the speed of light weaving a net to catch Slothrop. Who
else? He sweeps his cape back with a wink, tips his helmet
and smiles. In a conjuror's flourish he's out with card,
ticket 'n' bilingual pass, giving them some line about a
command performance in that Potsdam.

One of the sentries takes the pass and nips into his
kiosk to make a phone call. The others stand staring at
Tchitcherine's boots. No one speaks. The call is taking a
while. Scarred leather, day-old breads, cheekbones in the
sun. Slothrop's trying to think of a few card tricks he can
do, sort of break the ice, when the sentry sticks his head
out. "Stiefeln, bitte."

Boots? What would they want with—*yaaahhh!* Boots,
indeed, yes. We know beyond peradventure who has to be
on the other end, don't we. Slothrop can hear all the man's
metal parts jingling with glee. In the smoky Berlin sky,
somewhere to the left of the Funkturm in its steel-wool
distance, appears a full-page photo in *Life* magazine: it is
of Slothrop, he is in full Rocketman attire, with what appears to be a long, stiff sausage of very large diameter
being stuffed into his mouth, so forcibly that his eyes are
slightly crossed, though the hand or agency actually holding the stupendous wiener is not visible in the photo.
A SNAFU FOR ROCKETMAN, reads the caption—"Barely off
the ground, the Zone's newest celebrity 'fucks up.' "

We-e-e-ll, Slothrop slides off the boots, the sentry takes
them inside to the telephone—the others lean Slothrop up
against the arch and shake him down, finding nothing but
the reefer Säure gave him, which they expropriate. Slothrop waits in his socks, trying not to think ahead. Glancing around for cover, maybe. Nothing. Clear field of fire
for 360 degrees. Smells of fresh asphalt patch and gun oil.
The jeep, crystal verdigris, waiting: the road back to
Berlin, for the moment, deserted. . . . Providence, hey
Providence, what'd you do, step out for a beer or something?

Not at all. The boots reappear, smiling sentry right
behind them. "Stimmt, Herr Schlepzig." What does irony

sound like in Russian? These birds are too inscrutable for
Slothrop. Tchitcherine would've known enough not to arouse
any suspicion by asking to see those boots. Nah, it
couldn't've been him on the phone. This was probably
some routine search for that contraband, was all. Slothrop
is being seized right now by what the Book of Changes
calls Youthful Folly. He swirls his green cape a few more
times, chisels a stubby Balkan army off of one of the
tommyguns, and moseys away, southward. The officer's
jeep stays where it is. The tank has vanished.

> Jubilee Jim, just a-peddlin' through the country,
> Winkin' at the ladies from Stockbridge up to Lee—
> Buy your gal a brooch for a fancy gown,
> Buggy-whip rigs for just a dollar down,
> Hey come along ev'rybody, headin' for the Jubi-lee!

Two miles down the road, Slothrop hits that canal
Säure mentioned: takes a footpath down under the bridge
where it's wet and cool for a minute. He sets off along the
bank, looking for a boat to hijack. Girls in halters and
shorts lie sunning, brown and gold, all along this dreaming
grass slope. The clouded afternoon is mellowed to wind-
softened edges, children kneeling beside the water with
fishing lines, two birds in a chase across the canal soaring
down and up in a loop into the suspended storm of a
green treetop, where they sit and begin to sing. With distance the light gathers a slow ecru haze, girls' flesh no
longer bleached by the zenith sun now in gentler light
reawakening to warmer colors, faint shadows of thigh-
muscles, stretched filaments of skin cells saying touch . . .
stay. . . . Slothrop walks on—past eyes opening, smiles
breaking like kind dawns. What's wrong with him? Stay,
sure. But what keeps him passing by?

There are a few boats, moored to railings, but always
somebody with an eye out. He finally comes on a narrow
flat-bottomed little rig, oars in the locks and ready to go,
nothing but a blanket upslope, a pair of high heels, man's
jacket, stand of trees nearby. So Slothrop climbs right in,
and casts off. Have fun—a little nasty here—*I* can't, but
I can steal your *boat!* Ha!

He hauls till sundown, resting for long stretches, really
out of condition, cape smothering him in a cone of sweat

so bad he has to take it off finally. Ducks drift at a wary distance, water dripping off of bright orange beaks. Surface of the canal ripples with evening wind, sunset in his eyes streaking the water red and gold: royal colors. Wrecks poke up out of the water, red lead and rust ripening in this light, bashed gray hullplates, flaking rivets, unlaid cable pointing hysterical strands to all points of the compass, vibrating below any hearing in the breeze. Empty barges drift by, loose and forlorn. A stork flies over, going home, below him suddenly the pallid arch of the Avus overpass ahead. Any farther and Slothrop's back in the American sector. He angles across the canal, debarking on the opposite bank, and heads south, trying to skirt the Soviet control point the map puts someplace to his right. Massive movement in the dusk: Russian guardsmen, green-capped elite, marching and riding, pokerfaced, in trucks, on horseback. You can feel the impedance in the fading day, the crowding, jittering wire loops, Potsdam warning stay away . . . stay away. . . . The closer it comes, the denser the field around that cloaked international gathering across the Havel. Bodine's right: a gnat can't get in. Slothrop knows it, but just keeps on skulking along, seeking less sensitive axes of suspicion, running zigzags, aimed innocuously south.

Invisible. It becomes easier to believe in the longer he can keep going. Sometime back on Midsummer Eve, between midnight and one, fern seed fell in his shoes. He is the invisible youth, the armored changeling. Providence's little pal. *Their* preoccupation is with forms of danger the War has taught them—phantoms they may be doomed now, some of them, to carry for the rest of their lives. Fine for Slothrop, though—it's a set of threats he doesn't belong to. They are still back in geographical space, drawing deadlines and authorizing personnel, and the only beings who can violate their space are safely caught and paralyzed in comic books. They think. They don't know about Rocketman here. They keep passing him and he remains alone, blotted to evening by velvet and buckskin— if they do see him his image is shunted immediately out to the boondocks of the brain where it remains in exile with other critters of the night. . . .

Presently he cuts right again, toward the sunset. There's

still that big superhighway to get across. Some Germans
haven't been able to get home for 10, 20 years because
they were caught on the wrong side of some Autobahn
when it went through. Nervous and leadfooted now, Slothrop comes creeping up to the Avus embankment, listening to traffic vacuuming by above. Each driver thinks he's
in control of his vehicle, each thinks he has a separate
destination, but Slothrop knows better. The drivers are out
tonight because They need them where they are, forming
a deadly barrier. Amateur Fritz von Opels all over the
place here, promising a lively sprint for Slothrop—snarling
inward toward that famous S-curve where maniacs in white
helmets and dark goggles once witched their wind-faired
machinery around the banked brick in shrieking drifts
(admiring eyes of colonels in dress uniforms, colonels'
ladies in Garbo fedoras, all safe up in their white towers
yet belonging to the day's adventure, each waiting for his
own surfacing of the same mother-violence underneath . . .).

Slothrop frees his arms from the cape, lets a lean gray
Porsche whir by, then charges out, the red of its taillights
flashing along his downstream leg, headlights of a fast-
coming Army truck now hitting the upstream one and
touching the grotto of one eyeball to blue jigsaw. He
swings sideways as he runs, screaming, "Hauptstufe!"
which is the Rocketman war-cry, raises both arms and the
sea-green fan of the cape's silk lining, hears brakes go on,
keeps running, hits the center mall in a roll, scampering
into the bushes as the truck skids past and stops. Voices
for a while. Gives Slothrop a chance to catch his breath
and get the cape unwound from around his neck. The
truck finally starts off again. The southbound half of the
Avus is slower tonight, and he can jog across easy, down
the bank and uphill again into trees. Hey! Leaps broad
highways in a single bound!

Well, Bodine, your map is perfect here, except for one
trivial detail you sort of, uh, forgot to mention, wonder
why that was. . . . It turns out something like 150 houses
in Neubabelsberg have been commandeered and sealed
off as a compound for the Allied delegates to the Potsdam
Conference, and Jolly Jack Tar has stashed that dope
right in the middle of it. Barbed wire, searchlights, sirens,

security who've forgotten how to smile. Thank goodness, which is to say Säure Bummer, for this special pass here. Stenciled signs with arrows read ADMIRALTY, F.O., STATE DEPARTMENT, CHIEFS OF STAFF. . . . The whole joint is lit up like a Hollywood premiere. Great coming and going of civilians in suits, gowns, tuxedos, getting in and out of BMW limousines with flags of all nations next to the windscreens. Mimeographed handouts clog the stones and gutters. Inside the sentry boxes are piles of confiscated cameras.

They must deal here with a strange collection of those showbiz types. Nobody seems too upset at the helmet, cape, or mask. There are ambiguous shrugging phone calls and the odd feeble question, but they do let Max Schlepzig pass. A gang of American newspapermen comes through in a charabanc, clutching on to bottles of liberated Moselle, and they offer him a lift part way. Soon they have fallen to arguing about which celebrity he is. Some think he is Don Ameche, others Oliver Hardy. Celebrity? what is this? "Come on," sez Slothrop, "you just don't know me in this getup. I'm that Errol Flynn." Not everybody believes him, but he manages to hand out a few autographs anyhow. When they part company, the newshounds are discussing the candidates for Miss Rheingold 1946. Dorothy Hart's advocates are the loudest, but Jill Darnley has a majority on her side. It's all gibberish to Slothrop—it will be months yet before he runs into a beer advertisement featuring the six beauties, and find himself rooting for a girl named Helen Rückert: a blonde with a Dutch surname who will remind him dimly of someone. . . .

The house at 2 Kaiserstrasse is styled in High Prussian Boorish and painted a kind of barf brown, a color the ice-cold lighting doesn't improve. It is more heavily guarded than any other in the compound. Gee, Slothrop wonders why. Then he sees the sign with the place's stenciled alias on it.

"Oh, no. No. Quit fooling." For a while he stands in the street shivering and cursing that Seaman Bodine for a bungler, villain, and agent of death. Sign sez THE WHITE HOUSE. Bodine has brought him straight to the dapper, bespectacled stranger who gazed down the morning Fried-

richstrasse—to the face that has silently dissolved in to
replace the one Slothrop never saw and now never will.

The sentries with slung rifles are still as himself. The
folds of his cape are gone to corroded bronze under the
arc-lighting. Behind the villa water rushes. Music strikes
up inside and obliterates the sound. An entertainment. No
wonder he got in so easy. Are they expecting this magician, this late guest? Glamour, fame. He could run in and
throw himself at somebody's feet, beg for amnesty. End
up getting a contract for the rest of his life with a radio
network, o-or even a movie studio! That's what mercy is,
isn't it? He turns, trying to be casual about it, and goes
moseying out of the light, looking for a way down to that
water.

The shore of the Griebnitz See is dark, starlit, strung
with wire, alive with roving sentries. Potsdam's lights,
piled and scattered, twinkle across the black water. Slothrop has to go in up to his ass a few times to get past
that wire, and wait for the sentries to gather around a
cigarette at one end of their beat before he can make a
dash, cape-flapping and soggy, up to the villa. Bodine's
hashish is buried along one side of the house, under a certain juniper bush. Slothrop squats down and starts scooping up dirt with his hands.

Inside it is some do. Girls are singing "Don't Sit Under
the Apple Tree," and if it ain't the Andrews Sisters it may
as well be. They are accompanied by a dance band with
a mammoth reed section. Laughing, sounds of glassware,
multilingual chitchat, your average weekday night here at
the great Conference. The hash is wrapped in tinfoil inside a moldering ditty bag. It smells really good. Aw,
jeepers—why'd he forget to bring a pipe?

Actually, it's just as well. Above Slothrop, at eye level,
is a terrace, and espaliered peach trees in milky blossom.
As he crouches, hefting the bag, French windows open
and someone steps out on this terrace for some air. Slothrop freezes, thinking *invisible, invisible....* Footsteps
approach, and over the railing leans—well, this may
sound odd, but it's Mickey Rooney. Slothrop recognizes
him on sight, Judge Hardy's freckled madcap son, three-
dimensional, flesh, in a tux and am-I-losing-my-mind face.

Mickey Ronney stares at Rocketman holding a bag of hashish, a wet apparition in helmet and cape. Nose level with Mickey Rooney's shiny black shoes, Slothrop looks up into the lit room behind—sees somebody looks a bit like Churchill, lotta dames in evening gowns cut so low that even from this angle you can see more tits than they got at Minsky's . . . and maybe, maybe he even gets a glimpse of that President Truman. He *knows* he is seeing Mickey Rooney, though Mickey Rooney, wherever he may go, will repress the fact that he ever saw Slothrop. It is an extraordinary moment. Slothrop feels he ought to say something, but his speech centers have failed him in a drastic way. Somehow, "Hey, you're Mickey Rooney," seems inadequate. So they stay absolutely still, victory's night blowing by around them, and the great in the yellow electric room scheming on oblivious.

Slothrop breaks it first: puts a finger to his mouth and scuttles away, back around the villa and down to the shore, leaving Mickey Rooney with his elbows on that railing, still watching.

Back around the wire, avoiding sentires, close to the water's edge, swinging the ditty bag by its drawstring, some vague idea in his head now of finding another boat and just rowing back up that Havel—sure! Why not? It isn't till he hears distant conversation from another villa that it occurs to him he might be straying into the Russian part of the compound.

"Hmm," opines Slothrop, "well in that case I had better—"

Here comes that wiener again. Shapes only a foot away—they might have risen up out of the water. He spins around, catches sight of a broad, clean-shaven face, hair combed lionlike straight back, glimmering steel teeth, eyes black and soft as that Carmen Miranda's—

"Yes," no least accent to his English whispering, "you were followed all the way." Others have grabbed Slothrop's arms. High in the left one he feels something sharp, almost painless, very familiar. Before his throat can stir he's away, on the Wheel, clutching in terror to the dwindling white point of himself, in the first windrush of anaesthesia, hovering coyly over the pit of Death. . . .

□

A soft night, smeared full of golden stars, the kind of night
back on the pampas that Leopoldo Lugones liked to write
about. The U-boat rocks quietly on the surface. The only
sounds are the chug of the "billy-goat," cutting in now
and then below decks, pumping out the bilges, and El
Ñato back on the fantail with his guitar, playing Buenos
Aires tristes and milongas. Beláustegui is down working on
the generator. Luz and Felipe are asleep.

By the 20 mm mounts, Graciela Imago Portales lounges
wistfully. In her day she was the urban idiot of B.A.,
threatening nobody, friends with everybody across the
spectrum, from Cipriano Reyes, who intervened for her
once, to Acción Argentina, which she worked for before
it got busted. She was a particular favorite of the literati.
Borges is said to have dedicated a poem to her ("El labe-
rinto de tu incertidumbre/ Me trama con la disquietante
luna . . .").

The crew that hijacked this U-boat are here out of all
kinds of Argentine manias. El Ñato goes around talking
in 19th-century gaucho slang—cigarettes are "pitos," butts
are "puchos," it isn't caña he drinks but "la tacuara," and
when he's drunk he's "mamao." Sometimes Felipe has to
translate for him. Felipe is a difficult young poet with any
number of unpleasant enthusiasms, among them romantic
and unreal notions about the gauchos. He is always sucking up to El Ñato. Beláustegui, acting ship's engineer, is
from Entre Ríos, and a positivist in the regional tradition.
A pretty good knife-hand for a prophet of science too,
which is one reason El Ñato hasn't made a try yet for the
godless Mesopotamian Bolshevik. It is a strain on their
solidarity, but then it's only one of several. Luz is currently with Felipe, though she's supposed to be Squalidozzi's girl—after Squalidozzi disappeared on his trip to
Zürich she took up with the poet on the basis of a poignant
recitation of Lugones's "Pavos Reales," one balmy night
lying to off Matosinhos. For this crew, nostalgia is like
seasickness: only the hope of dying from it is keeping
them alive.

Squalidozzi did show up again though, in Bremerhaven.
He had just been chased across what was left of Germany
by British Military Intelligence, with no idea why.

"Why didn't you go to Geneva, and try to get through
to us?"

"I didn't want to lead them to Ibargüengoitia. I sent
someone else."

"Who?" Beláustegui wanted to know.

"I never got his name." Squalidozzi scratched his shaggy
head. "Maybe it was a stupid thing to do."

"No further contact with him?"

"None at all."

"They'll be watching us, then," Beláustegui sullen.
"Whoever he is, he's hot. You're a fine judge of character."

"What did you want me to do: take him to a psychiatrist
first? Weigh options? Sit around for a few weeks and
think about it?"

"He's right," El Ñato raising a large fist. "Let women
do their thinking, their analyzing. A man must always go
forward, looking Life directly in the face."

"You're disgusting," said Graciela Imago Portales.
"You're not a man, you're a sweaty *horse*."

"Thank you," El Ñato bowing, in all gaucho dignity.

Nobody was yelling. The conversation in the steel space
that night was full of quiet damped *s*s and palatal *y*s, the
peculiar, reluctant poignancy of Argentine Spanish, brought
along through years of frustrations, self-censorship, long
roundabout evasions of political truth—of bringing the
State to live in the muscles of your tongue, in the humid
intimacy just inside your lips . . . pero ché, no sós argentino. . . .

In Bavaria, Squalidozzi was stumbling through the outskirts of a town, only minutes ahead of a Rolls Royce with
a sinister dome in the roof, green Perspex you couldn't see
through. It was just after sunset. All at once he heard
gunshots, hoofbeats, nasal and metallic voices in English.
But the quaint little town seemed deserted. How could
this be? He entered a brick labyrinth that had been a
harmonica factory. Splashes of bell-metal lay forever un-
rung in the foundry dirt. Against a high wall that had
recently been painted white, the shadows of horses and
their riders drummed. Sitting watching, from workbenches

and crates, were a dozen individuals Squalidozzi recognized right away as gangsters. Cigar-ends glowed, and
molls whispered back and forth in German. The men ate
sausages, ripping away the casings with white teeth, well
cared for, that flashed in the light from the movie. They
were sporting the Caligari gloves which now enjoy a summer vogue in the Zone: bone white, except for the four
lines in deep violet fanning up each gloveback from wrist
to knuckles. All wore suits nearly as light-colored as the
teeth. It seemed extravagant to Squalidozzi, after Buenos
Aires and Zürich. The women crossed their legs often:
they were tense as vipers. In the air was a grassy smell, a
smell of leaves burning, that was strange to the Argentine
who, terminally homesick, had only the smell of freshly
brewed maté after a bitter day at the racetrack to connect it with. Crowned window frames gave out on the
brick factory courtyard where summer air moved softly.
The filmlight flickered blue across empty windows as if it
were breath trying to produce a note. The images grew
blunt with vengeance. "Yay!" screamed all the zootsters,
white gloves bouncing up and down. Their mouths and
eyes were as wide as children's.

The reel ended, but the space stayed dark. An enormous figure in a white zoot-suit stood, stretched, and
ambled right over to where Squalidozzi was crouching,
terrified.

"They after you, amigo?"

"Please—"

"No, no. Come on. Watch with us. It's a Bob Steele.
He's a good old boy. You're safe in here." For days, as it
turned out, the gangsters had known Squalidozzi was in
the neighborhood: they could infer to his path, though he
himself was invisible to them, by the movements of the
police, which were not. Blodgett Waxwing—for it was
he—used the analogy of a cloud chamber, and the vapor
trail a high-speed particle leaves. . . .

"I don't understand."

"Not sure I do either, pal. But we have to keep an eye
on everything, and right now all the hepcats are going
goofy over something called 'nuclear physics.' "

After the movie, Squalidozzi was introduced to Gerhardt von Göll, also known by his *nom de pègre*, "Der
Springer." Seems von Göll's people and Waxwing's were in

the course of a traveling business conference, rumbling
the roads of the Zone in convoy, changing trucks and
busses so often there was no time for real sleep, only
cat-naps—in the middle of the night, the middle of a
field, no telling when, you'd have to pile out, switch vehicles and take off again along another road. No destinations, no fixed itinerary. Most of the transportation was
furnished through the expertise of veteran automotive
jobber Edouard Sanktwolke, who could hot-wire anything
on wheels or caterpillar tracks—even packed around a
custom-built ebony case full of the rotor arms, each in its
velvet recess, to every known make, model, and year, in
case the target's owner had removed that vital part.

Squalidozzi and von Göll hit it off right away. This film
director turned marketeer had decided to finance all his
future movies out of his own exorbitant profits. "Only way
to be sure of having final cuts, ¿verdad? Tell me, Squalidozzi, are you too pure for this? Or could your anarchist
project use a little help?"

"It would depend what you wanted from us."

"A film, of course. What would you like to do? How
about *Martín Fierro?*"

Keep the customer happy. Martín Fierro is not just the
gaucho hero of a great Argentine epic poem. On the
U-boat he is considered an anarchist saint. Hernández's
poem has figured in Argentine political thinking for years
now—everybody's had his own interpretation, quoting
from it often as vehemently as politicians in 19th-century
Italy used to from *I Promessi Sposi*. It goes back to the
old basic polarity in Argentina: Buenos Aires vs. the provinces, or, as Felipe sees it, central government vs. gaucho
anarchism, of which he has become the leading theoretician. He has one of these round-brim hats with balls hanging from it, he has taken to lounging in the hatchways,
waiting for Graciela—"Good evening, my dove. Haven't
you got a kiss for the Gaucho Bakunin?"

"You look more like a Gaucho Marx," Graciela drawls,
and leaves Felipe to go back to the treatment he's working
on for von Göll, using El Ñato's copy of *Martín Fierro*,
which has long been thumbed into separate loose pages,
and smells of horses, each of whose names El Ñato, tear-
fully *mamao*, can tell you. . . .

A shadowed plain at sundown. An enormous flatness.

Camera angle is kept low. People coming in, slowly, singly or in small groups, working their way across the plain, in to a settlement at the edge of a little river. Horses, cattle, fires against the growing darkness. Far away, at the horizon, a solitary figure on horseback appears, and rides in, all the way in, as the credits come on. At some point we see the guitar slung on his back: he is a payador, a wondering singer. At last he dismounts and goes to sit with the people at the fire. After the meal and a round of caña he reaches for his guitar and begins to strum his three lowest strings, the bordona, and sing:

> Aquí me pongo a cantar
> al compás de la vigüela,
> que el hombre que lo desvela
> una pena estrordinaria,
> como la ave solitaria
> con el cantar se consuela.

So, as the Gaucho sings, his story unfolds—a montage of his early life on the estancia. Then the army comes and conscripts him. Takes him out to the frontier to kill Indians. It is the period of General Roca's campaign to open the pampas by exterminating the people who live there: turning the villages into labor camps, bringing more of the country under the control of Buenos Aires. Martín Fierro is soon sick of it. It's against everything he knows is right. He deserts. They send out a posse, and he talks the sergeant in command over to his side. Together they flee across the frontier, to live in the wilderness, to live with the Indians.

That's Part I. Seven years later, Hernández wrote a *Return of Martín Fierro*, in which the Gaucho sells out: assimilates back into Christian society, gives up his freedom for the kind of constitutional Gesellschaft being pushed in those days by Buenos Aires. A very moral ending, but completely opposite to the first.

"What should I do?" von Göll seems to want to know. "Both parts, or just Part I?"

"Well," begins Squalidozzi.

"I know what *you* want. But I might get better mileage out of two movies, if the first does well at the box office. But will it?"

"Of course it will."

"Something that anti-social?"

"But it's everything we believe in," Squalidozzi protests.

"But even the freest of Gauchos end up selling out, you know. That's how things are."

That's how Gerhardt von Göll is, anyway. Graciela knows the man: there are lines of liaison, sinister connections of blood and of wintering at Punta del Este, through Anilinas Alemanas, the IG branch in Buenos Aires, on through Spottbilligfilm AG in Berlin (another IG outlet) from whom von Göll used to get cut rates on most of his film stock, especially on the peculiar and slow-moving "Emulsion J," invented by Laszlo Jamf, which somehow was able, even under ordinary daylight, to render the human skin transparent to a depth of half a millimeter, revealing the face just beneath the surface. This emulsion was used extensively in von Göll's immortal *Alpdrücken*, and may even come to figure in *Martín Fierro*. The only part of the epic that really has von Göll fascinated is a singing-duel between the white gaucho and the dark El Moreno. It seems like an interesting framing device. With Emulsion J he could dig beneath the skin colors of the contestants, dissolve back and forth between J and ordinary stock, like sliding in and out of focus, or wipe—how he loved wipes! from one to the other in any number of clever ways. Since discovering that Schwarzkommando are really in the Zone, leading real, paracinematic lives that have nothing to do with him or the phony Schwarzkommando footage he shot last winter in England for Operation Black Wing, Springer has been zooming around in a controlled ecstasy of megalomania. He is convinced that his film has somehow brought them into being, "It is my mission," he announces to Squalidozzi, with the profound humility that only a German movie director can summon, "to sow in the Zone seeds of reality. The historical moment demands this, and I can only be its servant. My images, somehow, have been chosen for incarnation. What I can do for the Schwarzkommando I can do for your dream of pampas and sky. . . . I can take down your fences and your labyrinth walls, I can lead you back to the Garden you hardly remember. . . ."

His madness clearly infected Squalidozzi, who then

eventually returned to the U-boat and infected the others. It seemed what they had been waiting for. "Africans!" daydreamed the usually all-business Beláustegui at a staff meeting. "What if it's true? What if we've really come back, back to the way it was before the continents drifted apart?"

"Back to Gondwanaland," whispered Felipe. "When Río de la Plata was just opposite South-West Africa ... and the mesozoic refugees took the ferry not to Montevideo, but to Lüderitzbucht...."

The plan is to get somehow to the Lüneburg Heath and set up a small estancia. Von Göll is to meet them there. By the gun-mounts tonight, Graciela Imago Portales dreams. Is von Göll a compromise they can tolerate? There are worse foundations than a film. Did Prince Potemkin's fake villages survive Catherine's royal progress? Will the soul of the Gaucho survive the mechanics of putting him into light and sound? Or will someone ultimately come by, von Göll or another, to make a Part II, and dismantle the dream?

Above and beyond her the Zodiac glides, a north-hemisphere array she never saw in Argentina, smooth as an hour-hand. . . . Suddenly there's a long smash of static out of the P.A., and Beláustegui is screaming, "Der Aal! Der Aal!" The eel, wonders Graciela, the *eel*? Oh, yes, the torpedo. Ah, Beláustegui is as bad as El Ñato, he feels his own weird obligation to carry on in German sub-mariner slang, it is just precisamente a seagoing Tower of Babel here—the *torpedo*? why is he screaming about the torpedo?

For the good reason that the U-boat has just appeared on the radar screen of the U.S.S. *John E. Badass* (smile, U-boat!), as a "skunk" or unidentified pip, and the *Badass*, in muscular postwar reflex, is now lunging in at flank speed. Reception tonight is perfect, the green return "fine-grained as a baby's skin," confirms Spyros ("Spider") Telangiecstasis, Radarman 2nd Class. You can see clear out to the Azores. It is a mild, fluorescent summer evening on the sea. But what's this on the screen now, moving fast, sweep by sweep, broken as a drop of light from the original pip, tiny but unmistakable, in toward the unmoving center of the sweep, closer now—

"Bakerbakerbaker!" hollers somebody down in Sonar, loud and scared, over the phones. It means hostile torpedo on the way. Coffee messes go crashing, parallel rulers and dividers sliding across the glass top of the dead-reckoning tracer as the old tin can goes heeling over around onto an evasion pattern that was already obsolete during the Coolidge administration.

Der Aal's pale tunnel of wake is set to intersect the *Badass*'s desperate sea-squirm about midships. What intervenes is the drug Oneirine, as the hydrochloride. The machine from which it has emerged is the coffee urn in the mess hall of the *John E. Badass*. Playful Seaman Bodine—none other—has seeded tonight's grounds with a massive dose of Laszlo Jamf's celebrated intoxicant, scored on Bodine's most recent trip to Berlin.

The property of time-modulation peculiar to Oneirine was one of the first to be discovered by investigators. "It is experienced," writes Shetzline in his classic study, "in a subjective sense . . . uh . . . well. Put it this way. It's like stuffing wedges of silver sponge, *right, into*, your *brain!*" So, out in the mellow sea-return tonight, the two fatal courses do intersect in space, but not in time. Not nearly in time, heh heh. What Beláustegui fired his torpedo at was a darkrust old derelict, carried passively by currents and wind, but bringing to the night something of the skull: an announcement of metal emptiness, of shadow, that has spooked even stronger positivists than Beláustegui. And what passed into visual recognition from the small speeding pip on the *Badass*'s radar screen proved to be a corpse, dark in color, perhaps a North African, which the crew on the destroyer's aft 3-inch gun mount spent half an hour blowing to pieces as the gray warship slid by at a safe distance, fearful of plague.

Now what sea is this you have crossed, exactly, and what sea is it you have plunged more than once to the bottom of, alerted, full of adrenalin, but caught really, buffaloed under the epistemologies of these threats that paranoid you so down and out, caught in this steel pot, softening to devitaminized mush inside the soup-stock of your own words, your waste submarine breath? It took the Dreyfus Affair to get the Zionists out and doing, finally: what will drive you out of your soup-kettle? Has it already happened? Was it tonight's attack and deliverance? Will you go to the Heath, and begin your settlement, and wait there for your Director to come?

□

Under a tall willow tree beside a canal, in a jeep, in the shade, sit Tchitcherine and his driver Džabajev, a teenage Kazakh dope fiend with pimples and a permanently surly look, who combs his hair like the American crooner Frank Sinatra, and who is, at the moment, frowning at a slice of hashish and telling Tchitcherine, "Well, you should have taken more than this, you know."

"I only took what his freedom is worth to him," explains Tchitcherine. "Where's that pipe, now?"

"How do *you* know what his freedom is worth to him? You know what I think? I think you're going a little Zone-happy out here." This Džabajev is more of a sidekick, really, than a driver, so he enjoys immunity, up to a point, in questioning Tchitcherine's wisdom.

"Look, peasant, you read the transcript in there. That man is one unhappy loner. He's got problems. He's more useful running around the Zone thinking he's free, but he'd be better off locked up somewhere. He doesn't even know what his freedom *is*, much less what it's worth. So *I* get to fix the price, which doesn't matter to begin with."

"Pretty authoritarian," sneers young Džabajev. "Where's the matches?"

It's sad, though. Tchitcherine likes Slothrop. He feels that, in any normal period of history, they could easily be friends. People who dress up in bizarre costumes have a savoir-vivre—not to mention the sort of personality disorder—that he admires. When he was a little boy, back in Leningrad, Tchitcherine's mother sewed by hand a costume for him to wear in a school entertainment. Tchitcherine was the wolf. The minute he put on the head, in front of the mirror by the ikon, he knew himself. He was the wolf.

The Sodium Amytal session nags at the linings of Tchitcherine's brain as if the hangover were his own. Deep, deep—further than politics, than sex or infantile terrors . . .

a plunge into the nuclear blackness.... Black runs all through the transcript: the recurring color black. Slothrop never mentioned Enzian by name, nor the Schwarzkommando. But he did talk about the Schwarzgerät. And he also coupled "schwarz-" with some strange nouns, in the German fragments that came through. Blackwoman, Blackrocket, Blackdream.... The new coinages seem to be made unconsciously. Is there a single root, deeper than anyone has probed, from which Slothrop's Blackwords only appear to flower separately? Or has he by way of the language caught the German mania for name-giving, dividing the Creation finer and finer, analyzing, setting namer more hopelessly apart from named, even to bringing in the mathematics of combination, tacking together established nouns to get new ones, the insanely, endlessly diddling play of a chemist whose molecules are words....

Well, the man is a puzzle. When Geli Tripping first sent word of his presence in the Zone, Tchitcherine was only interested enough to keep a routine eye on him, along with the scores of others. The only strange item, which grew stranger as surveillance developed, was that he seemed to be alone. To date Slothrop has still not recorded, tagged, discovered, or liberated a single scrap of A4 hardware or intelligence. He reports neither to SPOG, CIOS, BAFO, TI, nor any American counterpart—indeed, to no known Allied office. Yet he is one of the Faithful: the scavengers now following industriously the fallback routes of A4 batteries from the Hook of Holland all across Lower Saxony. Pilgrims along the roads of miracle, every bit and piece a sacred relic, every scrap of manual a verse of Scripture.

But the ordinary hardware doesn't interest Slothrop. He is holding out, saving himself for something absolutely unique. Is it the Blackrocket? Is it the ooooo? Enzian is looking for it, and for the mysterious Schwarzgerät. There is a very good chance that Slothrop, driven by his Black-phenomenon, responding to its needs though they be hidden from him, will keep returning, cycle after cycle, to Enzian, until the mission is resolved, the parties secured, the hardware found. It's a strong hunch: nothing Tchitcherine will ever put into writing. Operationally he's alone as Slothrop is out here—reporting, if and when, direct to

Malenkov's special committee under the Council of People's Commissars (the TsAGI assignment being more or less a cover). But Slothrop is his boy. He'll be followed, all right. If they lose him why they'll find him again. Too bad he can't be motivated personally to go get Enzian. But Tchitcherine is hardly fool enough to think that all Americans are as easy to exploit as Major Marvy, with *his* reflexes about blackness. . . .

It's a shame. Tchitcherine and Slothrop could have smoked hashish together, compared notes on Geli and other girls of the ruins. He could have sung to the American songs his mother taught him, Kiev lullabies, starlight, lovers, white blossoms, nightingales. . . .

"Next time we run across that Englishman," Džabajev looking curiously at his hands on the steering-wheel, "or American, or whatever he is, find out, will you, where he *got* this shit?"

"Make a note of that," orders Tchitcherine. They both start cackling insanely there, under the tree.

□

Slothrop comes to in episodes that fade in and out of sleep, measured and serene exchanges in Russian, hands at his pulse, the broad green back of someone just leaving the room. . . . It's a white room, a perfect cube, though for a while he can't recognize cubes, walls, lying horizontal, anything too spatial. Only the certainty that he's been shot up yet again with that Sodium Amytal. *That* feeling he knows.

He's on a cot, still in Rocketman garb, helmet on the floor down next to the ditty bag of hash—*oh*-oh. Though it requires superhuman courage in the face of doubts about whether or not he can really even move, he manages to flop over and check out that dope. One of the tinfoil packages looks smaller. He spends an anxious hour or two undoing the top to reveal, sure enough, a fresh cut, raw green against the muddy brown of the great chunk. Footsteps ring down metal stairs outside, and a heavy door slides to below. Shit. He lies in the white cube, feeling groggy, feet crossed hands behind head, doesn't care espe-

cially to go anyplace. . . . He dozes off and dreams about
birds, a close flock of snow buntings, blown in a falling-
leaf of birds, among the thickly falling snow. It's back in
Berkshire. Slothrop is little, and holding his father's hand.
The raft of birds swings, buffeted, up, sideways through
the storm, down again, looking for food. "Poor little guys,"
sez Slothrop, and feels his father squeeze his hand through
its wool mitten. Broderick smiles. "They're all right. Their
hearts beat very, very fast. Their blood and their feathers
keep them warm. Don't worry, son. Don't worry. . . ."
Slothrop wakes again to the white room. The quiet. Raises
his ass and does a few feeble bicycle exercises, then lies
slapping on new flab that must've collected on his stomach
while he was out. There is an invisible kingdom of flab, a
million cells-at-large, and they all know who he is—soon
as he's unconscious, they start up, every one, piping in high
horrible little Mickey Mouse voices, hey fellas! hey c'mon,
let's all go over to Slothrop's, the big sap ain't doing anything but laying on his ass, c'mon, oboy! "Take that,"
Slothrop mutters, "a-and that!"

Arms and legs apparently working, he gets up groaning,
puts his helmet on his head, grabs the ditty bag and leaves
by the door, which shudders all over, along with the walls,
when he opens it. Aha! Canvas flats. It's a movie set.
Slothrop finds himself in a dilapidated old studio, dark
except where yellow sunlight comes through small holes in
the overhead. Rusted catwalks, creaking under his weight,
black burned-out klieg lights, the fine netting of spider
webs struck to graphwork by the thin beams of sun. . . .
Dust has drifted into corners, and over the remains of other
sets: phony-gemütlich love nests, slant-walled and palm-
crowded nightclubs, papier-mâché Wagnerian battlements,
tenement courtyards in stark Expressionist white/black,
built to no human scale, all tapered away in perspective
for the rigid lenses that stared here once. Highlights are
painted on to the sets, which is disturbing to Slothrop,
who keeps finding these feeble yellow streaks, looking up
sharply, then all around, for sources of light that were
never there, getting more agitated as he prowls the old
shell, the girders 50 feet overhead almost lost in shadows,
tripping over his own echoes, sneezing from the dust he
stirs. The Russians have pulled out all right, but Slothrop

isn't alone in here. He comes down a metal staircase
through shredded webs, angry spiders and their dried
prey, rust crunching under his soles, and at the bottom
feels a sudden tug at his cape. Being still a little foggy
from that injection, he only flinches violently. He is held
by a gloved hand, the shiny kid stretched over precise
little knuckles. A woman in a black Parisian frock, with a
purple-and-yellow iris at her breast. Even damped by the
velvet, Slothrop can feel the shaking of her hand. He
stares into eyes rimmed soft a black ash, separate grains
of powder on her face clear as pores the powder missed or
was taken from by tears. This is how he comes to meet
Margherita Erdmann, his lightless summer hearth, his safe-
passage into memories of the Inflationszeit stained with
dread—his child and his helpless Lisaura.

   She's passing through: another of the million rootless.
Looking for her daughter, Bianca, bound east for Swinemünde, if the Russians and Poles will let her. She's in
Neubabelsberg on a sentimental side-trip—hasn't seen the
old studios in years. Through the twenties and thirties she
worked as a movie actress, at Templehof and Staaken too,
but this place was always her favorite. Here she was directed by the great Gerhardt von Göll through dozens of
vaguely pornographic horror movies. "I knew he was a
genius from the beginning. I was only his creature." Never
star material, she admits freely, no Dietrich, nor vamp à
la Brigitte Helm. A touch of whatever it was they wanted,
though—they (Slothrop: "They?" Erdmann: "I don't
know. . . .") nicknamed her the Anti-Dietrich: not destroyer of men but doll—languid, exhausted. . . . "I
watched all our films," she recalls, "some of them six or
seven times. I never seemed to *move*. Not even my face.
Ach, those long, long gauze close-ups . . . it could have
been the same frame, over and over. Even running away—
I always had to be chased, by monsters, madmen, crimi-
nals—still I was so—" bracelets flashing—"stolid, so . . .
monumental. When I wasn't running I was usually
strapped or chained to something. Come. I'll show you."
Leading Slothrop now to what's left of a torture chamber,
wooden teeth snapped from its rack wheel, plaster masonry
peeling and chipped, dust rising, dead torches cold and
lopsided in their sconces. She lets wood chains, most of

the silver paint worn away now, slither clattering through
her kid fingers. "This was a set for *Alpdrücken*. Gerhardt
in those days was still all for exaggerated lighting." Silver-
gray collects in the fine wrinkles of her gloves as she dusts
off the rack, and lies down on it. "Like this," raising her
arms, insisting he fasten the tin manacles to her wrists and
ankles. "The light came from above and below at the
same time, so that everyone had two shadows: Cain's and
Abel's, Gerhardt told us. It was at the height of his
symbolist period. Later on he began to use more natural
light, to shoot more on location." They went to Paris,
Vienna. To Herrenchiemsee, in the Bavarian Alps. Von
Göll had dreamed of making a film about Ludwig II. It
nearly got him blacklisted. The rage then was all for
Frederick. It was considered unpatriotic to say that a
German ruler could also be a madman. But the gold, the
mirrors, the miles of Baroque ornament drove von Göll
himself a little daft. Especially those *long corridors....*
"Corridor metaphysics," is what the French call this condition. Oldtime corridor hepcats will chuckle fondly at descriptions of von Göll, long after running out of film, still
dollying with a boobish smile on his face down the golden
vistas. Even on orthochromatic stock, the warmth of it
survived in black and white, though the film was never
released, of course. *Das Wütend Reich,* how could they sit
still for that? Endless negotiating, natty little men with
Nazi lapel pins trooping through, interrupting the shooting, walking facefirst into the glass walls. They would
have accepted anything for "Reich," even "Königreich,"
but von Göll stood fast. He walked a tightrope. To compensate he started immediately on *Good Society,* which it's
said delighted Goebbels so much he saw it three times,
giggling and punching in the arm the fellow sitting next
to him, who may have been Adolf Hitler. Margherita
played the lesbian in the cafe, "the one with the monocle,
who's whipped to death at the end by the transvestite,
remember?" Heavy legs in silk stockings now with a hard,
machined look, slick knees sliding against each other as
the memory moves in, exciting her. Slothrop too. She
smiles up at his tautening deerskin crotch. "He was beautiful. Both ways, it didn't matter. You remind me of him a
little. Especially . . . those boots. . . . *Good Society* was our

second film, but this one," *this one*? "*Alpdrücken,* was our first. I think Bianca is his child. She was conceived while we were filming this. He played the Grand Inquisitor who tortured me. Ah, we were the Reich's Sweethearts—Greta Erdmann and Max Schlepzig, Wonderfully Together—"

"Max Schlepzig," repeats Slothrop, goggling, "quit fooling. *Max Schlepzig?*"

"It wasn't his real name. Erdmann wasn't mine. But anything with Earth in it was politically safe—Earth, Soil, Folk . . . a code. Which they, staring, knew how to decipher. . . . Max had a very Jewish name, Something-sky, and Gerhardt thought it more prudent to give him a new one."

"Greta, somebody also thought it prudent to name *me* Max Schlepzig." He shows her the pass he got from Säure Bummer.

She gazes at it, then at Slothrop briefly. She's begun to tremble again. Some mixture of desire and fear. "I knew it."

"Knew what?"

Looking away, submissive. "Knew he was dead. He disappeared in '38. They've been busy, haven't They?"

Slothrop has picked up, in the Zone, enough European passport-psychoses to want to comfort her. "This is forged. The name's just a random alias. The guy who made it probably remembered Schlepzig from one of his movies."

"Random." A tragic, actressy smile, beginnings of a double chin, one knee drawn up as far as these leg irons will let her. "Another fairy-tale word. The signature on your card is Max's. Somewhere in Stefania's house on the Vistula I have a steel box full of his letters. Don't you think I know that Latin *z*, crossed engineer-style, the flower he made out of the *g* at the end? You could hunt all the Zone for your 'forger.' They wouldn't let you find him. They want you right here, right now."

Well. What happens when paranoid meets paranoid? A crossing of solipsisms. Clearly. The two patterns create a third: a moiré, a new world of flowing shadows, interferences. . . . " 'Want me here'? What for?"

"For me." Whispering out of scarlet lips, open, wet. . . . Hmm. Well, there's this hardon, here. He sits on the rack, leans, kisses her, presently unlacing his trousers and peeling them down far enough to release his cock bounding up with a slight wobble into the cool studio. "Put your helmet on."

"O.K."

"Are you very cruel?"

"Don't know."

"Could you be? Please. Find something to whip me with. Just a little. Just for the warmth." Nostalgia. The pain of a return home. He rummages around through inquisitional props, gyves, thumbscrews, leather harness, before coming up with a miniature cat-o'-nine-tails, a Black Forest elves' whip, its lacquered black handle carved in a bas-relief orgy, the lashes padded with velvet to hurt but not to draw blood. "Yes, that's perfect. Now on the insides of my thighs...."

But somebody has already educated him. Something... that dreams Prussian and wintering among their meadows, in whatever cursive lashmarks wait across the flesh of their sky so bleak, so incapable of any sheltering, wait to be summoned.... No. No—he still says "their," but he knows better. His meadows now, his sky... his own cruelty.

All Margherita's chains and fetters are chiming, black skirt furled back to her waist, stockings pulled up tight in classic cusps by the suspenders of the boned black rig she's wearing underneath. How the penises of Western men have leapt, for a century, to the sight of this singular point at the top of a lady's stocking, this transition from silk to bare skin and suspender! It's easy for non-fetishists to sneer about Pavlovian conditioning and let it go at that, but any underwear enthusiast worth his unwholesome giggle can tell you there is much more here—there is a cosmology: of nodes and cusps and points of osculation, mathematical kisses... *singularities!* Consider cathedral spires, holy minarets, the crunch of trainwheels over the points as you watch peeling away the track you didn't take... mountain peaks rising sharply to heaven, such as those to be noted at scenic Berchtesgaden... the edges of steel razors, always holding potent mystery... rose thorns that prick us by surprise... even, according to the Russian mathematician Friedmann, the infinitely dense point from which the present Universe expanded.... In each case, the change from point to no-point carries a luminosity and enigma at which something in us must leap and sing, or withdraw in fright. Watching the A4 pointed at the sky—just before the last firing-switch closes—watching that singular point at the very top of the Rocket, where the fuze is.... Do all these points imply, like the Rocket's, an annihilation? What is that, detonating in the sky above the cathedral? beneath the edge of the razor, under the rose?

And what's waiting for Slothrop, what unpleasant surprise, past the tops of Greta's stockings here? laddering suddenly, the pallid streak flowing downthigh, over intricacies of knee and out of sight.... What waits past this whine and crack of velvet lashes against her skin, long red stripes on the white ground, her moans, the bruise-colored flower that cries at her breast, the jingling of the hardware holding her down? He tries not to tear his victim's stockings, or whip too close to her stretched vulva, which shivers, unprotected, between thighs agape and straining, amid movements of muscle erotic, subdued, "monumental" as any silver memory of her body on film. She comes once, then perhaps again before Slothrop puts the whip down and climbs on top, covering her with the wings of his cape, her Schlepzig-surrogate, his latest reminder of Katje ... and they commence fucking, the old phony rack groaning beneath them, Margherita whispering *God how you hurt me* and *Ah, Max* ... and just as Slothrop's about to come, the name of her child: strained through her perfect teeth, a clear extrusion of pain that is not in play, she cries, *Bianca.* ...

□

... yes, bitch—yes, little bitch—poor helpless *bitch* you're coming can't stop yourself now I'll whip you again till you *bleed.* ... Thus Pökler's whole front surface, eyes to knees: flooded with tonight's image of the delicious victim bound on her dungeon rack, filling the movie screen—close-ups of her twisting face, nipples under the silk gown amazingly erect, making lies of her announcements of pain—

bitch! she loves it . . . and Leni no longer solemn wife, embittered source of strength, but Margherita Erdmann underneath him, on the bottom for a change, as Pökler drives in again, into her again, yes, bitch, yes. . . .

Only later did he try to pin down the time. Perverse curiosity. Two weeks since her last period. He had come out of the Ufa theatre on the Friedrichstrasse that night with an erection, thinking like everybody else only about getting home, fucking somebody, fucking her into some submission. . . . God, Erdmann was beautiful. How many other men, shuffling out again into depression Berlin, carried the same image back from *Alpdrücken* to some drab fat excuse for a bride? How many shadow-children would be fathered on Erdmann that night?

It was never a real possibility for Pökler that Leni might get pregnant. But looking back, he knew that had to be the night, *Alpdrücken* night, that Ilse was conceived. They fucked so seldom any more. It was not hard to pinpoint. *That's how it happened. A film. How else? Isn't that what they made of my child, a film?*

He sits tonight by his driftwood fire in the cellar of the onion-topped Nikolaikirche, listening to the sea. Stars hang among the spaces of the great Wheel, precarious to him as candles and good-night cigarettes. Cold gathers along the strand. Child phantoms—white whistling, tears never to come, range the wind behind the wall. Twists of faded crepe paper blow along the ground, scuttling over his old shoes. Dust, under a moon newly calved, twinkles like snow, and the Baltic crawls like its mother-glacier. His heart shrugs in its scarlet net, elastic, full of expectation. He's waiting for Ilse, for his movie-child, to return to Zwölfkinder, as she has every summer at this time.

Storks are asleep among two- and three-legged horses, rusted gearwork and splintered roof of the carousel, their heads jittering with air-currents and yellow Africa, dainty black snakes a hundred feet below meandering in the sunlight across the rocks and dry pans. Oversize crystals of salt lie graying, drifted in the cracks of the pavement, in the wrinkles of the dog with saucer eyes in front of the town hall, the beard of the goat on the bridge, the mouth of the troll below. Frieda the pig hunts a new place to nestle and snooze out of the wind. The plaster witch, wire

mesh visible at her breasts and haunches, leans near the
oven, her poke at corroded Hansel in perpetual arrest.
Gretel's eyes lock wide open, never a blink, crystal-heavy
lashes batting at the landings of guerrilla winds from the
sea.

If there is music for this it's windy strings and reed
sections standing in bright shirt fronts and black ties all
along the beach, a robed organist by the breakwater—itself
broken, crusted with tides—whose languets and flues
gather and shape the resonant spooks here, the candle-
flame memories, all trace, particle and wave, of the sixty
thousand who passed, already listed for taking, once or
twice this way. Did you ever go on holiday to Zwölfkinder?
Did you hold your father's hand as you rode the train up
from Lübeck, gaze at your knees or at the other children
like you braided, ironed, smelling of bleach, boot-wax,
caramel? Did small-change jingle in your purse as you
swung around the Wheel, did you hide your face in his
wool lapels or did you kneel up in the seat, looking over
the water, trying to see Denmark? Were you frightened
when the dwarf tried to hug you, was your frock scratchy
in the warming afternoon, what did you say, what did you
feel when boys ran by snatching each other's caps and too
busy for you?

She must have always been a child on somebody's list.
He only avoided thinking about it. But all the time she
was carrying her disappearance in her drawn face, her
reluctant walk, and if he hadn't needed her protection so
much he might have seen in time how little she could
protect anything, even their mean nest. He couldn't talk
to her—it was arguing with his own ghost from ten years
ago, the same idealism, the adolescent fury—items that
had charmed him once—a woman with spirit!—but which
he came to see as evidence of her single-mindedness, even,
he could swear, some desire to be actually destroyed. . . .

She went out to her street-theatre each time expecting
not to come back, but he never really knew that. Leftists
and Jews in the streets, all right, noisy, unpleasant to look
at, but the police will keep them channeled, she's in no
danger unless she wants to be. . . . Later, after she left, he
got a little drunk one forenoon, a little sentimental, and
went out at last, his first and last time, hoping that some-

how the pressures of Fate or crowd hydrodynamics might bring them together again. He found a street full of tan and green uniforms, truncheons, leather, placards fluttering unstable in all modes but longitudinal, scores of panicked civilians. A policeman aimed a blow at him, but Pökler dodged, and it hit an old man instead, some bearded old unreconstructed geezer of a Trotskyite ... he saw the strands of steels cable under black rubber skin, a finicky smile on the policeman's face as he swung, his free hand grasping his opposite lapel in some feminine way, the leather glove of the hand with the truncheon unbuttoned at the wrist, and his eyes flinching at the last possible moment, as if the truncheon shared his nerves and might get hurt against the old man's skull. Pökler made it to a doorway, sick with fear. Other police came running as some dancers run, elbows close to sides, forearms thrusting out at an angle. They used firehoses to break up the crowd, finally. Women slid like dolls along the slick cobbles and on tram rails, the thick gush catching them by belly and head, its brute white vector dominating them. Any of them might have been Leni. Pökler shivered in his doorway and watched it. He couldn't go out in the street. Later he thought about its texture, the network of grooves beween the paving stones. The only safety there was antscaled, down and running the streets of Ant City, bootsoles crashing overhead like black thunder, you and your crawling neighbors in traffic all silent, jostling, heading down the gray darkening streets. ... Pökler knew how to find safety among the indoor abscissas and ordinates of graphs: finding the points he needed not by running the curve itself, not up on high stone and vulnerability, but instead tracing patiently the xs and ys, P (atü), W (m/sec), T_i (° K), moving always by safe right angles along the faint lines. ...

When he began to dream about the Rocket with some frequency, it would sometimes not be a literal rocket at all, but a street he knew was in a certain district of the city, a street on a certain small area of the grid that held something he thought he needed. The coordinates were clear in his mind, but the street eluded him. Over the years, as the Rocket neared its fullness, about to go operational, the coordinates switched from the Cartesian x and y of the laboratory to the polar azimuth and range of the weapon as deployed: once he knelt on the lavatory floor of his old rooming house in Munich, understanding that if he faced exactly along a certain compass-bearing his prayer would be heard: he'd be safe. He wore a robe of gold and orange brocade. It was the only light in the room. Afterward he ventured out into the house, knowing people slept in all the rooms, but feeling a sense of desertion. He went to switch on a light—but in the act of throwing the switch he knew the room had really been lit to begin with, and he had just turned everything out, *everything*. . . .

The A4 operational-at-last hadn't crept up on him. Its coming true was no climax. That hadn't ever been the point.

"They're using you to kill people," Leni told him, as clearly as she could. "That's their only job, and you're helping them."

"We'll all use *it*, someday, to leave the earth. To transcend."

She laughed. "Transcend," from Pökler?

"Someday," honestly trying, "they won't have to kill. Borders won't mean anything. We'll have all outer space. . . ."

"*Oh* you're blind," spitting it as she spat his blindness at him every day, that and "Kadavergehorsamkeit," a beautiful word he can no longer imagine in any voice but hers. . . .

But really he did not obey like a corpse. He *was* political, up to a point—there was politics enough out at the rocket field. The Army Weapons Department was showing an ever-quickening interest in the amateur rocketeers of the Verein für Raumschiffahrt, and the VfR had recently begun making available to the Army records of their experiments. The corporations and the universities—the Army said—didn't want to risk capital or manpower on developing anything as fantastic as a rocket. The Army had nowhere to turn but to private inventors and clubs like the VfR.

"Shit," said Leni. "They're all in on it together. You really can't see that, can you."

Within the Society, the lines were drawn clear enough. Without money the VfR was suffocating—the Army had the money, and was already financing them in round-about ways. The choice was between building what the Army wanted—practical hardware—or pushing on in chronic poverty, dreaming of expeditions to Venus.

"Where do you think the Army's getting the money?" Leni asked.

"What does it matter? Money is money."

"*No!*"

Major Weissmann was one of several gray eminences around the rocket field, able to talk, with every appearance of sympathy and reason, to organized thinker and maniac idealist alike. All things to all men, a brand-new military type, part salesman, part scientist. Pökler, the all-seeing, the unmoving, must have known that what went on in the VfR committee meetings was the same game being played in Leni's violent and shelterless street. All his training had encouraged an eye for analogies—in equations, in theoretical models—yet he persisted in thinking the VfR was special, preserved against the time. And he also knew at first hand what happens to dreams with no money to support them. So, presently, Pökler found that by refusing to take sides, he'd become Weissmann's best ally. The major's eyes always changed when he looked at Pökler: his slightly prissy face to relax into what Pökler had noticed, in random mirrors and display windows, on his own face when he was with Leni. The blank look of one who is taking another for granted. Weissmann was as sure of Pökler's role as Pökler was of Leni's. But Leni left at last. Pökler might not have had the will.

He thought of himself as a practical man. At the rocket field they talked continents, encirclements—seeing years before the General Staff the need for a weapon to break ententes, to leap like a chess knight over Panzers, infantry, even the Luftwaffe. Plutocratic nations to the west, communists to the east. Spaces, models, game-strategies. Not much passion or ideology. Practical men. While the military wallowed in victories not yet won, the rocket engineers had to think non-fanatically, about German reverses, German defeat—the attrition of the Luftwaffe and its decline in power, the withdrawals of fronts, the need for weapons with longer ranges. . . . But others had the money, others gave the orders—trying to superimpose their

lusts and bickerings on something that had its own vitality,
on a *technologique* they'd never begin to understand. As
long as the Rocket was in research and development, there
was no need for them to believe in it. Later, as the A4
was going operational, as they found themselves with a
real rocket-in-being, the struggles for power would begin
in earnest. Pökler could see that. They were athletic, brainless men without vision, without imagination. But they
had power, and it was hard for him not to think of them
as superior, even while holding them in a certain contempt.

But Leni was wrong: no one was using him. Pökler was
an extension of the Rocket, long before it was ever built.
She'd seen to that. When she left him, he fell apart. Pieces
spilled into the Hinterhof, down the drains, away in the
wind. He couldn't even go to the movies. Only rarely did
he go out after work and try to fish lumps of coal from
the Spree. He drank beer and sat in the cold room, autumn
light reaching him after impoverishments and fadings,
from gray clouds, off courtyard walls and drainpipes,
through grease-darkened curtains, bled of all hope by the
time it reached where he sat shivering and crying. He
cried every day, some hour of the day, for a month, till a
sinus got infected. He went to bed and sweated the fever
out. Then he moved to Kummersdorf, outside Berlin, to
help his friend Mondaugen at the rocket field.

Temperatures, velocities, pressures, fin and body con-
figurations, stabilities and turbulences began to slip in, to
replace what Leni had run away from. There were pine
and fir forests out the windows in the morning, instead of
a sorrowful city courtyard. Was he giving up the world,
entering a monastic order?

One night he set fire to twenty pages of calculations.
Integral signs weaved like charmed cobras, comical curly
*d*s marched along like hunchbacks through the fire-edge
into billows of lace ash. But that was his only relapse.

At first he helped out in the propulsion group. No one
was specializing yet. That came later, when the bureaus
and paranoias moved in, and the organization charts became plan-views of prison cells. Kurt Mondaugen, whose
field was radio electronics, could come up with solutions
to cooling problems. Pökler found himself redesigning in-

strumentation for measuring local pressures. That came in handy later at Peenemünde, when they often had to lead over a hundred measuring tubes from a model no more than 4 or 5 centimeters' diameter. Pökler helped in working out the Halbmodelle solution: bisecting the model lengthwise and mounting it flat-side to the wall of the test chamber, bringing the tubes through that way to all the manometers outside. A Berlin slum-dweller, he thought, knew how to think in half-rations . . . but it was a rare moment of pride. No one could really claim credit 100% for any idea, it was a corporate intelligence at work, specialization hardly mattered, class lines even less. The social spectrum ran from von Braun, the Prussian aristocrat, down to the likes of Pökler, who would eat an apple in the street—yet they were all equally at the Rocket's mercy: not only danger from explosions or falling hardware, but also its dumbness, its dead weight, its obstinate and palpable mystery. . . .

In those days, most of the funding and attention went to the propulsion group. Problem was just to get something off the ground without having it blow up. There were minor disasters—aluminum motor casings would burn through, some injector designs would set up resonant combustion, in which the burning motor would try to shriek itself to pieces—and then, in '34, a major one. Dr. Wahmke decided to mix peroxide and alcohol together *before* injection into the thrust chamber, to see what would happen. The ignition flame backed up through the conduit into the tank. The blast demolished the test stand, killing Dr. Wahmke and two others. First blood, first sacrifice.

Kurt Mondaugen took it as a sign. One of these German mystics who grew up reading Hesse, Stefan George, and Richard Wilhelm, ready to accept Hitler on the basis of Demian-metaphysics, he seemed to look at fuel and oxidizer as paired opposites, male and female principles uniting in the mystical egg of the combustion chamber: creation and destruction, fire and water, chemical plus and chemical minus—

"Valency," Pökler protested, "a condition of the outer shells, that's all."

"Think about it," said Mondaugen.

There was also Fahringer, an aerodynamics man, who

went out in the pine woods at Peenemünde with his Zen
bow and roll of pressed straw to practice breathing, draw
and loosing, over and over. It seemed rather rude at a
time when his colleagues were being driven insane by
what they called "Folgsamkeitfaktor," a problem with
getting the Rocket's long axis to follow the tangent, at all
points, to its trajectory. The Rocket for this Fahringer was
a fat Japanese arrow. It was necessary in some way to become one with Rocket, trajectory, and target—"not to *will*
it, but to surrender, to step out of the role of firer. The act
is undivided. You are both aggressor and victim, rocket
and parabolic path and . . ." Pökler never knew what the
man was talking about. But Mondaugen understood. Mondaugen was the bodhisattva here, returned from exile in
the Kalahari and whatever light had found him there, returned to the world of men and nations to carry on in a
role he'd chosen deliberately, but without ever explaining
why. In Südwest he had kept no journals, written no letters home. There had been an uprising by the Bondel-
swaartz in 1922, and general turmoil in the country. His
radio experiments interrupted, he sought refuge, along with
a few score other whites, in the villa of a local landowner
named Foppl. The place was a stronghold, cut off on all
sides by deep ravines. After a few months of siege and
debauchery, "haunted by a profound disgust for everything European," Mondaugen went out alone into the
bush, ended up living with the Ovatjimba, the aardvark
people, who are the poorest of the Hereros. They accepted him with no questions. He thought of himself,
there and here, as a radio transmitter of some kind, and
believed that whatever he was broadcasting at the time
was at least no threat to them. In his electro-mysticism, the
triode was as basic as the cross in Christianity. Think of
the ego, the self that suffers a personal history bound to
time, as the grid. The deeper and true Self is the flow
between cathode and plate. The constant, pure flow. Signals—sense-data, feelings, memories relocating—are put
onto the grid, and modulate the flow. We live lives that
are waveforms constantly changing with time, now positive, now negative. Only at moments of great serenity is
it possible to find the pure, the informationless state of
signal zero.

"In the name of the cathode, the anode, and the holy grid?" said Pökler.

"Yes, that's good," Mondaugen smiled.

Closest to the zero among them all, perhaps, was the African Enzian, the protégé of Major Weissmann. At the Versuchsanstalt, behind his back, he was known as Weissmann's Monster, probably less out of racism than at the picture the two of them made, Enzian towering a foot over Weissmann, who was balding, scholarly, peering up at the African through eyeglass lenses thick as bottles, skipping now and then to keep up as they stalked over the asphalt and through the labs and offices, Enzian dominating every room and landscape of those early Rocket days. . . . Pökler's clearest memory of him is his first, in the testing room at Kummersdorf, surrounded by electric colors—green nitrogen bottles, a thick tangle of red, yellow and blue plumbing, Enzian's own copper face with the same kind of serenity that now and then drifted into Mondaugen's—watching in one of the mirrors the image of a rocket engine beyond the safety partition: in the stale air of that room snapping with last-minute anxieties, nicotine craving, unreasonable prayer, Enzian was *at peace*. . . .

Pökler moved to Peenemünde in 1937, along with some 90 others. They were invading Gravity itself, and a beachhead had to be laid down. Never in his life, not even as a laborer in Berlin, did Pökler work so hard. The vanguard spent the spring and summer converting a little island, the Greifswalder Oie, into a testing station: resurfacing road, stringing cable and telephone line, putting up living quarters, latrines and storage sheds, excavating bunkers, mixing concrete, endlessly stevedoring in crates of tools, bags of cement, drums of fuel. They used an ancient ferryboat for cargo runs between the mainland and the Oie. Pökler remembers the worn red plush and scratched lacquer inside the dim cabins, the neglected brightwork, the asthmatic cry of her steam-whistle, odors of sweat, cigarette smoke and Diesel fuel, the trembling of arm and leg muscles, the tired joking, the exhaustion toward the end of each day, his own new calluses struck to gold by the late sun. . . .

The sea was mostly calm and blue that summer, but in

the autumn the weather turned. Rain swept in from the north, the temperature plunged, wind tore into storage tents, giant waves boomed all night long. The water was white for fifty meters out from shore. Spray feathered landward off the curls of the big breakers. Pökler, billeted at a fisherman's cottage, came in from his evening walks behind a fine mask of salt. Lot's wife. What disaster had he dared to look back on? He knew.

He reverted that season to childhood, to the wounded dog. During those wet and solitary walks he brooded about Leni: he concocted scenarios in which they would meet again, in some elegant or dramatic setting—ministry, theatre lobby—two or three jeweled and beautiful women hanging to him, generals and industrialists springing to light his American cigarettes and listening to his offhand solutions to problems Leni would only vaguely understand. The most satisfying of these fantasies would come while Pökler was on the toilet—he'd tap his feet, fanfares would whisper through his lips as he felt that pleasant anticipation. . . .

But the burden of his poor Berlin self lingered. He had spoken of it, listened, probed, and yet it would not dissolve or flee, it persisted, beggar in all the doorways of his life, beseeching silently with eyes, with hands quite sure of their guiltmaking craft. Busywork at Peenemünde and good company at Herr Halliger's inn on the Oie—all marking time till good firing weather—and Pökler more vulnerable than he'd ever been. His cold and womanless nights, the card and chess games, the all-male beer-drinking sessions, the nightmares he had to find his own way up out of because there was no other hand now to shake him awake, nobody to hold him when the shadows came on the window shade—all caught up with him that November, and maybe he allowed it to. A protective reflex. Because something scary was happening. Because once or twice, deep in the ephedrine pre-dawns nodding ja, ja, stimmt, ja, for some design you were carrying not in but *on* your head and could feel bobbing, out past your sidevision, bobbing and balanced almost—he would become aware of a drifting-away . . . some assumption of Pökler into the calculations, drawings, graphs, and even what raw hardware there was . . . each time, soon as it happened, he would panic, and draw back into the redoubt of waking Pökler, heart pounding, hands and feet aching, his breath catching in a small voiced *hunh*— Something was out to get him, something here, among the paper. The fear of extinction named Pökler knew it was the Rocket, beckoning him in. If he also knew that in something like this extinction he could be free of his loneliness and his failure, still he wasn't quite convinced. . . . So he hunted, as a servo valve with a noisy input will, across the Zero, between the two desires, personal identity and impersonal salvation. Mondaugen saw it all. He could see into Pökler's heart. In his compassion, not surprisingly, he had no free advice for his friend. Pökler would have to find his own way to his zero signal, his true course.

By '38 the Peenemünde facility was taking shape, and Pökler moved over to the mainland. With hardly more to go on than Stodda's treatise on steam turbines, and helpful data now and then from universities at Hannover, Darmstadt, Leipzig and Dresden, the propulsion group were testing a rocket engine of $1\frac{1}{2}$ tons' thrust, 10 atmospheres' combustion pressure, and 60 seconds' duration. They were getting exhaust velocities of 1800 meters per second, but the value they were aiming for was 2000. They called it the magic number, and they meant it literally. As some gamblers on the stock market know when to place stop orders, feeling by instinct not the printed numbers but the *rates of change,* knowing from first and second derivatives in their skin when to come in, stay or go, so there are engineering reflexes tuned always to know, at any moment, what, given the resources, can be embodied in working hardware—what is "feasible." On the day that a 2000 m/sec exhaust became feasible, the A4 itself suddenly came in reach. The danger then lay in being seduced by approaches that were too sophisticated. No one was immune. Hardly a designer there, including Pökler, didn't come up with at least one monster rig, some Gorgon's head writhing with pipes, tubes, complicated folderol for controlling pressures, solenoids on top of pilot valves on auxiliary valves on backup valves—hundreds of pages on valve nomenclature were printed as appendices to these weird proposals, all promising huge pressure differences between the inside of the chamber and the nozzle exit—beautiful, as long as you didn't care much about those millions of moving parts behaving together too reliably. But to get a dependable working motor, one the military could use in the field to kill people, the real engineering problem now was to keep things as simple as possible.

The model currently being fired was the A3, christened not with champagne, but with flasks of liquid oxygen by the playful technicians. Emphasis had begun to shift from propulsion to guidance. Telemetry on the flight tests was still primitive. Thermometers and barometers were sealed in a watertight compartment with a movie camera. During flights the camera photographed the needles swinging on the gauges. After the flight the film was recovered, and the data played back. Engineers sat around looking at movies of dials. Meantime Heinkels were also dropping iron models of the Rocket from 20,000 feet. The fall was photographed by Askania cinetheodolite rigs on the ground. In the daily rushes you would watch the frames at around 3000 feet, where the model broke through the speed of sound. There has been this strange connection between the German mind and the rapid flashing of successive stills to counterfeit movement, for at least two centuries—since Leibniz, in the process of inventing calculus, used the same approach to break up the trajectories of cannonballs through the air. And now Pökler was about to be given proof that these techniques had been extended past images on film, to human lives.

He had returned to his quarters about sundown, too tired or preoccupied to be much affected by the furnace of colors in the flower gardens, the daily changes to the skyline of the Station, even the absence of noise today from the testing stands. He smelled the ocean, and could almost imagine himself as someone who lives year-round at a seaside resort, but seldom gets to the beach. Now and then, over in Peenemünde-West, a fighter plane took off or landed, the motors softened by distance to tranquil purring. A late sea-breeze flickered. He had no warning other than a smile from a colleague who lived a few cubicles away and was coming down the barracks stairs as Pökler was going up. He entered his own cubicle and saw her sitting on the bed, her toes pointed in next to a flow-

ered carpetbag, skirt pulled over her knees and eyes
anxiously, fatally, looking into his.

"Herr Pökler? I am your—"

"Ilse. Ilse. . . ."

He must have picked her up, kissed her, drawn the curtain. Some reflex. She was wearing in her hair a ribbon
of brown velvet. He remembered her hair as lighter,
shorter—but then it does grow, and darken. He looked
slantwise into her face, all his emptiness echoing. The vacuum of his life threatened to be broken in one strong inrush
of love. He tried to maintain it with seals of suspicion, looking for resemblances to the face he'd last seen years ago
over her mother's shoulder, eyes still puffy from sleep
angled down across Leni's raincoated back, going out a
door he'd thought closed for good—pretending not to find
resemblances. Perhaps pretending. *Was* it really the same
face? he'd lost so much of it over the years, that fat,
featureless child's face. . . . He was afraid now even to
hold her, afraid his heart would burst. He said, "How long
have you been waiting?"

"Since lunchtime." She'd eaten in the canteen. Major
Weissmann had brought her up on the train from Stettin,
and they had played chess. Major Weissmann was a slow
player, and they hadn't finished the game. Major Weissmann had bought her sweets, and had asked her to say
hello and sorry he couldn't stay long enough to see
Pökler—

Weissmann? What was this? A blinking, tentative fury
grew in Pökler. They must have known everything—all
this time. His life was secretless as this mean cubicle, with
its bed, commode and reading-light.

So, to stand between him and this impossible return, he
had his anger—to preserve him from love he couldn't
really risk. He could settle for interrogating his daughter.
The shame he felt was acceptable, the shame and coldness. But she must have picked it up, for she sat now
very still, except for nervous feet, her voice so subdued he
missed parts of her answers.

They had sent her here from a place in the mountains,
where it was chilly even in summer—surrounded by
barbed wire and bright hooded lights that burned all
night long. There were no boys—only girls, mothers, old

ladies living in barracks, stacked up in bunks, often two
to a pallet. Leni was well. Sometimes a man in a black
uniform came into the barracks and Mutti would go away
with him, and stay away for several days. When she came
back she didn't want to talk, or even to hug Ilse the way
she usually did. Sometimes she cried, and asked Ilse to
leave her alone. Ilse would go off and play with Johanna
and Lilli underneath the barracks next door. They had
scooped a hideout there in the dirt, furnished with dolls,
hats, dresses, shoes, old bottles, magazines with pictures,
all found out near the barbed wire, the treasure pile, they
called it, a huge refuse dump that always smoldered, day
and night: you could see its red glow out the window from
the top bunk where she slept with Lilli, nights when Leni
was away. . . .

But Pökler was hardly listening, he had the only datum
with any value: that she was somewhere definite, with a
location on the map and authorities who might be con-
tacted. Could he find her again? Fool. Could he somehow
negotiate her release? Some man, some Red, must have
got her into this. . . .

Kurt Mondaugen was the only one he could trust,
though Pökler knew before they spoke that the role Mondaugen had chosen would keep him from helping. "They
call them re-education camps. They're run by the SS. I
could talk to Weissmann, but it might not work."

He had known Weissmann in Südwest. They had shared
the months of siege inside Foppl's villa: Weissmann was
one of the people who had driven Mondaugen, finally,
away to live in the bush. But they had found a rapprochement here, among the rockets, either for sunblasted holy-
man reasons it was not for Pökler to understand or because
of some deeper connection which had always been
there. . . .

They stood on the roof of one of the assembly buildings,
the Oie across the water six miles away clearly visible,
which meant a change in the weather tomorrow. Steel was
being hammered somewhere out in the sunlight, hammered in cadences, purified as the song of some bird. Blue
Peenemünde shivered around them in all directions, a
dream of concrete and steel masses reflecting the noon
heat. The air rippled like camouflage. Behind it something

else seemed to carry on in secret. At any moment the illusion they stood on would dissolve and they would fall to earth. Pökler stared across the marshes, feeling helpless. "I have to do something. Don't I?"

"No. You have to wait."

"It's not right, Mondaugen."

"No."

"What about Ilse? Will she have to go back?"

"I don't know. But she's here now."

So, as usual, Pökler chose silence. Had he chosen something else, back while there was time, they all might have saved themselves. Even left the country. Now, too late, when at last he wanted to act, there was nothing to act on.

Well, to be honest, he didn't spend much time brooding about past neutralities. He wasn't that sure he'd outgrown them, anyway.

They took walks, he and Ilse, by the stormy shore—fed ducks, explored the pine forests. They even allowed her to watch a launching. It was a message to him, but he didn't understand till later what it meant. It meant that there was no violation of security: *there was no one she could tell who mattered.* The noise of the Rocket ripped at them. For the first time then she moved close, and held him. He felt that he was holding on to her. The motor cut off too soon, and the Rocket crashed somewhere over in Peenemünde-West, in Luftwaffe territory. The dirty pillar of smoke drew the screaming fire engines and truckloads of workers by in a wild parade. She took in a deep breath, and squeezed his hand. "Did you make it do that, Papi?"

"No, it wasn't supposed to. It's supposed to fly in a big curve," motioning with his hand, the parabola trailing behind encompassing testing stands, assembly buildings, drawing them together as the crosses priests make in the air quarter and divide the staring congregations behind them. . . .

"Where does it go?"

"Wherever we tell it to."

"May I fly in it someday? I'd fit inside, wouldn't I?"

She asked impossible questions. "Someday," Pökler told her. "Perhaps someday to the Moon."

"The *Moon* . . ." as if he were going to tell her a story. When none followed she made up her own. The engineer

in the next cubicle had a map of the Moon tacked to his
fiberboard wall, and she spent hours studying it, deciding
where she wanted to live. Passing over the bright rays of
Kepler, the rugged solitude of the Southern Highlands, the
spectacular views at Copernicus and Eratosthenes, she
chose a small pretty crater in the Sea of Tranquillity called
Maskelyne B. They would build a house right on the rim,
Mutti and she and Pökler, gold mountains out one window
and the wide sea out the other. And Earth green and blue
in the sky....

Should he have told her what the "seas" of the Moon
really were? Told her there was nothing to breathe? His
ignorance frightened him, his ineptitude as a father....
Nights in the cubicle, with Ilse curled a few feet away in
a canvas army cot, a little gray squirrel under her blanket,
he'd wonder if she wasn't really better off as ward of the
Reich. He'd heard there were camps, but saw nothing
sinister in it: he took the Government at their word, "re-
education." *I've made such a mess of everything ... they
have qualified people there ... trained personnel ... they
know what a child needs ...* staring up at the electric
scatter from this part of Peenemünde mapping across his
piece of ceiling priorities, abandoned dreams, favor in the
eyes of the master fantasists in Berlin, while sometimes Ilse
whispered to him bedtime stories about the moon she
would live on, till he had transferred silently to a world
that wasn't this one after all: a map without any national
borders, insecure and exhilarating, in which flight was as
natural as breathing—but I'll fall ... no, rising, look down,
nothing to be afraid of, this time it's good ... yes, firmly
in flight, it's working ... yes....

Pökler may be only witnessing tonight—or he may really
be part of it. He hasn't been shown which it is. Look at
this. There is about to be expedited, for Friedrich August
Kekulé von Stradonitz, his dream of 1865, the great Dream
that revolutionized chemistry and made the IG possible.
So that the right material may find its way to the right
dreamer, everyone, everything involved must be exactly
in place in the pattern. It was nice of Jung to give us the
idea of an ancestral pool in which everybody shares the
same dream material. But how it is we are each visited as
individuals, each by exactly and only what he needs?

Doesn't that imply a switching-path of some kind? a
bureaucracy? Why shouldn't the IG go to séances? They
ought to be quite at home with the bureaucracies of the
other side. Kekulé's dream here's being routed now past
points which may arc through the silence, in bright reluctance to live inside the moving moment, an imperfect, a
human light, over here interfering with the solemn binary
decisions of these agents, who are now allowing the cosmic
Serpent, in the violet splendor of its scales, shining that is
definitely *not* human, to pass—without feeling, without
wonder (after you get a little time in—whatever *that*
means over here—one of these archetypes gets to look
pretty much like any other, oh you hear some of these new
hires, the seersucker crowd come in the first day, "Wow!
Hey—that's th-th' *Tree o' Creation!* Huh? Ain't it!
Je-eepers!" but they calm down fast enough, pick up the
reflexes for Intent to Gawk, you know self-criticism's an
amazing technique, it shouldn't work but it does. . . .) Here,
here's the rundown on Kekulé's problem. Started out to
become an architect, turned out instead to be one of the
Atlantes of chemistry, most of the organic wing of that
useful edifice bearing down on top of his head forever—
not just under the aspect of IG, but of World, assuming
that's a distinction you observe, heh, heh. . . . Once again
it was the influence of Liebig, the great professor of chemistry on whose name-street in Munich Pökler lived while
he attended the T.H. Liebig was at the University of
Giessen when Kekulé entered as a student. He inspired the
young man to change his field. So Kekulé brought the
mind's eye of an architect over into chemistry. It was a
critical switch. Liebig himself seems to have occupied the
role of a gate, or sorting-demon such as his younger contemporary Clerk Maxwell once proposed, helping to concentrate energy into one favored room of the Creation at
the expense of everything else (later witnesses have suggested that Clerk Maxwell intended his Demon not so
much as convenience in discussing a thermodynamic idea
as a parable about the *actual existence* of personnel like
Liebig . . . we may gain an indication of how far the repression had grown by that time, in the degree to which
Clerk Maxwell felt obliged to code his warnings . . . indeed some theorists, usually the ones who find sinister

meaning behind even *Mrs.* Clerk Maxwell's notorious "It
is time to go home, James, you are beginning to enjoy
yourself," have made the extreme suggestion that the Field
Equations themselves contain an ominous forewarning—
they cite as evidence the disturbing intimacy of the Equations with the behavior of the double-integrating circuit in
the guidance system of the A4 rocket, the same double-
summing of current densities that led architect Etzel Ölsch
to design for architect Albert Speer an underground factory at Nordhausen with just that symbolic shape...).
Young ex-architect Kekulé went looking among the molecules of the time for the hidden shapes he knew were
there, shapes he did not like to think of as real physical
structures, but as "rational formulas," showing the relation-
ships that went on in "metamorphoses," his quaint 19th-
century way of saying "chemical reactions." But he could
visualize. He *saw* the four bonds of carbon, lying in a tetra-
hedron—he *showed* how carbon atoms could link up one
to another, into long chains. . . . But he was stumped when
he got to benzene. He knew there were six carbon atoms
with a hydrogen attached to each one—but he could not
see the shape. Not until the dream: until he was made to
see it, so that others might be seduced by its physical
beauty, and begin to think of it as a blueprint, a basis for
new compounds, new arrangements, so that there would
be a field of aromatic chemistry to ally itself with secular
power, and find new methods of synthesis, so there would
be a German dye industry to become the IG. . . .

Kekulé dreams the Great Serpent holding its own tail in
its mouth, the dreaming Serpent which surrounds the World.
But the meanness, the cynicism with which this dream is
to be used. The Serpent that announces, "The World is a
closed thing, cyclical, resonant, eternally-returning," is to
be delivered into a system whose only aim is to *violate*
the Cycle. Taking and not giving back, demanding that
"productivity" and "earnings" keep on increasing with
time, the System removing from the rest of the World
these vast quantities of energy to keep its own tiny desperate fraction showing a profit: and not only most of humanity—most of the World, animal, vegetable and mineral, is
laid waste in the process. The System may or may not
understand that it's only buying time. And that time is an

artificial resource to begin with, of no value to anyone or anything but the System, which sooner or later must crash to its death, when its addiction to energy has become more than the rest of the World can supply, dragging with it innocent souls all along the chain of life. Living inside the System is like riding across the country in a bus driven by a maniac bent on suicide . . . though he's amiable enough, keeps cracking jokes back through the loudspeaker, "Good morning folks, this is Heidelberg here we're coming into now, you know the old refrain, 'I lost my heart in Heidelberg,' well I have a friend who lost both his *ears* here! Don't get me wrong, it's really a nice town, the people are warm and wonderful—when they're not dueling. Seriously though, they treat you just fine, they don't just give you the key to the city, they give you the bung-starter!" u.s.w. On you roll, across a countryside whose light is forever changing—castles, heaps of rock, moons of different shapes and colors come and go. There are stops at odd hours of the mornings, for reasons that are not announced: you get out to stretch in lime-lit courtyards where the old men sit around the table under enormous eucalyptus trees you can smell in the night, shuffling the ancient decks oily and worn, throwing down swords and cups and trumps major in the tremor of light while behind them the bus is idling, waiting—*passengers will now reclaim their seats* and much as you'd like to stay, right here, learn the game, find your old age around this quiet table, it's no use: he is waiting beside the door of the bus in his pressed uniform, Lord of the Night he is checking your tickets, your ID and travel papers, and it's the wands of enterprise that dominate tonight . . . as he nods you by, you catch a glimpse of his face, his insane, committed eyes, and you remember then, for a terrible few heart-beats, that of course it will end for you all in blood, in shock, without dignity—but there is meanwhile this trip to be on . . . over your own seat, where there ought to be an advertising plaque, is instead a quote from Rilke: "Once, only once . . ," One of Their favorite slogans. No return, no salvation, no Cycle—that's not what They, nor Their brilliant employee Kekulé, have taken the Serpent to mean. No: what the Serpent means is—how's this— that the six carbon atoms of benzene are in fact curled around into a closed ring, *just like that snake with its tail in its mouth*, GET IT? "The aromatic Ring we know today," Pökler's old prof, Laszlo Jamf, at this point in the spiel removing from his fob a gold hexagon with the German formée cross in the center, a medal of honor from IG Farben, joking, in his lovable-old-fart manner, that he likes to think of the cross not as German so much as standing for the tetravalency of carbon—"but *who*," lifting his open hands on each beat, like a bandleader, "who, sent, the *Dream*?" It is never clear how rhetorical any of Jamf's questions are. "Who sent this new serpent to our ruinous garden, already too fouled, too crowded to qualify as any locus of innocence—unless innocence be our age's neutral, our silent passing into the machineries of indifference— something that Kekulé's Serpent had come to—not to destroy, but to define to us the loss of . . . we had been given certain molecules, certain combinations and not others . . . we used what we found in Nature, unquestioning, shamefully perhaps—but the Serpent whispered, *'They can be changed,* and new molecules assembled from the debris of the given. . . .' Can anyone tell me what else he whispered to us? Come—who knows? You. Tell me, *Pökler*—"

His name fell on him like a thunderclap, and of course it wasn't Prof.-Dr. Jamf after all, but a colleague from down the hall who had pulled reveille duty that morning. Ilse was brushing her hair, and smiling at him.

His daytime work had started to go better. Others were not so distant, and more apt to look in his eyes. They'd met Ilse, and been charmed. If he saw anything else in their faces, he ignored it.

Then one evening he returned from the Oie, a little drunk, a little anxious-elated over a firing the next day, and found his cubicle empty. Ilse, her flowered bag, the clothing she usually left strewn on the cot, had all vanished. Nothing left but a wretched sheet of log paper (which Pökler found so useful for taming the terror of exponential curves into the linear, the safe), the same kind she'd drawn pictures of her Moonhouse on. "Papi, they want me back. Maybe they'll let me see you again. I hope so. I love you. Ilse."

Kurt Mondaugen found Pökler lying on her cot breathing what he imagined were colors of her hair on the pillow. For a while then he went a little insane, talked of killing Weissmann, sabotaging the rocket program, and quitting his job and seeking asylum in England. . . . Mondaugen sat, and listened to all of it, touched Pökler once or twice, smoked his pipe, till at last, at two or three in the morning, Pökler had talked through a number of unreal options, cried, cursed, punched a hole into his neighbor's cubicle, through which he heard the man snoring on oblivious. Cooled by then to a vexed engineer-elitism—"They are fools, they don't even know what sine and cosine are and they're trying to tell *me*"—he agreed that yes, he must wait, and let them do what they would do. . . .

"If I set up a meeting with Weissmann," Mondaugen did suggest, "could you be graceful? calm?"

"No. Not with him. . . . Not yet."

"When you think you are ready, let me know. *When* you're ready, you'll know how to handle it." Had he allowed himself a tone of command? He must have seen how much Pökler needed to be at someone's command. Leni had learned to subdue her husband with her face, knew what cruel lines he expected of her mouth, what tones of voice he needed . . . when she left him she left an unemployed servant who'd go with the first master that called, just a

VICTIM IN A VACUUM!

Nur . . . ein . . . Op-fer!
Sehr ins Vakuum,
("Won't somebody take advantage of me?")
Wird niemand ausnut-zen mich, auch?
("Just a slave with nobody to slave for,")
Nur ein Sklave, ohne Her-rin, (*ya*-ta ta-*ta*)
("A-and who th' heck wants at be, free?")
Wer zum Teufel die Freiheit, braucht?

(All together now, all you masochists out there, specially those of you don't have a partner tonight, alone with those fantasies that don't look like they'll ever come true—want you just to join in here with your brothers and sisters, let each other know you're alive and sincere, try to break through the silences, try to reach through and connect. . . .)

Aw, the sodium lights-aren't, so bright in Berlin,
I go to the bars dear, but nobody's in!
Oh, I'd much rather bee
In a Greek trage-dee,
Than be a VICTIM IN A VACUUM to-nite!

Days passed, much like one another to Pökler. Identical
morning plunges into a routine dreary as winter now. He
learned to keep an outward calm, at least. Learned to feel
the gathering, the moving toward war that is unique to
weapons programs. At first it simulates depression or non-
specific anxiety. There may be esophagal spasms and unrecoverable dreams. You find you are writing notes to
yourself, first thing in the morning: calm, reasoned assur-
ances to the screaming mental case inside—1. It is a combination. 1.1 It is a scalar quantity. 1.2. Its negative aspects are distributed isotropically. 2. It is not a conspiracy.
2.1 It is not a vector. 2.11 It is not aimed at anybody.
2.12 It is not aimed at *me* . . . u.s.w. The coffee begins to
taste more and more metallic. Each deadline is now a
crisis, each is more intense than the last. Behind this job-
like-any-other-job seems to lie something void, something
terminal, something growing closer, each day, to mani-
festation. . . . ("The new planet Pluto," she had whispered
long ago, lying in the smelly dark, her long Asta Nielsen
upper lip gibbous that night as the moon that ruled her,
"Pluto is in my sign now, held tight in its claws. It moves
slowly, so slowly and so far away . . . but it will burst out.
It is the grim phoenix which creates its own holocaust . . .
deliberate resurrection. Staged. Under control. No grace,
no interventions by God. Some are calling it the planet of
National Socialism, Brunhübner and that crowd, all trying
to suck up to Hitler now. They don't know they are telling
the *literal truth*. . . . Are you awake? Franz. . . .")
As war drew closer, the game of priorities and politick-
ing grew more earnest, Army vs. Luftwaffe, the Weapons
Department vs. the Ministry of Munitions, the SS, given
their aspirations, vs. everybody else, and even a simmering
discontent that was to grow over the next few years into
a palace revolt against von Braun, because of his youth
and a number of test failures—though heaven knew, there
were always enough of those, they were the raw material

of all testing-station politics. . . . In general, though, the test results grew more and more hopeful. It was impossible not to think of the Rocket without thinking of *Shicksal,* of growing toward a shape predestined and perhaps a little otherworldly. The crews launched an uncontrolled series of A5s, bringing some of them down by parachute, reaching a height of five miles and nearly to the speed of sound. Though the guidance people had still a long way to go, they had by this point switched over to vanes made of graphite, brought the yaw oscillations down to five degrees or so, and grown measurably happier about the Rocket's stability.

At some point during the winter, Pökler came to feel that he could handle a meeting with Weissmann. He found the SS man on guard behind eyeglasses like Wagnerian shields, ready for unacceptable maxima—anger, accusation, a moment of office-violence. It was like meeting a stranger. They had not spoken since the days at Kummersdorf, at the old Raketenflugplatz. In this quarter-hour at Peenemünde, Pökler smiled more than he had in the year previous: spoke of his admiration for Poehlmann's work in devising a cooling system for the propulsion.

"What about the hot spots?" Weissmann asked. It was a reasonable question, but also an *intimacy.*

It came to Pökler that the man didn't give a damn about heating problems. This was a game, as Mondaugen had warned—ritualized as jiu-jitsu. "We've got heat-flow densities," Pökler feeling as he usually did when he sang, "on the order of three million kcal/m^2h°C. Regenerative cooling is the best interim solution right now, but Poehlmann has a new approach"—showing him with chalk and slate, trying for the professional manner—"he feels that if we use a film of alcohol on the *inside* of the chamber, we can reduce the heat transfer by a considerable amount."

"You'll be injecting it."

"Correct."

"How much fuel is that going to reroute? How's it going to affect the engine efficiency?"

Pökler had the figures. "Right now injection is a plumber's nightmare, but with the delivery schedules as they are—"

"What about the two-stage combustion process?"

"Gives us more volume, better turbulence, but there's also a non-isotropic pressure drop, which cuts into our efficiency. . . . We're trying any number of approaches. If we could depend on better funding—"

"Ah. Not my department. We could do with a more generous budget ourselves." They both laughed then, gentleman scientists under a stingy bureaucracy, suffering together.

Pökler understood that he had been negotiating for his child and for Leni: that the questions and answers were not exactly code for something else, but in the way of an evaluation of Pökler personally. He was expected to be-have a certain way—not just to play a role, but to live it. Any deviations into jealousy, metaphysics, vagueness would be picked up immediately: he would either be cor-rected back on course, or allowed to fall. Through winter and spring the sessions with Weissmann became routine. Pökler grew into his new disguise—Prematurely Aged Adolescent Whiz—often finding that it could indeed take him over, keeping him longer at reference books and firing data, speaking lines for him he could never have planned in advance: gentle, scholarly, rocket-obsessed language that surprised him.

In late August he had his second visit. It should have been "Ilse returned," but Pökler wasn't sure. As before, she showed up alone, unannounced—ran to him, kissed him, called him Papi. But . . .

But her hair, for one thing, was definitely dark brown, and cut differently. Her eyes were longer, set differently, her complexion less fair. It seemed she'd grown a foot taller. But at that age, they shoot up overnight, don't they? If it *was* "that age. . . ." Even as Pökler embraced her, the perverse whispering began. Is it the same one? Have they sent you a different child? Why didn't you look closer last time, Pökler?

This time he asked how long they were going to let her stay.

"They'll tell me. And I'll try to let you know." And would there be time for him to recalibrate from his little squirrel who dreamed of living on the Moon to this dark, long-legged, Southern creature, whose awkwardness and

need of a father were so touching, so clear even to Pökler,
at this their second (or was it first, or third?) meeting?

Hardly any news of Leni. They had been separated, Ilse
said, during the winter. She'd heard a rumor that her
mother had been moved to a different camp. So, so. Present a pawn, withdraw the queen: Weissmann, waiting to
see how Pökler would react. This time he had gone too
far: Pökler laced up his shoes and calmly enough went out
looking for the SS man, cornered him in his office, denounced him before a panel of kindly, dim governmental
figures, the speech eloquently climaxing as he threw chessboard and pieces all into Weissmann's arrogantly blinking
face.... Pökler's impetuous, yes, a rebel—but Generaldirektor it's his kind of fire and honestly we *need*—

The child had suddenly come into his arms, to kiss him
again. For free. Pökler forgot his troubles and held her to
his heart for a long time, without speaking....

But that night in the cubicle, only breathing—no moon-
wishes this year—from her cot, he was awake wondering,
one daughter one impostor? same daughter twice? two im-
postors? Beginning to work out the combinations for a third
visit, a fourth.... Weissmann, those behind him, had
thousands of these children available. As the years passed,
as they grew more nubile, would Pökler even come to fall
in love with one—would she reach the king's row that way
and become a queen-substitute for lost, for forgotten Leni?
The Opponent knew that Pökler's suspicion would always
be stronger than any fears about real incest.... They
could make up new rules, to complicate the game indefinitely. How could any man as empty as Pökler felt
that night be flexible enough for that?

Kot—it was ridiculous—hadn't he seen her go by from
every angle in their old city rooms? Carried, asleep, crying,
crawling, laughing, hungry. Often he had come home too
tired to make it to the bed, and had lain on the floor with
his head under the one wood table, curled, beaten, wondering if he could even sleep. The first time Ilse noticed, she
crawled over and sat staring at him for a long time. She
had never seen him still, horizontal, with his eyes shut....
He drifted toward sleep. Ilse leaned over and bit him in
the leg, as she bit crusts of bread, cigarettes, shoes, anything that might be food. —I'm your father. —You're

inert and edible. Pökler screamed and rolled out of the
way. Ilse began to cry. He was too tired to want to think
about discipline. It was Leni finally who calmed her down.

He knew all Ilse's cryings, her first attempts at words,
the colors of her shit, the sounds and shapes that brought
her tranquillity. He ought to know if this child was his
own or not. But he didn't. Too much had happened between. Too much history and dream. . . .

Next morning his group leader handed Pökler a furlough
chit, and a paycheck with a vacation bonus. No travel
restrictions, but a time limit of two weeks. Translation:
Will you come back? He packed some things, and they got
on the train for Stettin. The sheds and assembly buildings,
the concrete monoliths and steel gantries that were the
map of his life flared backward, shadowing into great
purplish chunks, isolated across the marshland one from
another, in parallax away. Would he dare not to come
back? Could he think so far ahead?

He'd left their destination up to Ilse. She chose Zwölfkinder. It was the end of summer, nearly the end of peacetime. The children knew what was coming. Playing refugee, they crowded the railway carriages, quieter, more
solemn than Pökler had expected. He had to keep fighting
an urge to start babbling each time Ilse's eyes turned from
the window toward his own. He saw the same thing in all
their eyes: he was strange to them, to her, and growing
stranger, and he knew of no way to reverse it. . . .

In a corporate State, a place must be made for innocence, and its many uses. In developing an official version of innocence, the culture of childhood has proven invaluable. Games, fairy-tales, legends from history, all the
paraphernalia of make-believe can be adapted and even
embodied in a physical place, such as at Zwölfkinder.
Over the years it had become a children's resort, almost a
spa. If you were an adult, you couldn't get inside the city
limits without a child escort. There was a child mayor, a
child city council of twelve. Children picked up the papers,
fruit peelings and bottles you left in the street, children
gave you guided tours through the Tierpark, the Hoard
of the Nibelungen, cautioning you to silence during the
impressive re-enactment of Bismarck's elevation, at the
spring equinox of 1871, to prince and imperial chancellor

. . . child police reprimanded you if you were caught alone, without your child accompanying. Whoever carried on the real business of the town—it could not have been children—they were well hidden.

A late summer, a late, retrospective blooming. . . . Birds flew everywhere, the sea warmed, the sun shone on into the evenings. Random children took your shirt cuff by mistake, and trudged along for minutes before discovering you were not their adult, and then wandered off with backward smiles. The Glass Mountain twinkled rose and white in the hot sun, the elf king and his queen made a royal progress every noon with a splendid retinue of dwarves and sprites, handing out cakes, ices and candies. At each intersection or square, bands played—marches, folk-dances, hot jazz, Hugo Wolf. Children went streaming like confetti. At the drinking fountains, where soda water sparkled deep inside the fanged mouths of dragons, of wild lions and tigers, the queues of children waited, each for his moment of danger, leaning halfway into the shadow, into the smell of wet cement and old water, into the mouth of the beast, to drink. In the sky, the tall ferris wheel spun. From Peenemünde they had come 280 kilometers, which was to be, coincidentally, the operational range of the A4.

Among all there was to choose from, Wheel, myths, jungle animals, clowns, Ilse found her way to the Antarctic Panorama. Two or three boys hardly older than she wandered through the imitation wilderness, bundled up in sealskins, constructing cairns and planting flags in the August humidity. Watching them made Pökler sweat. A few "sled dogs" lay suffering in the shade of the dirty papier-mâché sastrugi, on plaster snow that had begun to crack. A hidden projector threw images of the aurora on a white scrim. Half a dozen stuffed penguins also dotted the landscape.

"So—you want to live at the South Pole. Have you given up so easily on"—*Kot*—idiot, that was a slip—"on the Moon?" He'd been good up till then about cross-examining. He couldn't afford to know who she was. In the false Antarctic, in ignorance of what had attracted her there, uneasy and dripping sweat, he waited for her answer.

She, or They, let him off. "Oh," with a shrug, "who wants to live on the Moon?" They never brought it up again.

Back at their hotel, they were handed the key by an eight-year-old desk clerk, rose in a whining elevator run by a uniformed child, to a room still warm from the day's heat. She closed the door, took off her hat and scaled it over to her bed. Pökler collapsed on his own bed. She came over to take off his shoes.

"Papi," gravely unlacing, "may I sleep next to you tonight?" One of her hands had come lightly to rest on the beginning of his bare calf. Their eyes met for half a second. A number of uncertainties shifted then for Pökler and locked into sense. To his shame, his first feeling was pride. He hadn't known he was so vital to the program. Even in this initial moment, he was seeing it from Their side—every quirk goes in the dossier, gambler, foot-fetishist or soccer fan, it's all important, it can all be used. Right now we have to keep them happy, or at least neutralize the foci of their unhappiness. You may not understand what their work really is, not at the level of the data, but you're an administrator after all, a leader, your job is to get results . . . Pökler, now, has mentioned a "daughter." Yes, yes we know it's disgusting, one never can tell what they have locked up in there with those equations, but we must all put off our judgments for now, there'll be time after the war to get back to the Pöklers and their dirty little secrets. . . .

He hit her upside the head with his open hand, a loud and terrible blow. That took care of his anger. Then, before she could cry or speak, he had dragged her up on the bed next to him, her dazed little hands already at the buttons of his trousers, her white frock already pulled above her waist. She had been wearing nothing at all underneath, nothing all day . . . *how I've wanted you,* she whispered as paternal plow found its way into filial furrow . . . and after hours of amazing incest they dressed in silence, and crept out into the leading edge of faintest flesh dawn, everything they would ever need packed inside her flowered bag, past sleeping children doomed to the end of summer, past monitors and railway guards, down at last to the water and the fishing boats, to a

fatherly old sea-dog in a braided captain's hat, who wel-
comed them aboard and stashed them below decks, where
she snuggled down in the bunk as they got under way
and sucked him for hours while the engine pounded, till
the Captain called, "Come on up, and take a look at your
new home!" Gray and green, through the mist, it was
Denmark. "Yes, they're a free people here. Good luck to
both of you!" The three of them, there on deck, stood
hugging. . . .

No. What Pökler did was choose to believe she wanted
comfort that night, wanted not to be alone. Despite Their
game, Their palpable evil, though he had no more reason
to trust "Ilse" than he trusted Them, by an act not of faith,
not of courage but of conservation, he chose to believe
that. Even in peacetime, with unlimited resources, he
couldn't have proven her identity, not beyond the knife-
edge of zero tolerance his precision eye needed. The years
Ilse would have spent between Berlin and Peenemünde
were so hopelessly tangled, for all of Germany, that no
real chain of events could have been established for sure,
not even Pökler's hunch that somewhere in the State's oversize paper brain a specific perversity had been assigned
him and dutifully stored. For every government agency,
the Nazi Party set up a duplicate. Committees fissioned,
merged, generated spontaneously, disappeared. No one
would show a man his dossier—

It was not, in fact, even clear to him that he had made
a choice. But it was in those humming moments in the
room smelling of a summer day, whose light no one had lit
yet, with her round straw hat a frail moon on the bed-
spread, lights of the Wheel slowly pouring red and green
over and over outside in the dark, and a group of school-
boys singing in the street a refrain from before their time,
their sold-out and cruelly handled time—Juch-heierasas-sal
o tempo-tempo-ra!—that board and pieces and patterns at
least all did come clear for him, and Pökler knew that
while he played, this would have to be Ilse—truly his
child, truly as he could make her. It was the real moment
of conception, in which, years too late, he became her
father.

Through the rest of the furlough, they strolled about
Zwölfkinder, always hand in hand. Lanterns swaying from

the trunks of elephants' heads on top of tall pillars lit their
way . . . over spidery bridges looking down at snow-leop-
ards, apes, hyenas . . . along the miniature railway, between
the corrugated pipe legs of steel-mesh dinosaurs, down to
the patch of African desert where every two hours exactly
the treacherous natives attacked an encampment of General von Trotha's brave men in blue, all the parts played
by exuberant boys, and a great patriotic favorite with
children of all ages . . . up on the giant Wheel so naked, so
void of grace, there for only the clear mission: to lift and
to frighten. . . .

On their last night—though he didn't know it, for they
would take her as abruptly and invisibly as before—they
stood looking in again at stuffed penguins and false snow,
and around them the artificial aurora flickered.

"Next year," squeezing her hand, "we'll come back
here, if you like."

"Oh yes. Every year, Papi."

Next day she was gone, taken back into the coming war,
leaving Pökler alone in a country of children, to go back
to Peenemünde after all, alone. . . .

So it has gone for the six years since. A daughter a year,
each one about a year older, each time taking up nearly
from scratch. The only continuity has been her name, and
Zwölfkinder, and Pökler's love—love something like the
persistence of vision, for They have used it to create for
him the moving image of a daughter, flashing him only
these summertime frames of her, leaving it to him to build
the illusion of a single child . . . what would the time scale
matter, a 24th of a second or a year (no more, the engineer thought, than in a wind-tunnel, or an oscillograph
whose turning drum you could speed or slow at will . . .)?

Outside the Peenemünde wind-tunnel, Pökler has come
to stand at night, next to the the great sphere, 40 feet high,
listening to the laboring pumps as they evacuate the air
from the white sphere, five minutes of growing void—
then one terrific gasp: 20 seconds of supersonic flow . . .
then the fall of the shutter, and the pumps starting up
again . . . he has listened, and taken it to imply his own
cycle of shuttered love, growing empty over the year for
two weeks in August, engineered with the same care. He
has smiled, and drunk toasts, and traded barracks humor

with Major Weissmann, while all the time, behind the music and the giggling, he could hear the flesh of pieces moved in darkness and winter across the marshes and mountain chains of the board . . . watched run after run the Halbmodelle results out of the wind tunnel, showing how the net normal force would be distributed over the Rocket's length, for hundreds of different Mach numbers—seen the true profile of the Rocket warped and travestied, a rocket of wax, humped like a dolphin at around caliber 2, necking down toward the tail which was then stretched up, impossibly, in a high point with a lower shoulder aft of it—and seen how his own face might be plotted, not in light but in net forces acting upon it from the flow of Reich and coercion and love it moved through . . . and known that it must suffer the same degradation, as death will warp face to skull. . . .

In '43, because he was away at Zwölfkinder, Pökler missed the British air raid on Peenemünde. Returning to the station, as soon as he came in sight of the "foreign workers' " quarters at Trassenheide razed and smashed, bodies still being dug from the wreckage, a terrible suspicion began, and would not be put down. Weissmann was *saving* him for something: some unique destiny. Somehow the man had known the British would bomb that night, known even in '39, and so arranged the tradition of an August furlough, year after year but all toward protecting Pökler from the one bad night. Not quite balanced . . . a bit paranoid, yes, yes . . . but the thought purred on in his brain, and he felt himself turning to stone.

Smoke seeped from the earth, charred trees fell, as he watched, at no more than a breath from the direction of the sea. Powdered dust rose up at every footfall, turning clothes white, faces to masks of dust. The farther up the peninsula, the less damage. A strange gradient of death and wreckage, south to north, in which the poorest and most helpless got it worst—as, indeed, the gradient was to run east to west, in London a year later when the rockets began to fall. Most of the casualties had been among "foreign workers," a euphemism for civilian prisoners brought in from countries under German occupation. The wind tunnel and the measuring house were untouched, the pre-production works only slightly damaged. Pökler's colleagues were outside Scientist Housing, which had been hit—phantoms moving in morning fog still not burned off, washing up in buckets of beer because the water was still out. They stared at Pökler, failing, enough of them, to keep accusation out of their faces.

"I wish I could have missed this."

"Dr. Thiel is dead."

"How was fairyland, Pökler?"

"I'm sorry," he said. It wasn't his fault. The others were silent: some watching, some still in shock from the night.

Mondaugen showed up then. "We're exhausted. Could you come with me to Pre-production? A lot has to be sorted out, we need a hand." They shuffled along, each in his own dust-cloud. "It was terrible," Mondaugen said. "All of us have been under some strain."

"They sounded like *I'd* done it."

"You feeling guilty because you weren't here?"

"I'm wondering why I wasn't here. That's all."

"Because you were in Zwölfkinder," replied the enlightened one. "Don't invent complications."

He tried not to. That was Weissmann's job, wasn't it, Weissmann was the sadist, he had responsibility for coming up with new game-variations, building toward a maximum cruelty in which Pökler would be unlaid to nerves vessels and tendons, every last convolution of brain flattened out in the radiance of the black candles, nowhere to shelter, entirely his master's possession . . . the moment in which he is defined to himself at last. . . . This is what Pökler could feel waiting now, a room he'd never seen, a ceremony he couldn't memorize in advance. . . .

There were false alarms. Pökler was almost sure once during the winter, during the test series at Blizna. They had moved east into Poland, to fire over land. The shots from Peenemünde were all out to sea, and there'd been no way to observe the re-entry of the A4. Blizna was almost exclusively an SS project: part of Maj.-Gen. Kammler's empire-building. The Rocket at that point was plagued by an airburst problem in its terminal phase—the vehicle blew apart before reaching the target. Everyone had an idea. It might be an overpressure in the liquid-oxygen tank. Perhaps, because the Rocket coming down was lighter by 10 tons of fuel and oxidizer, the shift in the center of

gravity was making it unstable. Or perhaps the insulation
on the alcohol tank was at fault, somehow allowing residual fuel to be burned on re-entry. This was Pökler's
reason for being there. By then he was no longer in the
propulsion group, or even working as a designer—he was
in the Materials office, expediting the procurement of
various plastics for insulation, shock absorption, gasketry—
exciting stuff. The orders to Blizna were strange enough to
be Weissmann's work: the day Pökler went out to sit in
the Polish meadows at the exact spot where the Rocket
was supposed to come down, he was certain.

Green rye and low hills for miles all around. Pökler was
by a small trench, in the Sarnaki target area, pointing his
binoculars south toward Blizna like everybody else: waiting. Erwartung in the crosshairs, with the just-sprung rye
blowing, its gentler nap being brushed up by the wind . . .
look down at this countryside, down through Rocket-miles
of morning space: the many shades of forest green, Polish
farmhouses white and brown, dark eels of rivers catching
the sun at their curves . . . and at the very center down
there, in the holy X, Pökler, crucified, invisible at first look,
but in a moment . . . *now* beginning to resolve as the fall
gathers momentum—

But how can he believe in its reality up there? Insects
whine, the sun is almost warm, he can gaze off at the red
earth and millions of blowing stalks, and fall nearly into a
light trance: in shirtsleeves, with his bony knees pointing
up, the gray suit jacket wrinkled years beyond last pressing
bundled under his ass to soak up the dew. The others
he came out with are dotted here about Ground Zero,
blithe Nazi buttercups—binoculars sway from slate-colored
horsehide straps around their necks, the Askania crew
fuss with their equipment, and one of the SS liaison men
(Weissmann isn't here) keeps looking at his watch, then
at the sky, then the watch, the crystal becoming, in brief
flashes on/off, a nacreous circle binding together the hour
and the fleecy sky.

Pökler scratches at a graying 48-hour beard, bites at lips
very chapped, as if he has spent most of the late winter
outside: he has a winter look. Around his eyes, over the
years, has grown a ruinous system of burst capillaries,
shadows, folds, crowsfeet, a ground that by now has

gathered in the simple, direct eyes of his younger and
poorer days . . . no. Something was in them, even then,
something others saw and knew they could use, and
found how to. Something Pökler missed. He's spent enough
of his life looking into mirrors. He really ought to remember. . . .

The airburst, if it happens, will be in visual range.
Abstractions, math, models are fine, but when you're down
to it and everybody's hollering for a fix, this is what you
do: you go and sit exactly on the target with indifferent
shallow trenches for shelter, and you watch it in the silent
firebloom of its last few seconds, and see what you will
see. Chances are astronomically against a perfect hit, of
course, that is why one is safest at the center of the
target area. Rockets are supposed to be like artillery shells,
they disperse about the aiming point in a giant ellipse—
the Ellipse of Uncertainty. But Pökler, though trusting as
much as any scientist in uncertainty, is not feeling too secure
here. It is after all his own personal ass whose quivering
sphincter is centered right on Ground Zero. And there is
more to this than ballistics. There is Weissmann. Any number of chemists and materials people know as much about
insulation as Pökler . . . why should he have been picked,
unless . . . somewhere in his brain now two foci sweep together and become one . . . zero ellipse . . . a single point . . .
a live warhead, secretly loaded, special bunkers for everyone else . . . yes that's what he wants . . . all tolerances in the
guidance cooperating toward a perfect shot, right on top
of Pökler . . . ah, Weissmann, your end game lacks finesse—
but there were never spectators and judges not in all this
time, and who ever said the end could not be this brutal?
Paranoia has rushed Pökler, drowned him to the temples
and scalp. He may have shit, he can't tell. His pulse thuds
in his neck. His hands and feet ache. The black-suited
blond enforcers look on. Their metal insignia twinkle. Low
hillsides lie under early sun. All the field glasses stare
south. The Aggregat is on route, nothing can be changed.
No one else here cares for the penetralia of the moment,
or last mysteries: there have been too many rational
years. The paper has piled too thick and far. Pökler cannot
reconcile, not really, his dream of the perfectly victimized
with the need bred into him to take care of business—nor

see how these may be one and the same. The A4 must, after all, go out in the field very soon, this failure rate *must* be brought down, and so those who've come are here, and if there is a massive failure of vision this morning in the Polish meadow, if no one, not even the most paranoid, can see anything at all beyond the stated Requirements, certainly it's not unique to this time, this place, where the eyes cupped against the black binoculars are looking only for the day's "reluctant virgin"—as the witty rocketeers have dubbed their problem rockets—to announce herself . . . to note where, forward to aft, the trouble may be, the shape of a vapor trail, the sound of the burst, anything that might help. . . .

At Sarnaki, as the records tell it, the rocket came down that day with the usual double-blast, a streak of white condensation in the blue sky: another premature airburst. Steel fragments fell, a hundred feet away from the Zero point, slashing into the rye like hail. Pökler saw the explosion, no more than anyone else. He was never sent out again. The SS people watched him get to his feet, and stretch, and slowly move off with the others. Weissmann would get his report. New varieties of torture would be coming.

But inside Pökler's life, on no record but his soul, his poor harassed German soul, the time base has lengthened, and slowed: the Perfect Rocket is still up there, still descending. He still waits—even now, alone at Zwölfkinder waiting for "Ilse," for this summer's return, and with it an explosion that will take him by surprise. . . .

In the spring, when the winds at Peenemünde had shifted around to the southwest, and the first birds were back, Pökler was transferred to the underground factory at Nordhausen, in the Harz. Work at Peenemünde, after the British raid, had begun to fall off. The plan—again Kammler's—was now to disperse testing and production around Germany, to prevent another and possibly fatal Allied attack. Pökler's duties at the Mittelwerke were routine: materials, procurement. He slept in a bunk next to a wall of dynamited stone painted white, with a bulb over his head burning all night long. He dreamed that the bulb was a representative of Weissmann, a creature whose bright filament was its soul. They held long dream-dia-

logues whose substance Pökler could never remember. The
bulb was explaining the plot to him in detail—it was
more grand and sweeping than Pökler could ever have
imagined, it seemed many nights to be purely music, his
consciousness moving through the soundscape at bay, observing, compliant, still precariously safe, but not for long.

At the time there were rumors of an estrangement growing between Weissmann and his "monster," Enzian. The
Schwarzkommando by then had grown away from the SS
structure, much as the SS itself had from the German
Army. Their power now lay not in absolute weaponry but
in information and expertise. Pökler was happy to hear
that Weissmann was having his troubles, but at a loss how
to use it to any advantage. When his orders to Nordhausen
had come through, he'd had a flash of despair. Was the
game adjourned then? He might never see Ilse again. But
a memo had come, telling him to report to Weissmann in
his office.

The hair at Weissmann's temples was graying and dis-
arranged. Pökler saw that one earpiece of his glasses was
held on with a paper clip. His desk was a litter of documents, reports, reference books. It was a surprise to see
him looking less diabolical than harassed as any civil
servant under pressure. His eyes were aimed in Pökler's
direction, but the lenses distorted them.

"You understand that this transfer to Nordhausen is
voluntary."

Pökler understood, with relief and two seconds of actual
love for his protector, that the game was still on. "It will
be something new."

"Yes?" Partly a challenge, but partly interested too.

"Production. We've been so involved here with the re-
search-and-development end. It's not a weapon for us so
much as a 'flying laboratory,' as Dr. Thiel said once—"

"Do you miss Dr. Thiel?"

"Yes. He wasn't in my section. I didn't know him well."

"A shame he got caught in the raid. We all move in an
Ellipse of Uncertainty, don't we?"

Pökler allowed himself a look at the cluttered desk,
quick enough to be taken either for nervousness or as a
comeback—Weissmann, looks like you have your own
Ellipse all right—"Oh, I don't have the time usually to
worry. At least the Mittelwerke is underground."

"The tactical sites won't be."

"Do you think I might be sent—"

Weissmann shrugged and favored Pökler with a big fake smile. "My dear Pökler, how can anyone predict where you'll go? We'll see how it all develops."

Later, in the Zone, with his guilt become a sensual thing, prickling at his eyes and membranes like an allergy, it would seem to Pökler that he could not, even by that day in Weissmann's office, have been ignorant of the truth. That he had known the truth with his senses, but allowed all the evidence to be misfiled where it wouldn't upset him. Known everything, but refrained from the only act that could have redeemed him. He should have throttled Weissmann where he sat, corrugations of skinny throat and Adam's apple sliding under Pökler's palms, thick eyeglasses sliding off as the weak little eyes go blearing helplessly after their final darkener. . . .

Pökler helped with his own blindness. He knew about Nordhausen, and the Dora camp: he could *see*—the starved bodies, the eyes of the foreign prisoners being marched to work at four in the morning in the freezing cold and darkness, the shuffling thousands in their striped uniforms. He had known too, all along, that Ilse was living in a re-education camp. But it wasn't till August, when the furlough arrived as usual in its blank kraft envelope, and Pökler rode northward through the gray kilometers of a Germany he no longer recognized, bombed and burned, the wartime villages and rainy purple heath, and found her at last waiting in the hotel lobby at Zwölfkinder with the same darkness in her eyes (how had he missed it till now? such swimming orbits of pain) that he could finally put the two data together. For months, while her father across the wire or walls did his dutiful hackwork, she had been prisoner only a few meters away from him, beaten, perhaps violated. . . . If he must curse Weissmann, then he must also curse himself. Weissmann's cruelty was no less resourceful than Pökler's own engineering skill, the gift of Daedalus that allowed him to put as much labyrinth as required between himself and the inconveniences of caring. They had sold him convenience, so much of it, all on credit, and now They were collecting.

Trying, a bit late for it, to open himself to the pain he should have been feeling, he questioned her now. Did she

know the name of her camp? Yes, Ilse confirmed—or was
told to answer—that it was Dora. The night before she
left to come here she'd seen a hanging. Evening was the
hour for the hangings. Did he want to hear about it? Did
he want to hear about it. . . .

 She was very hungry. They spent the first few days eating, whatever Zwölfkinder had to sell. There was less than
the year before, and it was much more expensive. But the
enclave of innocence still enjoyed a high priority, so there
was something.

 Not so many children this year, though. The engineer
and girl had the place practically to themselves. The Wheel
and most of the other rides stood motionless. Petrol shortage, a child guard informed them. Luftwaffe flights roared
overhead. Nearly every night the sirens cried out, and
they watched the searchlights come on in Wismar and in
Lübeck, and sometimes heard the bombs. What was Pökler
doing in this dream world, this lie? His country waited to
be crushed between invaders from east and west: back at
Nordhausen the hysteria had risen to epic scale, as the
first rockets were about to go out into the field, about to
fulfill engineering prophecies old as peacetime. Why, at
this critical moment, had they let Pökler off? Who else
these days was getting furloughs? And what was "Ilse"
doing here, wasn't she supposed to be too old by now for
fairy tales? her new breasts so visible now beneath her
frock, her eyes so nearly empty drifting without real interest toward random boys destined for the Volkssturm,
older boys, no more interested in her. They dreamed of
their orders, of colossal explosions and death—if they even
saw her it was sidewise, sly . . . *her Father will tame her
. . . her teeth will bite the pole . . .* someday I will have a
herd of them for myself . . . but first I must find my Captain . . . somewhere out in the War . . . first they must deliver me from this little place. . . .

 Who was that, going by just then—who was the slender
boy who flickered across her path, so blond, so white he
was nearly invisible in the hot haze that had come to
settle over Zwölfkinder? Did she see him, and did she
know him for her own second shadow? She was conceived
because her father saw a movie called *Alpdrücken* one
night and got a hardon. Pökler in his horny staring had

missed the Director's clever Gnostic symbolism in the lighting scheme of the two shadows, Cain's and Abel's. But Ilse, some Ilse, has persisted beyond her cinema mother, beyond film's end, and so have the shadows of shadows. In the Zone, all will be moving under the Old Dispensation, inside the Cainists' light and space: not out of any precious Göllerei, but because the Double Light was always there, outside all film, and that shucking and jiving moviemaker was the only one around at the time who happened to notice it and use it, although in deep ignorance, then and now, of what he was showing the nation of starers. . . . So that summer Ilse passed herself by, too fixed at some shadowless interior noon to mark the intersection, or to care.

She and Pökler hardly talked this time: it was their mutest holiday together. She walked broodful, her head down, her hair hooding her face, brown legs kicking at refuse the undermanned garbage detail hadn't picked up. Was it her time of life, or did she resent being under orders to spend time with a dull and aging engineer at a place she'd outgrown years ago?

"You don't really want to be here, do you?" They sat by a polluted stream, throwing bread to ducks. Pökler's stomach was upset from ersatz coffee and tainted meat. His head ached.

"It's here or the camp," her face stubbornly aside. "I don't really want to be anywhere. I don't care."

"Ilse."

"Do you like it here? Do you want to be back under your mountain? Do you talk to the elves, Franz?"

"No, I don't *enjoy* it where I am"—*Franz?*—"but I have, I have my job. . . ."

"Yes. So do I. My job is being a prisoner. I'm a professional inmate. I know how to get favors, who to steal from, how to inform, how to—"

Any minute she'd say it . . . "Please—*stop it* Ilse—" this time Pökler got hysterical and did slap her. Ducks surprised at the sharp report about-faced and waddled away. Ilse gazed back at him, no tears, eyes room after room strung into the shadows of an old prewar house he could wander for years, hearing voices and finding doors, hunting himself, his life as it might have been. . . . He could not bear indifference from her. Close to losing control, Pökler committed then his act of courage. He quit the game.

"If you don't want to come back next year," even though "next year" meant so little by that point in Germany, "you don't have to. It would be better if you didn't."

She knew immediately what he'd done. She pulled one knee up, and rested her forehead there, and thought. "I'll come back," she said very quietly.

"You?"

"Yes. Really."

He did, then, let everything go, every control. He veered into the wind of his long isolation, shuddering terribly. He cried. She took his hands. The floating ducks watched. The sea cooled under the hazy sun. An accordion played somewhere back in the town. From behind the decaying mythical statues, sentenced children shouted to each other. Summer ended.

Back at the Mittelwerke he tried, and kept trying, to get into the Dora camp and find Ilse. It didn't matter any more about Weissmann. The SS guards each time were courteous, understanding, impossible to get past.

The work load now was incredible. Pökler was getting less than two hours' sleep a day. News of the war reached under the mountain only as rumors and shortages. Procurement philosophy had been "triangular"—three possible sources for the same part, in case one one was destroyed. Depending what didn't come from where, or how late it was, you knew which factories had been bombed, which rail connections taken out. Toward the end you had to try and fabricate many of the components locally.

When Pökler had time to think, he was met by the growing enigma of Weissmann's silence. To provoke him, or the memory of him, Pökler went out of his way to talk to officers in Major Förschner's security detail, looking for news. None of them responded to Pökler as anything more than a nuisance. They'd heard rumors that Weissmann was no longer here but in Holland, in command of his own rocket battery. Enzian had dropped out of sight, along with many key Schwarzkommando. Pökler grew more and more certain that this time the game was really over, that the war had caught them all, given new life-death priorities and no more leisure for torturing a minor engineer. He was able to relax some, move through the day's routine, wait for the end, even allow himself to hope that the thousands in Dora would soon be free, among them Ilse, some acceptable Ilse. . . .

But in the spring, he did see Weissmann again. He woke from a dream of a gentle Zwölfkinder that was also Nordhausen, a city of elves producing toy moon-rockets, and there was Weissmann's face at the edge of his bunk, watching him. He seemed to have aged ten years, and Pökler hardly recognized him.

"There isn't much time," Weissmann whispered. "Come with me."

They moved through the white, sleepless bustle of the tunnels, Weissmann walking slowly and stiffly, both men silent. In one of the office spaces, half a dozen others were waiting, along with some SS and SD. "We've already obtained permission from your groups," Weissmann said, "to release you for work on a special project. This will be the highest possible security. You'll be billeted separately, eat separately, and speak to no one who is not present in this room." They all looked around to see who that might be. No one they knew. They looked back at Weissmann.

He wanted a modification worked into one rocket, only one. Its serial number had been removed, and five zeros painted in. Pökler knew immediately that this was what Weissmann had been saving him for: this was to be his "special destiny." It made no sense to him: he had to develop a plastic fairing, of a certain size, with certain insulating properties, for the propulsion section of the rocket. The propulsion engineer was the busiest on the project, rerouting steam and fuel lines, relocating hardware. Whatever the new device was, nobody saw it. According to the rumor, it was being produced elsewhere, and was nicknamed the Schwarzgerät, because of the high secrecy surrounding it. Even the weight was classified. They were through inside of two weeks, and the "Vorrichtung für die Isolierung" was on its way to the field. Pökler reported back to his regular supervisor, and the routine went on as before. He never saw Weissmann again.

The first week in April, with American units supposed

to be arriving at any moment, most of the engineers were
packing, collecting addresses of co-workers, drinking farewell toasts, drifting through the emptying bays. There was
a graduation feeling in the air. It was hard not to whistle
"Gaudeamus igitur." Suddenly the cloistered life was about
to come to an end.

A young SS guard, one of the last to leave, found
Pökler in the dusty cafeteria, handed him an envelope,
and left without a word. It was the usual furlough form,
superseded now by the imminent death of the Government—and a travel permit to Zwölfkinder. Where the
dates should have been, someone had written, almost
illegibly, "after hostilities end." On the back, in the same
hand (Weissmann's?) a note to Pökler. *She has been released. She will meet you there.* He understood that this
was payment for the retrofit work he'd done on the 00000.
How long had Weissmann been keeping him deliberately
on ice, all so he'd have a plastics man he could depend
on, when the time came?

On the last day, Pökler walked out the south end of the
main tunnels. Lorries were everywhere, all engines idling,
farewell in the spring air, tall trees sunlit green on the
mountainsides. The Obersturmbannführer was not at his
post when Pökler went into Dora. He was not looking for
Ilse, or not exactly. He may have felt that he ought to
look, finally. He was not prepared. He did not know. Had
the data, yes, but did not know, with senses or heart. . . .

The odors of shit, death, sweat, sickness, mildew, piss,
the breathing of Dora, wrapped him as he crept in staring
at the naked corpses being carried out now that America
was so close, to be stacked in front of the crematoriums,
the men's penises hanging, their toes clustering white and
round as pearls . . . each face so perfect, so individual; the
lips stretched back into death-grins, a whole silent audience
caught at the punch line of the joke . . . and the living,
stacked ten to a straw mattress, the weakly crying, coughing, losers. . . . All his vacuums, his labyrinths, had been
the other side of this. While he lived, and drew marks on
paper, this invisible kingdom had kept on, in the darkness
outside . . . all this time. . . . Pökler vomited. He cried some.
The walls did not dissolve—no prison wall ever did, not
from tears, not at this finding, on every pallet, in every

cell, that the faces are ones he knows after all, and holds
dear as himself, and cannot, then, let them return to that
silence. . . . But what can he ever do about it? How can
he ever keep them? Impotence, mirror-rotation of sorrow,
works him terribly as runaway heartbeating, and with
hardly any chances left him for good rage, or for turning. . . .

Where it was darkest and smelled the worst, Pökler
found a woman lying, a random woman. He sat for half
an hour holding her bone hand. She was breathing. Before he left, he took off his gold wedding ring and put it
on the woman's thin finger, curling her hand to keep it
from sliding off. If she lived, the ring would be good for
a few meals, or a blanket, or a night indoors, or a ride
home. . . .

□

Back to Berlin, with a terrific thunderstorm blowing over
the city. Margherita has brought Slothrop to a rickety
wood house near the Spree, in the Russian sector. A
burned-out Königstiger tank guards the entrance, its paint
scorched, treads mangled and blasted off of the drive
sprocket, its dead monster 88 angled down to point at the
gray river, hissing and spiculed with the rain.

Inside are bats nesting in the rafters, remains of beds
with a moldy smell, broken glass and bat shit on the bare
wood floor, windows boarded up except where the stove
is vented through because the chimney's down. On a rocking chair lies a moleskin coat, a taupe cloud. Paint from
some long-ago artist is still visible over the floor in wrinkled splashes of aged magenta, saffron, steel blue, reverse
deformations of paintings whose whereabouts are unknown.
Back in a corner hangs a tarnished mirror, birds and flowers painted in white all around its frame, reflecting Margherita and Slothrop and the rain out the open door. Part
of the ceiling, blown away when the King Tiger died, is
covered now with soggy and stained cardboard posters all
of the same cloaked figure in the broad-brimmed hat, with
its legend DER FEIND HÖRT ZU. Water drips through in half
a dozen places.

Greta lights a kerosene lamp. It warms the rainlight with a handful of yellow. Slothrop builds a fire in the stove while Margherita ducks down under the house, where it turns out there's a great stash of potatoes. Jeepers, Slothrop hasn't seen a potato for months. There's onions in a sack too, and even wine. She cooks, and they both sit there just pigging on those spuds. Later, without paraphernalia or talk, they fuck each other to sleep. But a few hours later Slothrop wakes up, and lies there wondering where he's going.

Well, to find that Säure Bummer, soon as this rain lets up, give the man his hashish. But what then? Slothrop and the S-Gerät and the Jamf/Imipolex mystery have grown to be strangers. He hasn't really thought about them for a while. Hmm, when *was* that? The day he sat with Säure in the café, smoking that reefer . . . oh, that was day before yesterday, wasn't it? Rain drips, soaking into the floor, and Slothrop perceives that he is losing his mind. If there is something comforting—religious, if you want—about paranoia, there is still also anti-paranoia, where nothing is connected to anything, a condition not many of us can bear for long. Well right now Slothrop feels himself sliding onto the anti-paranoid part of his cycle, feels the whole city around him going back roofless, vulnerable, uncentered as he is, and only pasteboard images now of the Listening Enemy left between him and the wet sky.

Either They have put him here for a reason, or he's just here. He isn't sure that he wouldn't, actually, rather have that *reason*. . . .

The rain lets up at midnight. He leaves Margherita to creep out in the cold city with his five kilos, having kept for himself the one Tchitcherine plundered from. Russian troops are singing in their billets. The salt ache of accordion music cries on in back of them. Drunks materialize, merry and pissing in the center grooves of cobbled alleys. Mud occupies some streets like flesh. Shell craters brim with rainwater, gleaming in the lights of midwatch work crews clearing debris. Shattered Biedermeier chair, mateless boot, steel eyeglass frame, dog collar (eyes at the edges of the twisting trail watching her sign, for blazing), wine cork, splintered broom, bicycle with one wheel missing, discarded copies of *Tägliche Rundschau*, chalcedony doorknob dyed blue long ago with ferrous ferrocyanide, scattered piano keys (all white, an octave on B to be exact—or H, in the German nomenclature—the notes of the rejected Locrian mode), the black and amber eye from some stuffed animal. . . . The strewn night. Dogs, spooked and shivering, run behind walls whose tops are broken like fever charts. Somewhere a gas leak warps for a minute into the death and after-rain smells. Ranks of blackened window-sockets run high up the sides of gutted apartment buildings. Chunks of concrete are held aloft by iron reinforcing rod that curls like black spaghetti, whole enormous heaps wiggling ominously overhead at your least passing brush by. . . . The smooth-faced Custodian of the Night hovers behind neutral eyes and smile, coiled and pale over the city, humming its hoarse lullabies. Young men spent the Inflation like this, alone in the street, no place to go into out of the black winters. Girls stayed up late on stoops or stitting on benches in lamplight by the rivers, waiting for business, but the young men had to walk by, ignored, hunching overpadded shoulders, money with no relation to anything it could buy, swelling, paper cancer in their billfolds. . . .

The Chicago Bar is being guarded outside by two of their descendants, kids in George Raft suits, many sizes too big, too many ever to grow into. One keeps coughing, in uncontrolled dying spasms. The other licks his lips and stares at Slothrop. Gunsels. When he mentions Säure Bummer's name, they move together in front of the door, shaking their heads. "Look, I'm supposed to deliver him a package."

"Don't know him."

"Can I leave a message?"

"He's not here." The cougher makes a lunge. Slothrop sweeps aside, gives him a quick veronica with his cape, sticks his foot out and trips the kid, who lies on the ground cursing, all tangled up in his long keychain, while his pardner goes pawing inside of his flapping suitcoat for what Slothrop surmises to be a sidearm, so him Slothrop kicks in the balls, and screaming "Fickt nicht mit der Raketemensch!" so they'll remember, kind of a hiyo Silver here, he flees into shadows, among the heaps of lumber, stone and earth.

He takes a trail he thinks Säure led them along the other night—keeps losing it, wandering into windowless mazes, tangles of barbed wire holidayed by the death-storms of last May, then into a strafed and pitted lorry-park he can't find his way out of for half an hour, a rolling acre of rubber, grease, steel, and spilled petrol, pieces of vehicles pointing at sky or earth no differently than in a peacetime American junkyard, fused into odd, brown *Saturday Evening Post* faces, except that they are not folksy so much as downright sinister . . . yes it's really the Saturday Evening *Post*, all right: they are the faces of the tricorned messengers coming in from out of the long pikes, down past the elms, Berkshire legends, travelers lost at the edge of the Evening. Come with a message. They unwrinkle, though, if you keep looking. They smooth out into timeless masks that speak their entire meaning, all of it right out on the surface.

It takes an hour to find Säure's cellar. But it's dark, and it's empty. Slothrop goes in, lights the light. Looks like either a bust or a gang war: printing press vanished, clothes tossed all around, and some very strange clothes at that, there is, for example, a wickerware suit, a *yellow* wickerware suit actually, articulating along armpit, elbow, knee and groinlines . . . oh, hmm, well, Slothrop runs a quick search of his own here, looking inside shoes, not really shoes, some of them, but footgloves with individual *toes*, not, however, sewn but *cast* from some unpleasant variegated resin such as bowling balls are made of . . . behind the peeling scraps of wallpaper, up in the rolled-up windowshade, among the hatchings of one or two phony Reichsmarks let spill by the looters—fifteen minutes of this, finding nothing . . . and the white object on the table watching him out of its staring shadows the whole time. He feels its stare before he spots it finally: a chesspiece two inches high. A white knight, molded out of plastic— a-and wait'll Slothrop finds out what *kind* of plastic, boy!

It's a horse's skull: the eye-sockets are hollow far down into the base. Inside one of them is a tightly rolled ciga-rette paper with a message from Säure. "Raketemensch! Der Springer asks me to give you this, his symbol. Keep it—by it shall he know you. I am at Jacobistrasse 12, 3er Hof, number 7. As B/4, Me. I?" Now "As B/4" was John Dillinger's old signoff. Everybody in the Zone this summer is using it. It indicates to people how you feel about certain things. . . .

Säure has included a map showing how to get to where he is. It's clear back in the British sector. Groaning, Slothrop pushes on back out in the mud and early morning. Around the Brandenburg Gate, a slight drizzle starts up again. Chunks of the Gate still lie around in the street—leaning shell-spalled up in the rainy sky, its silence is colossal, haggard as he pads by flanking it, the Chariot gleaming like coal, driven and still, it is the 30th century and swashbuckling Rocketman has just landed here to tour the ruins, the high-desert traces of an ancient European order. . . .

The Jacobistrasse and most of its quarter, slums, survived the street-fighting intact, along with its interior darkness, a masonry of shadows that will persist whether the sun is up or down. Number 12 is an entire block of tenements dating from before the Inflation, five or six stories and a mansarde, five or six Hinterhöfe nested one inside the other—boxes of a practical joker's gift, nothing in the center but a last hollow courtyard smelling of the same cooking and garbage and piss decades old. Ha, ha!

Slothrop moseys toward the first archway. Streetlight throws his caped shadow forward into a succession of these arches, each labeled with a faded paint name, Erster-Hof, Zweiter-Hof, Dritter-Hof u.s.w., shaped like the entrance to the Mittelwerke, parabolic, but more like an open mouth and gullet, joints of cartilage receding waiting, waiting to swallow . . . above the mouth two squared eyes, organdy whites, irises pitch black, stare him down . . . it laughs as it has for years without stopping, a blubbery and percussive laugh, like heavy china rolling or bumping under the water in the sink. A brainless giggle, just big old geometric me, nothin' t' be nervous about, c'mon in. . . . But the pain, the twenty, twentyfive years of pain paralyzed back in that long throat . . . old outcast, passive, addicted to survival now, waiting the years out, waiting for vulnerable saps like Slothrop here to expose itself to, laughing and crying and all in silence . . . paint peels from the Face, burned, diseased, long time dying and how can Slothrop just walk down into such a schizoid throat? Why, because it is what the guardian and potent Studio wants from him, natürlich: Slothrop is the character juvenile

tonight: what's kept him moving the whole night, him and
the others, the solitary Berliners who come out only in
these evacuated hours, belonging and going noplace, is
Their unexplained need to keep some marginal population
in these wan and preterite places, certainly for economic
though, who knows, maybe emotional reasons too. . . .

Säure's on the move too, though inside, prowling his
dreams. It looks like one big room, dark, full of tobacco
and kif smoke, crumbled ridges of plaster where walls
have been knocked out, straw pallets all over the floor, a
couple on one sharing a late, quiet cigarette, somebody
snoring on another . . . glossy Bosendorfer Imperial concert grand piano over which Trudi, wearing only an army
shirt, leans, a desperate muse, bare legs long and stretching, "*Please* come to bed Gustav, it'll be light soon." The
only answer is a peevish strumming among the lower
strings. Säure is on his side, quite still, a shrunken child,
face long worked at by leaps from second-story windows,
"first rubdowns" under gloved and womanish sergeants'
fists in the precinct stations, golden light in the afternoons
over the racetrack at Karlshorst, black light from the pavements of boulevards at night finely wrinkled like leather
stretched over stone, white light from satin dresses, glasses
stacked shining in front of bar mirrors, sans-serif Us at the
entrances to underground stations pointing in smooth
magnetism at the sky to bring down steel angels of exalta-
tion, of languid surrender—a face that in sleep is awe-
somely old, abandoned to its city's history. . . .

His eyes open—for an instant Slothrop is only shadowed
green folds, highlighted helmet, light-values still to be put
together. Then comes the sweet nodding smile, everything's
O.K., ja, howdy Rocketman, was ist los? Though the unregenerate old doper is not quite kindly enough to keep
from opening the ditty bag right away and peering in,
eyes like two pissholes in a snowbank, to see what he has.

"I thought you'd be in the slam or something."

Out with a little Moroccan pipe and Säure sets to flatten-
ing a fat crumb of hashish, humming the popular
rumba

A little something from Moroc-co,
With just a lit-tle bit of sock-o,

"Oh. Well, Springer blew the whistle on our counterfeiting operation. Kind of a little temporary hitch, you understand."

"I don't. You're supposed to be ace buddies."

"Not nearly. And he moves in higher orbits." It is something very complicated having to do with American yellow-seal scrip being discontinued in the Mediterranean theatre, with the reluctance of Allied forces here to accept Reichsmarks. Springer has a balance-of-payments problem too, and he's been speculating heavily in Sterling, and . . .

"But," sez Slothrop, "but, uh, where's my million marks, then, Emil?"

Säure sucks yellow flame flowing over the edge of the bowl. "It is gone where the woodbine twineth." Exactly what Jubilee Jim Fisk told the Congressional committee investigating his and Jay Gould's scheme to corner gold in 1869. The words are a reminder of Berkshire. With nothing more than that to go on, it occurs to Slothrop that Säure can't possibly be on the Bad Guys' side. Whoever They are, Their game has been to extinguish, not remind.

"Well, I can sell by the ounce from what I have," Slothrop reckons. "For occupation scrip. That's stable, isn't it?"

"You aren't angry. You really aren't."

"Rocketman is above all that shit, Emil."

"I have a surprise for you. I can get you the Schwarzgerät you asked about."

"You?"

"Springer. I asked him for you."

"Quit fooling. Really? Jeepers, that's so swell of you! How can I—"

"Ten thousand pounds sterling."

Slothrop loses a whole lungful of smoke. "Thanks Emil. . . ." He tells Säure about the run-in with Tchitcherine, and also about how he saw that Mickey Rooney.

"Rocketman! Spaceman! Welcome to our virgin planet. We only want to be left in some kind of peace here, O.K.? If you kill us, don't eat us. If you eat, don't digest. Let us come out the other end again, like diamonds in the shit of smugglers. . . ."

"Look"—remembering now the tip that that Geli gave him long ago in Nordhausen—"did your pal Springer mention he was hanging out in Swinemünde these days, anyplace like that?"

"Only the price of your instrument, Rak. Half the money in front. He said it would cost him at least that much to track it down."

"So he doesn't know where it is. Shit, he could have us all on the hook, bidding us up, hoping somebody's fool enough to front him some dough."

"Usually he delivers. You didn't have any trouble, did you, with that pass he forged?"

"Yaaahhh—" Oh. Oh, wow, aha, yes been meaning to ask you about this little Max Schlepzig item here— "Now then." But meantime Trudi has abandoned Gustav in the piano and comes over now to sit and rub her cheeks against the nap of Slothrop's trousers, dear naked legs whispering together, hair spilling, shirt half unbuttoned, and Säure has at some point rolled over and gone groaning back into sleep. Trudi and Slothrop retire to a mattress well away from the Bosendorfer. Slothrop settles back sighing, takes his helmet off and lets big sweet and saftig Trudi have her way with him. His joints are aching with rain and city wandering, he's half blitzed, Trudi is kissing him into an amazing comfort, it's an open house here, no favored senses or organs, all are equally at play . . . for possibly the first time in his life Slothrop does not feel obliged to have a hardon, which is just as well, because it does not seem to be happening with his penis as much as with . . . oh mercy, this is embarrassing but . . . well his *nose* actually seems to be erecting, the mucus beginning to flow yes a nasal hardon here and Trudi has certainly noticed all right, how could she help but . . . as she slides her lips over the throbbing snoot and sends a yard of torrid tongue up one of his nostrils . . . he can feel each pink taste-bud as she penetrates even farther, pulling aside the vestibule walls and nose-hair now to accommodate her head, then shoulders and . . . well she's halfway in, might as well—pulling up her knees, crawling using the hair for hand and footholds she is able to stand at last inside the great red hall which is quite pleasantly lit, no walls or ceiling she can really discern but rather a fading to seashell and springtime grades of pink in all directions. . . .

They fall asleep in the roomful of snoring, with low-pitched twangs out of the piano, and the rain's million-legged scuttle in the courtyards outside. When Slothrop wakes up it's at the height of the Evil Hour, Trudi is in some other room with Gustav rattling coffee cups, a tortoise-shell cat chases flies by the dirty window. Back beside the Spree, the White Woman is waiting for Slothrop. He isn't especially disposed to leave. Trudi and Gustav come in with coffee and half a reefer, and everybody sits around gabbing.

Gustav is a composer. For months he has been carrying on a raging debate with Säure over who is better, Beethoven or Rossini. Säure is for Rossini. "I'm not so much for Beethoven qua Beethoven," Gustav argues, "but as he represents the German dialectic, the incorporation of more and more notes into the scale, culminating with dodecaphonic democracy, where all notes get an equal hearing. Beethoven was one of the architects of musical freedom—he submitted to the demands of history, despite his deafness. While Rossini was retiring at the age of 36, womanizing and getting fat, Beethoven was living a life filled with tragedy and grandeur."

"So?" is Säure's customary answer to that one. "Which would you rather do? The point is," cutting off Gustav's usually indignant scream, "a person feels *good* listening to Rossini. All you feel like listening to Beethoven is going out and invading Poland. Ode to Joy indeed. The man didn't even have a sense of humor. I tell you," shaking his skinny old fist, "there is more of the Sublime in the snare-drum part to *La Gazza Ladra* than in the whole Ninth Symphony. With Rossini, the whole point is that lovers always get together, isolation is overcome, and like it or not that is the one great centripetal movement of the World. Through the machineries of greed, pettiness, and the abuse of power, *love occurs*. All the shit is transmuted to gold. The walls are breached, the balconies are scaled—listen!" It was a night in early May, and the final bombardment of Berlin was in progress. Säure had to shout his head off. "The Italian girl is in Algiers, the Barber's in the crockery, the magpie's stealing everything in sight! The World is rushing together. . . ."

This rainy morning, in the quiet, it seems that Gustav's German Dialectic has come to its end. He has just had the word, all the way from Vienna along some musicians' grapevine, that Anton Webern is dead. "Shot in May, by the Americans. Senseless, accidental if you believe in accidents—some mess cook from North Carolina, some late draftee with a .45 he hardly knew how to use, too late for WW II, but not for Webern. The excuse for raiding the house was that Webern's brother was in the black market. Who isn't? Do you know what kind of myth *that's* going to make in a thousand years? The young barbarians coming in to murder the Last European, standing at the far end of what'd been going on since Bach, an expansion of music's polymorphous perversity till all notes were truly equal at last. . . . Where was there to go after Webern? It was the moment of maximum freedom. It all had to come down. Another Götterdämmerung—"

"Young fool," Säure now comes cackling in from out in Berlin, trailing a pillowcase full of flowering tops just in from that North Africa. He's a mess—red-drenched eyes, fatbaby arms completely hairless, fly open and half the buttons gone, white hair and blue shirt both streaked with some green horrible scum. "Fell in a shell-hole. Here, quick, roll up some of this."

"What do you mean, 'young fool,'" inquires Gustav.

"I mean you and your musical mainstreams," cries Säure. "Is it finally over? Or do we have to start da capo with Carl Orff?"

"I never thought of that," sez Gustav, and for a moment it is clear that Säure has heard about Webern too, and trying in his underhanded way to cheer Gustav up.

"What's wrong with *Rossini*?" hollers Säure, lighting up. "*Eh*?"

"Ugh," screams Gustav, "ugh, ugh, Rossini," and they're at it again, "you wretched antique. Why doesn't anybody go to concerts any more? You think it's because of the war? *Oh* no, *I'll* tell you why, old man—because the halls are full of people like you! *Stuffed* full! Half asleep, nodding and smiling, farting through their dentures, hawking and spitting into paper bags, dreaming up ever more ingenious plots against their children—not just their own, but *other people's* children too! just sitting around, at the concert with all these other snow-topped old rascals, just a nice background murmur of wheezing, belching, intestinal gurgles, scratching, sucking, croaking, an entire opera house crammed full of them right up to standing room, they're doddering in the aisles, hanging off the tops of the highest balconies, and you know what they're *all listening to,* Säure? eh? They're all listening to Rossini! Sitting there drooling away to some medley of predictable little tunes, leaning forward elbows on knees muttering, 'C'mon, c'mon then Rossini, let's get all this pretentious fanfare stuff out of the way, let's get on to the *real good tunes!'* Behavior as shameless as eating a whole jar of peanut butter at one sitting. On comes the sprightly *Tancredi* tarantella, and they stamp their feet in delight, they pop their teeth and pound their canes—'Ah, ah! *that's* more like it!'"

"It's a *great* tune," yells Säure back. "Smoke another one of these and I'll just play it for you here on the Bosendorfer."

To the accompaniment of this tarantella, which really is a good tune, Magda has come in out of the morning rain, and is now rolling reefers for everybody. She hands Säure one to light. He stops playing and peers at it for a long time. Nodding now and then, smiling or frowning.

Gustav tends to sneer, but Säure really turns out to be an adept at the difficult art of papyromancy, the ability to prophesy through contemplating the way people roll reefers—the shape, the licking pattern, the wrinkles and folds or absence thereof in the paper. "You will soon be in love," sez Säure, "see, this line here."

"It's long, isn't it? Does that mean—"

"Length is usually intensity. Not time."

"Short but sweet," Magda sighs. "Fabelhaft, was?" Trudi comes over to hug her. They are a Mutt and Jeff routine, Trudi in heels is a foot or so taller. They know how it looks, and travel around in the city together whenever they can, by way of intervening, if only for a minute, in people's minds.

"How do you like this shit?" sez Säure.

"*Hübsch,*" allows Gustav. "A trifle *stahlig,* and perhaps the infinitesimal hint of a *Bodengeschmack* behind its *Körper,* which is admittedly *süffig.*"

"I would rather have said *spritzig,*" Säure disagrees, if that indeed is what it is. "Generally more *bukettreich* than last year's harvests, wouldn't you say?"

"Oh, for an Haut Atlas herbage it does have its *Art*. Certainly it can be described as *kernig*, even—as can often be said of that *sauber* quality prevailing in the Oued Nfis region—authentically *pikant*."

"Actually I would tend to suspect an origin somewhere along the southern slope of Jebel Sarho," Säure sez—"note the *Spiel*, rather *glatt* and *blumig*, even the suggestion of a *Fülle* in its *würzig* audacity—"

"No no no, *Fülle* is overstating it, the El Abid Emerald we had last month had *Fülle*. But this is obviously more *zart* than that."

The truth is they are both so blitzed that neither one knows what he's talking about, which is just as well, for at this point comes a godawful hammering at the door and a lot of achtungs from the other side. Slothrop screams and heads for the window, out onto the roof and over, scrambling down a galvanized pipe to the next streetward courtyard. Back in Säure's room the heat come busting in. Berlin police supported by American MPs in an adviser status.

"You will show me your papers!" hollers the leader of the raid.

Säure smiles and holds up a pack of Zig-Zags, just in from Paris.

Twenty minutes later, somewhere in the American sector, Slothrop is ambling past a cabaret where blank-faced snowdrops are lounging in front and inside, and a radio or phonograph somewhere is playing an Irving Berlin medley. Slothrop goes hunching paranoiacally along the street, here's "God Bless America," a-and "This Is the Army, Mister Jones," and they are his country's versions of the Horst Wessel Song, although it is Gustav back at the Jacobi-strasse who raves (nobody gonna pull an Anton Webern on him) to a blinking American lieutenant-colonel, "A parabola! A trap! You were never immune over there from the simple-minded German symphonic arc, tonic to dominant, back again to tonic. Grandeur! Gesellschaft!"

"Teutonic?" sez the colonel. "Dominant? The war's over, fella. What kind of talk is that?"

In from the soggy fields of the Mark comes a cold drizzle blowing. Russian cavalry are crossing the Kurfür-stendamm, driving a herd of cows to slaughter lowing and muddy, eyelashes beaded with the fine rain. In the Soviet sector, girls with rifles slung across bouncing wool-covered breasts are waving the traffic around with bright orange pennants. Bulldozers growling, trucks straining push over teetering walls, and little kids cheer at each wet crash. Silver tea-services ring on fronded terraces where water drips, waiters in lean black coats wheel and tilt their heads. An open victoria splashes by, two Russian officers covered with medals sitting with their ladies in silk frocks and great floppy-brimmed hats trailing ribbons in the breeze. On the river, ducks with green heads glittering drift among shock-waves of one another's passage. Wood-smoke scatters out the dented pipe of Margherita's house. Inside the door, the first thing Slothrop sees is a high-heeled shoe come flying straight at his head. He twitches out of the way in time. Margherita is kneeling on the bed, breathing rapidly, staring. "You left me."

"Had some chores." He rummages in covered cans on a shelf over the stove, finds dried clover tops for tea.

"But you left me alone." Her hair blows in a gray-black cloud around her face. She is prey to interior winds he never felt.

"Only for a little while. Do you want tea?" Starting outside with an empty can.

"What's a little while? For God's sake, haven't you been alone?"

"Sure." Dipping up water from a rain barrel outside the door. She lies, shaking, her face working, helpless.

Slothrop puts the can on to boil. "You were sleeping pretty soundly. Isn't it safe here? Is that what you mean?"

"Safe." A terrible laughter. He wishes she wouldn't. The water has begun to creak. "Do you know what they were doing to me? What they were piling on my breasts? The *names they were calling me?*"

"Who, Greta?"

"When you left I woke up. I called to you but you didn't come back. When they were sure you'd left, they came in. . . ."

"Why didn't you try to stay awake?"

"*I was awake!*" Sunlight, switched on, breaks through. At the harsh lighting she turns her face away.

While he makes tea, she sits on the bed, cursing him in

German and Italian, in a voice always just at the edge of
falling apart. He hands her a cup. She knocks it out of his
hand.

"Look, take it easy, all right?" He sits down next to her
and blows on his tea. The cup she refused stays on its
side where it is. The dark stain steams into the wood
planks. Faraway clover rises, disperses: a ghost. . . . After
a while she takes his hand.

"I'm sorry I left you alone."

She starts to cry.

And cries all day. Slothrop falls asleep, keeps drifting
up to her sobs, and to feel her, always in touch, some part
of her, some part of him. . . . In a dream from this time,
his father has come to find him. Slothrop has been wandering at sundown by the Mungahannock, near a rotting old
paper mill, abandoned back in the nineties. A heron rises
in silhouette against luminous and dying orange. "Son," a
falling tower of words tumbling over and over themselves,
"the president died three months ago." Slothrop stands
and curses him. "Why didn't you tell me? Pop, I loved
him. You only wanted to sell me to the IG. You sold me
out." The old man's eyes fill with tears. "Oh son . . ." trying to take his hand. But the sky is dark, the heron gone,
the empty skeleton of the mill and the dark increase of the
river saying *it is time to go* . . . then his father is gone too,
no time to say good-by, though his face stays, Broderick
who sold him out, long after waking, and the sadness Slothrop brought into it, fool loudmouth kid. Margherita is
leaning over him, brushing tears from his face with the
tips of her nails. The nails are very sharp, and pause
often when they approach his eyes.

"I'm afraid," she whispers. "Everything. My face in the
mirror—when I was a child, they said not to look in the
mirror too often or I'd see the Devil behind the glass . . .
and . . ." glancing back at the white-flowered mirror behind them, "we have to cover it, please, can't we cover
it . . . that's where they . . . *especially at night*—"

"Easy." He moves to put as much of their bodies in
touch as he can. He holds her. The tremor is strong, and
maybe uncalmable: after a while Slothrop has started to
tremble too, in phase. "Please, take it easy." Whatever
possesses her needs touch, to drink touch insatiably.

The depth of this frightens him. He feels responsible for her safety, and often trapped. At first they stay together days at a clip, till he has to go out dealing, or foraging. He doesn't sleep much. He finds himself by reflex telling lies—"It's all right," "There's nothing to worry about." Sometimes he manages to be alone out by the river, fishing with a piece of string and one of her hairpins. They manage a fish a day, on lucky days two. They are goofy fish, anything swimming in Berlin waters these days has to be everybody's last choice. When Greta cries in her sleep for longer than he can listen to, he has to wake her. They will try to talk, or to screw, though he's less and less often in the mood, and that makes her worse because she feels he's rejecting her, which indeed he is. Whippings seem to comfort her, and they let him off the hook. Sometimes he's too tired even for that. She keeps provoking him. One night he puts in front of her a broiled fish, an unwholesome yellow loach with brain damage. She can't eat it, she'll get sick.

"You have to eat."

She moves her head aside, first one side, then the other.

"Oh boy, what a sad story, listen cunt, you ain't the only one's ever suffered—you been out *there* lately?"

"Of course. I keep forgetting how *you* must have suffered."

"*Shit* you Germans are crazy, you *all* think the world's against you."

"I'm not German," just remembering, "I'm a Lombard."

"Close enough, sweetheart."

With a hiss, nostrils wide, she grabs the little table and wrenches it away, plates, silverware, fish flying *splot* against the wall where it commences to drip down toward the woodwork, still, even in death, getting all the lousy breaks. They sit in their two straight chairs, a meter and a half of perilously empty space between. It is the warm, romantic summer of '45, and surrender or not, the culture of death still prevails: what Grandmother called "a crime of passion" has become, in the absence of much passion over anything today, the technique of preference in resolving interpersonal disputes.

"Clean it up."

She flicks a pale bitten thumbnail from one of her top

teeth and laughs, that delightful Erdmann laugh. Slothrop, shaking, is about to say, "You don't know how close you are—" Then, by chance, he happens to get a look at her face. Of course she knows how close she is. "O.K., O.K." He throws her underwear around the room till he finds the black girdle he's looking for. The metal clips of the suspenders raise dark little curved welts over fading earlier bruises on her buttocks and thighs. He has to draw blood before she cleans up the fish. When she's finished she kneels and kisses his boots. Not exactly the scenario she wanted but close enough, sweetheart.

Getting closer every day, and he's afraid. He's never seen anything like it. When he goes out to the city she begs to be tied with her stockings, star-fashion, to the bedposts. Sometimes she'll leave the house, and stay away for days, coming home with stories about Negro MPs beating her with nightsticks, screwing her in the asshole, how much she loved it, hoping to trigger some race/sex reaction, something a little bizarre, a little different. . . .

Whatever it is with her, he's catching it. Out in the ruins he sees darkness now at the edges of all the broken shapes, *showing from behind them.* Light nests in Margherita's hair like black doves. He will look at his chalk hands, and along the borders of each finger, darkness will gutter and leap. In the sky over the Alexanderplatz he has seen Oberst Enzian's KEZVH mandala, and the face of Tchitcherine on more than one random snowdrop. Across the façade of the Titaniapalast, in red neon through a mist one night he saw DIE, SLOTHROP. One Sunday out at Wannsee, an armada of sails all bent the same way, patiently, dreamlike into the wind, passing forever against the other shore, a crowd of little kids in soldier hats folded from old army maps plotted to drown and sacrifice him. He escaped only by murmuring *Hauptstufe* three times.

The house by the river is an enclosure that acts as a spring-suspension for the day and the weather, allowing only mild cycling of light and heat, down into evening, up again into morning to the midday peak but all damped to a gentle sway from the earthquake of the day outside.

When Greta hears shots out in the increasingly distant streets, she will think of the sound stages of her early career, and will take the explosions as cue calls for the titanic sets of her dreams to be smoothly clogged with a thousand extras: meek, herded by rifle shots, ascending and descending, arranged into patterns that will suit the Director's ideas of the picturesque—a river of faces, made up yellow and white-lipped for the limitations of the film stock of the time, sweating yellow migrations taken over and over again, fleeing nothing, escaping nowhere. . . .

It's early morning now. Slothrop's breath is white on the air. He is just up from a dream. Part I of a poem, with woodcuts accompanying the text—a woman is attending a dog show which is also, in some way, a stud service. She has brought her Pekingese, a female with a sickeningly cute name, Mimsy or Goo-Goo or something, here to be serviced. She is passing the time in a garden setting, with some other middle-class ladies like herself, when from some enclosure nearby she hears the sound of her bitch, coming. The sound goes on and on for much longer than seems appropriate, and she suddenly realizes that the sound is her own voice, this interminable cry of dog-pleasure. The others, politely, are pretending not to notice. She feels shame, but is helpless, driven now by a need to go out and find other animal species to fuck. She sucks the penis of a multicolored mongrel who has tried to mount her in the street. Out in a barren field near a barbed-wire fence, winter fires across the clouds, a tall horse compels her to kneel, passively, and kiss his hooves. Cats and minks, hyenas and rabbits, fuck her inside automobiles, lost at night in the forests, out beside a waterhole in the desert.

As Part II begins, she has discovered she's pregnant. Her husband, a dumb, easygoing screen door salesman, makes an agreement with her: her own promise is never stated, but in return, nine months from now, he will take her where she wants to go. So it is that close to the end of her term he is out on the river, an American river, in a rowboat, hauling on the oars, carrying her on a journey. The key color in this section is violet.

Part III finds her at the bottom of the river. She has drowned. But all forms of life fill her womb. "Using her as mermaid" (line 7), they transport her down through these green river-depths. "It was down, and out again./ Old Squalidozzi, ploughman of the deep,/ At the end of his day's sowing/ Sees her verdigris belly among the weeds" (lines 10–13), and brings her back up. He is a classically-bearded Neptune figure with an old serene face. From out of her body streams a flood now of different creatures, octopuses, reindeer, kangaroos, "Who can say all the life/ That left her womb that day?" Squalidozzi can only catch a glimpse of the amazing spill as he bears her back toward the surface. Above, it is a mild and sunlit green lake or pond, grassy at the banks, shaded by willows. Insects whine and hover. The key color now is green. "And there as it broke to sun/ Her corpse found sleep in the water/ And in the summer depths/ The creatures took their way/ Each to its proper love/ In the height of afternoon/ As the peaceful river went. . . ."

This dream will not leave him. He baits his hook, hunkers by the bank, drops his line into the Spree. Presently he lights up an army cigarette, and stays still then for a long while, as the fog moves white through the riverbank houses, and up above the warplanes go droning somewhere invisible, and the dogs run barking in the backstreets.

□

When emptied of people, the interior is steel gray. When crowded, it's green, a comfortable acid green. Sunlight comes in through portholes in the higher of the bulkheads (the *Rücksichtslos* here lists at a permanent angle of 23°27'), and steel washbowls line the lower bulkheads. At the end of each sub-latrine are coffee messes and hand-cranked peep shows. You'll find all the older, less glamorous, un-Teutonic-looking women in the enlisted men's machines. The real stacked and more racially golden tomatoes go to the officers, natürlich. This is some of that Nazi fanaticism.

The *Rücksichtslos* itself is the issue of another kind of fanaticism: that of the specialist. This vessel here is a Toiletship, a triumph of the German mania for subdividing. "If the house is organic," argued the crafty early Toiletship advocates, "family lives in the house, family's organic, house is outward-and-visible sign, you see," behind their smoked glasses and under their gray crewcuts not believing a word of it, Machiavellian and youthful, not quite ripe yet for paranoia, "and if the bathroom's part of the house—house-is-or*ganic*! ha-hah," singing, chiding, pointing out the broad blond-faced engineer, hair parted in the middle and slicked back, actually blushing and looking at his knees among the good-natured smiling teeth of his fellow technologists because he'd been about to forget that point (Albert Speer, himself, in a gray suit with a smudge of chalk on the sleeve, all the way in the back leaning akimbo the wall and looking remarkably like American cowboy actor Henry Fonda, has *already* forgotten about the house being organic, and nobody points at *him*, RHIP). "Then the Toiletship is to the Kriegsmarine as the bathroom is to the house. Because the Navy is organic, we all know *that*, hahah!" [General, or maybe Admiral, laughter.] The *Rücksichtslos* was intended to be the flagship of a whole Geschwader of Toiletships. But the steel quotas were diverted clear out of the Navy over to the A4 rocket program. Yes, that does seem unusual, but Degenkolb was heading up the Rocket Committee by then, remember, and had both power and will to cut across all branches of the service. So the *Rücksichtslos* is one-of-a-kind, old warship collectors, and if you're in the market you better hurry 'cause GE's already been by to have a look. Lucky the Bolshies didn't get it, huh, Charles? Charles, meantime, is making on his clipboard what look like studious notes, but are really observations of the passing scene such as *They are all looking at me*, or *Lieutenant Rinso is plotting to murder me*, and of course the ever-reliable *He's one of them too and I'm going to get him some night*, well by now Charles's colleague here, Steve, has forgotten about the Russians, and discontinued his inspection of a flushing valve to take a really close look at that *Charles*, you can't pick your search team, not if you're just out of school and here I am, in the asshole of nowhere, not much more than a gofer to this—what is he, a fag? What am *I*? What does GE want me to be? Is this some obscure form of company punishment, even, good God, permanent *exile*? I'm a career man, they can keep me out here 20 years if they want, 'n' nobody'll ever know, they'll just keep writing it off to overhead. Sheila! How'm I gonna tell Sheila? We're engaged. This is her

picture (hair waved like choppy seas falling down Rita
Hayworth style, eyes that if it were a color snap would
have yellow lids with pink rims, and a mouth like a hot
dog bun on a billboard). Took her out to Buf-falo Bayou,

> Lookin' for a little fun—
> Big old bayou mosquito, oh my you
> Shoulda seen what he done!
> Poked his head up, under her dress,
> Give a little grin and, well I guess,
> Things got rough on Buf-falo Bayou,
> Skeeter turn yer meter, down,
> All—right—now!
>   Ya ta, ta-ta, ya-ta-ta, ta-ta
> Lookin' for a little fun,
> Ev-rybody!

Oh ya know, when you're young and wholesome
["Ev'rybody," in this case a Toiletshipload of bright hornrimmed
shoe-pac'd young fellas from Schenectady, are singin' along behind
this recitative here] and a good church-goin' kid, it's sure a mournful thing to get suddenly ganged by a pack of those Texas mosquitoes,
it can set you back 20 years. Why, there's boys just like you wan-
derin' around, you may've seen one in the street today and never
known it, with the mind of a infant, just because those mosquitoes
got to him and did their unspeakable thing. And we've laid down
insecticides, a-and bombed the bayous with citronella, and it's no
good, folks. They breed faster'n we can kill 'em, and are we just
gonna tuck tail and let them *be* there out in Buffalo Bayou where my
gal Sheila had to look at the loathsome behavior of those—things,
we gonna allow them even to *exist?*

>   —And,
> Things got rough on, Buf-falo Bayou,
> Skeeter turn yer meter, down,
> Hubba hubba—
> Skeeter turn yer meter, down!

Well, you can't help but wonder who's really the more
paranoid of the two here. Steve's sure got a lot of gall
badmouthing Charles that way. Among the hilarious graffiti
of visiting mathematicians,

$$\int \frac{1}{(\text{cabin})}\, d\,(\text{cabin}) = \log \text{cabin} + c = \text{houseboat},$$

that sort of thing, they go poking away down the narrow
sausage-shaped latrine now, two young/old men, their
feet fade and cease to ring on the sloping steel deck, their
forms grow more transparent with distance until it's im-

possible to see them any more. Only the empty compartment here, the S-curved spokes on the peep-show machines, the rows of mirrors directly facing, reflecting each other, frame after frame, back in a curve of very great radius. Out to the end of this segment of curve is considered part of the space of the *Rücksichtslos*. Making it a rather fat ship. Carrying its right-of-way along with it. "Crew morale," whispered the foxes at the Ministry meetings, "sailors' superstitions. Mirrors at high midnight. *We* know, don't we?"

The officers' latrines, by contrast, are done in red velvet. The decor is 1930s Safety Manual. That is, all over the walls, photograffiti, are pictures of Horrible Disasters in German Naval History. Collisions, magazine explosions, U-boat sinkings, just the thing if you're an officer trying to take a shit. The Foxes have been busy. Commanding officers get whole suites, private shower and sunken bathtub, manicurist (BDM volunteers, mostly), steam room, massage table. To compensate though, all the bulkheads, and the overhead, are occupied by enormous photographs of Hitler at various forms of play. The toilet paper! The toilet paper is covered square after square with caricatures of Churchill, Eisenhower, Roosevelt, Chiang Kai-shek, there was even a Staff Caricaturist always on duty to custom-illustrate blank paper for those connoisseurs who are ever in search of the unusual. Wagner and Hugo Wolf were patched into speakers from up in the radio shack. Cigarettes were free. It was a good life on board the Toiletship *Rücksichtslos*, as it plied its way from Swinemünde to Helgoland, anyplace it was needed, camouflaged in shades of gray, turn-of-the-century style with sharp-shadowed prows coming at you from midships so you couldn't tell which way she was headed. Ship's company actually lived each man inside his stall, each with his own key and locker, pin-ups and library shelves decorating the partitions . . . and there were even one-way mirrors so you could sit at your ease, penis dangling toward the ice-cold seawater in your bowl, listen to your VE-301 People's Receiver, and watch the afternoon rush, the busy ringing of feet and talk, card games inside the group toilets, dealers enthroned on real porcelain receiving visitors, some of them lined up back outside the compartment (quiet

queues, all business, something like the queues in banks),
toilet-lawyers dispensing advice, all kinds of visitor coming
and going, the U-boat crews hunching in, twitching eyes
nervously every second or two at the overhead, destroyer
sailors larking at the troughs (*gigantic* troughs! running
the whole beam of the ship, even, legend has it, off into
mirror-space, big enough to seat 40 or 50 aching assholes
side by side, while a constant river of salt flushing water
roared by underneath), lighting wads of toilet paper, is
what they especially liked to do, setting them flaming
yellow in the water upstream and cackling with glee as
one by one down the line the sitters leaped off the holes
screaming and clutching their blistered asses and inhaling
the smell of singed pubic hair. Not that the crew of the
Toiletship itself were above a practical joke now and then.
Who can ever forget the time shipfitters Höpmann and
Kreuss, at the height of the Ptomaine Epidemic of 1943,
routed those waste lines into the ventilation system of the
executive officer's stateroom? The exec, being an old
Toiletship hand, laughed good-naturedly at the clever
prank and transferred Höpmann and Kreuss to icebreaker
duty, where the two Scatotechnic Snipes went on to erect
vaguely turd-shaped monoliths of ice and snow all across
the Arctic. Now and then one shows up on an ice floe
drifting south in ghostly grandeur, exciting the admiration
of all.

A good ship, a good crew, Merry Xmas and turn to.
Horst Achtfaden, late of the Elektromechanische Werke,
Karlshagen (another cover name for the testing station at
Peenemünde), has really no time for naval nostalgia. With
the technical spies of three or four nations after him, he
has had the disastrous luck to've been picked up by the
Schwarzkommando, who for all he knows now constitute
a nation of their own. They have interned him in the
Chiefs' Head. He has watched voluptuous Gerda and her
Fur Boa go through the same number 178 times (he has
jimmied the coin box and figured a way to override it)
since they put him in here, and the thrill is gone. What do
they want? Why are they occupying a derelict in the
middle of the Kiel Canal? Why don't the British *do* something about this?

Look at it this way, Achtfaden. This Toiletship here's

a wind tunnel's all it is. If tensor analysis is good enough
for turbulence, it ought to be good enough for history.
There ought to be nodes, critical points . . . there ought to
be super-derivatives of the crowded and insatiate flow
that can be set equal to zero and these critical points
found. . . . 1904 was one of them—1904 was when Admiral
Rozhdestvenski sailed his fleet halfway around the world
to relieve Port Arthur, which put your present captor
Enzian on the planet, it was the year the Germans all but
wiped out the Hereros, which gave Enzian some peculiar
ideas about survival, it was the year the American Food
and Drug people took the cocaine out of Coca-Cola, which
gave us an alcoholic and death-oriented generation of
Yanks ideally equipped to fight WW II, and it was the
year Ludwig Prandtl proposed the boundary layer, which
really got aerodynamics into business and put you right
here, right now. 1904, Achtfaden. Ha, ha! *That's* a better
joke on you than any singed asshole, all right. Lotta good
it does *you*. You can't swim upstream, not under the present dispensation anyhow, all you can do is attach the
number to it and *suffer*, Horst, fella. Or, if you can tear
yourself away from Gerda and her Fur Boa, here's a
thought—find a non-dimensional coefficient for yourself.
This is a wind-tunnel you're in, remember? You're an
aerodynamics man. So—

Coefficients, ja, ja. . . . Achtfaden flings himself discon-
solately on the scarlet VD toilet way down at the very
end of the row. He knows about coefficients. In Aachen
once, for a while, he and his colleagues could stand in the
forward watchtower: look out into the country of the
barbarians through Hermann and Wieselsberger's tiny
window. Terrific compressions, diamond shadows writhing
like snakes. Often the sting was bigger than the model
itself—the very need to measure interfered with the observations. That should have been a clue right there. No
one wrote then about supersonic flow. It was surrounded
by myth, and by a pure, primitive terror. Professor Wagner
of Darmstadt predicted that at speeds above Mach 5, air
would liquefy. Should pitch and roll frequencies happen
to be equal, the resonance would throw the projectile into
violent oscillations. It would corkscrew to destruction.
"Lunar motion," we called it. "Bingen pencils" we would

call the helical contrails in the sky. Terrified. The Schlieren shadows danced. At Peenemünde the test section measured 40 × 40 cm, about the size of a tabloid page. "They pray not only for their daily bread," Stresemann had said, "but also for their daily illusion." We, staring through the thick glass, had our Daily Shock—the only paper many of us read.

You come in—just hit town, here in the heart of downtown Peenemünde, hey, whatcha do for fun around here? hauling your provincial valise with a few shirts, a copy of the *Handbuch,* perhaps Cranz's *Lehrbuch der Ballistik.* You have memorized Ackeret, Busemann, von Kármán and Moore, some Volta Congress papers. But the terror will not go away. This is faster than *sound,* than the words she spoke across the room so full of sunlight, the jazz band on the radio when you could not sleep, the hoarse *Heils* among the pale generators and from the executive-crammed galleries overhead . . . the Gomerians whistling from the high ravines (terrific falls, steepness, whistling straight down the precipice to a toy village lying centuries, miles below . . .) as you sat out on the counter of the KdF ship alone, apart from the maypole dancing on the white deck, the tanned bodies full of beer and song, paunches in sunsuits, and you listened to Ur-Spanish, whistled not voiced, from the mountains around Chipuda . . . Gomera was the last piece of land Columbus touched before America. Did he hear them too, that last night? Did they have a message for him? A warning? Could he understand the prescient goatherds in the dark, up in the Canarian holly and the faya, gone dead green in the last sunset of Europe?

In aerodynamics, because you've only got the thing on paper at first, you use dimensionless coefficients: ratios of this to that—centimeters, grams, seconds neatly all canceling out above and below. This allows you to use models, arrange an airflow to measure what you're interested in, and scale the wind-tunnel results all the way up to reality, without running into too many unknowns, because these coefficients are good for *all* dimensions. Traditionally they are named after people—Reynolds, Prandtl, Péclet, Nusselt, Mach—and the question here is, how about an Achtfaden number? How's chances for that?

Not good. The parameters breed like mosquitoes in the

bayou, faster than he can knock them off. Hunger, compromise, money, paranoia, memory, comfort, guilt. Guilt gets a minus sign around Achtfaden though, even if it is becoming quite a commodity in the Zone. Remittance men from all over the world will come to Heidelberg before long, to major in guilt. There will be bars and nightclubs catering especially to guilt enthusiasts. Extermination camps will be turned into tourist attractions, foreigners with cameras will come piling through in droves, tickled and shivering with guilt. Sorry—not for Achtfaden here, shrugging at all his mirror-to-mirror replications chaining out to port and starboard—he only worked with it up to the point where the air was too thin to make a difference. What it did after that was none of his responsibility. Ask Weichensteller, ask Flaum, and Fibel—they were the re-entry people. Ask the guidance section, they pointed it where it was going. . . .

"Do you find it a little schizoid," aloud now to all the Achtfaden fronts and backs, "breaking a flight profile up into segments of responsibility? It was half bullet, half arrow. *It* demanded this, we didn't. So. Perhaps you used a rifle, a radio, a typewriter. Some typewriters in Whitehall, in the Pentagon, killed more civilians than our little A4 could have ever hoped to. You are either alone absolutely, alone with your own death, or you take part in the larger enterprise, and you share in the deaths of others. Are we not all one? Which is your choice," Fahringer now, buzzing and flat through the filters of memory, "the little cart, or the great one?" mad Fahringer, the only one of the Peenemünde club who refused to wear the exclusive pheasant-feather badge in his hatband because he couldn't bring himself to kill, who could be seen evenings on the beach sitting in full lotos position staring into the setting sun, and who was first at Peenemünde to fall to the SS, taken away one noon into the fog, his lab coat a flag of surrender, presently obscured by the black uniforms, leather and metal of his escort. Leaving behind a few joss sticks, a copy of the *Chinesische Blätter für Wissenschaft und Kunst,* pictures of a wife and children no one had known about . . . was Peenemünde his mountain, his cell and fasting? Had *he* found his way free of guilt, fashionable guilt?

"*Atmen . . . atman . . .* not only to breathe, but also the

soul, the breath of God . . ." one of the few times Achtfaden can remember talking with him alone, directly,
"*atmen* is a genuinely Aryan verb. Now tell me about the
speed of the exhaust jet."

"What do you want to know? 6500 feet per second."

"Tell me how it changes."

"It remains nearly constant, through the burning."

"And yet the relative airspeed changes drastically,
doesn't it? Zero up to Mach 6. Can't you see what's happening?"

"No, Fahringer."

"The Rocket creating its own great wind . . . no wind
without both, Rocket and atmosphere . . . but inside the
venturi, breath—furious and blazing breath—always flows
at the same unchanging speed . . . can't you really see?"

Gibberish. Or else a *koan* that Achtfaden isn't equipped
to master, a transcendent puzzle that could lead him to
some moment of light . . . almost as good as:

—What is it that flies?

—Los!

Rising from the Wasserkuppe, rivers Ullster and Haune
tilting around into map-shapes, green valleys and mountains, the four he has left below gathering up the white
shock cords, only one looking up, shading his eyes—Bert
Fibel? but what does the name matter, from this vantage?
Achtfaden goes looking for the thunderstorm—*under,
through the thunder* playing to a martial tune inside his
head—crowding soon in gray cliffs to the right, the
strokes of lightning banging all the mountains blue, the
cockpit briefly filled with the light . . . right at the edge.
Right here, at the interface, the air will be rising. You
follow the edge of the storm, with another sense—the
flight-sense, located nowhere, filling all your nerves . . . as
long as you stay always right at the edge between fair
lowlands and the madness of Donar it does not fail you,
whatever it is that flies, this carrying drive toward—*is* it
freedom? Does no one recognize what enslavement gravity
is till he reaches the interface of the thunder?

No time to work out puzzles. Here come the Schwarzkommando. Achtfaden has wasted too much time with
luscious Gerda, with memories. Here they come clattering
down the ladders, fast oogabooga talk he can't even guess
at, it's a linguistic wilderness here, and he's afraid. What do

they want? Why won't they leave him in peace—they have their victory, what do they want with poor Achtfaden?

They want the Schwarzgerät. When Enzian actually pronounces the word aloud, it's already redundant. It was there in his bearing, the line of his mouth. The others back him, rifles slung, half a dozen African faces, mobbing the mirrors with their darkness, their vein-heavy red-white-and-blue eyes.

"I only was assigned to part of it. It was trivial. Really."

"Aerodynamics isn't trivial," Enzian calm, unsmiling.

"There were others from Gessner's section. Mechanical design. I always worked out of Prof.-Dr. Kurzweg's shop."

"Who were the others?"

"I don't remember."

"So."

"Don't hit me. Why should I hide anything? It's the truth. They kept us cut off. I didn't know anybody at Nordhausen. Just a few in my own work section. I swear it. The S-Gerät people were all strangers to me. Until that first day we all met with Major Weissmann, I'd never seen any of them. No one used real names. We were given code-names. Characters from a movie, somebody said. The other aerodynamics people were 'Spörri' and 'Hawasch.' I was called 'Wenk.'"

"What was your job?"

"Weight control. All they wanted from me was the shift in CG for a device of a given weight. The weight was classified top secret. Forty-something kilos. 45? 46?"

"Station numbers," raps Andreas from over Enzian's shoulder.

"I can't remember. It was in the tail section. I do remember the load was assymmetrical about the longitudinal axis. Toward Vane III. That was the vane used for yaw control—"

"We know that."

"You'd have to talk to 'Spörri' or 'Hawasch.' They'd be the ones who worked that problem out. Talk to Guidance." *Why did I say—*

"Why did you say that?"

"No, no, it wasn't my *job,* that's all, guidance, warhead, propulsion . . . ask them. Ask the others."

"You meant something else. Who worked on guidance?"

"I told you, I didn't know any of their names." The dust-covered cafeteria in the last days: The machinery in the adjoining halls, that once battered eardrums pitiless as a cold-chisel day and night, is silenced. The Roman numerals on the time clocks stare from the walls of the bays, among the glass windowpanes. Telephone jacks on black rubber cords dangle from brackets overhead, each connection hanging over its own desk, all the desks perfectly empty, covered with salt-dust sifted from the ceiling, no phones to plug in, no more words to be said.... The face of his friend across the table, the drawn and sleepless face now too pointed, too lipless, that once vomited beer on Achtfaden's hiking boots, whispering now, "I couldn't go with von Braun ... not to the Americans, it would only just keep on the same way ... I want it really to be over, that's all ... good-by, 'Wenk.'"

"Stuff him down the waste lines," Andreas suggests. They are all so black, so sure....

I must be the last one ... somebody's sure to have him by now ... what can these Africans do with a name ... they could have got it from anybody....

"He was a friend. We knew each other before the war, at Darmstadt."

"We're not going to hurt him. We're not going to hurt you. We want the S-Gerät."

"Närrisch. Klaus Närrisch." A new parameter for his self-coefficient now: betrayal.

As he leaves the *Rücksichtslos*, Achtfaden can hear behind him, metallic, broadcasting from another world, ripped by static, a radio voice. "Oberst Enzian. M'okamanga. M'okamanga. M'okamanga." There is urgency and gravity in the word. He stands by the canalside, among steel wreckage and old men in the dusk, waiting for a direction to go. But where is the electric voice now that will ever call for him?

□

They have set out by barge along the Spree-Oder Canal, headed at last for Swinemünde, Slothrop to see what Geli Tripping's clew will lead him to in the way of a Schwarzgerät, Margherita to rendezvous with a yachtful of refugees from the Lublin regime, among whom ought to be her daughter Bianca. Stretches of the canal are still blocked—in the night Russian demolition crews can be heard blasting away the wrecks with TNT—but Slothrop and Greta can summon, like dreamers, draft shallow enough to clear whatever the War has left in their way. Off and on it rains. The sky will begin to cloud up about noon, turning the color of wet cement—then wind, sharpening, colder, then rain that must be often at the edge of sleet, blowing at them head-on up the canal. They shelter under tarps, among bales and barrels, tar, wood and straw smells. When the nights are clear, peepers-and-frogs nights, star-streaks and shadows at canalside will set travelers' eyes to jittering. Willows line the banks. At midnight coils of fog rise to dim out even the glow of the bargee's pipe, far away up, or down, the dreaming convoy. These nights, fragrant and grained as pipesmoke, are tranquil and good for sleep. The Berlin madness is behind, Greta seems less afraid, perhaps all they needed was to be on the move. . . .

But one afternoon, sliding down the long mild slope of the Oder toward the Baltic Sea, they catch sight of a little red and white resort town, wiped through in broad smudges by the War, and she clutches to Slothrop's arm.

"I've been here . . ."

"Yeah?"

"Just before the Polish invasion . . . I was here with Sigmund . . . at the spa. . . ."

On shore, behind cranes and steel railings, rise fronts of what were restaurants, small factories, hotels, burned now, windowless, powdered with their own substance. The name of the town is Bad Karma. Rain from earlier in the day has streaked the walls, the pinnacles of waste and the coarse-cobbled lanes. Children and old men stand on shore waiting to take lines and warp the barges in. Black dumplings of smoke are floating up out of the stack of a white river steamer. Shipfitters are slamming inside its hull. Greta stares at it. A pulse is visible in her throat. She takes her head. "I thought it was Bianca's ship, but it isn't."

In close to the quay, they swing ashore, grabbing on to an iron ladder held in the old stone by rusted bolts, each one staining the wall downward in a wet sienna fan. On

Margherita's jacket a pink gardenia has begun to shake.
It isn't the wind. She keeps saying, "I have to see. . . ."

Old men are leaning on railings, smoking pipes, watching Greta or looking out at the river. They wear gray
clothes, wide-bottom trousers, wide-brim hats with rounded
crowns. The market square is busy and neat: tram tracks
gleam, there's a smell of fresh hosing down. In the ruins
lilacs bleed their color, their surplus life out over the
broken stone and brick.

Except for a few figures in black, sitting out in the sun,
the Spa itself is deserted. Margherita by now is spooked
as badly as she ever was in Berlin. Slothrop tags along,
in his Rocketman turnout, feeling burdened. The Sprudelhof is bounded on one side by a sand-colored arcade: sand
columns and brown shadows. A strip just in front is
planted to cypresses. Fountains in massive stone bowls are
leaping: jets 20 feet high, whose shadows across the
smooth paving of the courtyard are thick and nervous.

But who's that, standing so rigid by the central spring?
And why has Margherita turned to stone? The sun is out,
there are others watching, but even Slothrop now is bris-
tling along his back and flanks, chills flung one on the
fading cluster of another, up under each side of his jaw
. . . the woman is wearing a black coat, a crepe scarf covering her hair, the flesh of thick calves showing through
her black stockings as nearly purple, she is only leaning
over the waters in a very fixed way and watching them
as they try to approach . . . but the *smile* . . . across ten
meters of swept courtyard, the smile growing confident in
the very white face, all the malaise of a Europe dead and
gone gathered here in the eyes black as her clothing, black
and lightless. *She knows them.* Greta has turned, and tries
to hide her face in Slothrop's shoulder. "By the well," is
she whispering this? "at sundown, that woman in
black. . . ."

"Come on. It's all right." Back to Berlin talk. "She's just
a patient here." Idiot, idiot—before he can stop her she's
pulled away, some quiet, awful cry in the back of her
throat, and turned and begun to run, a desperate tattoo
of high heels across the stone, into the shadowed arches of
the Kurhaus.

"Hey," Slothrop, feeling queasy, accosts the woman in
black. "What's the big idea, lady?"

But her face has changed by now, it is only the face of
another woman of the ruins, one he would have ignored,
passed over. She smiles, all right, but in the forced and
business way he knows. "Zigaretten, bitte?" He gives her
a long stub he's been saving, and goes looking for Margherita.

He finds the arcade empty. All the doors of the Kurhaus
are locked. Overhead passes a skylight of yellow panes,
many of them fallen out. Down the corridor, fuzzy patches
of afternoon sun stagger along, full of mortar dust. He
climbs a broken flight of steps that end in the sky. Odd
chunks of stone clutter the way. From the landing at the
top, the Spa stretches to country distances: handsome trees,
graveyard clouds, the blue river. Greta is nowhere in
sight. Later he will figure out where it was she went. By
then they will be well on board the *Anubis,* and it will
only make him feel more helpless.

He keeps looking for her till the darkness is down and
he's come back by the river again. He sits at an open-air
café strung with yellow lights, drinking beer, eating
spaetzle and soup, waiting. When she materializes it is a
shy fade-in, as Gerhardt von Göll must have brought her
on a time or two, not moving so much as Slothrop's own
vantage swooping to her silent closeup stabilized presently
across from him, finishing his beer, bumming a cigarette.
Not only does she avoid the subject of the woman by the
spring, she may have lost the memory already.

"I went up in the observatory," is what she has to say
finally, "to look down the river. She's coming. I saw the
boat she's on. It's only a kilometer away."

"The what now?"

"Bianca, my child, and my friends. I thought they'd
have been in Swinemünde long ago. But then nobody's on
timetables any more. . . ."

Sure enough, after two more bitter cups of acorn coffee
and another cigarette, here comes a cheerful array of
lights, red, green, and white, down the river, with the
faint wheeze of an accordion, the thump of a string bass,
and the sound of women laughing. Slothrop and Greta
walk down to the quay, and through mist now beginning
to seep up off the river they can make out an ocean-going
yacht, nearly the color of the mist, a gilded winged jackal
under the bowsprit, the weather-decks crowded with chat-

tering affluent in evening dress. Several people have
spotted Margherita. She waves, and they point or wave
back, and call her name. It is a moving village: all summer it has been sailing these lowlands just as Viking ships
did a thousand years ago, though passively, not maraud-
ing: seeking an escape it has not yet defined clearly.

The boat comes in to the quay, the crew lower an
access ladder. Smiling passengers halfway down are already stretching out gloved and ringed hands to Margherita.

"Are you coming?"

"Uh . . . Well, should I?"

She shrugs and turns her back, steps gingerly off the
landing and on board, skirt straining and glossy a moment
in the yellow light from the café. Slothrop dithers, goes to
follow her—at the last moment some joker pulls the
ladder up and the boat moves away, Slothrop screams,
loses his balance and falls in the river. Head first: the
Rocketman helmet is pulling him straight down. He tugs
it off and comes up, sinuses burning and vision blurred,
the white vessel sliding away, though the churning screws
are moving his direction, beginning to suck at the cape, so
he has to get rid of that, too. He backstrokes away and
then cautiously around the counter, lettered in black:
ANUBIS *Świnoujście*, trying to keep away from those screws.
Down the other side he spots a piece of line hanging, and
manages to get over there and grab hold. The band up on
deck is playing polkas. Three drunken ladies in tiaras and
pearl chokers are lounging at the lifelines, watching Slothrop struggle up the rope. "Let's cut it," yells one of
them, "and see him fall *in* again!" "Yes, let's!" agree her
companions. Jesus Christ. One of them has produced a
huge meat cleaver, and is winding up all right, amid much
vivacious laughing, at about which point somebody grabs
hold of Slothrop's ankle. He looks down, observes sticking
out a porthole two slender wrists in silver and sapphires,
lighted from inside like ice, and the oily river rushing by
underneath.

"In here." A girl's voice. He slides back down while she
tugs on his feet, till he's sitting in the porthole. From
above comes a heavy thump, the rope goes falling and the
ladies into hysterics. Slothrop squirms on inside, water

squeegeeing off, falls into an upper bunk next to a girl maybe 18 in a long sequined gown, with hair blonde to the point of pure whiteness, and the first cheekbones Slothrop can recall getting a hardon looking at. Something has definitely been happening to his brain out here, all right. . . .

"Uh—"

"Mmm." They look at each other while he continues to drip water all over. Her name, it turns out, is Stefania Procalowska. Her husband Antoni is owner of the *Anubis* here.

Well, husband, all right. "Look at this," sez Slothrop, "I'm soaking wet."

"I noticed. Somebody's evening clothes ought to fit you. Dry off, I'll go see what I can promote. You can use the head if you want, everything's there."

He strips off the rest of the Rocketman rig, takes a shower, using lemon verbena soap in which he finds a couple of Stefania's white pubic hairs, and is shaving when she gets back with dry clothes for him.

"So you're with Margherita."

"Not sure about that 'with.' She find that kid of hers?"

"Oh indeed—they're already deep into it with Karel. This month he's posing as a film producer. You know Karel. And of course *she* wants to get Bianca into the films worse than anything."

"Uh . . ."

Stefania shrugs a lot, and every sequin dances. "Margherita wants her to have a legitimate career. It's guilt. She never felt her own career was anything more than a string of dirty movies. I suppose you heard about how she got pregnant with Bianca."

"Max Schlepzig, or something."

"Or something, right. You never saw *Alpdrücken?* In that one scene, after the Grand Inquisitor gets through, the jackal men come in to ravish and dismember the captive baroness. Von Göll let the cameras run right on. The footage got cut out for the release prints of course, but found its way into Goebbels's private collection. I've seen it—it's frightening. Every man in the scene wears a black hood, or an animal mask . . . back at Bydgoszcz it became an amusing party game to speculate on who the child's father was. One has to pass the time. They'd run the film and ask Bianca questions, and she had to answer yes or no."

"Yup." Slothrop goes on dousing his face with bay rum.

"Oh, Margherita had her corrupted long before she came to stay with us. I wouldn't be surprised if little Bianca sleeps with Karel tonight. Part of breaking into the business, isn't it? Of course it will have to be all business— that's the least a mother can do. Margherita's problem was that she always enjoyed it too much, chained up in those torture rooms. She couldn't enjoy it any other way. You'll see. She and Thanatz. And whatever Thanatz brought in his valise."

"Thanatz."

"Ah, she didn't tell you." Laughing. "Miklos Thanatz, her husband. They get together off and on. Toward the end of the war they had a little touring show for the boys at the front—a lesbian couple, a dog, a trunk of leather costumes and implements, a small band. They entertained the SS troops. Concentration camps . . . the barbed-wire circuit, you know. And then later, in Holland, out at the rocket sites. This is the first time since the surrender they've been together, so I wouldn't actually expect to see too much of her. . . ."

"Oh, yeah, well, I didn't know that." Rocket sites? The hand of Providence creeps among the stars, giving Slothrop the finger.

"While they were away, they left Bianca with us, at Bydgoszcz. She has her bitchy moments but she's really a charming child. I never played the father game with her. I doubt she had a father. It was parthenogenesis, she's pure Margherita, if pure is the word I want."

The evening clothes fit perfectly. Stefania leads Slothrop up a companionway and out on deck. The *Anubis* moves now through starlit countryside, the horizon broken now and then by silhouettes of a windmill, haycocks, a row of pig arks, some line of trees set on a low hill for the wind. . . . There are ships we can dream across terrible rapids, against currents . . . our desire is wind and motor. . . .

"Antoni." She has brought Slothrop to an enormous figure in Polish cavalry fatigues and with a lot of maniacal teeth.

"American?" pumping Slothrop's hand. "Bravo. You nearly complete the set. We are the ship of all nations now. We've even got a Japanese on board. An ex-liaison man from Berlin who didn't quite get out by way of Russia. You'll find a bar on the next deck. Anything wandering around"—hugging Stefania to him—"except this one, is fair game."

Slothrop salutes, gathers they would like to be alone, and finds the ladder to the bar. The bar is hung with festive garlands of flowers and light bulbs, and crowded with dozens of elegantly-decked guests, who have just now, with the band accompanying, broken into this up-tempo song:

Welcome Aboard!

Welcome aboard, gee, it's a fabulous or-gy
That you just dropped in on, my friend—
We can't recall just how it star-ted,
But there's only one way it can end!
The behavior is bestial, hardly Marie-Celestial,
But you'll fit right in with the crowd,
If you jettison all of those prob-lems,
And keep it hysterically loud!

There are mo-thers, with their lo-vers,
Stealing rot-ters, from their daught-ers,
Big erec-tions, predilec-tions
That you wouldn't believe,
So put your brain on your sleeve,
And come a-
         board the *Titanic*, things'll really be manic,
Folks'll panic the second that sunken ice*berg* is knocked,
Naughty 'n' noisy, and very Walpurgisnacht,
That's how the party will end,
So—welcome aboard, welcome aboard, my friend!

Well here's couples moaning together in the lifeboats, a drunk's gone to sleep in the awning over Slothrop's head, fat fellows in white gloves with pink magnolias in their hair are dancing tummy-to-tummy and murmuring together in Wendish. Hands grope down inside satin gowns. Waiters with brown skins and doe eyes circulate with trays on which you are likely to find any number of sub-stances and paraphernalia. The band is playing a medley

of American fox-trots. The Baron de Mallakastra sifts a
sinister white powder into the highball of Mme. Sztup. It
is the same old shit that was going on back at Raoul de la
Perlimpinpin's place, and for all Slothrop knows it's the
same party.

He gets a glimpse of Margherita and her daughter, but
there is a density of orgy-goers around them that keeps
him at a distance. He knows he's vulnerable, more than
he should be, to pretty little girls, so he reckons it's just as
well, because that Bianca's a knockout, all right: 11 or 12,
dark and lovely, wearing a red chiffon gown, silk stockings and high-heeled slippers, her hair swept up elaborate
and flawless and interwoven with a string of pearls to
show pendant earrings of crystal twinkling from her tiny
lobes . . . help, help. Why do these things have to keep
coming down on him? He can see the obit now in *Time*
magazine—Died, Rocketman, pushing 30, in the Zone,
of lust.

The woman who tried to chop Slothrop down with the
cleaver is now seated on a bitt, holding a half-liter of
some liquid which has already seeped into and begun to
darken the orchid garnishing it. She is telling everybody a
story about Margherita. Her hair has been combed or
styled in a way that makes it look like a certain cut of
meat. Slothrop's drink, nominally Irish whisky and water,
arrives and he moves in to listen.

". . . her Neptune is afflicted. Whose isn't? some will
ask. Ah. But as residents on *this* planet, usually. Greta
lived, most of the time, *on* Neptune—her affliction was
more direct, purer, clearer than we know it here.

"She found Oneirine on a day when her outpost in England, the usual connection for Chlordyne, failed. Beside
the Thames, as geraniums of light floated in the sky too
slow to tell—brass light, tanned-skin and mellow peach
light, stylized blooms being drafted on and on among the
clouds, to fade here, to regenerate there—as this happened
to the day's light, he fell. A fall of hours, less extravagant
than Lucifer's, but in the same way part of a deliberate
pattern. Greta was meant to find Oneirine. Each plot
carries its signature. Some are God's, some masquerade as
God's. This is a very advanced kind of forgery. But still
there's the same meanness and mortality to it as a falsely

made check. It is only more complex. The members have names, like the Archangels. More or less common, humanly-given names whose security can be broken, and the names learned. But those names are not magic. That's the key, that's the difference. Spoken aloud, even with the purest magical intention, *they do not work*.

"So he fell from their grace. So there was no Chlordyne. So she happened to meet V-Mann Wimpe in the street, in Berlin, under a theatre marquee whose sentient bulbs may have looked on, a picturesque array of extras, witnesses to grave and historic encounters. So she had come to Onei-rine, and the face of her afflicted home planet was re-arranged in the instant."

Oneirine Jamf Imipolex A4. . . .

"That silly bitch," observes a voice at Slothrop's elbow, "tells it worse every time."

"Beg pardon?" Slothrop looks around and finds Miklos Thanatz, full beard, eyebrows feathering out like trailing edges of hawks' wings, drinking absinthe out of a souvenir stein on which, in colors made ghastly by the carnival lights on deck, bony and giggling Death is about to sur-prise two lovers in bed.

There is no problem steering him onto the subject of the Rocket—"I think of the A4," sez he, "as a baby Jesus, with endless committees of Herods out to destroy it in infancy— Prussians, some of whom in their innermost hearts still felt artillery to be a dangerous innovation. If you'd been out there . . . inside the first minute, you saw, you grew docile under its . . . it really did possess a Max Weber charisma . . . some joyful—and *deeply* irrational—force the State bureaucracy could never routinize, against which it could not prevail . . . they did resist it, but they also allowed it to happen. We can't imagine anyone *choosing* a role like that. But every year, somehow, their numbers grow."

But the tour with General Kammler's rocketeers is what Slothrop, perversely, wants—wants?—to know about, "Well I've been to that Nordhausen, sure, seen the bits and pieces. But never a fully-assembled A4. That must really be something, huh?"

Thanatz is holding out his stein for a refill. The waiter, deadpan, dribbles water down a spoon to turn the absinthe

milky green while Thanatz caresses his buttocks, then
moves away. It is not clear if Thanatz has been thinking
about his answer. "Yes, fueled, alive, ready for firing . . .
fifty feet high, trembling . . . and then the fantastic, virile
roar. Your ears nearly burst. Cruel, hard, thrusting into the
virgin-blue robes of the sky, my friend. Oh, so phallic.
Wouldn't you say?"

"Uh . . ."

"Hmm, ja, you would have got on with them out at the
batteries, they were sedate, like you. More studious than
your infantry or Panzer types, attentive to the point of
fanaticism. Oh, with notable exceptions of course. One
lives for notable exceptions. . . . There was a boy." Drunk
reminiscence? Is he faking this? "His name was Gottfried.
God's peace, which I trust he's found. For us I hold no
such hope. We are weighed in the balance and found wanting, and the Butcher has had His thumb in the scales . . .
you think I'm jaded. So did I, until that terrible week. It
was a time of dissolution, falling back across the Nieder-
sächsisch oil fields. Then I understood I was but a dewy
child. The battery commander had become a screaming
maniac. He called himself 'Blicero.' He'd begun to talk the
way the captain in *Wozzeck* sings, his voice breaking suddenly up into the higher registers of hysteria. Things were
falling apart, and he reverted to some ancestral version of
himself, screamed at the sky, sat hours in a rigid trance,
with his eyes rolled clear up into his head. Breaking without warning into that ungodly coloratura. White blank
ovals, the eyes of a statue, with the gray rain behind them.
He had left 1945, wired his nerves back into the pre-
Christian earth we fled across, into the Urstoff of the
primitive German, God's poorest and most panicked creature. You and I perhaps have become over the generations
so Christianized, so enfeebled by Gesellschaft and our
obligation to its celebrated 'Contract,' which never did
exist, that we, even we, are appalled by reversions like
that. But deep, out of its silence, the Urstoff wakes, and
sings . . . and on the last day . . . it is shameful . . . through
that whole terrible day, I had an erection . . . don't judge
me . . . it was out of my control . . . *everything* was out of
control—"

About here they are interrupted by Margherita and

Bianca, playing stage mother and reluctant child. Whispers to the bandleader, funseekers crowding eagerly around a cleared space where Bianca now stands pouting, her little red frock halfway up her slender thighs, with black lace petticoats peeping from beneath the hem, surely it's going to be something sophisticated, bigcity, and wicked, but what's she doing with her finger posed aside of one dimpled cheek like this—at which point comes the band's intro, and pre-vomit saliva begins to gush into Slothrop's mouth, along with a horrible doubt into his brain about how he is going to make it through the next few minutes.

Not only is her song "On the Good Ship Lollipop," but she is also now commencing, without a trace of shame, to *grunt* her way through it, in perfect mimickry of young Shirley Temple—each straining baby-pig inflection, each curl-toss, unmotivated smile, and stumbling toe-tap . . . her delicate bare arms have begun to grow fatter, her frock shorter—is somebody fooling with the lights? But the billowings of asexual child-fat have not changed her eyes: they remain as they were, mocking, dark, her own. . . .

Much applause and alcoholic bravo-ing when it's finally over. Thanatz abstains, fatherly head wagging, great eyebrows in a frown. "She's never going to be a woman if this goes on. . . ."

"And *now*, liebling," Margherita with a rare, and somewhat phony, smile, "let's hear 'Animal Crackers in My Soup'!"

"'Super Animals in My Crack,'" hollers a humorist from the crowd.

"No," groans the child.

"Bianca—"

"You bitch," spike heel ringing on the steel deck. It's an act. "Haven't you humiliated me enough?"

"Not nearly enough," pouncing on her daughter, grabbing her by the hair and shaking her. The little girl has fallen to her knees, struggling, trying to get away.

"Oh, delightful," cries the meat-cleaver lady, "Greta's going to punish her."

"How *I'd* like to," murmurs a striking mulatto girl in a strapless gown, pushing forward to watch, tapping Slothrop's cheek with her jeweled cigarette holder as satin haunches whisper across his thigh. Someone has provided

Margherita with a steel ruler and an ebony Empire chair.
She drags Bianca across her lap, pushing up frock and
petticoats, yanking down white lace knickers. Beautiful
little-girl buttocks rise like moons. The tender crevice
tightens and relaxes, suspender straps shift and stretch as
Bianca kicks her legs, silk stockings squeak together, erotic
and audible now that the group have fallen silent and
found the medium of touch, hands reaching out to breasts
and crotches, Adam's apples bobbing, tongues licking lips
. . . where's the old masochist and monument Slothrop
knew back in Berlin? It's as if Greta is now releasing all
the pain she's stored up over the past weeks onto her
child's naked bottom, the skin so finely grained that white
centimeter markings and numerals are being left in mirror-
image against the red stripes with each blow, crisscrossing,
building up a skew matrix of pain on Bianca's flesh. Tears
go streaming down her inverted and reddening face, mixing with mascara, dripping onto the pale lizard surfaces of
her mother's shoes . . . her hair has loosened and spills to
the deck, dark, salted with the string of little seed pearls.
The mulatto girl has backed up against Slothrop, reaching
behind to fondle his erection, which has nothing between
it and the outside but somebody's loosely-pleated tuxedo
trousers. Everyone is kind of aroused, Thanatz is sitting
up on the bar having his own as yet unsheathed penis
mouthed by one of the white-gloved Wends. Two of the
waiters kneel on deck lapping at the juicy genitals of a
blonde in a wine velvet frock, who meantime is licking
ardently the tall and shiny French heels of an elderly lady
in lemon organza busy fastening felt-lined silver manacles
to the wrists of her escort, a major of the Yugoslav artillery
in dress uniform, who kneels with nose and tongue well
between the bruised buttocks of a long-legged ballerina
from Paris, holding up her silk skirt for him with docile
fingertips while her companion, a tall Swiss divorcée in
tight-laced leather corselette and black Russian boots, un-
does the top of her friend's gown and skillfully begins to
lash at her bared breasts with the stems of half a dozen
roses, red as the beads of blood which spring up and soon
are shaking off the ends of her stiff nipples to splash into
the eager mouth of another Wend who's being jerked off
by a retired Dutch banker sitting on the deck, shoes and

socks just removed by two adorable schoolgirls, twin
sisters in fact, in identical dress of flowered voile, with
each of the banker's big toes inserted now into a downy
little furrow as they lie forward along his legs kissing his
shaggy stomach, pretty twin bottoms arched to receive in
their anal openings the cocks of the two waiters who have
but lately been, if you recall, eating that juicy blonde in
that velvet dress back down the Oder River a ways. . . .

As for Slothrop, he ends up coming between the round
shuddering tits of a Viennese girl with hair the color of a
lioness's pelt and emerald eyes with lashes thick as fur, his
sperm surging out into the hollow of her arched throat
and among all the diamonds of her necklace, burning age-
lessly through the haze of his seed—and it *feels*, at least,
like everybody came together, though how could that be?
He does notice that the only person not connected, aside
from Antoni and Stefania, seems to be the Jap liaison man,
who's been sitting alone, one deck up, watching. Not
masturbating or anything, just watching, watching the
river, the night . . . well, they're pretty inscrutable, you
know, those Japs.

There is a general withdrawing from orifices after a
while, drinking, doping and gabbing resume, and many
begin to drift away to catch some sleep. Here and there
a couple or threesome linger. A C-melody saxophone
player has the bell of his instrument snuggled between the
widespread thighs of a pretty matron in sunglasses, yes
sunglasses at night, this is some degenerate company Slothrop has fallen in with all right—the saxman is playing
"Chattanooga Choo Choo," and those vibrations are just
driving her wild. A girl with an enormous glass dildo inside which baby piranhas are swimming in some kind
of decadent lavender medium amuses herself between
the buttocks of a stout transvestite in lace stockings and a
dyed sable coat. A Montenegran countess is being fucked
simultaneously in her chignon and her navel by a pair of
octogenarians who wear only jackboots and are carrying
on some sort of technical discussion in what seems to be
ecclesiastical Latin.

The sun is still hours away, down the vast unreadable
underslope of Russia. Fog closes in, and the engines slow.
Wrecks slide away under the keel of the white ship.

Springtime corpses caught in the wreckage twist and flow
as the *Anubis* moves by overhead. Under the bowsprit, the
golden jackal, the only being aboard that can see through
the fog, stares ahead, down the river, toward Swinemünde.

□

Slothrop here's been dreaming about Llandudno, where
he spent a rainy furlough once drinking bitter in bed
with a tug skipper's daughter. Also where Lewis Carroll
wrote that *Alice in Wonderland*. So, they put up a statue
of the White Rabbit in Llandudno. White Rabbit's been
talking to Slothrop, serious and crucial talk, but on the
way up to waking he loses it all, as usual. He lies staring
at ducts and raceways overhead, asbestos-covered elbows,
pipes, gages, tanks, switchboards, flanges, unions, valve-
wheels and all their thickets of shadow. It's noisy as hell.
Sunlight filters down the hatches, so that must mean it's
morning. In a corner of his vision now, he catches a flutter
of red.

"You mustn't tell Margherita. Please." That Bianca. Hair
down to her hips, cheeks smudged, eyes hot. "She'll kill
me."

"What time is it?"

"The sun's been up for hours. Why do you want to
know?"

Why does he want to know. Hmm. Maybe he'll go back
to sleep, here. "Your mother upset with you, or something?"

"Oh, she's gone out of her mind, she just accused me
of having an affair with Thanatz. *Mad*ness, of course we're
good *friends*, but that's all . . . if she paid *any* attention to
me she'd know that."

"She sure was paying attention to your ass there, kid."

"Oh, dear," lifting her dress, turning so she can also
watch Slothrop back over a shoulder. "I can still feel *that*.
Did she leave marks?"

"Well, you'll have to come closer."

She moves toward him, smiling, pointing toes each step.
"I watched you sleep. You're very pretty, you know.
Mother also said you're cruel."

"Watch this." He leans to bite her gently on one cheek of her ass. She squirms, but doesn't move away.

"Mm. There's a zipper there, could you . . ." She shrugs, twists as he unzips her, red taffeta slides down and off and sure enough there's one or two lavender bruises starting to show up on her bottom, which is perfectly shaped, smooth as cream. Small as she is, she's been further laced into a tiny black corset, which compresses her waist now to the diameter of a brandy bottle and pushes pre-subdeb breasts up into little white crescents. Satin straps, adorned with intricately pornographic needlework, run down each thigh to hold up stockings with tops of dark Alençon lace. The bare backs of her legs come brushing softly across Slothrop's face. He starts taking giant, ass-enthusiast bites now, meantime reaching around to play with cuntlips and clit, Bianca's little feet shifting in a nervous dance and scarlet nails digging sharp as needles underneath her stocking tops and into her legs as he goes planting hickeys, red nebulae across her sensitive spaces. She smells like soap, flowers, sweat, cunt. Her long hair falls to the level of Slothrop's eyes, fine and black, the split ends whispering across the small of her white back in and out of invisibility, like rain . . . she has turned, and sinks to her knees to undo his pleated trousers. Leaning, brushing hair back behind her ears, the little girl takes the head of Slothrop's cock into her rouged mouth. Her eyes glitter through fern lashes, baby rodent hands race his body unbuttoning, caressing. Such a slender child: her throat swallowing, strummed to a moan as he grabs her hair, twists it . . . she has him all figured out. Knows exactly when to take her mouth away and stand up, high-heeled Parisian slippers planted to either side of him, swaying, hair softly waving forward to frame her face, repeated by the corset darkly framing her pubic mound and belly. Raising bare arms, little Bianca lifts her long hair, tosses her little head to let the mane shiver down her back, needle-tipped fingers drifting then down slowly, making him wait, down over the satin, all the shiny hooks and laces, to her thighs. Then her face, round with baby-fat, enormous night-shadowed eyes comes swooping in as she kneels, guides his penis into her and settles slow, excruciating till he fills her, stuffs her full. . . .

Now something, oh, kind of *funny* happens here. Not

that Slothrop is really aware of it now, while it's going on—but later on, it will occur to him that he was—this may sound odd, but he was somehow, actually, well, *inside his own cock*. If you can imagine such a thing. Yes, inside the metropolitan organ entirely, all other colonial tissue forgotten and left to fend for itself, his arms and legs it seems *woven* among vessels and ducts, his sperm roaring louder and louder, getting ready to erupt, somewhere below his feet ... maroon and evening cuntlight reaches him in a single ray through the opening at the top, refracted through the clear juices flowing up around him. He is enclosed. Everything is about to come, come incredibly, and he's helpless here in this exploding *emprise* ... red flesh echoing ... an extraordinary sense of *waiting to rise*. . . .

She posts, his pretty horsewoman, face to the overhead, quivering up and down, thightop muscles strung hard as cable, baby breasts working out the top of her garment ... Slothrop pulls Bianca to him by her nipples and bites each one very hard. Sliding her arms around his neck, hugging him, she starts to come, and so does he, their own flood taking him up then out of his expectancy, out the eye at tower's summit and into her with a singular detonation of touch. Announcing the void, what could it be but the kingly voice of the Aggregat itself?

Somewhere in their lying-still are her heart, buffeting, a chickadee in the snow, her hair, draping and sheltering both their faces, little tongue at his temples and eyes on and on, silk legs rubbing his flanks, cool leather of her shoes against his legs and ankles, shoulderblades rising like wings whenever she hugs him. What happened back there? Slothrop thinks he might cry.

They have been holding each other. She's been talking about hiding out.

"Sure. But we'll have to get off sometime, Swinemünde, someplace."

"No. We can get away. I'm a child, I know how to hide. I can hide you too."

He knows she can. He knows. Right here, right now, under the make-up and the fancy underwear, she *exists*, love, invisibility. . . . For Slothrop this is some discovery. But her arms about his neck are shifting now, apprehensive. For good reason. Sure he'll stay for a while, but eventually he'll go, and for this he is to be counted, after all, among the Zone's lost. The Pope's staff is always going to remain barren, like Slothrop's own unflowering cock.

So when he disentangles himself, it is extravagantly. He creates a bureaucracy of departure, inoculations against forgetting, exit visas stamped with love-bites . . . but coming back is something he's already forgotten about. Straightening his bow tie, brushing off the satin lapels of his jacket, buttoning up his pants, back in uniform of the day, he turns his back on her, and up the ladder he goes. The last instant their eyes were in touch is already behind him. . . .

Alone, kneeling on the painted steel, like her mother she knows how horror will come when the afternoon is brightest. And like Margherita, she has her worst visions in black and white. Each day she feels closer to the edge of something. She dreams often of the same journey: a passage by train, between two well-known cities, hit by that same nacreous wrinkling the films use to suggest rain out a window. In a Pullman, dictating her story. She feels able at last to tell of a personal horror, tell it clearly in a way others can share. That may keep it from taking her past the edge, into silver-salt dark closing ponderably slow at her mind's flank . . . when she was growing out her fringes, in dark rooms her own unaccustomed hair, beside her eyes, would loom like a presence. . . . In her ruined towers now the bells gong back and forth in the wind. Frayed ropes dangle or slap where her brown hoods no longer glide above the stone. Her wind keeps even dust away. It is old daylight: late, and cold. Horror in the brightest hour of afternoon . . . sails on the sea too small and distant to matter . . . water too steel and cold. . . .

Her look now—this deepening arrest—has already broken Slothrop's seeing heart: has broken and broken, that same look swung as he drove by, thrust away into twilights of moss and crumbling colony, of skinny clouded-cylinder gas pumps, of tin Moxie signs gentian and bittersweet as the taste they were there to hustle on the weathered sides of barns, looked for how many Last Times up in the rearview mirror, all of them too far inside metal and combustion, allowing the days' targets more reality than

anything that might come up by surprise, by Murphy's
Law, where the salvation could be.... Lost, again and
again, past poor dam-busted and drowned Becket, up and
down the rut-brown slopes, the hayrakes rusting in the
afternoon, the sky purple-gray, dark as chewed gum, the
mist starting to make white dashes in the air, aimed earth-
ward a quarter, a half inch ... she looked at him once, of
course he still remembers, from down at the end of a
lunchwagon counter, grill smoke working onto the windows patient as shoe grease against the rain for the plaid,
hunched-up leaky handful inside, off the jukebox a quick
twinkle in the bleat of a trombone, a reed section, planting
swing notes precisely into the groove between silent mid-
point and next beat, jumping it *pah* (hm) *pah* (hm) *pah*
so exactly in the groove that you knew it was ahead but
felt it was behind, both of you, at both ends of the counter,
could feel it, feel your age delivered into a new kind of
time that may have allowed you to miss the rest, the
graceless expectations of old men who watched, in bifocal
and mucus indifference, watched you lindy-hop into the
pit by millions, as many millions as necessary.... Of course
Slothrop lost her, and kept losing her—it was an American
requirement—out the windows of the Greyhound, passing
into beveled stonery, green and elm-folded on into a failure of perception, or, in a more sinister sense, of will (you
used to know what these words mean), she has moved on,
untroubled, too much Theirs, no chance of a beige summer spook at *her* roadside....

Leaving Slothrop in his city-reflexes and Harvard crew
sox—both happening to be red-ring manacles, comicbook
irons (though the comic book was virtually uncirculated,
found by chance near nightfall by a hopper at a Berkshire sandbank. The name of the hero—or being—was
Sundial. The frames never enclosed him—or it—for long
enough to tell. Sundial, flashing in, flashing out again,
came from "across the wind," by which readers understood "across some flow, more or less sheet and vertical:
a wall in constant motion"—over there was a different
world, where Sundial took care of business they would
never understand).

Distant, yes these are pretty distant. Sure they are. Too
much closer and it begins to hurt to bring her back. But
there is this Eurydice-obsession, this *bringing back out*

of . . . though how much easier just to leave her there, in fetid carbide and dead-canary soups of breath and come out and have comfort enough to try only for a reasonable fascimile—"Why bring her back? Why try? It's only the difference between the real boxtop and the one you draw for Them." No. How can he believe that? It's what They want him to believe, but how can he? No difference between a boxtop and its image, all right, their whole economy's based on *that* . . . but she must be more than an image, a product, a promise to pay. . . .

Of all her putative fathers—Max Schlepzig and masked extras on one side of the moving film, Franz Pökler and certainly other pairs of hands busy through trouser cloth, that *Alpdrücken* Night, on the other—Bianca is closest, this last possible moment below decks here behind the ravening jackal, closest to you who came in blinding color, slouched alone in your own seat, never threatened along any rookwise row or diagonal all night, you whose interdiction from her mother's water-white love is absolute, you, alone, saying *sure I know them,* omitted, chuckling *count me in,* unable, thinking *probably some hooker* . . . She favors you, most of all. You'll never get to see her. So somebody has to tell you.

□

Halfway up the ladder, Slothrop is startled by a bright set of teeth, beaming out of a dark hatchway. "I was watching. I hope you don't mind." Seems to be that Nip again, who introduces himself now as Ensign Morituri, of the Imperial Japanese Navy.

"Yeah, I . . ." why is Slothrop drawling this way? "saw ya watching . . . last *night too,* mister. . . ."

"You think I am a voyeur. Yes you do. But it isn't that. There is no thrill, I mean. But when I watch people, I feel less alone."

"W'l hell, Ensign . . . why don'tcha just . . . join in? *They're* always lookin' fer . . . company."

"Oh, my goodness," grinning one of them big polyhedral Jap grins, like they do, "then I would feel *more* alone."

Tables and chairs have been set out under orange-and-red-stripe awnings on the fantail. Slothrop and Morituri have got the place almost to themselves, except for some girls in two-piece swimsuits out to catch some sun before it goes away. Cumulonimbus are building up dead ahead. You can hear thunder in the distance. The air is coming awake.

A steward brings coffee, cream, porridge and fresh oranges. Slothrop looks at the porridge, doubtful. "I'll take it," Ensign Morituri grabbing the bowl.

"Oh, sure." Slothrop notices now how this Nip also has this wide handle-bar mustache. "Aha, aha. I'm hep to you. A porridge fan! Shameful. A latent Anglophile—yeah, you're blushing." Pointing and hollering ha, ha, ha.

"You've found me out. Yes, yes. I've been on the wrong side for six years."

"Ever try to get away?"

"And find out what you people are really like? Oh, my golly. What if phile changes then to phobe? Where would I be?" He giggles, spits an orange pit over the side. Seems he put in a few weeks' training on that Formosa, in Kamikaze school, but they washed him out. No one ever told him why, exactly. Something to do with his attitude. "I just didn't have a good attitude," he sighs. "So they sent me back here again, by way of Russia and Switzerland. This time with the Propaganda Ministry." He would sit most of the day watching Allied footage for what could be pulled and worked into newsreels to make the Axis look good and the other side look bad. "All I know about Great Britain comes from that raw material."

"Looks like German movies have warped other outlooks around here too."

"You mean Margherita's. Did you know, that's how we met! A mutual friend at Ufa. I was on holiday at Bad Karma—just before the Polish invasion. The little town where you joined us. It was a spa. I watched you fall in the water. Then you climbed aboard. I also watched Margherita watching you. Please don't be offended, Slothrop, but it might be better to stay away from her right now."

"Not at all. I know something creepy is going on." He tells Morituri about the incident in the Sprudelhof, and Margherita's flight from the apparition in black.

The Ensign nods, grim, twisting half his mustache up

so it points in a saber at one eye. "She didn't tell you
what happened there? Golly, Jack, you had better
know. . . ."

ENSIGN MORITURI'S STORY

Wars have a way of overriding the days just before
them. In the looking back, there is such noise and gravity.
But we are conditioned to forget. So that the war may
have more importance, yes, but still . . . isn't the hidden
machinery easier to see in the days leading up to the
event? There are arrangements, things to be expedited . . .
and often the edges are apt to lift, briefly, and we see
things we were not meant to. . . .

They'd tried to talk Margherita out of going to Hollywood. She went, and she failed. Rollo was there when
she returned, to keep the worst from happening. For a
month he impounded sharp objects, kept her at ground
level and away from chemicals, which meant she didn't
sleep much. She would drop off and wake up hysterical.
Afraid to go to sleep. Afraid she wouldn't know how to
get back.

Rollo did not have a keen mind. He meant well, but
after a month of her he found he couldn't take any more.
Actually it surprised everyone that he'd lasted so long.
Greta was handed over to Sigmund, hardly improved, but
perhaps no worse.

The trouble with Sigmund was the place he happened
to be living in, a drafty, crenelated deformity overlooking
a cold little lake in the Bavarian Alps. Parts of it must
have dated back to the fall of Rome. That was where
Sigmund brought her.

She had got the idea somewhere that she was part
Jewish. Things in Germany by then, as everyone knows,
were very bad. Margherita was terrified of being "found
out." She heard Gestapo in every puff of air that slipped
in, among any of a thousand windways of dilapidation.
Sigmund spent whole nights trying to talk it away. He
was no better at it than Rollo. It was around this time
that her symptoms began.

However psychogenic these pains, tics, hives and
nauseas, her suffering was real. Acupuncturists came down

by Zeppelin from Berlin, showing up in the middle of the
night with little velvet cases full of gold needles. Viennese
analysts, Indian holy men, Baptists from America trooped
in and out of Sigmund's castle, stage-hypnotists and Co-
lombian *curanderos* slept on the rug in front of the fireplace. Nothing worked. Sigmund grew alarmed, and before long as ready as Margherita to hallucinate. Probably
it was she who suggested Bad Karma. It had a reputation
that summer for its mud, hot and greasy mud with traces
of radium, jet black, softly bubbling. Ah. Anyone who's
been sick in that way can imagine her hope. That mud
would cure anything.

   Where was anybody that summer before the War?
Dreaming. The spas that summer, the summer Ensign
Morituri came to Bad Karma, were crowded with sleep-
walkers. Nothing for him to do at the Embassy. They
suggested a holiday till September. He should have known
something was up, but he only went on holiday to Bad
Karma—spent the days drinking Pilsener Urquelle in the
café by the lake in the Pavilion Park. He was a stranger,
half the time drunk, silly beer-drunk, and he hardly spoke
their language. But what he saw must have been going on
all over Germany. A premeditated frenzy.

   Margherita and Sigmund moved along the same mag-
nolia-shaded paths, sat out in rolling-chairs to hear concerts of patriotic music . . . when it rained they fidgeted
over card games in one of the public rooms of their Kurhaus. At night they watched the fireworks—fountains,
spark-foaming rockets, yellow starbursts high over Poland.
That oneiric season. . . . There was no one in all the spas
to read anything in the patterns the fires made. They
were only gay lights, nervous as the fantasies that flickered
from eye to eye, trailing the skin like the ostrich fans of
50 years ago.

   When did Sigmund first notice her absences, or when
did they become for him more than routine? Always she
gave him plausible stories: a medical appointment, a chance
meeting with an old friend, drowsiness in the mud-baths,
while time raced by. It may have been unaccustomed sleep
that got him suspicious at last, because of what her wakefulness had put him through in the South. The stories about
the children in the local newspapers could have made no

impression, not then. Sigmund only read headlines, and rarely at that, to fill up a dead moment.

Morituri saw them often. They would meet and bow, exchange Heil Hitlers, and the Ensign would be permitted a few minutes to practice his German. Except for waiters and barmen, they were the only people he spoke with. Out at the tennis courts, waiting in line at the pump room under the cool colonnade, at an aquatic *corso*, a battle of flowers, a Venetian fête, Sigmund and Margherita hardly changed, he with his—Morituri thought of it as his American Smile, around the amber stem of his dead pipe . . . his head like a flesh Christmas ornament . . . how long ago it was . . . she with her yellow sunglasses and Garbo hats. The flowers were all that changed about her day to day: morning glory, almond blossom, foxglove. Morituri grew to look forward so to these daily meetings. His wife and daughters clear on the other side of the world, himself exiled in a country that bewildered and oppressed him. He needed the passing zoogoers' civility, the guidebook words. He knows he stared back, every bit as curious. In their European slickness, they all fascinated him: the white-plumed old ladies in the lying-out chairs, the veterans of the Great War like serene hippopotamuses soaking in the steel baths, their effeminate secretaries chattering shrill as monkeys across the Sprudelstrasse, while far down the arches of lindens and chestnuts you could hear the endless roar of carbon dioxide at the bubbling spring, coming out of solution in great shuddering spheres . . . but Sigmund and Margherita fascinated him most of all. "They seemed as alien here as I was. We each have antennas, don't we, tuned to recognize our own. . . ."

One forenoon, by accident, he met Sigmund, alone, a tweed statue on his walking stick in front of the Inhalatorium, looking as if he'd lost his way, no real place to go, no desire. Without premeditation, then, they began to talk. The time was right. They moved off presently, strolling through the crowds of sick foreigners, while Sigmund told of his troubles with Greta, her Jewish fantasy, her absences. The day before, he had caught her out in a lie. She'd come in very late. Her hands had taken a fine tremor that wouldn't stop. He'd begun to notice things. Her shoes, beaded with drying black mud. A seam in her dress

widened, nearly ripped, though she'd been losing weight.
But he hadn't the courage to have it out with her.

Morituri, who had been reading the papers, for whom
the connection had sprung up like a monster from the
tamed effervescences of the Trinkhalle, but who did not
have the words, German or otherwise, to tell Sigmund,
Morituri, the Beer Ensign, began to follow her then. She
never looked back, but she knew he was there. At the
weekly ball in the Kursaal he felt, for the first time, a
reticence among them all. Margherita, eyes he was accustomed to seeing covered with sunglasses naked now,
burning terribly, never took her gaze from him. The Kur-
Orchestra played selections from *The Merry Widow* and
Secrets of Suzanne, out-of-date music, and yet, when bits
of it found Morituri years later in the street, over the
radio, they never failed to bring back the unwritten taste
of that night, the three of them at the edge of a deepness
none could sound . . . some last reprise of the European
thirties he had never known . . . which are also for him a
particular room, a salon in the afternoon: lean girls in
gowns, mascara all around their eyes, the men with faces
shaven very smooth, film-star polished . . . not operetta but
dance music here, sophisticated, soothing, a bit "modern,"
dipping elegantly in the up-to-date melodic lines . . . an
upstairs room, with late sunlight coming in, deep carpets,
voices saying nothing heavy or complex, smiles informed
and condescending. He was awakened that morning in a
soft bed, he looks forward to an evening at a cabaret
dancing to popular love songs played in just such a mannered and polished style. His afternoon salon with its held
tears, its smoke, its careful passion has been a way-station
between the comfortable morning and the comfortable
night: it was Europe, it was the smoky, citied fear of
death, and most perilous it was Margherita's scrutable
eyes, that lost encounter in the Kursaal, black eyes among
those huddled jewels and nodding old generals, in the
roar from the Brodelbrunnen outside, filling the quiet
spaces in the music as machinery was soon to fill the sky.

Next evening, Morituri followed her out for the last time.
Down the worn paths, under the accustomed trees, past
the German goldfish pool that reminded him of home,
across the golf links, the day's last white-mustached men

struggling up out of traps and hazards, their caddies standing at allegorical attention in the glow of the sunset, the bundled clubs in Fascist silhouette.... Twilight came down on Bad Karma that night pallid and violent: the horizon was a Biblical disaster. Greta had dressed all in black, a hat with a veil covering most of her hair, purse slung by a long strap over one shoulder. As choices of a destination narrowed to one, as Morituri ran into snares the night began to lay out for him, prophecy filled him like the river wind: where she had been on her absences, how the children in those headlines had—

They had arrived at the edge of the black mud pool: that underground presence, old as Earth, partly enclosed back at the Spa and a name given to.... The offering was to be a boy, lingering after all the others had gone. His hair was cold snow. Morituri could only hear fragments of what they said. The boy wasn't afraid of her at first. He might not have recognized her from his dreams. It would have been his only hope. But they had made that impossible, his German overseers. Morituri stood by in his uniform, waiting, unbuttoning the jacket so that he could move, though he didn't want to. Certainly they were all repeating this broken act from an earlier time....

Her voice began its rise, and the boy his trembling. "You have been in exile too long." It was a loud clap in the dusk. "Come home, with me," she cried, "back to your people." Now he was trying to break away, but her hand, her gloved hand, her claw had flown out and seized his arm. "Little piece of Jewish shit. Don't try to run away from me."

"No . . ." but at the very end rising, in a provocative question.

"You know who I am, too. My home is the form of Light," burlesquing it now, in heavy Yiddish dialect, actressy and false, "I wander all the Diaspora looking for strayed children. I am Israel. I am the Shekhinah, queen, daughter, bride, and mother of God. And I will take you back, you fragment of smashed vessel, even if I must pull you by your nasty little circumcised penis—"

"No . . ."

So Ensign Morituri committed then the only known act of heroism in his career. It's not even in his folder.

She had gathered the boy struggling, one glove busy between his legs. Morituri rushed forward. For a moment
the three of them swayed, locked together. Gray Nazi
statuary: its name may have been "The Family." None of
the Greek stillness: no, they *moved*. Immortality was not
the issue. That's what made them different. No survival,
beyond the senses' taking of it—no handing-down.
Doomed as d'Annunzio's adventure at Fiume, as the Reich
itself, as the poor creatures from whom the boy now tore
loose and ran off into the evening.

Margherita collapsed by the edge of the great lightless
pool. Morituri knelt beside her while she cried. It was
terrible. What had brought him there, what had understood and moved in so automatically, fell back now to
sleep. His conditioning, his verbal, ranked and uniformed
self took over again. He knelt shivering, more afraid than
he'd ever been in his life. It was she who led their way
back to the Spa.

She and Sigmund left Bad Karma that night. The boy
may have been too frightened, the light too faint, Morituri himself may have had strong protectors, for God
knows he was visible enough there—but no police came.
"It never occurred to me to go to them. In my heart, I
knew she had murdered. You may condemn me for it. But
I saw what I'd be handing her over to, and it came to
the same thing, in official custody or not, you see." The
next day was 1 September. There was no longer any way
for children to vanish mysteriously.

The forenoon has gone dark. Rain spits in under the
awning. The bowl of porridge has stayed all untouched
in front of Morituri. Slothrop is sweating, staring at the
bright remains of an orange. "Listen," it has occurred to
his agile brain, "what about Bianca, then? Is she going
to be safe with that Greta, do you think?"

Frisking his great mustache, "What do you mean? Are
you asking, 'Can she be saved?' "

"Oh, pip, pip, old Jap, come off it—"

"Look, what can *you* save her from?" His eyes are pry-
ing Slothrop away from his comfort. Rain is drumming
now on the awnings, spilling in clear lacework from the
edges.

"But wait a minute. Oh, shit, that *woman* yesterday, in that Sprudelhof—"

"Yes. Remember Greta also saw you coming up out of the river. Now think of all the folklore among these people about radioactivity—these travelers from spa to spa, season after season. It's grace. It's the holy waters of Lourdes. This mysterious radiation that can cure so much—might it be the *ultimate* cure?"

"Uh . . ."

"I watched her face as you came aboard. I was with her at the edge of one radioactive night. I know what she saw this time. One of those children—preserved, nourished by the mud, the radium, growing taller and stronger while slowly, viscous and slow, the currents bore him along underground, year by year, until at last, grown to manhood, he came to the river, came up out of the black radiance of herself to find her again, Shekhinah, bride, queen, daughter. And mother. Motherly as sheltering mud and glowing pitchblende—"

Almost directly overhead, thunder suddenly breaks in a blinding egg of sound. Somewhere inside the blast, Slothrop has murmured, "Quit fooling."

"Are you going to risk finding out?"

Who is this, oh *sure* it's a Jap ensign, looking at me like this. But where are Bianca's arms, her defenseless mouth. . . . "Well in a day or two we'll be in Swinemünde, right?" talking to keep from—get up from the table then, you asshole—

"We'll all just keep moving, that's all. In the end it doesn't matter."

"Look, you've got kids, how can you say that? Is that all you want, just to 'keep moving'?"

"I want to see the war over in the Pacific so that I can go home. Since you ask. It's the season of the plum rains now, the Bai-u, when all the plums are ripening. I want only to be with Michiko and our girls, and once I'm there, never to leave Hiroshima again. I think you'd like it there. It's a city on Honshu, on the Inland Sea, very pretty, a perfect size, big enough for city excitement, small enough for the serenity a man needs. But these people are not returning, they are leaving their homes you see—"

But one of the knots securing the rain-heavy awning to

its frame has given way, white small-stuff unlacing rapidly, whipping around in the rain. The awning sags, funneling rainwater at Slothrop and Morituri, and they flee below decks.

They get separated in a crowd of newly-risen roisterers. There is hardly a thing now in Slothrop's head but getting to Bianca. At the end of the passageway, across a score of empty faces, he spots Stefania in white cardigan and slacks, beckoning. It takes him five minutes to thread his way to her, by which time he's picked up a brandy Alexander, a party hat, a sign taped to his back urging whoever reads it, in Low Pomeranian, to kick Slothrop, lipstick smudges in three shades of magenta, and a black Italian maduro someone has thoughtfully already lit.

"You may look like the soul of conviviality," Stefania greets him, "but it doesn't fool me. Under that cheerful mask is the face of a Jonah."

"You mean, uh, the, uh—"

"I mean Margherita. She's locked herself in the head. Hysterical. Nobody can bring her out."

"So you're looking at me. How about Thanatz?"

"Thanatz has disappeared, and so has Bianca."

"Oh, shit."

"Margherita thinks you've done away with her."

"Not me." He gives her a quick rundown of Ensign Morituri's tale. Some of her élan, her resilience, go away. She bites a fingernail.

"Yes, there were rumors. Sigmund, before he vanished, leaked just enough to titillate people, but never got specific. That was his style. Listen, Slothrop. Do you think Bianca's in any danger?"

"I'll try to find out." He is interrupted here by a swift kick in the ass.

"Unlucky you," crows a voice behind them. "I'm the only one on board who reads Low Pomeranian."

"Unlucky you," Stefania nods.

"All I wanted was a free ride to Swinemünde."

But like Stefania sez, "There's only one free ride. Meantime, start working off the fare for this one. Go see Margherita."

"You want me to—come on."

"We don't want anything to happen."

One of the General Orders aboard this vessel. Nothing shall happen. Well, Slothrop politely sticks the rest of his cigar between Mme. Procalowska's teeth and leaves her puffing on it, fists jammed in her sweater pockets.

Bianca isn't in the engine room. He moves around in pulsing bulblight, among asbestos-packed masses, burning himself once or twice where insulation's missing, looking into pale recesses, shadows, wondering about his own insulation here. Nothing but machinery, noise. He heads for the ladder. A scrap of red is waiting for him . . . no, only her frock, with a damp trace of his own semen still at the hem . . . this loud humidity has kept it there. He crouches, holding the garment, smelling her smell. I'm a child, I know how to hide, and I can hide you. "Bianca," he calls, "Bianca, come out."

Gathered about the door to the head, he finds an assortment of upper-class layabouts and drunks blocking the passageway along with a litter of bottles and glassware, and a seated circle of cocaine habitués, crystal birds flying up into forests of nose hair off the point of a gold and ruby dagger. Slothrop pushes through, leans on the door and calls Margherita's name.

"Go away."

"You don't have to come out. Just let me in."

"I know who you are."

"Please."

"They were very clever, sending you as poor Max. But it won't work now."

"I'm through with Them. I swear it. I need you, Greta." Bullshit. For what?

"They'll kill you, then. Go away."

"I know where Bianca is."

"What have you done with her?"

"Just—will you let me in?" After a full minute's silence, she does. A funseeker or two tries to push in, but he slams the door and locks it again. Greta is wearing nothing but a black chemise. Strokes of black hair curl high on her thighs. Her face is white, old, strained.

"Where is she?"

"Hiding."

"From me?"

"From Them."

A quick look at him. Too many mirrors, razors, scissors, lights. Too white. "But *you're* one of Them."

"Quit it, you know I'm not."

"You are. You came up out of the river."

"Well, that's cause I fell *in*, Greta."

"Then They made you."

He watches her playing, nervous, with strands of her hair. The *Anubis* has begun to rock some, but the sickness rising in him is for his head, not his stomach. As she begins to talk, nausea begins to fill him: a glowing black mudslide of nausea. . . .

□

It was always easy for men to come and tell her who to be. Other girls of her generation grew up asking: "Who am I?" For them it was a question full of pain and struggle. For Gretel it was hardly even a question. She had more identities than she knew what to do with. Some of these Gretels have been only the sketchiest of surfaces— others are deeper. Many have incredible gifts, antigravity, dreams of prophecy . . . comatic images surround their faces, glowing in the air: the light itself is actually crying tears, weeping in this stylized way, as she is borne along through the mechanical cities, the meteorite walls draped in midair, every hollow and socket empty as a bone, and the failing shadow that shines black all around it . . . or is held in staring postures, long gowns, fringe and alchemical symbol, veils flowing from leather skullcaps padded concentric as a bike-racer's helmet, with crackling-tower and obsidian helix, with drive belts and rollers, with strange airship passages that thread underneath arches, solemnly, past louvers and giant fins in the city mist. . . .

In *Weisse Sandwüste von Neumexiko* she played a cowgirl. First thing, they'd asked, "Can you ride?" "Of course," she'd answered. Never been closer than roadside ditches in time of war to any horse in her life, but she needed the work. When the moment came to saddle up, it never occurred to her to be afraid of the beast pressing up between her thighs. It was an American horse named Snake.

Trained or not, it could have run away with her, even killed her. But they pranced the screen full of the Sagittarian fire, Gretel and that colt, and her smile never drew back.

Here is one of the veils she has shed, a thin white scum, a caustic residue from one recent night in Berlin. "While you were asleep, I left the house. I went out in the street, without my shoes. I found a corpse. A man. A week's gray beard and old gray suit. . . ." It was lying still and very white behind a wall. She lay down beside it and put her arms around it. There was frost. The body rolled toward her and the wrinkles stayed frozen in the cloth. She felt its bristled face rub her own cheek. The smell was no worse than cold meat from the icebox. She lay, holding it, till morning.

"Tell me how it is in your land." What woke her? Boots in the street, an early steamshovel. She can hardly hear her tired whispering.

Corpse answers: "We live very far beneath the black mud. Days of traveling." Though she couldn't move its limbs easily as a doll's, she could make it say and think exactly what she wished.

For an instant too she did wonder—not quite in words— if that's how her own soft mind might feel, under the fingers of Those who . . .

"Mm, it's snug down here. Now and then you can pick up something from Them—a distant rumbling, the implied silhouette of some explosion, conducted here through the earth overhead . . . but nothing, ever, *too close*. It's so dark that things glow. We have flight. There's no sex. But there are fantasies, even many of those we used to attach to sex—that we once modulated its energy with. . . ."

As the dizzy debutante Lotte Lüstig, she found herself during a flood, disguised as a scrubwoman, proceeding downriver in a bathtub with rich playboy Max Schlepzig. Every girl's dream. Name of the movie was *Jugend Herauf!* (a lighthearted pun, of course, on the then popular phrase "Juden heraus!"). Actually, all the bathtub scenes were process shots—she never did get to go out *on the river* in the bathtub with Max, all that was done with doubles, and in the final print it survives only as a very murky long shot. The figures are darkened and deformed, resembling apes, and the quality of the light is peculiar, as if the whole scene were engraved on dark metal such as lead. Greta's double was actually an Italian stunt man named Blazzo in a long blonde wig. They carried on a romance for a while. But Greta wouldn't go to bed with him, unless he wore that *wig!*

Out on the river the rain lashes: the rapids can now be heard approaching, still impossible to see, but real, and inevitable. And the doubles both experience an odd, ticklish fear now that perhaps they are really lost, and that there is really no camera on shore behind the fine gray scribbling of willows . . . all the crew, sound-men, grips, gaffers have left . . . or never even arrived . . . and what was that the currents just brought to knock against our snow-white cockle shell? and what was that thud, so stiffened and so mute?

Bianca is usually silver, or of no color at all: thousands of times taken, strained through glass, warped in and out the violet-bleeding interfaces of Double and Triple Protars, Schneider Angulons, Voigtländer Collinears, Steinheil Orthostigmats, the Gundlach Turner-Reichs of 1895. For Greta it is her daughter's soul each time, an inexhaustible soul. . . . This scarf of an only child, tucked in waist-high, always out vulnerable to the wind. To call her an extension of her mother's ego is of course to invite the bitterest sarcasm. But it's possible, now and then, for Greta to see Bianca in other children, ghostly as a double exposure . . . clearly yes very clearly in Gottfried, the young pet and protégé of Captain Blicero.

"Pull down my straps for a moment. Is it dark enough? Look. Thanatz said they were luminous. That he knew each one by heart. They're very white today, aren't they? Hmm. Long and white, like cobwebs. They're on my ass too. Around the insides of my thighs. . . ." Many times, afterward, after the blood had stopped and he had put on the alcohol, Thanatz would sit with her lying across his knees, and read the scars down her back, as a gypsy reads a palm. Life-scar, heart-scar. Croix mystique. What fortunes and fantasies! He was so exalted, after the whippings. So taken away by the idea that they *would* win out, escape. He'd fall asleep before the wildness and hope had quite left him. She loved him most at those moments, just before sleep, her own dorsal side aflame, his little head heavy on her breast, while scar-tissue formed silently on her, cell by cell, in the night. She felt almost safe. . . .

Each time the lash struck, each attack, in her helplessness to escape, there would come to her a single vision, only one, for each peak of pain. The Eye at the top of the pyramid. The sacrificial city, with figures in rust-colored robes. The dark woman waiting at the end of the street. The hooded face of sorrowing Denmark, leaning out over Germany. The cherry-red coals falling through the night. Bianca in a Spanish dancer's costume, stroking the barrel of a gun. . . .

Out by one rocket site, in the pine woods, Thanatz and Gretel found an old road that no one used any more. Pieces of pavement were visible here and there among the green underbrush. It seemed that if they followed the road they would come to a town, a station or outpost . . . it wasn't at all clear what they would find. But the place would be long deserted.

They held hands. Thanatz wore an old jacket of green suede, with patches on the sleeves. Gretel wore her camel's-hair coat and a white kerchief. In places, pine needles were drifted across the old roadway, so deep as to silence their footsteps.

They came to a slide where years ago the road had been washed away. Gravel spilled salt-and-pepper downhill toward a river they heard but couldn't see. An old automobile, a Hannomag Storm, hung there, nose-down, one door smashed open. The lavender-gray metal shell had been picked clean as the skeleton of a deer. Somewhere in these woods was the presence that had done this. They skirted the wreck, afraid to come too near the spidered glass, the hard mortality in the shadows of the front seat.

Remains of houses could be glimpsed, back in the trees. There was now a retreat of the light, though it was still before noon, and the forest grew no thicker here. In the middle of the road, giant turds showed up, fresh, laid in

twists like strands of rope—dark and knotted. What could
have left them?

At the same instant, she and Thanatz both realized that
for hours now they must have been walking through the
ruin of a great city, not an ancient ruin, but brought down
inside their lifetime. Ahead of them, the path curved on,
into trees. But something stood now between them and
whatever lay around the curve: invisible, impalpable . . .
some *monitor*. Saying, "Not one step farther. That's all.
Not one. Go back now."

It was impossible to move any farther into it. They
were both terrified. They turned, feeling it at their backs,
and moved away quickly.

Back at the Schußstelle they found Blicero in his final
madness. The trunks in the cold little clearing were
stripped of bark, bleeding with beads of gum from the
rocket blasts.

"He could have banished us. Blicero was a local deity.
He wouldn't even have needed a piece of paper. But he
wanted us all to stay. He gave us the best there was, beds,
food, liquor, drugs. Something was being planned, it involved the boy Gottfried, that was as unmistakable as the
smell of resin, first thing those blue hazy mornings. But
Blicero would tell us nothing.

"We moved into the Heath. There were oilfields, and
blackened earth. *Jabos* flew over in diamond shapes, hunting us. Blicero had grown on, into another animal . . . a
werewolf . . . but with no humanity left in its eyes: that
had faded out, day after day, and been replaced by gray
furrows, red veins in patterns that weren't human. *Islands:*
clotted islands in the sea. Sometimes even the topographic
lines, nested on a common point. 'It is the map of my
Ur-Heimat,' imagine a shriek so quiet it's almost a whisper,
'the Kingdom of Lord Blicero. A white land.' I had a
sudden understanding: he was seeing the world now in
mythical regions: they had their maps, real mountains,
rivers, and colors. It was not Germany he moved through.
It was his own space. But he was taking *us* along with
him! My cunt swelled with blood at the danger, the chances
for our annihilation, delicious never knowing when it
would come down because the space and time were

Blicero's own. . . . He did not fall back along roads, he did not cross bridges or lowlands. We sailed Lower Saxony, island to island. Each firing-site was another island, in a white sea. Each island had its peak in the center . . . was it the position of the Rocket itself? the moment of liftoff? A German Odyssey. Which one would be the last, the home island?

"I keep forgetting to ask Thanatz whatever became of Gottfried. Thanatz was allowed to stay with the battery. But I was taken away: driven in a Hispano-Suiza with Blicero himself, out through the gray weather to a petrochemical plant that for days had stalked us in a wheel at our horizon, black and broken towers in the distance, clustered together, a flame that always burned at the top of one stack. It was the Castle: Blicero looked over, about to speak, and I said, 'The Castle.' The mouth smiled quickly, but absent: the wrinkled wolf-eyes had gone even beyond these domestic moments of telepathy, on into its animal north, to a persistence on the hard edge of death I can't imagine, tough cells with the smallest possible flicker inside, running on nothing but ice, or less. He called me Katje. 'You'll see that your little trick won't work again. Not now, Katje.' I wasn't frightened. It was madness I could understand, or else the hallucinating of the very old. The silver stork flew wings-down into our wind, brow low and legs back, Prussian occipital knot behind: on its shiny surfaces now appeared black swirls of limousines and staff cars in the driveway of the main office. I saw a light plane, a two-seater, at the edge of the parking lot. The faces of the men inside seemed familiar. I knew them from films, the power and the gravity were there—they were important men, but I only recognized one: Generaldirektor Smaragd, from Leverkusen. An elderly man who used a cane, a notorious spiritualist before the War, and, it seemed, even now. 'Greta,' he smiled, groping for my hand. 'Ah, we're all here.' But his charm was shared by none of the others. They'd all been waiting for Blicero. A meeting of nobles in the Castle. They went into the board room. I was left with an assistant named Drohne, high forehead, graying hair, always fussing with his necktie. He'd seen every one of my films. We moved off into the machinery. Through the windows of the board room I saw them at a round conference table, with something in the center. It was gray, plastic, shining, light moving on its surfaces. 'What is it?' I asked, vamping Drohne. He took me out of earshot of the others. 'I think it's for the F-Gerät,' he whispered."

"*F?*" sez Slothrop, "F-Gerät, you sure of that?"

"Some letter."

"S?"

"All right, S. They are children at the threshold of language with these words they make up. It looked to me like an ectoplasm—something they had forced, by their joint will, to materialize on the table. No one's lips were moving. It was a séance. I understood then that Blicero had brought me across a frontier. Had injected me at last into his native space without a tremor of pain. I was free. Men crowded behind me in the corridor, blocking the way back. Drohne's hand was sweating on my sleeve. He was a plastics connoisseur. Flipping his fingernail against a large clear African mask, cocking his ear—'Can you hear it? The true ring of Polystyrene . . .' and going into raptures for me over a heavy chalice of methyl methacrylate, a replica of the Sangraal. . . . We were by a tower reactor. A strong paint-thinner smell was in the air. Clear rods of some plastic came hissing out through an extruder at the bottom of the tower, into cooling channels, or into a chopper. The heat was heavy in the room. I thought of something very deep, black and viscous, feeding this factory. From outside I heard motors. Were they all leaving? Why was I here? Plastic serpents crawled endlessly to left and right. The erections of my escort tried to crawl out the openings in their clothes. I could do whatever I wanted. Black radiant and deep. I knelt and began unbuttoning Drohne's trousers. But two others took me by the arms and dragged me off into a warehouse area. Others followed, or entered from other doors. Great curtains of styrene or vinyl, in all colors, opaque and transparent, hung row after row from overhead. They flared like the northern lights. I felt that somewhere beyond them was an audience, waiting for something to begin. Drohne and the men stretched me out on an inflatable plastic mattress. All around, I watched a clear crumbling of the air, or of the light. Someone said 'butadiene,' and I heard *beauty dying*. . . . Plastic rustled and snapped around us, closing us in, in ghost white. They took away my clothes and dressed me in an exotic costume of some black polymer, very tight at the waist, open at the crotch. It felt alive on me. 'Forget leather, forget satin,' shivered Drohne. 'This is Imipolex, the material of the future.' I can't describe its perfume, or how it felt—the luxury. The moment it touched them it brought my nipples up swollen and begging to be bitten. I wanted to feel it against my cunt. Nothing I ever wore, before or since, aroused me quite as much as Imipolex. They promised me brassieres, chemises, stockings, gowns of the same material. Drohne had strapped on a gigantic Imipolex penis over his own. I rubbed my face against it, it was so delicious. . . . There was an abyss between my feet. Things, memories, no way to distinguish them any more, went tumbling downward through my head. A torrent. I was evacuating all these, out into some void . . . from my vertex, curling, bright-colored hallucinations went streaming . . . baubles, amusing lines of dialogue, objets d'art . . . I was letting them all go. Holding none. Was this 'submission,' then—letting all these go?

"I don't know how long they kept me there. I slept, I woke. Men appeared and vanished. Time had lost meaning. One morning I was outside the factory, naked, in the rain. Nothing grew there. Something had been deposited in a great fan that went on for miles. Some tarry kind of waste. I had to walk all the way back to the firing site. They were all gone. Thanatz had left a note, asking me to try to get to Swinemünde. Something must have happened at the site. There was a silence in that clearing I'd felt only once before. Once, in Mexico. The year I was in America. We were very deep in the jungle. We came on a flight of stone steps, covered with vines, fungus, centuries of decay. The others climbed to the top, but I couldn't. It was the same as the day with Thanatz, in the pine forest. I felt a silence waiting for me up there. Not for them, but for me alone . . . my own personal silence. . . ."

□

Up on the bridge of the *Anubis*, the storm paws loudly on the glass, great wet flippers falling at random in out of the night *whap!* the living shape visible just for the rain-

bow edge of the sound—it takes a certain kind of maniac,
at least a Polish cavalry officer, to stand in this pose behind such brittle thin separation, and stare each blow full
in its muscularity. Behind Procalowski the clinometer bob
goes to and fro with his ship's rolling: a pendulum in a
dream. Stormlight has turned the lines of his face black,
black as his eyes, black as the watchcap cocked so tough
and salty aslant the furrows of his forehead. Light clusters,
clear, deep, on the face of the radio gear . . . fans up softly
off the dial of the pelorus . . . spills out portholes onto the
white river. Inexplicably, the afternoon has been going on
for longer than it should. Daylight has been declining for
too many hours. Corposants have begun to flicker now in
the rigging. The storm yanks at rope and cable, the cloudy
night goes white and loud, in huge spasms. Procalowski
smokes a cigar and studies charts of the Oder Haff.

All this light. Are the Russian lookouts watching from
shore, waiting in the rain? Is this arm of the passage being
kept in grease-pencil, X by dutiful X, across some field of
Russian plastic, inside where cobwebs whiten the German
windows nobody needs to stand at, where phosphor grass
ripples across the A-scopes and the play you feel through
the hand-crank in the invisible teeth is the difference between hit and miss. . . . Vaslav—is the pip you see there
even a ship? In the Zone, in these days, there is endless
simulation—standing waves in the water, large drone-birds,
so well-known as to have nicknames among the operators,
wayward balloons, flotsam from other theatres of war
(Brazilian oildrums, whisky cases stenciled for Fort-Lamy),
observers from other galaxies, episodes of smoke, moments
of high albedo—your real targets are hard to come by.
Too much confusion out here for most replacements and
late draftees. Only the older scope hands can still maintain
a sense of the appropriate: over the watches of their Dura-
tions, jittering electric green for what must have seemed,
at first, forever, they have come to understand distribution . . . they have learned a visual mercy.

How probable is the *Anubis* in this estuary tonight? Its
schedule has lapsed, fashionably, unavoidably: it should
have been through Swinemünde weeks ago, but the Vistula
was under Soviet interdiction to the white ship. The Russians even had a guard posted on board for a while, till

the Anubian ladies vamped them off long enough to single
up all lines—and so the last reprise of Polish homeland
was on, across these water-meadows of the north, radio
messages following them in clear one day and code the
next, an early and shapeless situation, dithering between
executioner's silence and the Big Time. There are international reasons for an Anubis Affair right now, and also
reasons against, and the arguments go on, too remote to
gather, and orders are changed hour to hour.

Pitching and rolling furiously, the *Anubis* drives northward. Lightning flickers all around the horizon, and
thunder that reminds the military men on board of drumfire announcing battles they're not sure now if they survived or still dream, still can wake up into and die. . . .
Weather decks shine slick and bare. Party litter clogs the
drains. Stale fat-smoke goes oozing out the galley porthole
into the rain. The saloon's been set up for baccarat, and
filthy movies are showing in the boiler room. The second
dog watch is about to come on. The white ship settles,
like the soul of a kerosene lamp just lit, into its evening
routine.

Partygoers stagger fore and aft, evening clothes decorated with sunbursts of vomit. Ladies lie out in the rain,
nipples erect and heaving under drenched silk. Stewards
skid along the decks with salvers of Dramamine and bicarbonate. Barfing aristocracy sag all down the lifelines. Here
comes Slothrop now, down a ladder to the main deck,
bounced by the rolling off of alternate manropes, feeling
none too keen. He's lost Bianca. Gone fussing through the
ship doubling back again and again, can't find her any
more than his reason for leaving her this morning.

It matters, but how much? Now that Margherita has
wept to him, across the stringless lyre and bitter chasm of
a ship's toilet, of her last days with Blicero, he knows as
well as he has to that it's the S-Gerät after all that's following him, it and the pale plastic ubiquity of Laszlo
Jamf. That if he's been seeker and sought, well, he's also
baited, and bait. The Imipolex question was planted for
him by somebody, back at the Casino Hermann Goering,
with hopes it would flower into a full *Imipolectique* with
its own potency in the Zone—but They knew Slothrop
would jump for it. Looks like there are sub-Slothrop needs

They know about, and he doesn't: this is humiliating on the face of it, but now there's also the even more annoying question, *What do I need that badly?*

Even a month ago, given a day or two of peace, he might have found his way back to the September afternoon, to the stiff cock in his pants sprung fine as a dowser's wand trying to point up at what was hanging there in the sky for everybody. Dowsing Rockets is a gift, and he had it, suffered from it, trying to fill his body to the pores and follicles with ringing prurience . . . to enter, to be filled . . . to go hunting after . . . to be shown . . . to begin to scream . . . to open arms legs mouth asshole eyes nostrils without a hope of mercy to its intention waiting in the sky paler than dim commercial Jesus. . . .

But nowadays, some kind of space he cannot go against has opened behind Slothrop, bridges that might have led back are down now for good. He is growing less anxious about betraying those who trust him. He feels obligations less immediately. There is, in fact, a general loss of emotion, a numbness he ought to be alarmed at, but can't quite . . .

Can't . . .

Russian transmissions come crackling out of ship's radio, and the static blows like sheets of rain. Lights have begun to appear on shore. Procalowski throws a master switch and cuts off all the lights of the *Anubis*. St. Elmo's fire will be seen spurting at moments from crossends, from sharp points, fluttering white as telltales about the antennas and stays.

The white ship, camouflaged in the storm, will slip by Stettin's great ruin in silence. Rain will slacken for a moment to port and reveal a few last broken derricks and charred warehouses so wet and gleaming you can almost smell them, and a beginning of marshland you can smell, where no one lives. And then the shore again will be invisible as the open sea's. The Oder Haff will grow wider around the *Anubis*. No patrol boats will be out tonight. Whitecaps will come slamming in out of the darkness, and break high over the bow, and brine stream from the golden jackal mouth . . . Count Wafna lurch aft in nothing but his white bow tie, hands full of red, white, and blue chips that spill and clatter on deck, and he'll never cash them in . . .

the Countess Bibescue dreaming by the fo'c'sle of Bucharest four years ago, the January terror, the Iron Guard on the radio screaming *Long Live Death,* and the bodies of Jews and Leftists hung on the hooks of the city slaughter-houses, dripping on the boards smelling of meat and hide, having her breasts sucked by a boy of 6 or 7 in a velvet Fauntleroy suit, their wet hair flowing together indistin-guishable as their moans now, will vanish inside sudden whiteness exploding over the bow . . . and stockings ladder, and silk frocks over rayon slips make swarming moirés . . . hardons go limp without warning, bone buttons shake in terror . . . lights be thrown on again and the deck become a blinding mirror . . . and not too long after this, Slothrop will think he sees her, think he has found Bianca again—dark eyelashes plastered shut and face running with rain, he will see her lose her footing on the slimy deck, just as the *Anubis* starts a hard roll to port, and even at this stage of things—even in his distance—he will lunge after her without thinking much, slip himself as she vanishes under the chalky lifelines and gone, stagger trying to get back but be hit too soon in the kidneys and be flipped that easy over the side and it's adios to the *Anubis* and all its screaming Fascist cargo, already no more ship, not even black sky as the rain drives down his falling eyes now in quick needlestrokes, and he hits, without a call for help, just a meek tearful *oh fuck,* tears that will add nothing to the whipped white desolation that passes for the Oder Haff tonight. . . .

□

The voices are German. Looks like a fishing smack here, stripped for some reason of nets and booms. Cargo piled on deck. A pink-faced youth is peering down at Slothrop from midships, rocking in, rearing back. "He's wearing evening clothes," calling in to the pilot house. "Is that good or bad? You're not with the military government, are you?"

"Jesus, kid, I'm drowning. I'll sign a *form* if you want." Well, that's Howdy Podner in German. The youth reaches out a pink hand whose palm is crusted with barnacles, and

hauls him on up, ears freezing, salty snot pouring out his
nose, flopping onto a wood deck that reeks with generations of fish and is scarred bright from more solid cargo.
The boat gets under way again with this tremendous surge
of acceleration. Slothrop is sent rolling wetly aft. Behind
them a great roostertail foams erect against the rain.
Maniacal laughter blows aft from the pilot house. "Hey
who, or what, is in command of this vessel, here?"

"My mother," the pink boy crouching beside him with
an apologetic and helpless look. "The terror of the high
seas."

This apple-cheeked lady is Frau Gnahb, and her kid's
name is Otto. When she's feeling affectionate she calls him
"the Silent Otto," which she thinks is very funny, but it
dates her. While Slothrop gets out of the tuxedo and hangs
it up inside to dry, wrapping himself in an old army
blanket, mother and son tell him how they run black
market items all along the Baltic coast. Who else would be
out tonight, during a storm? He has a trustworthy face,
Slothrop does, people will tell him anything. Right now
seems they're headed for Swinemünde to take on cargo for
a run tomorrow up the coast of Usedom.

"Do you know a man in a white suit," quoting Geli
Tripping from a few eras back, "who's supposed to be on
the Strand-Promenade in that Swinemünde every day
around noon?"

Frau Gnahb takes a pinch of snuff, and beams. "Everybody does. He's the white knight of the black market, as I
am queen of the coastal trade."

"Der Springer, right?"

"Nobody else."

Nobody else. Up in his pants pocket Slothrop is still
packing around the chesspiece old Säure Bummer gave
him. By it shall Springer know him. Slothrop falls asleep
in the pilot house, gets in two or three hours, during which
Bianca comes to snuggle in under his blanket with him.
"You're really in that Europe now," she grins, hugging him.
"Oh my goo'ness," Slothrop keeps saying, his voice exactly
like Shirley Temple's, out of his control. It sure is embarrassing. He wakes to sunlight, gulls squealing, smell of
number 2 fuel oil, the booming of wine barrels down
racketing planks to shore. They are docked in Swine-

münde, by the sagging long ash remains of warehouses. Frau Gnahb is supervising some offloading. Otto has a tin can of honest-to-God Bohnenkaffee simmering. "First I've had in a while," Slothrop scorching his mouth.

"Black market," purrs the Silent Otto. "Good business to be in."

"I was in it for a while. . . ." Oh, yes, and he's left the last of that Bodine hashish, hasn't he, several fucking ounces in fact, back on the *Anubis*, wasn't that clever. See the sugar bowl do the Tootsie Roll with the big, bad, Devil's food cake—

"Nice morning," Otto remarks.

Slothrop puts his tux back on, wrinkled and shrunken and almost dry, and debarks with Otto to find Der Springer. It seems to be Springer who's chartered today's trip up the coast. Slothrop keeps looking around for the *Anubis*, but she's nowhere in sight. In the distances, gantries huddle together, skeletal, presiding over the waste that came upon this port so sudden. The Russian assault in the spring has complicated the layout here. The white ship could be hiding behind any of these heaps of dock-yard wreckage. Come out, come out. . . .

The storm has blown away, the breeze is mild today and the sky lies overhead in a perfect interference-pattern, mackerel gray and blue. Someplace military machines are rooting and clanking. Men and women are hollering near and far in Russian. Otto and Slothrop dodge them down alleys flanked by the remains of half-timbered houses, stepped out story by story, about to meet overhead after centuries of imperceptible toppling. Men in black-billed caps sit on stoops, watching hands for cigarettes. In a little square, market stalls are set up, wood frames and old, stained canvas shimmering when the breeze passes through. Russian soldiers lean against posts or benches talking to girls in dirndls and white knee-socks, all nearly still as statues. Market wagons stand unhitched with tongues tilted to the ground and floors covered with burlap and straw and traces of produce. Dogs sniff among the mud negatives of tank treads. Two men in dark old blue uniforms work their way along with hose and broom, cleaning away garbage and stone-dust with salt water pumped up from the harbor. Two little girls chase round

and round a guady red kiosk plastered with chromos of
Stalin. Workers in leather caps, blinking, morning-faced,
pedal down to the docks with lunchboxes slung on handle
bars. Pigeons and seagulls feint for scraps in the gutters.
Women with empty string bags hurry by light as ghosts.
A lone sapling in the street sings with a blockful of birds
you can't see.

Just as Geli said, out on the steel-littered promenade,
kicking stones, watching the water, eyes idly combing the
beach for the odd watch or gold eyeglass frame, waiting
for whoever will show up, is The Man. About 50, bleak
and neutral-colored eyes, hair thick at the sides of his head
and brushed back.

Slothrop flashes the plastic knight. Der Springer smiles
and bows.

"Gerhardt von Göll, at your service." They shake hands,
though Slothrop's is prickling in an unpleasant way.

Gulls cry, waves flatten on the strand. "Uh," Slothrop
sez, "I have this kind of trick ear, you'll have to—you say
Gerhardt von what now?" This mackerel sky has begun to
look less like a moiré, and more like a chessboard. "I guess
we have a friend in common. Well, that Margherita Erdmann. Saw her last night. Yup. . . ."

"She's supposed to be dead." He takes Slothrop's arm,
and they all begin to stroll along the promenade.

"W-well you're supposed to be a movie director."

"Same thing," lighting American cigarettes for everybody. "Same problems of control. But more intense. As to
some musical ears, dissonance is really a higher form of
consonance. You've heard about Anton Webern? Very sad."

"It was a mistake. He was innocent."

"Ha. Of course he was. But mistakes are part of it too—
everything fits. One *sees how* it fits, ja? learns patterns,
adjusts to rhythms, one day you are no longer an actor,
but free now, over on the other side of the camera. No
dramatic call to the front office—just waking up one day,
and knowing that Queen, Bishop, and King are only
splendid cripples, and pawns, even those that reach the
final row, are condemned to creep in two dimensions, and
no Tower will ever rise or descend—no: *flight has been
given only to the Springer!*"

"Right, Springer," sez Otto.

Four Russian privates come wandering out of a bank of

ruined hotel-fronts, laughing across the promenade, over the wall down to the water where they stand throwing smooth stones, kicking waves, singing to each other. Not much of a liberty town, Swinemünde. Slothrop fills von Göll in on Margherita, trying not to get personal. But some of his anxiety over Bianca must be coming through. Von Göll shakes his arm, a kindly uncle. "There now. I wouldn't worry. Bianca's a clever child, and her mother is hardly a destroying goddess."

"You're a comfort, Springer."

The Baltic, restless Wehrmacht gray, whispers along the beach. Von Göll tips an invisible Tyrolean to old ladies in black who've come out in pairs to get some sun. Otto goes chasing seagulls, hands out in front of him silent-movie style looking to strangle, but always missing his bird. Presently they are joined by a party with a lumpy nose, stoop, week's growth of orange and gray whiskers, and oversize leather trenchcoat with no trousers on under-neath. His name is Närrisch—the same Klaus Närrisch that aerodynamics man Horst Achtfaden fingered for the Schwarzkommando, the very same. He is carrying by the neck an unplucked dead turkey. As they thread their way among chunks big and little of Swinemünde and the battle for it last spring, townspeople begin to appear out of the ruins, and to straggle close on von Göll's landward flank, all eying this dead bird. Springer reaches inside his white suit jacket, comes out with a U.S. Army .45, and makes a casual show of checking its action. His following promptly dwindles by a half.

"They're hungrier today," observes Närrisch.

"True," replies the Springer, "but today there are fewer of them."

"Wow," it occurs to Slothrop, "that's a shitty thing to say."

Springer shrugs. "Be compassionate. But don't make up fantasies about them. Despise me, exalt them, but remember, we define each other. Elite and preterite, we move through a cosmic design of darkness and light, and in all humility, I am one of the very few who can comprehend it *in toto*. Consider honestly therefore, young man, which side you would rather be on. While they suffer in perpetual shadows, it's . . . always—"

BRIGHT DAYS (FOX-TROT)

—bright days for the black mar-ket,
That silver 'n' gold makes-it shine!
From the Cor-al Sea to, the sky, blue, Baltic,
Money's the mainspring, that makes it *all* tick—like a
Blinkin' beacon, there's a pricetag peekin'
From each décolletage dee-vine—
Be she green or scar-let, even Mom's a har-lot, it's the
Good Lord's grand design . . .
A-and it's sunny days-for, the black, black ma(a)rket,
Cause silver and gold makes it shii-iine!

Närrisch and Otto joining in here on three-part harmony, while the idle and hungry of Swinemünde look on,
whitefaced as patient livestock. But their bodies are only
implied: wire racks for prewar suits and frocks, too ancient, too glassy with dirt, with passage.

Leaving the promenade, they pause at a street corner
while a detachment of Russian infantry and horsemen
marches by. "Gee, they're pouring in," notes Otto. 'Where's
the circus?"

"Up the coast, kid," sez Närrisch.

"What's up the coast," inquires Slothrop.

"*Look out,*" warns Närrisch, "*he's a spy.*"

"Don't call me 'kid,' " Otto snarls.

"Spy's ass," sez Slothrop.

"He's all right," Springer pats them all on the shoulders,
Herr Gemütlich here, "the word's been out on him for a
while. He isn't even armed." To Slothrop: "You're welcome to come along with us, up the coast. It might be
interesting for you." But Slothrop is no dummy. He notices
how he is getting funny looks from everybody now, including that Springer.

Among the cargo headed up the coast are six chorus
girls, wearing feathers and spangles under old cloth coats
to save trunk space, a small pit band at different levels of
alcoholic slumber, manymany cases of vodka, and a troupe
of performing chimpanzees. Otto's nautical-piratical
mother has one of these chimps cornered inside the pilot
house, where they are going at it, the Frau with her insults, the chimp reaching now and then trying to slap her
with his floppy banana peel. Ulcerous impresario G. M. B.

Haftung is trying to get Otto's attention. He has a record of always making his appeals to the wrong personnel. "That's Wolfgang in there! He'll murder her!" Wolfgang's his prize chimp, somewhat unstable, does a fair Hitler imitation but has this short attention span.

"Well," vaguely, "he'd better watch out for my Mom."

Framed here in her lozenge of hatchway, it's much clearer just how extensively this old woman has been around: she is leaning, lifting, big sweet smile just as toothy as can be, right into that Wolfgang, *cooing* at him: "Deine *Mutter* . . ."

"Say, *she's* never seen one of those critters before," Slothrop turning to Otto, surprising the youth with a faceful of, call it amiable homicide, "has she—"

"Ach, she's fantastic. She knows by instinct—*exactly how* to insult *anybody*. Doesn't matter, animal, vegetable— I even saw her insult a *rock* once."

"Aw, now—"

"Really! Ja. A gigantic clummmp of felsitic debris, last year, off the coast of Denmark, she criticized its," just about to fall into one of those mirthless laughs we edge away from, "its *crystalline structure,* for twenty minutes. Incredible."

Chorus girls have already pried open a case of vodka. Haftung, brushing hair that grows only in memory across the top of his head, rushes over to scream at them. Boys and girls, all ages, tattered and thin, trail across the brow, stevedoring. Against the fair sky, chimps swing from spars and antenna, above them seagulls glide by and stare. Wind rises, soon a whitecap here and there will start to flicker out in the harbor. Each child carries a bale or box of a different shape, color, and size. Springer stands by, pince-nez clipped in front of agate eyes, checking off his inventory in a green morocco book, snails in garlic sauce, one gross . . . three cases cognac . . . tennis balls, two dozen . . . one Victrola . . . film, *Lucky Pierre Runs Amok,* three reels . . . binoculars, sixty . . . wrist-watches . . . u.s.w., a checkmark for each child.

Presently all has been stowed below decks, chimps fall asleep, musicians wake up, girls surround Haftung and call him names, and pinch his cheeks. Otto makes his way along the side, hauling in lines as the children cast them

off. As the last one is flung away, its eye-splice still in
midair framing a teardrop vista of gutted Swinemünde,
Frau Gnahb, sensing the release from land through her
feet, gets under way in the usual manner, nearly losing a
chimp over the fantail and sending Haftung's half-dozen
lovelies sprawling in a winsome tangle of legs, bottoms
and breasts.

Crosscurrents tug a the boat as it moves out the widen-
ing funnel of the Swine, toward the sea. Just inside the
breakwaters, where it foams through breaches bombed
underwater in the spring *look* out, Frau Gnahb, with no
change of expression, swings her wheel full over, goes
barreling straight at the Sassnitz ferry *whoosh* veers away
just in time, cackling at passengers staggering back from
the rail, gaping after her. "Please, Mother," silent Otto
plaintive in the window of the pilot house. In reply the
good woman commences bellowing a bloodthirsty

SEA CHANTY

I'm the Pirate Queen of the Baltic Run, and nobody
    fucks with me—
And those who've tried are bones and skulls, and lie
    beneath the sea.
And the little fish like messengers swim in and out
    their eyes,
Singing, "Fuck ye not with Gory Gnahb and her
    desperate enterprise!"

I'll tangle with a battleship, I'll massacre a sloop,
I've sent a hundred souls to hell in one relentless
    swoop—
I've seen the Flying Dutchman, and each time we pass,
    he cries,
"Oh, steer me clear of Gory Gnahb, and her desperate
    enterprise!"

Whereupon she grips her wheel and accelerates. They
find themselves now leaping toward the side of a half-
sunken merchantman: black concave iron splashed with
red-lead, each crusted rivet and pitted plate closing in,
looming over— The woman is clearly unbalanced. Slothrop shuts his eyes and hangs on to a chorus girl. With a

whoop from the pilot house, the little boat is put over hard to port, missing collision by maybe a few coats of paint. Otto, caught daydreaming of death, staggers wildly by heading over the side. "It's her sense of humor," he points out, on the way past. Slothrop reaches out grabs him by the sweater, and the girl grabs Slothrop by the tail of his tuxedo.

"She gets into something a little illegal," Otto a moment later catching his breath, "you see what happens. I don't know what to do with her."

"Poor kid," the girl smiles.

"Aw," sez Otto.

Slothrop leaves them, always happy to see young people get together, and joins von Göll and Närrisch on the fantail. Frau Gnahb has angled, wallowing, around to the northwest. Presently they are heading up the coast, through white-streaked, salt-smelling Baltic.

"Well. Where we going, fellas?" jovial Slothrop wants to know.

Närrisch stares. "That is the isle of Usedom," von Göll explains, gently. "It is bounded on one side by the Baltic Sea. It is also bounded by two rivers. Their names are the Swine, and the Peene. We were just on the Swine River. We were in Swinemünde. Swinemünde means 'mouth of the Swine River.'"

"All right, all right."

"*We* are headed around the island of Usedom, to a place that is at the mouth of the Peene River."

"Let's see, so that would be called . . . wait . . . Peenemünde, right?"

"Very good."

"So?" There is a pause. "Oh. Oh, *that* Peenemünde."

Närrisch, as it turns out, used to work up there. He's apt to brood some at the idea of Russians occupying the place.

"There was a liquid-oxygen plant I had my eye on, too," Springer a little down with it himself, "I wanted to start a chain—we're still angling for the one in Volkenrode, at the old Goering Institute."

"There's a bunch of those LOX generators under Nordhausen," Slothrop trying to be helpful.

"Thanks. The Russians have that too, you'll recall.

That's a problem: if it weren't so against Nature I'd say they don't know what they want. The roads heading east are jammed day and night with Russian lorries, full of materiel. All kinds of loot. But no clear pattern to it yet, beyond strip-it-and-pack-it-home."

"Jeepers," clever Slothrop here, "do you reckon they've found that S-*Gerät* yet, huh, Mr. von Göll?"

"Ah, cute," beams the Springer.

"He's an OSS man," groans Närrisch, "tell you, we ought to rub him out."

"S-Gerät's going for £10,000 these days, half of that in front. You interested?"

"Nope. But I did hear at Nordhausen that you already have it."

"Wrong."

"Gerhardt—"

"He's all *right*, Klaus." The look is one Slothrop's had before, from auto salesmen signaling their partners *got a real idiot here, Leonard, now don't spook him please*. "We planted the story deliberately in Stettin. Wanted to see how a Colonel Tchitcherine will respond."

"Fuck. Him again? He'll respond, all right."

"Well, that's what we're going up to Peenemünde today to find out."

"Oh, boy." Slothrop goes on to tell about the run-in at Potsdam, and how Geli thought Tchitcherine didn't care about Rocket hardware nearly so much as working out some plot against that Oberst Enzian. If the two marketeers are interested, they don't show it.

The talk has drifted on into that kind of slack, nameful recapitulating that Slothrop's mother Nalline loved to float away on in the afternoons—Helen Trent, Stella Dallas, Mary Noble Backstage Wife. . . .

"Tchitcherine is a complex man. It's almost as if . . . he thinks of Enzian as . . . another *part* of him—a black version of something inside *himself*. A something he needs to . . . liquidate."

NÄRRISCH: Do you think there might be some . . . some *political* reason?

VON GÖLL (shaking his head): I just don't know, Klaus. Ever since what happened in Central Asia—

NÄRRISCH: You mean—

VON GÖLL: Yes . . . the Kirghiz Light. You know, it's funny—he's never *wanted* to be thought of as an imperialist—

NÄRRISCH: None of *them* do. But there's the girl. . . .

VON GÖLL: Little Geli Tripping. The one who thinks she's a witch.

NÄRRISCH: But do you really think she means to go through with this—this plan of hers, to find Tchitcherine?

VON GÖLL: I think . . . *They* . . . do. . . .

NÄRRISCH: But Gerhardt, she *is* in love with him—

VON GÖLL: He hasn't been dating her, has he?

NÄRRISCH: You can't be implying—

"Say," splutters Slothrop, "what th' heck're you guys *talkin'* about, anyway?"

"Paranoia," Springer snaps reproachfully (as folks will snap when interrupted at a game they enjoy). "You wouldn't understand that."

"Well excuse me, got to go vomit now," a klassic komeback among charm-school washouts like our Tactful Tyrone here, and pretty advanced stuff on dry land, but not out here, where the Baltic is making it impossible not to be seasick. Chimps are all doing their vomiting huddled under a tarp. Slothrop joins at the rail a miserable lot of musicians and girls. They instruct him in fine points such as not vomiting into the wind, and timing it for when the ship rolls toward the sea, Frau Gnahb having expressed the hope that no one would get any vomit on her ship with the kind of glacial smile Dr. Mabuse used to get, especially on a good day. She can be heard in the pilot house now, bellowing her sea chanty. "Ööööö," goes Slothrop over the side.

And this is how their desperate enterprise goes a-rollicking up the coast of Usedom, under a hazy summer sky. On shore, the green downs roll up in two gentle steps: above them is a chain of hills thick with pines and oaks. Little resort towns with white beaches and forlorn jetties wheel abeam rheumatically slow. Military-looking craft, probably Russian PT boats, will be seen now and then lying dead in the water. None challenge the Frau's passage. The sun is in and out, turning the decks a stark moment's yellow around everyone's shadow. There's a late time of day when all shadows are thrown along the same east-northeast bear-

ing as the test rockets were always fired out to sea from
Peenemünde. The exact clock time, which varies through
the year, is known as Rocket Noon . . . and the sound that
must at that moment fill the air for its devout can only be
compared with a noontime siren the whole town believes
in . . . and guts resonate, hard as stone. . . .

Before you sight it, you can feel the place. Even draped
over a gunwale, cheek against a fender smelling of tar, eyes
tearing and insides sloshing as the sea. Even barren and
scorched as Rossokovsky and the White Russian Army left
it in the spring. It's a face. On the maps, it's a skull or a
corroded face in profile, facing southwest: a small marshy
lake for the eye-socket, nose-and-mouth cavity cutting in
at the entrance to the Peene, just below the power station
. . . the draftsmanship is a little like a Wilhelm Busch
cartoon face, some old fool for mischievous boys to play
tricks on. Tapping his tanks for grain alcohol, scratching
great naughty words across fields of his fresh cement, or
even sneaking in to set off a rocket in the middle of the
night. . . .

Low, burned-out buildings now, ash images of camouflage nets burned onto the concrete (they had only a minute to glow, like a bürger's silk mantle—to light this
coastal indoors, this engineers' parlor full of stodgy shapes
and neutral tones . . . didn't it only flare? no need to put
right, nothing monitory, no new levels to be reached . . .
but who would that be, watching so civil and mild over
the modeltop? face all in these chromo sunset colors, eyes
inside blackrim lenses which, like the flaring nets, now are
seen to have served as camouflage for who but the Bicycle
Rider in the Sky, the black and fatal Edwardian silhouette
on the luminous breast of sky, of today's Rocket Noon,
two circular explosions inside the rush hour, in the death-
scene of the sky's light. How the rider twirls up there,
terminal and serene. In the Tarot he is known as The Fool,
but around the Zone here they call him Slick. It's 1945.
Still early, still innocent. Some of it is).

Charred helpless latticework: what was wooden now
only settles, without strength. Green human shapes flash in
the ruins. The scale is very confusing, along here. The
troops look larger than they should. A zoo? a shooting
gallery? Why, some of both. Frau Gnahb wallows in closer

to land, proceeds up the marshy shoreline at half speed.
Signs of occupation increase: lorry-parks, tents, a corral
teeming with horses pied, sorrel, snow-white, red as blood.
Wild summer ducks up exploding, wet and showery, out
of green reeds—they swing aft over the boat and descend
in its wake, where they bob quacking in two-foot excursions. High in the sunlight, a white-tailed eagle is soaring.
Smoothlipped bomb and shell craters hold blue sea water.
Barracks have had their roofs blown away: spinal and rib-
wise and sunwhite the bones of these creatures that must
have held in their time half the Jonahs of falling Europe.
But trees, beech and pine, have begun to grow in again
where spaces were cleared and leveled for housing or
offices—up through cracks in the pavement, everywhere
life may gain purchase, up rushes green summer '45, and
the forests are still growing dense on the upland.

Passing now the great blackened remains of the Development Works, most of it strewn at ground level. In
series, some ripped and broken, others largely hidden by
the dunes, Närrisch reverently telling them one by one,
come the concrete masses of the test stands, stations of the
cross, VI, V, III, IV, II, IX, VIII, I, finally the Rocket's
own, from which it stood and flew at last, VII and X.
Trees that once screened these from the sea now are only
stalks of charcoal.

Pulling around the northern curve of the peninsula, test-
stand wall and earthworks receding—moving now past
Peenemünde-West, the Luftwaffe's old territory. Far away
to starboard, the cliffs of the Greifswalder Oie shimmer
through the blue haze. Concrete launching-ramps used to
test the V-1 or buzzbomb point at the sea. Runways
pocked with craters, heaped with rubble and wrecked
Messerschmitts swing by, down the peninsula: over the
skull's arc, south again toward the Peene, there—above the
rolling hills, miles off the port bow, the red brick tower
of the cathedral in Wolgast, and closer in the half-dozen
stacks of the power station, smokeless over Peenemünde,
have survived the lethal compression-loads of March. . . .
White swans drift in the reeds, and pheasants fly over the
tall pines inland. A truck motor snarls somewhere into life.

Frau Gnahb brings her boat around in a tight turn,
through an inlet, to the dock. The summer calm lies over

everything: rolling-stock inert on its tracks, one soldier sitting against an orange-topped oil drum trying to play an accordion. Maybe only fooling around. Otto lets go of his chorus girl's hand. His mother cuts the engines, and he steps broadly to the dock and jogs along, making fast. Then there's a brief pause: Diesel fumes, marsh birds, quiet idleness. . . .

Somebody's staff car, racketing around the corner of a cargo shed, slides to a stop, bouncing forth out of its rear door a major even fatter than Duane Marvy, but with a kindlier and dimly Oriental face. Gray hair like sheep's wool comes twisting down all around his head. "Ah! von Göll!" arms outstretched, wrinkled eyes shiny with—is it real tears? "von Göll, my dear friend!"

"Major Zhdaev," Springer nods ambling over the brow, as behind the major now this truckload of troops in fatigues seems to be pulling up here, kind of odd they should be toting those submachine guns and carbines just for some stevedoring. . . .

Right. Before anyone can move, they've leaped out and made a cordon around Zhdaev and the Springer, pieces at the ready. "Do not be alarmed," Zhdaev waving and beaming, strolling backward to the car with his arm around the Springer, "we are detaining your friend for a bit. You may proceed with your work and go. We'll see that he gets safely back to Swinemünde."

"What the devil," Frau Gnahb comes growling out of the pilot house. Haftung shows up, twitching, putting hands in various pockets and taking them out again: "Who are they arresting? What about my contract? Will anything happen to us?" The staff car pulls away. Enlisted men begin filing on board.

"Shit," ponders Närrisch.

"You think it's a bust?"

"I think Tchitcherine is responding with interest. Just as you said."

"Aw, now—"

"No, no," hand on sleeve, "he's right. You're harmless."

"Thanks."

"I warned him, but he laughed. 'Another leap, Närrisch. I have to keep leaping, don't I?'"

"Well what do you want to do now, cut him loose?"

There is some excitement amidships. The Russians have

thrown back a tarp to reveal the chimps, who are covered with vomit, and have also broken into the vodka. Haftung blinks and shudders. Wolfgang is on his back, sucking at a gurgling bottle he is clutching with his feet. Some of the chimps are docile, others are looking for a fight.

"Somehow . . ." Slothrop *does* wish the man would quit talking this way, "I owe him—*that* much."

"Well I don't," Slothrop dodging a sudden plume of yellow chimpanzee vomit. "He ought to be able to take care of himself."

"His talk's grandiose enough. But he's not paranoid *in his heart*—in this line of work, that's a disaster."

One of the chimps now bites a Soviet corporal in the leg. The corporal screams, unslinging his Tokarev and firing from the hip, by which time the chimp has leaped for a halyard. A dozen more of the critters, many carrying vodka bottles, head en masse for the gangplank. "Don't let them get away," Haftung hollers. The trombone player sticks his head sleepily out a hatch to ask what's happening and has his face walked over by three sets of pink-soled feet before grasping the situation. Girls, spangles aflame in the afternoon sun, feathers all quivering, are being chased forward and aft by drooling Red Army personnel. Frau Gnahb pulls on her steam whistle, thereby spooking the rest of the chimps, who join the stampede to shore. "Catch them," Haftung pleads, "somebody." Slothrop finds himself between Otto and Närrisch, being pushed ashore over the brow by soldiers chasing after chimps or girls, or trying to wrangle the cargo ashore. Among splashes, cursing, and girlish shrieks from the other side of the boat, chorus girls and musicians keep appearing and wandering back and forth. It is difficult to perceive just what the fuck is happening here.

"Listen." Frau Gnahb leaning over the side.

Slothrop notices a canny squint. "You have a plan."

"You want to pull a diversionary feint."

"What? What?"

"Chimps, musicians, dancing girls. Decoys all over. While the three of *you* sneak in and grab Der Springer."

"We can hide," Närrisch looking around gangster-eyed. "Nobody'll notice. Ja, ja! The boat can take off, as if *we* were *on board!*"

"Not me," sez Slothrop.

"Ha! Ha!" sez Frau Gnahb.

"Ha! Ha!" sez Närrisch.

"I'll lie to at the northeast corner," this madmother continues, "in the channel between the little island and that
triangular part that's built up on the foreshore."

"Test Stand X."

"Catchy name. I think here'll be enough of a tide by
then. Light a fire. Otto! Cast me off now."

"Zu Befehl, Mutti!"

Slothrop and Närrisch go dash behind a cargo shed, find
a boxcar, and hide inside. Nobody notices. Chimps are
running by in several directions. The soldiers chasing them
seem by now to be really pissed off. Someplace the clarinet player is blowing scales on his instrument. The boat's
motor sputters up into a growl, and screws go churning
away. A while later, Otto and his girl come climb in the
boxcar, out of breath.

"Well, Närrisch," Slothrop might as well ask, "where'd
they take him, do you think? eh?"

"From what I could see, Block Four and that whole
complex to the south were deserted. My guess is the assembly building near Test Stand VII. Under that big
ellipse. There are underground tunnels and rooms—ideal
for a headquarters. Looks like most of it survived pretty
well, even though Rossokovsky had orders to level the
place."

"You got a piece?" Närrisch shakes his head no. "Me
neither. What kind of a black-market operator are you,
anyway? no piece."

"I used to be in inertial guidance. You expect me to
revert?"

"W-well what are we supposed to use, then? Our wits?"

Out the slats of the car, the sky is darkening, the clouds
turning orange, tangerine, tropical. Otto and his girl are
murmuring in one corner. "Scrub that one," Närrisch with
sour mouth. "Five minutes away from his mother, he's a
Casanova."

Otto is earnestly explaining his views on the Mother
Conspiracy. It's not often a sympathetic girl will listen.
The Mothers get together once a year, in secret, at these
giant conventions, and exchange information. Recipes,
games, key phrases to use on their children. "What did

yours use to say when she wanted to make you feel guilty?"

" 'I've worked my fingers to the bone!' " sez the girl.

"Right! And she used to cook those horrible casseroles, w-with the potatoes, and onions—"

"And ham! Little piece of ham—"

"You see, you see? That *can't* be accidental! They have a contest, for Mother of the Year, breast-feeding, diaper-changing, they *time* them, casserole competitions, ja—then, toward the end, they actually begin to use the *children*. The State Prosecutor comes out on stage. 'In a moment, Albrecht, we are going to bring your mother on. Here is a Luger, fully loaded. The State will guarantee you absolute immunity from prosecution. Do whatever you wish to do— anything at all. Good luck, my boy.' The pistols are loaded with blanks, natürlich, but the unfortunate child does not know this. Only the mothers who get shot at qualify for the finals. Here they bring in psychiatrists, and judges sit with stopwatches to see how quickly the children will crack. 'Now then, Olga, wasn't it *nice* of Mutti to break up your affair with that long-haired poet?' 'We understand your mother and you are, ah, *quite close*, Hermann. Re-member the time she caught you *masturbating into her glove*? Eh?' Hospital attendants stand by to drag the children off, drooling, screaming, having clonic convul-sions. Finally there is only one Mother left on stage. They put the traditional flowered hat on her head, and hand her the orb and scepter, which in this case are a gilded pot roast and a whip, and the orchestra plays *Tristan und Isolde*."

☐

They come out into the last of the twilight. Just a sleepy summer evening in Peenemünde. A flight of ducks passes overhead, going west. No Russians around. A single bulb burns over the entrance to the cargo shed. Otto and his girl wander hand in hand along the dock. An ape comes scampering up to take Otto's free hand. To north and south the Baltic keeps unrolling low white waves. "What's happening," asks the clarinet player. "Have a banana,"

tuba player with his mouth full has a good-sized bunch
stowed in the bell of his ax.

Night is down by the time they get started. They head
inland, Springer's crashout party, along the railroad tracks.
Pine trees tower to either side of the cinder embankment.
Ahead fat pinto rabbits scurry, only their white patches
visible, no reason to suppose rabbits is what they are.
Otto's friend Hilde comes gracefully down out of the
woods with his cap that she's filled to the brim with round
berries, dusty blue, sweet. The musicians are packing
vodka bottles in every available pocket. That's tonight's
meal, and Hilde kneeling alone at the berry bushes has
whispered grace for them all. In the marshes now you can
hear the first peepers start up, and the high-frequency
squeals of a bat out hunting, and some wind in the upper
trees. Also, from farther away, a shot or two.

"Are they firing at my apes?" Haftung chatters. "That's
2000 marks apiece. How am I ever going to get that back?"

A family of mice go dashing across the tracks, and right
over Slothrop's feet. "I was expecting just a big cemetery.
I guess not."

"When we came we only cleared out what we needed
to," Närrisch recalls. "Most of it stayed—the forest, the
life . . . there are probably still deer up in there, someplace. Big fellows with dark antlers. And the birds—
snipes, coots, wild geese—the noise from the testing drove
them out to sea, but they'd always come back in when it
was quiet again."

Before they reach even the airfield they have to scatter
twice into the woods, first for a security patrol, then for a
steam-engine come puffing up from Peenemünde-East, its
headlight cutting through a fine night-haze, some troops
with automatics hanging on to steps and ladders. Steel
grinding and creaking by in the night, the men shooting
the breeze as they pass, no feeling of tension to it. "They
might be after us anyway," Närrisch whispers. "Come on."

Through a patch of woods, and then cautiously out onto
the open airfield. A sharp sickle of moon has risen. Apes
scuttle along in the bonelight, arms dangling. It's a nervous passage. Everybody's a perfect target, there's no cover
except for airplanes strafed where they stood into relics—
rusted stringers, burned paint, gullwings driven back into
the earth. Lights from the old Luftwaffe complex glow to

the south. Trucks purr now and then along the road at the far edge of the airfield. There's singing from the barracks, and someplace a radio. The evening news from somewhere. Too far to hear the words or even the language, only the studious monotone: the news, Slothrop, going on without you. . . .

They make it across the tarmac to the road, and crouch in a drainage ditch, listening for traffic. Suddenly, to their left, yellow runway lights come on, a double row of them chaining to the sea, brightness bouncing up and down a couple-three times before it settles in. "Somebody coming in," Slothrop guesses.

"More likely going out," snaps Närrisch. "We'd better hurry."

Back in the pine woods now, heading up a road of packed dirt toward Test Stand VII, they start to pick up stray girls and chimpanzees. Pine smells wrap them: old needles lie at the margins of the road. Downhill, lights appear as the trees begin thinning out, then the test-stand area comes in view. The assembly building is something like a hundred feet high—it blocks out the stars. There's a tall bright band where sliding doors are open, and light scatters outside. Närrisch grabs Slothrop's arm. "It looks like the major's car. And the motor's running." Lotta searchlights, too, set up on fences topped with barbed wire—also what look like a division of security roaming around.

"Guess this is it," Slothrop a little nervous.

"Ssh." Sound of a plane, a single-engine fighter, circling to make its approach low over the pines. "Not much time." Närrisch gathers the others around and issues his orders. Girls are to go in from the front, singing, dancing, vamping the woman-hungry barbarians. Otto will try to knock out the car, Haftung will get everybody rounded up and ready to rendezvous with the boat.

"Tits 'n' ass," mutter the girls, "tits 'n' ass. That's all we are around here."

"Ah, shaddap," snarls G. M. B. Haftung, which is his usual way of dealing with the help.

"Meanwhile," continues Närrisch, "Slothrop and I will go in after Springer. When we have him, we'll try to get them to shoot. That will be *your* signal to run like hell."

"Oh, definitely some shooting," sez Slothrop, "a-and how

about this?" He has just had a brilliant idea: fake Molotov cocktails, a switch on Säure Bummer's old routine. He holds up a vodka bottle, pointing and grinning.

"But that stuff won't even hardly burn."

"But they'll *think* it's gasoline," beginning to pluck ostrich feathers from the costume of the nearest girl. "And just imagine how secure it will make *us* feel."

"Felix," the clarinet player asks the tuba player, "what have we fallen among?" Felix is eating a banana, and living for the moment. Presently he has wandered off in the woods with the rest of the band, where they can be heard moving around in circles, tootling and blatting at each other. Hilde and Slothrop are making Phony Phire-bombs, the other girls have taken off, Zitz und Arsch, downslope.

"So we'll present a plausible threat," Närrisch whispers, "we'll need matches. Who's got matches?"

"Not me."

"Me either."

"Gee, my lighter's out of flints."

"Kot," Närrisch throwing up his hands, "Kot," walking off into the trees, where he collides with Felix and his tuba. "You don't have any matches either."

"I have a Zippo," replies Felix, "and two Corona Coronas, from the American officers' club in—"

A minute later, Närrisch and Slothrop, hands each cupped around the coal of one Havana's finest, are sneaky-Peteing like two cats in a cartoon off toward Test Stand VII, with vodka-bottle bombs stuck in their belts and ostrich-feather wicks trailing behind in the sea breeze. The plan is to climb the pine-topped sand-and-scrub embankment around the test stand, and come in on the Assembly Building from behind.

Now Närrisch here's a guidance man, a guidance man is he. And ev'ry day at Rocket Noon, there's death, and revelry. . . . But Närrisch has managed, in his time, to avoid nearly all of it.

In fact, no two people have been so ill-equipped to approach a holy Center since the days of Tchitcherine and Džaqyp Qulan, hauling ass over the steppe, into the North, to find their Kirghiz Light. That's about ten years' gap. Giving this pastime about the same vulnerability to record-

breakers as baseball, a sport also well-spidered with white
suggestions of the sinister.

Holy-Center-Approaching is soon to be the number one
Zonal pastime. Its balmy heyday is nearly on it. Soon more
champions, adepts, magicians of all ranks and orders will
be in the field than ever before in the history of the game.
The sun will rule all enterprise, if it be honest and sporting. The Gauss curve will herniate toward the excellent.
And tankers the likes of Närrisch and Slothrop here will
have already been weeded out.

Slothrop, as noted, at least as early as the *Anubis* era,
has begun to thin, to scatter. "Personal density," Kurt
Mondaugen in his Peenemünde office not too many steps
away from here, enunciating the Law which will one day
bear his name, "is directly proportional to temporal bandwidth."

"Temporal bandwidth" is the width of your present,
your *now*. It is the familiar "Δt" considered as a dependent
variable. The more you dwell in the past and in the future,
the thicker your bandwidth, the more solid your persona.
But the narrower your sense of Now, the more tenuous
you are. It may get to where you're having trouble remembering what you were doing five minutes ago, or even—as
Slothrop now—what you're doing *here*, at the base of this
colossal curved embankment. . . .

"Uh," he turns slackmouth to Närrisch, "what are
we . . ."

"What are we what?"

"What?"

"You said, 'What are we . . . ,' then you stopped."

"Oh. Gee, that was a funny thing to say."

As for Närrisch, he's too locked in to business. He has
never seen this great Ellipse any other way but the way
he was meant to. Greta Erdmann, on the contrary, saw
the rust-covered eminences here bow, exactly as they did
once, in expectancy, faces hooded, smooth cowlings of
Nothing . . . each time Thanatz brought the whip down on
her skin, she was taken, off on another penetration toward
the Center: each lash, a little farther in . . . till someday,
she knows, she will have *that first glimpse of it*, and from
then on it will be an absolute need, a ruling target . . .
wh-wh-wh-*whack* the boneblack trestling of water towers

above, bent to the great rim, visible above the trees in light that's bleak and bruise-purple as Peenemünde sunsets in the chill slow firing-weather . . . a long look from the top of some known Low Country dike into a sky flowing so even and yellowed a brown that the sun could be anywhere behind it, and the crosses of the turning windmills could be spoke-blurs of the terrible Rider himself, Slothrop's Rider, his two explosions up there, his celestial cyclist—

No, but even *That* only flickers now briefly across a bit of Slothropian lobe-terrain, and melts into its surface, vanishing. So here passes for him one more negligence . . . and likewise groweth his Preterition sure. . . . There is no good reason to hope for any turn, any surprise *I-see-it*, not from Slothrop. Here he is, scaling the walls of an honest ceremonial plexus, set down on a good enough vision of what's shadowless noon and what isn't. But oh, Egg the flying Rocket hatched from, navel of the 50-meter radio sky, all proper ghosts of place—forgive him his numbness, his glozing neutrality. Forgive the fist that doesn't tighten in his chest, the heart that can't stiffen in any greeting. . . . Forgive him as you forgave Tchitcherine at the Kirghiz Light. . . . Better days are coming.

Slothrop is listening to faraway peripatetic tuba and clarinet being joined in on now by trombone and tenor sax, trying to pick up a tune . . . and to the bursts of laughter from soldiers and girls . . . sounds like a party down there . . . maybe even some stag dames . . . "Say, why don't we, uh . . . what was your—" Närrisch, leather scarecrow, trying to ignore Slothrop's behavior, has decided to dismantle his fire-bomb: he uncorks the vodka and waves it under his nose before taking a belt. He beams, cyinical, salesmanwise, up at Slothrop. "Here." A silence under the white wall.

"Oh, yes I was thinking it was gasoline, but then it's fake, so it's really vodka, right?"

But just over the embankment, down in the arena, what might that have been just now, waiting in this broken moonlight, camouflage paint from fins to point crazed into jigsaw . . . is it, then, really never to find you again? Not even in your worst times of night, with pencil words on your page only Δt from the things they stand for? And inside the victim is twitching, fingering beads, touching wood, avoiding any Operational Word. Will it really never come to take you, now?

Near the water towers, they have started to climb, up toward the rim. Sand leaks into their shoes and hisses away down the slope. At the top, back through the trees, they get a quick look at the lighted runway, the fighter now landed, surrounded by groundcrew shadows fueling, servicing, turning her around. Down the penninsula lights glow in patches, curves, zigzags, but over on this side, from the old Development Works south, it's pitch black.

They push through pine branches and down again, into the Egg, sacked of its German hardware, long converted to a Russian motor pool. The corner of the huge Assembly Building, as they come down, rises to face them across a hundred yards of jeeps and lorries. Down to the right is a three- or four-level test frame with a round, kind of quonset top, and underneath the frame is a long pit shaped like a shallow V. "Cooling duct," according to Närrisch. "They're probably under there. We have to go in through here."

They have come halfway down the slope to a pump house, built into the earthworks, for the cold water that used to carry off the tremendous heat from the test firings. It is stripped now, hollow and dark inside. Slothrop isn't two steps over the doorsill when he walks into somebody.

"Beg your pardon," though it comes out less than calmly.

"Oh, that's all right." Russian accent. "I don't mind at all." He backs Slothrop outside again, oh, a *mean* looking junior sergeant here about 8 or 9 feet high.

"Well, now—" at which point Närrisch comes walking into them.

"Oh." Närrisch blinks at the sentry. "Sergeant, don't you hear that music? Why aren't you back at the Assembly Building, with your comrades? There are, I understand, a number of eager fräuleins *entertaining* them," nudge nudge, "in a most enchanting state of deshabille, too."

"I suppose that's all perfectly divine," replies the sentry, "for *some* people."

"*Kot . . .*" So much for tactics.

"And besides, this is out of *bounds,* you big sillies."

Sighing. Närrisch raises his bottle aloft, brings it down, or up, *thunk* on the sentry's nape, dislodging the man's helmet liner, is what happens. "Naughty," the Russian, somewhat nettled, stoops to retrieve his headgear. "*Really* I ought to put you *both* under apprehension."

"Enough chit-chat," snarles Slothrop, brandishing his glowing cigar and "Molotov cocktail." "Hand over that gun there, Ivan, or I turn you into a *human flare!*"

"You're *mean*," sulks the sentry, unslinging his Deg-tyarov a little too quickly—Slothrop dodges aside, aims his usual swift kick to the groin, which misses, but does knock loose the weapon, which Närrisch is thoughtful enough to dive for. "Beasts," whimpers the Russian, "oh, nasty, aw-ful . . ." scampering off into the night.

"Two minutes," Närrisch already inside the pump house. Slothrop grabs the automatic from him and follows at a run, accelerating down a sloping corridor. Their feet ring faster, sharper, on the concrete, down to a metal door: behind it they can hear Springer singing and babbling like a drunk. Slothrop pushes off his safety and Närrisch goes busting in. A pretty blonde auxiliary in black boots and steel-rimmed glasses is sitting here taking down shorthand notes of everything she hears from Springer, who leans happily grandiose against a cold-water pipe four feet high that runs the length of the room.

"Drop that pencil," orders Slothrop. "All right, where's that Major Zhdaev?"

"He's in conference. If you'd care to leave your name—"

"Dope," Närrisch screams, "they have given him some kind of *dope!* Gerhardt, Gerhardt, speak to me!"

Slothrop recognizes the symptoms. "It's that Sodium Amytal. It's O.K. Let's go."

"I expect the Major to be back any moment. They're upstairs in the guardroom, smoking. Is there a number where he can reach you?"

Slothrop has slid under one of Springer's arms, Närrisch under the other, when there's this loud hammering on the door.

"Smoking? Smoking *what?*"

"*This way, Slothrop.*"

"Oh." They hustle Springer out another door, which Slothrop bolts and wrassles a heavy filing cabinet up

against, then they drag Springer up a flight of steps into
a long, straight corridor, lit by six or seven bulbs, the
spaces between which are very dark. Along either side,
floor to ceiling, run thick bundles of measurement cabling.

"We're done for," Närrisch wheezes. It's 150 yards to
the measurement bunker, and no cover but the shadows
between the bulbs. All these birds gotta do is spray a
pattern.

"She baffs at nothing, the heterospeed," cries Gerhardt
von Göll.

"Try to walk," Slothrop scared shit, "come on, man, it's
our *ass!*" Smashing echoes after them down the tunnel. A
muffled burst of autometic fire. And another. All at once,
two faint pools of light ahead, Zhdaev materializes, on the
way back to his office. He has a friend with him, who
smiles when he sees Slothrop 40 yards away, a big steel
smile. Slothrop lets go of Springer and runs up into the
next light, piece at the ready. The Russians are blinking at
him in a puzzled way. "Tchitcherine! Hey."

They stand facing, each at his lit circle. Slothrop recalls
that he has the drop on them. He smiles in half-apology,
tips the muzzle at them, moves closer. Zhdaev and Tchitcherine, after a discussion which seems unnecessarily long,
decide they will raise their hands.

"Rocketman!"

"Howdy."

"What are you doing in a Fascist uniform like that?"

"You're right. Think I'll join the Red Army, instead."
Närrisch leaves Springer sagging against a row of sleek
rubber and silver-mesh cables, and comes up to help disarm the two Russians. Troops back down the tunnel are
still busy busting the door down.

"You guys want to undress, here? Say Tchitcherine,
how'd you like that hashish, by the way?"

"Well," taking off his trousers, "we were all up there in
the *budka* just now smoking some . . . Rocketman, your
timing is fantastic. Zhdaev, isn't he something?"

Slothrop slides out of his tux. "Just see you don't get a
hardon here now, fella."

"I'm serious. It's your Schwarzphänomen."

"Quit fooling."

"You don't even know about it. It choreographs you.

Mine's always trying to *destroy* me. We should be ex-
changing *those,* instead of uniforms."

The disguise business grows complicated. Zhdaev's
jacket with the gold-starred *pogoni* on the shoulders gets
draped around the Springer, who is now humming everyone a Kurt Weill medley. Zhdaev puts on Springer's white
suit, and then him and Tchitcherine get tied up with their
own belts, a-and neckties. "Now—the idea," Slothrop explains, "being that you, Tchitcherine, will be posing as me,
and the major there—" At which point the door back
down the tunnel comes blasting open, two figures with
wicked Suomi subs, drums on them as big as that Gene
Krupa's, come flying through. Slothrop stands in the light
in Tchitcherine's uniform, and waves dramatically, pointing
at the two hogtied officers. "Make it good," he mutters to
Tchitcherine, "I'm trusting you now, but look out I have
a great passive vocabulary, I'll know what you're saying."

It's O.K. with Tchitcherine, but confusing. "I'm supposed to be who, now?"

"Oh, shit . . . look, just tell them to go check out the
pump house up there, it's urgent." Slothrop gestures and
lip-synchs while Tchitcherine talks. It seems to work. The
two actually salute, and go back through the door they
just shot down.

"Those apes," Tchitcherine shakes his head. "Those
black apes! How did you know, Rocketman? Of course
you didn't, but the Schwarzphänomen did. A great touch.
Two of them, looking at me through the window. And I
thought—well, you know: I thought just about what you
thought I'd think. . . ."

But by this time Slothrop is way out of earshot. Springer
by now is able to stumble at a fast walk. They get as far
as the measurement bunker without running into anybody.
Out a door of bulletproof glass, behind their own reflections, is the old test frame, windows broken out, camouflage in German Expressionist ripples streaming gray and
black all over it. The two soldiers are sure enough up
there poking around that pump house, finding nothing.
Presently they disappear inside again, and Närrisch opens
the door. "Hurry." They edge outside, into the arena.

It takes a while to get back up the slope and into the
woods. Otto and Hilde show up. They've finessed Zhdaev's
car and driver out of a rotor arm. So there are four of

them now to try and lift warbling payload Gerhardt von
Göll up these few crummy feet of sand embankment here,
gotta be the most ill-designed propulsion system this test
stand has seen in a while. Otto and Hilde tug at Springer's
arms, Närrisch and Slothrop push from the ass end. About
halfway up Springer blows a tremendous fart that echoes
for minutes across the historic ellipse, like now to do for
you folks my anal impression of the A4. . . .

"Oh, fuck you," Slothrop snarls.

"An erect green steed of planetoid and bone," nods the
Springer in reply.

Music and chatter back by the Assembly Building have
all died away now, and an unpleasant calm has replaced
them. Up over the top at last and into the woods, where
Springer rests his forehead against a tree trunk and commences vomiting violently.

"Närrisch, we're risking our ass for *this slob?*"

But Närrisch is busy helping squeeze his friend's stomach. "Gerhardt, are you all right? What can I do?"

"Beautiful," chokes Springer, vomit trickling down his
chin. "Ahh. Feels great!"

Along come chimps, musicians, dancing girls. Drifting
in to rendezvous. Over the last dune and down to the
packed cinder triangle of Test Stand X, and the sea. The
musicians for a while play a kind of march tune. Past the
foreshore, the tide has left them a strip of sand. But Frau
Gnahb is nowhere in sight. Haftung is holding hands with
an ape. Felix shakes spit out of his tuba. A honey-haired
chorus girl, whose name he never does get, puts her arms
around Slothrop. "I'm scared."

"Me too." He hugs her.

All hell breaks loose—sirens whoop-whooping, searchlights starting to probe the woods up above, truck motors
and shouted commands. The crashout party move off the
cinders, and crouch in marsh grass.

"We've collected one automatic and two sidearms,"
Närrisch whispers. "They'll be coming at us from the
south. It'll only take one of us to go back up and hold
them." He nods and begins checking his hardware.

"You're crazy," hisses Slothrop, "they'll kill you." Commotion now from over by Test Stand VII. Headlights are
appearing, one after another, along the road up there.

Närrisch taps Springer on the chin. It isn't clear if

600   GRAVITY'S RAINBOW

Springer knows who he is. "Lebe wohl," anyway, Springer.
... Nagants stuck in overcoat pockets, automatic cradled
in his arms, Närrisch takes off at a crouching run along
the beach, and doesn't look back.

"Where's the boat?" Haftung in a white panic. Ducks,
alarmed, are quacking at each other down here. Wind
moves in the grass. When searchlights move by, pine
trunks uphill flare, deeply shining, terrible ... and at
everyone's back, the Baltic shakes and streams.

Shots from uphill—then, maybe from Närrisch in reply,
a burst of automatic fire. Otto is holding his Hilde close.
"Anybody read Morse Code?" the girl next to Slothrop
wants to know, "because there's been a light going over
there, see, at the tip of that little island? for a few minutes now." It's three dots, dot, dot, three more dots. Over
and over.

"Hmm, SEES," ponders Felix.

"Maybe they're not dots," sez the tenor-sax player,
"maybe they're *dashes*."

"That's funny," sez Otto, "that would spell OTTO."

"That's your name," sez Hilde.

"Mother!" screams Otto, running out in the water and
waving at the blinking light. Felix commences booming
tuba notes across the water, and the rest of the band joins
in. Reed shadows come stabbing across the sand, as the
spotlights swoop down. A boat engine roars into hearing.
"Here she comes," Otto jumping up and down in the
marsh.

"Hey, Närrisch," Slothrop squinting, trying to find him
back there in light that was always too weak, "come on.
Fall back." No answer. But more shooting.

Running-lights off, the boat comes barreling in at flank
speed, Frau Gnahb has decided to ram Peenemünde? no,
now she puts everything full astern—bearings shriek,
screw-foam geysers, the boat slews around to a stop.

"Get on board," she bellows.

Slothrop's been hollering for Närrisch. Frau Gnahb
leans on her steam-whistle. But no answer. "Shit, I've got to
get him—" Felix and Otto grab Slothrop from behind,
drag him back to the boat kicking and cursing. "They'll kill
him, you assholes, lemme go—" Dark shapes come spilling
over the dune between here and Test Stand VII, orange

flickers at their midsections, the sound of rifle fire following a second later.

"They will kill *us*." Otto heaves Slothrop over the side, and tumbles in after. Spotlights find and skewer them now. The firing is louder—nipples and spatters in the water, slugs hammering into the boat.

"Everybody here?" the Frau's fangs bared in a grin. "Fine, fine!" A last ape reaches up, Haftung catches his hands, and he dangles, feet in the water, for several yards as they light out, all ahead full, till he can finally clamber up and over. Gunfire follows out to sea, out of range, at last out of earshot.

"Hey Felix," sez the tenor sax player, "you think there's any gigs in Swinemünde?"

John Dillinger, at the end, found a few seconds' strange mercy in the movie images that hadn't quite yet faded from his eyeballs—Clark Gable going off unregenerate to fry in the chair, voices gentle out of the deathrow steel *so long, Blackie* . . . turning down a reprieve from his longtime friend now Governor of New York William Powell, skinny chinless condescending jerk, Gable just wanting to get it over with, "Die like ya live—all of a sudden, don't drag it out—" even as bitchy little Melvin Purvis, staked outside the Biograph Theatre, lit up the fatal cigar and felt already between his lips the penis of official commendation—and federal cowards at the signal took Dillinger with their faggots' precision . . . there was still for the doomed man some shift of personality in effect—the way you've felt for a little while afterward in the real muscles of your face and voice, that you *were* Gable, the ironic eyebrows, the proud, shining, snakelike head—to help Dillinger through the bushwhacking, and a little easier into death.

Närrisch now, huddled inside a broken few meters of concrete drainage pipe, after doubling back under the wall of Test Stand VII, bracing curled now in the smell of old storm water, trying not to breathe loud enough to smack echoes into any betrayal—Närrisch hasn't been to a movie since *Der Müde Tod*. That's so long ago he's forgotten its ending, the last Rilke-elegiac shot of weary Death leading the two lovers away hand in hand through

the forget-me-nots. No help at all from that quarter. Tonight Närrisch is down to the last tommygun of his career,
foreign and overheated . . . and blisters on his hands he
won't have to worry about tomorrow. No sources of mercy
available beyond the hard weapon, the burning fingers—a
cruel way to go out for a good guidance man who always
put in fair time for fair wages. . . . He had other offers
. . . could've gone east with the Institute Rabe, or west to
America and $6 a day—but Gerhardt von Göll promised
him glamour, jackpots, a flashy dame on his arm, say, why
not on *both* arms?—after poor linear Peenemünde, who
could blame him?

It wasn't ever necessary to see around the entire Plan . . .
really that's asking too much of anyone . . . not true? This
S-Gerät strategy he's going out of his way to die for tonight, what does he know of the Springer's *full* intentions
in the affair? It is reasonable to Närrisch that he, being
smaller, he should be the sacrifice, if it helps Springer
survive, even survive another day . . . wartime thinking,
ja, ja . . . but too late to change. . . .

Did the S-Gerät program at Nordhausen in its time ever
hint that so many individuals, nations, firms, communities
of interest would come after the fact? Of course he was
flattered then at being chosen to work on the modification
to the guidance, minor as it was . . . hardly worth the special treatment . . . still, it was his first high historical moment and he sourly figured it to be his last, up until meeting with Springer's recruiting team, back during the rainier
part of June. . . . Conferences in cafés and entrances to
churchyards around Braunschweig (stucco arches, vines
dripping onto thin collars) without an umbrella but with
that light, belled hope inside—a field, crowded with lines
of force, to expand, to fill, to keep him in good health and
spirits . . . Berlin! The Chicago Cabaret! "Cocaine—or
cards?" (an old movie line the gunsels loved to use that
summer) . . . the *Big Time!*

But the ringing bright thing inside brought him here,
instead: here, down in a pipe, to only a handful more of
minutes. . . .

The idea was always to carry along a fixed quantity, A.
Sometimes you'd use a Wien bridge, tuned to a certain
frequency A_t, whistling, heavy with omen, inside the elec-

tric corridors . . . while outside, according to the tradition
in these matters, somewhere a quantity B would be gathering, building, as the Rocket gathered speed. So, up till
assigned Brennschluss velocity, "v_1^*," electric-shocked as
any rat into following this very narrow mazeway of clear
space—yes, radio signals from the ground would enter the
Rocket body, and by reflex—literally by electric signal
traveling a reflex arc—the control surfaces twitch, to steer
you back on course the instant you'd begin to wander off
(how could you've kept from lapsing, up here, into that
radiant inattention, so caught up in the wind, the sheer
altitude . . . the unimaginable fires at your feet?) . . . so,
for that tightly steered passage, all was carried on in the
sharpest, most painful *anticipation*, with B always growing, as palpably cresting as the assault of tidal wave that
stills every small creature and hones the air down to a
cold stir. . . . Your quantity A—shining, constant A, carried
as they must have once packed far overland at night the
Grail, in their oldtime and military bleakness of humor . . .
and one morning a wide upper lip steelwool gray with the
one day's growth, the fatal, the terrible sign, he shaved
smooth every day, it meant that this *was* the Last Day—
and, too, with only the grim sixth sense, as much faith as
clear reception, that the B of Many Subscripts just over
the electric horizon was really growing closer, perhaps this
time as "B_{1w}," the precession angle of the gyro, moving
invisibly but *felt*, terrifically arousing, over the metal frame
toward angle A_{1w} (which is how they have set you the
contacts: to close, you must see, at that exact angle). Or
as "B_{1L}," another integrating, not of gyro rate but of the
raw current flow itself, bled from the moving coil inside
the poles, the "fettered" pendulum . . . they thought this
way, Design Group, in terms of captivity, prohibition . . .
there was an attitude toward one's hardware more brutal
and soldierly than most engineers' got the chance to
be. . . . They felt quite the roughshod elite, Driwelling,
and Schmeil, with the fluorescent lights shining on his
bared forehead night after night. . . . Inside their brains
they shared an old, old electro-decor—variable capacitors
of glass, kerosene for a dielectric, brass plates and ebonite
covers, Zeiss galvanometers with thousands of fine-threaded
adjusting screws, Siemens milliammeters set on slate sur-

faces, terminals designated by Roman numerals, Standard Ohms of manganese wire in oil, the old Gülcher Thermosäule that operated on heating gas, put out 4 volts, nickel and antimony, asbestos funnels on top, mica tubing. . . .

Wasn't that life more decent than gangstering? A cleaner sort of friendship . . . less devious, anyway. . . . There we *saw* how we had to fit in . . . the machinery itself determined that . . . everything was so clear then, paranoia was all for the enemy, and never for one's own. . . .

—What about the SS?

—Oh, they were the enemy, I'd say. . . . [Laughter.]

No, Klaus, don't drift away, please, not onto dreams of kindly Soviet interrogation that will end in some ermine bed, some vodka-perfumed stupor, you know that's foolish. . . .

B, B-sub-N-for-Närrisch, is nearly here—nearly about to burn through the last whispering veil to equal "A"—to equal the only fragment of himself left by them to go through the moment, the irreducible doll of German styrene, shabbier, less authentic than any earlier self . . . a negligible quantity in this last light . . . this tattoo of hunters' boots, and rifle bolts in oiled keyways. . . .

□

Here come Enzian, Andreas, and Christian, coming on like Smith, Klein, 'n' French, crashing into the basement room—field-gray kit, newspaper shoes, rolled trouser-cuffs, hands and bare forearms shining with motor oil and gear grease, toting carbines in a show of force. But no Empty Ones here to see them. It's too late. Just the mute bed, and the brown ellipse her blood made on the torn ticking. And washing-blue in grainy splashes in the corners, under the bed . . . ther signature, their challenge.

"Where *is she*—" Christian is just this side of berserk. One word astray and he'll be off to kill the first Empty One he finds. Maria, his sister, is, was, may be—

"We'd better," Enzian already back out the door, "where's, uh . . . her husband, you know. . . ."

"Pavel." Christian wants to see his eyes, but Enzian won't turn.

Pavel and Maria meant to have the child. Then Josef Ombindi and his people started their visiting. They have learned their vulturehood from the Christian missionaries. They keep lists of all the women of child-bearing age. Any pregnancy is an invitation to hover, to tune in, to swoop. They will use threats, casuistry, physical seduction—there's an arsenal of techniques. Washing-blue is the abortifacient of choice.

"The refinery," suggests Andreas Orukambe.

"Really? I thought he'd sworn off that."

"Maybe not now." The girl's brother stares him hard as fists. *Enzian, old bastard, you really are out of touch. . . .*

They remount their motorcycles and head off again. Blasted drydocks, charcoal ribs of warehouses, cylindrical chunks of submarine that never got assembled, go ripping by in the darkness. British security are about, but that's another, encapsulated world. The British G-5 occupy their own space and Zone congruent but not identical to what these serious Schwarzkommando astride bikes unmuffled go blasting on through tonight.

Separations are proceeding. Each alternative Zone speeds away from all the others, in fated acceleration, redshifting, fleeing the Center. Each day the mythical return Enzian dreamed of seems less possible. Once it was necessary to know uniforms, insignia, airplane markings, to observe boundaries. But by now too many choices have been made. The single root lost, way back there in the May desolation. Each bird has his branch now, and each one is the Zone.

A crowd of DPs is milling by the ruin of an ornamental fountain, a score of them, eyes of ash, smudged into faces white as salt. The Hereros go swerving by them, halfway up a shallow flight of long steps dovetailing into the grade of the street, teeth slamming together upper and lower, cycle frames squeaking shrill, up and down the steps past wordless plosions of Slavic breath. Ashes and salt. A soundtruck appears around a wall a hundred meters away: the voice, University-bred and long tired of the message, recites, "Clear the streets. Go to your homes." Clear the—go to your *what?* There must be a mistake, it must be for some other town. . . .

Whir underneath an oil pipeline up on trestles running

down leftward to the water now, huge bolted flanges overhead softened by rust and oily dirt. Far out in the harbor rides an oil tanker, rocking serene as a web of stars. . . . *Zoom* uphill slantwise toward a rampart of wasted, knotted, fused, and scorched girderwork, stacks, pipes, ducting, windings, fairings, insulators reconfigured by all the bombing, grease-stained pebblery on the ground rushing by a mile a minute and wait, wait, say what, say *"reconfigured,"* now?"

There doesn't exactly dawn, no but there *breaks*, as that light you're afraid will break some night at too deep an hour to explain away—there floods on Enzian what seems to him an extraordinary understanding. This serpentine slag-heap he is just about to ride into now, this ex-refinery, Jamf Ölfabriken Werke AG, is *not a ruin at all. It is in perfect working order.* Only waiting for the right connections to be set up, to be switched on . . . modified, precisely, *deliberately* by bombing that was never hostile, but part of a plan both sides—*"sides?"*—had always agreed on . . . yes and now what if we—all right, say we *are* supposed to be the Kabbalists out here, say that's our real Destiny, to be the scholar-magicians of the Zone, with somewhere in it a Text, to be picked to pieces, annotated, explicated, and masturbated till it's all squeezed limp of its last drop . . . well we assumed—natürlich!— that this holy Text had to be the Rocket, orururumo orunene the high, rising, dead, the blazing, the great one ("orunene" is already being modified by the Zone-Herero children to "omunene," the eldest brother) . . . our Torah. What else? Its symmetries, its latencies, the *cuteness* of it enchanted and seduced us while the real Text persisted, somewhere else, in its darkness, our darkness . . . even this far from Südwest we are not to be spared the ancient tragedy of lost messages, a curse that will never leave us. . . .

But, if I'm riding through it, the Real Text, right now, if this is it . . . or if I passed it today somewhere in the devastation of Hamburg, breathing the ash-dust, missing it completely . . . if what the IG built on this site were not at *all* the final shape of it, but only an arrangement of fetishes, come-ons to call down special tools in the form of 8th AF bombers *yes* the "Allied" planes all would have been, ultimately, IG-built, by way of Director Krupp, through his English interlocks—the bombing was the exact industrial process of conversion, each release of energy placed exactly in space and time, each shockwave plotted in advance to bring *precisely tonight's wreck* into being thus decoding the Text, thus coding, recoding, derecoding the holy Text . . . If it is in working order, what is it meant to do? The engineers who built it as a refinery never knew there were any further steps to be taken. Their design was "finalized," and they could forget it.

It means this War was never political at all, the politics was all theatre, all just to keep the people distracted . . . secretly, it was being dictated instead by the needs of technology . . . by a conspiracy between human beings and techniques, by something that needed the energy-burst of war, crying, "Money be damned, the very life of [insert name of Nation] is at stake," but meaning, most likely, *dawn is nearly here, I need my night's blood, my funding, funding, ahh more, more.* . . . The real crises were crises of allocation and priority, not among firms—it was only staged to look that way—but among the different Technologies, Plastics, Electronics, Aircraft, and their needs which are understood only by the ruling elite . . .

Yes but Technology only responds (how often this argument has been iterated, dogged and humorless as a Gaussian reduction, among the younger Schwarzkommando especially), "All very well to talk about having a monster by the tail, but do you think we'd've had the Rocket if someone, some specific somebody with a name and a penis hadn't *wanted* to chuck a ton of Amatol 300 miles and blow up a block full of civilians? Go ahead, capitalize the T on technology, deify it if it'll make you feel less responsible—but it puts you in with the neutered, brother, in with the eunuchs keeping the harem of our stolen Earth for the numb and joyless hardons of human sultans, human elite with no right at all to be where they are—"

We have to look for power sources here, and distribution networks we were never taught, routes of power our teachers never imagined, or were encouraged to avoid . . . we have to find meters whose scales are unknown in the world, draw our own schematics, getting feedback, making

connections, reducing the error, trying to learn the real
function . . . zeroing in on what incalculable plot? Up
here, on the surface, coaltars, hydrogenation, synthesis
were always phony, dummy functions to hide the real,
the planetary mission yes perhaps centuries in the unrolling . . . this ruinous plant, waiting for its Kabbalists and
new alchemists to discover the Key, teach the mysteries to
others . . .

And if it isn't exactly Jamf Ölfabriken Werke? what if
it's the Krupp works in Essen, what if it's Blohm & Voss
right here in Hamburg or another make-believe "ruin," in
another city? Another *country?* YAAAGGGGHHHHH!

Well, this is stimulant talk here, yes Enzian's been
stuffing down Nazi surplus Pervitins these days like popcorn at the movies, and by now the bulk of the refinery—
named, incidentally, for the famous discoverer of Oneirine—is behind them, and Enzian is on into some other
paranoid terror, talking, talking, though each man's wind
and motor cuts him off from conversation.

Sort of a
Hoagy Carmichael
piano can be heard
in behind
this, here

> Just a daredevil Desox-yephedrine Daddy
> With m'pockets full o' happee daze,
> Zoomin' through the Zone, where the wild
>   dogs roam,
> Givin' all m'dreams away . . .
> Took the tubes outa my radi-yo,
> Don't mean a thing to me—
> Wouldn't spend a nickel on the Stars 'n'
>   Stripes, cause
> I'm doin' my own fer free. . . .
>
> Mouth keeps goin', nobody listenin',
> Gabbin' at a terrible pace—
> Aw, you're so sly, but I wave good-by,
> With a shit-eatin' grin on m'face!
>
> Don'tcha ephedrine of me, my honey,
> Swoon just to hear my name—
> In the curfew cells when all the lights are
>   gone, oh,
> Ev'ry thing'll be the same
> (Just light the candles)
> Ev-rything'll be the same. . . .

Last night in his journal, Enzian wrote: "The Mouth lately has been too much in service. Too little coming out of use to anybody. A defense. Oh God, oh God. Then they really are getting at me. Please I don't *want* to pontificate this way . . . I know what my voice sounds like—heard it at Peenemünde years ago on Weissmann's Dictaphone . . . chrome and Bakelite . . . too high, obnoxious, Berliner Schnauze . . . how they must wince inside whenever I begin to speak. . . .

"I could go tomorrow. I know how to be alone. It doesn't frighten me as much as they do. They take endlessly—but they never *use* what they take. What do they think they can take from me? They don't want my patriarchy, they don't want my love, they don't want my information, or my work, or my energy, or what I own . . . I don't own *anything*. There's no money any more—nobody's seen any out here for months, no it can't be money . . . cigarettes? I never have enough cigarettes. . . .

"If I left them, where could I go?"

Back among the reservoir tanks now, into the evening wind, skidding on this synthetic wastefield, all of it ungraded blackness . . . Christian's motor seems to be missing now and then, dithering toward a stall. Spot decision: if he breaks down let him walk. That way less trouble if Pavel's there, if he's not there pick up Christian on the way back and see about getting a truck out to repair it . . . keep it simple, that's the mark of a great leader, Enzian.

Christian doesn't break down, though, and Pavel turns out to be there, sort of. Well, not "there" the way Enzian in his current state of mind would consider for very long. But present, all right, along with an amazing collection of friends who always seem to show up whenever he comes to sniff Leunagasolin, such as, oh, the Moss Creature here, brightest green you can imagine, more burning than fluorescent, lurking over in a corner of the field tonight, shy, stirring like an infant now and then . . . or how about the Water Giant, a mile-high visitor made all of flowing water who likes to dance, twisting from the waist, arms blowing loosely along the sky. When the Ombindi people took Maria off to find their doctor in Hamburg, voices began calling—voices of the Fungus Pygmies who breed in the tanks at the interface between fuel and water-bottom

began to call to him. "Pavel! Omunene! Why don't you
come back, to see *us?* We miss you. Why have you stayed
away?" Not much fun for them down here at the Interface, competing with the bacteria who cruise by in their
country of light, these cellular aristocracy, approaching the
wall of hydrocarbons each for his share of God's abun-
dance—leaving their wastes, a green murmur, a divergently
unstable gabbling, a slime that grows with the days thicker,
more poisonous. It is a depressing thing indeed to be a
pygmy clustered together with thousands of others, hundreds of thousands, and have to live on the other side of
all this. You say other side? What do you mean? What
other side? You mean in the gasoline? (Clustered Pygmies,
playfully and to some well-known swing riff:) No-no, no,
no! —You mean in the water, then? (C.P.:) No-no, no,
no! —Well you gotta tell me please, 'fore I drop my
BVDs! We mean, explain the Pygmies, gathering their
little heads into a symmetrical cauliflower pattern, and
settling into a soft, wistful a cappella like kids around the
campfire with Bing Crosby in a baseball cap (yes these
Leunahalluzinationen have been known to get weird all
right, weirder than cultural shock, even, this here is *meta*-
shock's what it is, 3-sigma white faces in a ritual whose
mystery is deeper than north light over the Kalahari . . .)
we mean on the other side of the whole thing, the whole
bacteria-hydrocarbon-waste cycle. We can see the Interface from here. It's a long rainbow, mostly indigo, if that's
any help—indigo and Kelly green (Bing, directing, raises
up all these brainwashed little Irish faces in a moving
firelit crescendo) green . . . gasoline . . . between . . . submarine . . . fading, because by then Pavel was on his way
out to the refinery, forget this 2½ weeks of self-imposed
torture, Ombindi's men after him down by the glasswool
boiler pipes, men and women both trying to caress him,
pressure from both sides of the Tribal Suicide Question,
Enzian complaining, too entangled with the Rocket, too
encrimsoned in his feud with the Russian, to care much
about anyone outside himself . . . and here Pavel was trying
to stay away from this, from the breath of Mukuru, only
trying to be a good man—

The Moss Creature stirs. It has crept an alarming distance closer since Pavel last looked. A sudden overflow of

smooth cherry-red down the mountainside to his right (were there mountains? Where did the *mountains* come from?) and at once he knows, beyond deception or hope, that he has slipped into the North, that inhaling the breath of the first ancestor has taken him over into the terrible land, as he must have known it would, step by step over these last years, impossible to turn (what *is* turn? don't know which way to begin to move . . . don't know *how* to move . . .) too late, miles and changes too late.

And now his head in Christian's steel notch at 300 yards. Suddenly, this awful branching; the two possibilities already beginning to fly apart at the speed of thought—a new Zone in any case, now, whether Christian fires or refrains—jump, choose—

Enzian tries his best—knocks the barrel aside, has a few unpleasant words for the young revenger. But both men saw the new branches. The Zone, again, has just changed, and they are already on, into the new one. . . .

They ride on up to where Pavel's sniffing synthetic gasoline on the side of the lampless beige hill, under the tanks snailing whitely to heaven, here he is, one of the IG's happiest customers. . . .

Does Pavel know something the rest of us don't? If the IG wanted this to be a cover-up for something else, why not the breath of Mukuru?

Enzian can project himself back in the Erdschweinhöhle starting a new file on the IG—see it getting fatter and fatter as the interlocks develop, the books are audited, the witnesses come—not forward but sideways at least, always in shadows. . . . And if it should prove not to be the Rocket, not the IG? Why then he'll have to go on won't he, on to something else—the Volkswagen factory, the pharmaceutical companies . . . and if it isn't even in Germany then he'll have to start in America, or in Russia, and if he dies before they find the True Text to study, then there'll have to be machinery for others to carry it on. . . . Say, that's a swell idea—call the whole Erdschweinhöhle together, get up there say, *My people, I have had a vision* . . . no no but there *will* need to be more staff, if it's to be that big a search, quiet shifting of resources away from the Rocket, diversifying while making it look like an organic growth . . . and who to bring in on it? Christian—can he use the boy now, Christian's anger, will *It* use Christian regardless to help suppress Ombindi ... because if the Schwarzkommando mission in the Zone has been truly revealed just now, then there'll have to be something done about Ombindi, Empty Ones, doctrine of the Final Zero. More staff will mean more Zone-Hereros, not fewer—more information coming in about the enemy, more connections made will mean a greater threat to the people, will mean that tribal numbers will have to increase. Is there an alternative? no ... he would rather ignore Ombindi but the needs of this new Search will not allow him that comfort now ... the search will rule. ...

Somewhere, among the wastes of the World, is the key that will bring us back, restore us to our Earth and to our freedom.

Andreas has been talking with Pavel, who is still out with his strangely lighted companions, playing at this and that. Presently, with love and subterfuge, he gets the address of Ombindi's medical connection.

Enzian knows who he is. "Saint Pauli. Let's go. Your machine running a little rough, Christian?"

"Don't sweet-talk me," Christian explodes, "you don't care about me, you don't care about my sister, she's dying out there and you just keep plugging her into your equations—you—play this holy-father routine and inside that ego you don't even hate us, you don't care, you're not even *connected* any more—" He swings his fist at Enzian's face. He's crying.

Enzian stands there and lets him. It hurts. He lets it. His meekness isn't all politics, either. He can feel enough of the bone truth in what Christian said—maybe not all of it, not all at once, but enough.

"You just connected. Can we go after her, now?"

☐

Here is the good Frau, leaning over Slothrop from way down at the foot of the bed: her eye bright and cocky as a parrot's, a big white boss of eye cantilevered on old prickly arms and legs, a black kerchief above the roll of her pompadour in mourning for all her Hanseatic dead, underneath heaving iron fleets, under waves of the Baltic keel-edged and gray, dead under the fleets of waves, the prairies of the sea. . . .

Next thing is Gerhardt von Göll's foot nudging Slothrop in a less than tender way. The sun is up, and all the girls have gone. Otto grouches around deck with a broom and swab, removing yesterday's chimpanzee shit. Swinemünde.

The Springer is his old chipper self: "Fresh eggs and coffee in the pilot house—fall to. We're due out of here in 15 minutes."

"Well just belay that 'we,' Ace."

"But I need your help." Springer's wearing a suit of fine tweed this morning, very Savile Row, fits perfectly—

"Närrisch needed your help."

"You don't know what you're talking about." His eyes are steelies that never lose. His laugh, subtitled *Humoring the Fools*, is Mitteleuropäisch and mirthless. "All right, all right. How much do you want?"

"Everything's got a price, right?" But he's not being noble here, no, what it is is that his own price has just occurred to him, and he needs to shim the talk here, give it a second to breathe and develop.

"Everything."

"What's the deal?"

"A minor piracy. Pick up one package for me while I cover you." He looks at his watch, hamming it up.

"O.K., get me a discharge, I'll come with you."

"A what? A discharge? For *you*? Ha! Ha! Ha!"

"You ought to laugh more, Springer. It makes you look really cute."

"What *kind* of a discharge, Slothrop? *Honorable*, perhaps? Ah, ah-ha! Ha! Ha!" Like Adolf Hitler, Springer is easily tickled by what the Germans call Schadenfreude, the feeling of joy at another's misfortune.

"Quit fooling, I'm serious."

"Of *course* you are, Slothrop!" More giggling.

Slothrop waits, watches, sucking on an egg though he feels anything but sly this morning.

"Närrisch, you see, was supposed to go with me today. Now I'm stuck with you. Ha! Ha! Where do you want it delivered, this—ha—this discharge?"

"Cuxhaven." Slothrop has been having lately this dim

fantasy about trying to contact the Operation Backfire
people in Cuxhaven, to see if they'll help get him out.
They seem to be the only English connection to the
Rocket any more. He knows already it won't work. He and
Springer arrange a date anyhow.

"Be at a place called Putzi's. It's down the Dorum road.
Local dealers will be able to tell you where."

So it's out once again—out past the moles' wet embrace,
into the Baltic, crest to crest, and into nimbus piling sheet
on sheet bounces the jolly pirate bark, into a day already
squally and bitter, and getting worse. Springer stands outside the pilot house hollering in above the sound of heavy
seas that splash back over the bow and down the decks.
"Where do you make her?"

"If it's Copenhagen she's bound for," Frau Gnahb's
windburned face, permanent smile-creases all around her
eyes and mouth, beaming like the sun, "can't have more
than an hour on us. . . ."

Visibility this morning is too low to see the coast of
Usedom. Springer joins Slothrop at the rail looking at
nothing, breathing the closing smell of gray weather.

"He's all right, Slothrop. He's seen worse. Two months
ago in Berlin we got ambushed, right outside the Chicago.
He walked through crossfire from three Schmeissers to
offer our competitors a deal. Not a scratch."

"Springer, he was going round and round with half the
Russian Army up there."

"*They* won't kill him. They know who he is. He worked
in guidance, he was Schilling's best man, he knows more
about integrating circuits than anybody they'll find outside
of Garmisch now. The Russians are offering fantastic
salaries—better than the Americans—and they'll let him
stay in Germany, work at Peenemünde or the Mittelwerke,
just like he used to. He can even escape, if that's what he
wants, we have very good connections for that—"

"But what if they *did* shoot him?"

"No. They weren't supposed to."

"Springer, this ain't the fuckin' *movies* now, come on."

"Not yet. Maybe not quite yet. You'd better enjoy it
while you can. Someday, when the film is fast enough, the
equipment pocket-size and burdenless and selling at people's prices, the lights and booms no longer necessary

*then ... then ..." We now come in sight of mythical
Rügen off our starboard bow.* Its chalk cliffs are brighter
than the sky. There is mist in the firths, and among the
green oaks. Along the beaches drift pearl patches of fog.

*Our captain, Frau Gnahb, heads into the Greifswalder
Bodden, to comb the long firths for her quarry. After an
hour* (comical basoon solos over close-ups of the old recreant guzzling some horrible fermented potato-mash
lobotomy out of a jerrican, wiping her mouth on her
sleeve, belching) *of fruitless search, our modern-day
pirates head out to sea again, and up the eastern coast of
the island.*

Light rain has been falling. Otto breaks out slickers, and
a Thermos of hot soup. Clouds, a dozen shades of gray, go
scudding along the sky. Great misty heaps of rock, steep
cliffs, streams in deep gorges, gray and green and spires
of white chalk in the rain, go passing—the Stubbenkam-
mer, the King's Seat, and presently, off to port, Cape
Arkona where waves crash at the base of the cliffs and on
top the groves of white-trunked trees are blowing....
*The ancient Slavs put up a temple here, to Svetovid, their
god of fertility and war. Old Svetovid did business under
quite a number of aliases! Three-headed Triglav, five-
headed Porevit, SEVEN-faced Rugevit! Tell that to your
boss next time he talks about "wearing two hats!" Now, as
Arkona slides away off our port quarter—*

"There she is," Otto calls from the top of the pilot
house. Far far away, hauling out to sea from behind the
Wissow Klinken (the pale limestone latchkey with which
Providence today is probing the wards of Slothrop's heart),
barely visible in the rain, dips a tiny white ghost of a
ship. . . .

"Get a bearing," Frau Gnahb grabbing the wheel and
bracing her feet. "We want a *collision course!*" Otto
crouches by the pelorus, shivering.

"Here, Slothrop."

Luger? Box of rounds? "What ..."

"Came this morning with the egg delivery."

"You didn't mention—"

"He may be a little exercised. But he's a realist. Your
friend Greta and I knew him in Warsaw, in the old days."

"Springer—tell me Springer, now, what ship is that?"

Springer hands him some binoculars. In fine gold lettering, behind the golden jackal on the wraith-white bow, is the name he already knows. "O. . . . K.," trying to see through the rain into Springer's eyes, "you knew I was aboard. You're setting me up, now, right?"

"When were *you* on board?"

"Come on—"

"Look—Närrisch was going after the package today. Not you. We didn't even *know* you. Do you have to see conspiracies in everything? I don't control the Russians, and I didn't deliver him—"

"You're really pushing that innocence today, ain't you?"

"Quit bickering, idiots," hollers Frau Gnahb, "and clear—for *action!*"

Lazy and spectral pitches the *Anubis*, growing no clearer as they close with her. Springer reaches a megaphone out of the pilot house, and bawls, "Good day, Procalowski—permission to come aboard."

The answer is a gunshot. Springer hits the deck, slicker in rattling yellow flow, lies on his back with the megaphone pointing up funneling rain in his mouth: "We'll have to without permission, then—" Motioning Slothrop over, "Get ready to board." To Frau Gnahb, "We'll want to lash on."

"Fine but," one look at the evil leer now lighting up Otto's mother's face and it's clear that she didn't come out today for money, "when do I get to, to *ram* her?"

Alone on the sea with the *Anubis*. Slothrop has begun to sweat, unpleasantly. The green rocky coast of Rügen backdrops them, rising and falling through the squall. Zonggg another shot rattlesnaking off of a bulkhead. "Ram," orders the Springer. The storm comes down in earnest. Gleeful Frau Gnahb, humming through her teeth, spins the wheel, spokes blurring, prow swinging over aiming for midships. The blank side of the *Anubis* rushes in—is the Frau gonna bust on through it like a paper hoop? Faces behind portholes, cook peeling potatoes outside the galley, drunk in a frock coat sleeping on the rainy deck and sliding as the ship rolls . . . ah—ja, ja, a huge blue-flowered bowl of shredded potatoes at her elbow, a window, cast-iron flowers on spiral vine all painted white, a mild smell of cabbage and dishrags from under the sink, an apron bow snug and tight above her kidneys and lambs about her legs and ja little, oh, ja, here comes little—ah—here comes *herecomes* LITTLE—AHH—

OTTO! slams her boat into the *Anubis,* a most godawful earsplitting *Otto.* . . .

"Stand by." Springer's on his feet. Procalowski is turning away and increasing engine speed. Frau Gnahb moves up again on the yacht's starboard quarter, wallowing in her wake. Otto passes out grappling hooks, long in Hanseatic service, iron, pitted, functional-looking, as Mutti puts it all head full. Couples have wandered out under awnings on the *Anubis* to watch the fun, pointing, laughing, gaily waving. Girls, their nude breasts beaded with rain, blow kisses while the band plays a Guy Lombardo arrangement of "Running Between the Raindrops."

Up the slippery ladder goes salty and buccaneering Slothrop, hefting his grappling hook, letting out line, keeping an eye on that Otto—wind up, spin like a lasso, wheeee—clank. Springer and Otto at bow and stern are grappling on at the same time, hauling in as the vessels hit, bounce, hit . . . but the *Anubis,* softwhite, has slowed, sprawled, allowed . . . Otto gets line around chocks forward and up around the scrimshawed railing of the yacht—then dashes aft, sneakers splashing, ribbed footprints left behind then rained out, to repeat the lashing there. A newly-arranged river roars, white and violent, backward between the two ships. Springer is already up on the yacht's main deck. Slothrop tucks Luger in belt and follows.

Springer with the classic gangster head-move gestures him up the bridge. Slothrop moves through groping hands, greetings in broken Russian, puffs of alcoholic breath, around to the ladder on the port side—climbing, edging quietly onto the bridge. But Procalowski is only sitting in the captain's chair smoking one of Springer's *amis* with his cap tilted back, and Springer's just at the punch line to one of his giant repertoire of German toilet jokes.

"What the devil, Gerhardt," Procalowski waving a thumb. "The Red Army's working for you too?"

"Hello again, Antoni." The three silver stars on each of his epaulets twinkle howdy, but it's no good.

"I don't know you." To the Springer: "All right. It's in the engine room. Starboard side, down behind the generator," which is Slothrop's cue to leave.

At the bottom of the ladder he meets Stefania coming along the passageway. "Hi. Sorry we have to meet again this way."

"Hello, I'm Stefania," shuttering a fast smile as she passes, "there's liquor next deck up, enjoy yourself," already gone, out in the rain. What?

Slothrop steps down through a hatchway, starts to climb down toward the engineering spaces. Somewhere above him three bells strike, slowly, a little hollow, with a slight echo. It's late ... *late*. He remembers where he is.

Just as he touches the deck, all the lights go out. Air blowers whine down in stillness. The engine room is down one more deck. Will he have to do this in the dark?

"I can't," out loud.

"You can," replies a voice close to his ear. He can feel its breath. He is smashed expertly at the base of the neck. Light loops through the pitch dark. His left arm has gone numb. "I'll leave you the other one," the voice whispers, "for climbing down to the engine room."

"Wait—" It feels like the pointed toe of a dancing-pump, in out of nowhere to hover a second and stroke the soft underside of his chin—then it flicks up, slamming his teeth shut on his tongue.

The pain is awful. He tastes blood. Sweat gathers next to his eyes.

"Move, now." When he hesitates he is pinched on the back of the neck. Oh, it hurts ... he holds to the ladder, night-blind, starting to cry ... then he thinks of the Luger, but before he can get to it he's been kicked viciously between hip and groin. The gun falls to the steel deck. Slothrop is down on one knee, groping, when the shoe descends lightly on his fingers. "You will need this hand for holding on to the ladder, remember? *Remember?*" Then the shoe is lifted, but only to kick him under the armpit. "Up, up."

Slothrop gropes to the next ladder, makes his stiff one-armed way down onto it. He feels the steel hatch-opening rise around him. "Don't try to come back up till you've done what you have to do."

"Thanatz?" Slothrop's tongue hurts. The name comes out clumsily. Silence. "Morituri?" No answer. Slothrop moves one foot up one rung.

"No, no. I'm still here."

As he edges downward, shaking, rung by rung, feeling prickles back into his arm. How can he go down? How can he go up? He tries to concentrate on the pain. His feet strike steel plate finally. Blindness. He moves to starboard, colliding at every step with shin-high edges, sharp projections . . . *I don't want to . . . how can I . . . reach down behind . . . bare hands . . . what if . . .*

A sudden whine to his right—something mechanical—he jumps, breath sucking very cold between teeth, nerves in back and arms off and on, skittering . . . he reaches a cylindrical barrier . . . might be the generator . . . stoops and begins to— His hand closes on stiff taffeta. He jerks it away, tries to get up, slams his head against something sharp . . . he wants to crawl back toward the ladder, but has lost all sense of direction now . . . he squats, turning in a circle, slowly . . . *let it end letitend. . . .* But his hands, pawing the deck, return to slippery satin.

"No." Yes: hooks and eyes. He breaks a fingernail, trying to lose them but they follow . . . lacing that moves, snake-sure, entangling, binding each finger. . . .

"No. . . ." He rises to a crouch, moves forward into something hanging from the overhead. Icy little thighs in wet silk swing against his face. They smell of the sea. He turns away, only to be lashed across the cheek by long wet hair. No matter which way he tries to move now . . . cold nipples . . . the deep cleft of her buttocks, perfume and shit and the smell of brine . . . and the smell of . . . *of . . .*

When the lights come back on, Slothrop is on his knees, breathing carefully. He knows he will have to open his eyes. The compartment reeks now with suppressed light—with mortal possibilities for light—as the body, in times of great sadness, will feel its real chances for pain: real and terrible and only just under the threshold. . . . The brown paper bundle is two inches from his knee, wedged behind the generator. But it's what's dancing dead-white and scarlet at the edges of his sight . . . and are the ladders back up and out really as empty as they look?

Back on the Frau's boat, Springer is out with a bottle of champagne courtesy of the *Anubis*, untwisting the bright wires and firing the cork in a farewell salvo. Slothrop's hands are shaking and he spills most of his. Antoni and Stefania watch from the bridge as the two vessels pull

apart, Baltic sky visible through the backs of their eyes.
Her white hair in filaments of foam, her cheeks sculptured
fog . . . cloud-man, fog-wife, they dwindle, aloof, silent,
back into the heart of the storm.

The Frau heads south, along the other coast of Rügen,
into the straits by way of the Bug. The storm keeps pace,
as night comes down. "We'll put in at Stralsund," her
scrawled face streaming with lube-green shadow, yellow
light, as the oil-lantern sways in the pilot house.

Slothrop reckons he'll get off there. Head for that Cuxhaven. "Springer, you think you'll have those papers for
me on time?"

"I can't guarantee anything," sez Gerhardt von Göll.

At Stralsund, on the quai, in the lamplight and the rain,
they say good-by. Frau Gnahb kisses Slothrop, and Otto
gives him a pack of Lucky Strikes. The Springer looks up
from his green notebook and nods auf Wiedersehen over
his pince-nez. Slothrop walks away, over the brow, into
the wet Hafenplatz, sea-legs trying to balance rolling he's
left behind, past booms and masts and strung tackle of
derricks, past a crew on the night shift offloading the
creaking lighters into wood wagons, bowed gray horses
kissing the grassless stones . . . good-bys in his pockets
warming his empty hands. . . .

□

Where is the Pope whose staff will bloom for me?
Her mountain vamps me back, with silks and scents,
Her oiled, athletic slaves, her languid hints
Of tortures transubstantiate to sky,
To purity of light—of bonds that sing,
And whips that trail their spectra as they fall.
At weather's mercy now, I find her call
At every turn, at night's foregathering.

I've left no sick Lisaura's fate behind.
I made my last confession as I knelt,
Agnostic, in the radiance of his jewel . . .
Here, underneath my last and splintering wind,
No song, no lust, no memory, no guilt:
No pentacles, no cups, no holy Fool. . . .

Brigadier Pudding died back in the middle of June of a
massive *E. coli* infection, whining, at the end, "Me little

Mary hurts . . ." over and over. It was just before dawn, as he had wished. Katje stayed on at "The White Visitation" for a while, roaming the demobbed corridors, smoky and still at the ends of all the emptied lattices of cages in the laboratory, herself part of the ash-colored web, the thickening dust and fly-pocked windows.

One day she found the cans of film, stacked carelessly by Webley Silvernail in what had been a music room, occupied now only by a disintegrating Wittmaier harpsichord no one played, quills and stops broken shamefully, strings left to sharp, flat, or corrode in the busy knives of weather pushing relentlessly into all the rooms. Pointsman happened that day to be up in London, working out of Twelfth House, lingering at alcoholic luncheons with his various industrialists. Was he forgetting her? Would she be free? Was she, already?

Out of apparently nothing more than the emptiness of "The White Visitation," she finds a projector, threads a reel and focuses the image on a water-stained wall, next to a landscape of some northern coomb, with daft aristocrats larking about. She sees a white-haired girl in Pirate Prentice's Chelsea maisonette, a face so strange that she has recognized the mediaeval rooms before she does herself.

When did they—ah, the day Osbie Feel was processing the Amanita mushrooms. . . . Fascinated, she stares at twenty minutes of herself in pre-Piscean fugue. What on earth did they use it for? The answer to that one's in the can too, and it isn't long before she finds it—Octopus Grigori in his tank, watching the Katje footage. Clip after clip: flickering screen and cutaways to Octopus G., staring—each with its typewritten date, showing the improvement in the creature's conditioned reflex.

Spliced on at the end of all this, inexplicably, is what seems to be a screen test of Osbie Feel, of all people. There is a sound track. Osbie is improvising a scenario for a movie he's written, entitled:

DOPER'S GREED

"We open with Nelson Eddy in the background, singing:

> Doper's greed,
> Oh, doper's greed!

It's the most disgustin' thing I ever seed!
When you're out there feelin' fine,
It'll turn you into swine,
If you ever get a taste of DOPER'S GREED!

"Now into town ride two trail-weary cowboys, Basil
Rathbone and S. Z. ('Cuddles') Sakall. At the entrance to
town, barring their way, stands the Midget who played
the lead in *Freaks*. The one with the German accent. He is
the town sheriff. He is wearing an enormous gold star that
nearly covers his chest. Rathbone and Sakall rein up, with
uneasy smiles on their faces.

"RATHBONE: That can't possibly be *real*, can it?

"SAKALL: Hoo, hoo! Of course that's real, you wretched
eddict, you vent 'n' chewed too much o' that veird *cectus*,
beck down the trail. You should hev smucked that nice
veed I had, I *tuld* you—

"RATHBONE (with his nervous Sickly Smile): Please—I
don't need a Jewish mother. I know what's real, and what
isn't real.

"(The Midget, meanwhile, is posturing in different
tough-hombre attitudes, and waving a brace of gigantic
Colts about.)

"SAKALL: Vhen you been out on the trail—and *you
know vhich* trail too, don't you you sniveling punk—for as
long as I have, you know ah real midget sheriff from ah
hallucinated vun.

"RATHBONE: I hadn't known either class existed. You
must obviously have seen midget sheriffs all over this
Territory, else you would hardly have invented the category. O-or would you? You know, you're just dodgy
enough to try anything.

"SAKALL: You forgot 'You old rascal.'

"RATHBONE: You old rascal.

"They laugh, draw their guns, and exchange a few playful shots. The Midget is rushing back and forth, furious,
emitting high-pitched German-accented Westernisms like
'This town ain't big enough for both of us!'

"SAKALL: Vell, ve're *both seeing* him. That means he's
real.

"RATHBONE: Joint hallucination is not unknown in our
world, podner.

"SAKALL: Who sez it's *joint* hallucination? Hoo, hoo! If it vas any kind of hallucination—I'm not saying it *is*, now—it vould be peyote. Or jimson veed, mebbe. . . .

"This interesting conversation goes on for an hour and a half. There are no cuts. The Midget is active the whole time, reacting to the many subtle and now and then dazzling points presented. Occasionally the horses will shit in the dust. It is not clear if the Midget knows that his reality is being discussed. Another of this film's artful ambiguities. Finally, Rathbone and Sakall agree that the only way to settle the argument is to kill the Midget, who gathers their intention and runs off screaming down the street. Sakall laughs so hard he falls off his horse into the horse trough, and we get a final closeup of Rathbone smiling, in his uncertain way. Fade up song:

> When you're out there feelin' fine,
> It'll turn you into swine,
> If you ever get a taste of Doper's Greed!"

There is a brief epilogue to this, with Osbie trying to point out that of course the element of *Greed* must be worked somehow into the plot line, in order to justify the title, but the film runs out in the middle of an "uh . . . .".

Katje by now is in a bewildered state, but she knows a message when she sees it. Someone, a hidden friend at "The White Visitation"—perhaps Silvernail himself, who's been less than fanatically loyal to Pointsman and his lot—has planted Osbie Feel's screen test deliberately here, where they knew she'd find it. She rewinds and runs the film again. Osbie is looking straight into the camera: straight at her, none of your idle doper's foolery here, he's *acting*. There's no mistake. It *is* a message, in code, which after not too long she busts as follows. Say that Basil Rathbone stands for young Osbie himself. S. Z. Sakall may be Mr. Pointsman, and the Midget sheriff the whole dark grandiose Scheme, wrapped in one small package, diminished, a clear target. Pointsman argues that it's real, but Osbie knows better. Pointsman ends up in the stagnant trough, and the plot/Midget vanishes, frightened, into the dust. A prophecy. A kindness. She returns to her open cell, gathers a few belongings in a bag, and walks out of "The

White Visitation," past the unclipped topiary hedges, growing back into reality, past peacetime's returned madmen sitting gently in the sun. Once, outside Scheveningen, she walked the dunes, past the waterworks, past the blocks of new flats replacing the torn-down slums, concrete still wet inside its shuttering, with the same hope of escape in her heart—moved, a vulnerable shadow, so long ago, toward her rendezvous with Pirate by the windmill called "The Angel." Where is he now? Is he still living in Chelsea? Is he even alive?

Osbie is at home, anyway, chewing spices, smoking reefers, and shooting cocaine. The last of his wartime stash. One grand eruption. He's been up for three days. He beams at Katje, a sunburst in primary colors spiking out from his head, waves the needle he's just taken out of his vein, clamps between his teeth a pipe as big as a saxophone and puts on a deerstalker cap, which does not affect the sunburst a bit.

"Sherlock Holmes. Basil Rathbone. I was right," out of breath, letting her bag fall with a thump.

The aura pulses, bows modestly. He is also steel, he is rawhide and sweat. "Good, good. There's the son of Frankenstein in it, too. I wish we could have been more direct, but—"

"Where's Prentice?"

"Out scouting up some transportation." He leads her to a back room fitted out with telephones, a cork board with notes pinned all over, desks littered with maps, schedules, *An Introduction to Modern Herero,* corporate histories, spools of recording wire. "Not very organized around here yet. But it's coming along, love, it's coming."

Is this what she thinks it is? Wakened from how many times and pushed away because it won't do to hope, not this much? Dialectically, sooner or later, some counterforce would have had to arise . . . she must not have been political enough: never enough to keep faith that it would . . . even with all the power on the other side, that it really would. . . .

Osbie has pulled up folding chairs: hands her now a mimeographed sheaf, rather fat it is, "One or two things, here, you should know. We hate to rush you. But the horse trough is waiting."

And presently, his modulations having flowed through
the rooms in splendid (and for a while distracting) dis-
plays of bougainvillea red and peach, it seems he has
stabilized for the moment into the not-quite-worldly hero of
a lost Victorian children's book, for he answers, after her
hundredth version of the same question, "In the Parliament
of Life, the time comes, simply, for a division. We are
now in the corridors we have chosen, moving toward the
Floor. . . ."

□

Dear Mom, I put a couple of people in Hell today. . . .

—Fragment, thought to be from
the *Gospel of Thomas*
(Oxyrhynchus papyrus number classified)

Who would have thought so many would be here? They
keep appearing, all through this disquieting structure,
gathered in groups, pacing alone in meditation, or studying the paintings, the books, the exhibits. It seems to be
some very extensive museum, a place of many levels, and
new wings that generate like living tissue—though if it all
does grow toward some end shape, those who are here
inside can't see it. Some of the halls are to be entered at
one's peril, and monitors are standing at all the approaches
to make this clear. Movement among these passages is
without friction, skimming and rapid, often headlong, as on
perfect roller skates. Parts of the long galleries are open
to the sea. There are cafés to sit in and watch the sunsets—or sunrises, depending on the hours of shifts and
symposia. Fantastic pastry carts come by, big as pantechni-
cons: one has to *go inside,* search the numberless shelves,
each revealing treats gooier and sweeter than the last . . .
chefs stand by with ice-cream scoops at the ready, awaiting
only a word from the saccharomaniac client to swiftly mold
and rush baked Alaskas of any size and flavor to the ovens
. . . there are boats of baklava stuffed with Bavarian cream,
topped with curls of bittersweet chocolate, broken almonds, cherries as big as ping-pong balls, and popcorn in
melted marshmallows and butter, and thousands of kinds

of fudge, from liquorice to divinity, being slapped out on
the flat stone tables, and taffy-pulling, all by hand, that
sometimes extends around corners, out windows, back in
another corridor—er, excuse me, sir, could you hold this
for a moment? thank *you*—the joker is gone, leaving Pirate
Prentice here, newly arrived and still a bit puzzled with it
all, holding one end of a candy clew whose other end
could be anywhere at all . . . well, he might as well follow
it . . . prowling along looking quite wry, reeling in taffy by
the yard, occasionally stuffing a bit in his mouth—mm,
peanut butter and molasses—well, its labyrinthine path
turns out, like Route One where it passes through the heart
of Providence, to've been set up deliberately to give the
stranger a tour of the city. This taffy trick is a standard
orientation device here it seems, for Pirate now and then
will cross the path of some other novice . . . often they'll
have a time getting their strands of taffy disentangled,
which has also been planned as a good, spontaneous way
for the newcomers to meet. The tour now takes Pirate out
into an open courtyard, where a small crowd has formed
around one of the Erdschweinhöhle delegates in a rip-
roaring argument with some advertising executive over
what else but the Heresy Question, already a pebble in the
shoe of this Convention, and perhaps to be the rock on
which it will founder. Street-entertainers go by: self-
taught tumblers doing amazing handsprings on pavement
that seems dangerously hard and slippery, choirs of kazoos
playing Gilbert & Sullivan medleys, a boy and girl who
dance not along the level street but up and down, usually
at the major flights of steps, whenever there's a queue to
be waited through. . . .

Gathering up his ball of taffy, which by now is growing
quite cumbersome, Pirate passes Beaverboard Row, at it is
known: comprising the offices of all the Committees, with
the name of each stenciled above the doorway—A4 . . . IG
. . . OIL FIRMS . . . LOBOTOMY . . . SELF-DEFENSE . . .
HERESY . . .

"Naturally you're seeing this all through a soldier's eyes,"
she's very young, insouciant, wearing a silly small young-
woman's hat of the period, her face clean and steady
enough for the broad-shouldered, high-waisted, no-neck
profile they're all affecting these days. She moves along

beside him taking long and graceful steps, swings her arms, tosses her head—reaches over to grab some of his taffy, and touching his hand as she does so.

"For you it's all a garden," he suggests.

"Yes. Perhaps you're not such a stick after all."

Ah, they do bother him, these free women in their teens, their spirits are so contagious,

I'll tell you it's just —out, —ray,
    —juss,
Spirit is so —con, —tay, —juss,
Nobody knows their a-ges . . .

Walkin' through bees of hon —ney,
Throwin' away —that —mon, —ney,
Laughin' at things so —fun —ny,
Spirit's comin' through —to, —you!

Where did the swing band come from? She's bouncing up and down, she wants to be jitterbugged, he sees she wants to lose her gravity—

Nev —ver, —mind, whatcha hear from your car,
Take a lookit just —how —keen —they are,
Nev —ver, —mind, —what, your calendar say,
Ev'rybody's nine months old today! Hey,
Pages are turnin' pages,
Nobody's in —their, —ca, —ges,
Spirit's just so —con, —ta, —gious—
Just let the Spirit —move, —for, —you!

The only office not physically touching the others on Beaverboard Row, intentionally set apart, is a little corrugated shack, stovepipe coming out the top, pieces of automobile lying around rusted solid in the yard, piles of wood under rain-colored and failing canvas, a house trailer with its tires and one wheel tilted forlorn in the spanging of the cold rain at its weathered outsides . . . DEVIL'S ADVOCATE's what the shingle sez, yes inside is a Jesuit here to act in that capacity, here to preach, like his colleague Teilhard de Chardin, against return. Here to say that critical mass cannot be ignored. Once the technical means of control have reached a certain size, a certain degree of *being connected* one to another, the chances for freedom are over for good. The word has ceased to have meaning. It's a potent case Father Rapier makes here, not without great moments of eloquence, moments when he himself is clearly moved . . . no need even to be there, at the office, for visitors may tune in from anywhere in the Convention to his passionate demonstrations, which often come in the midst of celebrating what hep humorists here are already calling "Critical Mass" (get it? not too many did in 1945, the Cosmic Bomb was still trembling in its earliness, not yet revealed to the People, so you heard the term only in the very superhepcat-to-hepcat exchanges). "I think that there is a terrible possibility now, in the World. We may not brush it away, we must look at it. It is possible that They will not die. That it is now within the state of Their art to go on forever—though we, of course, will keep dying as we always have. Death has been the source of Their power. It was easy enough for us to see that. If we are here once, only once, then clearly we are here to take what we can while we may. If They have taken much more, and taken not only from Earth but also from us—well, why begrudge Them, when they're just as doomed to die as we are? All in the same boat, all under the same shadow . . . yes . . . yes. But is that really true? Or is it the best, and the most carefully propagated, of all Their lies, known and unknown?

"We have to carry on under the possibility that we die *only* because They want us to: because They need our terror for Their survival. We are their harvests. . . .

"It must change radically the nature of our faith. To ask that we keep faith in Their mortality, faith that They also cry, and have fear, and feel pain, faith They are only pretending Death is Their servant—faith in Death as the master of us all—is to ask for an order of courage that I know is beyond my own humanity, though I cannot speak for others. . . . But rather than make that leap of faith, perhaps we will choose instead to turn, to fight: to demand, from those for whom we die, our own immortality. They may not be dying in bed any more, but maybe They can still die from violence. If not, at least we can learn to withhold from Them our fear of Death. For every kind of vampire, there is a kind of cross. And at least the physical things They have taken, from Earth and from us, can be dismantled, demolished—returned to where it all came from.

"To believe that each of Them *will* personally die is also to believe that Their system will die—that some chance of renewal, some dialectic, is still operating in History. To affirm Their mortality is to affirm Return. I have been pointing out certain obstacles in the way of affirming Return. . . ." It sounds like a disclaimer, and the priest sounds afraid. Pirate and the girl have been listening to him as they linger outside a hall Pirate would enter. It isn't clear if she will come in with him. No, he rather thinks not. It is exactly the sort of room he was afraid it would be. Jagged holes in the walls, evidently where fixtures have been removed, are roughly plastered over. The others, waiting for him it seems, have been passing the time with games in which pain is the overt commodity, such as Charley-Charley, Hits 'n' Cuts, and Rock-Scissors-and-Paper. From next door comes a sound of splashing water and all-male giggling that echoes a bit off of the tiles. "And *now*," a fluent wireless announcer can be heard, "it's *time* for? Drop—The *Soap!*" Applause and shrieks of laughter, which go on for a disagreeably long time.

"Drop the Soap?" Sammy Hilbert-Spaess ambles over to the thin dividing wall, puts his nose around the end of it to have a look.

"Noisy neighbors," remarks German film director Gerhardt von Göll. "Doesn't this sort of thing ever stop?"

"Hullo, Prentice," nods a black man Pirate doesn't recognize, "we seem to be old school tie." What *is* this, who are all these— His name is St.-Just Grossout. "For most of the Duration, the Firm had me trying to infiltrate the Schwarzkommando. I never saw anyone else trying to. It sounds a bit paranoiac, but I think I was the only one. . . ." This forthright breach of security, if that's what it is, takes Pirate a little aback.

"Do you think you could—well, give me a sort of sitrep on all this?"

"Oh, Geoffrey. Oh, my." Here comes Sammy Hilbert-Spaess back from watching the shower-room frolic, shaking his head, pouched and Levantine eyes continuing to stare straight down his nose, "Geoffrey, by the time you get *any* summary, the whole thing will have changed. We could shorten them for you as much as you'd like, but you'd be losing so much resolution it wouldn't be worth it, really it wouldn't. Just look *around* you, Geoffrey. Have a nice look, and see who's here."

Pirate is surprised to find Sir Stephen Dodson-Truck more fit than he ever looked in his life. The man is *actively at peace*, in the way of a good samurai—each time he engages Them fully expecting to die, without apprehension or remorse. It is an amazing change. Pirate begins to feel hope for himself. "When did you turn?" He knows Sir Stephen won't be offended at his asking. "How did it happen?"

"Oh, no, don't let *this* one fool you?" who in the world is this, with this greasy pompadour combed nearly as high again as his face, through which shows the peened, the tenderized soul of a fighter who's not only taken dives, but also thought heavily about them all the way down. It is Jeremiah ("Merciful") Evans, the well-known political informer from Pembroke. "No, our little Stevie's not ready for sainthood *quite* yet, are we my fine chap?" Slapping him, playful, clubbing slaps on the cheek: "Eh? eh? eh?"

"Not if they've thrown me in wiv v' likes o' you," replies the knight, churlishly. But it's hard to say really who's provoking whom, for Merciful Evans now bursts into song, and a terrible singer he is, a discredit to his people, in fact—

> Say a prayer for the common informer,
> He came out of a quim, just like yoooou—
> Yes be kind what you chortle,
> For narks are as mortal
> As any, Kilkenny to Kew . . .
> And the next time you sigh in your comfort,
> Ask yourself how he's doing, today—
> Is it worse being sold,
> For those handfuls of gold,
> Than to sigh all your real-life, away?

"I don't know that I'm going to like it in here," Pirate, an unpleasant suspicion growing on him, looking about nervously.

"The worst part's the shame," Sir Stephen tells him. "Getting through that. Then your next step—well, I talk like an old hand, but that's really only as far as I've come, up through the shame. At the moment I'm involved with the 'Nature of Freedom' drill you know, wondering if *any* action of mine is truly my own, or if I always do only what

They want me to do . . . regardless of what I *believe*, you
see . . . I've been given the old Radio-Control-Implanted-
In-The-Head-At-Birth problem to mull over—as a kind of
koan, I suppose. It's driving me really, clinically insane. I
rather imagine that's the whole point of it. And who
knows what comes *next?* Good God. I don't find out, of
course, till I break through this one. . . . I don't mean to
discourage you so soon—"

"No, no, I've been wondering something else—are all
you lot my Group or something? Have I been *assigned*
here?"

"Yes. Are you beginning to see why?"

"I'm afraid I am." With everything else, these are, after
all, people who kill each other: and Pirate has always been
one of them. "I'd been hoping for—oh, it's foolish, a bit
of mercy . . . but I was at the all-night cinema, around the
corner from Gallaho Mews, the intersection with the extra
street, the one you can't always see because it comes in at
such a strange angle . . . I had a bad stretch of time to get
through, poison, metallic time . . . it smelled as sour as a
burned pot . . . all I wanted was a place to sit a while, and
they don't care who you are really, what you eat or how
long you sleep or who—whom you get together with. . . ."

"Prentice, really it's all right," it's St.-Just Grossout,
whom the others call "Sam Juiced" when they want to
shout him down, during the passages in here when there
is nothing for it but a spot of rowdyism.

"I . . . just can't . . . I mean if it is true, then," a laugh
it hurts him, deep in his windpipe, to make, "then I defected for nothing, didn't I? I mean, if I haven't really
defected at all. . . ."

The word reached him during a government newsreel.
FROM CLOAK-AND-DAGGER TO CROAK-AND-STAG-
GER, the sequin title twinkled to all the convalescent souls
gathered for another long night of cinema without schedule—shot of a little street-crowd staring in a dusty show-
window, someplace so far into the East End that no one
except those who lived there had ever heard of it . . .
bomb-tilted ballroom floor of the ruin slipping uphill behind like a mountain meadow, but dodgy as a trampoline
to walk upon, conch-twisting stucco columns tiled inward,
brass elevator cage drooping from the overhead. Right out

in front was a half-naked, verminous and hairy creature, approximately human, terribly pale, writhing behind the crumbled remains of plate glass, tearing at sores on his face and abdomen, drawing blood, scratching and picking with dirt-black fingernails. "Every day in Smithfield Market, Lucifer Amp makes a spectacle of himself. That's not so surprising. Many a demobilized soldier and sailor has turned to public service as a means of keeping at least body and soul together, if nothing else. What is unusual is that Mr. Amp used to work for the *Special Operations Executive. . . .*"

"It's quite good fun, actually," as the camera moves in for a close-up of this individual, "only took me a week to pick up the knack of it. . . ."

"Do you feel a sense of belonging now, that you hadn't when you came, or—have they still not accepted you out here?"

"They—oh the people, the people have been just wonderful. Just grand. No, no problems *there* at all."

At which point, from the bishopwise seat behind Pirate, came an alcohol smell, and warm breath, and a pat on the shoulder. "You hear? 'Used to work.' That's rich, that is. No one has ever left the Firm alive, no one in history— and no one ever will." It was an upper-class accent, one Pirate might have aspired to once in his rambling youth. By the time he decided to look back, though, his visitor was gone.

"Think of it as a handicap, Prentice, like any other, like missing a limb or having malaria . . . one can still live . . . one learns to get round it, it becomes part of the day—"

"*Being a d—*"

"It's all right. 'Being a—'?"

"Being a double agent? 'Got round'?" He looks at the others, computing. Everyone here seems to be at *least* a double agent.

"Yes . . . you're down here now, down here with us," whispers Sammy. "Get your shame and your sniffles all out of the way, young fellow, because we don't make a practice of indulging *that* for too long."

"It's a *shadow*," cries Pirate, "it's working under a shadow, forever."

"But think of the free-dom?" sez Merciful Evans. "I

can't even trust myself? can I. How much freer than that can a man be? If he's to be sold out by anyone? even by *himself* you see?"

"*I don't want that*—"

"You don't have a choice," Dodson-Truck replies. "The Firm know perfectly well that you've come here. They'll expect a full report from you now. Either voluntary or some other way."

"But I wouldn't . . . I'd never tell them—" The smiles they are putting on for him now are deliberately cruel, to help him through it a bit. "You don't, you really don't trust me?"

"Of course not," Sammy sez. "Would you—really—trust any of us?"

"Oh, no," Pirate whispers. This is one of his own in progress. Nobody else's. But it's still a passage They can touch quite as easily as that of any client. Without expecting to, it seems Pirate has begun to cry. Odd. He has never cried in public like this before. But he understands where he is, now. It will be possible, after all, to die in obscurity, without having helped a soul: without love, despised, never trusted, never vindicated—to stay down among the Preterite, his poor honor lost, impossible to locate or to redeem.

He is crying for persons, places, and things left behind: for Scorpia Mossmoon, living in St. John's Wood among sheet-music, new recipes, a small kennel of Weimaraners whose racial purity she will go to extravagant lengths to preserve, and husband Clive who shows up now and then, Scorpia living only a few minutes away by Underground but lost to Pirate now for good, no chance for either of them to turn again . . . for people he had to betray in the course of business for the Firm, Englishmen and foreigners, for Ion so naïve, for Gongylakis, for the Monkey Girl and the pimps in Rome, for Bruce who got burned . . . for nights up in partisan mountains when he was one with the smell of living trees, in full love with the at last undeniable beauty of the night . . . for a girl back in the Midlands named Virginia, and for their child who never came to pass . . . for his dead mother, and his dying father, for the innocent and the fools who *are* going to trust him, poor faces doomed as dogs who have watched us so amiably

from behind the wire fences at the city pounds ... cries
for the future he can see, because it makes him feel so
desperate and cold. He is to be taken from high moment
to high moment, standing by at meetings of the Elect,
witnessing a test of the new Cosmic Bomb—"Well," a wise
old face, handing him the black-lensed glasses, "there's
your Bomb ..." turning then to see its thick yellow exploding down the beach, across the leagues of Pacific waves ...
touching famous assassins, yes actually touching their
human hands and faces ... finding out one day how long
ago, how early in the game the contract on his own life
was let. No one knows exactly when the hit will come—
every morning, before the markets open, out before the
milkmen, They make Their new update, and decide on
what's going to be sufficient unto the day. Every morning
Pirate's name will be on a list, and one morning it will be
close enough to the top. He tries to face it, though it fills
him with a terror so pure, so cold, he thinks for a minute
he'll pass out. Later, having drawn back a bit, gathering
heart for the next sortie, it seems to him he's done with the
shame, just as Sir Stephen said, yes past the old shame
and scared now, full of worry for nothing but his own ass,
his precious, condemned, personal ass....

"Is there room here for the dead?" He hears the question before he can see her asking it. He isn't sure how she
came into this room. From all the others now flow impressions of male jealousy, a gruff sort of women-on-ships-is-
bad-luck chill and withdrawal. And here's Pirate left alone
with her and her question. He holds out to her the ball of
taffy he's been carrying, boobish as young Porky Pig holding out the anarchist's ticking bomb to him. But there's to
be no sweetness. They are here instead to trade some pain
and a few truths, but all in the distracted style of the
period:

"Come now," what sort of idiotic trouble does she think
she's in now? "you're not dead. I'll wager not even figura-
tively so."

"I meant, would I be allowed to bring my dead in with
me," Katje explains. "They *are* my credentials, after all."

"I rather liked Frans van der Groov. Your ancestor. The
dodo chap."

It's not quite what she meant by her dead. "I mean the

ones who owe their deadness directly to me. Besides, if Frans were ever to walk in here you'd only stand around, all of you, making sure he understood just how guilty he was. The poor man's world held an inexhaustible supply of dodoes—why teach him about genocide?"

"*You* could tell him a thing or two about *that*, couldn't you, girly?" sneers Evans, the tone-deaf Welsh stoolie.

Pirate is moving against Evans, forearms out from his sides saloon-fighter-style, when Sir Stephen intervenes: "There'll be talk like this all the time, Prentice, we're a case-hardened lot. You'd better start learning to make it work *for* you here. No telling how long we're in for, is there? The young woman has grown herself all the protection she needs, it seems to me. She doesn't want you to fight for her."

Well, he's right. She's put her warm hand on Pirate's arm, shaking her head twice with embarrassed small laughs, "I'm glad to see you anyway, Captain Prentice."

"No one else is. Think about it."

She only raises her eyebrows. It *was* a shitty thing to say. Remorse, or some late desire to be pure, rush into his blood like dope.

"But—" astonished to feel himself beginning to *collapse*, like a stack of rifles, around her feet, caught in her gravitation, distances abolished, waveforms unmeasurable, "Katje . . . *if I could never betray you*—"

He has fallen: she has lost her surface. She is staring at him amazed.

"Even if the price for that were . . . betraying others, hurting . . . or killing others—then it wouldn't matter who, or how many, no, not if I could be your safety, Katje, your perfect—"

"But those, those are the sins that might never happen." Here they are bargaining like a couple of pimps. Do they have any idea what they sound like? "*That's* easy enough to pledge, doesn't cost you a thing."

"Then even the sins I did commit," he protests, "yes I'd do *them* over—"

"But you can't do that, either—so you get off just as cheap. Hm?"

"I can repeat patterns," more grim than she really wants him to be.

"Oh, think . . ." her fingers are lightly in his hair, "*think* of the things you've done. Think of all your 'credentials,' and all of mine—"

"But that's the only medium we've *got* now," he cries, "our gift for bad faith. We'll have to build everything with it . . . deal it, as the prosecutors deal you your freedom."

"Philosopher." She is smiling. "You were never like that."

"It must have come from always being in motion. I've never felt *this stillness*. . . ." They are touching now, without urgency, still, neither of them, quite over the surprise. . . . "My little brother" (Pirate understands the connection she has made) "left home at 18. I liked to watch him sleeping at night. His long eyelashes . . . so innocent . . . I watched for hours. . . . He got as far as Antwerp. Before long he was loitering around parish churches with the rest of them. Do you know what I mean? Young, Catholic males. Camp followers. They got to depend on alcohol, many of them, at an early age. They would choose a particular priest, and become his faithful dog—literally wait all night at his doorstep in order to talk to him fresh from his bed, his linen, the intimate smells that had not yet escaped the folds of his garment . . . insane jealousies, daily jostling for position, for the favors of this Father or that. Louis began to attend Rexist meetings. He went out to a soccer field and heard Degrelle tell the crowd that they must let themselves be swept away by the flood, they must act, act, and let the rest take care of itself. Soon my brother was out in the street with his broom, along with the other guilty sarcastic young men with their brooms in their hands . . . and then he had joined Rex, the 'realm of total souls,' and the last I heard he was in Antwerp living with an older man named Philippe. I lost track of him. We were very close at one time. People took us for twins. When the heavy rocket attacks began against Antwerp I knew it could not be an accident. . . ."

Yes well Pirate's Chapel himself. "But I've wondered about the solidarity of your Church . . . you kneel, and she takes care of you . . . when you are acting politically, to have all that common momentum, taking you upward—"

"You never had that either, did you." She's been looking really *at him*—"none of the marvelous excuses. *We did everything ourselves.*"

No, there's no leaving shame after all—not down here—
it has to be swallowed sharp-edged and ugly, and lived
with in pain, every day.

Without considering, he is in her arms. It isn't for comfort. But if he is to keep dragging himself up the ratchet's
teeth one by one he does need to pause in human touch
for a bit. "What did it look like out there, Katje? I saw an
organized convention. Someone else saw it as a garden. . . ." But he knows what she'll say.

"There was nothing out there. It was a barren place.
I'd been most of the day looking for a sign of life. Then
at last I heard you all in here." So they have wandered to
a balcony, a graceful railing, no one can see them from
inside or out: and below them in the streets, streets they
have both lost now, are the People. There passes for
Pirate and Katje a brief segment of a much longer chron-
icle, the anonymous *How I Came to Love the People.* "Her
name was Brenda, her face was the bird under the protecting grin of the car in the rain that morning, she knelt
and performed fellatio on me, and I ejaculated on her
breasts. Her name was Lily, she was 67 last August, she
reads off the labels of beer bottles to herself out loud, we
coupled in the standard English position, and she patted
me on the back and whispered, 'Good friend.' His name
was Frank, his hair curled away from his face, his eyes
were rather sharp but pleasant, he stole from American
Army depots, he bum-fucked me and when he came inside me, so did I. Her name was Frangibella, she was
black, her face was broken out, she wanted money for
dope, her openness was a viper writhing in my heart, I
performed cunnilingus upon her. His name was Allan, his
buttocks were tanned, I said, where did you find the sun,
he answered, the sun is just around the corner, I held him
over the pillow and buggered him and he cried with love
till I, my piston pungently greased, exploded at last. Her
name was Nancy, she was six, we went behind a wall
near a crater full of ruins, she rubbed and rubbed against
me, her milky little thighs reaching in and out of my own,
her eyes were closed, her fair little nostrils moved upward,
backward forever, the slope of debris rushed down, steeply,
just beside us, we teetered at the edge, on and on, ex-
quisitely. Her name was—" well, all these and many more
pass for our young couple here, enough to make them

understand that horny Anonymous's intentions are nothing
less than a megalomaniac master plan of sexual love with
every individual one of the People in the *World*—and
that when every one, somewhat miraculously, is accounted
for at last, *that* will be a rough definition of "loving the
People."

"Take that, you frauds out there in the Branches," Pirate
wants to strike a humorous note, but doesn't. He is holding
Katje now as if, in a moment, music will start, and they
would dance.

"But the People will never love you," she whispers, "or
me. However bad and good are arranged for them, we will
always be bad. Do you know where that puts us?"

He does smile, crookedly as a man being theatrical about
something for the very first time. Knowing it for a movie
there's to be no going back from, in the same terminal class
as reaching for a gun, he turns his face upward, and looks
up through all the faintly superimposed levels above, the
milieux of every sort of criminal soul, every unpleasant
commercial color from aquamarine to beige, desolate as
sunlight on a day when you'd rather have rain, all the
clanging enterprise and bustle of all those levels, extending
further than Pirate or Katje can see for the moment, he
lifts his long, his guilty, his permanently enslaved face to
the illusion of sky, to the reality of pressure and weight
from overhead, the hardness and absolute cruelty of it,
while she presses her own face into the easy lowland between his shoulder and pectoral, a look on her face of
truce, of horror come to a détente with, and as a sunset
proceeds, the kind that changes the faces of buildings to
light gray for a while, to an ashy soft chaff of light bleating over their outward curves, in the strangely forgelike
glow in the west, the anxiety of pedestrians staring in the
tiny storefront window at the dim goldsmith behind his
fire at his work and paying them no attention, afraid because the light looks like it's going to go away forever this
time, and more afraid because the failure of light is not a
private thing, *everyone else in the street has seen it too* . . .
as it grows darker, the orchestra inside this room does, as a
matter of fact, strike up a tune, dry and astringent . . . and
candelabra have been lighted after all . . . there is Veal
Florentine ripening in the ovens tonight, there are drinks
on the House, and drunks in the hammocks,

And all the world's busy, this twi-light!
Who knows what morning-streets, our shoes have known?
Who knows, how many friends, we've left, to cry alone?
We have a moment together,
We'll hum this tune for a day . . .
Ev'ryone's dancing, in twi-light,
Dancing the bad dream a-way. . . .

And they do dance: though Pirate never could before,
very well . . . they feel quite in touch with all the others as
they move, and if they are never to be at full ease, still it's
not parade rest any longer . . . so they dissolve now, into
the race and swarm of this dancing Preterition, and their
faces, the dear, comical faces they have put on for this
ball, fade, as innocence fades, grimly flirtatious, and striving
to be kind. . . .

□

Fog thickens down the throats of the narrow gassen. In the
air is a a smell of salt water. The cobbled streets are wet
with last night's rain. Slothrop wakes up in a burned-out
locksmith's shop, under racks of sooty keys whose locks
have all been lost. He stumbles out, finds a pump in a
courtyard between brick walls and casement windows nobody stares out of, puts his head under the spout and
pumps the pump, soaking his head for as long as he thinks
he needs to. A ginger cat, meowing for breakfast, comes
stalking him, doorway to doorway. "Sorry, Ace." Doesn't
look like breakfast for either of them.

He hitches up Tchitcherine's pants and heads out of
town, leaving the blunt towers, the domes of copper corroded green swimming up in the mist, the high gables and
red tiles, gets a ride with a woman driving an empty farm
wagon. The horse's sandy forelock bobs and blows, and
the fog settles in behind.

This morning it looks like what Vikings must have seen,
sailing this great water-meadow south, clear to Byzantium,
all eastern Europe their open sea: the farmland rolls gray
and green as waves . . . ponds and lakes seem to have no
clear boundaries . . . the sight of other people against this
ocean sky, even the military, comes welcome as sails after
long days of passage. . . .

The Nationalities are on the move. It is a great frontier-less streaming out here. Volksdeutsch from across the Oder, moved out by the Poles and headed for the camp at Rostock, Poles fleeing the Lublin regime, others going back home, the eyes of both parties, when they do meet, hooded behind cheekbones, eyes much older than what's forced them into moving, Estonians, Letts, and Lithuanians trekking north again, all their wintry wool in dark bundles, shoes in tatters, songs too hard to sing, talk pointless, Sudetens and East Prussians shuttling between Berlin and the DP camps in Mecklenburg, Czechs and Slovaks, Croats and Serbs, Tosks and Ghegs, Macedonians, Magyars, Vlachs, Circassians, Spaniols, Bulgars stirred and streaming over the surface of the Imperial cauldron, colliding, shearing alongside for miles, sliding away, numb, indifferent to all momenta but the deepest, the instability too far below their itchy feet to give a shape to, white wrists and ankles incredibly wasted poking from their striped prison-camp pajamas, footsteps light as waterfowl's in this inland dust, caravans of Gypsies, axles or linchpins failing, horses dying, families leaving the vehicles beside the roads for others to come live in a night, a day, over the white hot Autobahns, trains full of their own hanging off the cars that lumber overhead, squeezing aside for army convoys when they come through, White Russians sour with pain on the way west, Kazakh ex-P/Ws marching east, Wehrmacht veterans from other parts of old Germany, foreigners to Prussia as any Gypsies, carrying their old packs, wrapped in the army blankets they kept, pale green farm-worker triangles sewn chest-high on each blouse bobbing, drifting, at a certain hour of the dusk, like candleflames in religious procession—supposed to be heading today for Hannover, supposed to pick potatoes along the way, they've been chasing these nonexistent potato fields now for a month—"Plundered," a one-time bugler limps along with a long splinter of railroad tie for a cane, his instrument, implausibly undented and shiny, swinging from one shoulder, "stripped by the SS, Bruder, ja, every fucking potato field, and what for? Alcohol. Not to drink, no, alcohol for the rockets. Potatoes we could have been eating, alcohol we could have been drinking. It's unbeliev-able." "What, the rockets?" "No! The SS, picking pota-

toes!" looking around for his laugh. But there are none
here to follow the brass and flourish of his less solemn
heart. They were infantrymen, and know how to snooze
between footfalls—at some hour of the morning they will
fall out by the side of the road, a moment's precipitate out
of the road chemurgy of these busy nights, while the invisible boiling goes on by, the long strewn vortices—
pinstripe suits with crosses painted on the back, ragged
navy and army uniforms, white turbans, mismatched socks
or none, Tattersall dresses, thick-knitted shawls with babies
inside, women in army trousers split at the knees, flea-
bitten and barking dogs that run in packs, prams piled
high with light furnishings in scarred veneer, hand-
mortised drawers that will never fit into anything again,
looted chickens alive and dead, horns and violins in weathered black cases, bedspreads, harmoniums, grandfather
clocks, kits full of tools for carpentry, watchmaking,
leatherwork, surgery, paintings of pink daughters in white
frocks, of saints bleeding, of salmon and purple sunsets
over the sea, packs stuffed with beady-eyed boas, dolls
smiling out of violently red lips, Allgeyer soldiers an inch
and a quarter to the man painted cream, gold and blue,
handfuls of hundred-year-old agates soaked in honey that
sweetened greatgrandfather tongues long gone to dust,
then into sulfuric acid to char the sugar in bands, brown
to black, across the stone, deathless piano performances
punched on Vorsetzer rolls, ribboned black lingerie, flowered and grape-crested silverware, faceted lead-glass de-
canters, tulip-shaped Jugendstil cups, strings of amber
beads . . . so the populations move, across the open
meadow, limping, marching, shuffling, carried, hauling
along the detritus of an order, a European and bourgeois
order they don't yet know is destroyed forever.

When Slothrop has cigarettes he's an easy mark, when
somebody has food they share it—sometimes a batch of
vodka if there's an army concentration nearby, the GI cans
can be looted for all kinds of useful produce, potato peels,
melon rinds, pieces of candy bars for sugar, no telling
what's going to go into these DP stills, what you end up
drinking is the throwaway fraction of some occupying
power. Slothrop drifts in and out of dozens of these quiet,
hungry, scuffling migrations, each time getting hard Benze-

drine jitters off of the faces—there aren't any he can really ignore, is the problem, they're all too *strong*, like faces of a racetrack crowd, each one urging *No, me—look at me, be touched, reach for your camera, your weapon, your cock....* He's stripped all the insignia off Tchitcherine's uniform, trying for less visibility, but very few people seem to care much about insignia....

Much of the time he's alone. He'll come on farmhouses, deserted in the night, and will sleep in the hay, or if there's a mattress (not often) in a bed. Wake to sun glittering off some small lake surrounded by green salted with blossoms of thyme or mustard, a salad hillside, sweeping up to pines in the mist. Sapling tomato-frames and purple foxgloves in the yards, huge birds' nests built up under the eaves of the thatched roofs, bird-choruses in the morning, and soon, one day, as the summer turns ponderously in the sky, the clang of cranes, on the move.

At a farmhouse in a river valley far south of Rostock, he comes in to shelter out of the midday rain, falls asleep in a rocking-chair on the porch, and dreams about Tantivy Mucker-Maffiick, his friend from long ago. He has come back, after all and against the odds. It's somewhere out in the country, English country, quilted in darkened green and amazingly bright straw-yellow, of very old standing rocks on high places, of early indenture to death and taxes, of country girls who walk out at night to stand naked on the tor and sing. Members of Tantivy's family and many friends have come, all in a mood of quiet celebrating, because of Tantivy's return. Everybody understands it's only a visit: that he will be "here" only in a conditional way. At some point it will fall apart, from thinking about it too much. There is a space of lawn cleared for dancing, with a village band and many of the women dressed in white. After a spell of confusion about the day's schedule of events, the meeting takes place—it seems to be underground, not exactly a grave or crypt, nothing sinister, crowded with relatives and friends around Tantivy who looks so *real*, so untouched by time, very clear and full of color ... "Why, Slothrop."

"Oh—where've you *been*, gate?"

" 'Here.' "

" ' "Here" ' ? "

"Yes, like that, you've got it—once or twice removed like that, but I walked in the same streets as you, read the same news, was narrowed to the same spectrum of colors. . . ."

"Then didn't you—"

"*I* didn't *do* anything. There was a change."

The colors in here—stone facing, flowers worn by guests, the strange chalices on the tables—carry an under-breath of blood spilled and turned black, of gentle carbonizing in the blank parts of the cities at four o'clock on Sunday afternoon . . . it makes crisper the outlines of Tantivy's suit, rather a gigolo suit of unspeakably foreign cut, certainly nothing he ever would have thought of wearing. . . .

"I guess we don't have much time . . . I know this is shitty, and really selfish but I'm so alone now, and . . . I heard that just after it happens, sometimes, you'll sort of hang around for a while, sort of look after a friend who's 'here.' . . ."

"Sometimes." He is smiling: but his serenity and distance are the stretch of an impotent cry past Slothrop's reach.

"Are you looking after me?"

"No, Slothrop. Not you. . . ."

Slothrop sits in the old weathered rocker looking out at a rolling line of hills and the sun just come down out of the last of the rainclouds, turning the wet fields and the haycocks to gold. Who passed by and saw his sleeping, his face white and troubled nodded on the breast of his muddy uniform?

As he moves on he finds these farms haunted, but amiably. The oakwork creaks in the night, honest and wooden. Unmilked cows low painfully in distant fields, others come in and get drunk on fermented silage, barging around into the fences and piles of hay where Slothrop dreams, uttering moos with drunken umlauts on them. Up on the rooftops the black and white storks, long throats curved to the sky, heads upside down and looking backwards, clatter their beaks in greeting and love. Rabbits come scurrying at night to eat whatever's good in the yards. Trees, now—Slothrop's intensely alert to trees, finally. When he comes in among trees he will spend time touching them, studying them, sitting very quietly near them and understanding that each tree is a creature, carrying on its individual life, aware of what's happening around it, not just some hunk of wood to be cut down. Slothrop's family actually made its money killing trees, amputating them from their roots, chopping them up, grinding them to pulp, bleaching that to paper and getting paid for this with more paper. "That's really insane." He shakes his head. "There's insanity in my family." He looks up. The trees are still. They know he's there. They probably also know what he's thinking. "I'm sorry," he tells them. "I can't do anything about those people, they're all out of my reach. What can I do?" A medium-size pine nearby nods its top and suggests, "Next time you come across a logging operation out here, find one of their tractors that isn't being guarded, and take its oil filter with you. That's what you can do."

Partial List of Wishes on Evening Stars for This Period:

Let me find that chicken coop the old lady told me about.
Let Tantivy really be alive.
Let this fucking zit on my back go away.
Let me go to Hollywood when this is over so that Rita Hayworth can see me and fall in love with me.
Let the peace of this day be here tomorrow when I wake up.
Let that discharge be waiting for me in Cuxhaven.
Let Bianca be all right, a-and—
Let me be able to take a shit soon.
Let that only be a meteor falling.
Let these boots hold out at least to Lübeck.
Let that Ludwig find his lemming and be happy and leave me in peace.

Well, Ludwig. Slothrop finds him one morning by the shore of some blue anonymous lake, a surprisingly fat kid of eight or nine, gazing into the water, crying, shuddering all over in rippling fat-waves. His lemming's name is Ursula, and she has run away from home. Ludwig's been chasing her all the way north from Pritzwalk. He's pretty sure she's heading for the Baltic, but he's afraid she'll mistake one of these inland lakes for the sea, and jump into that instead—

"One lemming, kid?"

"I've had her for two years." he sobs, "she's been fine, she's never tried to— I don't know. Something just came over her."

"Quit fooling. Lemmings never do anything alone. They need a crowd. It gets contagious. You see, Ludwig, they overbreed, it goes in cycles, when there are too many of them they panic and run off looking for food. I learned that in college, so I know what I'm talking about. Harvard. Maybe that Ursula's just out after a boy friend or something."

"She would have let me know."

"I'm sorry."

"Russians aren't sorry about anything."

"I'm not a Russian."

"Is that why you took off all your insignia?"

They look at each other. "Uh, well, you need a hand finding that lemming?"

This Ludwig, now, may not be completely Right in the Head. He is apt to drag Slothrop up out of sleep in the middle of the night, waking half the DP encampment, spooking the dogs and babies, absolutely sure that Ursula is out there, just beyond the circle of the fire, looking in at him, seeing him but not the way she used to. He leads Slothrop into detachments of Soviet tankers, into heaps of ruins high-crested as the sea, that collapse around and, given a chance, on top of you the minute you step in, also into sucking marshes where the reeds pull away in your fingers when you try to grab them, and the smell is of protein disaster. This is either maniac faith, or something a little darker: it does dawn on Slothrop at last that if there's any impulse to suicide around here it ain't Ursula's, it's that *Ludwig's*—why, the lemming may not even exist!

Still . . . hasn't Slothrop, once or twice, seen something? scooting along ahead down gray narrow streets lined with token saplings in one or another of these Prussian garrison-towns, places whose whole industry and meaning was soldiering, their barracks and stone walls deserted now— or-or crouching by the edge of some little lake, watching clouds, white sails of gaff-riggers against the other shore so green, foggy, and far away, getting secret instruction from waters whose movements in lemming-time are oce-

anic, irresistible, and slow enough, solid-looking enough at
least to walk out on safely. . . .

"That's what Jesus meant," whispers the ghost of Slothrop's first American ancestor William, "venturing out on
the Sea of Galilee. He saw it from the lemming point of
view. Without the millions who had plunged and drowned,
there could have been no miracle. The successful loner
was only the other part of it: the last piece to the jigsaw
puzzle, whose shape had already been created by the
Preterite, like the last blank space on the table."

"*Wait* a minute. You people didn't *have* jigsaw puzzles."

"Aw, shit."

William Slothrop was a peculiar bird. He took off from
Boston, heading west in true Imperial style, in 1634 or -5,
sick and tired of the Winthrop machine, convinced he
could preach as well as anybody in the hierarchy even if
he hadn't been officially ordained. The ramparts of the
Berkshires stopped everybody else at the time, but not
William. He just started climbing. He was one of the
very first Europeans in. After they settled in Berkshire, he
and his son John got a pig operation going—used to drive
hogs right back down the great escarpment, back over the
long pike to Boston, drive them just like sheep or cows.
By the time they got to market those hogs were so skinny
it was hardly worth it, but William wasn't really in it so
much for the money as just for the trip itself. He enjoyed
the road, the mobility, the chance encounters of the day—
Indians, trappers, wenches, hill people—and most of all
just being with those pigs. They were good company.
Despite the folklore and the injunctions in his own Bible,
William came to love their nobility and personal freedom,
their gift for finding comfort in the mud on a hot day—
pigs out on the road, in company together, were everything Boston wasn't, and you can imagine what the end
of the journey, the weighing, slaughter and dreary pigless
return back up into the hills must've been like for William.
Of course he took it as a parable—knew that the squealing bloody horror at the end of the pike was in exact
balance to all their happy sounds, their untroubled pink
eyelashes and kind eyes, their smiles, their grace in cross-
country movement. It was a little early for Isaac Newton,
but feelings about action and reaction were in the air.

William must've been waiting for the one pig that wouldn't die, that would validate all the ones who'd had to, all his Gadarene swine who'd rushed into extinction like lemmings, possessed not by demons but by trust for men, which the men kept betraying . . . possessed by innocence they couldn't lose . . . by faith in William as another variety of pig, at home with the Earth, sharing the same gift of life. . . .

He wrote a long tract about it presently, called *On Preterition*. It had to be published in England, and is among the first books to've been not only banned but also ceremonially burned in Boston. Nobody wanted to hear about all the Preterite, the many God passes over when he chooses a few for salvation. William argued holiness for these "second Sheep," without whom there'd be no elect. You can bet the Elect in Boston were pissed off about that. And it got worse. William felt that what Jesus was for the elect, Judas Iscariot was for the Preterite. Everything in the Creation has its equal and opposite counterpart. How can Jesus be an exception? could we feel for him anything but horror in the face of the unnatural, the extracreational? Well, if he is the son of man, and if what we feel is not horror but love, then we have to love Judas too. Right? How William avoided being burned for heresy, nobody knows. He must've had connections. They did finally 86 him out of Massachusetts Bay Colony—he thought about Rhode Island for a while but decided he wasn't that keen on antinomians either. So finally he sailed back to Old England, not in disgrace so much as despondency, and that's where he died, among memories of the blue hills, green maizefields, get-togethers over hemp and tobacco with the Indians, young women in upper rooms with their aprons lifted, pretty faces, hair spilling on the wood floors while underneath in the stables horses kicked and drunks hollered, the starts in the very early mornings when the backs of his herd glowed like pearl, the long, stony and surprising road to Boston, the rain on the Connecticut River, the snuffling good-nights of a hundred pigs among the new stars and long grass still warm from the sun, settling down to sleep. . . .

Could he have been the fork in the road America never took, the singular point she jumped the wrong way from?

Suppose the Slothropite heresy had had the time to consolidate and prosper? Might there have been fewer crimes in the name of Jesus, and more mercy in the name of Judas Iscariot? It seems to Tyrone Slothrop that there might be a route back—maybe that anarchist he met in Zürich was right, maybe for a little while all the fences are down, one road as good as another, the whole space of the Zone cleared, depolarized, and somewhere inside the waste of it a single set of coordinates from which to proceed, without elect, without preterite, without even nationality to fuck it up. . . . Such are he vistas of thought that open up in Slothrop's head as he tags along after Ludwig. Is he drifting, or being led? The only control in the picture right now is the damned lemming. If she exists. The kid shows Slothrop photos he's packing in his wallet: Ursula, eyes bright and shy, peeking out from under a pile of cabbage leaves . . . Ursula in a cage decked with a giant ribbon and swastika'd seal, first prize in a Hitler Youth pet show . . . Ursula and the family cat, watching each other carefully across a tiled stretch of floor . . . Ursula, front paws dangling and eyes drowsy, hanging out the pocket of Ludwig's Nazi cub-scout uniform. Some part of her is always blurred, too quick for the shutter. Even knowing when she was a baby what they'd be in for someday, still Ludwig has always loved her. He may be thinking that love can stop it from happening.

Slothrop will never find out. He loses the fat young lunatic in a village near the sea. Girls in full skirts and flowered kerchiefs are out in the woods gathering mushrooms, and red squirrels flash through the beeches. Streets curve on into town, foreshortening too fast—it's wideangle, smalltown space here. Lamps are clustered up on the poles. Street cobbles are heavy and sand-colored. Drayhorses stand in the sun flourishing their tails.

Down an alleyway near the Michaeliskirche, a little girl comes tottering under an enormous pile of contraband fur coats, only her brown legs visible. Ludwig lets out a scream, pointing at the coat on top. Something small and gray is worked into its collar. Artificial yellow eyes gleam unwholesomely. Ludwig runs hollering Ursula, Ursula, grabbing for the coat. The little girl lets out a flurry of curses.

"You killed my lemming!"

"Let go, idiot." A tug-of-war among the blurry patches of sun and shadow in the alley. "It isn't a lemming, it's a gray fox."

Ludwig stops yelling long enough to look. "She's right," Slothrop points out.

"I'm sorry," Ludwig snivels. "I'm a little upset."

"Well, could you help me carry these as far as the church?"

"Sure."

They each take an armful of furs and follow her through the bumpy gassen of the town, in a side entrance, down several flights to a subbasement of the Michaeliskirche. There in the lamplight, the first face Slothrop sees, inclined over a Sterno fire tending a simmering pot, is that of Major Duane Marvy.

□

YAAAGGGGHHHH— Slothrop hefts his armload of coats, ready to throw them and flee, but the Major's just all smiles. "Hi there, comrade. You're just in time for some o' Duane Marvy's Atomic Chili! Whyntcha pull up a *pew* 'n' sit down? *Yaah*-ha-ha-ha! Little What's-her-name here," chuckling and copping a feel as the girl deposits her delivery with the enormous stash of furs that occupies most of this room, "she's kind of indiscreet sometimes. I hope you don't feel like that we're doing anything illegal, I mean in your zone and everything."

"Not at all, Major," trying for a Russain accent, which comes out like Bela Lugosi. Marvy is out with his pass anyhow, most of which is hand-written, with here and there a seal stamped onto it. Slothrop squints at the Cyrillic handwriting at the bottom and makes out Tchitcherine's signature. "Ah. I have coordinated with Colonel Tchitcherine on one or two occasions."

"Hey'd ya hear what happened up in Peenymunde? Buncha 'suckers just come in hijacked Der Springer right out f'm under the Colonel's nose. Yeah. You know Der Springer? Bad ass, comrade. That 'sucker got so many arns in the far don't leave much for free-enterprisers like me 'n' old Bloody Chiclitz."

Old Bloody Chiclitz, whose mother, Mrs. Chiclitz, named

him Clayton, has been lurking behind a stack of mink capes with a .45 aimed at Slothrop's stomach. "Say he's O.K., buddy," Marvy calls. "Y'all bring us s'more that champagne why don'tcha." Chiclitz is about as fat as Marvy and wears hornrimmed glasses, and the top of his head's as shiny as his face. They stand there with their arms around each other's shoulders, two smiling fat men. "Ivan, you're lookin' at 10,000 calories a day, right here," indicating the two paunches with his thumb, and winking. "Chiclitz here goam be the Royal Baby," and they both collapse with laughter. But it is true. Chiclitz has actually figured out a way to cash in on redeployment. He is about to wangle with Special Services the exclusive contract for staging the equator-crossing festivities for every troop ship that changes hemispheres. And Chiclitz himself will be the Royal Baby on as many as he can, that's been written in. He dreams of the generations of cannon fodder, struggling forward on their knees, one by one, to kiss his stomach while he gobbles turkey legs and ice-cream cones and wipes his fingers off in the polliwogs' hair. Officially he is one of the American industrialists out here with the T-Force, scouting German engineering, secret weaponry in particular. Back home he owns a toy factory in Nutley, New Jersey. Who can ever forget the enormously successful Juicy Jap, the doll that you fill with ketchup then bayonet through any of several access slots, whereupon it flies to pieces, 82 of them, realistically squishy plastic, all over the room? or-or Shufflin' Sam, the game of skill where you have to shoot the Negro before he gets back over the fence with the watermelon, a challenge to the reflexes of boys and girls of all ages? Right now business is taking care of itself, but Chiclitz has his eyes on the future. That's why he's running this fur operation, with the Michaeliskirche serving as a depot for the whole region. "Retrenchment. Got to get capitalized, enough to see me through," splashing champagne into gold communion chalices, "till we see which way it's gonna go. Myself, I think there's a great future in these V-weapons. They're gonna be really big."

The old church smells of spilled wine, American sweat, and recently burned cordite, but these are raw newer intrusions that haven't done away with the prevailing

Catholic odor—incense, wax, centuries of mild bleating from the lips of the flock. Children come in and go out, bringing furs and taking them away, chatting with Ludwig and presently inviting him along to check out the freight cars down at the marshaling yards.

There are about 30 kids on Chiclitz's payroll. "My dream," he admits, "is to bring all these kids back to America, out to Hollywood. I think there's a future for them in pictures. You heard of Cecil B. De Mille, the producer? My brother-in-law's pretty close to him. I think I can teach them to sing or something, a children's chorus, negotiate a package deal with De Mille. He can use them for the real big numbers, religious scenes, orgy scenes—"

"Ha!" cries Marvy, dribbling champagne, eyeballs bulging. "You're *dreaming* all right, old buddy! You sell those kids to Cecil B. De Mille it's f'damn sure they ain't goam be *singin'*. He'll use them little 'suckers for *galley slaves! Yaah*-ha-ha—yeah they'll be chained to th' oars, just haulin' ass, rowin' old Henry Wilcoxon away into th' sunset to fight them Greeks or Persians or somebody."

"Galley slaves?" Chiclitz roars. "Never, by God. For De Mille, young fur-henchmen can't be rowing!"

Out at the edge of town are the remains of an A4 battery, left where it stood as the troops fled south, trying to escape British and Russian pincers. Marvy and Chiclitz are going to have a look, and Slothrop is welcome to come along. But first there is the matter of Duane Marvy's Atomic Chili, which turns out to be a test of manhood. The champagne bottle is there within easy reach, but drinking from it will be taken as a sign of weakness. Once Slothrop would have been suckered in, but now he doesn't even have to think it over. While the two Americans, blinded, noses on fire and leaking incredible quantities of snot, undergo what the authoritative *A Cheapskate's Guide to the Zone* aptly describes as "a Götterdämmerung of the mucous membranes," Slothrop sits guzzling champagne like soda pop, nodding, smiling, and mumbling *da, da* now and then for authenticity's sake.

They ride out to the site in a green, grinning Ford staff car. Marvy soon as he slides behind the wheel turns into a fanged dipsomaniac—*eeeeerrrrr* leaving rubber enough to condom a division, zero to 70 before the echo's died, trying to run down bicyclists right 'n' left, stampeding the livestock, whilst Bloody Chiclitz, whooping happily, a champagne bottle in each fist, urges him on—Marvy bellowing "San Antonya Rose," his fav'rite song, Chiclitz screaming out the window admonitions like "Fuck not with the Kid, lest instead of fucker thou become fuckee," which takes a while and draws only a few bewildered Fascist salutes from old ladies and little children at the roadside.

The site is a charred patch becoming green with new weeds, inside a copse of beech and some alder. Camouflaged metal stands silent across a ghostly crowd of late dandelions, gray heads nodding together waiting for the luminous wind that will break them toward the sea, over to Denmark, out to all points of the Zone. Everything's been stripped. The vehicles are back to the hollow design envelopes of their earliest specs, though there's still a faint odor of petrol and grease. Forget-me-nots are growing violent blue violent yellow among the snarl of cables and hoses. Swallows have built a nest inside the control car, and a spider has begun filling in the web of the Meillerwagen boom with her own. "Shit," sez Major Marvy. "Fuckin' Rooskies done stole *ever*thing, no offense, comrade." They go kicking through green and purple weeds, rusted food tins, old sawdust and chips of wood. Surveying stakes, each with a tatter of white nailed on top, still chain away toward the guide-beam transmitter 12 kilometers away. Eastward. So it must've been the Russians they were trying to stop. . . .

Red, white, and blue winks from the dusty deck of the control car. Slothrop drops to one knee. The Schwarzkommando mandala: KEZVH. He looks up to see Marvy giving him a sly fat smile.

"Why shore. I shoulda known. You don't have no *insignia* on. Sheeeee . . . you're-you're like th' Soviet CIC! Ain'tcha." Slothrop stares back. "Hey. Hey, who're you tryin' to git? Huh?" The smile vanishes. "Sa-a-a-y, I shore hope it ain't Colonel Tchitcherine, now. He's a *good* Rooskie, you know."

"I assure you," holding up the mandala, cross to vampire, "my only interest is in dealing with the problem of *these* black devils."

Back comes the smile, along with a fat hand on Slothrop's arm. "You all set to go round 'n' round with thim, whin y'r comrades git here?"

"Round, and round? I am not sure that I—"

"*You* know. Come on. Why all thim *boogies*'t's camped outside o' town! Hey, Ivan, god-*damn* 'at's goam be fun. I spint all day today cleanin' my Colt's," caressing the sidearm in its holster. "Goam make me a coonskin cap outa one o' thim 'suckers, 'n' I don't have to tell you what part's goam be danglin' down there in back, do Uh? Hah?" Which tickles Bloody Chiclitz so much he like to chokes laughing.

"Actually," Slothrop making it up as he goes along, "my mission is coordinating intelligence," whatever that means, "in operations such as this. I am down here, in fact, to reconnoiter the enemy position."

"Enemy's right," Chiclitz nods. "They got guns and everything. Only thing a coon ought to have in his hands is a *broom!*"

Marvy is frowning. "You, you ain't expecting us to go out there *with* you, now. We can tell you how to git there, comrade, but you're *crazy* to go out there alone. Why don'tcha wait'll tonight? Scheduled to stort about midnight, ain't it? You can wait till then."

"It is essential that I gather certain information in advance," pokerface, pokerface, good, good . . . "I do not have to tell you how important this is . . ." a pregnant Lugosi pause, "to *all* of us."

Well, that gets him directions out to the Schwarzkommando and a lift back into town, where the businessmen pick up a couple of those Eager Fräuleins and go roistering off into the sunset. Slothrop stands in their exhaust, muttering.

Next time it won't be any custard pie, you asshole. . . .

Takes him an hour to get out to the camp on foot across a wide meadow whose color is deepening now as if green dye flowed and seeped into its nap . . . he is aware of each single grassblade's shadow reaching into the shadows east of it . . . pure milk-colored light sweeps up in a bell-curve above the sun nearly down, transparent white flesh, fading up through many blues, powdery to dark steel at the zenith . . . why is he out here, doing this? Is this Ursula the lemming's idea too, getting mixed up in

other people's private feuds when he was supposed to
be . . . whatever it was . . . uh. . . .

Yeah! yeah what happened to Imipolex G, all that Jamf
a-and that S-Gerät, s'posed to be a hardboiled private eye
here, gonna go out all alone and beat the odds, avenge
my friend that They killed, get my ID back and find that
piece of mystery hardware but now aw it's JUST LIKE—

LOOK-IN' FAWR A NEEDLE IN A HAAAAY-STACK!
Sssss—searchinfrasomethin' fulla moon-beams,
(Something) got ta have yooooou!

Feet whispering through weeds and meadow grass, hum-
ming along exactly the breathless, chin-up way Fred
Astaire did, reflecting on his chances of ever finding Ginger
Rogers again this side of their graceful mortality. . . .

Then, snapping back—no no, wait, you're supposed to
be planning soberly now, weighing your options, deter-
mining your goals at this critical turning point in your . . .

Ya—*ta-ta*, LOOKIN' F'R A NEEDLE IN A—

Nonono come *on*, Jackson, quit fooling, you got to *concentrate*. . . . The S-Gerät now—O.K. if I can find that
S-Gerät 'n' how Jamf was hooked in, if I can find that out,
yeah yeah Imipolex now . . .

   —searchin' for a (hmm) cellar full o' saffron . . .

Aw . . .

At about which point, as if someone's simple longing has
made it appear, comes a single needle-stroke through the
sky: the first star.

Let me be able to warn them in time.

They jump Slothrop among the trees, lean, bearded,
black—they bring him in to the fires where someone is
playing a thumb-harp whose soundbox is carved from a
piece of German pine, whose reeds are cut from springs of
a wrecked Volkswagen. Women in white cotton skirts
printed with dark blue flowers, white blouses, braided
aprons, and black kerchiefs are busy with pots and tin-
ware. Some are wearing ostrich-egg-shell necklaces knife-
hatched in red and blue. A great cut of beef drips from a
wooden spit over a fire.

Enzian isn't there, but Andreas Orukambe is, nervous as wire, wearing a navy pullover and army fatigue trousers. He remembers Slothrop. "Was ist los?"

Slothrop tells him. "Supposed to be here at midnight. Don't know how many there are, but maybe you'd better clear out."

"Maybe." Andreas is smiling. "Have you eaten?"

The argument, go or stay, proceeds over supper. It is not the tactical decision-making Slothrop was taught in officer school. There seem to be other considerations, something the Zone Hereros know about and Slothrop doesn't.

"We have to go where we go," Andreas explains to him later. "Where Mukuru wants us to go."

"Oh. Oh, I thought you were out here looking for something, like everybody else. The ooooo, what about that?"

"That is Mukuru's. He hides it where he wants us to seek."

"Look, I have a line on that S-Gerät." He gives them Greta Erdmann's story—the Heath, the gasoline works, the name Blicero—

That rings a bell. A gong, in fact. Everybody looks at everybody else. "Now," Andreas very careful, "that was the name of the German who commanded the battery that used the S-Gerät?"

"I don't know if they *used* it. Blicero took the woman to a factory where it was either put together, or a part of it was made, from some plastic called Imipolex G."

"And she didn't say where."

"Only 'the Heath.' See if you can find her husband, Miklos Thanatz. He may have seen the actual firing, if there was one. Something out of the ordinary went on about then, but I never got to find out what."

"Thank you."

"It's O.K. Maybe you can tell me something now." He brings out the mandala he found. "What's it mean?"

Andreas sets it on the ground, turns it till the K points northwest. "Klar," touching each letter, "Entlüftung, these are the female letters. North letters. In our villages the women lived in huts on the northern half of the circle, the men on the south. The village itself was a mandala. Klar is fertilization and birth, Entlüftung is the breath, the soul. Zündung and Vorstufe are the male signs, the activities, fire and preparation or building. And in the center, here, Hauptstufe. It is the pen where we kept the sacred cattle. The souls of the ancestors. All the same here. Birth, soul, fire, building. Male and female, together.

"The four fins of the Rocket made a cross, another mandala. Number one pointed the way it would fly. Two for pitch, three for yaw and roll, four for pitch. Each opposite pair of vanes worked together, and moved in opposite senses. Opposites together. You can see how we might feel it speak to us, even if we don't set one up on its fins and worship it. But it was waiting for us when we came north to Germany so long ago . . . even confused and uprooted as we were then, we *knew* that our destiny was tied up with its own. That we had been passed over by von Trotha's army so that we would find the Aggregat."

Slothrop gives him the mandala. He hopes it will work like the mantra that Enzian told him once, mba-kayere (I am passed over), mba-kayere . . . a spell against Marvy tonight, against Tchitcherine. A mezuzah. Safe passage through a bad night. . . .

□

The Schwarzkommando have got to Achtfaden, but Tchitcherine has been to Närrisch. It cost him Der Springer and three enlisted men in sick bay with deep bites. One severed artery. Närrisch trying to go out Audie Murphy style. A knight for a bishop—Närrisch under narcohypnosis raved about the Holy Circle and the Rocketfin Cross. But the blacks don't know what else Närrisch knew:

(a) there was a radio link *from* the ground *to* the S-Gerät but not the other way round.

(b) there was an interference problem between a servo-actuator and a special oxygen line running aft to the device from the main tank.

(c) Weissmann not only coordinated the S-Gerät project at Nordhausen, but also commanded the battery that fired Rocket 00000.

Total espionage. Bit by bit this mosaic is growing. Tchitcherine, bureauless, carries it around in his brain. Every chip and scrap belongs. More precious than Ravenna, something goes erecting against this starch-colored sky. . . .

Radio link + oxygen = afterburner of some kind. Ordinarily it would. But Närrisch also spoke of an asymmetry, a load inside near vane 3 that complicated roll and yaw control almost impossibly.

Now wouldn't an afterburner there also give an asymmetrical burning pattern, and heat fluxes greater than the structure could take? Damn, why hasn't he picked up *any* of the propulsion people? Do the Americans have them all?

Major Marvy, bowie knife in his teeth and two Thompsons propped on either hip, as dumbfounded in the clearing as the rest of the attack party, is in no mood to talk. Instead he is sulking, and drinking vodka out of Džabajev's bottomless canteen. But *had* any propulsion engineers assigned to the S-Gerät showed up at Garmisch, Marvy would have let him know. That's the arrangement. Western intelligence, Russian trigger-fingers.

Oh, he *smells* Enzian . . . even now the black may be looking in out of the night. Tchitcherine lights a cigarette, greenbluelavender flare settling to yellow . . . he holds the flame longer than necessary, thinking *let him. He won't. I wouldn't. Well . . . maybe I would. . . .*

But it's come a quantum-jump closer tonight. They are going to meet. It will be over the S-Gerät, real or fantasized, working or wasted—they will meet face to face. *Then . . .*

Meantime, who's the mysterious Soviet intelligence agent that Marvy talked to? Paranoia for you here, Tchitcherine. Maybe Moscow's been tipped to your vendetta. If they are gathering evidence for a court-martial, it won't be any Central Asia this time. It'll be Last Secretary to the embassy in Atlantis. You can negotiate narcotics arrests for all the drowned Russian sailors, expedite your own father's visas to far Lemuria, to the sun-resorts of Sargasso where the bones come up to lie and bleach and mock the passing ships. And just before he rides out on the noon current, brochures tucked between ribs, traveler's checks wadded in a skull-socket, tell him of his black son—tell him about the day with Enzian in the creeping edge of autumn, cold as the mortal cold of an orange kept under shaved ice on

the terrace of the hotel in Barcelona, si me quieres
escribir you already know where I'll be staying . . . cold at
the tip of your peeling-thumb, terminally-approaching
cold. . . .

"Listen," Marvy by now a little drunk and peevish,
"when we gonna *git* those 'suckers?"

"It's coming, you can be sure."

"Butchyew don't know the kinda pressure *I'm* gettin'
f'm Paris! F'm headquarters! It's fantastic! There's people
in high places wanna wipe thim 'suckers out, *now*. All's
they got to do's mash on a button 'n' I never git to see no
Mexican whores again's long's I *live*. Now you can *see*
what these coons're try'n t'do, *somebody* got to stop them
'fore they *do*, *shit*—"

"This intelligence man you saw—both our governments
easily could have the same policy—"

"You ain't got General Electric breathin' over your
shoulder, fella. Dillon, Reed . . . Standard Awl . . . shit. . . ."

"But that's just what you folks *need*," Bloody Chiclitz
interjects. "Get some business people in there to run it
right, instead of having the government run everything.
Your left hand doesn't know what your *right* hand's *doing!*
You know *that?*"

What's this? A political debate now? Not enough humiliation missing the Schwarzkommando, no, you didn't think
you were going to get off *that* easy. . . .

"A-and what about Herbert Hoover?" Chiclitz is screaming. "He came over and *fed* you people, when you were
starving! They *love* Hoover over here—"

"Yes—" Tchitcherine breaks in: "what *is* General Electric
doing out here, by the way?"

A friendly wink from Major Marvy. "Mister Swope was
ace buddies with old FDR, you see. Electric Charlie's in
there now, but Swope, he was one-thim Brain Trusters.
Jews, most of'm. But Swope's O.K. Now GE has connections with Siemens over here, they worked on the V-2
guidance, remember—"

"Swope's a Jew," sez Chiclitz.

"Naahh—Bloody, yew don' know whatcher talkin'
about—"

"I'm *telling* you—" They fall into a drawling juicers'
argument over the ethnic background of the ex-chairman

of GE, full of poison and sluggish hate. Tchitcherine listens
with only one ear. An episode of vertigo is creeping on
him. Didn't Närrisch, under the drug, mention a Siemens
representative at the S-Gerät meetings in Nordhausen?
yes. And an IG man, too. Didn't Carl Schmitz of the IG
sit on Siemens's board of directors?

No use asking Marvy. He is too drunk by now to stay
on any subject. "Ya know I was purty ignorant whin Uh
come out here. Sheeit, I used t'think I. G. Farben was
somebody's name, you know, a *fella*—hello, this I. G.
Farben? No, this is his wife, *Mizzus* Farben! *Yaaah*-ha-ha-
ha!"

Bloody Chiclitz is off on his Eleanor Roosevelt routine.
"The othuh day, my son Idiot—uh, Elliot—and I, were
baking cookies. Cookies to send to the boys overseas. When
the boys received the cookies we sent them, they would
bake cookies, and send some back to us. That way, *everybody* gets his cookies!"

Oh, Wimpe. Old V-Mann, were you right? Is your IG
to be *the very model of nations?*

So it comes to Tchitcherine here in the clearing with
these two fools on either side of him, among the debris
of some numberless battery's last stand, cables paralyzed
where winch-operators levered them to stillness, beer bottles lying exactly where they were thrown by the last men
on the last night, everything testifying so purely to the
shape of defeat, of operational death.

"Say, there." It appears to be a very large white Finger,
addressing him. Its Fingernail is beautifully manicured: as
it rotates for him, it slowly reveals a Fingerprint that
might well be an aerial view of the City Dactylic, that
city of the future where every soul is known, and there
is noplace to hide. Right now, joints moving with soft,
hydraulic sounds, the Finger is calling Tchitcherine's attention to—

☞ *A Rocket-cartel.* A structure cutting across every
agency human and paper that ever touched it. Even to
Russia . . . Russia bought from Krupp, didn't she, from
Siemens, the IG. . . .

Are there arrangements Stalin won't admit . . . doesn't
even *know about?* Oh, a State begins to take form in the
stateless German night, a State that spans oceans and sur-

face politics, sovereign as the International or the Church of Rome, and the Rocket is its soul. IG Raketen. Circus-bright, poster reds and yellows, rings beyond counting, all going at once. The stately Finger twirls among them all. Tchitcherine is certain. Not so much on outward evidence he has found moving through the Zone as out of a personal doom he carries with him—always to be held at the edges of revelations. It happened first with the Kirghiz Light, and his only illumination then was that fear would always keep him from going all the way in. He will never get further than the edge of this meta-cartel which has made itself known tonight, this Rocket-state whose borders he cannot cross. . . .

He will miss the Light, but not the Finger. Sadly, most sadly, everyone else seems to be in on it. Every scavenger out here is in IG Raketen's employ. All except for himself, and Enzian. His brother, Enzian. No wonder They're after the Schwarzkommando . . . and. . . .

And when They find out I'm not what They think . . . and why is Marvy looking at me like this now, his eyes bulging . . . oh, don't panic, don't feed his insanity, he's just this side of . . . of . . .

□

To Cuxhaven, the summer in deceleration, floating on to Cuxhaven. The meadows hum. Rain clatters in crescent swoops through the reeds. Sheep, and rarely a few dark northern deer, will come down to browse for seaweed at the shore which is never quite sea nor quite sand, but held in misty ambivalence by the sun. . . . So Slothrop is borne, afloat on the water-leas. Like signals set out for lost travelers, shapes keep repeating for him. Zonal shapes he will allow to enter but won't interpret, not any more. Just as well, probably. The most persistent of these, which seem to show up at the least real times of the day, are the stair-step gables that front so many of these ancient north-German buildings, rising, backlit, a strangely *wet* gray as if risen out of the sea, over these straight and very low horizons. They hold shape, they endure, like monuments to Analysis. Three hundred years ago mathematicians were learning to break the cannonball's rise and fall into stairsteps of range and height, Δx and Δy, allowing them to grow smaller and smaller, approaching zero as armies of eternally shrinking midgets galloped upstairs and down again, the patter of their diminishing feet growing finer, smoothing out into continuous sound. This analytic legacy has been handed down intact—it brought the technicians at Peenemünde to peer at the Askania films of Rocket flights, frame by frame, Δx by Δy, flightless themselves . . . film and calculus, both pornographies of flight. Reminders of impotence and abstraction, the stone Treppengiebel shapes, whole and shattered, appear now over the green plains, and last a while, and go away: in their shadows children with hair like hay are playing Himmel and Hölle, jumping village pavements from heaven to hell to heaven by increments, sometimes letting Slothrop have a turn, sometimes vanishing back into their dark gassen where elder houses, many-windowed and sorrowing, bow perpetually to the neighbor across the way, nearly touching overhead, only a thin lead of milk sky between.

At nightfall the children roam the streets carrying round paper lanterns, singing *Laterne, Laterne, Sonne, Mond und Sterne* . . . spheres in country evenings, pale as souls, singing good-by to another summer. In a coastal town, near Wismar, as he's falling to sleep in a little park, they surround Slothrop and tell him the story of Plechazunga, the Pig-Hero who, sometime back in the 10th century, routed a Viking invasion, appearing suddenly out of a thunderbolt and chasing a score of screaming Norsemen back into the sea. Every summer since then, a Thursday has been set aside to celebrate the town's deliverance—Thursday being named after Donar or Thor, the thunder-god, who sent down the giant pig. The old gods, even by the 10th century, still had some pull with the people. Donar hadn't quite been tamed into Saint Peter or Roland, though the ceremony did come to be held at the town's Roland-statue near the Peterskirche.

This year, though, it's in jeopardy. Schraub the shoe-maker, who has taken the role of Plechazunga for the past 30 years, got drafted last winter into the Volksgrenadier and never came back. Now the white lanterns come crowding around Tyrone Slothrop, bobbing in the dark. Tiny fingers prod his stomach.

"You're the fattest man in the world."

"He's fatter than anyone in the village."

"Would you? Would you?"

"I'm not *that* fat—"

"Told you somebody would come."

"And taller, too."

"—waitaminute, would I what?"

"Be Plechazunga tomorrow."

"Please."

Being a soft touch these days, Slothrop gives in. They roust him up out of his grass bed and down to the city hall. In the basement are costumes and props for the Schweinheldfest—shields, spears, horned helmets, shaggy animal skins, wooden Thor's hammers and ten-foot lightning bolts covered with gold leaf. The pig costume is a little startling—pink, blue, yellow, bright sour colors, a German Expressionist pig, plush outside, padded with straw inside. It seems to fit perfectly. Hmm.

The crowd next morning is sparse and placid: old people and children, and a few silent veterans. The Viking invaders are all kids, helmets sloping down over their eyes, capes dragging the ground, shields as big as they are and weaponry twice as high. Giant Plechazunga images with white stock and red and blue cornflowers woven onto the wire-mesh frames, line the square. Slothrop waits hidden behind the Roland, a particularly humorless, goggle-eyed, curly-headed, pinch-waisted specimen. With Slothrop is an arsenal of fireworks and his assistant Fritz, who's about 8, and a Wilhelm Busch original. Slothrop is a little nervous, unaccustomed as he is to pigherofestivals. But Fritz is an old hand, and has thoughtfully brought along a glazed jug of some liquid brain damage flavored with dill and coriander and distilled, unless *Haferschleim* means something else, from oatmeal.

"Haferschleim, Fritz?" He takes another belt, sorry he asked.

"Haferschleim, ja."

"Well, Haferschleim is better than none, ho, ho. . . ." Whatever it is, it seems to work swiftly on the nerve centers. By the time all the Vikings, to a solemn brass chorale from the local band, have puffed and struggled up to the statue, formed ranks, and demanded the town's surrender,

Slothrop finds his brain working with less than the usual keenness. At which point Fritz strikes his match, and all hell breaks loose, rockets, Roman candles, pinwheels and—PLECCCHHAZUNNGGA! an enormous charge of black powder blasts him out in the open, singeing his ass, taking the curl right out of his tail. "Oh, yes, that's right, uh . . ." Wobbling, grinning hugely, Slothrop hollers his line: "I am the wrath of Donar—and this day you shall be my anvil!" Away they all go in a good roaring chase through the streets, in a shower of white blossoms, little kids squealing, down to the water, where everybody starts splashing and ducking everybody else. Townspeople break out beer, wine, bread, Quark, sausages. Gold-brown Kartoffelpuffer are lifted dripping hot from oil smoking in black skillets over little peat fires. Girls commence stroking Slothrop's snout and velvet flanks. The town is saved for another year.

A peaceful, drunken day, full of music, the smell of salt water, marsh, flowers, frying onions, spilled beer and fresh fish, overhead little frost-colored clouds blowing along the blue sky. The breeze is cool enough to keep Slothrop from sweating inside this pig suit. All along the shoreline, blue-gray woods breathe and shimmer. White sails move out in the sea.

Slothrop returns from the brown back room of a pipe-smoke-and-cabbage café, and an hour's game of hammer-and-forge with—every boy's dream—TWO healthy young ladies in summer dresses and woodsoled shoes to find the crowd begun to coagulate into clumps of three and four. Oh, shit. Not now, come on. . . . Tight aching across his asshole, head and stomach inflated with oat mash and summer beer, Slothrop sits on a pile of nets and tries, fat chance, to will himself alert.

These little vortices appearing in a crowd out here usually mean black market. Weeds of paranoia begin to bloom, army-green among the garden and midday tranquillities. Last of his line, and how far-fallen—no other Slothrop ever felt such fear in the presence of Commerce. Newspapers already lie spread out on the cobbles for buyers to dump out cans of coffee on, make sure it's all Bohnenkaffee, and not just a thin layer on top of ersatz. Gold watches and rings appear abruptly sunlit out of dusty

pockets. Cigarettes go flashing hand to hand among the
limp and filthy and soundless Reichsmarks. Kids play
underfoot while the grownups deal, in Polish, Russian,
north-Baltic, Plattdeutsch. Some of the DP style here, a
little impersonal, just passing through, dealing on route,
in motion, almost as an afterthought . . . where'd they all
come from, these gray hustlers, what shadows in the
Gemütlichkeit of the day were harboring them?

Materializing from their own weird office silence, the
coppers show up now, two black 'n' white charabancs full
of bluegreen uniforms, white armbands, little bucket hats
with starburst insignia, truncheons already unsheathed,
black dildos in nervous hands, wobbling, ready for action.
The eddies in the crowd break up fast, jewelry ringing to
the pavement, cigarettes scattered and squashed under the
feet of stampeding civilians, among the instant litter of
watches, war medals, silk-stuffs, rolls of bills, pinkskinned
potatoes all their eyes staring in alarm, elbow-length kid
gloves twisted up fingers clutching at sky, smashed light
bulbs, Parisian slippers, gold picture-frames around still-
lifes of cobbles, rings, brooches, nobody gonna claim any
of it, everybody scared now.

No wonder. The cops go at busting these proceedings
the way they must've handled anti-Nazi street actions
before the War, moving in, mmm ja, with these flexible
clubs, eyes tuned to the finest possibilities of threat, smelling of leather, of the wool-armpit rankness of their own
fear, jumping little kids three-on-one, shaking down girls,
old people, making them take off and shake out even
boots and underwear, jabbing and battering in with tireless truncheonwork among the crying kids and screaming
women. Beneath the efficiency and glee is nostalgia for the
old days. The War must've been lean times for crowd control, murder and mopery was the best you could do, one
suspect at a time. But now, with the White Market to be
protected, here again are whole streets full of bodies eager
for that erste Abreibung, and you can bet the heat are
happy with it.

Presently they have Russian reinforcements, three truckloads of young Asiatics in fatigues who don't seem to know
where they are exactly, just shipped in from someplace
very cold and far to the east. Out of their slatsided rigs

like soccer players coming on field, they form a line and
start to clear the street by compressing the crowd toward
the water. Slothrop is right in the middle of all this,
shoved stumbling backward, pig mask cutting off half his
vision, trying to shield whom he can—a few kids, an old
lady who was busy earlier moving cotton yardage. The
first billy-clubs catch him in the straw padding over his
stomach, and don't feel like much. Civilians are going
down right and left, but Plechazunga's holding his own.
Has the morning been only a dress rehearsal? Is Slothrop
expected to repel *real* foreign invaders now? A tiny girl is
clutching to his leg, crying the Schweinheld's name in a
confident voice. A grizzled old cop, years of home-front
high living and bribes in his face, comes swinging a club at
Slothrop's head. The Swine-hero dodges and kicks with
his free leg. As the cop doubles over, half a dozen yelling
civilians jump on, relieving him of hat and truncheon.
Tears, caught by the sun, leak out of his withered eyes.
Then gunfire has started somewhere, panicking everybody,
carrying Slothrop half off his feet, the kid around his leg
torn loose and lost in the rush forever.

Out of the street onto the quai. The police have quit
hitting people and begun picking up loot off of the street,
but now the Russians are moving in, and enough of them
are looking straight at Slothrop. Providentially, one of the
girls from the café shows up about now, takes his hand
and tugs him along.

"There's a warrant out for you."

"A what? They're doing pretty good without any paperwork."

"The Russians found your uniform. They think you're a
deserter."

"They're right."

She takes Slothrop home with her, in his pig suit. He
never hears her name. She is about seventeen, fair, a young
face, easy to hurt. They lie behind a sperm-yellowed bedsheet tacked to the ceiling, very close on a narrow bed
with lacquered posts. Her mother is carving turnips in the
kitchen. Their two hearts pound, his for his danger, hers
for Slothrop. She tells how her parents lived, her father
a printer, married during his journeymanship, his wonder-
years now stretched out to ten, no word where he's been

since '42, when they had a note from Neukölln, where he
had dossed down the night with a friend. Always a friend,
God knows how many back rooms, roundhouses, print
shops he slept single nights in, shivering wrapped in back
numbers of *Die Welt am Montag*, sure of at least shelter,
like everybody in the Buchdrucherverband, often a meal,
almost certainly some kind of police trouble if the stay
lasted too long—it was a good union. They kept the German Wobbly traditions, they didn't go along with Hitler
though all the other unions were falling into line. It
touches Slothrop's own Puritan hopes for the Word, the
Word made printer's ink, dwelling along with antibodies
and iron-bound breath in a good man's blood, though the
World for him be always the World on Monday, with its
cold cutting edge, slicing away every poor illusion of
comfort the bourgeois takes for real ... did he run off
leaflets against his country's insanity? was he busted,
beaten, killed? She has a snapshot of him on holiday,
someplace Bavarian, waterfalled, white-peaked, a tanned
and ageless face, Tyrolean hat, galluses, feet planted perpetually set to break into a run: the image stopped, preserved here, the only way they could keep him, running
room to room down all his cold Red suburbs, freemason's
night to night ... their aproned and kitchen way of going
evening or empty afternoon in to study the Δx's and Δy's
of his drifter's spirit, on the run—study how he was changing inside the knife-fall of the shutter, what he might've
been hearing in the water, flowing like himself, forever,
in lost silence, behind him, already behind him.

Even now, lying bedside a stranger in a pig disguise,
her father is the flying element of Slothrop, of whoever
else has lain here before, flightless, and heard the same
promise: "I'd go anywhere with you." He sees them walking a railroad trestle, pines on long slanted mountains all
around, autumn sunlight and cold, purple rainclouds, midafternoon, her face against some tall concrete structure,
the light of the concrete coming down oblique both sides
of her cheekbones, blending into her skin, blending with
its own light. Her motionless figure above him in a black
greatcoat, blonde hair against the sky, himself at the top
of a metal ladder in a trainyard, gazing up at her, all
their shining steel roads below crisscrossing and peeling

off to all parts of the Zone. Both of them on the run. That's what she wants. But Slothrop only wants to lie still with her heartbeat awhile . . . isn't that every paranoid's wish? to perfect methods of immobility? But they're coming, house to house, looking for their deserter, and it's Slothrop who has to go, she who has to stay. In the streets loudspeakers, buzzing metal throats, are proclaiming an early curfew tonight. Through some window of the town, lying in some bed, already browsing at the edges of the fields of sleep, is a kid for whom the metal voice with its foreign accent is a sign of nightly security, to be part of the wild fields, the rain on the sea, dogs, smells of cooking from strange windows, dirt roads . . . part of this unrecoverable summer. . . .

"There's no moon," she whispers, her eyes flinching but not looking away.

"What's the best way out of town?"

She knows a hundred. His heart, his fingertips hurt with shame. "I'll show you."

"You don't have to."

"I want to."

Her mother gives Slothrop a couple of hard rolls to stash inside his pig suit. She'd find him something else to wear, but all her husband's clothes have been traded for food at the Tauschzentrale. His last picture of her is framed in the light of her kitchen, through the window, a fading golden woman, head in a nod over a stove with a single pot simmering, flowered wallpaper deep-orange and red behind her averted face.

The daughter leads him over low stone walls, along drainage ditches and into culverts, southwesterly to the outskirts of the town. Far behind them the clock in the Peterskirche strikes nine, the sightless Roland below continuing to gaze across the square. White flowers fall one by one from the images of Plechazunga. Stacks of a power station rise, ghostly, smokeless, painted on the sky. A windmill creaks out in the countryside.

The city gate is high and skinny, with stairsteps to nowhere on top. The road away goes curving through the ogival opening, out into the night meadows.

"I want to go with you." But she makes no move to step through the arch with him.

"Maybe I'll be back." It's no drifter's lie, both of them
are sure that someone will be, next year at about this
time, maybe next year's Schweinheld, someone close
enough . . . and if the name, the dossier are not exactly
the same, well, who believes in those? She's a printer's
kid, she knows the medium, she even learned from him
how to handle a Winkelhaken pretty good, how to set up
a line and take it down, "You're a May bug," she whispers,
and kisses him good-by, and stands watching him go, a
sniffling still girl in pinafore and army boots by the isolated gate. "Good night. . . ."

Docile girl, good night. What does he have for her
but a last snapshot of a trudging pig in motley, merging
with the stars and woodpiles, something to put beside
that childhood still of her father? He impersonates flight
though his heart isn't in it and yet he's lost all knowledge
of staying. . . . Good night, it's curfew, get back inside,
back in your room . . . good night. . . .

He keeps to open country, sleeping when he's too tired
to walk, straw and velvet insulating him from the cold.
One morning he wakes in a hollow between a stand of
beech and a stream. It is sunrise and bitter cold, and
there seems to be a warm tongue licking roughly at his
face. He is looking here into the snout of another pig,
very fat and pink pig. She grunts and smiles amiably,
blinking long eyelashes.

"Wait. How about this?" He puts on the pig mask. She
stares for a minute, then moves up to Slothrop and kisses
him, snout-to-snout. Both of them are dripping with dew.
He follows her on down to the stream, takes off the mask
again and throws water at his face while she drinks beside
him, slurping, placid. The water is clear, running lively,
cold. Round rocks knock together under the stream. A
resonant sound, a music. It would be worth something to
sit day and night, in and out, listening to these sounds of
water and cobbles unfold. . . .

Slothrop is hungry. "Come on. We got to find breakfast." Beside a small pond near a farmhouse, the pig
discovers a wood stake driven into the ground. She begins
snuffling around it. Slothrop kicks aside loose earth and
finds a brick cairn, stuffed with potatoes ensiled last year.
"Fine for you," as she falls to eagerly, "but I can't eat that

stuff." Sky is shining in the calm surface of the water.
Nobody seems to be around. Slothrop wanders off to check
the farmhouse. Tall white daisies grow all over the yard.
Thatch-hooded windows upstairs are dark, no smoke comes
from the chimneys. But the chicken-house in back is occupied. He eases a big fat white hen up off of her nest,
reaches gingerly for the eggs—PKAWW she flies into a
dither, tries to peck Slothrop's arm off, friends come shooting in from outside raising a godawful commotion, at
which point the hen has worked her wings through the
wood slats so she can't get back in and is too fat below
the wingpits to get the rest of the way out. So, there she
hangs, flapping and screaming, while Slothrop grabs three
eggs then tries to push her wings back inside for her. It
is a frustrating job, especially trying to keep the eggs
balanced. The rooster is in the doorway hollering Achtung,
Achtung, discipline in his harem is shot to hell, noisy
white tumbleweed hens are barrelassing all over the inside
of the coop, and blood is flowing from Slothrop in half a
dozen places.

Then he hears a dog barking—time to give up on this
hen—comes outside sees a lady in her Wehrmacht auxiliary
outfit 30 meters away leveling a shotgun and the dog
charging in growling, teeth bared, eyes on Slothrop's
throat. Slothrop goes scrambling around the henhouse just
as the gun kicks off a good-morning blast. About then the
pig shows up and chases off the dog. Away they go, eggs
cradled in pig mask, lady yelling, hens raising hell, pig
galloping along beside. There's a final shotgun blast, but
by then they're out of range.

About a mile farther on they pause, for Slothrop's
breakfast. "Good show," thumping the pig affectionately.
She crouches, catching her breath, gazing at him while
he eats raw eggs and smokes half a cigarette. Then they
set off again.

Soon they have begun to angle toward the sea. The pig
seems to know where she's going. Far away on another
road, a great cloud of dust hangs, crawling southward,
maybe a Russian horse convoy. Fledgling storks are trying out their wings over the haystacks and fields. Tops of
solitary trees are blurred green, as if smudged accidentally
by a sleeve. Brown windmills turn at the horizon, across
miles of straw-sprinkled red earth.

A pig is a jolly companion,
Boar, sow, barrow, or gilt—
A pig is a pal, who'll boost your morale,
Though mountains may topple and tilt.
When they've blackballed, bamboozled, and burned you,
When they've turned on you, Tory and Whig,
Though you may be thrown over by Tabby or Rover,
You'll never go wrong with a pig, a pig,
You'll never go wrong with a pig!

By nightfall they have entered a wooded stretch. Fog
drifts in the hollows. A lost unmilked cow complains somewhere in the darkness. The pig and Slothrop settled down
to sleep among pines thick with shreds of tinfoil, a cloud
of British window dumped to fox the German radars in
some long-ago raid, a whole forest of Christmas trees,
tinsel rippling in the wind, catching the starlight, silent,
ice-cold crownfire acres wild over their heads all night.
Slothrop keeps waking to find the pig snuggled in a bed
of pine needles, watching over him. It's not for danger,
or out of restlessness. Maybe she's decided Slothrop needs
looking after. In the tinfoil light she's very sleek and con-
vex, her bristles look smooth as down. Lustful thoughts
come filtering into Slothrop's mind, little peculiarity here
you know, hehheh, nothing he can't handle. . . . They fall
asleep under the decorated trees, the pig a wandering
eastern magus, Slothrop in his costume a gaudy present
waiting for morning and a child to claim him.

Next day, about noon, they enter a slow-withering city,
alone on the Baltic coast, and perishing from an absence
of children. The sign over the city gate, in burned bulbs
and empty sockets, reads ZWÖLFKINDER. The great wheel,
dominating the skyline for miles out of town, leans a little
askew, grim old governess, sun catching long streaks of
rust, sky pale through the iron lattice that droops its long
twisted shadow across the sand and into the plum sea.
Wind cat-howls in and out the doorless halls and houses.

"Frieda." A voice calling from the blue shadow behind
a wall. Grunting, smiling, the pig stands her ground—
look who I brought home. Soon a thin freckled man,
blond, nearly bald, steps out into the sun. Glancing at
Slothrop, nervous, he reaches to scratch Frieda between
the ears. "I am Pökler. Thank you for bringing her back."

"No, no—she brought me."

"Yes."

Pökler is living in the basement of the town hall. He has some coffee heating on a driftwood fire in the stove.

"Do you play chess?"

Frieda kibitzes. Slothrop, who tends to play more by superstition than strategy, is obsessed with protecting his knights, Springer and Springer—willing to lose anything else, thinking no more than a move or two ahead if that, he alternates long lethargic backing and filling with bursts of idiot razzle-dazzle that have Pökler frowning, but not with worry. About the time Slothrop loses his queen, "Sa-a-a-y, waitaminute, did you say *Pökler?*"

Zip the man is out with a Luger as big as a house—really fast guy—with the muzzle pointing right at Slothrop's head. For a moment Slothrop, in his pig suit, thinks that Pökler thinks that he, Slothrop, has been fooling around with Frieda the Pig, and that there is about to be a shotgun, or Luger, wedding here—in fact the phrase *unto thee I pledge my trough* has just arrived in his brain when he realizes that what Pökler's *actually* saying is, "You'd better leave. Only two more moves and I'd've had you anyway."

"Lemme at least tell you my story," blithering fast as he can the Zürich information with Pökler's name on it, the Russian-American-Herero search for the S-Gerät, wondering meantime, in parallel sort of, if that Oberst Enzian wasn't right about going native in the Zone—beginning to get ideas, fixed and slightly, ah, erotic notions about Destiny are you Slothrop? eh? tracing back the route Frieda the pig brought him along, trying to remember forks where they might have turned another way. . . .

"The Schwarzgerät." Pökler shakes his head. "I don't know what it was. I was never that interested. Is that really all you're after?"

Slothrop thinks that over. Their coffee cups take sunlight from the window and bounce it back up to the ceiling, bobbing ellipses of blue light. "Don't know. Except for this kind of personal tie-in with Imipolex G. . . ."

"It's an aromatic polyimide," Pökler putting the gun back in his shirt.

"Tell me about it," sez Slothrop.

Well, but not before he has told something of his Ilse and her summer returns, enough for Slothrop to be taken again by the nape and pushed against Bianca's dead flesh. ... Ilse, fathered on Greta Erdmann's silver and passive image, Bianca, conceived during the filming of the very scene that was in his thoughts as Pökler pumped in the fatal charge of sperm—how could they not be the same child?

She's still with you, though harder to see these days, nearly invisible as a glass of gray lemonade in a twilit room ... still she is there, cool and acid and sweet, waiting to be swallowed down to touch your deepest cells, to work among your saddest dreams.

□

Pökler does manage to tell a little about Laszlo Jamf, but keeps getting sidetracked off into talking about the movies, German movies Slothrop has never heard of, much less seen ... yes here's some kind of fanatical movie hound all right— "On D-Day," he confesses, "when I heard General Eisenhower on the radio announcing the invasion of Normandy, I thought it was really Clark Gable, have you ever noticed? the voices are *identical.* ..."

In the last third of his life, there came over Laszlo Jamf—so it seemed to those who from out in the wood lecture halls watched his eyelids slowly granulate, spots and wrinkles grow across his image, disintegrating it toward old age—a hostility, a strangely *personal* hatred, for the covalent bond. A conviction that, for synthetics to have a future at all, the bond must be improved on— some students even read "transcended." That something so mutable, so *soft,* as a sharing of electrons by atoms of carbon should lie at the core of life, *his* life, struck Jamf as a cosmic humiliation. *Sharing?* How much stronger, how everlasting was the *ionic* bond—where electrons are not shared, but *captured. Seized!* and held! polarized plus and minus, these atoms, no ambiguities ... how he came to love that clarity: how stable it was, such mineral stubbornness!

"Whatever lip-service we may pay to Reason," he told

Pökler's class back at the T.H., "to moderation and compromise, nevertheless there remains the lion. A lion in
each one of you. He is either tamed—by too much mathematics, by details of design, by corporate procedures—or
he stays wild, an eternal predator.

"The lion does not know subtleties and half-solutions.
He does not accept *sharing* as a basis for anything! He
takes, he holds! He is not a Bolshevik or a Jew. You will
never hear relativity from the lion. He wants the absolute.
Life and death. Win and lose. Not truces or arrangements,
but the joy of the leap, the roar, the blood."

If this be National Socialist chemistry, blame that some-
thing-in-the-air, the Zeitgeist. Sure, blame it. Prof.-Dr.
Jamf was not immune. Neither was his student Pökler.
But through Inflation and Depression, Pökler's idea of "the
lion" came to have a human face attached to it, a movie
face natürlich, that of the actor Rudolf Klein-Rogge,
whom Pökler idolized, and wanted to be like.

Klein-Rogge was carrying nubile actresses off to rooftops
when King Kong was still on the tit with no motor skills
to speak of. Well, one nubile actress anyway, Brigitte
Helm in *Metropolis*. Great movie. Exactly the world Pökler and evidently quite a few others were dreaming about
those days, a Corporate City-state where technology was
the source of power, the engineer worked closely with the
administrator, the masses labored unseen far underground,
and ultimate power lay with a single leader at the top,
fatherly and benevolent and just, who wore magnificent-
looking suits and whose name Pökler couldn't remember,
being too taken with Klein-Rogge playing the mad inventor that Pökler and his codisciples under Jamf longed
to be—indispensable to those who ran the Metropolis, yet,
at the end, the untamable lion who could let it all crash,
girl, State, masses, himself, asserting his reality against
them all in one last roaring plunge from rooftop to
street. . . .

A curious potency. Whatever it was the real visionaries
were picking up out of the hard tessitura of those days
and city streets, whatever Käthe Kollwitz saw that brought
her lean Death down to hump Its women from behind,
and they to love it so, seemed now and then to have
touched Pökler too, in his deeper excursions into the Mare

Nocturnum. He found delight not unlike a razor sweeping
his skin and nerves, scalp to soles, in ritual submissions to
the Master of this night space and of himself, the male
embodiment of a technologique that embraced power not
for its social uses but for just those chances of surrender,
personal and dark surrender, to the Void, to delicious and
screaming collapse. . . . To Attila the Hun, as a matter of
fact, come west out of the steppes to smash the precious
structure of magic and incest that held together the kingdom of the Burgundians. Pökler was tired that night, all
day out scavenging for coal. He kept falling asleep, waking to images that for a half a minute he could make no
sense of at all—a close-up of a face? a forest? the scales
of the Dragon? a battle-scene? Often enough, it would
resolve into Rudolf Klein-Rogge, ancient Oriental thana-
tomaniac Attila, head shaved except for a topknot, bead-
strung, raving with grandiloquent gestures and those
enormous bleak eyes. . . . Pökler would nod back into sleep
with bursts of destroying beauty there for his dreams to
work on, speaking barbaric gutturals for the silent mouths,
smoothing the Burgundians into something of the meekness, the grayness of certain crowds in the beerhalls back
at the T.H. . . . and wake again—it went on for hours—
into some further progression of carnage, of fire and
smashing. . . .

On the way home, by tram and foot, his wife bitched
at Pökler for dozing off, ridiculed his engineer's devotion
to cause-and-effect. How could he tell her that the dramatic connections were really all there, in his dreams?
How could he tell her anything?

Klein-Rogge is remembered most of all for his role as
Dr. Mabuse. You were meant to think of Hugo Stinnes,
the tireless operator behind the scenes of apparent Inflation, apparent history: gambler, financial wizard, arch-
gangster . . . a fussy bürgerlich mouth, jowls, graceless
moves, a first impression of comic technocracy . . . and yet,
when the rages came over him, breaking through from
beneath the rationalized look, with his glacial eyes become
windows into the bare savanna, then the real Mabuse sur-
faced, vital and proud against the gray forces surrounding him, edging him toward the doom he must've known
he couldn't escape, the silent inferno of guns, grenades,

streets full of troops attacking his headquarters, and his own madness at the end of the secret tunnel. . . . And who brought him down but matinee idol Bernhardt Goetzke as State Prosecutor von Wenk, Goetzke who played tender, wistful bureaucratic Death in *Der Müde Tod*, here too running true to form, too tame, too gentle for the jaded Countess he coveted—but Klein-Rogge *jumped in*, with all claws out, drove her effeminate husband to suicide, seized her, threw her on his bed, the languid bitch—*took her!* while gentle Goetzke sat in his office, among his papers and sybarites—Mabuse trying to hypnotize him, drug him, bomb him to death in his own office—nothing worked, each time the great Weimar inertia, files, hierarchies, routines, kept saving him. Mabuse was the savage throwback, the charismatic flash no Sunday-afternoon Agfa plate could ever bear, the print through the rippling solution each time flaring up to the same annihilating white (Piscean depths Pökler has cruised dream and waking, beneath him images of everyday Inflation dreariness, queues, stockbrokers, boiled potatoes in a dish, searching with only gills and gut—some nervous drive toward myth he doesn't even know if he believes in—for the white light, ruins of Atlantis, intimations of a truer kingdom). . . .

Metropolitan inventor Rothwang, King Attila, Mabuse der Spieler, Prof.-Dr. Laszlo Jamf, all their yearnings aimed the same way, toward a form of death that could be demonstrated to hold joy and defiance, nothing of bourgeois Goetzkian death, of self-deluding, mature acceptance, relatives in the parlor, knowing faces the children can always read. . . .

"You have the two choices," Jamf cried, his last lecture of the year: outside were the flowery strokings of wind, girls in pale-colored dresses, oceans of beer, male choruses intensely, movingly lifted as they sang *Semper sit in flores/ Semper sit in flo-ho-res* . . . "stay behind with carbon and hydrogen, take your lunch-bucket in to the works every morning with the faceless droves who can't wait to get in out of the sunlight or move *beyond*. Silicon, boron, phosphorus—these can replace carbon, and can bond to nitrogen instead of hydrogen—" a few snickers here, not unanticipated by the playful old pedagogue, be he always in flower: his involvement in getting Weimar to subsidize

the IG's Stickstoff Syndikat was well known—"move beyond life, toward the inorganic. Here is no frailty, no
mortality—here is Strength, and the Timeless." Then his
well-known finale, as he wiped away the scrawled C—H
on his chalkboard and wrote, in enormous letters, Si—N.

The wave of the future. But Jamf himself, oddly, did
not move on. He never synthesized those new inorganic
rings or chains he had prophesied so dramatically. Had
he only remained behind in the trough, academic generations swelling away just ahead, or had he known something Pökler and the others didn't? Were his exhortations
in the lecture hall some kind of eccentric joke? He stayed
with C—H, and took his lunchbucket to America. Pökler
lost touch with him after the Technische Hochschule—
so did all his old pupils. He was now under the sinister
influence of Lyle Bland, and if he was still seeking to
escape the mortality of the covalent bond, Jamf was doing
it in the least obvious way there was.

□

If that Lyle Bland hadn't joined the Masons, he'd still
probably be up to those nefarious tricks of his. Just as
there are, in the World, machineries committed to injustice
as an enterprise, so too there seem to be provisions active
for balancing things out once in a while. Not as an enterprise, exactly, but at least in the dance of things. The
Masons, in the dance of things, turned out to be one of
these where Bland was concerned.

Imagine the fellow's plight—got so much money he
don't know what to do with it all. Don't go screaming,
"Give it to me!" either. He's given it to you, though in
roundabout ways you might need a good system of search
to unsnarl. Oh, has he given it to you. By way of the
Bland Institute and the Bland Foundation, the man has
had his meathooks well into the American day-to-day since
1919. Who do you think sat on top of the patent for that
100-miles-per-gallon carburetor, eh? sure you've heard that
story—maybe even snickered along with paid anthropolo-
gists who called it Automotive Age Myth or some shit—
well, turns out the item was real, all right, and it was Lyle

Bland who sprang for those academic hookers doing the snickering and the credentialed lying. Or how about the great Killer Weed advertising campaign of the thirties, who do you think worked hand-in-glove (or, as grosser individuals have put it, penis-in-mouth) with the FBI on that one? And remember all those guy-goes-to-the-doctor-can't-get-a-hardon jokes? Planted by Bland, yup—half a dozen basic variations, after having done depth studies for the National Research Council that indicated an unacceptable 36% of the male work force wasn't paying enough attention to their cocks—not enough genital obsession there, and it was undermining the efficiency of the organs doing the *real work.*

Psychological studies became, in fact, a Bland specialty. His probe into the subconscious of early-Depression America is considered a classic, and widely credited with improving the plausibility of Roosevelt's "election" in 1932. Though many of his colleagues found a posture of hatred for FDR useful, Bland was too delighted to go through the motions. For him, FDR was exactly the man: Harvard, beholden to all kinds of money old and new, commodity and retail, Harriman and Weinberg: an American synthesis which had never occurred before, and which opened the way to certain grand possibilities—all grouped under the term "control," which seemed to be a private code-word—more in line with the aspirations of Bland and others. A year later Bland joined the Business Advisory Council set up under Swope of General Electric, whose ideas on matters of "control" ran close to those of Walter Rathenau, of German GE. Whatever Swope's outfit did, it did in secret. Nobody got to see its files. Bland wasn't about to tell anybody, either.

He had gotten to be buddies, after World War I, with the office of the Alien Property Custodian. Their job was to dispose of confiscated German interests in the U.S. A lot of Midwestern money was involved here, which is what got Bland embroiled in the Great Pinball Difficulty, and so into the Masons. Seems that through something called the Chemical Foundation—cover names in those days had no style to them—the APC had sold Bland a few of Laszlo Jamf's early patents, along with the U.S. agency of Glitherius Paint & Dye, a Berlin firm. A few years later,

in 1925, in the course of being put together, the IG
bought back 50% of American Glitherius from Bland, who
was using his end of it as a patent-holding company.
Bland got cash, securities, and controlling interest in a
Glitherius subsidiary in Berlin being run by a Jew named
Pflaumbaum, yesyes, the same Pflaumbaum Frank Pökler
worked for till the placed burned down and Pökler went
back out on the streets. (Indeed, there were those who
could see Bland's hand in that disaster, though the Jew
got blamed, fucked under by the courts, attached till he
was bankrupt, and, in the fullness of time, sent east along
with many others of his race. We would also have to
show some interlock between Bland and the Ufa movie-
distribution people who sent Pökler out with his advertising bills to Reinickendorf that night, to his fateful meeting
with Kurt Mondaugen and the Verein für Raumschiffahrt
—not to mention *separate* connections for Achtfaden, Närrisch, and the other S-Gerät people—before we'd have a
paranoid structure worthy of the name. Alas, the state of
the art by 1945 was nowhere near adequate to that kind
of data retrieval. Even if it had been, Bland, or his suc-
cessors and assigns, could've bought programmers by the
truckload to come in and make sure all the information
fed out was harmless. Those like Slothrop, with the greatest interest in discovering the truth, were thrown back on
dreams, psychic flashes, omens, cryptographies, drug-
epistemologies, all dancing on a ground of terror, contra-
diction, absurdity.)

After the Pflaumbaum fire, lines of power among Bland
and his German colleagues had to be renegotiated. It
dragged on for a few years. Bland found himself in Depression in St. Louis, talking with one Alfonso Tracy,
Princeton '06, St. Louis Country Club, moving into petro-
chemicals in a big way, Mrs. Tracy dithering in and out
of the house with yardage and armloads of flowers, preparing for the annual Veiled Prophet Ball, Tracy himself
preoccupied with the appearance of some individuals down
from Chicago in flashy pinstripe suits, two-tone shoes and
snap-brim fedoras, all talking in accents staccato as a
Thompson.

"Oh, do I need a good electronics man," Tracy moaned.
"What do you do with these wops? The whole shipment

was bad, and now they won't take it back. If I step out of line, they'll murder me. They'll rape Mabel, they'll go back to Princeton some dark night a-and *castrate* my *kid!* You know what I think it is, Lyle? A *plot!*"

Vendettas, jeweled gauntlets, subtle poisons come infiltrating this well-mannered parlor with the picture of Herbert Hoover on the piano, the pinks in the Nieman-Marcus bowl, the Bauhaus-style furniture like alabaster slabs of a model city (you expect little HO trains to come whirring out from under the davenport, cans 'n' reefers on and on across the carpet's ash-colored lowland . . .). Alfonso Tracy's long face, creased either side of the nose and on around the mustache line, dragged down by worries, thirty years without a genuine smile ("Even Laurel & Hardy doesn't work for me any more!"), morose with fright in his easy chair. How could Lyle Bland not be touched?

"Got just the fella," sez he, touching Tracy's arm, compassionate. Always good to have an engineer on tap. This one did some just top-notch electronic-surveillance designs once for the then-fledgling FBI, on a contract the Bland Institute landed a few years ago and subbed part of out to Siemens over there in Germany. "Have him in tomorrow on the Silver Streak. No problem, Al."

"Come on out and have a look," sighs Tracy. They hop in the Packard and drive out to the green little river town of Mouthorgan, Missouri, which is a railroad station, a tanning factory, a few frame houses, and dominating the area a gigantic Masonic hall, not a window on the whole massive monolith.

After a lot of rigmarole at the door, Bland is finally allowed in and led through velvet poolrooms, elaborate polished-wood gambling setups, chrome bars, soft bedrooms, on to a large warehouse section in back, which is crammed ten high with more pinball machines than Bland's ever seen in one place in his *life,* Oh Boys, Grand Slams, World Serieses, Lucky Lindies as far as the eye can reach.

"And every one is fucked up," sez melancholy Tracy. "Look at this." It's a Folies-Bergères: four-color lovelies doing the cancan all over it, zeros happening to coincide with eyes, nipples, and cunts, one of your racy-type games here, a little hostile toward the ladies but *all in fun!* "You got a nickel?" *Chungg,* boing there goes the ball just missing a high-scoring hole, hmm looks like a permanent warp there *ahnnnggghk* knocks a flasher worth 1000 but only 50 lights up on the board—"You *see?*" Tracy screams as the ball heads like a rock for the bottom, outside chance to get with a flipper *zong* flipper flips the other fucking *way,* and the board lights up TILT.

"Tilt?" Bland scratching his head. "You didn't even—"

"They're *all* like that," Tracy watering with frustration. "You try it."

The second ball isn't even out of the chute before Bland gets another TILT, again without having applied any English. Third ball gets *stuck* somehow against a solenoid and (helphelp, it's hollering, wounded high little voice, oh I'm being *electrocuted...*) dingdingding, gongs and racing numbers up on the board, 400,000, 675,000 *bong* a million! greatest Folies-Bergères score in history and climbing, the poor spherical soul against the solenoid thrashing, clonic, horrible (yes they're sentient all right, beings from the planetoid Katspiel, of veryvery elliptical orbit—which is to say it passed by Earth only once, a long time ago, nearly back at the grainy crepuscular Edge, and nobody knows where Katspiel is now or when, or if, it'll be back. It's that familiar division between return and one-shot visitation. If Katspiel had enough energy to leave the sun's field forever, then it has left these kind round beings in eternal exile, with no chance of ever being gathered back home, doomed to masquerade as ball bearings, as steelies in a thousand marble games—to know the great thumbs of Keokuk and Puyallup, Oyster Bay, Inglewood—Danny D'Allesandro and Elmer Ferguson, Peewee Brennan and Flash Womack... where are they now? where do you think? they all got drafted, some are dead on Iwo, some gangrenous in the snow in the forest of Arden, and their thumbs, first rifle inspection in Basic, GI'd, driven deep back into childhood as little finger sweat-cams off M-1 operating handle, thumb pushing down follower still deep in breech, bolt sshhOCK! whacks thumb oh shit yes it hurts and good-by to another unbeatable and legendary thumb, gone for good back to the summer dust, bags of chuckling glass, bigfooted basset hounds, smell of

steel playground slides heating in the sun), well here
come these cancan girls now, Folies-Bergères maenads,
moving in for the kill, big lipstick smiles around blazing
choppers, some Offenbach galop come jigging in now out
of the loudspeakers that are implicit in this machine's
design, long gartered legs kicking out over the agony of
this sad spherical permanent AWOL, all his companions
in the chute vibrating their concern and love, feeling his
pain but helpless, inert without the spring, the hustler's
hand, the drunk's masculinity problems, the vacuum hours
of a gray cap and an empty lunchbox, needing these to
run their own patterns down the towering coils, the deep
holes with their promises of rest that only kick you
wobbling out again, always at the mercy of gravity, finding now and then the infinitesimally shallow grooves of
other runs, great runs (twelve heroic minutes in Virginia
Beach, Fourth of July, 1927, a drunken sailor whose ship
went down at Leyte Gulf ... flipped up off the board,
your first three-dimensional trip is always your best, when
you came down again it wasn't the same, and every time
you'd pass anywhere near the micro-dimple you made
when you fell, you'd get a rush ... sobered, a few, having
looked into the heart of the solenoid, seen the magnetic
serpent and energy in its nakedness, long enough to be
changed, to bring back from the writhing lines of force
down in that pit an intimacy with power, with glazed
badlands of soul, that set them apart forever—check out
the portrait of Michael Faraday in the Tate Gallery in
London, Tantivy Mucker-Maffick did once, to fill up a
womanless and dreary afternoon, and wondered then how
eyes of men could grow so lambent, sinister, so educated
among the halls of dread and the invisible ...) but now
the voices of the murder-witness coquettes grow shrill,
with more of a blade's edge, the music changes key,
pitching higher and higher, the ruffled buttocks bumping
backward more violently, the skirts flipping redder and
deeper each time, covering more of the field, eddying to
blood, to furnace finale, and how's the Katspiel Kid gonna
get out of this one?

Well, wouldn't you know it, just as things look worst,
Providence plants a short—*statatatah!* the lights go out
leaving a diminishing red glow on the shaven cheeks and

chins of the two operators cringing before the girls' destroying kooch-dance, the solenoid jitters to silence, the
chrome ball, released, rolls traumatized back to the comfort of its friends.

"They're *all* like this?"

"Oh, was I took," groans Alfonso Tracy.

"It comes and goes," consoles Bland, and here we get a
reprise of Gerhardt von Göll's "Bright Days for the Black
Market," with allowances made for time, place and color:

> There'll al-ways—be another dollar,
> Any way it hap-pens!
> If they catch ya nap-pin',
> Wake up-with, the dew on the grass
> 'n' you can hand 'em their ass—
> You can make another dollar,
> Third eye up on that py-ra-mid,
> Oh give a listen kid,
> It's just winkin' at you, singin', "Piss on through!"
>
> There's a will, there's a way,
> Doesn't happen, ev'ry day,
> But if ya got-the-brains, those mid-night-trains
> 'll never whistle your dreams away, hey—
>
> Just flip another dollar,
> Heads or tails it'll be all right,
> You can lose the fight, but
> That ever-lovin' War goes on and on, ya know,
> Just follow that dollar and vo-dee, o-do-do!

All the baggy-pants outfielders, doughboys in khaki,
cancan girls now sedate, bathing beauties even more so,
cowboys and cigar-store Indians, google-eyed Negroes,
apple-cart urchins, lounge lizards and movie queens, card-
sharps, clowns, crosseyed lamppost drunks, flying aces,
motorboat captains, white hunters on safari and Negroid
apes, fat men, chefs in chefs' hats, Jewish usurers, XXX
jug-clutching hillbillies, comic-book cats dogs and mice,
prizefighters and mountaineers, radio stars, midgets, ten-in-
one freaks, railroad hobos, marathon dancers, swing bands,
high-society partygoers, racehorses and jockeys, taxidanc-
ers, Indianapolis drivers, sailors ashore and wahines in
hula skirts, sinewed Olympic runners, tycoons holding big

round bags with dollar signs, all join in on a second grand chorus of the song, all the boards of the pinball machines flashing on and off, primary colors with a touch of acid to them, flippers flipping, bells ringing, nickels pouring out of the coinboxes of the more enthusiastic, each sound and move exactly in its place in the complex ensemble.

Outside the temple, the organization reps from Chicago lurk, play morra, drink Canadian blends out of silver hip-flasks, oil and clean .38s and generally carry on in their loathsome ethnic way, Popish inscrutability in every sharp crease and shadowy jowl. No way to tell if someplace in the wood file cabinets exists a set of real blueprints telling exactly how all these pinball machines were rewired—a randomness deliberately simulated—of if it has happened at real random, preserving at least our faith in Malfunction as still something beyond Their grasp . . . a faith that each machine, individually, has simply, in innocence, gone on the blink, after the thousands of roadhouse nights, end-of-the-world Wyoming thunderstorms that come straight down on your hatless head, truckstop amphetamines, tobacco smoke clawing at insides of eyelids, homicidal grabs after some way out of the year's never-slackening shit . . . have players forever strangers brought about, separately, alone, each of these bum machines? believe it: they've sweated, kicked, cried, smashed, lost their balance forever—a single Mobility you never heard, a unity unaware of itself, a silence the encyclopedia histories have blandly filled up with agencies, initials, spokesmen and deficits enough to keep us from finding them again . . . but for the moment, through the elaborate theatrical foofooraw of Mob 'n' Masons, it has concentrated here, in the back of the Mouthorgan temple, an elegant chaos to bend the ingenuity of Bland's bought expert, Silver-Streaking Bert Fibel.

Last we saw of Fibel he was hooking, stretching, and running shock cord for that Horst Achtfaden back in his gliding days, Fibel who stayed on the ground, and saw his friend on to Peenemünde—*saw him on?* isn't that a slice of surplus paranoia there, not *quite* justified is it—well, call it Toward a Case for Bland's Involvement with Achtfaden Too, if you want. Fibel worked for Siemens back when it was still part of the Stinnes trust. Along with his

design work he also put in some time as a Stinnes intelligence agent. There are also still loyalties to Vereinigte
Stahlwerke in effect, though Fibel happens to be working
now at the General Electric plant in Pittsfield, Massachusetts. It's in Bland's interest to have an agent in the Berkshires, can you guess why? Yup! to keep an eye on
adolescent Tyrone Slothrop, is why. Nearly ten years after
the original deal was closed, IG Farben is still finding it
easier to subcontract the surveillance of young Tyrone
back to Lyle Bland.

This stonefaced kraut Fibel is a genius with solenoids
and switches. How all this machinery got "out of the
glue," as they say over there, is a sinful waste of time
even to think about—he dives into topologies and color-
codes, the odor of rosin flux goes seeping into the poolrooms and saloons, a Schnipsel here and there, a muttered
also or two, and before you know it he's got most of
them working again. You can bet there's a lotta happy
Masons in Mouthorgan, Missouri.

In return for his good deed, Lyle Bland, who couldn't
care less, is made a Mason. He finds good fellowship, all
kinds of comfort designed to remind him of his virility,
and even a number of useful business contacts. Beyond
this, all is just as tight as that Business Advisory Council.
Non-Masons stay pretty much in the dark about What
Goes On, though now and then something jumps out,
exposes itself, jumps giggling back again, leaving you with
few details but a lot of Awful Suspicions. Some of the
American Founding Fathers were Masons, for instance.
There is a theory going around that the U.S.A. was and
still is a gigantic Masonic plot under the ultimate control
of the group known as the Illuminati. It is difficult to look
for long at the strange single eye crowning the pyramid
which is found on every dollar bill and not begin to
believe the story, a little. Too many anarchists in 19th-
century Europe—Bakunin, Proudhon, Salverio Friscia—
were Masons for it to be pure chance. Lovers of global
conspiracy, not all of them Catholic, can count on the
Masons for a few good shivers and voids when all else
fails. One of the best of the classic Weird Mason Stories
has Doctor Livingstone (living stone? oh, yes) come wandering into a native village in, not even the heart, but the

subconscious of Darkest Africa, a place, a tribe he's never seen before: fires in the silence, unfathomable stares, Livingstone ambles up to the village chief and flashes him a Masonic high sign—the chief recognizes it, *returns it*, all smiles, and orders every fraternal hospitality laid on for the white stranger. But recall that Dr. Livingstone, like Wernher von Braun, was born close to the Spring Equinox, and so had to confront the world from that most singular of the Zodiac's singular points. . . . Well, and keep in mind where those Masonic Mysteries came from in the first place. (Check out Ishmael Reed. He knows more about it than you'll ever find here.)

We must also never forget famous Missouri Mason Harry Truman: sitting by virtue of death in office, this every August 1945, with his control-finger poised right on Miss Enola Gay's atomic clit, making ready to tickle 100,000 little yellow folks into what will come down as a fine vapor-deposit of fat-cracklings wrinkled into the fused rubble of their city on the Inland Sea. . . .

By the time Bland joined up, the Masons had long, long degenerated into just another businessmen's club. A real shame. Business of all kinds, over the centuries, had atrophied certain sense-receptors and areas of the human brain, so that for most of the fellows taking part, the present-day rituals were no more, and even maybe a little less, than hollow mummery. Not for *all* of them, though. Now and then you found a throwback. Lyle Bland happened to be one.

The magic in these Masonic rituals is very, very old. And way back in those days, it *worked*. As time went on, and it started being used for spectacle, to consolidate what were only secular appearances of power, it began to lose its zip. But the words, moves, and machinery have been more or less faithfully carried down over the millennia, through the grim rationalizing of the World, and so the magic is still there, though latent, needing only to touch the right sensitive head to reassert itself.

Bland found himself coming home to Beacon Hill after meetings late at night, unable to sleep. He would lie down in his study on the davenport, not thinking about anything in particular, and come back with a jolt, his heart pounding terribly, knowing he'd just been *somewhere*,

but unable to account for the passage of time. The old
American Empire clock beat in the resonant hallway. The
Girandole mirror, passed on by generations of Blands,
gathered images in its quicksilver pool that Lyle couldn't
bring himself to face. In another room, his wife, varicose
and religious, groaned in her sleep. What was happening
to him?

Next meeting night, home on his back on the accustomed davenport, *Wall Street Journal* with nothing in
it he didn't already know, Lyle Bland rose up out of his
body, about a foot, face-up, realized where he was and
gaahh! *whoosh* back in again. He lay there, more terrified
than he'd ever been, even at Belleau Wood—not so much
because he'd left his body, but because he knew that this
was only a *first step*. The next step would be to roll over
in mid-air and look back. Old magic had found him. He
was off on a journey. He knew he couldn't keep from
going on with it.

It took him a month or two before he could make
the turn. When it happened, he felt it as a turn not so
much in space as in his own history. Irreversible. The
Bland who came back to rejoin the inert white container
he'd seen belly-up on the sofa, thousands of years beneath
him, had changed forever.

Before very long, he was spending most of his time on
that davenport, and hardly any at all down on State
Street. His wife, who never questioned anything, moved
vaguely through the rooms, discussing only household
affairs, sometimes getting an answer if Bland happened
to be inside his body, but most often not. Odd-looking
people began to show up at the door, without phoning.
Creeps, foreigners with tinted, oily skin, wens, sties, cysts,
wheezes, bad teeth, limps, staring or—worse—with
Strange Faraway Smiles. She let them in the house, all
of them, and the study doors were closed gently behind
them, in her face. She could hear nothing but a murmur
of voices, in what she guessed to be some foreign tongue.
They were instructing her husband in techniques of
voyage.

There have happened, though rarely, in geographical
space, journeys taken northward on very blue, fire-blue
seas, chilled, crowded by floes, to the final walls of ice.

Our judgment lapsed fatally: we paid more attention to the Pearys and Nansens who returned—and worse, we named what they did "success," though they failed. Because they came back, back to fame, to praise, they failed. We only wept for Sir John Franklin and Salomon Andrée: mourned their cairns and bones, and missed among the poor frozen rubbish the announcements of their victory. By the time we had the technology to make such voyages easy, we had long worded over all ability to know victory or defeat.

What did Andrée find in the polar silence: what should we have heard?

Bland, still an apprentice, hadn't yet shaken off his fondness for hallucinating. He knows where he is when he's there, but when he comes back, he imagines that he has been journeying underneath history: that history is Earth's mind, and that there are layers, set very deep, layers of history analogous to layers of coal and oil in Earth's body. The foreigners sit in his parlor, hissing over him, leaving offensive films of sebum on everything they touch, trying to see him through this phase, clearly impatient with what they feel are the tastes of a loafer and vulgarian. He comes back raving about the presences he has found out there, members of an astral IG, whose mission—as indeed Rathenau implied through the medium of Peter Sachsa—is past secular good and evil: distinctions like that are meaningless out there. . . .

"Yess, yess," all staring at him, "but then why keep saying 'mind and body'? Why make that distinction?"

Because it's had to get over the wonder of finding that Earth is a living critter, after all these years of thinking about a big dumb rock to find a body and psyche, he feels like a child again, he knows that in theory he must not attach himself, but still he is in love with his sense of wonder, with having found it again, even this late, even knowing he must soon let it go. . . . To find that Gravity, taken so for granted, is really something eerie, Messianic, extrasensory in Earth's mindbody . . . having hugged to its holy center the wastes of dead species, gathered, packed, transmuted, realigned, and rewoven molecules to be taken up again by the coal-tar Kabbalists of the other side, the ones Bland on his voyages has noted, taken boiled off, teased apart, explicated to every last permutation of useful magic, centuries past exhaustion still finding new molecular pieces, combining and recombining them into new synthetics—"Forget them, they are no better than the Qlippoth, the shells of the dead, you must not waste your time with them. . . ."

The rest of us, not chosen for enlightenment, left on the outside of Earth, at the mercy of a Gravity we have only begun to learn how to detect and measure, must go on blundering inside our front-brain faith in Kute Korrespondences, hoping that for each psi-synthetic taken from Earth's soul there is a molecule, secular, more or less ordinary and named, over here—kicking endlessly among the plastic trivia, finding in each Deeper Significance and trying to string them all together like terms of a power series hoping to zero in on the tremendous and secret Function whose name, like the permuted names of God, cannot be spoken . . . plastic saxophone reed *sounds of unnatural timbre*, shampoo bottle *ego-image*, Cracker Jack prize *one-shot amusement*, home appliance casing *fairing for winds of cognition*, baby bottles *tranquilization*, meat packages *disguise of slaughter*, dry-cleaning bags *infant strangulation*, garden hoses *feeding endlessly the desert* . . . but to bring them together, in their slick persistence and our preterition . . . to make sense out of, to find the meanest sharp sliver of truth in so much replication, so much waste. . . .

Lucky Bland, to be free of it. One night he called his whole family together around the davenport in the study. Lyle, Jr. came in from Houston, shivering with first-stage grippe from contact with a world where air-conditioning is not so essential to life. Clara drove down from Bennington and Buddy rode the MTA in from Cambridge. "As you know," Bland announced, "I have been taking these little trips lately." He was wearing a simple white smock, and holding a red rose. He looked unearthly, all were later to agree: his skin and eyes had a clarity which is seldom encountered, except on certain spring days, at certain latitudes, just before sunrise. "I have found," he continued, "that each time out, I have been traveling farther and farther. Tonight, I am going out for good. That is, I am not coming back. So I wanted to say good-by to you all, and let you know that you'll be provided for." He'd been to see his friend Coolidge ("Hot") Short, of the State Street law firm of Salitieri, Poore, Nash, De Brutus, and Short, and made sure all the family finances were in perfect order. "I want you to know that I love you all. I'd stay here if I could, but I have to go. I hope you can understand."

One by one, his family came up to say good-by. Hugs, kisses, handshakes done, Bland sank back into that davenport's last embrace, closed his eyes with a dim smile. . . . After a bit he felt himself beginning to rise. Those watching disagreed about the exact moment. Around 9:30 Buddy left to see *The Bride of Frankenstein,* and Mrs. Bland covered the serene face with a dusty chintz drape she'd received from a cousin who had never understood her taste.

□

A windy night. The lids of GI cans blow clanging across the parade ground. Sentries in their idleness are practicing Queen Anne salutes. Sometimes gusts of wind come that rock the jeeps on their springs, even the empty deuce 'n' a halfs and civilian bobtail rigs—shock absorbers groan, deeply, in discomfort . . . in the peaks of wind, living pine trees move, lined above the last sand dropoff into the North Sea. . . .

Walking at a brisk pace, but out of step, across the lorry-scarred spaces of the old Krupp works here, Doctors Muffage and Spontoon look anything but conspiratorial. You take them immediately for what they seem: a tiny beachhead of London respectability here in benighted Cuxhaven—tourists in this semicivilized colony of sulfa shaken into the wells of blood, syrettes and tourniquets, junkie M.O.s and sadistic corpsmen, a colony they were spared for the Duration, thank heaven, Muffage's brother being highly placed in a certain Ministry, Spontoon having been technically disqualified because of a strange hysterical stigma, shaped like the ace of spades and nearly the same color, which would appear on his left cheek at moments of high stress, accompanied by severe migraine.

Only a few months ago they felt themselves fully mobilized as any British civilian, and thus amenable to most Government requests. About the present mission, though, both now are deep in peacetime second thoughts. How quickly history passes these days.

"I can't think why he asked *us*," Muffage stroking his full Imperial (a gesture that manages only to look compulsive), speaking in a voice perhaps too melodious for a man of his mass, "he must *know* I haven't done one of these since '27."

"I assisted at a few whilst I was interning," Spontoon recalls. "That was during the great vogue they had at mental institutions, you know."

"I can name you a few National Institutions where it's still in vogue." The medicos share a chuckle, full of that British Weltschmerz that looks so uncomfortable on the faces of the afflicted. "See here, then, Spontoon, you'd rather assist me, is that it?"

"Oh, either way you know. I mean it's not as if there'll be some chap with a *book* standing there, you know, writing it all down."

"I wouldn't be too sure. Weren't you listening? Didn't you notice anything . . ."

"Enthusiastic."

"Obsessional. I wonder if Pointsman isn't *losing his grip*," sounding here remarkably like James Mason: "L(h)oo-ssing(?) hiss *khrip*."

They are looking at each other now, separate night scapes of Marston shelters and parked vehicles flowing darkly by together behind each face. The wind carries smells of brine, of beach, of petrol. A distant radio tuned to the General Forces Programme features Sandy MacPherson at the Organ.

"Oh, all of us . . ." Spontoon begins, but lets it lapse.

"Here we are."

The bright office is hung with crimson-lipped, sausage-limbed Petty Girl pin-ups. A coffee mess hisses in the corner. There's also a smell of rancid shoe-dubbing. A corporal sits with his feet on a desk, absorbed in an American Bugs Bunny comic book.

"Slothrop," in answer to Muffage's inquiry, "yes yes the Yank in the, the pig suit. Well, he's in and out all the time. Completely dotty. What are you lot then, M.I.6 or something?"

"Can't discuss it," raps Spontoon. Fancies himself a bit of a Nayland Smith, Spontoon does. "D'you know where we might find a General Wivern?"

"This time of night? Down at the alcohol dump, most likely. Follow the tracks, head for all the noise. If I weren't on duty, I'd be there m'self."

"Pig suit," frowns Muffage.

"Big bloody pig suit, yellow, pink, and blue, on my oath," replies the corporal. "You'll know him when you see him. You wouldn't have a cigarette, one of you gentlemen, by any chance."

Sounds of carousing reach them as they trudge along the tracks, past empty triple flats and tank cars. "Alcohol dump."

"Fuel for their Nazi rockets, I'm told. If they ever get one in working order."

Under a cold umbrella of naked light bulbs are gathered a crowd of Army personnel, American sailors, NAAFI girls, and German fräuleins. Fraternizing, every last one of them, shamefully, amid noise which becomes, as Muffage and Spontoon reach the edge of the gathering, a song, at whose center, with a good snootful, each arm circling a smiling and disheveled young tootsie, ruddy face under these lights gone an apoplectic mauve, and leading the glee, is the same General Wivern they last saw in Pointsman's office back at Twelfth House. From a tank car whose contents, ethanol, 75% solution, are announced in stark white stenciling along the side, spigots protrude here and there, under which an incredible number of mess cups, china mugs, coffeepots, wastebaskets, and other containers are being advanced and withdrawn. Ukuleles, kazoos, harmonicas, and any number of makeshift metal noisemakers accompany the song, which is an innocent salute to Postwar, a hope that the end of shortages, the end of Austerity, is near:

It's—
Mouthtrip-ping time!
Mouthtrip-ping time!
Time to open up that icebox door—

Oh yes it's
Mouthtrip-ping time,
Mouthtrip-ping time,
And once you've eaten some, you'll come, for more!
Ah, mouthtrip-ping time,
Mouthtrip-ping time!
It's something old, but also very new-w-w—
Life's so sublime,
In mouthtrip-ping time—
We hope you're all mouth*trip*-ping, tooooool

Next chorus is soldiers 'n' sailors all together for the first eight bars, girls for the second, General Wivern singing the next eight solo, and *tutti* to finish it up. Then comes a chorus for ukuleles and kazoos and so on while everyone dances, black neckerchiefs whipping about like the mustaches of epileptic villains, delicate snoods unloosening to allow stray locks of hair to escape their tight rolls, skirt-hems raised to expose flashing knees and slips edged in prewar Cluny lace a frail flight of smoky bat-wings here under the white electricity . . . on the final chorus the boys circle clockwise, girls anticlockwise, the ensemble opening out into a rose-pattern, from the middle of which dissipatedly leering tosspot General Wivern, tankard aloft, is hoisted briefly, like an erect stamen.

About the only one not participating here, aside from the two prowling surgeons, is Seaman Bodine, whom we left, you recall, carrying on in the bathtub at Säure Bummer's place back in Berlin. Impeccable tonight in dress whites, straight-faced and sober, he trudges among the merrymakers, thickly sprouting hair from jumper sleeves and V-neck, so much of it that last week he spooked and lost a connection just in from the CBI theatre with close to a ton of bhang, who mistook him for a seagoing version of the legendary *yeti* or abominable snowman. To make up some of what he blew on that one, Bodine is tonight promoting the First International Runcible Spoon Fight, between his shipmate Avery Purfle and an English Commando named St. John Bladdery. "Place yer bets, yes yes the odds are even, 50/50," announces suave croupier Bodine, pushing through the gathered bodies, many of them far from upright, one shaggy hand clutching a wad of occupation scrip. With the other, from time to time, he will tug the big collar of his jumper around and blow his nose on it, grommets on the hem of his T-shirt blinking, light bulbs dancing overhead in the wind he's raised, his own several shadows thrashing in all directions and merging with others.

"Greetings, gate, need an opiate?" Tiny red eyes in a vast pink Jell-o of a face, and an avaricious smile. It is Albert Krypton, corpsman striker of the U.S.S. *John E. Badass,* who now produces from inside a secret jumper pocket a glass vial full of white tablets. "Codeine, Jackson, it's beautiful—here."

Bodine sneezes violently and wipes the snot away with his sleeve. "Not for any fucking cold, Krypton. Thanks. You seen Avery?"

"He's in great shape. He was getting in some last-minute practice down the goat hole when I came over."

"Listen, old buddy," begins the enterprising tar. This decrypts into 3 ounces of cocaine. Bodine comes up with a few squashed notes. "Midnight, if you can. Told him I'd see him out at Putzi's after the fight."

"Solid. Hey, you checked under the barracks lately?" Seems the CBI returnees get together to play marbles with opium balls. You can pick up hundreds if you're any good. Corpsman Krypton pockets his money and leaves Bodine flexing his thumb and thinking about it, moves on copping feels, pausing to drink from a shell case of grain alcohol and grapefruit juice, whilst dealing the odd tablet of codeine. He has a brief paranoid episode as two red-hatted MPs show up, stroking their billy clubs and giving him, he fancies, pregnant looks. He slides into the night, peeling away, banking through dark sky. He is coming on to a proprietary mixture known as the Krypton Blue, and so it is a giddy passage to the dispensary, not without moments of deep inattention.

Inside, his connection, Pharmacist Birdbury, is conducting the last act of *La Forza del Destino* crackling in from Radio Luxembourg, and singing along. His mouth snaps shut as Krypton comes taxiing in. With him is what appears to be a gigantic, multicolored pig, the plush nap of its coat reversed here and there, which widens the possible range of colors. "*Micrograms,*" Krypton striking his head dramatically, "that's right, micrograms, not milligrams, Birdbury, gimme something, I've OD'd."

"*Ssh.*" The dispenser's high forehead wrinkling in and

out of operatical cross-furrows. Krypton goes back in among the shelves, and watches the lighted room through a bottle of paregoric till the opera's over. Comes back in time to hear the pig asking, "Well where else would he head for?"

"I got it third-hand," Birdbury laying down the hypodermic he's been using as a baton. "Ask Krypton here, he gets around a bit."

"Greetings, gate," sez Albert, "let's inoculate."

"I hear Springer is supposed to be coming in tonight."

"First I've heard. But go on out to Putzi's, why don't you. That's where all that sort of thing goes on."

The pig looks up at a clock on the wall. "Got a funny schedule tonight, is all."

"Look here, Krypton, there's a bigwig from SPOG due in here any moment, so whatever it was, you know...." They haggle over the three ounces of cocaine, the pig politely withdrawing to leaf through an old *News of the World.* Presently, taping the last of the crystal-stuffed bottles to his bare leg, Krypton invites everyone to the runcible spoon fight. "Bodine's holding some big money, folks in from all over the Zone—"

"*Seaman* Bodine?" inquires the amazed plush pig.

"The king of Cuxhaven, Porky."

"Well I ran him an errand once in Berlin. Tell him Rocketman sez howdy."

Krypton, bellbottom pulled up, opening one bottle just to see what he has, pauses, goggling. "You mean that *hash*?"

"Yup."

Krypton snuffs a big fingerful of the flaky white into nostrils right 'n' left. The world goes clarifying. Bitter snot begins to form in a stubborn fist at the back of his throat. Already the Potsdam Pickup is part of the folklore of the Zone. Would this pig here be trying to cash in on the glory of Rocketman (whose existence Krypton has never been that sure of)? Cocaine suspicions, cringing and mean as rats ... shining bottles of a thousand colors, voices from the radio, the drape and hand of the pig's shag coat as Krypton reaches out to stroke ... no, it's clear that the pig isn't looking for anything, isn't a cop, isn't dealing, or about to hustle anybody.... "Just wanted to see how it felt, you know," sez Krypton.

"Sure." Now the doorway is suddenly full of red hats, leather and brass. Krypton stands very still, the top to the open cocaine bottle in one hand.

"Slothrop?" sergeant in command comes edging into the room, hand resting on his sidearm. The pig looks over at Birdbury, who's shaking his head no, not me, as if he means it.

"Wasn't me, either," Krypton feels he ought to mention.

"Well somebody blew the whistle," the pig mutters, looking really hurt.

"Stand by," whispers Albert. To the MP: "Excuse me," moseying straight over to the wall switch, which he flicks off, Slothrop at once dashing through all the shouting past Birdbury's desk *wham* into a tall rack of medicines his straw stomach bounces him off of, but which then falls over on somebody else with a stupendous glass crash and scream—on down a pitchblack aisle, arms out to guide him, to the back exit, where he meets Krypton.

"Thanks."

"Quick."

Outside they cut eastward, toward the Elbe and the docks, pounding along, skidding in mudpuddles, stumbling over lorry-ruts, wind sweeping among the Quonsets to bat them in the face, cocaine falling in little white splashes from underneath Krypton's left bellbottom. Behind them the posse are hollering and shining flashlights, but don't seem to know where they've gone. Good. "Follow the yellow-brick road," hums Albert Krypton, on pitch, "follow the yellow-brick road," what's this, is he actually, yes he's *skipping....*

Presently, out of breath, they arrive at the pier where the *Badass* and its division, four haze-gray piglets, are tied up, to find the runcible spoon fiight just under way at the center of a weaving, cheering crowd of civilian and military drunks. Stringy Avery Purfle, sideburns slick as seal's fur in the pallid light, Adam's apple working in and out at a nervous four or five cycles a minute, shuffles around his opponent, the serene and oxlike St. John Bladdery, both with runcible spoons in the on-guard position, filed edges bright.

Krypton stashes Slothrop in a garbage bin and goes looking for Seaman Bodine. After a number of short, glittering feints, Purfle dodges in, quick as a fighting-cock.

With a high slash that Bladdery tries to parry in third, Purfle rips through the Commando's blouse and draws blood. But when he goes to jump back, it seems thoughtful Bladdery has brought his combat boot down on the American's low dress shoe, nailing him where he stands.

Promoter Bodine and his two combatants are burning crystals of awareness in this poisoned gray gathering: a good half of the crowd are out in the foothills of unconsciousness, and the rest are not exactly sure what's going on. Some think that Purfle and Bladdery are really mad at each other. Others feel that it is meant to be comedy, and they will laugh at inappropriate moments. Now and then the odd beady eyes will appear up in the night superstructures of the warships, staring, staring. . . .

Purfle and Bladdery have made simultaneous thrusts and are now *corps à corps*—with a scrape and clank the runcible spoons are locked, and elbows tense and set. The outcome rests with scrawny Purfle's gift for trickery, since Bladdery appears ready to hold the position all night.

"Rocketman's here," Krypton tugging at Bodine's damp wrinkled collar, "in a *pig suit*."

"Not now, man. You got the, ah—"

"But but the heat's after him, Bodine, where can we hide him?"

"Who cares, it's some asshole, is all. A fake. Rocketman wouldn't be *here*."

Purfle yanks his runcible-spoon hand back, leaning to the side, twisting his own weapon to keep its tines interlocked with those of Bladdery's, pulling the commando off-balance long enough to release his own foot, then deftly unlinking the spoons and dancing away. Bladdery recovers his footing and moves heavily in pursuit, probing in with a series of jabs then shifting the spoon to his other hand and surprising Purfle with a slash that grazes the sailor's neck, missing the jugular, but not by much. Blood drips into the white jumper, black under these arclights. Sweat and cold shadows lie darkly in the men's armpits. Purfle, made reckless by the pain, goes flying at Bladdery, a flurry of blind wild pokes and hackings, Bladdery hardly needing to move his feet, weaving from the knees up like a great assured pudding, finally able to grab Purfle's spoon hand at the wrist and twirl him about, like jitterbugging a girl, around in front of him, his own knife-edge now up and bi-

secting Purfle's Adam's apple, ready to slice in. He looks
up, around, wheezing, sweaty, seeking some locus of
power that will thumb-signal him what to do.

Nothing: only sleep, vomiting, shivering, a ghost and
flowered odor of ethanol, solid Bodine counting his money.
Nobody really watching. It then comes to Bladdery and
Purfle at once, tuned to one another at the filed edge of
this runcible spoon and the negligible effort it will take to
fill their common world with death, that nobody said anything about a fight to the finish, right? that each will get
part of the purse whoever wins, and so the sensible course
is to break it up now, jointly to go hassle Bodine, and find
some Band-Aids and iodine. And still they linger in their
embrace, Death in all its potency humming them romantic
tunes, chiding them for moderate little men . . . *So far and
no farther, is that it? You call that living?*

An MP car, horn and siren and lights all going, approaches. Reluctantly, Purfle and Bladdery do relax, and,
sighing out of puffed cheeks, part. Bodine, ten feet away,
tosses over the heads of the awakening crowd a fat packet
of scrip which the Commando catches, riffle-splits, and
gives half of to Purfle, who's already on route to the gangplank of his gray mother the *John E. Badass,* where the
quarterdeck watch are looking more lively, and even a
card game in the ship's laundry breaking up so everybody
can go watch the big bust. Drunkards ashore begin to mill,
sluggish and with no sense of direction. From beyond the
pale of electric light comes a rush of girls, shivering,
aroused, beruffled, to witch St. John Bladdery away under
cover of pretty-pastel synthetics and amorous squeals.
Bodine and Krypton, hipwriggling and cursing their way
through the crowd, stumbling over wakers and sleepers,
stop by the dumpster to collect Slothrop, who rises from a
pile of eggshells, beer cans, horrible chicken parts in yellow gravy, coffee grounds and waste paper spilling or
clattering off of him, raises his mask, and smiles howdy at
Bodine.

"Rocketman, holy shit, it really is. What's happening,
ol' buddy?"

"Been double-crossed, need a ride to Putzi's." Lorries
have been showing up, into whose canvas shadows MPs
are beginning to load everybody slower-moving than they
are. Now two civilians, one with a beard, come charging

down the pier, hollering, "A pig suit, a pig suit, there, look," and, "You—Slothrop—stay where you are."

Not about to, Slothrop with a great clank and crunch rolls out of the garbage and at a dead run follows Bodine and Krypton, chickenfat flowing away, eggshells flying off behind him. A Red Cross Clubmobile or canteen truck is parked down at the next nest of destroyers, its light spilling neatly square on the asphalt, a pretty girl with a Deanna Durbin hairdo framed inside against stacks of candy bars, cigarettes, chock-shaped sandwiches in waxed paper.

"Coffee, boys?" she smiles, "how about some sandwiches? We're sold out of everything tonight but ham," then seeing Slothrop, "oh, dear, I'm sorry. . . ."

"Keys to the truck," Bodine coming up with a Cagney sneer and nickel-plated handgun, "c'mon," cocking the hammer.

Tough frown, shoulderpadded shrug. "In the ignition, Jackson." Albert Krypton climbs in the back to keep her company while Slothrop and Bodine jump in front and get under way in a tight, screeching U-turn just as the two civilians come running up.

"Now who th' hell's zat," Slothrop looking back out the window at their shouting shapes diminishing, "did you check that one bird with the ace of spades on his cheek?"

Bodine swerves past the disturbance around the *John E. Badass* and gives everybody the obligatory finger. Slothrop slouches back in the seat, putting the pig mask up like a knight's beaver, reaching over to pry a pack of cigarettes out of Bodine's jumper pocket, lighting one up, weary, wishing he could just sleep. . . . In back of him suddenly the Red Cross girl shrieks, "My God, what's that?"

"Look," Krypton patiently, "you get some on the end of your finger, right, then you close off one half of your nose, a-and—"

"It's cocaine!" the girl's voice rising to an alarming intensity, "is what it is! It's heroin! You're *dope fiends!* and you've kidnapped *me!* Oh. my God! This is a, don't you realize, its a *Red Cross Clubmobile!* It's the property of the Red Cross! Oh, you can't *do* this! I'm with the Red Cross! Oh, help me, somebody! They're dope fiends! Oh, please! Help! Stop and let me out! Take the truck if you want, take everything in it, but oh please don't—"

"Steer a minute," Bodine turning around and pointing his shiny pistol at the girl.

"You can't shoot me," she screams, "you hoodlum, who do you think you are, hijacking Red Cross property! Why don't you just—go somewhere and—sniff your dope and—leave *us alone!*"

"Cunt," advises Seaman Bodine, in a calm and reasonable tone, "you are wrong. I *can* shoot you. Right? Now, you happen to be working for the same warm and wonderful organization that was charging fifteen cents for coffee and doughnuts, at the Battle of the fucking *Bulge,* if you really wanna get into who is stealing what from who."

"Whom," she replies in a much smaller voice, lower lip quivering kind of cute and bitchy it seems to Slothrop, checking it out in the rear-view mirror as Bodine takes over the wheel again.

"Oho, what's this," Krypton watching her ass, "what have we here," shifting under its khaki skirt as she stands with long legs braced for their rattling creaking 60 or 70 miles an hour and Bodine's strange cornering techniques, which look to be some stylized form of suicide.

"What's your name?" Slothrop smiling, an avuncular pig.
"Shirley."
"Tyrone. Howdy."

"Tra-la-la," Krypton now looting the cash register, gobbling Hershey bars and stuffing his socks with packs of smokes, "love in bloom." About then Bodine slams on the brakes and goes into a great skid, ass end of their truck slewing toward an icy-lit tableau of sentries in white-stenciled helmet liners, white belts, white holsters, a barricade across the road, an officer running toward a jeep hunched up and hollering into a walkie-talkie.

"Roadblock? What the shit," Bodine grinding it into reverse, various goodies for the troops crashing off of their shelves as the truck lurches around. Shirley loses her footing and staggers forward, Krypton grabbing for her as Slothrop leans to take the handgun off the dashboard, finding her half-draped over the front seat when he gets back around to the window. "Where the fuck is low now? What is it, a Red Cross gearbox, you got to put a nickel in someplace to get it in gear, *hey Shirley?*"

"Oh, goodness," Shirley squirming over into the front

between them, grabbing the shift, "like this, you drip."
Gunshots behind them.

"Thank you," sez Bodine, and, leaving rubber in a
pungent smoking shriek, they're off again.

"You're really hot, Rocketman, wow," Krypton lying in
back offering ankle and taped cocaine bottle to Shirley
with a smile.

"Do tell."

"No thanks," sez Shirley. "I'd really better not."

"C'mon . . . aw . . ."

"Were those snowdrops back there?" Slothrop squinting
into the lampshine ahead, "GIs? What're GIs doing here
in the British sector, do you know?"

"Maybe not," Bodine guesses, "maybe only Shore Patrol,
c'mon, let's not get any more paranoid than we *have*
to. . . ."

"Look, see, I'm doing (snuff) it and I'm not growing
(snuff) fangs or anything. . . ."

"Well, I just don't know," Shirley kneeling backwards,
breasts propped on the back of the seat, one big smooth
country-girl hand on Slothrop's shoulder for balance.

"Look," Bodine sez, "is it currency, or dope, or what?
I just like to know what to expect, cause if the heat's
on—"

"Only on me, far as I know. This is nothing to do with
dealing, it's a whole different drill."

"She's the rose of no-man's laaaand," sings Albert Krypton, coaxing.

"Why you going to Putzi's?"

"Got to see that Springer."

"Didn't know he was coming in."

"Why does everybody keep saying that?"

"Rebebber, dow," Shirley talking with only one nostril
here, "dot too *buch*, Albert, just a teensy bit."

"Just that nobody's seen him for a while."

"Be inhaling now, good, good, O.K., *now*. Umm, there's
a little still, uh, kind of a booger that's blocking it . . . do
it again, right. Now the other one."

"Al*bert*, you said only one."

"Look, Rocky, if you do get busted—"

"Don't want to think."

"Jeepers," sez Shirley.

"You like that? Here, just do a little more."

"What'd you do?"

"Nothing. Wanted to talk to somebody at that SPOG. Find out what was happening. We were just supposed to talk, you know, off the record, tonight in the dispensary. Neutral ground. Instead The Man shows up. Now there are also these other two creeps in civvies."

"You a spy, or something?"

"Wish I was even *that*. Oh boy. I should've known better."

"Well it sounds pretty bad." And Seaman Bodine drives along not liking it much, brooding, growing sentimental. "Say," presently, "if they do, well, catch up with you, I could get in touch with your Mom, or something."

"My—" A sharp look. "No, no, no . . ."

"Well, somebody."

"Can't think of a soul."

"Wow, Rocketman. . . ."

Putzi's turns out to be a sprawling, half-fortified manor house dating from the last century, off the Dorum road and seaward down a sandy pair of wheel-tracks with reeds and tough dune grass growing in between, the house perched like a raft atop a giant comber of a sandhill that sweeps upward from a beach whose grade is so subtle that it becomes water only by surprise, tranquil, salt-pale, stretching miles into the North Sea like clouds, here and there more silver, long cell or skin shapes, tissue-thin, stilled under the moon, reaching out toward Helgoland.

The place never got requisitioned. Nobody has ever seen the owner, or even knows if "Putzi" is anybody real. Bodine drives the truck right on into what used to be the stable and they all get out, Shirley hoorahing in the moonlight, Krypton mumbling oboy, oboy through big mouthfuls of that frau bait. There is some password and security hassle at the door, on account of the pig getup, but Slothrop flashes his white plastic knight and that works. Inside they find a brightly lit and busy combination bar, opium den, cabaret, casino and house of ill repute, all its rooms swarming with soldiers, sailors, dames, tricks, winners, losers, conjurors, dealers, dopers, voyeurs, homosexuals, fetishists, spies and folks just looking for company, all talking, singing or raising hell at a noise level the house's silent walls seal off completely from the outside. Perfume, smoke, alcohol, and sweat glide through the house in turbulences too gentle to feel or see. It's a floating celebration no one's thought to adjourn: a victory party so permanent, so easy at gathering newcomer and old regular to itself, that who can say for sure which victory? which war?

Springer is nowhere in sight, and from what Slothrop can gather from random questioning won't be by till later, if at all. Now this happens to be the very delivery date for that discharge they arranged sailing in with Frau Gnahb to Stralsund. And tonight, of all nights, after a week of not bothering him, the police decide to come after Slothrop. Oh yes, yes indeed NNNNNNNN Good Evening Tyrone Slothrop We Have Been Waiting For You. Of Course We Are Here. You Didn't Think We Had Just Faded Away, No, No Tyrone, We Must Hurt You Again If You Are Going To Be That Stupid, Hurt You Again and Again Yes Tyrone You Are So Hopeless So Stupid And Doomed. Are You Really Supposed To Find Anything? What If It Is Death Tyrone? What If We Don't Want You To Find Anything? If We Don't Want To Give You Your Discharge You'll Just Go On Like This Forever Won't You? Maybe We Want You Only To Keep On. You Don't Know Do You Tyrone. What Makes You Think You Can Play As Well As We Can? You Can't. You Think You're Good But You're Really Shit And We All Know It. That Is In Your Dossier. (Laughter. Humming.)

Bodine finds him sitting inside a coat closet, chewing on a velvet ear of his mask. "You look bad, Rocky. This is Solange. She's a masseuse." She is smiling, quizzical, a child brought to visit the weird pig in his cave.

"I'm sorry. I'm sorry."

"Let me take you down to the baths," the woman's voice a soapy sponge already caressing at his troubles, "it's very quiet, restful. . . ."

"I'll be around all night," Bodine sez. "I'll tell you if Springer shows."

"This is some kind of a plot, right?" Slothrop sucking saliva from velvet pile.

"*Everything* is some kind of a plot, man," Bodine laughing.

"And yes but, the arrows are pointing all different ways," Solange illustrating with a dance of hands, red-pointed fingervectors. Which is Slothrop's first news, out loud, that the Zone can sustain many other plots besides those polarized upon himself . . . that these are the els and busses of an enormous transit system here in the Raketenstadt, more tangled even than Boston's—and that by riding each branch the proper distance, knowing when to transfer, keeping some state of minimum grace though it might often look like he's headed the wrong way, this network of all plots may yet carry him to freedom. He understands that he should not be so paranoid of either Bodine or Solange, but ride instead their kind underground awhile, see where it takes him. . . .

Solange leads Slothrop off to the baths, and Bodine continues to search for his customer, 2½ bottles of cocaine clinking and clammy against his bare stomach under his skivvy shirt. The Major isn't at any of the poker or crap games, nor attending the floor show wherein one Yolande, blonde and shining all over with baby oil, dances table to table picking up florin pieces and sovereigns, often hot from the flame of some joker's Zippo, between the prehensile lips of her cunt—nor is he drinking, nor, according to Monika, Putzi's genial, cigar-smoking, matelassé-suited madame, is he screwing. He hasn't been by to hassle the piano player for "San Antonio Rose." It takes Bodine half an hour before colliding with the man finally, reeling out the swinging doors of a pissoir, groggy from a confrontation with the notorious Eisenkröte, known throughout the Zone as the ultimate test of manhood, before which bemedaled and brevetted Krautkillers, as well as the baddest shit-on-my-dick-or-blood-on-my-blade escapees from the grossest of Zonal stockades, all have been known to shrink, swoon, chicken out, and on occasion vomit, yes right where they stood. For it is indeed an Iron Toad, faithfully rendered, thousand-warted and some say faintly smiling, a foot long at its longest, lurking at the bottom of a rank shit-stained toilet and hooked up to the European Grid through a rheostat control rigged to deliver varying though not lethal surges of voltage and current. No one knows who sits behind the secret rheostat (some say it's the half-mythical Putzi himself), or if it

isn't in fact hooked up to an automatic timer, for not everybody gets caught, really—you can piss on the Toad without anything at all happening. But you just never know.
Often enough to matter, the current will be there—pi-
ranha-raid and salmon-climb up the gold glittering fall of
piss, your treacherous ladder of salts and acids, bringing
you back into touch with Mother Ground, the great, the
planetary pool of electrons making you one with your
prototype, the legendary poor drunk, too drunk to know
anything, pissing on some long-ago third rail and ful-
minated to charcoal, to epileptic night, his screams not even
his own but the electricity's, the amps speaking through
his already shattering vessel, shattered too soon for them
even to begin to say it, voice their terrible release from
silence, nobody listening anyhow, some watchman poking
down the track, some old man unable to sleep out for a
walk, some city drifter on a bench under a million June
bugs in green nimbus around the streetlight, his neck relaxing and tightening in and out of dreams and maybe it
was only a cat screwing, a church bell in a high wind, a
window being broken, no direction to it, not even alarming, replaced swiftly by the old, the coal-gas and Lysol,
silence. And somebody else finds him next morning. Or
you can find him any night at Putzi's if you're man enough
to go in piss on that Toad. The Major has got off this time
with only a mild jolt, and is in a self-congratulating mood.

"Ugly 'sucker tried his best," wrapping an arm about
Bodine's neck, "but got his warty ol' ass handed to him
tonight, damn 'f he didn't."

"Got your 'snow,' Major Marvy. Half a bottle shy, sorry,
it's the best I could do."

"That's all reet, sailor. I know so many nose habits between here 'n' Wiesbaden you'd need three *ton* 'n' that
wouldn't last the 'suckers a day." He pays off Bodine, full
price, overriding Bodine's offer to prorate for what's
missing. "Call it a little lagniappe, goodbuddy, that's
Duane Marvy's way o' doin' thangs. *Damn* that ol' toad's
got my pecker to feelin' pretty good now. Damn 'f I
wouldn't like to stick it inside one them little whores. Heyl
Boats, where can I find me some *pussy* around here?"

The sailor shows him how to get downstairs to the
whorehouse. They take you into a kind of private steam

bath first, you can screw right there if you want, doesn't cost any extra. The madame—hey! ha, ha! looks like some kind of a dyke with that stogie in her face! raises an eyebrow at Marvy when he tells her he wants a nigger, but thinks she can get hold of one.

"It isn't the House of All Nations, but we do aim for variety," running the tortoise end of her cigar-holder down a call-sheet, "Sandra is engaged for the moment. An exhibition. In the meantime, here is our delightful Manuela, to keep you company."

Manuela is wearing only a high comb and black-lace mantilla, shadow-flowers falling to her hips, a professional smile for the fat American, who is already fumbling with uniform buttons.

"Hubba, hubba! Hey, she's pretty sunburned herself. Ain'tcha? You got a leetle mulatto in there, a leetle Mayheecano, honey? You sabe español? You sabe fucky-fucky?"

"Si," deciding tonight to be from the Levante, "I am Spanish. I from Valencia."

"Va-len-cia-a-a," sings Major Marvy, to the well-known tune of the same name, "Señorita, fucky-fucky, sucky-sucky sixty-ni-i-ine, la-lalala *la*-la *la*-la laaa . . ." dancing her in a brief two-step about the grave center of the waiting madame.

Manuela doesn't feel obliged to join in. Valencia was one of the last cities to fall to Franco. She herself is really from the Asturias, which knew him first, felt his cruelty two years before the civil war even began for the rest of Spain. She watches Marvy's face as he pays Monika, watches him in this primal American act, paying, more deeply himself than when coming, or asleep, or maybe even dying. Marvy isn't her first, but almost her first, American. The clientele here at Putzi's is mostly British. During the War—how many camps and cities since her capture in '38?—it was German. She missed the International Brigades, shut away up in her cold green mountains and fighting hit-and-run long after the Fascists had occupied all the north—missed the flowers, children, kisses, and many tongues of Barcelona, of Valencia where she's never been, Valencia, this evening's home. . . . Ya salimos de España. . . . Pa' luchar en otros frentes, ay, Manuela, ay, Manuela. . . .

She hangs his uniform neatly in a closet and follows her trick into heat, bright steam, the walls of the seething room invisible, feathered hairs along his legs, enormous buttocks and back beginning to come up dark with the dampness. Other souls move, sigh, groan unseen among the sheets of fog, dimensions in here under the earth meaningless—the room could be any size, an entire city's breadth, paved with birds not entirely gentle in twofold rotational symmetry, a foot-darkened yellow and blue, the only colors to its watery twilight.

"Aaahhh, hot damn," Marvy slithering fatly down, sleek with sweat, over the tiled edge into the scented water. His toenails, cut Army-square, slide under last. "Come on, everybody in the pool," a great happy bellow, seizing Manuela's ankle and tugging. Having taken a fall or two on these tiles, and seen a girl friend go into traction, Manuela comes along gracefully, falling hard enough astraddle, bottom hitting his stomach a loud smack, to hurt him, she hopes. But he only laughs again, loudly abandoned to the warmth and buoyancy and sounds encompassing—anonymous fucking, drowsiness, ease. Finds himself with a thick red hardon, and slips it without ado into the solemn girl half-hidden inside her cloud of damp black Spanish lace, eyes anyplace but on his, aswing now through the interior fog, dreaming of home.

Well, that's all reet. He isn't fucking her eyes, is he? He'd rather not have to look at her face anyhow, all he wants is the brown skin, the shut mouth, that sweet and nigger submissiveness. She'll do anything he orders, yeah he can hold her head under the water till she drowns, he can bend her hand back, yeah, break her fingers like that cunt in Frankfurt the other week. Pistol-whip, bite till blood comes . . . visions go swarming, violent, less erotic than you think—more occupied with thrust, impact, penetration, and such other military values. Which is not to say he isn't enjoying himself innocently as you do. Or that Manuela doesn't find herself too, in some casual athletic way, liking the ride up and down the stubborn red shaft of Major Marvy, though her mind is on a thousand other things now, a frock of Sandra's that she covets, words to various songs, an itch below her left shoulderblade, a tall English soldier she saw as she came through the bar around suppertime, his brown forearm, shirt rolled to the elbow, against the zinc top of the table. . . .

Voices in the steam. Alarms, many feet clopping in shower shoes, silhouettes moving by, a gray cloudy evacuation. "What in thee hell," Major Marvy about to come, rising on his elbows distracted, squinting in several directions, rapidly getting a softoff.

"Raid," a voice going past. "MPs," shivers somebody else.

"Gaaahh!" screams Major Marvy, who has just recalled the presence of 2½ ounces of cocaine in his uniform pockets. He rolls, walrus-heavy, Manuela sliding away and off his limpening nervous penis, hardly aroused but enough of a professional to feel the price includes a token *puto* and *sinvergüenza* now. Scrambling up out of the water, skidding on the tiles, Duane Marvy, bringing up the rear, emerges into an ice-cold changing-room to find the last of the bathers fled, the closets stone-empty except for one multicolored velvet something or other. "Hey where's my uniform!" stomping on the floor, fists at his sides, face very red. "Oh you motherless bastards," thereupon throwing several bottles and ashtrays, breaking two windows, attacking the wall with an ornate umbrella stand, feeling better for it in his mind. He hears combat boots crashing overhead and in rooms nearby, girls screaming, a phonograph record knocked screeching into silence.

He checks out this plush or velvet rig, finds it to be a pig costume complete with mask, considers slyly that no MP would bother an innocent funseeking pig. As humorless limey voices move closer through the rooms of Putzi's, he rips frantically at silk lining and straw padding to make room for his own fat. And, struggled at last inside, whew, zipped up, mask hiding face, safe, clownish-anonymous, pushes out through bead curtains, then upstairs to the bar, only to run spang into a full division of the red-hatted 'suckers coming his way, all in step, swear to God.

"Here's our elusive swine, gentlemen," pocked face, blunt and ragged mustache, pointing a pistol right at his head, others moving up quickly. A civilian comes pushing through, spade-shape blazing dark on his smooth cheek.

"Right. Dr. Muffage is outside with the ambulance, and we'd like two of your chaps for a moment, sergeant, till we're all secure."

"Certainly, sir." Wrists weak from steam and comfort gathered skillfully behind his back before he can even get mad enough to start yelling at them—cold steel, ratcheting like a phone number being dialed late at night, with no hope in hell of any answer ever. . . .

"Goddamn," he finally gets out, mask muffling his voice, giving it an echo that hurts his ears, "what'n thee hell's wrong with you, boy? Don't you know who I am?"

But oh-oh, waitaminute—if they've found the uniform, Marvy ID and cocaine in the same set of pockets, maybe it isn't such a hot idea to tell them his name just yet. . . .

"Leftenant Slothrop, we presume. Come along, now."

He keeps silent. Slothrop, O.K., we'll just wait, see what the score is, square the dope thing later, play dumb, say it must've been planted. Maybe even find him a Jewish lawyer good enough to nail the 'suckers for false arrest.

He's escorted out the door and into the idling ambulance. The bearded driver gives him only a quick over-the-shoulder glance, then lets in the clutch. Before he can think to struggle, the other civilian and the MPs have quickly strapped Marvy at knees and chest to a stretcher.

A pause by an Army lorry to let the MPs off again. Then they continue on. Toward Cuxhaven. Marvy thinks. Nothing but night, moon-softened blackness out the window. Can't tell. . . .

"Sedation now?" Ace of Spades crouches beside him, shining a pocket flashlight over ampoules in his kit, rattling syringes and points.

"Mm. Yes, we're almost there."

"I don't see why they couldn't have given us hospital space for this."

The driver laughs. "Oh yes, I can just see *that*."

Filling the hypodermic slowly, "Well we *are* under orders . . . I mean there's nothing—"

"Dear *chap*, it's not the most respectable operation."

"Hey," Major Marvy tries to raise his head. "Operation? What's this, boy?"

"Ssh," ripping away part of one pigsuit sleeve, baring Marvy's arm.

"I don't want no needle—" but it's already in the vein and discharging as the other man seeks to calm him. "I mean you really got the wrong fella, you know?"

"Of course, Leftenant."

"Hey, hey, hey. No. Not me, I'm a *major*." He should be more emphatic about this, more convincing. Maybe it's the 'sucking pig mask in the way. Only he can hear his voice, now given back entirely to himself, flatter, metallic . . . they can't hear him. "Major Duane Marvy." They don't believe him, don't believe his name. Not even *his name*. . . . Panic strikes him, deeper than the sedative has reached, and he begins to buck truly in terror against the straps, feeling small muscles along his chest stretch into useless twinges of pain, oh God, beginning to scream now with all his might, no words, only cries, as loud as the strap across his chest will let him.

"For pity's sake," the driver sighs. "Can't you shut him up, Spontoon?"

Spontoon has already ripped the pig mask away, and replaces it now with one of gauze, which he holds on with one hand while dripping ether with the other—whenever the thrashing head comes within range. "Pointsman has taken leave of his senses," he feels obliged to say, irritated out of all patience, "if he calls *this* a 'calm imperturbable.' "

"All right, we're on the strand now. No one in sight." Muffage drives down toward the water, the sand just solid enough to hold the ambulance, everything very white in the small moon, which is at its zenith . . . perfect ice. . . .

"Oh," Marvy moans. "Oh fuck. Oh no. Oh Jesus," the words in long drugged diminuendo, struggles against his bonds weakening as Muffage parks them at last, an olive-drab derelict tiny on this broad beach, the enormous slick stretching away moonward, to the threshold of the north wind.

"Plenty of time," Muffage looking at his watch. "We're catching the C-47 at one. They said they could hold up for a bit." Sighs of comfort before turning to their task.

"That man's connections," Spontoon shaking his head, removing the instruments from their disinfectant solution and laying them on a sterile cloth beside the stretcher. "My, my. Let's hope he never turns to a life of crime, eh?"

"Fuck," groans Major Marvy softly, "oh, fuck me, will you?"

Both men have scrubbed, and donned masks and rubber gloves. Muffage has switched on a dome light which stares

down, a soft radiant eye. The two work quickly, in silence,
two wartime pros used to field expediency, with only an
occasional word from the patient, a whisper, a white
pathetic grope in his ether-darkness after the receding
point of light that's all he has left of himself.

It's a simple procedure. The crotch of the velvet costume
is torn away. Muffage decides to dispense with shaving
the scrotum. He douses it first with iodine, then squeezes
in turn each testicle against the red-veined and hairy bag,
makes the incision quickly and cleanly through skin and
surrounding membranes, popping the testicle itself out
through the wound and welling blood, pulling it out with
the left hand till the cords hard and soft are strung visible
under the light. As if they are musical strings he might, a
trifle moon-mad, strum here on the empty beach into appropriate music, his hand hesitates: but then, reluctantly
bowing to duty, he severs them at the proper distances
from the slippery stone, each incision then being bathed
in disinfectant, and the two neat slits, side by side, finally
sutured up again. The testicles are plopped into a bottle of
alcohol.

"Souvenirs for Pointsman," Muffage sighs, stripping off
the surgical gloves. "Give that one another shot. It might
be better if he sleeps through, and someone back in London
explains this to him."

Muffage starts up the motor, backs in a half-circle and
slowly heads back up toward the road, the vast sea lying
still behind.

Back at Putzi's, Slothrop curls in a wide crisp-sheeted
bed beside Solange, asleep and dreaming about Zwölfkinder, and Bianca smiling, he and she riding on the wheel,
their compartment become a room, one he's never seen, a
room in a great complex of apartments big as a city, whose
corridors can be driven or bicycled along like streets: trees
lining them, and birds singing in the trees.

And "Solange," oddly enough, is dreaming of Bianca
too, though under a different aspect: it's of her own child,
Ilse, riding lost through the Zone on a long freight train
that never seems to come to rest. She isn't unhappy, nor is
she searching, exactly, for her father. But Leni's early
dream for her is coming true. She will not be used. There
is change, and departure: but there is also help when least
looked for from the strangers of the day, and hiding, out

among the accidents of this drifting Humility, never quite to be extinguished, a few small chances for mercy. . . .

Upstairs, one Möllner, valise full of his night's treasures —an American major's uniform and papers, and 2½ ounces of cocaine—explains to the shaggy American sailor that Herr von Göll is a very busy man, attending to business in the north, as far as he knows, and has not commissioned him to bring to Cuxhaven any kind of papers, no military discharges, passports—nothing. He's sorry. Perhaps the sailor's friend is mistaken. Perhaps, again, it's only a temporary delay. One appreciates that forgeries take time.

Bodine watches him leave, unaware of what's inside that valise. Albert Krypton has drunken himself unconscious. Shirley comes wandering in, bright-eyed and restless, wearing a black garter belt and stockings. "Hmm," she sez, with a certain look.

"Hmm," sez Seaman Bodine.

"And anyway, it was only *ten* cents at the Battle of the Bulge."

□

So: he has traced Weissmann's battery from Holland, across the salt marshes and lupine and bones of cows, to find *this*. Lucky he's not superstitious. He'd be taking it for a prophetic vision. There is of course a perfectly rational explanation, but Tchitcherine has never read *Martín Fierro*.

He watches from his temporary command post in a copse of jumpers on a low hill. Through the binoculars he sees two men, one white, one black, holding guitars. Townspeople are gathered in a circle, but these Tchitcherine can crop out, leaving in his elliptical field a scene with the same structure as the male-female singing contest in the middle of a flat grassland in Central Asia well over a decade ago—a coming-together of opposites that signaled then his own approach to the Kirghiz Light. What does it signal this time?

Over his head, the sky is streaked and hard as marble. He knows. Weissmann installed the S-Gerät and fired the 00000 somewhere close by. Enzian can't be far behind. It will be here.

But he has to wait. Once that would have been un-

bearable. But since Major Marvy dropped out of sight,
Tchitcherine has been a little more cautious. Marvy was a
key man. There is a counterforce in the Zone. Who was
the Soviet intelligence man who showed up just before the
fiasco in the clearing? Who tipped the Schwarzkommando
off to the raid? Who got rid of Marvy?

He's been trying hard not to believe too much in the
Rocket-cartel. Since his illumination that night, Marvy
drunk, Bloody Chiclitz declaiming on the virtues of Herbert
Hoover, Tchitcherine has been watching for evidence.
Gerhardt von Göll, with his corporate octopus wrapping
every last negotiable item in the Zone, must be in it, consciously or otherwise. Tchitcherine last week was on the
point of flying back to Moscow. He'd seen Mravenko, one
of the VIAM people, briefly in Berlin. They met in the
Tiergarten, two officers ostensibly strolling in the sun.
Work crews shoveled cold patch into holes in the pavement, banging it flat with shovels. Bicycle riders ratcheted
by, skeleton-functional as their machines. Small clusters
of civilians and military were back under the trees, sitting
on fallen trunks or lorry wheels, stirring through bags and
valises, dealing. "You're in trouble," Mravenko said.

He'd been a remittance man too, back in the thirties,
and the most maniacal, systemless chess player in Central
Asia. His tastes ran low enough to include even blindfold
chess, which Russian sensibilities find unutterably gross.
Tchitcherine sat down at the board each time more upset
than the last, trying to be amiable, to jolly the madman
into some kind of rational play. Most often he'd lose. But
it was either Mravenko or the Semirechie winter.

"Do you have any idea what's going on?"

Mravenko laughed. "Does anybody? Molotov isn't telling
Vishinsky. But they know things about you. Remember
the Kirghiz Light? Sure you do. Well, they found out about
that. *I* didn't tell them, but they got to somebody."

"It's ancient history. Why bring it up now?"

"You're regarded as 'useful,' " Mravenko said.

They looked at each other, then, for a long time. It was
a death sentence. Usefulness out here ends as quickly as
a communiqué. Mravenko was afraid, and not entirely for
Tchitcherine, either.

"What will *you* do, Mravenko?"

"Try not to be very useful. They're not perfect, though."
Both men knew this was meant to be comfort, and isn't
working too well. "They don't really know what *makes*
you useful. They go on statistics. I don't think you were
supposed to survive the War. When you did, they had to
look at you more closely."

"Maybe I'll survive this, too." And that was when he got
the idea of flying to Moscow. But just about then word
came in that Weissmann's battery couldn't be traced any
further than the Heath. And the renewed hope of meeting
Enzian stopped him from going—the seductive hope that's
leading him further each day from any chance of continuing on past the other side of that meeting. He never supposed he would. The real question is: will they get him
before he gets Enzian? All he needs is a little more time
. . . his only hope is if they're looking for Enzian too, or
the S-Gerät, and using him the same way he thinks he's
using Slothrop. . . .

The horizon is still clear: has been all day. Cypress-
shaped junipers stand in the rust and hazy distances, still
as monuments. The first purple flowers are showing on the
heather. It is not the busy peace of late summer, but the
peace of a burial ground. Among the prehistoric German
tribes, that's what this country was: the territory of the
dead.

A dozen nationalities, dressed as Argentine estancieros,
crowd around the soup-kitchen commissary. El Ñato is
standing on the saddle of his horse, Gaucho style, looking
off into the German pampas. Felipe is kneeling out in the
sun, making his noontime devotionals to the living presence of a certain rock back in the wasteland of La Rioja,
on the eastern slopes of the Andes. According to an Argentine legend from the last century, María Antonia Correa
followed her lover into that arid land, carrying their newborn child. Herders found her a week later, dead. But the
infant had survived, by nursing from her corpse. Rocks
near the site of the miracle have since been the objects of
yearly pilgrimages. But Felipe's particular rock embodies
also an intellectual system, for he believes (as do M. F.
Beal and others) in a form of mineral consciousness not
too much different from that of plants and animals, except
for the time scale. Rock's time scale is a lot more stretched

out. "We're talking frames per century," Felipe like everybody else here lately has been using a bit of movie language, "per millennium!" Colossal. But Felipe has come
to see, as those who are not Sentient Rocksters seldom do,
that history as it's been laid on the world is only a fraction,
an outward-and-visible fraction. That we must also look to
the untold, to the silence around us, to the passage of the
next rock we notice—to its aeons of history under the long
and female persistence of water and air (who'll be there,
once or twice per century, to trip the shutter?), down to
the lowland where your paths, human and mineral, are
most likely to cross. . . .

Graciela Imago Portales, dark hair parted in the middle
and drawn back from her forehead, wearing a long black
riding skirt and black boots, sits shuffling cards, stacking
herself flushes, full houses, four of a kind, just for her own
amusement. The supernumeraries have brought next to
nothing to play with. She knew it would come to this:
she'd thought once that by using it only in games, money
would lose its reality. Wither away. Has it, or is she playing a game with herself? It seems Beláustegui has been
watching her more closely since they got here. She doesn't
want to threaten his project. She's been to bed with the
solemn engineer a few times (though at first, back in B.A.,
she'd have sworn to you she couldn't have drunk him even
with a silver straw), and she knows he's a gambler too. A
good pair, wired front-to-front: she picked it up the first
time he touched her. The man knows his odds, the shapes
of risk are intimate to him as loved bodies. Each moment
has its value, its probable success against other moments
in other hands, and the shuffle for him is always moment-
to-moment. He can't afford to remember other permutations, might-have-beens—only what's present, dealt him
by something he calls Chance and Graciela calls God. He
will stake everything on this anarchist experiment, and if
he loses, he'll go on to something else. But he won't hold
back. She's glad of that. He's a source of strength. She
doesn't know, if the moment came, how strong she'd be.
Often at night she'll break through a fine membrane of
alcohol and optimism to see really how much she needs
the others, how little use, unsupported, she could ever be.
The sets for the movie-to-be help some. The buildings

are real, not a false front in sight. The boliche is stocked
with real liquor, the pulpería with real food. The sheep,
cattle, horses, and corrals are real. The huts are weather-
proof and are being slept in. When von Göll leaves—if he
ever comes—nothing will be struck. Any of the extras who
want to stay are welcome. Many of them only want to rest
up awhile for more DP trains, more fantasies of what home
was like before the destruction, and some dream of getting
somewhere. They'll move on. But will others come? And
what will the military government think of a community
like this in the middle of their garrison state?

It isn't the strangest village in the Zone. Squalidozzi has
come in out of his wanderings with tales of Palestinian
units strayed all the way from Italy, who've settled down
farther east and started up Hasidic communes, on the
pattern of a century and a half ago. There are onetime
company towns come under the fleet and jittery rule of
Mercury, dedicated now to a single industry, mail delivery,
eastward and back, in among the Soviets and out, 100
marks a letter. One village in Mecklenburg has been taken
over by army dogs, Dobermans and Shepherds, each one
conditioned to kill on sight any human except the one who
trained him. But the trainers are dead men now, or lost.
The dogs have gone out in packs, ganged cows in the fields
and brought the carcasses miles overland, back to the
others. They've broken into supply depots Rin-Tin-Tin
style and looted K-rations, frozen hamburger, cartons of
candy bars. Bodies of neighboring villagers and eager
sociologists litter all the approaches to the Hund-Stadt.
Nobody can get near it. One expeditionary force came
armed with rifles and grenades, but the dogs all scattered
in the night, slender as wolves, and no one could bring
himself to destroy the houses and shops. No one wanted to
occupy the village, either. So they went away. And the
dogs came back. If there are lines of power among themselves, loves, loyalties, jealousies, no one knows. Someday
G-5 might send in troops. But the dogs may not know of
this, may have no German anxieties about encirclement—
may be living entirely in the light of the one man-installed
reflex: Kill The Stranger. There may be no way of distin-
guishing it from the other given quantities of their lives—
from hunger or thirst or sex. For all they know, kill-the-

stranger was born in them. If any have remembered the blows, the electric shocks, the rolled-up newspapers no one read, the boots and prods, their pain is knotted in now with the Stranger, the hated. If there are heresiarchs among the dogs, they are careful about suggesting out loud any extra-canine source for these sudden eruptions of lust to kill that take them over, even the pensive heretics themselves, at any first scent of the Stranger. But in private they point to the remembered image of one human, who has visited only at intervals, but in whose presence they were tranquil and affectionate—from whom came nourishment, kind scratches and strokings, games of fetch-the-stick. Where is he now? Why is he different for some and not for others?

There is a possibility, among the dogs, latent so far because it's never been seriously tested, of a crystallizing into sects, each around the image of its trainer. A feasibility study, in fact, is going on even now at staff level in G-5, to see whether original trainers might not be located, and this crystallizing begun. One sect might try to protect its trainer against attacks from others. Given the right combinations and an acceptable trainer-loss figure, it might be cheaper to let the dogs finish themselves off than to send in combat troops. The study has been contracted to, of all people, Mr. Pointsman, who is now restricted to one small office at Twelfth House, the rest of the space having been taken over by an agency studying options for nationalizing coal and steel—given him more out of sympathy than anything else. Since the castrating of Major Marvy, Pointsman has been officially in disgrace. Clive Mossmoon and Sir Marcus Scammony sit in their club, among discarded back copies of *British Plastics*, drinking the knight's favorite, Quimporto—a weird prewar mixture of quinine, beef-tea and port—with a dash of Coca-Cola and a peeled onion. Ostensibly the meeting is to finalize plans for the Postwar Polyvinyl Chloride Raincoat, a source of great corporate fun these days ("Imagine the look on some poor bastard's face when the whole *sleeve* simply falls out of the shoulder—" "O-or how about mixing in something that will actually *dissolve* in the rain?"). But Mossmoon really wants to discuss Pointsman: "What shall we do with Pointsman?"

"I found the most darling boots in Portobello Road,"

pipes Sir Marcus, whom it's always hard to get around to talking business. "They'll look stunning on you. Blood-red cordovan and halfway up your thighs. Your naked thighs."

"We'll give it a go," replies Clive, neutral as can be (though it's a thought, old Scorpia's been so damned bitchy lately). "I could use a spot of relaxation after trying to explain Pointsman away to the Higher Levels."

"Oh, the *dog* chap. I say, have you ever thought about a Saint Bernard? Big, shaggy darlings."

"On occasion," Clive keeps at it, "but mostly I think about Pointsman."

"Not your sort, darling. Not at all. And he *is* getting on, poor chap."

"Sir Marcus," last resort, usually the willowy knight demands to be called Angelique, and there seems no other way to get his attention, "if this show prangs, we're going to see a national crisis. I've got Ginger Groupers jamming my switchboard and my mailbox day and night—"

"Mm, I'd like to jam your male box, Clivey—"

"—*and* 1922 Committee coming in the windows. Bracken and Beaverbrook go *on*, you know, it isn't as if the election put them out of a job or something—"

"Dear *chap*," smiling angelically, "there isn't going to *be* any crisis. Labour wants the American found as much as we do. We sent him out to destroy the blacks, and it's obvious now he won't do the job. What harm can he cause, roaming around Germany? For all we know he's taken ship for South America and all those adorable little mustachios. Let it *be* for a while. We've got the Army, when the time is right. Slothrop was a good try at a moderate solution, but in the end it's always the Army, isn't it?"

"How can you be so sure the Americans will ever condone that?"

A long disagreeable giggle. "Clive, you're such a little boy. You don't know the Americans. I do. I deal with them. They'll want to see how we do with *our* lovely black animals—oh dear, ex Africa semper aliquid novi, they're so big, so *strong*—before they try it on their own, ah, target groups. They may *say* a good many harsh things if we fail, but there'll be no sanctions."

"Are we going to fail?"

"We're all going to fail," Sir Marcus primping his curls, "but the Operation won't."

Yes. Clive Mossmoon feels himself rising, as from a bog of trivial frustrations, political fears, money problems: delivered onto the sober shore of the Operation, where all is firm underfoot, where the self is a petty indulgent animal that once cried in its mired darkness. But here there is no whining, here inside the Operation. There is no lower self. The issues are too momentous for the lower self to interfere. Even in the chastisement room at Sir Marcus's estate, "The Birches," the foreplay is a game about who has the real power, who's had it all along, chained and corseted though he be, outside these shackled walls. The humiliations of pretty "Angelique" are calibrated against their degree of fantasy. No joy, no real surrender. Only the demands of the Operation. Each of us has his place, and the tenants come and go, but the places remain. . . .

It wasn't always so. In the trenches of the First World War, English men came to love one another decently, without shame or make-believe, under the easy likelihoods of their sudden deaths, and to find in the faces of other young men evidence of otherwordly visits, some poor hope that may have helped redeem even mud, shit, the decaying pieces of human meat. . . . It was the end of the world, it was total revolution (though not quite in the way Walter Rathenau had announced): every day thousands of the aristocracy new and old, still haloed in their ideas of right and wrong, went to the loud guillotine of Flanders, run day in and out, on and on, by no visible hands, certainly not those of the people—an English class was being decimated, the ones who'd volunteered were dying for those who'd known something and hadn't, and despite it all, despite knowing, some of them, of the betrayal, while Europe died meanly in its own wastes, men loved. But the life-cry of that love has long since hissed away into no more than this idle and bitchy faggotry. In this latest War, death was no enemy, but a collaborator. Homosexuality in high places is just a carnal afterthought now, and the real and only fucking is done on paper. . . .

4

The Counterforce

What?

—RICHARD M. NIXON

□

Bette Davis and Margaret Dumont are in the curly-Cuvil-
liés drawing-room of somebody's palatial home. From outside the window, at some point, comes the sound of a
kazoo, playing a tune of astounding tastelessness, probably
"Who Dat Man?" from *A Day at the Races* (in more
ways than one). It is one of Groucho Marx's vulgar friends.
The sound is low, buzzing, and guttural. Bette Davis
freezes, tosses her head, flicks her cigarette. "What," she
inquires, "is *that?*" Margaret Dumont smiles, throws out
her chest, looks down her nose. "Well it *sounds*," she
replies, "like a ka*zoo*."

For all Slothrop knows, it *was* a kazoo. By the time he's
awake, the racket has faded in the morning. Whatever it
was, it woke him up. What it was, or is, is Pirate Prentice,
in a more or less hijacked P-47, on route to Berlin. His
orders are terse and clear, like those of the others, agents
of the Pope, Pope got religion, go out 'n' find that minnesinger, he's a good guy after all. . . .

Well, it's an older Jug, one with a greenhouse canopy.
The barred field of sight gives Pirate twinges of memory
in his neck muscles. The plane seems permanently out of
trim to him, though he still fiddles now and then with
different tabs. Right now he's trying the War Emergency
Power to see how it works, even though there seems to be
no War, no Emergency, keeping an eye on the panel,
where RPMs, manifold pressure, and cylinder-head temperature are all nudging their red lines. He eases it down
and flies on, and presently is trying a slow roll over Celle,
then a loop over Brunswick, then, what the hell, an Immelmann over Magdeburg. On his back, molars aching in a
grin, he starts his roll a hair too slow, just this side of
one-thirty, and nearly stalls it, jolts over a set of surprise
points—finish it as an ordinary loop or go for the Immelmann?—already reaching for ailerons, forget the damn
rudder, a spin isn't worth worrying about . . . but at the
last second does give the pedal just a touch anyway, a
minor compromise (I'm nearly forty, good God, is it happening to me *too?*) and rolls himself upright again. It had
to be the Immelmann.

721

Oh I'm the Eagle of Tooting,
Bombing and shooting,
And nobodee can bring me down!
Old Kaiser Bill, you're over the hill,
Cause I'm comin' into your home town!
Tell all the fräuleins and mademoiselles
To keep a light in the window for me . . .
Cause I'm the Eagle of Tooting, just rooty-toot-tooting,
And flyin' on to victo-reel

By now, Osbie Feel ought to be in Marseilles, already
trying to contact Blodgett Waxwing. Webley Silvernail is
on route to Zürich. Katje will be going to Nordhausen . . .
Katje. . . .

No, no, she hasn't told him everything she's been up to.
It's none of his business. However much she told him,
there'd always be the bit of mystery to her. Because of
what he is, because of directions he can't move in. But
how is it both of them kept from vanishing from each
other, into the paper cities and afternoons of this strange
peace, and the coming Austerity? Could it be there's something about ad hoc arrangements, like the present mission,
that must bring you in touch with the people you need to
be with? that more formal adventures tend, by their nature, to separation, to loneliness? Ah, Prentice. . . . What's
this, a runaway prop? no, no, check the fuel-pressure—
here's the gauge needle wobbling, rather low, tank's run
dry—

Little in-flight annoyance for Pirate here, nothing serious. . . . Out of his earphones now and then, ghost-voices
will challenge or reprimand him: air traffic people down in
their own kingdom, one more overlay on the Zone, antennas strung in the wilderness like redoubts, radiating
half-spheres of influence, defining invisible corridors-in-the-
sky that are real only for them. The Thunderbolt is painted
Kelly green. Hard to miss. Pirate's idea. Gray was for the
War. Let them chase. Catch me if you can.

Gray was for the War. So, it seems, was Pirate's odd
talent for living the fantasies of others. Since V-E Day,
nothing. But it's not the end of his psychic difficulties. He
is still being "haunted," in the same marginal and uncertain way, by Katje's ancestor Frans van der Groov, dodo
killer and soldier of fortune. The man never quite arrives,
nor quite leaves. Pirate is taking it personally. He is the

Dutchman's compatible host, despite himself. What does Frans see in him? Has it to do—of course it does—with the Firm?

He has warped a skein of his dreams into Pirate's own, heretical dreams, exegeses of windmills that turned in shadow at the edges of dark fields, each arm pointing at a spot on the rim of a giant wheel that turned through the sky, stop and go, always exactly with the spinning cross: "wind" was a middle term, a convention to express what really moved the cross . . . and this applied to all wind, everywhere on Earth, shrieking between the confectionery pink and yellow mountains of Mauritius or stirring the tulips at home, red cups in the rain filling bead by clear bead with water, each wind had its own cross-in-motion, materially there or implied, each cross a unique mandala, bringing opposites together in the spin (and tell me now, Frans, what's this wind I'm in, this 25,000-foot wind? What mill's that, grinding there below? What does it grind, Frans, who tends the stone?).

Far beneath the belly of the Thunderbolt, brushed on the green countryside, pass the time-softened outlines of ancient earthworks, villages abandoned during the Great Dying, fields behind cottages whose dwellers were scythed down without mercy by the northward march of black plague. Behind a scrim, cold as sheets over furniture in a forbidden wing of the house, a soprano voice sings notes that never arrange themselves into a melody, that fall apart in the same way as dead proteins. . . .

"It's as clear as the air," rants Gustav the composer, "if you weren't an old fool you'd see it—I know, I know, there's an Old Fools' Benevolent Association, you all know each other, you vote censures against the most troublesome under-70s and my name's at the head of the list. Do you think I care? You're all on a different frequency. There's no way you'll get interference from us. We're too far separated. We have our own problems."

Cryptozoa of many kinds scurry through crumbs, pubic hairs, wine-splashes, tobacco ash and shreds, a litter of dram cocaine vials, each with a red Bakelite top bearing the seal of Merck of Darmstadt. The bugs' atmosphere ends about an inch from the floor, an ideal humidity, darkness, stability of temperature. Nobody bothers them.

There is an unspoken agreement about not stomping on bugs in Säure's place.

"You're caught in tonality," screams Gustav. "Trapped. Tonality is a game. All of them are. You're too old. You'll never move beyond the game, to the Row. The Row is enlightenment."

"The Row is a game too." Säure sits grinning with an ivory spoon, shoveling incredible piles of cocaine into his nose, going through his whole repertoire: arm straight out swinging in a giant curve *zoom* precisely to the nostril he's aiming at, then flicking in the lot from two feet away without losing a crystal . . . then a whole bunch gets tossed up in the air like a piece of popcorn and nose-gobbled *ngkok* on target, inside where it's smooth as a Jo block, not a cilium in sight there since the Liebknecht funeral, if not before . . . hand-to-hand shifts of spoon two or three times, faster than ivory ever moved in air . . . rails disappearing in a wink without benefit of a tube to guide them. "*Sound* is a game, if you're capable of moving that far, you adenoidal closet-visionary. That's why I listen to Spohr, Rossini, Spontini, I'm choosing *my* game, one full of light and kindness. You're stuck with that stratosphere stuff and rationalize its dullness away by calling it 'enlightenment.' You don't what what enlightenment is, Kerl, you're blinder than I am."

Slothrop moseys down the trail to a mountain stream where he's left his harp to soak all night, wedged between a couple of rocks in a quiet pool.

"Your 'light and kindness' are the jigging of the doomed," sez Gustav. "You can smell mortality in every one of those bouncy little tunes." Surly, he decapitates a vial of cocaine with his teeth, and spits the red debris in among the shimmering bugs.

Through the flowing water, the holes of the old Hohner Slothrop found are warped one by one, squares being bent like notes, a visual blues being played by the clear stream. There are harpmen and dulcimer players in all the rivers, wherever water moves. Like that Rilke prophesied,

> And though Earthliness forget you,
> To the stilled Earth say: I flow.
> To the rushing water speak: I am.

It is still possible, even this far out of it, to find and make audible the spirits of lost harpmen. Whacking the water out of his harmonica, reeds singing against his leg, picking up the single blues at bar 1 of this morning's segment, Slothrop, just suckin' on his harp, is closer to being a spiritual medium than he's been yet, and he doesn't even know it.

The harp didn't show up right away. His first days in these mountains, he came across a set of bagpipes, left behind in April by some Highland unit. Slothrop has a knack for doping things out. The Imperial instrument was a cinch. In a week he mastered that dreamy tune Dick Powell sang in the movies, "In the Shadows Let Me Come and Sing to You," and spent most of his time playing that, WHANGde*didd*le de-dee, WHANG de *dum*—de-doooooo . . . over and over, on the bagpipes. By and by he began to notice that offerings of food were being left near the lean-to he'd put up. Mangel-wurzels, a basket of cherries, even fresh fish. He never saw who was leaving them. Either he was supposed to be a bagpiper's ghost, or just purely sound itself, and he knew enough about solitudes and night-voices to figure what was going on. He quit playing the bagpipes, and next day he found the harp. It happens to be the same one he lost in 1938 or -9 down the toilet at the Roseland Ballroom, but that's too long ago for him to remember.

He's kept alone. If others have seen him or his fire, they haven't tried to approach. He's letting hair and beard grow, wearing a dungaree shirt and trousers Bodine liberated for him from the laundry of the *John E. Badass.* But he likes to spend whole days naked, ants crawling up his legs, butterflies lighting on his shoulders, watching the life on the mountain, getting to know shrikes and capercaillie, badgers and marmots. Any number of directions he ought to be moving in, but he'd rather stay right here for now. Everyplace he's been, Cuxhaven, Berlin, Nice, Zürich, must be watched now. He could still make a try at finding Springer, or Blodgett Waxwing. Why does he have this obsession with getting papers? What th' fuck are *papers*, anyhow? He could try one of the Baltic ports, wait around for Frau Gnahb to put in, and get over to that Denmark or that Sweden. DPs, offices burned, records

lost forever—papers might not mean so much in Europe
... waitaminute, so much as *where*, Slothrup? Huh? America? Shit. C'mon—

Yup, still thinking there's a way to get back. He's been
changing, sure, changing, plucking all the albatross of
self now and then, idly, half-conscious as picking his nose
—but the one ghost-feather his fingers always brush by is
America. Poor asshole, he can't let her go. She's whispered
love me too often to him in his sleep, vamped insatiably
his waking attention with come-hitherings, incredible promises. One day—he can see a day—he might be able finally
to say *sorry*, sure and leave her ... but not just yet. One
more try, one more chance, one more deal, one more
transfer to a hopeful line. Maybe it's just pride. What if
there's no place for him in her stable any more? If she has
turned him out, she'll never explain. Her "stallions" have
no rights. She is immune to their small, stupid questions.
She is exactly the Amazon Bitch your fantasies have called
her to be.

Then there's Jamf, the coupling of "Jamf" and "I" in the
primal dream. Who can he go to with *it*? it will not bear
that much looking into, will it? If he gets too close, there
will be revenge. They might warn him first, They might
not.

Omens grow clearer, more specific. He watches flights of
birds and patterns in the ashes of his fire, he reads the
guts of trout he's caught and cleaned, scraps of lost paper,
graffiti on the broken walls where facing has been shot
away to reveal the brick underneath—broken in specific
shapes that may also be read....

One night, on the wall of a public shithouse stinking
and ripe with typhoid, he finds among initials, dates, hasty
pictures of penises and mouths open to receive them,
Werewolf stencils of the dark man with the high shoulders
and the Homburg hat, an official slogan: WILLST DU V-2,
DANN ARBEITE. If you want the V-2, then work. Good Evening Tyrone Slothrop ... no, no, wait, it's O.K., over on
the other wall they've also painted WILLST DU V-4, DANN
ARBEITE. Lucky. The brimming voices recede, the joke
clarifies, he is only back with Goebbels and the man's in-
ability to let a good thing be. But it had taken an effort
to walk around and look at that other wall. Anything

could've been back there. It was dusk. Plowed fields,
power lines, ditches and distant windbreaks went for miles.
He felt brave and in control. But then another message
caught his eye:

ROCKETMAN WAS HERE

His first thought was that he'd written it himself and
forgot. Odd that that should've been his first thought, but
it was. Might be he was starting to implicate himself,
some yesterday version of himself, in the Combination
against who he was right then. In its sluggish coma, the
albatross stirred.

Past Slothrops, say averaging one a day, ten thousand
of them, some more powerful than others, had been going
over every sundown to the furious host. They were the
fifth-columnists, well inside his head, waiting the moment
to deliver him to the four other divisions outside, closing
in. . . .

So, next to the other graffiti, with a piece of rock, he
scratches this sign:

Slothrop besieged. Only after he'd left it half a dozen
more places did it dawn on him that *what he was really
drawing was the A4 rocket,* seen from below. By which
time he had become tuned to other fourfold expressions—
variations on Frans van der Groov's cosmic windmill—
swastikas, gymnastic symbols FFFF in a circle symmetrically upside down and backward, Frisch Fromm Fröhlich
Frei over neat doorways in quiet streets, and crossroads,
where you can sit and listen in to traffic from the Other
Side, hearing about the future (no serial time over there:
events are all there in the same eternal moment and so
certain messages don't always "make sense" back here:
they lack historical structure, they sound fanciful, or
insane).

The sand-colored churchtops rear up on Slothrop's horizons, apses out to four sides like rocket fins guiding the

streamlined spires ... chiseled in the sandstone he finds waiting the mark of consecration, a cross in a circle. At last, lying one afternoon spread-eagled at his ease in the sun, at the edge of one of the ancient Plague towns he becomes a cross himself, a crossroads, a living intersection where the judges have come to set up a gibbet for a common criminal who is to be hanged at noon. Black hounds and fanged little hunters slick as weasels, dogs whose breeds have been lost for 700 years, chase a female in heat as the spectators gather, it's the fourth hanging this spring and not much spectacle here except that this one, dreaming at the last instant of who can say what lifted smock, what fat-haunched gnädige Frau Death may have come sashaying in as, gets an erection, a tremendous darkpurple swelling, and just as his neck breaks, he actually *comes* in his ragged loin-wrapping creamy as the skin of a saint under the purple cloak of Lent, and one drop of sperm succeeds in rolling, dripping hair to hair down the dead leg, all the way down, off the edge of the crusted bare foot, drips to earth at the exact center of the crossroad where, in the workings of the night, it changes into a mandrake root. Next Friday, at dawn, the Magician, his own moving Heiligenschein rippling infrared to ultraviolet in spectral rings around his shadow over the dewy grass, comes with his dog, a coal-black dog who hasn't been fed for a few days. The Magician digs carefully all around the precious root till it's held only by the finest root-hairs—ties it to the tail of his black dog, stops his own ears with wax then comes out with a piece of bread to lure the unfed dog *rrrowf!* dog lunges for bread, root is torn up and lets loose its piercing and fatal scream. The dog drops dead before he's halfway to breakfast, his holy-light freezes and fades in the million dewdrops. Magician takes the root tenderly home, dresses it in a little white outfit and leaves money with it overnight: in the morning the cash has multiplied tenfold. A delegate from the Committee on Idiopathic Archetypes comes to visit. "Inflation?" the Magician tries to cover up with some flowing hand-moves. " 'Capital'? Never heard of that." "No, no," replies the visitor, "not at the moment. We're trying to think ahead. We'd like very much to hear about the basic structure of this. How bad was the scream for instance?" "Had m'ears plugged up, couldn't hear it." The delegate flashes a fraternal business smile. "Can't say as I blame you. . . ."

Crosses, swastikas, Zone-mandalas, how can they not speak to Slothrop? He's sat in Säure Bummer's kitchen, the air streaming with kif moirés, reading soup recipes and finding in every bone and cabbage leaf paraphrases of himself . . . news flashes, names of wheelhorses that will pay him off for a certain getaway. . . . He used to pick and shovel at the spring roads of Berkshire, April afternoons he's lost, "Chapter 81 work," they called it, following the scraper that clears the winter's crystal attack-from-within, its white necropolizing . . . picking up rusted beer cans, rubbers yellow with preterite seed, Kleenex wadded to brain shapes hiding preterite snot, preterite tears, newspapers, broken glass, pieces of automobile, days when in superstition and fright he could *make it all fit*, seeing clearly in each an entry in a record, a history: his own, his winter's, his country's . . . instructing him, dunce and drifter, in ways deeper than he can explain, have been faces of children out the train windows, two bars of dance music somewhere, in some other street at night, needles and branches of a pine tree shaken clear and luminous against night clouds, one circuit diagram out of hundreds in a smudged yellowing sheaf, laughter out of a cornfield in the early morning as he was walking to school, the idling of a motorcycle at one dusk-heavy hour of the summer . . . and now, in the Zone, later in the day he became a crossroad, after a heavy rain he doesn't recall, Slothrop sees a very thick rainbow here, a stout rainbow cock driven down out of pubic clouds into Earth, green wet valleyed Earth, and his chest fills and he stands crying, not a thing in his head, just feeling natural. . . .

☐

Double-declutchingly, heel-and-toe, away goes Roger Mexico. Down the summer Autobahn, expansion joints booming rhythmic under his wheels, he highballs a pre-Hitler Horch 870B through the burnt-purple rolling of the Lüneburg Heath. Over the windscreen mild winds blow down on him, smelling of junipers. Heidschnucken sheep out there rest as still as fallen clouds. The bogs and broom go speeding by. Overhead the sky is busy, streaming, a living plasma.

The Horch, army-green with one discreet daffodil painted halfway up its bonnet, was lurking inside a lorry at the Elbeward edge of the Brigade pool at Hamburg, shadowed except for its headlamps, stalked eyes of a friendly alien smiling at Roger. Welcome there, Earthman. Once under way, he discovered the floor strewn with rolling unlabeled glass jars of what seems to be baby food, weird unhealthy-colored stuff no human baby could possibly eat and survive, green marbled with pink, vomit-beige with magenta inclusions, all impossible to identify, each cap adorneed with a smiling, fat, cherubic baby, seething under the bright glass with horrible botulism toxins 'n' ptomaines ... now and then a new jar will be produced, spontaneously, under the seat, and roll out, against all laws of acceleration, among the pedals for his feet to get confused by. He knows he ought to look back underneath there to find out what's going on, but can't quite bring himself to.

Bottles roll clanking on the floor, under the bonnet a hung-up tappet or two chatters its story of discomfort. Wild mustard whips past down the center of the Auto-bahn, perfectly two-tone, just yellow and green, a fateful river seen only by the two kinds of rippling light. Roger sings to a girl in Cuxhaven who still carries Jessica's name:

> I dream that I have found us both again,
> With spring so many strangers' lives away,
> And we, so free,
> Out walking by the sea,
> With someone else's paper words to say. ....
>
> They took us at the gates of green return,
> Too lost by then to stop, and ask them why—
> Do children meet again?
> Does any trace remain,
> Along the superhighways of July?

Driving now suddenly into such a bright gold bearding of slope and field that he nearly forgets to steer around the banked curve. ...

A week before she left, she came out to "The White Visitation" for the last time. Except for the negligible rump of PISCES, the place was a loony bin again. The barrage-balloon cables lay rusting across the sodden meadows, going to flakes, to ions and earth—tendons that sang in the violent nights, among the sirens wailing in thirds smooth as distant wind, among the drumbeats of bombs, now lying slack, old, in hard twists of metal ash. Forget-me-nots boil everywhere underfoot, and ants crowd, bustling with a sense of kingdom. Commas, brimstones, painted ladies coast on the thermoclines along the cliffs. Jessica has cut fringes since Roger saw her last, and is going through the usual anxiety—"It looks utterly horrible, you don't have to say it. . . ."

"It's utterly swoony," sez Roger, "I love it."

"You're making fun."

"Jess, why are we talking about *haircuts* for God's sake?"

While somewhere, out beyond the Channel, a barrier difficult as the wall of Death to a novice medium, Leftenant Slothrop, corrupted, given up on, creeps over the face of the Zone. Roger doesn't want to give him up: Roger wants to do what's right. "I just can't leave the poor twit out there, can I? They're trying to destroy him—"

But, "Roger," she'd smile, "it's *spring*. We're at peace."

No, we're not. It's another bit of propaganda. Something the P.W.E. planted. Now gentlemen as you've seen from the studies our optimum time is 8 May, just before the traditional Whitsun exodus, schools letting out, weather projections for an excellent growing season, coal requirements beginning their seasonal decline, giving us a few months' grace to get our Ruhr interests back on their feet—no, he sees only the same flows of power, the same impoverishments he's been thrashing around in since '39. His girl is about to be taken away to Germany, when she ought to be demobbed like everyone else. No channel upward that will show either of them any hope of escape. There's *something* still on, don't call it a "war" if it makes you nervous, maybe the death rate's gone down a point or two, beer in cans is back at last and there *were* a lot of people in Trafalgar Square one night no so long ago . . . but Their enterprise goes on.

The sad fact, lacerating his heart, laying open his emptiness, is that Jessica believes Them. "The War" was the
condition she needed for being with Roger. "Peace" allows
her to leave him. His resources, next to Theirs, are too
meager. He has no words, no technically splendid embrace, no screaming fit that can ever hold her. Old Beaver,
not surprisingly, will be doing air-defense liaison over
there, so they'll be together in romantic Cuxhaven. Ta-ta
mad Roger, it's been grand, a wartime fling, when we came
it was utterly incendiary, your arms open wide as a
Fortress's wings, we had our military secrets, we fooled
the fat old colonels right and left but stand-down time
must come to all, yikes! I must run sweet Roger really it's
been dreamy. . . .

He would fall at her knees smelling of glycerine and
rose-water, he would lick sand and salt from her ATS
brogans, offer her his freedom, his next 50 years' pay from
a good steady job, his poor throbbing brain. But it's too
late. We're at Peace. The paranoia, the danger, the tune-
less whistling of busy Death next door, are all put to
sleep, back in the War, back with her Roger Mexico
Years. The day the rockets stopped falling, it began to end
for Roger and Jessica. As it grew clear, day after safe day,
that no more would fall ever again, the new world crept
into and over her like spring—not so much the changes
she felt in air and light, in the crowds at Woolworth's, as
a bad cinema spring, full of paper leaves and cotton-wool
blossoms and phony lighting . . . no, never again will she
stand at their kitchen sink with a china cup squeaking in
her fingers, its small crying-child sound defenseless, meekly
resonating BLOWN OUT OF ATTENTION AS THE
ROCKET FELL smashing to a clatter of points white and
blue across the floor. . . .

Those death-rockets now are in the past. This time she'll
be on the firing end, she and Jeremy—isn't *that* how it
was always meant to be? firing them out to sea: no death,
only the spectacle, fire and roar, the excitement without
the killing, isn't that what she prayed for? back in the
fading house, derequisitioned now, occupied again by
human extensions of ball-fringe, dog pictures, Victorian
chairs, secret piles of *News of the World* in the upstairs
closet.

She's meant to go. The orders come from higher than she can reach. Her future is with the World's own, and Roger's only with this strange version of the War he still carries with him. He can't move, poor dear, it won't let him go. Still passive as he'd been under the rockets. Roger the victim. Jeremy the firer. "The War's my mother," he said the first day, and Jessica has wondered what ladies in black appeared in his dreams, what ash-white smiles, what shears to come snapping through the room, through their winter . . . so much of him she never got to know . . . so much unfit for Peace. Already she's beginning to think of their time as a chain of explosions, craziness ganged to the rhythms of the War. Now he wants to go rescue Slothrop, another rocket-creature, a vampire whose sex life actually *fed* on the terror of that Rocket Blitz— ugh, creepy, creepy. They ought to lock him up, not set him free. Roger *must* care more about Slothrop than about her, they're two of a kind, aren't they, well—she hopes they'll be happy together. They can sit and drink beer, tell rocket stories, scribble equations for each other. How jolly. At least she won't be leaving him in a vacuum. He won't be lonely, he'll have something to occupy the time. . . .

She has wandered away from him, down the beach. The sun is so bright today that the shadows by her Achilles tendon are drawn sharp and black as seams up the heel of a silk stocking. Her head, as always, is bent forward, away, the bare nape he's never stopped loving, will never see again, unprotected as her beauty, her innocence of how forever in peril it moves through the World. She may know a little, may think of herself, face and body, as "pretty" . . . but he could never tell her all the rest, how many other living things, birds, nights smelling of grass and rain, sunlit moments of simple peace, also gather in what she is to him. Was. He is losing more than single Jessica: he's losing a full range of life, of being for the first time at ease in the Creation. Going back to winter now, drawing back into his single envelope. The effort it takes to extend any further is more than he can make alone.

He hadn't thought he'd cry when she left. But he cried. Snot by the cubic yard, eyes like red carnations. Presently, every time his left foot hit the ground walking he'd get a jolt of pain through half his skull. Ah, this must be what they mean by the "pain of separation!" Pointsman kept showing up with armloads of work. Roger found himself unable to forget Jessica, and caring less about Slothrop.

But one day Milton Gloaming popped in to deliver him from his unmoving. Gloaming was just back from a jaunt through the Zone. He'd found himself on a task force with one Josef Schleim, a defector of secondary brilliance, who had once worked for the IG out of Dr. Reithinger's office, VOWI—the Statistical Department of NW7. There, Schleim had been assigned to the American desk, gathering for the IG economic intelligence, through subsidiaries and licensees like Chemnyco, General Aniline and Film, Ansco, Winthrop. In '36 he came to England to work for Imperial Chemicals, in a status that was never to be free from ambiguities. He'd heard of Slothrop, yes indeed... recalled him from the old days. When Lyle Bland went out on his last transmural journey, there'd been Green Reports flapping through the IG offices for weeks, Geheime Kommandosache, rumors coupling and uncoupling like coal-tar molecules under pressure, all to do with who was likely to take over the Slothrop surveillance, now that Bland was gone.

This was toward the beginning of the great struggle for the IG's intelligence machinery. The economic department of the foreign office and the foreign department of the economic office were both after it. So were the military, in particular the Wehrwirtschaftstab, a section of the General Staff that maintained OKW's liaison with industry. The IG's own liaison with OKW was handled by Vermittlungsstelle W, under Drs. Dieckmann and Gorr. The picture was further confused by the usual duplicate Nazi Party offices, Abwehr-Organizations, set up throughout German industry after 1933. The Nazis' watchdog over the IG was called "Abteilung A" and was set up in the same office building as—in fact, it appeared perfectly congruent with—the IG's own Army liaison group, Vermittlungsstelle W. But Technology, alas, braid-crowned and gold-thighed maiden, always comes up for grabs like this. Most likely the bitching and bickering of Army vs. Party was what finally drove Schleim over the hill, more

than any moral feelings about Hitler. In any case, he remembers Slothrop surveillance being assigned to a newly
created "Sparte IV" under Vermittlungsstelle W. Sparte I
was handling nitrogen and gasoline, II dyes, chemicals,
buna rubber, pharmaceuticals, III film and fibers. IV
handled Slothrop and nothing else, except—Schleim had
heard tell—one or two miscellaneous patents acquired
through some dealings with IG Chemie in Switzerland. An
analgesic whose name he couldn't recall, and a new plastic,
some name like Mipolam . . . "Polimex," or something. . . .

"Sounds like that would've come under Sparte II," was
Gloaming's only comment at the time.

"A few directors were upset," Schleim agreed. "Ter
Meer was a Draufgänger—he and Hörlein both, go-ahead
fellows. They might have got it back."

"Did the Party assign an Abwehr man to this Sparte
IV?"

"They must have, but I don't know if he was SD or SS.
There were so many of them around. I can remember
some sort of rather thin chap with thick eyeglasses coming
out of the office there once or twice. But he wore civilian
clothes. Couldn't tell you his name."

Well now what'n the bloddy 'ell. . . .

"Surveillance?" Roger is fidgeting heavily, with his hair,
his necktie, ears, nose, knuckles, "IG Farben had Slothrop
under surveillance? Before the War? What *for*, Gloaming."

"Odd, isn't it?" Cheerio *boing* out the door without
another word, leaving Roger alone with a most disagreeable light beginning to grow, the leading edge of a revelation, blinding, crescent, at the periphery of his brain. IG
Farben, eh? Mr. Pointsman has been chumming, almost
exclusively these days, with upper echelon from ICI. ICI
has cartel arrangements with Farben. The bastard. Why,
he must have known about Slothrop all along. The Jamf
business was only a front for . . . well say what the hell
is going *on* here?

Halfway up to London (Pointsman has repossessed the
Jaguar, so Roger's on a motorcycle from the PISCES pool,
which consists now only of the cycle and one Morris with
virtually no clutch) it occurs to him that Gloaming was
sent around deliberately by Pointsman, as some obscure
tactic in this Nayland Smith campaign he seems to be into

(Pointsman owns a matched set of all the books in Sax Rohmer's great Manichaean saga, and is apt these days to pop in at any time, usually while Roger is sleeping or trying to take a quiet shit, and actually *stand* there, in front of the toilet, reading aloud a pertinent text). Nothing is beyond Pointsman, he's worse than old Pudding was, no shame at all. He would use anyone—Gloaming, Katje Borgesius, Pirate Prentice, no one is (Jessica) exempt from his (*Jessica?*) Machiavellian—

Jessica. Oh. Yes ofcourseofcourse Mexico you fucking *idiot* . . . no wonder the 137th gave him the runaround. No wonder her orders came from Too High. He had even, lamb frolicking about the spit, asked *Pointsman* to see what he could do. . . . Fool. Fool.

He arrives at Twelfth House on Gallaho Mews in a homicidal state of mind. Bicycle thieves run down the back streets, old pros wheeling them three abreast at a good pace. Young men with natty mustaches preen in the windows. Children loot the dustbins. Courtyard corners are drifted with official papers, the shed skin of a Beast at large. A tree has inexplicably withered in the street to a shingly black corpse. A fly lands belly-up on the front fender of Roger's motorcycle, thrashes ten seconds, folds its veined and sensitive wings, and dies. Quick as that. First one Roger has ever seen. P-47s fly over in squadron box formations, four checkmarks apiece RedWhiteBlue-Yellow on the unamended form of the whitish sky, squadron after squadron: it is either some military review, or another war. A plasterer is busy around the corner, smoothing over a bomb-scarred wall, plaster heaped on his hawk luscious as cream cheese, using an unfamiliar trowel inherited from a dead friend, still, these first days, digging holes like an apprentice, the shiny knife-edge not yet broken to his hand, the curl of it a bit more than his own strength could have ever brought it to . . . Henry was a larger bloke. . . . The fly, who was not dead, unfolds its wings and zooms off to fool somebody else.

All right Pointsman stomping into Twelfth House, rattling the corkboards down the seven hallways and flights, receptionists making long arms for the telephone *dammit now where are you*—

Not in his office. But Géza Rózsavölgyi is, and tries to

give Roger a hard time. "You are *ma*-king a *spec*-tacle of your-*self*, young *man*."

"Shurrup you Transylvanian twit," snarls Roger, "I'm looking for the boss, see, one funny move out of you and it's your last taste of O-negative, Jackson, those fangs won't even be able to gum *oatmeal* when I'm through wiv you—" Alarmed Rózsavölgyi, retreating around the water cooler, tries to pick up a swivel chair to defend himself with. The seat falls off, and Rózsavölgyi is left with only the base, which happens, embarrassingly, to be shaped like a cross.

"Where is he," Mexican standoff, Roger gritting his teeth *do not succumb to hysteria, it is a counter-productive luxury you cannot, in your present great vulnerability, afford.* . . . "Come on you sod, tell me or you'll never see the inside of a coffin again—"

In runs a short but spunky secretary, bit of a chubbette here, and commences belting Roger in the shins with the excess-profits tax records from 1940 to '44 of an English steel firm which happened to share a patent with Vereinigte Stahlwerke for an alloy used in the liquid-oxygen couplings for the line running aft to the S-Gerät in A4 number 00000. But Roger's shins are not set up for this kind of information. The secretary's glasses fall off. "Miss Müller-Hochleben," reading her nametag, "you look *beastly* without your glasses. Put ssem back on, at vunce!" this comic Nazi routine being inspired by her surname.

"I can't find them," German accent all right, "I don't see too well."

"*Well*, we'll see if we can't *help* you here—ah! what's this? Miss Müller-Hochleben!"

"Ja. . . ."

"What do they look like, these eyeglasses?"

"They are white—"

"With clever little *rhinestones* all around the rims, Fräulein? eh?"

"Ja, ja, und mit—"

"And running down all the earpieces too, a-and *feathers?*"

"Ostrich feathers. . . ."

"*Male* ostrich feathers, dyed a stunning peacock blue, sprouting off the edges?"

"That is my eyeglasses, ja," sez the groping secretary, "where are they, please?"

"Right *here!*" bringing his foot down CRUNCH, smashing them to bright arctic gatherings all over Pointsman's rug.

"*I-say*," offers Rózsavölgyi from a far corner: the one corner of the room, by the way, which is not brightly lit, yes kind of an optic anomaly here, just a straight, square room, no odd-shaped polyhedrons in Twelfth House . . . and still, this strange, unaccountable prism of shadow in the corner . . . more than one visitor has popped in to find Mr. Pointsman not at his desk where he ought to be but standing in the shadow-corner—most disturbingly *facing into it.* . . . Rózsavölgyi is not himself that fond of the Corner, he's tried it a few times but only came out shaking his head: "Mis-ter *Point*sman, I-don't *like* it in there, at *all.* What *poss*-ible kind, of a *thrill* can *an*-yone *get,* from *such* an *unwhole*some *experience.* Eh?" raising one crookedly wistful eyebrow. Pointsman had only looked apologetic, not for himself but *to* something for Rózsavölgyi, and said gently, "This is one spot in the room where I feel alive," well bet your ass one or two memos went up toward Ministerial level over *that* one. If they reached the Minister himself, it was probably as office entertainment. "Oh yes, yes," shaking his wise old head of sheep's wool, high, almost Slavic cheekbones crinkling his eyes up into an inattentive but polite laughter, "yes Pointsman's famous Corner, yes . . . wouldn't be surprised if it was *haunted,* eh?" Reflex laughs from the underlings present, though only grim smiles from the overlings. "Get the S.P.R. in, to have a look," giggles someone with a cigar. "*The* poor bloke will think he's back in the *War* again." "Hear, hear," and, "That's a good one, all right," ring through the layering smoke. Practical jokes are all the rage among these particular underlings, a kind of class tradition.

"You say *what,*" Roger has been screaming for a while.

"*I-say,*" sez Rózsavölgyi, again.

"You say, 'I say'? Is that it? Then you should have said, 'I say, "I say." ' "

"I did."

"No, no—you said, 'I say,' *once,* is what you—"

"A-*ha!* But I *said* it *again.* I-*said* it . . . *twice.*"

"But that was after I asked you the question—you can't tell me the two 'I say's were both part of the same statement," unless, "that's asking me to be unreasonably," unless it's really true that, "credulous, and around *you* that's a form of," that we're the *same person,* and that the whole exchange was ONE SINGLE THOUGHT yaaaggghhh and that means, "insanity, Rózsavölgyi—"

"My glasses," snivels Fräulein Müller-Hochleben, now crawling around the room, Mexico scattering the glass splinters with his shoe so that now and then the unfortunate girl will cut a hand or a knee, beginning to trail dark little feathers of blood for inches at a time, eventually —assuming she were to last long enough—dotting in Pointsman's rug like the train of a Beardsley gown.

"You're doing *fine,* Miss Müller-Hochleben!" cries Roger encouragingly, "and as for *you,* you—" but is stopped on noticing how Rózsavölgyi now is nearly invisible in the shadow, and how the whites of his eyes are actually *glowing* white, jittering around in the air, winking-out-coming-back . . . it is costing Rózsavölgyi an effort to stay in this shadow-corner. It is not, at all, his sort of place. For one thing, the rest of the room seems to be at more of a distance, as through the view-finder on a camera. And the walls—they don't appear to be . . . well, *solid,* actually. They flow: a coarse, a viscous passage, rippling like a standing piece of silk or nylon, the color watery gray but now and then with a surprise island in the flow, some color absolutely foreign to this room: saffron spindles, palm-green ovals, magenta firths running comblike into jagged comicbook-orange chunks of island as the wounded fighter-plane circles, jettisons the tanks, then the silver canopy, sets the flaps to just above a stall, wheels up as the *blue* (suddenly, such a violent blue!) rushes in just before impact throttle closed *uhhnnhh!* oh shit the *reef,* we're going to smash up on the—oh. Oh, there's no reef? We—we're *safe?* We are! Mangoes, I see mangoes on that tree over there! a-and there's a girl—there's a *lotta* girls! Lookit, they're all gorgeous, their tits point straight out, and they're all swingin' those grass skirts, playin' ukuleles and singing (though why are the voices so hard and tough, so nasally like the voices of an American chorus line?)—

White man welcome ta Puke-a-hook-a-look-i I-i-i-island!
One taste o' my pa-paya and y'll never wanna go
    a-waaaay!
Moon like a yel-low ba-na-na,
Hangin' over, my ca-ba-na,
And lotsa hula, hula games to play—
Oh the stars are fallin' over Puke-a-hook-a-look-i Island,
And the lava down the mountain's runnin' scrump-shus as
    a cherry pie—
Even Sweet Leilani in the Little Grass Shack
Loves a coconut monkey and a missionary snack,
Looky-looky, sugar cookie, you're on Puke-a-hook-a-look-i
    I-i-i-island!

O-*boy*, o-*boy*—go-ing to *nail* me, one, of those *lit*-tle *is*-land
love-lies, *spend*, the *rest* . . . of my *life*, *eat*-ing pa-*pay*-as,
fra-grant as the *cunt*, of young para*dise*—
    When paradise was young. The pilot is turning to
Rózsavölgyi, who is still strapped in safety harness behind
him. The face is covered with helmet, goggles that reflect
too much light, oxygen mask—a face of metal, leather,
isinglass. But now the pilot is raising the goggles, slowly,
and whose eyes are these, so familiar, smiling hello, I know
you, don't you know me? Don't you *really* know me?
    Rózsavölgyi screams and backs out of the corner, shiver-
ing, blinded now in the overhead lights. Fräulein Müller-
Hochleben is crawling around and around in the same
circle, faster and faster, nearly a blur, croaking hysterically. Both have reached the exact level Roger's subtle
psychological campaign here was intended to work them
up to. Quietly but firmly: "Right. Now for the last time,
where is Mr. Pointsman?"
    "Mossmoon's office," they reply, in unison.
    Mossmoon's office is a roller-skate ride away from White-
hall, and guarded by room after room of sentinel girls,
each of them wearing a frock of a radically different color
from the others (and this goes on for a while, so you can
imagine what 3-sigma colors these are to begin with, if
that many can be so "radically different," you know, like
that—oh, colors such as lizard, evening star, pale Atlantis
to name a few), and whom Roger romances, bribes, threatens, double-talks and (sigh) yes punches his way through
till finally "Mossmoon," pounding on this gigantic oak

door, carved like the stone doorways of certain temples, "Pointsman, the jig's up! In the name of whatever marginal decency enables you to get through the day without being shot dead by the odd armed stranger, open this door." This is quite a long speech, and the door actually opens halfway through, but Roger finishes it up anyhow. He's looking into a room of incandescent lemon-lime subdued drastically, almost to the milky point of absinthe-and-water, a room warmer than this tableful of faces really deserves, but perhaps it's Roger's entrance that deepens the color a bit now as he runs and jumps on the polished table, over the polished head of a director of a steel company, skidding 20 feet down the waxed surface to confront the man at the end, who sits with a debonair (well, snotty) smile on his face. "Mossmoon, I'm on to you." Has he actually come inside, in among the hoods, eye-slits, gold paraphernalia, the incense and the thighbone scepter?

"That's *not* Mossmoon," Mr. Pointsman clearing his throat as he speaks, "Mexico *do* come down off the table won't you... gentlemen, one of my old PISCES colleagues, brilliant but rather unstable, as you may've noted —oh, Mexico, *really*—"

Roger has unbuttoned his fly, taken his cock out, and is now busy pissing on the shiny table, the papers, in the ashtrays and pretty soon on these poker-faced men themselves, who, although executive material all right, men of hair-trigger minds, are still not quite willing to admit that this is happening, you know, in any world that really touches, at too many points, the one *they're* accustomed to... and actually the fall of warm piss is quite pleasant as it sweeps by, across ten-guinea cravats, creative-looking little beards, up into a liver-spotted nostril, across a pair of Army-issue steel-rim eyeglasses, slashing up and down starched fronts, Phi Beta Kappa keys, Legions of Honour, Orders of Lenin, Iron Crosses, V.C.s, retirement watchchains, Dewey-for-President lapel pins, half-exposed service revolvers, and even a sawed-off shotgun under the shoulder there....

"Pointsman," the cock, stubborn, annoyed, bucks like an airship among purple clouds (very dense purple, as pile velvet that color) at nightfall when the sea-breeze promises a difficult landing, "I've saved you for last. But—goodness, I don't seem to have any urine left, here. Not even a drop.

I'm so sorry. Nothing left for you at all. Do you understand? If it means giving my *life*," the words have just come out, and maybe Roger's exaggerating, but maybe not, "there will be nothing *anywhere* for you. What you get, I'll take. If you go higher in this, I'll come and get you, and take you back down. Wherever you go. Even should you find a spare moment of rest, with an understanding woman in a quiet room, I'll be at the window. I'll always be just outside. You will never cancel me. If you come out, I'll go in, and the room will be defiled for you, haunted, and you'll have to find another. If you stay inside I'll come in anyway—I'll stalk you room to room till I corner you in the last. You'll have the last room, Pointsman, and you'll have to live in it the rest of your scum, prostituted life."

Pointsman won't look at him. Won't meet his eyes. That's what Roger wanted. The security police show up as an anticlimax, although aficionados of the chase scene, those who cannot look at the Taj Mahal, the Uffizi, the Statue of Liberty without thinking chase scene, chase scene, wow yeah Douglas Fairbanks scampering across that moon minaret there—these enthusiasts may find interest in the following:

Roger dives under the table to unbutton his fly and the zealous flatties leap at each other over the top of the table, colliding and cursing, but Roger has gone scuttling down the horsehide, hobnailed, pinstriped, Mom's-argyle-socked sublevel of these conspirators above, a precarious passage, any one foot could kick untelegraphed and wipe him out—till he arrives back at the bald steel-magnate, reaches up, grabs him by the necktie or the cock, whichever it's easiest to get a hold on, and drags the man down under the table.

"Right. Now, we're going to get out of here, and you're my hostage, *get it*?" He emerges dragging the livid executive by his necktie or cock, pulling him like a child's sleigh strangling and apoplectic out the door, past the modally unusual rainbow of sentinel-ladies now intimidated-*looking* at least, sirens already wailing in the street MANIAC ASSAULTS OIL PARLEY *Ousted After* ——*ing on Conferees* and he's out of the elevator by now running down a back corridor to a central-heating complex *zoom!* over the heads of a couple of black custodians who are passing back and forth a cigarette rolled from some West African narcotic herb, stuffs his hostage into a gigantic furnace which is banked for the spring (too bad), and flees out the back way down an aisle of plane trees into a small park, over a fence zippety zop, fastfoot Roger and the London cops.

There's nothing back at "The White Visitation" he really needs. Nothing he can't let go. Clothes on his back and the pool motorcycle, a pocket full of spare change and anger unlimited, what more does a 30-year-old innocent need to make his way in the city? "I'm fucking *Dick Whittington!*" it occurs to him zooming down Kings Road, "I've come to London! I'm your Lord Mayor. . . ."

Pirate is home, and apparently expecting Roger. Pieces of his faithful Mendoza lie about the refectory table, shining with oil or bluing, wads, patches, rods, bottles occupy his hands, but his eager eyes are on Roger.

"No," cutting into a denunciation of Pointsman when Milton Gloaming's name comes up, "it's a minor item, but stop right there. Pointsman didn't send him. *We* sent him."

"We."

"You're a novice paranoid, Roger," first time Prentice has ever used his Christian name and it touches Roger enough to check his tirade. "Of course a well-developed They-system is necessary—but it's only half the story. For every They there ought to be a We. In our case there is. Creative paranoia means developing at least as thorough a We-system as a They-system—"

"Wait, wait, first where's the Haig and Haig, be a gracious host, second what is a 'They-system,' I don't pull Chebychev's Theorem on you, do I?"

"I mean what They and Their hired psychiatrists call 'delusional systems.' Needless to say, 'delusions' are always officially defined. We don't have to worry about questions of real or unreal. They only talk out of expediency. It's the *system* that matters. How the data arrange themselves inside it. Some are consistent, others fall apart. Your idea that Pointsman sent Gloaming takes a wrong fork. Without any contrary set of delusions—delusions about ourselves, which I'm calling a We-system—the Gloaming idea might have been all right—"

"Delusions about ourselves?"

"Not real ones."

"But officially defined."

"Out of expediency, yes."

"Well, you're playing Their game, then."

"Don't let it bother you. You'll find you can operate quite well. Seeing as we haven't won yet, it isn't really much of a problem."

Roger is totally confused. At this point, in wanders who but Milton Gloaming with a black man Roger recognizes now as one of the two herb-smokers in the furnace room under Clive Mossmoon's office. His name is Jan Otyiyumbu and he's a Schwarzkommando liaison man. One of Blodget Waxwing's apache lieutenants shows up with his girl who's not walking so much as dancing, very fluid and slow, a dance in which Osbie Feel, popping out of the kitchen now with his shirt off (and a Porky Pig tattoo on his stomach? How long has Feel had *that*?) correctly identifies the influence of heroin.

It's a little bewildering—if this is a "We-system," why isn't it at least thoughtful enough to interlock in a reasonable way, like They-systems do?

"That's exactly it," Osbie screams, belly-dancing Porky into a wide alarming grin, "*They're* the rational ones. We piss on Their rational arrangements. Don't we . . . Mexico?"

"Hoorah!" cry the others. Well taken, Osbie.

Sir Stephen Dodson-Truck sits by the window, cleaning a Sten. Outside, blowing over its dorsal and summer stillness, London today can feel advance chills of Austerity. There isn't a word in Sir Stephen's head right now. He is completely involved with the weapon. He no longer thinks about his wife, Nora, although she's out there, in some room, still surrounded by her planetary psychics, and aimed herself now toward a peculiar fate. In recent weeks, in true messianic style, it has come clear to her that her real identity is, literally, the Force of Gravity. *I am Gravity, I am That against which the Rocket must struggle, to which the prehistoric wastes submit and are transmuted to the very substance of History.* . . . Her wheeling freaks, her seers, teleporters, astral travelers and tragic human interfaces all know of her visitation, but none see any way for her to turn. She must prove herself now—find deeper forms of renunciation, deeper than Sabbatai Zvi's apostasy before the Sublime Porte. It is a situation no

without its chances for a grood practical joke now and then
—poor Nora will be suckered into séances that wouldn't
fool your great-aunt, visits from the likes of Ronald
Cherrycoke in a Jesus Christ getup, whistling down the
wires into a hidden ultraviolet baby spot where he will
start fluorescing in most questionable taste, blithering odd
bits of Gospel together, reaching down from his crucified
altitudes to actually cop feels of Nora's girdled behind
. . . highly offended, she will flee into hallways full of
clammy invisible hands—poltergeists will back toilets up
on her, ladylike turds will bob at her virgin vertex, and
screaming *ugh*, ass dripping, girdle around her knees, she
will go staggering into her own drawing-room to find no
refuge even there, no, someone will have caused to materialize for her a lesbian elephant soixante-neuf, slimy trunks
pistoning symmetrically in and out of juicy elephant
vulvas, and when she turns to escape this horrible exhibition she'll find some playful ghost has latched the door
behind her, and another's just about to sock her in the face
with a cold Yorkshire pudding. . . .

In Pirate's maisonette, everyone is singing now a
counterforce traveling song, with Thomas Gwenhidwy,
who has not fallen to the dialectic curse of Pointsman's
Book after all, accompanying on what seems to be a rose-
wood crwth:

They've been sleeping on your shoulder,
They've been crying in your beer,
And They've sung you all Their sad lullabies,
And you thought They wanted sympathy and didn't care
    for souls,
And They never were about to put you wise.
But I'm telling you today,
That it ain't the only way,
And there's shit you won't be eating any more—
They've been paying you to love it,
But the time has come to shove it,
And it isn't a resistance, it's a war.

"It's a war," Roger sings, driving into Cuxhaven, wondering offhand how Jessica has cut her hair for Jeremy,
and how that insufferable prig would look with a thrust
chamber wrapped around his head, "it's a war . . ."

Light one up before you mosey out that door,
Once you cuddled 'em and kissed 'em,
But we're bringin' down Their system,
And it isn't a resistance, it's a war. . . .

□

These pine limbs, crackling so blue and watery, don't seem
to put out any heat at all. Confiscated weapons and ammo
lie around half-crated or piled loose inside the C-Company
perimeter. For days the U.S. Army has been out sweeping
Thuringia, busting into houses in the middle of the night.
A certain lycanthropophobia fear of Werewolves occupies
minds at higher levels. Winter is coming. Soon there won't
be enough food or coal in Germany. Potato crops toward
the end of the War, for example, all went to make alcohol
for the rockets. But there are still small-arms aplenty, and
ammunition to fit them. Where you cannot feed, you take
away weapons. Weapons and food have been firmly linked
in the governmental mind for as long as either has been
around.

On the mountainsides, patches will flash up now and
then, bright as dittany in July at the Zippo's ceremonial
touch. Pfc. Eddie Pensiero, a replacement here in the
89th Division, also an amphetamine enthusiast, sits huddling nearly on top of the fire, shivering and watching the
divisional patch on his arm, which ordinarily resembles a
cluster of rocket-noses seen out of a dilating asshole, all
in black and olive-drab, but which now looks like something even stranger than *that*, which Eddie will think of
in a minute.

Shivering is one of Eddie Pensiero's favorite pastimes.
Not the kind of shiver *normal* people get, the goose-on-
the-grave passover and gone, but shivering that *doesn't*
stop. Very hard to get used to at first. Eddie is a connoisseur of shivers. He is even able, in some strange way,
to *read* them, like Säure Bummer reads reefers, like Miklo
Thanatz reads whip-scars. But the gift isn't limited just
to Eddie's *own* shivers, oh no, they're *other* people's
shivers, too! Yeah they come in one by one, they come in
all together in groups (lately he's been growing in hi

brain a kind of discriminator circuit, learning how to separate them out). Least interesting of these shivers are the
ones with a perfectly steady frequency, no variation to
them at all. The next-to-least interesting are the freqency-
modulated kind, now faster now slower depending on information put in at the other end, wherever that might be.
Then you have the irregular waveforms that change both
in frequency and in amplitude. They have to be Fourier-
analyzed into their harmonics, which is a little tougher.
There is often coding involved, certain subfrequencies, certain power-levels—you have to be pretty good to get the
hang of these.

"Hey Pensiero." It is Eddie's Sergeant, Howard ("Slow")
Lerner. "Getcher ass offa dat fire."

"Aww, Sarge," chatters Eddie, "c'mon. I wuz just tryin'
ta get wawm."

"No ick-skew-siz, Pensiero! One o' th' koinels wants his
hair cut, *right now,* an' yer *it!*"

"Ahh, youse guys," mutters Pensiero, crawling over to
his sleeping bag and looking through his pack for comb
and scissors. He is the company barber. His haircuts,
which take hours and often days, are immediately recognizable throughout the Zone, revealing as they do the
hair-by-hair singlemindedness of the "benny" habitué.

The colonel is sitting, waiting, under an electric bulb.
The bulb is receiving its power from another enlisted man,
who sits back in the shadows hand-pedaling the twin
generator cranks. It is Eddie's friend Private Paddy
("Electro") McGonigle, an Irish lad from New Jersey, one
of those million virtuous and adjusted city poor you know
from the movies—you've seen them dancing, singing,
hanging out the washing on the lines, getting drunk at
wakes, worrying about their children going bad, I just
don't know any more Faather, he's a good b'y but he's
runnin' with a crool crowd, on through every wretched
Hollywood lie down to and including this year's big hit,
A Tree Grows in Brooklyn. With his crank here young
Paddy is practicing another form of Eddie's gift, though
he's transmitting not receiving. The bulb appears to burn
steadily, but this is really a succession of electric peaks
and valleys, passing by at a speed that depends on how
fast Paddy is cranking. It's only that the wire inside the

bulb unbrightens slow enough before the next peak shows
up that fools us into seeing a steady light. It's really a
train of imperceptible light and dark. *Usually* imperceptible. The message is never conscious on Paddy's part. It is
sent by muscles and skeleton, by that circuit of his body
which has learned to work as a source of electrical power.

Right now Eddie Pensiero is shivering and not paying
much attention to that light bulb. His own message is
interesting enough. Somebody close by, out in the night,
is playing a blues on a mouth harp. "Whut's *dat?*" Eddie
wants to know, standing under the white light behind the
silent colonel in his dress uniform, "hey, McGonigle—you
hear sump'n?"

"Yeah," jeers Paddy from behind the generator, "I hear
yer dischodge, flyin' away, wit' big *wings* comin' outa th'
ass end. Dat's whut *I* hear! Yuk, yuk!"

"Aw, it's th' *bunk!*" replies Eddie Pensiero. "Y-you don't
hear no dischodge, ya big dumbheaded Mick."

"Hey, Pensiero, ya know whut a Eye-talian *submarine*
sounds like, on dat new sonar? Huh?"

"Uh . . . whut?"

"*Pinnngg*guinea-guinea-guinea wopwopwop! *Dat's* whut!
Yuk, yuk, yuk!"

"Fuck youse," sez Eddie, and commences combing the
colonel's silver-black hair.

The moment the comb contacts his head, the colonel
begins to speak. "Ordinarily, we'd spend no more than 24
hours on a house-to-house sweep. Sundown to sundown,
house to house. There's a quality of black and gold to
either end of it, that way, silhouettes, shaken skies pure as
a cyclorama. But these sunsets, out here, I don't know.
Do you suppose something has exploded somewhere?
Really—somewhere in the East? Another Krakatoa? Another name at least that exotic . . . the colors are so different now. Volcanic ash, or any finely-divided substance,
suspended in the atmosphere, can diffract the colors
strangely. Did you know that, son? Hard to believe, isn't
it? Rather a long taper if you don't mind, and just short
of combable on top. Yes, Private, the colors change, and
how! The question is, are they changing *according to
something?* Is the sun's everyday spectrum being modulated? Not at random, but systematically, by this unknown

debris in the prevailing winds? Is there information for us? Deep questions, and disturbing ones.

"Where are you from, son? I'm from Kenosha, Wisconsin. My folks have a little farm back there. Snowfields and fenceposts all the way to Chicago. The snow covers the old cars up on blocks in the yards . . . big white bundles . . . it looks like Graves Registration back there in Wisconsin."

"Heh, heh. . . ."

"Hey Pensiero," calls Paddy McGonigle, "ya still hearin' dat sound?"

"Yeah uh I t'ink it's a mouth-organ," Pensiero busily combing up single hairs, cutting each one a slightly different length, going back again and again to touch up here and there . . . God is who knows their number. Atropos is who severs them to different lengths. So, God under the aspect of Atropos, she who cannot be turned, is in possession of Eddie Pensiero tonight.

"I got *your* mouth organ," jeers Paddy, "right here! Look! A wop clarinet!"

Each long haircut is a passage. Hair is yet another kind of modulated frequency. Assume a state of grace in which all hairs were once distributed perfectly even, a time of innocence when they fell perfectly straight, all over the colonel's head. Winds of the day, gestures of distraction, sweat, itchings, sudden surprises, three-foot falls to the edge of sleep, watched skies, remembered shames, all have since written on that perfect grating. Passing through it tonight, restructuring it, Eddie Pensiero is an agent of History. Along with the reworking of the colonel's head runs the shiver-borne blues—long runs in number 2 and 3 hole correspond, tonight anyway, to passages in the deep reaches of hair, birch trunks in a very humid summer night, approaches to a stone house in a wooded park, stags paralyzed beside the high flagged walks. . . .

Blues is a matter of lower sidebands—you suck a clear note, on pitch, and then bend it lower with the muscles of your face. Muscles of your face have been laughing, tight with pain, often trying not to betray *any* emotion, all your life. Where you send the pure note is partly a function of that. There's that secular basis for blues, if the spiritual angle bothers you. . . .

"I didn't know where I was," relates the colonel. "I kept

climbing downward, along these big sheared chunks of
concrete. Black reinforcing rod poking out . . . black rust.
There were touches of royal purple in the air, not bright
enough to blur out over their edges, or change the substance of the night. They dribbled down, lengthening out,
one by one—ever seen a chicken fetus, just beginning? oh
of course not, you're a city boy. There's a lot to learn, out
on the farm. Teaches you what a chicken fetus looks like,
so that if you happen to be climbing around a concrete
mountain in the dark, and see one, or several, up in the
sky reproduced in purple, you'll know what they look
like—that's a heap better than the city, son, there you
just move from crisis to crisis, each one brand-new, nothing to couple it back onto. . . ."

Well, there he is, cautiously edging along the enormous
ruin, his hair at the moment looking *very* odd—brushed
forward from one occipital spot, forward and up in great
long points, forming a black sunflower or sunbonnet
around his face, in which the prominent feature is the
colonel's long, crawling magenta lips. Things grab up for
him out of crevices among the debris, sort of fast happy
lunge out and back in, thin pincer arms, nothing personal,
just thought I'd *grab a little night air,* ha, ha! When they
miss the colonel—as they always seem to do—why they
just zip back in with a gambler's ho-hum, well, maybe
next time. . . .

Dammit, cut off from my regiment here, gonna be captured and cremated by dacoits! *Oh Jesus there they are
now,* unthinkable Animals running low in the light from
the G-5 version of the city, red and yellow turbans,
scarred dope-fiend faces, faired as the front end of a '37
Ford, same undirected eyes, same exemption from the
Karmic Hammer—

A '37 Ford, exempt from the K.H.? C'mon quit fooling.
They'll all end up in junkyards same as th' rest!

Oh, *will they,* Skippy? Why are there so many on the
roads, then?

W-well gee, uh, Mister Information, th-th' War, I mean
there's no new cars being built right now so we all have to
keep our Old Reliable in tiptop shape cause there's not too
many mechanics left here on the home front, a-and we
shouldn't hoard gas, and we should keep that A-sticker
prominently displayed in the lower right—

Skippy, you little fool, you are off on another of your senseless and retrograde journeys. Come back, here, to the points. Here is where the paths divided. See the man back there. He is wearing a white hood. His shoes are brown. He has a nice smile, but nobody sees it. Nobody sees it because his face is always in the dark. But he is a nice man. He is the pointsman. He is called that because he throws the lever that changes the points. And we go to Happyville, instead of to Pain City. Or "Der Leid-Stadt," that's what the Germans call it. There is a mean poem about the Leid-Stadt, by a German man named Mr. Rilke. But we will not read it, because *we* are going to Happyville. The pointsman has made sure we'll go there. He hardly has to work at all. The lever is very smooth, and easy to push. Even you could push it, Skippy. If you knew where it was. But look what a lot of work he has done, with just one little push. He has sent us all the way to Happyville, instead of to Pain City. That is because he knows just where the points and the lever are. He is the only kind of man who puts in very little work and makes big things happen, all over the world. He could have sent you on the right trip back there, Skippy. You can have *your* fantasy if you want, you probably don't deserve anything better, but Mister Information tonight is in a kind mood. He will show you Happyville. He will begin by reminding you of the 1937 Ford. Why is that dacoit-faced auto still on the roads? You said "the War," just as you rattled over the points onto the wrong track. The War *was* the set of points. Eh? Yesyes, Skippy, the truth is that the War is keeping things alive. *Things.* The Ford is only one of them. The Germans-and-Japs story was only one, rather surrealistic version of the real War. The real War is always there. The dying tapers off now and then, but the War is still killing lots and lots of people. Only right now it is killing them in more subtle ways. Often in ways that are too complicated, even for us, at this level, to trace. But the right people are dying, just as they do when armies fight. The ones who stand up, in Basic, in the middle of the machine-gun pattern. The ones who do not have faith in their Sergeants. The ones who slip and show a moment's weakness to the Enemy. These are the ones the War cannot use, and so they die. The right ones survive. The others, it's said, even *know* they have a short

life expectancy. But they persist in acting the way they
do. Nobody knows why. Wouldn't it be nice if we could
eliminate them completely? Then no one would have to
be killed in the War. That would be fun, wouldn't it,
Skippy?

Jeepers, it sure *would*, Mister Information! Wow, I-I
can't wait to see Happyville!

Happily, he doesn't have to wait at all. One of the
dacoits comes leaping with a whistling sound, ecru silk
cord strung buzzing tight between his fists, eager let's-get-
to-it grin, and just at the same moment a pair of arms
comes up out of a fissure in the ruins, and gathers the
colonel down to safety just in time. The dacoit falls on his
ass, and sits there trying to pull the cord apart, muttering
oh shit, which even dacoits do too.

"You are under the mountain," a voice announces. Stony
cave-acoustics in here. "Please remember from this point
on to obey all pertinent regulations."

His guide is a kind of squat robot, dark gray plastic
with rolling headlamp eyes. It is shaped something like a
crab. "That's Cancer in Latin," sez the robot, "and in
Kenosha, too!" It will prove to be addicted to one-liners
that never quite come off for anyone but it.

"Here is Muffin-tin Road," announces the robot, "note
the smiling faces on all the houses here." Upstairs windows are eyes, picket fence is teeth. Nose is the front door.

"Sa-a-a-y," asks the colonel, taken by a sudden thought,
"does it ever *snow* here in Happyville?"

"Does what ever snow?"

"You're evading."

"I'm evading-room vino from Visconsin," sings this boorish machine, "and you oughta see the nurses run! So what
else is new, Jackson?" The squat creature is actually *chewing gum*, a Laszlo Jamf variation on polyvinyl chloride,
very malleable, even sending out detachable molecules
which, through an ingenious Osmo-elektrische Schalter-
werke, developed by Siemens, is transmitting, in code, a
damn fair approximation of Beeman's licorice flavor to the
robot crab's brain.

"Mister Information *always* answers questions."

"For what he's making, I'd even question answers.
Does it ever snow? Of *course* it snows in Happyville. Lotta
snowmen'd sure be sore if it didn't!"

"I recall, back in Wisconsin, the wind used to blow right up the walk, like a visitor who expects to be let in. Sweeps the snow up against the front door, leaves it drifted there. . . . Ever get that in Happyville?"

"Old stuff," sez the robot.

"Anybody ever open his front door, while the wind was doing that, eh?"

"Thousands of times."

"*Then,*" pounces the colonel, "if the door is the house's *nose,* and the door is open, a-and all of those snowy-white crystals are blowing up from Muffin-tin Road in a big cloud right into the—"

"*Aagghh!*" screams the plastic robot, and scuttles way into a narrow alley. The colonel finds himself alone in a brown and wine-aged district of the city: sandstone and adobe colors sweep away in a progress of walls, rooftops, streets, not a tree in sight, and who's this come strolling down the Schokoladestrasse? Why, it's Laszlo Jamf himself, grown to a prolonged old age, preserved like a '37 Ford against the World's ups and downs, which are never more than damped-out changes in smile, wide-pearly to wistfully gauze, inside Happyville here. Dr. Jamf is wearing a bow tie of a certain limp grayish lavender, a color for long dying afternoons through conservatory windows, minor-keyed lieder about days gone by, plaintive pianos, pipesmoke in a stuffy parlor, overcast Sunday walks by canals . . . here the two men are, dry-scratched precisely, attentively on this afternoon, and the bells across the canal are tolling the hour: the men have come from very far away, after a journey neither quite remembers, on a mission of some kind. But each has been kept ignorant of the other's role. . . .

Now it turns out that this light bulb over the colonel's head here is the same identical Osram light bulb that Franz Pökler used to keep next to in his bunk at the underground rocket works at Nordhausen. Statistically (so Their story goes), every n-thousandth light bulb is gonna be perfect, all the delta-q's piling up just right, so we shouldn't be surprised that this one's still around, burning brightly. But the truth is even more stupendous. This bulb is *immortal!* It's been around, in fact, since the twenties, has that old-timery point at the tip and is less pear-shaped than more contemporary bulbs. Wotta history, this bulb, if only it could speak—well, as a matter of fact, it *can* speak. It is dictating the muscular modulations of Paddy Mc-Gonigle's cranking tonight, this is a loop here, with feedback through Paddy to the generator again. Here it is,

THE STORY OF BYRON THE BULB

Byron was to've been manufactured by Tungsram in Budapest. He would probably have been grabbed up by the ace salesman Géza Rózsavölgyi's father Sandor, who covered all the Transylvanian territory and had begun to go native enough to where the home office felt vaguely paranoid about him throwing some horrible spell on the whole operation if they didn't give him what he wanted. Actually he was a salesman who wanted his son to be a doctor, and that came true. But it may have been the bad witch-leery auras around Budapest that got the birth of Byron reassigned at the last minute to Osram, in Berlin. Reassigned, yes. There is a Bulb Baby Heaven, amiably satirized as if it was the movies or something, well Big *Business*, ha, ha! But don't let Them fool you, this *is* a bureaucracy first, and a Bulb Baby Heaven only as a sort of sideline. All overhead—yes, out of its own pocket the Company is springing for square leagues of organdy, hogsheads of IG Farben pink and blue Baby Dye, hundred-weights of clever Siemens Electric Baby Bulb Pacifiers, giving the suckling Bulb the shape of a 110-volt current without the least trickle of power. One way or another, these Bulb folks are in the business of providing the appearance of power, power against the night, without the reality.

Actually, B.B.H. is rather shabby. The brown rafters drip cobwebs. Now and then a roach shows up on the floor, and all the Babies try to roll over to look (being Bulbs they *seem* perfectly symmetrical, Skippy, but don't forget the contact at the top of the thread) going uh-guh! uhhhh-*guh!*, glowing feebly at the bewildered roach sitting paralyzed and squashable out on the bare boards, rushing, reliving the terror of some sudden blast of current out of nowhere and high overhead the lambent, all-seeing Bulb. In their innocence, the Baby Bulbs don't know what to make of this roach's abreaction—they feel his fright, but don't know what it is. They just want to be his friend. He's interesting and has good moves. Everybody's excited except for Byron, who considers the other Bulb Babies a bunch of saps. It is a constant struggle to turn their thoughts on anything meaningful. Hi there Babies, I'm Byron-the-Bulb! Here to sing a little song to you, that goes—

> Light-up, and-shine, you—in-cande-scent Bulb Ba-bies!
> Looks-like ya got ra-bies
> Just lay there foamin' and a-screamin' like a buncha
>   little demons,
> I'm deliv'rin' unto you a king-dom of roa-ches,
> And no-thin' ap-proaches
> That joyful feelin' when-you're up-on the ceilin'
> Lookin' down—night and day—on the king-dom you
>   sur-vey,
> They'll come out 'n' love ya till the break of dawn,
> But they run like hell when that light comes on!
> So shine on, Baby Bulbs, you're the wave of the fu-ture,
> And I'm here to recruit ya,
> In m'great crusade,
> Just sing along Babies—come-on-and-join-the-big-
>   pa-rade!

Trouble with Byron's he's an old, old soul, trapped inside the glass prison of a Baby Bulb. He hates this place, lying on his back waiting to get manufactured, nothing to listen to on the speakers but Charleston music, now and then an address to the Nation, what kind of a setup's that? Byron wants to get out of here and *into it*, needless to say he's been developing all kinds of nervous ailments, Baby Bulb Diaper Rash, which is a sort of corrosion on his screw threads, Bulb Baby Colic, a tight spasm of high resistance someplace among the deep loops of tungsten wire, Bulb Baby Hyperventilation, where it actually feels like his vacuum's been broken though there is no organic basis. . . .

When M-Day finally does roll around, you can bet Byron's elated. He has passed the time hatching some really insane grandiose plans—he's gonna organize all the Bulbs, see, get him a power base in Berlin, he's already hep to the Strobing Tactic, all you do is develop the knack (Yogic, almost) of shutting off and on at a rate close to

the human brain's alpha rhythm, and you can actually
trigger an *epileptic fit!* True. Byron has had a vision against
the rafters of his ward, of 20 million Bulbs, all over
Europe, at a given sychronizing pulse arranged by one of
his many agents in the Grid, all these Bulbs beginning to
strobe *together*, humans thrashing around the 20 million
rooms like fish on the beaches of Perfect Energy— Attention, humans, this has been a warning to you. Next time,
a few of us will *explode*. Ha-ha. Yes we'll unleash our
Kamikaze squads! You've heard of the Kirghiz Light? well
that's the ass end of a firefly compared to what we're
gonna—oh, you haven't heard of the—oh, well, too bad.
Cause a few Bulbs, say a million, a mere 5% of our number, are more than willing to flame out in one grand burst
instead of patiently waiting out their design hours. . . . So
Byron dreams of his Guerrilla Strike Force, gonna get
Herbert Hoover, Stanley Baldwin, all of them, right in the
face with one coordinated blast. . . .

Is Byron in for a rude awakening! There is already an
organization, a human one, known as "Phoebus," the international light-bulb cartel, headquartered in Switzerland.
Run pretty much by International GE, Osram, and Associated Electrical Industries of Britain, which are in turn
owned 100%, 29% and 46%, respectively, by the General
Electric Company in America. Phoebus fixes the prices
and determines the operational lives of all the bulbs in the
world, from Brazil to Japan to Holland (although Philips
in Holland is the mad dog of the cartel, apt at any time
to cut loose and sow disaster throughout the great Combination). Given this state of general repression, there
seems noplace for a newborn Baby Bulb to start but at the
bottom.

But Phoebus doesn't know yet that Byron is immortal.
He starts out his career at an all-girl opium den in Charlot-
tenburg, almost within sight of the statue of Wernher
Siemens, burning up in a sconce, one among many bulb
witnessing the more languorous forms of Republican dec
adence. He gets to know all the bulbs in the place, Benit
the Bulb over in the next sconce who's always planning an
escape, Bernie down the hall in the toilet, who has al
kinds of urolagnia jokes to tell, his mother Brenda in th
kitchen who talks of hashish hush puppies, dildos rigge

to pump floods of paregoric orgasm to the capillaries of the womb, prayers to Astarte and Lilith, queen of the night, reaches into the true Night of the Other, cold and naked on linoleum floors after days without sleep, the dreams and tears become a natural state. . . .

One by one, over the months, the other bulbs burn out, and are gone. The first few of these hit Byron hard. He's still a new arrival, still hasn't accepted his immortality. But on through the burning hours he starts to learn about the transience of others: learns that loving them while they're here becomes easier, and also more intense—to love as if each design-hour will be the last. Byron soon enough becomes a Permanent Old-Timer. Others can recognize his immortality on sight, but it's never discussed except in a general way, when folklore comes flickering in from other parts of the Grid, tales of the Immortals, one in a kabbalist's study in Lyons who's supposed to know magic, another in Norway outside a warehouse facing arctic whiteness with a stoicism more southerly bulbs begin strobing faintly just at the thought of. If other Immortals *are* out there, they remain silent. But it is a silence with much, perhaps, everything, in it.

After Love, then, Byron's next lesson is Silence.

As his burning lengthens toward 600 hours, the monitors in Switzerland begin to keep more of an eye on Byron. The Phoebus Surveillance Room is located under a little-known Alp, a chilly room crammed full of German electro hardware, glass, brass, ebonite, and silver, massive terminal blocks shaggy with copper clips and screws, and a cadre of super-clean white-robed watchers who wander meter to meter, light as snowdevils, making sure that nothing's going wrong, that through no bulb shall the mean operating life be extended. You can imagine what it would do to the market if *that* started happening.

Byron passes Surveillance's red-line at 600 hours, and immediately, as a matter of routine, he is checked out for filament resistance, burning temperature, vacuum, power consumption. Everything's normal. Now Byron is to be checked out every 50 hours hereafter. A soft chime will go off in the monitoring station whenever it's time.

At 800 hours—another routine precaution—a Berlin agent is sent out to the opium den to transfer Byron. She is wearing asbestos-lined kid gloves and seven-inch spike heels, no not so she can fit in with the crowd, but so that she can reach that sconce to unscrew Byron. The other bulbs watch, in barely subdued terror. The word goes out along the Grid. At something close to the speed of light, every bulb, Azos looking down the empty black Bakelite streets, Nitralampen and Wotan Gs at night soccer matches, Just-Wolframs, Monowatts and Siriuses, every bulb in Europe knows what's happened. They are silent with impotence, with surrender in the face of struggles they thought were all myth. *We can't help,* this common thought humming through pastures of sleeping sheep, down Autobahns and to the bitter ends of coaling piers in the North, *there's never been anything we could do....* Anyone shows us the meanest hope of transcending and the Committee on Incandescent Anomalies comes in and takes him away. Some do protest, maybe, here and there, but it's only information, glow-modulated, harmless, nothing close to the explosions in the faces of the powerful that Byron once envisioned, back there in his Baby ward, in his innocence.

He is taken to Neukölln, to a basement room, the home of a glassblower who is afraid of the night and who will keep Byron glowing and on watch over all the flint bowls, the griffins and flower-ships, ibexes in mid-leap, green spider-webs, somber ice-deities. This is one of many so-called "control points," where suspicious bulbs can be monitored easily.

In less than a fortnight, a gong sounds along the ice and stone corridors of the Phoebus headquarters, and faces swivel over briefly from their meters. Not too many gongs around here. Gongs are special. Byron has passed 1000 hours, and the procedure now is standard: the Committee on Incandescent Anomalies sends a hit man to Berlin.

But here something odd happens. Yes, damned odd. The plan is to smash up Byron and send him back right there in the shop to cullet and batch—salvage the tungsten, of course—and let him be reincarnated in the glassblower's next project (a balloon setting out on a journey from the top of a white skyscraper). This wouldn't be too bad a deal for Byron—he knows as well as Phoebus does how many hours he has on him. Here in the shop he's watched enough glass being melted back into the structureless pool from which all glass forms spring and re-spring, and wouldn't mind going through it himself. But he is trapped on the Karmic wheel. The glowing orange batch is a taunt, a cruelty. There's no escape for Byron, he's doomed to an infinite regress of sockets and bulbsnatchers. In zips young Hansel Geschwindig, a Weimar street urchin—twirls Byron out of the ceiling into a careful pocket and Ge-ssssschhhh*win*dig! out the door again. Darkness invades the dreams of the glassblower. Of all the unpleasantries his dreams grab in out of the night air, an extinguished light is the worst. Light, in his dreams, was always hope: the basic, mortal hope. As the contacts break helically away, hope turns to darkness, and the glassblower wakes sharply tonight crying, "Who? *Who?*"

Phoebus isn't exactly thrown into a frenzy. It's happened before. There is still a procedure to follow. It means more overtime for some employees, so there's that vague, full-boweled pleasure at the windfall, along with an equally vague excitement at the break in routine. You want high emotion, forget Phoebus. Their stonefaced search parties move out into the streets. They know more or less where in the city to look. They are assuming that no one among their consumers knows of Byron's immortality. So the data for *Non*-immortal Bulbsnatchings ought to apply also to Byron. And the data happen to hump up in poor sections, Jewish sections, drug, homosexual, prostitute, and magic sections of the capital. Here are the most logical bulbsnatchers, in terms of what the crime is. Look at all the propaganda. It's a *moral* crime. Phoebus discovered—one of the great undiscovered discoveries of our time—that consumers need to feel a sense of sin. That guilt, in proper invisible hands, is a most powerful weapon. In America, Lyle Bland and his psychologists had figures, expert testimony and money (money in the Puritan sense—an outward and visible O.K. on their intentions) enough to tip the Discovery of Guilt at the cusp between scientific theory and fact. Growth rates in later years were to bear Bland out (actually what bore Bland out was an honorary pallbearer sextet of all the senior members of Salitieri, Poore, Nash, De Brutus and Short, plus Lyle, Jr., who was sneezing. Buddy at the last min-

ute decided to go see *Dracula*. He was better off). Of all
the legacies Bland left around, the Bulbsnatching Heresy
was perhaps his grandest. It doesn't just mean that somebody isn't buying a bulb. It also means that same somebody is not putting any power in that socket! It is a sin
both against Phoebus and against the Grid. Neither one is
about to let *that* get out of hand.

So, out go the Phoebus flatfoots, looking for the snatched
Byron. But the urchin has already left town, gone to Hamburg, traded Byron to a Reeperbahn *prostitute* so he can
shoot up some morphine—the young woman's customer tonight is a cost-accountant who likes to have light bulbs
screwed into his asshole, and this john has also brought a
little *hashish to smoke,* so by the time he leaves he's forgotten about Byron still there in his asshole—doesn't ever,
in fact, find out, because when he finally gets around to
sitting down (having stood up in trolleys all the way
home) it's on his own home toilet and plop! there goes
Byron in the water and flusssshhhh! away down the waste
lines to the Elbe estuary. He is just round enough to get
through smoothly all the way. For days he floats over the
North Sea, till he reaches Helgoland, that red-and-white
Napoleon pastry tipped in the sea. He stays there for a
while at a hotel between the Hengst and the Mönch, till
being brought back one day to the mainland by a very old
priest who's been put hep to Byron's immortality in the
course of a routine dream about the taste of a certain
1911 Hochheimer ... suddenly here's the great Berlin
Eispalast, a booming, dim iron-trussed cavern, the smell o
women in the blue shadows—perfumes, leathers, fur skat-
ing-costumes, ice-dust in the air, flashing legs, jutting
haunches, desire in grippelike flashes, helplessness at the
end of a crack-the-whip, rocketing through beams of sun
light choked with the powdered ice, and a voice in the
blurred mirror underfoot saying, "Find the one who ha
performed this miracle. He is a saint. Expose him. Expedit
his canonization. . . ." The name is on a list the old ma
presently draws up of about a thousand tourists who'v
been in and out of Helgoland since Byron was found o
the beach. The priest begins a search by train, footpat
and Hispano-Suiza, checking out each of the tourists o
his list. But he gets no farther than Nürnberg, where h

valise, with Byron wrapped inside in an alb, is ripped off by a transsectite, a Lutheran named Mausmacher who likes to dress up in Roman regalia. This Mausmacher, not content with standing in front of his own mirror making papal crosses, thinks it will be a really bizarre kick to go out to the Zeppelin field to a Nazi torchlight rally in full drag, and walk around blessing people at random. Green torches flaring, red swastikas, twinkling brasses and Father Mausmacher, checking out tits 'n' asses, waistlines 'n' baskets, humming a clerical little tune, some Bach riff, smiling as he moves through the Sieg Heils and choruses of "Die Fahne Hoch." Unknown to him, Byron slides out of the stolen vestments onto the ground. He is then walked past by several hundred thousand boots and shoes, and not one so much as brushes him, natch. He is scavenged next day (the field now deathempty, columned, pale, streaked with long mudpuddles, morning clouds lengthening behind the gilded swastika and wreath) by a poor Jewish ragpicker, and taken on, on into another 15 years of preservation against chance and against Phoebus. He will be screwed into mother (*Mutter*) after mother, as the female threads of German light-bulb sockets are known, for some reason that escapes everybody.

The cartel have already gone over to Contingency Plan B, which assumes a seven-year statute of limitations, after which Byron will be considered legally burned out. Meanwhile, the personnel taken off of Byron's case are busy tracking a long-lived bulb that once occupied a socket on the porch of an army outpost in the Amazon jungle, Beatriz the Bulb, who has just been stolen, mysteriously, by an Indian raiding party.

Through his years of survival, all these various rescues of Byron happen as if by accident. Whenever he can, he tries to instruct any bulbs nearby in the evil nature of Phoebus, and in the need for solidarity against the cartel. He has come to see how Bulb must move beyond its role as conveyor of light-energy alone. Phoebus has restricted Bulb to this one identity. "But there are other frequencies, above and below the visible band. Bulb can give heat. Bulb can provide energy for plants to grow, illegal plants, inside closets, for example. Bulb can penetrate the sleeping eye, and operate among the dreams of men." Some bulbs

listened attentively—others thought of ways to fink to
Phoebus. Some of the older anti-Byronists were able to
fool with their parameters in systematic ways that would
show up on the ebonite meters under the Swiss mountain:
there were even a few self-immolations, hoping to draw
the hit men down.

Any talk of Bulb's transcendence, of course, was clear
subversion. Phoebus based everything on bulb efficiency—
the ratio of the usable power coming out, to the power put
in. The Grid demanded that this ratio stay as small as
possible. That way they got to sell more juice. On the
other hand, low efficiency meant longer burning hours, and
that cut into bulb sales for Phoebus. In the beginning
Phoebus tried increasing filament resistance, reducing the
hours of life on the sly and gradually—till the Grid noticed
a fall-off in revenues, and started screaming. The two
parties by and by reached an accord on a compromise
bulb-life figure that would bring in enough money for
both of them, and to go fifty-fifty on the costs of the anti-
bulbsnatching campaign. Along with a more subtle attack
against those criminal souls who forswear bulbs entirely
and use candles. Phoebus's long-standing arrangement with
the Meat Cartel was to restrict the amount of tallow in
circulation by keeping more fat in meat to be sold regardless of cardiac problems that might arise, and redirecting
most of what was trimmed off into soap production. Soap
in those days was a booming concern. Among the consumers, the Bland Institute had discovered deep feelings
about shit. Even at that, meat and soap were minor interlocks of Phoebus. More important were items like tungsten.
Another reason why Phoebus couldn't cut down bulb life
too far. Too many tungsten filaments would eat into available stockpiles of the metal—China being the major world
source, this also brought in very delicate questions of
Eastern policy—and disturb the arrangement between
General Electric and Krupp about how much tungsten
carbide would be produced, where and when and what the
prices would be. The guidelines settled on were $37–$90 a
pound in Germany, $200–$400 a pound in the U.S. This
directly governed the production of machine tools, and
thus all areas of light and heavy industry. When the War
came, some people thought it unpatriotic of GE to have

given Germany an edge like that. But nobody with any power. Don't worry.

Byron, as he burns on, sees more and more of this pattern. He learns how to make contact with other kinds of electric appliances, in homes, in factories and out in the streets. Each has something to tell him. The pattern gathers in his soul (*Seele*, as the core of the earlier carbon filament was known in Germany), and the grander and clearer it grows, the more desperate Byron gets. Someday he will know everything, and still be as impotent as before. His youthful dreams of organizing all the bulbs in the world seem impossible now—the Grid is wide open, all messages can be overheard, and there are more than enough traitors out on the line. Prophets traditionally don't last long—they are either killed outright, or given an accident serious enough to make them stop and think, and most often they do pull back. But on Byron has been visited an even better fate. He is condemned to go on forever, knowing the truth and powerless to change anything. No longer will he seek to get off the wheel. His anger and frustration will grow without limit, and he will find himself, poor perverse bulb, enjoying it. . . .

Laszlo Jamf walks away down the canal, where dogs are swimming now, dogs in packs, dogs heads bobbing down the scummy canals . . . dogs' heads, chess knights, also may be found invisible in the air over secret airbases, in the thickest fogs, conditions of temperature, pressure and humidity form Springer-shapes the tuned flyer can feel, the radars can see, the helpless passengers can almost glimpse, now and then, out the little window, as through sheets of vapor . . . it is the kind Dog, the Dog no man ever conditioned, who is there for us at beginnings and ends, and journeys we have to take, helpless, but not quite unwilling. . . . The pleats in Jamf's suit go weaving away like iris leaves in a backyard wind. The colonel is left alone in Happyville. The steel city waits him, the even cloud-light raising a white streak down each great building, all of them set up as modulations on the perfect grid of the streets, each tower cut off at a different height— and where is the Comb that will move through *this* and

restore the old perfect Cartesian harmony? where are the
great Shears from the sky that will readjust Happyville?

There is no need to bring in blood or violence here. But
the colonel does have his head tilted back now in what
may truly be surrender: his throat is open to the pain-
radiance of the Bulb. Paddy McGonigle is the only other
witness, and he, a one-man power system with dreams of
his own, wants the colonel out of the way as much as
anyone. Eddie Pensiero, with the blues flooding his shaking muscles, the down, mortal blues, is holding his scissors
in a way barbers aren't supposed to. The points, shuddering in the electric cone, are aiming downward. Eddie
Pensiero's fist tightens around the steel loops his fingers
have slid out of. The colonel, with a last tilt of his head,
exposes his jugular, clearly impatient with the—

□

She comes riding into town on a stolen bicycle: a white
kerchief at her crown, fluttering behind in points, a distinguished emissary from a drained and captured land,
herself full of ancient title, but nothing in the way of usable
power, not even a fantasy of it. She's wearing a lean white
dress, a tennis dress from prewar summers, falling now not
in knife-edge pleats but softer, more accidental, half-crisp,
touches of blue in its deeper folds, a dress for changes in
the weather, a dress to be flowed upon by shadows of
leaves, by a crumble of brown and sun-yellow moving
across it and on as she coasts preoccupied but without
private smiles, under the leafy trees that line the road of
hard-packed dirt. Her hair is wound, in braids, up on her
head, which she holds not too high nor what used to be
called "gravely," but toward (say against) a particular
future, for the first time since the Casino Hermann Goering
. . . and she's not of our moment, our time, at all.

The outermost sentry peers from his rusty-boned cement
ruin, and for two full pedal-swings they are both, he and
Katje, out in the daylight, blending with packed earth,
rust, blobbing perforations of sunlight cold gold and slick
as glass, the fresh wind in the trees. Hyperthyroidal African eyes, their irises besieged as early cornflowers by the

crowding fields of white ... Ooga-*booga!* Gwine jump on dis *drum* hyah! Tell de res' ob de trahb back in de village, yowzah!

So, DUMdumdumdum, DUMdumdumdum, O.K., but still there's no room in her demeanor for even curiosity (of course weren't there going to be drums, a chance for violence? A snake jumping off of a limb, a very large presence ahead among the thousand bowing treetops, a scream inside herself, a leap upward into primal terror, surrendering to it and so—she has dreamt—regaining her soul, her long-lost self ...). Nor will she waste more than token glances now on the German lawns rushing so deeply away into green hazes or hills, the pale limbs of marble balusters beside sanitarium walks that curve restlessly, in a fever, a stifling, into thickets of penis-budded sprig and thorn so old, so without comfort that eyes are drawn, seized by the tear-glands and dragged to find, to find at all cost, the path that has disappeared so suddenly ... or to look behind to hold on to some trace of the spa, a corner of the Sprudelhof, the highest peak of the white-sugar bandstand, something to counteract Pan's whisper inside the dark grove *Come in ... forget them. Come in here. ...* No. Not Katje. She has been into the groves and thickets. She has danced naked and spread her cunt to the horns of grove-dwelling beasts. She has left the moon in the soles of her feet, taken its tides with the surfaces of her brain. Pan was a lousy lover. Today, in public, they have no more than nervous glances for each other.

What does happen now, and this is quite alarming, is that out of nowhere suddenly appear a full dancing-chorus of Herero men. They are dressed in white sailor suits designed to show off asses, crotches, slim waists and shapely pectorals, and they are carrying a girl all in silver lamé, a loud brassy dame after the style of Diamond Lil or Texas Guinan. As they set her down, everyone begins to dance and sing:

> Pa—ra—nooooiiiia, Pa-ra-noia!
> Ain't it grand ta see, that good-time face, again!
> Pa-ra-*noi*-ya, boy oh boy, yer
> Just a bit of you-know-what
> From way back when!
> Even Goya, couldn't draw ya,

Not the way you looked, just kickin' in that door—
Call a lawyer, Paranoia,
Lemme will my ass to you, for-ever-more!

Then Andreas and Pavel come out in tap shoes (liberated from a rather insolent ENSA show that came through
in July) to do one of those staccato tap-and-sing numbers:

Pa- ra- noi— (clippety-clippety-clippety cl[ya,]op!)
Pa- ra- noi— (shuffle*stomp!* shuffle*stomp!* shuffle*stomp!*
    [and] cl[ya,]op! clickety cl[Ain't]ick) it grand (clop)
    ta (clop) see (clippy*clop*) yer good-time face again! etc.

Well, Katje realizes long before the first 8 bars of all this
that the brazen blond bombshell is none other than herself: *she* is doing a dance routine with these black sailors-
ashore. Having gathered also that she is the allegorical
figure of Paranoia (a grand old dame, a little wacky but
pure heart), she must say that she finds the jazzy vulgarity
of this music a bit distressing. What she had in mind was
more of an Isadora Duncan routine, classical and full of
gauzes, and—well, *white*. What Pirate Prentice briefed her
on was folklore, politics, Zonal strategies—but *not blackness*. When that was what she most needed to know about.
How can she pass now through so much blackness to redeem herself? How can she expect to find Slothrop? among
such *blackness* (subvocalizing the word as an old man
might speak the name of a base public figure, letting it
gutter out into *real* blackness: into being spoken no more).
There is that stubborn, repressive heat to her thoughts. It
is none of your *heavy* racist skin-prickling, no, but a feeling
of one more burden, along with the scarcity of food in the
Zone, the chicken-coop, cave or basement lodgings at sun-
fall, the armed-occupation phobias and skulkings as bad
as Holland last year, comfortable in here at least, lotos-
snuggly, but disastrous out in the World of Reality she still
believes in and will never give up hoping to rejoin someday. All that's not bad enough, no, *now* she must also
endure blackness. Her ignorance of it must see her
through.

With Andreas she is charming, she radiates that sensuality peculiar to women who are concerned with an absent
lover's safety. But then she must see Enzian. Their firs

meeting. Each in a way has been loved by Captain Blicero. Each had to arrive at some way of making it bearable, just bearable, for just long enough, one day by one. . . .

"Oberst. I am happy—" her voice breaks. Genuinely. Her head inclines across his desk no longer than is necessary to thank, to declare her passivity. The *hell* she's happy.

He nods, angles his beard at a chair. This, then, is the Golden Bitch of Blicero's last letters from Holland. Enzian formed no image of her then, too taken up, too gagged with sorrow at what was happening to Weissmann. She seemed then only one of the expected forms of horror that must be populating his world. But, ethnic when he least wants to be, Enzian came after a while to think of her as the great Kalahari rock painting of the White Woman, white from the waist down, carrying bow and arrows, trailed by her black handmaiden through an erratic space, stone and deep, figures of all sizes moving to and fro. . . .

But here is the true Golden Bitch. He's surprised at how young and slender she is—a paleness as of having begun to leak away from this world, likely to vanish entirely at any too-reckless grab. She knows her own precarious thinness, her leukemia of soul, and she teases with it. You must want her, but never indicate it—not by eyes or move—or she will clarify, dead gone as smoke above a trail moving into the desert, and you'll never have the chance again.

"You must have seen him more recently than I." He speaks quietly. She is surprised at his politeness. Disappointed: she was expecting more force. Her lip has begun to lift. "How did he seem?"

"Alone." Her brusque and sideways nod. Gazing back at him with the best neutrality she can be sure of in the circs. She means, You were not with him, when he needed you.

"He was always alone."

She understands then that it isn't timidity, she was wrong. It is decency. The man wants to be decent. He leaves himself open. (So does she, but only because everything that might hurt has long been numbed out. There's small risk for Katje.) But Enzian risks what former lovers risk whenever the Beloved is present, in fact or in word: deepest possibilities for shame, for sense of loss renewed, or humiliation and mockery. Shall she mock? Has he made that too easy—

and then, turning, counted on her for fair play? Can she be as honest as he, without risking too much? "He was dying," she tells him, "he looked very old. I don't even know if he left Holland alive."

"He—" and this hesitation may be (a) in consideration of her feelings, or (b) for reasons of Schwarzkommando security, or (c) both of the above . . . but then, hell, the Principle of Maximizing Risk takes over again: "he got as far as the Lüneberg Heath. If you didn't know, you ought to."

"You've been looking for him."

"Yes. So has Slothrop been, though I don't think Slothrop knows that."

"Slothrop and I—" she looks around the room, her eyes skitter off metal surfaces, papers, facets of salt, cannot come to rest anywhere. As if making a desperate surprise confession: "Everything is so remote now. I don't really know why they sent me out here. I don't know any more who Slothrop really was. There's a failure in the *light*. I can't *see*. It's all going away from me. . . ."

It isn't yet time to touch her, but Enzian reaches out gives a friendly chin-up tap on the back of her hand, a military now-see-here. "There *are* things to hold to. None of it may look real, but some of it is. Really."

"*Really*." They both start laughing. Hers is weary-European, slow, head-shaking. Once she would have been assessing as she laughed, speaking of edges, deeps, profit and loss, H-hours and points of no return—she would have been laughing *politically*, in response to a power-predicament, because there might be nothing else to do. But now she's only laughing. As she once laughed with Slothrop, back at the Casino Hermann Goering.

So she's only been talking with Enzian about a common friend. Is this how the Vacuum feels?

"Slothrop and I" didn't work too well. Should she have said "Blicero and I"? What would *that* have got her into with the African?

"Blicero and I," he begins softly, watching her over burnished cheekbones, cigarette smoldering in his curled right hand, "we were only close in certain ways. There were doors I did not open. Could not. Around here, I play an omniscient. I'd say don't give me away, but it wouldn't matter. Their minds are made up. I am the Berlin Snoot supreme, Oberhauptberlinerschnauze Enzian. I know it all, and they don't trust me. They gossip in a general way about me and Blicero, as yarns to be spun—the truth wouldn't change either their distrust or my Unlimited Access. They'd only be passing a story along, another story. But the truth must mean something to you.

"The Blicero I loved was a very young man, in love with empire, poetry, his own arrogance. Those all must have been important to me once. What I am now grew from that. A former self is a fool, an insufferable ass, but he's still human, you'd no more turn him out than you'd turn out any other kind of cripple, would you?"

He seems to be asking her for real advice. Are these the sort of problems that occupy his time? What about the Rocket, the Empty Ones, the perilous infancy of his nation?

"What *can* Blicero matter to you?" is what she finally asks.

He doesn't have to think for long. He has often imagined the coming of a Questioner. "At this point, I would take you to a balcony. An observation deck. I would show you the Raketen-Stadt. Plexiglass maps of the webs we maintain across the Zone. Underground schools, systems for distributing food and medicine. . . . We would gaze down on staffrooms, communications centers, laboratories, clinics. I would say—"

"All this will I give you, if you will but—"

"*Negative.* Wrong story. I would say: This is what I have become. An estranged figure at a certain elevation and distance . . ." who looks out over the Raketen-Stadt in the amber evenings, with washed and darkening cloud sheets behind him—"who has lost everything else but this vantage. There is no heart, anywhere now, no human heart left in which I exist. Do you know what that feels like?"

He is a lion, this man, ego-mad—but despite everything, Katje likes him. "But if he were still alive—"

"No way to know. I have letters he wrote after he left your city. He was changing. Terribly. You ask what he could matter to me. My slender white adventurer, grown twenty years sick and old—the last heart in which I might have been granted some being—was changing, toad to prince, prince to fabulous monster.... 'If he is alive,' he may have changed by now past our recognition. We could have driven under him in the sky today and never seen. Whatever happened at the end, he has transcended. Even if he's only dead. He's gone beyond *his* pain, *his* sin— driven deep into Their province, into control, synthesis and control, further than—" well, he was about to say "we" but "I" seems better after all, "I haven't transcended. I've only been elevated. That must be as empty as things get: it's worse than being told you won't have to die by someone you can't believe in....

"Yes he matters to me, very much. He is an old self, a dear albatross I cannot let go."

"And me?" She gathers that he expects her to sound like a woman of the 1940s. "And me," indeed. But she can think of no other way offhand to help him, to allow him a moment of comfort....

"You, poor Katje. Your story is the saddest of all." She looks up to see exactly how his face will be mocking her. She is stunned to see tears instead running, running over his cheeks. "*You've only been set free,*" his voice then breaking on the last word, his face brushing forward a moment into a cage of hands, then uncaging again for a try at her own gay waltztime gallows laugh. Oh, no, is *he* about to go goofy on her too? What she needs right now in her life, from *some* man in her life, is stability, mental health and strength of character. Not this. "I told Slothrop he was free, too. I tell anybody who might listen. I will tell them as I tell you: you are free. You are free...."

"How can my story be sadder that that?" Shameless girl, she isn't humoring him, she's actually flirting with him now, any technique her crepe-paper and spider-italics young ladyhood ever taught her, to keep from having to move into his blackness. Understand it isn't *his* blackness, but her own—an inadmissible darkness she is making believe for the moment is Enzian's, something beyond even the center of Pan's grove, something not pastoral at all, but of the city, a set of ways in which the natural forces are turned aside, stepped down, rectified or bled to ground and come out very like the malignant dead: the Qlippoth that Weissmann has "transcended," souls whose journey across was so bad that they lost all their kindness back in the blue lightning (the long sea-furrows of it rippling), and turned to imbecile killers and jokers, making unintelligible honks in the emptiness, sinewed and stripped thin as rats—a city-darkness that is her own, a textured darkness in which flows go in all directions, and nothing begins, and nothing ends. But as time passes things get louder there. It is shaking itself into her consciousness.

"Flirt if you want," Enzian now just as smooth as that Cary Grant, "but expect to be taken seriously." Oh, *ho.* Here's whatcha came for, folks.

Not necessarily. His bitterness (all properly receipted in German archives which may, however, be destroyed now) runs too deep for her, really. He must have learned a thousand masks (as the City will continue to mask itself against invasions we often do not see, whose outcomes we never learn, silent and unnoticed revolutions in the warehouse districts where the walls are blank, in the lots where the weeds grow thick), and this, no doubt, this Suave Older Exotic, is one of them.

"I don't know what to do." She gets up in a long, long shrug and begins to stalk gracefully in the room. Her old style: a girl about 16 who thinks everyone is staring at her. Her hair falls like a hood. Her arms often touch.

"You don't have to come into this any further than locating Slothrop," he finally gets around to telling her. "All you *have* to do is tag along with us, and wait till he shows up again. Why bother yourself with the rest?"

"Because I feel," her voice, perhaps by design, very small, "that 'the rest' is exactly what I *ought* to be doing. I don't want to get away with some shallow win. I don't just want to—I don't know, pay him back for the octopus, or something. Don't I have to know *why* he's out here, what I did to him, for Them? How can They be stopped? How long can I get away with easy work, cheap exits? *Shouldn't* I be going all the way in?"

Her masochism [Weissmann wrote from The Hague] is reassurance for her. That she can still be hurt, that she is human and can cry at pain. Because, often, she will forget. I can only try to guess how terrible that must be. . . . So, she needs the whip. She raises her ass not in surrender, but in despair—like your fears of impotence, and mine: can it still . . . will it fail. . . . But of true submission, of letting go the self and passing into the All, there is nothing, not with Katje. She is not the victim I would have chosen to end this with. Perhaps, before the end, there will be another. Perhaps I dream. . . . I am not here, am I, to devote myself to *her* fantasies!

"You are meant to survive. Yes, probably. No matter how painful you want to make it for yourself, still you're always going to come through. You're free to choose exactly how pleasant each passage will be. Usually it's given as a reward. I won't ask for what. I'm sorry, but you seem really not to know. That's why your story *is* saddest of all."

"*Reward*—" she's getting mad. "It's a life-sentence. If you call that a reward, then what are you calling me?"

"Nothing political."

"You black bastard."

"Exactly." He has allowed her to speak the truth. A clock chimes in the stone corner. "We have someone who was with Blicero in May. Just before the end. You don't have to—"

"Come and listen, yes, Oberst. But I will."

He rises, crooks her his official and gentlemanly arm, smiling sideways and feeling like a clown. Her own smiling is upward like mischievous Ophelia just having glimpsed the country of the mad and itching now to get away from court.

Feedback, smile-to-smile, adjustments, waverings: what it damps out to is *we will never know each other.* Beaming, strangers, la-la-la, off to listen to the end of a man we both loved and we're strangers at the films, condemned to separate rows, aisles, exits, homegoings.

Far away in another corridor a loud drill-bit strains, smokes, just before snapping. Cafeteria trays and steelware rattle, an innocent and kind sound behind familiar regions of steam, fat at the edge of souring, cigarette smoke, washwater, disinfectant—a cafeteria in the middle of the day. There are things to hold on to. . . .

□

You will want cause and effect. All right. Thanatz was washed overboard in the same storm that took Slothrop from the *Anubis.* He was rescued by a Polish undertaker

in a rowboat, out in the storm tonight to see if he can get
struck by lightning. The undertaker is wearing, in hopes it
will draw electricity, a complicated metal suit, something
like a deep-sea diver's, and a Wehrmacht helmet through
which he has drilled a couple of hundred holes and inserted nuts, bolts, springs and conductive wands of many
shapes so that he jingles whenever he nods or shakes his
head, which is often. He's a digital companion all right,
everything gets either a yes or a no, and two-tone checker-
boards of odd shape and texture indeed bloom in the rainy
night around him and Thanatz. Ever since reading about
Benjamin Franklin in an American propaganda leaflet,
kite, thunder and key, the undertaker has been obsessed
with this business of getting hit in the head by a lightning
bolt. All over Europe, it came to him one night in a flash
(though not the kind he wanted), at this very moment,
are hundreds, who knows maybe thousands, of people
walking around, who have been struck by lightning and
survived. What stories *they* could tell!

What the leaflet neglected to mention was that Benjamin Franklin was also a Mason, and given to cosmic forms
of practical jokesterism, of which the United States of
America may well have been one.

Well, it's a matter of continuity. Most people's lives
have ups and downs that are relatively gradual, a sinuous
curve with first derivatives at every point. They're the
ones who never get struck by lightning. No real idea of
cataclysm at all. But the ones who do get hit experience
a singular point, a discontinuity in the curve of life—do
you know what the time rate of change *is* at a cusp? *Infinity*, that's what! A-and right across the point, it's *minus*
infinity! How's *that* for sudden change, eh? Infinite miles
per hour changing to the same speed *in reverse*, all in the
gnat's-ass or red cunt hair at the Δt across the point.
That's getting hit by lightning, folks. You're *way* up there
on the needle-peak of a mountain, and don't think there
aren't lammergeiers cruising there in the lurid red altitudes
around, waiting for a chance to snatch you off. Oh yes.
They are piloted by bareback dwarves with little plastic
masks around their eyes that happen to be shaped just
like the infinity symbol: ∞. Little men with wicked eyebrows, pointed ears and bald heads, although some of

them are wearing outlandish headgear, not at all the usual
Robin Hood green fedoras, no these are *Carmen Miranda*
hats, for example, bananas, papayas, bunches of grapes,
pears, pineapples, mangoes, jeepers even *watermelons—*
and there are World War I spike-top Wilhelmets, and baby
bonnets and crosswise Napoleon hats with and without *N*
on them, not to mention little red suits and green capes,
well here they are leaning forward into their cruel birds'
ears, whispering like jockeys, out to nab you, buster, just
like that sacrificial ape off of the Empire State Building,
except that they won't let you fall, they'll carry you away
to the places they are agents of. It will *look* like the world
you left, but it'll be different. Between congruent and
identical there seems to be another class of look-alike that
only finds the lightning-heads. Another world laid down on
the previous one and to all appearances no different.
Ha-*ha!* But the lightning-struck know, all right! Even if
they may not *know* they know. And that's what this undertaker tonight has set out into the storm to find.

Is he interested in all those other worlds who send their
dwarf reps out on the backs of eagles? Nope. Nor does he
want to write a classic of anthropology, with the lightning-
struck grouped into a subculture, even secretly organized
handshakes with sharp cusp-flicks of fingernails, private
monthly magazine *A Nickel Saved* (which looks perfectly
innocent, old Ben Franklin after inflation, unless you know
the other half of the proverb: ". . . is a stockpile of nickel."
Making the *real* quote nickel-magnate Mark Hanna's:
"You have been in politics long enough to know that no
man in public owes the public anything." So the real title
is *Long Enough,* which Those Who Know, know. The text
of each issue of the magazine, when transformed this way,
yields many interesting messages). To outsiders it's just a
pleasant little club newsletter—Jed Plunkitt held a barbecue for the Iowa Chapter the last weekend in April.
Heard about the Amperage Contest, Jed. Tough luck! But
come next Barbecue, you'll be back good as new. . .
Minnie Calkins (Chapter 1.793) got married Easter Sunday to a screen-door salesman from California. Sorry to say
he's not eligible for Membership—at least not yet. But
with all those *screen doors* around, we'll sure keep our
fingers crossed! . . . Your Editor has been receiving many

many "Wha hoppen?" 's concerning the Spring Convention in Decatur when all the lights failed during the blessing. Glad to report now that trouble was traced finally to a giant transient in the line, "Kind of an electrical tidal wave," sez Hank Faffner, our engineer-on-the-scene. "Every bulb in the place burned out, a ceilingful of sooty, sterile eggs." Quite a poet, Hank! Now if you can only find out where that spike *came* from—

But does the Polish undertaker in the rowboat care about busting this code, about secret organizations or recognizable subcultures? No, he doesn't. The reason he is seeking these people out is that he thinks it will help him *in his job*. Can you dig *that*, gates? He wants to know how people behave before and after lightning bolts, so he'll know better how to handle bereaved families.

"You are perverting a great discovery to the uses of commerce," sez Thanatz, stepping ashore. "You ought to be ashamed of yourself." He is no more than five minutes into the empty town at the edge of the marsh when nockle KKAHH-*UHNN!* nocklenockle nockle an enormous blast of light and sound hits the water back where the undertaker, peeved at what he takes to be no gratitude, is hauling away.

"Oh," comes his faint voice. "*Oh*, ho. Oh-ho-ho-*ho!*"

"Nobody lives here but us." A solid figure, a whispering silhouette, charcoal-colored, has materialized in Thanatz's path. "We do not harm visitors. But it would be better if you took another way."

They are 175s—homosexual prison-camp inmates. They have come north from the Dora camp at Nordhausen, north till the land ended, and have set up an all-male community between this marsh and the Oder estuary. Ordinarily, this would be Thanatz's notion of paradise, except that none of the men can bear to be out of Dora— Dora was home, and they are homesick. Their "liberation" was a banishment. So here in a new location they have made up a hypothetical SS chain of command—no longer restricted to what Destiny allotted then for jailers, they have now managed to come up with some really *mean ass* imaginary Nazi playmates, Schutzhäftlingsführer to Block-führer, and chosen an internal hierarchy for themselves too: Lager and Blockältester, Kapo, Vorarbeiter, Stuben-

dienst, Läufer (who is a runner or messenger, but also
happens to be the German name for a chess bishop ... if
you have seen him, running across the wet meadows in
very early morning, with his red vestments furling and
fluttering darkened almost to tree-bark color among the
watery downs, you will have some notion of his real purpose here inside the community—he is carrier of holy
strategies, memoranda of conscience, and when he approaches over the reedy flats of morning you are taken
by your bowed nape and brushed with the sidebands of a
Great Moment—for the Läufer is the most sacred here, it
is he who takes messages out to the ruinous interface between the visible Lager and the invisible SS).

At the top of the complex is Schutzhäftlingsführer Blicero. The name has found it way this far east, as if carrying on the man's retreat for him, past the last stand in the
Lüneburg Heath. He is the Zone's worst specter. He is
malignant, he pervades the lengthening summer nights.
Like a cankered root he is changing, growing toward
winter, growing whiter, toward the idleness and the
famine. Who else could the 175s have chosen for their
very highest oppressor? His power is absolute. And don't
think he isn't really waiting, out by the shelled and rusty
gasworks, under the winding staircases, behind the tanks
and towers, waiting for the dawn's first carmine-skirted
runner with news of how the night went. The night is his
dearest interest, so he must be told.

This phantom SS command here is based not so much
on the one the prisoners knew at Dora as on what they
inferred to be the Rocket-structure next door at the Mittelwerke. The A4, in its way, was also concealed behind an
uncrossable wall that separated real pain and terror from
summoned   deliverer.   Weissmann/Blicero's   presence
crossed the wall, warping, shivering into the fetid
bunkrooms, with the same reach toward another shape as
words trying to make their way through dreams. What the
175s heard from their real SS guards there was enough to
elevate Weissmann on the spot—they, his own brother-
elite, *didn't know* what this man was up to. When prisoners came in earshot, the guards stopped whispering. But
their fear kept echoing: fear not of Weissmann personally,
but of the time itself, a time so desperate that *he* could

now move through the Mittelwerke as if he owned it, a time which was granting him a power different from that of Auschwitz or Buchenwald, a power they couldn't have borne themselves. . . .

On hearing the name of Blicero now, Thanatz's asshole tightens a notch. Not that he thinks the name was planted here or anything. Paranoia is not a major problem for Thanatz. What does bother him is *being reminded at all*— reminded that he's had no word, since the noon on the Heath when ooooo was fired, of Blicero's status—alive or dead, powerlord or fugitive. He isn't sure which he prefers. As long as the *Anubis* kept moving, there was no need to choose: the memory would have been left so far behind that one day its "reality" wouldn't matter any more. Of course it happened. Of course it didn't happen.

"We think he's out there," the town spokesman is telling Thanatz, "alive and on the run. Now and then we hear something—it could fit Blicero easily enough. So we wait. He will find us. He has a prefabricated power base here, waiting for him."

"What if he doesn't stay?" pure meanness, "what if he laughs at you, and passes by?"

"Then I can't explain," the other beginning to step backward, back out into the rain, "it's a matter of faith."

Thanatz, who has sworn that he will never seek out Blicero again, not after the ooooo, feels the flat of terror's blade. "Who is your runner?" he cries.

"Go yourself," a filtered whisper.

"Where?"

"The gasworks."

"But I have a message for—"

"Take it yourself. . . ."

The white *Anubis*, gone on to salvation. Back here, in her wake, are the preterite, swimming and drowning, mired and afoot, poor passengers at sundown who've lost the way, blundering across one another's flotsam, the scrapings, the dreary junking of memories—all they have to hold to—churning, mixing, rising, falling. Men overboard and our common debris. . . .

Thanatz remains shaking and furious in the well-established rain, under the sandstone arcade. I should have sailed on, he wants to scream, and presently does. "I

wasn't supposed to be left with you discards. . . ." Where's
the court of appeals that will hear his sad story? "I lost my
footing!" Some mess cook slipped in a puddle of elite
vomit and spilled a whole galvanized can full of creamed
yellow chicken nausea all over that starboard weather
deck, Thanatz didn't see it, he was looking for Margherita.
. . . Too bad, les jeux sont faits, nobody's listening and the
Anubis is gone. Better here with the swimming debris,
Thanatz, no telling what'll come sunfishing by, ask that
Oberst Enzian, he knows (there is a key, among the
wastes of the World . . . and it won't be found on board
the white *Anubis* because they throw everything of value
over the side).

So—Thanatz is out by the gasworks, up against a tar
wall, mackerel eyes bulging out of wet cool collar-shadows,
all black and white, really scared, breath smoking out
corners of his mouth as green dawn begins to grow back
among the gassen. *He won't be here, he's only dead* only
dead? Isn't this an "interface" here? a meeting surface for
two worlds . . . sure, but *which two*? There's no counting
on any positivism to save him, that didn't even work back
in Berlin, before the War, at Peter Sachsa's sittings . . . it
only got in the way, made others impatient with him. A
screen of words between himself and the numinous was
always just a tactic . . . it never let him feel any freer.
These days there's even less point to it. He knows Blicero
exists.

It wasn't a dream. Don't you wish it could be. Another
fever that sooner or later will break, releasing you into the
cool reality of a room . . . you don't have to perform that
long and complicated mission after all, no, you see it was
only the fever . . . it wasn't real. . . .

This time it is real, Blicero, alive or dead, is real.
Thanatz, a little crazy now with fear, wants to go provoke
him, he can't wait any more, he has to see what it will take
to get Blicero across the interface. What screaming ass-
wiggling surrender might bring him back. . . .

All it brings is the Russian police. There's a working
agreement about staying inside the limits of the 175-Stadt
that of course no one told Thanatz about. The gasworks
used to be a notorious hustling spot till the Russians made
a series of mass busts. A last fading echo of the 175-Stadt

Chorale goes skipping away down the road singing some horrible salute to faggotry such as

> Yumsy-numsy 'n' *poopsie-poo*,
> If *I'm* a degenerate, *so* are *you*. . . .

"Nowadays all we get are you tourists," sez the natty civilian with the white handkerchief in his breast-pocket, snickering in the shadow of his hat brim. "And, of course, the odd spy."

"Not me," Thanatz sez.

"Not you, eh? Tell me about it."

Something of a quandary, all right. In less than half a day, Thanatz has moved from no need to worry or even *think* about Blicero, to always needing some formulation of him at hand to please any stray curious cop. This is one of his earlier lessons in being preterite: he won't escape any of the consequences he sets up for himself now, not unless it's by accident.

For example, at the outskirts of Stettin, by accident, a Polish guerrilla group, just arrived back from London, mistakes the police car for one transporting an anti-Lublin journalist to prison, shoots out the tires, roars in, kills the driver, wounds the civilian interrogator, and escapes lugging Thanatz like a sack of potatoes.

"Not me," Thanatz sez.

"Shit. He's right."

They roll him out of the car door into a DP encampment a few miles farther on. He is herded into a wire enclosure along with 1,999 others being sent west to Berlin.

For weeks he rides the freights, hanging in shifts to the outside of his assigned car while inside someone else sleeps on the straw space he vacated. Later they change places. It helps to stay awake. Every day Thanatz sees half a dozen DPs go on the nod and fall off the train, and sometimes it's funny to watch, but too often it's not, though DP humor is a very dependent thing. He is rubber-stamped on hands, forehead, and ass, deloused, poked, palpated, named, numbered, consigned, invoiced, misrouted, detained, ignored. He passes in and out the paper grasp of Russian, British, American and French body-job-

bers, round and round the occupation circuit, getting to
recognize faces, coughs, pairs of boots on new owners.
Without a ration card or Soldbuch, you are doomed to
be moved, in lots of 2,000, center to center, about the
Zone, possibly forever. So, out among the ponds and fenceposts of Mecklenburg somewhere, Thanatz discovers that
he is exempt from nothing. His second night on the rails
his shoes are stolen. He comes down with a deep
bronchial cough and a high fever. For a week no one
comes to look at him. For two aspirins he has to suck
off the orderly in charge, who has grown to enjoy rough-
bearded cheeks flaming at 103° against his thighs, the
furnace breath under his balls. In Mecklenburg Thanatz
steals a cigarette butt from a sleeping one-armed veteran,
and is beaten and kicked for half an hour by people whose
language he has never heard before, whose faces he never
gets a look at. Bugs crawl over him only slightly irritated
that he's in their way. His daily bread is taken away by
another DP smaller than he is, but with the *look* of some
right to it, a look Thanatz at best can only impersonate—
and he's afraid to go after the little rag-coated liver-
colored back, the munching haystack head . . . and others
are watching: the woman who tells everyone that Thanatz
molests her little girl at night (Thanatz can never meet
her eyes because yes he wants to, pull down the slender
pretty pubescent's oversize GI trousers stuff penis between
pale little buttocks reminding him so of Bianca take bites
of soft-as-bread insides of thighs pull long hair throatback
Bianca make her moan move her head how she loves it)
and a beetlebrowed Slav too, who has forced Thanatz to
go hunting cigarette butts for him after lights out, to give
up his sleep not so much to the chance of finding a real
butt as to the Slav's right to demand it—the Slav is watching too—in fact, a circle of enemies have all observed
the taking of the bread and Thanatz's failure to go after
it. Their judgment is clear, a clarity in their eyes Thanatz
never saw back on the *Anubis*, an honesty he can't avoid,
can't shrug off . . . finally, finally he has to face, literally
with his own real *face*, the transparency, the *real light*
of . . .

   Little by little his memory of that last rocket-firing on
the Heath grows clearer. The fevers fire-polish, the pain

removes impurities. An image keeps recurring—a muddy brown almost black eyeball reflecting a windmill and a jagged reticule of tree-branches in silhouette . . . doors at the sides of the windmill open and shut quickly, like loose shutters in a storm . . . in the iris sky one cloud, the shape of a clamshell, rises very purple around the edges, the puff from an explosion, something light ocher at the horizon . . . closer in it seems snarling purple around a yellow that's brightening, intestines of yellow shadowed in violet spilling outward, outward in a bellying curve toward us. There are, oddly (not to cut this picturesque scene off, but) oddly enough, get this, no windmills on the Lüneburg Heath! Thanatz even checked around real fast just to make sure, nope, no windmills, O.K., so, how come Blicero's eye, looking out on the Heath, is reflecting a windmill, huh? Well, to be honest, *now* it isn't reflecting a windmill, it's reflecting a bottle of gin. No bottle of gin out here on the Heath either. But it *was* reflecting a windmill. What's this? Could it be that Blicero's eyes, in which Greta Erdmann saw maps of his Kingdom, are for Thanatz reflecting the past? *That would* be strange. Whatever went on on those eyeballs when you weren't looking would just be lost. You'd only have fragments, now and then. Katje, looking back over her shoulder at fresh whip-marks. Gottfried in the morning lineup, body all over Wandervogellimp, wind blowing his uniform in great ripples back from the bough-curves of his thighs, hair flying in the wind, saucy sideways smile, mouth a little open, jaw forward, eyelids down. Blicero's own reflection in the oval mirror, an old face—he is about to don a wig, a Dragon Lady pageboy with bangs, and he pauses, looking in, face asking what? what did you say? wig held to the side and slightly lower so as to be another face in heavy wig-shadows nearly invisible . . . but looking closer you can see bone-ridges and fat-fields begin to emerge now, an ice-glaze white bobbing, a mask hand-held, over the shadows in the hollow hood-space—*two faces* looking back now, and Thanatz, are you going to judge this man? Thanatz, haven't you loved the whip? Haven't you longed for the brush and sigh of ladies' clothes? Haven't you wanted to murder a child you loved, joyfully kill something so helpless and innocent? As he looks up at you, at the last pos-

sible minute, trusting you, and smiles, purses his lips to
make a kiss *just as the blow* falls across his skull . . . isn't
that best of all? The cry that breaks in your chest *then,*
the sudden, solid arrival of loss, loss forever, the irreversible end of love, of hope . . . no denying what you finally
are . . . (but so much fear at taking it in, the serpent face
—at opening your arms and legs and letting it *enter* you,
into your true face *it'll kill you if it*—)

He is telling the Schwarzkommando this now, all this
and more. After a week of shouting *I know,* of crying *I've
seen the Schwarzgerät* whenever a black face appears
behind the flowing wire fences, at the cinderbanks or the
crossings, word has got around. One day they come for
him: he is lifted from the straw as black with coal-dust as
they—lifted easy as an infant, a roach flicked in kindness
off of his face—and transported shivering, gathered moaning south to the Erdschweinhöhle where now they are all
sitting around a fire, smoking and munching, eyes riveted
on blue Thanatz, who has been gabbing for seven hours
nonstop. He is the only one privileged, in a way, to tell
this much of the story, he's the fella who lost out, the
loser,

> Just a fool-who-never-wins, at love,
> Though-he-plays, most-ev', ry night . . .
> A loser-to-the-Ones, Above,
> Who stack-the-cards, of wrong, and right. . . .
> Oh the loser never bets-it-all, and-he never-plays,
>   to win,
> He knows if-once, you don't-succeed, you can al-ways
>   lose-again!
> Just a loser at-the-game, of love . . .
> Spending night after night a-lo-o-o-one!

He lost Gottfried, he lost Bianca, and he is only beginning,
this late into it, to see that they are the same loss, to the
same winner. By now he's forgotten the sequence in time.
Doesn't know which child he lost first, or even—hornet
clouds of memory welling up—even if they aren't two
names, different names, for the same child . . . but then in
the crash of others' flotsam, sharp edges, and high-spin
velocities you understand, he finds he can't hold on to this
thought for long: soon he's floundering in the open water

again. But he'll remember that he held it for a little, saw
its texture and color, felt it against the side of his face
as he woke from a space of sleeping near it—that the two
children, Gottfried and Bianca, *are the same....*

He lost Blicero, but it wasn't quite as real. After the last
firing, the unremembered night-hours to Hamburg, the
hop from Hamburg to Bydgoszcz in a purloined P-51
Mustang was so clearly Procalowski-down-out-of-the-sky-
in-a-machine, that Thanatz came to imagine he had disposed of Blicero too only in that same very conditional,
metallic way. And sure enough, the metal has given way
to flesh, and sweat, and long chattering night encounters,
Blicero cross-legged stammering down at his crotch I
cuh-cuh-cuh-cuh— "Can't," Blicero? "Couldn't"? "Care"?
"Cry"? Blicero that night was offering all his weapons, laying
down all maps of his revetments and labyrinths.

Thanatz was really asking: when mortal faces go by,
sure, self-consistent and never seeing me, are they real?
Are they souls, really? or only attractive sculpture, the
sunlit faces of clouds?

And: "How can I love them?"

But there's no answer from Blicero. His eyes go casting
runes with the windmill silhouettes. A number of con-
tributed scenes do now flash by for Thanatz. From Ensign
Morituri, a banana-leaf floor somewhere near Malabacat
in the Philippines, late '44, a baby squirms, rolls, kicks in
drops of sunlight, raising dust off the drying leaves, and
the special-attack units roar away overhead, Zeros bearing
comrades away, finally as fallen cherry-blossoms—that favorite Kamikaze image—in the spring ... from Greta Erdmann, a world below the surface of Earth or mud—it
crawls like mud, but cries like Earth, with layer-pressed
generations of gravities and losses thereto—losses, failures,
last moments followed by voids stringing back, a series of
hermetic caves caught in the suffocated layers, those forever lost ... from someone, who'll ever know who? a flash
of Bianca in a thin cotton shift, one arm back, the smooth
powdery hollow under the arm and the leaping bow of
one small breast, her lowered face, all but forehead and
cheekbone in shadow, turning this way, the lashes now
whose lifting you pray for ... will she see you? a sus-

pension forever at the hinge of doubt, this perpetuate doubting of her love—

They'll help him through it. The Erdschweinhöhlers will sit up all night with this nonstop intelligence briefing. He is the angel they've hoped for, and it's logical he should come now, on the day when they have their Rocket all assembled at last, their single A4 scavenged all summer piece by piece clear across the Zone from Poland to the Low Countries. Whether you believed or not, Empty or Green, cunt-crazy or politically celibate, power-playing or neutral, you had a feeling—a suspicion, a latent wish, some hidden tithe out of your soul, *something*—for the Rocket. It is that "something" that the Angel Thanatz now illuminates, each in a different way, for everybody listening.

By the time he's done, they will all know what the Schwarzgerät was, how it was used, where the 00000 was fired from, and which way it was pointed. Enzian will smile grimly, and groan to his feet, the decision already made for him hours ago, and say, "Well, let's have a look at the timetables now." Erdschweinhöhle rival, Empty One Josef Ombindi, grips him by the forearm—"If there's anything . . ." Enzian nods. "See if you can work us out a tight security watch, 'kurandye." He hasn't called Ombindi *that* for a while. Nor is it a small concession to give the Empty Ones control of the watch lists, at least for the duration of this journey . . .

. . . which has already begun, as one and a half levels below, men and women are busy with tackle, lines, and harness easing rocket sections each onto its dolly, more Schwarzkommando waiting in leather and blueflowered files up the ramps to the outside, along the present and future vectors strung between wood rails and grooves, Empty, Neutral and Green all together now, waiting or hauling or supervising, some talking for the first time since the dividing along lines of racial life and racial death began, how many years ago, reconciled for now in the only Event that could have brought them together (*I* couldn't, Enzian knows, and shudders at what's going to happen after it's over—but maybe it's only meant to last its fraction of a day, and why can't that be enough? try to let it be enough . . .).

Christian comes past, downhill adjusting a web belt, not quite swaggering—night before last his sister Maria visited him in a dream to tell him she wished no revenge against anyone, and wanted him to trust and love the Nguarorerue—so their eyes now meet not quite amused nor quite yet in a challenge, but knowing more together than they ever have so far, and Christian's hand at the moment of passing cocks out half in salute, half in celebration, aimed toward the Heath, northwesterly, Kingdom-of-Deathward, and Enzian's goes out the same way, iya, 'kurandye! as, at some point, the two palms do slide and brush, do touch, and it is touch and trust enough, for this moment. . . .

□

Unexpectedly, this country is pleasant, yes, once inside it, quite pleasant after all. Even though there is a villain here, serious as death. It is this typical American teenager's own *Father*, trying episode after episode to kill his son. And the kid knows it. Imagine that. So far he's managed to escape his father's daily little death-plots—but nobody has said he has to *keep* escaping.

He's a cheerful and a plucky enough lad, and doesn't hold any of this against his father particularly. That ol' Broderick's just a murderin' fool, golly what'll he come up with next—

It's a giant factory-state here, a City of the Future full of extrapolated 1930s swoop-façaded and balconied skyscrapers, lean chrome caryatids with bobbed hairdos, classy airships of all descriptions drifting in the boom and hush of the city abysses, golden lovelies sunning in roofgardens and turning to wave to you as you pass. It is the Raketen-Stadt.

Down below, thousands of kids are running in windy courtyards and areaways, up and down flights of steps, skullcaps on their heads with plastic propellers spinning in the wind rattling and blurred, kids running messages among the plastic herbage in and out of the different softplastic offices—Here's a memo for you Tyrone, go and find the Radiant Hour (Weepers! Didn't know it was lost!

Sounds like ol' Pop's up to somma those *tricks* again!), so it's out into the swarming corridors, full of larking dogs, bicycles, pretty subdeb secretaries on roller skates, produce carts, beanies whirling forever in the lights, cap-gun or water-pistol duels at each corner, kids dodging behind the sparkling fountains WAIT *that's a real gun,* this is a real bullet zinnnggg! good try, Pop, but you're not quite as keen as The Kid today!

Onward to rescue the Radiant Hour, which has been abstracted from the day's 24 by colleagues of the Father, for sinister reasons of their own. Travel here gets complicated—a system of buildings that move, by right angles, along the grooves of the Raketen-Stadt's street-grid. You can also raise or lower the building itself, a dozen floors per second, to desired heights or levels underground, like a submarine skipper with his periscope—although certain paths aren't available to you. They are available to others, but not to you. Chess. Your objective is not the King—there is no King—but momentary targets such as the Radiant Hour.

Bing in pops a kid with beanie spinning, hands Slothrop another message and spins off again. "The Radiant Hour is being held captive, if you want to see her on display to all interested customers be present at this address 11:30 a.m."—in the sky a white clockface drifts conveniently by, hmm only half an hour to gather together my rescue team. Rescue team will consist of Myrtle Miraculous flyin' in here in a shoulderpadded maroon dress, the curlers still up in her hair and a tough frown fer draggin' her outa Slumberland . . . next a Negro in a pearl-gray zoot and Inverness cape name of Maximilian, high square pomaded head and a superthin mustache come zooming here out of his "front" job, suave manager of the Club Oogabooga where Beacon Street aristocracy rubs elbows ev'ry night with Roxbury winos 'n' dopefiends, yeah hi Tyrone, heah Ah is! H'lo Moitle baby, hyeah, hyeah, hyeah! Whut's de big rush, mah man? Adjusting his carnation, lookin' round th' room, everybody's here now except for that *Mar-cel* but hark the familiar music-box theme yes it's that old-timery sweet Stephen Foster music and sure enough in through the balcony window now comes Marcel, a mechanical chess-player dating back to the Second Empire, actually built a century ago for the great conjuror Robert-Houdin, very serious-looking French refugee kid, funny haircut with the ears perfectly outlined in hair that starts abruptly a quarter-inch strip of bare plastic skin away, black patent-shiny hair, hornrim glasses, a rather remote manner, unfortunately much too literal with humans (imagine what happened the first time Maximilian come hi-de-hoing in the door with one finger jivin' in the air sees metal-ebonite-and-plastic young Marcel sitting there and say, "Hey man gimme some *skin*, man!" well not only does Marcel give him a heavy time about skin, skin in *all* its implications, oh no that's only at the superficial level, *next* we get a long discourse on the concept of "give," that goes on for a while, then, then he starts in on "Man." That's really an exhaustive one. In fact Marcel isn't anywhere near finished with it *yet*). Still, his exquisite 19th-century brainwork—the human art it took to build which has been flat lost, lost as the dodo bird—has stood the Floundering Four in good stead on many, many go-rounds with the Paternal Peril.

But where inside Marcel is the midget Grandmaster, the little Johann Allgeier? where's the pantograph, and the magnets? Nowhere. Marcel really is a mechanical chessplayer. No fakery inside to give him any touch of humanity at all. Each of the FF is, in fact, gifted while at the same time flawed by his gift—unfit by it for human living. Myrtle Miraculous specializes in performing miracles. Stupendous feats, impossible for humans. She has lost respect for humans, they are clumsy, they fail, she does want to love them but love is the only miracle that's beyond her. Love is denied her forever. The others of her class are either homosexuals, fanatics about law 'n' order, off on strange religious excursions, or as intolerant of failure as herself, and though friends such as Mary Marvel and Wonder Woman keep inviting her to parties to meet eligible men, Myrtle knows it's no use. . . . As for Maximilian, he has a natural sense of rhythm, which means *all* rhythms, up to and including the cosmic. So he will never be where the fathomless manhole awaits, where the safe falls from the high window shrieking like a bomb —he is a pilot through Earth's baddest minefields, if we only stay close to him, be where he is as much as we

can—yet Maximilian's doom is never to go any further into
danger than its dapperness, its skin-exciting first feel. . . .

Fine crew this is, getting set to go off after the Radiant
—say what? what's Slothrop's *own* gift and Fatal Flaw?
Aw, *c'mon*—uh, the Radiant Hour, collecting their equipment, Myrtle zooming to and fro materializing this and
that:

The Golden Gate Bridge ("How about that one?" "Uh,
let's see the other one, again? with the, you know, uh . . ."
"The Brooklyn?" "—kind of old-fashioned looking—" "The
Brooklyn Bridge?" "Yeah, that's it, with the pointed . . .
whatever they are . . .").

The Brooklyn Bridge ("See, for a chase-scene, Myrtle,
we ought to observe proportions—" "Do tell." "Now if we
were gonna be in high-speed automobiles, well, sure, we
might use the Golden Gate . . . but for zooming through
the air now, we need something older, more intimate,
human—").

A pair of superlatively elegant Rolls Royces ("Quit
fooling, Myrtle, we already agreed, didn't we? No automobiles . . .").

A small plastic baby's steering wheel ("Aw all right, I
know you don't respect me as a leader but listen can't
we be reasonable . . .").

Any wonder it's hard to feel much confidence in these
idiots as they go up against Pernicious Pop each day?
There's no real direction here, neither lines of power nor
cooperation. Decisions are never really *made*—at best they
manage to emerge, from a chaos of peeves, whims, hallucinations and all-round assholery. This is less a fighting
team than nest full of snits, blues, crotchets and grudges,
not a rare or fabled bird in the lot. Its survival seems,
after all, only a mutter of blind fortune groping through
the heavy marbling of skies one Titanic-Night at a time.
Which is why Slothrop now observes his coalition with
hopes for success and hopes for disaster about equally
high (and no, that *doesn't* cancel out to apathy—it makes
a loud dissonance that dovetails inside you sharp as
knives). It does annoy him that he can be so divided, so
perfectly unable to come down on one side or another.
Those whom the old Puritan sermons denounced as "the
glozing neuters of the world" have no easy road to haul

down, Wear-the-Pantsers, just cause you can't see it doesn't mean it's not there! Energy inside is just as real, just as binding and inescapable, as energy that shows. When's the last time you felt *intensely lukewarm?* eh? Glozing neuters are just as human as heroes and villains. In many ways they have the most grief to put up with, don't they? Why don't you, right now, wherever you are, city folks or out in the country, snuggled in quilts or riding the bus, just turn to the Glozing Neuter nearest you, even your own reflection in the mirror, and . . . just . . . sing,

> How-dy neighbor, how-dy pard!
> Ain't it lone-ly, say ain't it hard,
> Passin' by so silent, day-after-day, with-out, even
>   a smile-or, a friendly word to say? Oh, let me
> Tell ya bud-dy, tell ya ace,
> Things're fal-lin', on their face—
> Maybe we should stick together part o' the way, and
> Skies'll be bright-er some day!
> Now *ev'rybody*—

As the 4 suit up, voices continue singing for a while, depending how much each one happens to care—Myrtle displaying generous expanses of nifty gam, and Maximilian leering up beneath the fast-talking young tomato's skirts, drawing bewildered giggles from adolescent Marcel, who may be a bit repressed.

"Now," Slothrop with a boobish, eager-to-please smile, "time for that *Pause that Refreshes!*" And he's into the icebox before Myrtle's "Oh, Jesus" has quite finished echoing . . . the light from the cold wee bulb turning his face to summerlight blue, Broderick and Nalline's shadow-child, their unconfessed, their monster son, who was born with hydraulic clamps for hands that know only how to reach and grab . . . and a heart that gurgles audibly, like a funny fatman's stomach . . . but look how lost, how unarrested his face is, was, that 1½ seconds in the glow from the folksy old icebox humming along in Kelvinator-Bostonian dialect, "Why cummawn in, T'rone, it's nice and friendly heeah in my stummick, gawt lawtsa nice things, like Mawxies, 'n' big Baby Rooths. . . ." Walking now in among miles-down-the-sky shelves and food-mountains or food-cities of Iceboxland (but look out, it can get

pretty Fascist in here, behind the candy-colored sweet
stuff is thermodynamic elitism at its clearest—bulbs can
be replaced with candles and the radios fall silent, but the
Grid's big function in this System is iceboxery: freezing
back the tumultuous cycles of the day to preserve this
odorless small world, this cube of changelessness), climbing over the celery ridges where the lettered cheese glasses
loom high and glossy in the middle distance, slippin' on
the butter dish, piggin' on the watermelon down to the
rind, feelin' yellow and bright as you skirt the bananas,
gazing down at verdigris reaches of mold across the
crusted terrain of an old, no longer identifiable casserole
—*bananas!* who-who's been putting bananas—

> In-the-re-frig er a-tor!
> O no-no-no, no-no-no!

Chiquita Banana sez we shouldn't! Somethin' awful'll happen! Who would do that? It couldn't be Mom, and
Hogan's in *love* with Chiquita Banana, Tyrone's come in
the room plenty of times found his brother with banana
label glued on his erect cock for ready reference, lost in
masturbatory fantasies of nailing this cute but older Latin
lady *while she's wearing her hat,* gigantic fruit-market hat
and a big saucy smile [Ay, ay, how passionate you
Yankees are! . . . a-and it couldn't've been Pop, no Pop
wouldn't, but if it (is it getting cold in here?) wasn't any
of us, then (what's happening to the Spike Jones record
of "Right in the Führer's Face" playing back out in the
living room, why's the sound fading?) . . . unless I did it
without knowing (look around, something's squeaking on
its hinges) and maybe that means I'm going crazy (what's
this *brightening the bulblight,* what's—) SLAM well whoever it is that's been wantonly disregarding United Fruit's
radio commercials has also just closed young Tyrone in
that icebox, and now he'll have to count on Myrtle to get
him out. Embarrassing as heck.

"Good thinking, boss man."

"Gee, M.M., I don't know what happened. . . ."

"Do you ever? Grab on to my cape."

Whoosh—

"Whew. Well," sez Slothrop, "uh, are we all . . . ?"

"That Radiant Hour's probably light-years away by now," sez Myrt, "and *you* have a snot icicle hanging outa your nose." Marcel springs to the controls of the mobile building, keys in to Central Control a request for omni-directional top-speed clearance, which sometimes comes through and sometimes not, depending on a secret process among the granters of permission, a process it is one of the 4's ongoing mandates to discover and impart to the world. This time they get Slow Crawl, Suburban Vectors, lowest traffic status in the Raketen-Stadt, involved only once in recorded history, against a homosexual child-murdering Indian liked to wipe off his organ afterwards on the Flag and so on—"Shit!" hollers Maximilian at Slothrop, "Slow Crawl, Suburban *Vectors!* whut th' fuck we s'posed to *do* man, *swim* or some shit?"

"Uh, Myrtle ..." Slothrop approaches gold-snooded M.M. a little deferent, "uh, do you think you could ..." Jesus they run through this same routine every time—doesn't Myrtle wish Sniveling Slothrop would cut this wishy-washy malarkey 'n' be a *man* fer once! She lights a cigarette, lets it droop from one corner of her mouth, juts out the opposite hip and sighs, "On the beam," exasperated already with this creep—

And *Los!* the miracle is done, they're now zipping along the corridor-streets of the Raketen-Stadt like some long-necked sea monster. Little kids boil up like ants on the webby arches of viaducts high over the city dripping stone like Spanish moss petrified in mid-collapse, kids up over the airy railings and onto the friendly back of the sleek city-cruising monster. They climb window to window, too full of grace ever to fall. Some of them, naturally, are spies: that honey-curled little cutie in the blue checked pinafore and blue knee-socks, up there under the gargoyle at the window listening in to Maximilian, who began drinking heavily as soon as the building started to move, and is now carrying on a long denunciation of Marcel under the thin scholarly disguise of trying to determine if the Gallic Genius can truly be said to have any "soul." Young lady under gargoyle is taking it all down in short-hand. These are valuable data for the psychological war-fare effort.

For the first time now it becomes apparent that the 4

and the Father-conspiracy do not entirely fill their world.
Their struggle is not the only, or even the ultimate one.
Indeed, not only are there many *other* struggles, but
there are also *spectators*, watching, as spectators will do,
hundreds of thousands of them, sitting around this dingy
yellow amphitheatre, seat after seat plunging down in rows
and tiers endless miles, down to the great arena, brown-
yellow lights, food scattered on the stone slopes up higher,
broken buns, peanut shells, bones, bottles half-filled with
green or orange sweet, fires in small wind-refuges, set in
angles where seats have been chiseled away, shallow de-
pressions in the stone and a bed of cherry embers where
old women are cooking hashes of the scavenged bits and
crumbles and gristly lumps of food, heating them in thin
frying pans of gray oil-water bubbling, as the faces of children gather around to wait for food, and in the wind the
dark young man, the slippery young knife who waits for
your maid outside the iron gate each Sunday, who takes
her away to a park, a stranger's automobile and a shape
of love you can never imagine, stands now with his hair
untended in the wind, his head averted from the fire,
feeling the cold, the mountain cold, at his temples and
high under his jaw ... while beside other fires the women
gossip, one craning over now and then to look miles downward at the stage, to see if a new episode's come on yet
—crowds of students running by dark as ravens, coats
draped around shoulders, back out into a murky sector of
seats which traditionally are never entered (being reserved
for the Ancestors), their voices fading still very intense,
dramatic, trying to sound good or at least acceptable. The
women go on, playing cards, smoking, eating. See if you
can borrow a blanket from Rose's fire over there, it's
gonna be cold tonight. Hey—and a pack of Armies while
you're out—and come right back, hear me? Of course the
cigarette machine turns out to be Marcel, who else, in
another of his clever mechanical disguises, and inside one
pack is a message for one of the spectators. "I'm sure you
wouldn't want Them to know about the summer of 1945.
Meet me in the Male Transvestites' Toilet, level L16/39C,
station Metatron, quadrant Fire, stall Malkuth. You know
what time. The usual Hour. Don't be late."

What's this? What're the antagonists doing here—infiltrating their own audience? Well, they're not really. It's

somebody else's audience at the moment, and these nightly spectacles *are* an appreciable part of the darkside-hours life of the Rocket-capital. The chances for any paradox here, really, are less than you think.

Maximilian is way down in the bottom of the orchestra pit posing as the C-melody saxophone player, complete with Closet Intellectual Book, *The Wisdom of the Great Kamikaze Pilots,* with illustrations by Walt Disney— screaming, hairy-nosed, front teeth in white dihedral, slant-eyed (long, elaborate *curlicued* shapes) round black licorice dog-nosed *Japs,* zoomin' through ev'ry page! and any time he's not playing that saxophone, you can be sure Maximilian will be, to the casual observer, immersed in this diffuse, though rewarding, work. Myrtle meantime is back in the candycane control room, manning the switchboard and ready to swoop in at any time to save the others, who are sure (through their own folly if nothing else) to be in deep trouble soon. And Slothrop himself lurks in the Transvestites' Toilet, in the smoke, the crowds, the buzzing fluorescent lights, piss hot as melted butter, making notes of all the dealing going on among the stalls, bowls 'n' urinals (you've got to look butch but not *that* butch and another thing no metal showing at any *vital spots,* she'll knock off ten marks for every one she sees, and the only bonuses she gives are spelled out here: blood drawn no first try, that's an extra 20—) wondering if the cigarette-pack message got through and if they'll come in person or if Pop'll send a hit man to try for a first-round KO.

Well, there is the heart of it: the monumental yellow structure, out there in the slum-suburban night, the never-sleeping percolation of life and enterprise through its shell, Outside and Inside interpiercing one another too fast, too finely labyrinthine, for either category to have much hegemony any more. The nonstop revue crosses its stage, crowding and thinning, surprising and jerking tears in an endless ratchet:

THE LOW-FREQUENCY LISTENER

The German U-boats communicated on a wave length of 28,000 meters, which is down around 10 kc. A half-wave antenna for that'd halfta be 9 miles high, or long, and even folded here and there it is still some antenna. It is located at Magdeburg. So is the headquarters of the German branch of Jehovah's Witnesses. So, for a time, is Slothrop, attempting to get through to the Argentine anarchist U-boat, now in unknown waters. The reason why is no longer clear to him. He was either visited again in some way by Squalidozzi, or he came upon Squalidozzi one day by accident, or he found, in some lint-picking attentionless search through pockets, rags or bedroll, the message he was given, back at the green edge of Aries, at the Café l'Éclipse long ago in Geneva. All he knows is that finding Squalidozzi, right now, is his overriding need.

The Keeper of the Antenna is a Jehovah's witness named Rohr. He's just out of the Ravensbrück camp after being in since '36 (or '37, he can't remember). With that much camp time in, he's politically reliable enough for the local G-5 to put him, nights, in control of the network of longest wavelength in the Zone. Although this could be accidental, more likely there is some eccentric justice lately begun to operate out here which it would behoove Slothrop to look into. There are rumors of a War Crimes Tribunal under way in Nürnberg. No one Slothrop has listened to is clear who's trying whom for what, but remember that these are mostly brains ravaged by antisocial and mindless pleasures.

But the only people—if any—apt to be communicating these days on 28,000 meters (the distance from Test Stand VII at Peenemünde to the Hafenstraße in Greifswald, where Slothrop in early August may see a particular newspaper photo), except for freak Argentine anarchists, are the undenazified Nazis still wandering around in unaccounted-for submarines holding their own secret shipboard tribunals against enemies of the Reich. So the closest thing in the Zone to an early Christian is put on to listen for news of unauthorized crucifixions.

"Someone the other night was dying," Rohr tells him, "I don't know if he was inside the Zone or out at sea. He wanted a priest. Should I have got on and told him about priests? Would he've found any comfort in that? It's so painful sometimes. We're really trying to be Christians. . . ."

"My folks were Congregationalist," Slothrop offers, "I

think." It's getting harder to remember either of them, as Broderick progresses into Pernicious Pop and Nalline into ssshhhghhh ... (into what? *What* was that word? Whatever it is, the harder he chases, the faster it goes away).

MOM SLOTHROP'S LETTER TO AMBASSADOR KENNEDY

Well *hi* Joe how've ya *been*. Listen: Jew-zeppy—we're getting edgy about our youngest again. Would you try bothering a few of those jolly old London connections just *once more?* (Promise!!) Even if it's old news it'll be good news for Poppy and I. I still remember what you said when the awful word about the PT boat came in, before you knew how Jack was. I'll never forget your words then. It's every parent's dream, Joe, that it is.

Oh, and Hozay (whoops, don't mind that, the pen just skidded as you can see! Naughty Nalline's on her *third* martini, we'll have you know). Poppy and I heard your wonderful speech at the GE plant over in Pittsfield the other week. You're in the groove, Mister K! How true! we've *got* to modernize in Massachusetts, or it'll just keep getting worse and worse. They're supposed to be taking a strike vote *here* next week. Wasn't the WLB set up to *prevent* just that? It isn't starting to break down, is it, Joe? Sometimes, you know these fine Boston Sundays, when the sky over the Hill is *broken* into clouds, the way white bread appears through a crust you hold at your thumbs and split apart. ... You know, don't you? Golden clouds? Sometimes I think—ah, Joe, I think they're pieces of the Heavenly City falling down. I'm sorry—didn't mean this to get so gloomy all so sudden, it's just ... but it *isn't* beginning to fall apart, is it, my old fellow Harvard-parent? Sometimes things aren't very clear, that's all. Things *look* like they're going against us, and though it always turns out fine at the end, and we can always look *back* and say oh of course it *had* to happen that way, otherwise so-and-so wouldn't have happened—still, *while* it's happening, in my heart I keep getting this terrible fear, this empty place, and it's very hard at such times really to believe in a Plan with a shape bigger than I can see. ...

Oh, anyway. Grumpy old thoughts away! Shoo! Martini

Number Four, comin' up!

Jack's a fine boy. Really I love Jack like Hogan and
Tyrone, just like a son, my own son. I even love him like
I *don't* love my sons, ha-ha! (she croaks) but then I'm a
wicked old babe, you know that. No hope for the likes of
me. . . .

ON THE PHRASE "ASS BACKWARDS"

"Something I have never understood about your language, Yankee pig." Säure has been calling him "Yankee
pig" all day now, a hilarious joke he will not leave alone,
often getting no further than "Yank—" before collapsing
into some horrible twanging phthisic wheeze of a laugh,
coughing up alarming ropy lungers of many colors and
marbling effects—green, for example, old-statue green at
leafy dusk.

"Sure," replies Slothrop, "you wanna learn English, me
teachee you English. Ask me anything, kraut." It is
exactly the kind of blanket offer that's always geeting
Slothrop in trouble.

"Why do you speak of certain reversals—machinery
connected wrong, for instance, as being 'ass backwards'?
I can't understand that. Ass usually *is* backwards, right?
You ought to be saying 'ass forwards,' if backwards is
what you mean."

"Uh," sez Slothrop.

"This is only one of many American Mysteries," Säure
sighs, "I wish somebody could clear up for me. Not you,
obviously."

Säure got a lotta gall picking on other people's language like this. One night, back when he was a second-
story man, he had the incredible luck to break into the
affluent home of Minnie Khlaetsch, an astrologer of the
Hamburg School, who was, congenitally it seems, unable
to pronounce, even perceive, umlauts over vowels. That
night she was just coming on to what would prove to be an
overdose of Hieropon, when Säure, who back in those
days was a curly-haired and good-looking kid, surprised
her in her own bedroom with his hand around an ivory
chess Läufer with a sarcastic smile on its face, and filled
with good raw Peruvian cocaine still full of the Earth—

"Don't call for help," advises Säure flashing his phony acid bottle, "or that pretty face goes flowing off of its bones like vanilla pudding." But Minnie calls his bluff, starts hollering for help to all the ladies of the same age in her building who feel that same motherly help-help-but-make-sure-there's-time-for-him-to-rape-me ambivalence about nubile cat burglars. What she means to scream is "Hübsch Räuber! Hübsch Räuber!" which means "Cute-looking robber! Cute-looking robber!" But she can't pronounce those umlauts. So it comes out "Hubschrauber! Hubschrauber!" which means "Helicopter! Helicopter!" well, it's 1920-something, and nobody in earshot even knows what the word means, Liftscrewer, what's that?—nobody except one finger-biting paranoid aerodynamics student in a tenement courtyard far away, who heard the scream late in Berlin night, over tramclashing, rifle shots in another quarter, a harmonica novice who has been trying to play "Deutschland, Deutschland Über Alles" for the past four hours, over and over missing notes, fucking up the time, the breathing ü . . . berall . . . es . . . indie . . . e . . . then longlong pause, oh come on asshole, you can find it—*Welt* sour, ach, immediately corrected . . . through all this to him comes the cry Hubschrauber, liftscrewer, a helix through cork air over wine of Earth falling bright, yes he knows *exactly*—and can this cry be a prophecy? a warning (the sky full of them, gray police in the hatchways with ray-guns cradled like codpieces beneath each whirling screw *we see you from above there is nowhere to go it's your last alley, your last stormcellar*) to stay inside and not interfere? He stays inside and does not interfere. He goes on to become "Spörri" of Horst Achtfaden's confession to the Schwarzkommando. But he didn't go to see what Minne was hollering about that night. She would've OD'd except for her boy friend Wimpe, an up-and-coming IG salesman covering the Eastern Territory, who'd blown into town after unexpectedly dumping all of his Oneirine samples on a party of American tourists back in hilltop Transylvania looking for a new kind of thrills —it's me Liebchen, didn't expect to be back so—but then he saw the sprawled satin creature, read pupil-size and skin-tint, swiftly went to his leather case for stimulant and syringe. That and an ice-filled bathtub got her back O.K.

"'Ass' is an intensifier," Seaman Bodine now offers, "a in 'mean ass,' 'stupid ass'—well, when something is very backwards, by analogy you'd say 'backwards ass.'"

"But 'ass backwards' is 'backwards ass' backwards," Säure objects.

"But gee that don't make it mean forwards," blink Bodine with a sincere little break in his voice as if somebody's just about to hit him—actually this is a bit of private fun for the spirited salt, it is a William Bendix imitation. Let the others do Cagney and Cary Grant, Bodine specializes in supporting roles, he can do a perfect Arthur Kennedy-as-Cagney's-kid-brother, how about that. O-or Cary Grant's faithful Indian water-bearer, Sam Jaffe. He is a white-hat in the navy of life, and that extends to vocal impressions of the fake film-lives of strangers.

Säure meantime is into something like this with instrumental soloists, or trying, teaching himself kind of by trial and error, currently ee-ee-aw-aw-ing his way through some hypothetical Joachim playing his own cadenza from the long-suppressed Rossini violin concerto (op. posth.), and in the process driving the household mad. One morning Trudi just goes stomping away into an 82nd Airborne mass jump over the conquered city, a million fleecy canopies in the sky, falling slow as white ash behind around the silhouette of her good-by stomp. "He's driving me crazy." "Hi Trudi, where you going?" "I just told you—crazy!" and don't think this wretched old horny dopefiend doesn't love her, because he does, and don't think he isn't praying, writing down his wishes carefully on cigarette papers, rolling up in them his finest sacramental kif and smoking them down to a blister on the lip, which is the dopefiend's version of wishing on an evening star, hoping in his heart she's just off on another stomp, please only a stomp, let it be over inside the day just one more time, he writes on each good-night's reefer, that's all, I won't ask again, I'll try not to, you know me, don't judge me too hard, please ... but how many more of these stomps can there be, One's going to be the last. Still he keeps on ee-ee-aw-awing with the Rossini, radiating his mean, lean, living-at-theedge street-longevity, no he can't seem to stop it, it's an old man's habit, he hates himself but it just comes on him no matter what attention he brings to the problem, b

can't stop drifting back into the catchy cadenza. . . . Seaman Bodine understands, and is trying to help. To set up
a useful interference, he has composed his own *counter-
cadenza*, along the lines of those other pop tunes with
classical names big around 1945 ("My Prelude to a Kiss,"
"Tenement Symphony")—every chance he gets, Bodine
will croon it to the new weekly arrivals, Lalli just in from
Lübeck, Sandra who's run away from the Kleinbürger-
strasse, here's vile Bodine with his guitar ambling pelvis-
wiggling down the hallway after each naughty defector,
each choice little sexcrime fantasy made flesh, singing
and picking a moving rendition of:

My Doper's Cadenza

If you hear, a "box" so sweet,
Play-in' tunes-with, a peppy beat,
That's just MY DOPER'S, CADEN-ZA-A-A-A!

Mel-o-dees, that getcha so,
Where'd they *come* from? *I* don't know!
(h-ha) It's just MY DOPER'S CADEN-ZA(A)A-A-A!

This is the "ca-denza" part—	Now I know it's not as keen as old Rossini *[snatch of La Gazza Ladra here]*,
	Nor as grand as Bach, or Beethoven-or-Brahms *(bubububoo[oo] oo [sung to opening of Beethoven 5th, with full band])*,
	But I'd give away the fames, of a hundred Harry James . . . wait, fame? of a hundred *Jame?* Jameses . . . uh . . . fameses? Hmm
[scherzoso]	. . . I-hi-hif this little-song, can-bring, you-to-my arms!

Dum de dum, de-dum de dee,
Oh, it's better than a symphonee—
It's MY DOPER'S CADENZA, to yoooouuu!

These days, the tenement is known as "Der Platz," and
is nearly filled up, all the way in to the last central courtyard, with friends of Säure's. The change is unexpected—
a lot more vegetation seems to be growing now in the

tenement dirt, an ingenious system of home-carpentered light ducts and mirrors adjusted throughout the day send sunlight, for the first time, down into these back courts, revealing colors never seen before ... there's also a rain-structure, to route the rain among flumes, funnels, splash-reflectors, waterwheels, nozzles, and weirs to make a system of rivers and waterfalls to play in this summer ... the only rooms that can still be locked from the inside are reserved for isolates, fetishists, lost stumblers-in out of the occupation who need loneliness like the dopefiend needs his dope ... speaking of which, everywhere in the complex now you can find army dope of all kinds stashed, from cellars to mansarde floors are littered with wire loops and plastic covers from ½-grain syrettes of morphine tartrate squeezed toothpaste-tube empty, broken amyl nitrite containers looted from anti-gas kits, olive-drab tins of Benzedrine ... work is proceeding on an anti-police *moat* around the entire tenement: to keep from drawing attention, this moat here is the first in history being dug from inside out, the space directly below the Jacobistrasse, slowly, paranoiacally, is hollowed, sculpted, carefully shored up under the thin crust of street so the odd tram won't find itself in unscheduled plunge—though it *has* been known to happen, out in the late night with interior tram-lights warm-colored as clear broth, out on the Peripheral runs through long stretches of unlighted park or along singing fences of storage depots all at once like a mouth pursing MF the blacktop buckles and you're down in some dripping paranoids' moat, the night-shift staring in with huge denizen-of-the-underground eyes, faced not with *you* so much as with the agonizing problem of deciding *is* this a real bus, or are these "passengers" really *police agents in disguise* well it's a touchy business, touchy.

Somewhere in Der Platz now, early morning, somebody's two-year-old, a baby as fat as a suckling pig, has just learned the word "Sonnenschein." "Sunshine," sez the baby, pointing, *"Sunshine,"* running into the other room.

"Sunshine," croaks some grownup morning-voice.

"Sunshine!" hollers the baby, tottering off.

"Sunshine," a smiling-girl voice, maybe his mother.

"Sunshine!" the baby at the window, showing her, showing anybody else who'll look, *exactly*.

Shit 'n' Shinola

"Now," Säure wants to know, "you will tell me about the American expression 'Shit from Shinola.'"

"What is this," screams Seaman Bodine, "I'm being set *tasks* now? This is some *Continuing Study* of American Slang or some shit? Tell me you old fool," grabbing Säure by throat and lapel and shaking him asymmetrically, "you're one of Them too, right? Come *on*," the old man Raggedy Andy in his hands, a bad morning of suspicion here for the usually mellow Bodine, "Stop, stop," snivels the amazed Säure, amazement giving way, that is, to a sniveling conviction that the hairy American gob has lost his mind. . . .

Well. *You've* heard the expression "Shit from Shinola." As in, "Aw, he don't know Shit from Shinola! 'bout that." Or, "Marine—you don't know Shit from Shinola!" And you get sent to the Onion Room, or worse. One implication is that Shit and Shinola are in wildly different categories. You would envision—maybe just because they smell different—no way for Shit and Shinola to coexist. Simply impossible. A stranger to the English language, a German dopefiend such as Säure, not knowing either word, might see "Shit" as a comical interjection, one a lawyer in a bowler hat, folding up papers tucking them in a tan briefcase might smiling use, "Schitt, Herr Bummer," and he walks out of your cell, the oily bastard, forever . . . or *Scchhit!* down comes a cartoon guillotine on one black & white politician, head bouncing downhill, lines to indicate amusing little spherical vortex patterns, and you thought yes, like to see that all right, yes cut it off, one less rodent, *schitt ja!* As for Shinola, we pass to universitarians Franz Pökler, Kurt Mondaugen, Bert Fibel, Horst Achtfaden and others, their Schein-Aula is a shimmering, Albert Speer-style alabaster open-air stadium with giant cement birds of prey up at each corner, wings shrugged forward, sheltering under each wing-shadow a hooded German face . . . from the outside, the Hall is golden, the white gold precisely of one lily-of-the-valley petal in 4 o'clock sunlight, serene at the top of a small, artificially-graded hill. It has a talent, this Seeming-Hall, for posing up there in attractive profiles, in front of noble clouds, to suggest persistence, through returns of spring, hopes for love, meltings of snow and ice, academic Sunday tranquillities, smells of grass just crushed or cut or later turning to hay . . . but inside the Schein-Aula all is blue and cold as the sky overhead, blue as a blueprint or a planetarium. No one in here knows which way to look. Will it begin above us? Down *there?* Behind us? *In the middle of the air?* and how soon. . . .

Well there's one place where Shit 'n' Shinola do come together, and that's in the men's toilet at the Roseland Ballroom, the place Slothrop departed from on his trip down the toilet, as revealed in the St. Veronica Papers (preserved, mysteriously, from that hospital's great holocaust). Shit, now, is the color white folks are afraid of. Shit is the presence of death, not some abstract-arty character with a scythe but the stiff and rotting corpse itself inside the whiteman's warm and private own *asshole,* which is getting pretty intimate. That's what that white toilet's for. You see many brown toilets? Nope, toilet's the color of gravestones, classical columns of mausoleums, that white porcelain's the very emblem of Odorless and Official Death. Shinola shoeshine polish happens to be the color of Shit. Shoeshine boy Malcolm's in the toilet slappin' on the Shinola, working off whiteman's penance on his sin of being born the color of Shit 'n' Shinola. It is nice to think that one Saturday night, one floor-shaking Lindy-hopping Roseland night, Malcolm looked up from some Harvard kid's shoes and caught the eye of Jack Kennedy (the Ambassador's son), then a senior. Nice to think that young Jack may have had one of them Immortal Light-bulbs then go on overhead—did Red suspend his rag-popping just the shadow of a beat, just enough gap in the moiré there to let white Jack see through, not through to but through *through* the shine on his classmate Tyrone Slothrop's shoes? Were the three ever lined up that way —sitting, squatting, passing through? Eventually Jack and Malcolm both got murdered. Slothrop's fate is not so clear. It may be that They have something different in mind for Slothrop.

An Incident in the Transvestites' Toilet

A small ape or orangutan, holding something behind his back, comes sidling unobserved among net-stockinged legs, bobby sox rolled down to loop under ankle bones, subdeb beanies tucked into rayon aquamarine waist-sashes. Finally he reaches Slothrop, who is wearing a blonde wig and the same long flowing white cross-banded number Fay Wray wears in her screentest scene with Robert Armstrong on the boat (considering his history in the Roseland toilet, Slothrop may have chosen this gown not only out of some repressed desire to be sodomized, unimaginably, by a gigantic black ape, but also because of an athletic innocence to Fay that he's never spoken of except to point and whisper, "Oh, look . . ."—some honesty, pluck, a cleanness to the garment itself, its enormous sleeves so that wherever you pass is visibly where you've been . . .).

> At that first moment, long before our flight:
> Ravine, tyrannosaurus (flying-mares
> And jaws cracked out of joint), the buzzing serpent
> That jumped you in your own stone living space,
> The pterodactyl or the Fall, no—just . . .
> While I first hung there, forest and night at one,
> Hung waiting with the torches on the wall.
> And waiting for the night's one Shape to come,
> I prayed then, not for Jack, still mooning sappy
> Along the weather-decks—no. I was thinking
> Of Denham—only him, with gun and camera
> Wisecracking in his best bum actor's way
> Through Darkest Earth, making the unreal reel
> By shooting at it, one way or the other—
> Carl Denham, my director, my undying,
> *Carl* . . .
> Ah, show me the key light, whisper me a line. . . .

We've seen them under a thousand names . . . "Greta Erdmann" is only one, these dames whose job it is always to cringe from the Terror . . . well, home from work they fall asleep just like us and dream of assassinations, of plots against good and decent men. . . .

The ape reaches up taps Slothrop on the ass, hands him what he's been carrying yaahhgghh it's a round black iron anarchist *bomb*'s what it is, with *lit fuse* too. . . . Ape goes scampering away. Slothrop just stands there, in the glassed

and humid rooms, his makeup starting to run, consterna-
tion in his eyes clear as marbles and lips pressed into a
bee-stung well-what-th'-heck-'m-I-s'posed-t'-do-*now*? He
can't *say* anything, the contact still hasn't showed and his
voice would blow his disguise. . . . The fuse is burning
shorter and shorter. Slothrop looks around. All the washbowls and urinals are occupied. Should he just put the
fuse out in front of somebody's *cock*, right in the stream
of piss . . . uh, but wouldn't that look like I was propo-
sitioning them or something? Gee, sometimes I wish I
wasn't so indecisive . . . m-maybe if I picked somebody
weaker than me . . . but then it's the little guys got the
reflexes, remember—

He is rescued from his indecision by a very tall, fat,
somewhat Oriental-looking transvestite, whose ideal, screen
and personal, seems to be little Margaret O'Brien. Somehow
this Asiatic here is managing to look pigtailed and wistful
even as he snatches the sputtering bomb away from Slothrop, runs heaves it into an empty toiletbowl and flushes
it, turning back to Slothrop and the others with an air of
civic duty well done when suddenly—

KRUPPALOOMA comes this giant *explosion:* water
leaps in a surprised blue-green tongue (ever seen a toilet
hollering, "Yikes!"?) out of every single black-lidded bowl,
pipes wrench and scream, walls and floor shudder, plaster
begins to fall in crescents and powder-sheets as all the
chattering transvestites fall silent, reach out to touch anyone nearby as a gesture of preparation for the Voice out
of the Loudspeaker, saying:

"That was a sodium bomb. Sodium explodes when
it touches water." So the fuse was a *dummy,* the dirty
rat. . . . "You saw who threw it in the toilet. He is a
dangerous maniac. Apprehend him, and there'll be a
large reward. Your closet *could* make Norma Shearer's
look like the wastebasket in Gimbel's basement."

So they all leap on the poor protesting Margaret
O'Brien devotee, while Slothrop, for whom the humiliation and (presently, as the arrival of the police grows
later and later) the sexual abuse and torture were really
intended (Gotta hand it to ya, Pop!) slips away, loosening
as he nears the outside the satin ties of his gown, dragging
reluctantly, off of his grease-chevroned head, the shining
wig of innocence. . . .

A MOMENT OF FUN WITH TAKESHI AND ICHIZO, THE KOMICAL KAMIKAZES

Takeshi is tall and fat (but doesn't braid his hair like that Margaret O'Brien) Ichizo is short and skinny. Takeshi flies a Zero, while Ichizo flies an Ohka device, which is a long bomb, actually, with a cockpit for Ichizo to sit in, stub wings, rocket propulsion and a few control surfaces back aft. Takeshi only had to go to Kamikaze School for two weeks, on Formosa. Ichizo had to go to Ohka school for six *months*, in Tokyo. They are as different as peanut butter and jelly, these two. No fair asking which is which.

They are the only two Kamikazes out here at this air base, which is rather remote actually, on an island that nobody, well, really *cares* much about, any more. The fighting is going on at Leyte . . . then on to Iwo Jima, moving toward Okinawa, but always too far away for any sortie from *here* to reach. But they have their orders, and their exile. Not much to do for kicks but go wandering on the beaches looking for dead Cypridinae. These are crustaceans with three eyes, shaped like a potato with cat-whiskers at one end. Dried and powdered, Cypridinae are also a great source of light. To make the stuff glow in the dark, all you do is add water. The light is blue, weird multishaded blue—some green in it, and some indigo—amazingly cool and nocturnal blue. On moonless or overcast nights, Takeshi and Ichizo take off all their clothes and splash each other with Cypridina light, running and giggling under the palm trees.

Every morning, and sometimes evening too, the Scatterbrained Suicidekicks mosey down to the palm-thatched radar shack to see if there's any American targets worth a crash-dive, anywhere inside their flying radius. But it's the same story every time. Old Kenosho the loony radarman who's always brewing up a batch of that sake back in the transmitter room, in a still he's hooked up to a magnetron tube in some fiendish-Nip way that defies Western science, every time the fellas show up this drunken old reprobate starts cackling, "No dying today! No dying today! So solly!" pointing at all the blank PPI scopes, green radii sweeping silent round and round trailing clear webs of green shampoo, nothing but surface return for more miles than you can fly, and of the fatal mandala both hearts would leap to, green carrier-blob screened eight-fold in a circle of destroyer-strokes, nothing . . . no, each morning's the same—only the odd whitecap and old hysterical Kenosho, who by now is on the floor gagging on saliva and tongue, having his Seizure, an eagerly awaited part of each daily visit, each fit trying to top the one before, or at least bring in a new twist—a back-flip in the air, a gnaw or two after Takeshi's blue-and-yellow patent wingtips, an improvised haiku:

> The lover leaps in the *volcano!*
> It's ten feet deep,
> And inactive—

as the two pilots mug, giggle, and jump around trying to avoid the grizzled old radarman's thrashings—*what?* You didn't like the haiku. It wasn't *ethereal* enough? Not Japanese at all? In fact it sounded like something *right outa Hollywood?* Well, Captain—yes you, Marine Captain Esberg from Pasadena—*you,* have just had, the Mystery Insight! (gasps and a burst of premonitory applause) and so *you*—are our *Paranoid . . . For The Day.* (band burst into "Button Up Your Overcoat," or any other suitably paranoid up-tempo tune, as the bewildered contestant is literally yanked to his feet and dragged out in the aisle by this M.C. with the gleaming face and rippling jaw). Yes, it *is* a movie! Another World War II situation comedy, and your chance, to find out what it's *really like,* because *you*—have *won* (drumroll, more gasps, more applauding and whistling) an all-expense, one-way trip for *one,* to the movie's actual location, exotic Puke-a-hook-a-look-i *Island!* (the orchestra's ukulele section taking up now a tinkling reprise of that "White Man Welcome" tune we last heard in London being directed at Géza Rózsavölgyi) on a giant TWA Constellation! You'll while your nights away chasing vampire mosquitoes away from your *own throat!* Getting blind *lost,* out in the middle of torrential tropical downpours! Scooping rat turds out of the enlisted men's water barrel! But it won't be all nighttime giddiness and excitement, Captain, because daytimes, up at five a.m. sharp, you'll be out making the acquaintance of the Kamikaze *Zero* you'll be flying! getting all checked out on those *controls,* making sure

you know *just where* that bomb-safety-release is! A-ha-
hand of *course,* trying to stay out of the way, of those
two *Nonsensical Nips,* Takeshi and Ichizo! as they go
about their uproarious weekly adventures, seemingly oblivious to your presence, and the frankly ominous implications of your day's routine. . . .

STREETS

Strips of insulation hang up in the morning fog, after
a night of moon brightening and darkening as if by itself,
because the blowing fog was so smooth, so hard to see.
Now, when the wind blows, yellow sparks will spill away
with a rattlesnake buzz from the black old fraying wires,
against a sky gray as a hat. Green glass insulators go
cloudy and blind in the day. Wood poles lean and smell
old: thirty-year-old wood. Tarry transformers hum aloft.
As if it will really be a busy day. In the middle distance
poplars just emerge out of the haze.

It could have been the Semlower Strasse, in Stralsund.
The windows have the same ravaged look: the insides of
all the rooms seem to've been gutted black. Perhaps there
is a new bomb that can destroy only the *insides* of structures . . . no . . . it was in Greifswald. Across some wet railroad tracks were derricks, superstructure, tackle, smells of
canalside . . . Hafenstrasse in Greifswald, down over his
back fell the cold shadow of some massive church. But
isn't that the Petritor, that stunted brick tower-arch
straddling the alleyway ahead . . . it could be the Slü-
terstrasse in the old part of Rostock . . . or the Wandfärber-
strasse in Lüneburg, with pulleys high up on the brick
gables, openwork weathercocks up at the very peaks . . .
why was he looking *upward?* Upward from any of a score
of those northern streets, one morning, in the fog. The
farther north, the plainer things grow. There's one gutter,
down the middle of the alley, where the rain runs off.
Cobbles are laid straighter and there aren't as many
cigarettes to be had. Garrison-churches echo with starlings. To come into a northern Zone town is to enter a
strange harbor, from the sea, on a foggy day.

But in each of these streets, some vestige of humanity,
of Earth, has to remain. No matter what has been done to
it, no matter what it's been used for. . . .

There were men called "army chaplains." They preached inside some of these buildings. There were actually soldiers, dead now, who sat or stood, and listened. Holding on to what they could. Then they went out, and some died before they got back inside a garrison-church again. Clergymen, working for the army, stood up and talked to the men who were going to die about God, death, nothingness, redemption, salvation. It really happened. It was quite common.

Even in a street used for that, still there will be one time, one dyed afternoon (coaltar-impossible orange-brown, clear all the way through), or one day of rain and clearing before bedtime, and in the yard one hollyhock, circling in the wind, fresh with raindrops fat enough to be chewed ... one face by a long sandstone wall and the scuffle of all the doomed horses on the other side, one hair-part thrown into blue shadows at a turn of her head —one busful of faces passing through in the middle of the night, no one awake in the quiet square but the driver, the Ortsschutz sentry in some kind of brown, official-looking uniform, old Mauser at sling arms, dreaming not of the enemy outside in the swamp or shadow but of home and bed, strolling now with his civilian friend who's off-duty, can't sleep, under the trees full of road-dust and night, through their shadows on the sidewalks, playing a harmonica ... down past the row of faces in the bus, drowned-man green, insomniac, tobacco-starved, scared, not of tomorrow, not yet, but of this pause in their night-passage, of how easy it will be to lose, and how much it will hurt. ...

At least one moment of passage, one it will hurt to lose, ought to be found for every street now indifferently gray with commerce, with war, with repression ... finding it, learning to cherish what was lost, mightn't we find some way back?

In one of these streets, in the morning fog, plastered over two slippery cobblestones, is a scrap of newspaper headline, with a wirephoto of a giant white cock, dangling in the sky straight downward out of a white pubic bush. The letters

MB DRO
ROSHI

appear above with the logo of some occupation newspaper, a grinning glamour girl riding astraddle the cannon of a tank, steel penis with slotted serpent head, 3rd Armored treads 'n' triangle on a sweater rippling across her tits. The white image has the same coherence, the hey-lookit-me smugness, as the Cross does. It is not only a sudden white genital onset in the sky—it is also, perhaps, a Tree. . . .

Slothrop sits on a curbstone watching it, and the letters, and girl with steel cock waving hi fellas, as the fog whitens into morning, and figures with carts, or dogs, or bicycles go by in brown-gray outlines, wheezing, greeting briefly in fog-flattened voices, passing. He doesn't remember sitting on the curb for so long staring at the picture. But he did.

At the instant it happened, the pale Virgin was rising in the east, head, shoulders, breasts, 17° 36' down to her maidenhead at the horizon. A few doomed Japanese knew of her as some Western deity. She loomed in the eastern sky gazing down at the city about to be sacrificed. The sun was in Leo. The fireburst came roaring and sovereign. . . .

LISTENING TO THE TOILET

The basic idea is that They will come and shut off the water first. The cryptozoa who live around the meter will be paralyzed by the great inbreak of light from overhead . . . then scatter like hell for lower, darker, wetter. Shutting the water off interdicts the toilet: with only one tankful left, you really can't get rid of much of anything any more, dope, shit, documents, They've stopped the inflow/outflow and here you are trapped inside Their frame with your wastes piling up, ass hanging out all over Their Movieola viewer, waiting for Their editorial blade. Reminded, too late, of how dependent you are on Them, for neglect if not good will: Their neglect is your freedom. But when They do come on it's like society-gig Apollos, striking the lyre

ZONGGG

Everything freezes. The sweet, icky chord hangs in the air . . . there is no way to be at ease with it. If you try the "Are you quite finished, Superintendent?" gambit, the man will answer, "No, as a matter of fact . . . no, you nasty little wet-mouthed prig, I'm not *half* finished, not with you. . . ."

So it's good policy always to have the toilet valve cracked a bit, to maintain some flow through the toilet so when it *stops* you'll have that extra minute or two. Which is not the usual paranoia of waiting for a knock, or a phone to ring: no, it takes a particular kind of mental illness to sit and listen for a cessation of noise. But—

Imagine this very elaborate scientific lie: that sound cannot travel through outer space. Well, but suppose it *can*. Suppose They don't want us to know there is a medium there, what used to be called an "aether," which can carry sound to every part of the Earth. The Soniferous Aether. For millions of years, the sun has been roaring, a giant, furnace, 93 millionmile roar, so perfectly steady that generations of men have been born into it and passed out of it again, without ever hearing it. Unless it changed, how would anybody know?

Except that at night now and then, in some part of the dark hemisphere, because of eddies in the Soniferous Aether, there will come to pass a very shallow pocket of no-sound. For a few seconds, in a particular place, nearly every night somewhere in the World, sound-energy from Outside is shut off. The roaring of the sun *stops*. For its brief life, the point of sound-shadow may come to rest a thousand feet above a desert, between floors in an empty office building, or exactly around a seated individual in a working-class restaurant where they hose the place out at 3 every morning . . . it's all white tile, the chairs and tables riveted solid into the floor, food covered with rigid shrouds of clear plastic . . . soon, from outside, rrrnnn! clank, drag, squeak of valve opening oh yes, ah yes, Here Are The Men With The Hoses To Hose The Place Out—

At which instant, with no warning, the arousing feather-point of the Sound-Shadow has touched you, enveloping you in sun-silence for oh, let us say 2:36:18 to 2:36:24, Central War Time, unless the location is Dungannon, Virginia, Bristol, Tennessee, Asheville or Franklin, North Carolina, Apalachicola, Florida, or conceivably in Murdo Mackenzie, South Dakota, or Phillipsburg, Kansas, or Stockton, Plainville, or Ellis, Kansas—yes sounds like a

Roll of Honor don't it, being read off someplace out on the prairie, foundry colors down the sky in long troughs, red and purple, darkening crowd of civilians erect and nearly-touching as wheat stalks, and the one old man in black up at the microphone, reading off the towns of the war dead, Dungannon ... Bristol ... Murdo Mackenzie ... his white hair blown back by a sculpting thine-alabaster-cities wind into leonine wreathing, his stained pored old face polished by wind, sandy with light, earnest outboard corners of his eyelids folding down as one by one, echoing out over the anvil prairie, the names of death-towns un-reel, and surely Bleicheröde or Blicero will be spoken any minute now. . . .

Well, you're *wrong*, champ—these happen to be towns all located on the borders of *Time Zones*, is all. Ha, ha! Caught *you* with your hand in your pants! Go on, show us *all* what you were doing or leave the area, we don't need your kind around. There's nothing so loathsome as a sen-timental surrealist.

"Now—the eastern towns we've listed are on Eastern War Time. All the other towns along the interface are on Central. The western towns just read off are on Central, while the other towns along *that* interface are on Moun-tain. . . ."

Which is all our Sentimental Surrealist, leaving the area, gets to hear. Just as well. He is more involved, or "unhealthily obsessed," if you like, with the moment of sun-silence inside the white tile greasy-spoon. It seems like a place he has been (Kenosha, Wisconsin?) already, though he can't remember in what connection. They called him "the Kenosha Kid," though this may be apocryphal. By now, the only other room he can remember being in was a two-color room, nothing but the two exact colors, for all the lamps, furniture, drapes, walls, ceiling, rug, radio, even book jackets in the shelves—*everything* was either (1) Deep Cheap-Perfume Aquamarine, or (2) Creamy Choco-late FBI-Shoe Brown. That may've been in Kenosha, may not. If he tries he will remember, in a minute, how he got to the white tiled room half an hour before hose-out time. He is sitting with a coffee cup half full, heavy sugar and cream, crumbs of a pineapple Danish under the saucer where his fingers can't reach. Sooner or later he'll have to move the saucer to get them. He's just holding off. But it isn't sooner and it isn't later, because

the sound-shadow comes down on him,

settles around his table, with the invisible long vortex surfaces that brought it here swooping up away like whorls of an Aetheric Danish, audible only by virtue of accidental bits of sound-debris that may happen to be caught in the eddying, voices far away out at sea *our position is two seven degrees two six minutes north,* a woman crying in some high-pitched language, ocean waves in gale winds, a voice reciting in Japanese,

> Hi wa Ri ni katazu,
> > Ri wa Ho ni katazu,
> > > Ho wa Ken ni katazu,
> > > > Ken wa Ten ni katazu,

which is the slogan of a Kamikaze unit, an Ohka outfit—it means

> > Injustice cannot conquer Principle,
> > Principle cannot conquer Law,
> > Law cannot conquer Power,
> > Power cannot conquer Heaven.

Hi, Ri, Ho, Ken, Ten go Jap-gibbering away on the long solar eddy and leave the Kenosha Kid at the riveted table, where the roaring of the sun has stopped. He is hearing, for the first time, the mighty river of his blood, the Titan's drum of his heart.

Come into the bulbshine and sit with him, with the stranger at the small public table. It's almost hosing-out time. See if you can sneak in under the shadow too. Even a partial eclipse is better than never finding out—better than cringing the rest of your life under the great Vacuum in the sky they have taught you, and a sun whose silence you never get to hear.

What if there is no Vacuum? Or if there is—what if They're *using* it on you? What if They find it convenient to preach an island of life surrounded by a void? Not just the Earth in space, but your own individual life in time? What if it's *in Their interest* to have you believing that?

"He won't bother us for a while," They tell each other. "I just put him on the Dark Dream." They drink together,

shoot very very synthetic drugs into skin or blood, run incredible electronic waveforms into Their skulls, directly
into the brainstem, and backhand each other, playfully,
with openmouth laugh—*you know, don't you* is in those
ageless eyes . . . They speak of taking So-and-So and
"putting him on the Dream." They use the phrase for each
other too, in sterile tenderness, when bad news is passed,
at the annual Roasts, when the endless mindgaming
catches a colleague unprepared—"Boy, did we put *him*
on the Dream." *You* know, don't you?

WITTY REPARTEE

Ichizo comes out of the hut, sees Takeshi in a barrel
under some palm leaves taking a bath and singing "Doo-
doo-doo, doo-doo," some koto tune, twanging through his
nose—Ichizo screams runs back inside reemerging with a
Japanese Hotchkiss machine gun, a Model 92, begins setting
it up with a lot of jujitsu grunting and eyepopping. About
the time he's got the ammo belt poised, ready to riddle
Takeshi in the tub,

TAKESHI: Wait a minute, wait a minute! What's all this?

ICHIZO: Oh, it's *you! I*—thought it was General Mac-
Arthur, in his—rowboat!

Interesting weapon, the Hotchkiss. Comes in many
nationalities, and manages to fit in ethnically wherever it
goes. American Hotchkisses are the guns that raked
through the unarmed Indians at Wounded Knee. On the
lighter side, the racy 8 mm French Hotchkiss when fired
goes haw-haw-haw-haw, just as nasal and debonair as a
movie star. As for our cousin John Bull, a lot of British
Hotchkiss heavies were either resold privately after World
War I, or blowtorched. These melted machine guns will
show up now and then in the strangest places. Pirate
Prentice saw one in 1936, during his excursion with
Scorpia Mossmoon, at the Chelsea home of James Jello,
that year's king of Bohemian clowns—but a minor king,
from a branch prone to those loathsome inbred diseases,
idiocy in the family, sexual peculiarities surfacing into
public view at most inappropriate times (a bare penis
dangling out of a dumpster one razor-clear and rainwashed
morning, in an industrial back-street about to be swarmed
up by a crowd of angry workers in buttontop baggy caps

carrying spanners three feet long, Kelly crowbars, lengths
of chain, here's bareass Crown Prince Porfirio with a giant
halo of aluminum-shaving curls on his head, his mouth
made up with black grease, his soft buttocks squirming
against the cold refuse picking up steel splinters that sting
deliciously, his eyes sultry and black as his lips, but oh
dear what's this, oh how embarrassing here they come
around the corner he can smell the rabble from here,
though they are not too sure about Porfirio—the march
pauses in some confusion as these most inept revolutionaries fall to arguing whether the apparition is a diversionary
nuisance planted here by the Management, or whether he's
real Decadent Aristocracy to be held for real ransom and
if so how much ... while up on the rooftops, out from the
brick and corrugated doorways begin to appear brown
Government troops manning British Hotchkisses which
were *not* melted down, but bought up by machinegun
jobbers and sold to a number of minor governments around
the world). It may have been in memory of Crown Prince
Porfirio that day of massacre that James Jello kept a melted
Hotchkiss in his rooms—or it may've been only another
flight of grotesquerie on dear James's part you know, he's
so unaware. . . .

HEART-TO-HEART, MAN-TO-MAN

—Son, been wondering about this, ah, "screwing in"
you kids are doing. This matter of the, shooting electricity
into head, ha-ha?

—*Waves*, Pop. Not just raw *electricity*. That's fer drips!

—Yes, ah, waves. "Keying waves," right? ha-hah. Uh,
tell me, son, what's it like? You know *I've* been something
of a doper all m'life, a-and—

—Oh Pop. Cripes. It isn't like *dope* at all!

—Well we got off on some pretty good "vacations" we
called them then, some pretty "weird" areas they got us
into 's a matter of fact—

—But you always came back, didn't you.

—What?

—I mean it was always understood that *this* would still
be here when you got back, just the same, exactly the
same, right?

—Well ha-ha guess that's why we called 'em *vacations*,

son! Cause you always do come back to old Realityland, don't you.

—*You* always *did*.

—Listen Tyrone, you don't know how dangerous that stuff is. Suppose someday you just plug in and go away and never come back? Eh?

—Ho, ho! Don't I wish! What do you think every electrofreak dreams about? You're such an old fuddyduddy! A-and who sez it's a dream, huh? M-maybe *it exists.* Maybe there *is* a Machine to take us away, take us completely, suck us out through the electrodes out of the skull 'n' into the Machine and live there forever with all the other souls it's got stored there. *It* could decide who it would suck out, a-and when. Dope never gave *you* immortality. *You* hadda come back, every time, into a dying hunk of smelly *meat!* But *We* can live forever, in a clean, honest, purified Electroworld—

—Shit that's what I get, havin' a double Virgo fer a son. . . .

SOME CHARACTERISTICS OF IMIPOLEX G

Imipolex G is the first plastic that is actually *erectile.* Under suitable stimuli, the chains grow cross-links, which stiffen the molecule and increase intermolecular attraction so that this Peculiar Polymer runs far outside the known phase diagrams, from limp rubbery amorphous to amazing perfect tessellation, hardness, brilliant transparency, high resistance to temperature, weather, vacuum, shock of any kind (slowly gleaming in the Void. Silver and black. Curvewarped reflections of stars flowing across, down the full length of, round and round in meridians exact as the meridians of acupuncture. What are the stars but points in the body of God where we insert the healing needles of our terror and longing? Shadows of the creature's bones and ducts—leaky, wounded, irradiated white—mingling in with its own. *It* is entangled with the bones and ducts, its own shape determined by how the Erection of the Plastic shall proceed: where fast and where slow, where painful and where slithery-cool . . . whether areas shall exchange characteristics of hardness and brilliance, whether some areas should be allowed to flow over the surface so that the passage will be a caress, where to orchestrate sudden discontinuities—blows, wrenchings—in among these more caressive moments).

Evidently the stimulus would have had to be electronic. Alernatives for signaling *to* the plastic surface were limited:

(a) a thin matrix of wires, forming a rather close-set coordinate system over the Imipolectic Surface, whereby erectile and other commands could be sent to an area quite specific, say on the order of ½ cm²,

(b) a beam-scanning system—or several—analogous to the well-known video electron stream, modulated with grids and deflection plates located as needed on the Surface (or even below the outer layer of Imipolex, down at the interface with What lies just beneath: with What has been inserted or What has actually *grown itself a skin of Imipolex G,* depending which heresy you embrace. We need not dwell here on the Primary Problem, namely that everything below the plastic film does after all lie in the Region of Uncertainty, except to emphasize to beginning students who may be prone to Schwärmerei, that terms referring to the Subimipolexity such as "Core" and "Center of Internal Energy" possess, outside the theoretical, no more reality than do terms such as "Supersonic Region" or "Center of Gravity" in other areas of Science),

(c) alternatively, the projection, *onto* the Surface, of an electronic "image," analogous to a motion picture. This would require a minimum of three projectors, and perhaps more. Exactly how many is shrouded in another order of uncertainty: the so-called Otyiyumbu Indeterminacy Relation ("Probable functional derangement γ_R resulting from physical modification ϕ_R (x,y,z) is directly proportional to a higher power p of sub-imipolectic derangement γ_B, p being not necessarily an integer and determined empirically"), in which subscript R is for Rakete, and B for Blicero.

□

Meantime, Tchitcherine has found it necessary to abandon his smegma-gathering stake-out on the Argentine anarchists. The heat, alias Nikolai Ripov of the Commissariat for

Intelligence Activities, is in town and closing in. The faithful Džabajev, in terror or disgust, has gone off across the cranberry bogs on a long wine binge with two local derelicts, and may never be back. Rumor sez he is cutting a swath these days across the Zone in a stolen American Special Services getup, posing as Frank Sinatra. Comes into town finds a tavern and starts crooning out on the sidewalk, pretty soon there's a crowd, subdeb cuties each a $65 fine and worth every penny dropping in epileptiform seizures into selfless heaps of cable-stitching, rayon pleats and Xmastree appliqué. It works. It's always good for free wine, an embarrassment of wine, rolling Fuder and Fass in a rumbling country procession through the sandy streets, wherever the Drunkards Three find themselves. Never occurs to anybody to ask what Frank Sinatra's doing flanked by this pair of wasted rumdums. Nobody doubts for a minute that it *is* Sinatra. Town hepcats usually take the other two for a comedy team.

While nobles are crying in their nights' chains, the squires sing. The terrible politics of the Grail can never touch them. Song is the magic cape.

Tchitcherine understands that he is finally alone now. Whatever is to find him will find him alone.

He feels obliged to be on the move, though there's no-place for him to go. Now, too late, the memory of Wimpe, longago IG Farben V-Mann, finds him. Tags along for the run. Tchitcherine was hoping he might find a dog. A dog would have been ideal, a perfect honesty to calibrate his own against, day to day, till the end. A dog would have been good to have along. But maybe the next best thing is an albatross with no curse attached: an amiable memory.

Young Tchitcherine was the one who brought up political narcotics. Opiates of the people.

Wimpe smiled back. An old, old smile to chill even the living fire in Earth's core. "Marxist dialectics? That's *not* an opiate, eh?"

"It's the antidote."

"No." It can go either way. The dope salesman may know everything that's ever going to happen to Tchitcherine, and decide it's no use—or, out of the moment's velleity, lay it right out for the young fool.

"The basic problem," he proposes, "has always been

getting other people to die for you. What's worth enough for a man to give up his life? That's where religion had the edge, for centuries. Religion was always about death. It was used not as an opiate so much as a technique—it got people to die for one particular set of beliefs about death. Perverse, natürlich, but who are you to judge? It was a good pitch while it worked. But ever since it became impossible to die for death, we have had a secular version—yours. Die to help History grow to its predestined shape. Die knowing your act will bring a good end a bit closer. Revolutionary suicide, fine. But look: if History's changes *are* inevitable, why *not* not die? Vaslav? If it's going to happen anyway, what does it matter?"

"But you haven't ever had the choice to make, have you."

"If I ever did, you can be sure—"

"You don't know. Not till you're there, Wimpe. You can't say."

"That doesn't sound very dialectical."

"I don't know what it is."

"Then, right up till the point of decision," Wimpe curious but careful, "a man could still be perfectly pure . . ."

"He could be anything. *I* don't care. But he's only real *at* the points of decision. The time between doesn't matter."

"Real to a Marxist."

"No. Real to himself."

Wimpe looks doubtful.

"I've been there. You haven't."

Shh, shh. A syringe, a number 26 point. Bloods stifling in the brownwood hotel suite. To chase or worry this argument is to become word-enemies, and neither man really wants to. Oneirine theophosphate is one way around the problem. (Tchitcherine: "You mean *thio*phosphate, don't you?" Thinks *indicating the presence of sulfur.* . . . Wimpe: "I mean *theo*phosphate, Vaslav," *indicating the Presence of God.*) They shoot up: Wimpe eying the water-tap nervously, recalling Tchaikovsky, salmonella, a fast medley of whistlable tunes from the *Pathétique*. But Tchitcherine has eyes only for the point, its German precision, its fine steel grain. Soon he will come to know a circuit of aic

stations and field hospitals, as good for postwar nostalgia
as a circuit of peacetime spas—army surgeons and dentists
will bond and hammer patent steel for life into his suffering flesh, and pick out what has entered it by violence
with an electromagnetic device bought between the wars
from Schumann of Düsseldorf, with a light bulb and ad-
justable reflector, 2-axis locking handles and a complete
set of weird-shaped Polschuhen, iron pieces to modify the
shape of the magnetic field . . . but there in Russia, that
night with Wimpe, was his first taste—his initiation into
the bodyhood of steel . . . no way to separate this from
the theophosphate, to separate vessels of steel from the
ungodly insane rush. . . .

For 15 minutes the two of them run screaming all over
the suite, staggering around in circles, lined up with the
rooms' diagonals. There is in Laszlo Jamf's celebrated
molecule a particular twist, the so-called "Pökler singularity," occurring in a certain crippled indole ring, which
later Oneirinists, academician and working professional
alike, are generally agreed is responsible for the hallucinations which are unique to this drug. Not only audiovisual,
they touch all senses, equally. And they recur. Certain
themes, "mantic archetypes" (as Jollifox of the Cambridge
School has named them), will find certain individuals
again and again, with a consistency which has been well
demonstrated in the laboratory (see Wobb and Whoaton,
"Mantic Archetype Distribution Among Middle-Class University Students," *J. Oneir. Psy. Pharm.*, XXIII, pg. 406–
453). Because analogies with the ghost-life exist, this
recurrence phenomenon is known, in the jargon, as "haunting." Whereas other sorts of hallucinations tend to flow by,
related in deep ways that aren't accessible to the casual
dopefiend, these Oneirine hauntings show a definite nar-
rative continuity, as clearly as, say, the average *Reader's
Digest* article. Often they are so ordinary, so conventional—Jeaach calls them "the dullest hallucinations known
to psychopharmacology"—that they are only recognized
as hauntings through some radical though plausible violation of possibility: the presence of the dead, journeys by
the same route and means where one person will set out
later but arrive earlier, a printed diagram which no
amount of light will make readable. . . . On recognizing

that he is being haunted, the subject enters immediately into "phase two," which, though varying in intensity from subject to subject, is always disagreeable: often sedation (0.6 mg atropine subcut.) will be necessary, even though Oneirine is classified as a CNS depressant.

About the paranoia often noted under the drug, there is nothing remarkable. Like other sorts of paranoia, it is nothing less than the onset, the leading edge, of the discovery that *everything is connected*, everything in the Creation, a secondary illumination—not yet blindingly One, but at least connected, and perhaps a route In for those like Tchitcherine who are held at the edge. . . .

TCHITCHERINE'S HAUNTING

As to whether the man is or isn't Nikolai Ripov: he does arrive the way Ripov is said to: heavy and inescapable. He wants to talk, only to talk. But somehow, as they progress, into the indoor corridor-confusions of words, again and again he will trick Tchitcherine into uttering heresy, into damning himself.

"I'm here to help you see clearly. If you have doubts, we should air them, honestly, man to man. No reprisals. Hell, don't you think I've had doubts? Even *Stalin's* had them. We all have."

"It's all right though. It isn't anything I can't handle."

"But you're *not* handling it, or they wouldn't have sent me out here. Don't you think they *know* when someone they care for is in trouble?"

Tchitcherine doesn't want to ask. He strains against it with the muscles of his heart-cage. The pain of cardiac neurosis goes throbbing down his left arm. But he asks, feeling his breath shift a little, "Was I supposed to die?"

"When, Vaslav?"

"In the War."

"Oh, Vaslav."

"You wanted to hear what was troubling me."

"But don't you see how they'll take that? Come, bring it all the way out. We lost twenty million souls, Vaslav. It's not an accusation you can make lightly. They'd want documentation. Even your life might be in danger—"

"I'm not accusing anyone . . . please don't . . . I only want to know if I am supposed to die for them."

"No one wants you to die." Soothing. "Why do you think that?"

So it is coaxed out of him by the patient emissary, whining, desperate, too many words—paranoid suspicions, unappeasable fears, damning himself, growing the capsule around his person that will isolate him from the community forever. . . .

"Yet that's the very heart of History," the gentle voice talking across twilight, neither man having risen to light a lamp. "The inmost heart. How could everything you know, all you've seen and touched of it, be fed by a lie?"

"But life after death . . ."

"There is no life after death."

Tchitcherine means he's had to fight to believe in his mortality. As his body fought to accept its steel. Fight down all his hopes, fight his way into the bitterest of freedoms. Not till recently did he come to look for comfort in the dialectical ballet of force, counterforce, collision, and new order—not till the War came and Death appeared across the ring, Tchitcherine's first glimpse after the years of training: taller, more beautifully muscled, less waste motion than he'd ever expected—only in the ring, feeling the terrible cold each blow brought with it, only then did he turn to a Theory of History—of all pathetic cold comforts—to try and make sense of it.

"The Americans say, 'There are no atheists in foxholes.' You were never of the faith, Vaslav. You had a deathbed conversion, out of fear."

"Is that why you want me dead now?"

"Not dead. You're not much use dead." Two more olive-drab agents have come in, and stand watching Tchitcherine. They have regular, unremarkable faces. This is, after all, an Oneirine haunting. Mellow, ordinary. The only tipoff to its unreality is—

The radical-though-plausible-violation-of-reality—

All three men are smiling at him now. *There is no violation.*

It's a scream, but it comes out as a roar. He leaps at Ripov, nearly nails him with his fist too, but the others, with faster reflexes than he counted on, have come up either side to hold him. He can't believe their strength. Through the nerves of hip and ass he feels his Nagant being slid from its holster, and feels his own cock sliding

out of a German girl he can't remember now, on the last
sweetwine morning he saw her, in the last warm bed of
the last morning departure. . . .

"You're a child, Vaslav. Only making believe that you
understand ideas which are really beyond you. We have
to speak very simply for you."

In Central Asia he was told of the functions of Moslem
angels. One is the examine the recently dead. After the
last mourner has gone, angels come to the grave and
interrogate the dead one in his faith. . . .

There is another figure now, at the edge of the room.
She is Tchitcherine's age, and in uniform. Her eyes don't
want to say anything to Tchitcherine. She only watches.
No music heard, no summer journey taken . . . no horse
seen against the steppe in the last daylight. . . .

He doesn't recognize her. Not that it matters. Not at
this level of things. But it's Galina, come back to the
cities, out of the silences after all, in again to the chain-
link fields of the Word, shining, running secure and always
close enough, always tangible. . . .

"Why were you hunting your black brother?" Ripov
manages to make the question sound courteous.

Oh. Nice of you to ask, Ripov. Why *was* I? "When it
began . . . a long time ago—at first . . . I thought I was
being punished. Passed over. I blamed him."

"Now?"

"I don't know."

"What made you think he was *your* target?"

"Who else's would he be?"

"Vaslav. Will you never *rise above*? These are old bar-
barisms. Blood lines, personal revenge. You think this has
all been arranged for you, to ease your little, stupid lusts."

All right. All right. "Yes. Probably. What of it?"

"*He isn't your target.* Others want him."

"So you've been letting me—"

"So far. Yes."

Džabajev could have told you. That sodden Asiatic is
first and last an enlisted man. *He* knew. Officers. Fucking
officer mentality. You do all the work, then *they* come in,
to wrap it up, to get the glory.

"You're taking it away from me."

"You can go home."

Tchitcherine has been watching the other two. He sees now that they are in American uniform, and probably haven't understood a word. He holds out his empty hands, his sunburned wrists, for a last application of steel. Ripov, in the act of turning to leave, appears surprised. "Oh. No, no. You have thirty days' survivor's leave. You have survived, Vaslav. You're to report to TsAGI when you get back to Moscow, that's all. There'll be another assignment. We'll be taking German rocket personnel out to the desert. To Central Asia. I imagine they'll need an old Central Asia hand out there."

Tchitcherine understands that in *his* dialectic, his own life's unfolding, to return to Central Asia is, operationally, to die.

They have gone. The woman's iron face, at the very last, did not turn back. He is alone in a gutted room, with the plastic family toothbrushes still in their holders on the wall, melted, strung downward in tendrils of many colors, bristles pointing to every black plane and corner and soot-blinded window.

☐

The dearest nation of all is one that will survive no longer than you and I, a common movement at the mercy of death and time: the ad hoc adventure.

—Resolutions of the Gross Suckling Conference

North? What searcher has ever been directed *north?* What you're supposed to be looking for lies south—those dusky natives, right? For danger and enterprise they send you west, for visions, east. But what's north?

The escape route of the *Anubis.*

The Kirghiz Light.

The Herero country of death.

Ensign Morituri, Carroll Eventyr, Thomas Gwenhidwy, and Roger Mexico are sitting at a table on the redbrick terrace of Der Grob Säugling, an inn by the edge of a little blue Holstein lake. The sun makes the water sparkle. The housetops are red, the steeples are white. Everything is miniature, neat, gently pastoral, locked into the rise

and fall of seasons. Contrasting wood ×s on closed doors.
The brink of autumn. A cow sez moo. The milkmaid farts
at the milk pail, which echoes with a very slight clang,
and the geese honk or hiss. The four envoys drink watered
Moselle and talk mandalas.

The Rocket was fired southward, westward, eastward.
But not northward—not so far. Fired south, at Antwerp,
the bearing was about 173°. East, during testing at Peenemünde, 072°. Fired west, at London, about 260°. Working it out with the parallel rulers, the missing (or, if you
want, "resultant") bearing comes out to something like
354°. This would be the firing implied by all the others, a
ghost-firing which, in the logic of mandalas, either has occurred, most-secretly, or will occur.

So the conferees at the Gross Suckling Conference here,
as it will come to be known, sit around a map with their
instruments, cigarettes and speculations. Sneer not. Here is
one of the great deductive moments in postwar intelligence.
Mexico is holding out for a weighting system to make
vector lengths proportional to the actual number of firings
along each one. Thomas Gwenhidwy, ever sensitive to
events in geographical space, wants to take the 1944
Blizna firings (also eastward) into account, which would
pull the arrow northward from 354°—and even closer to
true north if the firings at London and Norwich from
Walcheren and Staveren are also included.

Evidence and intuition—and maybe a residue of un-
civilizable terror that lies inside us, every one—point to
000°: true North. What better direction to fire the oooooP

Trouble is, what good's a bearing, even a mythic-sym-
metric bearing, without knowing where the Rocket was
fired from to begin with? You have a razor-edge, 280 km
long, sweeping east/west across the Zone's pocked face,
endlessly sweeping, obsessive, dithering, glittering, unbearable, never coming to rest. . . .

Well, Under The Sign Of The Gross Suckling. Swaying
full-color picture of a loathsomely fat drooling infant. In
one puddinglike fist the Gross Suckling clutches a dripping
hamhock (sorry pigs, nothing personal), with the other
he reaches out for a human Mother's Nipple that emerges
out into the picture from the left-hand side, his gaze arrested by the approaching tit, his mouth open—a gleeful

look, teeth pointed and itching, a glaze of FOODmunch-
munchyesgobblemmm over his eyes. Der Grob Säugling,
23rd card of the Zone's trumps major. . . .

Roger likes to think of it as a snap of Jeremy as a child.
Jeremy, who Knows All, has forgiven Jessica her time with
Roger. He's had an outing or two himself, and can understand, he's of liberal mind, the War after all has taken
down certain barriers, Victorianisms you might say (a tale
brought to you by the same jokers who invented the
famous Polyvinyl Chloride Raincoat) . . . and what's this,
Roger, he's trying to *impress* you? his eyelids make high,
amiable crescents as he leans forward (smaller chap than
Roger thought) clutching his glass, sucking on the most
tasteless Pipe Roger has ever seen, a reproduction in brier
of Winston Churchill's *head* for a bowl, no detail is spared,
even a *cigar in its mouth* with a little hole drilled down it
so that some of the smoke can actually seep out the end
. . . it is a servicemen's pub in Cuxhaven here, the place
used to be a marine salvage yard, so the lonesome soldiers
sit dreaming and drinking among all that nautical junk,
not at the same level as in one's usual outdoor café, no,
some are up in tilted hatchways, or dangling in boat-
swain's chairs, crow's-nests, sitting over their bitter among
the chain, tackle, strakework, black iron fittings. It's night.
Lanterns have been brought out to the tables. Soft little
nocturnal waves hush on the shingle. Late waterfowl cry
out over the lake.

"But will it ever get *us*, Jeremy, you and me, that's the
quesshun. . . ." Mexico has been uttering these oracular—
often, as at the Club today for lunch, quite embarrassing—
bits of his ever since he showed up.

"Er, will *what* ever get me, old chap?" It's been old
chap all day.

"Haven't—ch'ever felt something wanted to *gesh* you,
Jeremy?"

"Get me." He's drunk. He's insane. I obviously can't let
him near Jessica these math chaps they're like oboe players
it affects the *brain* or something. . . .

Aha, *but*, once a month, Jeremy, even Jeremy, dreams:
about a gambling debt . . . different sorts of Collectors keep
arriving . . . he cannot remember the debt, the opponent
he lost to, even the game. He senses a great organization

behind these emissaries. Its threats are always left open,
left for Jeremy to complete ... each time, terror has come
welling up through the gap, crystal terror. . . .

Good, good. The other sure-fire calibration test has already been sprung on Jeremy—at a prearranged spot in a
park, two unemployed Augustes leap out in whiteface and
working-clothes, and commence belting each other with
gigantic (7 or 8 feet long) foam rubber penises, cunningly
detailed, all in natural color. These phancy phalli have
proven to be a good investment. Roger and Seaman Bodine (when he's in town) have outdrawn the ENSA shows.
It is a fine source of spare change—multitudes will gather
at the edges of these north German villages to watch the
two zanies whack away. Granaries, mostly empty, poke up
above the rooftops now and then, stretching a wood gal-
lowsarm against the afternoon sky. Soldiers, civilians, and
children. There is a lot of laughter.

Seems people can be reminded of Titans and Fathers,
and laugh. It isn't as funny as a pie in the face, but it's at
least as pure.

Yes, giant rubber cocks are here to stay as part of the
arsenal. . . .

What Jessica said—hair much shorter, wearing a darker
mouth of different outline, harder lipstick, her typewriter
banking in a phalanx of letters between them—was:
"We're going to be married. We're trying very hard to
have a baby."

All at once there is nothing but this asshole between
Gravity and Roger. "I don't care. Have his baby. I'll love
you both—just come with me Jess, please ... I need
you. . . ."

She flips a red lever on her intercom. Far away a buzzer
goes off. "Security." Her voice is perfectly hard, the word
still clap-echoing in the air as in through the screen door
of the Quonset office with a smell of tide flats come the
coppers, looking grim. Security. Her magic word, her spell
against demons.

"Jess—" shit is he going to *cry?* he can feel it building
like an orgasm—

Who saves him (or interferes with his orgasm)? Why,
Jeremy himself. Old Beaver shows up and waves off the
heat, who go surly, fangflashing back to masturbating into

Crime Does Not Pay Comics, gazing dreamy at guardroom pinups of J. Edgar Hoover or whatever it was they were up to, and the romantic triangle are suddenly all to have *lunch* together at the *Club. Lunch* together? Is this Noel Coward or some shit? Jessica at the last minute is overcome by some fictitious female syndrome which both men guess to be morning-sickness, Roger figuring she'll do the most spiteful thing she can think of, Jeremy seeing it as a cute little private yoo-hoo for 2-hoo. So that leaves the fellas alone, to talk briskly about Operation Backfire, which is the British program to assemble some A4s and fire them out into the North Sea. What else are they going to talk about?

"Why?" Roger keeps asking, trying to piss Jeremy off. "Why do you want to put them together and fire them?"

"We've captured them, haven't we? What does one *do* with a rocket?"

"But why?"

"Why?" Damn it, to *see*, obviously. Jessica tells me you're—ah—a *math chap?*"

"Little sigma, times P of s-over-little-sigma, equals one over the square root of two pi, times e to the minus s squared over two little-sigma squared."

"Good Lord." Laughing, hastily checking out the room.

"It is an old saying among my people."

Jeremy knows how to handle *this*. Roger is invited to dinner in the evening, an intimate informal party at the home of Stefan Utgarthaloki, an ex-member of management at the Krupp works here in Cuxhaven. "You're welcome to bring a guest, of course," gnaws the eager Beaver, "there's a lot of snazzy NAAFIs about, it wouldn't be too difficult for *you* to—"

"Informal means lounge suit, eh?" interrupts Roger. Too bad, he hasn't got one. The prospects of being nabbed tonight are good. A party that includes (a) an Operation Backfire figure, (b) a Krupp executive, must necessarily then include (c) at least one ear to the corporate grapevine that's heard of the Urinating Incident in Clive Mossmoon's office. If Roger only knew what Beaver and his friends *really* have in mind!

He does take a guest: Seaman Bodine, who has caused to be brought him from the Panama Canal Zone (where the lock workers wear them as a uniform, in amazing tropical-parrot combinations of yellow, green, lavender, vermilion) a zoot suit of unbelievable proportions—the pointed lapels have to be *reinforced with coat-hanger stays* because they extend so far outboard of the rest of the suit—underneath his purple-on-purple satin shirt the natty tar is actually wearing a corset, squeezing his waist in to a sylphlike 42 inches to allow for the drastic suppression of the jacket, which then falls to Bodine's knees *quintuple-vented* in yards of kilt-style pleats that run clear back up over his ass. The pants are belted under his armpits and pegged down to something like ten inches, so he has to use hidden zippers to get his feet through. The whole suit is blue, not suit-blue, no—really BLUE: *paint-blue*. It is immediately noticed everywhere it goes. At gatherings it haunts the peripheral vision, making decent small-talk impossible. It is a suit that forces you either to reflect on matters as primary as its color, or feel superficial. A subversive garment, all right.

"Just you and me, podner?" sez Bodine. "Ain't that kind of cutting it a little close?"

"Listen," Roger chuckling unhealthily at what's also just occurred to him, "we can't even bring those big rubber cocks along. Tonite, we're going to have to use our *wits!*"

"Tell you what, I'll just send a motorcycle out to Putzi's, round us up a goon squad, and—"

"You know what? You've lost your sense of adventure. Yeh. You didn't use to be like this, you know."

"Look old buddy," pronouncing it in Navy Dialect: budd*ih*, "c'mon, budd*ih*. Putcherself in my shoes."

"I might, if they weren't ... *that* ... shade of yellow—"

"Just a humble guy," the swarthy doughboy of the deep scratching in his groin after an elusive crab with a horn finger, rippling the ballooning pleats and fabric of his trousers, "just a freckleface kid from Albert Lea, Minnesota, down there on Route 69 where the speed limit's lickety-split all night long, just tryin' t' make it in the Zone here, kind of a freckle-face kid used a safety pin through a cork for a catwhisker and stayed up listened to the voices coast to coast before I was 10 and none of them ever recommended gettin' into any of them *gang wars*, budd*ih*. Be glad you're still so fuckin' naïve, Rog, wait'll

you see your first European-gangster hit, they like to use
3 rounds: head, stomach, and heart. You dig that *stomach?*
Over here stomach's no second-class organ, podner 'n'
that's a good autumn kind of thought to keep in mind."

"Bodine, didn't you desert? *That's* a death-sentence, isn't
it?"

"Shit, I can square *that.* But I'm only a cog. Don't go
thinking I know everything. All I know is my trade. I can
show you how to wash coke and assay it, I can feel a gem
and tell you from the temperature if it's a fake—the fake
won't suck as much heat from your body, 'glass is a reluctant vampire,' ancient dealers' saying, a-and I can spot
funnymoney easy as E on an eye chart, I got one of the
best visual memories in the Zone—" So, Roger drags him
off, monologuing, in his zoot suit, to the Krupp wingding.

Coming in the door, first thing Bodine notices is this
string quartet that's playing tonight. The second violin
happens to be Gustav Schlabone, Säure Bummer's frequent unwelcome doping partner, "Captain Horror," as he
is affectionately but not inaccurately known around Der
Platz—and playing viola is Gustav's accomplice in
suicidally depressing everybody inside 100 meters' radius
wherever they drop in (who's that tapping and giggling at
your door, Fred and Phyllis?), André Omnopon, of the
feathery Rilke mustaches and Porky Pig tattoo on stomach
(which is becoming the "hep" thing lately: even back in
the Zone of the Interior the American subdebs all think
it's swoony). Gustav and André are the Inner Voices tonight. Which is especially odd because on the program is
the suppressed quartet from the Haydn Op. 76, the so-
called "Kazoo" Quartet in G-Flat Minor, which gets its
name from the *Largo, cantabile e mesto* movement, in
which the Inner Voices are called to play kazoos instead
of their usual instruments, creating problems of dynamics
for cello and first violin that are unique in the literature.
"You actually need to shift in places from a spiccato to a
détaché," Bodine rapidly talking a Corporate Wife of
some sort across the room toward the free-lunch table piled
with lobster hors d'oeuvres and capon sandwiches—"less
bow, higher up you understand, soften it—then there's also
about a thousand ppp-to-fff blasts, but only the one, the
notorious One, going the other way. . . ." Indeed, one rea-

son for the work's suppression in this subversive use of
sudden fff quieting to ppp. It's the touch of the wandering sound-shadow, the Brennschluss of the Sun. They
don't want you listening to too much of that stuff—at least
not the way Haydn presents it (a strange lapse in the
revered composer's behavior): cello, violin, alto and treble
kazoos all rollicking along in a tune sounds like a song
from the movie *Dr. Jekyll and Mr. Hyde,* "You Should
See Me Dance the Polka," when suddenly in the middle
of an odd bar the kazoos *just stop completely,* and the
Outer Voices fall to plucking a non-melody that tradition
sez represents two 18th-century Village Idiots vibrating
their lower lips. At each other. It goes on for 20, 40 bars
this feeb's pizzicato, middle-line Kruppsters creak in the
bowlegged velvet chairs, bibuhbuhbibuhbuh this does not
sound like *Haydn,* Mutti! Reps from ICI and GE angle
their heads trying to read in the candlelight the little programs lovingly hand-lettered by Utgarthaloki's partner in
life, *Frau* Utgarthaloki, nobody is certain what her first
name is (which is ever so much help to Stefan because it
keeps them all on the defensive with her). She is a blonde
image of your mother dead: if you have ever seen her
travestied in beaten gold, the cheeks curving too far, deformed, the eyebrows too dark and whites too white, some
zero indifference that in the end is truly evil in the way
They've distorted her face, then you know the look: Nalline
Slothrop just before her first martini is right here, in spirit
at this Kruppfest. So is her son Tyrone, but only because
by now—early Virgo—he has become one plucked albatross. Plucked, hell—*stripped.* Scattered all over the Zone.
It's doubtful if he can ever be "found" again, in the conventional sense of "positively identified and detained."
Only feathers . . . redundant or regenerative organs, "which
we would be tempted to classify under the 'Hydra-Phä-
nomen' were it not for the complete absence of hostility. . . ."—Natasha Raum, "Regions of Indeterminacy in
Albatross Anatomy," *Proceedings of the International Society of Confessors to an Enthusiasm for Albatross Nosology,* Winter 1936, great little magazine, they actually
sent a correspondent to *Spain* that winter, to cover that
there are issues devoted entirely to analyses of world
economics, all clearly relevant to problems of Albatross

Nosology—does so-called "Night Worm" belong among the Pseudo-Goldstrassian Group, or is it properly considered—indications being almost identical—a more insidious form of Mopp's Hebdomeriasis?

Well, if the Conference knew better what those categories concealed, they might be in a better position to disarm, de-penis and dismantle the Man. But they don't. Actually they do, but they don't admit it. Sad but true. They are as schizoid, as double-minded in the massive presence of money, as any of the rest of us, and that's the hard fact. The Man has a branch office in each of our brains, his corporate emblem is a white albatross, each local rep has a cover known as the Ego, and their mission in this world is Bad Shit. We do know what's going on, and we let it go on. As long as we can see them, stare at them, those massively moneyed, once in a while. As long as they allow us a glimpse, however rarely. We need that. And how they know it—how often, under what conditions. . . . We ought to be seeing much popular-magazine coverage on the order of The Night Rog and Beaver Fought Over Jessica While She Cried in Krupp's Arms, and drool over every blurry photo—

Roger must have been dreaming for a minute here of the sweaty evenings of Thermidor: the failed Counterforce, the glamorous ex-rebels, half-suspected but still enjoying official immunity and sly love, cameraworthy wherever they carry on . . . doomed pet freaks.

They will use us. We will help legitimize Them, though They don't need it really, it's another dividend for Them, nice but not critical. . . .

Oh yes, isn't that *exactly* what They'll do. Bringing Roger now, at a less than appropriate time and place here in the bosom of the Opposition, while his life's first authentic love is squirming only to get home and take another wad of Jeremy's sperm so they'll make their day's quota—in the middle of all that he has to walk (*ow*, uck) right into the interesting question, which is worse: living on as Their pet, or death? It is not a question he has ever imagined himself asking seriously. It has come by surprise, but there's no sending it away now, he really does have to decide, and soon enough, plausibly soon, to feel the terror in his bowels. Terror he cannot think away.

He has to choose between his life and his death. Letting it sit for a while is no compromise, but a decision to live, on Their terms. . . .

The viola is a ghost, grainy-brown, translucent, sighing in and out of the other Voices. Dynamic shifts abound. Imperceptible lifts, platooning notes together or preparing for changes in loudness, what the Germans call "breath-pauses," skitter among the phrases. Perhaps tonight it is due to the playing of Gustav and André, but after a while the listener starts actually hearing the pauses instead of the notes—his ear gets tickled the way your eye does staring at a recco map until bomb craters flip inside out to become muffins risen above the tin, or ridges fold to valleys, sea and land flicker across quicksilver edges—so the silences dance in this quartet. A-and wait'll those *kazoos* come on!

That's the background music for what is to transpire. The plot against Roger has been formulated with shivering and giddy glee. Seamen Bodine is an unexpected bonus. Going in to dinner becomes a priestly procession, full of secret gestures and understandings. It is a very elaborate meal, according to the menu, full of relevés, poissons, entremets. "What's this 'Überraschungsbraten' here?" Seaman Bodine asks right-hand dinner companion Constance Flamp, loose-khakied newshound and toughtalkin' sweetheart of ev'ry GI from Iwo to Saint-Lô.

"Why, just what it sez, Boats," replies "Commando Connie," "that's German for 'surprise roast.'"

"I'm hep," sez Bodine. She has—maybe not meaning to—gestured with her eyes—perhaps, Pointsman, there is such a thing as the kindness-reflex (how many young men has she seen go down since '42?) that now and then, also beyond the Zero, survives extinction. . . . Bodine looks down at the far end of the table, past corporate teeth and polished fingernails, past heavy monogrammed eating-tools and for the first time notices a stone barbecue pit, with two black iron hand-operated spits. Servants in their prewar livery are busy layering scrap paper (old SHAEF directives, mostly), kindling, quartered pine logs, and coal luscious fist-sized raven chunks of the kind that once left bodies up and down the sides of the canals, once, during the Inflation, when it was actually held that mortally dear.

magine. . . . At the edge of the pit, with Justus about to
ight the taper, as Gretchen daintily laces the fuel with GI
ylene from down in the dockyards, Seaman Bodine ob-
erves Roger's head, being held by four or six hands up-
ide down, the lips being torn away from the teeth and
he high gums already draining white as a skull, while one
f the maids, a classic satin-and-lace, impish, torturable
oung maid, brushes the teeth with American toothpaste,
arefully scrubbing away the nicotine stains and tartar.
Roger's eyes are so hurt and pleading. . . . All around,
guests are whispering. "How quaint, Stefan's even thought
f head cheese!" "Oh, no, it's *another* part *I'm* waiting to
get my teeth in . . ." giggles, heavy breathing, and what's
hat pair of very blue peg pants all ripped . . . and what's
his staining the jacket, and what, up on the spit, red-
ening to a fat-glazed crust, is turning, whose face is
about to come rotating around, why it's—

"No ketchup, no ketchup," the hirsute bluejacket search-
ng agitatedly among the cruets and salvers, "seems to be
o . . . what th' fuck kind of a place is this, *Rog*," yelling
own slantwise across seven enemy faces, "hey, budd*ih*
ou find any *ketchup* down there?"

Ketchup's a code word, okay—

"Odd," replies Roger, who clearly has seen exactly the
ame thing down at the pit, "I was just about to ask *you*
he same question!"

They are grinning at each other like fools. Their auras,
or the record, are green. No shit. Not since winter of
42, in convoy in a North Atlantic gale, with accidental
ons of loose 5-inch ammo rolling all over the ship, the
German wolf pack invisibly knocking off sister ships right
nd left, at Battle Stations inside mount 51 listening to
Pappy Hod tell disaster jokes, really funny ones, the whole
gun crew clutching their stomachs hysterically, gasping for
ir—not since then has Seaman Bodine felt so high in the
good chances of death.

"Some layout, huh?" he calls. "Pretty good food!" Con-
ersation has fallen nearly silent. Politely curious faces
re turning. Flames leap in the pit. They are not "sensi-
ive flames," but if they were they might be able now to
letect the presence of Brigadier Pudding. He is now a
member of the Counterforce, courtesy of Carroll Eventyr.

Courtesy is right. Séances with Pudding are at least as trying as the old Weekly Briefings back at "The White Visitation." Pudding has even more of a mouth on him than he did alive. The sitters have begun to whine: "Aren't we *ever* to be rid of him?" But is is through Pudding's devotion to culinary pranksterism that the repulsive stratagem that follows was devised.

"Oh, I don't know," Roger elaborately casual, "I can't seem to find any *snot soup* on the menu. . . ."

"Yeah, I could've done with some of that *pus pudding,* myself. Think there'll be any of that?"

"No, but there might be a scum soufflé!" cries Roger, "with a side of—*menstrual marmalade!*"

"Well I've got eyes for some of that rich, meaty *smegma stew!*" suggests Bodine. "Or howbout a *clot casserole?*"

"I say," murmurs a voice, indeterminate as to sex, down the table.

"We could plan a better meal than *this,*" Roger waving the menu. "Start off with afterbirth appetizers, perhaps some clever little *scab sandwiches* with the crusts trimmed off of course . . . o-or booger biscuits! Mmm, yes, spread with mucus mayonnaise? and topped with a succulent bit of slime sausage. . . ."

"Oh *I* see," sez Commando Connie, "it has to be all*litera*-tive. How about . . . um . . . *discharge dumplings?*"

"We're doing the soup course, babe," sez cool Seaman Bodine, "so let me just suggest a canker consommé, or perhaps a barf bouillon."

"Vomit vichyssoise," sez Connie.

"You got it."

"Cyst salad," Roger continues, "with little cheery-red squares of abortion aspic, tossed in a subtle dandruff dressing."

There is a sound of well-bred gagging, and a regional sales manager for ICI leaves hurriedly, spewing a long crescent of lumpy beige vomit that splatters across the parquetry. Napkins are being raised to faces all down the table. Silverware is being laid down, silver ringing the fields of white, a puzzling indecision here again, the same as at Clive Mossmoon's office. . . .

On we go, through fart fondue (skillfully placed bubbles of anal gas rising slowly through a rich cheese viscosity, yummm), boil blintzes, Vegetables Venereal in slobber sauce. . . .

A kazoo stops playing. "Wart waffles!" Gustav screams.

"Puke pancakes, with sweat syrup," adds André Omnopon, as Gustav resumes playing, the Outer Voices meantime having broken off in confusion.

"And spread with pinworm preserves," murmurs the cellist, who is not above a bit of fun.

"Hemorrhoid hash," Connie banging her spoon in delight, *"bowel burgers!"*

Frau Utgarthaloki jumps to her feet, upsetting a platter of stuffed sores—*beg* pardon, no they're deviled eggs—and runs from the room, sobbing tragically. Her suave metal husband also rises and follows, casting back at the troublemakers virile stares that promise certain death. A discreet smell of vomit has begun to rise through the hanging tablecloth. Nervous laughter has long embrittled to badmouth whispering.

"A choice of gangrene goulash, or some scrumptious creamy-white *leprosy loaf*," Bodine in a light singsong "le-pro-sy [down a third to] loaf," playfully hounding the holdouts, shaking a finger, c'mon ya little rascals, vomit for the nice zootster. . . .

"Fungus fricassee!" screams Roger the Rowdy. Jessica is weeping on the arm of Jeremy her gentleman, who is escorting her, stiff-armed, shaking his head at Roger's folly, away forever. Does Roger have a second of pain right here? Yes. Sure. You would too. You might even question the worth of your cause. But there are nosepick noodles to be served up buttery and steaming, grime gruel and pustule porridge to be ladled into the bowls of a sniveling generation of future executives, pubic popovers to be wheeled out onto the terraces stained by holocaust sky or growing rigid with autumn.

"Carbuncle cutlets!"

"With *groin gravy!*"

"And ringworm relish!"

Lady Mnemosyne Gloobe is having a seizure of some kind, so violent that her pearls break and go rattling down the silk tablecloth. A general loss of appetite reigns, not to mention overt nausea. The flames in the pit have dwindled. No fat to feed them tonight. Sir Hannibal Grunt-Gobbinette is threatening, between spasms of yellow bile foaming out his nose, to bring the matter up in Parliament. "I'll see you two in the Scrubs if it kills me!" Well . . .

A gentle, precarious soft-shoe out the door, Bodine waving his wide-brim gangster hat. Ta-ta, foax. The only guest still seated is Constance Flamp, who is still roaring out dessert possibilities: "Crotch custard! Phlegm fudge! Mold muffins!" Will she catch hell tomorrow. Pools of this and that glitter across the floor like water-mirages at the Sixth Antechamber to the Throne. Gustav and the rest of the quartet have abandoned Haydn and are all following Roger and Bodine out the door, kazoos and strings accompanying the Disgusting Duo:

> Oh gimme some o' that acne, à-la-mode,
> Eat so much-that Ah, jes' ex-plode!
> Say there budd*ih* you can chow all night, on
> Toe-jam tarts 'n' Diarrhea Dee-lite. . . .

"I have to tell you," Gustav whispering speedily, "I feel so awful about it, but perhaps you don't want people like me. You see . . . I was a Storm Trooper. A long time ago. You know, like Horst Wessel."

"So?" Bodine's laughing. "Maybe I was a Melvin Purvis Junior G-Man."

"A what?"

"For Post Toasties."

"For whom?" The German actually thinks Post Toasties is the name of some American Führer, looking vaguely like Tom Mix or some other such longlip bridlejaw cowboy.

The last black butler opens the last door to the outside, and escape. Escape tonight. "Pimple pie with filth frosting, gentlemen," he nods. And just at the other side of dawning, you can see a smile.

□

In her pack, Geli Tripping brings along a few of Tchitcherine's toenail clippings, a graying hair, a piece of bedsheet with a trace of his sperm, all tied in a white kerchief, next to a bit of Adam and Eve root and a loaf of bread baked from wheat she has rolled naked in and ground against the sun. She has left off tending her herd of toads on the witches' hillsides, and has passed her white wand to another apprentice. She is off to find her gallant Attila. Now there are a good few hundred of these young women in the Zone who're smitten with love for Tchitcherine, all of them sharp as foxes, but none quite as stubborn as Geli—and none are witches.

At noon she comes to a farmhouse with a floor of blue and white tiles in the kitchen, elaborate old china plates hung like pictures, and a rocking-chair. "Do you have a photo of him?" the old woman handing her a tin army plate with the remains of her morning's Bauernfrühstück. "I can give you a spell."

"Sometimes I can call up his face in a cup of tea. But the herbs have to be gathered carefully. I'm not that good at it yet."

"But you're in love. Technique is just a substitute for when you get older."

"Why not stay in love always?"

The two women watch each other across the sunny kitchen. Cabinets with glass panes shine from the walls. Bees buzz outside the windows. Geli goes and pumps water from the well, and they brew some strawberry-leaf tea. But Tchitcherine's face doesn't appear.

The night the blacks started off on their great trek, Nordhausen felt like a city in a myth, under the threat of some special destruction—engulfment by a crystal lake, lava from the sky . . . for an evening, the sense of preservation there was lost. The blacks, like the rockets in the Mittelwerke, had given Nordhausen continuity. Now the blacks are gone: Geli knows they are on collision course with Tchitcherine. She doesn't want duels. Let the university boys duel. She wants her graying steel barbarian alive. She can't bear to think that she may already have touched him, felt his scarred and historied hands, for the last time.

Behind, pushing her, is the town's somnolence, and at night—the strange canaried nights of the Harz (where canary hustlers are busy shooting up female birds with male hormones so they'll sing long enough to be sold to

the foreign suckers who occupy the Zone)—full of too
many spells, witch-rivalries, coven politics . . . she knows
that's not what magic is about. The Hexes-Stadt, with its
holy mountains cropped in pale circles all up and down
their green faces by the little tethered goats, has turned
into just another capital, where the only enterprise is
administrating—the feeling there is of upstairs at the
musicians' union—no music, just glass-brick partitions,
spittoons, indoor plants—no *practicing* witches left. You
either come to the Brocken-complex with a bureaucratic
career in mind, or you leave it, and choose the world.
There are the two distinct sorts of witch, and Geli is the
World-choosing sort.

Here is the World. She is wearing gray men's trousers
rolled to the knee that flap around her thighs as she walks
by the rye fields . . . walking, with her head down, pushing
hair out of her eyes often. Sometimes soldiers come by,
and give her rides. She listens for news of Tchitcherine,
of the trekking Schwarzkommando. If it feels right, she
will even ask about Tchitcherine. The variety of the rumors
surprises her. *I'm not the only one who loves him . .*
though *their* love of course is friendly, admiring, unsexual
. . . Geli's the only one in the Zone who loves him completely. Tchitcherine, known in some circles as "the Red
Doper," is about to be purged: the emissary is none other
than Beria's top man, the sinister N. Ripov himself.

Bullshit, Tchitcherine's already dead, didn't you hear
he's been dead for months . . .

. . . they've had somebody impersonating him till all the
others in his Bloc are taken care of . . .

. . . no, he came into Lüneburg last weekend, my mate'
seen him before, no mistake, it's him . . .

. . . he's lost a lot of weight and takes a heavy body
guard everywhere he goes. At least a dozen. Oriental
mostly . . .

. . . fully equipped with Judas Iscariot no doubt. *Tha*
one's hard to believe. A dozen? Where does anybody fin
that many people he can trust? Especially out at th
edge like he is—

"What edge?" They're rattling along in the back of a
2½-ton lorry through very green rolling country . . .
storm is blowing up mute purple, veined in yellow, behin

hem. Geli's been drinking wine with this scurvy lot of
ommies, a demolition squad who've been out all day
learing canals. They smell of creosote, marsh-mud, am-
aonia from the dynamite.

"Well *you* know what he's doing."

"The rockets?"

"I wouldn't want to be in his place, that's all."

Up on the crest of a hill, an army surveying party is
estoring a damaged road. One silhouette leans peering
hrough a transit, one holds a bob. A bit apart from the
nstrument man another engineer stands with his arms out
straight to the sides, his head moves sighting along either
pointed hand, then the arms swoop together . . . if you
close your eyes, and have learned to let your arms move
by themselves, your fingers will touch making a perfect
right angle from where they were . . . Geli watches the tiny
act: it is devotional, graceful, and she *feels the cross* the
man has made on his own circle of visible earth . . .
unconsciously a mandala . . . it is a sign for her. He is
pointing her on her way. Later that evening she sees an
eagle flying across the marshes, in the same direction.
It's golden-dark, almost night. The region is lonely and
Pan is very close. Geli has been to enough Sabbaths to
handle it—she thinks. But what is a devil's blue bite on
the ass to the shrieking-outward, into stone resonance,
where there is no good or evil, out in the luminous spaces
Pan will carry her to? Is she ready yet for anything so
real? The moon has risen. She sits now, at the same spot
where she saw the eagle, waiting, waiting for something
to come and take her. Have you ever waited for *it*? wondering whether it will come from outside or inside? Finally
past the futile guesses at what might happen . . . now and
then re-erasing brain to keep it clean for the Visit . . . yes
wasn't it close to here? remember didn't you sneak away
from camp to have a moment alone with What you felt
stirring across the land . . . it was the equinox . . . green
spring equal nights . . . canyons are opening up, at the
bottoms are steaming fumaroles, steaming the tropical life
there like greens in a pot, rank, dope-perfume, a hood of
smell . . . human consciousness, that poor cripple, that
deformed and doomed thing, is about to be born. This is
the World just before men. Too violently pitched alive in

constant flow ever to be seen by men directly. They are
meant only to look at it dead, in still strata, transputrefied
to oil or coal. Alive, it was a threat: it was Titans, was an
overpeaking of life so clangorous and mad, such a green
corona about Earth's body that some spoiler *had* to be
brought in before it blew the Creation apart. So we, the
crippled keepers, were sent out to multiply, to have dominion. God's spoilers. Us. Counter-revolutionaries. *It is
our mission to promote death.* The way we kill, the way
we die, being unique among the Creatures. It was something we had to work on, historically and personally. To
build from scratch up to its present status as reaction
nearly as strong as life, holding down the green uprising.
But only nearly as strong.

Only nearly, because of the defection rate. A few keep
going over to the Titans every day, in their striving sub-
creation (how can flesh tumble and flow so, and never be
any less beautiful?), into the rests of the folk-song Death
(empty stone rooms), out, and through, and down under
the net, down to the uprising.

In harsh-edged echo, Titans stir far below. They are all
the presences we are not supposed to be seeing—wind
gods, hilltop gods, sunset gods—that we train ourselves
away from to keep from looking further even though
enough of us do, leave Their electric voices behind in the
twilight at the edge of the town and move into the constantly parted cloak of our nightwalk till

Suddenly, Pan—leaping—its face too beautiful to bear,
beautiful Serpent, its coils in rainbow lashings in the sky
—into the sure bones of fright—

Don't walk home at night through the empty country.
Don't go into the forest when the light is too low, even
too late in the afternoon—it will get you. Don't sit by the
tree like this, with your cheek against the bark. It is
impossible in this moonlight to see if you are male or
female now. Your hair spills, silver white. Your body under
the gray cloth is so exactly vulnerable, so fated to
degradation time and again. What if he wakes and finds
you've gone? He is now always the same, awake or asleep
—he never leaves the single dream, there are no more
differences between the worlds: they have become one
for him. Thanatz and Margherita may have been his last

ies with the old. That may be why they stayed so long, t was his desperation, he wanted to hold on, he needed hem . . . but when he looks at them now he doesn't see hem as often any more. They are also losing what reality hey brought here, as Gottfried lost all of his to Blicero ong ago. Now the boy moves image to image, room to room, sometimes out of the action, sometimes part of it . . . whatever he has to do, he does. The day has its logic, ts needs, no way for him to change it, leave it, or live outside it. He is helpless, he is sheltered secure.

It's only a matter of weeks, and everything will be over, Germany will have lost the War. The routines go on. The boy cannot imagine anything past the last surrender. If he and Blicero are separated, what will happen to the flow of days?

Will Blicero die *no please don't let him die.* . . . (But he will.) "You're going to survive me," he whispers. Gottfried kneels at his feet, wearing the dog collar. Both are in army clothes. It's a long time since either of them dressed as a woman. It is important tonight they they both be men. "Ah, you're so smug, you little bastard. . . ."

It is only another game isn't it, another excuse for a whipping? Gottfried keeps silent. When Blicero wants an answer, he says so. It happens often that he only wants to talk, and that may go on for hours. No one has ever talked to Gottfried before, not like this. His father uttered only commands, sentences, flat judgments. His mother was emotional, a great flow of love, frustration and secret terror passed into him from her, but they never really talked. This is so more-than-real . . . he feels he must keep every word, that none must be lost. Blicero's words have become precious to him. He understands that Blicero wants to give, without expecting anything back, give away what he loves. He believes that he exists for Blicero, even if the others have all ceased to, that in the new kingdom they pass through now, he is the only other living inhabitant. Was it this he expected to be taken by, taken into? Blicero's seed, sputtering into the poisoned manure of his bowels . . . it is waste, yes, futility . . . but . . . as man and woman, coupled, are shaken to the teeth at their approaches to the gates of life, hasn't he also felt more, worshipfully more past these arrangements for penetration, the style, garments of flaying without passion, sheer hosiery perishable as the skin of a snake, custom manacles and chains to stand for the bondage he feels in his heart... all become theatre as he approached the gates of that Other Kingdom, felt the white gigantic muzzles some-where inside, expressionless beasts frozen white, pushing him away, the crust and mantle hum of mystery so beyond his poor hearing... there have to be these too, lovers whose genitals *are* consecrated to shit, to endings, to the desperate nights in the streets when connection proceeds out of all personal control, proceeds or fails, a gathering of fallen—as many in acts of death as in acts of life—or a sentence to be alone for another night.... Are they to be denied, passed over, all of them?

On his approaches to it, taken inward again and again, Gottfried can only try to keep himself open, to loosen the sphincter of his soul. ...

"And sometimes I dream of discovering the edge of the World. Finding that there *is* an end. My mountain gentian always knew. But it has cost me so much.

"America *was* the edge of the World. A message for Europe, continent-sized, inescapable. Europe had found the site for its Kingdom of Death, that special Death the West had invented. Savages had their waste regions, Kalaharis, lakes so misty they could not see the other side. But Europe had gone deeper—into obsession, addiction, away from all the savage innocences. America was a gift from the invisible powers, a way of returning. But Europe refused it. It wasn't Europe's Original Sin—the latest name for that is Modern Analysis—but it happens that Subsequent Sin is harder to atone for.

"In Africa, Asia, Amerindia, Oceania, Europe came and established its order of Analysis and Death. What it could not use, it killed or altered. In time the death-colonies grew strong enough to break away. But the impulse to empire, the mission to propagate death, the structure of it, kept on. Now we are in the last phase. American Death has come to occupy Europe. It has learned empire from its old metropolis. But now we have *only* the structure left us, none of the great rainbow plumes, no fittings of gold, no epic marches over alkali seas. The savages of other continents, corrupted but still resisting in the name of life, have gone on despite everything . . . while Death and Europe are separate as ever, their love still unconsummated. Death only rules here. It has never, in love, become *one with.* . . .

"Is the cycle over now, and a new one ready to begin? Will our new Edge, our new Deathkingdom, be the Moon? I dream of a great glass sphere, hollow and very high and far away . . . the colonists have learned to do without air, it's vacuum inside and out . . . it's understood the men won't ever return . . . they are all men. There are ways for getting back, but so complicated, so at the mercy of language, that presence back on Earth is only temporary, and never 'real' . . . passages out there are dangerous, chances of falling so shining and deep. . . . Gravity rules all the way out to the cold sphere, *there is always the danger of falling.* Inside the colony, the handful of men have a frosty appearance, hardly solid, no more alive than memories, nothing to touch . . . only their remote images, black and white film-images, grained, broken year after hoarfrost year out in the white latitudes, in empty colony, with only infrequent visits from the accidental, like me. . . .

"I wish I could recover it all. Those men had once been through a tragic day—ascent, fire, failure, blood. The events of that day, so long ago, had put them into exile forever . . . no, they weren't really spacemen. Out here, they wanted to dive between the worlds, to fall, turn, reach and swing on journeys curved through the shining, through the winter nights of space—their dreams were of rendezvous, of cosmic trapeze acts carried on in loneliness, in sterile grace, in certain knowledge that no one would ever be watching, that loved ones had been lost forever . . . .

"The connections they hoped for would always miss by trillions of dark miles, by years of frozen silence. But I wanted to bring you back the story. I remember that you used to whisper me to sleep with stories of us one day living on the Moon . . . are you beyond that by now? You've got much older. Can you feel in your body how strongly I have infected you with my dying? I was meant to: when a certain time has come, I think that we are all meant to. Fathers are carriers of the virus of Death, and sons are the infected . . . and, so that the infection may be more certain, Death in its ingenuity has contrived to make the father and son beautiful to each other as Life has made male and female . . . oh Gottfried of course yes you are beautiful to me but I'm dying . . . I want to get through it as honestly as I can, and your immortality rips at my heart—can't you see why I might want to destroy that, oh that *stupid clarity* in your eyes . . . when I see you in morning and evening ranks, so open, so ready to take my sickness in and shelter it, shelter it inside your own little ignorant love. . . .

"Your love." He nods several times. But his eyes are too dangerously spaced beyond the words, stunned irreversibly away from real Gottfried, away from the weak, the failed smells of real breath, by barriers stern and clear as ice, and hopeless as the one-way flow of European time. . . .

"I want to break out—to leave this cycle of infection and death. I want to be taken in love: so taken that you and I, and death, and life, will be gathered, inseparable, into the radiance of what we would become. . . ."

Gottfried kneels, numb, waiting. *Blicero is looking at him.* Deeply: his face whiter than the boy has ever seen it. A raw spring wind beats the canvas of their tent. It's near sunset. In a moment Blicero must go out to take evening reports. His hands rest near a mound of cigarette butts in a mess tray. His myopic witch's eyes, through the thick lenses, may be looking into Gottfried's for the first time. Gottfried cannot look away. He knows, somehow, incompletely, that he has a decision to make . . . that Blicero expects something from him . . . but Blicero has always made the decisions. *Why is he suddenly asking* . . .

It all poises here. Passageways of routine, still cogent enough, still herding us through time . . . the iron rockets waiting outside . . . the birth-scream of the latest spring torn across rainy miles of Saxony, route-sides littered with last envelopes, stripped gears, seized bearings, rotted socks and skivvies fragrant now with fungus and mud. If there is still hope for Gottfried here in this wind-beat moment, then there is hope elsewhere. The scene itself must be read as a card: what is to come. Whatever has happened since to the figures in it (roughly drawn in soiled white, army gray, spare as a sketch on a ruined wall) it is preserved, though it has no name, and, like The Fool, no agreed assignment in the deck.

□

Here's Enzian ramrodding his brand-new rocket through the night. When it rains, when the mist is heavy, before the watch can quite get tarps over, the glossy skin of the rocket is seen to've turned to dark slate. Perhaps, after all, just before the firing, it will be painted black.

It is the 00001, the second in its series.

Russian loudspeakers across the Elbe have called to you. American rumors have come jiving in to the fires at night and summoned, against the ground of your hopes, the yellow American deserts, Red Indians, blue sky, green cactus. How did you feel about the old Rocket? Not now that it's giving you job security, but back then—do you remember any more what it was wheeling them out by hand, a dozen of you that morning, a guard of honor in the simple encounter of your bodies with its inertia ... all your faces drowning in the same selfless look—the moirés of personality softening, softening, each sweep of surf a little more out of focus till all has become subtle grades of cloud—all hatred, all love, wiped away for the short distance you had to push it over the winter berm, aging men in coatskirts flapping below your boottops, breaths in white spouts breaking turbulent as the waves behind you. . . . Where will you all go? What empires, what deserts? You caressed its body, brute, freezing through your gloves, here together without shame or reticence you twelve struggled, in love, on this Baltic shore—not Peenemünde perhaps, not official Peenemünde ... but once, years ago ... boys in white shirts and dark vests and caps ... on some beach, a children's resort, when we were younger ... at Test Stand VII the image, at last, you couldn't leave—the way the wind smelled salt and dying, the sound of winter surf, the premonition of rain you could feel at the back of your neck, stirring in the clipped hairs. . . . At Test Stand VII, the holy place.

But young men have all grown older, and there's little color in the scene ... they are pushing into the sun, the

glare strikes them squinting and grinning, bright here as
the morning shift at Siemens with the centaurs struggling
high on the wall, the clock without numerals, bicycles
squeaking, lunchpails and lunchbags and the lowered faces
of the trudging dutiful streams of men and women into
the dark openings . . . it resembles a Daguerreotype taken
of early Raketen-Stadt by a forgotten photographer in
1856: this is the picture, in fact, that killed him—he died
a week later from mercury poisoning after inhaling fumes
of the heated metal in his studio . . . well, he was a habitué
of mercury fumes in moderate doses, he felt it did his
brain some good, and that may account for pictures like
"Der Raketen-Stadt": it shows, from a height that is
topographically impossible in Germany, the ceremonial
City, fourfold as expected, an eerie precision to all lines
and shadings architectural and human, built in mandalic
form like a Herero village, overhead a magnificent sky,
marble carried to a wildness of white billow and candes-
cence . . . there seems to be building, or demolition, under
way in various parts of the City, for nothing here remains
the same, we can see the sweat in individual drops on the
workers' dark necks as they struggle down in the bone-
damp cellars . . . a bag of cement has broken, and its
separate motes hang in the light . . . the City will always
be changing, new tire-treads in the dust, new cigarette
wrappers in the garbage . . . engineering changes to the
Rocket create new routes of supply, new living arrangements, reflected in traffic densities as viewed from this
unusual height—there are indeed tables of Functions to
get from such City-changes to Rocket-modifications: no
more than an extension, really, of the techniques by which
Constance Babington-Smith and her colleagues at R. A. F.
Medmenham discovered the Rocket back in 1943 in recco
photographs of Peenemünde.

    But remember if you loved it. If you did, how you loved
it. And how much—after all you're used to asking "how
much," used to measuring, to comparing measurements,
putting them into equations to find out how much more,
how much of, how much when . . . and here in your common drive to the sea feel as much as you wish of that
dark double-minded love which is also shame, bravado,
engineers' geopolitics—"spheres of influence" modified to
toruses of Rocket range that are parabolic in section . . .

... not, as we might imagine, bounded below by the line of the Earth it "rises from" and the Earth it "strikes" No But Then You Never Really Thought It Was Did You Of Course It Begins Infinitely Below The Earth And Goes On Infinitely Back Into The Earth it's only the *peak* that we are allowed to see, the break up through the surface, out of the other silent world, violently (a jet airplane crashing into faster-than-sound, some years later a spaceship crashing into faster-than-light) Remember The Password In The Zone This Week Is FASTER—THAN, THE-SPEED-OFLIGHT Speeding Up Your Voice Exponentially—Linear Exceptions Made Only In Case of Upper Respiratory Complaints, at each "end," understand, a very large transfer of energy: breaking upward into this world, a controlled burning—breaking downward again, an uncontrolled explosion ... this lack of symmetry leads to speculating that a presence, analogous to the Aether, flows through time, as the Aether flows through space. The assumption of a Vacuum in time tended to cut us off one from another. But an Aether sea to bear us world-to-world might bring us back a continuity, show us a kinder unverse, more easy-going. ...

So, yes yes this is a scholasticism here, Rocket state-cosmology ... the Rocket does lead that way—among others—past these visible serpent coils that lash up above the surface of Earth in rainbow light, in steel tetany ... these storms, these things of Earth's deep breast we were never told ... past them, through the violence, to a numbered cosmos, a quaint brownwood-paneled, Victorian kind of Brain War, as between quaternions and vector analysis in the 1880s—the nostalgia of Aether, the silver, pendulumed, stone-anchored, knurled-brass, filigreed elegantly functional shapes of your grandfathers. These sepia tones are here, certainly. But the Rocket has to be many things, it must answer to a number of different shapes in the dreams of those who touch it—in combat, in tunnel, on paper—it must survive heresies shining, unconfoundable ... and heretics there will be: Gnostics who have been taken in a rush of wind and fire to chambers of the Rocket-throne ... Kabbalists who study the Rocket as Torah, letter by letter—rivets, burner cap and brass rose, its text is theirs to permute and combine into new revelations, always unfolding ... Manichaeans who see two Rock-

ets, good and evil, who speak together in the sacred
idiolalia of the Primal Twins (some say their names are
Enzian and Blicero) of a good Rocket to take us to the
stars, an evil Rocket for the World's suicide, the two
perpetually in struggle.

But these heretics will be sought and the dominion of
silence will enlarge as each one goes down ... they will
all be sought out. Each will have his personal Rocket.
Stored in its target-seeker will be the heretic's EEG, the
spikes and susurrations of heartbeat, the ghost-blossomings
of personal infrared, each Rocket will know its intended
and hunt him, ride him a green-doped and silent hound,
through our World, shining and pointed in the sky at his
back, his guardian, executioner rushing in, *rushing
closer*. . . .

Here are the objectives. To make the run over tracks
that may end abruptly at riverside or in carbonized trainyard, over roads even the unpaved alternates to which are
patrolled now by Russian and British and American troops
in a hardening occupation, a fear of winter bleaching the
men all more formal, into braces of Attention they ignored
during the summer, closer adherence now to the paperwork as colors of trees and brush begin their change, as
purple blurs out over miles of heath, and nights come
sooner. To have to stay out in the rains of early Virgo:
the children who stowed away on the trek against all
orders are down now with coughs and fevers, sniffling at
night, hoarse little voices inside oversized uniform jackets.
To brew tea for them from fennel, betony, Whitsun roses,
sunflowers, mallow leaves—to loot sulfa drugs and penicillin. To avoid raising road-dust when the sun has dried
the ruts and crowns again by noon. To sleep in the fields.
To hide the rocket sections under haystacks, behind the
single wall of a gutted railroad shed, among rainy willow,
down beside the river beds. To disperse at any alarm, or
often at random, just for drill—to flow like a net, down
out of the Harz, up the ravines, sleeping in the dry glazed
spaces of deserted spas (official pain, official death watching all night from the porcelain eyes of statues), digging
in nights' perimeters, smelling pine needles boots and
trench-shovels have crushed. . . . To keep faith that it is
not trek this time, nor struggle, but truly Destiny, the

00001 sliding like an oiled bolt into the receivership of the railway system prepared for it last spring, a route only apparently in ruins, carefully crafted by the War, by special techniques of bombardment, to take this most immachinate of techniques, the Rocket—the Rocket, this most terribly potential of bombardments. . . .

The 00001 goes disassembled, in sections—warhead, guidance, fuel and oxidizer tanks, tail section. If they all make it to the firing site, it will have to be put back together there.

"Show me the society that never said, 'I am created among men,'" Christian walks with Enzian in the fields above the encampment, "'to protect you each from violence, to give shelter in time of disaster'—but Enzian, what protection *is* there? what can protect us from *that*," gesturing down the valley at the yellow-gray camouflage netting they can both, X-ray eyed for this one journey, see through. . . .

Enzian and the younger man somehow have drifted into these long walks. Nothing deliberate on either side. Is this how successions occur? Each man is suspicious. But there are no more of the old uncomfortable silences. No competing.

"It comes as the Revealer. Showing that no society can protect, never could—they are as foolish as shields of paper. . . ." He must tell Christian everything he knows, everything he suspects or has dreamed. Proclaiming none of it for truth. But he must keep nothing back for himself. Nothing is his to keep. "They have lied to us. They can't keep us from dying, so They lie to us about death. A cooperative structure of lies. What have They ever given us a return for the trust, the love—They actually say 'love' —we're supposed to owe Them? Can They keep us from even catching cold? from lice, from being alone? from *anything*? Before the Rocket we went on believing, because we wanted to. But the Rocket can penetrate, from the sky, at any given point. Nowhere is safe. We can't believe Them any more. Not if we are still sane, and love the truth."

"We are," nods Christian. "We do." He isn't looking at Enzian to confirm it, either.

"Yes."

"Then . . . in the absence of faith . . ."

One night, in the rain, their laager stops for the night at
a deserted research station, where the Germans, close to
the end of the War, were developing a sonic death-mirror.
Tall paraboloids of concrete are staggered, white and
monolithic, across the plain. The idea was to set off an
explosion in front of the paraboloid, at the exact focal
point. The concrete mirror would then throw back a
perfect shock wave to destroy anything in its path. Thousands of guinea pigs, dogs and cows were experimentally
blasted to death here—reams of death-curve data were
compiled. But the project was a lemon. Only good at
short range, and you rapidly came to a falloff point where
the amount of explosives needed might as well be deployed
some other way. Fog, wind, hardly visible ripples or snag
in the terrain, anything less than perfect conditions, could
ruin the shock wave's deadly shape. Still, Enzian can envision a war, a place for them, "a desert. Lure your enemy
to a desert. The Kalahari. Wait for the wind to die."

"Who would fight for a desert?" Katje wants to know.
She's wearing a hooded green slicker looks even too big
for Enzian.

"*In*," Christian squatting down, looking up at the pale
curve of reflector they've come to the base of and have
gathered at in the rain, sharing a smoke, taking a moment
away from the rest of the trek, "not 'for.' What he's
saying is 'in.'"

Saves trouble later if you can get the Texts straight
soon as they're spoken. "Thank you," sez Oberst Enzian.

A hundred meters away, huddled into another white
paraboloid, watching them, is a fat kid in a gray tanker
jacket. Out of its pocket peer two furry little bright eyes.
It is fat Ludwig and his lost lemming Ursula—he has
found her at last and after all and despite everything. For
a week they have been drifting alongside the trek, just
past visibility, pacing the Africans day by day . . . among
trees at the tops of escarpments, at the fires' edges at
night Ludwig is there, watching . . . accumulating evidence
or terms of an equation . . . a boy and his lemming, out
to see the Zone. Mostly what he's seen is a lot of chewing
gum and a lot of foreign cock. How else does a foot-loose
kid get by in the Zone these days? Ursula is preserved

Ludwig has fallen into a fate worse than death and found it's negotiable. So not all lemmings go over the cliff, and not all children are preserved against snuggling into the sin of profit. To expect any more, or less, of the Zone is to disagree with the terms of the Creation.

When Enzian rides point he has the habit of falling into reveries, whether the driver is talking or not. In night without headlamps, a mist coarse enough to be falling, or now and then blown like a wet silk scarf in the face, inside and outside the same temperature and darkness, balances like these allow him to float just under waking, feet and arms bug-upwards pushing at the rubbery glass surface-tension between the two levels, sticking in it, dream-caressed at hands and feet become super-sensitive, a good home-style horizontalless drowse. The engine of the stolen truck is muffled in old mattresses tied over the hood. Henryk the Hare, driving, keeps a leery eye on the temperature gauge. He's called "the Hare" because he can never get messages right, as in the old Herero story. So reverences are dying.

A figure slips into the road, flashlight circling slowly. Enzian unsnaps the isinglass window, leans out into the heavy mist, and calls "faster than the speed of light." The figure waves him on. But in the last edge of Enzian's glance back, in the light from the flash *rain is sticking to the black face in big fat globules,* sticking as water does to black grease-paint, but not to Herero skin—

"Think we can make a U-turn here?" The shoulders are treacherous, and both men know it. Back in the direction of camp the line of slow-rolling lowlands is lit up by a thud of apricot light.

"Shit," Henryk the Hare jamming it in reverse, waiting for orders from Enzian as they grind slowly backwards. The one with the flashlight may have been the only look-out, there may be no enemy concentration for miles. But—

"There." Beside the road, a prone body. It's Mieczislav Omuzire, with a bad head wound. "Get him in, come on." They load him into the back of the idling truck, and cover him with a shelter half. No time to find out how bad it is. The blackface sentry has vanished for good. From the direction they're backing in comes the stick-rattle of rifle fire.

"We're going into this *backwards?*"

"Have *you* heard any mortar fire?"

"Since the one? No."

"Andreas must have knocked it out then."

"Oh, *they'll* be all right, Nguarorerue. I'm worrying about *us.*"

Orutyene dead. Okandio, Ekori, Omuzire wounded, Ekori critically. The hostiles were white.

"How many?"

"Dozen maybe."

"We can't count on a safe perimeter—" blue-white flashlight blobbing ellipse-to-parabola across the shaking map, "till Braunschweig. If it's still there." Rain hits the map in loud spatters.

"Where's the railroad?" puts in Christian. He gets an interested look from Andreas. It's mutual. There's a good deal of interest here lately. The railroad is 6 or 7 miles northwest.

The people come empty their belongings next to the Rocket's trailer rigs. Saplings are being axed down, each blow loud and carrying . . . a frame is being constructed, bundles of clothing, pots and kettles stuffed here and there under the long tarpaulin between bent-sapling hoops, to simulate pieces of rocket. Andreas is calling, "All decoys muster by the cook wagon," fishing in his pockets for the list he keeps. The decoy trek will move on northward, no violent shift in direction—the rest will angle east, back toward the Russian Army. If they get just close enough, the British and American armies may move more cautiously. It may be possible to ride the interface, like gliding at the edge of a thunderstorm . . . all the way to the end between armies East and West.

Andreas sits dangling feet kicking heels against tailgate *bong . . . bong . . .* tolling departure. Enzian looks up, quizzical. Andreas wants to say something. Finally: "Christian goes with you, then?"

"Yes?" Blinking under rain-beaded eyebrows. "Oh, for God's sake, Andreas."

"Well? The decoys are supposed to make it too, right?"

"Look, take him with *you,* if you want."

"I only wanted to find out," Andreas shrugs, "what's been settled."

"You could have asked me. Nothing's been 'settled.'"

"Maybe not by you. That's your game. You think it'll preserve you. But it doesn't work for *us*. We have to know what's really going to happen."

Enzian kneels and begins to lift the heavy iron tailgate. He knows how phony it looks. Who will believe that in his heart he wants to belong to them out there, the vast Humility sleepless, dying, in pain tonight across the Zone? the preterite he loves, knowing he's always to be a stranger.... Chains rattle above him. When the edge of the gate is level with his chin, he looks up, into Andreas's eyes. His arms are braced tight. His elbows ache. It is an offering. He wants to ask, How many others have written me off? Is there a fate only I've been kept blind to? But habits persist, in their own life. He struggles to his feet, silently, lifting the dead weight, slamming it into place. Together they slip bolts through at each corner. "See you there," Enzian waves, and turns away. He swallows a tablet of German desoxyephedrine then pops in a stick of gum. Speed makes teeth grind, gum gets chewed by grinding teeth, chewing on gum is a technique, developed during the late War by women, to keep from crying. Not that he wants to cry for the separation. He wants to cry for himself: for what they all must believe is going to happen to him. The more they believe it, the better chance there is. His people are going to demolish him if they can....

Chomp, chomp, hmm good evening ladies, nice job on the lashings there Ljubica, chomp, how the head Mieczislav, bet they were surprised when the bullets *bounced off!* heh-heh chomp, chomp, evening "Sparks" (*Ozohande*), anything from Hamburg yet on the liquid oxygen, damned Oururu better come through-ru, or we gonna have a bad-ass time trying to lay low till he do-ru—oh shit who's *that*—

It's Josef Ombindi's who it is, leader of the Empty Ones. But till he stopped smiling, for a few second there, Enzian thought it was Orutyene's ghost. "The word is that the Okandio child was killed too."

"Not so." Chomp.

"She was my first try at preventing a birth."

"So you maintain a deadly interest in her," chomp, chomp. He knows that's not it, but the man annoys him.

"Suicide is a freedom even the lowest enjoy. But you would deny that freedom to a people."

"No ideology. Tell me if your friend Oururu is going to have the LOX generator ready to roll. Or if there is a funny surprise, instead, waiting for me in Hamburg."

"All right, no ideology. You would deny *your* people a freedom even *you* enjoy, Oberst Nguarorerue." Smiling again like the ghost of the man who fell tonight. Probing for the spot, jabbing what? what? want to say *what*, Oberst? till he sees the tiredness in Enzian's face, and understands it is not a trick. "A freedom," whispering smiling, a love song under black skies edged all around in acid orange, a commercial full of Cathar horror at the practice of imprisoning souls in the bodies of new-borns, "a freedom you may exercise soon. I hear your soul talking in its sleep. I know you better than anyone."

Chomp, chomp, oh I had to give him the watch lists didn't I. Oh, am I a fool. Yes, he can choose the night. . . . "You're a hallucination, Ombindi," putting just enough panic into his voice so that if it doesn't work it'll still be a good insult, "I'm projecting my own death-wish, and it comes out looking like you. Uglier than I ever dreamed." Giving him the Spaceman Smile for a full 30 seconds, after only 10 seconds of which Ombindi has already begun to shift his eyes, sweat, press his lips together, look at the ground, turn away, look back, but Enzian prolongs it, no mercy tonight my people, Spaceman Smile turning everything inside a mile radius to frozen ice-cream colors NOW that we're all in the mood, how about installing the battery covers *any*way, Djuro? That's right, X-ray vision, saw right through the tarp, write it down as another miracle . . . you there Vlasta, take the next radio watch, forget what it says on the list, there's never been any more than routine traffic logged with Hamburg, and I wanna know why, wanna know what *does* come through when Ombindi's people are on watch . . . communication on the trek command frequency is by CW dots and dashes—no voices to betray. But operators swear they can tell the individual sending-hands. Vlasta is one of his best operators, and she can do good hand-imitations of most of Ombindi's people. Been practicing up, just in case.

The others, who've been all along wondering if Enzian

was *ever* going to move on Ombindi, can tell now by the
look on his face and the way he's walking through—So,
with little more than touches to the brim of his forage cap,
signaling Plan So-and-So, the Ombindi people are quietly,
without violence, relieved of all watch duties tonight,
though still keeping their weapons and ammo. No one has
ever taken those away. There's no reason to. Enzian is
no more vulnerable now than he ever was, which was
plenty.

The fat boy Ludwig is a white glowworm in the mist.
The game is that he's scouting for a vast white army,
always at his other flank, ready to come down off of the
high ground at a word from Ludwig, and smear the blacks
into the earth. But he would never call them down. He
would rather go with the trek, invisible. There is no
hustling for him down there. Their journey doesn't include
him. They have somewhere to go. He feels he must go
with them, but separate, a stranger, no more or less at
the mercy of the Zone. . . .

□

It's a bridge over a stream. Very seldom will traffic come
by overhead. You can look up and see a whole slope of
cone-bearing trees rushing up darkly away from one side
of the road. Trees creak in sorrow for the engineered
wound through their terrain, their terrenity or earthhood.
Brown trout flick by in the stream. Inside the culvert,
other shelterers have written on the damp arc of wall. *Take
me, Stretchfoot, what keeps you? Nothing worse than
these days. You will be like gentle sleep. Isn't it only
sleep? Please. Come soon— Private Rudolf Effig, 12.iv.45.*
A drawing in Commando blackface-grease, of a man looking closely at a flower. In the distance, or smaller, appears
to be a woman, approaching. Or some kind of elf, or
something. The man isn't looking at her (or it). In
the middle distance are haystacks. The flower is shaped
like the cunt of a young girl. There is a luminary looking
down from the sky, a face on it totally at peace, like the
Buddha's. Underneath, someone else has written, in English: *Good drawing! Finish!* and underneath that, in

another hand, *It IS finished, you nit. And so are you.*
Nearby, in German, *I loved you Lisele with all my heart*
—no name, rank, unit or serial number. . . . Initials, tic-
tac-toe games you can tell were played alone, a game of
hangman in which the mystery word was never filled in:
GE _ _ RAT _ _ and the hanged body visible almost at the
other end of the culvert, even this early in the day, because it's a narrow road, and no real gradient of shadow.
A bicycle is incompletely hidden in the weeds at the side
of the road. A late butterfly pale as an eyelid winks aimlessly out over the stalks of new hay. High up on the
slope, someone is swinging an ax-blade into a living tree
. . . and here is where and when the young witch finds
Vaslav Tchitcherine at last.

He's sitting by the stream, not dejected, nor tranquil,
just waiting. A passive solenoid waiting to be sprung. At
her step, his head lifts, and he sees her. She is the first
presence since last night he's looked at and seen. Which
is her doing. The charm she recited then, fastening the
silk crotch torn from her best underpants across the
eyes of the doll, *his* eyes, Eastern and liquid, though they'd
been only sketched in clay with her long fingernail, was
this:

May he be blind now to all but me. May the burning
sun of love shine in his eyes forever. May this, my own
darkness, shelter him. By all the holy names of God, by
the Angels Melchidael, Yahoel, Anafiel, and the great
Metatron, I conjure you, and all who are with you, to go
and do my will.

The secret is in the concentrating. She inhibits everything else: the moon, the wind in the junipers, the wild
dogs out ranging in the middle of the night. She fixes
on Tchitcherine's memory and his wayward eyes, and lets
it build, pacing her orgasm to the incantation, so that
by the end, naming the last Names of Power, she's screaming, coming, without help from her fingers, which are
raised to the sky.

Later she breaks a piece of the magic bread in half,
and eats one part. The other is for Tchitcherine.

He takes the bread now. The stream rushes. A bird
sings.

Toward nightfall, the lovers lying naked on a cold

rass bank, the sound of a convoy approaches on the ittle road. Tchitcherine pulls on his trousers and climbs ip to see if he can beg some food, or cigarettes. The black aces pass by, mba-kayere, some glancing at him curiously, thers too involved with their own exhaustion, or with eeping a tight guard on a covered wagon containing the varhead section of the 00001. Enzian on his motorcycle tops for a moment, mba-kayere, to talk to the scarred, inshaven white. They're in the middle of the bridge. They alk broken German. Tchitcherine manages to hustle half a pack of American cigarettes and three raw potatoes. The wo men nod, not quite formally, not quite smiling, Enzian puts his bike in gear and returns to his journey. Tchitcherine lights a cigarette, watching them down the oad, shivering in the dusk. Then he goes back to his young girl beside the stream. They will have to locate ome firewood before all the light is gone.

This is magic. Sure—but not necessarily fantasy. Cerainly not the first time a man has passed his brother by, it the edge of the evening, often forever, without knowng it.

◻

By now the City is grown so tall that elevators are longaaul affairs, with lounges inside: padded seats and benches, nack bars, newsstands where you can browse through a vhole issue of *Life* between stops. For those faint hearts vho first thing on entering seek out the Certificate of Inpection on the elevator wall, there are young women in reen overseas caps, green velvet basques, and tapered ellowstripe trousers—a feminine zootsuit effect—who've een well-tutored in all kinds of elevator lore, and whose ob it is to set you at ease. "In the early days," pipes young Mindy Bloth of Carbon City, Illinois, smiling vacantly way in profile, close by the brass moiré of diamond-blurs assing, passing in vertical thousands—her growing-up ace, dreamy and practical as the Queen of Cups, never quite looks for you, is always refracted away some set ngle in the gold-brown medium between you . . . it's norning, and the flower man at the rear of the elevator,

down a step or two, behind the little fountain, has brought
lilacs and irises fresh and early—"before the Vertical
Solution, all transport was, in effect, two-dimensional—ah,
I can guess *your* question—" as a smile, familiar and un-
refracted for this old elevator regular, passes between girl
and heckler—" 'What about *airplane flight*, eh?' That's
what you were going to ask wasn't it!" as a matter of fact
he was going to ask about the Rocket and everyone
knows it, but the subject is under a curious taboo, and
polite Mindy has brought in now a chance for actual
violence, the violence of repression—the bleached colors
of a September morning sky opposite the sunrise, and the
filing-edge of a morning wind—into this intimate cubic
environment moving so smoothly upward through space
(a bubble rising through Castile soap where all around
it's green lit by slow lightning), past levels already a-
bustle with heads seething brighter than sperm and eggs
in the sea, past some levels left dark, unheated, somehow
forbidden, looking oddly *wasted*, levels where nobody's
been since the War aaaaa-*ahhh!* howling past, "a common
aerodynamic effect," explains patient Mindy, "involving
our own boundary layer and the shape of the orifice as
we pass it—" "Oh you mean that before we get to it,"
hollers another heckler, "it's a different *shape?*" "Yup, and
after we go by it too, Mac," Mindy brushes him off,
broadly mugging the same thing with her mouth, purse-
relax-smile—these jagged openings howling, hauling forlorn and downward, already stories gone beneath the
soles of your shoes, a howl bent downward like a harmonica note—but why don't any of the *busy* floors make a
sound going by? where the lights are shining warm a
Xmas-week parties, floors that beckon you into densitie
of glass faceting or screening, good-natured coffee-urn
grousing, well golly, here goes another day, howdy Marie
where you ladies hiding the drawings on the SG-1 . .
what do you mean *Field Service* has them . . . again
doesn't Engineering Design have any rights, it's like watch
ing your child run away, to see a piece of equipment ge
set out to the Field (*Der Veld*). That it is. A broken hear
a mother's prayer. . . . Slowly, the voices of the Lübec
Hitler Youth Glee Club fade in behind (nowadays th
boys sing at officers' clubs all across the Zone under thei

road name, "The Lederhoseners." They are dressed appro-
priately, and sing—when the house feels right—with their
backs turned to the audiences, their sly little faces turned
over shoulders to flirt with the fighting men:

> But sharper than a Mother's tears
> Are the beatings Mutti gave to me . . .

with a beautifully coordinated wiggle then to each pair of
buttocks gleaming through leather so tight that the
clenching of gluteal muscles is plainly visible, and you
can bet there isn't a cock in the room doesn't stir at the
sight, and scarcely an eye that can't hallucinate that
maternal birch smacking down across each naked ass, the
delicious red lines, the stern and beautiful female face,
smiling down through lowered lashes, only a glint of light
off of each eye—when you were first learning to crawl,
it was her calves and feet you saw the most of—they
replaced her breasts as sources of strength, as you learned
the smell of her leather shoes, and the sovereign smell
rose as far as you could see—to her knees, perhaps—
depending on fashion that year—to her thighs. You were
infant in the presence of leather legs, leather feet . . .).

"Isn't it possible," Thanatz whispers, "that we all learned
that classical fantasy at Mother's knees? That somewhere
tucked in the brain's plush album is always a child in
Fauntleroy clothes, a pretty French maid begging to be
whipped?"

Ludwig shifts his rather fat ass under Thanatz's hand.
Both have perimeters they are not supposed to cross. But
they have crept away anyhow, to a piece of the interface,
a cold thicket they've pounded down a space in the middle
of, to lie on. "Ludwig, a little S and M never hurt
anybody."

"Who said that?"

"Sigmund Freud. How do I know? But why are we
taught to feel reflexive shame whenever the subject comes
up? Why will the Structure allow every other kind of
sexual behavior but *that* one? Because submission and
dominance are resources it needs for its very survival.
They cannot be wasted in private sex. In *any* kind of sex.
It needs our submission so that it may remain in power.

It needs our lusts after dominance so that it can co-opt us into its own power game. There is no joy in it, only power. I tell you, if S and M could be established universally, at the family level, the State would wither away."

This is Sado-anarchism and Thanatz is its leading theoretician in the Zone these days.

It is the Lüneburg Heath, at last. Rendezvous was made last night with the groups carrying fuel and oxidizer tanks. The tail-section group has been on the radio all morning, trying to get a position fix, if the skies will only clear. So the assembly of the 00001 is occurring also in a geographical way, a Diaspora running backwards, seeds of exile flying inward in a modest view of gravitational collapse, of the Messiah gathering in the fallen sparks. . . . Remember the story about the kid who hates kreplach? Hates and fears the dish, breaks out in these horrible green hives that shift in relief maps all across his body, in the mere presence of kreplach. Kid's mother takes him to the psychiatrist. "Fear of the unknown," diagnoses this gray eminence, "let him watch you *making* the kreplach, that'll ease him into it." Home to Mother's kitchen. "Now," sez Mother, "I'm going to make us a delicious surprise!" "Oh boy!" cries the kid, "that's *keen*, Mom!" "See, now I'm sifting the flour and salt into a nice little pile." "What's that, Mom, hamburger? oh, boy!" "Hamburger, and *onions*. I'm frying them here, see, in this frying pan." "Gee, I can hardly wait! This is exciting! What're ya doin' *now*?" "Making a little volcano in the flour here, and breaking these eggs into it." "Can I help ya mix it up? Oh, boy!" "Now, I'm going to roll the dough out, see? into a nice flat sheet, now I'm cutting it up into squares—" "This is ter*rif*, Mom!" "Now I spoon some of the hamburger into this little square, and now I fold it over into a tri—" "GAAHHHH!" screams the kid in absolute terror— "*kreplach!*"

As some secrets were given to the Gypsies to preserve against centrifugal History, and some to the Kabbalists, the Templars, the Rosicrucians, so have this Secret of the Fearful Assembly, and others, found their ways inside the weatherless spaces of this or that Ethnic Joke. There is also the story about Tyrone Slothrop, who was sent into the Zone to be present as his own assembly—perhaps, heavily paranoid voices have whispered, *his time's assembly*—and there ought to be a punch line to it, but there isn't. The plan went wrong. He is being broken down instead, and scattered. His cards have been laid down, Celtic style, in the order suggested by Mr. A. E. Waite, laid out and read, but they are the cards of a tanker and feeb: they point only to a long and scuffling future, to mediocrity (not only in his life but also, heh, heh, in his chroniclers too, yes yes nothing like getting the 3 of Pentacles upside down covering the significator on the second try to send you to the tube to watch a seventh rerun of the Takeshi and Ichizo Show, light a cigarette and try to forget the whole thing)—to no clear happiness or redeeming cataclysm. All his hopeful cards are reversed, most unhappily of all the Hanged Man, who is supposed to be upside down to begin with, telling of his secret hopes and fears. . . .

"There never was a Dr. Jamf," opines world-renowned analyst Mickey Wuxtry-Wuxtry—"Jamf was only a fiction, to help him explain what he felt so terribly, so immediately in his genitals for those rockets each time exploding in the sky . . . to help him deny what he could not possibly admit: that he might be in love, in sexual love, with his, and his race's, death.

"These early Americans, in their way, were a fascinating combination of crude poet and psychic cripple. . . ."

"We were never that concerned with Slothrop *qua* Slothrop," a spokesman for the Counterforce admitted recently in an interview with the *Wall Street Journal*.

INTERVIEWER: You mean, then, that he was more a rallying point.

SPOKESMAN: No, not even that. Opinion even at the start was divided. It was one of our fatal weaknesses. [I'm sure you want to hear about fatal weaknesses.] Some called him a "pretext." Others felt that he was a genuine, point-for-point microcosm. The Microcosmists, as you must know from the standard histories, leaped off to an early start. We—it was a very odd form of heretic-chasing, really. Across the Low Countries, in the summer. It went on in fields of windmills, marshlands where it was almost too dark to get a decent sight. I recall the time Christian found an old alarm clock, and we salvaged the radium, to

coat our plumb-bob strings with. They shone in the twilight. You've seen them holding bobs, hands characteristically gathered near the crotch. A dark figure with a
stream of luminescent piss falling to the ground fifty
meters away . . . "The Presence, pissing," that became a
standard joke on the apprentices. A Raketen-Stadt Charlie
Noble, you might say. . . . [Yes. A cute way of putting it.
I am betraying them all . . . the worst of it is that I know
what your editors want, *exactly* what they want. I am a
traitor. I carry it with me. Your virus. Spread by your
tireless Typhoid Marys, cruising the markets and the
stations. We did manage to ambush some of them. Once
we caught some in the Underground. It was terrible. My
first action, my initiation. We chased them down the tunnels. We could feel their fright. When the tunnels
branched, we had only the treacherous acoustics of the
Underground to go on. Chances were good for getting
lost. There was almost no light. The rails gleamed, as they
do aboveground on a rainy night. And the whispers *then*
—the shadows who waited, hunched in angles at the
maintenance stations, lying against the tunnel walls, watching the chase. "The end is too far," they whispered. "Go
back. There are no stops on this branch. The trains run
and the passengers ride miles of blank mustard walls, but
there are no stops. It's a long afternoon run. . . ." Two of
them got away. But we took the rest. Between two station-
marks, yellow crayon through the years of grease and
passage, 1966 and 1971, I tasted my first blood. Do you
want to put this part in?] We drank the blood of our
enemies. That's why you see Gnostics so hunted. The
sacrament of the Eucharist is really drinking the blood of
the enemy. The Grail, the Sangraal, is the bloody vehicle.
Why else guard it so sacredly? Why should the black
honor-guard ride half a continent, half a splintering
Empire, stone night and winter day, if it's only for the
touch of sweet lips on a humble bowl? No, it's mortal sin
they're carrying: to swallow the enemy, down into the slick
juicery to be taken in by all the cells. Your officially
defined "mortal sin," that is. A sin against you. A section
of your penal code, that's all. [The true sin was yours: to
interdict that union. To draw that line. To keep us worse
than enemies, who are after all caught in the same fields of
shit—to keep us strangers.

We drank the blood of our enemies. The blood of our friends, we cherished.]

Item S-1706.31, Fragment of Undershirt, U.S. Navy issue, with brown stain assumed to be blood in shape of sword running lower left to upper right.

Not included in the Book of Memorabilia is this foot-note. The piece of cloth was given to Slothrop by Seaman Bodine, one night in the Chicago Bar. In a way, the eve-ning was a reprise of their first meeting. Bodine, smolder-ing fat reefer stuck in under the strings at the neck of his guitar, singing mournfully a song that's part Roger Mexico's and part some nameless sailor stuck in wartime San Diego:

Last week I threw a pie at someone's Momma,
Last night I threw a party for my mind,
Last thing I knew that 6:02 was screamin' over my head,
Or it might've been th' 11:59 . . .

[Refrain]:

Too many chain-link fences in the evening,
Too many people shiverin' in the rain,
They tell me that you finally got around to have your
 baby,
And it don't look like I'll see your face again.

Sometimes I wanna go back north, to Humboldt County—
Sometimes I think I'll go back east, to see my kin . . .
There's times I think I almost could be happy,
If I knew you thought about me, now and then. . . .

Bodine has a siren-ring, the kind kids send away cereal boxtops for, cleverly arranged in his asshole so it can be operated at any time by blowing a fart of a certain mag-nitude. He's gotten pretty good at punctuating his music with these farted WHEEEEeeee's, working now at getting them in the right key, a brand-new reflex arc, ear-brain-hands-asshole, and a return toward innocence too. The merchants tonight are all dealing a bit slower. Sentimental Bodine thinks it's because they're listening to his song. Maybe they are. Bales of fresh coca leaves just in from the Andes transform the place into some resonant Latin warehouse, on the eve of a revolution that never

will come closer than smoke dirtying the sky above the
cane, sometimes, in the long lace afternoons at the
window.... Street urchins are into a Busy Elf Routine,
wrapping each leaf around a betel nut, into a neat little
packet for chewing. Their reddened fingers are living
embers in the shadow. Seaman Bodine looks up suddenly,
canny, unshaven face stung by all the smoke and unaware-
ness in the room. He's looking straight at Slothrop (being
one of the few who can still see Slothrop as any sort of
integral creature any more. Most of the others gave
up long ago trying to hold him together, even as a concept—"It's just got too remote"'s what they usually say).
Does Bodine now feel his own strength may someday
soon not be enough either: that soon, like all the others,
he'll *have* to let go? *But somebody's got to hold on, it
can't happen to all of us—no, that'd be too much* ...
Rocketman, Rocketman. You poor fucker.

"Here. Listen. I want you to have it. Understand? It's
yours."

Does he even hear any more? Can he see this cloth,
this stain?

"Look, I was there, in Chicago, when they ambushed
him. I was there that night, right down the street from
the Biograph, I heard the gunfire, everything. Shit, I was
just a boot, I thought this was what liberty was all about,
so I went running. Me and half Chicago. Out of the bars,
the toilets, the alleys, dames holding their skirts up so
they could run faster, Missus Krodobbly who's drinking
her way through the Big Depression, waitin' till the sun
shines thru, and whatta you know, there's half my graduating class from Great Lakes, in dress blues with the
same bedspring marks as mine, and there's longtime hookers and pockmark fags with breath smelling like the
inside of a motorman's glove, old ladies from Back of the
Yards, subdebs just out of the movies with the sweat still
cold on their thighs, gate, *everybody* was there. They were
taking off clothes, tearing checks out of checkbooks,
ripping off pieces of each other's newspaper, just so they
could soak up some of John Dillinger's blood. We went
crazy. The Agents didn't stop us. Just stood with smoke
still curling out of their muzzles while the people all
went down on that blood in the street. Maybe I went

along without thinking. But there *was something else.* Something I must've needed ... if you can hear me ... that's why I'm giving this to you. O.K.? That's Dillinger's blood there. Still warm when I got it. They wouldn't want you thinking he was anything but a 'common criminal'— but Their head's so far up Their ass—he still did what he did. He went out socked Them right in the toilet privacy of Their banks. Who cares what he was *thinking* about, long as it didn't get in the way? A-and it doesn't even matter why *we're* doing this, either. Rocky? Yeah, what we need isn't right reasons, but just the *grace.* The physical grace to keep it working. Courage, brains, sure, O.K., but without that grace? forget it. Do you—please, are you listening? This thing here works. Really does. It worked for me, but I'm out of the Dumbo stage now, I can fly without it. But you. Rocky. You. . . ."

It wasn't their last meeting, but later on there were always others around, doper-crises, resentments about burns real or intended, and by then, as he'd feared, Bodine was beginning, helpless, in shame, to let Slothrop go. In certain rushes now, when he sees white network being cast all directions on his field of vision, he understands it as an emblem of pain or death. He's begun to spend more of his time with Trudi. Their friend Magda was picked up on first-degree mopery and taken back to Leverkusen, and an overgrown back court where electric lines spit overhead, the dusty bricks sprout weeds from the cracks, shutters are always closed, grass and weeds turn to bitterest autumn floor. On certain days the wind brings aspirin-dust from the Bayer factory. The people inhale it, and grow more tranquil.

They both feel her absence. Bodine finds presently that his characteristic gross laugh, *hyeugh, hyeugh,* has grown more German, *tjachz, tjachz.* He's also taking on some of Magda's old disguises. Good-natured and penetrable disguises, as at a masked ball. It is a transvestism of caring, and the first time in his life it's happened. Though nobody asks, being too busy dealing, he reckons it's all right.

Light in the sky is stretched and clear, exactly like taffy after no more than the first two pulls.

"Dying a weird death," Slothrop's Visitor by this time may be scrawled lines of carbon on a wall, voices down a chimney, some human being out on the road, "the object of life is to make sure you die a weird death. To make sure that *however it finds you*, it will find you under *very weird* circumstances. To live that kind of life. . . ."

Item S-1729.06, Bottle containing 7 cc. of May wine. Analysis indicates presence of woodruff herb, lemon and orange peel.

Sprigs of woodruff, also known as Master of the Woods, were carried by the early Teutonic warriors. It gives success in battle. It appears that some part of Slothrop ran into the AWOL Džabajev one night in the heart of downtown Niederschaumdorf. (Some believe that fragments of Slothrop have grown into consistent personae of their own. If so, there's no telling which of the Zone's present-day population are offshoots of his original scattering. There's supposed to be a last photograph of him on the only record album ever put out by The Fool, an English rock group—seven musicians posed, in the arrogant style of the early Stones, near an old rocket-bomb site, out in the East End, or South of the River. It is spring, and French thyme blossoms in amazing white lacework across the cape of green that now hides and softens the true shape of the old rubble. There is no way to tell which of the faces is Slothrop's: the only printed credit that might apply to him is "Harmonica, kazoo—a friend." But knowing his Tarot, we would expect to look among the Humility, among the gray and preterite souls, to look for him adrift in the hostile light of the sky, the darkness of the sea. . . .)

Now there's only a long cat's-eye of bleak sunset left over the plain tonight, bright gray against a purple ceiling of clouds, with an iris of darker gray. It is displayed above, more than looking down on, this gathering of Džabajev and his friends. Inside the town, a strange convention is under way. Village idiots from villages throughout Germany are streaming in (streaming from mouth as well as leaving behind high-pitched trails of color for the folks to point at in their absence). They are expected to pass a resolution tonight asking Great Britain for Commonwealth status, and perhaps even to apply for membership in the UNO. Children in the parish schools are being asked to pray for their success. Can 13 years of Vatican collaboration have clarified the difference between what's holy and what is not? Another State is forming in the night, not without theatre and festivity. So tonight's prevalence of Maitrinke, which Džabajev has managed to score several liters of. Let the village idiots celebrate. Let their holiness ripple into interference-patterns till it clog the lantern-light of the meeting hall. Let the chorus line perform heroically: 16 ragged staring oldtimers who shuffle aimlessly about the stage, jerking off in unison, waggling penises in mock quarter-staffing, brandishing in twos and threes their green-leaved poles, exposing amazing chancres and lesions, going off in fountains of sperm strung with blood that splash over glazed trouser-pleats, dirt-colored jackets with pockets dangling like 60-year-old breasts, sockless ankles permanently stained with the dust of the little squares and the depopulated streets. Let them cheer and pound their seats, let the brotherly spit flow. Tonight the Džabajev circle have acquired, through an ill-coordinated smash-and-grab at the home of Niederschaumdorf's only doctor, a gigantic hypodermic syringe and needle. Tonight they will shoot *wine*. If the police are on the way, if far down the road certain savage ears can already pick up the rumble of an occupation convoy across the night kilometers, signaling past sight, past the first headlamp's faintest scattering, the approach of danger, still no one here is likely to break the circle. The wine will operate on whatever happens. Didn't you wake up to find a knife in your hand, your head down a toilet, the blur of a long sap about to smash your upper lip, and sink back down to the old red and capillaried nap where none of this could possibly be happening? and wake again to a woman screaming, again to the water of the canal freezing your drowned eye and ear, again to too many Fortresses diving down the sky, again, again. . . . But no, never real.

A wine rush: a wine rush is defying gravity, finding yourself on the elevator ceiling as it rockets *upward*, and no way to get down. You separate in two, the basic Two, and each self is aware of the other.

THE OCCUPATION OF MINGEBOROUGH

The trucks come rolling down the hill, where the State highway narrows, at about three in the afternoon. All

their headlights are on. Electric stare after stare topping
the crest of the hill, between the maple trees. The noise
is terrific. Gearboxes chatter as each truck hits the end of
the grade, weary cries of "Double-clutch it, idiot!" come
from under the canvas. An apple tree by the road is in
blossom. The limbs are wet with this morning's rain, dark
and wet. Sitting under it, with anyone else but Slothrop,
is a barelegged girl, blonde and brown as honey. Her name
is Marjorie. Hogan will come home from the Pacific and
court her, but he'll lose out to Pete Dufay. She and
Dufay will have a daughter named Kim, and Kim will
have her braids dipped in the school inkwells by young
Hogan, Jr. It will all go on, occupation or not, with or
without Uncle Tyrone.

There's more rain in the air. The soldiers are mustering
by Hicks's Garage. In the back lot is a greasy dump, a pit,
full of ball-bearings, clutch plates, and pieces of transmission. In the parking lot below—shared with the green-
trimmed candy store, where he waited for the first slice
of very yellow schoolbus to appear each 3:15 around the
corner, and knew which high-school kids were easy marks
for pennies—are six or seven old Cord automobiles, in
different stages of dustiness and breakdown. Souvenirs of
young empire, they shine like hearses now in the premonition of rain. Work details are already putting up barri-
cades, and a scavenging party has invaded the gray
clapboards of Pizzini's Store, standing big as a barn on the
corner. Kids hanging around the loading platform, eating
sunflower seeds out of burlap sacks, listen to the soldiers
liberating sides of beef from Pizzini's freezer. If Slothrop
wants to get home from here, he has to slide into a pathway next to the two-story brick wall of Hicks's Garage, a
green path whose entrance is concealed behind the trash-
fire of the store, and the frame shed where Pizzini keeps
his delivery truck. You cut through two lots which aren't
platted exactly back to back, so that actually you're skirting one fence and using a driveway. They are both amber
and black old ladies' houses, full of cats alive or stuffed,
stained lampshades, antimacassars and doilies on all the
chairs and tables, and a terminal gloom. You have to
cross a street then, go down Mrs. Snodd's driveway beside
the hollyhocks, through a wire gate and Santora's back

yard, over the rail fence where the hedge stops, across your own street, and home. . . .

But there is the occupation. They may already have interdicted the kids' short cuts along with the grown-up routes. It may be too late to get home.

BACK IN DER PLATZ

Gustav and André, back from Cuxhaven, have unscrewed the reed-holder and reed from André's kazoo and replaced them with tinfoil—punched holes in the tinfoil, and are now smoking hashish out of the kazoo, finger-valving the small end pa-pa-pah to carburete the smoke—turns out sly Säure has had ex-Peenemünde engineers, propulsion-group people, working on a long-term study of optimum hashpipe design, and guess what—in terms of flow rate, heat-transfer, control of air-to-smoke ratio, the perfect shape turns out to be that of the classical *kazoo!*

Yeah, another odd thing about the kazoo: the knuckle-thread above the reed there is exactly the same as a thread in a light-bulb socket. Gustav, good old Captain Horror, wearing a liberated pair of very yellow English shooting-glasses ("Helps you find the vein easier, I guess"), likes to proclaim this as the clear signature of Phoebus. "You fools think the kazoo is a subversive instrument? Here—" he always packs a light bulb on his daily rounds, no use passing up an opportunity to depress the odd dopefiend . . . deftly screwing the light bulb flush against the reed, muting it out, "You see? Phoebus is even behind the *kazoo.* Ha! ha! ha!" Schadenfreude, worse than a prolonged onion fart, seeps through the room.

But what Gustav's light bulb—none other than our friend Byron—wants to say is no, it's not that way at all, it's a declaration of brotherhood by the Kazoo for all the captive and oppressed light bulbs. . . .

There is a movie going on, under the rug. On the floor, 24 hours a day, pull back the rug sure enough there's that damn movie! A really offensive and tasteless film by Gerhardt von Göll, daily rushes in fact from a project which will never be completed. Springer just plans to keep it going indefinitely there, under the rug. The title is *New Dope,* and that's what it's about, a brand new kind of dope that nobody's ever heard of. One of the most annoying characteristics of the shit is that the minute you take it you are rendered incapable of ever telling anybody what it's like, or worse, where to get any. Dealers are as in the dark as anybody. All you can hope is that you'll come across somebody in the act of taking (shooting? smoking? swallowing?) some. It is the dope that finds *you,* apparently. Part of a reverse world whose agents run around with guns which are like vacuum cleaners operating in the direction of life—pull the trigger and bullets are sucked back out of the recently dead into the barrel, and the Great Irreversible is actually reversed as the corpse comes to life to the accompaniment of a backwards gunshot (you can imagine what drug-ravaged and mindless idea of fun the daily sound editing on this turns out to be). Titles flash on such as

GERHARDT VON GÖLL BECOMES SODIUM AMYTAL FREAK!

And here he is himself, the big ham, sitting on the toilet, a . . . well what appears to be an unusually large infant's training toilet, up between the sitter's legs rises the porcelain head of a jackal with what, embarrassingly, proves to be a *reefer,* in its rather loosely smiling mouth—"Through evil and eagles," blithers the Springer, "the climate blondes its way, for they are no strength under the coarse war. No not for roguery until the monitors are there in blashing sheets of earth to mate and say medoshnicka bleelar medoometnozz in bergamot and playful fantasy under the throne and nose of the least merciful king. . . ." well, there is a good deal of this sort of thing, and a good time to nip out for popcorn, which in the Platz turn out to be morning-glory seeds popped into little stilled brown explosions. None of the regular company here actually watch the movie under the rug much—only visitors passing through: friends of Magda, defectors from the great aspirin factory in Leverkusen, over in the corner there dribbling liberated cornstarch and water on each other's naked bodies, giggling unhealthily . . . devotees of the I Ching who have a favorite hexagram tattooed on each toe, who can never stay in one place for long, can you guess why? Because they always have I

Ching feet! also stumblebum magicians who can't help leaving themselves wide open for disastrous visits from Qlippoth, Ouijaboard jokesters, poltergeists, all kinds of astral-plane tankers and feebs—yeah they're all showing up at Der Platz these days. But the alternative is to start keeping some out and not others, and nobody's ready for that. . . . Decisions like that are for some angel stationed very high, watching us at our many perversities, crawling across black satin, gagging on whip-handles, licking the blood from a lover's vein-hit, all of it, every lost giggle or sigh, being carried on under a sentence of death whose deep beauty the angel has never been close to. . . .

WEISSMANN'S TAROT

Weissmann's Tarot is better than Slothrop's. Here are the real cards, exactly as they came up.

Significator: Knight of Swords
Covered by: The Tower
Crossed by: Queen of Swords
Crowning: King of Cups
Beneath: Ace of Swords
Before: 4 of Cups
Behind: 4 of Pentacles
Self: Page of Pentacles
House: 8 of Cups
Hopes and Fears: 2 of Swords
What will come: The World

He appears first with boots and insignia shining as the rider on a black horse, charging in a gallop neither he nor horse can control, across the heath over the giant grave-mounds, scattering the black-faced sheep, while dark stands of juniper move dreamily, death-loving, across his path in a parallax of unhurrying fatality, presiding as monuments do over the green and tan departure of summer, the dust-colored lowlands and at last the field-gray sea, a prairie of sea darkening to purple where the sunlight comes through, in great circles, spotlights on a dancingfloor.

He is the father you will never quite manage to kill. The Oedipal situation in the Zone these days is terrible. There is no dignity. The mothers have been masculinized

to old worn moneybags of no sexual interest to anyone,
and yet here are their sons, still trapped inside inertias of
lust that are 40 years out of date. The fathers have no
power today and never did, but because 40 years ago we
could not kill them, we are condemned now to the same
passivity, the same masochist fantasies *they* cherished in
secret, and worse, we are condemned in our weakness to
impersonate men of power our own infant children must
hate, and wish to usurp the place of, and fail.... So
generation after generation of men in love with pain and
passivity serve out their time in the Zone, silent, redolent
of faded sperm, terrified of dying, desperately addicted
to the comforts others sell them, however useless, ugly or
shallow, willing to have life defined for them by men
whose only talent is for death.

Of 77 cards that could have come up, Weissmann is
"covered," that is his present condition is set forth, by
The Tower. It is a puzzling card, and everybody has a
different story on it. It shows a bolt of lightning striking a
tall phallic structure, and two figures, one wearing a
crown, falling from it. Some read ejaculation, and leave it
at that. Others see a Gnostic or Cathar symbol for the
Church of Rome, and this is generalized to mean any
System which cannot tolerate heresy: a system which, by
its nature, must sooner or later fall. We know by now
that it is also the Rocket.

Members of the Order of the Golden Dawn believe
The Tower represents victory over splendor, and avenging
force. As Goebbels, beyond all his professional verbalizing,
believed in the Rocket as an avenger.

On the Kabbalist Tree of Life, the path of The Tower
connects the sephira Netzach, victory, with Hod, glory or
splendor. Hence the Golden Dawn interpretation. Netzach
is fiery and emotional, Hod is watery and logical. On the
body of God, these two Sephiroth are the thighs, the pillars
of the Temple, resolving together in Yesod, the sex and
excretory organs.

But each of the Sephiroth is also haunted by its proper
demons or Qlippoth. Netzach by the Ghorab Tzerek, the
Ravens of Death, and Hod by the Samael, the Poison of
God. No one has asked the demons at either level, but
there may be just the wee vulnerability here to a sensa-

tion of falling, the kind of very steep and out-of-scale fall
we find in dreams, a falling more through space than
among objects. Though the different Qlippoth can only
work each his own sort of evil, activity on the path of The
Tower, from Netzach to Hod, seems to've resulted in the
emergence of a new kind of demon (what, a dialectical
Tarot? Yes indeedyfoax! A-and if you don't think there are
Marxist-Leninist magicians around, well *you* better think
again!). The Ravens of Death have now tasted of the
Poison of God . . . but in doses small enough not to sicken
but to bring on, like the Amanita muscaria, a very peculiar
state of mind. . . . They have no official name, but they
are the Rocket's guardian demons.

Weissmann is crossed by the Queen of his suit. Perhaps
himself, in drag. She is the chief obstacle in his way. At his
foundation is the single sword flaming inside the crown:
again, Netzach, victory. In the American deck this card
has come down to us as the ace of spades, which is a bit
more sinister: you know the silence that falls on the room
when it comes up, whatever the game. Behind him, moving out of his life as an influence, is the 4 or Four of
Pentacles, which shows a figure of modest property
desperately clutching on to what he owns, four gold
coins—this feeb is holding two of them down with his
feet, balancing another on his head and holding the fourth
tightly against his stomach, which is ulcerous. It is the
stationary witch trying to hold her candy house against the
host of nibblers out there in the dark. Moving in, before
him, comes a feast of cups, a satiety. Lotta booze and
broads for Weissmann coming soon. Good for him—although in his house he is seen walking away, renouncing
eight stacked gold chalices. Perhaps he is to be given only
what he must walk away from. Perhaps it is because in the
lees of the night's last cup is the bitter presence of a
woman sitting by a rocky shore, the Two of Swords, alone
at the Baltic edge, blindfolded in the moonlight, holding
the two blades crossed upon her breasts . . . the meaning is
usually taken as "concord in a state of arms," a good
enough description of the Zone nowadays, and it describes
his deepest hopes, or fears.

Himself, as the World sees him: the scholarly young
Page of Pentacles, meditating on his magic gold talisman.

The Page may also be used to stand for a young girl. But Pentacles describe people of very dark complexion, and so the card almost certainly is Enzian as a young man. And Weissmann may at last, in this limited pasteboard way, have become what he first loved.

The King of Cups, crowning his hopes, is the fair intellectual-king. If you're wondering where he's gone, look among the successful academics, the Presidential advisers, the token intellectuals who sit on boards of directors. He is almost surely there. Look high, not low.

His future card, the card of what will come, is The World.

THE LAST GREEN AND MAGENTA

The Heath grows green and magenta in all directions, earth and heather, coming of age—

No. It was spring.

THE HORSE

In a field, beyond the clearing and the trees, the last horse is standing, tarnished silver-gray, hardly more than an assembling of shadows. The heathen Germans who lived here sacrificed horses once, in their old ceremonies. Later the horse's role changed from holy offering to servant of power. By then a great change was working on the Heath, kneading, turning, stirring with fingers strong as wind.

Now that sacrifice has become a political act, an act of Caesar, the last horse cares only about how the wind starts up this afternoon: rises at first, and tries to stick, to catch, but fails . . . each time, the horse feels a similar rising in his heart, at the edges of eye, ear, brain. . . . Finally, at the sure catching of the wind, which is also a turning in the day, his head rises, and a shiver comes over him— possesses him. His tail lashes at the clear elusive flash of the wind. The sacrifice in the grove is beginning.

ISAAC

There is an Aggadic tradition from around the 4th century that Isaac, at the moment Abraham was about to sacrifice him on Moriah, saw the antechambers of the Throne. For the working mystic, having the vision and passing through the chambers one by one, is terrible and complex. You must have not only the schooling in counter-signs and seals, not only the physical readiness through exercise and abstinence, but also a hardon of resolution that will never go limp on you. The angels at the door-ways will try to con you, threaten you, play all manner of cruel practical jokes, to turn you aside. The Qlippoth, shells of the dead, will use all your love for friends who have passed across against you. You have chosen the active way, and there is no faltering without finding the most mortal danger.

The other way is dark and female, passive, self-aban-doning. Isaac under the blade. The glittering edge widen-ing to a hallway, down, up which the soul is borne by an irresistible Aether. Gerhardt von Göll on his camera dolly, whooping with joy, barrel-assing down the long corridors at Nymphenburg. (Let us leave him here, in his transport, in his innocence. . . .) The numinous light grows ahead, almost blue among all this gilt and glass. The gilders worked naked and had their heads shaved bald—to get a static charge to hold the fluttering leaf they had first to run the brush through their pubic hair: genital electricity would shine forever down these gold vistas. But we have long left mad Ludwig and his Spanish dancer guttering, fading scarlet across the marble, shining so treacherously like sweet water . . . already that lies behind. The ascent to the Merkabah, despite his last feeble vestiges of man-hood, last gestures toward the possibility of magic, is irreversibly on route. . . .

PRE-LAUNCH

A giant white fly: an erect penis buzzing in white lace, clotted with blood or sperm. Deathlace is the boy's bridal costume. His smooth feet, bound side by side, are in white satin slippers with white bows. His red nipples are erect. The golden hairs on his back, alloyed German gold, pale yellow to white, run symmetric about his spine, run in arches fine and whirled as the arches of a fingerprint, as filings along magnetic lines of force. Each freckle or mole is a dark, precisely-set anomaly in the field. Sweat gathers at his nape. He is gagged with a white kid glove. Weiss-

mann has engineered all the symbolism today. The glove
is the female equivalent of the Hand of Glory, which
second-story men use to light their way into your home: a
candle in a dead man's hand, erect as all your tissue will
grow at the first delicious tongue-flick of your mistress
Death. The glove is the cavity into which the Hand fits,
as the 00000 is the womb into which Gottfried returns.

Stuff him in. Not a Procrustean bed, but modified to
take him. The two, boy and Rocket, concurrently designed.
Its steel hindquarters bent so beautifully . . . he fits well.
They are mated to each other, Schwarzgerät and next
higher assembly. His bare limbs in their metal bondage
writhe among the fuel, oxidizer, live-steam lines, thrust
frame, compressed air battery, exhaust elbow, decomposer,
tanks, vents, valves . . . and one of these valves, one test-
point, one pressure-switch is the right one, the true
clitoris, routed directly into the nervous system of
the 00000. She should not be a mystery to you,
Gottfried. Find the zone of love, lick and kiss . . .
you have time—there are still a few minutes. The
liquid oxygen runs freezing so close to your cheek, bones
of frost to burn you past feeling. Soon there will be the
fires, too. The Oven we fattened you for will glow. Here
is the sergeant, bringing the Zündkreuz. The pyrotechnic
Cross to light you off. The men are at attention. Get ready,
Liebchen.

HARDWARE

He's been given a window of artificial sapphire, four
inches across, grown by the IG in 1942 as a mushroom-
shaped boule, a touch of cobalt added to give it a greenish tint—very heat-resistant, transparent to most visible
frequencies—it warps the images of sky and clouds outside, but pleasantly, like Ochsen-Augen in Grandmother's
day, the days before window-glass. . . .

Part of the vaporized oxygen is routed through Gottfried's Imipolex shroud. In one of his ears, a tiny speaker
has been surgically implanted. It shines like a pretty ear-
ring. The data link runs through the radio-guidance system, and the words of Weissmann are to be, for a while,
multiplexed with the error-corrections sent out to the

Rocket. But there's no return channel from Gottfried to the ground. The exact moment of his death will never be known.

CHASE MUSIC

At long last, after a distinguished career of uttering, "My God, we are too late!" always with the trace of a sneer, a pro-forma condescension—because of course he *never* arrives too late, there's always a reprieve, a mistake by one of the Yellow Adversary's hired bunglers, at worst a vital clue to be found next to the body—now, finally, Sir Denis Nayland Smith *will* arrive, my God, too late.

Superman will swoop boots-first into a deserted clearing, a launcher-erector sighing oil through a slow seal-leak, gum evoked from the trees, bitter manna for this bitterest of passages. The colors of his cape will wilt in the afternoon sun, curls on his head begin to show their first threads of gray. Philip Marlowe will suffer a horrible migraine and reach by reflex for the pint of rye in his suit pocket, and feel homesick for the lacework balconies of the Bradbury Building.

Submariner and his multilingual gang will run into battery trouble. Plasticman will lose his way among the Imipolex chains, and topologists all over the Zone will run out and stop payments on his honorarium checks ("perfectly deformable," indeed!) The Lone Ranger will storm in at the head of a posse, rowels tearing blood from the stallion's white hide, to find his young friend, innocent Dan, swinging from a tree limb by a broken neck. (Tonto, God willing, will put on the ghost shirt and find some cold fire to hunker down by to sharpen his knife.)

"Too late" was never in their programming. They find instead a moment's suspending of their sanity—but then it's over with, whew, and it's back to the trail, back to the *Daily Planet. Yes Jimmy, it must've been the day I ran into that singularity, those few seconds of absolute mystery . . . you know Jimmy, time—time is a funny thing. . . .* There'll be a thousand ways to forget. The heroes will go on, kicked upstairs to oversee the development of bright new middle-line personnel, and they will watch their system falling apart, watch those singularities begin to come more and more often, proclaiming another dispensation out of the tissue of old-fashioned time, and they'll call it cancer, and just won't know what things are coming to, or what's the meaning of it all, Jimmy. . . .

These days, he finds he actually misses the dogs. Who would have thought he'd ever feel sentimental over a pack of slobbering curs? But here in the Sub-ministry all is so odorless, touchless. The sensory deprivation, for a while, did stimulate his curiosity. For a while he kept a faithful daily record of his physiological changes. But this was mostly remembering about Pavlov on his own deathbed, recording himself till the end. With Pointsman it's only habit, retro-scientism: a last look back at the door to Stockholm, closing behind him forever. The entries began to fall off, and presently stopped. He signed reports, he supervised. He traveled to other parts of England, later to other countries, to scout for fresh talent. In the faces of Mossmoon and the others, at odd moments, he could detect a reflex he'd never allowed himself to dream of: the tolerance of men in power for one who never Made His Move, or made it wrong. Of course there are still moments of creative challenge—

Yes, well, he's an ex-scientist now, one who'll never get Into It far enough to start talking about God, apple-cheeked lovable white-haired eccentric gabbing from the vantage of his Laureate—no he'll be left only with Cause and Effect, and the rest of his sterile armamentarium . . . his mineral corridors do not shine. They will stay the same neutral nameless tone from here in to the central chamber, and the perfectly rehearsed scene he is to play there, after all. . . .

COUNTDOWN

The countdown as we know it, 10-9-8-u.s.w., was invented by Fritz Lang in 1929 for the Ufa film *Die Frau in Mond*. He put it into the launch scene to heighten the suspense. "It is another of my damned 'touches,' " Fritz Lang said.

"At the Creation," explains Kabbalist spokesman Steve Edelman, "God sent out a pulse of energy into the void. It presently branched and sorted into ten distinct spheres or aspects, corresponding to the numbers 1–10. These are known as the Sephiroth. To return to God, the soul must negotiate each of the Sephiroth, from ten back to one. Armed with magic and faith, Kabbalists have set out to conquer the Sephiroth. Many Kabbalist secrets have to do with making the trip successfully.

"Now the Sephiroth fall into a pattern, which is called the Tree of Life. It is also the body of God. Drawn among the ten spheres are 22 paths. Each path corresponds to a letter of the Hebrew alphabet, and also to one of the cards called 'Major Arcana' in the Tarot. So although the Rocket countdown appears to be serial, it actually conceals the Tree of Life, which must be apprehended all at once, together, in parallel.

"Some Sephiroth are active or masculine, others passive or feminine. But the Tree itself is a unity, rooted exactly at the Bodenplatte. It is the axis of a particular Earth, a new dispensation, brought into being by the Great Firing."

"But but with a new axis, a newly spinning Earth," it occurs to the visitor, "what happens to astrology?"

"The signs change, idiot," snaps Edelman, reaching for his family-size jar of Thorazine. He has become such a habitual user of this tranquilizing drug that his complexion has deepened to an alarming slate-purple. It makes him an oddity on the street here, where everybody else walks around suntanned, and red-eyed from one irritant or another. Edelman's children, mischievous little devils, have lately taken to slipping wafer capacitors from junked transistor radios into Pop's Thorazine jar. To his inattentive eye there was hardly any difference: so, for a while, Edelman thought he must be developing a tolerance, and that the Abyss had crept intolerably close, only an accident away—a siren in the street, a jet plane rumbling in a holding pattern—but luckily his wife discovered the prank in time, and now, before he swallows, he is careful to scrutinize each Thorazine for leads, mu's, numbering.

"Here—" hefting a fat Xeroxed sheaf, "the Ephemeris. Based on the new rotation."

"You mean someone's actually found the Bodenplatte? The Pole?"

"The delta-t itself. It wasn't made public, naturally. The 'Kaisersbart Expedition' found it."

A pseudonym, evidently. Everyone knows the Kaiser has no beard.

STRUNG INTO THE APOLLONIAN DREAM . . .

When something real is about to happen to you, you go toward it with a transparent surface parallel to your own front that hums and bisects both your ears, making eyes very alert. The light bends toward chalky blue. Your skin aches. At last: something real.

Here in the tail section of the 00000, Gottfried has found this clear surface before him in fact, literal: the Imipolex shroud. Flotsam from his childhood are rising through his attention. He's remembering the skin of an apple, bursting with nebulae, a look into curved reddening space. His eyes taken on and on, and further. . . . The plastic surface flutters minutely: gray-white, mocking, an enemy of color.

The day outside is raw and the victim lightly dressed, but he feels warm in here. His white stockings stretch nicely from his suspender-tabs. He has found a shallow bend in a pipe where he can rest his cheek as he gazes into the shroud. He feels his hair tickling his back, his bared shoulders. It's a dim, whited room. A room for lying in, bridal and open to the pallid spaces of the evening, waiting for whatever will fall on him.

Phone traffic drones into his wired ear. The voices are metal and drastically filtered. They buzz like the voices of surgeons, heard as you're going under ether. Though they now only speak the ritual words, he can still tell them apart.

The soft smell of Imipolex, wrapping him absolutely, is a smell he knows. It doesn't frighten him. It was in the room when he fell asleep so long ago, so deep in sweet paralyzed childhood . . . it was there as he began to dream. Now it is time to wake, into the breath of what was always real. Come, wake. All is well.

ORPHEUS PUTS DOWN HARP

LOS ANGELES (PNS)—Richard M. Zhlubb, night manager of the Orpheus Theatre on Melrose, has come out against what he calls "irresponsible use of the harmonica." Or, actually, "harbodica," since Manager Zhlubb suffers from a chronic adenoidal condition, which affects his speech. Friends and detractors alike think of him as "the Adenoid." Anyway, Zhlubb states that his queues, especially for midnight showings, have fallen into a state of near anarchy because of the musical instrument.

"It's been going on ever since our Bengt Ekerot / Maria Casarès Film Festival," complains Zhlubb, who is fiftyish and jowled, with a permanent five-o'clock shadow (the worst by far of all the Hourly Shadows), and a habit of throwing his arms up into an inverted "peace sign," which also happens to be semaphore code for the letter U, exposing in the act uncounted yards of white French cuff.

"Here, Richard," jeers a passerby, "I got your French cuff, right here," meanwhile exposing himself in the grossest possible way and manipulating his foreskin in a manner your correspondent cannot set upon his page.

Manager Zhlubb winces slightly. "That's one of the ringleaders, definitely," he confides. "I've had a lot of trouble with him. Him and that Steve Edelman." He pronounces it "Edelbid." "I'b dot afraid to dabe dabes."

The case he refers to is still pending. Steve Edelman, a Hollywood businessman, accused last year of an 11569 (Attempted Mopery with a Subversive Instrument), is currently in Atascadero under indefinite observation. It is alleged that Edelman, in an unauthorized state of mind, attempted to play a chord progression on the Department of Justice list, out in the street and in the presence of a whole movie-queue of witnesses.

"A-and now they're all doing it. Well, not 'all,' let me just clarify that, of course the actual lawbreakers are only a small but loud minority, what I meant to say was, all those like Edelman. Certainly not all those good folks in the queue. A-ha-ha. Here, let me show you something."

He ushers you into the black Managerial Volkswagen, and before you know it, you're on the freeways. Near the interchange of the San Diego and the Santa Monica, Zhlubb points to a stretch of pavement: "Here's where I got my first glimpse of one. Driving a VW, just like mine. Imagine. I couldn't believe my eyes." But it is difficult to keep one's whole attention centered on Manager Zhlubb.

The Santa Monica Freeway is traditionally the scene of every form of automotive folly known to man. It is not white and well-bred like the San Diego, nor as treacherously engineered as the Pasadena, nor quite as ghetto-suicidal as the Harbor. No, one hesitates to say it, but the Santa Monica is a freeway for freaks, and they are all out today, making it difficult for you to follow the Manager's entertaining story. You cannot repress a certain shudder of distaste, almost a reflexive Consciousness of Kind, in their presence. They come gibbering in at you from all sides, swarming in, rolling their eyes through the side windows, playing harmonicas and even *kazoos,* in full disrespect for the Prohibitions.

"Relax," the Manager's eyes characteristically aglitter. "There'll be a nice secure home for them all, down in Orange County. Right next to Disneyland," pausing then exactly like a nightclub comic, alone in his tar circle, his chalk terror.

Laughter surrounds you. Full, faithful-audience laughter, coming from the four points of the padded interior. You realize, with a vague sense of dismay, that this is some kind of a stereo rig here, and a glance inside the glove compartment reveals an entire *library* of similar tapes: CHEERING (AFFECTIONATE), CHEERING (AROUSED), HOSTILE MOB in an assortment of 22 languages, YESES, NOES, NEGRO SUPPORTERS, WOMEN SUPPORTERS, ATHLETIC—oh, come now—FIRE-FIGHT (CONVENTIONAL), FIRE-FIGHT (NUCLEAR), FIRE-FIGHT (URBAN), CATHEDRAL ACOUSTICS. . . .

"We have to talk in *some* kind of code, naturally," continues the Manager. "We always have. But none of the codes is that hard to break. Opponents have accused us, for just that reason, of contempt for the people. But really we do it all in the spirit of fair play. We're not monsters. We know we have to give them *some* chance. We can't take hope away from them, can we?"

The Volkswagen is now over downtown L.A., where the stream of traffic edges aside for a convoy of dark Lincolns, some Fords, even GMCs, but not a Pontiac in the lot. Stuck on each windshield and rear window is a fluorescent orange strip that reads FUNERAL.

The Manager's sniffling now. "He was one of the best. I couldn't go myself, but I did send a high-level assisant. Who'll ever replace him, I wonder," punching a sly button under the dash. The laughter this time is sparse male *oh-hoho's* with an edge of cigar smoke and aged bourbon. Sparse but loud. Phrases like "Dick, you character!" and "Listen to *him*," can also be made out.

"I have a fantasy about how I'll die. I suppose you're on *their* payroll, but that's all right. Listen to this. It's 3 a.m., on the Santa Monica Freeway, a warm night. All my windows are open. I'm doing about 70, 75. The wind blows in, and from the floor in back lifts a thin plastic bag, a common dry-cleaning bag: it comes floating in the air, moving from behind, the mercury lights turning it white as a ghost... it wraps around my head, so super-fine and transparent I don't know it's there really until too late. A plastic shroud, smothering me to my death. ..."

Heading up the Hollywood Freeway, between a mys-teriously-canvased trailer rig and a liquid-hydrogen tanker sleek as a torpedo, we come upon a veritable caravan of harmonica players. "At least it's not those tambourines," Zhlubb mutters. "There aren't as many tambourines as last year, thank God."

Quilted-steel catering trucks crisscross in the afternoon. Their ripples shine like a lake of potable water after hard desert passage. It's a Collection Day, and the garbage trucks are all heading north toward the Ventura Freeway, a catharsis of dumpsters, all hues, shapes and batterings. Returning to the Center, with all the gathered fragments of the Vessels. ...

The sound of a siren takes you both unaware. Zhlubb looks up sharply into his mirror. "You're not holding, are you?"

But the sound is greater than police. It wraps the con-crete and the smog, it fills the basin and mountains further than any mortal could ever move... could move in time. ...

"I don't think that's a police siren." Your guts in a spasm, you reach for the knob of the AM radio. "*I don't think—*"

The Clearing

"Räumen," cries Captain Blicero. Peroxide and perman-ganate tanks have been serviced. The gyros are run up. Observers crouch down in the slit trenches. Tools and

fittings are stashed rattling in the back of an idling lorry.
The battery-loading crew and the sergeant who screwed
in the percussion pin climb in after, and the truck hauls
away down the fresh brown ruts of earth, into the
trees. Blicero remains for a few seconds at launch position, looking around to see that all is in order. Then
he turns away and walks, with deliberate speed, to the
fire-control car.

"Steuerung klar?" he asks the boy at the steering panel.

"Ist klar." In the lights from the panel, Max's face is
hard, stubborn gold.

"Treibwerk klar?"

"Ist klar," from Moritz at the rocket motor panel. Into
the phone dangling at his neck, he tells the Operation
Room, "Luftlage klar."

"Schlüssel auf SCHIESSEN," orders Blicero.

Moritz turns the main key to FIRE. "Schlüssel steht auf
SCHIESSEN."

Klar.

There ought to be big dramatic pauses here. Weissmann's head ought to be teeming with last images of
creamy buttocks knotted together in fear (not one trickle
of shit, Liebchen?) the last curtain of gold lashes over
young eyes pleading, gagged throat trying to say too late
what he should have said in the tent last night . . . deep in
the throat, the gullet, where Blicero's own cock's head has
burst for the last time (but what's this just past the
spasming cervix, past the Curve Into The Darkness The
Stink The . . . The White . . . The Corner . . . Waiting . . .
Waiting For—). But no, the ritual has its velvet grip on
them all. So strong, so warm. . . .

"Durchschalten." Blicero's voice is calm and steady.

"Luftlage klar," Max calls from the steering panel.

Moritz presses the button marked VORSTUFE. "Ist durch-
geschaltet."

A pause of 15 seconds while the oxygen tank comes up
to pressure. A light blazes up on Moritz's panel.

Entlüftung. "Belüftung klar."

The ignition lamp lights: Zundung. "Zundung klar."

Then, "Vorstufe klar." Vorstufe is the last position from
which Moritz can still switch backward. The flame grows
at the base of the Rocket. Colors develop. There is a period
of four seconds here, four seconds of indeterminacy. The

ritual even has a place for that. The difference between a
top-grade launch officer and one doomed to mediocrity is
in knowing exactly when, inside this chiming and fable-
crowded passage, to order Hauptstufe.

Blicero is a master. He learned quite early to fall into
a trance, to wait for the illumination, which always comes.
It is nothing he's ever spoken of aloud.

"Hauptstufe."

"Hauptstufe ist gegeben."

The panel is latched forever.

Two lights wink out. "Stecker 1 und 2 gefallen," Moritz
reports. The Stotz plugs lie blasted on the ground, tossing
in the splash of flame. On gravity feed, the flame is bright
yellow. Then the turbine begins to roar. The flame suddenly turns blue. The sound of it grows to full cry. The
Rocket stays a moment longer on the steel table, then
slowly, trembling, furiously muscular, it begins to rise.
Four seconds later it begins to pitch over. But the flame is
too bright for anyone to see Gottfried inside, except now
as an erotic category, hallucinated out of that blue violence, for purposes of self-arousal.

ASCENT

This ascent will be betrayed to Gravity. But the Rocket
engine, the deep cry of combustion that jars the soul,
promises escape. The victim, in bondage to falling, rises
on a promise, a prophecy, of Escape. . . .

Moving now toward the kind of light where at last the
apple is apple-colored. The knife cuts through the apple
like a knife cutting an apple. Everything is where it is, no
clearer than usual, but certainly more present. So much
has to be left behind now, so quickly. Pressed down-and-
aft in his elastic bonds, pressed painfully (his pectorals
ache, an inner thigh has frozen numb) till his forehead is
bent to touch one knee, where his hair rubs in a touch
crying or submissive as a balcony empty in the rain,
Gottfried does not wish to cry out . . . he knows they can't
hear him, but still he prefers not to . . . no radio back to
them . . . *it was done as a favor, Blicero wanted to make it
easier for me, he knew I'd try to hold on—hold each voice,
each hum or crackle—*

He thinks of their love in illustrations for children, in

last thin pages fluttering closed, a line gently, passively
unfinished, a pastel hesitancy: Blicero's hair is darker,
shoulder-length and permanently waved, he is an adolescent squire or page looking into an optical device and
beckoning the child Gottfried with a motherly or eager-to-
educate look . . . now he is far away, seated, at the end of
an olive room, past shapes going out of focus, shapes
Gottfried can't identify as friend or enemy, between him
and—where did he—it's already *gone*, no . . . they're beginning to slide away now faster than he can hold, it's like
falling to sleep—they begin to blur CATCH you can hold
it steady enough to see a suspender-belt straining down
your thighs, white straps as slender as the legs of a fawn
and the points of the black . . . the black CATCH you've
let a number of them go by, Gottfried, important ones you
didn't want to miss . . . you know this is the *last time* . . .
CATCH when did the roaring stop? Brennschluss, when
was Brennschluss *it can't be this soon* . . . but the burnt-out
tail-opening is swinging across the sun and through the
blonde hair of the victim here's a Brocken-specter, someone's, something's shadow projected from out here in the
bright sun and darkening sky into the regions of gold, of
whitening, of growing still as underwater as Gravity dips
away briefly . . . what is this death but a whitening, a carrying of whiteness to ultrawhite, what is it but bleaches,
detergents, oxidizers, abrasives— Streckefuss he's been
today to the boy's tormented muscles, but more appro-
priately is he Blicker, Bleicheröde, Bleacher, Blicero, extending, rarefying the Caucasian pallor to an abolition of
pigment, of melanin, of spectrum, of separateness from
shade to shade, it is *so white that* CATCH the dog was a
red setter, the last dog's head, the kind dog come to see
him off *can't remember what red meant*, the pigeon he
chased was slateblue, but they're both white now beside
the canal that night the smell of trees *oh I didn't want to
lose that night* CATCH a wave between houses, across a
street, both houses are ships, one's going off on a long, an
important journey, and the waving is full of ease and
affection CATCH last word from Blicero: "The edge of
evening . . . the long curve of people all wishing on the
first star. . . . Always remember those men and women
along the thousands of miles of land and sea. The true
moment of shadow is the moment in which you see the

point of light in the sky. The single point, and the Shadow
that has just gathered you in its sweep..."

Always remember.

The first star hangs between his feet.

Now—

DESCENT

The rhythmic clapping resonates inside these walls,
which are hard and glossy as coal: Come-*on!* Start-the-
show! Come-*on!* Start-the-*show!* The screen is a dim page
spread before us, white and silent. The film has broken, or
a projector bulb has burned out. It was difficult even for
us, old fans who've always been at the movies (haven't
we?) to tell which before the darkness swept in. The last
image was too immediate for any eye to register. It may
have been a human figure, dreaming of an early evening
in each great capital luminous enough to tell him he will
never die, coming outside to wish on the first star. But it
was *not a star*, it was falling, a bright angel of death. And
in the darkening and awful expanse of screen something
has kept on, a film we have not learned to see... it is
now a closeup of the face, a face we all know—

And it is just here, just at this dark and silent frame,
that the pointed tip of the Rocket, falling nearly a mile
per second, absolutely and forever without sound, reaches
its last unmeasurable gap above the roof of this old
theatre, the last delta-t.

There is time, if you need the comfort, to touch the
person next to you, or to reach between your own cold
legs... or, if song must find you, here's one They never
taught anyone to sing, a hymn by William Slothrop, centuries forgotten and out of print, sung to a simple and
pleasant air of the period. Follow the bouncing ball:

> There is a Hand to turn the time,
> Though thy Glass today be run,
> Till the Light that hath brought the Towers low
> Find the last poor Pret'rite one...
> Till the Riders sleep by ev'ry road,
> All through our crippl'd Zone,
> With a face on ev'ry mountainside,
> And a Soul in ev'ry stone....

Now everybody—

ABOUT THE AUTHOR

THOMAS PYNCHON is known almost exclusively through his writing. In all other respects, he craves and guards his privacy. The public facts about his life are therefore few and far between. He was born in 1937 and attended Cornell University, where he published his first story, "Mortality and Mercy in Vienna," in EPOCH. Soon after leaving Cornell, he published three short stories— "Under the Rose," in NOBLE SAVAGE #3; "Entropy," in THE KENYON REVIEW; *and* "Low-Lands," in NEW WORLD WRITING #16—which earned him an immediate reputation among the narrow but intense circle of short story readers. His novel *V.* won the coveted William Faulkner Foundation First Novel Award in 1963. His second novel, *The Crying of Lot 49,* appeared in 1966. Since then he has published "The Secret Investigation" in THE SATURDAY EVENING POST, and an essay on Los Angeles in THE NEW YORK TIMES MAGAZINE. *GRAVITY'S RAINBOW,* his third and most recent novel, was published in 1973. Mr. Pynchon is currently rumored to spend his time primarily in California and Mexico.

RELAX!

SIT DOWN

and Catch Up On Your Reading!

- [ ] **THE HARRAD EXPERIMENT** by Robert Rimmer (4690—$1.
- [ ] **THE FRENCH CONNECTION** by Robin Moore (5369— 9
- [ ] **HER** by Anonymous (6669—$1.
- [ ] **THE BELL JAR** by Sylvia Plat (7178—$1.
- [ ] **THE EXORCIST** by William Peter Blatty (7200—$1.
- [ ] **WHEELS** by Arthur Hailey (7244—$1.
- [ ] **RAGA SIX** by Frank Lauria (7249—$1.
- [ ] **HIM** by Anonymous (7369—$1.
- [ ] **THE DAY OF THE JACKAL** by Frederick Forsyth (7377—$1.
- [ ] **THE FRIENDS OF EDDIE COYLE** by George Higgins (7504—$1.
- [ ] **THE TERMINAL MAN** by Michael Crichton (7545—$1.
- [ ] **MEMOIRS OF AN EX-PROM QUEEN** by Alix Shulman (7565—$1.
- [ ] **THE LEVANTER** by Eric Ambler (7603—$1.
- [ ] **SHEILA LEVINE IS DEAD AND LIVING IN NEW YORK** by Gail Parent (7633—$1.
- [ ] **THE ODESSA FILE** by Frederick Forsyth (7744—$1

Buy them at your local bookstore or use this handy coupon for order